The Age of Justice

RAY DACOLIAS

The Age of Justice

ISBN 978-1-942721-04-8

Contents

The Other Half

Father lay on the cool, dirt floor of the mud hut, gazing at the waning, twinkling lights in the ebony sky, waving away an irksome swarm of buzzing mosquitoes from himself and his wife. "Today, we will be blessed," he whispered to Mother, who lay next to him; "we will find food." He felt the diffident nod of her head on his thin chest. "I will go to a Red Cross station," he murmured, glancing at his sleeping son, and then, reaching over with his skinny arm, chased away a thick, black cloud of flies from him.

Mother rose up. "It is too dangerous," she said, "along the road; the UN has pulled out—even they fear this place, now." But she was too weak to sit up any longer, and so lay down again. "Everyone comes to rescue, but they all go back to their rich, safe countries; but we are still here, we are real, not some sad picture on a piece of paper to make people weep." She checked herself, nearly shouted, and then clutched her heart. "We are people, we are here, with no way out; how can we survive, Father, how?" And she wept. "I can't even feed my child, anymore; I have failed him—I am a bad mother."

"I will go to the Red Cross station, and bring back maize flour, and beans, and yams; we will eat like kings and queens, and then leave for the border; and it is not you who are bad, good Mother—it is those who rule over us."

"But why, why must we live like this, Father, like refugees, like animals, like things that do not matter, and forgotten, and neglected?" The authentic want for understanding, the pain and ache to know, suffused her strained voice.

He did not reply immediately, but continued to stare at the burst of a beryl-blue, drenched, dappled and lean dawn, feeling the blast of hot air sweeping through the ripening sky. "Today, we will be blessed."

He arose and went outside to the village well, pulled up the brown rope to reveal the sodden, old wooden bucket, dipped his long, black, skinny fingers into the mud-colored, germ-ridden, foul-smelling liquid, splashed his face and neck, looked up at the women who were coming to get water for drinking and cooking, and watched them fill their white buckets and then turn away without evincing any palpable disgust, any outrage, or pleading faces; their cries for equality and justice had withered when they finally accepted that there would be no resolve to their woes, and thus they were condemned to die an early and horrific death. He turned toward the open dirt road. "It is not so far to the Red Cross station," he thought, and began to walk, in his long white robes and brown leather sandals, his short-black-haired head exposed to the ravages of the sun. He wiped the profuse sweat off his glistening forehead. "My family depends on me." He paused at the bloated graveyard. "Is this life—more of them, than us? How will the world go forward this way?"

More women had gathered around the well. "Omar came back from a food drop in Ethiopia yesterday," one of the women said as she filled her plastic bucket. "The rebels had already raided the government trucks." She yearned to talk of lighter things, for she, as well as the others, did not wish to feed the cold aura of death that lay like a black, stinking fog on the encampment. One baby had died of cholera only yesterday.

"Yes, I heard about it," said another woman, much younger and prettier. "The Militia are moving east; that's what my man told me." But now, she would keep the direction of the conversation away from such difficult news, if only to help them forget the daily fear of waking up and finding one more dead or dying loved one, and begin again.

"One of the men at the drop told Hadiya a big, big, silly story about American women—you know her: Hadiya will talk you far into midnight with her fantastic tales; well, this man told her that American women are as big as camels, and that they eat more food every day than an entire village, and," she learned forward, bringing them all toward her, as if all were attracted by the strong gravitational pull of her revelation, "ah, but I have heard," she continued, still smiling, and wanting very much to interject what tidbit of gossip she had learned about the "huge females of the Western Hemisphere," "that these giants will sometimes starve themselves to take off layers of their new body." The women around her gasped and held their hearts fast. She was pleased. "Yes, yes, it is true, I tell you, for Tadewi told me—they starve themselves and lose their layers of blubber off their bodies like a snake sheds its skin." But the women were having great difficulty comprehending such a creature—one that would gorge and disgorge—for it was not part of their language proper, as they had no name for it, no grammar, no concept, no background information, no vocabulary, no proper context for such a disturbingly grotesque vision; how can you tell a man who has never had legs, and also lives among those who have none, that there are those who purposely destroy their fully equipped bodies and now thus are incapable of doing what he has dreamed his entire life of doing: of running and jumping and leaping for joy, wild and free? Some of the women dared to giggle, if only to forget their troublesome heritage.

"I do not believe any of this," one of the younger women said, watching the next group of women gathering for water; "it is exaggeration, if you ask me." She considered herself educated, as she had attended school for six months when she was eleven, until her father had sold her for ten oxen and three camels to a forty-year-old man, who, after their wedding, refused to allow her to attend school; subsequently, she had run away, married another man, and eventually had come to this camp. "I've seen American women in pictures—very slender, very beautiful."

The woman who had related the story frowned, shook her head, and then smiled slyly. "Ah, but I have proof, don't you know, ladies," she said, seeing their incredulous faces, cunningly, and then, pulling out a crumpled black and white picture, proudly held it up.

The women gasped.

"Why, it isn't human—it looks like someone patched together pictures of large, fat and lazy animals onto a woman's head."

"Oh my, its arms are as big as my waist," another sighed, in disbelief.

"I saw a hippopotamus in Kenya," an older woman said, nodding her head; "it is as big as that."

"Maybe it is a hippopotamus with a painted woman's face on it," said the woman who had first aired the suspicion of the fake picture.

The owner of the remarkable photograph waved off their ridiculous explanations. "No, no, the man at the food drop was American, and he assured Hadiya that this was not only a real woman, but an average woman in his country."

"Oh, I don't believe it, Hadara," the older woman protested strongly, "if we tied you down for a year and stuffed you with food the whole time, you still wouldn't get close to looking like that, that, that…hippopotamus!"

Now, all of the women laughed.

Two of their husbands had gone to other villages for work only a month ago, and had not yet returned. The faces of the two women, pinched by famine and despair, scrubbed raw by injustice and a great gnawing depression that sank into the very marrow of their brittle bones, now wore the veil of a growing merriment; but joy was soon flushed out of them by the deluge of misery the women swam in, misery that oozed about them and swallowed up their malnourished children, misery that buzzed the boiling air like hungry locusts, like human locusts come to wreak havoc upon innocent human crops.

The next day, in the steaming hot, lazy morning, in the stale breath of a dead breeze, a rank smell seized the inhabitants of the encampment.

The human locusts had arrived.

Pounding hooves of horses raced up on the scurrying people, the masters of the sweating animals astride them like desert sheikhs, robed in layers of white and black clothing and pouring into the small community with black rifles held tightly in their thorn-like limbs.

"Gather round and pay homage to General Makki's army," one of the creatures shouted.

The frightened people walked out from their feeble shelters, standing like trembling penitents before their threatening lords.

"Pay tribute, you lazy worms," the fat creature shouted at the masses before him. "Line up with your food, your money, your gifts."

The people dutifully put their precious food in large, white canvas bags held out by the adjutants of the big-mouthed creature, and when all was collected, he ordered the people to stand before him while his fellow locusts surveyed the haul. "What? Twelve pounds of sweet potatoes, a half-sack of rice, three dinar coins—that is an insult—a banana, and no meat! Not even a turquoise bracelet that our beloved General might wear in fond remembrance of his unappreciated village? Yes, you there, woman, approach me, quickly!"

Mother walked haltingly toward this raider of encampments, thinking only of her husband, who had been gone for two days, and her son, whom she had furtively sent on a course behind the tents, toward the sloping hills. She stood, head bowed, listening to the great insect-head spout invectives against her and her supposedly lazy, deceitful, uncaring people. "But I have not eaten for two days, and…"

"Excuses," the human insect roared; "you're hiding food and tribute!" And then any reflection of what is good and fair in his voice dissipated when he shouted, "The sentence for such insolence is death."

She stared at him, her sunken eyes too tired to rage, and when she spoke softly but firmly, her words came from ancient stories and ancient themes she had heard all her life: "Justice will come for you; it is the way of the world."

A fierce shot rang out and she soon lay in a crumpled death pose.

"Take the women," the leader of the human locusts shouted in his blood frenzy, "and kill the men."

Thus, the slaughterhouse began, but did not last long, for such butchering of helpless human beings by the will of soulless creatures is executed without moral constraints; as it turned out, the human locusts turned their carnal lusts upon the screaming, terrified women, and raped all of them, killed them all, mutilated them all, and then gathered the tents and threw them onto the dead bodies, and lit it all on fire.

In a day's time, only shreds of scorched canvas, burnt poles, and ashes and charred bone remained of Refuge Encampment Forty-Three in Zone Three.

Father and Mother's son had continued to wander in the boiling desert, hiding for two days from raiding patrols, and eating insects, and drinking water squeezed from cactus and deep, unclean holes, and sleeping in the far recesses of dark caves; on the third day, he was found crying, agitated, dehydrated and hungry by a group of men on horses; they took him to their camp, fed him, clothed him, tended to his wounds, and then took him to their commander.

"Boy, have you seen the raiders of General Makki?" the man with the skin as black as coal asked. "Did they burn your village?"

"Yes, sir," the boy replied, meekly.

"Do you know in which direction they proceeded?"

"Yes, sir, for I watched them."

"Silence, boy; answer only with words to justify a response."

The boy frowned upon this, as he had never known such verbal abuse, for his mother and father had raised him with a free hand, sparing his grief in a land made of grief where it heaps up more every day. "To the north," he said.

"Good," the man said, smiling, his bright white teeth showing as he did so, and then, looking to his men, "We go tonight." He clapped his large hands together. "The boy works like the others."

Kofi fell into his tasks without complaint, joining the other captured boys in bringing water and food to the soldiers, and cleaning their rifles and making fires and preparing meals, and attending to every need of his new masters with a mature industriousness, lest the sting of the whip prompt him to the task.

Kofi did not understand what was transpiring in the camp, what it meant when the various commanders quoted radical prophets and revolutionaries; when the soldiers moved rapidly from camp to camp, when he saw men returning bloody from battle, when they gathered around the fire at night and swore allegiance to their sacred cause; when he saw the captured women thrown into tents; when he saw the dead bodies of women left behind in the rock-encircled fire pits, just as if they had been caught game, cleaned, cooked and skinned of all their value, as if everything brought here or wandering in here was Providence and to be consumed by the soldiers; he only now knew that he ate, and ate to his intense greedy pleasure, good, hard, clean flatbread and warm beer, and hot cornmeal and ripe, zesty red beans and sometimes a sliver of tough hare, or a cupful of oh-so-delicious camel milk that poured so sweetly into his dry mouth that hung so greedily open and held back like a baby bird for its mother-nur-turer, and so satisfyingly cleansed the gritty dust from his parched throat that everything else faded away into obscurity and he did not care what he had to do to attain it and keep it funneling into his growing body; thus, food ranked high above his known world, so high that all other activities and memories fell to dust, to the mounds of the blurred and dissipating past.

He gladly cleaned the wounds of the soldiers, fetched water in peril-ous territory, took verbal and physical beatings when he erred in his duties, cleaned clothes and prepared rifles and bullets, and yes, anything a slave would do, if only he could continue to eat and feel the immense secret power growing within him, a new paradigm surging within his bony frame, awak-ening a sleeping strength that whispered, "This is life, boy, this is how you should feel; you are, thus, alive!" And he felt cunning to have fooled his mas-ters into feeding him for so little work.

The other children cried for their mothers, cried when they were whipped, cried when they had to stand guard in the black-as-pitch night, especially when enemy patrols were lurking about; they cried when their fellows were captured or shot or blown up; crying softly or crying loud, the boys sobbed a river all the harsh, hot, day long and into the cold, lonely, unforgiving night; Kofi wept in silence, never allowing the other boys to see him, and especially was careful not to let the soldiers see him weep, for he too often had seen the whiners and criers herded forth into the path of destruction.

There were times when the soldiers had to cross the miserable hard ground of rock or yellow sand wherein they knew danger lay, and the commander had given a rule to his men, and it was this: that children were expendable in this holy war.

Kofi had learned early about which ones were selected to walk point; the soldiers, with their AK-47s slung over their slender shoulders, would let their ever-present scowls evaporate as they talked to the chosen boys in kind, soothing voices. These boys were just like the dog who is incessantly whipped and abused by his Master's strident voice, and one day finds his Master's voice sickeningly sweet and pleasing as it beckons him forward, but then instinctively steps backward in distrust; these boys stood in confusion as the men talked to them of promises of extra food and cool water and toys on the other side of the clearing. "No," the boys would timidly reply, "no, thank you, please." But the men, prodding the reluctant boys on, just like a smiling father would when encouraging his son to ride a bicycle for the first time, would merely assume the false mask of assurance and compassion. The boys had to comply, and so they went forward; and this particular time, there were five of them, walking continuously over the baked and scarred desert floor. Faster, the soldiers yelled, toys and candy and games on the other side of the hill, and even a television—so run, boys, run for your silly lives!

Kofi, watching curiously from a safe distance, acknowledged that the boys were now running and laughing with glee and had forgotten all of their apprehension with each successful step that took them closer to the slowly materializing prizes. "I know all of them: why, that is Osman, Salva, and that is Sadiq, and…" The first explosion that tore Osman to shredded bits of flesh and bone ransacked Kofi's thoughts, and he stood, his heart beating loudly, his breath fast, his trembling body drenched in perspiration as he watched in horror as the other boys screamed like scared rabbits who are approaching the howling noise that comes from the coyote's den.

"Help us, help us, soldiers," the remaining boys shouted in their mad desperation as they froze, staring at the smoke and destruction before them.

The big, gangly soldier with the broad smiled waved them on. "It's fine, boys, it's fine, go on; we just must have missed one of the mines; anyway, it's more food and toys for you, now." He leaned over and whispered to his comrades as the two men lip up cigarettes. "On, go on, you'll be fine," he shouted, casually, as if telling his son to get back onto the bicycle after falling and ride some more.

"Okay, Lam, okay," the boys said.

"Hey," he said, irritated now, "don't be calling me by my name—just go on—go!"

A little further on, and with no more explosions, the three boys were beginning to smile through the blood and drifting smoke.

And then, boom went a mine, and one of the scrawny boys was blown to scattered bits and chunks.

"Ah, man," the big soldier said, shaking his head as he slapped a pack of cigarettes into the greedy palm of his fellow, "I always pick the loser." But the remaining two boys, completely hysterical now, were running back toward the men. "No, back, back, you little fools," he said, laughing, waving them away, and then he cursed, raised his rifle and released a barrage of bullets in front of them. "What a waste of ammunition," he muttered, watching the obedient boys retreating, "so, hurry up—and don't forget, toys and candy; chocolate, lots of chocolate," and he turned toward his comrade, "Do you think they know what ice cream is, eh? No, oh well, I will say it anyway," and he turned again toward them after he took a long drag on his cigarette, "ice cream, ice cream, too—so, go on, you little fools, you pitiful insects," and then his voice lowered in tone as he imagined the words dying right before they reached their intended target, "you who are fodder for our holy cause."

Boom, boom, went the land mines, and gone, gone went the last little boys.

Kofi wept like he had when he had lost his own brothers; but it was what the two soldiers then said that stabbed his heart and wounded him.

"Well," casually spoke the soldier, shrugging his shoulders, and now aiming his weapon toward the bloodied corpses, "now we know it's a bad crossing."

"Yes," the other one said, as he too aimed his rifle, "and we saved a few bullets, and got rid of five useless workers." Consequently, they opened fire on the minefield, ripping up the ground and exploding the remaining metallic land sharks.

Kofi stared at the two men with an indescribable, immature enmity scorched on his tortured face.

The features of one day were indistinguishable from the next, for every day in this army, the soldiers lived only to fight, and the children lived only to serve them; an injured boy, a dead boy, a physically weak girl, an emotionally crippled girl, all were indistinguishable from another as seen through the bloodstained prism of the fanatic lens of the man who ruled with an iron fist and whose every word was obeyed without hesitation by his fanatical adherents: the General.

There is a young boy, perhaps eight or nine, Kofi thought, upon observing a youngster as he was herded into the camp for the first time. He reminds me of myself, he decided, observing the youth for some duration; perhaps he needs a friend. Kofi introduced himself to the boy, who hesitatingly, through the cracks of pain and sorrow, said his name was Mohan. "I'll look after you, Mohan," he said, bravely. "I've been here a long time—six months, I think." It had been a year.

When Mohan stumbled carrying the heavy wooden water bucket, he should have been whipped, but Kofi caught him; when Mohan picked up the wrong rifle for the screaming soldier, he should have been thrashed, but

Kofi selected the right rifle and handed it to him; every error committed by the youth, Kofi corrected; every ache, Kofi soothed; and every time he did, he felt more authentically alive and connected to what life had once meant to him. He was fond of calling him "little brother," and often walked with his arm around the slim shoulders of his friend as he explained existence in the camps. He was soon forgetting all about his past life.

If Kofi turned left, Mohan did not follow and erred; if Kofi turned right, Mohan did not follow and erred again, and so many mistakes so early on in the difficult career of a boy-slave attendant caught the attention of the tall and bony soldier whose task it was to overseer the shearing and pruning of the children; it had been only two weeks when, one dry, hot morning, he summoned Mohan and two other boys to his green tent. "I have a very important mission for you—it could be a promotion, I don't know; I will talk to the General myself if you perform admirably." He suppressed a sly smile. The boys stood tall and at attention. "The General has selected you three brave boys to deliver a most important message to a man in town." He held up a small brown box that was wrapped in white cloth and brown twine. "This package must be in the hands of the man by eight in the a.m., tomorrow; do you know what this means—please to nod your head." Satisfied, he gave them the carefully drawn directions to the place where the man would be. The boys, excited and as proud as if they had been selected for a great honor, saluted their superior, and quickly set off, running at full speed out of the encampment. He then summoned Kofi and bade him follow the boys to make certain the package was delivered.

Kofi shadowed the boys from a safe distance, wondering why they simply did not run away. He tracked them over rock hills and through deep gullies and into the periphery of a small town; he watched the boys helping each other navigate the landmarks they were familiar with; he watched them turn left at the old, burned-out warehouse, laughingly touch the tall, brown telephone pole, throw rocks, kick cans, and then march right up to the two-story building and exuberantly race up its stone steps. Kofi viewed this from a safe distance, anxious as to their fate.

Twenty minutes elapsed, and he saw nothing; and then, there was movement at one of the windows of the second story; he stood horrified as a small body was hurled through the broken glass and landed with a sickening thud on the cracked concrete below. High-pitched squeals and screams, like those of a pig being stuck with a hog poker, punched through the jagged window like a sonic blast; in a moment, three men, two with rifles, came angrily down the steps with the two remaining messengers; he heard their every blood-soaked intonation and pitch.

"Who sent you, you little monsters," the big man, who was unarmed, shouted at the two trembling boys. He shoved their faces into the dead body of their comrade, laughing as the boys excreted waste over themselves, and then grunted, "Well, this is one time you won't have to worry about a whipping for urinating on yourselves," and he nodded to the men as a man does who stands over vermin that must be violently killed. There was no hesitation as the two men shot each boy in the head in a bored manner. "Finish it; we need free advertising for our adopted policy, 'no limits, no boundaries, and success cannot help but find its way to you,'" he said, smiling; "A good little slogan to sell any product, eh?" as he watched the men drag the three corpses away. "And far enough so I don't have to smell that unpleasantness of it all—well, that is why I pay you to do the dirty work; anyway, your nose gets deadened to the stench in no time." He smoothed his short, black hair and returned to his office.

Kofi could not feel his body; he was, that is to say, his senses were encased in his small, round head, watching from an undetermined distance that he could not measure, features of moral degradation he could not measure, which shut down his humanity and caused it to shutter in disbelief and shame and humiliation, which he also could not measure; it confused him and silenced his mind, for though he had witnessed so many horrors and cruelty, these murderers should have seemed as natural to the scenery as a cactus of green or a hill of pebbles and dirt among the barren yellow sand; but a new thought arose, curling like a black vapor in his leaking brain: was it possible this was the way of the horrible world? And then he saw the man come down again and approach the men after they had soaked the dead boys with precious fuel and lit them on fire.

"Well," the man said, with a hearty smile, "I seriously thought to relieve myself upon them so people also might say, 'hey, he isn't bad, he urinated on someone who was on fire.'" He roared with laughed as he slapped the hands of his compatriots and spat largely on the burning bodies, mockingly holding his fat, squat nose, and then said, "I should have done it for one less flush—water is too precious in these parts, eh? But I have higher standards now, as I am in charge," and he laughed again, as it seemed he enjoyed a good joke at the expense of others.

The eyes of Kofi's limp body fell to gaze at the two men in front of the now purple-smoking blaze, two men talking as if at a holiday barbecue, two men who were actually conversing about their girlfriends and children. Kofi thought of his own family, but then this casual mix of flagrant villainy that was mixed into the normal stream of things took his throbbing head, which had been struggling to rise above the ugly morass of life to see what could be seen, and stuffed it down into the stinking mire.

And then the building exploded, and the two men looked upward, seeing their boss flung out like a bloodied and broken rag doll through the broken window onto the makeshift funeral below.

"Well, I am in charge now," one of the men casually said to his comrade.

"Eh, you? I have rank," the other protested.

But before the formal talks could ensue, the first man took out a small black revolver and shot his fellow three times in the head, and then plopped the still-twitching body onto the heaping orange blaze.

Kofi had been crying, but his face was too cold to feel the small liquid representatives of human sorrow; he had been trying to think, but his mind was drained of electrical currency; he had been trying to feel, but a bitter and heavy balm had been rubbed onto his wounded black skin, and he could feel neither cold nor heat, wind, nor the stillness of the sizzling air. He was stone, now, a stone statue of a boy; but he was salt, too, a white salt pillar who had seen what he should never have seen; and he was dying—not physically, as most people graciously do in civilized countries where they chose to die: he was dying by losing his humanity sloughed off layer by layer, peeled like a purple onion, unraveling the finely spun shield of humanity that had been woven round him to reveal a hard, oily, tightly coiled set of steel talons and claws that had no master but the narcotic of supreme self-propelled survival.

Bloody murder played a loud revelry in his waning thoughts; murder, effective and binding, promoting clarity, promising resolution; charming murder chained him to the descending dungeon that drops to the outer regions of abomination; he stood at the pit of the slimy, black abyss, breathing in the sweet mists of beckoning murder that caressed the land like a nursing mother, as if it were essential, life-giving, regenerating; this temptress, Murder, was his maternal guide now, issuing dark visions of dead enemies, and golden visions of precious freedom for himself. Murder stood at the red, moss-covered pit, cloaked in white gauze, but covered in bright red blood, and murmured in a weird, gurgling, hoarse tone, "Above me, only sky." It pointed upward with its meaty fingers at the steady drizzle of blood-red that fell only upon its white-robed and covered head, and then let its giant tattooed arm point to the ground. "Below me, only land; and yet, without me, the world grows fat and lazy, like a house pet." The fine red mist slowed to a trickle, and then halted, causing Murder to look upward, its deformed hand shaking violently against the healing sky. And then Murder's diseased face lost its thick, crusty scales, and black scabs dropped off its protruding forehead, and its mangled hands grew straight, its face grew comely, its hood came off as its now-handsome head and its clothes shone in resplendent glory. "Help me," it cried, its arms outstretched to Kofi, who too held out his arms in sympathy and tears; but then the blood rain commenced with a single droplet, which gave voice to the body it had once inhabited, who cried out, "I am Mohan, and I should not have died"; and Murder felt its power diminish; but as the foul rain poured, again Murder's heart beat stronger, its black blood now coursing quickly throughout its steel veins. "Real power to bring change to this land you love," it shouted, clenching its hairy, lumpy fists, and Kofi quickly pulled his hands away.

"But I am you in the Light," Kofi protested, remembering his parents' lessons.

"No," Murder growled, "you are me, now!"

"I am in you in the Light," Kofi pleaded, falling backward a step.

"You are me in both worlds," Murder whispered, in a graveled voice; "men choose."

"You are mine enemies."

"Man is Darkness and the Light."

Kofi stepped backward, and murmured, "I have seen what you should be," and he paused as Murder leaned toward him. "I choose the Light." Murder let out a ghoulish scream, its figure afire as it was sucked into the burning flame of the closing abyss.

The pit vanished. Kofi stared up at the black ceiling of night, fell onto his chafed knees, raised his puny arms skyward, and prayed.

Survival in the Desert

Kofi walked on land that had once been fertile and covered in dense forests and freshwater lakes, and now was hard-baked clay, dry desert, squeezed of life and ambition; he followed trails of tribesmen who traveled for miles with white plastic containers, and then stood behind them as they patiently waited at steel water pumps for hours; he had no jerrican, only a small tin cup he had found, but he filled it with the precious cool water and drank it, and then refilled it, and drank it, and again, until his thirst was quenched, and then moved on. No one grumbled about his multiple refills, no one seemed to see him, no one at all—they were just waiting their turn with the patience of Job; he watched them as they marched back to their villages with the five-gallon containers perfectly balanced upon their heads. He followed them at a safe distance, to let them know he did not want their water, only their company; when he felt his imposition upon them increase, when they began to shove worried glances at him, he would wander off and attach himself to other villagers.

Once he found a tribe following a route along the barren desert to a place where trees had grown aplenty thousands of years ago, but now contained only wood chips and twigs and bits of bark, which was even insufficient as fuel for cooking; thus, villagers walked or rode donkeys to other regions where small forests still thrived, gathered wood, and came back. So, he would collect as much wood as possible, bundle it in twine, put it atop his head, and follow the people back, sometimes to the village, oftentimes to market, where such a precious commodity brought some money or food. This was life, he knew, this was the world, he thought; there are those who have little, those who have less, and those who take from both by force. This was the life he knew, life as if it were a delicate mustard seed in his hand, life as a tiny, helpless, blind creature at the mercy of the wind, and with one small puff of air, it would.

He joined a wagon train of refugees en route to the border, but was reluctant to stay with them, always paralleling them, sleeping apart from their camp—he would be, must be, safe, always; one night, he was startled from sleep by the howling screeches of marauding rebels, and he watched the slaughter of their victims as if through a glass darkly, as if he were detached and not a part of it at all, a spectator of another gruesome fact of this stark land; and he sat and wept; later, he joined a long line of villagers going to a United Nations encampment, but chose not to stay with them, always paralleling them, sleeping apart from the camp—he would be, must be, safe, always; on another night—do not cowards always strike at night against unsuspecting Innocents—he was startled awake to find these poor people trapped in the bloody snare of the government-sponsored rebels, who soon slaughtered them like diseased sheep; and he still wept, even though he knew this was and is the world, and could not fathom it to be any other way.

"This is life, then," he murmured, drying his tears with his torn and stained, raggedy shirt, "this is life, then? Is there no other terrible world but ours? But, at least, I will not be a part of the killing." He moved on.

He had attended school for six months when he was nine, but that was three years ago. "I have seen other worlds, but I think they are not real," he decided, as he walked along the underside of a large hill, hugging its dark and curved shoulders. "How could other people not come to help us? O God," he looked up at the black garden with its sparkling jewels decorating it, and he felt as if others too were looking up at such beauty; "if only I could live over there, where people live in big houses and do not kill each other for food and water and wood—I have heard it is so, even though I am not sure if I believe it; but if it were so, are they wondering about me, and would they help me?" He wept for his beloved mother and father, he wept for every tribe and village he saw massacred, he wept for little Mohan, whom he had known only a month but had accepted as a little brother. He embraced himself in his lacerating anguish, for he yearned for companionship; he felt the welts of self-beating upon his heart as he knelt on the hard ground, and then let his head fall to the cool soil. "O, how I wish I could live in a land of plenty; I would be so good, so grateful for the smallest thing, even a small hut and a few cows, and a small plot of land; I would ask for nothing more, for such great wealth would make me so very proud." But he knew his supplication went with his salty tears right into the dry, cracked, pale earth; he stood up, looking around at the thin vapors of a drifting, boundless, sooty dome of sky. "I hear something," he murmured, hearing slight footsteps from the east. "Who could that be?" he asked himself, scampering to the side of a small hill to hide, just as a defenseless creature does when it hears the savage pounding of the coming predator.

He heard labored breath, sloppy footsteps, and painful moans, but still hid in his tiny fortress; presently, a thin form was sketched out by the luminous moonlight, and he saw a young girl staggering across the wastelands; she fell.

He leaped to the fallen form and, determining that she was dehydrated, administered water in small portions to her bloody, cracked lips, and stroked her hot forehead. "You will be all right, girl," he whispered to her, looking at her bloodied clothes, yet there were no visible wounds about her body. He lay next to her all night and into the red edge of dawn, and she awoke under the protection of the small jutting hilltop that was momentarily their home.

The red sun rose and dressed the girl in a dazzling costume of shimmering, gauzy light; her face was radiant with the luster of youth and a natural loveliness that poured over him like a mighty wave.

"She will leave me," he thought, watching her awaken; "it is too late for me to have a companion of such great beauty and elegance."

But when she opened her luminous eyes and smiled at him, he felt a surge of joy throughout his body. "Hello," she said, weakly, in his native tongue, "did you save me?" He blushed innocence as she squeezed his hand. "Thank you," she whispered; "I am Naomi," but she fell into another long slumber, so great was her weariness.

Kofi felt a gentle calm settle into his fragile heart. "I do not understand it, but I must try," he murmured, caressing her forehead with a soft, damp rag. "I do not know why, but she must live," he whispered, observing her pretty face as if for the first time; "I do not know how, but I will find a way," he thought, observing her feminine features as if he had never seen such a marvel before; "this time, she will live, somehow, and this time, I must provide the way." He remembered the talk of soldiers and men, how they boasted about defending their own family and home, and how his own mother and father had failed. "She is with me, now, and this time, she will live."

He adorned her in his finest thoughts, dressing her as an angelic being who was incapable of hurtful acts, and capable of much joy; he tended to her wounds, fed her, washed her face, and combed her short, black, curly hair. He scoured the barren land for edible nutrition; he worked at campsites and bought her food and clothes, and walked for endless miles to fill a canteen with water, and always what little he had, he gave to her in her delirium; he gave to her what little he needed, he gave up all of it so she might live, she who was so handsome, and innocent, so alone; all of his hurt and pain and loneliness would dissipate if only she might live and care for him and be his companion; and to this goal he worked assiduously, protecting her, as she regained her strength from the smallest biting insect and cut or bruise, and the blasting sandstorms, as they hid from the terrorizing hordes of men who rode on horseback or camels, or who drove in Jeeps or simply walked on foot; and so they moved on, and he hid her, taught her and, above all things, loved her as if she were the real world he had always sought, a world he might understand to help him understand the world he did not.

The Story of Naomi

Naomi had lived in a small encampment of nomads who were escaping rebels who had destroyed their village; she lived with her father and mother, and her sister, Musa; her father had been picking marula during the months of December and March, and then selling the prized green fruit in town for his employer; her mother and sister had a job in a local factory, stitching and sewing garments together in a large warehouse made of tin and capital greed, for sixteen hours a day in a hot, humid climate, receiving few breaks and even less compassion from their employer; one late Friday afternoon, a big man with a fine gray suit had come from a big corporation in the United States of America and walked into the local office of this regional clothes manufacturer and complained that the prices he paid for these cheap shirts were too high. "How can we compete with other retail chains if their overhead is smaller than ours?" he bellowed, walking around the dusty room and peering through the metal shades into the dark gloom of the factory and somehow not seeing these hard workers as human beings, but rather as laboring chattel, like cows to give milk, or oxen for the fields, or cattle to be fattened up for slaughter. "How much are we paying these lazy peasants?"

"Two-fifty a day," the nervous manager had said, sweat beading on his shiny, bony black forehead.

"Two-fifty? Why, Feke pays his people a buck fifty, less if they show up late or leave early, or damage any goods." He was lying, of course, but he knew Feke would soon be paying that amount after this session was done.

"One-fifty, you say?" The manager frowned. "I may lose workers; they do not make enough as it is…"

The big man with the clean-shaven face and jet-black hair that was greased from stem to stern laughed like one who may not own the bank but was speaking for the banker to the desperate merchant who needed the loan. "Lose workers, you say? Well, where do you think they are going to go to work instead, eh?"

The manager rubbed his chin. "I suppose…I suppose we could lower it to two dollars a day." The man still had uncomfortable particles of debris from his years as a day laborer in the harsh fields and the deep and dirty coal mines, and still had a small degree of sympathy.

"One seventy-five," the big man with the clumsy gestures and perfumed, soapy, alabaster skin said calmly; "and here are the statistics to show the profits you and I will make at that living wage for these ungrateful wretches—where else can they get a job like this, huh?"

"Livable wage," the manager repeated, wanting to believe in such a sustainable illusion.

"Sure, sure, look here, partner," the big man said assuredly, and then began to speak rapidly as he pulled out charts and graphs, and laid them carefully one upon another like coils of a rattlesnake.

The owner was soon called in; hands were shaken, alcohol consumed, egos balanced, money exchanged, and the dastardly deal was executed.

The mother and sister of Naomi could do nothing but accept the new terms at the factory, as they had as many rights as penned pigs waiting for slaughter. "We must work to eat, and there is no better work than this," the mother had told her family the day of this terrible news.

"But have we no more rights than an animal on a tether?" Riva had argued. "Must we be like cattle, to be bought and sold and traded, as if we had no immortal soul?"

Her father, standing next to her in the small hut of mud, straw and sticks, slapped her hard across her radiant face. "You are cattle to be bought and sold," he had shouted, "and no more wicked Western ideas from your friends will be leaked from your stupid mouth; the West is corrupt, full of heretics who have no morals; we have our holy book to teach us right from wrong." Riva had brooded revenge, and that night had snuck out to meet the rebellious youths who preached Freedom and Justice and Equality from the stories they had heard and read about in distant Democracies.

"In America, girls dress any way they choose, and go out with whomever they choose, and their parents let them," Kiupita, her best friend, had whispered among the group. "A missionary told me so, and she would not lie about such things; she seemed so sincere."

The heart and soul of every youth yearns to break from the tight constraints of parents and rigid rules of society, and when that society finally draws them into an inevitable clash of indomitable wills, the youths become entangled in a mass of smoking, twisted, burning restrictions and boundaries, and the more they struggle to free themselves, the deeper they are absorbed into the fuming wreckage; so, when these flaming youths of sixteen, of fifteen, and of fourteen heard of such boundless liberties, it was as if they felt the restrictive chains of convention loosen; passion inflamed their strong bodies and poured fiery juices into their thirsty hearts, for they had never had the chance to taste even the smallest of liberties, and now they were fairly ready to burst forth like a verdant sprout through hard soil.

"Oh, to be in such a place," Kiupita said, a small thrill of hope cautiously assembling itself upon her sweet face.

"And the girls are free to marry whomever they desire."

But this was too much for these girls, who had known only the lurid pageantry of families bartering away their daughters for profit.

"Oh, I want to believe it," Kiupita said. "But," she despaired, "already I have heard my father talk of giving me away to a local farmer…" She could not refrain from sobbing. "For thirty cows—thirty cows, his own daughter, his own flesh and blood," she said, choking on her sorrow, "to a fifty-year-old man…"

The black plague of fate descended upon them and smothered their democratic whimsies, robbing their natural ardor for hope; Freedom was a fairy tale in a faraway land, an impossible-to-imagine place drawn in glossy pictures in big books that proclaimed equality for all, but their land was here, now and forever, as far away from the land of opportunity as the earth from the stars; for they knew that their elder sisters had been sold for cash, cows and convenience, and had also dreamed of escape and respect, but had been condemned to be free only from birth until the first signs of ovulation.

Kiupita stood up, her fists thrust into the air. "I want to live in freedom," she shouted, looking up at the great expanse of black sky. "Is God so cruel that he intended us to be nothing more than slaves; is this not the modern century, where slavery does not exist? Is there not something greater than our land, greater than us," and she looked to her friends; "must we submit, are we cattle, have we no rights—why, why must we suffer while others do not?" And then she shouted, her voice hoarse with passion, "Why must we suffer!"

The next day, she heard her parents talking about giving her away to a farmer, and she felt the thrill of rebellion bear up in her and, later that night, attempted to run away, but was caught by her father, who beat her relentlessly until he was too tired to lift his hand against his own battered flesh and blood; after she healed, she began an affair with a boy in her village, and encouraged him to run away with her, to which he reluctantly agreed, but it was mainly due to wanderlust, as he had no real intention of doing so, and so put her off.

A month hence, she was sold for twenty cows, two camels, an old rusted wagon—complete with two aged oxen—and ten bales of hay. Her father beamed with pride at the deal he had secured from his forty-nine-year-old soon-to-be brother-in-law.

Justice is an idea that is born in a tiny seed and is planted in every desert and field, every mountain and pasture, every valley and plateau, but dies without nourishment from selfless dedication of those courageous souls who are willing to embrace it at a harsh cost; to live, it needs those willing to not step aside, not fall back, not walk away forever; to grow, it puts forth slender roots to pierce the noble hearts of its paramours and inspire them to sacrifice for the furthering of its ideal; to flourish, the sacrifice of the few must inspire in the hearts and minds of the many to firmly establish that without it, there can be no peace or harmony in the world. Justice is born with every child, part of their inner landscape of concepts and realities; yea, all seek it for themselves, but for others, already in chains, perhaps it is ignored, and forgotten, so that only a few will follow its shining path to encompass all Mankind.

Those who have plenty will risk little for Justice they have long had; those who have very little will risk their very lives to taste its magic elixir. Kiupita had tasted the sweet nectar of Justice, if only in her lofty dreams, and so, when she was bound and gagged and then hoisted onto a dusty wooden cart like a wild hog and delivered to her soon-to-be-husband, who smiled lewdly as he saw his young, fleshly prize, the horror of every societal wrong that enslaved her aligned itself in her passionate heart: first, and the treachery of it all—for youth seeks youth, passionate fires burn for each other, virgin flowers grow together; then, the debauchery of it all—that she was to be bequeathed to a fat, greasy, unkempt, mongrel thing of decaying oldness, like when an old, gnarled male dog is mated with a flowering young female and sabotages all the natural Beauty in the world; and finally the iniquity of it all: that her culture condoned and applauded this unseemly act merely because it was beholden to an ancient ritual that seemed to live and breathe and grow with every injury and outrage done to young girls.

She raged against his pockmarked, hairy, grizzly, sloppy, sloth-filled body with all the inner strength of her blazing youth and the available serum of Justice now coursing in her hot blood; alas, she was a child still, and needing to be about the business children attend to: giggling and dreaming of boys her age, and attending school and enjoying the intricacies that the teenage years bring, of simply being, simply marveling at the joys of life, simply loving life and discovering herself and the world around her, before the responsibilities of adulthood and family weighed heavily upon her and increased her roles in society; yet, here she was, battling the whole society of her native people, where even, in this atrocious war, the elder females—in their blind faith to obey without scrutiny the practices born of a cruel past, and thus continuing to perpetuate a shame upon their progeny—proceeded to tug and pull her, with their bloody hands joined to the bloodied hands of their ignorant and savage ancestors, violently down to the hard, barren ground and take out their shameful true weapon of mass destruction, which was any instrument used to bring wanton terror into the hearts and minds of the female human species. So, now, the four village women, who were now mere automatons, faithful to a faithless paradigm of oppressing their own kind, sought to cut and snip and mutilate the tender area on the screaming girl that would normally allow her to feel pleasure during moments of sexual congress; once the deed was accomplished, the women, dressed in their proud native dress, continued to be amazed that the girl had not been taken care of long ago, and boasted about how proud they were to have been "fixed," so long ago. The girl was taken away to a private place where she might further transgress the boundaries of childhood into adulthood.

Riva was to be next, but when they came for her, she struggled mightily against them, and soon lay drenched in sweat and shame in the midst of the haughty crowd of sneering women. "In America," she thought, not able to exhale this loitering vapor out of her injured mind, "girls do as they please; they have freedoms; they do not submit to such degradation, they do not; they are not molested by those who have power only over each other; they are their own…" She sobbed as she lay bruised and battered on the field of dirt and weeds and cow dung, her dreams of romance and a husband of love, and babies and happiness, becoming evanescent. Cold water was splashed upon her. "Up, you troublesome wretch," an elder woman shouted, hustling the limp girl to be cleaned and prepared for the great event.

But Justice, sweet, sweet Justice, blew her the fragrance of Law, of Natural Law and God's Law, into her feverish, desperate heart, and she reared up against her captors, screaming, "In America, girls are not molested by old hags who have power only over each other and exercise it in tyranny," and she spat at them and hissed at them, and threw rocks and dirt at them, and then dashed out into the black, starry night toward what had once been her illusory solace. As she approached the small thatched hut, her birthplace, she felt as if she were struggling against the raw waves of betrayal emanating from her home. "But I mustn't go back there, either," she thought. O, how alone she felt, walking in the inky, impenetrable darkness of a culture that willingly imprisoned her entire gender, to shape her, and control her, and subdue her; and yet, how could she deny its existence? She ran now on the swirling currents of hope that Justice would shield her from retaliation, that her own kin might now realize how wrong they had been to acquiesce in silence about her plight; she wandered into the home of her aunt, declaring her intent to run away from her captor and cross over into new lands. "He wished to humiliate me," she screamed, collapsing upon the dirt floor; "my own father wanted this for me—and every girl who does not protest encourages these barbaric acts against us; O, what will I do, where can I go? Save me!"

Her aunt picked up the frightened girl and placed her on a small chair. "Riva," she said, softly, "listen to me," bending down in front of her; "you need to close your eyes, and take deep breaths, and think of where you are now." Her words were like a calming salve. "These men are monsters." She thought of her own coerced genital mutilation and subsequent marriage to an older man, but she had been saved by the man's early death, and had managed to avoid another unpleasant marriage by her outspoken opinions on the natural right of women—and subsequently, no man had desired her, for what they could not overcome, they reasoned would overcome them.

But the intricate web upon which her culture rested had already felt a tremor caused by Riva, and eavesdropping neighbors, who were fervent supporters of having their own genitals destroyed if only to please their filthy husbands, had scurried off like gossiping old hens to curry favor with those who rejoiced over every mutilation as if they were following divine law that would ultimately reward them for their unconscious zealotry.

In due time, then, these withered elder women of the village amassed like a lynch mob outside of this humble domicile of Riva's aunt, and soon burst in. "Get up, you rebellious brat," the oldest of them howled, grabbing Riva, despite the aunt's fervent protestations, by her long, beautiful black hair, and hurling her outside. "You will be taught not to run away from us again." The girl was held down and one of the women began to beat her with a leather whip.

The entire village woke up.

The four elder women, standing in front of the pleased groom-to-be, slowly circled the curled-up girl as the villagers gathered round; there, the parents of Riva, who, after being told of the circumstances before them, spat largely upon their own daughter; there, in the small encircling crowd, stood trembling her friends, sobbing and lamenting a similar fate; and there, in the dreaded silence, stood a sobbing Naomi, held back by her aunt.

The violent whipping continued, but now Riva was held down by four more women. "You will obey," the women chanted, each taking a turn on the whip, and then looking with bold authority at the young and sobbing girls around them. "You will obey," they grunted, and crack went the whip on the bare legs of the victim. "Obey," they screamed, like wild creatures, and crack went the black leather whip on the bare arms of the crying girl; "if you had had this done when a child…if only we had not listened to those interfering missionaries, who bribed us to go against our faith, and brought us humiliation and shame."

When this atrocity was over—done without anesthesia, and using a razor dulled only by the last ten unwilling victims, and given the good seal of approval by the entire adult residence of this still Stone-Age village, save the Aunt—Naomi broke free and fell upon her beloved sister.

Riva, weeping, was bloodied, but not bowed; battered, but not broken; bested, but not beaten, and rose up in her fiery defiance and stood tall in her willful disobedience, as she cried to her tormentors, "Too late, too late, too late," and she flung her head back and became fully erect, despite her puny physical wounds, for her spiritual powers were stronger; "I have been with a boy; yes, yes, yes," she screamed, looking round at the shocked and disgusted faces of her accusers, "I have been with a boy of my own age, and not with some dirty, filthy old man who lusts after my young flesh," and she spat largely on the ground. "Thief, thief, thief!" and she pointed to the glaring faces about her: "Stealing my life because you are ignorant peasants," and then she shouted so loud and hard at them that they were startled, and fell back, as she pointed at them; "shame, shame, shame on all of your black hearts, you horrible, wretched, pathetic, ugly old hags."

"The girl is no good now, for she is poisoned," the soon-to-be bridegroom now complained to his once-future father-in-law; "I will please take back my camels and oxen."

The father cursed, and cursed Riva. "She cost us a good living," he moaned to his wife. "She is no good to us, now, either."

"Get up, Naomi," her mother commanded, grabbing her daughter by the arm. "Your sister has shamed us, and now she is dead to us."

"No," Naomi cried, struggling to get away.

"You will obey," her mother shouted, yanking her up and slapping her and then dragging her.

"You think you own us," Riva shouted, approaching her parents, "but we are not born for your pleasure, but for our own sakes; you do not have the right to treat us like property."

The rest of the village barred her way from following her family, and so she turned and ran clear away from them.

Later that night, Naomi heard her parents' plans of marketing her now, just as if Riva had been found to be a sick dog and now Naomi a healthy one, and she went numb as the chilling specter of marriage to the old, fat, lascivious man spilled its diseased guts inside her spinning head.

She escaped while others slept, still wearing her bloodstained clothes, first searching for her sister, running to other huts, running away from screeching voices, running wildly until she no longer recognized the terrain nor the people, running now toward the shining light of the full moon, running on and on and on until she finally stumbled and fell, but then got up and ran and ran some more, falling, weeping, rising, walking, hearing searching voices, and then running, running, on and on and on until finally she lay from exhaustion and fell to rest. For three days, she journeyed into the boiling desert, eventually crumbling into the arms of her now and future savior, Kofi.

And what became of her beloved sister, she who yearned for those simple yet elegant joys promised and freely given to young girls in Democracies the world over?

No one wanted her; she was not even allowed to stay with her aunt, who was beaten for harboring the girl; and so she stumbled from village to village, a social leper, as disgraced as an unrepentant criminal who had committed unheard-of crimes. She was fifteen years of age, and utterly alone, starving and cold and feverish, when men, not rebels, not an army of criminals, not a band of marauding madmen, but men of her own ilk who perceived women as fallen and lost and redeemed only by their association with them, and who knew her: it was they who found her and escorted her to a small home and set her up in a room where she was beaten and coerced to lend her flesh to the fulfillment of their endless lusts. She endured a fortnight in this insane asylum, until she managed to regain her senses, and then, rather easily, hung herself with a long, white cloth strip of her dress. And what was the reaction of the men but a shrug of the shoulders, and to take down the corpse and throw it into a pit and bury it, and climb back comfortably and with ease into a world that sees women as a species between man and ape, equal to a slave, to be bought or sold, bartered or traded, with the rights of a donkey or camel, an object that is a means to an end for the sake of almighty man of this and any region that calculated the life of woman with such utter disdain and disregard.

And somewhere in the world, there rants a smug scholar who states that we must honor all cultures and their customs: "Who are we to judge their actions through our eyes?" But it was too late to ask Riva; had she known she would not die in vain, perhaps she would have died easier, or chosen to live; but that is not reality, and reality is now as she lay upon countless other corpses of her sisters around the world in a mass grave that gets deeper and deeper every hot day that is not filled with the tender mercies accorded to human beings at the least by the right of natural law, and fills up more and more every cold night when fellow human beings ignore the plight of their brothers and sisters, and turn to the fanatical strains of errant philosophies or faiths that violate the sanctity of the natural rights of human beings.

But this is not a story about those who willingly accept the indefensible crimes of any society or simply turn their collective faces away and stick their shrinking souls into a convenient dark and safe place; no, definitively not—it is about those who see the world without borders, one world, one people, one nation, and who will risk all to defend one set of immutable, inviolate, infinite laws of Justice that govern their every word and deed and thought, and that, without hesitation or exception.

One Man Comes

When all the world seems destitute of human compassion, and the cherished love of humanity seeps into the scorched, hard earth; when the world seems devoid of law, and Justice evaporates on the lips of innocent victims, if two people are able to find each other and love each other and stay loyal to each other long enough, it is conceivable they might create a world of Hope and Justice and Love. Kofi and Naomi were stitching a universe together from a paradigm hardened by prejudice and ignorance, atom by molecule by element, by thought and word and deed, allowing the natural elements of Love and Hope and Justice to guide them. They extracted these principles and laws from the limitless panorama of life that had been cast down, crushed, and thoroughly mixed together, gathered it and sought to put it back again without knowledge of its boundaries to its south or north, east or west; and as no facet of life stands alone, but supported by other concepts and experience, they filled in the substantial unknown vistas with what little experience they had, and through the glorious eyes that independence brings.

"There is the world and us," he would say to her, smiling, holding her hand as they walked.

"And we, the better half," she would say, gleefully.

The constraints of society now existed in a void outside of the virgin sphere that inhabited them.

"We can start our own village," she would say.

"My Queen," he would return.

"My King," she would reply, and kiss him affectionately.

They expressed their fondness and love and devotion to each other through romantic commingling; their young bodies flushed delight from these frequent and intense interludes; it was their world, their rules, their choices, and they abided by their own judgments on any rules broken; she sobbed, he held her; he shouted and asked for forgiveness, and she hugged him; every tear dried, every pain soothed, every problem solved. Freedom tingled in their joyful hearts like a new birthing song.

A year passed, and their love for each other grew like a healthy red rose bathed by the golden rays of the sun as they came to know each other and rely upon the other and respect each other. They worked to survive, joining caravans that were going to labor camps; they worked in the International Red Cross camps, distributing food; they worked on farms, hauling produce to market; they worked in the mines; they helped to haul the ubiquitous jerricans that the people filled with precious water, which the women then tied to their backs or balanced on top of their heads, or the men hauled the larger ones on their pushcarts, as many as fifty cans, consisting of over two and fifty gallons, four hundred pounds total, for many leagues, while they strained and sweated under their taskmaster, the unrelenting, scorching sun; yet, this was water that was often infected with the dreaded Guinea worm, the "fiery serpent," so named as it moves throughout its host body, and it was in such places that Kofi and Naomi learned how to properly detach this parasite from the human body as it burst through the skin. Yes, they would watch the villagers, after noticing a blister on the victim, submerge the affected area in water to entice the creature to lay its eggs, and then take the slimy creature and carefully wrap it around a stick, sometimes for hours, or working on it intermittently for days, or even weeks, until it was totally free of the body, for otherwise, it would break, and if its body were to stay inside the host and putrefy, it might cause a problem if it were wrapped around a vital area like a bone or vein; but even then, when the Guinea worm was successfully removed, if it happened to come out at a joint, there was always the chance that the joint would be permanently disabled.

And they were always careful to tell the people around them that they were brother and sister, for they had discerned from listening to their elders that unmarried couples were not allowed to be physically intimate; consequently, their tender flesh united in the dark shadows and veiled places, thus heightening the excitement and thrill of pouring all of their energy and lust for life into pleasing each other.

They hid in abandoned grass huts when rebels came to murder; they hid in abandoned mines when the government troops came to slaughter; they hid in small holes and larger holes and behind rocks and in front of sloping hills when the rebels and the government troops butchered at will. They coupled after human life around them had been eviscerated as easily as one throws twigs into a fire to increase its furnace, thus ameliorating this unrestrained vileness and gore that sought to encircle their hearts and burn it to soot and ash.

One day they came upon a smoldering field and beheld bloating, rotting corpses: women who had been often and over a long period of time raped and then tortured and mutilated, and children who had been many times raped, and then tortured and mutilated, and men who had been tortured and mutilated with an unmatched zeal and want for delivering pain and destruction by their assassins; and as they breathed in the acrid stench of death into their flaring nostrils, they wept as they held each other close, walking past the bodies of people they had once lived with; but to run from such a massacre would only invite nightmares for them, so they forced themselves to look at every body, kneeling in front of each victim and certain to say the name of the person, and praying and blessing them. But then, Naomi looked up, her ears pricked up.

"Did you hear that?" she said, standing up suddenly.

Kofi looked about, straining to hear as he too stood up.

"Again," she whispered, pointing toward the end of the refugee camp, and they advanced with the greatest circumspection until they determined the origin of the noise.

"Why, it's children," she exclaimed, running to the two crying infants, and sweeping them into her arms; "you are safe now, my darlings."

But they were not safe, for each had been infected with the ubiquitous Guinea worm, but Kofi and Naomi, having seen its removal done so often, were able to extract it without harm from the two children; and thus, a bond between the four was born, one that is rarely created in modern industrial nations, for it was a bond begun by having to fend for each other, without outside help, without anyone caring for them, and by caring for themselves, and saving each other, as it once was everywhere, so very long ago.

Kofi did not know how the children would be fed. "But had not my parents somehow managed?" he thought, watching his young mistress coming toward him with the two-year-olds; he wanted to weep as he thought of his own family. "But I mustn't, not now, she wants me, she expects me to be strong—like a man," he thought, holding fast the small, dirty, naked children in his skinny arms.

"You are the father now, and I, the mother," Naomi said, proudly, as they walked away from the stinking carnage.

It is an enigma how those starving and struggling to survive in a brutal world can inherit lost souls and adequately clothe and feed and protect them, but it is undeniably true: those things that did not lead to sustenance and once had seemed important now fell away as Kofi and Naomi sharpened their resolve for all of their new family to survive.

When, in the past, they had walked warily past villages that had been bombed and wiped out by marauding armies, now they boldly ventured into them, seeking any shred of food and material the conqueror worms had left behind; when, in the past, they had conceived dead bodies as taboo, they now considered them gold mines for bits of food, a hidden coin, a piece of clothing, anything visible that would fill their need; restrictions on perilous ventures fell away as they skirted along the periphery of the battle zones, invading rebel and government camps when they were deserted and stealing food and personal necessities. "We must take from those who created our family," Kofi would often say to his young sweetheart and the two children, who, although they did not understand fully, would nod their round heads almost as if they understood and approved.

One day, at the beginning of Summer, they came into an encampment that existed between the porous borders of two countries, one in the throes of tyranny, the other in the throes of a struggling Democracy; the people had arrived here after having fled government troops and the rebels who had worked for the President of the country. The International Red Cross frequented the tiny enclave, bringing canvas tents and woolen blankets, food and medicine, but more importantly, hope and love.

Kofi and Naomi, with the two children standing beside them, introduced themselves as brother and sister, and the tiny ones as orphans of war.

"What is that to us," the village elder said; "how are you unique in the world? We are all nomads, outcasts from even our own villages; we do not have enough food even for ourselves, so back to your wanderings." He was dressed in a jellabiya, a long, loose robe of white with an immah, a white scarf, and a sarwal, loose pants, and walked with a wooden cane; he had absolute authority over his own people. "God will take care of you if you follow his sacred laws," he said, waving his hand over them and, turning his back on them, began to walk away.

"Children." They heard a kind female voice, seeming to surround the brutality of the lingering words and subdue them. "We have food for you."

The village elder glared at the Red Cross woman, holding out his fragile, wrinkled hand. "How can we feed them when we haven't food enough for our own?"

"It is all our food, Mikasi," the woman replied, her deep British accent coloring the air with an aroma that unsettled him: that of Liberty. She smiled and hugged the four youngsters as if they were her own.

Mikasi spoke in bitter tones. "I recognize them—they are from the tribe of Masalit, they are the bane of our land, who have caused all who are not Arab to be persecuted," and he departed, scowling.

She had learned to avoid confrontations with anyone she considered unreasonable and not subject to alteration in their dogmatic, intellectual doctrines, and by speaking succinctly and to the point, and never denying their sacred beliefs, but neither embracing them, thus leaving someone like Mikasi no vulnerable area in her to attack. The man who ran the Red Cross here, who was now elsewhere, had taught her how to deal with the religious zealots, not only of this region, but of any region.

"Come, youngsters." She spoke in their native tongue of Kush Arabic. "Come with me," and she, holding the hands of the two toddlers, led them to a tent wherein lay in meager piles boxes of rations. She passed out the soft biscuits and poured a bowl of hot lentil soup for her newest guests, and watched them eat heartily. "So, tell me your story; where are you from?" she began, folding her hands and sitting upon a white canvas bag of mesa flour; she had learned long ago not to ask specific questions, such as the whereabouts of family members — for a child to be alone here, meant the family was dead, there.

"Do the armies come through here?" Kofi asked, scooping up the lentil soup with the yellow biscuit.

"No, dear," the blond-haired woman replied, "they do not come to the border areas."

She nodded behind herself. "The armies of the country on the other side will not permit intrusions into their sovereign territory."

Kofi looked up at her, curiosity about his face. "What is that, 'sovereign'?"

"It can mean a few things; but here, it means a country that is independent—that means no other country controls them; do you understand?"

"Oh," he replied, nodding, and eating some more, and then said, "Well, we are going that way," and he pointed toward the border; "we have a plan," and he looked to Naomi, and both of them smiled, and he took her hand.

Naomi smiled. "It is a very simple plan, kind lady—to walk until there are no more armies, where there are no more wars." She tilted her head in innocence. "Surely, there must be such a place in all of Africa?"

"And if not in Africa, then we will go anywhere in the whole wide world to find such a wonderful country," Kofi said.

"Yes, Kofi and Naomi, there are such places," the woman began, "in Africa, and in the whole wide world; but you just cannot just walk through each country until you find one; it is not practical."

"And what else are we to do?" Kofi said, angrily. "Stay here and wait to be killed by rebels or government troops? We want to be happy—how can we be happy if we have to hide all day from bad men and hunt for food like dogs?"

"Miss, what of your country—is it good? Did you have to live like a wild animal when you were a child?" Naomi asked.

"I come from the United Kingdom, Great Britain—and yes, it is a good country; and no, I did not have to live as you have; I had a good home and family."

"How far to this Great Britain, Miss?" Naomi asked, in childlike wonder, nudging the arm of Kofi. "Maybe we would like to go there."

Eleanor smiled and placed her slender hand on the girl's bony shoulder. "Very far."

Kofi smiled. "We have time, do we not, family?" he said, looking to his adopted brother and sister, who both laughed for the sheer joy of eating and talking without anguish and fear mixed in with their food and drink; and to hear such simple, joyous laughter reminds even those who have grown older of the simple pleasures in life, and so Eleanor laughed, and so too did Kofi and Naomi.

Eleanor placed the children in a tent and bid them goodnight.

During the warm, breezy night, Kofi and Naomi crept stealthily out of their green canvas house and crept quietly to the perimeter of the camp, where they engaged in acts of sexual congress.

But in the exhaustion and ecstasy of their coupling, there arose a strange dread, and both of them soon felt a strong grip upon their persons, whereupon they were violently dragged across the rough terrain amid the growing tumult in the camp.

"Defilers, defilers," a chant began by the people, "defilers of the holy book," the chant finished.

Cut and battered and bruised, the young lovers, naked still, were deposited in the center of the encampment by the chief elder, Mikasi, and two of his willing henchmen.

"You see before you a harlot and her lover, masquerading as brother and sister, so they can carry on their immoral acts." He spat upon them as the agitated crowd of the faithful observed the improvised court proceedings. "This is why we are attacked; this is why we are chased from our homes; we allow the wicked among us to practice their sins, corrupting our youth." The crowd shouted its hearty approval. "To disobey the sacred laws of the Holy Scripture is to invite the wrath of the Almighty upon us; I say to you, my people, cleanse this camp of these two defilers and bring the blessings of God upon us."

"Death, death," the violent refrain began, the people having already become as one in spirit and mind on this issue, and accepting of the indictment delivered by their holy leader.

Mikasi knew that the longer he waited, the greater the chance of failure, so he hastened his quest. "I will lead them," he raged.

"Death by stoning, as it is written in the Holy Scriptures," he shouted, gesturing to his loyal men to gather up the requisite ammunition to carry out the execution.

The two young lovers lay like two frightened lambs in the midst of a war council of ravenous wolves.

"No one is going to stone anyone," a voice of surpassing authority cut into his lingering order, and then the woman to whom it belonged appeared, cool, calm, and striding slowly toward them. She had been outside the camp when she had heard the commotion, and had still not reached them when she continued, "God has not ordered the stoning of the two children," she continued, her face severe, her voice austere, and then, coming upon the children, put over them a blanket she had picked up on the way; "second of all," and now she addressed the entire, agitated crowd, "you are under the jurisdiction of the United Nations, and they will have no murders this night or any other night," and she looked directly at her chief nemesis, and her voice was strong and proud, "and neither will I." She stood before the children like a mother protector, a shield she would not relinquish easily. Eleanor of Britannia looked boldly round. "You'll bring no harm to any Innocent in the presence of the International Red Cross; we are here to prevent such tragedies, not allow them."

Mikasi spoke as if his words were strummed daily in the high vault of heaven by angelic beings. "Your people are across the border, Western invader, Western—infidel."

Two men grabbed her from behind, securing her arms, but she stomped the bare foot of one man and kicked the shin of another, and presently she was free.

"This isn't your affair, white woman."

"All injustice is my affair, Mikasi," she cried, bending down toward the children, but then a large stone smote the back of her head, and she fell, dazed.

"Take the heretic outside of the ring of judgment," Mikasi commanded his loyalists, "and there, she will know how we discipline rebellious women." He turned his attention to the children who still embraced each other in terror under the white blanket, and motioned to the others to pick up their punitive stones. He raised his stone up as he looked on high and cried, "In the name of God, we cleanse this camp of the unrighteous," and reared back his arm to heave the missile.

But the rock was lifted easily out of his grasp, and he turned around while shock came upon him.

"Big rock," the man said, in a matter-of-fact tone, yet a tone that spoke of authority and power; he was holding the object in his hand as he walked toward the two trembling children, who still huddled together with hands over their heads; "there'll be no stoning today; everyone back to their tents."

"This is not your business!" Mikasi shouted.

"Well," began the man with equanimity filling his voice, "the Council may take up this matter in the morning, but now, the hour is getting late," and already, the gentleness and certainty of his words had cooled the bubbling morass of insanity and settled the minds of the adherents to Mikasi, and thus, he separated himself from him, by leading with the spirit of reason and goodness; he then gestured behind himself, "and besides, we have corn-meal and cassava and lentils to unpack; and, oh, I forgot—letters from the province are here: many letters from your families," but he said it with such a genuine smile and nod of his head that the once-maddened and enraged people paid no heed to him when he bent down and helped up the children, for they were already heading toward the food and letters. "Roka, would you bring me another blanket; they must be cold." He stroked the heads of the children, and then told, casually, four men and three women to help with the unpacking of the radios. It was this final announcement that diffused the lingering anger in the crowd and dispersed the rest of the remaining few toward the newest shipments, that they might hear of news concerning their plight. "John," he said, casually, "check on Eleanor; she seems to have a nasty bump on her head," and so John did, the very man who had thrown the rock; and then this new man looked once again upon the children, and smiled. "We have to confront our sins with honesty, or fail as a people," he whispered, helping them up.

After proper clothes were brought to Kofi and Naomi, and they were attended to by two Red Cross personnel who had just arrived, the man with the brown beard and imperturbable manner walked over to his fallen friend, who had already received aid from her fellow Red Cross coworkers.

"It's the ones you can't see you have to worry about," he said, inspecting her wound as she sat before him.

"Enemies in front of me, how novel," she moaned; "I outran the pauser, reason, and jumped into the fray," and, rubbing her head, "this will help me to remember I am not in some provincial town in merry old England, taking a summer walk along the river Thames."

"Well, Eleanor," he said, gently helping her stand, and then, warmly embracing her, whispered, "don't let your proud English heritage get too bruised."

"But I can't help but want them punished for what they were going to do to those innocent children; and as for me, well, I know what I want done…"

They were walking back toward the Red Cross tents, he supporting her with his strong arms around her shoulders, when he said, "We all want Justice," and then shook his brown-haired head, "but how do you convince a country where beliefs that have been practiced for centuries are morally wrong, and therefore indict them as willing accomplices in those crimes, and worse still, accessories, who aid by spreading this fanatical doctrine; our primary mission here, our only mission, is to bring succor to those in need; we are caretakers, not revolutionaries; it is our vow, our cross to bear, to stay between the conflicts, and judge only in our minds."

"Yes, I know, but still, I want Justice, sweet, sweet, avenging Justice."

He was silent, thinking of his past. "Justice is in Heaven, Eleanor; here, we have the collective weight of unprincipled men who function with the help of too many willing allies to crush the world; so, we help those who are crushed to the bottom, and if we can help them rise, why, then, we have done a great service to Mankind." He stopped walking and looked directly into her luminous eyes. "There must always be those who are willing to join in the good fight not with bullets and brawn, but selfless devotion of love for their fellow human being."

"But I am here now, Robert, I am here, on earth, with these unprincipled men and women all around me; is it not said that Justice is the rightful sovereign of the world?"

"Yes," he returned, sensing her increasing frustration, and so put his arms around her as they walked back to the tent, as a father might do to comfort his anxious daughter, "but you have to remember our singular role here—it is not to dispense judgment, but help the weak and infirm, and defend those Innocents that we can; to save a life through the blessings of peace, even if it is through supplication and cajoling, is to be placed as a pleasing aroma before the altar of our Faith."

"But is this not judgment, Robert, defending children from murderers like Mikasi?"

"Yes," he said, nodding his head. "I suppose it is, but it is without violence, and it is the charge of the International Red Cross to help lift up the fallen, give solace to the wounded, care for the dying."

She stopped and held him out from her, staring into his handsome face. "You are like me, Robert; you want to see thugs like Mikasi punished, who tries to blame other tribes for his tribe being persecuted; you want Justice as much as any man—no, more, because unlike most men, you have truly seen what the insidious nature of injustice and how it spreads like a narcotic among people."

"Yes," he said, quickly, "I do, I do want social justice for every wrong, for every child hurt, for every woman violated, but it isn't my role, not here, not now, not in the vow I have taken; these people will have to deal with their own debasers, not us, because if outsiders impose our will upon them without their invitation, it becomes one more problem, one more Westerner to blame, and the Red Cross would lose its credibility as a neutral observer that proffers aid to any who need it, regardless of their creed or philosophy; no, Eleanor, I want to help with the sick and dying, and leave the Law to the winners..."

"You can't believe that!"

"Oh, but I do; otherwise, I'd have a gun in my hand; and where would we be if peacekeepers became makers of war? Who would tend to the dying on the battlefield, as we did at Napata last month; there, we moved unmolested, because we had the symbol of neutrality with us, and if the other side needs our aid, they had better respect us, or they will lie dying in their own blood." He inhaled deeply and gazed into the clear, cerulean sky, and then said, in a profound state, "Go out at once into the streets and lanes of the city and bring in here the poor and crippled and the blind and lame." He looked again to her. "If not where, where then; if not us, who then; if not now, when then?"

She was frowning, as the frustrated young will do when they seek a rebuttal against philanthropic ideals they cannot combat, and said, "Well, you were right about Napata; but," she was still forming an opinion, and hesitated for a moment, "in this land, we have groups who do not respect the authority of the Red Cross, and would love to kill our people just to show that they are no respecters of law save their own, and because, in their mania, they think they will win, and will not ever need our humanitarian service or be dragged before the Court of Justice for recompense of their crimes."

He smiled, and placed his strong arms around her shoulders once more. "That is why I like you, Eleanor—your unbridled and undying passion for Virtue." Even as he watched her smile, and knew he had redirected and cast her abject worries into the sleeping shadows behind her, he struggled to believe what he had told her.

United Nations soldiers, in their multilayered uniforms and smart hats, paraded about the various camps, and even though they were hamstrung from firing their weapons upon the indigenous populations, they had a curious effect upon the villagers by causing them to lay to rest any anxious thoughts against their enemies.

Certain forces maintained a triad of shifting power in Southern Kush: the black Muslims and Christians and animists, mostly agriculturalists, who were more concerned with clan and tribe, and eschewed the idea of an Islamic state; the Arab government of Southern Kush—who were somewhat independent although still a part of Kush and who had recently embraced Islamic law, and their army; and the newly arrived Arab pastoralists who had left their own region due to drought and famine, and who had begun to encroach upon the western provinces of the non-Arabic Zaghawa, Masalit, and Fur tribes, the latter of which had no love for these Arabs.

The Arab government of Southern Kush and its army, and the Arab army of raiders, the Militia, coordinated their efforts to exterminate or flush their enemies from the central and southern regions, but rarely did they visit the border regions for fear of intervention from unfriendly countries and opposition groups; now, however, when bloodlust cradled them in its intoxicating grip, they could not refrain from shifting their strategy, especially when ripe opportunities appeared, just like a flock of ducks flying over and presenting themselves easily to the crouched hunter who sits in a marsh of tall reeds. But a fourth player also had emerged: the many rebel groups who had momentarily held the southern capital to establish a non-Arab government, but who had been recently defeated.

It was October and the morning blazed a red haze across the distant horizon; it is said that on the flat plain of a compact desert floor, a skilled craftsman versed in the art of scouting can hear the soft steps of game a mile away; thus, it came as no surprise when many of the men in the encampment were aroused by the intuitive knowledge of something fast and furious, and vast in number, coming their way.

"It is the Militia," the men shouted, looking about for escape.

"To the border," some screamed.

"No," Robert shouted, coming from his tent, and quickly assessing the dangers. "The land to the border is too far, and unprotected." He ran toward the frightened assemblage of people. "There has been talk of government troops on the other side pushing back fleeing villagers."

"That is just talk," Mikasi shouted; "if the Militia find us here, we are all dead."

"Dead you'll be if you leave for the border; stay here, for we have the protected status of the Red Cross and United Nations soldiers."

"Useless," Mikasi returned, his eyes aflame with anger; "more colorful targets for the Militia; to the border," he yelled, sweeping his long, black-robed arm over his head.

"They're coming," a man cried, running down a small hill, "a mile away."

Panic ate into the already weakened resolve of the agitated crowd.

"We must go," Mikasi shouted, and led a large contingent of villagers toward the southern border. "Let these fools slow down the Militia with their worthless lives."

Forty-two people fled; sixty-three people stayed.

The thundering footsteps permeated the dry air, causing emotional mayhem in the minds of the trembling villagers. "Should we go?" some asked. "No," some stated; "we must stay with Mr. Heimdall." "Why? Is it too late to go?" others shouted in their delirium, and some began to ran toward the southern border, but were restrained by their loved ones.

Marauders—whom the people spoke of in whispers, who had been cutting a murderous swath across the burning land; desert pirates who brought a new edict flown with a black flag and an image of a white skull and cross-bones that was proudly soaked with the blood of their victims—were now approaching.

The Militia surrounded the encampment, sending a few soldiers on camels after the escaping villagers. A black-bearded man on horseback and wearing black and white flowing robes, his head covered in white cloth and in his arms a long, black steel rifle, came toward Robert. "Who is in charge here?" he demanded, his black eyes burning with indignation as his twenty-five men positioned themselves near tents and on the periphery of the camp.

Robert, with an absence of fear in his countenance, walked forward, speaking in the man's native language, Kush Arabic. "No one is in charge here; we have villagers, International Red Cross and United Nation personnel, all living here peacefully; it is peace I have, and peace I offer you."

The man sneered contempt and bellowed, "I was going to allow your leader to live and bring our message to the rest of your foreign swine, and it is this," he rose up on his black steed and shouted, "there is no peace or safety for the Masalit, Zaghawa, and Fur people, not near the border, not across the border; our Muslim ally has taken siege of the southern capital of infidels—Islamic law rules now!" He interlaced his thin, dark hands, glared at Robert, and hissed, "We are under Islamic law, as we have always been; we have you in a trap." Gunshots were heard in the near distance, bringing pleasure to the fat face of the man. "The end is at hand for the Zaghawa and the Fur and the Masalit." He motioned to his men to dismount.

"You have no authority to be here," Robert said. "We have UN monitors and Red Cross people who make reports; I urge you to leave peaceably."

"Make reports?" he laughed, looking at his smiling adjutants. "Do dead people make reports, eh?"

"You would not kill them."

He gestured about. "And what law, meddling Westerner, is here to stop me? Here," he shouted, "we are law," and he pointed with sweeping gestures all about, and then to the man in front of him, "not you!"

One of his own men asked about the United Nation soldiers, and the leader laughed. "What laws you supposedly civilized nations have; you send soldiers here to protect people, but will not let them fire a single shot; now, there is true diplomacy, and that is why the West is so corrupt and weak; and look," he sat up again on his sweaty horse, "where are those UN cowards, those women, eh? Fled to the border with the other cowards, I am sure." He spat. "Dead cowards now, I am quite sure. You, white woman," he shouted, his coal-black eyes sparkling lust, "you will fetch a handsome sum in the slave market." He was stroking his long, black beard now. "We will not damage you too much before you go before the bidders."

Robert held Eleanor fast to himself.

The leader motioned to his men to begin the process of conquest, first on foot, and later upon their camels and horses; and then he looked back to the two people before him, nodding as does the one who has no doubts as to the outcome of a carefully planned-out slaughter of Innocents.

The Heroic Quest Begins

But then a voice, hard and cold and clear, savage and strong and scintillating, rang out like the peal of a brass bell: "Who stands before you, but Sun Tzu, Clausewitz, and Jomini," and then emitted a satisfying grunt, "and in the name of International Law, I am ordering you to cease and desist your present hostile activities, and immediately leave the premises." Everyone in attendance looked about, expecting to see a new army of men coming into focus; alas, it was only three of the United Nations soldiers approaching the Militia. The men, walking in a casual manner, planted themselves next to Robert.

The big, well-muscled soldier issued a knowing glance at Eleanor, and then created a grim mask that promised grievous harm as he looked up at the mounted rebels. "I am looking at what I do not believe," he said, shaking his head; "you are in willful defiance of my plain and succinct verbal command."

The leader, stroking his beard, his eyes illuminated by amusement, laughed, which ignited his men to do likewise, and then said, after tossing his head back and looking down at the soldier as if he were addressing an impudent slave who blocked his path, "You think you represent the UN soldiers? You imperialist dog, you represent the corrupt arm of the Western powers who interfere in our affairs; and who are you but three blind beggars," and he gesticulated about, "and we are so many? And you," he pointed harshly, "who is not even allowed to fire his weapon; why, you are like a man wearing a dress—hiding behind what cannot save you." He spat at the feet of the three soldiers.

Once again, the soldier glanced at Eleanor and then winked at her, and she felt a strong flush of physical attraction for this noble-looking, fair-haired youth. Looking again to his adversary, he smiled, and then said, in a thick, Irish accent, "You must have mistaken us for United Nations workers," and then he and the other men removed their outer layer of clothing to reveal bullet belts and knives and a Glock 17 pistol all about their person, and concurrently raised their Heckler & Koch G36 combat rifles they had concealed and pointed them at the leader and his men, and then he said in a harsh growl, "I know how brave you are about having others sacrifice themselves for your holy wars, but I have a distinct hunch that you, in particular, want to live."

The leader of this Militia unit waved away the rifles of his men that were pointed at the soldiers, and then smiled. "Do you think you will live today? Kill me, and you die; let us go, and you die."

"Never trust a man who answers his own questions," the youth said to his fellows.

In the distance, five riders, coming from the direction of the fleeing villagers, were galloping back to the camp.

"More of my loyal men to fight, fool," the leader said.

But as the men approached, they threw off their white robes to reveal attire similar to the three soldiers.

"So," the leader snarled, "now you have eight—humph!" and he gestured about, "while we have thirty-one, still."

The soldier with the long, flaxen hair and muscular arms raised his right hand in small concentric circles, and presently, fifteen more of his men appeared outside of the encampment, surrounding the Militia who were on the inside of the periphery. He thrust his hand in the direction the raiders had come from.

"You will die!" shouted the leader.

The youth was standing still, his face stoic, his posture erect, his words dripping with raw, undiluted power, when he said, "It is not who puts on his armor after battle, it is he who takes it off," and his face glowed with bravery and surpassing certitude.

Robert watched in wonder as the Militia rode away.

"I have kept my part of the bargain," the soldier said to Robert; "I gave them a chance."

"You know him?" Eleanor asked, incredulous.

"Horses," the youth shouted to his men, and four of them came riding up, each with an additional horse; and after he mounted, his eyes radiant with the anticipation of heated combat, his countenance lit by the flame of vengeance, he looked upon Robert.

"Yes," Robert said, looking up at him, "you were true to your word."

The youth nodded, and then looked toward the Militia, who even now were turning round; he then looked to Eleanor, his face smoldering with passion, and then looked to his men, who were on the ready, and in attack formation: three main groups, that soon separated as the central group went forward, and the two groups went to flank the enemy who were regrouping in a saddle between two low ridges; and thus the fight began as the main support group divided into two units and began to fire down upon the enemy, and those on the flank covered any possible exit routes of the Militia.

Robert and Eleanor watched silently from the safety of a small hill; in less than an hour, the battle was over, and in another hour, the soldiers had come back to the camp, triumphant, all of them alive, none of them wounded.

The man, soaked in the thick perspiration of battle, walked up to Robert, tossed him a large, camel-leather pouch full of gold coins, all the while gazing with coolness and bravado at Eleanor, and then walked past them to assemble with his fellows.

"Who is he?" Eleanor asked, as if in a trance, staring at the handsome youth.

"I met him across the border with his men; it was they who told me about the military victory of the Arab forces in the South and their new, Islamic allies, and the bloodlust that would come here; he offered to defend us."

"And still, you brokered a deal with him, if possible, to forestall a fight?"

His countenance was still smitten by the torment of misdeeds all around him, and his analytical mind had begged mercy to escape these horrors by following one path of passive resistance; yet, now, his thinking had led him to an epiphany as he watched the battle; and now, he was ashamed, yet emboldened by penitence and a new philosophy.

"Yes," he began, looking at her as if for the first time, "before," and he looked at the forty men eating and drinking near the tents, and heard their good cheer, and celebration of brotherhood, and boasting victory over a palpable, evil force that needed to be expunged from the surface of the earth as if it were a virulent microbe; "before I came here, I had great wealth, a high position in American society, I was influential in politics—but I grew frustrated at the increasing injustice in the world, even as so many prospered, yet too many suffered; there was so much pain, so much sorrow, that seemed entirely unnecessary and too easily preventable if one just cared enough to put down their own ego and look beyond their own back yard, that I felt sinful about living in such grandeur and splendor and importance—but a shallow grandeur, an artificial splendor, an ephemeral and meaningless importance that seemed to matter only in the world I had created, one of exorbitant wealth and easy living and problems once solved that would make life even greater; the scales of Justice seemed tilted, as if too few were on one side, and weighing down the world with their own histories and ambitions and goals that benefited only them, and any other benefit to another was just incidental; while on the other side were the rest of humanity, poised high up in the air, their hands held out in supplication, trapped, discouraged, and abused by their sovereigns, and other sovereigns' interest was only in exploiting them; and I was as guilty as the rest, if not more; and so, I vowed to dedicate myself to helping the poorest of the poor who had never a chance for success or failure, those who would never turn away a piece of bread or a cup or rice or an article of clothing; and so, for two years, I have toiled to bring succor to the oppressed and the hungry and the infirm, but it just seems so overwhelming, too much work for relief organizations, if only because there is too much internal corruption in these forgotten and shattered countries." He frowned, inhaled deeply, and let out a slow expulsion of breath with a deep sigh. "It just seems as if we have been pouring trillions of dollars into a bottomless cup that they hold out before us; and who gets the money, and the food and the blankets, and the medical supplies? I will tell you, Eleanor: the corrupt regimes take it, and the rebels, and the armies, and the territorial lords, and the robbers and looters and anyone else who thinks they can spin it into gold; they take it all, and yes, a few crumbs of our donations trickle down to those in need, like drops of bread and wine from the open mouth of a gorging King; it's all so wrong, all of it, I can see that now; I should never have asked Conall and his men to even attempt to make peace with men who might come here—like the Militia or the army, such zealots who know only disloyalty and dishonor and cowardice; I should not have placed us in danger and restrictions on him and his men, true warriors, true warrior princes, as this is what they know: honor and loyalty and bravery." Eleanor looked toward the rowdy, celebratory men with a countenance of seeking answers, and then back again to Robert, with a countenance of better understanding. "In the West, we call them mercenaries, dogs of war, soldiers of fortune; but really, they are a new breed of warrior—I have heard stories about them: they do not fight for a King or country, or any corporation or wealthy monarch, but for Justice, for the sweet, sweet lady of Justice that we all crave deep within our souls because we know in our hearts and minds she exists and we will search her out until we see her and feel her fair, gentle hand laid upon us like a soothing balm; yes, these men have taken it upon themselves the iron crucible I did—but they use a weapon to defend the meek and give them what is their due, weapons that must be used now because this is the kind of world that exists here; yes, a new breed of warriors are they; and like the chivalrous knights of old, they have taken a blood oath to defend the oppressed and infirm and weak against tyranny, a sacred vow that allows them no personal monetary gain, no fleshly indulgence with the people they succor, and brings no harm to them, an inviolate edict written by the word of Holy Scripture; so, truly, I say to you, even though they appear young, they are as men of old in the ancient literature and the Holy Scriptures: Moses, David, Samson, Odysseus, Aeneas, Beowulf, Shaka, striving to be pure of heart, and bold for Justice and Mercy." He seemed to remember a pleasant memory from a long-ago, benevolent past, for his face grew gentle and radiated innocence. "Now, I know I was wrong; my money can do more good helping the right people to do good than me stumbling about in the desert trying to bargain with madmen who want to stone innocent children to death; yes, I am done here, at least; I know now that might—righteous and good—will help heal the land." He watched her gaze once again at Conall, and he smiled. "You are young, and there is so much for you to discover." He embraced her. "I will leave soon, and take Kofi and Naomi and the two little ones with me; at least I will save a few."

Within a week, the two youngsters were with a charitable organization who would soon place them in a good home in a safe region of northern Kenya.

That night, Robert met privately with Conall, and they talked of many things, of near and distant futures of armies and arms, of histories past and present, of soldiers of virtue, of their blood oaths and the sacred vow they prayed unto God. "Great oaths were uttered by men of great courage who then extended their strong hands to their brothers; let this day be celebrated in the minds and hearts of our posterity," Conall declared, shaking the hand of Robert as the two men approached the border. "The deed is done, sealed in blood." They embraced as only men who are eternally indebted to each other can, with full admiration and complete trust in each other. Conall watched as ten of his men escorted Heimdall and his four refugees to a safe haven in the neighboring country. "Now," he thought, "there is an army to build," but then his visage lit with desire at the memory of the innate loveliness of Eleanor; "but that woman," and he remembered certain verses he had once read, "she has imprisoned my heart with her transformative beauty." He inhaled deeply, and could smell her wondrous perfume though he had barely stridden past her, and waxed poetic, "There is something missing in my life that she carries like a flame in her soul mountain; aye, she melts my warrior's armor into a heap of tender red roses." He offered a primal scream into the sable mist, like a caged wolf that sees his captor before him. "She is a love liquor to savor for more than a night." He growled and grunted in deep anguish. "I have an army to build, a war to fight, and no unsoiled flower, no matter how fair, must extinguish my sacred mission." But he was lying to himself and he knew it; he avoided her for a full passing of night and day, feeding his starving passion with hollow promises, and when his hunger burned too bright, he drew near to her small chamber, and after much sharing of passions and philosophies and philanthropic ideals, took residence therein.

Flaming youth ignited their intense passion and engulfed the paramours, sending them into a warm and sensual embrace. The scintillating delights of the flesh wept a thick veil of ecstasy over them as they kissed and stroked each other, as their bodies whispered joyous longings and promises, as they slowly danced under the twinkling starlight.

Every night the paramours met and exchanged the natural vows of piety to the altar of pure love, and every morning they awoke, fresh from a romantic dream of the other, and filled the morning with happiness when they met the other with a kiss; now they were living inside a protected sphere of innocent love, and they felt the natural hum and harmony of nature, as if they too now were part of it, part of what is and what must be, and what is good and honorable and harmonious, and attained by saving each other, completing each other, increasing each other, by creating a better whole where before only two disparate parts existed, and by doing so, increasing the fortune of the world.

"But I am a Christian man," Conall had told her, "and so God judges us with our every thought and deed; expect no good thing if we betray His commandments."

"And I am a Christian woman," she had said, holding his hand and looking ardently into his dark eyes, "we will yet wait, and be twice blessed."

"We will wait and be blessed by God," he said, stroking her soft, rosy cheek, and the downy skin of her slender arms.

They were married, by one of the workers who was also a minister, with great ceremony in the midst of his comrades-in-arms and her fellows, married under the great canopy of celestial night, married according to the sacred laws of their chosen Faith.

But there were grave matters stirring in the region, and Conall and his men, although they had moved the dead bodies of the rebels to a place of less political unrest and violence, needed to move on. The young bride and groom had their first argument the night before he prepared to leave.

"You are my husband, and I need to be by your side," Eleanor insisted as she lay in his strong arms by the crackling, yellow flames of the campfire.

"You are my wife, and you will be by my side when we have gained more men, and are better able to defend ourselves."

"But husband," she said, fondly, joyous to hear the fresh title of her lover spoken by her own lips, "you are like a mighty lion," and she laughed, playing with his long, yellow mane of thick, curly hair; "who can raise a hand against you and yet live?"

Her kissed her in a long, sensuous, lustful embrace, and then said, in the romance language they both loved, which they had immersed themselves in as of late, gazing with ardor into her luminous eyes, "You are a good wife, to have such confidence in your husband, but my beloved, do you see how I am now? Am I ready for battle? Do I hold my heavy sword and shield in hand, ready to slay the enemy without mercy? No, for now my heart is filled with gladness and delicate thoughts." He looked about, to be certain his men had heard nothing. He whispered, stroking her long, soft, blond hair, "A soldier cannot wear both the honey-scented perfume of his woman and heavy armor into battle; no, he must wear the steel trappings of combat, he must not mingle those things that make him hesitate in war; I must be smeared with the venom and spilled blood of those fallen before me, and I must hear the hymn of the warrior's song, the hard voice of the conqueror, the mean philosophy of the dedicated soldier, filling my every thought, fueling my every deed, hastening me on to victory."

She sat up abruptly, her face burning with defiance. "Conall," she demanded, "why did you marry me, if I will only weaken your resolve to better kill men on the battlefield? Why not marry your horse!" She jumped up, and taking her female storm of reason with her, stood next to his trusty mount. "I am sorry, Conchobar," she whispered to him, eyeing her husband, "it is not your fault your master does not desire me now, and dares trifle with my heart." She stood, stroking the long, smooth nose of the black stallion.

The wrath of Conall was assuaged as he watched his faithful horse nestle his magnificent head next to his mistress and, motioning her to come inside the tent—which she willingly did, although turning her back to him—he said, while sitting, "Eleanor, my darling wife, did you not join the Red Cross to bring succor to those in the greatest need? Will you now abandon your vow to follow a trail of notorious men across this accursed continent? And how will I protect you while I am fighting those miscreants?" He scrutinized her quizzical expression, and nodded his head in mental agreement. "It is my vow to protect you above all things earthly, and how will I accomplish such a task if you are close enough to breathe air soiled in blood and death by my enemies? Is this the place for my beloved, at the center of a violent storm, where I could not fully consider your safety? And what if they found you, how could I live within the confines of my own tortured mind," and his voice broke as pathos poured faith and honor over his fervent words; "if they even touched you, even once, if they harmed you," and he stared with a countenance radiating a frightening power; "if they hurt you," and he abruptly leaped up as she turned full around to see his magnificent form sweating and heaving passion; "let any man lay his hand upon you and I will crush him as easily as if he were a fallen leaf." She could feel his explosive power burst upon her tingling skin, and the ecstasy of his fidelity lit a great torch in her bursting heart; her lips trembled, her arms shook, her body rocked in anticipation of his lusty form approaching her; he seized her and held her close as his flaming visage spoke for his burning heart, "For you, I would blot out the sun if you were too hot, for what is the sun, but merely a tool for our benefit," and he held her closer to his face; "for you, if you were cold, I would gladly burn the greatest treasures of man to warm you, for what are mere treasures, but to use for our benefit," and his lips neared her lips; "for you, I would deliver myself unto the hands of death if it gave you one more second of precious life, for what is the existence of the one, except to benefit the other." They kissed, as if in a great famine for love, as if they kissed for the first time, as her hot tears and sweet scents mingled on their warm bodies as they fell to the cool ground.

Young lovers resolve their conflicts with words and bodies and emotion, and each time a break between them is healed, their love is strengthened.

Those Who Fight

The men, having gathered intelligence on Militia attacks in the southern provinces, departed in the morning upon their trusty mounts; a silence of acknowledgement rode among them, knowing their leader, Conall, had left his young bride at the Red Cross encampment; for in small armies such as these, where there are no artificially imposed divisions of rank and jurisdiction, where every decision and desire is discussed *in toto*, the lamentation of one man spreads melancholy to them all.

It was the skill and bravery of Conall in battle, and his natural ability to command those who willingly chose to follow him, that allowed him to be their leader; and no one challenged this tacit agreement, no one questioned his authority, no one questioned his decisions and tactics, because they sensed that he had been born in the consecrated temple of battle, and with every thought and deed and word, he showed his cunning and expert strategy, so that they knew victory could not but come, and come famously.

The men rode on, checking their weapons, scrutinizing the horizon and the sloping brown hills around them with a wary eye.

Rustem of Iran, riding his faithful steed, Rakhsh, sped up and came to rest near Conall, pointing ahead of them. Conall, seeing nothing, raised his military binoculars, and spied their two scouts approaching. He signaled to Rustem, who, with only a gentle tap upon the glistening black nape of Rakhsh, caused his horse, as if indeed the horse and rider were of the same mind, to gallop ahead.

Came swiftly upon their noble steeds were Tyr, a youth from the northern provinces of Germany, and Enkidu, a native youth of Iraq.

"Ho, there," Rustem called out, focusing his acute vision on the approaching riders, "present yourselves."

The two men, riding side by side, let down the white cloth veil from their mouth and nose, and raised their rifles up and down, thrice, the proper signal; still Rustem spied them with great circumspection, and only relaxed the grip on his Barrett M82A1 rifle when the two youths sped past him; he scanned the flat horizon behind them first with his rifle scope and then with his naked eyes, ever watchful for aberration in the symmetrical landscape, scrutinizing every puff of dust, every nuance on the desert terrace; yea, he was as if an inert mass whose penetrating gaze bore deep into the dull hue and flat, burning surface of the desert. And then he saw it, something irregular, a black dot dispersing over a faraway small ridge, and Rakhsh, already sensing his master's restlessness, began to move forward.

Swiftly, Rakhsh brought Rustem to the exact spot wherein the anomaly had been, and the Iranian jumped down to inspect the imprint of camel hooves in the thick sand; he scanned the area, and after walking along the footprints, determined that the rider and camel must have disappeared around a nearby mountain side. "Government Militia," he decided, studying the nature of the hoofprint; "different from the government troops." He pressed ahead, keeping a safe distance from his quarry. The trail wound around the small mountain and then over the cracked, parched slabs of hard desert floor and down a valley, where he soon found a mass of displaced people toiling away in a huge mud pit.

He rode down to the edge of the misshapen hole, cautiously eyeing the people as they stared at his noble bearing. He stopped to admire the resolve of these workers. "Never have I seen such dedication to existence, such struggle for mere existence as I see in this poor land," he mused.

"Sir," a young boy called to him as he neared, "are thou government troop or Militia?"

Rustem observed a hideous red and infected swelling of the boy's right eye. "Trachoma," he decided, and gazed around at the other people in the gloomy swamp of mud. "There, a boy with a missing arm," he thought, "and there, a young girl with a missing leg." He saw men with fingers missing, women with sores and wounds about their sagging bodies, and as his compassion for these Innocents was magnified, his covenant with Justice increased; and then said, in the native tongue of the child, "I am neither, young man."

"Then, who art thou, a new kind of rebel, a foreigner come to save us poor Africans? Mama tells me men with guns are like these and we mustn't talk to any of them, but hold our head down and look to the ground and pray they do not kill us."

"You stand here, a brave youth, talking to me—how comes that, eh?"

The boy smiled. "You have a kindly and brave face, sir."

Rustem smiled for a moment, and then said, "I am not government troop, nor that accursed Militia," sitting taller now on his black leather saddle as he continued to scan the lazy horizon and then, turning his attention to the boy again, leaned down, and whispered, "So, tell me true, why dost thou speak to me?"

The boy shrugged his bony shoulders and lifted up his hands as if in capitulation as he said, "It is true what I said earlier about thee, O great warrior; but I cannot lie to men such as thee—a man came by not too long ago, and gave me this shiny, new dinar; see," and after reaching into his dirty pants pocket, he retrieved said coin and held it up for inspection; "if I were to ask who you were, but not to tell you why; he said, sir, if I found out, he would give me a five dinar."

Rustem had already grabbed his rifle and swung it up and around to the level of his waist as he spied the horizon. "So, why tell me now, eh?"

The boy shrugged his shoulders again. "Sir, I decided that you were a better man than he; and well," he said, smiling largely, "I decided that you would give me more if I told you; and besides, he was, after all, Militia, who killed my good Papa and brother and sister; and, after all, Mama says they are all spiders in human skin, and have no right to live." His countenance dropped as he frowned. "I have no love for them, even for a dinar, or five dinars."

"Where did he go?" There was urgency in his voice now, and the boy understood it easily.

Pointing to the north, he said, "That way, good sir." He looked up at the esoteric man on the handsome black stallion. "Do you wish to kill him?"

Rustem breathed easier, but still looked about. "How old are you, boy?"

"Ten, sir."

Even a trained eye would not have guessed accurately, for his malnourished body ruined natural markers of age.

"Ten, eh? Well, boy, your mind should be on other things than killing."

The boy stared intensely at the black-bearded man for what seemed the longest time. "But, sir, how can I, in this land? Mama says we wake up to horror and go to bed with death."

Rustem beheld the misery and toil of the camp before him; he watched as the slender men and women spilled water from steel drums over the side of the hacked and cut areas of the crudely carved mud lake; there, inside the brown slush, a tiny child waged war against a shovel bigger than his own frail body, frustration splashing upon his face as he tried to scrape the gooey mud into a plastic white carton; there, on the banks of the lake, men and women were molding the hardening mud into the rectangular-shaped bricks that would bring them more pay than selling the water they had acquired from far-off water pumps.

"Human beings," Rustem mused, "be they faced with starvation, toil night and day, like slaves; be they bestowed with riches, laze in the hot sun, growing fat as bloated walruses; where is the Justice in that? People rise or sink to their level of need; it is, unfortunately, the way of the world." A disturbing thought interrupted his reverie. "Boy, let me see that coin."

The boy frowned. "Sir, I fear you stealing it from me, although I still think you a nobleman, otherwise my heart would be glad to share its shiny new self with thee."

Rustem smiled briefly as he withdrew a fifty-dinar coin from his pocket and dropped it into the outstretched hands of the astonished child. "Fair trade, eh?" The boy happily assented, and reached up the coin to the stolid warrior, who still held the horizon sharp in focus; but when he beheld the bold design of the bronze coin, he leaped from his horse, retrieved all of his weapons and ammunition, and shouted, "Go, Rakhsh, gallop as swiftly as the hot winds and bring back my brethren," and he slapped the muscular rump of his noble steed, and watched him speed away. "Quick," he said to the boy, "take me to those in authority."

"None give orders here," the boy returned, flustered now with excitement; "all work together as slaves, and none are above or below the other."

Rustem, slinging his M82A1 rifle over his shoulder, and holding his Heckler &Koch G36, the assault rifle of choice of his brethren, in his right hand, began to run toward the workers, shouting, "The Militia is coming; into the pits, all of you." These displaced villagers, having lived in abject fear for so long, and having seen the wanton slaughter of the Militia, abandoned their work and obediently jumped into the lake of muck, huddling together against its steep embankment.

Rustem, standing still, facing the direction of the coming monolith of murder and mayhem, readied his Light Fifty rifle.

One Stands Alone

In the not-so-very-far distance, behind a small sandbar, lay twenty-nine heavily armed men, all of whom were watching, with great curiosity, the spectacle below; they lay, wrapped in their long, white robes, their rifles on the ready, each man peering through military binoculars to the event unfurling at the mud pit; no one wished to speak, for fear of dissolving the excitement of the unknown and the unexpected.

And then one of them, Abebe, a Kenyan, spoke in Swahili, his youth betrayed in his query. "Moses," he began, in utter reverence and wonder, "will the foreigner truly stand alone?"

Moses, still studying the enigmatic and silent figure who was now transfixed in his defiant stance at the head of the lake of mud, looked to his men, and then back through his binoculars.

"Yes," he said, in a voice deep with the intonations of wisdom, deep with the presage of experience with such men, "he has determined the accuracy and rifle range of his enemy, and as he is equipped with a superior rifle—it looks like a Barrett M82A1—he knows he can achieve this remarkable feat that is more than fifteen hundred meters away…"

"But who is he?" Jon Paul asked, frowning. "How comes a man who willfully awaits an entire army?"

"He feigns rescue," said another man, huddled a few feet away.

"You are always the pessimist, Henry," Jon Paul returned; "no heroes for you."

"No heroes in Africa; especially no white savior," he said, bitterly.

"Well, then, what are we?" said the soft-spoken Abebe.

"We, Abebe, are rebels, and rebels are not heroes."

Moses lay, silent, still studying the iron nerves of the white-clothed man down the hill; he did not care what his men said before or after battle, as long as during battle, they fought like fearless and skilled warriors.

"What do you think, Abdul?" he whispered to his second-in-command, nodding to the distant figure below.

Abdul, said, his face relaxed, his eyes keen on the lone figure, "I think he is the future."

Rustem stood, his rifle at the ready, his sharp eyes penetrating the hazy horizon, the dusty red flood of twilight draping the land, his lean body unmoving, his supreme equanimity throughout his body keeping him loose and ready to spring into action; he could hear the frightened, labored breathing of the people who hid, like lambs from the stalking wolf, in the brown muck; then, his acute senses picked up the slightest discordant movement when he leaned his ear to the ground, and then looked up and saw a small chute of sand spray, a billowing cloud hanging and drifting and blowing, and disintegrating behind the fierce riding of horses. He removed his white hood, and then everything not directly originating from the coming fury before him, all sights and sounds and smells, fell away.

They were coming like madmen bent on wild destruction, and still he did not move, but waited, watching silently as the riders advanced so swiftly, waiting, patiently discerning their distance from him and seeing the coming horde in a succinct grid pattern of latitude and longitude, watching as they breached the first zone of possible firing.

There was much to consider as he stood there, and this was the first dilemma: that he could not achieve maximum composure by lying down, or at least having a bench rest for his rifle, nor have a spotter with a scope spotter, but he must needs stand; but it was what it was, and he had been here before, and so merely stood, unflagging, unmoved, undeterred; so, after stuffing his ear with sealing wax, he looked through the PM II scope, and encountered the burning mirage radiating from the desert floor, which was not to be confused by the mirage caused by the steel barrel as it heated up after repeated firing, for which there was a mirage shield; he had already zeroed the rifle at three hundred yards, where the aim actually hit the target, which is to say that bullets do not travel in straight lines forever, but as soon as they leave the gun, travel in an arc, slowly descending until impact; but he would use the MOA and MIL of his scope to establish the proper range and accommodate the necessary factors included for the perfect shot: first, he knew that the camels were about six feet high, and the men astride them, measured from hip to head, probably added another three feet, so he considered nine feet as the height of his moving target, and he would make the necessary adjustments to his scope; there was wind drift of what he decided was about ten miles per hour that would deflect the bullet down and to the right, coming from three o'clock, and he must assign it full value, knowing that if it had come at twelve or six o'clock, he could have ignored it, or at other points, assigning it less wind value, so he would aim far to the left, and he would make the necessary adjustments on the scope; he supposed that it was one hundred degrees Fahrenheit, so the scope must go down; he was at an altitude of not quite two thousand feet, so, consequently, the scope must go up; the barometric pressure was normal—he had, like any good soldier, he had researched this, so he need not make any adjustment; the ground was relatively flat; the Coriolis effect was minimal, as the area was not much north of the equator, so he did not factor this in his aim; and as he proceeded to raise the rifle, an errant and, for all practical purposes, impossible bullet shot from the rifle of a rider coming from the east hit the knob of the scope and disabled it. And though no good marksman would dare enter the battlefield with only one scope, during the last firefight he had been in, his spare scope had been damaged when Rakhsh was felled, so that now he was without benefit of modern conveniences, but it was no matter to him. He quickly dispatched this lone rider.

His father had been a premier sniper in the Iraq-Iran war, and with more than two hundred official kills, and a documented shot of more than two thousand yards with the Barrett M82A1; and as he had taught Rustem to shoot in diverse places of every kind of terrain and interfering environmental factors and unusual circumstances and every type of moving and still target, he had been certain to instruct him in the ways of "sensory shooting," as the original shooters did (where was the scope for Daniel Boone's Kentucky rifle) to the point where Rustem could hit an object at any distance, despite the weather conditions or altitude or wind drift or temperature, or any other natural factor to determine, without benefit of technological aids to guide the bullet.

Thus freed from the harness of artificial instruments, he raised his rifle, sighted the closest piece of flowing black cloth in the landscape, found the rider, felt the rhythm of the up and down movement, and let his senses indwell on the fluid interaction woven between each rider: the fact that they rose as one—the action of the superior influencing the action of the inferior, as if they were birds flying in "V" formation, obliged by Nature to assume a particular pattern despite the hazards ahead—he assessed their posture and their determined near-straight line toward him; he then allowed his telescopic sight to wander over each rider all the way to the last man, where he hesitated, his intense concentration dwelling on the roiling, jarring movement of the rider, and he felt the swirling wind about himself as he looked through the scope that was raised high and far to the left, as he breathed slowly, in and out, in and out, oxygenating his body, falling into a deep trance where he listened to his steady breathing, becoming one with it, until, finally, he felt a pause at the bottom of his breath, and certain that to pull the trigger now would not affect the stability of the rifle, only then did he slowly squeeze it. The shot went slightly to the right and beyond the man, and so he timed the next opportune moment and fired once more: the trailing man was violently propelled over the back of his black horse.

And then it began, the shooting of the Militia, in one seamless stream from end to beginning; the first man to fall was in the last formation, and far to the right, and there were four more long, zigzagging lines, each rider in close quarter to the other, and shooting their raised rifles, expelled bullets far left, far right, and far short of their intended target.

Rustem, his mind attuned to the shifting wave of the charging riders, shot his rifle again, and again, in rapid succession, and a man fell, again, and again, but on the far left of the last formation, and then the other man, on the far right, fell backward over his horse, dead.

The other riders came on, undaunted, firing their weapons willy-nilly, the bullets launched from a bouncing position but being planted into the ground like a garden of hot lead seeds.

Bullets pierced the quietude about Rustem, digging small pockets in the dry, cracked sand and blasting into the pools of brown mud, scattered about like bird droppings, as if blindly dropped from above.

The Militia, consumed by rage and waving their rifles in between shots, were screaming for the blood of this infidel, and rode straight on, not cognizant of the blazing bullets that whistled past them and plucked their fellows off their horses with the precision of a master surgeon.

Rustem fired three more bursts from his rifle, and three more times, three riders, near the back, in front of a line of riderless, charging horses, fell over and dead onto the unforgiving desert floor; when a rider sought to contact another rider about the fallen comrades, Rustem shot him dead; he then concentrated on the men in the front of the howling pack, and one by one he first shot their arms, which they used to lift their rifles, and then he shot the rifles from their dead grip.

He was carving a holiday bird, shifting from one meaty morsel to the next, one slice at a time, and when it was all over, only the choicest cuts that created his own unique design would remain.

One by one the black-cloaked Militia fell, to the side, backward, landing free and clear, trampled, lying dead, leaving their horses to journey on without them.

Bullets slowly ceased to sting the air about Rustem as he carefully drew in the dwindling battalion of renegade soldiers, as he slew, at will, the exact men he sought, until, finally, the horses, without riders, galloped past him, and the three men he had chosen to merely wound and disarm stopped before him in obedience to his raised rifle; in the fury of the onslaught, these men had not perceived all the deaths of their comrades and, watching the other horses still running in the distance, shock and outrage visited their dark visages.

One of them—to be exact, the Captain of the brigade—sneered, and shouted, breathless, to Rustem, "So, what will you do now against us, coward!" He drew his sword from its leather sheath, as did the other two, all using their remaining good arm. "Out of bullets, infidel? Fight us, fight us man to man!"

Rustem, his face as smooth as a lake of calm, said, "No." He let fall his rifle to his side.

"He is out of bullets," the Captain laughed; "coward with a gun."

Rustem looked intensely at the Captain. "No."

"Eh, then you have bullets, but no nerve," the Captain returned, waving his silver sword about.

"I promised your last dance to another, 'luewih jahat,'" he cried, in the language of the people who had huddled in the mud pits; and he reached in and produced the rusty white coin with the skull and crossbones, and the initials "MOD" on it, "when I saw this coin."

"Ha! Militia of Death! Yes, I gave it to the crippled boy here," he said, with arrogance traversing his face like a snake swallowing a mouse, and he looked about, with disdain now upon his countenance. "So, where are the weak infidels? After we have killed you, we will slaughter them and rob them of their last penny, and defile their women, and butcher their bodies, and leave their filthy carcasses for the hungry vultures." The three men raised their swords to attack, uttering profane declarations against the race of the man who still stood tall in their midst, but then they were suddenly reduced in size and their plans dashed when the first of the mud-caked shovels was raised against them.

It was a feeding frenzy, truly, like lambs able to break the bones and tear the flesh of the red-eyed black wolf who has preyed mercilessly upon their meek flock.

There was not a man, woman or child who had not been sprayed with the black ashes of dead family, dead relatives, dead friends who had been eagerly and gleefully murdered by the marauding Militia; and there was not a man, woman or child there who had not witnessed and admired the chivalry of their benefactor as he withstood the attack of an entire squadron; nor were there any there who had not heard and understood this offering to them of their tormentors and once-certain, future murderers; thus enamored with the honor of Justice, the collective refugees, who had come from far and wide as they looked about for the barest of sustenance, easily took up their newly found tools and applied them, with grunting force, to the bony skulls and squirming bodies of their detested enemy.

When the deed was done, and the people, resting wearily upon their weapons as they gazed at their handiwork, a cloud of dust arose in the near distance; Rustem looked at it and smiled. "Comes, Rakhsh, and my fellows," he whispered, and presently, they did come, galloping up to him, and he embraced his loyal steed, stroking his long, sweaty, black nose and, cupping his hands, fed him water from the yellow canteen from his black saddle.

Conall, having dispatched scouts to survey the death toll from Rustem's shooting, dismounted, while his compatriots surveyed the scene with great circumspection; and then slapping Rustem upon his broad shoulders, he said, with admiration, "An eagle hunting mice."

"And with an audience," said Yoshitsune of Japan, his muscular arms crossed over themselves as he, sitting still upon his horse, bent closer to the two men, "about one click at three o'clock."

"Who would watch as a lone man fights an army," Horatius of Italy said, his horse next to Yoshitsune, "but cowards or villains."

Conall casually surveyed the area of their outlying position. "We are exposed if they mean engagement, but I think not."

"How so?" said Horatius.

Yoshitsune said, "Who watches their fellow soldier die just to see the strength of the enemy—it is possible, but unlikely."

"Ruthless men," Horatius said.

"But shrewd and cunning men," Yoshitsune said.

"Our foes attack like ravenous dogs, with no forethought to the consequences of their wanton slaughter."

Yoshitsune nodded his black-haired head. "And these men lay in wait, like the cunning lioness who watches the tiger fight the panther, and assesses the strength of both."

They raised their collective heads as two of their comrades came back.

"All dead," Tyr said, as if in approval of Rustem's actions.

Enkidu stared at Rustem in awe and admiration, and then said to the others, "No sign of Militia; only our shy guests who repose up yonder," and gave a barely perceptible nod behind himself.

"Do we arouse them from their gentle repose?" Horatius asked, taking out his spyglasses.

"And by this, show them our prowess of reconnaissance," Tyr suggested.

Horatius, looking through his beige binoculars, said, coolly, "Something wicked this way comes," and all the men looked to the sand dunes behind them.

They mounted their horses and arranged themselves in battle formation, four squads, one center, a left flank and right flank, and a trailing squad to face the coming storm, each man on the ready to fight, his rifle in hand, his eyes keen, his equanimity cool; they watched as the small band of thirty-one men rode on their purebred Arabian horses slowly toward them, in a wide horizontal pattern, halting just a few horse-steps away from physical engagement.

But before he left, Rustem approached the people, who were still gazing at him as if he were a great warrior to be admired and revered, and asked them who was the mother of the boy he had first met here; and upon greeting her, he took out ten silver coins and place them tenderly in her scarred, callused, mud-caked hands. "The boy deserves to see," he said, and the woman raised his hand to her lips, and kissed it, and wept tears over it. He then gently lifted up that now-precious hand and, nodding to her, and her kin and kind, turned and rode swiftly away, all the while these poor, humble people, caught in the eternal struggle between ruler and ruled, now had hope that somewhere, perhaps, there were men of valor who had come to fight a fight few had attempted.

Moses—swaddled in the jellabiya of his country, as were most of his men, but unlike the men before him, who wore traditional white head cloths that covered their necks, and long tunics—with his black Heckler & Koch G36 assault rifle laid in horizontally across his lap, an SR-25 semi-automatic sniper rifle slung over his left shoulder, an SIG Sauer P226 pistol in a black leather holster hanging at his right hip, and a bow and arrow attached to the side of his saddle; and his men were similarly armed, or a variant thereof—sitting atop his horse, whom he called, "Son of Al Khamasa," said, with exceeding authority and certitude, gesturing toward Rustem, "Rarely have I seen such marksmanship and bravery displayed for so small a prize," and nodded to the gathered people of the mud pit, who now sat in silent deference to the august men in their presence. "My countryman," he continued, nodding toward a sneering and smug Henry, "says you accomplish no mean feat, using a superior weapon; but ah," and he punched the air so quickly that it fairly popped, "I say you did it without benefit of the scope—what say you?" Rustem tossed him his PM II scope. "Ha! I knew it as I measured your shots—unbelievable, and when? Impossible!" and, smiling largely, Moses threw the scope back to its owner.

"Your horse is magnificent," Rustem said.

Moses patted the bulge between the eyes of Son of Al Khamasa—who was designated as a sabino due to the white patterns about its brown, sleek body—and then said, "The Bedouin call this the 'jibbah,' believing it helps the horse survive better in the desert."

"More sinus capacity," Rustem said, nodding.

"Exactly—and you are a man who knows what he rides." Moses gazed upon Rakhsh with admiration. "You are a passionate horseman, and would not choose a horse less than magnificent." Moses then looked around at the intense and silent figures before him, and he smiled. "Who leads you?" He nodded. "You must forgive me; Africans are always curious about strangers in their land."

"What do you seek?" Yoshitsune said, in an unassuming manner.

"Ah, the leader," Moses said, smiling, and nodded; "we want to know your intentions in our country: are you here to stay, or do you bring gifts?"

"I was not born here, but I live here now," Enkidu said, angrily, his hand resting near the brown holster on his left hip that housed his Glock 17 pistol, which most of his comrades also carried, or a variant thereof; "thou are not my landlord."

Moses looked the youth up and down. "So, you do, boy; then, why are you here with these mercenaries?"

"We're orphans, adopted by Mother Africa," Tyr said, smirking, and waving to his comrades with his rifle, "and these are my adopted brothers."

"Yes," Moses said, nodding, "a league of assassins, killing our people without legal authority."

"Killing those who need killing," Enkidu cried.

All of the men present were touched by the flame of his fiery passion, and were pricked for combat.

"So, you say; but your man," Moses said, matter-of-factly, and pointed to Rustem, "kills like an eagle hunting mice."

Conall, in his mind, acknowledged the coincidence of this metaphor.

"We don't need your permission to fight injustice wherever we find it," Yoshitsune said.

"You are not the law here, Asian."

"There are no laws here, African," Horatius said, still as stone.

"So, who determines law, here?" Moses cried.

"Justice," Conall said, with the simple power of evenness of mind and body.

Moses, nodding his head, looked at the newest speaker, and moved his horse toward him. All of the soldiers were tense with readiness. "How goes it if my countrymen came to your precious land and let our sense of Justice guide us to whom we would kill?"

Conall never wavered in his steely gaze. "My land needs no such allies against corruption; but if we did, I would gladly welcome them and fight by their side as we did when we fought the Normans and the English; when the Irish were considered savages and treated as such for hundreds of years by our conquerors; when we fought in our Civil War and our War of Independence from our oppressors; yes, we would have welcomed any who chose the side of Freedom."

"An answer for every question, a remedy for every problem," Moses said, thrusting his anger into the discussion; "the true mark of an imperialist; well, I am here to tell you, we have seen what outside influences have done to our country, and to us, even now, and I tell you," he cried, waving his cloaked arm about, "leave the problems of Africa to Africans." It was as if his bald words had opened a rusted, tightly shut door behind which the honor of his countrymen had been locked since colonial times; and now, once unleashed, he felt the effulgent flood of a new path of shining possibilities engulf him; he sat erect in his saddle, his handsome visage beaming pride and patriotism.

It was a time where men of great might and uncertain speech deferred to those born with the special talent of conversation and negotiation; all of Conall's men, most of them with a dry tongue in response to the African's, looked to their Irish Hercules to defend them.

Conall, his head held high, leaned back in his brown leather saddle, his head nodding imperceptibly. "You are correct, my prince, whose brave and daring exploits are renown throughout Africa," he began, keenly observing the proud and noble countenance of Moses; "many countries have brought shame upon themselves as they plundered your lands for wealth; I have studied the history of your continent, and I know the sorrows brought here by unrestrained avarice and unmitigated power; but that door has been closed, and a new door opened, and I gladly walk through it to amend the horrors and injustices of the past; all of us, every man here," he gestured toward his men, "gave up hearth and home to come here and bring succor to those in need, no matter who they are; no matter their race, religion or creed; no matter what happened in the past, or what will happen in the future." He scrutinized the face of his anxious host.

"Do you see my people in your country taking arms against those they perceive as an enemy? Your sovereign nations would not allow it; your arrogant nations deign to treat us like children who cannot fend for ourselves and who must be taught Democracy from their sacred texts, and give us money but tell us where it must go, and what we can and cannot do with it, and who we must listen to, and who we must follow; this is not your personal backyard to play in when you are bored, mercenary—this is Africa, Irishman, and we do not need your guidance on how to heal the woes you created and carved up here in blood and pain."

Conall was still unmoved. "Were you a traveler in my native land, and walking along the grassy path with your lady, and beheld a most grievous crime being committed, would you not, being a man of moral courage, act to abate it?" He saw the silence as acquiescence. "Valor arises when injustice reigns; and injustice arises only when cowardice reigns; this, then is our mission, to act on what we see, as we too are men of moral courage, and we will go where we are needed: on any continent, where iniquity flourishes unchecked—as we have already done." He paused, gazing with an ardent desire at his listener. "Where men suffer, there shall we be."

Moses, his head held high, now moved his head askew. "Talk," he said, scornfully.

Conall, his eyes diverted for a brief moment to the red horizon, looked again to the grave African. "My men talk with their guns." The Africans raised their weapons, but Moses waved them away. "I extended courtesy to you in your land, but when a land is under siege by the forces of darkness, men of might and valor are united," and he lifted back his head, "and once more courtesy I give you; that you ride quickly to the south." His men cast stealthy glances about themselves. "We will ride to the north to split the Militia."

Moses' men began to look anxiously around, shaming him. "Be still," he cried, admiring the training of Conall's men to evince no physical reaction to the danger, as he watched them slowly back away. "Where are these Militia?"

"Everywhere."

Moses gazed furtively about, and soon, he saw the host of drone soldiers dotting the tips of the brown hills that were parallel to them. "How came you to this conclusion?"

"I smelled their rotting moral filth in the hot breezes," he returned, as his own horse continued to slowly move away.

"Why do you go north, and send us south?" he replied, too moving his horse away.

"Did you not lend support to your soldiers by leaving men in the rear?"

"Of course," he said, rising uncomfortably in his black leather saddle.

"Good; then they will give you cover." He waved to his men. "We go together, slowly, until I signal you."

Moses, being a true soldier, recognized the bearing of another true soldier, and his experience in battle allowed him to recognize a true soldier who understood strategy and tactics; thus, he demurred, a quality of a great leader, and followed the band of foreigners.

The horse-riding Militia covered both sides of the straight, flat land on which the two small armies rode, and they moved as the armies moved.

When Conall saw the two Militia forces begin to quicken their pace, he issued the command to Moses and his men to ready themselves; and then, to his men, he said, "Faster." The horses were trotting now, and the Militia responded in kind, and upon seeing this, he said to Moses, "We go fast, and you with us, and then you count to ten and reverse course and go home," and before Moses could question this stratagem, Conall and his men urged their horses to gallop and were away, dragging the Africans with them, and then Moses shouted orders to his men.

"…Ten."

Moses and his men abruptly reversed course and fled south.

The race was on. The Militia, bewildered, and thus hesitant, split their forces in pursuit of their quarry, but soon gave up, as was their custom in the face of even or uncertain odds.

Conall and his men watched as the soldiers, holding their long, slender rifles on high, disappeared behind a mocha-colored mountain of stone.

Something Wicked

Sometimes, tiny, parasitic creatures will attach themselves to a large host, oftentimes sucking nourishment without a promise of return favors, sometimes offering a symbiotic relationship by cleaning unwanted invaders from the host body.

There was a considerable amount of black-skinned, tiny-brained, small creatures mounted on bigger, sometimes brown, sometimes black creatures, the latter of whom were moving at a leisurely pace in the unyielding heat of the desert; it was obvious that these smaller creatures were unkind to the sweaty slave under their puny legs, and it was also obvious that the bigger creatures realized this, for sometimes they refused the commands of their masters, and always suffered the worse for it.

As it was, the smaller creatures were communicating to their fellows, making their needs known to each other—which is to say, they were speaking about bodily waste removal, sustenance, relaxation, recreation, sleep; and by doing thus, at this point in this brief description of their journey, they were as yet indistinguishable from any other creature on earth had they the remarkable talent of speech; but as no further description of their physical features was forthcoming, what were these creatures, one could only imagine—but they had to be more than tics on a horse, fleas on a dog, worms on a camel; or so it appeared.

Surely, they were sentient creatures, and if so, at what level, and what were their origins? Which classification of the five kingdoms of life did they fit into: plant, animal, Protista, fungi, eubacteria, archaebacteria? Let us use a universal language decoder for all life-forms, and perhaps more clues will render a verdict to the reader as to their identity.

Let us scrutinize their every nuance of speech, every intonation and timbre and tone, every movement of their body, their posture and the relationship of their roles as their oily forms slithered about on their slowly walking, aggravated, indentured servants.

They, these sometimes bent-over, oft-laid-back small creatures, communicated their chronic need for the sugary pulp of the fruit, the fatty, crunchy taste of the nut, the savory, hot juices of the dead organism; so, reader, what say ye, at this point: be they chirping cricket on the back of a humble snail? Be they wily lizards riding the back of their green-skinned cousin, the iguana?

Let there be more pinholes in this shroud over them, and allow in pieces of illuminating light, and then more questions will be proffered.

The small creatures with the bony heads were fond of conversing on the desperate need for the fermented fruit of the vine; and the obsessive need and nature of copulation, in an almost obsessive neurosis, as if they needed both things more than food and water. One more clue, then, one more pinhole casting a drop of white light upon their smooth skin; and what do we see in this profile, thus? By the holes produced, we see an outline of something crooked, twisted, and bent; something beating to the pulse of a horrific, terrorized, wailing scream; something with an embedded vein in which runs the black, ill humor of the malcontent; something dark, brooding, vulgar, mean and nasty.

And then the small creatures introduced a new topic, albeit it one they had frequently worn as an expression of pleasure upon their ebony faces; it was the subject of murder, most foul, and most extraordinary and without restraint; now, reader, we see a shriek of pinholes that let in so many shreds of light that something hideous begins to manifest itself upon the face of the grinning creatures. May you now guess their life-form? These creatures murdered, and murdered well, murdered without compunction or reason, murdered as it if it were a basic need to be satisfied and full of themselves, as if it were a necessity to live, and flourish, and enjoy their life.

Yes, you know who they were: they were men; yes, yes, you know now because only man—with his special gift of thought—murders, and plans murders, and delights in it, seethes and basks and revels in it until it is his darling paramour; but, say ye, what category of men were they, and for what purpose did they exceed the limits of moral reason, and how did they apportion the facts of such murders in their minds? This may be easily answered, as one has only to carefully listen to their bantering dialogue for a brief time, the time it takes for the mangled shadows of a falling man they had mercilessly murdered to pass by them; but you, the inquisitive reader, will want to know more about this particular species of men, who talked of murder the way civilized men talk in a lackadaisical manner about excreting their waste, the way men boast about fornication, the way men loudly belch and emit gas and swear loudly as if it were an official legacy of their gender; these men treated murder as a singular species, courting it as a coy mistress that depended on the circumstances in which it was performed, which depended upon their mood, their ego, their hunger; yes, they inhaled murder as if it were a vital nutrient, murder shooting down into their muscle and bone and blood, murder encoded in their fractured DNA; murder, murder, vicious murder used for energy by their every voracious cell, and to staunch the bleeding, ever-widening, insatiable wound in their tormented minds that begged for an identity that could be carved only from the indiscriminate termination of human life.

Listen, then, and learn the special code of these willing disciples who worshiped the issuing of death.

Had they names, these laughing, crackling, short-haired creatures? Unrepentant murder, once committed, once acted-upon as a commitment to a decree, once embraced as a doctrine of life, proudly blossoms as a personal emblem of honor, and blurs the individual identity of men and imparts to them one common identity that becomes their dress, their face, their name, their language, their mind, heart and soul, their birthplace, their family, their country; blackheart is a their newly fashioned name; yes, the hearts of such men are sooty rich, without a spot of white, black-pitch thick, where no point of light might enter; shriveled hearts with no moral guide, no moral desires to do good, no honor, no love, no virtues easily recognized by even the most practiced sociologist; ah, you say, is there not some goodness in all men, even those who do harm to Innocents; are they not kind to their own kind, and their own family, and animals, and give presents to those around them? Does this evince some kind of portal through which their lost souls can be reclaimed? But, reader, one must ask: do they wish to be reclaimed; do they even acknowledge that what they do is heinous and diabolical?

And what rank had these creatures, what had they done to achieve such a terrible reckoning upon the world: had they been government soldiers in a great war to protect home and hearth; were they sanctioned by any official government agency; what had they done to achieve such a terrible status as inhuman butchers of anything they chose to eliminate in the same manner one kills any predator that threatens their own? Why, they simply decided to do it, and as no official, legitimate, or government agency—that is to say, recognized by the universal laws of Man as honorable and righteous and democratically elected—or other peoples actively took up arms and opposed them, they then continued on in their passionate embrace to efface from the land those they deemed unfit to breathe the same air and drink the same water as they. But the real horror was that they had been sanctioned by their country's leaders, who deemed themselves official but were not recognized by any legitimate government outside of their own allies, and this, then, was the true terror, for it meant that no government army in this country would come to help their victims—in fact, too many would help these rebels in their quest for mass slaughter.

There was one such blackheart, wearing the traditional garments of his particular make-believe, fantasy unit of pretend soldiers—that being khaki pants and long-sleeved brown shirt and green and brown beret, and carrying, like an additional appendage grown out of its skinny body, an AK-47 rifle—who was delivering an oratory on the meat and marrow of his past endeavors.

And every time the creature spoke, he initiated a rupture in the dry air that splintered the fabric of time and space around him, a rupture that sent invisible shock waves that were perverted in their very nature, sharp waves seducing any weak vessel near them and capturing it and remaking it in his own wicked image; and when he spoke, he chattered like the voracious sewer rat that gnaws on a rotting carcass, his four big incisors moving up and down like fiery pistons, his chopping words like a sharp scythe, his red ocher tongue darting and diving like a poisonous spider, his purple lips smacking each other like greasy hyena's lips, and the result was words soaked in venom, like that of a poisonous snake that can paralyze its victims with a terrible hiss.

"Hey, hey, you," he began, directing his comments to no one in particular, as do those who think themselves superior to any who hear their words, his long, happy-smiling face bobbing up and down like an apple in a vat of putrid water; "did you see how that fat one fell into the well?" He punctured the hot air with his barbed words. "She smashed against the brick—smack, smack—crying like a stuck pig." But the reader may ask, at this juncture, what matter of living thing did the smiling man-crocodile speak of? "Did you hear it hit the bottom, and the crying just stopped after that; wasn't it funny, eh? I took a skinny one and she was clawing and screaming as I lifted her over the well and dangled her by her feet, and I lifted her up and down to tease her, eh? Sure, I did that, you saw that, I did that to these animals, sure, I did that, and then I got tired of her screaming and dropped her straight in so she wouldn't hit the sides, neither, but would hit—smack—the bit fat one—and she did—bull's-eye! And, you know, guess what, the moaning of the fat one stopped, wouldn't you know it! Ha!"

So, reader, what classification of living things was he describing? what type do you hope it is? It is yours to guess, but another deranged clue may suffice.

"And then I went inside the house and found the cowering old man and I said, 'Old man, you should not be in here cowering; you should be with your daughters, it is your duty, you know, to be there for them'; and so I pulled him along—oh, you all saw me doing it—and his old lady, fussing at me; well, I put the rifle butt into her head and that quieted her down—heh, heh! And then I told her I would settle accounts with her later for daring to bother me while I was working; well, anyway, I took the old man, dragging him by his hair to the well, and I said, 'all right, old man, you need to be with your family now, they need you,' and I stuffed him into the well, too. Ha, ha! And now, that left the old lady who was crying like a child on the ground, and making me madder every minute with her whining."

Reader, now you know what manner of living thing this man-insect was pouring down the brick well, but you knew all along, didn't you, but you just did not want to believe that human beings can so easily divorce themselves from their humanity.

He took out a high-tar, non-filter, dirty-white cigarette, lit it with a sulfur-head match, and took a long drag on it; this non-nutritive substance seemed also to be an essential part of his basic needs, as deduced by the man-dog's flaccid face and sloppy gaze shortly after the narcotic took effect; his narrow eyes glazed over with a thick fog, hiding a grizzly, black hole wherein all bad things went and never came out.

His voice was now a fuming caldron of boasting carnality.

"So, I took the old lady," he began again, his tone cool and deadly, "and I put her before the old well, and I stood there with my rifle in her crying face, and I says to her, 'Woman, you can join your family or let me have my way with you like we did with your pathetic, whining daughters.'" He smiled when he thought of the puny, frightened, trembling woman imploring him for sweet life. "But the stupid woman begged me for life, so I pulled her up by her hair and stuck her head into the mouth of the well and let her hear the screams of her family; and I asked her again." He issued a small chuckle as his small head nodded in fond remembrance. "Of course, she agreed—which I sort of did not like, 'cause often I like them to fight me, like the daughters did, it brings more pleasure—and so I had my way with her, right there against the well, so the old man could hear the cries of the woman he loves with a real man." He laughed, then, like a naughty boy who shares his spoils with his friends. "But I am not selfish, eh, my good friends?" This was the cue of his fellow man-rodents to cheerfully acknowledge their part in this gruesome telling, and each of his twenty riding mates, with pride and honor, concurred on their physical violation of the woman whose shattered mind had been bursting out of her throbbing head; but once their boasting was done, they quickly quieted to allow their revered Captain to continue his stark narrative and his starring role therein.

As he continued in his cocksure drawl, this chirping man-cricket, this escaped residue from the burning shores of perdition, this animal in human skin, his feverish words flinging around his men like a creeping, black scab of fungus rot, enveloping them until it became them, and lo, they thrived upon its toxic vapors.

"And then," he said, scratching his soft belly, "you know, I got tired of this limp whore, and so—who was it; ah, I believe it was you," and everyone watched as the young Ali, proud as a new pup licked by his father, sat up straight in the saddle, "who decided to teach the screaming whore a lesson." Ali, being too young to fully understand his role in the intricacies of this family drama, was about to speak, but was quickly waved off by one of the older man-fleas; the Captain now spoke in words that were born in the red conflagration of burning bodies. "So, I took this stupid whore," he seemed to grain great satisfaction with every vicious and unclean diatribe uttered against the memory of the helpless woman, and now his tone became hard and mean, as if angry at some injury to his personal honor and beliefs, "this infidel, this animal, and I took a rag, and soaked it with kerosene oil, and stuffed it straight into her stupid mouth and tied it tight—and then lit it on fire; and then I pushed the wailing whore into the well, and then me and my boys laughed and had a good smoke hearing them screams echoing down in the pit and smelling that awful smell." He laughed hard, holding his round belly. "That family screamed like goats at slaughter time—hey, hey, you, you," he suddenly cried, his face lit with mirth, "can you imagine the fool who drinks from that well?"

These Militia felt the cleansing effect of their deep-rooted laughter, for they had been in the field for two days cleansing their sector of squatters and villagers, and they needed a hard flush of release from such hard toil. And now they were on their way to attack an Internally Displaced Persons' refugee camp.

But what does murder most heinous and lacking of natural checks and balances, and sung to its own hymn and following its own ordinances and statutes, do to such creatures? It emboldens them to act, for murder begets murder, and murder once absolved of any guilt, once worn as natural dress, creates a sense of legitimacy and power to do as one pleases, as if one now has the natural right to take human life as much as one has to give it; and when the foul deed is done, it is done without moral filter or restraint, without worry or woe, and without moral conscience afterward: for it is now considered as normal as waking or sleeping, or eating and drinking, or birth or death: just one more aspect viewed and arrived at with a different compass and route.

Comes One

The camp was arranged in rectangular shapes, fences of bundled yellow straw stacked four feet high, and inside them were the small straw and mud huts with their cone-shaped roofs, and inside these huts were the members of this Internally Displaced Persons' refugee camp, hiding in the naked open from their pursuers, the Militia.

The black dome of sky these people wore like a funeral wreath, the white flakes of distinct light twinkling at the top and spilling down to the curved sides of the far horizon.

Three women of the Masalit tribe were on the dirt floor of their tiny hut, their faces undone by the horrors of their unrelenting tormentors.

"We are forgotten by the world," said Onnab, leaning against the soft, earthen wall, rubbing her big, pregnant belly.

"No, Onnab, this is not true," said Sara; "the Civilian Police Force soldiers tell me that they saw men of other nations here filming our crisis so they can get aid for us."

"Humph," Celia said, massaging her gray hairs; "the world mourns for us, and from how far away, and in their nice, comfortable homes watching television; oh, yes, I have heard such stories from aid workers—it is shameless, I tell you; and to feel better, they put a few pieces of money in an envelope and mail it to a charity that is supposed to help and feed us poor Africans—shameless, I tell you; but do they mourn next to my dead husband and dead babies, or do they wipe their tears in front of their television? You know the truth—so, stop lying to yourselves and realize we are alone."

"Oh, Celia, how can you say that?" Onnab protested meekly. "The CPF soldiers say many countries are negotiating peace for us."

"Don't tell me about the CPF soldiers—what good are they, eh?" Celia cried. "Like wooden dolls, with wooden guns that shoot wooden bullets—they stood by while my man was murdered by the Militia," and she threw up her hands in disdain and disgust. "Oh yes, I can hear those shameful fools now: 'we cannot intervene, we can only observe.' And what good is that—so, they observe my man being murdered; how does that help, I ask you?"

"But it isn't their fault they can't fire their guns."

"So, why are the fools here?" she cried. "What good are soldiers without bullets? It is like a stream without water, or a cow without milk..." But she became silent as she and Onnab looked at Nyaring, who lay along the curve of the hut's base, unmoving, her pretty face masking a sorrow at what was not seen, her massive burn scars upon her legs at what was seen.

Those dispossessed souls who lose their loved ones to unwonted violence are of one family, and when they come across the other for the first time, they recognize each other, just as two long-lost sisters might, through familiar features of suffering; but they do not see a similar facial structure or body composition, but the newly carved features of their wounded spirit, the drooping posture that carries the weight of the dead upon it, the gait of the body that is slowed as if their dead were still tied to it; it is the wandering, aimless direction they go, as if they are cut loose in their anarchic world after being anchored on solid ground; it is their eyes, the desolate eyes of those who lament, which are a black void that sees only darkness and dread, into which all light and lust for life is lost forever.

Nyaring had awoken one humid morning to the calamitous shrieks that are uttered by people who are being terrorized into the small arena of a cruel and unjust death; she had leaped out of bed and peeped out of the hole in her hut and witnessed the Militia, riding on their horses, randomly shooting the people in her village in the same manner farmers might raid the hole of vegetation-destroying rabbits; they shot them with their mounted machine guns, they shot them with their automatic rifles and pistols; they shot whomever and whatever and whenever they saw a fleeing target, whether the villager was standing or sitting or crawling or running, whether the people were old or middle-aged or young, whether the Masalit was begging or praying or lying, or if it was an animal: dog or goat or cow; and more mirth was gained from these assassins as more passionate became the running, the imploring, the screaming of the victims; the whooping, careless, whimsical Militia men sprayed bullets with the joyous abandon of a band of brothers who douse their family members with cool water in the midst of a summer swelter.

There must be some way out of here, she reasoned, but her emotional mind was not privy to this query, for it was safely tucked away in her sanctum sanctorum of solace; yes, the inviolate soul had spoken thus, and it meant its words for sanctuary of her beloved country from the chaotic world she knew, but mostly it yearned for the serenity of heaven.

As it was, then, right there and nowhere else, she was tucked tight into a ferocious bloodletting that was part of a grandeur scheme beyond the narrow meaning of war, even beyond the broader definition of war, and into the living blasphemy that is the Island of Genocide, created every time a megalomaniac has a psychotic and insane thought and acts upon it—and not enough good people decide not to stop him—where only the damning and the damned exist in a hallucinatory, macabre slaughterhouse that is always building and never fills up and seems never to be permanently removed.

She was a poor lambkin caught asleep by a hungry bear, and with every scream and shout and implore for mercy by her own people, she felt the icy fingers of death creep over her hot skin; she felt faint, her knees buckled, and she collapsed to the hard desert floor, glassy-eyed, paralyzed by absolute fear and terror. The rude chants of her tormentors cracked in the air like bullets tossed into a roaring fire; someone fell at the entry point of her hut, and his head turned toward her. "Papa," echoed inside her numb body, and she watched as he reached his hand toward her, but then the sharp shadow of a long sword was flung over the yellow canvas door, and her father cried out in anguish as the weapon plunged into his body. She watched him reach out toward her, and she was amazed, as she could not feel her own movements as her own hand reached out to take his; but then, yes, before he died, he performed a miraculous deed.

His quivering mouth could not utter words, but his left hand could send a message that painted a vivid picture for her to remember; he took a handful of bright red blood from his fresh wound and brought his trembling hand over to her yellow shirt, and smeared it; his mouth sought to tell her, his loving eyes sought to show her his father's natural and good love, sought to comfort her as she stared into his kindly face. He managed to spread two handfuls of his own blood upon her, and then he died, quietly, nobly, proudly.

She felt her hands reaching out to his stomach wounds, and then taking the viscous blood and pouring it over herself like it was a protective shield, began to paint a portrait of a credible corpse.

Voices hissed and rumbled throughout the camp as the gunshots slowly died down; sometimes, she heard a shout from the red-eyed madman, who had just discovered a live victim, and then she would hear the awful report of the rifle, and then the terrible silence that meant another life had been too easily taken away; it went on like this for many minutes, the rambling discourse from the plunderers as they checked the bodies and hollered and laughed and whooped; but sometimes when the howl of the surprised murderer rose up and cleft the sanguinary air, it was followed by the loud bang of the rifle, and often proceeded by the slow stab of the long sword.

As it was, she lay as one dead, to everything, so when the human beast came to check her hut, it threw a casual glance first across the dead man with the authentic fatal wounds and blood-soaked clothes, and then its glowing red eyes glided over to the young woman lying next to him with the similar blood marks upon her still form. Its reptilian brain was satisfied that she was also dead; but what did it matter, the creature thought, as it lit the straw with the torch; and then it stood back, pausing to make sure the structure was burning, and then ran eagerly, because it enjoyed incinerating the infidels, and ran proudly, because it had been selected for the important task of igniting the initial fires; and it was young and proud and eager, for this was his future.

Then, horrible, terrible heat from the consuming fire began to oppress Nyaring, and the thick, black, poisonous smoke began to smother her, but she could do nothing but lie there because the combustible voices of the assassins were still in the killing fields, whooping and delighting at the raging conflagration of the burning heaps of freshly mutilated bodies, and even some live bodies that had pathetically hung on for dear life; they exulted in it as would any conquering army; yet, they were mistaken, as they had conquered nothing, for the body is not to be conquered, and the soul impervious to such a harvest of iniquity.

So, let it be stated, here and now, good citizens, whose outrage at such atrocities compel them to cry for vengeance, that soldiers who kill citizens in this beleaguered land—whose actions by the very definition of the word are not justified as they are not engaged in defensive combat—will be henceforth hunted down by the Elite Forces of Righteousness to the dry, and wet, and frozen, and rugged, and smooth, and hilly, and crowded, and sparse, and barren ends of the earth, and there, slain.

She pressed her face flush to the dirt and cupped her hands over her mouth as the black smoke swirled around her; she pulled in her legs and arms to her trembling body as the bright, jagged, red-orange flames of the blistering fire flickered and crackled and roared their unquenchable desire for fuel; and still, the caustic voices of this menacing tide would not blessedly recede into the noiseless tapestry of a faraway distance, where their images would shrink and their presence would finally melt into the sinking, crimson horizon. The burning flames touched her legs and her agonizing screams were intercepted and smothered into the hard ground.

How many frenzied cries from terrorized Innocents have been planted in the virgin soil over the millennia, terrible screams originating from tortured souls that cried for Justice, unheard screams that sunk slowly into the deepest, congested layers of the earth, unrequited screams that settled into a graveyard of stilled voices that exist as a silent shrine against those comfortable people who will not rise up and fight against the palpable agencies of evil. We, as a race, first we are born, and choose, most of us, one distinct philosophy or another to live by; and then for some, at one point or several, some prepare to die for a cause, and then, ultimately, for someone or something, we do die, while others simply die never wishing to stand against anything that might risk a premature death; and for Nyaring, she was preparing to die, and when this logical, human revelation struck her, the pain of the fire against her slight body propelled her up and out of the hut and into the fresh open air, where she fully expected to die, where she wanted to die, where her entire village had died. Could she do no less? Where was her fidelity and piety to family? All were dead now except her, all having been mutilated or raped or tortured, or some perverted combination thereof, and because of this, she sought to join them. She yearned for death, having freed herself from the fragile cage of life, wherein lies our cowardly grip and implacable vision of our own self-worth; she chased the grand illusion of patriotic death in the fervent desire that it would comply and relieve her of all her worldly obligations.

But, O death, it is not humble, and will not receiveth all who kneel at its frozen bosom; death will not be mocked, nor abused, nor abandoned, at least not yet.

She stood, her frantic eyes searching the frenetic, smoky, debauched arena of devastation around her, her senses jumbled, her mind unable to sort out the numerous creatures who inhabited the area; and then her swirling mind caught the slurred movement of something: was it animal or human, horse or man, bird, or the dead sky above falling in red flames upon her? She twirled around, dazed, her arms asleep at her sides, her scarred legs tumbling to the dry, dusty ground.

And then the images amassed about her, conformed to the shapes of large, festering pustules, but red, oozing pustules with human faces, and they were scabby faces embedded in a crust of bleeding poison; she stared and stared and focused and screwed up her tearing eyes, and watched in horror as the black jacket of pustule around the faces faded and in its stead proffered the long and skinny, opaque, mocking meat of these monsters who had been hatched from the temple of iniquity and chaos.

She fell; no, she collapsed to her burnt knees, her feeble body ready to yield up its spirit, swaying to and fro, her hands and dirtied face held up in supplication to the merciful heavens.

The things with the human faces stood within an absurd dreamlike aura of brightness and joy as they beheld the lone, defenseless and very comely young woman before them; oh, how iridescent were their smiles now, for they had reasoned that all pleasures had been exorcised from the burning camp, and pleasures, they reasoned, that had been exorcised all too quickly, as they were experiencing a profound depression that could be assuaged only by another injection of unfettered mayhem and debauchery. In the past, they had attempted to merely keep captured women and slowly drain them of their sensual energy, but it was never the same, and caused too many problems in the camps, and so had abandoned the idea, and merely gorged themselves sexually on every woman they encountered on raids and then simply killed them.

They moved toward her now, the same way a pack of voracious coyotes move upon a lost kitten in the dark woods, howling and screaming the taunt of the invincible vanquisher.

And then came a loud, piercing whistle, riding like fluffy white thistledown in the hot breezes, and this stripped the moving horde of its momentum, their rifles at the ready as they gazed about themselves.

Came into sight at the west end of the camp, a man with a wide-brimmed, yellow sombrero; he was wearing long, white cloth cotton pants and a long-sleeved pima cotton shirt, and it contrasted well with his swarthy, much-scarred skin, thick black beard, and now-burning coal-black eyes; within his crossed arms he was cradling an FN Minimi, which was covered by a white cloth—with a belt of two hundred chrome 5.56 x 45 mm bullets that extended from the underbelly of the silver-gray weapon and wrapped up and over his broad and brawny shoulders, in addition to many two-hundred-round magazines about his person—and was capable of spitting out fifteen hundred fiery projectiles per minute; there was a small brown cigar in his mouth that remained as of yet unlit, and his thick lips were still puckered as he whistled despite the irksome presence of it.

It seems that his large mouth could accommodate one thing going in and two things going out, but it was too early to tell if it could also accommodate the dispensing of words.

As it was, he was still walking, without compunction, toward the interlopers in the life of the refugee encampment; the very long and elongated barrel of the FN Minimi was now pointed at his wary and curious audience.

He came slowly to a halt, fidgeted, took a few more steps, mumbling to himself, nodding his head as he viewed the panoramic view of the place, took an additional step, nodded again as if he were weighing and measuring and feeling the texture of his environs, and then rested; both of his arms rested on the FN Minimi as he stood facing the agitated Militia.

And when he began to talk, his black-haired head swayed to the rhythms and gestures of his animated hands.

"I was walking along the road, not a care in the world, and minding my own private affairs," he began, speaking in Kush Arabic, "and I noticed this unfortunate occurrence…" His voice was rich with a deep baritone, his sharp accent traceable to the Mexican state of Chiapas. "And I said to myself: 'self, I said,'" and he made a scale with his hands that shifted up and down, "this is not good; where is the fair fight that even your dear father and mother taught you was demanded anywhere in the world?" He shook his head and frowned, and made a "tsk, tsk" sound, and then said, his hands moving in swirls against this rapt audience. "All of you against a tiny little girl, for shame; it is not so good; now, if it was her heart against all of your hearts, well, I think she would win, you know, very easily," and he looked at she whom he had come for, and he smiled reassuringly and nodded his round head. His handsome visage was never still, as he pursed his lips, frowned, and knit his thick, black brows; his shoulders shrugged again, his body rocked to and fro as if moved by his weighty words. "But, you know, this isn't a fair fight; so, I think I will help her, and my mistress, FN Minimi," which he briefly lifted up in a hearty salute, "she will help, too, for she has a kind heart, and a sharp tongue, and does not like it when the odds are overwhelming; well," scrunching up his swarthy face, he then said, quickly, "so, right now, she has something she wants to say to you, as a little reminder to have better manners toward a real lady."

The Militia, holding their automatic rifles in their sweaty palms, had been standing, trembling, waiting for a signal from their leader, who had been searching the area for more strangers coming to their little fantasy slaughterhouse.

But between the signal of the leader and the opportunity for the Militia to discharge their puny weapons against the magnificent FN Minimi, the Mexican had already hit the ground and aimed his faithful Beauty and began emptying its two hundred rounds, which burst like streaks of lightning bolts into the bewildered and panicking soldiers.

The Militia were dead in less than twenty seconds, and not only that, but shot through and through and chewed to unmerciful and bloody bits by the powerful projectiles digging into their soft and weak flesh.

Now, the Mexican was the consummate soldier, running now, with all senses on the alert, checking the perimeter, as he had done previously, and checking for movement of the fallen bodies; when he approached the scattered corpses, he grabbed their weapons and discharged them into their bodies. "No need to waste the bullets of my sweetheart on these disposable humans; she has expensive tastes." When he was satisfied all were dead, he turned to face the young woman and, slapping the FN Minimi over his shoulder, he took his cigar and tossed it onto the heap of the still-smoldering, dead Militia.

The Mexican was gentle and kind as he sat down next to Nyaring and stroked her scorched hair and held her shaking body; and whispering words of solace to her, he picked her up and, cradling her in his arms, began to walk toward the nearest sanctuary wherein he knew safety, like a bubbling stream in a barren wasteland, might bring life.

This, then, was Nyaring's memory, of a village swept up in the beast's talons and obliterated and violated, and the beast turning its red, flaming eyes to her but being crushed by a lone, mystical figure who brought her to safety; it was this haunting scream of unbound violence that roared like a harsh wind in her still-terrorized mind, but it was the saintly image of her mighty savior that quelled her internal fire, and gave her a measure of great relief, and planted the seed that would lead to the will to live, and by doing so, help others to live as they ought.

Conall and Rustem

Conall was riding his horse at the front of his trusted men, using his binoculars to search the horizon for Enkidu and Tyr, who had ridden ahead to scout for the Militia who had chased them and the band of Africans, as he was still not able to use the walkie-talkie radios that had proven to be of bad craftsmanship.

He was uneasy, pensive, stopping often and closing his eyes to sense the slightest flux of change in the broiling air. Yoshitsune came up to him, and the two men rode together, silence their third companion.

After some time, Conall said, gravely, "A soldier of Goodness must fight the forces of darkness—it is his moral duty; but only when it serves him well? Mustn't we attack at all costs, and only when success seems certain?" He expelled a long breath and screwed his eyes up to survey the smoky horizon. "For every moment we hold back, they might be murdering Innocents."

Yoshitsune, not yet thirty years of age, was not foolish enough to answer; instead, he listened intently, for he knew well the agony of leadership in battle.

"But the need to engage the enemy must be tempered by the wisdom of our Mission, and our limits and arms." He shook his blond head as he held his own rifle on high, inspecting it as if it were his own flesh and blood. The two men rode on for a great length without more words, until they both sighted Tyr and Enkidu riding up toward them, and then Conall whispered, "Heaven help us to keep our sacred vows to do what is right in the sight of God," and his horse began to gallop, as did Yoshitsune's, toward the fast-approaching scouts.

Enkidu and Tyr slowed their mighty steeds as they approached their comrades. "The Militia has joined with government troops for an attack on a displacement camp," Enkidu shouted as he dismounted, and, after receiving a canteen of cool water from Yoshitsune and eagerly draining it, explained that the recently formed and as yet poorly trained and armed Kush Liberation Army, or KLA—which had been part of a coalition that had briefly held the southern capital, and still was challenging the newly formed Kush government, which was now a theocracy—had been routed nearby, and retreated.

"We captured a scout," Tyr said, catching a beige canteen from Conall and soon emptying it.

The men gathered round to hear the reconnaissance report.

There was a displacement camp some twenty miles to the east that held refugees who had escaped from the ambitious slaughter of the government-sponsored terrorists, the Militia, and, on occasion, even their own government troops; these were refugee camps by the dozens all over this upside-down, backward, inside-out, unbalanced-and-unchecked, spiraling-down-into-the-decaying-heart-of-mayhem-and-chaos country, and camps that at first promised safety and food and shelter, camps that had a semblance of security in the form of UN peacekeepers, and the Civilian Police Force from the African Union Mission; but, unfortunately, the latter two were like a leopard who is sent to hunt although her claws and teeth had been shaven to mere nubs; but this farcical shield never stopped the Militia, which at first raided the camps alone, and then, boldly, in collusion with the government troops; but the government troops rarely were involved in such atrocities, leaving the blame to their unofficially hired butchers.

"Militia are moving toward them even now in Jeeps," Try said, pointing to the east; "about two hundred in all—they are about ten miles away."

"How many refugees?" Horatius asked, leaning over on his black saddle, his arms crossed.

"About two hundred," Enkidu answered, gravely.

The forty men, each of them, silently and expertly, as a proper guerilla soldier does, was already sizing up the potential battle.

Conall led by example.

He mounted his noble horse, Conchobar, who, along with the other horses, had recently been fed his special mix of legume-grass, whose black, sweaty mane he petted as he rose up in the black, leather saddle.

There was no need for talk, only action; and so the men of this small liberation army aimed their hearts and minds and courage in the direction of the enemy whose flagrantly immoral tactics had created a situation where they either slaughtered or were slaughtered; so yes, these forty who opposed them would have sweet Justice in victory, or die gloriously in battle doing what they knew was right before all the world, for, they had long ago reasoned, there must always be men who, in the midst of a retreating race of cowards, stand boldly and intransigent in the face of a menacing, rising red tide; these men, then, these men of a higher moral turpitude, needed only to look about to recognize each other and thenceforth join together and form a band of soulful, righteous brothers dedicated to the eternal struggle for freedom round the world; wherever they went, they fought the expanding rings of wickedness, suppressing its growth, heedless of inherent dangers, of the possibility of death, of the inevitability of pain; for it was their destiny to leave the comfort and safety of home and ride willingly into the black cauldron of the unknown and do battle with the cunning forces that hide in the cold shadows and slink among men of goodwill to wreak havoc on helpless and trusting Innocents.

As the men began to ride, Conall saw, coming from the west, a fast-approaching horse, and soon, recognizing it, halted, as did the other men.

It was Rakhsh, riderless and galloping with a maddened fury.

The great black steed stopped short of his target and came, panting, walking up to Conall, who greeted him with a gentle stroke upon his sweaty nose; Conall looked to the brown leather stirrup and saw the black ribbon tied to it, and then looked again at the direction from which Rakhsh had come, and felt a deadly chill numb his body, as he knew the different signs Rustem left on his horse: Rakhsh arriving alone meant that something untoward had happened to Rustem, and for the men to come posthaste; the black ribbon meant Rustem had had little time to write a message, and needed assistance in a great endeavor; and if he had had time to write a message, there was, naturally, little assistance needed.

Conall did not like it, as Rakhsh had come from the direction of the Red Cross camp. "Though it is far," he reasoned, but still, he felt a dire need to follow Rakhsh back.

"I will go to Rustem," he cried to his men; "I will join you when I am able." He nodded, with a look of confidence, and cast it toward Yoshitsune, who in turn nodded back.

Yoshitsune swept his right hand upward at his brethren. "Go," he shouted.

Conall watched the men rush toward battle. "Do I forgo duty for selfish reasons?" he thought, giving Rakhsh drink and sustenance. "Should I have had the men go with me to save her? Is this a command I have, or the rule of the fool who follows after his own advice? Does not iron sharpen iron? Do I avoid counsel only to consider my own opinions? Is this not the folly of the tyrant?" When Rakhsh was nourished, Conall glanced to the receding cloud of dust made by his loyal men, and felt a deep hurt and emptiness. "I must do what I am bound to, by love, and I have not the right to ask others to risk their lives, especially when they are gone to save a greater number of peoples." But despite this self-applied, internal balm, he could not soothe his anxiety; and so, slapping Rakhsh on his side, he watched the horse ride away, and soon was riding his faithful stallion, Conchobar, in close pursuit.

The fluid motion of Rakhsh across the soft desert floor was like the smooth movement of a drop of pure, sparkling water spilled across polished glass, every stride of his muscular legs powerful and purposeful, every step certain, every complete step elegant, balanced, coordinated; the profuse sweat beaded upon his coarse, black hair; his noble head bobbed up and down; his sleek body was like a shot missile, slicing through this yellow chamber of heat.

Conall, riding Conchobar close behind, kept his head and body low and his vision high, his mouth covered with a white cloth handkerchief, his right hand gripping his M24 sniper rifle as it sat snugly in its black leather sheath next to the Heckler & Koch G36 assault rifle.

In ten minutes of furious galloping Rakhsh rounded a small dune, then tossed up his glistening ebony head and began to slow upon seeing his master on the ready; as Rakhsh was nearly upon Rustem, who was now standing with arms raised, he transferred his speed to a trot, allowing Rustem to catch his black saddle horn, and accessing the cruising speed of Rakhsh, effected an adroit swing of his body up and over and onto the seat of the saddle. Conall pulled up alongside him, and the two men, conjoined seamlessly into the forward locomotion of the horses, who now ran in perfect harmony, accelerated together and swept away at a swift pace.

"I counted fifty Militia," Rustem shouted, "moving eastward." The Red Cross camp lay three miles to the east. He did not have to look at the face of his friend to know its worried expression. He pointed to a high rise of jagged, black basalt rocks that sat upon a hill of hard dirt.

In a few minutes, the two men were dismounting at the base of the craggy hill, rifles in hand, running up its steep side, and upon reaching the top of this bluff, each man looked through their high-resolution, extreme-magnification binoculars at the faraway cloud of moving dust.

Rustem switched on the infrared laser measuring device on his military tactical binoculars, but they proved inaccurate, so he relied on his senses. "Nearly a mile away," he said, and even as he let the plastic spyglasses drop from his eyes, he had been in motion, as had Conall, who had also dropped his binoculars and turned to move; these were men for whom idleness had no hold, men who, upon sighting the enemy or their objective, had a clearly described and drawn path for victory already established in their clear, cool, efficient heads.

No words were needed as Conall leaped past the large boulders and reached the ground in three huge bounds that few would have attempted; and upon touching the hot sands, he leaped upon Conchobar and directed him to pursue a winding course around the sloping hill and directly to the Red Cross site; once he had secured this strict line, he raised his fisted right hand up in the air to signal his solidarity with Rustem.

Rustem, with his Barrett M82A1 .50 caliber rifle draped lazily over his folded left arm and under his folded right arm, lifted his right hand in a salute of fidelity and brotherhood, raised his rifle and pointed it toward the Militia, placed the black metal telescopic sight before his left eye, then leaned his right side against a gray-colored granite rock.

Conall assumed a nearly flat position on Conchobar as the horse raced pell-mell in the direction of the Red Cross camp.

The lazy Militia, having no sense of urgency before the forthcoming attack—as they had no anxiety about counterattack from noncombatants, as this was merely a murder raid—were strutting along the desert, engaged in laughing and humor and pleasurable conversation; but, as it were, they were not wholly incautious when approaching a target, and so normally assigned two soldiers to survey the landscape around them.

"Look," one of the scouts cried, pointing to a fast-moving horse and rider in the far distance.

The men of the Militia caught sight of the horse galloping in the direction of the encampment, and the paranoid thought that any figure before them was against them prompted several of them to capture the image of the lone rider with their binoculars.

"Target practice," one of them shouted, eliciting laughter from his legions.

"He has hair like yellow straw," one of them cried.

The leader of this band of soldiers was smiling, too, but he realized the gravity of the situation and, watching his men take out their rifles, he said, "He is too far away; you need to ride out to him."

"One man," whined the lieutenant; "he is just one man riding toward the camp."

"One man with a weapon," the elder cried and, gesturing to three of his men, he said harshly, "Now, go."

The three soldiers obeyed and clicked their tongues, banged their heels on their horses, and sped away.

"Faster," the leader shouted, motioning to the other soldiers under his command as they assembled their horses into a tactically offensive formation.

The three soldiers rode their horses furiously for a minute, but the prize of shooting a swiftly moving man was just too great, so they halted and prepared to fire.

A bullet ripped into the first man, knocking him backward off his horse, and then another bullet exploded into the second man, felling him, and before the third man could react, a bullet seized him and tore him violently off his mount.

The leader of the Militia threw up his right hand as if to curse this unseen enemy. "Where are those shots coming from?" he yelled, and then, looking at the lone rider and pointing toward him, wrath and vengeance the sole arbiter of reason, he opened his mouth to declare war against this aggressor, when a slashing, spiraling bullet crashed into his body and lifted him up and over the side of his horse, dead.

"Fire," the lieutenant proclaimed, pointing to the lone soldier, and feeling very much a leader now, was about to send riders after the seen enemy, when a bullet tore into his head and dropped him with a thud to the hot sands.

"Dismount," the next soldier in command yelled, and all obeyed, pulling their horses down in front of them and lying behind them, nervously looking about for the seemingly omnipresent slayer.

"Shoot up at the rocks," someone yelled.

"Shoot the rider," another cried out.

The soldiers shot wildly, blindly, ferociously, and simultaneously at the two targets, but without discipline, as they had never been in combat with a formidable foe; but they soon realized that their rifles were simply inadequate to the task, and as they proffered wasted bullets to the heckling wind and searing sun, the fifty-caliber bullets from on high bore through the prostrate horses and dug unmercifully into the wiggling, crawling, whining soldiers.

"We need to ride," another man shouted, having, after much hesitation, nominated himself as their leader, and he ordered the first squad to attack the hill, and the other chase the lone rider; and then the soldiers who still had horses were to ride madly toward the Red Cross station.

Conchobar was riding across the hard-baked yellow crust, carrying his master, Conall, who was still bent forward, his right hand on his rifle, when a barrage of scattered steel missiles stung the air about horse and rider; Conchobar, wounded in the shoulder, began to stumble and slow, and Conall, sensing the injury to his steed, readied himself for the inevitable.

Conchobar crumpled and fell headlong, and as he did so, Conall managed to throw himself clear, and tumble forward, his head tucked in, his brawny shoulders absorbing the great impact from the wrinkled, pockmarked floor of the desert. Conall, bruised and battered, immediately sprang up and attended to his horse, who lay on his side, bloody and dirty, and who, presently, at his master's prodding, kept on the ground.

"Good boy," Conall whispered to him and, inspecting the wound, placed a healing ointment on it that he had extracted from the leathern bag around his waist; and nodding to himself, took out his two rifles, walked away a good distance, checked the weapons for damage, as all the while desperate and untamed bullets crackled and snipped the air about him; he set about assuming an erect posture, his M24 sniper rifle held shoulder high, his hands steady, his mind clear, his eyes sharp; he sighted the fast-approaching Militia, and gently squeezed the trigger; one soldier fell, and he pulled the trigger again, and before he saw the next soldier smashed from his horse, he was sighting another screaming, rifle-toting Militia through the scope, to which he squeezed the trigger once more, and felled another soldier, and then lined the widely scattered soldiers up, one, one, one after the other, and each time he pulled the trigger, each time a soldier was mortally wounded and struck with a violent blow off his horse.

Bullets buzzed about his still form like importunate hornets, like a colony of bees, like outraged wasps whose nest has been disturbed; but hornets, but bees, but wasps that bite and sting and whip their hot dagger-like tails; and so, in the inevitable emerging chaos of a multitude, a conflagration, a hurricane of wildly flying bullets, one bullet managed to pinch his left shoulder, splintering his supreme equanimity, pushing him slightly backward, but not down; and so he quickly regained his warrior sense and composure, and brought up his M24 rifle and re-sighted on the coming wave of maddened soldiers, and shot his weapon once more, again, and again, with adroit and expert skill, shooting his mighty cannon into this poisonous herd of barbaric invaders.

Meanwhile, Rustem, in order to achieve a better angle and trajectory for the greatest chance to direct his fifty-caliber gifts into their proper targets, stood, as fixed as a flesh-colored tree, the long, lean, black and mean Barrett M82A1 extended from his right shoulder and resting on a giant boulder just as if it were a part of his body—a third limb, a third arm, to be exact—and operated with the same dexterity and ease as his other limbs, and coordinated with his mind as if connected to it; and presently, he was picking the wailing Militia from their galloping horses with the facile exertion of picking peaches off a lavender-colored peach tree; one, two, three, four soldiers felt the combustible might of the little steel fairies and were dispatched to the rough earth; and then one, two, three, four more were lifted off their saddles in a rapid and perfectly choreographed backward ballet, and rudely pounded to the harsh terrain below. Rustem was a master craftsman living the life he was born to live, a man singular of demeanor as regards concentration, a soldier by nature who existed best in the hot guts of battle, and he stood, now, unflinching, uncaring as to the fate of the bullets that flung their lethal bodies around him. He fired again at the approaching soldiers, four successive shots, and then four successive Militia were smacked backward and to the ground as if they had been yanked by a heavy metal chain.

A bullet found its irksome self in his left thigh, and Rustem stumbled, shook his head, readjusted his aim, and fired again and again, blasting the enemy, who, with every passing second, approached the danger zone where their mediocre rifles and mediocre skills might finally find their strike zone. A second bullet, and then a third, hit him, the first on his right shoulder, the third on his left arm; he bent down, but would not let his knees touch the ground, shook his head, raised himself, readied the rifle, balancing it again now on the rocks, and shot once more, felling another soldier.

Conall could feel the loud roar of the bullets penetrating the sizzling air, and heard them smashing into the ground all about him; and still, standing erect, he fired ten successive shots at the swarming enemy; he would not think of her, not now, not of Eleanor, lest he lose his clear focus; another bullet pierced his right arm, and his weapon fell; but he quickly picked it up and lifted it to his left shoulder and continued to fire. "Eleanor," he thought, "I love you."

And then the terrific clamor of dozens of rifles burst into the battle, and Conall and Rustem still stood, firing, firing their weapons, fighting back in the name of Justice, prepared to die for a noble cause that united good men against the dark forces the world over; at this precise moment, they could feel the United Brotherhood of Justice standing as One, where other stalwart warriors were blocking malevolent armies that sought to plunder and pillage Innocents, where these brave officers of law and order were blocking the cunning exploits of these evil forces, each one of them good soldiers, good police officers, good men and women in every capacity and of every age, creed and color, who had sacrificed their own safety to deliver a world from an enveloping darkness.

Those born to be painters must paint, and so it is with those born to be writers, so they must write; and therefore, it logically follows that a born teacher must teach, a born sculptor must sculpt, a born doctor must doctor; and so, it must still logically follow that a born soldier must, undeniably, irrefutably, unconditionally, soldier, for he can do no other; and if all these people are Good, as Good as a person can possibly be, then they will paint and write and teach and sculpt and doctor that which reflects Virtue; and also, if they too are Good, these soldiers, they will fight as one who reflects Virtue.

> For gallant warriors who fell, adorn them in armor and ashes,
> anoint them in spice and oil, dress them in purple sashes;
> They fought in Justice's bosom, they died wearing her crown,
> Now bury them in hollowed soil, and tell of their great renown.

The Siege of of Refugee Camp Five

In the frozen heart of that great desert, the Artic, there is nothing but ice and snow and wind; stand at the center of the pole and turn one full revolution and an observer will see no mountains or hills, no landscape of green or oceans of blue, no streams or waterfalls, no rocks, no valleys, no visible animals or insects; yet, there is life there, somehow, minuscule life, digging in, grabbing hold, adapting, surviving and thriving; there is brown lichen on a frozen rock—tripe to explorers—and algae grows on permanent ice, and plankton grows heartily in the icy sea; and the white polar bear, the Artic fox, the Snowy Owl live there, too; and there are darling, tiny insects, who, placed on a bare human hand, will die from its mere warmth; and the Inuit live there—who once lived on the tundra in the tupiq which was made of caribou or seal skin and held up by frames of wood or animal bones—surviving by hunting the whale and the caribou, the walrus and the seal, and fish; every form of life has adapted, whether it subsisted exclusively while on the ice or near ice, or on tundra or in the water, life continued; it did not move or journey to warmer climates or gentler environs; no, it rooted itself here, in this harsh region, and the Inuit, they made it less harsh, less cold, less sterile, by choosing to live and work here and raise families and fight here—for the land, for their life, for what they know, for the only life they have ever known; and they live here, and yes, and sometimes suffer and sometimes work too hard and rest too little and sometimes think about the lot of the rest of the world; but, in the end, they settle here, and here, they and their progeny will always—whether of sticks or mud, snow or skin, and on ice or tundra—make their abode. Pray, why don't the people merely leave?

It is the same way around the world; no city, no town, no province or district or state or nation is perfect, and if people perpetually left every ghetto and unclean place in search of nirvana and utopia and paradise—but often taking the human aspects of it with them, thereby setting up a new one wherever they settle—then every ghetto and unclean place would simply have perpetually new residents and lose the memory of the old ones who could have improved conditions.

People, an irascible old philosopher once remarked, are like interchangeable automobile parts when they move—everywhere they go, their environs are not altered by their presence, if an equal amount and variety of parts are already there: if a chassis is already there, and an engine, a steel-frame body is already there, and they are the tire, and other parts exists there, and then it is a complete operating system; it is when too many big wheels and too many brand-new, raw rubber tires ramble in, and there are not enough solid engines and fine interiors to accommodate them, that authentic trouble begins.

In the incalescent furnace of the Sahara Desert, there is seemingly nothing but yellow sand and dry air and hot winds; stand at the center of this scorched sepulcher and turn one full revolution, and an observer will see no mountains or hills, no lands of green or oceans of blue, no streams or waterfalls, no rock, no valleys, no animals or insects; yet, there is life there, abounding, hearty, tenacious life, adapting, digging in, digging out, living inside, living outside, darting hither and thither in the shade, under the rock, inside the cave, inside this fortress of sand and rubble and rock, inside this seemingly living, breathing, encroaching organism that boasts a coastline of three thousand, two hundred miles and covers the greater northern part of Africa. There are great survivors: the Fig tree, the Olive, Myrtle and Cypress tree, and a phenomenon of Acacia forests; and brown-skinned, brown-and-white-horned gazelles, the brown rabbit, and the brown Barbary sheep and the long-earned Fennec fox. The crocodile, cousin of the lizard king, the dinosaur, rules in the south; there are camels, goats, donkeys, here; there are birds and locusts and butterflies, all adapting, all surviving; and the people, wherever scant vegetation and water sources exist, are herdsmen, are nomads, are laborers, one breath ahead of starvation and disease, shy of one misstep into the petrifying tomb to join their ancestors who too were slain by the unrelenting, unforgiving ecological ecosystem of this cruel and unrepentant taskmaster. Pray, why don't these people simply leave? They do leave, but many stay; many want to leave, but merely move into neighboring areas of a similar habitat; so, what is it that roots multitudes in this unforgiving domain—is it poverty, is it war, is it fidelity to land or country, to family or tribe; is it patriotism, is it courage and resilience and a fervent hope that change will one day come? And yet, there is always hope proffered by foreign interests, by foreign governments, by charitable organizations, by new leaders who promise economic progress and social justice; the helping and lifting hand is always out to the people of the Great Sahara, but sometimes the hand is of steel and bullets and pushes the Africans back down, or yanks them upward to do the bidding of their newest master; or the hand is polished and burnished to a glowing shine as it shades them from the boiling sun, but all the while on the other side of the giant porcelain appendage, the other hand of the giant is sucking the natural resources of the land with an assiduousness hitherto unknown, and stuffs not only its bank accounts but those of its relatives and friends, and concurrently crushes the resistance of the indigenous population with the same mercy masters once imparted to rebellious slaves.

It is true, then, that people are the same everywhere, but it is only partly true; although people may be biologically the same, they are not the same if they live in the unyielding grip of violent oppression, where their inborn emotions are being altered, where their brains inhale the pungent incense of false promises and their hearts grow forlorn; so, maybe it is only a little bit true that people are the same everywhere, as long as one tribe has plenty and health and joy and freedom, and another has little and disease and sorrow, and dwells inside a prison of oppression and wars and droughts and famines. Yes, people are the same, in Eden, but outside of this consecrated temple of Love and Peace and Beauty, in concert with the immutable laws and concepts and perceptions of Nature that are innate within him, every step a person takes, he collects things, and with every step again, he learns prejudices, and with more steps—with every step every Man takes in each direction, north and south and east and west and every mixture and variation in between—he forms opinions and ideas, and experiences things that influence and therefore shape him, and inevitably he settles in a land, and therein, as he dwells, he absorbs more ideas and philosophy about life; and soon, his mind is baking in a stone kiln, wherein it becomes hard and inflexible; but this occurs on one mountain, one hill, one plain, one plateau, and herein dwell many people of many origins and ideas, and each region becomes absorbed into a governing force that dictates life, and oft seeks to influence and subjugate the other region, or, simply, dominate their own, wherein tyranny germinates and is nourished by apathy and cowardice and greed and selfishness; so, when all is said and done, when all the travelers have settled in their own lands, a census that is taken evinces a government differing in degree and kind, some close in kind and degree, others as far apart as the ocean is to the desert.

People, people, people, O people, who seek Heaven in every hill and plain and mountain and plateau, sometimes they find peace, sometimes they find harmony, sometimes joy, sometimes freedom, and sometimes they find darkness, sometimes they find terror, sometimes tyranny, and sometimes, too many times, they find an empire of death and destruction that has been faithfully and fitfully created by wicked rulers who are expressing the perverse vision within themselves of an event only described and as of yet not born, the ineffable expression that is the slowly emerging image of the kingdom of Hell.

So, people live, some in darkness, some in light; some people hide in the darkness, some in the light, wanting only to survive, too afraid to have their precious flesh exposed to the forces who unjustly control them, content to have a crumb, even when a slice is what they have earned, but would cost them too much to oppose their masters, to whom they generally grovel, if only to continue in their fixed and safe lives; and then, there are some, very rare and enigmatic, who, for some deep and satisfying reason, take great pleasure in standing fully erect and defiant in full view and in front of their cruel taskmasters, and herein is rebellion inaugurated, and then ushers in its younger sovereign, war.

From whence comes this notion of war: from the moral failings of Man, or the immoral machinations of city-states; and if it cometh from Man, how does he transpose it to others, and is it a basic human trait when one refuses to follow a ruler they deem morally unfit into war? And in the case of the latter, how do nation-states fasten the collar of obedience on their citizens who willingly take up arms and proceed with undue enmity against a hitherto unknown enemy? And how does war commence, from on high or on low; does it originate with a righteous man who stands on the highest mountain and who brushes away the resentment of his purported wicked enemy onto the tiniest pebble, wherein this bitter dust collapses the intricate and fragile harmony of Nature and proceeds to cause upheaval down the entire side of the mountain; or does it originate on low, in the charred pits of aggression, in the spoiled cistern of jealousy, where one man takes a drink and infects himself with hysteria and mania for power?

Must there be war—must there? If the trees had thought and speech and movement, would they war—would they? If the animals had thought and speech, would they organize and slaughter for territory and land and riches in their history—would they? Is it Man alone, or because only he has a heart—no matter if it is oft cold and jealous and cruel; because only he has a mind—no matter if it is oft sullied with ignoble purpose; because only he has a soul—no matter if it is oft suffocated by the practice of deception and avarice?

And woe, woe, woe to every soldier in every war, who thinks himself right and true as he fights without wondering why; woe, woe, woe to every soldier whose heart leeches particles of Love into the air every time its master kills with eagerness and disdain; woe, woe, woe, for war needs nourishment, just like the forest and the jungle and the sea, it too needs to be sustained and renewed after every intricate cycle of life and death and rebirth; and for every drop of blood a soldier spills, War rejoices; and for every utterance of nasty vilification from a soldier about his brother enemy, War puts out its spiked, serried, and sharp tongue and tastes this intoxicating aroma from these verbal bombs as they explode with their parachutes of spittle-dripping venom into its gaping mouth, a webby, musty, rotting hole like the entrance into hulls of rusted, blown-up ships; and whenever a soldier takes great pride in decorating his heart and soul and mind when the hope of his enemy is slaughtered and cremated like so many plague-infected, dirty, stinking vermin, War puffs up its swelling bosom and raises up its sinewy wings and is lifted up higher and higher, pushed up by the hot gases of calumny and enmity into a sobering, blood-streaked sky, to fly o'er the land and spread its opiate of power and bloodlust, its boasting of conquering, its declaration to arms for survival, its urgency to act now with devotion to savagery and a discipline to destroy at all costs, and never to question or seek discernment, but merely to conquer, and that without mercy, this last horror its most dreaded weapon; yes, War promises to bathe Man in the finest scented waters and clothe him in the finest silken garments and feed his stupid flesh with the finest food, and entertain him with the finest artists, if only Man will adore it and worship it and hear its siren song, and lust for all of it, every drop and whimsy and whistle and sigh; but it all must be done by Man without question—without debate, either by print or spoken words, without thought, either by politician or officer, soldier, philosopher, laborer, teacher, student, or writer, or any citizen; no, War rewards only those who evince absolute fidelity to it, and it alone. So, in this fashion, War is very much like a virginal, beauteous, and wedded bride, and Man is the old, lustful, rapacious bridegroom.

And what revelation of War is this, that begets destruction of body and mind and spirit? It is the War of Iniquity, the Unjust War, the Unholy War, the War to appease its insatiable desire for its own nefarious existence.

But what, say you, of the War of Justice, the Righteous War, the War fought to repulse the unholy invader, the aggressive City-State, a War necessary for survival of the Nation; what of this?

What of this War, then, that unfurls a starry Flag over the proud and bold figures of soldiers who fight with what they perceive as a moral right at their side, and who, every time they kill the marauding, merciless enemy, hear the song of praise from those they protect; and lo, they fight with greater determination and fierceness and bravery than the enemy they perceive as unrighteous, with more resolve and grit as they perceive their fellows with the halo of Virtue about their heads, and see a dark reflection of every vile thing upon the brooding mask of their enemy, rendering them now as

Beasts: Beasts of the Field, Beasts that slither and crawl, bark and howl, lie and cheat, and commit every atrocity against Man and break every commandment of God; Beasts that snarl and whine and screech, who commit gruesome acts against their fallen foe and mutilate their dead bodies and the natural rights of soldiers who are prisoners of war, this enemy that must be destroyed, crushed underneath the heavy boot of Righteousness. And so, the War of Righteousness is waged by the Righteous soldier, and this War assumes the silver raiment of a King, and with every breath breathed by its progeny, it grows, and by every courageous act of the soldier, it grows, and by every unselfish act and pledge given and battle fought by its loyal soldiers, it rises; and as it rises, behold, its golden shimmer pervades their beloved Nation and swells the breast of every citizen, and captures the heart of every child; and in this way does it survive, in this way does it grow strong, in this way does it breed and go forth and stand by the great faiths of its hosts, seated on a newly built throne of sparkling jewels, between the exquisite virtues of Love and Goodness and Peace.

But who is to say what species of philosophy, what supposed shocking truths that spur on a country, what divine revelation of War belongs to whom? If each side embraces the eternal right to defend for any number of reasons, who is to say which side the nature of War belongs to? Shall we say that both sides are Just, or that both sides are wrong, or that one is right and the other one wrong? The philosopher sayeth, "Let Kings and Queens fight their own wars, and let the rest of us earn our daily bread and enjoy the fruits of our labors; is life not hard enough? Must we also suffer the whims of madmen, and their councilors, and wealthy, hiding-in-the-shadows-like-a-lurking-monster corporations that will profit from the blood and guts spilled, and bones broken and sinew torn, by innocent soldiers and civilians?"

There was a war, then, a war, like any other war, like a thousand thousand wars before it, that waxed and waned, and put good men and bad into their early grave, that hemmed and hawed when its human fuel, the young, robust blood of young men, ebbed low, this war of worlds colliding, just one more war where men were plucked from their homes and sent streaming into the blazing inferno of human carnage; and the men fought it for their beloved Motherland, as their breasts swelled with inordinate pride, and the men fought it for their Kings and Queens—be they presidents or primes ministers; the difference is only in the title—who read about it all from their ornate, high citadels in the sweet embrace of a too-faraway-to-imagine comfort and ease, and smug satisfaction of purpose.

In this war, there was a very peculiar battle, wherein the moral principles of the men over here were not impeached by the unprincipled men in power over there.

It had begun thusly.

The War had been raging for two long, bloody years, and neither side was even close to capitulating, for each side had the unfortunate but requisite, seemingly inexhaustible supply of men to be fed onto the heavy metal grate wherein they were shaken and shorn and squeezed through the jagged small holes so that their strong and youthful bodies might spill their red blood into the spongy brains of their ghoulish masters; it was small battle after battle, followed by a bigger battle and a counteroffensive and a retreat, and then came more recruits and more fresh blood to flow that turned the slovenly watermill in the minds of their absolutely mad-as-hatter generals, and politicians who bethought themselves generals, and journalists who thought they understood war because they had read about it or seen it or heard about it or perhaps seen it on television or in a movie, and they too were emotionally moved.

So, there was this battle being waged between the two combatants and each side had dug in for a long Winter's dying; it was not unlike any other battle in every other war, a protracted, too long, suffering affair of attrition; men dying, men wounded, men dead, men fighting, men in all degrees and gradations of fear and courage, and wearing an emotional camouflage because they thought their fellow was superior in his dealing with the unfettered wounds to his psyche; men cool, men hot, men trembling, men awake, men asleep, men dreaming, men seeking to live here, to experience life here, to eat and dream and talk and laugh and do something other than fight and kill and experience pain and suffering and everything bad associated with killing every day and being ready to kill at any minute, and stoking the fire to want to kill, always, seemingly forever, without interruption, without the chance to simply lie down and not worry about being pierced to the bone with shrapnel, without a moment of peace to simply be a human being and experience what they should: to be fully human and not lose a part of themselves forever; but all men hoping and praying and begging for the consummation of a siege they no longer understood or cared to understand and wanted to forget, forever.

Will the newest order brought by the courier say forward? Then forward they will gladly go, if only to end this intolerable quagmire. Will the order say retreat? Then the men will gladly retreat, not willing to return. Will the order say the war is over? Then the men will gladly leave and forget and live once again, and hold no animosity against those they fought. Will the order say stay and fight interminably until every man feels forgotten—like a speck of dust on the field map of an officer far from the front lines, which is flicked off to make room for a ceramic cup of steaming-hot coffee—until each and every man is drawn and quartered, until the ants, by commencing their laborious march to dissect the rotting meat inside the muddied, blood- and guts-stained soldier's uniforms, signal the other decomposers to engage in the ongoing feast?

So, why; so, why, now, why, and what for, why then, why so long, why no change, why, why, why, men on both sides asked and thought and howled as they fought magnificently and obediently while they stopped the sizzling flights of tumbling bullets and exploding shrapnel with their strong and youthful bodies, and honorably and patriotically aiming their weapons in the blurred direction of their blurring enemy; again and again they executed this with the aid of that restorative elixir, sleep, and in the cold rain and slush and sleet, and now white, crystalline snow, even in the midst of innocent snowflakes with their intricate and beautiful designs; yes, even in the midst of all of it, the men fought as if provoked to anger by some outside force, and shot bullets and launched bombs and valiantly stood their ground, still waiting, still listening, still hoping and praying for the final word to release them from their solitary gloom.

Yet, it did not come, but supplies were always dropped on high to both armies.

A fresh coat of paint will last as long as a primer agent is first placed on the bare wood, or it will slowly peel with the advent of harsh weather, and so too it is the same for the soldier: he wears obedience as long there is something strong enough to hold it as it is first laid; look then at a soldier who faithfully swallows orders without question and wears the emblem of obedience on his attentive person; it, obedience, will not adhere to his mind unless first he has developed trust and loyalty, which must come from his masters who rule over him and order him about as if he were born to be fodder for their absurd whims and changing predilections.

Does true obedience occur in coerced orders? No. Does true obedience occur in a day, a week, a month? No. A soldier obeys, at first, out of fear, out of obligation and acceptance, and perhaps loyalty and a willingness to believe in a greater purpose than he; but lead a soldier into the Valley of Desolation with duplicitous orders from dishonorable and treacherous leaders—lo, even orders born of the pestilence and pursuit of self-glory of their superiors—and any soldier, every soldier of good conscience, will shed his thin layer of obedience as his inner layer of trust dissolves, and self-preservation for himself and his fellow soldier will be resurrected.

The men of this battle obeyed because obedience was thought to be the geographical route that kept them from catastrophe, kept them from certain annihilation, rewarded them as they fought without question or hesitation; it was obedience that took the shape and heart and language of their superiors, but it was obedience that began to crumble, for the men now seemed forgotten—inconceivably, unbelievably, but undeniably, dismissed.

And still, they obediently fought on, watching their fellows trampled into the wet gush of blood and sweat and tears, for it was all they knew to do, now—fight, for were they not soldiers, and what could they do here but fight?

And then it happened, without collusion, without orchestration, without coercion: it merely and joyously took them, like a velvet sphere of Summer descending upon them and bursting its brilliant warmth over them and allowing golden sunshine into their sodden flesh and reviving their sagging spirt—it took them; it took them like a first, delicate kiss from a vivacious and bubbly girl, it took them; it took them like the time they realized they were no longer mere boys but grown and mature men, it took them; and it took them so fast and hard and easily that they yielded up every bid of doubt and resistance to it.

If all men laid down their arms save Kings,
Then the bells of freedom would ring;
And all the world would of freedom sing,
As they beheld them flee, those cowardly Kings

Comes a man, unflinching in his manner, uncaring of his physical and material impact upon this harrowing world; he liked to say he had one foot on earth and another in heaven. "And," he often told his Major, back in Ireland, "I sometimes wish for both feet on earth, and at other times, I pray for both feet in heaven; on earth, I cannot be a coward if I stay, as I know heaven awaits me; but if I pray for heaven, a coward am I in the wanting of it, as I would leave the good fight and my poor family behind; so, I end up staying, and lo, pity take the man who stands up against me, for if I fight and live, I rejoice, and if I fight and die, then, too, I rejoice; so, on the one hand am I serving this corporeal body, and on the other, I am making my abode in my Father's Kingdom."

Yet, it was such a philosophy that served him well in battle after battle in this African war, a fearless soldier, a revered Captain who promised his men that in whatever order he issued them, he would partake, regardless of the wishes of his superiors.

Captain Finn—his last name was McCool, but his men called him only by his last name without the attachment of the proper official ranking—had been on the radio listening to the last issuance of orders, when, forlorn and forsaken, he put down the black phone; he took off his light-green-and-brown-spotted helmet and laid it down slowly and carefully upon the mud hill on which he stood; he drew his large hands through his blond hair as he closed his dark blue eyes; he inhaled deeply and exhaled a long breath as he nodded his round head.

He opened his eyes, and began to speak, and when he did, his voice was infected with malaise. "Nothing." He looked at his Major. "No reinforcements." The Major cursed, then cursed his superiors, then cursed his untenable position. "Why?"

The Major said nothing, for there was nothing more to be said.

The men of the 133rd Infantry unit soon heard the hard news.

"Wait," echoed up and down the foxholes and bunkers; "we wait and nothing more," was whispered by the soldiers in and out of the trenches and behind the piled-up dirt and rock mounds, all of which they now called home; and they gazed about themselves, at the dead and dying, and the wounded, and instinctively looked toward the enemy. "We wait," wafted over them as if carried by a whistling, creaking wind that had passed over a freshly dug and empty cemetery, a foul scent that choked them like the purple smoke from a charred corpse, and then lifted up and blew over to the enemy side, where Captain Haidar—his last name was Wakesa, but his men called him only by his last name without the attachment of the official ranking—had been listening to the last issuance of orders, when he, forlorn and forsaken, put down the black phone; he took off his brown-and-green-spotted helmet and massaged his short, curly, black hair.

He looked over to his Major, and when he spoke, his voice was full of wrath. "No one is coming."

The Major spoke like a dying man waiting for medicine. "No one?"

The men of the 99th Infantry unit soon gained knowledge of the latest report, and everywhere they were—in the foxholes, in the bunkers and trenches, behind the high dirt and rock mounds that were now their homes—they heard the despondent cries of their future children they were eager to believe the world would never hear, the moans of their families, the wailing of their wives—in the ashy, burnt, tattered chorus of, "We wait, we wait, alone, we wait, while others decide our desperate fate…" and lo, this bitterness, this desolation of heart and mind and spirit, spilled into their nostrils and poisoned their will to fight, and colored their perception of the battlefield around them as a vast human wasteland with no logical and orderly purpose, and this foul aroma wafted over them and drifted to the other side.

Two men fighting each other in a tightly constructed ring,
two men coerced to fighting until one has nothing more to bring;
but two men fighting each other who are instantly repaired,
the two men fighting each other might never feel despair.

This, then, is what generals want for their battles, an inexhaustible supply of flesh stitched and repaired and sent back into the steel jaws of battle—and in doing so, welding the minds of the soldier to do battle no matter how insurmountable the task at hand.

But what happens to the soldier when he no longer feels the mock succor of his superior officers? What then, what will he do then, when his bitter oath to fight unto death is pried loose by doubt and positing disturbing and probing questions: why, why, why do we still fight; why now, for what; why, why are we here, and for whom?

Captain Finn stood before Major Dunham, the latter whose face was consumed by an approaching dread.

"Here," the Major began, pointing on his muddied map, but his voice had lost its color, its tone, its authority; his inflections, their sharpness and subtleties were blurred, "we concentrate our forces." But he was caught in an endless cycle, as if knowing the scene of a future accident, allowing it to happen, and then starting all over again; his fingers lingered too long on a crumpled and tattered map that he had too long possessed. He sighed, but said nothing out of the proper sequence of official dialogue, for he was a proper soldier, having canonized the living, breathing legal manual that he followed as strictly as if it were a book of mere facts and he merely computing and solving arithmetic problems.

"I have been thinking," Captain Finn said, and as he said it, Major Dunham glanced up at him as if Finn were his long-lost brother come to finally bring him to his long-lost home; Major Dunham begged to hear a miracle drop from Finn's lips like they a silver drop of liquid rain on a parched mouth, he truly did—yea, he longed for a contrarian presence, an alternative to the death sentence he held, he longed for a champion, but then he would have had to crush it as surely as a meddling fly near a sumptuous meal must be crushed. "Major, sir, I have reason to suspect we have been designated as expendable."

Dunham's face flushed crimson with revelation—he was glad his head was down; and his voice was hard and mean, betraying no hope or sentiment. "So, we all are; what of it?" He looked up, vexed now that someone other than he had breached the unimaginable and unspeakable. "I don't want that kind of talk around here, Finn." He respected Finn, admired him, praised him to his superiors for his bravery and tenacity and improvisation in the field of battle, but here, now, he, Major Dunham, was the living, breathing symbol of orders of the army, of strictly followed protocol, and none of it must ever be compacted or stretched or circumvented, at any time or for any reason—ever. His head hung low once more, his eyes aimed at the logistics map.

"Sir, I do not mean to provoke you. I merely was thinking of the men, sir; perhaps a little merriment before the next incursion—that is, if we are expendable," and then he hesitated; "unless you know otherwise."

The Major looked up at him, his countenance irritated now. "Are you saying our superior officers have designated us as fodder for a greater good in this stinking mire of a war, Finn?"

"Sir, what I am saying," he said, respectfully, looking up at the snow falling and then to the men trembling and back again to the Major, "that we might give these men some rest before the next engagement."

The Major cursed him. "Say it, Finn, say it: our commanders have left us to rot in this bleak canyon because it serves some purpose we may never know or care to know, because it will never make sense to us, and only serve to lessen our faith in those who design wars."

"May I speak freely, sir?"

The Major cursed him again. "Stop with the proper protocol, Finn, and speak as I want you to, as I demand the best Captain in the army to…"

"Very good, sir; well, sir, if you were to be asking, I would be saying that it is very possible that the strategies devised by officers who have greater knowledge of the war, mind you, may have changed since we were first sent here."

The Major abruptly laughed hard, smiting his thighs. "So help me, Finn, if you aren't the most accommodating and respectful soldier I have had the pleasure to fight beside." He slapped the broad shoulders of his officer, and said, "I have known you two years now, and never an unkind word about friend or foe from you, just good soldiering—and being a medic, if need be, too," and his face sobered and gained inordinate pride as his voice grew sentimental, "and a good and loyal friend to his men."

Finn's voice laid out now in genuine gratitude. "Thank you, sir, it means a great deal to me," and he looked down and shuffled his feet, for the fair complexion of his visage blushed, and then he raised his noble head when he reasoned he had reined in his pride. "So, sir, as I was saying, I would be pleased if we could reconnoiter to a place of levity and foolishness, as is the want of young men, for a brief interlude that might lift their flagging spirits."

The Major had been building a smile upon his light visage during this curious roundabout of talk, and finally, he burst into a hearty laugh; he smote his thighs once more, and cried, "Finn, you are a true child of virtue," and slapped him upon more upon his brawny shoulders; "you are the only officer I have ever known who treats his comrades with a dignity worthy of all people—equality to all; and a man, might I add, who is my equal in stratagem and military knowledge—good Finn." He smiled now, looking at the blushing soldier, who also smiled and once more lowered his humble head as he once more shuffled his feet in the loose black soil; but then his voice grew solemn again, as was befitting his august position. "Yes, Finn—Captain Finn," he continued, nodding his head, "take the minds of our good men on a brief reconnoiter with merriment—so," and he looked toward his weary men, his trembling men, his uncertain, his sometimes angry and confused men, "they might be regenerated men, if only for a brief interlude, and remember what they once were before they stepped into this accursed oblivion."

There was a grim figure standing beside each soldier—each man felt this cold shadow as if its icy presence came from blocking out every joy and happiness in life, for it was the grim shadow of beckoning, detestable, alluring, grotesque, and thrilling war.

Finn sat with his men in a tight circle. "Lads, I have a reconnoiter for us to engage—and I mean all of us," he began, in earnest, subterfuge being his willing accomplice; "I know it presages peril, but I volunteered our company."

"Did you have to be so obliging," Private Lawrence cried, and his words, like poisonous darts, shot out and sought the most vulnerable members of his brethren.

"Yes, sir, yes, Paul, that I did, and right I did it, and the Major was most agreeable, too."

At the precise moment of Private Lawrence's fervent remonstration, a fervent whooping and hollering erupted across the curling, wispy, foggy landscape.

"What is it, Captain, what is it," Private Ruskin asked, his countenance pained.

"Well, sir, well," Finn returned, feigning gloom, "the other troops must know we have the reconnoiter."

Private Lawrence stomped his large, muddied boot. "Well, don't that beat all—well, now, don't it," he shouted, "ain't that just fine, just fine," and he gesticulated all about with his large hands, and withdrew his helmet from his large head, "ain't we always the ones," and he looked in vain for approval, "well, ain't we, fellas?"

"Shoot, Paul, we might be, but that don't mean the Captain don't always look aft' us," Ruskin said, and he looked to his fellows; "isn't that right—don't we always come out in an agreeable situation?"

No contrarian view was espoused.

"Well, there you have it," Finn said; "Private Lawrence may stay behind, and no bad feelings about it." He looked to the lone dissenter. "Guard duty for you, then."

Private Lawrence issued a huge smile of gratitude. "Blessed be guard duty, even if I hate it more than 'bout anything."

"Well, all is settled, gentlemen," Finn said, and as he stood up, the men were already selecting their specific tools of war, and then he said, his voice brimming with mirth, "Stow that, you eager men," and they abruptly felt the icy shadow of the unknown recede. "Tonight, we reconnoiter to relax and recreation."

The men cheered as if told they had just been healed of a terminal illness.

The men cheered even as Private Lawrence screamed his most strident protestations; they hollered and whooped, they truly did, even as Private Lawrence shouted and cursed and began to slam his large wrath all about the place.

"I have stinking guard duty; but what about me?" But no one was interested, as they knew he had just a moment ago been the one who had cause for joy and had not been interested in their heavy burden; but then, he began to cry in such shrieks of agony and torment that the festivities abated, and the men looked to their leader, who presently spoke, thusly.

"Well, sir, well, Lawrence, you asked for it."

C Company laughed loud and long and hard, but it was laughter, loud and long and hard, that was derived from their dazzling and raucous history together; it may have been laughter other men heard, but to these men, it was irony on gossamer wings; it may have been smiles other men saw, but to these tortured and tired soldiers, it was also a secret memory of insubordination against another superior officer; it may have been a smooth, powerful gait these young men now displayed as they moved away, and it was.

But the riotous laughter was carved out of a long-ago scene wherein Captain Finn had first made his honorable intentions toward his own men known to this other higher-ranking officer.

It had been an extremely perilous and pounding battle for two weeks, and the men were mere shadows of themselves, their bright young portraits of courage and fortitude a peeling image that trailed them in fragments as they dragged their lethargic forms about the blood-soaked fields, but the newly arrived Colonel, combat experience absent from his résumé, who quickly realized the hold Finn had on his men, contrived to break it and cast himself as the sole chief to be listened to and adored, by overriding Finn on strategy and tactics in the field that, during the Colonel's one-month stay, had plainly resulted in the needless deaths of five men of C Company; and recently he had ordered a reconnoiter, one of many he had ordered, far too many, which compromised the safety of the men, and resulted in three more deaths, but more importantly, the Colonel had personally selected the soldiers against the advice of Finn, who had intimate knowledge of the strengths and weaknesses of them and who was best for which specific reconnoiter, as each reconnoiter was unique and needed a special set of talents from each soldier to be successful; but this time, Captain Finn had ignored the Colonel's personal choices and selected his own men, whom he knew would perform better on the chosen terrain; and the Colonel, leaving a buzzing bee in Finn's steel bonnet, and the red-hot iron poker from the roaring fire of jealousy on his brain, prodded him to now act, thusly.

"Let's go, men," Finn had commanded his four original volunteers, and they forthwith complied.

"What is this, Captain?" the Colonel had yelled, and scorched the air with his incendiary threats, and then cried, "You will cease and desist with that detachment of soldiers and take the four men I have chosen."

Finn, never one to be assailed without a proper rebuttal, offered a proper response by yielding to the wisdom of silence and acting as if no order had been given, and continued to walk away with his men; but this served only to enrage the Colonel, who, never one to take incremental steps in dealing with perceived insubordination, unstrapped his black revolver and pointed it at Finn. "Halt, Captain; that is an order." When this directive was bounced back to him by Finn's unyielding locomotion in the opposite direction, he pushed the revolver in the direction of one of the soldiers he had selected for this duty but who had refused to go. "Finn—I am giving an order for your boy to go. Finn, do you hear me, Finn? Insubordination in the field is grounds for the firing squad—Finn, Finn, Captain Finn, stop right there, you loathsome pirate." But when Finn did not turn around and merely walked on, the wild-eyed Colonel screamed, "Then I will have to shoot!"

A shot did ring out, but the bullet had been fired by Captain Finn, who had expertly sent the steel projectile into the steel barrel of the Colonel's pistol, knocking it to the ground.

The Colonel jumped back, shaking his empty, stinging hand and cursing as Finn approached him.

Finn spoke, his voice the essence of equanimity and certitude. "Now, Colonel, I am sure there is paperwork to be filled out, but it will just have to wait until this mission is over." He smiled and slapped the still-shaking Private Lawrence on the back, and looking to the frightened youth, said, "Get some sleep, Private, it will relax you—now, son, that is an order."

"You will be court-martialed for this, Finn, and you too, Private Lawrence," the Colonel had cried, but Finn, walking away again, ignored him.

When he came upon his four men, they were aghast, and one of them said, "Sir, are you not fearful of the Colonel?"

Finn, whistling now, was silent for a good while as he casually walked along the winding dirt path that led into the mountainous terrain, but then replied, "I have learned many things in life, youngster, and one of the most valuable is that I do what I must, and whatever the outcome is, I shan't cry over it."

Later, the Colonel, before he could properly press charges against Finn and the four soldiers who refused to go, was killed by an enemy sniper, but it must also be said that defiance on Finn's part to officers of superior rank had occurred a few times previous, but as it had happened with the Colonel, those officers in question—officers, it must be stated, who were clearly and notably marked as overflowing with the conceit of power and profound ignorance of military strategy and tactics—never seemed to complete their official charges against him, owning to one unusual circumstance or another that prevented them physically or mentally from completing the task, inciting rumors that his men had taken unusual steps to make it so.

As it was, Captain Finn and his men of Company C and the entire 133rd Infantry, sans the few soldiers designated as guards from each unit, were gathered for a celebratory respite in this grim business of legalized killing. There was a grand speech by Major Dunham about honor and liberty, and the right of a soldier to take a holiday even in the midst of war; and that he was ordering the men, on account of it being the most festive of holidays, to secure a bit of R & R, even for a brief interlude; and as no objection arose from any of the men, he smiled briefly, and then, with a wide gesture of his hand, released them temporarily from duty. But instead of experiencing a wave of whoops and hollers, from the same men who had already been informed by their immediate officers of the R & R order, he received a surfeit of morose symptoms, of obtuse gestures, and weary, bewildered faces; of beaten and bent postures and sagging, numb faces; of petrified hopes and anxious dreams and trembling bodies; he beheld it all, from one extreme of the spectrum to the other, men who were wholly incapable of fully transposing this incredulous proclamation past their warrior-built minds because even though they were dead beat and beaten to death in every way imaginable, they were still, in their surging minds, engineers on a speeding train that had no awake brakeman; finally one of the most abrasive of the men—in that he still found the inner strength to engage his superior officers in logical thought—said, with great circumspection, "Major, sir, are you ordering the men—here, right now here, sir," and he shoved the brown butt of his rifle into the mushy soil, "to—be more precise, sir—party on?"

The Major, sensing a common link floating between himself and the men, applied himself to it. "Yes, Private, that is exactly my meaning—party on. By thunder," he abruptly shouted, looking about, "if you don't do it now," and he clenched the fist he held on high, "if you don't take the goblet of peace and tranquility and partake of its humble power, now, right now," and it seemed, to the men who were still cognizant of the smallest, sometimes imperceptible inflection and tones, that his voice now fell as if slain with a treacherous arrow of war, as his once-weighty hands fell lightly to his sides, as his once-grim countenance fell to his burgeoning pride, "you will be more stone than flesh and blood, and that must never be." He took off his Kevlar-protected helmet, unhitched his rifle from his shoulder, and walked away.

Yes, there was still an abundance of questions to ask, but none were so pressing that they might superintend the immediacy of this command to step down from the gory mantle of battle, and exhaust their joyful spirit.

The men celebrated; first, by laying down their weapons, they felt a heavy burden removed, as if it had been a malignant growth that had molded their will to its fancy, yet they felt naked now, and strangely incomplete; and second, by laying down their worries, they too felt a heavy burden removed, as if it had been a malignant growth that had molded their will to its fancy, yet they felt even more naked, and strangely incomplete; and still they indulged in diverse kinds of luxury, as if the practice of it would awaken the memory of when they were still young and innocent.

They sat and talked, they sang old songs, they sat and ate, they sang new songs; and some, they stood alone and dreamed of other private worlds, while others, they walked alone, and dreamed of this old world that had been shaped in their idea of Peace and Paradise; but in the end, when all was said and done, all of them had fallen in love again, with being exquisitely, marvelously, and simply, quietly, human.

There was one man who had never intended to allow his mind repose, and so, after the stirring speech of the Major, had walked along the perimeter of the small encampment, encouraging the guards, in their vigilance, to be steadfast and true, walking until he found Private Lawrence, who was somewhat resigned to his assignment.

"Captain," he said, upon seeing Finn approach him, and as he spoke, his face portrayed shame and contrition, "how are you on this wonderful night, sir?" The two men shook hands in good faith. He briefly smiled through the self-pity he sought to extricate. "I hear the men laugh, and I feel their joy from here; it is good for them." He truly was a humbled and timid man after he had bellowed and quaked. He nodded. "I am happy for them." Such words spoken from any other soldier would have concealed a conceit, but Finn knew the character of all his men, for in war, there is no time for pretentions and putting on of airs.

"Close your eyes, Paul," Finn said, and watching, in amusement, as the Private instantly obeyed, he continued on, "but there is something you do not hear—listen carefully." He let silence abound for a moment, and then said, "What is it you do not hear?"

He opened his eyes. "Nothing, sir—I hear the joy of the men, what I reckon I should hear, of men who have momentarily shed their armor."

Finn slapped the muscular youth on his shoulders. "You're a good lad, Paul, you truly are," he said, with a smile of empathy and fidelity, and his voice was mellow and smooth, like a fragrant wind as it whistles through majestic trees, "but what you did not hear was the sound of your own joyous voice."

The brown eyes of the tall youth began to mist over, and he looked away. "Captain Finn," he lamented, "I am not worthy of such frivolity, as I condemned myself to this purgatory."

Finn smiled, and said, "Paul, you are young," and he nearly laughed, thinking of his own youth, "you are a good man."

"But sir," he replied, choking back tears, "I am not worthy of such a tribute; I bring shame to my family whenever I let my passions wander without restraint."

Finn placed his right hand on the shoulder of the youth, and began to walk him toward the festivities below. "We aren't ultimately judged by the words here, but deeds, and your deeds in combat I will measure against any man, and count on you as his equal, and for most, his better." And Finn walked Paul far enough away from his established spot that that the youth might not feel its weight pressing down upon him, and when they had achieved a good distance, he let loose the soldier in the direction of the merriment, and then turned around, with a smile, and walked back to the small hill to assume guard duty.

"O Lord," he began, looking up at the great expanse of slowly forming, high-arched ceiling of black sky, "how could I ever ask my men to do what I would not do? So, here I am, but not alone, for Thou art with me—wherever I go—and so I am never alone." He looked toward the faraway enemy camp. "Whither their soul leadeth them, to rebuke Thee or themselves, and in doing so, choose the Light or the Darkness." He raised his infrared binoculars and scanned the perimeter of those with whom he and his men had become inextricably bound through blood and anguish.

Captain Haidar stood in the black raiment of night, looking at the distant enemy camp through his infrared binoculars, watching for the slightest movement that would allow him to believe that someone was still out there. "Two days without engagement," he whispered, pulling the black spyglasses to search the far corner of the embankment. "What are they thinking? Have they not received orders for an assault? They are soldiers, as are we; they must fight, as we must; they have no freedom to refuse orders, as we do not; our men are exhausted, and our supplies low, and our commanders incapable of helping us; is it yet possible…" He stopped talking when he beheld a faint glint from a small hill, and so he focused in on it, and presently, he could see the silhouette of a soldier who was standing with binoculars to his eyes.

Captain Haidar looked up at the thinning membrane of night as dawn assembled in its golden blooms and spread its luminous wings across the cold land. He looked again to the soldier with the binoculars and thought he recognized an archaic signal. He lowered his spyglasses, his countenance a font of bewilderment, then looked again at the man, and then whispered, "Yes, it is true—'M,' he frowned, shaking his head; "'e,'" he looked down for a moment, as if the act of accepting the message was the very heart of treason, but then his curiosity and weariness prevailed and impelled his head upward, like a soaring bird on a column of warm air; "'r,'" he murmured, incredulous still, "'r'...'y,'" and there was a pause in the Morse code, and then, in slow but sure succession, "'C-h-r-i-s-t-m-a-s...'"

Captain Haidar lost his regularly scheduled pattern of breathing, and in its stead, came a labored and long expulsion of hot frustration and fascination. "Is he yet mad, this soldier?" he mumbled, even as he felt his left hand rising to one of the lenses, "to make contact with those he has sworn to kill, and with a message foreign to us?" And then his hand, as if independent of his mind, as if a secret courier of his conflicted heart, sent the same holiday greeting through manipulation of the shiny lens and the emerging gauzy beams of light; when the message was sent and done—irretrievably gone and unable to re-enter into the lens of history—his body burst into a cold, hard sweat, and he could think only of the disgrace of a court-martial and the humiliation of the firing squad; and yet, while his body shook, like a scrawny tree surrounded by a consuming fire, there was an approaching calm in this that presaged a kinder and more fruitful future; nevertheless, he was first and foremost an officer in his army, and an officer bound by the rules that defined and shaped his every action and thought on the battlefield; and so, after this most disturbing deed, he ordered a soldier to take his place, and pursued a direct course to his immediate superior officer.

"Major Chikere, sir," he began, saluting and standing now at attention, his body totally erect, head up, chest out, eyes forward like a proper soldier.

The Major was sitting on a small, black wooden stool, his head hung low, his large hands massaging his face, and when he spoke, his voice seemed to come not from interest, but from a mere physiological response to his name. "Yes, Captain."

"I am here to report a serious breach of professional soldiering ethics during a time of war."

The voice of the Major reflected weariness and lack of enthusiasm to care about such a discovery. "Who, Captain..."

"Me, sir, myself, Captain Haidar, I have committed a grievous offense against regulations regarding contact with enemy combatants."

"What, pray, how..." His head was still drooping down like a broken branch of a once-sturdy and mighty tree.

"Sir, I," Haidar began, but hesitated, his voice disturbed by remorse and grief, "I, upon receiving a holiday greeting from an unknown enemy soldier who stood across the field—he used his binoculars to send Morse code—sir,

I, to my shame, and discredit, did the same." He still stood at perfection attention. "I have placed myself under arrest, and await your orders, sir."

The Major, still sitting calmly and quietly on the stool, exhaled a long, arduous breath. "Captain Haidar," he began, his voice assuming the tone of one who merely proffers analysis without a promise of condemnation. "Sometimes I wonder if you are more British than African."

"My upbringing has no bearing on my treachery," the Captain returned, in earnest.

"And what was this astounding message?"

"Merry Christmas, sir."

The Major rubbed his aching neck and then his aching shoulder, and then said, in an aching voice, "What do you want of me, Captain Haidar?"

"I expect you to follow the proper protocol and bring me up on proper charges—sir."

The Major finally willed his head to rise up against the heavy waves of responsibility that had previously borne it into the wet soil, and he gazed at his Captain—still at attention—who was overrun with fidelity and honor, and he smiled, though he knew not why. "Haidar, for goodness' sake, at ease, before you give me a backache." He watched in amusement as Haidar barely let his posture relax. He laughed. "Haidar, my good man, you are too focused on the man before you to see his environs."

"Sir?"

"Haidar, have you done nothing more than what you have so honorably and honestly declared?" When he received a reply in the negative, he would craft his reply, having known Haidar intimately, as all soldiers knew each other in combat, as soldiers do when they rely upon each other for survival, where each soldier is allowed to act without the recently acquired mental filter that hides their true selves from each other—there is no time for falsehoods here—for if one wanted to sing, they sang; if one wanted to scream and yell in their furious indignation, they did; if one wanted to weep and wail over the dead body of a beloved comrade, they did so, and without shame, as if these soldiers knew that once their mission was done, they would resume the artifice of the stoic male once more, and lose forever this moment to simply be as they were when growing up—completely uninhibited, and challenging all conventions, and even encouraged to do so, if it meant survival and success. "Captain, your admission of fraternizing with the enemy is duly noted—but charges must be delayed at this time, as I need you more on the battlefield than in a makeshift stockade for real criminals."

 Ray Dacolias

Disappointment surfaced on the face of the Captain, written on a stone tablet and in melancholy verse. "But sir, regulations…"

The Major caught the last, timid thrust of legal dogma between his sharp incisors and crunched it and then swallowed it whole, leaving a vicious scowl upon his war-torn, burden-laden, weary face.

The Captain begged off.

Now that the Major had realigned his senses to seize again his once-dormant anger, he ignited a tinderbox of wrath with a facileness born from frustration and an impotence of power to do what he knew was right. "Did it ever occur to you," he stated, but it must be clear that he was speaking not to the Captain but to those invisible cowards who even now hid their fat, satiated selves far, far behind friendly lines and in the solace and sweet embrace of what they desired beyond the understanding of an ordinary citizen, "that we are all fodder for imbeciles and megalomaniacs who feast on power like a parasite on a bird? That we are a mere squiggle on a military map that was revised and erased and revised again, and then shelved and forgotten, in a forgotten battle, forgotten by ambitious men and women who would gladly sacrifice our lives for promotion and glory?"

The Captain, who had admired the superhuman tenacity of the Major to explicitly follow orders, and with great success even in the bleakest of times, was aghast; yes, he, the Captain, a lowly Captain, had had doubts about this war, this battle, this time lapse without definitive orders, but he had to obey, he knew; he could grumble and he knew the Major would only chastise him, but with the understanding that it was acceptable and no real challenge would come of it. "But who," he wondered, staring at the slumped, beaten figure of the Major, "would chastise him?"

The two men existed within a tight sphere of power that they could not share with any other soldier, and they knew that resolution must come from within; so, both men dared not move until an epiphany came upon one or both of them.

The answer seemed to come so quickly to the Major that its very essence propelled him upward; and his voice was pure jubilation. "Why, Captain Haidar, I do believe I have viewed this thing through a clouded prism; and now, Captain, O Captain," and he slapped his shocked comrade upon his bony shoulders, "it is as if," and he gazed out beyond to the luminous stars above, "it is as if the stars are shining Truth upon me." He moved forward and waved on Haidar, and the two men walked to the trenches, wherein soldiers were on duty, who immediately stood up and saluted, and were forthwith relieved and sent back to the camp; and presently the Major took his binoculars and peered through the round lenses toward the enemy encampment. "And here I shall stay," he murmured, scanning the hilly terrain, "with brick and mortar."

Soon, in the golden aura of a birthing dawn, he saw the signal, and yea, he signaled too, a holiday greeting; but then he altered the mild flavor of the message, and tossed in hot spices and a pungent aroma that no mouth could long abide without swallowing.

"O, Good and Noble Major, Good Major," the Captain urgently whispered, "what have I done to thee to hasten your demise?"

The Major smiled as he watched the encoded reply flash toward him. "You have helped me slay the beast therein, Good Captain Haidar."

"Sir, it is better that had I died than tempt you with my weakness of spirit; we are not men, but soldiers, bred and born on the battlefield; and to turn away from the spirit of the warrior is villainy."

The Major looked up, laughter shedding tears down his dark face. "Villainy! O, Captain, Captain, thou art a good fellow, even if thou art more European than African—ha!" He shook his head as he wiped his moist eyes. "Self-sacrifice for a noble cause is the template upon which civilizations thrive; but self-sacrifice for a lost cause is folly."

"But is not virtue a uni—"

But the Major had already exclaimed, once more setting his face to the spyglass, and in the mischievous womb of rebellion, "Eureka! In yonder hills break, the message of our fate."

"Sir," the Captain protested, mildly, "are you mocking my European education?"

The Major, smiling broadly now, glanced at him and, nodding his head, said, "Yes," and then looked once more through the binoculars. "When I was a child, I spoke like a European, thought like a European, and reasoned like a European; but when I became a man, I put away childish things."

The face of the Captain blanched shame and embarrassment.

The Major worked the signals for another minute, and then, standing upright, addressed his slumped and dejected Captain. "Oh, where are your roots, Haidar? An African forgets what he doesn't need—remember that! We do not need the conquerors' etiquette or conventions; now look," and he pointed toward the curvaceous hills that surrounded them like fierce guardians, "we have a moment here, and I intend to seize it," and he made a fist of his lifted-up and extended free hand, "but I cannot do this alone." He saw the malaise of doubt seeping into the face of Haidar. "Captain, will you finish what you have begun, like a true African—noble, proud, brave—or will you be like our conquerors, who always leave talks undone?"

"But you want," he returned, sadly, "you want to collaborate with our enemy, now…"

"No, that is where you are mistaken, my good and loyal friend; I want to negotiate peace with men whom I suppose to have been abandoned by their superiors—men who, like us, are now brothers from within this common refrain of sorrow, who must want to wage war against our common conquerors, from without."

"It is treason to do so, sir."

"No, treason is when you betray your own kind, like our generals have— it is they," he cried, "who have committed treason against us, they who have broken a sacred covenant of brotherhood to never abandon their own; it is they who have used us spitefully, who offer us as sacrifice; look," and he pointed out toward the break in the rolling hills, "they too must know what we know; think, Haidar, think: two sides coming to the same conclusion at the same time, driven by the same impulse of revelation—the treasonous acts of our own, treason most foul; I accuse them," and he pointed toward his faraway homeland, "so yes, I accuse our officers up and down the continent, of starting this war and sustaining this war and funding this war not for Independence or the National Defense of our Homeland—but for their self-interest, and dirty, filthy lucre, for the shine of power and glory and fame; they are lost in its eternal flame, and want us to die for their perverted vision as so many others have willingly and blindingly died in obedience—but I stand here today delivered from that twisted paradigm," and he suddenly shouted, "let others die, let others be expendable for the 'good of the state,' but as for me, who has given all I can give, as have my fellows, and faithfully, we want to live, we deserve to live—we deserve to live because we have executed our mission bravely and honorably—and what more can we do; and so our reward is to live; this may be treachery to our masters, but as they are treacherous, we are exonerated; but this is the true sentiment of the African people: to live when you must, and die when you must, and now, we must live; this is true pride, and patriotism; to die now would only serve our zealous generals and kings whom we are no longer obliged to serve, for their unrepentant sins have unmasked their true citizenry—that of warmonger, tyrant, despot: they are all cruel and interchangeable taskmasters, capable only of ruling any peoples who allow themselves to be cut down like helpless trees of the forest and burned for their own desires; so, I say to you now that to live is good, and it just may shorten this calamity to restore peace in our homeland." His passion fell and he averted his eyes from Haidar. "Go, go get Sergeant Henry."

Haidar screwed up his eyes. "Sir, you want me to retrieve that lazy slacker?"

"Go, go get him and leave me," he lamented, and waved Haidar away, his head down, his spirit struggling to fulfill the courage of his mind to question and rebel.

Captain Haidar, his face drained of pride, turned, sorrow his company as he walked back to the encampment, musing intensely upon the soliloquy of the Major, wondering how such a great man could utter such apparent gross violations, how such a revered man could suddenly appear beaten, how such a brave man could appear so cowardly; but then he looked into his own tormented soul and allowed himself to dwell there not as a soldier but as a man who might endure this legacy of pain and suffering for nothing other than the gain of madmen who moved him about like a cold statistic, for political posturing, and he realized that a soldier was simply a man like any other man taking orders, and had the right to refuse those orders if they were corrupted from on high; and that was why, he now knew, he had returned the signal to the enemy soldier; and so, ten minutes hence, after replacing Sergeant Henry at the watch, and now joined by the Major, used the binoculars to sound off a series of dots and dashes toward their brothers-in-peace, and when he received a swift reply, Captain Haidar, without hesitation, marched boldly and bravely out into the foggy plateau.

"Proud and bold," whispered the Major, watching the Captain walk away, and standing fully erect now, "like a good African—like a real African of old."

So, they are as brothers on one long stretch of undivided, borderless, unified land; but sectioned-off, fenced-off, lines drawn in fire and blood, bullets and enmity, the men are strangers, enemies made in a moment of ephemeral ideology, by whims, by happenstance, and sworn to kill each other through no fault of their own, but by the cunning calculus of a seething few who draw invisible, shifting boundaries in their fanatical minds; but two men of a greater knowledge of the world and its illusory scales of Right and Wrong during wars of convenience might see beyond the pale of injustice and behold an image cut clean of a finer cloth, in the billowing smoke and ash, of a Universal Truth that was immutable law long before Man drew his first arbitrary dividing line.

These two men, their minds drawn from two different cultures and histories, approached each other, without weapons, without pretense and prescription, without self-righteousness, yet with honor born illegitimately from war, and with Peace and Friendship in their hearts; they stopped in front of each other, and no one was there to tell them how to be men, for they stood in the hallowed crown of eternal brotherhood, united now by a need to put away those things that had made them forget who they had been.

They each extended a hand and grasped the hand of the other.

"Finn McCool, son of Cumal, my beloved father, and Dana, my beloved mother."

"Haidar Wakesa," he returned, smiling, "son of Isaac, my beloved father, and Augustina, my beloved mother."

The men unclasped the hands of the other that formerly would have held the weapon with which to end the life of the other if for no other reason than for the bored mind of a faraway official in faraway headquarters whose fancy could change at any moment and end this war and begin another.

Finn, his hands resting palms down on his large thighs, his face wearing a thoughtful expression, said, "Truce." He held up his hand again.

Haidar, his hands resting at his sides, and his face illuminated by hope, held out his hand. "Truce."

The two men shook the other's hand for an interval longer than expected, but not longer than necessary; just long enough to evince fidelity to the present parlay.

Then they let go of the other's strong grip.

Finn thumbed a direction back toward his lines. "My Major stands behind me, waiting."

"As does mine," Haidar returned, cautiously, as if he still was uncertain what it all meant; he wanted to say, he wanted to shout, he longed to convince even his enemy, whom had been designated and specifically designed as something reprehensible and monstrous and worthy of a sanguine death, that this meeting was wrong, totally and magnificently wrong, a violation of every code of conduct and every rule of warfare, and that the end result could be only that the soldiers would be useless afterward, contaminated by the outside influences of the real world that must never invade the insular world of an unrestrained killing field such as war; that later they would be unable to fire upon their ascribed enemy, unable to obey orders from officers, unable to furnish the iron will to kill on demand; that they would be disgraced, court-martialed, sent back home in fetters and shame, humiliated in their hometowns, painted in the broadest strokes as lepers in the press, discarded by the citizenry as the most despicable kind of coward and finally executed;

these words burned on his tongue and were set to flee from his mouth at every lull and soft word spoken.

"There will be conditions," Finn said.

"Yes." He had wanted to say his incendiary words now, to destroy what was building before him every moment they did not plunge their long knives into the soft bellies of each other, to convince his enemy of the emboldened truth of his words, to make his enemy understand that a soldier has no easy way out, that it wasn't for soldiers to decide strategy or tactics, or the outcomes of battle, that they were mere cogs in this lumbering, giant wheel that rolled and had been rolling downhill since time immemorial over the ever-building-up of easily disposable bodies; that the only roads home were death or armistice for a good and obedient soldier; but something in the gentle face of the man before him, the man, after all, who had originated the message, gave him over to doubt, and doubt was the slayer of foolishness, and gave rise to wisdom; still, he would wait for the proper moment.

The two men talked for a considerable length, of troublesome times, and logical lines of broken symmetry, of absent guardians and revelry, of the burgeoning orange sun and lives back home; of shameless orders and human misery for the benefit of power-mongers; but mostly, and absolutely, they spoke of a truce born in the womb of Justice, a Justice for men abused and abandoned, men slaughtered and shaken, men loyal and loving; it was men, they decided, who needed mending, men to be stitched together, flesh and sinew and bone, mind and body and spirit, men who had earned a divine absolution from battle and then set sail on a fantasy voyage on a mythical crystal ship that was adorned by virginal maidens, which would land on a pristine shore of an idyllic isle that they then rejuvenated; it was men, they reasoned, who were caught in the steel jaws of arrogant powerbrokers, who had to be free, as must any innocent animal caught in the snare of the inveterate, merciless poacher.

"They are poachers of men," Finn said with great pathos; "they seek us to do their bidding, and when they are through, and our bodies lie rotting and mangled, and our bones dried and cracked in the boiling sun, they seek others to do their bidding; and if they change course, it is all good and well because they have the power; and if they reverse course, it is all good and well because they no longer do the will of the people, for they are a nation unto themselves, and we are subservient without voice; so, I ask you, why should we die so these human gargoyles might gorge themselves upon our fresh, virile blood; so, when the time to fight comes and we say no, then maybe we will have peace."

"We die for their corrupt ideals," Haidar said, still waiting to defend his position of obedient, tacit, mechanical soldier prepared to live or die for on a caprice—be it left or right of an ideology, or up or down of an economic goal, today or on the morrow for an attempt to attain political prominence for their self-obsessed, self-deluded, self-absorbed, megalomaniacal leaders; yet, for every utterance now, and every silence in between, he lifted a brick of blood and sweat and mud toward a common shrine wherein his brethren of Freedom dwelled, and once he placed this living and breathing brick of great price into its carefully hewn position, he could not retrieve it.

It was too easily and smoothly decided, this truce, but it had followed a natural course; days before or days after, or in another war or with other men, and this truce would never have taken hold and been sealed, never been allowed to ferment and flourish and come to fruition; but it had, and now, each Captain, after signaling to the other with a hearty handshake that a tentative agreement had been agreed to, returned to their anxious Majors.

"Well, Finn," Major Dunham said, quietly smoking a cigarette while sitting upon a small, gray boulder, "is it a boy or a girl?"

Finn laughed. "Twins," he said, and they shook hands not as soldiers now, but as brothers.

As the men walked back to their respective troops, the Major said, melancholy filling the empty cavities in his ripped and ragged voice, "I can only hope, Captain Finn, that it is a time of peace, here, in this dimension, created by our own dynamic will, and not a time of war, there, out there, creeping toward us like the black plague."

"Sir, do you think the men will abide by the rules?" He had queried the Major, knowing the answer himself, but wanting him to grab hold of the dilemma that an obvious answer would create.

The Major pursed his thin lips and knit his dark, thick, brown brows. "They will, Finn, to a man; I know they will, with all their hearts, now, they will not dare rebut it; but tomorrow, and tomorrow, well, who knows the course their minds will take; but our greatest concern is from the commanders." Finn was about to denigrate the identity of their remote and safe superior officers and scoff at their chances of discovering this radical truce, but he prudently abstained, and allowed the higher authority vested in the Major to lend credence to his agnosticism toward them. "Ah, but how absurd," he let out a prolonged sigh, "such men who have what they want never risk anything for Honor and Justice, and can never know what they do not risk for and gain, and seek Glory only if they are assured of it—and by the actions of those who are expendable, we build their stairway to prestige with our too-willing corpses."

The assembled men listened with keen interest to the efficacious commentary falling from the pious lips of the Major, hard words that swept into them without the foul odor of deceit and machinations; but lo, they did not want to believe in what their hearts had secretly desired, for such a reality frightened them.

"Treason," one of the privates declared; "is it treason, sir?"

A murderous squall swept along the damp ground, tugging at the unsteady feet of the men, its filthy stench creeping up into the flaring nostrils of the soldiers. "No," the Major replied, and the tugging slowed; "no," the Major said again, more assuredly now, and the tugging abated. "It is a recess, where each side has agreed that no rules have been violated, and no orders disobeyed."

The Captain looked in shock at the Major, and then began a hearty laugh that lent itself to every man, soldier, and officer. The awful, fearful rot of the unknown then fell, like melting icicles from their cold noses, and the men, caught in the unfurling wave of authentic laughter, willingly fell into its warm trance, and hilarity ensued, as realization that the battle, so long fought that it seemed they had been born here and were fated to die here, as if this was the only geography and culture they knew, as if the outside world, and their family, had ceased.

Festivities commenced on the next calculated moment in time; the men, saddled still with heavy camouflaged backpacks, utility belts, and rifles, ascended to the highest highs of the undulating hills, and peered across the zone formerly known as the Drive-Thru cemetery, and sighted a great mass of their contrarian brothers whose eyes also wore an expressive suit of apprehension, and a countenance dismissive of this transitory treaty, and stood, thusly, for a great while, their minds given over to fantastic wonderings, thinking of every conceivable argument to stay and rest or go and forget, or pull up their M16A2 rifles and attack.

"How do we know we can trust 'em?" one of the soldiers asked, to no one in particular, but to everyone in general. "After all, they wanted our blood 'afore, and will want it aft'."

"Reckon they are asking the same questions, now," another answered to no one in particular, but to everyone in general; for this is the way it was now, that one speaker here was speaking for everyone else, there; because this war had come to mean survival, and they had fought for each other in a way that no outsider could ever imagine or hope to equal.

"The Major said so."

"The Captain, he has vouchsafed good tidings for us."

"We might never go over to where they are; it isn't like we are lonely, and need to know who they are; it will just make it that much more difficult to re-engage the conflict."

There was a sharp pause that was punctuated by absolute silence, and then one man, rubbing his stubble chin, said, "I wonder if they have cigarettes…"

"Beer, I could go for a cold glass, even in this dismal mess…"

"A radio, a little music, maybe, coming from a speaker, not related to this conflict…"

One of the men removed his gear, and then said, "A smoke, just a smoke—I'll be right back, really, don't wait up, girls," and he began to walk away, as if in a dream.

A man cursed. "Why not," he muttered, "we're all dead men, anyway," and he too dissembled his warrior's dress and allowed it to fall ungraciously to the puddled ground, and then walked out into the unprotected battlefield, which was still strewn with blood and shell casings and small craters speckled with the black, burnt shadows of spent bullets and exploded bombs.

A man cursed. "Why, not me, I don't trust 'em, they're not 'uman, they ain't."

"Who is, when he is a-fighting?" another answered, and he too began to release his auxiliary gear. "I need to believe in this, I do." And his desperate voice trailed off as he walked into the misty invisibleness of what they all thought could never be, the cold, neutral unknown, supposedly impossible for a soldier trained to relentlessly kill an unlimited bounty of living creatures before him who were at once designated as the enemy and inhuman and thus unfit to live.

The mental partitions so craftily constructed by their masters to keep the men in the tight clutches of a mechanical mayhem that would serve as their mental and spiritual compass slowly dissipated as they observed their fellows abandoning their second skin, their precious security blankets, their life preservers—their utility belts—to the hard ground; and lo, their simmering blood began to cool and their inflamed minds began to heal even as they encountered this eerie but unseen force that pressed against their mental and physical energies that for so long had been erected as something not passable unless through gross violence; and their hardened hearts slowly began to soften, and their eyes, full of gore and vulgarity fed to them from the gruesome ravages of war, gained this resplendent vista of repose and relaxation, and stayed cruel memories, and gained a sojourn through a pastoral valley where no one sought their deaths, and they called it Paradise.

By the day's end, the men breathed out black death and despair, and breathed in the sweet fruit of hope and humility.

Captain Finn and Captain Haidar stood on high together, on the alert for something wicked coming, an unknown variable that would threaten to destroy that which they had so miraculously achieved; and as they conversed on the products of war and its nefarious effects on their persons, they came to realize that each side consisted simply of men on one side, and men on another; men with common ground, men who had common thoughts, and common ideas; men separated by a wide distance of geography in a wasteland that was no longer newsworthy in a war that was no longer viable, or profitable, and which was now a liability for those who had masterminded it; they talked of loved ones and friends, of school days and aspirations, and soon realized that had they been born neighbors, then good friends might they have been, despite their ideological differences, for true friendship recognizes no creed or color or heritage as a barrier; genuine friendship surpasseth all things, as it no longer sees with the mind, but the heart; they had families back home, and loved ones, and careers waiting, and dreams of greater things; they realized that the propaganda of the press, of the military, of the politicians, concerning the culture of the other was skewed, vehemently altered to profane and disgrace their foe; they knew now they had been pawns in a power struggle between ideologues who dwelled in a den of thieves as they plundered and looted and pillaged the world for their own pleasure and profit; and as they conversed, as they drew closer in the bond of friendship, they felt the hard, unyielding sword of the warrior slowly melt in their hands and stream into the blood-soaked earth, and where once they would have feared such an event, now they welcomed it, and the burden of carrying out executions for their wardens slowly lifted off their tired and aching shoulders.

Comes the Serpent

They had been of several dialects and tribes, but they had put their cultural divide behind them and united as brothers in a strange land, a new land they had built with the benevolence of peace they now laid at the feet of their former enemies.

The men sat in groups prescribed by natural affinities that each man possessed, traits and preferences unfurled by excited participants; as it was, men of tobacco comprised one circle, men of sports another, men who loved the great outdoors, men who loved classic automobiles, men who adored women (which was nearly all, and so men who worshiped them eventually took up their own inner circle), men who worshiped God, men who loved music, men of leisure, men of literature, men of business, all of them slowly falling into the protective, nourishing womb of Mother Earth.

And so, they were as children again, in the deep folds of bliss, throwing off the mature cloak of enmity so expertly woven by their egregious masters, now playing in these dead fields, felicity and humanity sprouting up and prancing about them like naughty imps. One might have suspected, if one were not privy to the circumstances of the geography of the place, and could, although blind, hear all the voices as monotone, that these men were casual diners, by consent at the same banquet, privy to the same humor, the same culture, the same employ—and indeed, they were soldiers still, but functioning as one whole, and wanting peace and serenity for their afflicted soul.

In this primordial soup of human emotion, was there unease, was there distrust, were there the blisters of animosity as yet unhealed? Does not any wounded living thing heal slowly, with great difficulty at first, and depending upon the host, heal at various rates from wound to scab to whole again? And who were the hosts now, but men with deeply damaged and abused and smothered psyches, whose hearts had been violently seized and rent into unrecognizable patterns and places, so that even rest from battle might not restore its original shape; so, yes, many of the men of both allegiances sat in a black cloud of suspicion, not allowing even a single uttered word from their now-reposed, former-and-perhaps-regained-future enemy to penetrate their personally invoked dome of bitterness, words that struck this invisible barrier like bits of icy rain, only to slide mercilessly down its corrugated, undulating slopes; but who, on Earth, was better equipped to help these men heal than their own oppressors? Who is better able to offer forgiveness, who is better to accept forgiveness, than those who perceive they have been wronged, and those who perceive they have been the aggressor? But did these men open mouths and ask or speak of sins past or present; did they admit sins or accuse others of sin? No, wisely they did not, for in every word and gesture and intonation and posture of every man, the other man saw what he sought to see, read in the face of his present fellow what he sought to read, accepted what he wanted from the music and rhythm of words and the position of the body what he wanted to accept; is it not the way of all encounters between men of diverse horizons and zones, climates and customs, skin and creed, rank and position, that they seek to build bridges upon which they might cross and meet in Universal Brotherhood, for what does Man want except Peace and Harmony, Joy and Family, Friendship and Beauty, Health and Happiness, God and Love? And any other who seeks to take these virtues from him must be hunted, like a wild boar that has gored Innocents, and cornered and speared and skinned and roasted and eaten, for the urge to live in Goodness and Tranquility is always stronger than the one to live in anarchy and fear, even if one is to serve an objective that is nebulous of vision and suspicious in purpose.

No one spoke of this grand experiment of brotherhood, no one spoke of its duration, or punitive measures from their superiors, as each man merely lived the exhilarating moment, the first hour to the next, the first day to the second day, as if each second of luxurious freedom would be their last to cherish.

It was Winter, but their words brought Spring; it was cold, but their deeds brought warmth; it was raining, but their new nature, of lovers of forgiveness and forgetting, brought them shelter; and lo, presently all hostilities between the men fell away, just as scales constructed by ignorance blind a man, and fall off and reveal to him a Brave New World once he sees the light of Truth and Beauty and Justice.

Each man began this truce on the far spectrum of doubt, eyeing his nemesis with suspicion and dread; yet, with each shared picture of a loved one, they stepped closer toward each other; with each story of a loved one, they stepped closer toward each other; with each common theme of their life explored, with each event and human emotion shared—tragedy, death, birth, jobs, school, friends, paramours, marriage, graduation, miracles, prosperity, suffering, justice given, justice taken—they crept closer to common ground where they would dwell in illuminating light, where they might finally see the unvarnished soul of their brother, and in doing so, finally be able to recognize themselves, and realize that all men share common traits and common values, and know that all men are truly brothers.

In a month, all of the men had acquired this Theater of Innocence regained, this new birthing ground, this glittering palace wherein asylum had been assembled by an absence of acts of malice and deception; the men were now free, having formed a new tribe out of the singular conditions of their collective pasts; they no longer thought about the war, no longer perceived this war, or any war, or any battle, into which they might be coerced, or even be filled with promised adventure to fight an adversary who was now friend and never again could be a foe.

As the men lay in sweet repose in their marble temple of sacred Unity, something weird and disturbing came upon them; a faint whirring of a mechanical engine sifting through the warming air—it was nearing Spring now, Spring who held out her fragrant and lithe hands to bring succor to those who had endured the harshness of her mean sister, Winter.

And then the methodical twin hum of the approaching noise perked up the ears of a few men, stirring old memories of what such an intrusion might mean, but still, they soon lay down again to dine on the sumptuous feast of rest and relaxation that had sprouted in the cool soil from the disintegrated bodies of death and misery.

From both directions now, within seconds, came an abrupt thud of silence, and the men, eyes still closed as they sat in the cool shadow of sanctuary, were not alerted, alarmed or even anxious; then there came a clamor unlike any other vibration or tone, tenor or intonation that had occurred inside this cozy nest: a squealing, squawking, screaming, plaintive voice.

"What!"

It had the bad manners of rude authority ringing in its loud banging, a red tinge of outrage that no longer had claim on their gentle spirits, an old and forgotten memory associated with the stink and stench emitted from those in the clutches of absolute and irrevocable power.

"How dare you!"

It definitely was of human origin, decided the men, who were awake now and listening, with furrowed brow, and none too happy with the someone or something that the owner of the voice sought to control, much as a master yanks hard on the short chain of his beaten and bowed dog.

One of the freed men chanced to look up from his prostrate form, in which he had arms folded behind his neck and a fresh twig of parsley in his mouth as he was gazing up into the high vault of a deep cerulean sky, and his countenance now became a landscape upon which grew thistles and thorns. "How now?" he wondered, and looked out among the splendid hammocks and makeshift beds of yellow, crisp straw and the exaggeration of ease and the cultivation of merriment abounding, and he thus purged the drowsy vision that had so disturbed him.

"You men stand at attention when a superior officer addresses you!"

Now, this angry and rude sentiment certainly roused the men from their lazy stupor, and looking up, they beheld a funny-looking man, all adorned in green and brown finery, and shining medals hanging by boldly colored ribbons upon his stiff-cotton-clothed chest, and a furious scowl and his short hands on his fat hips, standing before them on a small mound, his loyal adjutant at his side.

The sweet aroma of solitude dissolved into the rancid smell of overdue and overripe, decaying orders.

Two of the Allied soldiers jumped to and saluted, while the other men were still too intimate with a victory so hard fought and won, which had recently released them from the inner confines of torment to the spacious hall of ecstasy, and they were not fain to yield up such a divine treasure "to no plain ol' yokel," a derivative, a fragment, an unfortunate relic of the inglorious past.

"Where is Major Dunham! I demand to see Major Dunham this instant!" The small man shouted his words across the dissolving sea of tranquility as if he were the cause of their sun rising and falling, as if his mere words along could build up or tear down all human obstacle any number of soldiers had created.

More and more men were beginning to have the plump memories of the last months turn lean all too quickly, and quickly they began to assemble themselves, and soon stood upright and proffered a fairly effective if not sloppy and half-hearted salute, while the Africans began to sweat anxiety and fear.

Major Dunham approached the small soldier who was now propped on high. "Yes, General, sir," he began, but without a salute, or a gushing chorus of admiration and respect, but as if he were talking to someone who had once mattered, to someone to whom he was now merely being polite, and generous; and his posture was poor, his hands stuffed now in his pockets, a green, tender twig dangling from his lips, and then he finished, "What can I do for you today, sir?"

"What! What do I…you are Major Dunham! You will salute an officer of superior rank," he cried, but he was so flustered now that he was looking about in dismay, with pursed lips and furrowed brow, at the mass of men lying about him, as if looking for answers he thought must be there. "Are these men your prisoners? Why are they not bound and guarded?" And he looked back to the Major when the final realization seized him, "Have you gone mad?"

The Major, eyes screwed up, his head askew, said, calmly, "You ask quite a few questions—and in such a tone for a man of your age; you need to work on reducing stress levels. Yes, sir," he shook his head and pulled in his lips, and gestured about, "you definitely need a long vacation if you can be rattled so easily by such a small disturbance."

The General would never have allowed an officer of inferior rank, who was clearly in violation of multiple rules of military protocol, to prattle on so, but he was in such profound shock at this extreme breach of military ethics, that he was temporarily stunned speechless—but that did not last for long, for his indignation soon usurped his strangling wrath.

"Major Hanson," he growled to his adjutant, as if his body was inflicted with pain, his teeth clenched tight, "Major Dunham is now under arrest." His green veins bulged alongside his small, round, bald head; his ruddy face trembled—ruddy from excessive drink and celebration of awards and promotions won through the destruction of land, flesh and structures that were important one day to his personal campaign and forgotten the next; his fleshy, red jowls shook, his colored-black, thin mustache twitched, and his beady, squinting eyes hid behind their oval glass barriers, racked by quick spasms.

"Well, sir, it is too bad for you; I do not recognize your authority here."

Practically nothing in existence, not animal, vegetable, or mineral, at that precise moment in time was capable of sewing shut, even with a red-hot needle and steel thread, the gaping mouth of the General; but then it happened, and a fissure in the fabric of reality seemed to have widened a bit more.

"He needs to be shot, General," a sonorous voice dug into the blushing silence, and soon the owner of the voice was revealed, just as a curtain is parted to show the newest character in a play, his fierce face and mercurial eyes promising destruction to all those who had gained his disfavor. He had walked in with a haughty disdain that promoted the idea that all of his men would rise upon seeing his magnificent form, but this did not transpire; he cursed a veritable gusher of impure vulgarities, so much so that, if these maledictions were seeds, they might soon be a thick ravenous grove of tawdry shoots and leaves one day; for he was as all men of an inflated importance and ego are in any job: he recognized only his dense, insular world that could drop its blaring siren on any garden of innocence and crush it and absorb its energy, and in so doing, he was like a black hole that drowned out all the light and voice and pulse of life and radiant heat near him, too often leaving only a dull, lifeless lump of cold flesh in his carnivorous wake.

So, it was no surprise, as he stood with his loyal adjutant, that this African General watched with glee as his troops, as if they were flat land and he a powerful quake detonated underneath them that caused them to rise up in the fashion of undulating hills; he unholstered his ivory-handled Vektor Z88 semiautomatic pistols, and pointed them at the scattered, befuddled troops, and then said to his nemesis—the only man he considered a rival, whom he had agreed to meet here, at this precise time—without even looking at him. "See here, General, this is how you discipline insubordination," he shouted, disdain bubbling in fissures across his dark face; and then, the apparent coziness of the two armies, with their proud and lazy looks painted so joyfully across their sloppy visages, provoked an epiphany in him, "and treason! Just look at these duplicitous, unrepentant, good-for-nothing scoundrels!"

The General of the Allied troops cast a reproving look over the men, and his squinting eyes enlarged, the same way a patient opens them once his doctor tells him he has a terminal illness. "What is this?" he cried, frowning, with knit brows and screwed-up eyes, and then repeated it, as if surely he did not believe his own words: "What is this? Can it be—our men, in collusion with the accursed enemy of our beloved country?"

Major Dunham, the other player in the dreary drama, held up the lantern of knowledge to his animated detractors, his voice as smooth as silk and calm as a frozen lake; and when he stated it thus, he wasn't further away from them than spitting distance on a hot day in Summer. "The only enemy I see here are you two brutish simpletons, sent by those murderous blunderers who live safely far behind the lines and who must finally have been woken up from their drunken stupor to see that the bloodbath pipeline had temporarily dried up," and then he lifted his head as if with a proud gaze. "For shame."

"You let," the African General said, looking now at the other General as if he were a brother, "an inferior officer speak like that in front of your men? Why, I would just as soon shoot this yellow cur than court-martial him—why waste everyone's time for a criminal who begs to die?"

"His men, eh?" the Major said, amused, looking at the big African. "And I'll mind you to refer to them as men, not his," and he waved behind and aside himself, "that includes what once was your men, as well—for we have thrown off the yoke of tyranny and slavery." He waved his hands across the mass of men, and lo, everywhere his hand pointed, the men sat down; and as he spoke his voice was adorned with natural power that settled the agitated minds of the men. "Behold, a new creature, the dawn of Man as he was meant to be: Free and Equal and Peaceful, and wearing the natural crown of Victory."

The Allied General burst out laughing, and then cried out, "Are you yet mad, you walking dead man? Do you think deserters and cowards find anything other than a rope around their skinny and stupid necks? I may," and he allowed his head to bob up and down as if to signify his grand gesture, "allow them to live, as long as they indict you as the mad Pied Piper who induced them to such disgrace and dishonor," and he smirked, as if to say that he always won, simply due to his meritorious ranking in a closed system.

                               Ray Dacolias

Major Chikere, knowing that Major Dunham had played his essential part, stepped into the tight dimensions of this power fray: his demeanor was fearless, his posture perfect, his elocution scrubbed clean of all ambiguity when he spoke in his rich, natural, full-bodied African tongue.

"You, sirs, seem to be confused about the state we are in; we are, in fact, a sovereign state now, and we do not recognize your authority—unless," and he raised up his hands, palms out, "you wish to address our demands; but first, you must proffer an apology for treating us so miserably and cowardly— an act unbecoming an officer—especially for two like yourselves, who really ought to have better manners."

The Allied General, arms folded, turned to look at his horrified mirror brother-in-arms, and said, smugly, "Well..."

The African General walked slowly up to Major Chikere, with a sick, perverted smile stuffed with diverse kinds of ill boding. "The only reason I do not shoot you right here and now, on this very spot, you wretched dog," and he spat at the Major, but his dry spittle managed only to bubble up and hang glide to the moist soil, "is that I myself will prosecute you, and gladly put the bullets in the executioners' rifles."

Major Chikere signed, shrugging his slender shoulders. "I had to try, you know." He shook his head. "I am afraid you have wasted precious petrol coming out here."

The African General, his face as grim as disease, looked to his mirror brother-in-arms. "You know, when I came upon your vehicle, I was right to set aside our fundamental differences, so we might conspire to punish these treasonous soldiers." The Allied General eagerly assented again.

Captain McCool approached Major Dunham and whispered to him that it was prudent, if the Major were of the same mind, to disarm the generals and their loyal, doglike adjutants; the Major concurred, and then suggested the plan to Major Chikere, who likewise concurred.

Captain Haidar, standing nearby, was also alerted about the plan, and so he and Captain McCool turned to face their men.

But then a loud voice, like a clanging bell to signal peril, burst out from the small mouth of the African General as he raised his pistol toward the sol- diers. "You soldiers, get up, get up, I tell you, you lazy, degenerate, congenital cowards, who have shamed all of Mother Africa; up, up, up, you traitorous, filthy degenerates!"

The Allied General, his pistol un-holstered and waving about, also commenced to ranting and raving like one unhinged from sense and decency, instead now hitched to hilarity that stewed in a bubbling froth of undiluted power. "You swine, you filthy Allied troops, you living disgrace, you rotten, filthy cowards, up on your feet—that is an order, you detestable deserters!"

Then, it just happened, in the same sequence that a father loses his temper and strikes his son—usually after a long, sustained period of obstinacy and ill humor by the child; it happened: the African General simply stopped waving his gun about as if it were a cigar, and then began to discharge rounds into the men before him; and the Allied General, in concert with his mirror brother-in-arms, aped him.

No one would ever know why the generals did thusly, attempting to intimidate hundreds of men to capitulate to their lone, puny presence, but later historians speculate that it had something to do with a lifelong presence of superiority and power encased in the feeble minds of these officers, and their absolute faith in the concept that their very word and presence, and glorious past they represented, alone, was sufficient to dominate and control an entire division, or any amount of soldiers under their command.

Captain Haidar and Captain McCool raised their pistols immediately and immediately each man aimed at his respective ex-commanding officer, and their now-armed adjutants, and killed them in a swift barrage of bullets; but it was too late, for the human damage was done.

Soldiers had been murdered. The arrangement that the two camps had agreed upon before the truce was violated, and the consequences were severe.

This pact simply stated that if a soldier from one side murdered another soldier from the other side, regardless of the extenuating circumstances, then he would lose his life—but if he murdered more than one, a soldier from his side, too, must die, to balance the scales of Justice.

Three soldiers now lay dead.

Judgment Day

Two African soldiers and one Allied soldier had died.

Universal Brotherhood lay smoldering in a fresh grave, dug by old memories.

As the dead were buried, the somber countenances of the men reflected their abrupt awakening from Paradise and their passing through the thick membrane of obscene reality, wherein they stood, naked, hearing the turbulent sounds emitting from the machinations of war, and the ballad it sang therein, and the promise of doom through its menacing shadow; and the stubble of enmity, which had once been long but they had shorn, began to grow again at their restless feet, and the sinister shadows it threw, all speckled and striped, dotted and curved, they welcomed and commanded to dip into the reservoir of horror and fear about them to fashion a new garment from the distressing molecules of tragedy in an idyllic pasture; and when this chrysalis was complete, lo, it was a waxen coffin filled with the oozing pus of anger and fury that had morphed into a weird and mocking chimera, and the men rallied against it like they would any wound, and their minds tore at it, and the coffin turned to a slender wood of mahogany and pine, and their melancholy minds tore at this, splinter by splinter, but the coffin still imprisoned them.

So, their hearts sang for liberation, "Free us, free us, free us from our solitary doom," but their minds sang of retribution, "One of them, for one of us; it is the natural law of equality and justice, and we will be well again."

It was now as if the history of the Truce was now erased.

"But we don't have to follow the Law," Captain Haidar, rubbing his bald head, said to Captain McCool; "it was a Law established by men bound by a code they no longer believe in."

Finn, his face grave with the revelation of grim truth, responded thusly, "But they believe it now, and then, and so do you, Haidar, and so do I; it is what we forfeited to gain so much—and did you think we could gain Paradise without sacrificing one Innocent Lamb for our transgressions?"

"No, no, we mustn't do it; I will not allow it," Haidar pleaded, and turned to face Major Dunham. "Tell him he is wrong; it is your job to lead—tell him."

"How can I," the Major answered, his countenance bowed by Providence, "tell him it is not so, when he and you and I and Major Chikere know it to be true."

"Look at the men, Haidar," Major Chikere said; "they sit like ravenous dogs waiting for the kill."

"But why didn't we leave, Major, why? Why don't we just simply leave now—yes!" he said, excitedly. "We have two dead generals and their adjutants, so, why don't we just leave and go away forever—yes, that will resolve everything—there is always a way out!"

The sad eyes of his friends were imprisoned by inevitabilities.

"It is I who crafted the Truce, I who gave it life, and I alone who must atone for this grievous sin," Finn said, solemnly. "It is I who will go." He smiled and nodded, as if in remembrance of promises to be kept. "And I willingly go—I want to go—this life," he murmured, gesturing about, "it is no longer mine, for mine home is now with God and his angels and saints in heaven."

"No," Haidar cried, "we will talk to the men, and explain to them…" The two Majors walked away, slowly, heads cast down, their bodies limp, their spirits demolished.

Finn, facing his friend, put his hands upon the slender shoulders of the youth. "This thing I do, this unselfish act, it is what the Scriptures have preached, that to lay down one's life for a friend, hath no greater love than this." He smiled warmly. "And you are my friend, Haidar, as much a brother as I could ever hope for, and I should want to die like this; better to have known good men such as you than to wage war against them for no good purpose other than the vanity and egotism of those who roam unrestrained and devour those meek of heart."

Pious tears glistened in Haidar's black eyes. "But not you, Finn, not you, of all the men here, you are the most kind and giving, possessing the most love for his fellow—for you to live would do the most good in this horrible world."

"But this is the most good I can do, now, to prevent more good men from dying, by yielding up the life of one lowly sinner."

"For these, truly?" Haidar whispered, weeping now. "Who even now clamor for your blood? Are they not savages only, deserving of no good thing?"

"Of what good or bad thing they deserve, I do not know or judge, but what they will receive is a promise kept, and they will see a man of God die unafraid, and unencumbered by the lusts of life that tempt all men to sin."

Haidar, as if he had caught himself being too weak, abruptly stood erect, and held his head on high. "No," he stated, firmly, "you will not do this terrible thing; there is always another way, there is—and I will find it, you will see, my good and loyal brother." He turned and began to walk toward the men, who even now were loosening themselves from their self-made trap, in the same manner a fox does as he gnaws his ensnared leg in order to gain freedom; but these men were escaping from one trap to another of more intricate design and calculation.

"Haidar," Finn called, "you mustn't do this thing."

He turned around. "They will listen," he shouted back to him, thrusting out his right hand toward him. "I will make them listen."

"They move as the mob now, Haidar, and the mob knows only blood and vengeance."

"So, I will give them their blood, their death!"

Finn walked up to his friend and said, gently, calmly, "No, Haidar, no, it is not your battle now, it is not your yoke now, but mine, so it must be for a greater good."

"You are my yoke, Finn, because of the time we have spent together and the memories we have shared and the merging of our worlds, we are brothers, good Finn, as much brothers as my own brothers; as much family as my own family; and in my world, we take care of our own."

"Haidar, Haidar, Haidar," Finn whispered, embracing him, "this act I do, I do out of Love; and this act I do, I am not alone, for God is with me; and the place I go to, beckons me even now, which is Paradise, where I shall await you, my good and loyal brother."

So consumed by pathos was Haidar that he could neither speak nor move, but wept and trembled.

Finn left Haidar and slowly walked to where Major Dunham and Major Chikere stood before the raging bellows of fire and smoke, of which the African men now raged, who even now pined for blood appeasement.

"Men of the 133rd Infantry," Major Dunham began, his voice so devoid of the good cheer and enthusiasm for life so apparent these last few months, that his men felt the blood drain from their faces, and their spirits fall, "in accordance with the binding laws of our Truce, one of our own men will willingly sacrifice his life to recompense for the loss of an African soldier." The men grumbled, but the Major held up his right hand to impede them. "If it was the other side, you would be asking for legitimacy to fulfill the agreed-to law; and I order you, in the name of the Allied Code of Conduct of Soldiers in the field of battle, not to take physical retaliation against those whom as of late, we have called friends."

The two camps, having already receded away from each other, now, as if enmity were a corrosive force that eroded the foundation of the bridge that had been so carefully built, stood in two easily distinguished camps—one black, one white.

Captain Finn walked up to Major Dunham, saluted him, unsheathed his revolver, handed it over to the Major, turned, and faced his beloved men, who even now wept; and from his mouth would come the most eloquent prose, finally polished pearls and sparkling diamonds of virtue and praise for them, and an explication for his selfless deed and his eager ascent into the celestial firmament and his coming into Glory and Rapture in the Garden of Paradise; yes, his edified speech would be like a sweet-tasting wine of conciliation to their lips, a perfumed wreath of peace his forgiving gospel would place upon their grieving hearts and minds; and as he opened his mouth to let loose his blessed messengers of Love and Beauty to unlock the chains of ignorance and ugliness around his men, a loud report startled him, and he looked to his left and saw Haidar crumpling to the ground, wounded.

"Haidar," he cried, and running to him, saw to his utter horror that the weapon used in this shooting was still in Haidar's left hand. "Haidar, no," he screamed, kneeling next to him; he lifted him up to rest his head against his body, and he saw the mortal wound to Haidar's chest. "Haidar, my brother, my brother, my good and noble brother."

And as Finn held his friend, whose body now shuddered in its death throes, the light around the encampment seemed to recede, and the warm air seemed to dissipate, and the hum of calm that had grown up in the soil seemed to sink back in; and now there was a ghastly blackness brought by the phantoms of battles past, and an icy wind from the breath of death, and a restless chord, a rising clamor of armor, echoes from soldiers as they were shot, as they screamed in terror, as they fell to the hard soil during battle.

Finn gently rocked Haidar in his arms, whispered now, lovingly, passionately, "Why, Haidar, O, Haidar, O Haidar, O, why?"

Haidar, opening his eyes and looking into the face of his brother, now felt the pulse of his energies halt, and his body relaxed, and his heart leaped, and his mind seized upon one thought, as he said, with great passion, "You are a greater Light in the world, my brother," and he died, as he had lived, in the cause of liberating others from the senseless tyranny of Man's feeble incursions into determining life and death for Innocents.

Finn looked to the invisible sky and sobbed like a man wounded unto his very sacrosanct soul.

And what of the men of the African Solidarity—how did they receive the passing of their hero? Why, they dropped to their knees, their faces poisoned by regret, their hearts decaying with guilt, their spirits writhing in grief; and presently, they held up their arms to the darkening sky and wailed; but this action was not sufficient to translate their sorrow; and so, as if in a planned union, they began to rent their uniforms, first their green and brown shirts, and these they tore to tatters, and flung them to the ground; and then they pulled off their green and brown trousers, and tore them asunder, and flung them to the ground; in heaps now did these shredded and shorn clothes lie, in large heaps next to each other, and the men continued to wail and grieve just as if they had lost a part of themselves, forever.

Finn laid Haidar on the soft soil, and he gazed upon the act of penitence of the African soldiers, and he felt a kinship with them, and leaving Haidar, he stood up, and slowly walked down a small slope, and approached the men, who abated their lamentations as they beheld him.

And then, without further action or word, Finn took off his dark brown shirt and pants, and then tore them asunder, and placed them upon the nearest pile of tattered brown and green uniforms; and lo, after he did this, the men of the Allied Nations too tore off their uniforms, and then placed them in the huge pile whereupon Finn had lain his garments.

Major Dunham and Major Chikere did likewise; they tore off their clothes and placed them, each on the respective pile of their brethren.

And then Finn walked back to Haidar, and picked him up, and walked back and laid him upon the pile whereupon he had placed his own garments; and he stood there, observing with love the face of his fallen friend, and his words were mourning, his words were sadness, his words were anguish and pain: "He had a noble soul, and in Heaven, it now resides; and now my wretched heart grieves, in hell until I die."

And he instinctively stepped back, just as Major Chikere instinctively stepped forward, fell upon the body of his friend, and wept for a long time, and then raised his head, and kissed Haidar upon his forehead, and then reached into the pocket of his own trousers, which lay upon the pile, and withdrew a box of matches and presently, he struck one of them, and lit the box, and placed it onto the clothes of his fallen comrade.

The men felt the rising heat and saw the flickering orange flames increase but they did not remove themselves too far from the conflagration; and they sat down, and knelt in prayer, while others simply wept; and when the fire had spent itself, and the body of their fallen friend was consumed, Finn stood up, and with a solemn repose, approached the ashes of his brother, and taking some of the warm, black soot onto his fingertips, applied it to his forehead; and lo, Dunham and Chikere, too, dipped their hand into the warm ash and applied it to their foreheads; and soon, all of the men had done the same.

They were no longer an army of soldiers, but an army of liberated men, the scrolls that contained their military history having been abolished on the funeral pyre; and were now in civilian clothes once more; as it was, they were released from this delirium of killing and enmity, and were wont to purge their wounded minds of the diabolical lies of their masters; now, they would gather themselves and go forth and explore a world hitherto and hidden from them, for what they had done here had changed their hearts and minds and spirits, and they needed to rediscover who they were and where they had been going before the great apocalypse came; thus, they went forth, unafraid, on the soft grass of Mother Earth, bathed in her velvet beams of Spring sunshine, and wearing an expression like a newborn babe.

Finn shook the hand of Chikere, and watched him leave, and then he turned toward Dunham, and nodded as he shook his hand, and then watched him leave; and then turned his attention to the burnt heap of soot and ashes, and said, melancholy, "I shall live as if you are at my side, my brother, as if what you would do, I should do, also, so that you might be proud of me." And so he too turned to leave, and walked straight away across a green gown Nature had woven in loving kindness, a gauzy, plush, fragrant meadow that was full of vibrant life and the shining promise of hope.

And left behind in the filthy gorge were the four dead bodies of the soldiers who lay in mangled fashion, left behind for the filthy vultures and the filthy insects and distant relatives, the rats and ants and flies and the rest of the decomposer family nest; and very curiously, the tasty cuisine that these impatient diners began were those who had many slimy objects upon their now pecked and eaten, and chewed upon, pomp and circumstance uniforms.

A Battle

The Militia and government troops were like a band of jackals that stand on a precipice that overlooks a dirt field where dying and rotting animal carcasses lie, and at once, together, as if of the same mind, spring down a steep slope and begin to devour the outer edges of the prepared feast; so it was for the Militia and government troops as they lined up refugee camps in their bloody sights—it was a slaughterhouse vision, a frenzied killing field, and they had had it time and again and with no little resistance from the indigenous people or newly but poorly trained Kush Liberation Army and other rebel groups that had been disbanded or were presently forming, whom they routed numerous times, or the pitiful, makeshift troops of foreign nations;

it was the latter notion—that they could rout so easily these bleeding-heart Western democracies—that pleased them the most.

The government troops and Militia—henchmen of the government leaders, assassins of the leaders, dagger-tipped appendages of monster-projections of, human steamrollers of, carnivorous soldiers with the sloppy, blood-drenched grin of their leaders, drunk with the purity and financial benefits of genocide—never once flinched when they read about the Western nations' condemnation of this Country's never-ending civil wars; lo, they were wont to read such articles, especially after they had engaged in a harsh cleansing of a small village or refugee encampment, in howling, carnal glee, just after they had plucked the life-force clean out of a group of villagers, where they had murdered the men and raped the women and young girls and mutilated the men and murdered and raped more women and enslaved the raped young girls, and boys, and then sold them to slavers or just kept them for themselves; in prideful obstinacy, just after they had smashed into a peaceful village, in their camouflaged Jeeps, and horses, and camels, and where they had felt their breasts swell with pride as they machine-gunned the people who fled in vain, and then took the steel machete—a weapon of choice because it made the deaths of their victims so personal, and imparted such power and glory to them—and hacked their prey to gory pieces, and where they would burn every structure and rape every female and murder or maim every man; and then loot every house and rob every villager, and pull out silver and gold fillings from the teeth of the people by using metal pliers; and by cutting off fingers and toes just to get the jewelry—in the same way a predator rips apart its prey to get at the nutritious organs; so, as it was, during such times, when they considered themselves Masters of the Universe, invincible, untouchable, meeting no physical resistance by an organized movement or guerilla troops or outside foreign entity, taking anything they wanted from anybody in every target village; and subsequently, they felt immortal, superhuman, partakers of a new empire of a genetically superior race of Africans; and they were coerced to laugh heartily at the empty rhetoric of foreign leaders and journalists and celebrities who expressed disdain for this ethnic cleansing, genocide-slaughterhouse-madhouse of all indigenous people not like them, that was disguised in the trappings of a civil war.

The government and Militia troops felt like gods as they purged the land of undesirables, the human debris, the human pollution of their country, and they knew that no one or nothing could or would dare to stand firm and oppose them.

Thus, as one particular tandem of those human bloodletters approached, in their sleek green Jeeps and trucks, a refugee encampment of hundreds of makeshift homes of canvas tents, their brains were flush with the molecules of lust for female flesh and the exhilarating rush from freely taking human life; if truth be told, these soldiers could think of no better place to be, no better men to be with, no better employ than this, to be rewarded with so much wealth as they fulfilled their carnal lusts and drank the undiluted wine of power of doing whatever they pleased with living, breathing, free human beings; they reasoned that the exalted state of nirvana had been achieved.

And then the encampment came into sight, and the troops commenced to howl and shout, in the same manner wild dogs howl and shout as they surround a helpless, small prey; and they commenced to empty steel cartridges into the burning air, knowing the villagers would now be trembling in terror and straining their senses for sanctuary; and knowing the desperate search for escape of these people was fruitless, the troops roared in glee, just as if they were noble soldiers come to exterminate trapped and diseased vermin that had ravaged the countryside; yes, these troops envisioned themselves as heroes, patriots, lovers of freedom, acting selflessly to rid the land of human parasites that carried the black death that comes from adhering to a different philosophy of living.

Yes, bravely and nobly, the troops reasoned, they sped into the now-convulsive village, openly mocking the unarmed, green-beret-wearing Civilian Police Force of the United African Nations as they descended upon the first of the fleeing people, and then left their vehicles, shouting and pointing their hot weapons as they felt their hot blood pump maddeningly into their hot and agitated bodies.

Nothing on earth, they reasoned, could stop their raping, looting, burning, mauling, terrorizing, enslaving campaign, now.

But they were wrong.

A lone figure came walking toward the encampment from a southwesterly direction, the burning and shining sun behind him; and lo, his body was arrayed with diverse weapons, and he was humming, then whistling, then singing a merry tune, and the demeanor of his swarthy, black-bearded, scarred face was unassuming and tranquil, as if he were indeed strolling alone in the clutch of a gladdened, Spring-has-sprung, life-beginning-anew morning.

The Militia and government troops were so astonished to a see a man, perhaps an adversarial soldier, walking toward them, that they all turned round, their weapons on the ready, their eyes focused on his strange and even bearing;

he was wearing a brown-rimmed sombrero and stone-washed white jeans and a long-sleeved, thick cotton shirt, and amber-colored snakeskin boots, and carrying a wicked-looking rifle in his relaxed and crossed arms that was covered by a beige cloth, as he stood just outside of the accuracy gun range of the troops.

Of course, they knew they could kill him if they wanted to, if he was an enemy, and even if he wasn't, they might still kill him, if only out of boredom and a yearning for real battle—as long as they were assured to win, and win easily.

The man, seemingly oblivious to the human carnage about to occur before him, reached into his pocket, an act causing no little anxiety for his rapt audience—and retrieved a small object, and proceeded to walk around in a circle while observing this plastic compass; he stroked his thick, black beard, and looked upward, to the right, his brown eyes squinting, and then frowned, and looked upward, to the left, and then looked back again at the compass; and, apparently satisfied, he took out a paper map and casually unfolded it onto the hard desert floor.

He rubbed his chin as he squatted, analyzing the map, and then soon folded it up and put it and the compass away, all to the utter amusement and disbelief of the soldiers.

But then, as if he had just noticed their presence, he looked directly at them, and shouted, politely, in their language, "Excuse me, sirs, but I seem to be lost, and it is so embarrassing for a man," and he pointed to his heavily armed chest, "such as myself, who prides himself on having good directional sense."

He paused for effect, the same way an artilleryman shoots the first shell for effect—to size up range, quality and strategy, but in this special case, also for psychological reasons.

One of the officers in charge shouted back, "Who are you? You don't belong here—you are on government land. Surrender your weapons." There was not the least betrayal of worry in his voice, for there were forty of his men, and only one foreigner-drifter.

He shrugged his shoulders, and said, in earnest, "I am looking for a land that does not yet know that the age of tyrants and despots is at an end."

Another voice crashed in from the West, also in their language, just like a shot cannon shell. "But where are your manners, mon ami? Have you no cool water for my parched throat, no olive oil to rub upon my feet, no fresh fruit for my starved belly?"

The soldiers of the Militia and government troops swung their instruments of death around, only to behold a seemingly weaponless man at about three hundred meters on a small hill north of them, a bespectacled, sandaled, white-robed, golden-haired, fair-skinned man who was smiling broadly and kindly.

"What say ye, eh, good sirs? A drop of water from your canteens, yes?" the newest stranger cried.

"Go away, you vagabond," the officer in charge yelled, "or we will cure your parched throat with lead and fire."

But before further discourse could occur between the soldiers and the two strangers, the distinct whirring sounds of an aircraft penetrated the scene, and all the players in this tense drama looked hence to the fast-approaching IAR 330L military helicopter from the east.

There was nothing to do now but gaze at the mighty metal scorpion as it lorded itself over the desert, flying low and generating great gusts of sand-storms in its wake; presently, it hovered near the soldiers, landed, the engines went down, and then vomited out a soldier of a higher rank, who looked with suspicion upon the two unwanted guests, and then shouted in a coarse manner, "Lieutenant, who are these men, and why haven't you taken care of this hostile place?"

"It is my fault, El Jefe," the stranger with the thick Mexican accent inter-vened. "I am a hunter, and I am lost."

The General—so ranked because he had bought and killed his way to this title, while never having served in the military before—his black sunglasses and violent sneer prominent upon his arrogant face, replied, as he adjusted his green beret, "What are you hunting, you filthy Mexican trash?"

The Mexican smiled, and patted his silver FN Minimi; and simultaneous-ly, the stranger from the North threw back his white cloak, and swung from behind him to reveal a keen, black, awesome-looking, early-version, hot-off-the-black-market IMI Negev, with one hundred and fifty hundred rounds of belted ammunition of 5.56 x 45 mm fed into the machine gun and strung over his strong shoulders, hanging out like a mischievous steel tongue, in company with two more two-hundred-round belts of ammunition over his other shoulder.

Then, he, the well-mannered, well-tempered, even-keeled, nodding Mexican, while rubbing his whiskered chin, replied, and with great convic-tion and certitude as he smiled, "I am hunting you."

And then there came a great shout of war from the two strangers, first from the Mexican, who launched a missile directly into the belly of the steel scorpion, blowing it into bits of hot shrapnel and smoking ash, and then from the stranger from the West, who let rip the 5.56 mm bullets into the panicking soldiers.

When the Mexican had switched the FN Minimi to firing bullets, and fell to the ground, and directed its deadly cargo into the frenzied soldiers, this, adjoined to the absolute ferocity of the bullets descending from IMI Negev, quickly and efficiently pulverized the targets into a bucket of twisted bone and sinew, and pots of blood, just as if they had been violently seized and tossed into a giant food blender; the fight—a minor scuffle, truly—did not long endure between the two opposing forces, for the soldiers were just ordinary soldiers, not bred for international combat, not trained for real soldiering, and were not, in fact, real soldiers, with no formal training or discipline, for these men were really just human butchers sent on chores to wipe out helpless Innocents the land over; so, as it was, the confrontation was over and done in less than a minute's time, as was entirely expected in such a contest, and the two strangers still lay, unscathed, unconcerned, unassuming; and then they, as if their life's path had led to this exact spot, converged on the heap of corpses.

The people of the encampment, knowing a battle was to ensue, had safely hidden, and then when it was over, crept out slowly and cautiously from their hiding places like the survivors of a tornado; but like the survivors of any catastrophe who are just happy to be alive, they experienced a rush of euphoria and accompanying weeping, which was transformed into gratitude for their saviors and the accompanying embracing; and it was apparent, perhaps not to the people, but to an outside observer, how embarrassed the two men were, and it was soon obvious that they had not done this wondrous thing to be adored or worshiped.

And then both men, after commenting on their fateful meeting a few miles away, prior to this engagement, exchanged a hearty handshake, these born warriors, and living a proclaimed warrior life unto death; using their warrior sense, simultaneously, they turned toward the east, and saw a multitude of horsemen approaching, seemingly riding the fury of the desert wind.

Yoshitsune halted the band of men as they neared the village from a westerly direction, and spied the macabre theater therein, and decided to ride henceforth, by himself, to investigate.

His mount was magnificent, his bearing noble as he sat erect in the black leather saddle with his large hands on hips; his handsome face, replete with black goatee, and jet-black hair combed straight back, and black, fierce eyes, sharp nose, and large muscular frame a painted portrait of man as warrior at his mature zenith, a master craftsman with sword and fist, rifle and missile, a soldier who had made the pilgrimage up the polished garnet steps to the marbled temple of warfare, and had made therein his abode, and understood the esoteric language of combat, and honor; he who had seen things not seen by ordinary Man, and had heard the tribute of heroes; yes, he was man above most, and below nearly none.

"You," he grunted, an explosion form deep within his powerful core, as he looked at the two men with his fuming, black eyes, "who do you give allegiance to?"

Finn, unperturbed, smiled, and said, "Well, sir," and still leaning upon his beloved FN, "if there is a more striking figure on horseback, I have not seen him—and I want to see such a one!"

Miguel smiled and chuckled and shrugged his slender shoulders, and then gestured about, first to the dead, and then to the still trembling living beings behind them. "Ask them."

Yoshitsune grumbled, as he nodded. "You are hard men," he said, in his sonorous voice, and dismounted.

Finn looked to the other horsemen who waited in the distance. "I have heard about your merry band of dissenters," and he took off his white Paddy cap and he bowed. "Sirs, I salute you."

Yoshitsune, hands still high on hips, grunted in satisfaction in concert with a barely imperceptible nod, and not even looking behind himself, waved his men in; and then nodded as he addressed the two men with praise that rarely fell from his lips, "As I salute you."

Finn reached out his hand and clasped the strong grip of Yoshitsune, as did Miguel.

Justice binds men together, whereas injustice tears them apart.

The rest of the band of brothers came upon the scene, and took leave of their mounts, and soon, all of the men were moving about the village—lo, even now as one, as if Finn and Miguel had already been initiated into this intimate family of pilgrims; and the people perceived Finn and Miguel as saviors, first, and then as liberators, and the other men, as protectors, for they too had heard the rumors and stories about an elite fighting unit that dared to challenge the might of the Militia and government troops. It was soon agreed upon by all parties that the camp should hasten its removal to a faraway place, and be sequestered in a different geographical and ethnic region; the freedom fighters would lead them along the perilous path.

In the meantime, Yoshitsune sent his two best scouts, Tyr and Enkidu, to discover the whereabouts and welfare of Conall and Rustem.

Yoshitsune, a keen observer of his surroundings, and especially of men, and especially of dangerous men, kept a keen eye on Miguel and Finn, and noticed that the latter often looked at him with an amused and wry look; and so, Yoshitsune, being possessed of a short temper, approached the bemused Irishman.

"Something," he growled, to which the former army scout howled.

"You," Finn cried, slapping the brawny former Special Ops police officer on his massive shoulders, "you're a chameleon; ha!" Yoshitsune harrumphed. Finn smote his own thighs and his head fell back as he roared with laughter. "You're an actor, by Avalon, a kabuki, if I were to guess—now," he smiled, largely, his blue eyes as blue as the deepest opal, and gleaming with mischief, "confess, good and noble sir!"

Yoshitsune feigned outrage, his chest thrust out as he huffed and puffed and stood up taller, and grimaced, and frowned, but only managed to encourage more merrymaking from his seeming antagonist.

"There," Finn laughed, pointing at the grim countenance of the Yoshitsune, "you're a kabuki born and bred, for certain!" and he placed his arm around him as the two began to walk. "I love acting—even though I could never do it myself, you know. It's the transformation of character that fascinates me—like when you pretend to be a samurai warrior," and he acted the part, "toward myself and Miguel," and he acted it out, "toward the villagers," and he acted this out, and then slapped the big Japanese on his back, "what a talent!"

Yoshitsune desperately sought to extend his carefully constructed, hard demeanor toward this stranger for a much longer time, as was his custom, to test the character of those he met, but he was brought down by the honest mirth and sincere heart of his protagonist; and as he thought about how Finn and Miguel had so bravely fought the Militia and government troops, he presently burst out into uninhibited laugher, startling the other men.

"Kabuki," he said, nodding his head, and slapping Finn on his shoulders; "good training for men such as we."

Finn then stared at him for a time so long it demanded an explanation; and finally, "Sir, you are an enigma—being Japanese and Chinese." He nodded, smiling amiably. "Now, that is a history worth telling, and the question is: which one is the 'real' you," and then winked, "or is it better the man remain a mystery to the world..."

Yoshitsune gazed upon him with amusement, and finally nodded. "You have a sharp eye, wayfarer," and then he paused, scrutinizing him carefully, "and a flatter's tongue, or are a genuine good soul." He looked wistfully toward the place of his birth. "Someday, I may tell those worthy of hearing this incredible tale."

The freedom fighters escorted the one hundred and nine villagers throughout a vast wasteland of barren desert and brown scrub brush and scattered remains of corpses, scattered heaps of personal belongings of people fleeing terror, scattered histories of people who had adopted a nomadic existence in a geographical region where these hounds of genocide hunted them, where they existed in one village, and escaped to the next, and then fled a burning encampment, and then ran from this utter bedlam and mayhem into anywhere and anyone, during any climate or any season, into the open embrace of any who promised not to hurt them. The freedom fighters marched boldly into the next refugee encampment, uninterested in the righteous indignation of the defanged, impotent African Union Mission Civilian Police Force officers.

One of the officers in charge of AUM CPF, his face as if stuffed into a bag of fresh manure, spoke: "You," he began, addressing Yoshitsune, whom he had quickly deduced was the leader, "have no authority here—you cannot just drop off these vagabonds and expect us to feed them and be responsible for them."

Yoshitsune, much to the amusement of Finn, grunted as he sat high upon his black steed, his hands high on his hips, looking at the dour man whom he considered an unfortunate symptom of a larger problem in Africa: a bumbling milksop; he grunted again, and looked elsewhere.

Finn, who sat on his horse next to Yoshitsune, laughed as he regarded the chagrined African. "Let me translate that for you, sir," he said and, leaning toward the man, whispered, cupping his hand to his mouth, "he thinks you're as useful as a gun without a trigger," and satisfied, he leaned back, smiling still, "he thinks you're a poser—a scarecrow in a cornfield," and he nodded his head, "and where there's hardly any corn left at all, and the crows are in abundance, and aren't the slightest bit scared of you," he was gesturing about now, animated, "not one least little bit—so, poser," and he assumed the position of a scarecrow, "do you follow me, mate? No offense, truly, it's just a job, but really, maybe you shouldn't be here at all, if all you do is collect data on how much ripe corn the greedy crows eat." He leaned down and slapped the outraged AUM officer on his back, and then whispered, inclining his head, "But it is a job, now, isn't it? Don't feel too bad, it puts food on the table, clothes on your back, and a roof over your head." He leaned back and smiled, in such a way that the AUM soldier was utterly befuddled, not knowing whether he was still being mocked. "Well, give credit where credit is due—at least you are trying; I do give you that much," he continued, pursing his lips, and then winking at the man; and then issuing a reassuring nod, he shook the man's trembling hand, and said aloud, "How about that—all that from a grunt, eh? Well, God be with you in your endeavors—you will need Him when the enemy comes swooping down upon you like liquid fire dripping from the sky," and then he moved on with his fellows.

"That will not make him fight," Yoshitsune said.

Finn replied, "Oh, I know that, but sometimes, certain things must be said, even to state the obvious—as if in the doing of it, all of it becomes official, and real, and accountable."

"Herein in a nether world," Horatius said to Arjuna, as the men watched the refugees, who had sought this camp, join their brethren, "do we give them life today, so that they might die tomorrow at the hands of those desert sharks?"

Arjuna spoke, his hand still clinging to his rifle, in a voice rich in the intonation and tone and flavor of his southern heritage. "Sharks, yes, they do not exist without feeding on innocent life, guzzling the river of blood they create—they are just following a biological urge, one could say, and have no reason for contrition." Horatius looked at the Indian, and saw a man possessed of an unfurling wrath leaping like red-hot cinders from his grim countenance. "Those swine who run the United Nations ought to call in major airstrikes against these descendants of serpents and spiders, but they say it is just a regional conflict that must be meted out by regional powers; ah, but I say, collect all the Innocents into one place and burn the rest of this abomination of the human species into smoke and ashes, and let these poor people get on with a chance to know what it is to be truly alive," and he clutched his fist and shook it mightily in the arid air. He abruptly turned toward Horatius. "Is it not so in your Western myths? Did not your God take a few good souls, and then drown iniquity? We have the same in the Epic of Gilgamesh; why, Horatius, is Man so afraid to designate what is evil, and in doing so, fight that palpable evil," and then he shouted as he gestured with his free right hand, "that boasts openly of its wicked plans to destroy and torture, to all who will listen? What has become of us, that we must be careful in war and sit down and mourn and grieve our losses and casualties even while we fight? Is there a civilized war, eh? We are civilized warriors and our enemy is a ruthless barbarian." He then stated with the punctuated finesse of an educated man, a scholar in the fierce act of reasoning and critical thinking, a man whose mind was trained to track and trap and devour a quarry that was illogical, unreasonable, and diabolical, "Look at the last wars of America—soldiers wearing surgical gloves, instead of carrying rifles; soldiers coerced to fire only at the enemy when the Innocents are not about; now," and he tossed up his arms, "I ask you, what kind of war is that? I have studied war, and I know the Second World War would have been prolonged and caused even more deaths had we been excessively worried about civilian casualties." He shook his round head, and a tuft of his thick, black, curly hair swayed upon his dark forehead, and his tone became otherworldly—anchored, as it were, to the spirit of ancient, immortal warriors and their honorable code earned through fighting. "When a necessary war comes, it is no longer a civilized world; it is a barbaric one, and where the war is, so too is barbarism—the soldiers are no longer civilized, nor their commander, nor their people; it is as if time has slipped and the wars of the past are aligned with us, giving us affirmation for the infliction of misery to come; the civilized world does not want war, but when it comes, we must let out all the stops or suffer longer and suffer more; and still, still," and he knit his thick, black eyebrows as his posture slumped, "we fight because we hope that our actions will one day prevent more misery, so that when another war does begin, it is no fault of ours; but that when they look to the past, they will see us," and his posture became erect, "and they will see what we have done, and how we did it famously."

Horatius knew that Arjuna had lived in a small village in southern India, and that later Arjuna had treated soldiers and civilians during the Indian-Pakistan conflict; but he did not know much more. He did not reply now.

The men, after surveying the perimeter of the encampment, moved out toward the direction in which their two fellows had ridden to the rescue; and still without new radios, Enkidu and Tyr came galloping up to them, and after delivering the disturbing yet relieving news about their two fallen friends, all of the men provoked their horses into a furious pace toward the Western provinces.

The Africans

Man in industrial nations came of age swaddled in health and wealth and peace, and still, the esoteric Truths and precepts of life are too often on a horizon too far distant, and in a metaphysical land they may never reach because of their inherent tenacity to rebel against any philosophy already in existence, while the temptation of easy living becomes, unbeknown to them, their adversary, and sloth and capitulation their earthly refuge; yes, they have every opportunity to find paradise, yet abandon the journey because of hardship, because of suffering, because of poverty, and so merge into the indistinguishable masses, percolating into the frenzied pace of existence until they are so divided by interests and desires and unreasonable craving for things, that they end up going nowhere but in tight concentric circles, much the same way that a caged hamster runs his snug little wheel so eagerly, thinking that one day, he will indeed wind up somewhere other than where he is destined always to be.

But then to grow up in the furnace of war and destruction, to live in the same open pit as corpses and mutilated citizens, to breathe in the same infected fumes as those sick and dying, to share the same language and heritage of those hunted and murdered like so many plague-infected rats, and then to discover that the heart of Man is not universally cruel, to know that things once bent can be straightened again, why, this, then is the crucible of the African youth: to know that there exists verse that does not prescribe cruelty but kindness, not malevolence but benevolence, not enmity but love; and once this testimony of Virtue and Justice has been injected into his bloodstream and fed into his ravenous heart and fills out his hollow frame, he must now pursue a course that will bring him above the bedlam so he might see what good things he can see.

Now, we turn to the fusion of diverse Africans organized and led by Moses, all of whom had not too long ago roamed this barren land to discover first their identity as men, next for the reality of their tribe, and then their sacred mission as a cohesive fighting unit whose sole existence was to defend the defenseless.

Moses, once he realized that the taste of rotten fruit from widespread destruction and the societal flattening of law and order in his mouth was unnatural and unnecessary, once he investigated the history of Africa, and once he met other radical youths of the same philosophical dendrites, felt as if a concrete slab had been lifted from his muscular chest, allowing him to breathe as if for the first time, freeing him to move beyond the walls of the feigned rosy sunbeams of youth and real fear built by his corrupt lords and masters, and peer into the tangled, mangled contusion that is the history of his homeland; and lo, after he had ingested large portions of it, he wished with all the fervor in his noble heart to revive his beloved country to its past greatness and innocence.

The world had registered him upon his birth as simply one more hungry mouth to feed, a baby doomed to die early from a long choice of horrible and early deaths—malnutrition, disease, war, murder, kidnapping, slavery—a baby better never born, and if born, better to die at birth than cause further depletion of waning resources and thereby bringing grief to his own mother; yes, better to die at birth and abate this eroding, slowly creeping practice of families who dwelled in abject poverty and still insisted on imposing no limits on the number of children they must rear.

His was a birth flame barely flickering in a land of groans and wailings, a baby of no consequence, another male in a family seven, a brief celebration of joy for the parents who soon fell back into the pool of gloom that consumed them; a year hence, his father having been killed by rebels, and four of his brothers and sisters having died because the food that is so abundant in many other parts of the world was absent, often uneaten commodity that overflows the garbage cans of industrial nations and sits in the wasted heaps outside of homes and restaurants and grocery stores; this precious sustenance that is voluntarily, mind you, taken by human beings in the richest countries, and with an uncanny, methodical, and deadly accuracy, stuffed into their gaping, eager mouths again and again, ad nauseam, and over again, and again and again once more; and once satiation begins to dissipate, once again and once more and just one last time they initiate the gorging ritual until the zealous participants—who are not in a scientific study to measure precisely how much foodstuff the human body can tolerate per day, but willing participants who throw food into their mouths much like a conveyor belt, in perpetuity; oh, if only a crumb had ever breached the rapidly forming rolls of blubber that constitute their rapidly expanding bodies, and fallen into a magical portal and traveled at lightning speed to those distant lands where unwilling participants in that great experiment known as mass starvation, where such seemingly insignificant bits of foodstuff could somewhat fill their bellies, which had been swollen by hunger, and save the lives of millions; but, alas, it is only a crumb, probably stale, too, and much too much for a citizen of super self-indulgence to worry their overstuffed, fattened, can't-see-the-crumb-under-our-noses heads.

So, as it was, Moses was destined to fall victim to the curse of having been born in the wrong geographical locale, languishing in the harsh heat, covered with filthy flies, waiting patiently at death's door—and then, well, and then, someone, somewhere, for some reason, decided to sponsor a child in a Third World country through a Christian charity, which meant, immediately, that that child would be the recipient of nutritious food, clean water, modern medicine, and a proper education; but his little brother and sister, Ahmed and Samya, would also benefit, and so too their mother.

Somewhere, then, an obscene hill of goods, a towering stack of things that soared into the clear blue sky, lost an infinitesimal amount of weight, its spot having been shifted over to a pockmarked, cracked, dry, hard chunk of destitute real estate, in the form of the main meal for the family, the stew, which might be kajaik, dried fish that is added to aseeda, a porridge made from corn or sorghum, or other stews that have dried meat, to which is added onions, spices and perhaps a little milk; or ful medames, which has fava beans, parsley, garlic, vegetable oil; or shahan ful, which has fava beans, and green onions, yogurt and feta cheese and spices; but added to this might be kissra, a thin, wheat bread. And also arriving were medical kits and clothing and personal necessities. Moses and his family—at least what was left of them—were saved.

Yes, Moses would survive, as would his entire family, who lived in a small, conical home that was made of mud and a thatched roof, all of them beneficiaries of the tiny fragment of wealth transferred to them from a far-away utopia; soon, he would be in school, and prove to be an exceptional student, capable of great understanding and exhibiting a voracious appetite for knowledge; every day of the week he would happily walk the five miles, with his brother and sister, to the small schoolhouse that the friendly foreigners had built; every day he would gladly take his place upon the dusty dirt floor and, with the green chalkboard on his tiny lap, and white chalk in his hand, he would look up silently with his big brown eyes, which were so full of wonder, and listen intently to the pretty African woman who had shorn the bountiful harvest of capitalism for the opportunity to effect change for the good in young lives; and no student ever made an unnecessary sound, not even once, for the children cherished the place as a sanctuary, a magical chamber descended from the intellectual sphere; a sacred spot, like a church or the gravesite of a loved one; and one never desecrated these things, especially when one was living on vapors and hope.

He would sometimes stay after school and help the Teacher, if only to be near someone who seemed to be from a mystical place where knowledge flowed so freely, and to ask her questions; if only to ask questions about the world, a world he did not know, and he would listen intently and hang upon her every word and close his eyes and commit these wondrous images to his astonishing memory; and as soon as he could read—and really, before that—he borrowed books and took them home and felt the rough black exterior of them and petted them and turned the pages of them and proceeded to read each word as if indeed it had been printed just for him—and it did not matter what the subject was or the length; he loved them all because any knowledge gained was like a shivering child in the snow who was grateful for any article of clothing, no matter its style or source; he loved them all—be it science or history or math; and then one joyous day, his Teacher handed him the world, a book of geography, and the final domino of limited borders that had surrounded him began to collapse.

And as it was already established, he would then tell Ahmed and Samya all that he had learned, and felt even more very much the Teacher.

"Mamma, have you been here," he excitedly asked his mother one day, as she boiled cassava in the big, black, iron pot that hung over the makeshift fireplace of earth and kindling; he was pointing to a picture of Uganda. No, she replied, gently, she had not. "Mamma, have you been here?" he asked, certain that she had at least been to Ethiopia, and when he received another reply in the negative, his smile became a frown. "But why, Mamma, why haven't you been there? It is so close! Look!"

Mother, when she looked at her child, looked through a veil darkly, at once flooded with myriad layers of pain, of past and present, and days conceived in suffering, bleak, impenetrable days when the world strove to divest her family of life, when every inanimate thing on the earth—the dry, cracked, wrinkled, desert sheath that swept o'er the land like a hardened, dead skin, the barren land, devoid of fine forests of plush, life-giving greenery, the dearth of precious water, animals, crops, insects—plotting against her, but these were of things seen; but of those things unseen were compassion, sympathy, empathy, leadership, charity, loving kindness, Justice, courage, mercy, solace, tranquility, order, unity, sanity, a time for simply living, a time to live without suffering, a time to fully understand what it is to truly live; and for those things of material substance that she saw above, counted among them were the boiling, shuddering waves of unceasing heat, the empty, bleak sky, the black night and its harvest of luminous star flowers, which seemed more a cold cemetery and the white flowers markers for the newly dead—and these were the things seen; but of those things not seen were tall buildings inhabited by her countrymen, who vowed to help their corrupt and impoverished country, and fine rows of houses with running water and modern plumbing, and the long shadow cast by someone, something, perhaps some image or somebody, who would wear a symbol of some great import and meaning, that would guarantee and generate life, liberty, and the pursuit of happiness for her dying people.

So, when she visited the eager image of her boy again, she was sodden and damaged with despair, and could barely smile, and lost her enthusiasm for all things fantastical. "It isn't real," she murmured, and kicked the sand beneath her, "this is real, because this is the place where you will be born and die—right here." She sighed and shrugged her bare, bony shoulders, and spoke in a voice drained of all hope. "Don't think about anywhere but here, child; it will only make you sad."

The boy shook his head, for, no, he did not understand, for he was a child, still, and children are the most resilient of creatures, resistant to any kind of fierce, emotional erosion imaginable —both artificial and natural; an island of optimism, a fortress of zealotry for success, that no force could long endure against; so, you see, once this imp of an idea manifested itself in his curious mind, he could not be compelled to depart from it, for in the restless heart of every restless boy is the yearning for great adventure and exploration, and to him, such places around him seemed like those mythical kingdoms he had lately heard or read of in school.

He turned the page. His mother gasped and her right hand clutched her throat. "There," she exclaimed, once she regained the use of her speech, "there it is."

And there it was, the heroic image she had once seen in a book when she was a child so long ago. "Sweet mercy," she whispered and, bending down, lent her hands about the glossy pages; she was afraid to directly touch the shining symbol, lest she diminish its grandiose eloquence.

Moses, watching his mother closely, observed the reverence that glowed crimson awe from her lithe face, and he proffered the book to her, and she hesitated in taking it, but eventually did, after cleaning her hands on her old, tattered apron, daring to caress the divine images of a flag of the ol' faithful, red, white and blue.

"America," she murmured, as if in the audience of a great power, a super-natural power, a power omnipotent and capable of reaching through inter-di-mensional space and unshackling freedom-loving people from their unnatural enslavers.

Moses beheld the sublime canvas that this intense longing for all things decent and fair painted upon her worn and forlorn face; he dared not speak, lest the magical spell that engulfed her be broken—he had rarely seen his mother as anything but a wrecked vessel of misery and cynicism.

If only, he reasoned, he might keep that good glow about her pretty face, he would sacrifice the very world itself to achieve it.

Then, she cleanly broke from her laborious chores and, taking the now-precious book in her thin, bony hands, sat down with him upon the grainy dirt floor; and when she spoke, reverence and wonder flowed out like a newly discovered, fresh, silvery stream in the dry, hot desert. "I have heard about America since a child; Teacher taught us, so very long ago." He frowned, for she had never mentioned that she had been to school, and he gazed up at the rare sparkle of pleasure in her soft brown eyes. "Miss Marian told us about big places—big, big places—big buildings full of food and drink," and she stretched out her hand toward the horizon, her voice suffused with reverence, "as far as the eye can see, without armies hunting them—and all kinds of food and drink too—and people walking around filling up metal carts with these foods and drinks and taking it to homes that had running water and cool air." She smiled at the pleasurable memory, and then smiled mischievously, "And nobody in America is skinny, because they are always eating this fine food in their fine, rich houses, and everybody has fine jobs and makes good money to buy all the food and drink they desire." The endearing smile that memory constructs of times that cannot be retrieved—thus making them special—lingered on her for the longest time. Moses dared not speak.

"I think I should like to be fat, like American women," she whispered, and she playfully extended her arms into a semicircle to illustrate the absurd idea; but when she sought to think of someone she knew who was fat, no immediate image came to mind. "And I would not worry about losing this fat, like these women do—yes, being big and fat would be good, because that would mean..." But then her merriment stalled, and she sought to revive it. "Yes, Moses, in other countries, too, there are big places with lots of food and drink, and many fine houses...and without armies hunting them," and then bitterness, like a fever, set in, "just not ours."

She slowly stood up, yielding the book to her son, and regained the cooking of the cassava root. "But that is not real," she said, melancholy, casting her eyes into the bubbling water; "every day is hard, and always will be; why will it change, the rest of the world has, and we have had plenty of time." Moses sat perfectly still, contemplating the revelation she had given him, and when he thought it safe to speak, he did so, and, like any child, cut through the scholarly route and marched right up to the biggest question, even though he could not possibly conceive of such marvels that were reserved for a select few.

"Mama, why don't we go to America?"

She did not become angry, but smiled, as she had done when she thought of her cursory childhood education. "Because," she replied, reassuringly, "this is our home."

And then, as it had been established, Moses would teach Ahmed and Samya about what he had learned, feeling very much the Teacher.

The next day at school, he asked his Teacher a multitude of questions regarding America, and the rest of the world, and why his country was not like America, and the rest of the world—why the world was the way it was, and why Asia was one world, and why Europe was another; why America was one universe, and why Africa another; and with every passing day, he gained knowledge about the history of such places, and why one world flowed with milk and honey, and another flowed with death and suffering, and how some worlds encroached upon one world so they might increase their flow of milk and honey if only to increase the flow of death and suffering of the other; this, these hard lessons about the unbridled enthusiasm for one nation to conquer another, or one group within a nation to subjugate another, made little sense to a child, who, as did nearly all children, harbored a proud and intense desire for fairness and equality toward all things and for all persons.

He wept, as he should have, when he read about the destruction of his own beloved continent; how the imperialist nations had seized it and carved it up as if its people were not even sentient creatures, or if the indigenous populations were granted even this small concession—were not even the animals and plants given this scientific distinction—then they were treated like creatures with malformed brains who were wholly incapable of experiencing outrage or expressing resentment or feeling long-lasting pain as they should; and even if the imperialist powers conceded such basic human emotions, his own people were still viewed as a populace incapable of achieving equanimity of political and economic stature and a sovereign nation incapable of sustaining equanimity of a peaceful and harmonious stature—as defined by their new overlords and overseers, masters and guardians, their European landlords.

It is said that all people have an innate desire for knowledge—and this may indeed be true, but too often people do not exhibit such a trait; is it, then, incorrect, this old adage, or are people simply desirous of those things they need to know—trivial to some, important for others—or are people consumed with extraneous clutter that exceeds the borders of their natural curiosity; whatever the reason, most human beings spread a lifetime chasing and capturing an empty vessel of nondescript, nonessential, meaningless babble-script, and they devour it and live in it and bathe in it and wrap themselves in its gauzy, oily membrane and display it proudly and happily even though it simultaneously suffocates their minds from acquiring real truth, real knowledge, real wisdom; so, this was their choice, to be unaware of themselves and their environs and the unfurling world beyond their immediate senses; but not so for Moses, for he was not a mere trifle or a floating will-o'-the-wisp in the wind, but an individual whose every thought and action had a profound impact upon his environs—because he saw farther, because he felt deeper, because—because he loved more and hated less and cared more deeply for those oppressed, those in pain, those suffering; perhaps, in the end, he was simply a mere mortal, the kind of future man all men are supposed to be but are not because they are too busy pursuing those possessions and ideas that have no merit or substance or lasting beneficial impact on humanity.

So, he grew in wisdom and stature and pride, and all those who knew him were amazed at his humility and kindness; but still, even as he attended school all those years, walking all those rugged miles with his brother and sister, and still working before school and after school, and on the weekends—the weekend was just another day here—his mother admonished him for the perils of pursuing one's dream when one is condemned by an ignoble past to a present life of brutal servitude.

"And Moses," his mother was certain to say, "don't forget to watch out for Ahmed and Samya on the way to school, and the way back; you know they look up to you, and will follow you in whatever you ask—and Moses, you know the safe path through the land of knives." She could never seem to speak the name of the monstrous things that lay nestled beneath the desert sands that waited to spring up and seize an Innocent.

But Moses was always sure, no matter how late he stayed with his Teacher, to keep his siblings close, and then escort them home, even at night, through an area that even his elders avoided in the daytime.

He dreamed now of America, of Europe, of tropical islands: places where impossible realities happened, where people roamed free, and food and drink were plentiful, and disease was managed, and poverty attended to, and children went to school and did not plow the fields or collect wood or pick the crops or fear being captured by rebel groups and transformed into a soldier; so, no, even though he dreamed of such fanciful Kingdoms, he could not properly conceive of them; so, yes, these illustrious pictures and big, black words on a white page were simply fairy tales to him, as much a fairy tale as "Anansi," which his Teacher had read, because he still could not imagine how civilized countries could sustain such great wealth in light of Africa's great suffering, as if these nations subsumed the plight of poor nations to placate their own spiritual guilt, and to exploit it still for its natural resources. It was these things and more he would discuss with Ahmed and Samya, feeling very much the Teacher.

"Why don't they just come over here and help us?" he asked his Teacher one fateful day. "Cannot America just come and share their plenty? Don't they know we are here and need them? I have a nice sponsor who helps my family, and good Christian people from Faith with Works who come to our village and help us."

His young, pretty, university-educated African mistress smiled when she replied. "Oh, but they have, Moses—they have." And here she nodded her head in a knowing way, as if it were the first time he could decipher her subtle clues. "I have waited for you to ask such a profound question, and since you are now fourteen years old, and nearly a man, you are old enough to hear the truth." She sat him down in front of her, and the two explored material not strictly approved by the school. "Let me tell you about multinational corporations," she began. She then led him down a bloody road, cluttered with dead bodies and mass graves and corrupt regimes, and martyrs and saints on one continent, and murderers and savages on another, where one avaricious empire-building country plundered and plowed, raped and ruined Africa, at once proud and plush, the land of paradise, Africa, which had now become the ever-deepening cesspool, the drought and famine capital of the world, the Mecca for tyrants and dictators and terrorists, a resort for malevolent generals and genocidal-practicing armies.

Moses was mesmerized, hypnotized, energized; outraged, polarized, mortified; and he could feel his blossoming youth spreading its newly formed and tough wings toward this new sun that was bursting with raw, vital energy, a sun of knowledge his Teacher had created and he would sustain with the fuel of curiosity; he bathed in its hot, soothing rays, felt its power seep into his very marrow, planting seeds of its own selfish making; he was boiling, roiling youth, newly armed with proper disdain and scorn, gaining answers to the misery and cruelty around him that he felt he could not have addressed; yea, by the cunning narrative of his radical young mistress, he was, in his mind, constructing a warrior who grew daily from the bits and chunks of fleshly knowledge thrown his way—a warrior first sprouting stout limbs with which to hold the growing uneasiness of its master; and then a dense white skeleton, and fine black flesh, and short, curly, black hair, and a noble, round head, and handsome visage—seemingly a growth spurt provided each time by hearing more vexing histories of foreign influence and meddling in his Mother Africa; and his muscles grew, physically as well as intellectually, with the rendering of more tales of betrayal by Africans who were allies of these shameless imperialists, and the warrior grew a fearsome heart that could not be bought, bowed or broken.

The streaming history of poor Africa betrayed and besieged by imperialist nations; poor Africa decimated, decapitated, destroyed, and held captive like a slave; beaten and whipped and kicked; poor Africa, unable to flourish because it still lay in the heavy chains of colonial oppression, was a hurtful trespass into his youthful and optimistic spirit, and he could only answer with wrath and want for revenge that was born from the shackles of immature youth; yes, he vowed, he would dig deep his feet, and clench fast his teeth, and with both muscular arms pull against this palpable, easily identified, boasting and arrogant villain, whom he would meet in the east, be he clothed in armor or cloth; he would meet it in the north, be his stomach empty or full; he would meet it in the south, be he with troops or alone; he would meet it in the west, be he healthy or ill; yea, he would meet it head on, and famously so; he would seek it out and stalk it like any proud warrior who protects his own, and rush at it and smite it and he would gain the victory if only because he was a child newly born of heavenly Justice; he could feel the divine gift of righteousness bear up in him as he read about the atrocities and horrors committed in a great variety of colossal tactics and stratagems achieved by countries that waved the radiant flag of civilization as they stepped over the bloodied corpses of their fallen victims so they might scoop up the filthy lucre that enraptured them and overfilled their coffers, which were made from the spilled blood and guts and bleached-white bones of their sacrificed victims.

He would have his revenge—he would live it and be its master and cherish it every day; yes, he often thought on his long walks home in the menacing dark, he had purpose now; and he felt very much like a newborn man.

But, alas, life was life at home, and he was only fourteen, and had to work the crop fields at night and weekends, and help his mother with chores about their scrawny stick, leaf, and mud hut; and still, he continued to tutor Ahmed and Samya in the ways of this mysterious world that unfurled before him.

And every day, in the cool of an early morning, raspberry dawn, when the day was crisp and not yet ruined by what inevitably must be, and the possibility of a miracle that might somehow transpire, after he had already labored two hours hauling wood, and the idea of the miraculous had already faded from view, his mother, already weary, said, "And don't forget, Moses, you need to walk home with your brothers and sisters," to which he easily assented, but this day, he was not listening, for his mind was already on the fiery sermons of his Teacher.

It was a Friday, and his Teacher was elaborating on the reprehensible act of Italy, when in 1935, moving to redress their humiliating defeat by Ethiopia in 1896, Mussolini and his loyal fascist troops invaded it, and successfully so, and how Emperor Haile Selassie—or Ras Tafari—pleaded passionately with the League of Nations for help, which, in turn, excluded the Ethiopian problem from its private discussions; and so, Ethiopia fell to the Italian war machine, the latter which was like the man who has a heavy black boot above the body of a tiny, tail-wagging puppy, and then, with a foreknowledge of impunity, lets his foot drop even as his neighbors look away and busy themselves with their own problems.

But, his Teacher said, school was now over, and it was time to go, and he, Moses must take his brother and sister home before dark, as was his filial duty.

"No," Moses cried, "I must hear the end, I must know the end." He turned toward his brother and sister, and said, gently, "You know the way, don't you? You know which roads to take, don't you? You are a big boy and girl now, are you not?" It was the silky-smooth voice of reassurance from a trusted source, the voice that repairs a psyche damaged by unrealized horrors and lifts the listener into a lazy and unguarded state of acceptance; yes, Ahmed and Samya recited, they knew the way, and could go it alone and would arrive there safely; and they in turn allayed his waning fears that he was irresponsible and placing his own blood kin in jeopardy; and presently, they set off, and as he watched them go, his mania for learning slapped him from behind and he knelt before his Teacher as if she were the Buddha, or Oracle at Delphi, or Holy Man in a sacred temple, as if she were the only font of knowledge ever conceived, and she proceeded to anoint him with more incendiary verse.

It was so late when he exited the stone building wherein he had been newly crowned with the spectacular catastrophes of European colonialism in Africa and its inevitable end, that he felt his own heart bleeding for his murdered and enslaved brethren. "Mama will surely be mad," he grumbled, beginning to run wildly, and as he ran, the further he distanced himself from the palace of indoctrination, his suppressed guilt rose up through gaps in his weak fortitude and pestered him with macabre visions. "Dead, they are all dead—blown up by mines," he shouted, and moved even faster along the sandy, serpentine, safe paths.

At every perceived angle he reasoned he saw mangled bodies, but in reality the images were clumps of brown bush on scattered lumps of sand hills that were dotted with dry twigs stuck in them, like upside limbs, or bumps of small, dead animal carcasses heaped and scattered in this open graveyard of this harsh desert; and when he sighed relief at every turn, his fears were assuaged, and he ran lighter, and happier.

And then there it was—a twisted, mangled figure too big and too unmistakably human to be misinterpreted; it was still and its head was driven—smashed, really—into the hard, yellow sand; and Moses stopped and gasped, but he would not yield up even a little cry, for he, and his fellow travelers upon these roads, had an acquired reflex not to produce noises of an appreciable level in the close proximity of war or warlike machines or even the relics of war; so, he stood, hand upon his quivering, bare chest, braving the walk toward the undeniably dead human; his mind began to paint illusions all about the corpse—convincing him it was too old or too big or wearing the wrong clothes to be his brother or sister—but it was too dark and the only sure identification would come from a rather too close and personal inspection of the still thing; he crept up, shaking and mumbling his prayers, fearful to look, fearful to look away, coercing his brown sandaled feet to move closer and closer and still closer and then one more step and then another and finally to stoop down and by the luminous stream of the bright moon, he saw an adult face, and he rejoiced.

He truly whooped, he did, he jumped high and jumped out low and somersaulted and rolled about with his strong legs wiggling and his big arms jiggling like a newborn baby at the sight of its beautiful birth mother; he laughed and he cried tears of mirth and he rolled in the cool sand until he felt the hilarity take an exodus from his weary body; and so, he arose, and once glancing at the contorted corpse and humbly apologizing to it, he continued his journey toward home, skipping and hopping and singing songs of joy and singing songs of praise to his faith; and then, feeling so refreshed and vital again, he broke into a fast pace all the way home, laughing all the while.

He rounded the small dome that was the last physical marker signaling his closeness to the small village he lived in, and as he did, he heard noises not indigenous to his ears, odd noises not able to fit into the tiny chambers of recorded memories in his brain: screeching, raw and banging clamor that decorated the scene in bursting anger and draped it in apprehension and slit the delicate balance of restful peace that night brings, and in its stead, the flourishing of agony that the watchful cloak of night brings from crimes and criminals.

He instinctively abated his jaunt, he halted in mid-step, he fell to the ground as would any youth who had been reared on war and warriors who were his boundaries and masters; yes, he crawled now, like a soldier back from patrol to his post, and he expertly moved toward the choral shrieks and hollering, but such horrific exultations they were, as if verse boasted by humans who were imbued with absolute reckoning over lives; so yes, by the primeval songs of the sinister voices and the accompanying laughs and obscenities, he recognized now for what its viral, drunken self really was—it was a cleansing tide that had come to this village, a swooping vulture to sterilize and capture, murder and terrorize—and this black, depraved darkness dripped a condemning, blistering, scorching blood upon the whole world.

He had to see it, see who was in the iron grip of their sharp, steel talons; he lifted his tear-stained face and could barely make out the outline of the Militia's green and brown uniforms, and he shuddered, and gasped, and shut his palpitating mouth with his trembling hand—he could feel his hot blood storming into his brain and severing his head from his senses; he was immobile now, as if he had been ignominiously planted into the hard soil and set to gaze upon the sanguinary destruction of his blessed memories.

The Militia were smiling and laughing, and if one were to have seen their faces only, a reasonable deduction might have been that they were in attendance at a merry and blessed celebration, not a well-designed, well-executed genocide: yes, a genocide, not as it applies to an entire race—not that this Militia did not approve of such a specific notion—but a genocide in that it applies to the utter destruction of an entire family; for what are humans but representatives of a small family structure within larger influences and institutions that it is intimately connected to in nearly every way and relies upon and who reply upon them—hamlets, towns, cities, territories, regions, states, countries, continents, hemispheres, planet—but in the very beginning and the ultimate end, a family: families that constitute the beginning of a village and the whole of a planet; so, to kill the identity of a single family creates chaos on the entire planet and imbalances it and drains nourishment from it and covers it in shame and curses.

There, in the center of his village, could he see this most egregious act that was practiced with such skill and solicitude by these raving miscreants and monsters, who resided in an open cesspool of damnation and abomination, and whom people shunned and were frightened of, even as it was practiced upon their neighbors and then, themselves—and the entire world stood by, declaring, "Fair fight, fair fight!" It is times such as these that a human being actually believes that he alone is a sane man in an insane world, as his internal moral compass determines that this horror before him is a violation of a natural law that is universal to all men, and therefore, must affect all men, and would logically follow that all good men would come to his aid; and thus, Moses died within his own mind as he knew no rescue would be coming, and could feel his outer self detaching and fleeing inside of himself and settling there atop a succession of exploded realities that oozed and stunk up the seizing quarters of his psyche; but he had to look, could not look away, for guilt that he had been away and safe from it all drove his vision to the very nucleus of the burgeoning lunacy.

He could not untangle merging memories in his mind—one of animals being slaughtered and abused during a sacrificial feast, and his kin and friends being slaughtered and abused now. "Are we not human," drifted into his mind, but he could do nothing with it, for what he saw was a practice hitherto unknown to his visual mind.

There, in the plain open, the Militia was pummeling an older man he knew, like young, virile men pummel a wild boar with sharp spears or young boys pummel a helpless goat that has been designated for killing; but no, Moses decided, or, his mind's eye envisioned, the old man was being attacked in the same vicious manner villagers would attack a snake that had bitten and poisoned a small child—with utter abandon and enthusiasm for the kill. And so it was, the Militia was kicking and stomping and rolling him around as if he were a murderous reptilian-predator-monster; presently, the soldiers, with the face of the bored hunter, shot him dead.

Yet, this mauling was only one in this obscene tapestry spread out before him; conical huts were set on fire, young men were being savagely beaten, young women savagely raped, old men and women savagely beaten, old women savagely raped, children shackled and savagely thrown toward and finally into the green and brown Jeeps.

An old, too-old woman, too old for the debauched sentiment of the shouting and crowing Militia, was being physically dismantled, the same way, Moses' mind later concluded, in precisely the same manner a swarm of yellow-backed hornets seizes any unfortunate wayfarer into their nest; yes, they thrashed and stomped on her, and once she was dead, one of the men lifted up a long, silver machete and brought it swiftly upon her skinny neck and severed her head from her body, and then took the bloody head and with the frozen mask of horror etched on it, threw it onto her husband's shaking lap, and then the soldier, laughing, cut off the head of the weeping, now-sprawled man.

Moses beheld, but now, at this moment and at too young an age, could not possibly process these heinous images and sounds and smells, for all of it was too far removed from the tight world of normality and decency and humanity he had thus far experienced; the images assembled and assembling before him were made of irregular, sloping, slanting pieces and roughly hewn angles that were being forcefully mashed together to fit the depraved vision of reality as practiced by these conquering beasts; yes, even though he heard stories of such depravity, he had never been visited by this macabre conflagration even in his tormented dreams; and as he could neither free nor help anyone here, he wept more.

And then he saw it, the final threat to wrap around his neck and choke him into complete submission to madness—there, in the midst of the bodies, now drenched in gasoline and burning, some dead, some still alive, he saw his blessed mother, huddled with his younger brother and sister.

The commander of the Militia, having dipped his tarry soul into the very germ and form of moral corruption and debauchery that he celebrated without restraint, yielded up a gleefully white smile that boasted of his supreme confidence in smothering all life he deemed heretical and thus a blight, and therefore unnecessary; but more importantly, it was a bright, glowing smile that spoke of a supreme certitude concerning his mocking dance with the seemingly mystic gift of impunity so bestowed upon his sect as they dealt with such indigenous people; and had any group arisen against him, any divine retribution fallen upon him for such actions, he reasoned—No! and thus was emboldened that he would be rewarded just as if he were defending his household against animal predators.

The commander looked at Moses' little brother, and said, teasingly, "Well, well, little man," his round, black visage illumined by the burning, crackling corpses in the orange-flamed-and-purple-smoke fire, "do you think to protect your mother by holding her?"

There is a saturation point for most things, and for acts of wickedness, as executed here, the minds of soldiers had been stuffed with the ripest, most delectable variety and breed of evil conceived; but now, their imagination set in, and proffered to unite atrocity with the lowest, most base and vile acts in their expanding registry of obscenities.

The commander ordered the woman stripped. Moses looked away, driving his tear-stained face into the fine, yellow sand.

"Now," the commander cooed, bending down to stare at the trembling boy, who had averted his eyes away from his mother, caught now in the mesmerizing gaze of his captor, "to save her life," and he began an unsavory description of a sexual union between mother and son.

The boy, sobbing, shaking in uncontrollable spasms, shook his head, and the commander, amused still, walked over to the woman and placed a long, serrated knife against her reddened throat, and once more ordered the boy to do what Nature and God cried that he must not do. The boy would not, could not, move.

The mother said in a voice that was crushed and squeezed by her assailants, "I love you, Ahmed, I love you so very much, my good son; and Samya, my daughter, I love you so very much," and paused as she thought of Moses and offered her love to him and protection not only for him but her other children, and then seized the hand of the commander and drove the knife into her own throat, and lay down, dead.

The commander frowned, disappointed, while Ahmed and Samya fell upon their beloved mother and embraced her.

Moses was murmuring, "I love you, Mama, I love you; I love you, Ahmed and Samya, I love you so very much," as he smelled the fuming wings of death and despair ice over his bursting heart; he watched now as the Militia dragged away his brother and sister, and roughly tossed them, tied up like runaway calves, into the back of one of the Jeeps with the other bound children; and presently, the men, whooping and hollering, and shooting their rifles into the swelling black night, drove away.

Moses rushed upon his mother and wept like a newborn baby over her still form.

He woke up with the amber cloak of dawn draping him, his arms round his mother's body; he stood up and beheld the wanton carnage, and still, his juvenile mind could not comprehend the complete annihilation of his village, of his people, of his family, of his world; yet, he knew what he must do, and so he retrieved a small shovel from one of the burned-out huts and, coming back to her, he proceeded to dig a grave for his beloved mother, and once he was done, he kissed her forehead and then placed her body into the hole and then covered her with the soft, yellow sand.

He did not just feel isolated and alone and forgotten, he felt as if he were suddenly old, too old, having ascended the slowly descending stairway to manhood too quickly, missing too many transitions, losing moments of youthful discovery, a prisoner on an unfamiliar road where he had no prerequisites for membership, and coerced to enter a dark forest he was not equipped to survive in; he looked about and saw the ostentatious sin of his enemies unfolded before him like a heinous vision illuminated in this cold light, and he reasoned that the longer the bodies lay unburied in his village, the longer the treacherous lie of his sworn enemy's work would remain firmly planted in the hard soil.

So, he would bury them all, now, all fifty-two of the bodies, formerly people of his extended family, who had collectively raised him and whose cherished memories would stay with him all the rest of his days; he toiled ceaselessly, carefully, angrily, bitter that he must do this himself, proud that he could do this himself, and between the digs he foraged for food and he searched for water and he listened for any sound of life beyond his camp; yes, he could have sought help; but no, he would do this alone, for they were his people, his private tragedy, his story now, a story that was being written daily in his grieving heart, a story that would mold and shape him and drive him, shift his ideas about the world, harden his resolve against injustice, focus his life-force on the cleansing of war from his land and the uniting of his people against all threats, from without: foreign armies that misunderstood regional conflicts and bungled their way into civil wars, foreign businesses that devastated natural resources, foreign institutions that wrought havoc; as well as from within: indigenous armies that fought for corrupt lucre and unlimited power, indigenous businesses that plundered and looted the land; indigenous institutions that bred corruption and vice; yea, his country would be great again, he dreamed, as he dug the graves, as it was so long ago, this land called Kush.

He had not thought about his education while he had labored to bury the dead, for it seemed unimportant now—not that it had not been, but he felt as if he were now imbued with sufficient education about the world to deal with it, as if his eyes had been not just violently cracked open, but wide and forever open, and held open by Fate until he would hold them open himself; he was, after all, a mere youth, gone from a juvenile existence pertaining not only to life but his own internal environs, to a great capacity to understanding life, and a limited knowledge about this world—he was, in fact, a surging teenager, full of animus and distrust against the established hierarchy, and frustrated because he felt so small and helpless and living in a world that seemed illogical, unreasonable, and nonsensical; and yet he still dreamed of a utopia.

Still, he had a desire to find his Teacher and bid her goodbye, and ask her why she had not wondered about him during his absence and come by; and so, after praying at the graves, which were completed after these seven feverish days, he set out to visit the small encampment wherein the medical tent and the Faith with Works charity staff and small school dwelled, and when he got there, he understood why she had not come: for the place had been torched, and all of the adults murdered, and the children who had been in attendance during classes taken away by the Militia; he would later learn that multiple Militia raiding parties had swept over his region that night, attacking villages, relief camps, relief agencies, murdering foreign aid workers and stealing dozens of children, who would become soldiers and aides in the military camps.

The books had been burned. He shook his head. "It is too late; I know now what I must do." He would not bury the bodies of those murdered here, for the vultures and hyenas and various decomposers had already set to work upon them; he set out to find his destiny while looking for his brother and sister: be it here, in his own ancestral homeland, or in Western Africa, in the savanna and rainforest, visiting the Igbo and Ibibio people of Nigeria, the Ashanti in Ghana, the Kru of Liberia—there were so many people and tribes and cultures he had learned about, he desired to see them all: be it in Eastern Africa, in the arid lands and fertile highlands and savanna, visiting the Kikuyu in Kenya, the Chaga in Tanzania, the Amhara in Ethiopia; he had read about so many in so short a time that he yearned to know them all: in West-Central Africa, the savannas and forests, visiting the Fang of Gabon, the Pygmies in the Congo, the Bamileke in Cameroon—he had read and heard so many amazing stories about them that he desired to live with and learn about all of them; in Central and Southern Africa, the grasslands of the dry savanna, visiting the heroic Khoikhoi and San—the Khoikhoi in south-western Africa, and the San, the Bushmen, in South Africa and surrounding countries—and the Bantu-speaking tribes, who live in many territories: he had read all of their histories, and continued to, as he collected books and oral histories during his long journey, and he wanted to hear their special song and taste their regional food and learn their ancestral dances and celebrate their unique identity and learn their long-guarded secrets of combat; and it was here during his wanderings that he had ventured into the Atlas Mountains of Morocco, and heard of the remarkable Yew tree that was used to make the longbow, and it was here that he had, with the guidance of local expert archer-craftsmen, learned how to carefully inspect these trees until he found that special form that would make a stave free of physical impurities, which he would then cut to no more than seven feet in length, and not more than six inches wide, although it would end up no higher than himself. He was taught to properly study the physiognomy of a stave as well as its anatomy, and then to craft the bow to fit his hand and body, and to make certain that its pull would not be more than sixty-five pounds. The barbed broadhead, made of spring or bar steel, was three inches long, and one and a quarter inches wide; he shaped it on rocks, and fastened it onto the end of the bamboo shaft with plant sinew, or, if possible, he used a metal tube that was put on the end and secured by pounding a hole through it with a thin steel rod and then by pounding a river through the tube and point; the feathers from ducks were preferred, but other birds worked nearly as well, and were fastened with plant fibers at the beginning of the shaft. When later Moses' men could not purchase or barter for a recurve or compound bow, their longbows were made of tress that had been felled by fire, be they Mahogany, Bamboo or Juniper; and when the bows were not in use, the men were loath to sling them over their shoulders, unless absolutely necessary when carrying a rifle; so when they traveled on horseback, its wooden structure would be pointed toward the ground, in the same fashion as when they walked with it.

And as he continued his many years' journey throughout the sub-Saharan divide, in the great expanse of yellow desert, he sought to dwell with the Algerians in Algeria, the Liberians in Libya, the Egyptians in Egypt, and all the cultures and customs, therein—he had heard about their grand and remarkable history and he felt pride when he envisioned himself touching the soil where once-mighty kingdoms thrived, long before the terrible invaders had come, always looking for Samya and Ahmed, never giving up hope.

A Time for Healing

The band of African rebels were riding their horses over the far-reaching, flat plateau, riding in a spread-out, platoon-column fashion, each man lending his keen eyesight on the left and right side, while the men trailing them looked behind, and the men in front looked ahead; it was a strategy of necessity, for they had killed many Militia troops, and were presently hunted far and wide by the incensed government.

Moses was riding, at point, next to Abdul, and very few words passed between them, for each man was harvesting a rich vein of memories, and presently, Moses took out a book and began to read it, as he often did when peril seemed restrained; soon, however, two of their scouts, fresh from a reconnoiter, came galloping up to them, with their faces agitated by excitement, and presently rested their horses next to their natural leader. They were still observing strict radio silence.

"We have seen a large division of Militia moving across the plateau—maybe forty men," said Julius, a youth of surpassing strength and comeliness.

"They are riding against the Red Cross relief camp at three klicks east," interjected Olaudah, smiling as he glanced at Julius, for he had stolen the report from his friend, and it brought him no little amusement to see Julius frowning. "They will be there in twenty minutes."

Moses, supremely adept at interrupting his previous reverie at will, awoke himself, and turned toward Abdul, and saw his calm reflection, and then looked behind to his men, and shouted, "Militia," and consequently, he saw them ride up and close into a tight circle around him. "Militia are going to attack a Red Cross camp." There, he let this disturbing news dangle before them, like a child teetering on the edge of a cliff, and their pronouncements upon it giving it life or death.

It is intellectually easier to condemn than condone, more economical to dismiss than embrace, more practical to ride away from danger than ride into it; but where would the world be if no one took a stance beyond their safe and comfortable home?

"The Red Cross is an abscess in Africa, the meddlers," Henry grumbled; "we don't need their cuddling—it is just more excuse for the international community to present us as infantile children who are incapable of wiping our own noses." He sat bolt upright, his face stern and void of pity. "I say, let them bleed." He laughed. "Why, they have bandages for it aplenty."

Moses, unimpressed with this attack by Henry, looked to his other men, and spoke not, for such was his manner and bearing, that when he sat on high in the black leather saddle of quiet and ready Son of Al Khamasa, his handsome countenance flared bright, and his sleek, muscular body tensed, as if it were about to spring into battle, and his men knew not to divulge their private thoughts.

"I lean toward Henry," one of the men said. "I say we fight the Militia when they are vulnerable, not waste our energies and risk our own skin to save these so-called do-gooders, who need to take care of their own business." Henry thus rose up in his saddle, looking about for more support.

"Yes, we should fight the Militia, after they have wiped out the Red Cross invaders," Henry said, nodding his head, and more emboldened than before, seeing other men nodding in quiet assent with his idea.

"Yes, yes," the other man rejoined, "we cannot police this land, looking to protect foreign influence at our peril."

"I say," Henry said, "that we must not intervene to help any foreign entity, be they citizen or soldier; they imposed themselves here, and knew the risks; let them be driven out, or we will never see the last of them." He looked about to his comrades. "We fight to protect our own people, and to establish a democratic government—but this cannot be done while one," he cried, "foreigner stands upon our soil without our implicit permission, for their past betrays their present intentions."

Many men concurred, and Henry sat strong, erect, his proud visage resolute with the unmistakable grievances of the past propping him up.

Abdul, careful in speech, slow to speak, and calm in his manner, then said, carefully, slowly, calmly, "We are sworn, by our very history, to protect all Innocents; it is not for us to decide who lives or dies, but by fighting the aggressor wherever we see him, before he engages Innocents, so that God decides who lives or dies; otherwise, if we do nothing, we blame God, but we must blame ourselves."

This simple philosophy thwarted a good number of the men who had attempted to reconcile their core beliefs with Henry's hard stance against anyone not born and raised African.

Henry let out a loud "harrumph" as he looked at Abdul. "You sound like those arrogant foreigners we met, those arrogant…Crusaders; yes, that is exactly who they are, resurrected from days of old to interfere in our business—but how perfectly charitable of you, willing to risk our mission for foreigners who come here only to rape, loot and pillage our land."

"I don't understand," Jon Paul said. "Why does it matter when we engage the Militia?"

Henry smiled, as if a special vision, available to only a few, glided before him. "Because, little lamb, after the Militia has massacred the foreigners, and raped them, and looted them, they will be like drowsy jackals after gorging on a kill—and we," and here he lifted up his long, slender arm, and shot it across his body, "will swoop down upon them and slaughter them; yes, little lamb, it is an obligation to our people to make certain we live, at all costs— because of who we are and what we have done—and intervening before the Militia gets to the foreigners reduces our chances of success and gets some of us killed, and for what? For people we did not ask to come here, and should receive no special protection—let them defend themselves!"

"So, you are like the vulture now," Abdul said, "purposely coming late to the battle."

"You seek to provoke me, Abdul, but I am not against you going to protect the foreigners—or anyone else; go, go if you like, be a fool, but ride with fools on a fool's errand."

It was as if two speeding meteors—each meteor consisting of a unique philosophy—had crashed into each other and absorbed the other's momentum, and then fallen silently to earth, burning up and drifting to the ground as sprinkles and bits of their former glorious self; in so meeting, each had annihilated the other's free-ranging prowess and thriving mission to spread their will if only by mere presence; so, it was with the two philosophies here, each having cancelled the other out by obstinate and bitter arguing, leaving one course to pursue.

Moses nodded his head, and put away the book he had been reading, *History of Western Civilization.* "Now, we go," he shouted, waved his hand in the direction his scouts had come from, and encouraged his horse to speed away; now, it is quite true that not one of this troop lingered, but all made great haste just as if they had been prepared for it all along, and the preceding squabbling had been but a necessary and stimulating instrument to play before the curtain of battle had risen before them.

It must be stated here, before too much biography is doted upon these hard men, that each of them would have fought anybody, anytime, anywhere for any good reason, however it related to protecting Innocents from the iron jaws of injustice—although, it is also true that some of them still adhered to a purist, and quite tenable, extremist view that Africa was for Africa and her woes must be resolved from within, and her foreign entities removed and kept from without; however, these men, at least for now, had never been able to reconcile their beliefs with reality, and so merely allowed their fanatical zeal of opposition to take the form of huffs and puffs, and moans and groans, and rumblings and grumblings, and not explicit action.

Moses and his thirty-nine men—they had absorbed more willing and qualified candidates recently—were charging from the north, riding through the scant scrub brush, and soon came upon the large band of Militia who were momentarily engaged in a firefight with enemy combatants.

"Look at that," exclaimed the lean and muscular Henry, amused as he pointed to the distant figure that was standing near a horse, and boldly facing the onslaught of Militia riders with his rifle. "The fool—the foolish foreigner."

"And there," Olaudah cried, looking through his binoculars at a man who stood on a faraway, rocky formation, too facing down numerous Militia riders with his rifle, "is it those European do-gooders?"

"Two against so many—magnificent!" Julius shouted, bursting with excitement. "Such bravery, such courage in the face of impossible odds—it is inspiring."

"Ha! Such foolishness!" Henry shouted, frowning now, and looking to Moses, cried out, "What are you doing?"

But Moses had already unsheathed his black, steel Heckler &Koch G-36 assault rifle and aimed it toward the Militia, who had stayed in a flat, loose formation as they shot at their foes; Moses commanded his men who held sniper rifles to target the Militia who were on horseback as they approached the wounded adversaries, and the others to target those who were still on foot, Henry being the next man to ready his rifle.

Moses took careful aim.

So, there Moses stood, a fully grown man now, having roamed the great part of Africa for a dozen years, laboring, moving, settling, moving, celebrating, pontificating, liberating; and learning and loving and listening, always listening to the tortured cries and stories of his people, always loving, so passionate was he, and learning about what a man is and what he should be and must be, not only in Africa but the whole wide world; he was tall, now, according to the dictates of his magnificent heritage, and lean and muscular and handsome, too, derived from a bountiful harvest of hard labor and walking, and learning how to combat-fight from masters of diverse forms, with hands and feet, stick and stone, knife and gun, bow and arrow, as he traversed the continent in search of his identity; his supple grip on the cool assault rifle magnified his extraordinarily calm nature when in the maelstrom of crisis; he squeezed the trigger slowly and methodically sent the 5.56 mm rounds on their appointed trajectory of mercy—like mischievous messengers they were—into the flock of murderous men, stinging them like angry wasps, driving the importunate metal and cylindrical bodies into the men's soft, vulnerable, black skin, and penetrating deep into tissue and bone and sinew, to deliver their deadly cargo. The soldiers dropped like fat, swatted flies.

One hundred rounds were fired, and so he effortlessly retrieved a full C-mag drum with one hand while pulling out an empty one, and sunk the full one into the underbelly of the rifle and resumed sending his steady stream of hot lead bullets sizzling on a sure and accurate flight path into the panicking soldiers, like bully-boys abruptly thrust into a fair fight; his men, doing likewise, combined, then, to bring a quick and final peace to a small region of the desert, wherein now lay some dozens of dead and expiring Militia.

Swift was the mounting of their horses, and swifter still, the men rode toward their mortal and sworn enemies, and upon reaching them, without the slightest hesitation or deliberation, delivered any still-suffering soul to the boatman at the shore of the nether world, while Moses rode to the fallen man on the desert floor, and others rode to the fallen man who lay among the jagged, pockmarked, black rocks.

Moses dismounted and knelt beside Conall, and as he held up the youth's head, a rare smile of admiration seeped through his hard countenance. "You would take on the whole Militia," he whispered, in a gentle voice.

Conall clasped the hand of his human savior. "As would you, good friend, to protect Innocents."

Moses inspected the two wounds. "Two bullets, only? Too few to slay a true warrior, as thou." If his own men had heard him speak thus, with such passion and respect for a foreigner-soldier, they would have been paralyzed by bewilderment.

Conall began to stand, and Moses, knowing the folly of trying to deny the will of strong men, assisted him.

"Help me to my horse—I must find out about Rustem."

"We will bring your friend," Moses replied, and pointed to his men, who, at that exact moment, were assisting the brave and valiant Rustem down the hill of boulders.

"Does he live?" Rustem asked as he was lifted off the bloodstained rocks.

Henry frowned, his big, black eyes screwed up in disbelief. "Does it matter, foreigner? What of your own wounds?" and yet, he handed the youth a small but powerful pair of binoculars, and Rustem peered through them but briefly, and then closed his eyes, and nodded. "So, he lives, and yet, you live, too, and who both should be dead, two challenging an army—foolish."

Rustem, his dark visage lit by a glorious grandeur of serenity, whispered, "Others may judge themselves with words, but I, with actions."

"Well," Henry rejoined, taken aback, watching Rustem being placed upon his faithful Rakhsh, "you think highly of yourself."

Rustem looked at the men who, in the far distance, were helping Conall. "I stand in the presence of angels and God, so I aspire to greater things."

No reply came from his antagonist, who did not believe in the supernatural at all.

Rustem came riding up to Conall, who too sat tall upon his black steed, Conchobar, who had sustained a minor wound, and the two men clasped hands, and nodded heads, and smiled, albeit briefly; and then allowed Julius, who had medical training, to observe their injuries, even in a cursory fashion, and pronounce the wounds clean, as the bullets had passed through, and could easily be patched up, and also attended to Conchobar.

"Now, we will go to the Red Cross camp," Conall said, turning now to Moses. "Thank you, and may God bless you in your great mission." These last words were delivered here as a singular event, a rare jewel found in a pit of worthless rock and earth, for in combat, men do what is necessary for themselves and for each other, all for victory, and there is no heartfelt expression of gratitude necessary or even expected.

Moses, hands on his muscular thighs, head held up high, posture erect, nodded his round head, his eyes gleaming with pride and brotherhood. "Now, we go."

There would be no argument from Conall or Rustem, for when a warrior proffers assistance to another warrior, custom and etiquette demand that it be accepted, as it has been done for many a millennium; yes, many of Moses' men grumbled and groaned, but their admiration and respect, and loyalty, and willing deference to him in all things war, which had served them so spectacularly well, silenced their verbal opposition; thus, the troop commenced their ride.

They had not traveled far when a thundering clamor from the west danced around their heads; Conall and Rustem knew its origins, and their breasts swelled with pride.

"It is all right," Conall said easily to Moses, who then waved away the rifles drawn by the other men, and the binoculars raised by them; "it is our friends."

Yoshitsune, leaving his men at a safe distance, stopped his galloping horse near this band of African rebels, and now cautiously approached the squadron that was presently linked by curiosity and wonder.

"They rescued us, Yoshitsune," Conall said, "they are allies."

Yoshitsune, leaning close to Conall, uttered in a low whisper, "The matter of the plane has been resolved," and then told him the curious tale of it, how it had begun, and how it would all end; and then introduced him to Finn, who presently shook hands with Conall.

Beannachtai, mo chara, conas a theann Eire?" asked Conall, reverently. Greetings, friend: how goes Ireland?

"Misses Eire a cuid leanai," Finn said, solemnly. Ireland misses Her children. "Aye, agus chailleann mé léi." Aye, and I miss Her.

Many of Moses' men chafed at the description Conall used that linked them with these foreign invaders, and they grumbled and mumbled to themselves, but suppressed their anger; Yoshitsune then turned round and signaled to his men to come hither; soon, there were happy greetings and hearty exchanges of relief as Conall and Rustem exchanged stories with their comrades, even as Arjuna, who had been trained in medicine back in his native India, and Finn, who had been a medic—and, thus, a doctor everywhere—treated the wounds of their two friends with little difficulty, and also checked on Conchobar; but not all of the Africans waxed wroth at the attitude and bearing of Conall and Rustem; there was a significant group, like the three Fulas from Cameroon, dressed in their long, flowing white robes, and pants of white cotton linen, and white turbans, with markings on their face that had been done in childhood, who themselves were, in the practice of everyday, ordinary life and often beyond, those devout few who prided themselves on evincing little emotion, even at the most dire of times—these men, Issa, Baba, and Omar, scrutinized the two wounded foreigners, looking closely for any overt sign of emotional suffering, any glimmer of physical pain that would swallow up the equanimity of a normal man, but saw nothing save an iron resolve in their faces, and these three men, who had lived a hard life, were in awe, and bowed in respect; and the three Zulus, Lunga, Themba and Jabulani—whose ancestors had valiantly fought against the European invaders, the British, in their homeland; these men who traced an ancestry back to warriors who had never capitulated no matter the odds of overwhelming peril; whose ancestors had established the land in South Africa and had held the land—scrutinized the fierce bond of brotherhood that continues to be woven after battle, by every selfless action and gesture and word by these men Henry had unknowingly christened the Crusaders, and were greatly impressed; and the Tuareg brothers, Mahmoud and Issouf and Ibrahim Zbiri, hardy Berber nomads—no, this is wrong to speak of them as merely hardy, for they are possessed of an undaunted fortitude, a magnificent constitution to not only exist in the spectacular, barren landscape of the Central Sahara, but adapt and thrive by mining the hidden jewels of this desert cauldron—as they wore their black tagelmust that covered their head and went down to their eyes and then up over their mouths—hence, they are known as the "People of the Veil"—and long black robes over their white cotton pants, as they rode upon their magnificent white camels, and listened to Albade Okonkwo, a Bororo of Niger, a member of those henceforth-called Crusaders, translate the story of how they had fared for months against their enemies, the Tuareg, their misty, soulful black eyes staring at this curious mix of men of diverse nationalities, felt as if indeed they were in the midst of their own kind.

As the two distinct divisions of warriors rode side by side and observed each other's manners and conversed and exchanged information and ideas—scholarly and common, cultural and universal, scientific and superstitious—these dynamic men, who had dedicated their lives—by doing so, they had indefinitely forsaken their own brethren at home—to fighting against the tyranny of injustice, began to feel a kinship, a common heritage that unites men the world over, a fervent longing to step up and move forward against the unrestrained forces of aggressive nation-states, tyrants and fanatics, not with pen and paper, not with empty words uttered from a safe distance, but on the battlefield, on the sanguinary front—forming the frontline, a human barrier, a shield for the Innocent, composed of their small offering to Mankind, a fragrant aroma that is produced when the Light refuses to yield to the Darkness, between the diabolical forces that seek to devour Innocent masses upon whom they prey for sustenance, just as a fungus spore lands upon the unsuspected ripe fruit to swallow it into its foul, pungent, spindly web of rot; just like the bloodsucking tick that attaches itself to the helpless animal, and slowly bleeds it dry, just like the opportune parasite that lives in the host and slowly absorbs its life energy, and keeps it barely alive so that it stays plump and healthy.

The journey to the International Red Cross encampment was some eight kilometers in distance, and there was no hurry now, since both Rustem's and Moses' scouts had declared the area devoid of the enemy; the two divisions of men had been suspicious of each other, many were taciturn, some angry, but by the journey's end, the two groups had begun to merge, as they realized they were merely two sides of the same philosophical and moral equation, two ideas becoming as one, as in any relationship where two minds are of one grandiloquent and noble mission, so that, if one were to observe from a distance, it began to appear as if a single division of warriors rode together.

Brotherhood is created when men come together to fight for a common good against a common enemy and for a just cause.

When the now-assimilated army of rebels approached the Red Cross camp, and when they were quickly recognized as the liberators and protectors of Innocents in the region, and when Eleanor recognized Conall as leading the troops, there was cheering and celebrations—because they had heard about a fast and approaching delegation born of nefarious intentions; because they had heard about neighboring villages destroyed—and Eleanor celebrated most of all, as she ran to meet her husband, and she cried, most of all, when she saw his wounds and kissed him and kissed his wounds, and then welcomed all of these men as if family, as she walked with her husband back to her relieved and joyous fellow workers and villagers.

Conall held her small hand and smelled the honey-blossom fragrance about her blond hair, and felt her silky-smooth soft skin against his, and observed her gentle, calm walk, and heard her sweet, loving, melodic voice, and the armor of warfare fell off him like scales of old skin; and the long, sharp sword of the soldier fell to the parched, desert floor; and the bejeweled cup that was full of the flaming wine of the spirit of battle fell from his dry lips to the yellow grains of sand, and he walked into the camp as a mere man.

The Red Cross station was disassembled with the greatest alacrity, in response to the story of how the marauding Militia had been prevented from their murderous intent.

Tyr and Enkidu came galloping up to Conall and delivered to him the findings of their latest reconnoiter, who then divested himself of this weighty news to his men, and to Moses and his men, and finally to the Red Cross and the villagers. "Armies are coming," he told them, "and they mean to dispossess the land of all enemies and foreigners in this territory." He looked northwest. "Therein lies salvation."

Eleanor embraced him, and thought, "And herein lies my salvation."

Retreat

There were two choices confronting the members of this Red Cross International group: they could split from the now-combined armed forces to free themselves from being targeted with a known enemy, or they could ride with the liberators, knowing that an attack was imminent; but in the final analysis, after the news from Tyr and Enkidu and from the two African scouts, Julius and Olaudah, was set upon each other and assimilated, there was only one logical choice.

"It's a raiding party," Conall whispered to Eleanor; "the Militia, the government troops, and the GLA."

The radiant beauty inherent in her remarkably symmetrical visage was drained of all hues and warmth, and the upheaval in her mind spilled a frozen grimace of terror. "God's Liberation Army," she said, as if a death blow had just been delivered to her, and she barely whispered, "Here…" She embraced him, to feel his great capacity to emit calm even though violent upheaval was all around them, and she murmured to him, "In thee I trust with all of our lives, for thou art like no other man, but man blessed by God to defend us against those who would otherwise murder without impunity."

He said nothing, but embraced her even longer.

Everyone in the southern part of this country knew of the God's Liberation Army, the GLA, how they had fought the government in their own country for ten years, and how they had joined with the government of this country to quell the resistance of the indigenous people in the guise of the various rebel groups.

Moses rode up to Conall, and Conall, after kissing the hand of his fair wife, walked up to him.

"Where do we mean to go?" Moses asked.

Conall smiled inwardly, but then he said, with great respect, "We mean to get to Nigeria and ask sanctuary for the Red Cross, and the villagers." He allowed his eyes to wander away from Eleanor and onto the austere face of his newly adopted brother. "What say you?"

Moses pursed his lips. "It is true that Chad would not receive us kindly."

"We can go neither go up—more government troops await us—nor down—Ugandan troops and more GLA—and Ethiopia is too far away, so to Nigeria…"

"You seek the sanctum of the Ténéré Desert."

"Have you not Tuareg with you?" He unfolded a multilayered, color-co-ordinated map of Africa, one that that had the design of a well-lived, personally traveled, indelibly ingrained scholar upon it, where every significant rock formation and sandstone region and dune region, plain and plateau, mountain and valley and canyon, aquifer and oasis was carefully depicted and noted, with generous footnotes, and cultural references, where every border of every country that touched the fiery edge of the Sahara was drawn, delineating the length and danger of every real border, and the appearance of false borders; where every people who inhabit this sprawling, spreading monolith lived, and their political alliances; and the desert itself, in kind, be it the Hoggar Desert in Algeria, with its volcanic rock structures, or the Fezzan Desert in Libya with its limestone and sandstone surfaces; it was all here, a personal survival guide for the intrepid adventurer who might choose a leisurely crawl across the hot face of this great divide between the known and the unknown, or who desires to dissolve onto its luteous-colored skin and lie with it awhile.

"Yes," Moses replied, too surveying the magnificent, multicolored, many pages of the old map, and he let his hands drift over the expertly drawn architecture, while his magnificently drawn mind pulled the loose pieces of the origin of the map together, "and to have drawn—no, to have lived—such a map; truly remarkable." He looked at Conall with intense curiosity. "Did you know this wanderer?"

Conall smiled in sweet remembrance. "They were my father and mother," he whispered, reverently, and pointed to the initials written with a unique, swirling flourish and style. "One day I will tell you of their adventures." But the urgency of the mission before them arose and his soft reflection dissipated.

"You have sent emissaries..." Moses asked, certain that Conall had considered every point of the political compass.

"Yes—to every country that borders ours, and only one of them offered asylum."

"Tyrants do not offer charity unless they can profit from it." Moses rose up in the saddle and looked at the slowly moving exodus of people, and he could feel the omnipresent sword of despotism pushing against them. "Africa, she just needs a chance to start fair, just a running start, an asylum from those who rule with violence, instead with those who rule with the consent of the people—to be clear of this terror, we only need a chance to begin anew..." His mind harkened back to his youth, remembering Ahmed and Samya, for whom he still searched, and to his sacred mission.

"And your people, have they no allies?"

"No, none," he replied, grimly, and then said, "but what of your people, have they no allies?"

"We did—when first we came here, we had many rendezvous points, in Chad and Ethiopia, and Uganda—but the camps and the civil wars there have destroyed hope of going there; so, it is time to leave..." But he left an opening for a good listener and communicator to complete his thought.

"...When there are no places to retreat to," Moses smartly finished. "We too have found our alliances broken, our allies captured, our friends gone; only the KLA remains, and they are presently in disarray."

The two men rode in an austere silence, for they, each one of them, was a commander, a leader by nature, each one of them a strategist, a tactician by instinct; and so, each of them could sense, with their keen eyes, a thickening of dust in the red, hazy horizon; with their ears, they could hear a subtle disturbance in the rhythmic pulse of the steady fluxions of the sweltering air, and burning sand; with their noses, they could smell the acrid odor of chaos drifting in the hot, swirling breezes; and on their sweaty skin, they could feel the morbid chill that comes only from the panting breath of the murderous hordes as they slaughter Innocents and yearn for more of this narcotic to sustain their iniquitous hearts; yes, Conall and Moses felt it on the outside and the inside, and in their strong bones and rich red blood and tough sinew, too, they felt the encroaching terror accumulating around them like a tightening noose, and marching in great haste toward them.

Conall told Moses of the situation with the plains, and of the weather forecast, and of the secrets buried in the desert, and the latter nodded, in admiration of the grand strategist who rode beside him.

A few moments later, a camouflaged Jeep appeared on a rising sand dune, with four government troops sitting in its metal guts, armed to their very green berets; the Crusaders and the Red Cross International and the villagers stood still and gazed at the evil portent before them; and then another Jeep appeared, and still another, both filled with green-uniformed, well-armed soldiers, followed by a dozen more Jeeps, on either side, and forty soldiers on horseback, and twenty more on camels, followed by fourteen more machine-gun-mounted Jeeps, and twenty-five soldiers on foot; and, finally, an 85-IIM tank—but these were only the forces on the ground, for in the air were coming two Mil Mi-24 attack helicopters.

Conall and Moses rode up to their men and halted their progression inside a small valley that had two high rock mountains before and after them, two solid fortifications to shield them from enemy fire that the scouts had found.

Yoshitsune, staring at the veil of darkness before him, said, in a deep, booming and confident voice, "They are standing in their graves."

No one present disagreed.

Flight

The jagged teeth of the Militia and government and GLA troops formed the upper jaw of the black wolf's gaping, saliva-dripping, yellow-fanged mouth, as they stood defiantly and proudly upon that sandy hill, peering down upon what they perceived as helpless peasants caught in a snare and about to be swallowed whole by their voracious appetite for wanton slaughter; then, slowly the lower jaw of this murderous *Canis lupus* formed as more Militia and government troops and GLA troops swept up behind the now-immobile human targets, more Jeeps and more men on camel and horseback, and an Olifant Mk 1B tank, with its overly ripened snooty glare engraved on its lengthened hull and multilayered armor, feeling all too proud of its adoring, grinning, all-too-confident hosts.

"Will they risk an international incident?" Enkidu asked, to no one in particular, and then to no one in particular, Finn answered, in words torn from the pages of a blood reckoning: "Murdering foreigners on their own soil, murdering Innocents here, murdering anyone they please they feel is no one's business, and as newsworthy as a man defending his own home against robbers."

If there had been an illusory fragment of hope for a peaceful withdrawal in the minds of the young warriors around him, it now lay shattered to tiny shreds.

And yet, one of the youngest Crusaders asked, "Is there no chance for a parlay?"

"Does the wolf ask for a truce with the cornered lamb?" Abdul said, sternly, spying the agitated faces of the subordinate soldiers through his spyglass.

"So, why don't they attack?" Abebe asked.

Scorn planted itself like a poisonous seed upon the face of Henry. "They want to see how foolish we are, if we will negotiate or capitulate, if only to preserve bullets and soldiers."

"They would kill us no matter the course we take," Jon Paul stated, disturbed.

"Yes, little lamb, kill us and roast us and eat us all before daybreak, and forget about us the next day—it is the way with men who have no souls," Henry said.

No one exhibited the briefest distortion of facial contour, not the tiniest tremble of digit or limb, not the slightest slouch in their fully erect posture, for it was as if they were witnessing the armies aft and afore them from a safe territory in which they were totally detached, as if the vile creatures before them were being viewed through a video screen as they sat a world away: a toothy piranha in a glass aquarium; a black adder behind a thick, steel cage; a white polar bear behind a high rock fence in a zoo.

There were two opposing forces, representing two opposing philosophies, about to war against each other, and the two opposing forces knew that there was no one, or no one thing, or no situation, that could resolve this conflict; and when such desperate and disparate men are engaged in such a weighty conflict, the aggressor will do any conceivable thing to win; this, then, was the new war—actually a resurrection of old and original wars: not modern wars of surrender and compromise, and conquer and assimilation, but wars that had actually never gone out of style for those barbarians who enjoyed fighting civilized troops who had been weaned on the idea that wars were to be kinder and gentler; this new soldier dreamed of wars of mass slaughter and genocide, of scorched earth and total annihilation without a breath of humanity ever befouling their mind, who smiled whenever their enemy wanted to talk peace—the only peace they wanted was the utter devastation of the perceived enemy; it was savage, brutal, unrelenting war born in blood feuds, in the minds of fanatical, religious despots, in the black hearts of megalomaniacal tyrants, a war come and gone and come again, always fermenting somewhere in some small nation, never completely destroyed, never completely wiped clean from the lament of history's filthy scrolls, always kept alive by some crazed, vicious bully, and nourished by his emotionally insecure but loyal adherents, and allowed to foment and spread by a weak, hesitant, indigenous population that could not bring themselves to put all available resources into finding and killing, and finally separating the poisonous head of their nemesis from its leviathan body; and ignored by an insular and infinitely wealthy outside world that tended to its own infinitely and singular meaningless existence, that simply did not understand that there is no such concept as pure isolation, for there is only one world, and the borders of Man are not abstract and finite. There was the mindset of one opposing force—the Militia and the government and GLA troops—of a heaving and puffing mind that saw its collective enemies as unholy and unclean, of a species deserving only of torture and death, a broken tribe of humans better left destroyed than healed, a crooked and false brood of followers who were seen as something much less than human and not much more than vile insects; and the other opposing force—the now-conjoined Freedom Rebels—they knew this, understood how their enemy saw them, and knew there was no other means of engagement than they having the most technologically advanced weapons of war, and the emboldened spirit and courage to never back down, and to never, ever, despite the seemingly overwhelming odds, admit defeat, for a defeat once given silences the loud knell of freedom ringing throughout the land.

And still, some of the Freedom Rebels wondered, sometimes aloud—but carefully, carefully chosen in times past and different places and with often-changing words, but now not so optimistic or realistic or even imaginable—if there were not some other way to effectively convert their enemy to peace and love, and if not, if the enemy truly was a collective creature that felt no remorse or was so indoctrinated with a uncompromising and hateful doctrine that there was no chance for redemption, then they must be aggressively hunted and killed to protect the millions of Innocents who were caught in the terrorizing glare of a dogma that preached death and destruction to any and all who opposed it; and thus, the Crusaders rendered their own doubts lifeless, and reinvigorated their pledge to fight these human monsters to the death, no matter the odds.

A big, black, ornery grizzly bear unleashes his hot fury and fierce growl when he spies an intruder in his clearly marked territory; so too does the black panther; so too the domesticated canine; even the most timid *Homo sapiens*, from inside his tame fortress, issues a plaintive wail when comes a palpable invader; so, what animal was venting its calamitous roar to now announce its approach, but the metallic and flying kind, with its purring, melodic, humming song sung by its sharply rotating steel wings and gunpowder talons; yes, two military helicopters were coming from behind the hill, and this time, the creatures incubating inside had orders not to reconnoiter or investigate, but to simply and efficiently eviscerate; and still, remarkably still, the visages of the Freedom Rebels, which should been inflated by fear and dread, were kept deflated by calm and serenity, and their bodies, which should been inflated by terror and worry into a volcanic trembling and shaking, were reduced to a relaxed and easy repose; ah, but their enemies appeared to have the trappings of fear and dread—visages wild and full of grimaces, and bodies rent by worry and terror, which shook like the slender reed in a windy gale, but it was the enchantment of anticipation, the thrill of knowing, the magical glitter of watching—anticipating and knowing and watching a foe that had been so clever and destructive to your forces, and difficult to track and kill, and who was about to die a cruel and agonizing death; what greater joy hath they than this, than to watch their hated enemy finally succumb to the promises that their sacred religions boasted—that the faithful will always prevail against the infidel?

A small button on the small electronic device in the hand of Conall flashed red, and he quickly signaled the other men; it would not be long now; no, not too long at all, until these despised foes around them were left in smoldering heaps and bits for the foragers and decomposers of the desert; and now, their faces became grim, not with regret, but with reality that is written in the long passages of battle: the witnessing of men—be they good or bad—men dying by the scores, the reality that explores ideas sunk deep into the tissues of these men, that perhaps, if their enemy had been born in another region, in another time, to a different family, that all of this would mute and fade into the annals of what should be; but no, these warriors knew that the enemy before them would always be thus, no matter where they were born, or what ideology they were exposed to, that they—and even if it wasn't all of them, then others, and always plenty of them—would find some radical cause to fight for; and thus, as long as there was injustice in the world, and Justice stepped up to meet it, then there would be war.

So, it all began, a fierce, sizzling, piercing tune that swept over the Freedom Rebels and those whom they guarded, and cradled them in soft, harmonic music, rocking them to and fro, telling them all would be well; then the men saw it—it was perfectly fine to look now in the direction of the coming star attraction—the blaring, smoking projectiles spitting fire into the clear blue sky and bearing down hard on the soldiers afore and aft them, and address the facile deaths of their enemy by multiple missiles that slapped the helpless soldiers and pounded the hard soil, and the numerous missiles that skipped over their heads and swept over the hill and smeared the horizon with a fiery conflagration of twisted metal and falling debris from the blown-to-smithereens, now-feeble helicopters and puny tanks.

So, it all ended, with the now-prone Crusaders applying their skill in the use of firing a weapon with great accuracy, discharging a bounty of bullets before and in front of them, and each man, by prearranged plan, knew just where to plant the metal seed for the most rewarding harvest; in a threefold manner, like a bomb burst, the explosions of firepower were over, and all of the enemy lay dead, and all of the rebels stood, alive and unharmed, and now watching the magnificent gray MiG-29 jet fighter heading down toward them, blasting their ears as it blew directly overhead; the horses and camels were not amused, but the men were, for they knew that their own, with the aid of others, had hijacked the jet, and now were their guide in the air, their guardian angel, their army of one, a supernatural winged avenger no ordinary desert army could defend against unless they had the most technologically advanced weaponry.

Yet, some of the villagers had been hit by fire, and those killed were forthwith buried, and those injured were given medical treatment.

The Red Cross International personnel and villagers moved out with their land guardians, moving up the hill and past the charred, smoking, burning, scattered chunks of bodies and twisted metal, and as much as they tried not to look—these avowed healers, succors of the dying and vanquished, and

Innocents—too many looked, and their spirits were broken that so many had had to die, so many who desperately sought to destroy them. The Crusaders discharged their bullets into all the bodies, and the subsequent smash and tear of the still-living bodies bled madness into the malleable brains of the meek. "Must you," one of the young women shouted as the men checked the corpses; "must you!" No good reply for such a macabre action could ever come that would appease any healer, or meek soul; so, a dreaded but necessary silence was the reply.

There was a great expanse of empty desert before them now, and a certain exhilaration grew in the breasts of these travelers, which spoke of a great desire to move swiftly from their current environs, as if there was truly no safe place from another country; the jet flew by as if to roar approval.

The travelers had not gone far when the alarm spread throughout the Crusaders, and soon, even the Red Cross and villagers knew what had happened; on the distant horizon, coming from a northern direction, came four fighter jets, fallen angels having recently escaped from the dark abyss; there was nothing for the mass of people to do but watch the fight unfurl before their anxious eyes.

Yes, the guardian jet sent R-73 missiles, and bullets through its 30 mm cannon, and the enemy jets reciprocated in kind; and the guardian jet flew magnificently and avoided the missiles, and took out two jets, but it was not to be, everyone knew; there was no possible way for the lone jet to forestall the inevitable, no matter how brave or adroit the pilot was; the people below viewed the screaming dogfight as if removed from its stark reality, as if it had nothing to do with them, as if they were not part of the battle at all, as if, they felt, it was not real at all, but play, not physical, but surreal, not whole, but a fragment of a picture hidden by their anxious minds; and so, just as the two jets converged on the lone pilot and were set to explode him into ruin and rubble, three more jets appeared from a northern direction, and the hearts of the people below sank, and their countenances were of those already dead and buried; and then, lo, two jets that were about to seize the lone pilot burst into flames, and the people below scrutinized the heavens for an angelic messenger, and soon saw it, a fast-approaching jet, coming from the same direction as the lone pilot had, and firing more missiles at the approaching enemy jets; but the guardian jet had been hit by an errant missile from one of the enemy jets before it was downed; and thus, the pilot bailed out, leaving the newest guardian pilot to face the oncoming winged spirits of darkness; and he did, flying directly toward them and firing his missiles and cannon fire and taking out one, and then surging straight up and up, so very high that he verily disappeared from sight, the two enemy jets in hot pursuance; and the ground became still, and the smell of sulfur was everywhere, and black ash rained down, and the people looked skyward, their hearts and minds living on the faith of the miraculous; and then, yes, and then, high, high above, far, far away, in the deepest valley of the liquid firmament, dim, tiny objects appeared, but they came courting without sound; and then, as if riding on a bolt of white lightning, the dueling three objects became clearer and filled the sizzling air with fury; it was the lone pilot followed by the two dark warriors, swerving and darting and diving and dashing in the infinite pools of iridescent blue, slicing and clearing and skewering the ethereal ring of flesh round the earth; and then, the lone jet zigged and the other two jets zagged, and the lone jet looped and anchored itself as if by a magical hinge, and the other objects labored to follow, and the one jet shot its mighty cannon fire and missiles into the two jets and immediately one jet broke into pieces and exploded in orange flames; and then, to the utter shock of those transfixed on the ground, the lone jet chased the last vulture jet, closer, closer, closer, closing its distance so fast and expertly that no one below had any momentum of an idea that the lone jet would, and did, deliberately ram into the back of the fleeing jet, and the impact was tremendous and glorious, and the outcome seemingly impossible, but now clear and done, and the land-dwellers watched in awe as the two mangled, dancing, twirling jets sank, like entwined, wounded eagles whose claws were dug into each other, to the hard desert floor below and then burst into a magnificent explosion of sound and fury. It was over.

The first pilot, Horatius, had long since—long as it relates to modern dogfights—landed safely and disengaged himself from his white parachute and joined his Freedom Rebel brethren, and was heartily congratulated on his skill and daring; but now, the entire mass of people gazed up at the sky and watched as the other pilot landed his parachute some distance away, and then began to move toward them, looking about, brushing himself off, smoothing back his rich, black, oily, curly hair, and taking out a fresh, thick brown Cuban cigar, lit it, and then took a long, luxurious drag of its wondrous, smoky, earthy flavors.

He first walked up to Conall and Rustem, who now rode side by side, and then saluted. "Miguel Esteban Vega Cervantes," he said, in earnest, the fat cigar now in his left hand, as it lay at his side, "asking permission to join your magnificent band of freedom fighters."

Conall smiled as he shook Miguel's outstretched hand, and said, with great admiration, "Welcome," and then watched in reverence as Miguel shook the hand of not only Rustem and the recently enjoined African brothers, but also the Crusaders he had already known, making each of them feel as if it was his honor and privilege to know and ride with them, and all the other travelers.

"One more," Abdul said.

Moses, nodding his head, said, suffused with a surpassing sentiment of brotherhood and joy, "More than one."

Pastoral Symphony

No land is ever what it should be, because no land is ever devoid of human presence, and people are wont to alter the ground upon which they walk and work and live—especially after, so long ago, foraging was abandoned for agriculture, and the people saw that what they had done was good, and vowed to stay.

Without human beings, forests and jungles, savannas and deserts, mountains and valleys, oceans and lakes and rivers exist in a delicate ecosystem that sustains a constantly shifting balance between foliage and fauna, insects and bacteria and fungi, elastic enough to regard natural catastrophes such as floods and raging fire, drought and volcanic tempers, earthquakes and powerful tornadoes, as short-term, minor inconveniences; for where there are floods, the land adjusts; for where there are droughts, the life-forms therein recede until such a time they are called again to thrive; for where there are volcanic bursts, the land takes a holiday until the rich, dense ash restores the plant life; but where there are people invading these privately pristine kingdoms, they seek to alter the equilibrium, and do not care to recognize it, and even if they do, do not restore it, but loot it and mob it and alter it to feed the insatiable appetite of their false god, avarice, and for more dwellings and recreation, and for their gargantuan hunger; they will plunder forests to make coal, they will, they will uproot and gouge and dig and chop with a hearty abandon the earth's own woody children that flourished for decades, and centuries, even for a millennium, in peaceful coexistence with their brother and sister life-forms, for precious, black coal, to drag the murdered trees to the smoking factories so they might be placed with a flux agent and ore, and when the whole mixture is heated, to yield up the precious and purity of black gold, smelted iron; yes, they will, and they will assiduously dig and rip and tear and pound the bruised and battered land after finding great quantities of precious minerals; yes, of course, certainly, they will, as Man chases the next slippery rung up society's slippery social economic ladder to attain an easier existence; and they will massacre land and sea, sky and space, even their own species, lo, even would they loot the high vault of heaven, the cosmic children of the universe, the stars and planets and their wayward children and orphaned relatives, if they could convert this raw elemental abundance into fantastic wealth—why, indeed Man would, Man, who dares defy heaven and earth in his eternal quest to be his own idol, his own prophet, his own god.

> O, when the virgin Earth began, and cradled innocent and newborn Man,
> She cuddled and covered him in soft warmth and fur;
> And then Man betrayed her, when first and again he raped her,
> O, how she forgave him, as only a mother can

Recede in time a half-million years and sit high above the great continent of Africa, and this is what you will see: you will not see what you would perceive as a paradise, but still a paradise; a better place to live than now, even though it was no utopia, but a more peaceful world; not a sanctuary, but a gentler society—for it was young, and not yet disturbed by foreign influence, and it was in balance, and not yet ravaged by blind forces from outside, and it was whole, not yet ravaged and discarded from within.

The land surface of Africa is largely devoid of nutrients to sustain vegetation, leaving only a small area that is fertile and cultivatable, and the warmth that occurs year-round is an incubation chamber for sleeping sickness, yellow fever, and malaria; the jungle covers a minority of the continent, but the plants engage in a strict diet of rich nutrients from rain and air, from vegetation living and dead, and thus, leaving precious nutrients in the sandy soil only for those animals who eat the fruit and leaf of the savanna, which is also rich in woods and tall flowering grasses and able to recycle nutrients throughout the year, and so invite a greater variety of life-forms; yet, none of this mattered to the indigenous natives, for where there was cultivable land, there they were; where there was fertile land, there they were, sowing seed, raising crops, tending livestock, building small villages, where the population growth did not exceed the offerings of their environments; to wit: where there was just enough water and good land for no more than two hundred people, then no more than two hundred people existed there, a population growth held back by disease and available food, and low birth rates and natural childbirth through breastfeeding, existing mostly in small clans, not in cities and states.

Here, then, is harmony; here, then, is stability; here, then, might paradise take root—like a fragile seed planted between boulders—but it must be nourished, just like the flower, and guided toward the warm white light, just like the flower, and like the flower, once it has grown over its natural obstacles, will be able to stand tall and proud; but where there is paradise, there are those with a wicked nature who crave it, thinking that paradise is any land where they can unfurl their treasonous acts; so, where one village lay unmolested, another lay devious and discontented, and seeking to seize its neighbor's bounty; and thus, it all began.

Where one village grazed on peace, another on war, and so raids by the latter occurred against the former, be it for goods, or crop, or people, or simply mayhem, and the cycle would begin; yet, it was not a war of nations, not a war of foreign empires waged on them, not a civil war, yet, and the people lived through it, and survived it, and overcame it, and lived again until the next raid.

Slavery broke bread with Man at his inauguration on earth, infesting his mind like a leech, sucking his character and returning poisonous shreds of its DNA back into his malleable brain, wearing him down, drilling tiny holes into his resistance, setting up a solid foundation, then carefully and craftily constructing reasons for its existence, and proclaiming its credo, "That the strong in mind and body should rule over the weak in mind and body." Husbands realized this, and so enslaved the minds and bodies of their wives; parents enslaved children; so, too, neighbor enslaved neighbor, through debt, for money, for power, through violence, through intimidation; and so, too, villages, and cities, and city-states, and nation-states engaged in slavery, for whatever reason necessary to achieve their ambitious goals to extend their boundaries and their identity beyond themselves.

Slavery began long before the European came to Africa, and it continued long after the European left; where there was labor in decline, there were villages to raid; where there was food in decline in a home, there were villagers willing to trade a child for grain; so, villagers were kidnapped, bought, exchanged and sold to slavers, and the drums of sorrow beat slowly, and steadily, building a partition between what could have been, and what was.

There was a village somewhere in Africa, not yet unceremoniously dropped into a designated country, for the soulless European plunderers had not yet taken up their long knives and drawn nonsensical and artificial borders through people and heritages and customs; and now a bloody knife, upon which the lives and fortunes of indigenous people hung like skins from lusty trappers, was poised above their heads; but as it was, this village was near the longest river on this continent, the River Congo; now, originally the European had dubbed this river the Zaire, a corruption of an African word for river, but later it received the title Congo, and it is Congo that still pulses strongly in the mind of the international community; as it was, there was this fine and tranquil village set in a cluster of Palm, Mangrove, and Mahogany and Okoume trees, and Oil Palms, ferns and bushes, and barnyard grasses alongside the magnificent river; in small huts of leaves and twigs and limbs and mud, families dwelled; it was a simple life, of fishing in the streams and river, of chopping down trees and picking orange yams and succulent mangoes, and meaty nuts and white tubers, hunting wild game and drawing fresh water from the pristine lakes, and cooking and preparing and grinding the food, and skinning and scraping and carving and stitching the clothes; and telling stories of past generations, and singing jubilant songs of their people, and seeing the strange and new, weird, pale creatures who were coming from lands unknown that were too far away to imagine.

There was always adventure for the little ones, spying the scandalously sly crocodile, the slithering brown water snake; counting the great diversity of colorful fish in the swirling, frothy river; scouting hiding places among the giant evergreen trees; climbing vines; playing tag with the eland and the banded mongoose, and the puku; and seeing the dazzling white-skinned creature with two arms and two legs and smooth, skin drooping about its soft body as it traversed on boat and land with its guides, and always asking probing questions about life on the Big River.

There were celebration days, days of marriage and births and youths becoming adults, days of bountiful harvests and plentiful health, days of singing songs of the old ways so they would not forget the old days; and these were days of dread and woe, disease and death, abductions, murder, raids, villages burned and looted, and during those days of joy and sorrow, in between and before and after, and coming soon and more often and beginning to press down more and more with their obnoxious and intrusive presence, the pestilence from the northern formations appeared, asking annoying, disturbing questions, proffering startling, absurd—but self-promoting for them; intellectually castrating, but wealth-generating for them; arrogant and debasing, but smothering to the natives—proposals; and the creepy, carnivorous creatures with the ready smiles—constructed from nothing you might trace or build upon; impossible to stay upon their mocking faces—kept coming back now, more in bunches, like bloodthirsty vultures to the kill, and more in large numbers, like an army of leafcutter ants to annihilate everything in their path, and leaving only barren, skeletal remains behind.

There was one clan of the Yombe that dwelled in the very fertile heart of the southern rain forest who lived according to the customs and dictates of past practices and beliefs.

Mwindo lived there, and happily did he thrive, for he was a child, and could create joy and wonder in nearly all of creation, never one to allow the imperfection in Man or Nature to disenthrall him. One fine day, after a brief, light rain that had awakened the flora and fauna of his environs, he was skipping along the muddy soil of the forest, hopping over the wet bush and plants; and finding the tall Cyperaceae, the sedge and papyrus grasses, he dove into its verdant grasp and slid, like a brave hunter, toward the shore, and soon spied a magnificent gray hippopotamus surfacing close to him; he lay mesmerized, yet still possessed of a clarity of mind that enabled him to properly yield a careful scrutiny of the watery beast; oftentimes, he lay like this for hours, as a profound reverence for the animals along this waterway lay deep within his innocent heart; he had never been much of a hunter—more of a tracker—like his older three brothers, and was even wont to leave when game was skinned and gutted by his elders, for he considered these animals his friends, his brothers and sisters also, and he honored them for their gracious company.

Few noises could disconnect this intense reverie he lay in, but this particular day, there came a discordant chorus of clamor from the direction of his village, awakening him from his pleasant trance, and he gazed back toward his home. The hippopotamus he had been studying, as if it too were on the same plane of benevolence as the boy, looked up, and soon purchased an escape route from the growing noise; Mwindo, however, immediately chased a path back, halting abruptly just outside the dirt periphery of his village, and beheld men adorned in shield and spear, and faces painted in grim death, hauling away children, stabbing remonstrative mothers, killing combative fathers; predator fish they were in a peaceful pond. Mwindo, fearful and trembling, watched as the warriors took his brother and sister, and then left as the villagers lay wounded, weeping and grieving.

The ache for Justice awakened in his juvenile soul as he ran to his parents, who still lived, but his small hut had been consumed by the fiery wrath of the savage kidnappers; and although he was still a young boy, his passions roared like a rainstorm, demanding retribution, yet he heard no such dialogue spoken of in the village, and even as he asked questions, his elders were busy rebuilding, just as if what had ruined the village was a consequence of Nature, like a flood or a fire, and there was no one seeking recompense for the damages; but Mwindo would have none of it, for he was a member of a singular club, a soldier born into the Rage of the Furies, where men who could not countenance or ignore acts of cruelty toward living things then sought out recompense against the perpetrators.

His father had taught him to track and hunt, the latter which he reluctantly did, so it was no trouble as Mwindo snuck out of the village that night, his hands still stained with the blood of his slain kin, to follow a quarry who was so full of itself that it never once considered covering its blundering trail; and soon, he had managed to find the home of the raiders. "Here, I shall wait," he thought, his senses sharp as he lay in the clutch of hearty bush that grew like faithful guardians around an enormous Iombi tree; so, here he lay, in the bosom of a vanishing night and a golden-crowned dawn, tucked away behind its wide brown trunk, listening to the shrieking cries and effusive hollering and song of his enemies; and as he dared to peer into the mania therein, his heart leaped at the general hilarity and chaos of the gyrating, bobbing, dancing revelers: he saw faces painted in cold, harsh hues, men and women adorned in ceremonial dress—feather and flowering robes and colorful jewelry—and their posture was madness, a dark energy lifted by a thin veil that permeated into every chanting observer; this raging fever, this calamitous riot of abusive cries and shouts, lasted deep into the cool night, until, suddenly, it abated, and a man, all ablaze in the splendor of the rich plumage and hides of the forest, approached the captives, his menacing glare leading him on, like a ship's prow driven by a strong wind, boring into the scared psyche of his trembling hostages, blinding them with a promise of pain and suffering emanating from his frightening stare; he encircled them slowly, and like a human spider, sprouting ropes of silken fear that bound them to its grizzly texture; the hearts of the prisoners were wont to die of fear and save their executioners the walk to the stake, many now upon their bloody knees, many now crying, lamenting, praying, fomenting pity—they were dead now, they knew, dead now walking, dead in a night, buried in the day, having been swallowed whole by the heartless human python and feeling his corrosive juices devour their skin and bone and muscle, to soot and ash and dust.

How came us here, O mistress of fate

Herein we lie, we suffer and wait.
No valiant rescue, therein we weep,
The world is cruel; our life, cheap.

This spiritual crank with the rows of beads hanging from his scrawny neck, this matchless administrator of pomp and nonsense waved his ordinary sticks and ordinary shells about as if they truly were portals into a magical dimension, and pronounced judgment in ordinary, even poor, verse that was starved for eloquence and a cerebral caddy; and one searing glance at his cowardly but obedient handmaidens, and they rushed forward, all eager and hyper-intent to deliver the proper crushing blows against the soft tissue and hard bone of their captives; and what, pray tell, was it all about, in what realm and rank was it for, and why, why, for what clearly stated purpose did others perpetuate that which they did not understand or question; and so the prisoners died, as was required of them: to die for some obscure notion, some foolish whim of their transitory masters, to amuse their jolly audience, their blood spilled to christen a new house, their brains dashed to appease an unseen god, their flesh cut for food and drink, and imagined solace.

By a lark, by some weird fancy, a few of the children, not to be designated as slaves, were henceforth marched pell-mell to the busy river and then unceremoniously tossed in to those trustworthy and patient aquatic attendant, the scaly, toothy, cunning crocodile, who quickly proffered up a rotating boat ride to its honored guests.

Boom, in went the first two screaming-bloody-murder children; splash, in went two more, and then two elderly people, and then hush, in went an unseen and impossibly cool youth who was soon swimming strongly and cleverly underwater to the aid of a struggling boy and girl; and in a thrice, he had them in tow, and was pulling them upstream and into the obscure clutches of the tall, thick green reeds, where the three treaded water as they listened to the death throes of their brethren, as they listened to the vulgar savages sing their way back to the celebratory forest, as they saw the mutilated bodies of the victims floating by and now bumping into them; and so, when this shipment of human horror had retreated far, far into the swampy forest, the three mind-blown children, in the midst of the blood and guts and old friends, hoisted themselves up and onto the muddy bank and with great stealth, ran and dived, crawled and slid, all the way back to their precious village, creeping, like the wily red fox, through the tall, verdant ferns, quiet, like the black leopard, wary of the slightest movement.

Alas, they were children, merely, and no formidable opponent to the advanced and sharpened wits of men who dined on cunning and deception the same way a hungry man dines on luscious fruit; and so, the three were caught, and by the same villagers who had already taken the brother and sister, and had seen Mwindo's stealthy operation, and had been so subdued by its daring that they allowed his subterfuge to last a little while; but now the game was over, and the three siblings were marched back to the raiding village, not to die, by virtue of Mwindo's cleverness, but to be sold as slaves to a neighboring chief for a debt, and were forthwith bound by sturdy twine and marched with fellow prisoners to their new abode.

The new village was some twenty miles away, and once the children arrived there they were struck by the absolute vastness of it, the great hustle and bustle of it, and the very idea that such a large amount of people could coexist together was startling; it was, in truth, ten times the size, in area and population, of their own village, but to them, it was a magnificent, panoramic vision too enormous and far apart for their minds to properly etch into a logical, sustainable, orderly sense; but none of that mattered, for they were slaves now, as had been too many of their ancestors in Africa—and yes, before the Arab world threw down its iron fist and transported millions along the Indian Ocean and Saharan routes, and even before the Europeans threw down their spiked iron fists and transported millions more, mostly to the Caribbean and Brazil, and a small minority to the New World and other countries in the Western hemisphere; so you see, the fault is not in the greed of foreign capitalists alone—for the African not only bound and sold his own to his own, but to everyone else with his bloody hand out—it is in the black heart of Man himself; but none of this mattered to Mwindo and his brother and sister, for they were to be domestic slaves: the sister had the potential to endure, but the males, seen as troublesome, would be soon sold to the Englishmen, who would transport them to the New World, or to the Portuguese, who would transport them to the Gold Coast and exchange them for the rare yellow mineral; it did not matter now, for their fate was determined by cruel geography and a cruel epoch, and rescue would not come from without, as in rich countries; it must come, as in poor countries, from within.

> One man down, he grovels and scrapes
> Another man down, he seeks escape;
> One man down, his hope toward men
> Another man down, his eyes toward heaven.

Mwindo could not live through physical restraint, for the natural horizons around him extended so far east and west, north and south, so high up and so deep down, that he had to cast off any fetters or die—it is called the need for a non-binding existence, a need to flow freely through natural flora and pristine aqua and up and down and across undulating green hills and mushy mud and dusty and yellowy sand; a need in him just like a vital organ pumping a hormone that juiced his hot temper as it flushed in his vital bloodstream; a need no different from a golden eagle to fly free, a bottlenose dolphin to swim free, a yellow and black cheetah to roam free; and like the eagle, the dolphin, and the cheetah, to not grant him such unlimited access to his environs would doom him; therefore, and with exceeding hope, he plotted escape from his walking captivity.

"But we live," his little sister, Nyokato whispered, as the three were tramping along the damp jungle floor.

"No," Mwindo whispered back, "we live when we are free." He looked ahead at the long line of captives afore and aft him, and motioned to his little brother, Kengo, to hush himself. "Soon," he continued, his fierce words now birthing the fierce desire of his fervent soul; and his voice trembled with a consuming fire; "we will run, and when we run, you will follow me, and not look back—not even once, not even when you hear footsteps right behind you." He looked up with scorn, carved like a warrior's mask into his immature face, to his captors. "Our people must be free—it is all we have ever known; it is our right."

As he uttered this eternal pledge, generations of heroes past echoed in his too-soon-to-be-mature voice, his father to his father before him, to every subsequent man who had lived within the precious circle of pride and prosperity, pursuing an existence of peace not yet stolen, not yet exceeded by avarice and deceit, not yet eaten by the worms of war, and tyranny from within; and the need to struggle free from the suffocation of natural rights, this too, too ancient oath blasted from the silver trumpet of Justice, this anointed Right vested in the ardent breast of Man, it cradled him, rocked him and drove him inexorably toward that shimmering Light of Liberty.

The human parade followed a path long ago established by the slavers; the route was always accessible near the Congo River, and always accessible near villages, for the slavers' only intent was to capture, subdue, and move indigenous natives up and down the waterways; there were drop-off points for certain chiefs, certain clans, certain European businessmen, and then the trade route was regained.

Mwindo could see that, at any moment, he and brother and sister would be parceled off, like young heifers, and their fates sealed, like inanimate objects; so, he initiated an action even he thought was an incautious move.

It was raining. It was a hard rain, a hard, pounding, cold rain that submerged every human creature in a mania to flee, to hide, to take refuge under the nearest tree, bush, or structure; this arrogant rain, its harsh smile, it spread, and splashed on the long line of captives and captors, and let fall a thick but transient veil of a dense blur across the jungle, sending the people into their own private thoughts concerning their own private world; but, it was in this powerful cover that Mwindo acted, knowing that this beating wall of streaming rivers would allow him to access an exclusive escape route; and so, taking the hands of Nyokato and Kengo, he led them in a furious crawl directly away from the line of lumbering slaves, slipping through the dense undergrowth just like a beast escaping from a brutish master.

Who better to navigate a swift course through tangled and hanging and clinging plants; who, truly, better to slip and slide on squishy, mucky, puddled mud and slick rocks; who but small, healthy children who had a greater motivation to live than their captor to capture them; and why, incidentally, do seemingly all captors expend so much energy to recapture those whom they have previously spent less energy on than first capturing? It is hubris, and sometimes, it can be argued, strictly financial, or purely strategic to prevent the escapee from revealing sensitive information, but mostly, and absolutely, it is about preserving and thus avoiding shame and embarrassment; and so, it was no different for these slavers, who, once they realized that three of their prisoners were gone, dispatched two of their best trackers to bring the misfits back.

Mwindo and Nyokato and Kengo ran, their hands free now, fueled by absent rain and the prevailing warm winds and shunshine and their prodigious youth and desire to return to their home and live free as they now knew they must; they would run for some time and break for nourishment; they would run for some time and then break to rest; and they would run for some time, and wonder at the distant noises around them, and they would huddle in fear and pray to their sleeping gods and pray that their parents might happen upon them and embrace them to their warm and familiar bodies and enwrap them in the magical cloak that imparts invulnerability that only parents can weave for their own precious blood.

They were creating a non-linear trail, crossing the Congo River on borrowed canoes, at shallow spots, climbing tree to tree, and then diving into the swirling waters and swimming to the other side, outrunning disturbed crocodiles and angry hippopotamuses, brushing next to river snakes, always moving, occasionally finding a water vine to quench their thirst, munching on ripe bananas, and tubers, and all kinds of nuts, and sleeping very little, as only the young and strong can do, hour after anxious hour, day after desperate day, always with a worried look behind them.

Then there came a time when they knew their path to home was lost, and so the three of them sat down in a clump of thick vegetation, waving away the incessant insects, and listening to the garrulous chatter of monkeys and birds and the supporting cast of ubiquitous noisemakers, Nyokato and Kengo began to cry, and although Mwindo would have none of it for himself, he allowed them to weep, and weep fully, until both of them lay fully asleep; and he watched them, wanting, too, to weep, but knowing that he certainly must not, lest he die, like so many runaway, potential slaves before him; therefore, he sat bolt upright, feeling very much a protector, projecting his keen senses, like a widely distributed net, about the periphery of the jungle; and by and by, he heard a faint echo of human voices about him, and he reasoned that it was a village, and after placing large, green banana leaves upon his siblings, he ventured forth to investigate, following the sounds of the excited voices to the edge of the River Congo; and behold, he saw a group of men and women, their faces placid, their postures marginally slumped, as if they were in a mild state of melancholy; and presently, Mwindo looked to where the gathered people gazed, and he saw a middle-aged man standing with an elderly, white-haired woman at the high-edged embankment; and without any proper admonition at all, he pushed the old woman forcefully, actually with a great salute to power gained from a burden lifted, and she flew briefly through the air and splashed unceremoniously into the foaming, rapidly moving water below; and then, slapdash, the middle-aged man turned, his face never once grim or remorseful, but peaceful, as if he had just unloaded a dead corpse, which had been slung and tied to his bent back and which he had had to haul around for eons, into the cleansing river; as it was, he and the people met, and turning as one, walked straight away from the still but briefly struggling and soon limp figure in the fast, swirling currents.

Mwindo never hesitated; he dove straight into the meat of the mighty river and swam to the submerged woman and grabbed her and towed her back to shore, and there tended to her until she regained consciousness, and then brought her back to where his siblings lay, whereupon she too fell fast asleep; and still, like the good sentinel, he would not yield to that slayer of wakefulness, sleep, who entices us every day into its benevolent kingdom where we assume our secret roles once more as sons and daughters, noble-women and noblemen, heroes and champions.

Quiet, elegant morning came and when all were awake, the woman just sat there, as if she were not quite certain what to do with her life, now suddenly regained; and when she did speak, her words were foreign to the children; but this was not a deterrent, and soon she was leading them, with hand gestures, to food, and they, with hand and feet gestures, made it known to her they were being pursued; and after a meal of cooked cassava and fish, which they had cleverly pilfered from the cooking pit of the village that had recently disinherited her, the woman, standing before them, gestured toward the north, and turned around and walked away, with the children in close proximity, she never once looking back at the small world that had once been her life, and then, so abruptly, a judgment of death.

By and by, as they walked away from the River Congo and into the sophisticated collage of plant growth, she came to understand, through various bodily gestures, that the children had been captured and meant to be slaves, and now escaped; and she, too, attempted to relate to them that she had been captured long ago and brought to this village they had just quit, had married one of the chiefs, and became just one of his many wives, and had lived there in utter subjugation and loyalty to her elders, until one day her own son, after the death of the chief and his ascension to the throne, decided that she was no longer useful, and thus she had been condemned to death, as had so many women and men before her, a tradition practiced so long that now it was merely a part of their customs, and so obeyed without question.

But Mwindo wondered, as they walked, how this old woman was going to disable the imminent attack of the pursuers; would it be through subterfuge, he pondered, perhaps by ushering the children into a secret place only she knew; would it be by cunning, he mused, by leading their antagonists into a trap wherein they would be killed or captured by someone or something; surely, he thought, for all of her years of living here, she would have a plan; but then, to his utter dismay, she, appearing exhausted, sat down upon a fallen tree, took out a ripe and succulent mango from her small leather satchel, motioned to the others to consume their food, and proceeded to eat with an unnerving ease; now, this was not at all unusual, to eat along the way, but presently, she lay down and drifted off into a long, deep sleep. Have we traveled so far as to need such rest? Mwindo thought; no, he knew, they had not gone so far, and he no longer knew if he should trust this woman, or abandon her, as, perhaps, her village had so rightly done; he gazed upon her tired, wrinkled, small, weak, never-moving, still body, and he could see her only as someone unburied from the grave, better dead, fruitless, cursed; and then he thought of his burgeoning youth, and his instinct was to flee, to take his brother and sister with him and just start racing away, far away from this decrepit slab of withering flesh and bones and sinew—but he did not, he did not yield to the wild impulse of anxious and ambitious youth, a talent that separated him from all others, for he was a true thinker, able to reason and analyze a situation without a dilution of raw emotion muddling his equanimity; I will stay for now, he decided as he stared at the disturbingly ancient-to-him form, for she must know things beyond my years, as did my parents, and I do not think she wishes any longer to die; and so, baptized into this exclusive community of believers in the miraculous, he too, and then Nyokato and Kengo, fell into a deep and pleasant slumber.

The mean voice rang out like a sudden thunderstorm, blowing a huge hole in the satisfying sleep of the four fugitives, and presently, they awoke, only to see their pursuers standing before them like smoldering volcanoes ready to erupt.

Here were two powerfully built men, their black muscles glistening in the harsh sunlight; designated trackers, who, upon finding their quarry, were happy to beat them, and if they were women, pleased to rape them; and if their victims were dying, glad to kill them, as they thrived on those who struggled against the stinging whip, the thick stick, the hard slap of the cold iron blade; for the more the victim struggled, the more these men grew in stature, deriving their very sustenance from them, and consequently, saw themselves as important and wanted, while watching themselves assume a unique identity in this violent, unruly world.

"Get up," one of them shouted to the children, but not to the old woman, whom they considered as useless as the old, rotting log upon which her head lay.

The children understood none of their words, but abruptly popped to, and stood at trembling attention.

"Go," the captors shouted, readying their bamboo sticks to strike as the children passed them.

And then a serene voice, riding on a tall wave of a seemingly out-of-place certitude, crested upon the glaring soldiers, and drenched them in doubt. "You will not leave here with the children; you will leave here with great riches." The men raised their green bamboo toward the children to halt.

"Speak fast, you foolish old woman," the biggest one said, "or you will soon be food for the worms."

The old woman stood up, but with her stood up wisdom, and upon her face was a veil of cunning and subterfuge no youth could decipher. "You will swear an oath to your ancestors that you will leave the children alone after I show you the cowries." She watched the poor avaricious fools animate to a salivating frenzy. "Swear." They quickly and easily swore the oath. "Follow me."

The old woman led the two behemoths, just as if she were a master who was casually walking two tethered and willing hogs to slaughter; the children, unable to understand the conservation, trailed behind, hopeful, yet still apprehensive.

The treasure trove was not too far removed from where the two opposing camps had met, and so, the old woman stood in a small clearing among the drooping, green mask of leaf, petal, fruit and flower of the African Nutmeg, and the clustered green flowers of the tall Tamarind tree with its massive, corrugated trunk, and then she pointed to a spot and encouraged the human hunters to dig, which they presently did, and their efforts quickly revealed a large wooden covering, which, once removed, revealed more dirt, which they then dug with equal fervor, which soon revealed another wooden covering, which they hastily removed; and behold, they saw a bounty of cowrie shells beyond their peasant imagining—the cowrie shell, the monetary unit upon which the European bought slaves, white and bright when properly polished, an innocent intermediary, sending the slave to the Gold Coast to barter precious gold for the slavers. Thousands of these small, resilient shells bought a human being for a living entombment, until, over the generations, the amount of shells needed reached the hundreds of thousands during the frenzy of capturing and selling the human commodity.

"You will allow the children to live," the old woman said, in earnest.

The men brandished their trusty wooden punishing tools, and a heavy scowl and then a toothy grin spread like a consuming contagion across their swarthy faces. "No," the leader said, and went back to dancing inside the hoard of riches.

"You have dishonored your ancestors, and you must now die; it is the law of our people."

"Woman," the leader shouted, "we make no vow before foreigners."

The old woman, sitting now, did not seem nonplussed by the ferocious growl of the two mighty men; in fact, she was more inspired by amusement, as evidenced by an amused smirk upon her wizened face. "But, this day, you will sleep with your ancestors."

The two men, stopping their scooping up of the beauteous shells, laughed loud and hard. "You will do this," the leader shouted, pointing his bamboo stick at her, "an old, dried-up carcass?"

"No," she smiled, "it is I who lived, and it is I who will live, and because you are young, you believe your physical strength is greater than what I know."

The two men jumped out of the bath of shiny cowrie baubles. "You will die, you old—" the leader began, but suddenly clutched his right arm with his left hand, his face frozen in shock and horror, and then his left arm became paralyzed, and as he looked to his fellow conspirator, he saw the same frail health befall him. "What…" he gasped, looking at the old woman, who now stood, with the scorn of contempt upon her face, and then he collapsed, as did his fellow, both of them dining on the wail of an unmerciful rush of a virulent toxin racing with a ravenous hunger throughout their inflamed nervous system.

The old woman stood before and then over them, and then squatted and urinated upon their convulsing bodies. "It is the bad medicine of the Justice tree," she whispered down to their numb minds, "in the dirt in which you dug." It was indeed the crushed poison of the Acokanthera tree. She then slowly stood up, walked over to the base of the Tamarind tree, extracted two small, oblong, flat slices of brown bark, turned around, and held them up for the vanquished men. "I prefer to dig with these."

The children were wrapped in a disaffected but horrible glee as they watched this slow disintegration of life; but then Mwindo broke ranks from the trance of watching their tormentors being eclipsed by episodes of violent jerking, screaming in agony and pleading for mercy as they were slowly consumed by this gnawing death; and even though his words were unintelligible to them, even the old woman heard the genuine sensitivity and kindness nestled therein. "I am sorry for you, I am; I am sorry we were not friends, I am; and I wish you a better journey." And so, after the two men were dragged, with great effort, by the four refugees to the river and dropped in, they stood, knowing they were, at least for the moment, free to pursue any path they chose.

Mwindo looked to the old woman, and then to his brother and sister, and back to the bodies floating downstream; and then, walking over to Nyokato and Kengo, he took the hand of his sister, who took the hand of her brother; and then he stretched out his hand to the old woman, who came to him and gently took his hand, and then they all proceeded forth, led by the old woman, who, although they could not yet understand her linguistically, with their hearts they clearly understood her, and that her name was Kahambu, and she was here to stay.

Adoption

Kahambu led the siblings through the outer perimeter of the jungle, but some-times in, and sometimes out, for four days, until they reached a small village of her ancestors that was nestled in the deep thicket and surrounded by a dense network of foliage; when she entered the ground upon which she had walked as a young girl, she stood still and was wont to weep; and then she fell to her knees and kissed the fertile soil and lifted up her hands and face to the icy blue sky and chanted a song to her ancestors; she stood up and began walking toward the shadows and forms of things past from which she had built an altar to wor-ship inside her resting and awake dreams; it was all there, the mud and wood thatched huts, the children playing, the men and women carrying food and water to and fro, and men tending to repairs, and women tending to cooking and cleaning; it was all the same except that the faces were different; she kept on walking, and villagers began to notice, and did not seem distressed; and then one elderly, white-haired woman took notice from her squatting position over a deep rock-pit oven, and her face frowned, and then she stood, staring at the approaching travelers, and suddenly, she dropped a wooden spoon, and shouted, her face radiant with joy. "Kahambu," she cried, and broke into a run.

Kahambu saw the woman coming toward her, as did the whole of the vil-lage, and soon, she knew, too, and whispered, "Makemba," and then shouted as if she were breaking free of the rigid dimensions of her impossible dreams, "Makemba," and rushed toward her sister.

There was a celebration in the village that night, of feasting, and dancing, and singing, for Kahambu had been lost so long ago, but was now found, and such miraculous events did not often frequent such humble people. The children were easily acknowledged and embraced in the kindly ways of the Bantu, and though they still yearned for more, when they found out later that their own village had been destroyed, they soon realized this was home, and they were here to stay.

Kahambu taught the children her language, Kikongo, and the culture and custom of her village, the history of her people, and made certain they were raised with all those traits necessary to flourish as adults, and the children loved her; and so time transpired, peaceful, blissful, eventful years, and the children were fully adopted as sons and daughters of these people, but Mwindo, now a fully mature man, strong, muscular, and athletic, who had bested all the village men in every physical contest of skill and daring, and hunting and tracking, could not forget the injustice that grew unimpeachably all around him, free to roam and destroy the lives of those it deemed unworthy.

"Kahambu," he said, one day, while she was peeling yams and shallots for the big, black, iron pot, "how can a man live in peace while others live in sorrow?"

"You are a man, Mwindo, and happy, here, but out there," she began, pointing to the outside world, "you are not a man, and could not be happy."

"But how can a man be happy when he does not do what he feels he must do?"

She smiled, and took his large hand in hers. "You will stay here, with your family, your people, where you are loved, and be happy."

He shook his head. "I cannot live in peace while others weep, knowing I can help them."

She nodded. "It is a problem with you, I have seen it." She smiled in sweet remembrance of his innate and flourishing goodness. "You saved an old, worthless woman, once..." Now, he took her hand. "You are not like anyone here, Mwindo—you are a warrior, forced to dig like a farmer."

"But I am not alone; there are others in the village." He told her of the passion of other men who longed to fight the slavers, and despite her entreaties to dissuade this seemingly foolish ambition, she failed, and acquiesced, knowing who he was, and what he must become.

It was then that it all began, with four men from the village of the Bantu practicing the art of deception, a good distance south of the recognizable perimeter of their home, against the slavers, who never had considered a change of route, as there had never been a reason to alter it—as there had never been opposition to them.

During the next six months, Mwindo and his men, and those he recruited who were saved from slavery—now numbering thirty-nine—intercepted twelve slave lines, freed the captives, killed their captors, took their booty, and buried it deep and far in the tangled, thickest, most forsaken and perilous territory. Mwindo and his raiders took to living in the jungle, so as not to endanger their villages, and they were certain to lure away slavers coming toward their homes, and then dispatch them; and so, after some time, when the European masters began to grumble, the slave masters began to search, and send more men, even armed troops, to scour the region for the raiders; but neither could they find them or anyone who had seen them, and so it was not too much longer after that the slavers reasoned that the village of the Bantu, unblemished and unprotected, was endearing to the raiders; and so, they came with a great force, and fought back the raiders, and descended upon the village, and murdered many, and raped many, and tortured and maimed many more; and burned and cut down and tore out many of the structures of the place; and then they stood, in the midst of this living, breathing, mocking nightmare in the warring cloud seeping from their screaming, bloody mouths, and cried out for the raiders to come, lest they annihilate all living creatures about them.

And so, into the burning huts and corpses, into the smoking corpses and ruins, into it walked one man—one man ready to make atonement for his failures and still save more Innocents; and he did not walk with a trembling gait or a coward's shadow, but with equanimity and bravery perched upon his brawny, bare shoulders; an intrepid man, a fearless man, a man ready and willing to die for a cause greater than himself and known to his heart, for all men such as he must live according to the dictates of their noble conscience that is in all people, but in most retreats and hides in the safe, dark recesses of their mind—or slowly succumbs to a mournless, feeble death.

So, he stood before his hated foe, triumphant yet defeated; glorious, yet surrounded by iniquity; free in mind and spirit, yet captured in body; he stood, physically adorned in a black and gold cloth of his admired animal kings, the panther and the lion, but wearing pride and honor upon his proud, handsome visage.

He was taken down, and tales will tell that it took the entire enemy force to subdue him, and he was tied and bound and shackled, but he did not cry out, not once, as the tales about him would attest; nor did he plea for his life or beg for mercy, but held to his faith of eternal Justice; and let it be known that even though there were many versions of his capture told in many languages and in many contexts, all of them agree that he did shout out, as he was taken out, tied head to foot by thick ropes: "Long live Freedom and Justice for all people!"

Legend has it that he escaped en route to the Gold Coast, recruited more runaway slaves and freed more, and continued his battle with the slavers, even though there was good evidence to suggest that he died defending a female slave who was being beaten while he was in captivity.

Be that as it may, after he was taken away, his village was utterly destroyed, the people murdered or sold into bondage; all but three, an old woman and her adopted daughter and son, all who had been admonished to leave—as had the entire village—by a secret courier only hours before the attack had occurred.

Kahambu, along with Nyokato and Kengo, headed north, journeying for weeks, evading slavers' patrols, and savage men, and wild animals, until they found a place far removed from the slave routes, a place serene and peaceful that rested near a pristine lake, a small village that took them in as their own; and it was here that Nyokato married, and Kengo married, and where Nyokato gave birth to a boy, and named him Mwindo, and as the boy grew up straight and tall and lean and muscular, she told him of his now widely known and revered uncle, and how he had fought the slavers; and in her heart, she wished that he would carry on her brother's work, but in her mother's nurturing bosom, she hoped that he would settle for the life of a farmer.

The boy did become a warrior, and left his village to fight the slavers, and recruited many ex-slaves into his band of brothers, and so the legacy of Mwindo continued, on and on, year after year, generation after generation, always producing a magnificent Mwindo to lead in the eternal struggle against oppression and injustice, and funded by a secret source, a seemingly endless source of cowrie shells that was buried deep in the most secluded and dangerous regions of the jungle.

Retreat

Hell is the servant of Man,
When the morals of Man surrender,
Flesh weds this bride and bridegroom
Where pride and vanity plunder

Yet, where Heroes march, boldly
forces of Good increase, swiftly
bands of Brothers fight, bravely
and hell is the widow of Man, rightly.

The Crusaders and the Red Cross personnel and villagers traveled without molestation from their enemies, as it seemed that their persecutors were simply behaving like an army of ants, whose only concern is to protect the hole and hill, and once the enemy leaves its perimeter, they dismiss him; but lo, this was not to be, for the fiery anthill the Crusaders had disrupted had powerful allies across the border in every direction, like a complex, connected network of ant tunnels, allowing the ants to then relentlessly pursue the invaders.

It was a new territory they had crossed into as they avoided conflict with border guards, but the same arid desert, a country that housed a multidimensional assortment of ethnic groups and their accompanying languages and dialects, customs and practices; now, in the Ennedi region, the Crusaders and their companions encountered nomads who were tending to their herds of cattle, men who lived here during the rainy months and then left during the dry season in search of water for their animals; they were the Gouran people, speaking Dazaga, and some of Moses' men conversed with them, and found that there was a village ahead that had provisions. The herdsmen offered them sweet dates from their whole cloth bags, and water from their guerbas to all who yearned for it—for they had no love for the enemy to their east, either.

This land here, among the rising sandstone peaks, had once been deemed ungovernable, and very few tourists, very few citizens, came here to visit, but the travelers were welcome, and here they dined on millet and fresh dates, and delicious, creamy goat milk, and tender goat meat, and despite their best efforts to recompense their hosts, their efforts were rebuffed, but the Red Cross personnel were able to give medicine to some of the tribespeople, and so the debt was somewhat repaid. The travelers soon departed, among much fanfare from their gracious, kindhearted hosts, and turned north toward the Tibesti Mountains, where sojourners are forewarned to circumvent.

The nomadic—and sometimes seminomadic—Toubou, the Rock People, who also speak Dazaga, dwell in the undulating folds and peaks of the volcanic mountains, tending to livestock, farming, cultivating grain and dates, driving salt caravans, and moving their tents to where they draw water from clear, cool, ebullient springs around them.

The travelers stopped in the midst of flourishing and verdant palm groves, and one of the Red Cross men moved toward the goatskin guerba hanging next to a red-brick well; Moses looked at the desperate man and then spoke, as if he were issuing an opinion on whether to buy a pair of handmade sandals.

"It is a custom here to be entirely unfriendly toward those who steal water from a family well." He saw the man back away in abject fear. "Customs, my friends—remember where you are at all times; never at home, always a guest."

Conall was observing movement near the scalloped hills, as he sat on his horse next to Moses. "Who of the Toubou watches us—the Teda or Daza?"

"Teda—it is their pasture we have violated; it is their boundary we have breached. The Daza are further south."

"So, why haven't they come in force?"

"Clans have notified other clans, and decisions are being made about the invaders."

"Who is their leader?"

"The Teda have a derde, a spiritual head, so it will be a decision…" He stopped talking as a group of men came riding up fast on camels. "And where there are twenty men…"

The Crusaders looked about, and saw that there were Teda men on small hills, emerging from behind large palm trees, now riding from every direction on swiftly moving camels, soon encapsulating them in a tight and well-armed circle.

One of the Teda, unarmed, wearing white cloth pants and shirt, a yellow robe, and a white head turban, dismounted and walked toward the Crusaders; and when he spoke, it was in a series of harsh grunts, wildly gesturing toward the west.

One of Moses' men translated. "He says we have no authority to be here, that we need to leave now."

Tyr and Enkidu came galloping on their horses to Conall, spoke to him in hushed tones, and then Conall turned toward Moses. "We have forces from without, and from within, coming now."

Moses turned back toward the Teda. "Tell him," he began, firmly, "we require passage through the Tibesti, and that we mean no harm, and we will gladly pay for passage." He would not ask for food, as it was a commodity too valuable.

The Teda cleft the air with his hand, and his mouth slammed shut after uttering a one-word, one-syllable shout.

No translation was necessary.

The Crusaders were agitated, and were not ready to walk backward, holding their pride in their sloppy hands, but to fight Innocents gave them further distress.

Conall allowed Moses to fully negotiate, hoping that the common African ancestry of his friend would assuage the wrath of the Teda.

Moses pointed toward the far border of Libya. "We need to go to the great sands, or many of my men will die," he began, and gestured toward the Red Cross personnel and villagers, "and many of these fine missionaries and citizens will die." He waited for the translation, scrutinizing the rugged, deep furrows on the face of the Teda. "We must go now, or many of your people will be hurt by our enemies."

The Teda demanded to know who was chasing them, and after he received the answer, he turned, waved, and shouted to his men around him, then turned back toward the Crusaders, and waved them to advance.

The travelers, surrounded by all sides by Teda, on foot and on camel, followed on a twisting course that drifted behind rising peaks and took them up on a winding path that drifted behind more rising peaks and then up on a rocky trail, until they reached a plateau at the base of an explosion of great boulders that sat at the base of a high mountain, whereupon the Teda slowly pulled back, bowing, as if confident that what was about to transpire did not need their humble presence.

Around them, out of the top huddle of these super rock formations, on top of a monstrously giant boulder on high, there appeared a figure, seemingly too tall to be so far away, and as he approached, effortlessly leaped from rock to rock as if he were more mountain goat than man, as if his legs were mighty coiled springs; and his figure seemed to grow too tall, too big for a man of this region, certainly too big for any man so adroit and agile; and then, there he was on an enormous boulder just before them, and he was clad not in the traditional long, white robe and turban of his culture, but in the garments of those ancient Southern people too far removed from here—black panther skin on massive legs, yellow leopard skin stretched across his rippled midsection, a golden lion's mane across his impossibly large shoulders, his feet adorned in antelope hide— and his face was beaming salutations and pleasure at the sight of his guests.

He opened his long, muscular arms wide, his brilliant smile widening as he did so, and then said, in a sonorous and booming voice, and, to his incredulous audience, in English, "Welcome to the Tibesti, my good friends." And nodding his giant head, with its short, black, woolen hair, said, smiling largely, "I am Mwindo."

Council

When he leaped off the gray stone and onto the black basalt surface below, it seemed as if he were a pastoral part of Nature come to life, so effortlessly did he catapult his behemoth self, so magnificently did he float through the ethereal air, that it seemed as if he controlled gravity itself.

He extended both of his hands, one giant hand each to Moses and Conall. "I have heard of and admired your derring-do," he said, hands on hips now, as he nodded. "It is an honor to have men and women such as you, here in my humble home," and then, as the other Teda appeared from behind other rocks from all around to bring solace to the weary travelers, he performed a most marvelous gesture: he proceeded to shake—with great enthusiasm—the hand of each of the Crusaders; but with some, like Arjuna, he placed his hands in a prayer position and put them against his chest as he bowed, then rose up and said, "Namaste," and then shook his hand; but then Arjuna had brought his hand again to this heart to indicate his genuineness, and Mwindo nodded, in pleasure and admiration, and spoke in awe of the Indian people and their historic struggles; and then Yoshitsune bowed to a forty-five degree angle to him, his arms at his sides, and then strongly shook his hands; and thus, as he shook all the hands of the Crusaders, did Mwindo express his sincere appreciation for the avowed dedication of these men to fight tyranny; and then he, with equal fervor and warmth, shook the hand of each of the Red Cross personnel, expressing his sincere appreciation for their avowed dedication and selfless attitude to attending to the needs of those so unjustly harmed and laid low to injury by war and famine and disease; and then he was especially kind and gentle as he shook the hands of the villagers, and praised their avowed dedication to resist injustice and insist on equal rights and liberty and fairness for all.

Soon, the travelers were sitting and eating and drinking, enjoying the generous hospitality of their gracious hosts.

"We have had many of your refugees," Mwindo said to Moses, "from your civil war."

There was a small circle of men present—Moses, Conall, Rustem, Arjuna, Yoshitsune, Horatius and Abdul—as Mwindo spoke, each man a representative of his particular culture, and yet representative of a man was who was adapting, changing, throwing out and taking in those customs and ideas that had once seemed alien or objectionable, obtuse or incomprehensible.

"We have heard of your services to our people, and we express our deepest gratitude," Moses returned, bowing slightly. "But we do not wish to bring harm to them—we only require safe passage into the great desert."

Mwindo thrust his jutting chin forward and clicked his tongue, a gesture of assent, and then, rubbing his bare chin, he said, "Why the desert, my good friends?"

Conall answered, "Our enemies are on all sides; many countries are hunting us; we had anticipated Nigeria to be a safe haven, but now the desert is our perceived sanctuary."

"And you have people to guide you?"

"Yes," Moses said, "we have Tuareg here, and we will stay with their people."

Mwindo sat in stillness for a long duration, his large frame draped in silence, and then his frowns smoothed, and he nodded his lion-like head. "I will go with you; it is all too important a journey."

The Crusaders present were honored that a freedom fighter of such renown, who had valiantly and incessantly fought any threat to his homeland—all other freedom fighters had heard of Mwindo, he who had been educated by missionaries and had mastered a dozen African languages, and English—would leave his own land and accompany them into the perils of the Sahara, and they could not, must not, would not refuse such a gracious offer; it did not matter which culture the men were from, for each intrinsically understood the glory and honor of doing not only what was right but doing it when it was not required or even expected; and being prepared to risk one's own life was the highest tribute to the soul of a warrior.

The travelers were fed and given drink, and those who needed appropriate clothes, such as Eleanor, were given them; but no rest could they take, for their pursuers were close behind.

Conall and Moses followed Mwindo to a large trunk that was stashed behind enormous green bushes, and watched in anticipation as their host lifted it up and extracted, as his guests had requested, two-way radios.

"I am so very sorry that your radios malfunctioned—but these," he said, and slapped their green metallic base, "will work just fine in the Libyan desert, and better than VHF, which loses power to the hot sands. Of course, you have only to worry about charging them, but that is a matter of course."

It was agreed that the Red Cross personnel and villagers would await the promise of the Red Cross International officials, who had been notified of their people's whereabouts earlier using these radios, and had promised to send two Transall C-160 military transport aircraft.

It is well established in the written annals of war that a righteous army, at once pursued and refusing to yield to its enemy, will not gain a hasty retreat with non-combatants—it is not done, nor, as intimated, spoken of; and so, when the two planes came seeking to evacuate the Innocents, the Crusaders guarded them as they were ushered into the steel belly of the planes and watched with measured relief as the planes took off from the hard soil of the prearranged meeting place in the Chadian region, each man full of pride that their battles had at least come to some good.

The Crusaders and Mwindo, and twelve of his men, turned and headed off toward the north, on foot, for camels could not accompany them on this rugged journey; but then a loud, whooshing sound broke their silent reverie, and all of them looked behind, in concert with apprehension, to the southern sky; it was a warrior sense born from living in the ash and soot and flame of combat, of living in the terrific clamor of battle, and much passionate living in between; of living in a transient peace and breathing in serene life and then receding back into war and listening to the smallest and easiest alteration in sound and image, by seeing the perversion of fighting every day, of its warping of reality and normality; so, by knowing what is and what should be and what must be and what should not be, each man knew that when he heard the eerie chime of the whooshing sound, its song was death, black and charred and burning, destruction come home to boast, and roost, as long as possible.

They saw it, they did, they, these hard men, saw in the far distance the fiery explosion of the first cargo plane, and they knew what, and who, and why, and they knew what would and must come next, despite their most desperate wish: the second plane, after receiving its own ground-to-air missile, exploded into flesh and fuel, bone and metal, fire and sinew, now falling in slow, hypnotic, dreamlike motion, like a blown-to-bits giant bird, fluttering tragically and helplessly in half-circles, rotating about noisily and languidly, belching black and orange smoke as it joined its fallen steel-winged brother on the hard, unforgiving ground.

It was only Eleanor who openly grieved now; yes, Eleanor, who should have been on the rescue plane but had stood in defiance against Conall's hard resistance, and who now hugged him and wept upon his shoulder.

And what was there to do now, but go on; and what was there to say now, but nothing, and what was there to grieve now, but much, yet all of it must wait, for all of them knew what route must be followed; and that words were no good, and weeping would leave only a stained trail of weak resolve; and had not all of them known what their enemies were capable of, did they not know, had not they seen it and read about it and heard about it and battled it, every atrocity and human perversion practiced against Innocents; so, the two downed planes were just more, just now, just beyond them, but to be ignored so they might turn their collective clear heads toward the rocky, volcanic mountains and lose therein their enemies and find safety in that desolate beach of desiccated heat, that slow-moving tide of yellow crystals that buried every living and stone thing in its smirking, arrogant path.

Across the Mountains

There were once seven very active and proud brothers, spouting fire and sulfur and creating a rocky, crinkled surface with squiggly, twisting, rippled lava-scarred roads; a big, black, basalt protrusion boasted its presence alongside smaller, more fragile and calmer ecosystems that quivered and shook each time one of the boys huffed and puffed and blew his magma top; but then one day, it all came to a slow, decisive end, as all material things must, and the boys settled down within themselves to retire and be content in the criss-crossing, zigzagging, canal-ridden, hill-swollen, peak-rising mass of modest peaks and valleys and mostly bare black rock it had mainly wrought in its hot-tempered tantrums; so that now, this region of land spread across one nation and extended its rocky foot into the Libyan desert, and the boys, if they were sentient beings, would have been overjoyed, even active, to know that human beings studied their elegantly engraved, haphazard, spiraling, swirling architecture, with its sharp spires and deep ravines and countless vein-like—like petrified, meaty leaves—tributaries that are oftentimes dry but sometimes wet, and that diverse animals live and play inside their private basalt bellies, and many plants flourish in the black, rich, fertile soil.

It was into this craggy, pockmarked, wild-woven asymmetrical rock puzzle that the Crusaders and Mwindo and his men entered—Mwindo and his men with longbows and arrows and guns, the Crusaders with guns, Moses and his men also with guns and longbows and arrows, and Eleanor, who simply carried a deeply flowing sorrow—marching slowly in the increasingly heavy rains.

Mwindo led the way over the sloping, wrinkled surface of the hills, up and over into the wet riverbeds, leaving easily traceable footprints, and then up and over hills that were thousands of feet high and covered with scrub brush, and into gorges and gullies and onto long stretches of hard basalt skin, and then back down into the riverbeds, and occasionally the travelers were picking sugary dates from the various palm trees that managed to survive and that held water, and acknowledging the wonder of life that will exist in any condition—seeing the scurrying, gray hyrax and brown hare and wild jackal here; and still, the troop moved on in the Tibesti-Jebel Uweinat, drinking water from goatskins or pale leather canteens; and mostly silent was this kind of warrior, for they were dormant now, impotent to fight an army that had, like a gathering storm, grown in power and force as it pursued them; but

Mwindo, at the beginning of the journey, had explained to the Crusaders how it would all come to pass, for, he had stated emphatically, were not these his mountains, and subject to his own dominant will when he desired an honorable action? For, he said, passionately, he had treated these mountains with respect, as a father would any child, even as he had fought armies, both foreign and domestic, on this sacred soil.

So, the stage was set, the players chosen, the outcome known by Mwindo, and there was nothing for the Crusaders to do but wait, which was intolerable, and trust, which seemed impossible, and to look beyond to the sprawling Sahara, which was inconceivable.

It came after driving themselves deeper into the bosom of the Tibesti, having traversed some of the volcanoes, and climbing up and down, and up and down again the striated and harsh slopes; they were walking inside the fissures of the cratered monolith, keeping inside a narrow, sandy riverbed with high rising rock sides that hung over them in puffy rock clusters, when Mwindo eventually halted their progress, for Tyr and Enkidu, and Jon Paul and Abebe, had just come running up with news of the approaching armies, but two of Mwindo's men had come running up from the northern trail, with other, more chilling news.

The Crusader's and Mwindo's men sat down in the cool shade of the vertical ridge overhand, and listened as he spoke in a relaxed, confident tone.

"I believe in destiny, my good friends—coincidence is for the Lost." He shook his giant's head. "No, no," he continued, waving his giant's hand, "you will see that it could have only happened in my world, in my," and he spread his giant arms apart, "backyard, and then you will believe, too, that we have been chosen for a special purpose, as I believe all men are; but as for us, we have been united for a greater purpose, as men ought to be in times of war."

He issued forth instructions, and soon, all were in readiness.

The rumbling sound came to their ears, and then the sound of the converging armies—come from behind, some who had gone ahead and had gone down into the wadi—and they waited, listening to the increasing roar of the coming deliverance; and they heard the cries and taunts of the closing armies, and still they clung to the highest point of the ravine, confidently staring ahead.

Then it came, the shouts of panic and horror of the armies ahead, and quickly these soldiers came barreling down the rocky corridor, running wildly, screaming for their deaf god; but soon, they were swept up into the huge wall of floodwater that scooped them up as easily as a child scoops up pebbles into his eager hands.

It was the rainy season in the desert, and the local people knew of the inherent danger of floods in the wadis.

The Crusaders watched as the soldiers who were coming up from the south, having been alerted by radio from their superiors to the approaching watery terror, turned to flee, but who too were engulfed and swallowed whole, like guppies rushing into the gaping mouth of a blue whale.

The waters soon receded, and before the Crusaders and Mwindo and his men had climbed out of the top and onto the rocky ground, Rustem with his Barrett M82A1, Moses with his SR-25, and Yoshitsune with his Heckler & Koch PSG-1 semiautomatic assault rifle, took out the Mil Mi-24 gunship attack helicopter that had been searching for them; and now, once atop, they quickly, all of the Crusaders, split up now, moved north and south along the waterway, looking for and killing survivors of the seasonal flash flood; soon, it was all over, and the travelers stood on free soil again, and commenced the journey once more to the great barren desert that patiently waited to engulf them in its own dry and dusty seasonal extravagance.

And as they walked, undisturbed, at ease, celebrating victory, Moses turned toward Conall, and said, with great awe, "He even commands the rivers to devour our enemies—he who says that any enemy of ours is his, also."

Conall could see the glimmer of piety in the dark eyes of this hard man.

And so what these men could not yet see was a blessed rare event forming, a polis—a moving, breathing brotherhood here, a blessedly rare event, a teleia philia; a friendship among equals who admire and honor and are loyal to each other, the bonds of its youth having been inextricably fastened this very fine Autumn day.

The Ténéré Desert

The sultry sands of the desert sit, crystalline and cubed,
Swirling puffs of purring wind bring slender wings, unfurled;
Onward tiny amber beads march, slowly and subdued
From Nature's burning crown they come, polished and bejeweled.

It is mostly rock and rubble and seemingly endless plain, although sand is its official representative courier; it covers millions of square miles, and its empire is contained only by ocean and mountains; in Arabic it means Land of Fear, and other names few people dare to mention; many countries have their soil contained within this arid wilderness, and have learned its customs and manners, its moods and passions, its compassion and wrath; and where there is even the slightest amount of vegetation and water, therein will people be found, working and living, adapting and thriving.

It is all so simple in the hot furnace of the African continent, where there is little or no water or rain for years, or the evaporation rate is extremely high, or if the temperature is at one hundred fifty-one degrees Fahrenheit, that life tends to crawl away on its trembling belly in any blurred direction.

But the Crusaders did not seek the sand and hammada most likely traveled, but the yellow grain and rocky plain most least likely traveled, to avoid the expanding tourist roads and sites, and border patrols and police checkpoints, and indigenous clans who traveled on the desert periphery—be they Tuareg, Toubou, Moors, Fula or Nubians—unless they were certain of the outcome, but they sought the extreme edges of desolation, the very flaming heart of the beast, until they were convinced their enemies had capitulated and removed themselves back to the safety and comfort of their own homes.

Who willingly walks into a roaring fire to follow an enemy who flees from thee? Who has more compulsion for such an act of bravado, a bad man or a good one?

Mwindo had sent ahead two of his men, to arrange for camels and special supplies to be waiting for the Crusaders at the base of the sandy plains of the Tibesti, but as the troop neared, no one was waiting for them; no one was in sight; there was nothing to indicate movement in the distance through their military binoculars.

"The Tuareg will be here," Mwindo assured Moses as they filled their canteens at one of the watering holes. "I have dealt with them before. I have read their sacred script, the Tifinagh—I have eaten their millet and sweet dates, and have drunk their tea and goat milk and camel milk; I have jousted with them using sword and spear; I have seen their babies born, and have buried their old ones; they will come, although it is far; they will be here—although the Tuareg Kel Azjar of Ghat are far away, they have caravans."

The three Tuareg brothers, Mahmoud, Ibrahim, and Issouf of the Kel Azjar, came up to Mwindo, and listened to him, and heard some of the men grumbling; Mahmoud, the eldest, spoke in soft tones of the names of the many deserts that spread out before and after: the Tinariwen.

"Tinariwen," he began, and Mwindo, who spoke a dozen languages fluently, translated, "is not a city, where men may rest and grow fat, it is a place where men who grow idle die—no man there is on holiday."

"What does he mean?" Arjuna inquired, clearly perplexed, as evidenced by his deep frown.

Mwindo relayed this question of Mahmoud, who did not hesitate to answer. "If a man is late, he is dead or dying, for he should have radioed in by now."

"Might they be lost—they left two days ago, and maybe they lost their radios?" asked Jon Paul.

After Mahmoud heard the translated words, he smiled, shaking his head. "The Teda—Mwindo knows, as do the Tuareg—use the dunes and sun and stars to find their way. It would be like a bird forgetting where its nest is while out hunting for food."

"I should have arranged to have my own people send our supplies," Mwindo said, grief circling his dark face, and he said it first in Tamahaq, and then in English. "Two of my men—my friends, my brothers—have died because of my carelessness: I, who should have known better; there is no excuse for such failure." His drooping posture seemed as if burdened with an invisible weight.

Conall, who spoke seven languages fluently and understood five more, after listening and learning from the Toubou around him the last few days, and knowing languages close enough to theirs, felt confident enough to speak now. "You could not endanger your own people, Mwindo, you know that—they will be watched. You did what was right," and he put his strong hand upon his brawny shoulder, "you are a leader, and your people follow you without hesitation," and then reminded of his secret—that he had had food and water and ammunition buried at various points in the Sahara before this adventure began.

They never saw the two Toubou men again.

The Crusaders would march on toward the mark, as they could not deny their heritage; they could not think of the worst conditions, for this would lessen their resolve, so they must think of the best of conditions, and act as if what they desired would be provided to them by whomever or whatever they considered their Master—God or Providence; and to one, God was this figure, and to another, that figure; and Providence, this way, and to another, that way, but all of them, despite their human foibles of inner timidity and fear, spoke outwardly of an intersecting path where God and Providence met and judged their hearts and minds, and in so doing sent these warriors the proper word, the right road, the proper silence, the right weapon, at the right time and at the proper place.

So it was that the men sallied forth due northeast, across the bare, gray stone and hard pebbles.

Mwindo bemoaned the gnawing encroachment of civilization on the Sahara.

"Do you know they plan an RV park some ten miles from here?" he said, to Moses. "It is enough that they had roads cutting through us—like a surgeon's knife—so sightseers can travel in their air-conditioned cars." He shook his head, and allowed his next words to catch fire and crash to the sizzling stone beneath his huge, sandaled feet.

"I know what you mean—I have seen tour guides leading car caravans through here, and I have seen motorcycles, too. It is a recreational site now, an oddity, a big tourist attraction—and we are the ignorant locals who makes trinkets for sale and begs for alms."

Mwindo laughed, and slapped the back of Moses.

The Crusaders walked on, some in pairs, others in groups, some alone, but all of them close to each other as they moved away from the stone surface, collecting water from dry riverbeds by digging deep into the moist soil, and then moving on to the ergs, these orange-red seas of sand, where no rational person would venture on foot, though it would provide a temporary solace for the travelers. Now, the characters and structure of the ergs provided the indigenous people with a map—regarding how to determine directions: the dunes usually maintain a southwesterly direction, but might face south if the compass turns to the east; they can be half-moon-shaped: barchan; or long and narrow: seif; and in the wind, they can sing—yes, they can emit a sonorous, booming, resonating drum sound as the tiny, crystalline gypsies march down the sandy slide; and sometimes, when the wind whips itself into a high fever pitch, a melodic, constant, eerie drumming floats in the smoky haze, and the local people whisper that it is the drummer of death, the Spirit of Raul. But it is also here where there might be a few precious blades of sweet grass nestled in the yellow grains, deep inside which water is found.

And it was also here, both in the Erg Ubari—which was farther north from the more southern Erg Murzuq, the two kin having been separated at birth by a dark slice of sandstone—that a project had begun that would seek to top the fossil aquifers that lie deep in its grainy bowels.

When the Crusaders entered the territories of the great wave of swirling sand pyramids, the scouts who were past it and behind it reported no enemy movement; and so, the travelers moved over the sloping, stippled dunes and down them, stepping lightly into the pliant field of braided quartz orphans that was ever shifting, ever filling in, omnipresent and shapeless, indefatigable and undefeatable, indefeasible and undeterred. They were now in the Fezzan region, where the dry air allows one's vision to penetrate further into the landscape of sand and striated, furrowed, pockmarked rock formations that gave them shade.

"Here," Mwindo said, as the Crusaders stood about him, "on this very spot once lived the giraffe, the buffalo, the elephant; near lakes, on grass and plateaus," and he picked up a handful of the yellow flakes of deposited rocks, and then let them slowly fall through his giant hands; and speaking directly to them, "and here, our solitary friend sits, not even asking for forgiveness." He nodded, and bent down, and stuck his hands into the belly of the beast, and then spoke, not to his brethren, but to the brethren of yellow grain below; "you ask for nothing, yet take everything—man, beast and plant; you give back nothing good, and Man insults you—but I, Mwindo," and he pounded his barrel chest, "do not step in front of you or bow before you, but listen to you and make peace with you." He lent his ear to the rippled sand as he laid down his goatskin guerba, and then lay down for nearly a minute, as did Mahmoud and Ibrahim, behind him; and presently, they stood up and announced that water was deep within these deeply orange-hued sands.

"But it is too deep for us to take," Mwindo said, calmly, and then he and the Tuareg brothers led the travelers further east, and then stopped at the base of a rather tall dune, and it was here that they dug, quickly revealing a set of steel pipes sticking out of the sand. "The engineers do not want the local people stealing their water," he said, removing the bronze caps from the hollow pipes, and then dug down a little further to reveal gray, circular handles with spokes, "but this water is everyone's water," and turned the spigot as he hoisted Eleanor's guerba to the mouth of the pipes, now bubbling with clean, cool water, and filled it; and then the others filled their guerbas, and they all drank slowly from the liquid gold of the life-giving spout.

"Man always thinks he can hide Nature from us, or make us pay," Mwindo said, and everyone was listening, even the indigenous desert people, who already knew most of what he spoke, for it was his knowledge of the Ténéré that had ensured their survival. It was here that he also told them how to make the solar still, a method where a hole is dug in the sand, and a cup is placed in the middle and a plastic sheet over the hole with a rock in the middle, which is slanted down, where the moisture that condenses on the inside in a few hours will perhaps render a cup of fresh, clean water, and even more if plants and leaves are placed inside; it was a good supplementary method his listeners would not soon forget, as was his lesson on watching for birds as a sign that water must be near.

The Crusaders moved on past the dark sandstone to the Erg Ubari, with its red-tinged sand, and then, too, Mwindo found more of the buried steel tubes that had been sunk deep into the ancient aquifers, and again, the travelers quenched their thirst and filled their guerbas and jerricans, and so continued on their journey, certain to avoid the routes of tribes and touring tourists, hotels and hostiles, airports, and air patrols by placing beige, camouflage blankets over themselves.

They trekked on due northeast, having gone nearly five hundred miles thus far, having found the jerricans and arms buried by Conall and his men in the desert, toward the Issaouane Erg in Algeria, with their mammoth dunes and small dunes and star dunes, where between them are areas swept free of sand, revealing a pale area of salt and mud, meandering gray streets among the ever-changing orange-soaked dunes; and just as they entered its borders, air patrols, far in the distance, appeared.

"It's not Algerian," Moses said, looking at the two airplanes through his binoculars, and then said, gravely, "it is Kush."

It was one hundred ten degrees Fahrenheit, yet a cold chill sifted through the rigid bodies of this audience; weapons were readied, but the Crusaders knew a good pilot would avoid flying in too close; and this time, there was no place to hide themselves.

But the Tuareg, with ears to the sand, stood up, and were fairly dancing and singing, and shouting praise to Allah and holding the leather, rectangular amulets that hung around their necks to ward off the Jinn.

Mwindo spoke to them, nodded, and said, cautiously, "It is too good to be true, but a storm approaches," and he pointed behind them to the morning sky. Moses looked to Conall, acknowledging now the private weather report he had given him.

Everyone now lay flat on the sand and covered their mouths and silently and anxiously awaited until the sandstorm, this gibleh, which could raise the temperature as much as thirty degrees in a few hours, and which soaked the men with these fine-as-talcum-powder grains, coercing everyone to breathe through the cloth spread across their nose and mouth, and to don goggles for their inflamed eyes, as the Hammer of God, this King of Khyber, which seemingly stretched up to the stars and was as wide as the desert itself, poured over them, drenching them and filling them and caressing them with its gritty, powdery, fine particles, pummeling their tender skin like miniature rocks slamming against them until they ached from head to foot; until, after what seemed like many tortured hours, it abated, and the travelers extracted themselves from their sand-drenched clothes, and beheld the translucent and brilliant clear blue sky, and saw no manmade violation anywhere.

But despite this miracle, the unseen enemy that had begun to hunt the Crusaders while in Kush, began to take form—and its head was doubt; its tail, uncertainty; its legs, desperation; its body, fear: it was the animal of illogic and superstition and ignorance, growling incessant charms into their waning psyches, and its silent refrain beat eagerly in their minds: "It is coming, it must come, you know it must come, the killing, the cleansing, the balancing of luck and happenstance with the cold fusion of reality and historical precedence—for no one does what we have done and lives unscathed or unpunished." But many of them did not believe it, despite the fantastic story of every Crusader living through numerous battles, and escaping through impossible impasses and being rescued by eerie coincidence engineered by Man and by Nature and then just, recently, by both; and although they did not believe that the inevitable deaths of their comrades was imminent, they could not explain this seemingly God-protected, Providence-provided adventure, thus far; so, they extolled God, if they so believed, and extolled Providence, if they chose; but in the end, they reasoned that somehow, no matter who or what had blessed them and placed them within an invincible aura, it all had to be because of what they, an honored few in an apathetic and crowded world, had chosen to give up: an easy and safe and certain, good life, for one that was hard and dangerous and uncertain, all in the name of the flame that stays lit only as long as warriors such as they fight persecution wherever and whenever it breathes and lives and destroys, a golden flame that bursts forth in luminous incandescence whenever a warrior such as these selflessly and bravely meets tyranny in the field of battle, the hallowed, eternal flame of Justice that illumines the sacred writ that sits at the altar of Virtue, and where the constant refrain is, "Force and right are the governors of this world; force till right is ready."

Desert Asylum

It must be remembered that it was the rainy season now, which was a real advantage to the travelers, as the temperature reached a ceiling of no more than one hundred fifteen degrees in the day, and a floor of sixty-five degrees in the night, unlike the hottest seasons, when precious rain would fall and float and flutter, teasing the guileless inhabitants beneath them, these tiny, pearl-shaped drops of water that would begin their beauteous fall, gently falling, so wondrously gliding down, until tragically and shockingly, they would evaporate right before they reached the open mouths and hopeful minds of the poor prisoners who were chained to the oppressive heat and hot sand and tormenting misery.

But this did not mitigate the harsh reality of traveling on foot in a region where hearty camels and plenty of food and drink and cool shade were a necessity for mere survival.

Two of Mwindo's scouts came back from the southwest and reported that a coalition of three African governments—this information had been gained through unfriendly persuasion from enemy agents—had been searching the Tuareg camps all over Algeria and Libya, and the Bororo camps in Niger and Nigeria, and yes, even the Toubou back in the Tibesti. There was a large bounty on the heads of the Crusaders, which increased if they were brought back dead; there were press releases portraying the Crusaders as an arm of the Imperialist American and European powers who were attempting to subvert democratically elected nations on the African continent; there were killings, many killings of Innocents of the Tuareg, the Bororo, and the Toubou; killings back in Kush, killings everywhere and dead bodies left to rot in the boiling sun like slaughtered animals who died at the whim of egregious hunters; and this movable-holocaust of bounty-hunter-mercenaries had hunted most conspicuously in Chad and the Central African Republic, and Niger, and least of all in the barren desert, affirming the idea of this escape as strategically correct.

Once more, this abhorrent and sad news confirmed the routes to be taken and the places and people to be avoided: that they must avoid all people and palpable watering holes and wells, and high structures that might bring shade, unless inside that structure there dwelled a sufficient hiding place.

The Crusaders felt drenched to their very tissue and bone and sinew in this alien, gnawing, intrusive heat, which dug holes into their swelling brains and established a pair of sizzling hooks that fished about for their undying resources of resiliency and then ripped them out and threw the gray blob onto this scalding membrane, this suffocating sepulcher, this drowning-homicidal-terrorist garden of harvest-reaping-agonizing death and wanton destruction.

And what provincial language, what gentle discourse, what elegant dialogue rose up from this fallow blot as these tiny imps of grain playfully hopscotched down the soft slopes and plucked their golden harp and played their eerie music of the dunes?

"You live, you live, you live!
Witness the world, they bow and die;
Witness you, you stand and defy
You deserve, you earned, life, life, life!"

It was time for Conall to speak, for he had begun all of this, and his wounds were nearly healed, as were Rustem's; and when he did speak, all of the Crusaders gathered close to him, as if he were an ordained prophet who had already seen the future and needed only to relate what he had beheld; and Eleanor sat before him, and then did Mwindo and Moses, as did the rest of the warriors, looking up to him with hopeful countenances.

He stood over six feet tall, wearing the flowing robes of distinct earth colors of the desert people, which allowed circulation to flow, and had a physique that looked as if hewn from opposing the most difficult obstacles imaginable and refusing to yield, functional muscles that had earned their mass from heaving and pulling and pushing and throwing against the supposedly immovable forces in the known universe; his blond hair was long and thick and was combed back over onto his muscular back and lay in a cascade of thick strands upon his massive tree-trunk-like shoulders; his handsome face was defiant, his steel-blue eyes burning, and arms and legs were like the thick, solid, hard limbs sprouting from a young, robust oak tree.

And when he spoke, his words were the language of mighty warriors from time immemorial, and its bold pitch and genuine quality drew an emblem of heroism on the spirit of his receptive listeners.

"This war we fight, we fight because we must, we cannot do otherwise; we have a Covenant with the poor, the Innocent, the persecuted of the world, to fight those who oppress them; and fight them, we will; where we are now, we must be, and whether we live or die here, it does not matter, for the world is what it is, and we are Ambassadors of Truth, but the Truth will never die unless those who have it written on their hearts and souls and minds do not heed it; and then it will die, and so too will the world, though it will live, but in truth, it will be dead, a living grave and good for no one who loves Freedom and Justice; so, here we are, prepared to live or die, but ready to fight and struggle against the growing forces of iniquity; we must not consider life or death for ourselves as one better than the other, but as inevitable as this war continues; and so, whether we live or die, it is in this world that others will hear our story and pick up the eternal, flaming sword of Justice, and fight; but the world will not have a hand in our living and dying, but God only; so, therefore, we must give tribute to He who created us and has allowed those who love Freedom to fight those who would take it from the world: it is He who determines our destiny; so, if we live or die, it is the will of God, and how can we oppose the Creator of the universe? All we can do is His will and pray that our path is to life and the fight against those who oppose His will and attempt to graciously accept take the freedoms He gave us from the beginning; thus, by doing his will, pleasing Him, and to know that if we live, we will live boldly and nobly and proudly, for it is His will, and if we are to die, we will die boldly and nobly and proudly, for it is His divine will."

There was much praying and singing after this, each man praying and singing to his own deity, each man confident that indeed his supernatural divinity heard and blessed them.

There were two wars now for the Crusaders: one against the combined governments of the three African nations that relentlessly sought them, and one against this arcane panorama of heat, sand and the increasing bell toll of what seemed their approaching funeral march; so, with every step they took, they were walking away from their pursuers, and into the same past history of besieged travelers who had succumbed to the flaming daggers of this desert biome.

After finding more of the food and water containers that had been strategically buried by Conall and his comrades in spots no human being would have considered feasible to travel to, they reached the Erg Oriental in Algeria in one week's time, enduring more sandstorms, and despite finding a few unattended wells, were still exhausted and depleted of water and food; but they were alone, having outmaneuvered an enemy who were now nowhere to be seen, here, in this island of desolation, where there were linear dunes, built by strong winds, and star dunes, with their outstretched limbs, and the well-maintained, well-scrubbed, gray streets between them; and it was at the base of the dune and edge of the dune street that the Crusaders sat to contemplate their position: they were east of the Ghadames oasis, where the Tuareg dwelled and even had a festival; they were west of the Tademaït Plateau, north of the plains of Oued Amador, near the Tassili N'Ajjer sandstone mountains wherein dwelled the Tuareg, and south of the Ouargla oasis; they were specks inside specks, outside of hills of specks atop dunes of specks, surrounded by mountains of specks, where no one would consider them to be; yet, it was prudent, for if they were this burning speck, this ashen, tattered, wind-tumbled, walking-stumbling speck, the surrounding enemy would expect them to go either left or right or up, or up or down to extricate themselves from their boiling oblivion; the more they beat and confused and perplexed their human enemy, the more they surrendered to their desert enemy, which had eroded them during this epic one-thousand-mile journey, as surely as waves smashing against a cliff snatch infinitesimal grains of rock.

It was a thousand miles across the most inaccessible and impossible landscape, weeks of walking and stumbling, and still retrieving the life-giving, buried food and water containers, and discovering the occasional hidden well, and celebrating every drop of water removed and poured carefully down their parched throats, and there they sat and lay, many wanting life, some wanting to die.

It was sunset now, and the darkening sky glowed a burnished gold, and painted the dunes in a blushing deep hue of orange and scarlet, and dark shadows from the top, sharp crests of the dunes swept down its rippled sides. The air was cool and abrasive, like drinking hot tea spiked with hot spices; this entire land—now draped in a black coat that was studded with a white-hot diamond sky and later blooming with a radiant, sapphire sky glow painted with a burning brush— had the agony and ecstasy of Prometheus, at once alive and chained in misery, and then at once alive and still chained but in physical peace; this dreadful pyre, fueled by the solar, stench-filled breath through a melting furnace: a crown of tarry-black thorns by day, a crown of milky-white stars by night; a bipolar host this, beating its guests one moment and in the next, putting on a soothing balm.

"There is a Garden of Eden near Fezzan; it is called the Sabha Oasis," Olaudah began, as they all lay at the base of a tall dune, listening intently to him as they gazed up at the gorgeous cosmos, his sincere tone filling the air with a naive whimsy; Mwindo and his men listened intently, for they too had been to the Libyan oasis, but now longed to hear it described with such passion that would make it all seem bright and new to them once more. "I was there as a boy, when my father and I left Niger and were looking for work—and we had been traveling for a very long time, and had lost our way. My father," he smiled in sweet remembrance, "would not admit that he was lost—but oh, he was—but I, like an obedient son, said not a word to him, but feigned agreement with whatever he said; well, we were so very lost, and just when we thought we might die of thirst, we came upon—can you believe it," and he slapped his hands together, "this most beautiful, lush palm grove; and in the middle of these gorgeous green trees," and here he closed his dark eyes and placed his folded arms behind his head, as his voice grew whispery and melodic, "was a most sparkling, most beautiful—the most beautiful crystal-blue lake I had ever seen; a miracle of Nature in the midst of certain death." He smiled again. "Or course, my father pretended as if the lake had been his aim all along, and as our camels slowly walked up to it, slowly we led them to the shore, and hobbled them; and then, in perhaps the only time I have seen my father so happy, he ran and leaped into that beautiful lake, and I too followed, where we both felt as if we had just rejoined the land of the living, and we both swam and jumped about just like two silly children who have never before been in such a paradise." He smiled again, paused, and then said, "You know, that was the only time that I felt equal to my father; hmm."

The minds of the men digested this joyous sentimental journey the same way the body digests a ripe, sugary medjool date, very slowly, and with satiation that lingers for a little while, and then disappears and begs the question: what will be next?

Many men followed by telling of their joyous memories, and the other men listened to the storytellers speak, and when necessary, politely waited as the respectful translator translated and the courteous and patient audience listened attentively, and then the patient storyteller would continue: of journeys in caravans where men and their camels travel with goods to barter for salt cakes, the White Gold of the Sahara, or medical plants, which they then transport during weeks and over hundreds of miles to trade at the market in Agadez to Bilma Niger, which is called the Taghlamt route; and the caravans that went from Timbutuku to Aoudenni, called the Azalai route; and there were the Bororo people, when they have their gerewol, where the young men and women court each other in a culture where Beauty—but a certain kind of physical attribute—is highly praised, and for those unfortunate to have been cursed with looks deemed ugly, life can be difficult (but does this not sound like an address of Anywhere, Earth?); of adventurous trips down the Congo and swimming away from aggressive crocodiles and outraged hippopotamuses; of safaris in Kenya and riding wild elephants, and running with the black-striped zebras and long-loping, striding giraffes on the grassy savanna; and living with the Kikuyu people and hearing their story of how long ago, Kikuyu was brought to the peak of Kirinyaga by the great spirit Ngai, and shown a place where he might build a home a near a group of fig trees, and where he might marry Mumbi, and have nine daughters, wherefrom the nine Kikuyu clans originated; there were so many marvelous stories from so many African cultures that it reminded the listeners of simple Beauty in a world that oftentimes seemed unconscionably Ugly.

The foreigners here, although feeling kinship, did not feel the current of invitation floating in the rarefied air, so they obeyed their cautious nature and deferred their time to tell their tales, for now.

There are times for extolling humanity and cherishing the past and celebrating life even during war, but such times are ephemeral and must not last long, lest those pleasant intervals serve to unravel the tight bond of courage won and intrepid actions so carefully crafted during battle; thus, when the stories ended and silence pervaded and the black powdered field of space, where its phosphorescent pebbles reigned above, the subject of possibilities entered into the small forum of candor and brotherhood that forever encircled them.

There is an ancient formula regarding the discussion of a topic of an incendiary nature: there should be first a layer of reassurance and certitude and praise atop it, and an equally positive layer below it, so that any negative layer laid in between this verbal sandwich might not appear so harsh, and that any discordant note uttered too early might break the solid foundation laid therein, or uttered too late, like a sneak attack, and against those too tired for rebuttal, would destroy the harmony and unity of this special brotherhood, and disunity now meant death later, as survival depended on one army acting as one; good leaders understand this, as do good men and women.

But the unannounced, unofficial leaders of this expedition must not speak first; this is paramount if the formula is to hold, for early praise from the originators of any plan always feels false.

"I must say," began Yoshitsune, a man who never backed down from man or beast, friend or foe, "when we came into this open-air penal colony, I cursed the world for creating it; but now that we are here, I know that I am here for a purpose, to test the mettle of men, and we thus far have proven superior, and have defeated our enemies."

No one could disagree, but many could now argue for pursuing other roads back.

"Well, first we have to ask ourselves if we are going to continue," Henry said, stating what he had wanted to say about this frying pan of a terrain he abhorred, and the mission, and this foreign legion his people had joined; but there came a stifling, quashing, devouring silence that lay upon him and suffocated the last of his lingering words, and suddenly he wished he had not spoken and that everyone would forget what he had begun and intended to say; even in the dim glow of the luminous moon, he could tell that the postures of his comrades had grown rigid and their faces tense, and so any doubts he had about broaching the subject now or in the near future died, like a wandering, dehydrated bird on a dry, cracked desert floor, for now.

It was nearly a full minute—it took that long for the silence emitted from the men to scrub clean the pollution of Henry's words, before another Crusader dared speak; and when he did, it was as if the foul soul of Henry's intended heresy had never poisoned the proceedings—behold, the sacrosanct properties of Virtue.

Abdul, careful and succinct in his manner, spoke, in a measured, deliberate, forceful cadence, and tone. "The idea of seeking a wellhead, which we have at great length discussed, must be abandoned, even though its taking would release even our most adamant enemies from finding us." He paused for a nearly imperceptible moment to gather any outspoken, low-flying, disgruntled-projectiles, but found none. "Therefore, we must risk places where we know water resides." He had said it so matter-of-factly that he did not appear weak, and thus obliterated the original plan and opened the door for others to casually work through; yet he himself would not, as he had merely created it with his earnestness, and his lack of guile.

"Dare we trust anyone to our fate?" Arjuna cried, sitting up now, and then listened to the translator. "I respect the Berbers, the Bororo, the Tuareg, here, but there," and he pointed out into the horizon, "can we trust the Berbers, the Bororo, the Tuareg? At home, I trust the Indian whom I know, but the Indian whom I do not know is my enemy," and he looked around with a disdainful scowl to project an air of authority, "and you should do the same, if you plan on living."

Henry desired to speak, but sensed that a hasty return now would remind the others of his recent heresy, and so took a deep breath and muted himself.

"What do we do if we find a well that is tended to; what then?" Jon Paul asked. "Do we ask, and if they refuse, what do we do? Do we take what we need and risk offending them and incurring their wrath?"

"And what if these nomads relate our position to our enemies?" Arjuna interjected. "How do we know the reward is not known to them?"

"Well, we cannot go back into the dunes and survive," Yoshitsune said, firmly. "We have exhausted all of the buried canisters of food and water, and we need an isolated geography of food and water and mountains," he nodded, and grunted, "then, we are home."

Conall and Moses and Mwindo sat, stone silent, scrutinizing the faces of their fellows, listening to every nuanced inflection, and rising and lowered tone, and fast or slow cadence, to decipher bald emotion masked in mere words.

The Tuareg brothers spoke, first Mahmoud, then Ibrahim, and finally, Issouf.

"We cannot steal water from another man's well—it is not done; we would be warred upon by even my own people." So spoke the first one. "You can trust only those whom you know in this land." So spoke the second one, and frowned, and then the last one said, ardently, as only someone could who has lived it, "Water is so precious."

"I believe, too, that we must find wells, and trust the owners to honor our request to not inform our enemies." Albade, the Bororo, echoed the sentiments of his nomadic brethren.

Henry cried out and threw down a handful of sand. "We cannot trust anybody," he began, a bitter wind blowing off his hot head. "That is why we are here in this desert prison; why, the typical African would sell his own mother for a meal, and they do, they're so unbelievable, and so poor it is immoral, so poor and desolate, they cannot be trusted—why, bribery and corruption rules the day here; there is no honor here, not in Mother Africa: it is surely an orphan, here, for her nourishing breast has gone dry long ago; no, I say we kill whoever gets in our way and take whatever we need, for when one lives in a cage with animals, one has no choice but to kill, or be killed."

His speech was akin to people dragging a lake with metal hooks, looking for dead bodies—he pulled up all the submerged and hidden thoughts of his comrades, and in doing so, blocked out others who might have slurred in the same fashion; his was a verbal minefield none dared cross now, lest they chose to be blown up with him; thus, he had single-handedly turned the debate toward the mission.

There were various arguments made for and against pursuing this path or that, trusting one culture or another, seizing wells or seeking permission, seeking asylum in a country, joining the Tuareg, engaging the enemy head on, living with the nomads; and still, Conall and Moses and Mwindo listened to the honest dialogue of their men, and watched how they tossed out ideas and reeled them in, complimented each other on theories, and respected their comrades' divergent thinking; and when the fuel of ideas ran low, and the men grew weary of the discussion, the three leaders stood before them, having not discussed with each other their plans for survival.

"We must first find a well," Moses began.

"And we must do no harm to its owners—it is against our creed," Conall said.

"Tassili N'Ajjer is not too far south of us," Mwindo said. "It is there we will find sanctuary."

The translator translated, and the countenances of the men reflected the tremendous weight of responsibility lifted from them.

"But Tassili N'Ajjer is a national park, a tourist site," Henry whined. It was good and fortunate that it had been he who had complained, for now he had destroyed any decent argument against going there.

The next day, in the cool embrace of morning, under a ruby-blushing, domed-sky cap winking across the awakening land, the Crusaders left for the mountainous terrain of Tassili N'Ajjer.

The Tuaregs

Thus did the Crusaders march southward toward the Tassili N'Ajjer mountains, still carrying their rifles and ammunition, much of it retrieved from the buried treasure vault, and the goatskins and radios, and carrying the charisma of heroism, which states that any soldier engaged in combat—but especially in combat where an enemy exists in overwhelming odds and possesses a preponderance of firepower and resources, and especially an enemy that is not only despised by that soldier, but by the vast portion of the world, civilized and not—must not now, past or future, practice the unflattering art of complaining or begging, nor evince timidity, nor moral turpitude of a chronic nature: lying, cheating, betraying or stealing and the like, for these are traits of a weak character, they who would perish under the increasing weight of obstacles and defeats; on the contrary, he must practice the venerable art of honor, nobility, self-sacrifice, humility, and mercy and the like; however, it must also be said that there are a great deal of soldiers across the vast regions who have decided they have these singular qualities of heroism, but they are oftentimes the ones who are perceived as the merciless, dishonorable empty-boasters, murderous hordes who strip the lands of decency, harmony and tranquility, and replace it with debauchery, slander, corruption, and every kind of filthy-germ breeding vice.

So, then, who is the final arbiter of Truth, here? It is said that a coin flipped into the air for heads or tails, to determine the outcome of a problem, may instead land on its edge and stand upright, but even if it does, eventually it will fall, revealing one winner, and one loser. Man flips the coin, and History judges the outcome; but some say that Man and History are but two sides of the same coin, held by God.

The Crusaders trekked on, this time having to cross a heavily armored beast—precisely, the coarse, golden sands and blistering heat and perfect symmetry of gloom which magnifies desolation that sits atop an omnivorous depression, and sinks fast and deep into the psyche of any traveler who is here too long in residence.

After some twenty miles, the Tuaregs led them to a well that was unoccupied, yet full of precious, clean water, and the Crusaders looked into the soul of the round, tan-colored, cracked, circular hole of rock and imagined paradise; but they had to be more wary than ever, more cognizant of the cultural shifts that occur when war is declared around them and on them; so, they sat, in two concentric circles round the gray stone well, delirious with thirst, weak from hunger, exhausted from marching, and they waited patiently, enshrouded in a sweaty, dirty cocoon the desert had fashioned upon them with every step they took in the soft, dry mush of the burning, yellow skin of the grinning, looming desert.

In a short time, a caravan of Tuareg men came riding upon camels, stopping at a distance to surveil the odd scene, and then when they had produced their firearms, they proceeded to the site.

The Tuareg brothers began to instruct the Crusaders on what was to occur: many of the men approaching were older, as evidenced by their relaxed posture and by their allowing the camel to walk in calm, which was good, as they would be easier to negotiate with, and only a few were younger, as evidenced by their proud, erect posture, and by their keeping the head of the camel held up high and back. As the men approached closer, it was evident, the brothers said, that their saddles were tahiasht, the kind used for everyday business, unless it was the tamzak—that was much more valuable; hence, these were not rich men.

Also, any visitor here must begin the conversation, and in a deferential tone, carefully weaving his way through the strict cultural guidelines that the Tuareg observed.

The Tuareg, some dressed in white, others in black, their faces covered with the tagelmust, came upon the Crusaders and halted, the sheru, their daggers, and taburek, their sticks, at their sides; the camels were restless and uneasy near the watering hole.

The leader of the band spoke in terms harsh and unyielding. "Who are you to come here and invade our property!"

The response from the Crusaders had been agreed upon and prepared long ago; Mahmoud, the eldest Tuareg brother, spoke, in absolute deference as the newcomer.

"As-salamu alaikum; we seek only the use of your well, and we are prepared to recompense for any water we draw."

The twenty Tuareg men were in a semicircle, outside of the other Crusaders, their weapons visible.

"Our water is for our men and our camels, not for tourists," the leader shouted through the white cotton veil covering his mouth.

"In the name of Allah, we seek compassion and mercy, for we have gone many days without food, and now have no water," Mahmoud said, respectfully, his eyes barely making contact with the looming figure before him.

Another Tuareg spoke, and the visible effect of his words upon the face of the leader was astonishing.

"You waited for permission to use the well—why?" he asked, suspiciously.

"It is our mission to harm no Innocent, and drawing water without consent would harm the owner of the well."

The leader of the Tuareg shifted his posture, and then said, his head held high, brow knit, "Who are you people?"

Mahmoud nodded to Conall, who then, without hesitation, stood up, his rifle still strapped behind his back, and said, in Tamahaq, "We are the ones who fight for Justice."

"The Crusaders," the leader returned, astonished.

"It is so," Conall replied, nodding; it was the first time anyone outside of his brethren had so uttered the Crusader name.

The Tuareg leader immediately shouted orders to his men to dismount and attend to the needs of his personal guests. The Crusaders watched in sweet anticipation as the wooden bucket was lowered on the rope to the bottom of the well and then hoisted up, whereupon Eleanor used a wooden ladle to scoop up the cool liquid and bring it to her dried and cracked lips, pour it down her parched throat and into her inflamed stomach, and her comrades lived every beautiful moment of it; her body flushed rejuvenating ecstasy.

Despite the other Crusaders proffering water first to their gracious hosts, they were kindly waved off, and so they too joined Eleanor in partaking of the translucent elixir.

The Tuareg leader ordered some of his men to have his own camels—who, after a prolonged period without water, often as long as fifty days, are able to drink nearly forty gallons of water at once—to another well; he ordered his men to bring taguella, a flatbread composed of millet and doused with sauce, goat's cheese, and figs, and then commanded his men to bring more provisions for the guests.

Mahmoud translated all of this for Conall, Mwindo and Moses, and he then introduced the three leaders. "Wa'alaikum-salaam," the Tuareg said, "I am Balil, of the Kel Ajjer, and I am honored to serve you; come, sit and eat."

"Wa'alaikum-salaam," Ibrahim returned, and then he translated for the other Crusaders, while Mahmoud sat in a small circle with the other four men.

"We have heard of your daring," Balil began, "fighting the three countries that regularly attack our people and take our possessions and kill our camels. Your bravery extends," and he gestured toward the distant, smoky horizon, "far and wide."

It was now time for Mwindo to speak.

"And we are honored by your generosity, Balil," he began, lifting his hands up, "while so many flee in our presence." He let his massive arms fall. "But we do not wish to bring harm to your people—by bringing us provisions, you might bring the eyes of our enemies upon you."

Balil listened patiently to him, nodded, and then said, grimacing, his gleaming black eyes studded with the pain and sorrow of his persecuted land, glowing with pathos, "The Three Nations came to our camps, searching them, killing our people, raping our women, poisoning our precious wells, accusing us of hiding you; they searched all over the mountains and deserts, but could not find you." He smiled and nodded. "No one could find you, for you were swallowed up by the great desert." He adjusted his white cloth tagelmust so that his mouth and nose were exposed. "We Tuaregs will help you find a safe passage; so, where do you go now, and whom will you fight?" He never once imagined that the men in front of him would abandon their epic struggle, for the men before him were like huge, granite columns that hold up the statue that represents Freedom—so noble was their bearing, so adamant were their countenances, so fiery was their robust youth, that he could think of nothing otherwise.

The three leaders had also discussed the possibilities of these men of the desert being involved in deception for the Three Nations, and a decision regarding trusting them would have to be made during a meeting, face to face with the nomads, listening to the inflection and tone and cadence of the speaker, scrutinizing body language, assessing the logistics of the surroundings, the known habits of the hosts, contrasted, and the movement or absence thereof, in the immediate area of other groups—all of these variables had to be internalized and tried and found feasible or unfeasible on the spot; here, then, lies the dividing line between warrior and mere general, leader and follower, counsel-maker and counsel-seeker; it is a genius born in Man, a talent recognized and nourished by innate prudence that is daily sharpened, and philosophical acumen that is daily cogitated upon; a burden embraced and carried to the fullest extent of its powers by a man who fears nothing except not doing what he must: such true leaders rise out of the midst, out of the abounding, indistinguishable masses, not because they desire power, fame and fortune, but because they are lifted up by the oppressed voices of their persecuted brethren, giving them a mission not to fulfill their own selfish wishes but the normal wishes of all men, everywhere, to be Free and Equal, and find the clear, crystalline path to pursue a virtuous life they choose unimpeded by any repressive authority or institution.

An authentic leader of men cannot deny his genetic heritage and unique species any more than an eagle can deny its majestic heritage above other birds in the grand canopy of cumulus clouds and cool wind and cerulean sky.

The three leaders of the Crusaders studied the face of Mahmoud, and understood his heritage here, and watched the face of Balil, and understood his heritage here, and they, as if one, and operating on the same intellectual plane, understood that Balil spoke freely and honestly, full of rage against his persecutors, which could be traced to his childhood, full of joy toward his guests, which could be traced to the customs and norms of his society; Balil had no room for guile, no plan for it, no place to build it and swap it for honesty and integrity.

It was decided, then, that these Tuaregs would help the Crusaders find sanctuary.

That night, after more food and water had come and the Crusaders feasted as they had not done in so very long, and now clothed in the traditional garments of the Tuareg, the two companies, Crusaders and Tuareg, now blended together as one, left for the traditional nomad routes, everyone riding a camel, but everyone saddled with the imminent peril of such a large assemblage of Tuareg—but since the Crusaders would not be divided up, the journey commenced.

The only hope to deflect suspicion from spies, turncoats, or enemies of any color, creed or nation lay in close proximity to their route to the Tassili N'Ajjer, where a large camp of Tuareg had erected tents and attended to their horses and camels, and brought their wives and children, for a festival; thus, it was hoped that any spy, turncoat or enemy would reason their large assemblage was en route to the great and rare celebration; as it was, a Tuareg from the host, two of Mwindo's men, one of Moses' men, and Enkidu and Tyr were dispatched to reconnoiter the area, and this time, the two-way radios, which they had labored to keep on their aching backs for so long, would finally be used.

The Crusaders, their minds sprung from the sand trap of this desert amphitheater, their tongues loosed from the dire grip of fear and suffering, their weary and sore legs and aching and exhausted bodies rested were at ease now; they talked in pairs mostly as they rode, and sometimes in threes, while Conall and Eleanor, in the scented, veiled, pristine room of reunited lovers, communicated through the language of romance; much laughter was heard among the troop, and singing, too, and smiting of thighs, and beating of breasts; yet, let it never be said that they were, despite this overt display of frivolity and mirth, mentally at ease—on the contrary: for every laugh, their sharp eyes drifted east, and for every remembrance of things past, their keen eyes turned west, and for every hard gesture and head rocked backward, their eyes drifted backward toward the south and then again north; so, yes, once a warrior in battle, always a warrior until the battle is won or lost, and if lost, then an idea on how to win; and for many warriors, despite any battle's end, they were forever and always seeking what was lost, or perhaps found.

> Liberty, god child of vigilance, bond slave of charity;
> Liberty, life shortened by injustice and poverty;
> Liberty, spilt blood and wars of honor sustain thee;
> Liberty, thou must live unto eternity

Arjuna, at ease somewhat—though utter ease, for him, seemed contrary to his nature—was talking cruelly of his homeland, tossing verbal hand grenades at its acceptance of ancient practices, customs and belief.

"The caste system has enchained my brethren," he scowled, his dark visage becoming a deeper shade of wrath, but then he snapped his fingers and shouted, "Ha!" and laughed loud and hard. "Why, a most amusing thought has occurred to me, my dearest brothers—and sister: you are my prisoners here, and have no option but to listen to my words." And as there was no denial of his revelation, he proceeded, much pleased with himself. "I begin this lecture with a brief history of proper terms."

"Oh, no, not pedantry," exclaimed Horatius, who rode behind Arjuna; his Italian accent was thick with whimsy; "just skip the boring parts and get to the meat and sauce!"

Arjuna ignored him. "Well, students, first of all, when speaking of religion in my country or India, we have our Muslims; yes, but not too many, and we have—but no!" he cried. "Technically, we do not have Hindus! Are you shocked to learn this remarkable fact, eh? Hindu was a word those unfortunate Persians fostered on us, just like Columbus named the indigenous natives 'Indian'; why, calling someone a Hindu merely meant 'Indians'; so, there you have it: our faith is Sanatana Dharma—not called 'Hinduism'—the eternal religion; but I know I cannot alone change outward perception that all Indians are Hindus who practice Hinduism, our way of life; yes, now, first lesson is over; any questions?"

"Yes," Horatius said, winking at Rustem, who was still unsettled riding his camel, "when are you getting to something we actually care about?"

"Quiet, heckler," Arjuna demanded. "Now, the second lesson commences."

Horatius deigned to moan. "If I have to hear this much longer, I would rather go back to the Oriental Ergs."

"Quiet, you insufferable wretch," Arjuna grumbled. "Have you no capacity for learning?"

"Yes, quite frankly, I do," Horatius replied, amused, "just not history that has been squeezed and dried out and left lifeless, like a dry, worthless orange."

The translators translated, and the men around the two antagonists were smiling.

Arjuna grumbled once more, and decided to ignore Horatius. "And even when I speak of India, what do I mean? There are the Muslims, the Jews, the Jain, the Christians, the Sikhs—we have our eight hundred languages, and one billion people, and a five-thousand-year-old history! I admire our history and yet loathe it, too—ah, but I digress; I need to speak of the Vedas, Karma, and Reincarnation."

And he did, retelling the epic story of how the Aryans traveled from Central Asia to India and gave them the Vedas, holy writ that is a manual for proper living, and the epic story of creation, and the complex life of the gods and goddesses; and how the caste system evolved from the Aryan society, and how reincarnation and karma have kept an iron ball and chain on the Indian people, keeping them subservient and meek within it.

When Arjuna turned to observe his unusually silent audience, he saw them feigning sleep, and heard their rhythmic and mocking snores.

"Outrageous!" he exclaimed. "You have disgraced my heritage!"

Horatius, opening his brown eyes, smiled mischievously. "Hey, I thought you did not have much love for them," he said, amid laughter from the inner circle around him.

Arjuna pounded his barrel chest. "You do not," he shouted, "hear me heaping abuse upon your ancestors!"

"Go right ahead, be my guest," Horatius said, gleefully, gesturing at him; "many of them were perfect scoundrels; in fact, I tend to think all of our ancestors were perfect scoundrels—we just take what little good they did and thank them for passing their seed along, and then we build statues, and write books and make up fairy tales about other rascals—like Aeneas, Romulus and Remus; but in the end, what does it matter, eh? We are still the same culture—you could call us having a long affair with leisure, where the clock slows down, and we enjoy life more than our more stressed cousins in the West." He shook his round head. "Yes, you should visit us, especially in the south—where I will personally give you a guided tour—for we Italians are all about living to the fullest and relaxing and experiencing life to the fullest now, and not worrying so much about a future that it seems we cannot rightly control."

"I admire your culture, but you need to honor your ancestors!"

Horatius waved him away, pursed his thick lips, and said, in earnest, "Let me get this straight about karma: you get what you deserve, and when you do—depending on your caste class—you come back either one up, or one down, or stay the same; is that right, Arjuna, my good friend, and local historian?"

Arjuna, somewhat appeased that Horatius had indeed listened to his story, said, calmer, "Yes, in your uneducated interpretation of a complex societal and philosophical and intellectual issue, you have it—yes."

"Well," Horatius replied, satisfied, "it seems that you admire old India and now desire a new India—no more calcified caste system; a true democracy where people are freer to move in social classes based on self-motivation."

Arjuna, refusing to be impressed and accept that he had been heard, and having nothing more he wished to instruct, begrudgingly grunted an affirmative response.

The translators continued their rapid translation of the dynamic conversation.

"My good man," Horatius continued, "you want the best of both worlds, but I don't think you can pick and choose," and here he slammed his two fisted hands together. "You want the best pieces after two worlds have collided—and I don't see how you possibly can, and survive."

"The caste system is slowly changing, but not fast enough," Arjuna said, feeling at ease now, and wanting to speak openly and engagingly about his homeland.

Horatius pulled alongside Arjuna, thoughtfully, and said, with genuine sincerity, "Tell me, Arjuna," he said, and he turned around and winked at his co-conspirators, "do you, sometimes, I mean," gesturing about, "feel like a caste-off?"

For the sake of his physical well-being, he turned his smiling face from his prey, and then, kicking his camel, sped away, laughing so loud as to alarm his immediate neighbors to the south; and as soon as the translators completed the last transmission of that wit, Horatius using hard gestures to evince a breaking away of something, they burst into laughter, as did the listening audience, joining those who had heard it straight from beginning to end.

"What! What!" Arjuna exclaimed. "I don't understand! What! What is so hilarious! Well, will someone who is not hysterical please tell me, you blithering idiots!" Rustem, with proper etiquette and decorum, leaned over and whispered an explanation to the aggrieved party, which was sufficient to burnish his dark visage crimson red. "That scoundrel," he cried; "he will come back as a camel and I will wed him to a donkey!"

But into this ring of joviality came the scouts from all corners of the compass, all of them bearing bad news, and done so in person, fearful of transmitting information—even in code—on the two-way radios.

Troops of the Enemy Three Countries had been dispersed into the area to look for the Crusaders, and had converged on the large tent gathering of the Tuareg.

A soldier paid to fight might have fled back to the hot embrace of the Great Ergs, or moved on to the mountains, but any soldier desirous of fighting would not flinch.

The Crusaders dismounted from their dromedaries, hobbled them as the Tuareg had shown them, and formed concentric circles, with the three natural leaders in the middle, and the Tuareg nomads, still upon their camels, scanning the horizon with the detached scopes from their rifles.

"From the description Balil has supplied us," Conall began, drawing a rough sketch of the Tuareg camp in the sand, "the tents are spread over an area four hundred meters long, and about two hundred meters wide, with about three hundred tents and a thousand people."

"The Enemy Three will kill them all as a warning," Mwindo said, full of wrath, "no matter what they find—they will with impunity, so this is why they simply kill to kill, to be more feared."

"Balil also said," Moses added, pointing to several points of the perimeter, "that guards will posted to prevent people from leaving."

The translators spoke on, the passion in their blood spilling like a knife wound in their hearts, and into their somber words.

"The camp is a one-hour ride from here," Conall said, checking his military watch, and casting his gaze over the dimming sky, looked down and proceeded to draw three separate lines approaching three separate directions into the camp. "Moses and his men are here," he pointed, to the northern route, "and Mwindo and his men are here," he pointed to the southern route, "and me and my men, here," and he pointed to the eastern route, "with the Tuareg divided up among us to lend authenticity to each caravan."

Finn said, with a wry grin, while crouching in the first inner circle, "You have provoked a memory of the old American West, Conall—soldiers and Indian wars: Benteen, Reno, and that self-absorbed braggart, Custer."

Conall put forth a half-smile. "An historian," he returned, looking at his fellow Irishman with admiration, and then looked back to the sand blueprint of the attack. "But this time, we fight the invaders and protect the indigenous people."

All of the men arose, thus reinforced and reanimated to the fight; and with some difficulty, many of the men, despite constant education from the Tuareg on proper camel etiquette, could not readily mount the temperamental beast: large spit and snapping teeth aimed their way, and absolute obstinacy to stand and deliver, much to the amusement of the Tuareg.

Moses looked to where the camp lay, and said, with exceeding certitude. "We should be there in time for the festival."

Engagement

The troops of the Enemy Three had adopted an attitude toward non-combatants that can be traced back to the first time a human being gazed upon a member of its own race in a manner that reduced the status of that human being to less than human, more on the value level of animals and insects; this imperious attitude, then, neither old or new, not apt to inhabit only one place or depart soon, is merely a reflex of the person during the commission of war and crime and related atrocities when the natural fetters of power are unleashed by unnatural means; practiced in large scope, and the world condemns the aggressor as great butchers and malevolent spirits, but practiced in small offerings, and the world condemns it but still alludes to the former caretaker of profound slaughterer as the ultimate model of gross iniquity; yet, one death so delivered by a soulless murderer on a battlefield or in a town represents the worst of mankind, and should be so condemned equally alongside other larger-scale murders—it is, then, not the quantity but the quality of the action, for a million smaller actions still pile up their victims alongside the biggest and boldest of the human butchers, both kindred brothers in kind, both equally guilty before the high court of Eternal Justice.

So it was that the Enemy Three troops had descended upon the gathering of tents not like locusts, for even locusts gain at least something—nourishment for themselves as they annihilate the land—but, like madmen, for these troops gained a kind of mental narcotic of nourishment from treating combatants and non-combatants as if they were rabid dogs that needed killing; yet, here they were, and invoking fear and anger in the hearts and minds of these nomadic people they considered not only vermin but that needed to be obliterated as a filthy race.

The Tuareg people could not divulge information they did not know, but this would never preclude these unyielding troops from raining mayhem upon the timid nomads, for it was a special kind of maddened and unrestrained mayhem they continuously sought to hoist upon everyone who seemed their enemy; here, they imagined that the Tuareg were concealing the whereabouts of the Crusaders, and so, the troops began to punish them, as if to assure the old proverb that "any excuse will serve a tyrant."

Free murder—that is, murder executed with no impunity—is like a drug to the mind and body, and like a drug, it must be done, and done often, or the mind and body has withdrawals and fits, and demands another gorging, a quick fix, to maintain its artificial high; thus, the troops, already fresh from yesterday's murders—and for them, there were always "yesterday's murders" following them around like a bloody cloud—began anew.

The commander of the troops—a soldier promoted to general by his superiors due to his ruthless dispatching of anyone perceived as the enemy; a man after their own heart—stood before the assembled Tuareg population, looking upon them as a man who has just discovered rats in his grain storage; he, this general, perceived the prisoners before him as simply tools to further his quest for the Crusaders, and he perceived, through the green and brown camouflage uniform and smart green and brown spotted beret he wore atop his round head, that anyone before him who did not cooperate fully during his interrogation sessions deserved, and would, die, horribly, perhaps swiftly, perhaps slowly, perhaps here, perhaps elsewhere, but die they would, as would their relatives and friends and animals, and destroyed would their homes be, and their wealth confiscated, their women humiliated, their children killed or sold into slavery; yea, every possession and every memory of those he perceived as denying his absolute authority to carry out his explicit mission would be evanescent, and carried off by the hot winds, leaving no trace of their existence, home or race to the forgotten graveyards of history, as admonition to any he considered a rebel.

This general was not unlike leaders of other marauding bands of human gargoyles that trample the rights and lives of Innocents, in that he needed to use creativity in the execution of what he considered desert excrement that needed to be plowed right back into the yellow sand and their flesh picked clean by the lean vultures and their bones bleached white by the boiling sun; yes, today he would kill swiftly, because it aroused his passion, and efficiently, because it was cost effective and economical, and at random, because it brought him ecstasy and, above all of it, notoriety, which further inflated his ego.

"You, there," he grunted, flicking his gloved hand toward one of the Tuareg men, "take these numbers and distribute them to your fellow curs." He listened with mock indifference as his translator imparted the information to the man. "What a race, the men wear the veil, these blue men of the desert, living like an animal—yes, an animal ruling an animal, they are; you," he snapped his bony fingers and summoned one of the Tuaregs, "lower your veil, you stinking, filthy peasant, so I can see if you are a man, or beast with a long snout—a camel, a hideous beast, that—pretending to be a man—and bow before me, you swine." He looked at the man's feet. "Hooves in there, you dirty beast?" He listened with delight as the translator issued the order to the Tuareg, who, in the tradition of free-standing people everywhere, responded in the negative—a course the General had anticipated, having already taken the sword of one of the nomads, and readied it in his hand, and then, without fanfare, swiftly brought it up and over and across the helpless man's neck, thus separating the head from the shoulders, which produced copious amounts of thick, red blood to pour out; but this did not deter him from bending over and shouting at the corpse that wiggled on the ground. "I give orders once—once—once, you miserable wretch!" And he signaled for his adjutant to lift up the still-bloody head and attend a casual walk with him alongside the ranks of the standing, trembling Tuareg. "When I tell you to remove your girlish veil, you dogs, I mean for you to do so, and now!" he cried, exasperated the more he thought of the audacity of someone defying his royal will be done; thus were the Tuareg induced to remove their alasho, the blue-indigo veil that went over the head and under the neck, as well as their tagelmust, and reveal their Berber race. "Good, good," the General said, as he walked up and down the long line, inspecting his prisoners, "no one of European descent here—so, first chore done." He considered himself a visionary, an artist of great intellect, who devised imaginative ways to capture, question, torture, degrade, rape and then kill his quarry, and every mission had to be quantitatively as well as qualitatively, different from the previous one, or he found that he soon tired of the job, the thrill of the chase, anticlimactic outcomes dulling his senses; he was rapturous at the idea of the assigned numbers and their psychological effect it would have on the nomads; it should also be stated that he had studied psychology in foreign universities, and had always been fascinated by the effect that psychological experiments had on lab animals; and so, he was conducting experiments in what he considered the biggest laboratory available to him, and with an endless supply of test subjects.

"General," one of his men cried out, running up to him, and handed him a two-way radio; a few minutes later, he was leaving the camp on his way to a rendezvous with his co-conspirators, leaving, in his opinion, his plundering operation to much less imaginative, much less skilled and undisciplined underlings. Alas, he was not heard from again, this was, after all, a region where the enemy was constantly changing sides, where the fortunes of soldiers shifted like the sloping desert sands.

The immense responsibility of life and death fell to the least acceptable plebeians in the troop, a small cadre of human vipers and carnivores who practiced bad deeds with the same zeal with which missionaries practiced good deeds, to wit: their zone of inhumanity widened and sharpened as soon as the General exited; immediately, they began on the women, taking them to the desert floor to have their way with them, and beating, raping, stabbing, shooting, maiming, and then taunting the Tuareg men, and butchering the children, the camels, and other animals.

It was then that caravans appeared from three directions, and the sentries alerted the plebian commanders, who halted the horrors, and waited in glee for new blood to spill and fresh meat to butcher from their fearful prey.

The three caravans were escorted in by the troops and brought forth to the plebian commander.

"You see what you have walked into, you Tuareg dog," one of the plebian commanders said, sneering at the long row of still-veiled men before him. "Now, tell us, have you seen these foreign Crusaders anywhere—and take down that veil, you filthy camel herder!"

As the translators began, one of the veiled men raised up his hand to halt the translator, and then spoke, in good, plain, although heavily accented English.

"I understand you—and yes, I have seen them."

"Where?" the plebian commander yelled, approaching the man. "And take down that veil, yellow dog!"

The man slowly lifted up his arms. "Why," he began, casually, and then, taking the white cloth across his face, "here," and let it down.

It was Conall.

The enemy troops were dead in the next instant; no one, not the pack of ravenous wolves who surround a flock of lambs, not a swarm of ants on a furry caterpillar, not a gang of criminals enclosing a group of innocent victims, think they can be defeated, so they consider conquest, not defeat, the foul deed done; and so it was here, as the Crusaders had pulled out their concealed rifles—weapons the Tuareg had ceased to carry years ago—so the element of surprise was with them.

The previous scene, viewed from afar, seen from on high, drawn by the minds of the people therein, evinced first, bloody mayhem, second, bloody mayhem, and third, bloody mayhem; yet, it was bloody mayhem that now had been violently stripped of its momentum and laid to rest.

The Crusaders had killed every Enemy Three Trooper while wounding only a few Tuareg, who were attended to by Arjuna and Finn and Julius, as it was a masterful, carefully planned and precise carving-away of disease that was threatening the healthy body; but, alas, Abdul had been killed.

A stray bullet, fired by the enemy and never intended in direction except up, had somehow been deflected from its true target and into the heart of Abdul. The Crusaders greatly mourned his loss, but even as they did so, they were accosted.

"Why have you brought this curse upon us?" cried out one of the Tuareg elders, who recognized the Crusaders, clutching his head and viewing the carnage around him. "We are a peace-loving people who lived a quiet life before you madmen came here!"

Many of the Tuareg were tending to their wounded, their dead, their scattered possessions, muttering to themselves, praying to their god, comforting one another, and unable to engage in a dialogue about heroes and villains.

Two more Tuareg men, lamenting the deaths of members of their family, joined in the verbal attack upon their too-late rescuers, and slowly, their emotional whirlwind began to gather in more men, and women, to vehemently protest the presence of this foreign brigade: by chanting, and cursing them, shaking their fists at them, spitting at them, some of them even promising to inform on their whereabouts if the Enemy Three troops came back, if it curried favor with them.

The Crusaders, mounting their horses, Moses leading Abdul's horse with its master's body draped across it, said nothing, and with their Tuareg guide, Balil, and all of his loyal men at his side, departed toward the east, retrieving the other Crusaders who had stayed on the periphery, and moved on until they reasoned they were out of eyesight of the tent dwellers; and after burying Abdul, turned toward the Tassili N'Ajjer mountains, which were in Algeria and above Niger, a safe haven, and above Niger, which was a roiling mix of rebels, good and bad, and governments, come and gone and come again, and mostly bad.

No one spoke of the battle at the Tuareg tents: there was nothing to say, as words, this time, were not capable of fully and honestly expressing how they felt, for they themselves were not certain; and every good soldier knew that dwelling on a battle where they had fought honorably and bravely, and yet the outcome was not appreciated by the citizenry, is folly, and must be abandoned, buried in the deepest memories, and utterly forgotten.

And even though Abdul was buried as a brother of a family of brothers, as one who would be truly missed, his memory would not be.

Tassili N'Ajjer

The lacerating effect of a sandscape burrowing into the conscious mind of the Crusaders—save those who already lived in this arid zone—was measured on the sensations they experienced as they trekked toward the mountainous horizon: they felt as if the yellow kernels of shorn rock filled their shoes, their clothes, their pockets; as if these miniature sentries of fallen grain lay like a second scratchy skin upon their own hair, in their eyes, nose, ears and mouth; as if these gangs of scars dripped from the hard faces of ancient rock were heaped up like a dam in their blood, their bones, their membranes; but as they gained ground toward their objective, and the infernal monotony of the sandy garment the desert wore sprang green leaks—small plants and shrubs—and bore more animals—the desert monitor, the fennec, the desert fox, and the sandy cat—they felt the heart of the desert that beat inside them shrivel, and felt the scabrous scales over their eyes fall like splintered glass to the hard soil below; and when they beheld the black hills before them and the green trees therein and the refreshing streams, a final tribute to the long journey in their minds opened up and their tongues moistened and their hearts leaped for joy; and when they were inside the Tassili N'Ajjer, each Crusader silently and fondly bid a melancholy farewell to their tormentor and protector, mistress and villainess, that remote planet revolving around an alien sun: the Great Sahara.

Out they stepped from a cataclysmic hemisphere of desolation and heat oppression and into a world of buoyant life and pleasing coolness; and when the travelers had penetrated past the tall cone-shaped mountainous monuments, and outlining rubble, and into the cradle of this hidden paradise, they simply sat and stared at the spectacular success of Creation in its efficiency to create a mosaic of diverse beauty in every corner of the world, each pastoral idyll of Nature in perfect symmetry with the tune and melodies of its environment, and then humbly receding into the next wellspring of lyrical theater, each chord replete with its own orchestra, its own drama—some tragic and other comedic, and still others epic and adventurous—proffering nothing and yet everything, like a magnanimous, teasing young lover, to her human paramours.

They were now in the cradle of this sanctuary, and although it did not have the great breadth of pristine and glassy lakes the Crusaders had dreamed of, and into which they would joyously have flung their roasted bodies, it did have small, crystal-clear, bubbling streams flowing in narrow riverbeds, and this, to them, was luxury itself.

It was a time to disrobe old memories of battles lost, and put on new ones for future battles won, not merely a rudimentary sustenance to their sagging spirits, not merely hiding and retreating for survival; it was a time of blood and guts, body and soul regeneration, and with every passing tranquil moment in this private, aromatic garden, they were piecing themselves together one bold, precise, intelligent thought at a time.

In this ancient cathedral towered the immovable guardians on either side of a sandy riverbed, mountains of rock, cleft and chiseled, hammered and rubbed, by the ancient river that slowly and meticulously sculpted and designed this mighty fortress into its own image—of deep furrows and frowns, and deep etchings full of squiggles and ripples, and tiny little overhangs; and big, jutting chins, vertical ascending spires, and vertical descending pyres; of cracks longwise and splits otherwise, and clusters of piled and squished stone rings, all crafted, all, all sliced and cut and pulled apart—all, every rock figure, nook and cranny, every rock statue, shelf and nest—by friends, water, wind and time.

And in this precious gem-hotel stood the verdant Cypress tree of Tamrit, thousands of years old, and as hearty and invincible as its stone brothers and liquid sisters.

Balil and his men, in a fond farewell, left the Crusaders, who watched, in awe and admiration, as they willingly rode their camels back into the open-air furnace, fully aware of the hostile world around them and its sweet beckoning to come hither, but the Tuareg were not unlike any other person born in one specific geographical location, and once adapted to it, were less likely to move away than the giant Cypress trees.

The Crusaders had provisions to last a week, but little ammunition, yet they were content; they set up camp and slept soundly that starry night, wrapped in a honey-scented cocoon of serenity and security, except the four scouts, who were sent to reconnoiter the place, but gained their rest when they came back, after others had taken their place.

In the morning, the Crusaders held a meeting, where guidelines were laid out and agreed upon as to where they might go and what they might do and how often they might check in, and who would have guard duty and when, and who would look after the camels, and when; the rules were rigid yet fair, and conceived in an atmosphere of rest and relaxation and recuperation that was much deserved, but also in light of the Enemy Three still hunting them; when the meeting was disbanded, most of the Crusaders, save Conall and Eleanor, who knew exactly where they were going and what they were going to do, simply mulled about, seemingly lost, as if they were not prepared to simply rest and relax.

"I feel like I'm in camp," Finn said, half-smiling, "left alone for the first time in a strange place."

"Camp—what is that?" Jon Paul asked, in earnest.

Finn smiled fully now, and placed his arm around the lad. "It is where young boys and girls go to play wilderness—I guess for you, it would be like a week in a metropolitan city."

The men eventually drifted away, some in pairs, some alone, some in groups, sometimes according to tribe, but not always, for deep ties had formed the last month; and there was much to explore, and the time here was indefinite.

Radio contact, even in the sophisticated code the Crusaders had adopted, which could be monitored by the enemy, was not allowed unless a life was in peril, and even then, was discouraged.

"Tyr and I saw these wonderful caves," Enkidu said, "about a mile west down the riverbed—that way."

"Drawings," Tyr said.

"Ancient drawings?" Abebe asked, excited.

"If only I had brought a can of spray paint," Olaudah shouted, "I would make my mark on those walls," and he beat his chest, mocking graffiti artists the world over.

A large contingency moved east.

"And ruin priceless artwork with mindless graffiti?" Abebe exclaimed, appalled.

"Artwork," Olaudah laughed, "it's just old graffiti—and have you seen cave drawings before? It looks like a ten-year-old with crayons who ran wild! And besides, my graffiti is tomorrow's 'ancient artwork.'"

"Well, I'll get there first, anyway," Abebe said, laughing, and proceeded to take off at a fast pace down the narrow rock corridor.

"Look at the crazy Kenyan run," Olaudah said, smiling. "A month in the desert and he still has the energy to run like a young and healthy gazelle."

"Did you know his brother was a world-class miler?" Jon Paul began. "And Abebe has more talent than even he." Everyone in the group grew silent, for it was the origins of each Crusader that each man had always yearned to know.

This, then, is Abebe's story, as narrated by Jon Paul, but it is also the world's story, as narrated by geography, circumstance, and genetics, and so, there is a dual narrative for balance and curiosity, and, perhaps, introspection.

There is a woman, tall and lean—but she is too lean, like a withering cornstalk—who is emerging from a small thatched hut; she is covered in the traditional dress of her country—the cloak of dire poverty—and in this case, a black-and-red-checkered, long cloth robe that she has modestly wound around her bony shoulders, and has allowed to hang to her bony ankles; the colorful dress is clean—the best clean she can achieve without adequate water—and has some holes, the best she can patch without proper needle and thread; she has her black hair in long, thin braids falling about her round black head, and around her skinny neck sit many wonderful necklaces: some are black beaded, some are red, or green, or yellow, but it is her finest jewelry, these penny shell necklaces, and it imparts to her a sense of femininity and luxuriant wealth; she wears copper earrings, and very old, very dried brown leather sandals; she wears no makeup—it is unknown here, and would be an anomaly, too, as it would only divert funds away from other things, as would perfume; in her lithe hands, she carries a small, chestnut-colored wooden bowl, into which she will put tiny treasures for her children.

Now, turn the spherical globe clockwise about a one-third revolution and then glide up to the northern hemisphere and settle in any state in the Union, in any middle-class region in America, and then glide down to the opening bell tolled at the beginning day of a typical family, and this is what you might find: there will be a woman, and tall and plump—but she is too plump, like an overstuffed pie that bulges out at the sides and falls over the crispy crust—who is emerging from a huge, stucco-covered, wood and cement two-story house; she is covered in the traditional dress of her country—the cloak of excess capital—and in this case, a sprawling one-piece pomegranate-purple-red sheath dress, which conveniently smooths out her burgeoning frame, from bulging shoulders above to fat ankles below; her thousand-times bleached and dyed blond hair, its brown roots showing, is properly cut short, and around her white, sagging-in-folds neck lie imitation white pearls—not her finest jewelry, yet it still signals her unique sense of style to herself, and others; she wears diamond earrings, a small gift from her husband, and very new, very smart and expensive black leather ankle boots; she wears a multitudinous deep, penetrating, multihued array of makeup that paints a virtual face—like a 3-D image—upon her actual flesh face; and she has bathed herself in so much perfume that it actually emanates from her like electromagnetic waves from an electrified magnet and copper coil. In her chubby hands, she carries a large black leather purse that contains the instruments by which she will purchase tasty treasures for her children.

We turn our eyes to Kenya once more, in a region far away from the biggest cities—north, south, east or west, it does not matter which direction, for in every direction that humans are capable of comprehending, that is far enough from urban wealth, there is the worst of living conditions; now the tall, lean woman begins her daily ritual of walking out toward the sterile desert—sterile as an operating room, where everything that might live other than the human attendants is purposely expunged—in hopes of finding today's treasure. She keeps her tired but keen, beryl-green eyes aimed at the ground as she walks, occasionally using a long stick she has recently procured to poke under rocks and piles of dirt; she walks for nearly three hours in the blast furnace of the rising, raging, red sun until she lets out a small exclamation of triumph; she throws her arms up in the air, and then brings them down and to the tiny grain of dried seed corn, and using the index finger and thumb of her left hand, slowly and solicitously picks it up and relays it to the small wooden bowl.

"One," she announces, in a timid, tender voice, for she is especially joyous that she will not now return to her home empty-handed, and full of shame, and failure.

Sometimes she stoops while walking, and sometimes she crawls, but mainly she just walks inside the womb of this startling cauldron of unrelenting, seemingly increasing, heat, as she hunts for precious drops of food; once, she sees a tiny black ant walking lazily atop the burnt soil, and she grows excited as she comes upon it and falls to her haunches and then reaches out her hand to pluck the precious kernel of corn from the now-confounded creature. "It is you or my children, little sir, and I choose them," she whispers, and she pauses as she watches the tiny worker swing about in panic, and she feels sorrow. "Forgive me, I did not want to, I know you have babies to feed, too." She shrugged her thin, bony shoulders. "Oh, would you also please show me your fine home—I would so like to see it." She smiles when the scurrying insect seems to have heard her and begins once more to move quickly in the same direction; in a half-hour, the woman has found the mother lode of corn grains, for the built-up, circular ant hill of the unsuspecting betrayer has led her to is fairly bursting with them inside; and soon, the proud woman is walking, and singing, carrying a bowl full of dusty, dirty kernels, toward home.

Turn round now and dive back to our woman of the Americas as she drives in her new family van toward the local come-and-get-all-you-want-but-don't-really-need—because after all, it's mostly not real food, but chemical fancies meant to decorate a plate—supermarket, the end of the road for the greatest planting of crops and feeding of animals in human history; it is not merely a shopping excursion, but a social excursion as well, for this modern woman of the modern world never allows a restive and thus potentially reflective moment to fertilize her brain and allow the static shape and paradigm of her inner psyche to germinate and allow ideas to sprout—no, she must, and will, never be alone with herself and do nothing but think: it is forbidden fruit; so, she must talk while driving (or is it driving while talking), and talk during eating and talk during work and talk during walking, and talk when the television is on, and talk when the children and the husband come home, and so then they too talk—talk, talk, they must, talk, talk, about this, about that, about nothing, and mainly, that—mostly fluff and nondescript hyperbole and trivial waste products of what once was considered important, and engage in frivolous activities that achieve nothing permanent or beneficial to their intellect or bodies.

She parks the silver surfer of the road and turns off the air-conditioning and turns off the newly acquired and curious-looking gadget, not quite a CB, closer to a walkie-talkie; plops her massive hulk onto the black pavement, complains of the eighty-degree heat, and begins to shuffle her weighty self toward the looming food distribution center, and once inside, procures a rolling, metallic basket with which to hold the day's massive catch.

The food that goes therein is bought based on price and color: what pleases the sense of smell and taste, and appearance; so in goes a pile of fluffy white bread and crumbly delicious dark chocolate bars and a mass of six-packs of sugary-saturated soda and a bunch of six-packs of alcohol—light beer, this time, and cold cuts and ice cream and frozen pizza and a gigantic bag of chocolate cookies and jars of marmalade jam and a bucket of candy bars and a number of pounds of full-fat hamburger and a dozen eggs and a gallon of whole milk and a couple squares of yellow cheese; and in addition to these staple items, she drops in five fresh corn husks, and a bag of apples that shines brighter than the tiled floor she waddles upon.

The checker checks in the food and the woman uses a credit card, and the transaction is now completed; she rushes home—all the while conversing on the clumsy walkie-talkie—in hopes of earning a front row seat in front of her morning talk shows that has her philosophers, her sages, her gurus that will guide her through her O-so-difficult modern life.

Close your eyes now and turn around a bit and look down and you will see our African heroine just stepping into the dome hut with her bountiful prize; her three children thrill to the find of the handsome corn kernels, and help her by grinding with small rocks this miraculous find into a fine, powdery mulch. Now, go fetch some water, Abebe, she says, hugging her little sir, and he smiles as he runs happily to the pathetic hole in the ground that is a kind of chunky, fetid, rainbow-colored soup that has imagined itself a source of drinking water and not a virulent, bubbling swamp creature rising its malignant head the Third World over to kill millions of children in the next year; still, Abebe scoops up a portion of the thick gunk into a broken, rusty tin can, and runs back to his beloved home, and once there, mother allows him—because, she says, he is such a very big boy now, despite his smaller-than-average-frame for a six-year-old—to pour the nasty liquid, which she tries to filter through an old mesh fish net that had been given to her by a charity group to shield her family from mosquitoes, into the bowl, and then Abebe, with big, round, brown eyes of wonder, eagerly watches as mother mixes the pale, yellow flour and water until it is a thick, gooey paste.

Lunch, mother says, and then observes, with sad eyes, as her three children hold out their tiny hands, into which she scoops out equal portions of the one-course meal; mother's meal, they see, will be the paste still clinging onto her too-slender fingers.

The children eat slowly as they attempt to make each fragment of the odorless, tasteless dabble of grain last for such a very long time; then the family sits in the cool shade of their home, with daughter on mama's comforting lap, as the two boys play with rocks and twigs in the soft dirt.

Later that night, father comes home—father, who really did look for a job in the nearest shanty town for two days, but, weak-willed father that he is, allowed his dwindling flesh to fall for the lust of female comfort, and he now carries an unwelcome visitor into his bloodstream, which will soon be passed along to his unsuspecting wife—an epidemic he is at the forefront of, ahead of the curve on for once in his life, but for all the wrong reasons.

And now, we quickly go back to the track homes in the States, and we find big Mama pulling into the driveway and then into the garage and then walking into the twenty-four-hours-a-day-air-conditioned, or heated, house, with a bag of groceries and asking her big boys for help, who decline as they seize hold of the blue box of cookies and plop down in front of the television and experience true nirvana on earth as they swallow—gorge, actually—on the creamy, buttery, crunchy, fatty, sugary concoction as they play ultraviolent violent video games on the twenty-seven-inch color picture screen.

Mother sighs, and sets about putting away the morning haul, forgetting momentarily about her modern-day Socrates of the television waves; but when she remembers, the phone rings and she answers it, and then, well, it is all over for an hour, for the caller is her sister.

Big father comes home, his Santa Claus gut leading through the doorway, his breath perfumed with rank molecules, his lips decorated with fragments of lipstick from the local, or, in this case, common loose woman—or, in this case, not so uncommon—of ill repute, not a prostitute but a woman whose mores now match the society at large, in other words, none and unstructured; still, he hugs his kids and wife and takes a skin shower, but, unfortunately, not a moral shower, and then reads the newspaper and watches some random sports shows; and then he and his brood of roly-poly humans take to the dinner table like it was their first supper and eat more food than was just recently thought possible and certainly has been established by medical authorities as excessive; and then proceed, like a devouring horde of voracious and maddened insects who actually have an excuse for their behavior, to waste more food atop this spiking-on-the-gorge-graph by not refusing to finish even third helpings; and still, they have room in their gargantuan-like stomachs for a wealth of more calories in their rich dessert; hey, it's just topping, after all.

Done, done, done for now, with these bulging-stomach creatures; so, sleep, sleep, sleep, for now, they do, satiated and stuffed, and satisfied that their lot and existence in life was secured and clarified.

So, if you please, we will go once more through the rarefied ether and down, down to the geography of the Kingdom of Nothingness and Despair, where Suffering and Sorrow grow like thorny weeds, and seem normal.

Father died a miserable, wasting, pinched-by-disease, awful, terrible, painful death, and Mother, who fought with every ounce of her ardent soul to stay alive for her darling children, too died from the acquired scourge, and the children watched them die, in the thatched hut, die in horrible grunts and gasps, and shuddering swallows, and bodily, sweaty spasms, and frightening, trembling shakes; and then practically unknown Uncle and Auntie came from a faraway village, and took the children and promised them love and room and board, but this really meant a trip to the local slavers, who bought the children for three hundred dollars each, and a neat, but used, red moped; and Auntie and Uncle were very pleased, until the children ran away from their new masters, and they had to give the money and moped back.

Abebe and his brother and sister were found by a societal safety net, a Christian organization—you know the kind: the kind certain people loathe and condemn by saying they are phonies and incompetent, and "besides, who knows where the money goes" kind, all so they can justify not giving one penny of their hard-earned money to them, and instead, purchase another, oh-so-important lottery ticket or six-pack of light beer, or inert brain cell gained from the purchase of just one more electronic video game that is curiously played by the child as well as the child-adult; as it was, the children were then placed in a good, clean, Christian home, where Abebe met Jon Paul.

Turn around and dive back into the land of opportunity and too-much-plenty, where Mother and Father and the kids are still, once again, eating; so, this family portrait is finished, as it must be with those condemned to mediocrity based on geography and location.

So, now Abebe and his brother and sister had clean water and plenty food, and it was all so strange that it took a long while for them to become accustomed to it all, but children are very resilient and malleable creatures; and these children flourished. In point of fact, Abebe and his brother, and with their sister, with Jon Paul, too, used to run daily to their school, which was five hilly miles away; now, this new family may have had good food and clean water, but they did not live in a tract home, but in a remote, urban setting, which was still paradise to the children.

Soon, Abebe's brother and sister were in high school, where the track and field coach, upon seeing their fast and easy gait, encouraged them to join his team, and they did, and were a sensation; and soon, Abebe's older brother received a scholarship to a distant, foreign college somewhere in the Americas, and went there, and broke long-distance running records, and their family was so very proud; and then he graduated and became a professional and began to win very big races, and sent portions of his earnings home.

And then one day, Abebe's brother was in Uganda, doing missionary work during the off-season with his sister, and they were kidnapped and murdered by rebels.

Jon Paul stopped his narration, and could no longer continue, so distraught was he.

It was a story told and heard in a thousand epochs and in a thousand versions, but the hearing of it, that it was about a friend, gave it a genuine identity; and it is true, "that people will fight for something they believe in and know is real—everything else is a fairy tale."

Quietude was their new companion as the men walked on around the bend and down the dry riverbed, and then, in a few minutes, they heard faint echoes.

"Help."

"Eh, what's this?" Henry whispered, laying his rifle out in front of his body, while the others, just like a highly structured and practiced military unit, naturally divided themselves up into units, some facing ahead, others behind, a few looking up; and when these last few men did, they laughed.

"Ha!" Finn cried, disturbing the intensity of his brothers, except Jon Paul, who too was looking up, and smiling, "the culprit is above us!"

Now, everyone was laughing except Henry, who exclaimed, as he looked on high, "Get down from there, you fool!"

It was Abebe, his curiosity having got the better of him, as he had, on a caprice, climbed up the rock mountain and then reached a position, he reasoned from which he could not climb up or down. "Help," he barely said, his face awash in fear and trepidation.

"No one is coming up to get you, you little idiot," shouted Henry, and when his comrades told Abebe that he indeed must come down on his own, Henry felt emboldened. "Well, if you don't come down now, you'll just have to come down later."

"Help, help, I'm going to fall," Abebe whispered, his body trembling, his hands shaking.

"Oh, now I am a babysitter," Henry grumbled, and just like that, he leaped to the jagged wall of protruding rocks and roots, scrambled up it as if he were more agile than a mere clumsy human, and in a few moments, he had reached a small ledge to the left of the youth. "When you challenge something, you don't back down," he said. "Now, get going—it is the only way you will ever learn to overcome your fears."

"I cannot do that," Abebe whispered, his voice shaken by fear; "please help me down."

"Up, up you go," Henry shouted, but the passionate protestations of the youth continued. "Then down you will go, coward," he said, and began to pull Abebe's left hand, then his right hand, and then his left foot, then his right, until Abebe was howling like a baby. "Up! Up! Or I will send you down on your square head!" But the youth would not yield his secure position, so Henry grunted, "So, I go done now, and you will watch," and he let go of his hands and leaned backward.

"No," cried Abebe, who shot out his left hand and clutched Henry's outstretched arms and then pulled him back in.

"If you could do that, you can do anything," Henry exclaimed. "So, watch me now, and follow me, now, and do as I do now—now!" And he commenced to climb upward, like a human lizard, so powerful were his adroit feet and hands; and when Abebe saw this, he abandoned his previous timidity, keeping his gaze upon the body of his master, and too began to climb, and soon, he and Henry were standing tall upon a narrow ledge, and bowing to the wild applause of the men below.

"I want to do that again," Abebe shouted, smiling largely.

"Some other day, boy," Henry sighed, and slapped the youth on his shoulder, and then the two men descended the ledge until they reached the sandy trail below, and joined the others once more.

Presently, they came upon Conall and Eleanor, who were walking hand in hand, and once the lovers were past them, Henry said, in complete honesty, "That is what I need—a woman." The other men supposed that their abstaining from responding would cremate his enticing idea and send the hot ashes to ride the breezy wind currents along the serpentine trail, but it only enabled him to elaborate further. "You know what I mean, and I don't mean a wife."

Miguel shrugged his strong shoulders. "Pretend."

Henry cussed and spat. "You can be heroes and saints, and I'll be a man of flesh and blood—who needs a woman."

The younger men in the group happily deferred to their elder on this subject.

"Henry, you are a free man," Finn said, walking next to Miguel, and winking at him, "and you'll make an outstanding husband for a good woman."

"And father, too," Miguel said, smiling now.

"What?" Henry shouted. "I want a woman—and I don't care where she comes from or who she is. I have physical needs; is there a clause in this ridiculous vow of abstinence?"

Finn slapped Henry on his shoulders. "Henry, my good man, just think of your family, and pray, and remember who you are not: ordinary."

It is a strange phenomenon, how human contact, in concert with the correct words and gestures and genuine countenance of another, can right a person who has temporarily tilted left; Henry grumbled more, and then let gradually the gnawing need for female flesh subside.

Then came the caves Abebe had spoken of, and already in attendance were some of the men, who had come from the opposite direction.

But the wall carvings were not in the caves, as in other countries, but in plain sight; there were large stone murals and small ones; drawings grouped together, drawings going up, others going down, some spreading from side to side, and all of them involving scenes from the lives of ancients, of camels and elephants, of trees and running horses, men tending their herds of sheep and cows, people working near their huts, and the great god, who rises, like a phantom, many times the height of the humans and animals around him; this was a moment for the Crusaders, amid the battles and suffering, to recover some of their humanity that had begun to crumble and threaten to wobble their moral foundation; and here, learn about the past, to remember a past, to enjoy something that was pure and simple and yet elegant and thrilling.

"When is your spray can, Olaudah," Abebe whispered, as if his loud words would somehow tear away a piece of this sacred history.

"Next time," he replied, also whispering, as if his loud words would upset the serenity and simplicity of the magical moment.

"Maybe, one day, someone will draw pictures about us," Abebe whispered.

Later that night, all of the Crusaders sat, arranged in concentric circles, around a campfire, talking about the day's events, speaking of the future and analyzing the past; they had gathered roots and tubers, and fruits, and hunted during the day, using spears and slingshots crafted from local material, and using the bow and arrow of Moses and his men, and of the Toubou, and then cooked and ate some of the game at night, never fearing that the fire would arouse suspicion, as they reasoned, based on intelligence-gathering from local geography, that too many indigenous groups burned fires and sometimes burned them inside Tassili N'Ajjer.

For two weeks, then, the Crusaders followed the same course—hunt and relax and explore and eat during the day, with guards posted atop mountain peaks in four locations, and guards posted at the westerly and easterly openings; and at night, the Crusaders gathered round the campfire and ate and talked, and while they spoke of things past, present and future, and their words, to the last man, were amiable, designed to comply with a tacit rule that desired no emotional confrontation until all of the them had regained their complete mental and physical health.

Each of the them had lost a minimum of thirty pounds—even though they had been prudent enough to eat more calories than normal for weeks so as to prepare their body for this inevitable wasting, as they had expected such an arduous journey soon—and muscle, too, and so one of the activities they were to engage in was calisthenics and vigorous exercises to regain physical prowess and mental confidence; there were daily barefoot runs and sprints in the soft sand, and fierce competitions, and pushups and pullups with large rocks atop them, and lifting of boulders and logs; long jumps and high jumps; rock climbing, handstands and handstand pushups, and balance-beam walking, and tumbling, and flipping forward and backward; and obstacle courses, and log- and boulder-carrying and -throwing; and martial arts sparring, and wrestling contests, and rope climbs, and team competitions with the Europeans against the Africans, and the Kenyans against the Chadians, and once, they even found a long-abandoned, long, thick rope that had obviously been used to lead camels, and an amazing tug-o'-war contest began, one that started in the morning and lasted until the night and was resumed the next day, where the men lost skin and blood and sweat and tears, but gained much laughter, and no one capitulated, ever, never yielding even after defeat, but challenging again and again, and every time the men pulled with their every gram of might and grit, they were pulling tighter the prickly tie that binds all good men who must grip that dagger-covered, dangling string and suffer pain and blood, but ultimately gain brotherhood.

There were even tournaments involving stick-fighting, at which the Tuareg were masters, and were impressed to learn that Conall—as was his brother, whom they desired to meet—had been an expert at sword fighting, and witnessed his great prowess and skill.

And the Muslims still prayed five times a day, their bodies bowed toward Mecca, to Allah, and those who practiced Sanatana Dharma prayed to their gods, and the Buddhists among them mediated and prayed; and the Christians, they too prayed, and all of the Crusaders respected the faith of their brethren, even while engaging in gentle discourse on the theology of their beliefs; and for those who had no religion, why, they just mediated upon a life long-ago since practiced, but longed for again.

And then one night, in the middle of the third week of their visit at what they now called the "Tassili N'Ajjer Resort," while the Crusaders were sitting in the concentric circles they had become accustomed to, the outer rings consisting of stacked logs and boulders, the sentries being posted, the men having just come back from feeding and tending to the camels, Henry flung a verbal cluster bomb that landed against the carefully constructed glass barrier that had insulated the men from petty bickering and destructive arguing.

The men were sipping tea made from local plants, when Henry, the walking powder keg, blurted out, as if his mind had tripped past reason and fallen on a pile of thorns and thistles that ignited irrationality and illogic within him, "Well, what about it, eh?" He was speaking in broken English, now, and the interpreters began for the few who still had difficulty understanding. "Here we are, hiding in the mountains, pursued by three—three," he shouted, holding up three fingers on his left, callused hand, "nations, and we have little ammunition, and food—eh," he shrugged his shoulders, and lifted up his hands as his round head bobbed to and fro. "Rabbit, I can eat—but what plans—what! Where do we go? We are the hunted—and what can we do— we, eighty-three men against the resources of nations! No one cares about our sacred cause! We are finished, I tell you—finished—and lucky to be alive, too; yes, lucky, and I say we disband and go home and be happy we survived; and as to African's problems?" And he grunted loudly. "They won't go away soon; don't worry," he gesticulated, "they will be there for some time, so if any do-gooder wants to pick up the sword and give it a go, be my honored guest— but please, leave African's problems to Africa—not meddling foreigners, who only make things worse; we don't need a nursemaid, especially not from the people who created our mess," and he waved off the repugnant idea, and then waved around him. "And that includes any foreigner here." He abruptly stood up, fully erect, his face flaming defiance. "And I am not afraid to say it—not afraid one little bit; and cowards, all of you, who believe it and don't say it— cowards, to let foreigners affect our fate! Shame!" and he waved them all off in one grand gesture, grunted loudly, and nodded, his face scrunched up in a terrible scowl, and then sat down again, as if he were a prince and about to be crowned King on his rock throne.

No one had attempted to quiet him, for all sensed it was time to engage in an oral fistfight, and they welcomed it; the men were healthy, their spirits revived, their minds sharp, and aching for any kind of battle; and so, it would begin here.

There was a momentary lull, hanging like a knotted noose in the crackling air, and few men wished to slip their rash necks into it, least of all the established leaders, who, according to the ancient tradition, allowed their willing subordinates ample time to purchase shares of their own philosophy in the arena of oration; and so it began, one man announcing his presence by laying bare his mind onto the mounting platform, while another man awaited and then either stabbed or built upon this opine, each side launching a definitive idea on the subject of their present military mission.

"Why are we here?" asked one.

"To fight tyranny," said another.

"Alone!" cried one.

"Why are you here, then?" shouted another.

"To protect the Innocents," interjected one.

"But where do we go from here, who do we fight, and how?" asked another, excitedly.

"We're done, we have done more than most," lamented another.

"We cannot do what an army cannot," added one.

"It is a miracle that we survived; it is finished," one said, as did many others, as if this last statement had broken the seal on the bursting spigot, and authentic sentiment now splashed upon the center stage.

The leaders had scrutinized not only the faces of the men, but of each other, too, waiting, allowing the men to build up and then tear down the idea of each other, and then regroup and come around and again on every important point; and then, and only then, like master Teachers who sit quietly at the front of the class listening to the fine speeches of their students, would they finally to speak, but it must be understood that when this auspicious moment occurred, it would signify that their men had exhausted all of their arguments, and now, now, only the leaders and their closest allies—who too reserved speech for later—would speak, and then all would be finished and the matter resolved.

So, when the last of the men had spoken, and a second lull opened up a hole in the furious colloquy, silence spread over the heads of the men, waiting like a messenger, and when no words erupted from one man and opportunity for interjection or rebuttal expired, it moved to the next man—now, all of this actually occurred simultaneously, and in a long minute, the men had quite happily yielded the now-lopsided, warped, fragile center stage to their commanders.

Moses was sitting in the first ring nearest the fire, his face aglow with the passion of his beliefs; he spoke, and when he did, his words were like sharp steel shafts that had been dipped into the orange flames before him.

The night above him was clear, a rich, deep, penetrating bowl of blue-black sky populated by the cosmos' glittering children, and a shimmering, silvery moon; the only sounds around him were the cries of ambitious birds and boasting animals, and the soft, whooshing sound of swirling wind that swept lazily along the narrow, winding passage.

"Our history is a history of suffering," he began, still sitting on a big log, his legs propped up on a smaller log, a stick in his right hand, which he stuck into the ground. "We existed for centuries in relative peace before the colonists came—before that, most of us lived in small villages, and our populations did not exceed our ability to produce food and sustain life; we lived in peace—but then the arrogant European came and he took our lands, just as the Americans took the Native Indians' land, and the British took the Aborigines' land, and the Spaniards took the land of those in the Americas; and they forced us to live their way, and broke our natural borders and united tribal groups who had never lived together, and then told us we were now one country; they creat-ed false borders and then left—left us with altered states, and chaos; so, I say to you, we must be free of foreign influence—foreign investment, foreign aid, foreign missionaries and foreign military intervention—and world organizations that cripple us. Can you imagine if African missionaries went to Britain to aid their poor, or sent troops to France to quell their unrest, or bullied the economy of America with threats and financial bribes—from the World Bank, the International Monetary Fund—to alter their political system; no, fellow Africans, Africa is for Africans, and must be rebuilt by Africans, for only we understand our history, our geography, our people, our customs, our values: they created the wound; we will heal it," and he picked up a gulp of sand and stood up; and his voice was clear and bold and full of fervor. "This is our land, and only we know how to reclaim it; our heritage, our history—our destiny." He sat down, and would now await discourse from the other side.

Many men, who had settled upon the razor's edge concerning this dilemma, decided Moses was indeed correct, and now could not possibly see any reasonable refutation coming from his opponents that would sway them; while other men, ignorant of many things he had spoken of, still understood and appreciated the central tenets of his speech.

There was a pattern of honor and cordiality established among these men who had lived and fought together, a respect bred from a willingness to die not only for each other but for their just cause; and right now, it plainly said that one who disagreed with Moses would speak.

"You are the future of Africa, this is certain," Conall said, and so it all began, possibly the erosion of one wall of philosophy, and by doing so, picking up sand and grit and pebbles and creating a new philosophy—the debris of the dying to create the world of the living, the same way planets are formed.

"Africa," he continued, calmly, sitting next to his beloved Eleanor, "is for Africans, and should be rebuilt by Africans, but I ask you, my good and noble Moses, is there a place at Her table for children of another culture? May we too dine at her feast as we help her flourish?"

Moses, his long, muscular arms resting upon his knees, replied, "You are my friend, Conall, and have proved yourself noble, a true son of Africa, though born to a different mother; but you are a soldier, and soldiers merely clear the way for the righteous path to be followed; yet, no foreign troops from other lands should set foot upon our native soil, and foreign intervention must cease, in order for our country—your country, too, now, as much as ours—to exist and flourish."

"And where do you think Africa would be without the colonial powers having come here?"

"It would be a paradise," Moses fairly sang, "a paradise on earth, people living in nature, in peace with themselves—that is why we need no foreign influence: foreign companies that corrupt, foreign aid that corrupts, foreign influence that disrupts."

Conall, with Master's degrees in world military history and political science, inhaled deeply and slowly, and then exhaled even slower and more deeply. "Africa was never a paradise, Moses—in myth it was, to serve the rants of tyrants so they might blame all of African's ills on the imperialists."

"I don't believe you, Conall—show me!" Moses returned, and in so doing, opened up the door for Conall to install the first chapter of his master's thesis on Africa into the caucus.

He never once hesitated. "It is by geography that Africa has lain with misery: first by the oldness of the land, and second by those who surrounded Her; yes, the Arabs and the Europeans came here for slaves, but not before Africa had been selling her own people into slavery long before that, and even during the new age of slavery, and to the Arabs and the Europeans—gladly they did this, and profited greatly, too; and after the Arabs left and the Europeans quit, they continued it, and still do today—right now, even as I speak, they practice this great evil under the sun; and while it is true that then most of Africa was composed of small clans, there were a very few states like Ethiopia, but there were bigger villages that preyed on smaller ones and raided them for slavery and the narcotic of mammon; and there was witchcraft and human sacrifice in certain villages; and yes, the Europeans came and plundered and stole and murdered, but the auxiliary benefit was modernity they brought, civilization and technology, too, some of which still stands; so I ask you, my brothers, do we want the Africa unspoiled by outsiders in the nineteenth century where people lived in the Stone Age—as too many still do? Would they have come round to the twenty-first century—yes, I am sure, as all nations do—and they would be better off without the Big Men of Africa ruling with an iron fist over them, a consequence of what the imperialist nations did; had I a time machine and the ability to stop such malicious endeavors, and then watch Africa flourish on Her own—yes, with all my heart, I would, but that cannot be; so, now, we must overcome what obstacles now with the resources we have to heal those old wounds; and there is still the problem of geography, and disease, and climate, to struggle against."

He abruptly abated his discourse, and then, in one seamless transition, as if the men were members of a relay team who were expert at surreptitious handoffs, Yoshitsune spoke; he was university educated with Master's degrees in international affairs and philosophy, giving no time at all for gainsayers, although the current for reprisals was growing stronger with each passing moment.

"The land of Africa is mostly impoverished. Only eight percent is available for cultivation, and only three percent is fertile—look at Africa, it is sand, where few plants grow, and forests that recycle only eight percent of biomass; there are no nutrients in the soil there; and you have a billion people, and with drought and famine and overpopulation, it is an unfortunate mix; and look at your diseases—malaria, sleeping sickness, and yellow fever—which devastate the people, and why is this so? Because there is year-round warmth—geography again—that creates conditions for bacteria to grow, because of this constant warmth; and the advanced age of Africa has allowed organic matter to decompose, creating a soil depleted of nutrients; and look at the present: only four percent of Africa is irrigated—compared to about one-third in South and East Asia—so, there is less of a chance for agriculture to flourish."

The interpreters were mad with translating the words of Yoshitsune, and the faces of many of the men were bewildered, and some men, who had no need of interpreters, asked for clarification, at which point Yoshitsune stood up and bowed deeply and humbly apologized.

"Let me begin again," he said, and this time, he used the moist sand below and rocks and sticks and his gestures to tell the story; he picked up a medium-sized rock and held it on high, and spoke in deep, penetrating, precise terms. "This is like Africa—old," and he sprinkled sand upon it, "mostly desert," and he put some twigs on it, "some savanna, some grass and plains, and flat land," and he put in a small plant; "with forests—but with poor, sandy soil." He held the rock on high. "Too much warmth here—in addition to the old age of Africa—has made the soil poor for crops, and too much warmth creates disease that kills millions." He threw down the rock in the center of this meeting, bent down, and drew a rough sketch of the African continent, and then drew lines inside of it as the men gathered around. "Africa has a small area of land for crops to grow, and very few crops have water access, as do villages, of course." He pointed to several places on the continent. "There are no waterways to carry goods our countries make, making it expensive to send to other countries, and we need dams—all very bad." He drew boundaries in the continent. "There are too many people, too few crops, too little water, too much disease, and too little freedom to fix the problem."

Men began to ask questions, and Yoshitsune answered them, about how Africa compared to other countries in trade, infrastructure, in governmental interventions that were successful, and he then quickly deferred to Horatius's sketch.

The Italian, with multiple degrees in economics, stood up, and then bent down and drew an elegant outline, almost like an architect's fine blueprint, of the world, as the men gathered around again like schoolchildren hungry for an education.

"America," he said, his brown eyes sparkling with enthusiasm, pointing to this heaving, churning, steamroller Zeus of economies, "if you take," and he lifted up his hand as if it were full of a tangible something, "all the money," and he rubbed his fingers together and took out two coins and jingled them together, "they make from things made and services given," and then he raised his head high, "and divided it by all the people there—voila! Each person is very rich! Very rich—ricco! Much money everywhere; but if you take Africa," and he bent down again, and all surrounding eyes bent down, too, as he put his big fist into the dirt continent, and then lifted it up, all eager eyes lifted up, too, "and all its things made and services given," and then he lowered his hands nearly to the very sandy soil itself, "very low—very little money, most people are very poor—most of the money is with the rulers: the tyrants, and their willing playmates, the avaricious, blood-soaked monsters, all!"

There were few men who did not now wear disconcerting crowns of thorns upon their tender heads.

"Well, what about Europe?" Jon Paul asked.

"Eh?" Horatius said, shrugging his shoulders, sticking his finger in the old world portrait, and then raised his hand up, "A little below our rich American illegitimate cousins—the ingrates!"

"Asia?" shouted Arjuna.

Horatius lowered his hand. "Less," he said, his pursed lips and knit brows reflecting his inner thoughts on the issue.

"Central and South America?" Miguel asked, solemnly.

Once again, he dove down and plucked an imaginary basket of goods and services from the lower extremity, the ignored brown-haired native stepchild of North America, and then raised his hand up to a place above where it had rested for Africa but far lower than Asia, and once more, he shrugged his shoulders and his animated face evinced concern for the plight of the people in those places. "Not so good."

"But why?" Abebe asked.

"Ah," Horatius replied, excited now, "I was hoping you would ask, Abebe, my good friend—hey, slap him on his back, eh? I am too far away!" and he laughed as Henry too willingly accommodated; and with that done, Horatius fell once more to his intricate reproduction of the continents, and he looked up at his eager audience. "A country makes money, but money goes here," and he gestured to his pocket, and then pointed to the drawing of Africa, "and not here." He drew a government building and a house some distance from it, and then pointed to the palace. "The money goes here and stays here, but does not get to here," and he dug in his index finger and began to carve a route to the house, "because the people in charge are corrupt—corrupt!" He restated the message in Italian, "Corrotto! And so no good roads get built," his finger stopped moving, "and people can't get to where they need to on terrible roads—you have seen those crooked, potholed, broken roads, eh?" Many of the Africans cheered. "Yes, you have, because they are there, and for no good reason except that the politician in charge needs a new jet and a new mansion and a fleet of new cars!" He waited for the translators, and curiously, so too did the others, for all at once, they jeered against the corruption described therein. "Bad roads, bad economy—difficult to deliver things, difficult to travel, difficult to get to the hospital: all very bad." He then laid his hands over the house and said, "No electricity to the houses, either," and he lifted his hand and poured sand upon the house. "No water to it, either, and the water that exists, as we know, is dirty and infected." He built a half-finished schoolhouse. "No schools, broken schools—but if you have more education, more money, it generally means less corruption—yes!" Cheers erupted from his attentive audience. "And we need," he continued, and then drew deep lines throughout the drawing of Africa, "waterways—all rich countries have major ports to take away and receive goods; we have few!"

"But don't the rich countries try to help us?" asked Olaudah, in earnest.

"Oh, yes, sure, and big banks, too," he said, and stretched his arms wide, "they all send money," and he smiled slyly, and then said, coyly, "and where do you think," as he reached for his pocket, "it all goes!"

"Corruption!" his worthy students cried.

"Yes! Bravo! You are excellent students!"

"But what of charities—they come and help," cried Arjuna, caught up in the growing enthusiasm.

Horatius looked to Tyr and Enkidu.

Enkidu spoke first, and as he did, Horatius stepped out of the light and into the shadows.

"Yes, they come," Enkidu began, stepping onto center stage, "they help— they helped me and my family; without them I would not be here, and all of you know they helped Moses and his family." Moses nodded. Enkidu looked at him and smiled, and then back again to his panoramic, three-hundred-sixty-degree audience, and continued, "And money comes to Africa, but," and he scooped up a portion of earth in his right hand, lifted up both hands, and then proceeded to pour the soil onto supplicating, splayed fingers, and everyone watched in silence as the sand slowly sifted through; "it does not come to us, but those in power." Now, he too bent down and placed his slender fingers inside Africa, and drew a line roughly dividing it in twain. "Almost half," his voice was full of melancholy now, like the dead air after a flood that has destroyed a city and drowned many, "of our people live on a dollar a day—a dollar," and he took out a dinar and placed it squarely in his palm, "that must take care of all their needs," and then he drew the world into sixths, and highlighted one of the panels, and now his voice was full of sorrow, "So too does one-sixth of the world—a dollar a day, and almost half live on less than two dollars a day," and now his voice grew angry, "while their rulers live in golden palaces and instigate wars for recreation and power and greed," and now he paused, so full of indignation was he; but then said, choking back pathos as he pointed to sand map, "and of those who earn less than one dollar a day, almost half of them live here, in sub-Saharan Africa—here!" He shook his head. "And what about illiteracy—again, here, we have nearly a fifty percent illiteracy rate: here, right here, and most children who even start school do not finish; and girls, well, it is estimated that about one-third of them do not even have a fifth-grade education—and yet...yet, women work more hours; and yes, they earn less income, too; this is not right, it is a tragedy, and a crime; so let us not forget why we are here, that once they are free, they have the chance to live as the rest of the industrialized world."

"So, we must kick out these tyrants!" one of the men shouted, and was greeted by cheers.

Tyr, in his light German accent, spoke as he stood next to Enkidu. "Since the colonial powers left," and now he bent down toward the map as Enkidu receded back into the inner circle. "There have been one hundred and fifty times," and he pointed to nearly every country in Africa, "a man has been removed from office—one man comes and destroys the country, and another comes and takes him out and then he ruins the country. It," he lifted up his hands to imitate the rain cycle, "is like the rain," and he moved his hands up; "water evaporates from the ground and goes into the clouds," and he acted out all of this, "and the clouds rain and it comes down to the parched ground and goes deep to the rivers below us and runs to the sea and then eventually rises up again to the clouds—it is like this in Africa: one man rises up and then rains his power upon us until he is exhausted and then another man rises up; it is an endless cycle, unbroken by Nature and Man." He then told them stories of certain men here and how they had become a leader in their country and then stolen from the treasuries and stolen from the corporations and then stolen from foreign companies and people and from the Church and from even a consumptive dog with an old bone in its drooling mouth; how then they gave money to relatives and friends, and businesses to relatives and friends, and land to relatives and friends, all the while feigning that they were the champion of the people come to save poor Africa from the mean imperialists and foreign domination or neighboring threats; but in reality, they were themselves the greatest peril to that country. He stopped, forlorn and forsaken, as if by the speaking of them, he had lived these ignominious deeds, and then his words became powerful and frightening to the distant ears of distant rulers. "But the cords of their sin," and he lifted up his hands and caught these man-made, sinewy fibers of iniquity, "shall be brought upon them," and he pretended to wrap them around the necks of these tyrants; "and in so doing, they shall judge themselves to be unrighteous, and worthy of death."

Many questions were proffered from the listeners, and many answers from the speakers were delivered, and many of the listeners seemed satisfied, until one candle for unity lit by this free-flowing forum was extinguished by a blast from a powerful verbal sandstorm.

"And how do we know all of this is true, eh? Foreigners telling us our own history; in charge of us, once again, telling us our business, once again—who are you people, anyway?" It was Henry, having already ignited his own short fuse and just now exploding his personal minefield on everyone. "Africa for Africans, remember?" Everyone was now looking his way. "Do we really need foreigners to offer us advice? What's next, eh?" He grabbed the inside of his flaring nostrils with two fingers of his left hand and then stuck out his jaw. "They lead us by the nose," he shouted, and thrust out his hand in a sweeping accusation against his antagonists. "You don't know who to trust in Africa, so how can you trust them, eh?" He looked at Moses. "How can you stand by and let these outsiders run things? Look at us!" He began to walk about, agitated, strengthened by some of his fellows, who, through nods and gestures, evinced their satisfaction with his harangue. "Where do we go from here? Why are we here? We are eighty-three men against armies—what have we done to ourselves?" He looked again to Moses. "You are our true leader—you tell us what we need to do." His chest was heaving and his face sweating as he stood with his hands on his hips, his breath hot and furious. "Am I the only one with guts, eh?" The translators may have translated, but it was tinged with timidity and hesitation.

Moses, not one to react swiftly to ultimatums, said, calmly, looking at no one in particular, "Sit." His men sat quickly, but the other men, as if to signal independence from his authority, did sit, but delayed the act, sitting at the same time as their respective leaders; now, Moses came to center stage, his countenance aflame with desire. "A wise man who does not listen to other wise men is no longer wise, but a fool unto himself—all of us," he cried, gesturing around the circle, "are of one blood now—African blood, sharing the same history, the same passion for Justice; we are all sons—and daughters, now," and he gestured, kindly, smiling, up toward Eleanor, "for any good son and daughter is prepared to give his and her life for his mother and father—our Africa—and everyone here has proved his and her loyalty to Her through selfless devotion to protecting Her dignity; now," his tone dropped from a high-flying eagle to a slowly descending white dove with a tender olive branch in its mouth, as he looked at the inner circle who had spoken, "these men," he pointed to them, "whom we trust with our lives, have told us of our history, many things new to us, and seem insulting to us..." He hesitated now, and the warrior sense in the men immediately received an electrical charge to commence a combative countdown, but then he continued. "If we were not brothers and sisters already—no good son or daughter casts insults at his mother; no! If the truth is harsh, then the remedy is possible; lies during war lead men to the grave; so, I say to you," and he looked especially at Conall, and approached him and placed his large hand upon the youth's broad shoulders; and now his voice was conciliatory and encouraging. "I say to you, my African brothers and sisters, tell us of your beginnings, and how you came to our beloved continent."

Conall stood and shook the hand of Moses, smiled, and nodded his head, and then took center stage as Moses resumed his seat in the inner circle.

The sky was now an enormous ebony mural, punctuated by a million points of brilliant lights that hovered above their heads, and it seemed sometimes as if there was more light attempting to stream in from behind this pastoral painting, as the origin of the Crusaders disclosed itself to them.

The Origin of the Crusaders

Conall was born in Kenmare, a place of steep, rolling green hills, and lush, vibrant pastures, in southern Ireland, in Kerry County; son to Michael and Jenny Cuchulain, and older brother to Dylan; his father's father had been a sheep farmer in Kerry County, as had his father before him, and it was the same for many previous generations, and Michael had started out as one, but when he decided to the university to study Agriculture and Biology to improve the family business, he met Jenny McFee, who was studying Medicine and Veterinary Science, and there began the discontinuance of the family heritage, for when two educated people in love look around the world and decide that it is not good that there are people who exist who are not as happy as they, then these two people, if they, for a moment, might rein in self-ambition, just might ascend to a grander height and seek to do something greater; and so it was to no little fanfare that the young couple, as soon as they graduated and then wed, and after allowing his older brothers and sisters to have his ancestral home, moved into her ancestral home in Glendalough, where her grandparents had worked in the mines; and then were off to stitch up the wounds that poverty and injustice had so ignominiously opened up around the tired globe.

Dylan, too, was born in Kenmare, as Michael and Jenny wished that their children should be born in their mother country, but once the children were out of the womb, the family was off again to bring succor to another destitute region of the Third World, where Michael and Jenny, now working for a Christian organization, helped farmers and local governments deal with poor crops, poor drinking water and poor sanitary standards. It was in these countries that Conall and Dylan came to love and respect the great diversity of people, and develop a profound respect for Freedom and Justice; it was here that they met the children of the local villagers and other missionaries, and learned many languages, cultures, traditions, customs, fighting and weapons styles, martial arts, and established many good friends, bonds in times of strife that would never be broken.

In the deepest squalor of India, the family became embedded; in the most barren stretch of the African desert, the family lived; in the most dens- est jungles of the Amazon, the family endured; and everywhere they went, despite the hardship and pain they saw, they were happy because there was a sense that their mission of mercy, no matter how horrible the environment or circumstances around them, gave them an internal joy that could be harnessed anywhere, anyplace, anytime—as when one does the right thing when the majority does the wrong thing or doesn't care or simply cannot recognize that the right thing exists, then one is justified in one's actions, at peace with oneself, at peace with the world, and overflowing with a spiritual joy that is inexpressible to those who have not surrendered their devouring appetite for material objects.

Conall and Dylan understood that their parents had foregone the status and luxuries of a prosperous civilization that are typically afforded to educated people who have attained a higher station in life, in order to bring solace to the weakest, the poorest, the humblest people in Creation, people afflicted with every species of disease and privation, caught in every tyrant's lust for power and wealth, and every corporation's greed, who were abandoned by—save charities—every governmental institution, country, town and city, and village, the lowest-ranking people on earth, people who had no political power, no medicine, little food, little clothing, little shelter, and because of these dwindling assets, were ignored in the wide world, and battered, beaten and shunned, segregated and used, murdered and left to rot in the boiling sun, the icy wind, the burning desert, the soaking rain; and so the world is guilty, the youths reasoned, and a co-conspirator, to casually deliver these unwanted sons and daughters as sacrifice to the gods of lust and gluttony, simply because these people had nothing of value to offer anyone, except their own forced labor and tormented lives; and as the Cuchulains knew this, they could not, in good conscience, turn away from those in need. So, they had decided: "We say we love each other, and it is an easy thing to do, to love and care for your own; and then if we say we love others, but are not ready to care for them, but in words only, and so by this we will be judged."

But they were a happy family, blissfully so, and especially the boys, who at an early age appreciated the great diversity of life in the world, and were the envy of every boy and girl because they literally had friends from the highest northern top of the world to the most southern bottom, from the furthest east to the most navigable west, and every port, isle, and island was an adventure; every jungle, forest and savanna a fantastic voyage of discovery; every desert, plain and mountain full of life lessons to be learned and passed on.

And O, the people the boys met! How spoiled the boys became on their journeys, as Pygmies in the Amazon, where Mother was helping the locals sustain their diminishing environment, showed them how to make a wooden blowgun and poisonous darts from gently squeezing certain species of yellow-colored frogs and attaining a precious few drops from atop his back (this last one the boys attempted to hide from their mother—but it failed, miserably, as boys should, sometimes, fail); as the Tuareg in the Sahara, where Father was helping the indigenous people build better wells, showed them how to ride a camel; as the Aztecs in Mexico, where Father was helping the people with crop rotation, showed the boys ancient ruins and ancient sacred texts; as the Mongolians, where Mother showed the people how to improve animal husbandry, showed the boys the secrets of living in the raw wild; and the boys made friends with the children of villages and missionary families who were always there and plentiful, and each one a precious history of the planet and precious cultural resource to absorb; and they learned from the adults of the villages wherever they journeyed, where Conall and Dylan were especially fascinated by the legends and myths related to them, often comparing them to their own, reciting such stories and making up new ones with themselves as the mortal heroes; and they had the finest martial-arts teachers, who had not been corrupted by a confluence of diluted and oft-wedded styles; yes, women and men who had been taught the ancient skill of combat by their masters who received it from their masters in an unbroken, unaltered, pure, graceful form— and it all came flowing easily into the eager minds and bodies of the robust, blond-haired youths who envisioned themselves as one day being Champions of the Meek. It should also be noted that neither their mother nor father ever sought to dissuade or preclude the boys from pursuing such matters—it was the nature of these parents, liberal and free, to see the inherent wisdom of their children being exposed to the greatest living concepts in the way of the warrior, but also philosophy, history, science, medicine, culinary arts, sports, exercise, dance, music, art, geography, in virtually all areas of human knowledge; and so, from a wide cross section of various Teachers who were experts in varying academic disciplines, their two budding boys were nourished on the nutritious sap of a million masters of every known way of thinking and doing things.

And along their epic journey down lonely rivers and up narrow mountain trails and into dense jungles and out to isolated communities, the boys met young children, sometimes the children of missionaries, sometimes the children of villagers, sometimes the children of the wind and rain and sleet and snow, children abandoned by mother and father, and society, drifting pieces of flotsam on an endless dry ocean of land with no direction or purpose or claim on the world other than maintenance of self, and quite often, by any means; the boys slowly developed a philosophy regarding the societal bleeding-out of individuals it no longer deemed productive, those no longer deemed necessary, who had been issued a death warrant upon their unclean hands: their philosophy that was in anguish over the excising of children due to wars, drought, famine, and disease, and soon they were dedicated to the radical and yet natural precept that all innocent people deserve a chance to live in a quiet and serene happiness.

As it was, along the way, they met Yoshitsune, when their parents were attending a conference in Japan on global hunger; and in the Philippines, where their parents were working with the local farmers, they met Tyr, and while their family was helping the farmers in Kenya, they met Enkidu, and while in Brazil, they met Horatius, all of whom had missionary parents; and many others they met, along the way or by traveling with families, and as better and quicker access to long-distance communication increased, the boys kept in contact more often and for longer periods of time; and by going hither and then there, and then thither, and then there, they would once again meet their new boyhood pals in person and they would rejoice, and talk of many things, but mainly of the injustice of the whole wide world and how those in supreme authority seemed to have forgotten their primary objective—to protect, serve, and lead through an inviolate faith in Freedom and Justice and Equality for all.

As the boys became men, and their friends, too, they raised up an unimpeachable plan that would, like an alluring lover, be waiting for them at the proper time—but the proper time could not be reached, the youths agreed, when they met together or talked on telephone conferences, until they went to university and attained the proper education and background to prepare them for the weighty tasks ahead; therefore, the course was carefully constructed and analyzed, and when the time came, each young man attended a university and pursued certain academic areas that would prepare their minds for the Mission, be it: political science, religious studies, geography, economics, medicine, cultural studies, history, law, military history—while continuing to condition their bodies with strenuous aerobic and weight-lifting activities, and practicing martial arts, and becoming proficient in the usage of weapons and strategies and tactics, becoming a master in equestrianism, rock climbing, and mountain climbing, and survival techniques—in many of which the Cuchulains had already established a foundation while being taught by the masters of each discipline—horse riding by the Mongolians, sword play by the Chinese and Japanese, knife-fighting by the Scots, stick-fighting by the Thai, and again, infusing survival techniques learned everywhere they journeyed; and so the stage was set and the play enacted, and soon, the youths were men and graduates—they had not yet resolved to take women disciples into their private adventure-world—and soon kissed their sweethearts goodbye, and hugged their parents and bid them a fond farewell, and met in Athens, Greece, and as they eyed the great splendor that modernity had wrought upon this ancient family, the men swore an oath that they would not taste fine food or drink, own fine clothes or cars, live in fine houses or apartments, or possess fine wealth of material goods until they had fought against tyranny and injustice with all their heart and soul and mind, and body, and to the best of their now-superhuman ability.

And they numbered thirty good men, and immediately set off to Africa, having already decided it was there that humanity had mostly forgotten its inherent and unalterable oath to let no Innocent fall without a struggle unto death; and so, it was there where they were needed most, and immediately.

And now was now, and the story told, the origin of the Crusaders known to all, and nothing left to do for the men around the campfire but retire for the night and think not only of their own origins, but the origins of the others.

War Council

It was decided the next day, that every night the Crusaders would meet and allow any of the men to relate his story to his brethren, and once this was done, that a decision, one that the men were contemplating, concerning their imminent plans would be discussed at length and in detail; thus, it commenced, and truly, every man there was anxious to describe his unique life and reasons for joining so elite a confederation of freedom fighters. The lives of these men traversed five continents and thirty-three countries, and involved cities, towns and villages, nomads and wanderers, rich men and poor, family men and men alone, educated men and illiterate men, religious men and skeptics, humorists and somber men, young men and a few older, and pragmatists, realists, stoics and nihilists, doctors, teachers, farmers and scientists; men of every creed and class, men of character of every present and past; men of diligence, men of whimsy, men of hope and men of apathy, but men, all men, willing to die for, sacrifice for, and kill for, exclude their own family and normalcy and material wealth for, for a chance, the very slight chance, to secure Justice and Freedom for the Innocent.

Now, when it came to telling the story of Miguel, it was determined, by a consensus, that he was averse to speaking of his past, and was wont to avoid all such gatherings for that very purpose, and so always volunteered for guard duty.

Antonio Juan de Bolivar told a tale of his brief life in Bolivia, how he and his itinerant parents had moved throughout the Americas and finally settled in Colombia, where his parents received work on a coffee farm, and where he went to school and still worked on the plantation; but it wasn't too soon that the rebel groups, who proliferate like mold on rotting fruit in this continent, began to operate in the local area, not only engaging in subversive tactics against the government but also in the transporting and refining and selling of the coca leaf extract to its eager and brain-numb, far North American cousins; it became dangerous for his family to move about, for fear of encountering government troops who were suspicious of any peasant as collaborator, and meeting rebels who encouraged paranoia itself by assuming that anyone not for them was a spy and therefore against them. One day, after a long session of picking the hearty brown bean on the sloping green hills of the Puerto Venus region, his family was walking home when a rebel faction, newly sprouted—and newly sprouted ones had a marketing problem of anonymity—came upon them, whereupon his mother and father then dispatched Antonio to the safety of the thick bushes, where he lay, trembling, listening to the rebels questioning his parents about government troops in the area; and then he heard a terrific report, like a cannon shot, and then a hysterical scream, like a living thing screams when it has its inner core, its life-force, ripped out of it; and then he remembered waking up and leaping to the road to find his father dead and his mother gone.

But his father was no peasant fool and had not only taught his son politics and manners, but also tracking methods and survival skills, because such talents and skills were a necessary investment in this violent and uncertain world; and so, the young boy of twelve set out to find his mother, which he did in one week's time; and in a day more, had mapped out the rebel outpost, and in two more days, penetrated the camp during the lazy, pitch-dark night of a pouring-down-hard rain, and slipped into the tent his mother was held in, and found her and hugged her and wept loving tears over her and promised her escape; but she would not go, she said, could not go back, she wept, because of awful things that he could not yet comprehend, and so she urged him to go, and grow up straight and tall and true, but he refused to go without her; and just then the commandant came in, but not before Antonio—with his great acuity of hearing that had been honed by hunting—leaped to the side, and in so doing, caught the man from behind and then plunged a long, silver, serrated knife into the back of the man, until he was—in leaping flights of joy and gratitude from victims in future days that were now averted—certainly dead.

Go now, his weeping mother pleaded, they will find out, go now, and my love and your father's love will be with you always and guide you always, and God go with you, and guide you, always; so, she implored her only child and progeny, go, go now and live—make your parents proud, and your country proud—do something for your country to make all good people look up to you—but go now, son, go, go my love, the only part of who I and your father once were, go, and your father's love and my love will be with you, and God's love.

She embraced him one last time and their tears streamed together from the same grieving wellspring and once touching each other, became as one warm stream of piety, and the tears fell into the aging, bottomless pit of their country's sorrowful and shameful history, keeping alive the hope that grew poorly as it reached its sickly branches toward the high recesses of the gaping hole above, wherein sat shards and shreds of incandescent light.

And then Antonio leaped out of the back of the tent, and as he ran, he heard a gunshot, and then another, and then two more, and then silence, and he hesitated, weeping, and turned to go back, but then saw his mother pulled out of the tent as she cried out, "Freedom, Freedom, Freedom for Colombia," as the men around her raised their guns and lowered their souls; and so he turned and ran again, and then heard the gunshots, many gunshots, too many gunshots intended for one woman, for his beloved mother, and he ran so far and so fast that soon he heard nothing but his own fear rattling about in the crackling jungle, and so he stopped, and fell down, weeping still, and fell to rest.

No words were spoken from the other Crusaders now, no noise emitted from them, no gestures, only their profound empathy and sorrow, and filial brotherhood.

"A week later," finally said the Wayuu Indian youth, his comely, swarthy face lifted up in hope, after sitting silent for some time, and there was now a rising emotion in his voice, "Conall and Dylan found me." And as he turned his head, his long brown hair moved upon his bare brown shoulders as he looked to acknowledge Conall with a nod. "I would like to see Dylan again, the rascal," he whispered, in fond remembrance.

"He doesn't leave the university until his studies are completed," Conall stated, smiling too, as he held the hand of his beloved, Eleanor.

"A fine swordsman, he, and gifted practitioner with the katana and wakizashi, where he has few equals," Antonio said.

"No finer than he; and he has become a master at kendo and Iaido, fencing and escrima—he has few equals," Conall returned, but then said, looking at Eleanor, "except, perhaps, for Eleanor's sister."

Eleanor smiled, knowing that her sister had been the supreme athlete in the family, and followed a course like Dylan.

But Antonio, conscious of the impetus to divulge the stories of the men, and having regained his emotional stability, continued on.

"I have talked to Miguel, and I know his story well, and he has told me that I may give it to you, if you choose to hear it." The men assented. He nodded.

Miguel and his elder brother, Roberto, both of Aztecan descent, were pilots in the air force of Mexico, stationed in the territory of Michoacan, in Cuernavaca, near the capital, Mexico City, and they had just arrived at the base.

"Hey, Roberto, phone call from Louisa," a man wearing green overalls shouted to the youths as they approached the tall hangar, and Miguel watched as his brother spoke on the phone.

"That is what we all need, Marco, a family—a wife, a child, a home; that is what we all need."

Marco shrugged his scrawny shoulders. "And a mistress, too, would be good, no?"

"No," Miguel said, shaking his head, striking the back of the mechanic with a hard slap, "no mistress," and he grabbed a hunk of the man's arm. "You're letting flesh think for you," and he put his hand to his heart and then to his mind, "let your heart and mind choose."

March pursed his lips. "Sure, I have," he said, lifting up his hands, "and I think I want a wife and a mistress."

Miguel studied the craggy face of the man. "Have you been drinking again, Marco?" His tone was a mist of apprehension settling with a stinging sensation upon the face of the accused.

Marco shrugged his shoulders as he rubbed a silver wrench with an oily, red rag, and then held up his index finger and thumb to form a small slice of space, and then said, "Poquito."

Miguel opened wide the man's bloodshot eyes and smelled the man's tequila-soaked breath. "We have told you about this, Marco—no drinking here; never! And in the morning—what possesses you, amigo?"

Roberto came back, and hearing the conversation, immediately took Marco by his shirt collar and escorted him off the base, and then came back, angrier than when he had left.

"He is finished here," Roberto said.

"He is a fine mechanic," Miguel answered.

"And a finer drunk." He picked up the greasy wrench. "Paco did not come in today, so it is us, little brother."

"Isn't it always?"

Their father had died long ago, and Roberto had helped raise Miguel and his sister, Conchita, while attending the University and working, and then after joining the military, and working; but now the world was upright and the road much smoother, for Roberto had a beautiful wife and two children, and Miguel was an officer, like his brother, and their mother still was back in the Sierra mountains in northwest Chihuahua, living comfortably.

"Well, what about Maria?" Roberto asked, as the two walked around the jets. "When, little chicken, when?"

"Hey, I am no chicken—just cautious!"

"Cautious, really? You have wooed her for two years!" He held up two fingers for emphasis. "Two years—and you act like a married couple!"

"I am afraid, if you must know."

"You," Robert said, laughing, "you are afraid of nothing! This is the kid who jumped off the La Quebrada cliffs and dived seventy feet into the water below—on a whim! This is the kid who beat all the village elders in a one-hundred-kilometer race when he was only sixteen! This is the kid who soloed in a plane with no lessons; you, afraid—no, little brother, never," and he waved it away. "I choose not to believe it."

"I don't fear the moment," he said fondly, "that I can beat and pound my chest and just do what my body tells me, but it is the moments after marriage that are like jumping off a cliff every day—all day long!"

"And sometimes you live, little brother..."

"...And sometimes you die, big brother!"

They laughed heartily, then, for it was a time to celebrate the good things of the world, of the Mexican world, that was shaking off the frozen revolution of the Institutional Revolutionary Party, the PRI, that had once put chains around their peasant feet, that now had a slowly emerging middle class, and oil discoveries, and a preferred hope and desire for better things.

Miguel watched his brother work on one of the two-seater F-5F Tiger II with its 20 mm guns and two laser-guided missiles, and he watched with admiration and respect, fully acknowledging him as his mentor and wise councilor.

Twenty miles away, on a rural road, two police cars were engaged in a high-speed pursuit of two black sedans, passing the burning husks of police cars that had been swallowed hole and chewed up like peanuts turned into peanut butter, with many dead and wounded bodies inside and outside the carnage; but the officers inside the speeding squad car would not dare to stop now, impossible to stop now, especially at this precise moment when so much responsibility had been laid upon their sinking shoulders, for it was not merely the sedans they were following, but a large, gray tanker truck.

And then, there it was, the state helicopter downed, impossibly downed, a majestic flying machine impossibly lying in a crumpled heap, its hull smashed, its wings twisted, its occupants dead from the surface-to-air missile that had just clipped its rotator blades and sent the big bird plummeting to its fiery death; but the two patrol cars did not stop now, not now, could not possibly conceive of even aiding wounded officers now, not even their own men, not when so much responsibility lay upon the shoulders of so few, for not only did they pursue the sedans and the tanker, but cars that played suicide blocker for a tanker that was filled with a highly flammable liquid that if ignited could take out a city block and leave a hole the size of the Arizona meteor crater.

So, you see, they had to catch the sedans and the tanker and abate the progress of this caravan of horrors, or all of it was lost, the entire way of life for this city, this State, this Country; but then the inevitable happened: the men in the sedans shot their cannons and the missiles took out the last two patrol cars, and all was lost, just as the officers had secretly known, for they knew what few others knew, that too often the criminal is better armed than the lawman.

But hope was not on a meter, not apt to expire as long as the heart of Justice beat inside the officers downed; indeed, one of the men, his name would be forever known, and recorded, as Diego Juan Ramirez Montoya, even as he lay crumpled in the steel clutches of death, picked up the dispatch radio and called in the report, and his heart sank as he heard that the only available police cars and helicopters were still twenty minutes away. He let the black radio fall with his bloody hand and then let his bloody head lay against the hot black cushions of his seat for a moment of desperate thought, and when the desperate thought swept around the possibilities, he saw one chance only, and so made the call on his CB radio.

"Diego," Roberto said, pleased to hear from his brother-in-law, but in a moment he was unable to talk anymore as his face turned ashen white, but then shouted toward the hangar, "Miguel, fire up the Tiger," his countenance still in the awful grip of incredulity and shock; and then his voice was wrapped in a tender embrace as he talked again on the two-way radio. "Yes, yes, I will tell Juanita; yes, yes, I will tell your children, too, and Margarita; yes, yes, I will, Diego, I will not fail, but I must go now, good friend." He slowly dropped the black phone to the receiver.

Miguel was running about, preparing the jet and glancing at the grave demeanor of Roberto, but he knew better than to ask questions now.

Roberto ran up to him. "We have to go now, with missiles ready, and machines guns, too, with one plane only!"

Miguel was caught up in the tumult of the unknown, the thrill of the unexpected and the expected resultant combat as he and Roberto got inside the blue-and-white sky bird and ignited the engine.

"We have no time for tower clearance, no time for command clearance— no time," Roberto cried, as he and his brother donned their black helmets and looked down the runway; and his voice was a calm shaft shot through a tempest storm. "Diego says there is a tanker full of an explosive liquid that is heading toward Rivera Elementary School in Cuernavaca, and that every police car and every helicopter failed to stop it, and that any reinforcements are too far away to stop them—ten minutes, Miguel, we have ten minutes to get there."

"Ten minutes," Miguel said, as if in a trance, as he nodded his head, and the jet increased in speed down the long runway.

"No chain of command now, little brother, no time now, it's just you and me, yes?"

"Yes, Roberto," he replied, obediently, and full of certitude regarding his brother's judgment and actions.

Yes, the proper authorities had notified their supervisors, and their supervisors had attempted to contact the base commander, but, you see, he was at his daughter's school watching her dance in a bright red and green and white dress while the music played and the children sang and the banners proclaimed Mexico's Independence Day; yes, it was this sacred holiday now and festivities were high and the citizens were vulnerable, and not at all thinking of ill tidings—not today, not on this special, prideful day, boasting of their victory over the Spanish in 1821.

There were kinks and gaps, loops and gaffes in this chain of command, and still, contact was made with a base commander, and jets were scrambled, but it was all too late—too late, much, much too late as the pilots, who noticed a jet missing, leaped into their iron mistresses and put fresh fire into their iron bellies.

And now, back to the F-5F Tiger II, which was blasting the thin air around it into shreds and slices of burnt marshmallow puffs behind it, with its spear-like steel nose piercing the air and its trapezoidal wings slashing through the icy, churning winds, at a top speed of over sixteen hundred miles per hour, and it was like a diving, swooping eagle commanding the deep blue sky.

The school sat like a baby eagle safely in its warm nest, secure in its little house and confident that Mother Mexico would always protect it.

And now, back to the terrorists in the tanker, who were part of a larger plot to teach certain government officials their particular code of immortality—they were confident in their tight compartment, and hopeful, too, that their long-ago, carefully-planned-out plot to harm as many Innocents as possible would be successful; they had even cut and jammed all communication to the school to ensure their ghoulish triumph.

But that swiftly approaching shaft shot from heaven's mighty bow was fast approaching its quarry, and soon sighted it in its radar as the antagonists neared the periphery of the school ground.

"Lock," Roberto said, sighting the black tanker in the missile radar.

"Ready," Miguel said, from the back seat.

It seemed too facile, the pitifully sluggish tanker against the mighty F-5F—no contest, as Roberto switched on the controls for the laser-guided missiles and then pushed the red button fire, no struggle at all; but then the sparrow did not fly, held fast in its belly, having been jammed and left hanging by a drunken mechanic—now, perhaps, there seemed a small struggle as Roberto, after checking the missile system and all the missiles, activated the 20 mm cannon.

The tanker moved a little closer to the jet, closer still to the inviolate school ground, looming a little larger and seeming more powerful.

And as Roberto, streaming with a bright and shining equanimity, sighted the target and pushed the red button to fire the cannon, it still seemed like no contest, no struggle at all, between a pathetic, barely moving mammoth tanker and a powerful F-5F fighter jet that was equipped with thousands of rounds of 20 mm bullets; but then the tiny steel messengers did not go forth, for they had been inadvertently jammed and hung into oblivion by that same not-so-romantic, drunk mechanic.

Now, it was a struggle; now, it was a contest between a hulking, fast-moving, nearly-to-its prey, dark tanker truck, and a defanged, declawed, helpless iron eagle.

But all was not lost, for it must be remembered that a hero falls in battle not for one war but a thousand wars fought in a thousand places in a thousand worlds by thousands of brave men and women who know they too must be prepared to die so that others will one day do the same in the never-ending, epic struggle for Freedom.

"Miguel," Roberto said, his gaze locked on the growing tanker, "you are my brother," his words were tucked safely under the wings of filial love.

"Yes," Miguel said, melancholy, gazing in frustration at the peril ahead.

"My brother, best friend, I love you, Miguel, my good brother."

"Yes," Miguel answered, too wanting to express his love for his brother but fearful of something lurking behind his vision.

Roberto reached back with his now-gloveless hand and clasped the gloved hand of Miguel. "Tell Mama I love her…" And then his hand came back and Miguel went up into the air…

"No," Miguel cried, in horror, screaming in panic and terror as he was swept up and away as he tried to watch the F-5F Tiger II scream down upon the enemy.

"No, Roberto, no," Miguel cried, as he became a human scream, without a body, a shrill, passionate shout thundering through the heavens that seemed to be a voice coming from an infinite, never-healing wound in history.

No, he cried, as he watched the magnificent stallion of the scalded sky bore like a guardian angel into the now-wicked-looking tanker; no, he cried, as the magnificent explosion sent flames bursting forth in burgeoning orange plumes; Roberto, he cried, as his white parachute of brotherly love drifted down to earth; Roberto, he cried, as he sped toward the burning wreckage, and ran straight into it, crying, Roberto, Roberto, Roberto, only to be repulsed by the extreme heat of the flames; but still, he searched for any sign of life, crying, Roberto, Roberto, Roberto; and then the next thing he remembered was being pulled from the smoky wall of carnage and being taken away by ambulance.

Today, at the exact site of the Battle for Freedom, "Batalla por la Libertad," right in the middle of the road, there stands a large bronze base, a small but exact bronze replica of the F-5F Tiger II with two bronze pilots inside it, and the inscription reads thus, "For those willing to die for a greater cause, Liberty and Democracy, Mexico honors you.

"Roberto Noel Vega Cervantes, born 1967, died 1993."

No one who has ever driven that dirt road and who has knowledge of why the structure exists ever once complained about detouring around the monument and off onto the shoulder, a road that was never widened to accommodate the statue, a sculpture that would never be touched by any human hand who knew why it was there.

Antonio stopped his tale.

A thousand stories told a thousand times on television and radio, cinema or print, may move the listener to shed a vicarious tear, but one that, before it can reach the ground, may penetrate the warm cheek of its host and descend into the bloodstream to be recycled again for the next time a sad song is played, so it might form in the abused duct to be shot out like a signal flare once more; but a story of woe and suffering told a by a teller known to the audience, even if the audience has heard many such stories—especially an audience beholden to each other—is a story that penetrates beyond fleeting bias for evincing ostentatious emotion.

And so what are we, but like a planet as it is formed: by being battered with a bombardment of space debris—we too, from birth to death, are bombarded with people and places and things, events and illusions and reality, and we grow, physically and intellectually and emotionally and spiritually, a massive collection of inner and outer physical scars that somehow combine to make us pleasing to each other, and only the most skilled onlooker can discern when and how and by whom we become who we are, and recognize our scarred self-brother and -sister, in each other.

No man wished to speak, for private pain is not always profitable for airing; and so, the Crusaders disbanded and went to rest, and the next night, after more exploration of the Tassili N'Ajjer region, and more games of competition, such as rope climb and stick-fighting and wrestling matches and foot races and rock and log moving and throwing, and all things gymnastics and muscle, strength, and endurance building, they met once more at the campfire.

Some of the men from Moses' legion stood up and announced that they intended to depart and return to their families.

"We have been here too long," Horatius whispered, as he leaned closer to Rustem.

"Complacency," Rustem whispered back.

"What chance have we—we, who are so few," Henry cried, still sitting; "can we take down a nation, where other bigger armies cannot? Can we continue to fight militias and armies and hope to survive? It is a miracle—praise the impossible—that we still live, so I say we take the miracle with us and go home."

"What's stopping you?" Arjuna shouted, standing and gesturing toward him, but it was a command, an invitation to leave. "What can I do to help you leave," and he threw Henry his canteen, "go!"

But Henry, spokesperson for the dissatisfied, was not yet satisfied. "We will go, but we want to know about the others."

"That isn't your concern, now, is it?" Arjuna shouted from the other side of the campfire. "Just take your fellow minions and go!"

Henry scowled. "You aren't in charge here, Indian; you're a temporary guest in Africa."

Arjuna smiled. "Yes, well, I wouldn't have to have come if you hadn't let it go to Sheol."

Henry stood up like a shot, cursing Arjuna, and pointing his outstretched hand against him. "It is foreigners like you who come here and corrupt our governments and enslave our people and kill them with poisonous factories— your kind, Indian," and he let his hand sweep over all the Crusaders, "and every foreigner here."

Thus began a tight-rope tug-o'-war where the participants hurled invectives into the antagonist's camp while attempting to stay aloft their slippery, shaky perch.

Moses walked away into the anonymity of the pitch-black night.

"So," a voice descended upon him, "what did you think would happen?"

Moses turned around and saw Conall coming up to him. He shook his head, and waved away the human storm behind him. "I am not thinking of this; this is the moment that must be; but what you and your men have recently taught me— it was pride that held me back from accepting it; and so yes, I know it to be true, now," and suddenly his voice was suffused with frustration, "yet our overarching mission, of Kush—will it all end now? Will our people suffer always?"

Conall spoke in a hard tone. "Did you think you would simply walk into Kush again and defeat the Militia and the government troops and take power with the KLA, a benevolent ruler; did you, Moses?"

Moses stood tall, his burning black eyes narrowing as he scrutinized his protagonist. "You think you know my will?"

"I know the will of men fighting tyranny—they want change now, they desire it with all of their being, they want an end to suffering so much that they are willing to forego the necessary steps to achieve lasting peace; well, change comes swiftly with despots, not so in Democracies."

"Who said we want Democracy, eh? What is Democracy but another form of control over the people, where aristocrats flourish and the poor suffer?"

"You need lessons, Moses, if you are to rule—yes, I said, to rule: I know it is your destiny—but you must not seize power by force; you must first liberate your people and let them decide."

"And who are you to decide my fate, eh? Yes, you have risked much to help our cause, all of you have," and he gestured toward the men, "but it is our destiny, not yours, and must be done our way, the way that feels right to Africa," and he clutched his heart as he inclined his impassioned face toward Conall, as if the very seeing of his ardent desire would sway him.

"And what way is that, Moses—as it has always been? To kill one man and then take his place, and even if you were not corrupt—as I know you are not—it would be your will, not the people's will; and it is they you must serve, or you might as well lay down your weapons now."

"Western ideas," Moses grunted, and then shouted, pointing to the soil, "do not take root here!"

Conall let humility and nobility seed his timbre and tone. "You are the future of your people, Moses, you will lead them—you Moses, will lead Africa back to greatness: it is your destiny—but you must look around the world first and study," he implored, passionately, "the history of the world, of governments, and economies, and political systems, what works, and what does not..."

"There is no time!"

"Yes, my impatient friend, there is time: from this moment till the end of time, it all starts now, with one great man changing what has ruined a continent—a man with a vision—to build a legacy other Nations will follow; someone, one day, must establish this new order in Africa—you Moses, you, are the one, but done the right way, not my way or the Western way, but the way of Natural Law, Moses, a form of government that allows for Truth, and then you go forward—but not before." He stepped closer to the silent, brooding African. "You have an incomplete education, Moses," and he put out his right hand; "let me and others help you complete it and watch you ascend to the proper place of power through the will of eternal Justice."

Moses, his face smoldering from the pangs of realization and shame, stood his ground. "I know what you say is right, Conall, I know it." He shook his hand and let it fall back as he beheld the grandeur of a clear ebony sky set against the jagged puffs and spirals of rock plumes. "Somewhere, Conall, now, somewhere, right this second, as our brethren argue the merits of retreat or attack, some men are sitting comfortably in their chairs and not worrying about the next raid on their home." He shook his head again and closed his eyes. "Nor do they worry about where their next meal will come from, or if they will have their home seized by a tyrant and have his family butchered like cattle." He looked at Conall with a mask worn by great men from centuries past—a mask hewn from the want of Freedom for all people, and his voice was strained with urgency born from the ravages of the present. "I want that for my people—all people—now, right now, I want them to be able to live a normal life like those in industrialized countries; but I know, I know that I must not allow my impatience to destroy our revolution."

Conall placed his hand upon the youth's shoulders. "We will have victory, Moses, and you, my friend, will not be alone, for wherever there is injustice, Justice will rise; and where this is, good men will hear the call, and be joined by others, for Man forever seeks to be free."

The two men shook hands, and spoke at length about what was to come.

Moses' words were dressed in wonder. "I have much to learn." He laughed. "I want to start now, right now!"

Conall laughed, too. "You teach me, and I will teach you, son of Africa."

"Son of Ireland," Moses returned, smiling largely.

They then turned toward the human conflagration behind them, both of them smiling, as if they understood the other's thoughts, and summoned Mwindo, who promptly came, and the three of them conferred; and they proceeded to walk back into the center ring and thus absorb all of the volatile emotions that were being bandied about, and thus enable the three leaders to emit a dazzling display of energy that diverted all eyes to them.

Moses would speak first, for whatever was to occur, he would have to finish it; his voice was sharp and clear, like a tossed spear through icy air, his words like sharp daggers while dissembling old arguments and weak prejudices, and after acknowledging the obvious route back to Mwindo's homeland first, he said, "We will march on the Democratic Republic of the Congo."

Every Crusader felt a flash of electric current purchase his utmost attention, sealing their mouths shut, sucking their arms to their sides, seating their leaden bodies to their rock thrones.

The DRC had always been the next objective, as it had been discussed in the desert and in this mountain resort, but never had anyone opened up a dam below this notion to allow it to flow freely into the open forum.

Leaders whom men willfully follow share common traits, and such leaders who lead together form a symbiotic relationship, as they begin to think strategically and socially as one, just as two separate muscle cells that beat to a different rhythm, when placed together beat as one.

"We will prepare our tactics," Moses said.

"We will reconnoiter the area and contact rebel groups," Conall said.

"We will gather arms and food and water, and radios," Mwindo said.

"And now, we will speak of this war we are making," Moses declared, perfectly in tune with Conall and Mwindo, none of the three men once interrupting the other as they proceeded to speak, as if they had been forged into one dynamic fighting organism, but three voices of it.

Thus, it all began, the formulation of how and when the Crusaders would resume their Sacred Mission; and as the ardent voices rose up like thunder promising rain in a parched land, nary a word nor syllable nor gesture of protest emanated from any of the valiant soldiers, but only the enthusiastic voices of warriors eager to do what they were born for—battle, in the never-ending struggle to free Innocents from the eternal chains of servitude.

Old Friends

In another week's time, the Crusaders, their health fully restored—all muscle tissue and emotional tissue, too, restored, their spirits revived, enthusiasm for fighting high, and their passion to combat the forces of darkness that were a pestilence in the land motivating them to live; and as the plan of action was known by all, every man understanding his unique role, they set to move out from this perfumed garden sanctuary for which they had developed a deep affection.

And during their entire stay, no outside visitor had touched this ancient soil, as any stray desert adventurer was, with proper diplomacy, dissuaded from entering.

It was a Monday, and the men were assembled around the cold campfire; it was afternoon, and swaths and streaks of puffy clouds were strewn across a bluebonnet-painted sky, and the Crusaders were packed and ready to go forth as the three leaders stood before them.

Conall spoke. "Today, we are eighty-three, tomorrow, six hundred, and the next day, six thousand, and then a city, a country, a continent, for liberation from bondage allows men to see the world as it should be, not as it is—it has always been so, it is so, and always must be so, until all men live without tyranny and injustice; and I say to you now, if you pray, pray now; if you think of your loved one, think of them now; if you have courage, summon it now, so that when battle comes and you are in the robust soul of Fury and Fire, you will find solace therein."

The men dispersed and sought favorite spots in the mountain park, under the ancient mammoth trees, in cool caves, next to rock walls, near pristine streams, on jagged cliffs and in groups, or alone, a few whispering, some talking, many silent; and thinking of sisters, friends, brothers, and lovers, country, Creator, mother and father, and this they did until ethereal, smoky, violet-immersed dusk perched upon their shoulders and woke them from this splendid reverie with a gentle kiss, and then they all came back to the campfire and took their respective seats.

A low shout wafted down from the mountain top where Finn sat with his infrared binoculars aimed skyward; and Miguel, as sentry near the north entrance, also alerted a Crusader who was some fifty meters away, who promptly ran to the campfire, and shouted in a hoarse whisper, "Plane."

The Crusaders took cover and waited until Finn decided radio contact was safe.

"Something landed in the fourth quadrant," he whispered into his two-way radio.

Miguel approached the beeping object that lay ensconced in the sandy soil as if it were a small rabbit, then he stooped and picked it up and marched it to the campfire and handed it to Conall.

The object was a small steel capsule with a tiny electronic beeper welded into its oblong-shaped body. Conall opened it, let drop a small scrap of paper into his waiting hand, turned it over and, upon reading it, smiled so largely and with so much joy that the men, who knew him to be possessing a mien of classic stoicism, were startled.

He looked up, still with this curious elation spread across his beaming visage, and briefly told the Crusaders about Robert Heimdall, and then, in pleasant remembrance, and nodding, held up the handwritten paper as if it were an object more powerful than any weapon.

Yea, it was.

"You," he read aloud, his voice booming with pride, "are not alone—R."

Eleanor, who instantly recognized, as had Conall, the single initial as her old friend's, hugged her husband.

Conall looked up, defiance and certitude in bounty upon his countenance, and cried in Arabic, and in the other relevant languages, with equal fervor, "Force and right are the governors of this world…"

"And force till right is ready," the Crusaders responded in English.

The journey back through the scowling Sahara began that night, but at least, a vastly shorter one this time.

"It is better," Abebe said to Jon Paul as they rode their yellow camels through the outer region of Tassili N'Ajjer, "not to know when Mister Robert will arrive to help us."

"That is the silliest thing I ever heard," Olaudah interjected. "I want to know exactly where he is right now."

"But it is exciting not knowing if he is here," he said, pointing north, "or there," and he pointed west, "especially if the enemy is also coming—what if we know he waits in Tibesti and we need him now? To me, it is also very exciting."

"Yes, I see," Jon Paul said, "there is always hope."

"Yes, yes, I see—how dumb is that," Olaudah said, laughing. "Be practical, Abebe, we need to know if we have reinforcements—this isn't a child's game."

"I don't trust this Mister R," Henry interjected, sneering, "especially an American—they're all imperialists…"

This cast a black pall over the Africans who were listening, and resurrected the anti-American sentiment as it was espoused by government officials and village elders who blamed all the ills of Africa on powerful "empire-building" nations.

The men rode on, and those who suffered abuse by their dromedaries came to give the spitting, squawking, biting beasts, with a cantankerous attitude, more respect.

"Where do you think he will meet us—how did he find us?" Eleanor asked Conall, as they rode together.

Conall was peering into the blank canopy of night above them. "Robert deals in advanced technology, specifically communications and visual technology, and I am certain he used satellite tracking to find us."

"Do you really think so? I mean," she replied, still holding his hand as they rode side by side, "why didn't the Country Three use it?"

"It is the same reason their economies suffer—Horatius has told me as much: these nations here do not create much new technology, nor acquire much from other nations—they are too closed, and have too many rulers and regulations that prevent their own firms from becoming modern, and most importantly, the rulers are too busy stuffing their own coffers to care about the future—and yes," he said, nodding as he acknowledged the outer reaches of the hemisphere, and he pointed above, "there are his eyes—ever present, watching over us—and I believe he will meet us in Chad."

"Why not before? Why not in Tibesti?"

"He isn't a citizen here, Eleanor; he has to be careful about aiding an army that is perceived as mercenaries."

"Robert is a good man," she mused, and then looked lovingly at her husband. "I have been fortunate to be have been around good men—I suppose it is the way it is here, that there must be good men here to do what needs be done—and for that, I have been truly blessed to have made their acquaintance."

He leaned over and kissed her. "And I have had the good fortune to know many good people here—I suppose it is the way it is here, that there must be good women to do what needs be done." She leaned over and kissed him, but then he said, "You know you cannot stay here, my love…"

"I can't leave you, Conall, I cannot—I cannot be the wife who runs far away to the safe States and anxiously awaits the news about her husband." Her emerald green eyes were moist with piety as she looked upon his grand figure. "I have never lived my life running away from problems, and you know I never will—so, please, my husband, tell me where to wait for you nearby, and I will."

He took her hand and kissed its smooth softness. "There is such a place, in Kenya—Abebe and Jon Paul have told me of it."

She was pleased that he had thought of it even during the battles.

"I do not want to burden you while you pursue this Mission."

"My love, without you, I may have not have survived."

They were silent for a good while as they rode underneath the valley of black sky, twinkling stars as if spun from the sweet breath of lovers in love, and as if stars spun from crystalline diamonds, and then she whispered, "My love, when it is all over, and the victory is assured, and you are sure, come to me."

"I will come to you, Eleanor of Britannia." Her smile increased his love for her. "Why, Eleanor, my darling wife, did you marry a man such as I?"

"When I first beheld you, there in the Red Cross camp, I felt as if I was looking at a part of my lost self, as if—as if I needed you, to better understand not only the world but myself."

"But the fighting," he protested, meekly.

"When one is in love," she whispered, her head slightly tilted as she adored him, "it no longer matters what the loved one does or where he comes from or how he came to be there," and her voice became joyous, and full of loving caresses, "because when two people really love each other, they become as new creatures—and the past disappears and the present is theirs to achieve, the future is theirs, to live in; we will grow as one as we share our lives through all kinds of times, good and bad; that is why I must be with you, because without you, no matter where or what you are doing, I am alone in my past, and my present, and my future," and she reached out to touch his face. "You are my destiny, Conall, and nothing no one can do or say can alter our wondrous union."

He kissed her lovely hand once more. A brief smile came to him, one that changed his entire physical posture from rigid and tense to relaxed and easy; and his hard countenance from highly alert and highly focused to a soft, murmuring, blessed tranquility and gentleness; and his mind from savage to caring; and his entire being sloughed off the warrior soldier in the theater of battle to adoring husband in the architecture of solace. "I love you, Eleanor, I love you." He could feel the lust for a calm life in the fragrant breezes of civilization wafting back into him, and he felt himself being pulled down from his mount and into the soft cushions of an established routine of a soft, normal and safe life.

He leaned over and kissed her and held her fast. "Temptation, my love: it argues against this life, it wants to subdue me and settle me into a life, ordinary—but I cannot, you know I cannot; I cannot do that any more than you could live a life ordinary; it is our fate, then, my love, my darling wife, to be in those places that people are repulsed by when they hear or read of them, places that make them shudder and gasp, and make them thankful they are living the good life ordinary; but not us, not yet, not now, for we cannot betray what internally drives us to do what we know we must, if we are to make peace with ourselves—we cannot deny the heritage of our hearts, that seeks to deliver others around us from their torment: it is who we are; where others talk, we act; where others stand aside, we go forward; where others imagine, we achieve; and so, we cannot rest now, not yet, not now, not until we feel we have pleased that part of ourselves that is more concerned with doing what is right than easy, the immortal soul that strives to be the Perfect; so, then, should we."

She was, and would always be, a good soldier's wife, which is to say, she understood she must never, under any circumstances—or for any reasons whatsoever—inquire as to the nature of warfare, of its organic effect on his psyche; and when he did make mention, as he had back in Tassili N'Ajjer, of hyper-violent, mind-altering, space-burning, history-warping actions that, once done, tilted the planet more toward Justice, she listened patiently and did not interrupt.

They rode for another thirty minutes before he spoke again, as they were communicating silently, in a way only two lovers can, by the heart only, their hands clasped with each other, their minds, too, and when he spoke, she discerned that his thoughts had gone back to that grim kingdom wherein dwelled prisoners and poets of battle.

"War," he began, his voice seeming to rise upon the hot vapors of lingering combat, "must be, for there will always be iniquity, and if it is not met with sufficient force, it spreads." His face was ravaged by uncertainty, and then was relaxed by justification, and paralyzed by fear, and then relaxed by enlightenment—it is a cycle all good warriors live as they move from battle to battle, this need to understand the taking of another life, and yet, every good warrior knows that too long under its tutelage, and one grows limp and hesitant. "War," he said, again, "neither makes you brave or afraid, strong or weak, great or small—but this, war, it makes you either right or wrong; and when you know you are right, you truly know, you cannot turn away—ever."

It was a conversation between two people whose private thoughts about each other lived in a temple of adoration and devotion.

After some rumination upon his words, she said, with great solicitude, "Righteousness guards the one whose way is blameless."

They contemplated the visage of each other, and as they read these facial muscles and noticed the slightest upheaval in this sober mask their conversation had manufactured, they burst out into laughter together, each of them shaking their head and frowning as if to make amends for digging too deep in the well of philosophical analysis.

But then she said, still smiling as she looked up at the brilliant sky, "What do you think we will be doing ten years from now—I mean," she said, shyly, "if we had a house?"

"We'll have a house, Eleanor, my love," he said, smiling, and then nodding, contemplating her query, and looking into the pitch-black horizon; and then, as if in a trance, "We will be doing the same thing Dylan and Rhiannon are doing now—helping the most oppressed, the poorest, the sickest..."

"Rhiannon is so different from me—she's just like you and Dylan, a true warrior—but you're right: my sister and your brother are volunteers in their community, just like we were at their age." She halted. "They're only seventeen years old—how young they seem to us, and they are only six years younger than us." She held his hand for some time as they listened to the snort of the camel and the soft crunch of its foot in the sand slush, and the low tone of talk of the men about them; but when they spoke again, all of this receded into a nether world that could not penetrate this house of joy and fidelity that their loving words had built over them. "Do you ever wonder what men and women of our age are doing—in the UK, America, in Ireland; what do they worry about?"

Now, he looked ahead of himself and behind himself—but chronologically speaking—and he considered her question. "Do you think," he said, looking at his beloved, "they ever think about people like us?" He watched her shake her head. "They consider themselves, but we consider the world—but one day, we will live among them."

"And we shall still consider the world as we watch our children grow."

"Yes," he said, nodding, and then smiled, as she too smiled. "I do not mean to say we are greater than others; it is just that this is where we must be right now, and others are where they are right now, and one day, may get to where we are, and we, where they are." He smiled again, and she could see his joy abound. "But we will, Eleanor, one day, see our children grow, we will."

She admired his humility, his sense of decency, as he was certain not to tear others down if only to build up his own image with their shattered pieces.

"One day, my love, we will have our honeymoon—one day," he whispered to her, and as they held hands and listened to the world, all they heard was their own beating hearts and soft breath and the happy times of their future lives together.

Reunion

Just as a man chases from his home a pack of rodents that was nesting in his attic, and then turns and walks away satisfied, so too did the Nations Three turn around and shake the dust off their bloody black boots after they reasoned the Crusaders had been chased out for good; therefore, there were no violent incidents along the route back to the Tibesti for the Crusaders, who continued to grow stronger in body and mind and spirit, and increase their resolve, and refine their battle plans.

When the travelers came upon the small, clustered rock appendages of the extinct volcano, they felt a pang of home, of sanctuary, of civilization beginning to rebuild itself alongside them and take back the false season they had lived in order to survive, for they had been away too long from the remnants of their brethren and hunted too long by the worst of their brethren; so, it was up the slender slopes of the perforated black stone walls and once again into the deep trenches and once more onto grained, black basalt top, and there—there were the Toubou waiting, like faithful servants, waiting in a catatonic seizure, crippled by crisis, wasted, listless, motionless as they waited for their leader.

Yes, Mwindo had heard of the Nations Three daring to violate the sanctity of his land and murdering his people, but he had constructed an inner prison in his mind and kept this heinous act without form, but now—now, his people told him what the marauding armies had done to the Toubou. It was not the first time he and his people had fought such invaders: he had been involved in the Chad civil war against Libya, and then fought the same government he supported when they attempted to cleanse the land of the Zaghawa people.

His best friend, Oueddei, spoke, as does one who recounts the horrors of iniquity visited upon Innocents—his voice punctured by the iron spikes of agony.

"They came, Mwindo, they came soon after you left, and demanded to know where you had gone—our own government allowed the wolf to come to its own flock—and when we told them we did not know—O, Mwindo, Mwindo," he began, but weeping now, the salty tears of anguish marching slowly down his face and onto his bare chest and then onto the still redstained ground; O, if only the pious tears of people of incomparable goodness could touch the spilled blood and resurrect the Innocent slain there. "We fought them when they got here, we did—we did, Mwindo, as you taught us, we fought them, but they were too many, like an ocean of sand in a fierce storm; we laid down our weapons, though we did not want to, but they would not believe us, and so they began to torture us, and when we did not tell them, O Mwindo, the things they did…" His head fell upon his scarred and still-healing chest, his spring of tears falling left and right as his face swayed to and fro, the silver pilgrims of mercy touching his now broken right arm, and then his now amputated left arm. "Mwindo, Mwindo, what could we do?" he continued, raising his head and lifting his right arm as evidence of his sincerity; and then said, with great shame, "We could no nothing but watch our own people suffer."

Mwindo had loosed the caretakers of his inner prison wherein dwelled denial of the murders, and from his giant head to his giant feet, he became as part of Tibesti—basalt, brooding, volcanic—as he gazed upon Oueddei as if his own body was being dissembled atom by torturous atom.

"Mwindo, Mwindo, but you are home now, and we celebrate your return," he said, the sad tears upon his battered visage transformed now to tears of joy as he dropped the wooden crutch under his right arm and momentarily balanced on his left leg and fell into the embrace of his leader.

Mwindo became unborn. He saw, in his mind's eye, his best friend whole, his best friend healthy, his best friend alive, and now he held a man who had lost a leg and an arm, and had gashes and bruises all over him, just as if something inhuman had attacked him.

One hundred and fifty-three of the Toubou people had died and two hundred and eighty-five were wounded in the wanton slaughter.

Mwindo sat at each grave site of the fallen; he wept sorrow over them, he cried shame, he begged forgiveness; he slept there, he fasted there, he wanted to die there; but in the end, in the fast-moving, uncomplicated, linear end, he had to overcome the agony and sense of failure and join the Crusaders to finish the quest, or truly die.

Thus, once the travelers had their supplies replenished, they moved on, toward Fada, where they might gain more knowledge of their enemies.

There were more happy reunions, and this occurred when the magnificent black stallion Rakhsh came galloping up to his master, Rustem, whereupon he embraced him and kissed his sweaty, long face and patted and rubbed him and praised his bold courage for evading the Nation Three Enemies, as did Conall with Conchobar, and Moses with Son of Al Khamasa, as did all the other masters of their horses, which had been hidden and cared for by loyal and local patriots.

The road to the small city of Fada—where most of the Crusaders now rode on their own horses, while some, like the Tuareg, still insisted upon the dromedary—was quiet, but soon they were halted, as if by an invisible force; for in the near distance lay the burnt and twisted wreckage of the rescue plane that had carried the Red Cross International personnel, of which nothing of value was left, as the Nation Three armies had picked it clean as does the vulture of a putrid carcass.

Eleanor moved past all of the silent and still rough riders and into the boundary of the dead, who lay in unnatural repose, having been upset in their posture by ravaging, two-legged monsters; she would not isolate herself from the presence of carnage, nor turn her eyes from viewing it. "I must be true to myself, and them," she whispered, and dismounted from her horse and walked among the field of fallen friends; and lo, a veil of grief descended over her face as she knelt near them, weeping; and when she had finished her lamentation, she mounted her horse and rode right through the graveyard and out into the grassy terrain, and the Crusaders, riding around the wreckage, rode toward her.

Twilight fell and the bashful stars were awakening as the Crusaders neared the Ennedi region, and they met the Daza, and gained intelligence about the enemy, and stayed there a night and a day, and then left, refreshed; but soon, a lone camel rider appeared, to whom Tyr and Enkidu, and two of Moses' men, and two of Mwindo's men were dispatched, and brought back the stranger.

He wore white cloth wrapped around his slender body. "Salamu alaikum," he began, addressing the three leaders. "I am a friend of your friend."

"Wa'alaikum-salaam," Moses returned, as did Mwindo.

Conall addressed the Toubou Daza in Arabic.

"Who is your friend, friend?"

"Ah, my friend is very private, Conall of Ireland."

Conall scrutinized the stranger. "Your friend knows us well, but we are without knowledge of your friend."

The man handed Conall a small, powder-blue scarf that had two black initials stitched inside it.

"A trap?" Moses said, casually, as if he were at market, and bartering for goods.

"A trap for the hunter," Conall returned, still staring at the dark complexion of the Daza's face. "Lead us."

And so they went, skirting the fringes of Fada, and leading toward the Guelta d'Archei, where the nomadic herders drove their animals to partake of the fresh, cool lake basin therein, the same gorge Mwindo had spoken of in his sumptuous vision while in the hot, closed mouth of the steaming desert.

When the Crusaders were a half-mile out from the gorge, they waited for Tyr and Enkidu and four scouts—two of Moses' and two of Mwindo's men—to reconnoiter the area, and soon, after sending codes on their radios, they came galloping up on their horses, signaling the all-clear.

A lone figure, donned in a white robe and carrying a slender brown walking stick, came riding a dromedary toward them, very slowly and assuredly, as if he were afraid of no peril; and after he dismounted, unwrapped the white cloth from his face; and Eleanor, upon seeing him, leaped off her steed and ran fast and straight into the arms of Robert Heimdall; but he quickly motioned the Crusaders to follow him.

The red clot in the sky of burnished gold had been dragged below the horizon by its increasing wariness and gradually yielded to the black blot of night, which was now full of bluster and boisterousness, and its conceited, white-hot crew presently set up shop to crow about their wondrous properties of glittering light.

The herders were gone now from the gorge as the Crusaders walked in and beheld its magnificent cinnamon-colored rock towers, which were set on either side of a serpentine blue stream and small sand inlets. The men who had heard Mwindo expound on his generous fantasy about diving into the ebullient waters expected him now to jump in, but he merely hobbled his camel and then sat, stone-faced against the broad back of the granite base.

Twenty men, dressed in traditional robes of white, proffered the Crusaders refreshments.

Robert Heimdall proceeded to introduce himself to every man there, in the language of each man, offered in the correct custom, and once this was accomplished, he stood before them as they sat in rows and groups on the banks of the crystalline, gently flowing inlet, and his face was hard, unlike the kindly face Eleanor had known, and when he talked, his voice was hard, unlike the gentle voice she had known.

"I have come here to help you because I am a citizen of the world, and I cannot look away from human violence perpetuated against Innocents—it is my duty and my natural right in accordance with natural law—so, I am here." He gestured behind himself at the numerous wooden crates. "I have what you brave men and women need—I say brave, but that falls far short of who you are; yes, you are brave, but something more: extraordinary." He was talking clearly and decisively in English, and oftentimes pausing for the translators to do their work; his posture, normally relaxed and welcoming, was inflamed with movement—straightening up and bending down and crouching; walking side to side, turning around to occasionally gaze upon the crates; he simply could not root himself in a position of calm, for his ideas were so far-reaching and diverse and punishing to his conscience that he was unable to allow himself any peace.

He was presently wringing his hands. "How—how can Man live and breathe and not help his neighbor in need? Isn't it our heritage, born as a divine decree to shield those persecuted—yes, even at the risk of our own peril—from harm?" His vocal patterns were operating in an absurd range—from nervous to excited, from joy to sorrow. "I know I failed—yes, failed your kinsmen, your fellows—by leaving, but ah, for a better purpose!" He lifted up his right hand and extended his index finger. "One man here," he said, urgently, and he pointed downward, "working with the Innocents is a miracle," and then he pointed toward the West, "but one man far away, supplying many brave men and women, saves scores—scores more."

His face was conciliatory. "I know some of you have doubts about your Mission—yes, I did when first I learned of it—but not now, no, not now, certainly no," and then he cried out, his face convulsing in it, born of a fierce desperation and frustration, "never again."

Eleanor had witnessed normal, rational angry responses from him before, but never to the point where wrath had seemed to gestate in him and fuel his sentiment.

His eyes were normally an isle of tranquility, translucent sapphire of calm, set inside a warmth of milky-white—but now, a storm had set in, and the azure rock was scorched with vengeance, the nacreous sclera suffused with pain.

"Man is a tyrant restrained by God," he said, in a guttural shout, "an abscess deep in the heart of Earth, a sanguinary two-legged beast who hunts its own and everyone else for unrighteous mammon and power." His face was the soul of grief—battered, broken and bruised—his voice seeping out from a deep, bleeding wound he had recently fallen through. "This dimension we live in is neither heaven nor hell, but built by the very foul breath of man—but man in one land is not man in another, and so the dissoluble bonds of brotherhood that exist are shattered, leaving one nation to live in joy and serenity and civility, and another heir to the unnatural elements that grow strong on the fumes and discords of shattered natural rights, who inhale justice and exhale tyranny; and so the law of man is bondage to the institutions that profane natural laws; and so, when a nation, free, does not preclude the violation of natural laws in these arsenals of chaos and bloodshed, other men must impose their will and purchase freedom for those oppressed—thus, establishing patriotism to a higher order and circumventing the finite laws of Man."

The translator had stopped translating; the Crusaders sat motionless, their minds fertile fields for his judicious tenets to take root.

He let his slender hands caress his sweaty face and massage his wet scalp as his head rose up and his tone came down; pain suffused in his speech now, like thorns, bleeding patriotism into the lives of these heroes. "The chains that anchored the last vestiges of humanity have been cut, creating alliances between hell and man; it happened, yes, it happened, and I was there, and I saw it and acknowledged it and demanded aid from the world but—nothing!"

The translators once again translated.

His visage illuminated a wrath of righteousness that had been frustratingly deterred as he moved about and stared directly into the opaque orbs of each man and emblazoned his startling image upon them. His voice was covered in the spilt blood of those longingly crying for Justice. "I was coming up the river in a motorboat at night, to see what I could see, about reports that seemed very disturbing and impossible to believe," he began, articulating smoothly and clearly, his words carved in an immutable script, "and the boat kept hitting big things in the water and the pilot kept ignoring this, so I said, 'Sir, lend me the light so as to see the impediments in the water,' and the pilot, holding a long, slender brown walking stick, said to me, 'No, sir; you won't want to,' so I said, 'I think I must, for to see the impediments therein.' And he said, 'No, it would not do you any good'; so I said to him, 'I will do it myself,' and I retrieved the big yellow lantern and aimed its luminous eye into the languid river—and I saw curious shapes there, that looked like weird dummies or mannequins, and so I said aloud, 'What kind of joke is this, to dump mannequins into the water?' But I think I knew but I did not care to believe it, and he says, 'But, sir, I told you not to expose the light to the water; it will only harm your Western ideals.' And I looked upon him in awe, and said, 'What are you telling me, sir, that I am so coddled I cannot comprehend or manage its burden in my consciousness?' And he said, consigned to sadness, 'Sir, this is not America; when we do harm here, it travels, and without boundary or restraint—it is too much for your civilized mind.' Still, I peered down again into the churning river water at the swollen, grotesque caricatures of real people, and my face seemed to have dropped into the murky depths and swam a while in it, for I realized man's basest instincts there. 'Sir,' I then said to the pilot, quite astonished, 'am I to understand these are human beings in the river?' 'Yes, sir,' he said, melancholy. 'From the killings?' I asked forthwith, which he replied, 'Yes, sir, from the killings.' I closed my eyes and felt my memories, what I held as up and down and right and left, tilt, and I felt the whole world tilt with me—so that, it was as if I were newly born and about to be re-oriented by what I was about to behold, and unable to make sense of the world around me; and when I beheld the face of the pilot—lit by the silvery moonbeams—I saw a human being unimpressed by this gross practice of man's inability to live in peace with persons of a different stripe—a face perfectly calm despite the increasing Holocaust around us—a man who should have been terrified at the puncture in the equilibrium of sanity and decency in his own country, a man who should have turned around and sped away from the undiluted horror; but no, he stared straight ahead, just as if he were charging the boat through clusters of seaweed and dead fish.

"He docked the boat and I remember walking over and around dead bodies that were piled up: dead women, dead men, dead children, dead babies—dead, dead, dead, all of them lying in their contorted death throes—and you could smell this pervasive odor of death—it seemed stronger than the scent of birth, but I know that was a lie, done by its perverse nature—pulling all of your senses in to smell its rank offering, and none of the bodies were moving; I know, I looked. My guide lit a cigarette as he walked around the corpses and asked me if I wanted a smoke, to which I said no, and so he shook his head, and kept the flashlight ahead of us so we would not stumble on who had once been his neighbors.

"We walked up a dirt path that was littered with more corpses, and the closer we got to the house on the hill, the more dead bodies we saw. I then asked him, 'Aren't you afraid of being killed the closer we get to the house?' to which he replied, nonchalantly, 'No—I am not one of them; retaliation from the other side will come soon enough, and that I am very much afraid of; but, you know, I won't be around for that hanging party.'

"I never once looked at him because I still wasn't sure what I was seeing—and yes, I had seen scores of dead bodies in battle, but this was no battle scene, no, it was different from that, it was… an open, living grave.

"And I heard nary a noise, not a muffle, not a whimper, a whisper nor a cry—nothing human, no dog barking, no bird singing—as if… as if the world itself had died, too.

"I ascended the hill, fear and horror my cold shadow as my eyes wandered over people recently living, and recently dying; and as I gained the top of the hill, I saw a house and noticed that it had been broken and smashed, with more bodies at its base: on the porch and in the window, and in the doorway there was a mother and baby.

"'You tell me when you want to quit,' the pilot said, and quickly I said to him, 'I will quit when I'm dead.' I had no intention of boasting, but I suppose my mind had prepared a courageous slogan for any questioning of my tentative manhood. The pilot shrugged his shoulders and took a long drag on his cigarette as we turned west and headed toward town. It was then I first heard the echoes of human voices; I hastened my pace and I soon passed the pilot, who seemed unmoved and did not quicken his pace. 'Sir, you will only confuse them, if you are not with me,' he said, calmly, and somehow I recognized the judicious tone of his admonition—even in this abject terror—and so visited upon my inner self a vision of cowardice, as I slowed down to walk with him.

"I was seeing through a night darkly—that is, no stars were present, as a malevolent black soot seemed to be canvassing the sky; and so, when I beheld a group of young people and commotion up ahead, it was unclear what their intent was: they might have been engaged in tag, or dancing, or any kind of tomfoolery; and then I noticed that my steps were sometimes slippery, and I begged the pilot, who had been aiming the light ahead of us, to shoot the light low, and it revealed blood—not streaks of it, but pools and streams, just as if it'd been raining the red liquid—and I instinctively looked up and wondered if the stars were gone for the thick blood they had gushed from its firmament's big, black, pregnant belly.

"We kept walking around more bodies, and then I could see keenly what the commotion was—mostly young men, and boys, too, and a few young women, were lifting up and bringing down their arms and lifting up and bringing them down like powerful pistons upon other men and women and boys and girls, who had her arms up in desperate supplication against these large steel machetes; and the attackers were hacking these poor defenseless people like they—these people—were overgrown weeds to be cleared from a cornfield—which is, I mean to say, they paid no heed it all to the cries of the victims, and indeed, put great gusto into performing these grisly and very personal executions.

"I began to run toward them—what else could I do, as I was a man—I ran, but the pilot, he put out his lazy hand and restrained me, and said, with a wet cigarette hanging from his lips, 'I wouldn't—not that, sir—you would just join the deceased, and I would lose my boat fees, and for what: you would run into a human chopping mill.' I looked at his smooth face with utter disdain, but I knew he was right, and I said nothing further as we aimed for the American Embassy some distance down the paved road.

"So, we changed course, before upsetting the incensed hackers—whom I could not help watching, as I could not help hearing the horrible screams of pain, and the horrible screams of begging—but all for naught; but, as it was, we turned left, and had made some headway without disturbance, when a young boy—maybe fifteen, not more—came running up to us, his face awash in utter madness, his machete raised and ready to do his master's will—insanity—when my pilot, cool as an ice floe, slowed the boy by an identity card he apparently had already placed in his own hand; and this abated the boy's strike like a magic wand, for the youth lowered his blade and actually smiled upon us, then turned and ran back into the bloody maelstrom; I looked at the pilot, but no words increased their path from my dry lips, so he spoke, strongly, dispassionately, 'Sir, the whole matter comes down to, sometimes, a simple card, since so many of both sides do look so much alike—as you will soon see, when I am side by side with them.'

"We made our way to the Embassy, past gangs of men armed with hatchets, who were killing their supposed enemy—even babies—and even raping women and then butchering them; and I walked past this and noticed that even the police officers were in on these most heinous deeds.

"I stepped inside the Embassy and the American official stared at me as I talked, looking me up and down, and when I followed his gaze, I noticed I was covered with blood from head to foot. I was attempting calm, but it wasn't to be. 'What is the stance of the American government on these killings?' I found myself shouting, to which the seemingly unperturbed, middle-aged, overweight, balding official, after lighting a cigarette, said, and in a voice I shall always remember for its literal transference of information, as if a living machine, 'We don't have one, you know; it's a local affair—stay out of it, let the local government run the entire matter; coffee?' 'Why, the government is in on it,' I shouted back. 'They are behind it all! We have to do something!' To which the official replied, barely lifting his thick brown eyebrows, 'And so, now, we are two,' and he reached over and grabbed a gun and tossed it to me. 'Have at it.'

"'How can you be so cavalier about the whole thing?' I cried, to which he barely smiled, as he sat on his desk, puffing on his cigarette. 'I live here.' By now, he and the pilot were both slumped against the desk, sucking on cigarettes, and I was wandering about the room, unable to contain my emotions, but also knowing that being here was useless; so, I turned around and started to leave.

"'The UN has troops,' the official said, to which I replied as I faced him, 'What for?' To which he smiled and nodded in understanding, and then I exited the obscene place.

"The pilot and I began walking west to see what we could see—anything resembling a sense of order, a coordinated defense against the slaughter; and finally we saw some foreign troops, armed, walking on the far side of the town, but doing no good thing at all, and so I yelled at them. 'You have weapons to protect Innocents—use them,' to which one of the men replied, 'we have orders to yield to the indigenous forces.' I remember wanting to scream at this inane reply, but I yielded to my increasing wrath and moved on, past the youths with machetes and clubs and knives, and their murdering, and their looting, and oftentimes dancing to the next victim, when we saw a group of boys—three, perhaps—crouched down in a semicircle, and as I approached them, I wanted to believe they were bringing succor to a fallen countryman.

"'What are you doing boys?' I asked.

"One of the boys turned, smiling, showing me a big black beetle that was covered in a cloud of big black ants. 'It is unfair to gang up on him,' the boy explained, and turning around, with a long stick, scooted the beetle free of its biting tormentors so it could scuttle away; but then the boys arose and I could plainly see blood-soaked machetes lying next to them, which were parallel to a young woman who was gasping for the very breath of life; and then, in one, abrupt, lashing movement, the three boys picked up their tools of their trade and began hacking away at the woman.

"I cried out—I could not help myself: 'Stop!'

"The boys turned swiftly and threatened me with violence. The pilot, equanimity and his walking stick ever present as his companions, had already taken out three candy bars, and then gave one to each boy and bid them run along, which, incredibly, they did. The woman presently expired, and I was holding her hand when she did.

"The pilot then said to me, 'Candy—as good a weapon as any, right now.'

"How, I wondered, as we continued on, could one naked continent be covered in the soot and ashes of such repugnant violence and corruption, while another is adorned with the garments of tender mercy and Freedom?

"Now, as we walked on, I could plainly see the silhouette of a church in the near distance, and as I was drawn to it, as would anyone during mayhem, as if mayhem is a respecter of faiths, as if mayhem might defer in one age to God and not in another; but still, I hastened my pace as we ascended the dirt hill inside and saw a large group of men engaged in animated debate, and as I understood their language, the closer we came to them, their discourse sharpened.

"An elder man replied, 'But machetes is worse.'

"'Yes, but spears is good, too, you know,' a smaller man declared.

"'Knives hurt more,' said one, 'and they bleed longer.'

"'Use the grenade,' another shouted.

"'No, no grenade—we save it.'

"'But my arms are tired, you know.'

"I was nearly upon them and still looking about for bloodied corpses but saw none.

"'This is tedious work—I want to kill them when they run,' a man laughed.

"'Machetes—it is fast and stronger,' the elder of the men cried; 'we need to move on—there are too many to kill in town.'

"The men agreed on the machete, apparently, and then I found myself upon them and inquired, quite without reflection, where their prey awaited; they viewed me with much suspicion, but upon seeing my pilot, relaxed, then all of them pointed to the church; I felt dizzy.

"'But not there, it is forbidden,' I said, bewildered.

"'Ha! It is the best place because they are trapped like the vermin they are! And they whimper and weep like beaten dogs!'

"And then I thought aloud, 'But you are doing the same thing men from centuries past have done—killing indiscriminately, speaking of methods of killing—why, why, yes, like Hitler and the Third Reich… and Mao Zedong and Joseph Stalin, and… Pol Pot, and Idi Amin,' and then madness seized me, and I commenced to charge them, but then I felt a hard object against my skull and I lost awareness of my surroundings.

"I awoke.

"'Well, sir, it is me, you know,' the pilot declared, smiling shyly at me. 'I poured the flashlight over your skull to save your life; no sir, you did not lose consciousness, you were only dazed for a good time; I am careful that way.'

"The horrible pain was there, but still I looked about, clutching my still-aching head, and upon seeing the open entrance of the church, I rose up, stumbled, and ran to the doors, turned and ran out and fell to the ground, trembling with terror.

"I saw the stars fall from the sky and the moon turned blood red.

"I arose and resolved to enter the slaughterhouse, and did so, and what I saw, I cannot transcribe properly, unless one has lived on a farm and has seen animals tethered to the butcher's block.

"There were heaps of mangled dead—cut, torn, ripped apart—dead: man, woman, boy, girl, and infants, too, murdered like diseased animals, with strength and great effort and passion and a passionate cause; yes, a cre-do suggesting justification of annihilation for those peculiar to the killers; I forced myself to look at every victim, to see the death mask of every face, so I might remember them—so someone might remember them—so I might remember this night in this horror, for the future, for those moments too far away from now when I find myself worrying over things not essential for living; and I did, I looked at each one and lifted bodies about and began to pull them out and leave them on the soft, wet grass.

"'Sir, it is better not to disturb the dead—it won't help them; it will only harm you,' the pilot said, bemused, while watching me and smoking his short cigarette as he sat upon a big tree stump.

"I was getting tired now, but I managed to ignore him—I hadn't the strength to contest a living will now, no, not at all; so I continued hauling out the bodies and laying them side by side.

"'Will you bury them, eh, sir, tell me that? We will be here all night, you know, watching you bury dead who need no burying; what good is it?'

"I was exhausted now, breathing deeply, my chest rising and falling in a rhythmic fury, and I looked over to him as my salty sweat poured into my eyes and mouth; my hands and clothes and shoes were painted in bright red blood, as I said, laying down a tiny baby and its detached parts next to it—like a macabre jigsaw puzzle, 'Burying is not for the dead,' and went on with my chores, and for some, as yet unknown reason, the pilot helping me, hauling out every lost body and limb until the entire lawn contained sixty-three bodies, but then I heard an impossible sound, a cry, a human plaintive wail, and I bounded up in a panic and searched the bodies but found no pulse of life therein. 'Inside, sir,' the pilot nodded toward the church and I ran into the place, and found a small girl wearing the red wellspring of her kinsman over her body as she shuddered and crouched in the dark recesses of the room; now, it seemed, there were no longer dead bodies outside, nor their spilt blood inside the sanctuary, for one miraculous discovery seemed to heal the diabolical split in the universe that hung over us.

"The girl was no more than four years old, covered in slash marks on her back, which bled profusely, and I carried her in my arms as the pilot and I ran to the local hospital in town; there was a doctor coming out of the door, and I cried to him in our desperation, much the same way a man in danger cries to a police officer, but when I approached him, I saw that his face was provoked to gall and bitterness.

"'I am through here,' he said, as if his heart and soul had hitherto left him, and he was a mere husk of cold flesh and brittle bone. I looked into his fiercely black, luminous eyes and saw the hope and joy of eternity slowly expiring. 'They killed them here, there.' He blinked as he gazed at the dying girl in my bloodied arms. 'They killed them anywhere they are—this is not war,' he whispered, frustration fueling his voice, and then despondency bit into his failing desires and shook it until—as if—his words had dripped from the very tormented soul of Africa as it lay upon the executioner's crowded chopping block. 'This is hell unleashed on earth, where no man dares to stop it; heaven knows what would happen if a good man tried.'

"I wanted to tell him I was a good man, that I'd come from luxury, back to Africa when I heard about the slaughter, but he turned and began to walk away. 'But the girl,' I implored.

"He turned and said, his face stoic, his clothes smeared with the blood of countless victims, 'Bury her—there is no one else left to help,' and he turned around and vanished out of sight into a creeping, swirling, anonymous mist.

"I ran up the stairs and saw the origin of his grief, for everywhere there was death—death in the hallway, death in hospital beds, death on operating tables—even the patients had been murdered, even here, in a hospital, as in the church; there was no safe place left.

"'Well,' the pilot said, bewildered, 'there is nowhere else to go for them, now, is there?'

"'No,' I said, numb, 'it is over for this country.'

"Outside again, we found two United Nations soldiers, and they announced to us that they had recently been given orders to leave, forthwith.

"'What good were you, anyway—like a lazy referee in a boxing match,' the pilot said, full of disdain that shocked me, 'where one fighter is crippled, and the other one, everyone knows, has the bloodlust.'

"The soldiers took offense and set upon the pilot, who resisted their assault with a curious mixture of martial arts and stick-fighting—it must be remembered he was carrying a walking stick—and the men, easily beaten, backed off, to which the pilot craftily replied, 'Do not fight a lion if you are not one yourself.' I looked upon my pilot with admiration and respect, as if seeing him for the first time.

"The soldiers turned to leave, but still I beseeched them, for the sake of the girl, in the name of heaven, to allow us to accompany them out of town; they, smirking, ignored my request, until I proffered them a substantial fee, to which they greatly took, like flies to honey; and so we were swept into their false shadow of safety—surely a shadow illumined by clever hands; but we managed to avoid further hostilities toward us, and made it safely out of the city, and I found an International Red Cross camp, and took the girl there and tended to her wounds.

"I thanked the pilot, paid him and bid him farewell; but then he responded, his voice alive with humility and melancholy, two talents I imagined his heart had no position on. 'If it is acceptable to you, I would stay with you, Robert Heimdall.'

"I was astounded, and shook his hands. 'I would like you to stay, Paul,' I said, and here he stays with me now."

Robert stood before the Crusaders, silent now, next to good and trusted friend, Paul, as the translators finished their weighty task.

"Rachel—for that is the name of the girl I found—lived, and at this moment is safe," he said, again, his face—the face of a benevolent benefactor, a healer, a negotiator—now became the spirit of war—hard, unyielding, unmerciful—as he thought of the Christian charity, the same one to which he had taken Naomi and Kofi, to which he now had taken the girl. "The universe must not fall," he shouted, and thrust his hand toward the soil, "not here, not now, not while one good man still stands," and he waved over them all and over Paul, "even eighty-three; God guide us all."

Farewells

When upon a warrior's task, man wields
Pride and honor, his sword and shield;
Into battle, refusing to yield,
Courage and loyalty, forged and steeled,
as he fights in bloodied fields.

Anything daunted was undaunted now, anything restrained unloosed, anything burdened unburdened, after the Crusaders heard the tale of Robert and Paul as the two had navigated themselves through a pitch-black, soot-and-ash, fire-and-brimstone, screeching oblivion, a world that had been detonated into existence by the purest and most high-quality iniquity, its human daggers having penetrated millions of Innocents and left them dead, dying, wounded and wasted, lying in rotting, stinking heaps, lying on rocks and poles and housetops, lying in hospital beds and church's seats, lying in houses, chairs and nearby fields, lying in ponds, rivers and streams, lying in every available nightmarish scene—lying there, a living testimony to the fetters that burn away from man's soul when he deciphers truth from deformed and perverted, and finite reasoning.

Place before a good man a place bereft of order, a moral desert, a living, haunted wasteland where human wolves roam and devour human lambs, that man will rise up, with sword and shield, and set out to do battle with the foe, for it is in his heart and soul and mind to do so, as it is in the heart and soul and mind of others, but many who choose to sit idle and detached from a safe distance, like spectators at a lynching, who suppress it out of laziness and selfishness and fear.

Thus, the Crusaders soon moved on, bidding Robert and Paul, who were going back into the killing fields to keep the cinders moist, farewell, and also Eleanor, who presently walked with her beloved alongside the cavern streams.

"Crocodiles," Conall said, as he pointed to one of the scaly reptiles skimming along the water.

When she spoke, her voice was buried in gloom. "At least, animals know who eats whom—they don't become what they are not. What kind of world would it be if the snake became the mouse, and the mouse the snake, all because of who ruled whom?" Her words were digging into the deep trenches of history to uncover any sensibility. "Order exists there, at least—unlike human beings, who cannot trust their neighbors, one day to the next." It was time now for her to weep, in the arms of a man of surpassing strength, on the shoulders of her husband, who was confidant and wise counselor. "On our left and right, we have friends, and the next day, they are our enemies behind us—how, Conall, how has this come to be?" Grief cradled her pain in its generous carriage. "You heard Robert: after they shot down the Red Cross planes, no one in the international community did anything—only words, Conall, they issued only words, but can words build a prison and courts for the murderers? Can words build troops, or feed the poor, stop these wars, or bring Justice? O, my husband, I feel we are so alone here, so alone, so very alone, against an insurmountable enemy while the greater part of the earth sleeps; and when they do awaken, politely turn their heads so they will not have to be reminded of their own humanity, and see their own failures."

The brown, toothy crocodiles wiggled along the shore, warily eyeing the strangers, then disappearing into their watery lair to hide and hunt.

When a soul, a real soul, a special soul that is born of love and joy there, and is bathed in resplendent rays that come from every act of kindness it renders to the world, experiences pain, genuine pain, a special pain that is born of love and joy there, and is bathed in the resplendent rays that come from every act of pain it sees in the world, and attempts to ameliorate its own pain, then that soul will cry out for understanding, and yearn for solace and seek to heal its wounds.

The soul of Eleanor wept sorrow, and reached out to its mate, its soul-mate, and in turn, its mate returned solace, for there are times when a grieving soul needs only to be heard and held.

A soul of love cannot long exist in disharmony, as it cannot perceive why the other world of free souls cannot too want peace and serenity, and also seek it in others, and seek to drain conflict, like a festering boil, from other tormented souls; and so, a true soul, a good soul crafted through noble, selfless acts, will, if need be, sacrifice itself, like a perfumed offering into a brood of unclean souls, and, in so doing, cleanse them of their outer filth so they might now better see the shining lamp on the majestic hill and embrace its inherent virtues.

For it is said, it is better that one suffers in order to save many from sorrow.

When again Eleanor spoke, her voice was melancholy, her face reflecting her sadness. "I know you can do much more than I, that only force can change now, and help free millions, while I can only help a minor few, but I still pray for Peace; why can't it just be Peace, Conall, just Peace and Liberty and Justice."

She wanted his reply so her heart might gain his wisdom.

His voice was like the oracle of history, his words wrapping gently around her.

"It takes one man—only one man—to bring about a scourge and destroy his country, but it takes many men to stop him and help rebuild it; and those who were born to fight must fight; and so here is the country, scourged, and here we are—many men and women—to help rebuild it, and this is the way of all things: an appointed time for everything, a time for every event under heaven—a time for war, and a time for peace."

The two young lovers walked back toward the congregation of men and found Robert sitting alone on the edge of the steep embankment of the silvery stream, watching the lazy reptiles rise and submerge in the cool, blue water, and sat down next to him.

His voice was solemn, and weary. "There shall always be crocodiles," he said, staring still into the water, nodding his head imperceptibly. "Yes, there shall always be crocodiles, it is the way of creation; there shall always be men of ignoble character, it too is the way of creation; to fret over this, to want something else—well, is to want heaven on earth." He smiled then, and the two lovers easily recognized the psychological profile of a man they had come to admire. "Yes, no crocodiles in heaven—at least those who prey on the weak—so, here, we must deal with them." He remained silent for a time as he dipped his bare feet into the sparkling liquid. "I know now that I can do more good helping those who directly fight lovers of iniquity than tend only to the needs of those affected by such beasts—but I will still care for them." A distant crocodile made lustful eyes at the dangling feet, and began to slowly paddle toward them. Robert looked at his audience, his vision stretched beyond its physical selves. "I have reanimated my businesses in America, and even now," he closed his eyes, "they thrive, turning out products to give me capital so I can give it where it is needed most—so much money," he opened his eyes and looked at the man and woman. "There is so much money in the world, and so much wasted—wasted on people who do not need it to spend on things people do not need; so much money," he whispered, passionately, and lifting his hands out, palms up, said, solemnly, "And I shall take it from the rich and trample their golden shrines to dust, and give it to the homeless so they might rebuild their homes." The crocodile was too close now and his long snout was opening, and the two lovers were about to utter an admonition but Robert raised up his feet and simultaneously threw a small morsel of food far down the stream, which the animal obediently chased. "The rich are despots unto the poor and uneducated, but against their own, well—but a man removed from his own, comfortable yard, and coerced to distinguish profit from avarice, safety from danger, is a strawman, ready to fall at the slightest breath."

All of them arose, and after he handed them letters, embraced them, and departed to join the others.

Eleanor opened the letter, which was stamped with an address from Rhode Island, USA, where Eleanor's family had moved ten years previous. "It is from Rhiannon," she said, smiling.

Conall opened his letter, which was stamped with an address from Kerry County, Ireland. "It is from Dylan," he said, smiling.

Presently, they were laughing, and managed to forget what grave task was before them.

"Rhiannon, my little sister, still writing to Dylan, and talking incessantly of their love for combat—O, the things of youth that bind them together," she said, smiling.

"Dylan, my little brother, writing to Rhiannon—talking about their love for all things martial arts," he said, smiling.

"And in love..." she said, incredulous but joyous.

"… With each other," he said, incredulous but joyous.

"To be so young—do they know what love is?" she asked, for she felt so old, now. "Yes, they might, if they come faithfully to Love—yes, if you honor it, one might."

He put his arms around her, and kissed her, and the both of them walked toward the rest of the men, where Eleanor blessed each of them and bid them a fond farewell, and then embraced and kissed Conall once more, and left with Robert and Paul to a safe haven in Kenya.

"She will soon be safe," Rustem said to Conall, watching the three travelers depart, placing his callused hand upon the big Irishman's brawny shoulders.

An hour later, the Crusaders were heading for the Central African Republic.

Descent into Darkness

It was young and strong, like a mighty army that spread its ambitious plague across the land, without concession for wealth or status or power of the recipient; having no mercy, reasonable or unreasonable, deserved or undeserved, as it entered into cities and towns, villages and hamlets without even the formality of announcing its malevolent presence, but as it was invisible to the naked eye, it avoided such conventions, and simply settled into the ever-present role as conqueror worm without remorse or conscience; it did not come to parlay, or seek vengeance or reparations for past wrongdoing, but simply to punish and wreak havoc, and without meditation on the age or gender of its victims, nor considering if they were good or bad, happy or sad, courageous or cowardly, but that all of them would bow before the plentiful gore this avenger brought to them and magnify the fear they would feel, the absolute horror that swept them up as if they were mere dust in the wind when they even heard mention of this seemingly unstoppable, inseparable-from-life-here, faceless invader that had embedded its lethal hooks into first a few, then some more, and then many, until it was more than intolerable, and so ubiquitous that every family was affected, every house with a member who was marked for a black death by this shadow creeper; and so the fallen lay in hospitals that were overflowing with them, they who were slowly and pathetically dying without a chance for recovery, where even those who had taken an oath to bring succor to the sick were afraid to touch them. And once the truth was learned about how so many were felled, the true terror shuddered the world, that in the beginning it was just one person who had unknowingly transmitted the contagion to the next victim, that many thought them somehow in on the plot to destroy the world, person to person, man to woman, woman to child; and no one seemed safe when the epidemic began, for the bodies of the suffering were everywhere, waiting for an agonizing death, one more misery here so that families might have more widows, and orphans, or might leave no one at all to carry on the name that had once stood all the ravages of time. So, the thing that came from the primordial forest to consume human flesh had landed first and hard in Africa, and that without prejudice.

The Crusaders were warriors, desirous to fight that which was tangible and a palpable evil that had risen by its own volition and needed to be subdued, but when they came upon the villages of the condemned, where the people were lying in their emaciated, perspiring, writhing death throes, and the women wailed, and the children cried, and entire generations were swallowed alive by this virulent contagion, they felt helpless, defeated, bewildered; what could they do, how could they help, as they were soldiers who used weapons to fight a physical enemy that could be defeated; but now they felt emasculated, drained of courage, helpless, wanting to quit the good fight if they were forced to watch Innocents die. But they vowed they would not run, not evince fear, not back away like common cowards, but as always when something wicked loomed before them, they would trust in God to protect them; and so, they would stop at these villages, and bring solace as much as they could to those sick and aggrieved, and attempt to learn about this illness, and from whence it came. They transmitted much of this information to he who had the resources to effect change with great expedition, and so Robert Heimdall, already in negotiations with African countries concerning this fast-spreading disease, pressed harder upon his insistence to allow his scientists and medical team to study this human holocaust without restriction, and he was granted it.

But even as more aid came from around the world to help battle this new threat to human health, the Crusaders, as they moved from place to place, could not help but feel as if they had failed, and many wept; yet, they comforted themselves with the reality that they were not here to oppose an enemy with physical weapons only, but were against even those things that are purely a product of the mind that appear as a debauchery and perversion of the soul, and any sordid condition that brings pain to Innocents, be it biological or social, for they must always be human, even when they fought with only kind words and deeds.

In the Jungle

That Africa is a continent covered mostly in rich, fertile, lush jungle is a false belief embraced only by foreigners, for the indigenous population, while they may not know the precise proportions, know it is not what has been too often written of in popular literature; for nearly half of Africa is desert, the rest composed of wooded savanna and grassland, and open plain and scrub.

It is with the precious, wondrous, vibrant life of the tropical forest that we now turn, to examine this great mix of flora and fauna, and the effect its unique structure and geographical placement has for a few momentary visitors.

Here, in this luscious, idyllic symphony of unspoiled existence, a refuge from the civilized world of tearing down and digging up and burning out, hustling, bustling, innocent life obediently goes on, as it only knows: to be reared, despite catastrophe and killings, to thrive, despite perils and tragedies, to reproduce, despite death and destruction—despite the steady encroachment of Man, it goes on, as it has in one unbroken timeline from its beginning to the present, as it is all it knows; it has no covert agenda, no cunning plans of conquest, no desire to expand, but merely to survive: these monkeys, these shrews and cheetahs, and many more; and eagles, and hawks and bats, and so many more; and hippopotamuses, and rhinoceroses and snakes, and so many, many more; of red cedars, and palm and rubber trees, and so many more in this infinite variety of unrestrained and elegant life that is integral to the continuance of the harmony of its environs, seeds of joy and health that, once planted, must never be eroded.

Man is capable of cohabiting with this magisterial gift, if he does not take too much, if he learns how to heal the land and give back when he does take, if he honors and respects the living jewels that ask nothing of him except respect and decency.

There are indigenous cultures that exist within the mangroves and the various kinds of forests and habitats, keeping the same existence their ancestors kept: simple and life-sustaining, evincing a deep appreciation and special understanding of their environs as they hunt and fish and climb trees and carve wood, or build structures; it is as much their rightful home as those in the city when they shop, garden, or build structures, for each resident adopts and learns and knows the perils and secret sanctuaries of his community, where they believe they have the right to live as long as they choose—as long as they achieve harmony with those around them.

In the city, one follows agreed-upon legal guidelines, and purchases a lot, and builds a house, and then obeys the rules of the neighborhood and local authorities so one might find solace and peace therein; but in the forest, one does not purchase the land, one merely selects and builds, whether on the ground or in a tree, and then seeks to live in peace and health with other cultures in the arduous existence of hunters and gatherers.

And then one day, when one particular group of forest men were out on their daily hunt in the wild, and the women were out to gather tubers and fruits and nuts, they saw what they had known existed, but which, until now, had had as much relevance for them as city folk if they sighted a grizzly bear in the park; for what they saw was not one soldier, but a mass of soldiers, and other men dressed in city clothes, many of whom were wearing white hard hats as they examined the soil about them.

The men with the wooden bow and arrows, who wore a mere short loincloth and who had had few contacts with people outside of their private biome, were bewildered as they watched the big and noisy machines scalping the earth as if it were its victim to be plundered, and the captured people from other villagers who had been enslaved to dig at the site. Some of the soldiers came up to them to explain what was occurring, but the men did not understand the language, and kept waving away the machines that were rattling the ground and tearing and ripping it apart so viciously and unabashedly, their ancestral flora and fauna, their ancestral family.

It is here that the soldiers raised their rifles and physically pushed the men back toward their dwindling sanctuary. Yet, this was like lions and panthers coming to herd out residents of the city. Therefore, the men of the forest continued to protest, albeit weakly, until they incurred the ire of one of the commanders of the soldiers' detail, who, already having a decidedly unfavorable impression toward these "savages," simply pulled out his pistol and shot two of the men dead, causing the rest to flee into the safety of their mother-nurturer-protector.

The men of the forest watched in horror as the soldiers ignored the two fallen hunters as if they stood next to two dead animals; so, they waited until the cover of night to retrieve their dead, and bring them back to their family. There was much grieving and wailing, and outrage, but the leaders of the small community knew the best course was to avoid any more confrontation with these uncompromising and uncivilized murderers.

But the killers had been bred on the pathogen that violence creates when applied to Innocents, and it is called fear, and what fear gives back to the killers: power, which hatches control, and domination. The land-grabbers had a grand vision that spread far throughout the forest and into and around the small thatched huts and villages there, and unlike in the city, where the law might come with the proper papers if a resident had violated the rules, the soldiers came with their own version of the law for those who had violated no laws, except that the people of the forest were a tiny stumbling block in their quest to mine the forest for its hidden treasures.

The soldiers, unbeknown to themselves—when do human butchers ever scrutinize their own actions?—followed the same path all killers follow: mayhem, debauchery, chaos, and a severe philosophy of madness that is quickly bestowed upon its adherents, and so it began: the soldiers moved in with an overwhelming force, and murdered indiscriminately, and fed their lustful desire for flesh by raping the women, and then burned the huts, and fairly razed the communities to cinder and ash. And then they left, satisfied that no reprisals could possibly come from such backward, Stone-Age peoples, and went back confidently to the site where the plundering of the land continued. But they had made a crucial mistake, thinking that even a "primitive" culture has no feelings or sense of outrage, or would even defend themselves against injustice, and fuel a want of revenge.

Now, at this time, there came a group of wanderers from another direction of this ancient forest, armed with similar weapons as the aforementioned soldiers, but some also with bows and arrows; and the surviving people of the forest, with utter anonymity, scrutinized this group for some time; and if they been able to understand the strange languages of these visitors, they might have heard the following conversations.

"These insects are killing me," one of the lighter-skinned men said, batting away more of the winged tormentors; "how did Tarzan put up with this?"

This provoked much laughter from the dark-skinned men, and one of them finally said, "That is because your Tarzan could never have existed here—he would have been eaten alive, and become as black as I am."

"But what about the natives? How do they do it?" And he slapped away more of the irksome creatures that buzzed about his face. "I would rather face combat than this infernal enemy!"

"Ha!" one of the dark-skinned men responded. "I told you to put on the insect repellent," which was a mixture of the *Corymbia citriodora* tree, and the *Lippia* and *Cymbopogon martinii* plants, "back there to repel the nuisance."

"But there is none left," another of the men cried.

"Even your own countrymen told you to cover your body with ash to deter mosquitoes…"

"Sure, I did that—but it made me itch! I can only take so much! And besides, what about poisonous insects; sleeping sickness, malaria, yellow fever—and parasites!"

"Oh, come now, you're becoming hysterical."

"No, no, I feel," he said, weakly now, rubbing his throat, "like I am coming down with something awful…"

"It's probably a cold, man…"

"How can you be so callous? Five of us have had malaria already—try fighting when you have it; it's no fun. Ask Horatius."

Horatius shook his head. "No fun," he muttered, remembering the lingering memory of fight and flight while doused with the awful poison drenching his body, as he looked carefully now at the suspiciously quiet and thick, difficult-to-penetrate-visually entanglement of flora that was all about him in every imaginable direction. "I would feel better if I could see more than ten meters in front of me…"

"And how about those little monsters back in the mangroves…" Julius began.

"Don't ever mention fire ants and army ants to me again, and as for spiders…they are a living nightmare! I can't wait to get to ground that doesn't move…" Jon Paul said, trembling at the thought of when he and his brethren, where many had been bitten and "re-routed," and gladly, to other places less dense with these tiny masters of their domain.

But then a strange quiet fell among them, for when they had altered their course in this past adventure in the wild, they had come upon a village and rested for a time there and had their wounds and fevers tended to; but here, three Crusaders not only abrogated their vow of chastity with local village women—thereby violating the hospitality of their hosts and incurring their wrath, and in doing so, contracting diseases transmitted in this fashion—they also contracted with these women to smuggle precious gems to a prearranged buyer. When these three men were then set before their brethren to plead their case, they did not evince remorse, but a longing to be freed from the strict code of the Crusaders. Their wish was granted. The Crusaders heard that these men were soon killed by the gem dealers, who were, in fact, soldiers of the very enemy they had been fighting.

Two other men had also lain with some of the village women, but they had shown absolute contrition for their acts, and they were allowed to remain with the Crusaders.

But silence cannot long reign when other matters are of more import.

"Where are Bahati and Denis, Tyr and Enkidu—Bahati and Denis are Kongo, for goodness' sake; they know this area better than anyone. What is taking them so long?" asked Henry, agitated and rubbing his aching and hot neck.

"Maybe they found a mall and had a latte," Horatius said, winking at Abebe, who smiled in return.

"Don't change the subject—I feel sick, and I'm not joking," Henry continued.

"But you're African—aren't you immune to everything that is contagious here; for goodness' sake, man, you live here," Horatius said, exaggerating, walking in from Henry, and smiling largely. "You haven't lived until you've had malaria; you build up an immunity afterward, so you might as well get it now while we're on holiday."

"I need quinine," Henry moaned, clutching his throat now.

"We are out, and we need artemisinin, too," Arjuna said, still walking behind him, "and we also need suramin compounds at the first signs of sleeping sickness."

"Maybe there is a pharmacy up ahead," Horatius said, laughing, looking to his left and right, his rifle on the ready.

"That's right, keep joking; you're immune to one-third of this walking nightmare," Henry said, massaging now his perspiring forehead. "I hope I don't have yellow fever."

"He must be out of his head, to forget about our vaccinations against yellow fever," Abebe whispered to Horatius.

Julius, like Finn, who often helped Arjuna with administering medical aid to the men, was walking near Arjuna, and upon closer inspection of him, looked to Moses and nodded.

Moses nodded to Arjuna, who sped up and attended to Henry, and as everyone now stopped, Arjuna said, "It is malaria."

"Great," Henry said, dejected, "as long as I can lie down right here," and he motioned to the leaf-covered and twig-cluttered trail, "and sleep it off..."

"That's not happening," Arjuna replied, putting his arm around Henry; "we can rest later."

Moses left his position in the line spoke privately with Mwindo, and then caught up with Conall, whispering as both men were studying the landscape, which had presently lowered its high decibels of incessant jungle chatter. "Do you feel it?"

"Yes," Conall said, watching the agitated men looking around.

"If they were hostile…" Moses began.

"… We would be dead already," Conall finished.

Just then, Bahati and Denis, Tyr and Enkidu came moving briskly along the trail, and presently Bahati said carefully, "We are surrounded," and then very succinctly explained why.

Moses and Conall and Mwindo waved everyone to lower their weapons.

"They trust no one," Bahati said; "men with guns are all the same to them."

"We need to show them we are different," Denis added.

"Do they speak Sango or Kikongo?" Moses asked and, receiving an affirmative response that indeed they spoke Kigongo ya leta, cried out in their native tongue, while looking about the tangled growth, "We are your brothers, here to help you fight to keep your homes."

This was met by absolute silence.

"These people do not trust outsiders," Bahati whispered to Moses, as he too scrutinized the thicket, "and even though I talked to one of their elders and told them who we are—and they know I was born near here—they know only that the outside world means death and destruction."

Henry was moaning now as his fever began to eat away at his resistance.

"Tell them," Moses said to Bahati and Denis, "that we have a very sick man here who has risked his life to help people just like them to live in peace, who now needs their hospitality that the people of the forest are known for."

Bahati explained, forthwith, this plea, and Denis packed it with more praise regarding the known kindness and gentleness of the people of the forest.

It wasn't too much time longer that the natives, who were previously invisible to their guests, appeared, armed with bow and arrow, bamboo blowgun, and darts that were tipped with poison from the Arrow frog, eyeing the intruders to their ancestral home with the greatest suspicion.

"At least they have not given us a taste of their pointed little friends," Miguel said, still holding tight his FN Minimi, while eyeing his nervous hosts.

"This is a good sign," Enkidu said.

"They aren't murderers—but they need reassurance," Tyr said.

Moses handed his weapons to Conall, and then placed his arms around Henry and walked him toward the forest people who now stood near the edge of the path; and nodding his head, and looking at one of the male elders directly in his dark eyes, said, "My brother, your brother; my home, your home; your fight, our fight."

The Bakongo man, who belonged to the Kongo tribe, stared hard at the guileless face of Moses, and then at the sickly Henry, then back to Moses, and then reached out his strong hand to feel the hot forehead and flushed face of the sick man, and his stern face crumbled, and compassion grew and settled there as it had formerly been before the land usurpers had arrived. "Come," he said to the men, waving them over to help the ill man, and scrutinizing Moses, further nodded, reaching out his hand to touch his arm. "Follow," and he turned to join his men, all of whom now had lowered their weapons.

The Crusaders did follow, albeit with great circumspection, ever watchful of not only their hosts, but the impenetrable vegetation all around them, uneasy that they were hemmed in, blinded in nearly all of their senses, and now led down an uncertain path; but they needed to trust Moses, as they had done before, and prayed he would succeed again.

The forest people had made a small encampment a few kilometers from their homes, which had been destroyed by the land-grabbers, and it was here that the Crusaders, upon hearing the entire history of these tranquil people, and the horrors recently visited upon them, became animated, and wrath blew its fiery crimson storm upon their faces.

"These killers need killing," Finn proclaimed.

"Justice," the other Crusaders cried in unison.

Yoshitsune sat cross-legged and quiet, eyes shut, and after carefully listening to the sorrowful narrative, began in a guttural tone, "I know such men as these killers," and all those about him grew attentive, and while he spoke, Moses signaled to Bahati and Denis to translate his words to their hosts. "Their souls perished, having putrefied from greed and lust for glory and power; their deceitful eyes see only riches: where we see Beauty, they see opportunity; where we see Joy, they see sorrow; where we see Peace, they see war; what we have, they want, and will brook no remonstrance, and will destroy with fire and terror, and that without mercy; they do not seek to build, but trample underfoot all the good things we have; so, we must requite them according to their evil deeds, lest they take all that is good and tear it asunder." He sat silent for an anxious moment, and then said, solemn, brooding, passionate, "It matters not what they seek here—they have broken the treaty of the natural rights of Man to live in harmony and tranquility, and their bloodlust will never die; so die they must, and with the greatest expediency." He sat there, now, unmoving, his eyes open now, and looking into a warring future in which he knew he must partake.

When Bahati and Denis had finished their translation for the mesmerized forest people, the elder among them arose, with tears in his eyes, walked over to Yoshitsune and placed his hands upon the big man's shoulders, and said, "You are a true Kakongo."

Thus was the powerful stage erected upon which the Crusaders would now play their important role, to serve a volley of war back to those who, as they sought for self-aggrandizement and power, had decided that violating the sanctity of human life was not an obstacle.

Henry received the medicine that the forest people had used successfully for ages, and meanwhile, much reconnoitering was done by the Crusaders and the Kakongo scouts, until sufficient intel was gathered to satisfy the beginning of a stratagem.

Though it did not matter for what reason these land usurpers were here—be it lumber, gold, diamonds, or other products of mining—for "murderers must be recompensed for their deeds," Moses said, it was discovered that indeed, they were in the forest mining for precious minerals. "Instead, they will find death, and that, without end," Moses had continued, and those who had seen him nestled in the tough, sinewy muscle of a living and breathing wrath before were amazed at his hardness now, but it was a layer of armor woven too about themselves that the men welcomed, as if by this current mission they felt stronger, more noble, and more alive.

"I hate injustice," Moses began, standing with Conall and Mwindo near the temporary encampment the day before their battle plans were to commence. "Africa seems to breed every species of it; why are we so cruel to each other; why cannot Man simply be content with what blessed gifts God has so graciously bestowed upon him?" His brothers-in-arms were silent, as they knew that this was Moses' hour of command: his words, his skills, his tactics. "These evil men come for you if they hate your tribe, or religion, or allegiance to others; they come for you if they desire your land, or wealth, or family; they are not as we: they cannot be tolerated, these soulless villains—and these villains here, who we know now are a business: that is all, a business connected to the Big Man of Africa, which is no doubt owned by him or one of his friends or relatives—they think they can take whatever they choose, from whomever they choose, whenever they choose; well," and he grasped harder his rifle, "they are to be recompensed, and without mercy."

The habits of the land usurpers were studied for weeks, and the final plan was laid out by Moses to the Crusaders and the Kongo people, and war was declared upon them. The initial assault would begin when the enemy was in soft repose.

When the soldiers who slept at the ever-expanding wound in the forest site awoke one day in the early, misty morning, they found, to their outrage, that the chained villages were gone; and then they inspected the bulldozers and tractors, which seemed intact; but when the working crew arrived, they were unable to start the engines, and upon closer examination, found that all manner of harsh debris had been poured into the tanks, and the engines damaged beyond simple on-site repairs. The foreman radioed in to his bosses and, after receiving the proper orders back, executed them. "Kill them all," he shouted to the soldiers, as surely as if he were instructing men to hunt and kill some sinister force that had done them grievous harm for no reason.

Twenty-eight soldiers entered a sliver of a biome largely unknown to them, yet thought by virtue of their exclusive doctrine of civilization as a natural right to usurp those they considered uncivilized, and the implicit approval of the King, to massacre any life-form they deemed unworthy, they would succeed; but they only succeeded in failing, and sending a message to their masters that to enter into another person's home with intent to harm would not go down easily.

The soldiers were never seen again.

Two days later, a squadron of one hundred heavily armed soldiers arrived: eighty to enter the forest, twenty to guard the excavating site. They entered in the early dawn, invigorated by a promise of a handsome monetary bonus from the zealous foreman for every dead body or head of the Kongo people brought back.

That night, the foreman awoke to screams and shouts coming from the interior of the now-breached forest edge, and five of the soldiers came stumbling back, three with arrows stuck in them, another dragging a soldier who been struck by a poisonous dart and who was now quite dead; and, subsequently, they described the scene of chaos and confusion in which the impenetrable jungle had seemed to come alive and reach out and grab them and strangle them and stab them and shoot them. And when the angry foreman demanded to know how many of the enemy they had killed, the soldiers could not rightly say.

The foreman, beside himself with rancor, called his boss, who called the owner, the brother-in-law of the now presiding-dictator-despot—until the next assassin took him out and assumed the role of the next Big Man of Africa—who then called the ruler, who then simply laughed, and ordered one of his generals to reckon with these "barbaric, Stone Age natives."

The General sent troops and artillery and aircraft as if he were planning to invade a major rebel camp. The Mil Mi-2 helicopter flew its first mission two days later, with two of the survivors of the second incursion into the forest in the snug belly of the green and brown mechanical beast.

When the chopper was over the region the two soldiers indicated was the attack site, the soldiers manning the 23 mm cannons let loose with a massive barrage of bullets that carpeted hundreds of square meters of the forest; and then, having stopped and readied their hot surprise, presently dumped the big tubs of deadly soup through the open cockpit, and watched in glee as the napalm burst its steel eggshell and spread its horrific orange fire onto the treetops, followed by a steady stream of 57 mm rockets that blanketed hundreds more meters of the forest.

But this was like fishing with a net in a sea of floating kelp beds, for the forest here was so dense, so thick with entangling, entwined vegetation, where sometimes rainwater takes several minutes to reach bottom and sunlight never touches the ground, that the naturally obtrusive effects of these ferocious weapons were blunted, most often their effect not reaching more than sixty meters from their impact site.

That being said, this blind stab at the forest people did happen to wound one Kongo and kill another, who were, against the order of Moses to stay out of the "kill zone," hunting there that morning. The wounds of the one were tended to, the other man buried: soon came an order from the Kongo elders to their people to listen and obey Moses, the warrior-prince.

The chopper continued its indiscreet assault throughout the day, and after two hundred troops were sent in and found no opposition, no sign of the enemy, and reported this to the foreman, he relayed this to the boss, who told the brother-in-law, who rejoiced, and personally thanked the reigning despot, who smiled, and patted the man on his back, proclaiming that "god is good."

But, somehow, this convenient god of his did not seem to care, or receive this convenient praise, or, perhaps, was waiting for a sacrifice of some kind, for, a week hence, after the huge number of soldiers were sent away, leaving only fifty soldiers behind to guard the site, the forces of the forest came alive once more.

During the bright, sunshiny day, out in the bold open spaces, as the bulldozers and tractors plunged and raped closer to the ancestral home of the forest people, and the newly captured villagers, now slaves, dug and tore into the soft ground, looking for the precious minerals there, a piercing noise split the air, proclaiming its defiant message, Go!, as the mighty steel-winged warrior burst into the engine of a bulldozer, bursting its critical inner mechanisms, which was soon followed by more of its powerful brothers and sister, smacking into the internal guts of the machines, ultimately disabling them. The foreman waxed wroth.

A communication line was soon established all the way up to the still-reigning Big Man, and he, now mildly vexed, ordered a sufficient number of soldiers to the area as if he were set to invade a small, rebellious city: five hundred strong, with accompanying weapons and aircraft.

Yet, even though the commanding officer of this battalion had the green light to use any means whatsoever to achieve the stated goals—eradication of any group opposing the will and whim of the King or his appointed officials— they encountered the same problem all invading armies have once coming into unfamiliar terrain: they have a tactical disadvantage, and no amount of firepower or manpower, as many imperial powers can attest, is able to prevail against such realities, as demonstrated: there were too many times when the soldiers, attempting to cut a swath through vegetation so thick they could neither see anything past a few meters or hear anything that was not, to their city-bred senses, an enigmatic jumble of eerie, confusing, unfamiliar sounds. For two days they ventured in, their best trackers attempting to follow the exact scent and markings of their prey, but that led them into the knotty, ropey, twisted intestines of the lushly scented, noisy, cluttered jungle, slowly taking them inside its stuffed and spiraling, inescapable-oblivion entrails, until they were thoroughly lost and bewildered inside this alien landscape.

On the third day, despite the diffident protestations of the men about entering the dark forest, that a thick fog had settled in to accompany the constant rain, the commanders said, amused, "You are in the mountains: what do you expect, to fight only when it suits you? Now go!" So, in they went, in the early morning, looking for an enemy they could not yet see, smell, track, or fight, but they were fitted with an unshakable arrogance that they would prevail against mere savages, who, irritatingly worse, had procured their brother-soldiers' weapons.

But this was more for the soldiers than unceremoniously being dumped into a discomfiting battle zone: it was asking them to negotiate their way deeper and deeper into a frightening and alien monolith that seemed to suck them in and intertwine them into its own fibrous character, to sink them slowly into a widening mire where extraction seemed increasingly impossible the further they moved from their "marker of civilization"—their campsite—all the while anointing them with its singular chemistry and diverse biology, and beginning to reconfigure their senses.

Sometime near the shimmering cloak of twilight, when the troops were frustrated at the lack of engagement, they were frustrated no longer, first contact coming in the forms of poison darts and expertly placed arrows, now digging into nineteen soldiers, causing their brethren to panic and fire in a maddened fury: up, down, left, right, and center, behind, and even at each other in this misty, clamorous, smothering, multilayered confusion. And when the desperate barrage was consummated—one that included grenades tossed and rocket-propelled grenades launched by them—silence managed to slip in for a moment, and clarity was restored to the mother forest. Search parties of five soldiers in three groups were sent in to look for bodies, but all this accomplished was the impossibility of these men ever coming back on their own initiative, as they were soon dead.

The commander forthwith called in airstrikes for two patrolling Mil Mi-2 helicopters to cleanse an area two hundred meters wide in the sections in front of his soldiers and to the left and right as they retreated; but, alas, as his soldiers fled, gunfire erupted in front of their meandering path, stopping their exit, and so fierce was it that the soldiers stopped, and, of course, could not go in the other direction; and so, the commander urged his troops back toward the camp, incurring massive losses as they battled this unseen, constantly shifting and moving and slippery foe to the edge of the forest, where they ran pell-mell like haunted, frightened peasants, back to the cover of their huge machinery. It was then that the commander was informed that the two helicopters had been downed by enemy fire. He promptly called his boss, who called the brother-in-law to the King, who personally visited the supreme ruler, the latter who was now infuriated beyond rational thinking that any of his loyal subjects could be so inexplicably "disloyal," and immediately called his General Chief of Staff, who then ordered a force sufficient to invade a small country.

When the Crusaders saw the enormity of the troops landing, at first monitoring this event with their radios confiscated off the dead bodies of the soldiers killed, but which was soon lost when the frequency was changed, they began their hasty retreat, as quickly as possible, through the thicket, accompanied by the Kongo people, who took even their women and children and those injured.

Yet the enemy was not approaching merely from behind, but landing men in small clearings in the trees, some of them getting entangled and being injured or killed before they even reached the ground, others successful while coordinating with the commanders in the field as the choppers patrolled above, and those in the main force were still moving forward.

But before this, when the Crusaders knew they must retreat, the three leaders conferred and decided to send a small contingency of men to the north to find the Freedom Rebels with whom they had briefly fought against the brutal armies of the King of this country. Abebe and Jon Paul would go, with two Kongo scouts for that seventy-five-mile journey, the men leaving with much hope and fanfare.

The next day, the four men returned, exhausted, saying that they could not get through the closing ring that was tightening around all of them. Two more Crusaders had contracted malaria; four sustained injuries that Arjuna, Finn and Julius could not properly treat; five had a fever of unknown origin with horrible rashes appearing in clusters over their bodies; three Kongo children had died; and the riotous sounds of the enemy were getting closer.

Three days later, after virtually nonstop marching following a fierce firefight that nearly exhausted all of their ammunition, the Crusaders were nearly broken, battered, some sick and wounded, seeing little hope, hearing only the sounds of the enemy patrols above or on the ground, and their arms weary from hacking away at the tangled growth with machetes they had procured before they had entered the jungle; and they were nearly out of ammunition. The guides, the Kongo people, were now in areas even they did not recognize. Finding food and water, at least, was easier, because the Kongo people knew where to look in any terrain with similar plants.

Eventually, the men were forced to rest, most of them sleeping, their heads resting on their backpacks, rifles in their sweaty, bloodied, callused hands.

Conall, Moses and the Mwindo stood on the periphery of the temporary encampment, staring into the great diversity of plant life.

"God is with us," Conall began, "as long as we fight his enemies on earth, we are protected; we will," he said, defiant, "prevail."

"How can you be so certain?" Mwindo said. "Good people die all the time at the hands of wicked men."

"Yes, it is so," Moses said, "but there must also be those who fight to protect His people, and we have elected to do so—we are the elect."

"It is our burden and glory," Conall said, closing his eyes and lifting his head to catch the faint glimmer of bombs bursting in the far distance.

"If He chooses that we die, then we die," Moses said, too closing his eyes and sniffing the air.

"If He chooses that we live, then we live," Conall said, now opening his eyes.

"I should like to talk to your God," Mwindo said, curiously. "I have many questions for him, for I have visited many people and heard of many gods; I should like to know why His story is true above all the others."

Conall smiled. "You will know who He is—when you see Him."

Tyr and Enkidu and two Kongo scouts came back from a long reconnoiter, tired, bruised, hungry and thirsty, but full of vital information on an encroaching enemy that had increased in force and weaponry, facts derived from the two Kongo scouts having ascended a Baobab to its canopy and surveyed a score of helicopters skirting the treetops and dropping off a multitude of soldiers, where they joined other battalions of soldiers as they made ready their assault. Too many to count, Tyr had said. And they are here to stay, Enkidu had added.

Moses, listening intensely, staring at the men, thanked them for their excellent report, and bid them take rest and nourishment, then turned to face the Mwindo and Conall, saying with an uncanny, most assuring confidence, and possessing a remarkable calm in his voice, "We will not die." He nodded. "Yes, we will yet live, for I can feel it," and he clutched his chest, "just as a man who sets upon building a house, but a storm halts his work, knowing his work is not yet done; I know we are not yet done, for a sanctuary we are building will not be destroyed, it is merely awaiting us to resume our sacred duty; for this blessed house we build is not for ourselves, but for the solace of others, and this is why God protects us; we are not here fighting for power or glory or mammon, but to do His divine will, and it is in He we must trust, and thus prevail; yes," he said, nodding again, placing one hand on his shoulder of Conall and Mwindo, "we will prevail, because God prevails." He smiled briefly. "When defeat seems inevitable, and our faith increases, it is then that victory comes, and God rewards the faithful; to think otherwise is to die."

So, the Crusaders, low on ammunition, but plentiful with food—there was always plenty of the white fruit of the Baobab to be had, and water that rested in bowed leaves—and the Kongo people, low on arrows and darts, some of whom were sick or wounded, moved out in the only viable direction, due east, and into rugged terrain without trails, where none of those present had ventured, and without the ability to send messages to the world outside, and where Moses had cried to them as they began, "We are not alone in this fight—never despair!"

The noise that had encircled them was distant, faint, bits and shreds of intermittent echoes, tied together by no rhythm, no logical course, grouped, or single, or scattered, and as time went on, as the travelers crept slowly through the dense brush, the sounds grew louder, more powerful, more distinct, signaling cohesion, coordination, calculation of purpose, this looming leviathan gaining momentum and strength all about them; and occasionally with this came the loud booms of the explosive cargo dumped willy-nilly into the forest from the searching helicopters above.

The Crusaders were one hundred miles from the border of a friendly country. They were hemmed in, outmanned, and without rescue in sight; they halted, and Moses spoke to them.

"We will not die, not one of us," he said with a determined countenance; "they will die," he pointed behind them. "This is faith; they have no faith, their faith in is their wicked leaders; but here, right now, we will do what we must to live until we are victorious; this we must believe." He gestured above. "There we shall place the women and children, the sick and wounded, where no man might think to seek a fleeing enemy; and we who can carry on, will fight; what say ye, Crusaders!"

"Yes," they cried, in unison.

It took some time, but soon the women and children and the sick and the wounded were carefully lifted up from one man to another to a different height of the tree where a Kongo man waited, until they finally reached a man who was near the top, where the ailing person was eventually laid to rest in a high bough that was near the canopy, replete with food and drink, and hidden deep within the thick limbs and giant leaves.

The remaining men, huddled now in the thicket, planned their strategy, and it was soon decided that in order to gain time, they would use several of the grenades they had taken from the soldiers they had killed, and place them as booby traps along the way, where the grenade was covered by leaves in places three feet apart, a piece of twine was attached to them, and the twined stretched at a height of approximately six inches across the path they had covered and finally secured to the sturdy stalk of a plant. Eight such traps were set at various points over a kilometer distance, but none near those who were left high up in the trees.

The troop of men moved out and, after a few hours of hacking a path, stopped, and Moses spoke, entranced still. "We fight until victory is won," he said, assuredly, standing fully erect, and then looking with scorn and contempt in the direction of their pursuers. "We will hunt the hunter," and he laid out his plan, hark: that the Kongo people should presently help the Crusaders to be absorbed into the very enigmatic heart of the forest that only they knew, and to equip the Crusaders with the knowledge and weapons and spirit the forest would graciously yield up as they fought to protect her honor and stature.

When the transformation of the Crusaders was done, when they were smeared with the natural oil of plants and dressed with their leafy green and brown sections to assimilate them into the natural flow and rhythm of the flora and fauna; when they had received newly carved bamboo dart guns and plenty of newly minted poison-tipped darts recently acquired from the ever-present Arrow frog, and practiced shooting them; when the Kongo men had finished carving new arrows, and the Crusaders, all now equipped with their bow and arrows, and blowguns, and their own combat knives, and spears they had fashioned out of fallen limbs, they then heard an explosion of one of the booby-trapped grenades.

"Perhaps two clicks away," Yoshitsune said.

"Good," Moses returned, in a fierce tone; "let us bring death upon these loathsome beasts."

And with that, the men moved out, waiting until nightfall to circle back to the approaching enemy. More grenade explosions were heard.

The Crusaders, despite knowing the insurmountable odds for them, would fight, for they, true warriors and dedicated to their sacred vow, could do no other, as surrender was antithetical to their way of life.

It was a dark, dappled, blotchy, ensnaring night, befuddled with a fog as if oozing from a gash in the fertile forest floor, the kind of cover that beckoned attack from the Crusaders; so, they struck.

There was a Kongo man teamed with each small group of Crusaders as they moved circumspectly throughout the forest, slowly, quietly, crawling in like animal life, undetected as they approached sentries posted about the various encampments.

Each time a guard was killed, his weapons and radio were confiscated, and his body taken to a spot a sufficient distance away, and covered in leaves, twigs and debris.

When the morning came, and the enemy commander counted fifty-seven of his soldiers missing, he became even more incensed, and ordered his men immediately to go forward and annihilate their antagonist, and once again changed the frequency of his radios.

During the night, the Crusaders decided that an attempt should be made to send the same two Crusaders and two Kongo men through the enemy lines, but the men soon returned, reporting that the encirclement of the soldiers was even thicker and larger than before, prompting the Crusaders to pull back even deeper into the forest, but soon they heard the enemy approaching from this direction; thus, they could neither go back nor forward, left nor right.

But Moses insisted, "We will fight until victory is won; you must believe we fight with the fire of God before us!" and so the men readied themselves for the final battle.

"We are not alone," Moses whispered to Conall and Mwindo; "we have never been alone."

Helicopters could be heard overhead, no longer shooting, but dropping men through any viable opening in the forest. The shouts of the soldiers were louder now, their crashing, stumbling movement growing in noise, their language more heated, their promises of vengeance more explicit.

The heavy fog lifted, the intermittent, cool rain continued, and suffused daylight awoke the wildlife of the forest. The battle was imminent. The Crusaders would essentially go nowhere.

They had crossed streams and pondered the possibility of hiding there, but their scouts had informed them that the soldiers were taking particular care to check the water; they traveled around trees, but knew that if they hid in them now, and were found out by the pursuers, their lives were certainly forfeit; they had moved over the land: the leaves and rotting vegetation, the rich, fertile soil, the giant, serpentine taproots of the trees, the twisting, turning vines, the thick brush where the green cycads and copper plants, like the Commelina zigzag, and Chevalierella grass resided in plenty upon the fertile skin of its earth mother, and it was this ancient family of life they knew they must now join, becoming one with such as the Wenge, Sapele and Ebony trees, but in the right places to maximize a sensible and agreeable blending-in and minimizing dectection, a plan they had considered when the women and wounded and sick were still with them, but had rejected, knowing that such a plan required alertness and possible temporary flight, as if in a deadly game of hide and seek. But now they would be adopted children of the spirit of the forest, in looks, in appeal, in substance—they would become more inanimate than animate, more plant than man, more cunning animal than timid, frightened beast, a living, breathing, new species assimilated into the sisterhood and brotherhood of the diverse life-forms about them.

And so it began, the careful transformation of man to a true child of the forest, and the Kongo men would dress the Crusaders now in the proper finery of the silky garments of their home.

Now came the dogged pursuers, chopping and smashing and peering into what they considered every nook and cranny, every crevice and crack, the foot soldier anxious for the handsome reward for the capture of the daring marauders.

The soldiers had been explicitly instructed to check for any connivance of camouflage, by poking a stick into the plants, checking tree stumps, poking the ground, and kicking deposits of decaying matter, like an efficient and meticulous machine that touches any part coming through its mighty gears; and yet, somehow, they missed their objective, simply walking right past it, or, in some instances, perhaps it is better to say, over it.

Yes, some of the Crusaders and Kongo men had gone underground, doing so by first finding a particular kind of Baobab tree that had many trunks fused together to form one colossal trunk whose diameter could not be covered up by a dozen men standing side by side, and whose height was even more, with its long and crooked limbs that grew from the sides, but mainly from the top, from which stretched out scaffolding branches, which had spindly twigs at its ends that were like searching fingers; and then, with a knife, digging at its base a deep enough impression for them to lie in and be covered up with dirt and debris; and lastly, covered themselves fully, with only the precious bamboo shoot sucking precious air as a life preserver. Once their partner Crusader was satisfied that the cover was complete, he then entered into the hollow womb of the towering, aging, giant Baobab and stood, waiting for the approaching storm, ready to see if his partner was detected. It was a gamble the Crusaders made because neither idea seemed reasonable—that the soldiers would miss a buried man or man inside the hollow trunks of a tree—but they hoped the ignorance of the soldiers' knowledge of the forest would aid their deception. But there were not enough such trees in this cluster, and the rest of the Crusaders and Kongo were buried at the base of towering Mahogany, Iroko or Limba trees, a partner helping, then moving to another man who would help him, the last man burying himself.

Then came the heavy pounding of footsteps in the black fog of night, and these soldiers, with guns and flashlights, were shouting, boasting, angry, and promising vengeance upon their enemy.

Even though the first wave of soldiers walked past the hidden men, this was meaningless, for it was like the Crusaders were stuffed inside an active beehive, so many of the enemy there were, seemingly touching everything, stepping on, prodding, poking, hitting, smashing, uncovering; certainly, the ruse would not have worked in the daytime, had the commanders of the soldiers been reasonable and allowed the troops to rest at night, but so implacable had been the King about capturing the rebels that he had ordered a day and night pursuit; and this had brought about lethargy, sloppiness, dullness of spirit, and apathy in the soldiers, and the want of sweet sleep over sweet monies. Yet this had been part of the Crusaders' calculation, a strategy to consider not only how to attack, how to evade, and when, but why, knowing the current mind and physical state of their relentless pursuers.

It really was not an effective or even a judicious method of concealment, this shallow burial, and being ensconced inside the shell of a fleshy tree, but they had nothing else but faith in their chosen God, praying that the righteous mission would shield them.

Yoshitsune was the first to be detected as he stood inside his wooden shelter, caught by the incidental glare of a searching flashlight of a curious soldier, who followed the beam into the woody chambers, only to be greeted by a sharp knife in his gut and a hand over his mouth as Yoshitsune held him tight until he died.

A soldier stumbled upon the loose dirt that covered Finn, and stepped upon it, aiming his flashlight at it as he frowned, and then using a long stick, stabbing at it; he felt a sharp pain in his back, and then death swept solely over him as Yoshitsune hauled him into his Baobab tree just as more soldiers came by.

The soldiers were scanning the trees and brush, and the ground with flashlights, and as they walked, bored now, they could not possibly scrutinize every square inch of terra firma—it was like any assigned task of searching: at first, one is highly alert, ready, waiting, helpful, but as time drags on, and no discoveries are made, one becomes lazy, and the accuracy to detect the slightest aberration is blurred, and ultimately replaced by complacency.

"Check the treetops," the commanders began to say, and soldiers began firing at the treetops; such had the Crusaders anticipated, as the enemy, now frustrated, would consider other escapes for their foe. Soldiers climbed trees, they shed their flashlights on them from on high, and fired their rifles at the canopy, too. Nothing, they all eventually shouted back.

But then it all fell apart for the Crusaders.

There were too many soldiers finding the men in their covert hiding plac-es, so quickly, the Crusaders and Kongo unearthed themselves as they heard the special prearranged, constant call of the African Cuckoo bird, and after more killing of soldiers, they joined together and set to move out against the flow of their enemy.

It was now hand-to-hand combat, each Crusader and Kongo using the knife or their hands to subdue a soldier, and then hastily grabbing rifles and pistols, ammunition, and grenades. This was a momentary occurrence, and could not be sustained, and soon, soldiers shouted of the discovery of their antagonists; now, it was a fast retreat for the hunted—as fast as possible through the brush, through the remaining four hundred and fifty-three soldiers before them.

But this was an impossible flight of successful evasion, for the enemy was too thick in number, and as skilled as the Crusaders and Kongo were, they were being detected, and shot at: three Kongo men and two Crusaders were wounded as the alarm went out and a maddened frenzy occurred as the other soldiers came to get the long-awaited prize.

Then, for some as-yet-unaccountable reason, more gunfire than could possibly be imagined occurred, coming from in front of the Crusaders, and the more they moved forward, the higher the volume of noise; but it was not aimed at them, and it soon became apparent that it was aimed at the soldiers, who quickly forgot about their immediate prize and turned to defend them-selves against a new and more daunting enemy.

Moses heard it on a radio he had taken from a soldier. There were other rebels in the forest. Instinctively, the Crusaders and Kongo lay low, not wish-ing to be caught in the crossfire, and the soldiers ran swiftly past them, but those who discovered them were quickly killed.

By daybreak, the battle was won by the newly arrived rebels, who had been joined by the Crusaders and Kongo as they pursued the last remaining soldiers.

The leader of the rebel group, which was five thousand strong, met with the Crusaders and Kongo people, and related to them what had occurred.

"When first the soldiers of the King attempted to murder the Kongo people, the international community was outraged; this outrage was led by a certain Mr. Heimdall."

"Sir Robert," the Crusaders cheered, and even those Crusaders who had been retrieved with the others from the treetops, who were still recovering from hunger and thirst in their cramped conditions, and even those wound-ed, whispered this praise.

"But the King would not relent, despite threatened UN sanctions, that he was aiding any illegal mining operation and seeking to genocide an indigenous people. It would be his downfall. Three rebel groups combined, and even now, we are fighting our way to the capital."

It was over, the Crusaders had prevailed, but they had lost three good and brave men: Bahati Tansi of the Democratic Republic of Congo, whose grandparents had been involved in winning independence for their country from Belgium; Oluwa Okafor of Nigeria, an Igbo, whose grandparents had fought in the Biafran War against Nigeria; and Raoul Gagnon of France, whose grandmother had served in the French underground during the Second World War; and there were six wounded, all of whom received medical treatment from the doctors of the rebel groups.

"What did I miss? Was the fighting good?" Henry asked, disappointed. "I sure hate to miss a good fight..."

"It makes you ornery when you do," Abebe said, sheepishly, as he handed him a woolen blanket.

Henry slapped him on his back. "I heard you had the chance to prove your superior genetic ability in running; well, next time you have the chance, you will soar, eh, boy?"

"Sure, Henry, I will."

Before the Crusaders departed, they helped the Kongo people rebuild their homes, this time in the trees; and afterwards, a celebration occurred, replete with a feast, dancing, music and singing; and after the Kongo gave handmade gifts and rare treasures of the forest to their honored guests, the Crusaders, with much affection, graciously accepted, and then retired into the seemingly grateful bosom of the jungle, heading toward the next maelstrom where persecuted and oppressed Innocents cried for Justice.

So, the Crusaders had accomplished the impossible, using impractical strategies and desperate tactics they never would have selected if not for the coerced theater of battle they were in; but they had adapted, and now felt more invincible than ever, for they knew that cold logistical facts dictated that they should have died, had no reason to survive such insurmountable odds, and knew that others in similar situations almost always died; so, their logical deduction involved the intervention of the supernatural, and to these men, this was their chosen God.

Diversion

The elephant is a magnificent creature, and we feel close to him because he reminds us so much of what makes us uniquely human.

As it was, there was a mess of men carefully watching one such group of these gentle giants, creeping upon them slowly, perhaps in the same manner scientists do when studying *Elephas maximus*, careful not to intrude on their current behavior, which, presently, was playful between the two elephant families that often met in this open savanna, as they touched each other upon greeting with their massive trunks, and rolled about in the dry dirt and sprayed water over each other from the edge of a cool lake. These men even carried instruments that would aid them in their endeavor, but alas, they were weapons of a sinister nature; and as the men raised them, their faces were raised in a sinister glee as they dreamed of the riches from the precious ivory and hide and meat that the market would bring them; and so, without hesitation, they opened fire upon the unsuspecting creatures, and slaughtered many, and upon approaching these elephants, some not yet dead, did not even deem it humane to finish the massacre, as if they even loathed these creatures that would make them wealthy.

As the men began the gruesome task of removing the ivory from the dead and dying, they were distracted by the approaching presence of a very big and very tall man, to whom they turned quickly and raised their rifles and shouted for him to immediately desist his locomotion toward them.

The big man raised his massive and muscular arms on high, shouting, "Ho there, I am merely a traveler on this road; have you any nourishment for me, as I am thirsty from my walk?"

"Go away if you know what is good for you," one of the men shouted, waving his rifle at the man; "we have nothing here for you."

But the man was undeterred and, smiling, said, "Have you not even a drop of water for me? Will you make me drink from the lake you have just fouled? Please show some hospitality."

When the slaughterers of the innocent behemoths realized the unarmed man was alone and not to be a threat, they reckoned him a pest, and just ignored him.

"Well, what have you there, anyway, eh?" the visitor said, observing the men setting to carve the white gold from the body of the victims. "Hunters, are you?"

One of the men abruptly stood up and aimed his rifle to the face of the man. "It is none of your business, now is it, giant; just go on your way, or you will have trouble."

The man frowned. "I certainly do not want trouble," he answered, and began to move on, but then stopped a few steps away, rubbing his chin as he turned, and saying, "But I was just thinking, at least you could kill the ones that are not dead."

"What!" the same assassin of these helpless creatures shouted as he was about his ghoulish business, raising his bloody knife. "What are you blabbing about; you sound like an old woman—now, you just get, or I will shoot you and remove your teeth and mount your big head over my hearth."

This kind of bravado talk much pleased his brethren, who laughed and congratulated him for his tough swagger.

"Well, you have made yourself clear," the man said, shrugging his shoulders, "you certainly do not care for the well-being of even those you fail to kill by your careless aim and then let needlessly suffer." But this time he was not turning to leave.

The assassin stood up, bewildered, and looking about, as if to look for an answer he was expecting, but then said to the man, waving his knife at him, "You are lucky to be alive, and to tell you the truth, if I knew you were not to be missed, I would kill you right now."

"So, why don't you, man," one of his fellow assassins said. "He may turn us in."

"Not if he wants to live," the assassin said, confidently, and then looking at the man, "You will leave now, or I will put you down like these dumb animals, and maybe you will not even be dead, but suffering for the longest time." This provoked much gaiety from his fellow butchers as they continued their arduous chores.

The man did not move, but replied, "I have just thought of something— what if these creatures you have so ignominiously killed and wounded had a fair chance at defense, what then, eh, my brave hunters?"

The leader of the animal butchers, the first man who had addressed the stranger, who was busy cutting out the hard, thick ivory tusk from his victim, became incensed, and uttered in a profoundly disturbed voice that was more of a grunt than a clear enunciation, not even looking at the man, "You better leave now, before I kill you for sure."

But the man would not relent, and after staring in silence for a moment, said, rather curiously, "I will make you a wager, and if I lose, you may kill me."

The leader said, "Why should I wait on that, when I can kill you anyway?"

The man nodded. "Each of you will hold up a coin between your thumb and forefinger and hold it on high, and if I cannot make them vanish, you may kill me."

The leader shook his head, and then smiled cockily and said, "I am going to kill me a human animal," and as he stood up, so did his peers, and they all took out a coin, their rifles still on the ready, and held it on high. "Now, magician, make them all disappear, or you will."

The big man smiled and slowly lifted his hands up, and then shouted, "So be it, unbeliever!"

And lo, the coins did disappear from the hands of the assassins, but concurrently with a clamorous report that shook the sizzling air as it whistled past their heads; the men knew that only the most extraordinary marksmen could extricate an object that small without a trace of injury to their hands, and their senses were brutalized, and laid them down to couple with shock and confusion, and render their false bravado back into disorganized fragments.

The big man then said, his voice mean and hard, "If you even attempt to point your weapons at me, you will die." But even with this admonition, one man tried, and that man failed, and was soon laid to waste in a bloody heap upon one of his still-writhing victims. "Do you see the folly of not following instructions? So, drop your weapons." The men reluctantly obeyed. The big man moved closer to them. "What I especially do not admire about you filthy poachers is not just that you do not play fair while you slaughter the children of Africa—and I do mean children, for these darling and gentle elephants are as much Africa as you or I; more than you, I dare say." He stood now next to the leader, who was sneering in contempt at him. "First, you must all apologize to those whom you have so egregiously decided to murder, especially to those whom you wounded and would not even relieve their *agony*." He stared at the men as they mumbled something unintelligible at the creatures, and then, bending down to those elephants that were suffering, and stroking the crinkly skin of their foreheads, he said in a mournful voice, "Did you know that these elephants are ruled by the eldest female, while the males leave and roam about alone or together," he moved to the next suffering elephant, and whispered softly, "and they bond with other families, and tend to their sick, and show sadness for their own." He nodded, smiling tenderly. "You should see them take care of their own—like a good family who protects each other from harm; they are so much like the best of us," and he moved to the next suffering elephant, and stroked its pain, "and they communicate through so many fantastic ways—through noise coming from their enormous mouths, or by vibrations on the ground, or smell, or by movement; yes, these elephants are good and gentle," he murmured, and then stood up, and looked with wrath at his agitated human audience. "Perhaps you have mistaken me for a man who must repeat himself; you will say your apology with sincerity, and this time you will bend down to face them." He watched as the men did so, and then, picking up a rifle, first killed the wounded elephants who were still alive, but sincerely apologizing to them first, then gathered up the other rifles, and one by one, broke them violently over a huge bolder, and then said to the trembling killers, "It is the law of the jungle that when a creature is wronged, he will have his chance for vengeance; it is written on the hearts of all creatures, and so it will be done," and he paused, "and I do not believe in coerced apologies." And with this, he walked away toward the forest, and when he reached its periphery, he let out a great barrage of hitherto-unknown-to-his-captive-human-audience, deep, sonorous and bellowing noises that seemed to originate from the very heart of the most elusive and unknown wild; and lo, a rumbling noise began, and then a thundering explosion that presaged a coming apocalypse for the frightened assassins, who soon knew what was to come, and so fled pell-mell, running like madmen even as the avengers came stampeding toward them, and soon catching them and then finally crushing them; and when this was done, these large, gray mammoths came back to their fallen brethren and, yes, seemed to grieve and wail over them just as we humans would do for our unjustly fallen.

The man left, and rejoined his brethren, who too grieved, not only for those fallen noble creatures, but that there exist two-legged creatures who, by their monstrous deeds against the innocent children of the earth, are more animal than those they slaughter without conscience or care, and seem oblivious of what they are doing to what they themselves are inextricably part of: blessed and sacrosanct Nature.

Balancing the Scales

Man constructs a home from the raw constituents of the forest that has been achieved through his own indomitable spirit and irreducible grit to endure; and he survives in the same raw manner, by hunting animals, tilling and planting various crops in the black, fertile soil, foraging for nuts and seeds, fruits and vegetables, and tubers, but never to the detriment of the land, never upsetting the delicate balance that brings harmony and peace; for, he instinctively knows, when something is taken up, something else must go in; what is taken down, another must be put up; what new life is brought must not usurp what life is native, so that the equilibrium inherent in each finely woven and interconnected ecosystem is not permanently disturbed, disfigured, or destroyed.

Now, as there are no other people about, Man wanders a forest that is perfumed and elegantly adorned in the finest raiment of vibrant hues of silky verdure and golden brown and rosy red and burnished gold, obeying the moral tenets of his faith, his conscience, all the sum total of his experiences; and consequently, he is free, as no other man is there to interfere with him, alter his environment in any adverse manner, or challenge his right to possess the land and pursue a joyous and healthy life; thus, Man, alone, exists in bliss and tranquility. This is Man in his natural and most productive and humble state, appreciative of the fruit of his hard labor, physically and mentally and morally strong, understanding the special relationship between Nature and Man: that there must not be radical and permanent chaos; and even though he has dominion over the land, he must not subjugate it to his superior will to devour and change, to subvert, degrade, punish, wreak havoc upon, poison, or pollute. Thus, it must be concluded that Man, here, in order to be free, has certain immutable rights afforded to him, chief among them being Liberty and Property, and a naturally derived Equality and Justice that enable him to pursue peace and therefore attain happiness; nor are there any other peoples to challenge him and abrogate these enlightened concepts that align with Eternal Laws.

Comes another man into the same vicinity of the wild, and conflict may arrive: struggle over land, or personal disputes; and with more people coming, more conflicts may arise, and moral infractions ensue: lies, thievery, kidnapping, murder, slavery, covetousness, fraud, arson, iniquity of all kinds, as the temptation for power and prestige and riches generates a devious imagination in the instigator. Now, Man will enact his own retribution, executed by his own conscience, he being the sole arbiter of how to carry out Justice, as he is, without an established code of jurisprudence, the undisputed law.

When a multitude of people inhabit the wood, then a civil government may come into being: to fashion rules in law, but they needs be in accordance with natural law, which firmly entrusts that Man is given his fundamental, indissoluble rights he inherited upon birth, that are available in his natural state; but that new civil government must protect and serve the people and arbitrate disputes to the best of its ability, and punish the guilty, and provide a safe haven for the people, and provide social services for them, so that people might have the opportunity to prosper and pursue a life they desire: joyous, free, equal, and safe.

A civil government, therefore, exists to serve the people, to ensure that they will not have their freedoms—as guaranteed by the eternal law of natural rights—abridged, obliterated, distorted, deluded, attacked, in any manner, either by allowing others to wage such attacks upon any citizen, or even by the government itself; any egregious act committed thereof by the government that causes harm to its citizenry constitutes a grave failure by that government, and it is in peril of being usurped, as it no longer is upholding the sacred pact that Nature bestowed upon the people, like a good Mother onto her good child, for it has been already implicitly deduced that Man, in Nature, is not subject to unfair and unnecessary harassment—which is to say unjust persecutors—that endangers his innate right and ability to live as he ought, viz, in peace and harmony, while hurting no one, and pursuing a prosperous life on the blessed land.

There was one such government that certainly failed to erect and maintain a partition between those whom it wished to persecute and those who would be persecuted: not only did this government refuse to protect all of its own people, it loosed upon them its restrictive and dogmatic vision of its adopted religion, which was also supported by rebels who embraced the same strict, Orthodox ideology, and so encouraged them to wage war upon several "unwanted" groups of ethnic people they considered subhuman, morally diseased, an unnatural blight, and therefore unworthy of life.

Now, there happened to be a horrible drought in this same country, but in one particular region, it was the most severe—the same area where the "undesirable" ethnic people lived a simple life as farmers; yet, this drought was perceived as an opportunity by the government to further eradicate more of these people, and so, following the dictates of a long-ago-established law that states the strong and arrogant shall seek to destroy the weak and humble, it sent rebels to steal these people's cattle, burn their crops and villages, torture and maim, and terrorize and kill as many of them as possible; all the while, a famine of epic proportions was growing, and even as the resistance groups arose—compelled, as it were, by a natural law that proclaims that a failed civil government must now have its bond severed with the people—the freedom fighters were mostly fighting battles for their own survival, and rarely were able to reach the poor farmers to defend and aid them.

As the famine worsened, world organizations, like the UN, and loving charities decided to bring succor, and were guaranteed access to the drought regions, but their airdrops of foodstuff were restricted to certain areas; and often, when the precious, life-giving cargo was delivered to these humanitarian organizations, the rebels, at the behest of the government, stole the supplies, and sold them to other ethnic people, or other rebel groups they worked with, or unsavory representatives of other countries.

So, now we have what should never have occurred, but factually is: a mass of Innocents dying for want of food and water and medicine, and it seemed there was no Champion to bring sweet, abounding mercy to them.

The ravenous body is its own apocalypse, a traumatic reckoning, the black, cold shadow of impending doom screeching, howling, ripping viciously into itself in a frustrating and vain attempt to survive, like a swarm of voracious rats run rampant inside the delicate tissues and glands and organs, gnawing and biting and chewing every tasty morsel, until, finally, after hollowing out all available sustenance, themselves starving, they tear into each other, and eat one another; and then, in a desperate attempt to stay alive, eats their own flesh and brittle bone; yea, the insular temple of the complex network of diverse cells, built so intricately from birth, its foundations laid out, and then expanded upon as the body grows, will now, as the ingestion of outside resources disappears, turn inward for sustenance, grinding its own muscles and tissues into a grisly, lumpy, gooey powder in a desperate attempt to survive.

And the body, no longer adept at resisting illness, yields: the heart suffers breakdown and begins to digest itself, the sallow skin is covered with hideous, scaly rashes, and an insidious scourge arises, and its name is scurvy; the list increases daily as the body burns, initially, blood glucose, then fatty acids, then protein; as the muscle is broken down to provide glucose, the primary fuel of the brain; as the writhing body begs for the vital, rich, sweet caress of precious food. But no, no food will come this time, for this time there will be no precious cargo from charitable agencies, for certain devious groups have conspired to prevent what is now perceived as a potent, life-giving medicine from reaching the victims; and so, Death, with its sooty and wide plumage, blocks out the boiling heat, and brings a chill to the inhabitants beneath it, rearing its slimy head, and grins a malicious, yellow-fanged grin, overjoyed at the uncanny luck it has had in this normally healthy desert region, and the willful delivery of so many into its greasy, spiked bosom, causing it to salivate and drip a black, stinking ooze, and sing its odious song: "One more, one more, open the grisly door, let them in, there is no original sin, rest your weary bones in my easy inn, we all can win; I'm no hog, one at a time, tell you true, yet here I am, may my humble self be with all of you." It would have blushed, but it had no memory of the act, and so was not certain how to accomplish it.

So, life proceeds out of the plundered body, faster than life can sustain it, and opportunistic death fastens its sharp hooks, already coated with the mottled blood and stringy flesh of other victims, into the weakened form, and begins to tug at it; and now, the outraged ribs, devoid of protective flesh around themselves, poke out in a frightening augury of what is to come. As the arms thin, more bone and muscle hang loosely down from the collapsing shoulders, and the stick-like legs, barely able to support the body's emaciated frame, are covered with infected sores, trembling, and barely able to move slowly about; and the yellow eyes are sunk in deep sockets, the tender abdomen swells, and edema occurs, and vomiting, and another disease comes, and they call it anemia; and the heart continues to falter, as Death, snickering and boasting, increases its mighty grip on the victims; so sings conquering Death, "'Tis so easy, how so easy, never would have considered such a lottery won in this age of high technology and vast plenty; there must be some who are working independently for me; well, bless them, one and all, keep feeding me, and I will feed them—bitter gall! Ho! Ha!"

So, Death finally annihilates one such body, and simultaneously, others, and more daily; the fresh corpses, young and old, pile up, as many as five hundred a day, for no good reason other than to appease the fanatical will of some in this land—one land of many lands—small compared to the rest of the known world, who have prevailed upon the meek will of the rest of the unaffected population, and the majority of people of the outside world to not intervene; so, there we have it, a tiny fraction of the population, albeit those in governance, dominate, and express their dominion over those they detest and abhor through punishment and torture, and now escort them toward a horrible, slow, agonizing demise. These Innocent people have no resources to fight this encroaching terror, and the vast citizenry of the rest of the known and properly functioning world, in terms of their democratic government, and mostly food-rich, cash-rich, military-rich society, says: "Shall we get involved, shall we? Well, here—here is a bit of food … no? It is refused by those in authority, or, if it is allowed, it is stolen by unsavory elements. Well, what to do, what to do; wait, wait, we have our own problems: partisan politics, how O simply exasperating; say, isn't the game on?; scandals aplenty, how perfectly dreadful and shocking; didn't the latest video game come out?; well, sir, how about those foreign wars we fight for no discernible or logical reason, other than to follow some unintelligible and nonsensical thinking that misinterprets the history of the country we have invaded, which we won't soon leave because it just might make us look weak, even though we are still strong; eh, what's that, have you binge-watched the latest television cable-show sensation? It's absolutely marvelous!"

So, who will come and dare to render null and void this alliance between those of seemingly illimitable power, who are bent on destroying those whom they so furiously despise, and their natural rebel allies, who also share this maniacal disdain for the persecuted people, and say: "This stops not tomorrow, but today, and not just today, but now, and right now, and anyone who thinks we are interfering, may they be damned to a worse fate for not trying to stop this accursed genocide."

It is not true that the desert is absolutely a sea of loose and abundant sand, heaps and heaps of the tiny amber crystals: this is the imagination of city folk, but the folks here know better; so, when people here go in search of food during this horrendous drought, they do not step exclusively onto mounds of sand, walk over dunes, trudge in the soft embrace of this lifeless gush, but often, as they track for miles in desperate attempts for nourishment, they step onto hard, desert pavement, for the wind has already taken away the small particles that are susceptible to its strong force; so the people see the rotting carcasses of animals everywhere, lying on a rough brown surface, and the exposed bones have been polished in the boiling sun, the meat having already been picked clean by the birds of prey, and what scraps remaining are finished by tiny insect scavengers. But these are the unburied dead, as they are animals only, and they are everywhere; but there are the buried human dead, in too many places, resting beneath piles of rocks, put there by their loved ones who are still looking for food and water all day; and where do they look, when no water or food is readily available for use, where no green thing hardly grows, nor a river or lake or stream may nourish and offer repose? They will eat what they before never tasted: the scavengers that dine on the decaying corpses of animals, these shameless vultures and hyenas, a new meal will they become for the wandering and desperate people, and when that filthy meat supply succumbs, they will continue to eat anything that is alive, be it root or bark, leaves or hides, or insects they find; they will suck the morrow of bleached bones dried, they will search for days for any crumb of food or drop of pre-cious water, until their exhausted bodies can go no farther. What else can they do, capitulate they will not, a proud, fierce people are they, to survive this horrible famine and killing drought.

There was a seven-year-old girl who weighed just twenty-eight pounds, and was closer to death than she was to life, simply because her fragile body could not get enough vital nourishment to keep her alive; and so she waited for res-cue, right there at the food aid distribution site, under the large, beige, canvas tent, in her grieving mother's bony arms, and even though the food had come, it was not to be. How is this possible? The other five thousand people who had come here for sustenance this morning now had to wait for an indeterminate amount of time, and as they sat, and lay, more of them died; on this particular Monday, eighty-six more died, and the frustrated aid workers, who were fast-ing—having given their only food to those who had the greatest need—some of whom were now weeping, others cursing, others weeping as well as cursing, lamented that they could do nothing but hope and pray for deliverance, as the many tons of aid, which had been so carefully boxed and then airlifted by the Boeing C-17 cargo plane to this very site the night before, had been stolen—every life-giving sack of grains and canned produce, vitamins and medicine, and clean water—by rebel forces who were involved in this most horrific civil war, where the government so hated the ethnic group of its despised enemy that it would starve them if it could, as a means to murder them.

"This is just horrible," a woman said bitterly, walking slowly up to a man who was under a small tent, her face indignant, her camera crew close behind her. "This lousy government won't allow another shipment for at least another week; why, these people can't wait that long! It's murder! And this cholera epidemic is killing as many as the famine! Oh, it isn't right, Jon—we need an interview with Dr. Badri, right now!"

"I tried, Jenny," he replied, "but she is too upset."

"You know the network wants this broadcast by seven o'clock tonight," she said, slender hands on slender hips, and then let her beige-colored, wide-brimmed hat, with the white string around her neck, fall onto her bare back. "I hate this, Jon—I hate the whole thing; I am frustrated that these people are dying because of an easily preventable and treatable disease, and a lack of food and water, it's not right…it's obscene," and pious tears began to well in her luminous eyes.

"I know," he said, and placed his arm around her waist. "It is an evil our Western minds simply cannot tolerate."

"Can't anything be done—can't we call someone?" She then rested her head upon his strong, slender shoulders, her long, auburn hair flowing gently down his back.

"I wish we could, but we are as helpless as everyone else."

"It isn't right! People dying of cholera simply because they cannot find clean water, and in these modern times? It's absolute insanity! Where is the Justice?"

At that precise moment, even as the last word escaped from her parched lips, two figures— with their faces covered, each wearing a long, white, loose-fitting, long-sleeved tunic, and headdress that fell over the shoulder and covered the neck; one tall and big, with the stride of a man; the other, smaller, and walking with the measured steps of a woman—came from behind a large, crescent-shaped mound of sand, moving swiftly toward the tent where Dr. Badri resided, were detained briefly by two armed men, and then allowed in; a few minutes later, they were seen leaving, and hurrying due east, back behind the yellow dunes.

"Who in the world was that?" Jenny said, pulling out a small notebook and pencil from the pocket of her light brown khaki shorts, and beginning to walk toward the tent of Dr. Badri; but once there, she was rebuffed by the two armed guards. "Who was that it was so readily admitted an audience with Dr. Badri?"

But the men refused to comply with her demands, and so she and her husband walked back to their tent, conferring all the while.

"I am guessing that they—I suppose it was a man and a woman—were representatives of the rebels come to barter for a return of the food," Jon said.

"Maybe—but you know as well as I do that they usually just sell it on the black market for quick cash, to further finance their egregious cause."

"You're probably right; the World Food Bank doesn't have the ready cash." He frowned, looking at the scores of fragile people who were sitting, standing, or lying, who were bathed in the sweltering heat, huddled together in their death throes, caring for each other, many caressing those loved ones who recently had died, all of them feeling an impending death that hovered above them, a weight that increased with every passing moment, a weight they knew should never have existed, but that there was nothing for them to do, now, but wait, and hope and pray for a miracle. "Maybe," he said, nodding, "maybe they are here to help."

"It can't be government troops, those monsters, even if it were done for a political ploy—no, they are not interested; so, who else could it be—another freedom rebel group?"

"No, not government troops." He gave her a knowing look. "And Freedom rebels are too far north."

"What about the Crusaders; the last I heard, they were in Nigeria about a week ago."

"You can't trust the grapevine here, too many wrong numbers and lines crossed—it is possible that information was given by the indigenous population to protect their folk heroes." He took out the keys to the rented, camouflaged Jeep.

"I'll get Marcus and Mutabazi," Jenny said, and in another minute, although the two men suggested that the two reporters delay following the figures for the purposes of safety, they were roundly rejected by their bosses; so, all four members of the big television network affiliate, and their gear, were presently in the Jeep and traveling in an easterly direction, but not for long.

After they had driven for several minutes, a lone, armed figure came from behind a large, sloping dune to rest directly in their path, causing their driver to suddenly bring the vehicle to a sudden halt.

It was one of the two mysterious people who had met briefly with Dr. Badri, and it was obvious, as he stood there, tall and lean—even though his face was still covered by his white headcloth—that he was indeed a man; and then he spoke, in English, in an accent easily traceable to this region. "You need to go back, reporters."

"Who are you to order us about?" Jon said, irritated now, standing up. "Are you a rebel?"

"You must not follow." The voice was harder now. "It is too dangerous."

"This is not for you to decide," Jenny said, her face full of defiance.

"You must give me your word you will not proceed further."

"No," Jon said, shaking his head, "we will most definitely..."

But the man, now waving his rifle, motioned to two others—one who was obviously a woman, the same woman who had been with him—both of whom who had been waiting behind the heaped-up dune; and presently they came out, and deflated all four tires of the Jeep.

He then threw a full canteen to the news crew. "You should start back now," and he and the others walked away.

"Are you the Crusaders?" Jenny said, but they did not respond, and soon, their camouflaged Jeep could be heard motoring away.

"Mutabazi," Jenny said, exiting the Jeep, "you heard him—you're from Rwanda: is he a Kushite?"

"Yes, I believe so," Mutabazi said, too exiting the vehicle.

"What do you think, Marcus?" Jon began. "You are Kenyan—is he Kushite?"

"Yes, sir."

"Marcus, you've heard all the stories," Jenny said. "Do you think they are the Crusaders?"

Marcus scratched his chin and screwed up his black eyes. "It is hard to tell, ma'am—you do hear so many stories about them that you begin to wonder if they are just a myth created by the locals; but, yes, it is possible…"

"What do you think, Mutabazi?" Jon asked him, and received a similar reply.

The four of them then began the short walk back to the camp, and as they neared it, encountered another Jeep, one occupied by one of their competitors.

"Need a ride?" said the big, burly, handsome man, smiling as he came to a halt next to them.

"Very funny, Mickey," Jenny said, then climbed into the Jeep, as did the other three.

"Just where in the world were you headed, or need I ask?" said Mickey.

"Where were you going?" Jon said, and then took a drink of water from the canteen.

"The same place you were."

"Really? You're going to visit a refugee camp?" Jenny said.

"Jon—Jenny really needs to work on trying to set another reporter off the scent; very disappointing."

"Give her a point for trying, Mickey," Jon said, smiling at his wife.

"All right," Jenny said, "probably the same place you were, but we had a small problem." She told him what had happened. "And now, please, Mickey, tell me how a veteran reporter such as yourself would proceed."

Mickey pulled off his wide-brimmed, straw sunhat, and slapped his bare knee and laughed uproariously. "Why do you think I delayed my following of the mystery figures?" He laughed again, throwing back his round head.

Jenny looked to Mutabazi and Marcus. "Mutabazi and Marcus told us to wait, but we didn't listen—rookie mistake."

"Mutabazi and Marcus know, don't you, fellows," Mickey said, slapping both of them on their brawny, bare, black shoulders. "They know we're not in some civilized place where people just get in their cars and drive to any destination of their choosing; it's all strategy here; one must be cunning to survive, you're not just driving carelessly along back in the States. Hey, Jenny, newsflash: you're in Africa…"

"Okay, Mickey, wise guy, you've embarrassed us enough," Jenny said, half-smiling. "Now we go, yes?"

"Yes," Mickey said, and they drove in an easterly direction, following the tracks of the Jeep ahead of them.

In about one hour of driving on the dusty, sandy dirt road, they turned a bend, and were met by two armed men and a woman. Mickey stopped the Jeep, and one man approached: the same man who had stopped the Jeep of Jenny and Jon.

"You do not listen," he grunted. "Now, you must come with us."

"Why should we?" Jon demanded.

The man came to rest right next to Jon. "If you do not, then you might be wounded or killed by what is to come."

"Will you force us to go with you?" Jenny asked, standing directly in front of the man.

"No," he said, angrily, "you do as you please; you are either our guests, or you will go back, on foot."

"Fine," Jenny said, and after consulting with the others, all five of them followed the three armed figures to the bottom of the ravine, where three more men—all similarly robed, and armed, their faces covered—offered food and drink to their guests.

"Why are you here," one of the men began, his black glistening skin around eyes that were deep set in a fiery blaze that the anticipation of imminent battle brings.

"Are you the Crusaders?" Jon said excitedly.

The man looked to Mickey and nodded. "He knows."

"You know?" Jenny said.

"Of course," he said, calmly. "Everyone knows but you."

Jenny, bewildered, now looked away from Mickey, and back again to the man. "Are you here to get the cargo back from the rebels?"

"It is as you say."

"We want to film you."

The man grunted. "That would be impossible."

"Then, we mean to write about you, an authentic story, the first detailed interview to be published about you."

"You do as you please," the man said, "but we have business to attend to; we will leave two men to stay with you, so you do not fear for your lives."

"Why won't you be interviewed?" Jenny said passionately. "You're living legends right here; the people love you."

The man stopped, turned around, looked at Mickey, and nodded toward him. "Ask him," and left, leaving the two men behind.

"You know them?" Jon said to Mickey.

"Of course," Mickey responded, sitting down now at the base of the dune, "plenty of reporters have met them, and helped them, too, evade capture by the corrupt governments and soulless rebels they fight."

"I don't believe it," Jon said, amazed. "Why haven't you reported about them—you would get a huge bonus, a literary prize…"

"Mutabazi and Marcus know."

"Marcus, you know, too?" Jenny said.

"Yes, ma'am, I know, too."

Jenny was aghast. "What! What! Tell the two dumb reporters from America what everyone except us seems to know!"

"Ma'am," Mutabazi began, "every culture has its heroes; well, we have ours, but if the authorities were to know who the Crusaders were, where they camped, how they operated, who their contacts were, how they moved, how they got their supplies, how they are always able to avoid capture, it would not only be their deaths, but the deaths of many other people who risked their lives for them, and the lives they would no longer save—because no one else is doing what they do."

"Oh, I don't believe that," she said, frowning, and waving his answer away with a smug facileness that only an outsider could do.

Jenny asked Marcus what he thought about it.

"It is true, ma'am," Marcus said; "the people would never give up a consistent and victorious force for good, such as those who stand between them and torture and death at the hands of their oppressors."

"So, these Crusaders just get a pass," she said, irritated still, and she raised two fingers and snapped them, "just like that," and then wiped her sweaty forehead. "They get to operate with complete anonymity; how do we know if they aren't somehow enriching their own pockets: they are just ordinary human beings, after all, susceptible to all the known vices like everyone else."

A chilly pall engulfed them, as the faces of the listeners, except Jon, fell to sorrow and shame.

"I agree with Jenny," Jon said. "They are a big story; we're reporters—no one is above the law; it's that simple; we don't make decisions on who to write about, everyone is fair game. This isn't the good old boys running the show."

Mickey stood up. "It isn't that simple, not here, not in Africa; you can't believe in the nobility of the Crusaders because you don't believe in heroes anymore; you're of a new, young, cynical generation that has been disappointed by the lies uncovered from the past about whom you thought were heroes, but turned out to be just ordinary, flawed but gifted men and women; well, yes, the Crusaders are just men—and maybe a woman or two—but they are not ordinary, not by a long shot; they are the exception to the rule, and believe me, brother and sister, they will never let you down, because," and he looked intensely at him, then her, "they really believe they are doing the work of God."

"Religious fanatics," Jenny said, taken aback. "What makes Africa such an ironic tragedy!"

"No," Mickey returned, sternly, "zealots harm Innocents, but the Crusaders consider themselves the humble servants of God, and no better than those they serve—in fact, they feel they are the servants of the people—and have vowed to obey His laws, where Love and Charity and Mercy reign, and would rather die than purposely hurt an Innocent."

"Well, I'll believe that when I see it," Jenny said, frowning. "In any case, we have a story to tell." She screwed up her hazel eyes. "So, why did you come, then, huh?"

"To babysit you," Mickey said, and then sat down again. "I have said too much already," and proceeded to pull the large, floppy, light brown hat over his eyes.

An hour later, gunfire began, a cataclysmic eruption, deafening to the five people who were still attended to by the two guards, even though they were a good distance from the combat.

"I want to see the action," Jenny said, anxious.

"So do I, but I want to live, too," Mickey said. "Be smart, and stay here, until the Crusaders do what needs be done."

In two hours' time, the last of the gunfire was silenced; an hour later, the same man whom they had followed appeared, his clothes wrinkled and covered in soil and fresh blood, the barrel of his rifle still hot from the intense fighting.

"You may go now," he said, and waved the two other men to leave.

"It's all over?" Jon said. "I want to see; did you lose anyone?"

But the man was no longer amiable, and his voice was ripped to shreds of pathos, and impatience. "Go!"

The five went back to the Jeep, and soon, even from there, with binoculars, they beheld the awful carnage: nearly one hundred rebel soldiers dead, as were the twenty-two government troops they were meeting to whom they were to sell the stolen cargo; the Crusaders were nearly done loading up the wooden crates onto the trucks of the soldiers.

"All dead," Jenny whispered. "Film this," she said to Marcus and Mutabazi, who did as they were ordered. "It may be unsettling, but this is, after all, war, and it is factual evidence."

"I did not think that you would be foolish enough to film this," Mickey said, and abruptly turned the car around.

"Wait," Jon cried, "the story will go out on all major newspapers: AP, UPI, AFP, Reuters…"

"I won't be a party to it," Mickey said, and punched the accelerator, and drove fast away from the gruesome field of spilled blood and guts, and the death of treachery, but also the continuing blossoms of hard-fought and -won, and great-sacrifices-made Justice. "I should destroy your film," he shouted, looking back at his guests.

"You really are taken by these Crusaders," Jon shouted. "Unbelievable…"

"Film or no film, we still have a story; a big story," Jenny said excitedly.

When they returned to the food aid camp, Jenny and Jon fairly ran to the tent of Dr. Badri to tell her of the wonderful news; and soon, the news spread to her desperate people, who began to grow animated, and once the trucks appeared on the clear, bright horizon, those who could smile smiled, those who could laugh laughed, and those who could raise their arms in delight did so.

As the Crusaders, driving the trucks or their own jeeps, arrived, Dr. Badri met them, and embraced the mystery man, first; and then lifted up her hands, praising all of the rescuers of the precious cargo, and for the captured money that once was to be used for the transaction by the now-dead parties, embracing and kissing all of the men, all the while weeping tears of joy; at first of joy, but then upon hearing of the death of the woman, tears of a profound sadness. And then word spread throughout the camp, that the Crusaders would stay until all the food was given out, and guard any more incoming cargo drops, and the people cheered.

And all the while Jenny and Jon stood next to Marcus and Mutabazi, the last two who were filming the unloading of the crates from the truck beds.

But then Dr. Badri, as she was helping to unpack the boxes, even as the desperate people lined up to receive the precious cargo, saw the film crew, and stood up horrified, and cried out in a loud and passionate voice, wrapped in abject fear, "You would film the Crusaders and endanger their very existence!" Her swarthy countenance was consumed with shock and genuine horror, for the Crusaders had already uncovered their faces.

The people of Kush, their starving bodies hollowed out from disease, some so ill they were barely able to stand, many of whose children had died from cholera or a lack of food or water, or disease, turned toward the film crew, and, as if of one gentle and sympathetic mind, arose, and forgoing the life-giving nourishment, gathered round the Crusaders and in front of them; and when one of the women began to sing out in a proud and defiant voice, "God protect our saviors," they all began to chant it, waving their skinny arms about, holding high their aching and throbbing heads, propping up each other's feverish bodies.

Marcus and Mutabazi stopped filming, and their cameras dropped to their sides as the two men stood still, ashamed, for they were born of this region where the heroes that do exist are betrayed by the true famine of the soul that is caused by a maniacal need for those psychotropic drugs, blood-soaked mammon and unfettered power, or are hunted and killed by the over-whelming forces of darkness that seem never to leave this once-gentle conti-nent, which seems forever marooned in despair and destruction.

And what of Jon and Jenny?

Jon stood there, his face blanched by shock, and then embarrassment covered it, like a heavy cloth, and his body was numb, and he could not speak, so humiliated was he, not just that a whole people of one tribe had united against him, but that he had had to be publicly humiliated to under-stand that what he had done was so morally repugnant, an act everyone else, even the simplest people, understood was wrong. And Jenny, she could see only the suffering these people had so heroically and courageously endured, and now willingly prolonged, to offer a show of loyalty and admiration for their beloved rescuers; she wept for the beautiful souls before her, whose lives had been so incredibly difficult, that they had endured so much for so long at the hands of their wicked oppressors, that these people were simply mere Innocents, who just wanted to live normal lives, but instead were caught up in the calculated and brutal machinations of an inhuman government that was involved in a never-ending battle for political power and cultural and economic hegemony.

Presently, the husband-and-wife team of reporters was holding up their cameras and taking out the film and crumpling it up and ripping it apart, all to the cheers of the Kushite people, who presently went back to the business of attaining their life-giving food and drink and medicine.

Mickey walked over to Jon, and the two men shook hands, and then Jenny smiled, wiped away her tears, and embraced him, and went in search of the mystery man she had first followed; and soon she found him; he was help-ing unpack the crates of food, opening the boxes, and distributing the cans and packages to the eager, smiling, and grateful people, all of whom were very generous in their hearts and kisses to all who issued them, but especially to the Crusaders. Jenny quietly joined him in handing out the packages, as did Jon, Marcus and Mutabazi, and Mickey, too, but said nothing, and she, too, received affection from the recipients, and she was still somewhat embarrassed to receive such genuine love.

When the aid packages had all been handed out, and the cumulus clouds were in shadow as a darkening sky cast her golden rays of a burnished sunset upon the stark land, Jenny, again finding the man she sought, who was now hauling away the wooden crates, followed him; and then, as she was alone, and normally straightforward and unabashed dealing with those she were to interview, was now nonetheless trembling, and said, "Sir, sir, may I have a word with you?"

The man turned around, stood straight up and tall, and said, firmly, "What do you want?"

She felt her face flush with shame. "I just wanted to say I apologize for trying to film all of you…"

"You have done so," he said, matter-of-factly, and turned to leave.

"I will not report about what the Crusaders have done here, but, please, at least tell me why—why you risk your lives to do this, since few others do." She felt somewhat foolish at this question, but she felt it had to be asked.

He nodded, and then gestured toward the people. "These are my people, yes, but they are everyone's people, even yours, even the people in their comfortable homes three thousand miles away; and my fellows who accompany me, they are of many people, yet they feel as I do: that all people who are oppressed are the responsibility of all freedom-loving people, especially those who are free, and we will not rest until people such as those about us are given a chance to experience what you and I have—Justice."

Jenny was trembling with excitement. "I will not report about you now, but one day, as you write about your exploits, when it is all over."

He grunted, and shook his head. "It will never be over, as long as evil men and women seek to do harm to Innocents."

"Do you worry," she said, hesitatingly, "that one day, men and women such as the Crusaders may not fight?"

He smiled, gently, looking around, and then nodded. "As long as there is Goodness in the world, we will fight, and we will win."

She smiled, too, and then, sensing that he needed to be elsewhere, put out her hand, which he easily shook. "I will pray for all of you."

"Thank you," he said, "and be safe," then turned, and walked toward a group of his comrades.

"What did she want, Henry?" Abebe asked, as he was stacking crates one upon another outside of the tents.

"Oh, just to talk, you know, about…things."

Abebe became sad. "I'm so sorry about Mikala, Henry; she was a good woman, and a good fighter."

Henry shrugged. "She was, yes; but it is as I said—this business is not for a woman to endure, and the conflict she would bring…" Yet, it was not true; in fact, he had argued the exact opposite to his fellows so that they would accept Mikala into their small warrior family. And then he said, in a profoundly sorrowful voice, "I too am sorry she is gone," and he turned away so that Abebe could not see his face flushing from a profound and deep sorrow; but, like his brethren, he now began to bury what he considered a weakness, his past affection for Mikala, in his dedicated work.

"Oh, yes, things, there are always things to talk about," Abebe said, deliberately changing the subject, and then smiling, and nodding, then slapping Henry on his strong shoulders. "Have you eaten—I'm starved!"

"Abebe, always hungry; it is because you're always running about!"

Abebe laughed, and then the two men walked away, Abebe with his arm draped over the shoulders of Henry, to join their brothers and continue dispersing the aid packages, and then deciding on where to set up a defensive posture on the periphery of encampment. And so it was for them here, as it was for them everywhere, wherever they went, they would have Justice, and do what needs be done, without harm to Innocents, to secure it; such were the dictates of their inviolate credo.

A History of the World

"I am called Babeth Grace, and I am Brandan; I live in Bambari, near the Ouaka River; I speak many languages, like Sango, our main language, which nearly all speak; French is our main language, too, but more for the city folk, and although I live in the forest, I too speak it, and if you are a Westerner and understand it, I will speak it as I tell you the history of my country. Come and sit, then—you and your friends are welcome; and as I speak and you translate my words, I shall pause, like a lady, for the missionaries long ago taught me manners and etiquette.

"I do not remember much about our long-ago past; the missionaries taught me that my country had people living in it even before the time of the great Egyptians and their pyramids, but there are no written words, and our history is recent, the only history we care about, like a new well brimming with fresh, cool water, among old wells that have gone dry and are forgotten—it is the way of the world: you are young and produce much good and then you grow old and lose your importance and are cast aside; I've seen it happen many times before; I am sure it will happen to me.

"My mother has told me, like her mother told her, and her mother before her, and like all mothers all the way back to when the first Earth mother rose up and kissed the sweet blue sky, that our world lived far away from other worlds, in peace, because we were small and unimportant; and then we came here, to escape the slavers, as did the Baya; and we lived here in harmony with many tribes, like the M'Baka and the Azande, and the Pygmy—oh, there were so many wonderful people, who lived in the rain forest. But then our French cousins came here, and their brothers and sisters came from other worlds, and decided to be our masters—I do not know why they did this; I suppose their own people would not let them do that to them, so they came here, knowing we had no weapons to fight them; it is as it always is: the strong conquer the weak because they can, not because they should. Then, we lost our blessed world.

"My grandmother told me that people will live with a foreign father and mother only as long as they treat them like sons and daughters, so when the French treated us like slaves, our people took back our land, but by then, O sorrow of sorrows, our rulers had learned too much at their white parents' knees.

"All I ever wanted was a good home—see it? It is made of mud and sticks, and giant palm leaves, and a roof of thatched grass, to keep out the rain, and for this, I'm very happy; and I've wanted good food—do you enjoy your gozo and ngunza: they are from the manioc tree, and the fish is from the river; and I have wanted many good friends—you see them around us? They are like my family, and I have wanted a good family: I have many brothers and sisters, and a good husband; and my health is good; and the crops are good, and we have all we need—this is all I ever wanted, until someone came along and said I wanted something else or needed more or I needed a ruler—why do we need anyone to rule over us? Do we not have all that one needs to live and be happy? But then along comes a spider who tells us we cannot be happy unless he rules over us and takes what few things we have from us.

"So, we gained our independence—so the Holy Sisters taught us—from France, but her greedy seed had been planted in many of our own men's minds, and so many men rose up to rule us—but they did not rule us, they enslaved us. There was one man, I can tell you, who took power, but could never have been one of us—he wanted more than gozo and ngunza and fish, home and friends and family: he wanted the very beautiful dirt below our feet.

"I will not speak his name—to do that keeps his history alive, which should be buried in the deepest pit with the snakes and crocodiles to watch over it and keep it there.

"I shall first tell you that he was a ruler for many years, that no man killed him—no brave men and all of my country stepped up, all stepped aside or back; no real warrior does that—and we were at war when this man ruled us, for he was a flying spear through our hearts the whole time.

"My grandmother has told me of the things he has done, and to me, the man is a nasty spider—so now I'll call him spider, because a real man could not kill his own people, for that is what he did, and did often; he would have his own people imprisoned who spoke against him and he would personally beat them and talk to them in prison—this spider did not seem to like people, and made up rules to capture them in his sticky web. He told the people that if they had no job, they must pay money or go to prison, and he put beggars in jail, too; he made us into beggars by stealing our money and then put us into jail because we became beggars—is there no Justice? Thieves have their ears cut off, and a hand, sometimes—yet he was the biggest thief of them all: he stole our money. He stole the money he collected from us and crowned himself emperor—an Emperor spider; I was there when he rode through town wearing a wreath of gold and robe of pearls and shiny, colorful beads, a grinning baboon—yes, this time he is a baboon, for flavor, you see—in a splendid coach drawn by white horses. I was there when he sat down on a throne of gold and had the crown of jewels placed upon his spider's head; and I wondered, who, who will stop him, who? Who will kill this spider who is not a man, so the person who kills him cannot be found guilty—and drain his black blood and bury him deep in the Ubangi River and let our world heal? But no one came forward, no man with a dagger, a gun, spear, a rock— any good way to stop the spider's black heart from pumping black blood that craves what little money and things we have; the people in the village said so that our country needs roads built, hospitals fixed, schools tended to, but because of the spider's coronation, it will not be—and as I said, one bullet would do it all.

"The spider lived on, even demanding that all of the schoolchildren here wear expensive uniforms made by his wife's company, and the schoolchildren protested, and the Teachers protested, and many others, too, and the spider's army came in and killed many, and arrested the children and placed them in small jails and beat and tortured them—and some say the spider was there helping the guards—and many children died, too; so the French fathers came in to replace a spider with another spider, and since then, more spiders have come along, but they never stay too long, because they are always being eaten by the next nasty spider.

"And now the rebels come through and say they need our support against the new ruling fighter, and they will reward us with many fine presents and good roads and new schools and decent jobs if they win, but if they hear that we are helping the ruling spider, they will come back and kill us; and oh, they say, we need to borrow your sons while we fight, and sometimes the village elders say no—and the last time they said this, they were all found hanging with a rope around their necks from a Kapok tree; and so now our villagers help the rebels, and when the ruling spider found out, he sent his army here and took twelve women and hung them from the same Kapok tree.

"It is always the same: one man rises up and rules over us and kills us and then another man rises up and kills him and promises to make things better but he still robs us and kills us—I don't know, but it seems to me that we do better without anyone rising up at all, and everyone just leaving us alone.

"I have heard that your men fought against the rebels who took our boys, and against the army that took our children—I will pray for you always, since now you have two armies hunting you until you reach the border; yes, food and supplies, and a safe passage through the forest will be given to you by our people, for your kindness will be honored and remembered; and so I bid you a pleasant journey and victory against those unholy things that lurk in the jungle..."

"Well, it is good to see you again! It has been some time since last we talked, and I missed you! I hope all of you are well! Now, what more could you do for our people... Who is it that stands behind you? Children! Our children! You have brought them back to us! All of our children are home again, and safe, and you also say that the men who took them away no longer live; O, merciful heavens above, this day shall be sung and recited forever in our village!

"O, if only one day that terrible spider could be caught in his own web! What! You will seek Justice for him! But this is too much to ask of you, even though you have done more than anyone would have thought possible; but, yes, yes, I see in your fiery eyes that you mean it, you good, good men of old; so now, yes, I will accept your promise, and rest easy, knowing that one day Justice may yet come to our wounded land.

"And now all of you shall go, and yes, I shall tell you my age—a whisper out of silly vanity: one hundred years old! Yes, one hundred years I have watched the stars and moon set over the best and worst of man.

"A gift for me? I cannot—but I will take it—and so goodbye, goodbye, goodbye, good and gracious men of courage, and go with more of our food and supplies for you, and our best guides; and a good and happy life, and a peaceful life I wish for you, my good, good, good men of courage, good men from eternity, men from many nations living as one family.

"Ah, but now I must cry, and as there is no one around me, I can, an old woman can now cry, for these men of strength to have such goodness and love in them is what men ought to be and like the men I knew of old, and now that I have met men such as these, I shall be pleased to die with pleasant visions of selfless men, good, good, good men in my heart, and your precious present: diamonds, diamonds, so many sparkling diamonds, that our village will prosper forever, and it is all because of the guardian men of eternity, who do what they ought, because they must."

Sorrow's Children

The road to Zaire was without incident for the Crusaders, as the village guides led them as surely as if they were leading their own kin to safety, and when the porous border was reached, the two groups bid each other a fond farewell.

And now the Crusaders were eighty-seven strong, having gained four more men in the Central African Republic; it must also be said that no man, or even a woman, after displaying sufficient fighting skills, need audition to join, as if this were a play, or take a test, as if this were school, or answer a question, as if this were a job, but merely stand before the members and demonstrate a heritage of Freedom and Charity for all, and be a lover of Justice and Equality, talents displayed through a fierce countenance, often attained through a history of being persecuted by a tyrant, and a stubborn willingness to fight for all who are oppressed.

If there was a territory where the European powers had manifested their ill tidings for Africa, it was here, in Zaire, where eons before, there had existed tribal groups throughout the Congo River basin, but then Leopold, King of Belgium, breathed in lust for wealth and power and dominion over a greater entity than his own; Leopold, a trivial player, an adjacent ruler to great kingdoms, sought to enlarge his own paltry image, and so breathed out orders for his countrymen to take the Congo area and by doing so condemn all of Africa, for this malevolent spirit that began there soon infected all of Europe, and so they too—Great Britain, France, Portugal, Italy, Spain, Germany— many already having invaded significant areas of Africa, now invaded in earnest, and soon all of Africa was colonized.

And when the colonial powers finally withdrew, it was if they withdrew a stinger that had been festering deep inside human tissue for one hundred years, leaving a vastly different, political, social economic, cultural, and financial landscape; and into the disturbed lake of calm came the big man of Africa; and so where the colonial powers had brought a semblance of modernization, the Big Man took it away, and where there was an infusion of infrastructure, he dismantled it, and where there was any societal gains, he depleted those, too.

But the people of Zaire were living with what was now, although a creation of the past, a new creature of their own blood and heritage, and still they had no desire but to live in peace and prosperity.

The Crusaders made camp in the northern provinces, where the Azande, who are Kushite, live, and when two of Moses' men and two of the Central African Republic men scouted the area, they came back with a father and son who had intimate knowledge of the region.

The father evinced the long chapters of struggle living inside the Ituri forest, the thick, vegetative womb of the Congo; his black skin was deeply creased and wrinkled, scarred and leathery, his expression wary and forlorn and exposing the temperament of his environs; his clothes were threadbare— consisting of a brown cotton shirt that had been dyed with the cola nut, and he held a crude bow and arrow in his small hands, as he and his son had been out hunting bushmeat.

He shook the hand of Moses as he sat down in the midst of the Crusaders' camp; surrounding the men were Red Cedars and Bamboo trees more than one hundred feet high, with a canopy of such dense foliage that no sunlight or rain ever penetrated it, with green creepers and furry moss wrapped around the five feet wide, magnificent trunk, which oozed a milky-white latex; red and black ants swarmed about the trees, and epiphytes flowers piggybacked onto other plants and gained nourishment from the heavy, liquid air, and rain, and assorted debris near them; and there were also birds and reptiles, monkeys and baboons, and bees and mosquitoes, spiders and caterpillars, and seemingly every land-dwelling insect about.

After being bitten past counting, Arjuna whined, "Give me that old mistress, the desert, sterile and hot."

"The same way you like your women," Horatius said, grinning mischievously; he was never too far away from his antagonist so as not to miss an opportunity for a verbal stabbing; Arjuna shook his head in utter disgust.

"I tell you," Muteba began, in Swahili, sitting down in front of his translator, Moses, "you've entered hell's sanctuary on earth, for no one here fights for us, but for themselves; where every rebel force is against us and against each other; and now other countries invade us, too, and fight government and the rebels, too; so, I tell you once more, you must go—I and my son stay because it is our homeland—but you must go to the country where you can help people or fight with liberating armies; so, go, go." He gesticulated toward the border.

Moses, his face proud and his posture unyielding, spoke, "There is no safe place, and we go where the people have no hope."

Muteba frowned, then smiled as he bowed his head, smiting his slender thighs. "Then you have come to the right place—Mkombozi—rescuer," and he proceeded to divulge a brief history of anarchist groups and alliances and foreign nations meddling in the current geography of their camps. "My son, Joseph, has told me these things, for he has journeyed far and wide to help his people."

Joseph, the youngest son of Muteba, his muscular body poised like a mighty hammer, his visage boasting ill will toward trespassers, spoke; his cadence spilled from his lips with the hard rhythm of a blacksmith striking blows against the iron anvil as he shapes his strong sword, wrath coloring his tone, revenge soaking the texture of his language.

"We live in a monster's belly and we throw down our shields, but this is a coward's dress we wear as we bow and scrape before the beast; we retreat to the old ways and pray to false gods, and still they come, and still they must die—Matisse and the rebels and the foreign armies." He smashed the ground with his large, fisted hand.

"My son is educated, he knows what should be—and this is his torment," Muteba said, nodding as he observed the youth, "and knows what the world has and we do not, and impatience swallows him like a hungry snake."

"We have heard of your army," Joseph said to Moses, "who oppose tyrants and succor the weak; I want to fight with you, as do many young men I know." He abruptly stood up. "We will fight unto the death with you."

Moses waved him to sit again. "Impatience brings vulnerability, Joseph, and we are no army, but men of goodwill who seek to right wrongs, and, as you say, defend the weak; every man in our ranks is trustworthy, and must be of good mettle, or is cast out, like sour milk."

Mwindo, closely observing the youth, spoke, "This is the country of my lineage, Joseph, and I see her die every day, bleeding from internal wounds, dug deeper into a watery grave, and ignored by the outside world—but first we must help those who need us most, people who love this land and whose children will one day rule a free Congo."

For two weeks, the Crusaders lived in obscurity under the great forest canopy, sending out scouts to gather intelligence on the area and to contact more indigenous people who were willing to deliver their unintended and unwanted leaders and insurgents to destruction; so, when all was in readiness, the Crusaders met in a war council and talked of the mission, having left their horses once more with loyal and trustworthy allies.

Moses spoke first, as the men around him, sitting on fallen logs, and boulders, some standing near Kapok trees, others squatting in clusters of flowers, remained silent.

"We can neither liberate nor defend the country here against the national armies, rebel groups, and foreign armies—so, ours must be a mission of mercy, to liberate and defend the people who are presently enslaved."

Some of the Crusaders cried for the blood of Matisse. Mwindo spoke.

"We are few, its armies tens of thousands; to kill him would be to cut off the head of the snake, but it would let in wolves that it had guarded against."

"There is no worthy successor here," Moses said. "It is a time in Africa where the people must fight until all these Big Men of iniquity are dead and buried."

All of them, to a man, felt as if they too were buried—buried by the avarice of the world, a weight that buried them deeper than the surface upon which men stood, opening a crater into which the greater mass of the poor and suffering slid, from where the oppressed reached up their supplicating hands for succor, to which those not oppressed and diseased and enslaved turned their backs and by doing so created a dark veil which covered the deepening and widening pit that was filled daily with the cracked and smashed-to-dust bones, and tears-filled blood; and these free people turned on devices of convenience to create a noise of sufficient magnitude to drown out the desperate pleas and cries of their oppressed brethren, and as these proffered clean water to their own, as they gave good, clean bread to their own, their whining words managed to trickle down through this heavy cover of freshly ripped away human skin that their sins of commission had helped to create, "What can I do for these people? What are they to me? Am I not only one? I cannot save the world! I help my own—here, you sister, money for more fancy clothes; here, you brother, money for more fancy cars; here, you son, money for more of the most technologically advanced of anything; here, you daughter, money for more of the most expensive of anything; I take care of my own and make sure they have everything they need and want so they might be happy and contented and fulfilled; for the desire of one thing quenched, and the beginning of wanting another thing and its desire met, and the pursuit of its fulfillment is what brings true joy, anything less is false imprisonment, and this will not do, and not do, absolutely." These defiant words hung like rotting fruit above the ever-expanding pit of despair into which the family of Earth was thrown, and when the fruit burst, its sticky, rancid juice rained down upon the hole, soaking the people there in melancholy despair. And when a hand did come down through the closely knit skin that was mingled with smeared blood across the sinking crater, was it benevolent, from within, from valiant men who vowed rescue of their own, or from without, from other nations who long inhaled liberty and were compelled to share its sweet air with the oppressed? No, it came by the hand of relentless and unchecked tyranny. From within, from men who ruled, men who sought to rule and by nations from without, rulers who sought more subjects to subjugate and resources to steal, and this iron fist crushed the Innocents like a woman crushes corn kernels in a stone bowl; and so now, there was only one league of daring champions who would not retreat from any hand reaching out to them in love and supplication—but would they take the blood-drenched knife-wielding hand of the contrite villain?

A plan was agreed upon, the course set, the men ready, and nothing for them to do but go forward; they left the next morning, fully rested, eager to fight, fully armed, and eager to bring, like a healing rain after a ravaging fire, solace to those who were covered and forgotten in the wet pulp of the ashy, sooty, burned-out forest garden.

The march through the dense forest was accompanied by the men assuming their individual and team roles in a visual rehearsal, living advances and retreats, seeing failures and successes, analyzing alternative routes when strategic plans were broken, questioning their fellow warriors on evasive techniques and designated rendezvous points, and remembering what Conall had said what seemed long, long past. "That when a man of superior ability steps in to engage you in physical combat, it is of no good use—either in practice or in theory—to attempt and control the man, or block his punches, or suffer ways to avoid his kick and move in to disable him; it is better to step back and back again and bypass his lunge and quickly pick up the nearest weapon—a rock, perhaps—and speed its trajectory at his uncontrollable rage, and then turn and run hard, and then stop, and if he follows, pelt him the more with your stone friends, until he quits the chase or you tumble him to the ground; so, in this way, you will have won now—you who lived where others died; so, you are an honorable warrior, alive to fight again, while other warriors imagined themselves honorable heroes, but were not only dishonorable fools in smart uniforms who followed the rules and customs of blockheads."

The physiognomy of the forest revealed itself to the Crusaders as they marched under its limb-thatched ceiling above, and trod on its mud-packed, foliage-rich floor below; they began to see what pictures in a book could never show, but the inner workings of the dark realm and the intricate relation of plants to each other and to animals and insects, and so to them, it was another alien landscape, like the great desert, that their bodies—but their minds perceived afterward—appreciated, the wondrous diversity of the surface of the earth that provided a refuge for every kind of man, woman and child, be it cold, hot, wet, or dry, watery, barren, icy or green, flat, hilly, above or below, beach, mountain, valley, desert or plain, as there was always a place to rest one's head where you might breathe in peace and quiet.

The forest was like a genteel creature that swaddled its human residents in its protective girdle.

The Ubuhinzi extremists, who had escaped from Kwanda after their failed genocide against the Umushumbas and Umuhigi, had manipulated aid agencies to give them and other Ubuhinzi refugees money and supplies, and with this money they bought more weapons and so continued their plan to wipe out the Umushumbas; and this day, they had cruised back over into Kwanda to kill more of them. They came upon a clearing that contained a small village.

When the Crusaders quietly slipped camouflaged binoculars to their eyes, they first practiced the art of suppression, holding in their natural inclinations to react as warriors at the site of sin incarnate; for it was the boasting spirit of chaos and anarchy, dining at a banquet of impunity and beckoning encouragement they beheld—but this was the natural order of things here, and why not; does not the wolf among a shepherd-less flock think this is the natural order of things, that he should stuff himself on the weak and infirm, until satiation and even beyond?

It was human beings in the brown and green uniforms the Crusaders saw, yet they beheld animals in human skin, for, they reasoned, no human being would debase and debauch a fellow creature as these were presently doing, and not with the gross profit of joyous laughter and revelry they displayed; yet, below, in the Umushumba village, the Ubuhinzi rebels were, by the dozens, gleefully raping women, raping young girls, raping men, raping young boys, murdering men, murdering old men, murdering women, murdering young girls, and in no way unrestrained whatsoever, as if in a state of retribution, generally plundering and burning and destroying every and any little thing in and out of sight, just as surely as if they had finally caught up with rabid animals that had devoured these soldiers' families.

"I estimate over nine hundred," Yoshitsune whispered to Conall, his visage torn to red rage.

His comrades concurred.

Conall issued orders of restraint, as did Moses and Mwindo, to the other Crusaders, through their new two-way radiophones, which had a constantly shifting scrambling and frequency, and radio silence.

"We cannot watch this," Arjuna nearly cried, but bit it down to a harsh whisper. "Our credo says we never back down when Innocents are being harmed."

"We counted on two hundred being there," Yoshitsune said. "This other division must have recently arrived."

"We will implement SAR," Conall said. The orders were issued.

Strike and Retreat protocol was based on the mathematical concept known as shearing the greatest amount of combatants in the least amount of time, and done by having each man select enemy troops in threes and pass information to the next man, who would then choose the next three soldiers in the line of fire, and so on; when the order to fire was issued, the man would shoot one bullet at each soldier, then proceed to fire once more, if need be, at the third soldier, then back to the second and first soldier; once this was accomplished, the men had ten free seconds to shoot any man trespassing in the same zone kill they had previously established, and then retreat to a pre-arranged rendezvous point.

The Crusaders were anchored upon a small rise above the small village, some two hundred meters in distance, when the orders were given.

One shot, two shots, three shots more; four shots, five shots, six shots out they pour; seven shots, eight shots, nine shots, done; eleven shots, twelve shots, thirteen shots, run; and they did—the Crusaders turned around and ran as if Mercury himself had attached his wings to their nimble feet. And what did they leave behind but one hundred and sixty-seven Ubuhinzi rebel soldiers stone-cold dead, forty-two rebel wounded soldiers squirming and screaming, the rest of the rebel soldiers securing their bazookas and rifles and rocket launchers and machine gun-mounted trucks, and scores and scores and scores of Umushumba villagers fleeing for the sanctuary of the O wondrously dense green forest—as the Crusaders knew they would.

The rebel Ubuhinzi soldiers had superior manpower and firepower, and access to dirt roads to circumvent the escape routes of their enemies, and scouts to track, a communication network with other rebel forces, and now coupled with unbound rancor aimed at the perpetrators of the attack against them; and so, rather quickly, and easily, pursued and gained on their attackers; and when they were about to come upon them, they found themselves in a special quandary.

The Crusaders had two rendezvous points—one designated if the assault was complete and the men had to split up later due to the threat of incoming rebels; and the second if the assault was incomplete, and the men had to depart prematurely, and so it was the second route that was being followed now, and as the rebels came into a clearing to which they assumed their attackers had fled, instead they found a healthy squad of more than a thousand government troops assembled for encampment—troops who had been warned anonymously that rebels were in the area hours before, and then just recently, had been given their exact traveling locations; thus, the two forces, like black and red ants, tangled, where most of the rebels were killed.

The Crusaders sat at the rendezvous point, each man silent, solemn, melancholy, listening to the gunfire, on the one hand satisfied that they had broken up the debauchery at the village, but feeling impotent that the proper job had not been done, and that too many good citizens were still in peril.

Through a Glass Darkly

It was in this way, using the Strike and Retreat protocol, that the Crusaders became effective in engaging the diverse rogue and government troops in Zaire, and for six months, they established themselves as a small but potent threat to the instability and corruption here; and here, for the first time, since Abdul, Crusaders died—Samir Amrani of Algeria, whose father had fought against the French and the liberation of his country, died valiantly while fighting government troops near Goma; and Alphonse Kyenge of the Democratic Republic of Congo, whose mother had become one of the first females to hold a Master's degree in her country, died while fighting rebel troops near Kindu; and Kabelo Tambo of South Africa, whose family had fled Apartheid in South Africa and immigrated to Kenya, died while giving cover fire for his retreating comrades as they fled government troops near Mbandaka, all of whom were forthwith buried with great sorrow.

There was one very strict and very much agreed-upon rule regarding fallen comrades, that a man down should, at all costs, be taken back, wounded, to rendezvous points, and similarly, if the man were dead, all reasonable attempts should be made to retrieve the body; however, if all of these attempts failed, then it was paramount—with as much import as bullets to a rifle—for each Crusader to carry no identification, pictures, or the kind, on their person, that would allow the enemy to identify him. Anonymity, Conall had said, is one of our greatest weapons, and as long as we are a faceless, nameless, country-less entity, we can move with ease throughout this place.

Three more men were wounded and were given medical treatment by Arjuna and Finn and Julius, and by local doctors; it was a fact soon established for the Crusaders that in a country where every force of men with weapons is intent on hurting citizens, and it can be established that a new force of men appears, and is there to defend the citizens, then these citizens will risk life and limb to help and shield such new men from harm, and supply them with clothing and food and medical aid and information, and, if need be, even weapons, or any other need; and so, it was in this manner that the Crusaders could gather superior intel on enemy troop movement, and disappear so quickly and easily, and evade capture, for, strictly speaking, other than these, unfortunately, requisite few, too many in such dire times, easily gave allegiance to members of the darker force; and so entire civilized populations of Innocents, their hearts and souls, minds and bodies, thirsty and hungry for Justice, considered the Crusaders the most viable resource in all the country.

The world had had its world wars, and Africa, as much an insular world as the one outside of its native borders, had its, and in Goma, it began—after the Umushumbas had regained power in Kwanda—with Ubuhinzi refugees going there to escape planned-and-executed-but-not-finished funeral arrangements by the new Kwandan Umushumba extremists; but before this collision of peoples, Kwanda and Uganda had already been in Zaire, sucking the viable hordes of mineral wealth.

When avenging armies are on the march, when they move with the fresh taste of bloodlust on their wet tongues, when they become addicted to killing and torturing and plundering and raping, they're likened to frenzied sharks in bloodied water or, perhaps, any people whose moral guide is finite, flawed, and ever-changing; namely: a bloodstained army following a bloodstained trail comes upon a blood-soaked group of refugees fleeing from its blood-soaked country and, leave no doubt, there will be more blood.

There was such an army of the Kwandan Umushumba, in alliance with local rebels, in pursuance of Ubuhinzi refugees from its country, and they came upon a civilian camp in the cradle of a scarlet-streaked dawn, with their quarry therein, and scorned attempts by UN peacekeepers to keep the soldiers at bay, and rounded up the refugees, nearly three hundred in all; and once the refugees stood, bowed and bewildered before them, the soldiers evinced pity, and announced that the president of their country had declared peace between the Ubuhinzis and the Umushumbas, and wished to have the displaced Ubuhinzi people come back home; and so, the people, hesitant until they heard a recording of such a declaration from their president, rejoiced, and willingly went with the army, and traveled some distance until the soldiers decided to camp for the night, and the soldiers gave the refugees food and bid them a hearty meal and a hearty festival to celebrate this newfound brotherhood.

Now, the Kwandan Umushumba soldiers could simply have murdered the Ubuhinzi refugees when first they found them, as they did not fear retribution from the neutral, and inept, UN nincompoops, suit-wearing mannequins, worse-than-nothing peacekeepers or any other group, indigenous or otherwise; no, they had to bring—no, lure—the quarry out, out, far, far, into the forest so as to transfer out a hopeless hope and bring in ascending joy of joys to these people to ignite their soul's dwindling fires, to bring fresh smiles of serenity on top of fresh wounds of terror; all to make this a kill of kills for the soldier, a memorable murder, a sadistic slaughter to heighten the narcotic-tipped thrill of extinguishing life in one's hand—but is this not the singular abomination of the addict, to plot for a higher high, to elevate the next plunge of the needle into a grandeur plain? So it was, now, and the soldiers began to evince glee, and their pupils began to dilate, and their hearts began to shrink in terror as their spongy minds sipped on the sweet venom of villainy and dined on the savory bouquet of absolute power and the promise of fleshly delights and unrestrained carnage.

When the white dove of peace descended upon the camp of the refugees, when the Ubuhinzi people were singing songs of brotherhood and love, when the soldier escorts joined in the festivities and the two disparate groups enjoined their cultures and embraced a nationalistic spirit of unity and held hands and dined on the fresh meat and laughed and danced around the roaring orange flame and black plume of billowing smoke, it slowly disintegrated, like an unraveling thread on a rope that wraps around the waist and joins two mountain climbers, with sudden hoots and hollers of the soldiers, and howls and baying at the silver disc in the clear Autumn sky, with screams and shouts, chants and vulgar epitaphs spewed through the creases and folds of a glowing white-hot iron mask of zealotry—and zealotry stripped of every known stripe and symbol of humanity, zealotry drained of virtue and reason, zealotry melted and set in a soulless, heartless, human-less cast, and worn by the soldiers, like a crown of boasting honor.

So, the soldiers stepped back, and raised up their weapons, and the refugees looked around, and raised up their hands; and then many Umushumba soldiers grabbed many Ubuhinzis and tossed them into the roaring fire, and thus it all began.

It was as if a large contingency of men who were hunting disease-carrying, baby-killing rodents had finally caught the little creatures and now were determined to liberate them from the ranks of the living; this the Kwandan Umushumba army did, and they did it this time, and long ago, and would again in their quest to cleanse Africa of the Ubuhinzi extremists. Soon, all of the refugees were dead, and the soldiers moved on to the next easy slaughterhouse.

The Crusaders, now ninety-eight, were camped near Goma, listening to the news of the battle around them through radio reports, when Tyr and Enkidu came up to Conall, and whispered to him, and in turn, he nodded, and then signaled to Moses and Mwindo, and soon all of the men were in confidence with the report of the last reconnoiter.

An hour hence, and a voice, foreign to the ears of the men, cut through the thicket. "Ho, there," the burly voice whipped through the camp, and a big, muscular, white-skinned—slowly baking to a lighter shade of bronze—glistening, bald-headed man, who was adorned with brown leather bullet belts strong across his bare chest like proud decorations, appeared, with thirty-two more mean, grim-looking disciples of grief and pain in tow. He had a stamp of arrogance on his youthful, round, ruddy face, as he—a walking multicolored, multi-paneled mural of dastardly acts depicted in stylish, colorful tattoos—approached.

"Who's in charge of this merry band of do-gooders, eh? Where's Robin Hood, huh? Where is that vigilante—yo," he cried, upon seeing the great bulwark of Conall standing like a monolith before him, "in the flesh!" And when no reply came back, he halted, and waved to his men in the distance. "Don't worry, Bruce Wayne, we've got your sentries all safe and sound," he cried, snapping his large, sausage-like fingers; "too easy, too tidy, I must admit—and a tad bit disappointing, too, I must admit." Four Crusaders were brought forth and deposited near Conall. "See, all good."

Conall too waved his hand and presently five men from this new band of soldiers were brought forth by seven Crusaders. "Tidy," he whispered, staring directly into the man's smirking face.

"Like I said—too easy," the rifle-toting, cigar-chopping, shirtless man said, and then signaled his men to bring in two more Crusaders, who had been on the second ring of the peripheral watch. The bald man smiled.

Conall, watching the man intently, lifted his hand again, and he could plainly see incredulity in the face of his antagonist, and then the sly smile, and the barely perceptible nod of acquiescence. Five more of these invaders were brought in by nine more Crusaders.

"Okay, Chief, you got me there—a third ring of security," he said, pointing at Conall with his free right hand. "Very cautious, and very paranoid—I like it." He grinned as large as if he were attending his own surprise birthday party.

"An arrogant American," Henry said, as if the threat of fifty armed men, stoic-looking on the outside and simmering in a roiling pot of blood-seeking vengeance on the inside, were not obvious to him. "I can tell by the conceit in the accent."

The man smiled and nodded his head in recognition. "It's always nice to be recognized," he began, still looking at Conall, and then averting his eyes to his accuser, he said, scornfully, "and I can tell you're an African," and he raised his free hand to cup his ear. "I can hear the charter of human rights floating in a cesspool."

Fortunately for the hot-tempered, react-first, think-later Henry, Moses was able to throw a hand against the lunging man's chest and restrain him.

It was palpable as night following day that the smirking man with the red and black dragons painted boldly across his sweaty barrel chest sought to speak only to Conall. "So, do we talk, big man," he said, "or dance?" and he coolly placed a brown cigar into his own wide mouth.

Conall caught up his rifle and the new band of fifty men felt the cold shadow of death sprint pass them, but then he gently put it down next to a log and then sat down upon the log and stared at his guests; yet, it must be mentioned that no other Crusader yielded up his own steel life preserver.

The big man smiled and then, waving at his crew, too placed his rifle down, as did his fellows, and as did his fellows, up on the cold wet ground or moss-covered logs or boulders, they sat and waited for further invitations.

The rest of the Crusaders disengaged themselves from their steel dolls, and too sat, albeit ready as a crouching tiger.

"Friends now, eh?" the man began and, taking out a match, lit the big cigar that still lingered between his thick lips, and said, with considerable swagger, as if these words had special merit the world over, "The name is Rex," and he hesitated, anticipating the rising tide of astonishment spreading out from his audience; and when it became an inpatient desire cresting on high, he said, heaving the last two words with extra muscle and bravado into the balmy air, "Michael T."

He had lobbed a compact grenade of deadly language, yet had received only bored stares. Yoshitsune, however, his face beset by amusement, said, in a rich, deep baritone, "Fancy the irony here—they finally find a dinosaur in Africa, but it's about to become extinct." His men about him grunted in assent, as others smiled, and some sneered.

And then Henry was compelled to interject, frowning, "Man, is that your stage name?"

Michael T. Rex ignored the men's jabs, and said to Conall, "Obviously, you do not have access to the latest news, or you're very boring people—very disappointing, either way, I am afraid," and then smiled slyly, "unless you know—and have known—exactly who I am and that I was coming, which is why you prepared your little reception committee." When he inspected the countenance of his hosts, he laughed, nodding his round head with the dia-mond-pierced ears, and black skull and bones emblazoned on his back. His black, shadowy eyes, eyes ringed by a black mascara of deceit and cunning, narrowed, as if too much light that carried the truth seekers from without might penetrate his heavily guarded veil, within. "You people are good—better than vigilantes; no Robin Hood are you, dressed to the nines in your Interceptor body armor and Kevlar helmets," and he pointed his big, scarred index finger at his host. "Yes—saviors to these poor peasants." But then he grunted, and smote his thighs. "Well, I won't talk all day to myself—speak, Irishman!"

A man atop a bluff holding the end of a stick that sits under a pile of large granite boulders, when launching said rocks, which will fall upon his helpless prey below, need not explicate much, and if at all, it need be to his fancy.

Conall clasped his hands together as he sat upon a throne of rock and wood, resting his elbows on a jutting stone shelf, and his chin on his hands as he studied his anxious guest; and when he spoke, his words were as if hewn from rock and wood, so sinewy tough and hard were they.

"You seek union," he began; "you offer recognition of past deeds as a badge of merit."

Michael smiled and laughed. "Now, I know I came to the right camp—getting to the point," and again he pointed to his host. "You and I are mercenaries in a corrupt land brimming with gold and diamonds—we have only to combine our forces, and in no time flat, we'll all be rich men."

"You and your men attacked the Umushumba refugees for resources?" He received an affirmative reply. "You are, indeed, mercenaries; while we are not."

Michael feigned surprise with the rise of his bushy blond, thick eyebrows. "Really? What are you, then, you who kill hundreds," and he cursed, "no thousands of Militia and government soldiers all across this godless dark continent—peacekeepers? Ha! You're killers," and he beat his own burly chest, "just like me," and he waved to his men, "just like us," and waved to all of the men present, "just like all of us—give two men a rifle each and let them loose here and I'll guarantee you they'll be in opposing forces quicker than you can spit," and he did, "and each man will say he is fighting for the holy cause and the good guys." He cursed, disgusted, his right foot digging into the soil, his head held down momentarily; and then he looked up, waving his hands about. "No, no, you're mercenaries, all right, any way you color it—that is your identity: a man for hire with a gun."

Conall sat, stoic-faced, and his body still, his glowing blue eyes concentrated on the facial tones and lines of the man before him. "You have no cause greater than yourself—except to gain wealth."

Michael shot out his arms in a wide gesture of incredulity. "And who doesn't—especially the present company included?" He frowned and smacked the heavy air with his large fist. "But I am not here for dictionary definitions of toy soldiers; I am here for a business proposition—a merger," and when he heard or saw no reply from his host, either by words or facial posturing, he continued on, somewhat encouraged; "we can't move in this quagmire without intelligence, and, baby," he shot his hand out toward Conall, "you are it; anywhere we go, we hear about your exploits—the villagers sing about you and protect you and supply you, the Militia and government troops hate you and hunt you when they are bothered by you; you're it, friend, and with my intel combined with yours, we've got a handsome sandwich with thick diamonds dripping with juicy dollars between two hot cross cobalt buns."

The reply was swift. "You pave your path with the blood of your victims. We build paths with the seeds of Hope and Freedom."

Michael T. Rex cursed loudly and stood up so abruptly that every man, save the three leaders of the Crusaders, lunged for their weapons. "Oh, stow that," he shouted, waving his men away from their fears, while never averting his steely gaze from Conall. "Are you going to sit there and tell me you aren't in this for cold, hard cash, really? Man, you're quoting a script from a dead revolution." He shook his head in disbelief. "Who is speaking falsely now—Crusaders; that is what they call you—ha! Killers for hire, like us; look, no one—and I mean no one—risks their flesh and blood to protect peasants who are living in the Stone Age; for what? What fortune can you gain from it? You can stay here as long as you like and chill all the bad guys from here to kingdom come, and the day after you leave, some rebel group will come in and take over and loot and pillage and rape and kill them all, anyway! This is Africa, man—Africa; it's a smelly carcass sitting atop a fortune in riches! Join us, Irishman!" he cried, as he thrust out his arms in supplication, and slowly sat down again.

Conall never flinched, never frowned, never wavered—his courage never floundered, his resolved never frail, his inner vision more strengthened and shining brighter, like a sword that glows red hot as it is pounded into shape by the master blacksmith.

"Can," he said, with supreme equanimity, "the darkness join the light? But of course—is not the world darkness on one-half and light on the other; it is the same with Man—and when Man understands he is light and darkness, it is only then that he can be who he truly is when he embraces a greater cause than himself: a warrior, not a lamb; a soldier, not a barbarian."

Michael swore again at the lyrical language he heard, and then laughed in disbelief. "Out there," he pointed away toward the capital, "you want a moral dilemma, eh? I've got one hundred of them for you! You want things black and white, and I'm telling you it is dirty gray and a dozen shades of filth—all up and down this living grave." His fleshly face grew angry with disgust. "Why, everyone is dirty here, in this dung heap, this discard of humanity; Africa is an empire afflicted with the plight of regressive human rights and no country cares to land in this sinking mire; oh, I have some university education," and he winked as he leaned back, "as you can plainly see—but I hide it behind guns and blood and a bad attitude." His hard countenance mellowed and his rigid posture softened and his tight grip on his rifle relaxed as he remembered who he was before crossing the threshold of civility and into the killing fields of barbarity; but then his iron resolution, like oxygen pouring in large blasts through his wide mouth, was inhaled deeply, and deeply he exhaled bitterness and savagery; and his past intellectual refinements in elocution, which had starved on a meager diet of interacting with blockheads and brutes, sought recognition, one refined through the brittle harvest of a past as a student union leader at Berkeley protesting apartheid and U.S. intervention in the Gulf and the U.S. giving a free pass to the Big Man of Africa simply because he espoused anti-Communist sentiment, but soon it became a wailing cry and gave birth to his character, which was forged in disappointment and betrayal; and now his rugged visage assembled a hard look and a stone veneer that no easy, soft thing could yet imagine. "Why, there's Ubuhinzi genociders in Ubuhinzi refugee camps getting food from international aid groups that they sell to arm themselves with and then make raids on the Umushumba across the border in Kwanda; and you've got the new Kwandan government with the Umushumbas in charge hunting down the Ubuhinzi—good night, what a mess! And to beat it all, they'll change positions every few decades, just to make it different." And he shook his head, frowning. "And then you've got the Liberation Army—the NLF of their pal across the border—Kanza men all, with that nut-job Kinizi in charge, chasing the genocidaires—and taking children and making them into soldiers, and murdering them and any other Ubuhinzi; so, Matisse here isn't looking so good—no one looks any good; no branch of a rotting tree looks good, especially a tree that needs to be uprooted and burnt to ashes—ash that fertilizes the soil and brings about a new Zaire—a tree gone that shows a clear vision for a new Zaire; death to all of them—death to all of the assassins." He had ridden a wave and reached its zenith and now he landed upon an uncharted zone where his soul confessed nothing in a heart that had been hardened to a lump of black coal. "And you aren't so noble—not so, no, not so good," and when he spoke, his tone was undressed and enclosed in armor and sword and shield. "Give your men diamonds, and their loyalty to nobility will collapse like a church in a storm that was built on sand; how long, Irishman," he held out his outstretched, upturned, giant right hand; "how long before they tire of wiping the noses of peasants for a bowl of cold cassava while they hear stories of great riches all around themselves—nobility, it's a ride in a hearse to the graveyard in this rotting, bursting tumor."

Conall had watched the man as if through myriad layers of past and present heroes and villains, as if in between he and the man there existed a rogue's gallery, a roster of gallant warriors whom he superimposed upon the image of the raging Michael T. Rex, contrasting light and darkness, their bold intentions lying side by side their wagging tongues, their soaring eloquence cataloguing their tone and pitch and rhythm, their decibels falling, their decibels falsely inflated, the decibels born from a soul distressed; and when he had cut and pasted every nuance and clamor, every shout and whisper, every posture and look, and lain ancient manuscripts and philosophies in translucent writ in his mind like layered three-dimensional panes of glass, and peered down through it and allowed his mind to sift through the raft of sagacious sayings and pulled out the most germane, and cutting, and inspirational, he then said, in words laid on a swiftly turning sharp blade that cut swiftly and easily through the tense, heavy air:

"Your throat is an open grave."

The round bowl of meaty, animated flesh—the face of Michael T. Rex— was drained of color and equanimity and was wounded by humiliation. Conall spoke further, in a tone of humility and honor.

"And behold I saw the tears of the oppressed and that they had not one to comfort them; and on the side of their oppressors was power, but they had no one to comfort them..." He paused, and then said, staring hard at the intense man, in his own distinct, human language, "You kneel as a child before your twin faiths—the idols of violence and power; your season in the sun has passed."

The Crusader's interpreters were whispering in a hushed, thrilling anticipation.

Michael T. Rex jumped up as if he had just been shot. "You dare stigmatize me as the villain? You're no Boy Scout!" he cried. He grabbed his rifle by his large, thick right hand, though its green steel barrel still pointed to the muddy soil below. "You dare utter Scripture like a priest, O great killer of men? Why, you're just another religious fanatic who thinks he is protected by his one and only, almighty, powerful God—bah! This continent is lousy with zealots like you—that's the problem with this lousy, stinking world: too many people who think they are the only ones with the answer-come-down-from-heaven, and just can't leave well enough alone; and to that, I say," and he spat largely. He dismissed him with the swift wave of his hand; all of his men were standing with him now, holding their rifles, as the Crusaders held theirs as they too stood on the ready; his face was a flaming seat of indignation, now. "We don't need you—you need us; you'll see, you'll come and beg us for merger." His posture stiffened as his round head fell back and his sweaty face relaxed. "Don't worry, we'll meet again—mighty and righteous Crusaders," he grunted, and he and his band of mercenaries exited the camp.

Three of the men who had recently joined the Crusaders and had not experienced the soul-edifying, brother-bonding adventures of the desert, whose newly minted emblem of honor and loyalty had not yet dried and bonded with the other men, removed themselves, with heads hung down and drooping body postures, into the incendiary mix of the bone-crushing and bloodletting legion of Michael T. Rex.

No man, having eaten a ripe fruit, spits it out, but bad fruit only; and when he eats a bad fruit and does not spit it out, but thinks it good food, only then is he condemned.

A War Council was convoked by the three leaders, and the men heartily assented; Conall, grim-faced and harsh of tone, spoke first.

"The conceit of power without purpose or authority metastasizes into the cancer of anarchy: that is what we have before us and what we must commit ourselves to live beyond—to exist in the inviolate shadow of Justice and Freedom; we must be beyond the temptation of corrupt men by our word, our oath, our character, our actions, our faith; every man must here be an incorruptible tower of strength that every other man can depend upon in battle and deeds and words, or we are merely a puff of smoke, to be carried in any direction the wind pleases; so, now, our renewed pledge must decide our faith, and it is this: that no man shall accept mammon for any action, or material possession, other than food and clothing in arms and innocuous substances not related to our Mission—books and beads, ornaments of sentimental value, gifts of friendship—and those things given from the heart by gracious people; faith and purity of heart is our shield; this is our truest ambition, to achieve glory through righteous acts and righteous living."

Moses spoke next, and his words and tone were no less harsh and grim. "A man who stumbles into the mire cannot walk again with us; he will be cast off—let this declaration be known."

Mwindo spoke, and his words were no less harsh and grim. "Any man who shuns our credo and code, and betrays us, and causes one of us to die, or an Innocent to die, must also die." His big, round eyes were like black lanterns illuming the spaces before him. "We fight, we fight as one; we die, we die as one; let no man despise us, and use us for his ill-gotten good fortune, lest he die, for we are only as good as the least of us, as we stand united and complete."

It was affirmed, once more, and once more, it was understood that on the one hand, were gross temptations of the flesh that was very far and wide, and without a seemingly measurable depth or height; and on the other hand, were glories of Virtue that, if only one were achieved, its height and breadth and width, and fields far and wide, would be measureless, and leading to greater Truths beyond the reach of the most revered soul.

The Perception of Truth

In a warring land where everyone who has a gun murders seemingly with impunity, when is there time for courts, and jurists, and judges? And where are the witnesses, the arresting officers, the jails? So, when anyone who wields a gun is a murderer during a time of war, he has condemned himself already; he has become his own walking trial and condemning judge, his own jury and executioner, his bloody hands his condemning witness, the bloodied trail of his victims his moving jail; in war, soldiers kill their soldier-enemy with impunity—it is universally permitted and universally accepted—but a soldier who murders Innocents forfeits his walking immunity and has invited punishment wherever Justice finds his cowardly soul lurking.

In this crowded sepulcher, the Innocents who were still clinging to life did everything and did it often to aid each other in their quest for survival, and when they understood that the more the Crusaders stood next to them, the greater the cushion of safety for them from the relentless Hunter, then they set up a communication network directed toward this quest; consequently, the Crusaders had the anxious ear of every man, woman and child in the jungle, and it was soon determined that Michael T. Rex and his battalion of mercenaries had merged with a splinter group of the Liberation Army and had begun attacking certain towns that had valuable mineral wealth; in the meantime, the genocidal Ubuhinzi continued to make raids on Umushumba villages across the border.

The NLF, the National Liberation Front, endowed with the delusion that they existed for a purpose higher than the head of man, never objected to conjoining with another rogue entity with the express purpose of relieving of life the Ubuhinzi genociders and their Ubuhinzi refugees who flanked them, and so adopted the squadron of Michael T. Rex, like proud, beaming parents; nor were they coy about assimilating indigenous parties into their prodigious swarm of soldiers, be they children or teens, young men or young women.

There was a small and serene village near the Kwandan border, consisting of fifty-seven persons living a simple life as farmers, yet the congregation of mud huts and empty stomachs contained natural resources vital to the NLF; the operation was simple wherever the Liberation Army, like virulent mold, encountered a setting of homes like this in its spreading path, it liberated them: from their children, who would be trained as soldiers; from their food, for consumption; and their paltry valuables, for avarice; and from their young men, to be used as mules for errands and for soldiering; and from their women, to be used for their bodies and labor, and for this, the army never missed a woman to subdue despite the protestations of the victims' relatives, friends or spouses.

There was a small and serene village of eighty-one near the Zaire border where persons lived a simple life as farmers and lived in thatched huts and on empty stomachs, which contained a natural target for the Ubuhinzi genociders—Umushumbas; the operation was simple wherever the genociders, like virulent bacteria, encountered a setting of houses like this in their destructive path, they did liberate them: from life, killing them all; from dignity, first by raping the females, regardless of age, and by torturing and killing them afterward, and torturing and still killing anyone who should oppose their carnal proclivities; but in addendum it is noted here, for the genociders exceeded the known boundaries of human debauchery by obeying that curious taskmaster inside their illicit thoughts, and that was to purge the history of every Umushumba and his possessions until no recognizable reminder stood, their gnawing desire the same as when locusts turn from pleasant and mild green to insatiable brown on the march, their souls turned from hazy white to tarry black.

And so emboldened by such facile successes, each party—the NLF and the genocidal Ubuhinzis—dressed in their self-righteous regalia eagerly moved separately on to the next lamb to be sacrificed for slaughter even as the charred lambs behind them still emitted acrid, black smoke.

Thus, the NLF made for the next village, scouting for irregularities, and gulping and smacking their lustful, greasy lips, proceeded on down the small hill to engorge themselves on the images of pleading parents they would berate, and the sobbing women they would rape.

So, too, did the genocidal Ubuhinzi move on to their next village, scouting for irregularities, and gulping and smacking their lustful, greasy lips, and proceeding across the open grass field to engorge their barking brains on the image of Umushumbas pleading for life and the females, from infant to elderly, screaming in terror for rescue from these eerily smiling, soulless hobgoblins.

When the silhouetted figures of the NLF—dark shadows cast in the rising specter of their manmade hell—swarmed upon the quiet village, they found a singular phenomenon awaiting them, and it was this: that the people there begged the soldiers to peacefully surrender or face the violent repercussions of refusal, which issued no little amusement in the black wellspring inside their black hearts, and produced a high fever to impart greater damage and longer-lasting torment upon their apparently—and seemingly impossibly—smug victims.

When the rapacious, blood-sucking, murderous, flesh-eating, diabolical, rape-killing seeds from the vomit of masochism and tyranny, these human princes of the underworld, the genocidal Ubuhinzi, came upon this village of solitude, they too beheld a strange phenomenon awaiting them, and it was this: that the people there begged the soldiers to peacefully surrender or face the harsh repercussions of refusal, which elicited no little amusement in their black wellspring of a heartless chamber, and erected a high fever to impart even greater damage and longer-lasting pain upon their present, seemingly smug victims.

Five hundred and eight NLF soldiers and their now allied mercenaries took a step toward their intended victims, but forty-seven fell down convulsing, as if struck by sudden disease, impelling the other soldiers to cast incredulous, fearful glances at their fallen comrades; and once shock throttled them and the crust of laziness broke off their bruised brains, they realized that—O, what is this—but forty-two more dropped their souls into the busy and widening claw of Hades, and the soldiers knew it was an assault; it had been arrogance that had precluded these dog soldiers—who wore the long neck chain that flowed back to their masters—from thinking anyone would dare attack them anywhere; they quickly dispersed and organized and began an offensive against this bold and unseen enemy who were apparently using silencers on their weapons. But it must be said that at least three of the men knew what they were up against, and as the NLF charged the hill and moved into the valley to chase a fleeing enemy, they, these ex-Crusaders, tried to slip away, but the NLF leaders, upon seeing the fleeing figures, decided the men were traitors, and shot them dead. Michael T. Rex and his mercenary brothers trembled, and regret ached in their nauseous guts like burrowing rats.

Seven hundred eighty-three genocidal Ubuhinzi penetrated the protective sphere set around the villagers, and for their trespass, forty-eight of them took a violent dive into the dusty soil, and as the rest turned to orient their dazed inner compasses, forty-one more joined their recently fallen brethren on the gloomy shores of damned; now, the rest of the soldiers dispersed and presently aimed themselves toward their unseen enemy and charged forward up the sloping hill and into the valley.

It shall be, Conall had said at the War Council, like tugging on the short chain of two rabid killer dogs and throwing them into a very small space together.

So it began, that the parceling of each group of marauding terrors begat a disturbing symphony that steered its listeners to the proper place at the proper time, a musical composition destined to be unfinished.

The two potent forces, the NLF and mercenaries and the genocidal Ubuhinzi, met in north-south terrain—chosen by their orchestrators—that was known for its wide-open spaces in a deep valley and its steep, unsteady hills, which were easy to descend and difficult to ascend, and numerous obtrusions in the high rocky cliffs, like a forehead, above which stood plenty of vegetation, like a tangled mat of hair—but, lo, no adjoining facial features below this curious phenomenon existed—and then two opposing sides espied each other and commenced a downpour of unceasing firepower with a zeal and determination that sought to suck the very soul from their avowed foe.

From a hillock, high above and due east, the rapid, maddening, screaming projectiles of hot tumbling lead and bursting rockets and grenades sizzled in the air, and slowly at first, caused the fleeing of life-forms; and so a new life-form was built, replete with musical speech and a special language; from high above on the wooded hilltops, and spread out wide in a semicircular fashion, with weapons drawn and eyes and ears alert, the Crusaders, still as stone pillars, stood grim-faced, as if observing two wild beasts mauling each other, patient, waiting to finish the task they had begun.

When one traps a nest of Black Mambas that have been killing your family, Mwindo had said in anticipating this moment, one makes sure none of them leave the trap alive.

The two antagonists, nearly exhausted now in manpower and ammunition, were sunk into this suicide nest and wearing a tight-fitting girdle of flying bullets that hemmed them in and swept them in and struck them down and forced them to the ground, to lie there fearful and terror-filled and not able to go up or down, or past or around, for now there was a new enemy who fired freely from above; and so the end of their days overcame them and laid a black wreath upon their trembling forms; and all the while a dark, gruesome collage was carved into the fortress walls; and soon, if one looked specifically, a little bit askance at this formation and ran his eyes to and fro from steep hill to steep hill and then looked straight on and focused and took all the ingredients therein and cooked them in an intellectual, briny stew, and then looked once more from left to right—to the dead and dying soldiers, too—and then to the other hill, one would see a horrific transformation occur: a death mask, with huge, hollow, deep-set, orange-flamed eyes and sunken, burned cheeks and a grisly, decaying smile, and from the grotesquely round mouth would come special lyrics constructed by the funeral bullets and cries of pain and pleas for succor, which sang in violent chorus: O, death, death, death, come for us, let us rest our weary heads upon your spongy, black bosom; O life, life, life, we forfeit your claim upon us, we have violated your sacrosanct decree.

And when all was over and said and done, and before the red and black vultures of the sky and the hungry scavengers of the land were notified of the imminent cuisine before them, the somber judges above the clamor and fray descended to the bloodied battlefield.

Nearly all of the two warring camps were dead and dying. Conall found Michael T. Rex lying with a rifle clutched to his wounded body, and then setting aside his own weapon and bullets, he bent down next to the man and propped his head up with his own shirt and there knelt beside him.

The man was gasping for breath, gasping for life, sputtering in his death throes as he attempted to speak; and then he did speak, in a raspy, strained, choking whisper. "In another world, Irishman, would I have played the villain…" His sweaty, bloodied face trembled and his wet, bloodied eyes closed tight as thunderbolts of pain ripped into him, and then he opened them once more as he summoned his last remaining strength. "Has Man no purpose but to play a role he was born to; is there no force within him to disoblige his heritage; you fight for a cause, I to fulfill my nature." His body shuddered and shook, and Conall grasped the man's hand. Michael T Rex smiled. "You wear the golden thread of immortal heroes, so why do so many men oppose you…" His mouth shuttered and his teeth clenched as a riptide of agony bore across his hulking landscape. "Why do men freely embrace sin, knowing they are condemned by it—why, why, why," and he sat up suddenly and gripped Conall, "why doesn't God stop us?"

Conall gazed into the dimming black eyes of the man, into the dying embers of a man's expiring life, and saw the once-proud, boastful fire of youth receding; and he saw the conceit of power deceased, and he saw the want for wealth buried, and he did see an unrehearsed, guileless, honorable imploring for mercy and love and forgiveness, and a hearty refutation of sin; and so Conall said, as he stared into the final seconds of a man's beginning eternity.

"Ask Him."

And so he did ask, and then he died.

Conall closed the eyes of the man and laid the arms of Michael T. Rex upon his chest and then retrieved his own shirt and then said in a melancholy reverie, "God knows who lives, and who dies, at the last moment."

Now, with all of the men in this absurd battle dead, the Crusaders meant to hastily quit this tragic place, because of the dead bodies therein, for some of these dead men would be presently assumed—through rumors and gossips weighed, packaged and shipped by the indigenous people—to be that importunate blend of foreign and domestic fighters that were known in the region as the Crusaders.

Absence of Malice

Is there only one body of water upon the surface of the earth, the sea, divided into many sections and imprisoned in innumerable streams and rivers and brooks, inlets and rivulets and tributaries, that seek to return to its one mother ocean; also, is there only one body of land covering the surface of the earth, at once whole, now divided and floating apart but destined to reunite one day? Therefore, is there only one ocean and one land, so no one can claim ownership of one drop of precious water or one handful of fertile soil without acknowledging the debt of the past and the reality of locations? And is there only one whole earth, and one people upon it to share its wonders and its burdens and to strive to keep her unspoiled?

Then, if there is one land but temporarily separated by geological forces, is there not one people, though temporarily separated by geological forces? And concerning the people who do live on the land, how have they managed to step back and away from each other—like the drifting landmasses, but through forces of mind—color of skin, political institutions, customs and traditions, philosophical inclinations, and choice of worship.

And concerning ownership of the land, who can say they own that which they did not make or capture? Who can say they own the green grass; the silky, red Rose; the giant, ancient Redwood with its massive buttressed trunks and reddish-brown bark; the multi-stage, slow-moving caterpillars who dream of flight and that one day become darling Monarch butterflies with feathery wings of orange and brown and then fly thousands of miles for their purest pleasures? Who, then, can own the rich, black soil of Indiana, the brownish, whitish Falcon with brown stripes, who is the prince of the sky; the sleepy, gently sloping hills of Spain covered with its clusters of white and purple flowers, the great Rocky Mountains that took forever to form and forever will continue to change, who can own them; who can own the ethereal air, the azure sky, the celestial firmament, who—is it Man: custodian and tenant, mere caretaker for a brief moment in the winter of infinity? And how can he say who owns it and for how long, and determine who claimed it first and when and how who should continue to be master of the land and all its humble creatures; and when a lease is up—for this is all anyone can ever say, that they lease the land from the original owners—the stars, the birthplace of the magical stuff the land is made of, and from before them, to the birthplace of the elements, the atoms, the subatomic particles, an argument among people that dies only when they die; so, perhaps it is best said that as long as one stands upon a piece of land and is strong enough to hold it, it is their land, that they are temporal custodians, the caregivers, until an outside agency or force takes it from them; and who takes it back then? Why, Nature: fire, flood, earthquakes, famine can; foreign armies can, the law can, insects and animals can, neighbors can, everybody and everyone who can, and will, if they have a desire for it, and then it is theirs to defend and hold until the next catastrophe or avaricious man comes; yet, if you believe God gives you the land, it is yours, for God supersedes all natural and manmade laws—but if you do not believe in God, or you do but choose to war against Him, then the struggle continues: and here are the wars of faith.

So, it is just one land but Man lays down borders and says it is now his land and no one else's and he will not share what is on his land with someone just across the artificial barrier that is really just the same soil; the insects and animals do not understand and do what they must; and the earth below moves and shakes, and the sky above blows and rains freely upon every creature and place without fear of trespass, but only Man plows a wooden stake into the hard ground and proclaims, "mine," and by this very act causes his neighbors to recede from him and embrace himself and his own and to guard his possessions.

So, now there are good places of exceeding wealth and gentle climate, and there are bad places of exceeding poverty and harsh climate, and people flock to the former and flee the latter; and the people of the first place soon forget the people of the second place, and the farther the distance between these two disparate worlds, the quicker the decline in memory and sympathy.

There is such a place in the world that just happens to have been raised on poor luck and poor geography; it is barren lands in hot climates and barren crops and hot diseases, it has too little technology and too many wars, too many invaders and too many poor, it has every wrong combination and every bad circumstance, and it has been forgotten like a stone ripped off one's neck and plunged into the sunlit sea.

It is Africa, and it is alone, and misunderstood, abandoned, and abolished from the memory of better worlds, left to drift alone, released from the hardship of life and destined to drown in a swamp of sorrow and sand; its woes are perceived as too complex and colossal to fix, its customs too esoteric to understand, its merit not seen as justifiable to save it from extinction; yes, it is as if an entire continent is extinct, and the funeral tune plays for it, an entire continent suspended in amber like an insect, a quagmire of self-destruction of misery inflicted from without and within; and who can want such a defective entity, who will willingly embrace such an ugly child to its own body; what mother would allow such a sickly infant to suckle at her healthy breasts as she fears that there will not be enough milk for her healthy own? For that is how the outside world sees the inside world of Africa, as if she were an infant, and not freshly born of the modern era, who can stand on her own within moments of birth, but a struggling, dirty, frozen revolution never joining the modern era, a child of the Stone Age who still prefers rock and wood to steel and concrete.

And so to assuage shreds of civilized-style guilt pangs, civilized people and nations send monies and supplies to the poor, sad images of the poor continent of confused, backward Africans, and instantly feel relieved of their heavy conscience-burden and so turn toward losing their own sobriety and things that they think really matter in life.

Now, the Crusaders were already there and were doing their part but knew that their actions, though noble, could help only a few, and sometimes those few they saved were overrun by any malevolent band who happened their way, and so they had only withdrawn a dagger in the soft belly of the region one day while letting a dozen others slip through in the next.

A War Council was convened by the Crusaders, and the news that the government troops thought them dead was heard, that they had sold their allegiance to the highest bidder and had joined the small liberation faction—it was the kind of lie that can hold true only in a country that has no stable news agency or government, no effective communication network and internal investigation of its own affairs, and one built and sustained on corruption and bribes and hearsay; so, the lie, once told by the local villagers and spread to the NLF and the Ubuhinzi rebels, became the hard, indisputable truth.

The Crusaders, sitting in the secluded forest camp, were free—they could walk away and go home, they could continue to fight—but they knew they were not free in their own minds, for such men, once a job has begun, do not leave until it is done; yet, they decided, instead of renewing the fight here, where the first African civil war was still in its infancy, they would travel west to Uganda and avail themselves of the culture and customs by laying down their weapons and picking up the tools of humility and peace in the small villages and towns, and in refugee camps and with international relief organizations, so they might, when once more they picked up their weapons, know much more about whom they fought for and whom they fought against.

In a month's time, they had reached the Ugandan border and slipped easily across it. It wasn't too much later that Zaire became the Democratic Republic of Congo.

> What is in a name, anyway, if it changes,
> the person remains the same;
> what if it is a country then:
> Are the rulers to blame?
> All is vanity, and there is nothing new under the sun.

What Grief Hath Wrought

With his eyes, he enslaved them
with his mind, he imprisoned them
with his mouth, he swallowed them
with his heart, he concealed them.

He was a god among stick and stone, dirt and dung; a god among peasants and princes, merchants and minors; a god among criminals and corporations; politicians and professionals; he was a Titan, a Zeus, a resurrected god of myth and legend, a king, a pharaoh, an emperor, a usurper-of-legend, a being apart, a soothsayer, a reborn hero-of-old, and he knew it and asked for it and reflected it in every mirror and sign and written word; this Carnegie, Mansa Musa I, and Rockefeller, in a land where such colossuses had existed, he was now the one, the only Morgan, Hetty Green and Fugger, the sole heir to the kingdom, the breath of life upon which every citizen subsisted, albeit breath fraught with the skeletal remains of their families and relations and friends, breath containing the remains of burned-out buildings, the sour, rancid, nasty breath of a host that consumed too much and gobbled his food whole and had rotting things deep within his prodigious borders and staggered throughout his country, his image large, his appetite unclenched, his giant shadow casting the people into darkness, light and heat gone with it, his excretions pouring upon their heads like poisonous, black rain, and he was invincible.

He was a Big Man of Africa, and he was here to heal the wounds that evil colonial empires had wrought, and right wrongs, and set straight the crooked rivers and clear the black sky of the last remnants of European hegemony; he was given the keys to the kingdom and the heart of every supplicating citizen pledging allegiance to him; and thus he began, with every variable controlled and set up and held fast in his big, free hands, a chance to rule over his alleged kin as Justice demanded, and finally to do what was needed.

At first glance, he did smile and bring promises of glad tidings to a land hungry for kindness and joy, and while they smiled back and hailed him as a conquering hero, he reached out his large hands and took out their outstretched ones and tied them behind their backs and more oft chopped them off and then threw off his sheep's clothing and set about his father's business, the spirit of infamy.

As a bird builds its nest twig by twig to hold its future fortunes, so too did this Big Man of Africa, taking not a twig, not even a log, but the entire forest, and inside one of his magnificent Crystal Cathedrals he had built throughout the world, he dropped his neatly packaged prizes.

What precious little valuables the people possessed, he now possessed; what precious little resources the people possessed, he now possessed; what precious little future, and joy, and peace, and hearth and home they possessed, he desired that too, so that whatever the people held or owned or prized, he wanted it and pursued it and took it, until he was satisfied that no good thing under his rule was hidden; so that finally and always he would stand atop the palatial palace of glittering gems and burnished gold and see only his image in every face and figure, house and horizon, sky and sun.

No one or thing might now exist apart from his iron, resolute will. The revolution never began, not even a stumble or a sideways step, but it now lay frozen, like an eagle in a black cloth bag.

His princely image lay atop the biggest and smallest hills and was painted on billboards and buildings; his face adorned every denomination of currency and rested on shirts and caps; his name was song in schools and churches, his royal decree was printed in every newspaper and magazine; his words were recited on street corners and coffee shops; his august portrait hung in every business, his heavy spirit hanging like a drenching shower on the burning, crushed heads of his people every day, and in every way; and in this way, just as the sea flows over new land and fills in its height and depth, and every length and breadth, so too he sought to be omnipresent to them, truly, a man greater than a king and more powerful than any assembly of legislators, above and beyond the law and philosophies of natural man, a new creature made from immortal skin and bones and blood sinew, and stuffed with the brilliance of the stars—and lo, there he was, truly, and entitled to be worshiped and prayed to, yea, a god in their insular world to lord over them.

When the people toiled, it was for his betterment, and as a sinkhole they dwelled in sank deeper, his giant's shadow engulfed more of them, until his form blotted out even the deep cerulean sky.

He built prisons from the crushed bones of his enemies; he built gallows with the hollowed-out books of law and justice; he hung prisoners with a noose made from the shredded skin of the massacred masses, and it seemed that no one dared oppose him, but those who did died, and those men who helped him received a handsome bride, and those women who helped him received a handsome bridegroom.

And what were these brides and bridegrooms, but of magnificent wealth and fertile soil and unbound power?

This Big Man of Africa took all the big businesses and services and all the big lands and placed their identities on playing cards and reshuffled the deck and then proceeded to redistribute them into several rows of black felt hats, each hat with the name of his brother, sister or mother, father, father-in-law, mother-in-law, general, uncle, cousin, friend, and there you have it, he had created an instant layer of thick and loyal human insulation around his ever-increasingly fat, never satiated self.

He starved his people until they began to die by the thousands, and when the sympathetic, empathetic, international aid agencies came weeping and wailing to his door with outstretched hands that were full of cash and food and medicine, why, he gingerly pocketed the cash and sold the precious food and medicine for more loot, laughing all the while, and marveling at his good fortune; and he was fond of saying "god is good."

When the economy of his country began to disintegrate because he had allowed the infrastructure to crumble and the government employees to go unpaid, and because he had directed the majority of the nation's income toward his greedy self and his co-conspirators, international bank agencies came boasting with mountains of freshly minted cash while asking for a solemn pledge that he would reform the economy in good faith; well, sir, he smiled and said, "yes, sir," and signed a document he had no more regard for than you and I would have if it allowed barn animals to nest in our clean, sanitary home.

So, thus reinforced by an incessant string of rich but blind and ignorant do-gooders, he proceeded to indulge any whim, laughing all the while.

When only a cup of rice would have sustained one life in this country, he bought a château in France; and when he looked around at a fly-covered baby who had died of starvation, slumped over its hollowed-out, worn-out mother, he bought two more châteaux in Belgium—dead and dying compatriots seemed to inspire him to bouts of gross indulgence; but why, why did the observation of his country kin suffering at his own hand stimulate his sensory organs to lavish himself to build a presidential palace that took vast amounts of government GDP, when that very same money, if strategically shifted to his ailing people, would have brought one of the greatest gifts one person can bestow upon another: the gift of life, the gift of health, the gift of peace, and not just one life or health or peace but millions? It is said that when a reporter asked him about the regions where the most perverse suffering existed, the Big Man of Africa, this unwanted savior, had remarked that such reports were gross exaggerations, and that he much preferred to give the reporter a tour of the presidential palace that he was so proud of; thus, we have the secret of his unique ability to focus his energies upon his vast wealth while surrounded by a sea of suffering citizens—he was the Big Man of Africa for the promises of illimitable mammon, much like a CEO of a powerful company; in point of fact, he saw his country as a company, the citizens as employees, and like any cunning and impersonal owner, the fall of employees into the meat grinder meant simply an irksome delay while the machine parts were cleaned and the dead body removed and a punishment and salary reduction for the immediate supervisor; there were no practical emotions of remorse or sympathy for the dead worker, only contempt and disgust that the poor fool had interrupted the steady stream of the incessant, round-the-clock profit mechanism known as slave-labor market capitalism, or, roughly translated, where the worker should be grateful to work while making vast sums of inordinate wealth for the all-powerful CEO.

So, the fortune of the people of this country descended while the fortune of the Big Man of Africa ascended, and when the plight of the people declined below sea level and their world began to fill with the noxious debris of human carnage sliding inevitably toward them, his fortunes climbed upon the highest highs, above even the puffy white clouds and into the celestial firmament; and lo, not even one of them, not even one brave soul elevated himself from the deepening pit to deliver a death blow to the round head of the dreaded Puff Adder who feigned human proportions—not one courageous, liberated, dedicated soul stepped up to save the people.

And so, by not opposing him, the people were pulling dirt away from the great depression, and over their own crushed heads.

One day, when the season of villainy in his country rose as the temperature rose, a daring, mocking soldier of coiled flesh and venomous speech slipped into the presidential palace and extracted the life-force of the Big Man of Africa; and without hesitation at all slipped the reptilian scales of abusive power over his own thin skin and easily assumed the role of the newest Big Man, and so promised reform and regeneration and so on, ad infinitum, until the distinction between ruler before and who ruled now was obscured, and the memory of the people saw only one long, solid line of unbroken foreign and domestic tyrants, and the complexion and height and weight of these despots disappeared into the fabric of their royal robes; yea, even their physical forms dissolved and became the incarnation of fear and chaos, a grotesque, multilayered creature of brick and mortar that hovered above the people like a menacing gargoyle.

And in which country in Africa did this occur; whose story is it that needs be told? But the better question is in which country did it not occur? So, merely pick one, and there you have it—the story is told, where only names differ, for Puff Adders, anywhere they are, devour their prey, and positively do not think about it, at all.

Night Commuters

Day was glorious and abounding with good tidings. The children loved the brightness of the Day, loved its luminous nature, praised its open, piercing, brilliant eye, adored its gentle stroke and kindly smile; yes, the children in this small village in the district of East Acholi seemed to revel in every moment of the Day as if they had never experienced its warm touch, as if they might never again see its azure smile and feel its white, tender kisses upon their bare, black skin.

When it was midday, the children were at the height of their harvest of hilarity, dancing, and singing songs, laughing, and shouting joy; and when it was midday, the children could not be deterred from such jubilation, and one could have easily argued a case against their joy, as the barefoot and scrawny children, clothed in rags and living in thatched huts and dirt floors, lived on the bottommost rung of poverty, having no access to adequate sanitation or clean water or constant and nutritious meals, and adequate medicine and proper protection from the savage elements and the savage animals therein; but when it was past midday and the yellow ball of gaseous fluff in the sky began to move past its high arc and settle into its inevitable downward descent on the rim of the dimming sky-dome, a droplet of gloom fell upon the happy children as if it were a presentiment of a severe plague; yet, dancing still, the children continued on, smiling and laughing but with an occasional imperceptible glance over their shoulders at the enveloping black curtain slowly descending.

When the shadows lengthened and the giant red ball of fire opened the door of the far horizon and began to slip inside its cozy covers, the children were already melancholy, as if a great burden had been placed in their yoke, as if they were resigned to some dreaded fear that came with the dying fuel of Day and the imminent reign of a slowly forming, melancholy gloaming.

And then it came, the unstoppable herald of night and the horror each blade of darkness brought cast a pall over the now-alert faces of the children, but faces soon bruised from the battering knowledge that a great terror was coming down the road for them and only them, not for their parents or treasure or for farm animals but to snatch them up and spirit them away into a populous netherworld where they would drown in the bracing, heavily metal, devouring, heavily shameful, menacing, heavily toxic air.

Farewells came then, and hugs and tears too, as the children's bodies—against the rule of their minds—moved on down the dirt road as if drawn by some mysterious locomotion; swifter, swifter, their tiny legs stepped to get farther, farther down the narrow path that now wound an abrupt left and headed directly toward the distant town.

Crimson-soaked dusk still proffered a thin veil of protection over them against the approaching terror, for any flicker of light, like the flicker of a candle flame aimed at a beast, exposed the ghouls who waited without.

Children from the Internally Displaced Persons' camps, the IDPs, soon joined them, and many of them, nearly all of them, joined hands and kept an eager vigilance about them, many of them, most of them, still trembling in fear as they perused the now eerie, unknown, thick green brush on either side of them.

When these children reached the town, they sought out those places that projected the most light and produced the most human traffic, so they went to bus depots and churches, and found stores still open, and there they stood, still looking about at the people wandering the street, as if in this crowd the terrible ghouls were still watching them.

It was now fully and irrevocably Night, no hope for Day now, no chance for a sliver of light bursting through the tarry cloak, and still the children trembled as they lay upon the asphalt streets and wooden benches and cement steps to await their blessed Dawn-Savior, for they knew the terror they had left behind was now replaced by the terror ahead.

Police officers walked by and around the children, citizens avoided them, other children peered at them with intense curiosity as they walked with their own parents through the town.

Now, it was fully adult Night, past its shallow infant roots, where the black molecules settled upon the observers and took their vision and directional compass, took their emotional equanimity and crushed it and laid the remains upon their squirming minds.

With sleep came only a slimming of the children's trepidation, as many of them had bad visions of the ghouls in their restless dreams.

And sometimes a shrill cry might shatter the quietude of the streets, and the children asleep would start up and huddle together as they desperately looked around for the victim; and often they saw it, they saw the city ghoul dragging away a small girl into its metallic four-wheeled lair or a dark alley to satiate its animalistic carnal needs; and when it was done and gone and it had released its victim, she might stagger back to the fold and fall to the sidewalk and sob as her loyal friends wept solace and grief over her.

But sometimes—as when that cunning thief, the black crow, comes a-stealing eggs or chicks from the sparrow's high nest, it can be beaten back if mother comes and vents her fury at him—so, too now, when the man stealer comes round to pluck innocence from a young girl, her older compatriots—and even daring young ones—might hiss and holler and kick and bite and scratch to chase the mummified soul away, but just sometimes, for often it is too late once the girl is snatched and sometimes impossible if there are a gang of these malevolent spirits.

Any loud noise, or soft noise, any disturbing noise or noise like an unfriendly intention, shook the children awake and cast them into a roiling sea where they bobbed up and down anxiously awaiting another threat, and when the noise proved innocuous and the night once again assumed its eerie cap, the children drifted off to slumber.

When the first sprays of a maroon, candy-coated street sky appeared, the children knew that their brief internment was nearly at an end, and when the mighty sun heaved its mighty orange-blazed hue onto the horizon, and the city began to awaken, the children silently cheered, and slowly arose, their tired bodies slowly beginning to move, some of them heading off to school and others back home.

Yet, the ghouls who inhabited the night represented one schema of encroaching human viper, while the open-air, sunshine ghouls represented quite another, so it was not uncommon for some of the children, as they tracked back in the cool morning, to be taken while on the road back home.

And what of the desperate fathers and mothers who waited the long, anxious night for the return of their sweet babies; what of their breaking hearts and pleading words for protection; and their plaintive wails, and expensive breath, that seemed, with every exultation, to rob them of their injured souls? But the same repulsing hot wind was the answer: suffer Man's grossest injustices without hope for Justice; and how long can a mother abide such brawling inequalities? How long, how long can a father suffer such uncensored vices, and feel impotent to keep safe his own, how long? Forever long, until things of Nature—climate, disease, and catastrophe—or of civilization—sin, disease, and catastrophe—disappear, but until then, Fate will sink its sharp fangs into the people to drain their last drop of joy and pride and resolution, wearing down their final resistance until they are as one dead.

And so it was, and so it went on night after night, this twisted menagerie of fleeing and hiding, hoping and praying by the people; and so it, this funeral procession, inevitably fell night after night over the high cliff of insensibility and into the sensible tide of a bloodied, moonlit sea. And so it was, and so it went on Day after Day, this cherished hour of fleeting freedom and joy, where the children were as happy as princes and princesses at their own coronation, insistent upon bearing any sorrowful thing and obstacle where they would pour their hearts out in guileless abandon and be who they were supposed to be and who Nature expected them to be and who the brethren around the world in their comfortable houses were, every happy Day and every peaceful Night.

And then the dishonorable process was banged again into "go," with the first smear of tarry molecules against a watermelon sky, and what could the players do but act the role that geography and world apathy had spun for them?

On the road well traveled by these children, as they came back from their temporary lodging, some went to school, some back home, and many others, who had already lost their homes to the caprice of this interminable civil war, took a diverging path to the IDP camps, and on this particular road were a brother and sister, who continued to hold the small hand of each other as they had since the journey had begun.

Nabulungi, being the eldest of the two, walked slightly ahead, eyes forward for any peril, holding the hand of Ojore, who too often allowed his toddler gaze to stray upon those things most important to his age, that being lizards, snakes, creepy crawling things, birds in the air, birds in the bush, and any bright and shiny object he considered prospect for holding and inspecting and possibly throwing or kicking.

She had the large, round, innocent brown eyes of the newborn creature who has not yet had the chance to damage another innocent life, and it was through these soft and gentle orbs that she perceived the world; her black hair was short and curly, and her nose was small and narrow, and her outlook on life was big and hopeful as she spun cheerful words out of her small mouth that they might form a barrier in front of them to catch the menace of life, and she would often bend down and kiss her brother's forehead and say blessings about him to form a shield of love and goodness against the unseen enemy. She had, perhaps through the uniqueness of her circumstances, learned that tone and pitch in her words could cradle Ojore in swaddling serenity; and to achieve this balance she would utter deeply, rich oaths of fidelity and higher notes of assurance and love to him, thus soothing his uneasiness; her voice was oft like a flowing melody, as she would sing verse and hum prose in such a continued pattern to him that his mind embraced it as musical notes; and in this way, she created an idyllic world of shapes and patterns, colors and contrasts, things living and magical, that he and he alone saw that comforted him and kept his small body from conversing with worry and fear.

She was nine and he was four.

But she was not the nine-year-old of wealthy countries, most of whom who are sheltered from any harmful and obscene thing, and trial and tribulation, but the nine-year-old living in a constant state of horror and degradation; and so she was not nine, but older, but not older in intelligence as measured by tests, but in the ways of Nature and the human heart and how the world is set up and how villains and heroes interact, and in this way, she was much, much older; but still, little Ojore was just four, too, too young to understand why the ogres of the world were not daily bound—and as Nabulungi would say to him after she heard an adult mention it—"and held before the world's courts and flung into the burning fires below."

And Nabulungi knew that there were many, many children such as she and her brother, and that every day such children were taken away by that growing-in-strength ogre and eaten by him, and when he smiled for the camera, remains of her friends could plainly be seen sticking between his sharp, yellow-fanged teeth; but what she did not know was that people around the world knew who the ogre was and exactly what he was doing and oftentimes encouraged him and his deadly pursuits with money and things; this last detail, perhaps, would have punctured a tiny hole in the fragile equilibrium she balanced their life upon.

But as it was, she and Ojore were once more entering the camp for displaced persons, which was a miserable sprawl of fragile structures placed in certain configurations to illustrate the illusion of a house, but the canopies of thatching grass and circular mud sides were really nothing more than discards from civilization's playground.

It was here that international aid workers came to deliver food and medicine and clothing, and to distribute that most important commodity in this moral abscess: Hope.

This IDP was situated in the north-eastern region of Karamoja in Uganda, in the midst of wooded savanna. Many of the people had abandoned homes that were not far from here; many of the children had no memory of home other than this one; and many more people came in every week to find shelter and safety from the encroaching, diabolical human storm.

At night, the Acholi would sit in their huts, some around campfires, and talk of the rumors they had heard about the anarchy that existed around them.

A tall, slender man with a bony cranium and skinny, long, leathery fingers, spoke in a wispy, hoarse voice. "The Karamojong chased me off my own land to gain my pasture for their cattle." His oblong-shaped skull swiveled back and forth. "When will it all end?"

Some of the other men acknowledged the ancient feud among the Karamojong.

"It is just one more thing that never seems to end," a young man said, his voice racked by melancholy. "In our country, we seem never to resolve problems, and gain more; it is beyond my understanding."

"It was not always that way," an elderly woman said, carefully, and so quietly that those around the campfire had to stop eating their cassava and beans and incline their heads toward her to hear her low, bird-like chirping; her face was a heap of gloom, her voice a heap of sorrow. "When in the day before we were taken over, in that happy day, when we had no borders and people lived simply, we had what we needed and we never had to worry about other clans or nations, for they were a world apart, and not about our business." A hurtful gaze came to her misty gray eyes, and a deep longing cradled her words in old, wrinkled cloth. "…A time that will never come again."

It would have been simply too impolite to utter words now and trample upon the significant history she had just uttered, so those around the smoldering fire politely waited until those images, like cinders leaping from its mother-fire, died in the cool, dusty soil.

"Well, I heard a UN peacekeeper talk about more mines that were found on the eastern side," a woman finally said, caution still in her words; "new mines."

It was worse news to make a bad situation intolerable, and all of the villagers there thought of someone they knew who had been a victim of these blind and buried soldiers.

"They don't care who they kill, these GLA parasites, killing their own people."

"And what has the Ugandan government done, eh?" a young man said, angrily. "Every time they go after Mulumba and fail, he punishes us."

Nothing they said this night was new, nor would any conversation on any night render different things to explore, for these people were captives in a secluded prison where real news from the outside was shorn from them like wool on a sheep.

A young girl, perhaps thirteen, came up to the small circle of Ugandan refugees, carrying a rusty tin tray with numerous foam cups upon it, and offered them warm tea, to which all of them politely assented; but then one of the men, a middle-aged man, said to her, "You were taken by the GLA—what was it like?"

There were newcomers in this group who expressed instant curiosity at the girl's possible answers, but upon inspecting the disapproving frowns of the majority of his elders, they withdrew their eager faces and sat mortified like the others.

"You should not be menacing the girl like that," an elderly woman said to the man, who subsequently blanched with shame, and the woman held the girl fast and stroked her hands.

A small girl and her little brother happened by the group and stood behind a seated, very tall man, and both of them placed their small hands upon his big, broad shoulders, one on each side.

"I'm not afraid to tell you," the young girl replied, focusing on the two children behind the giant; "it is the way it is and you need to know how it is," and then shifted her eyes to the big man, "so one day all of it will not be as it is now." She turned her penetrating stare to the others, and said, with a mature calmness, "If you do not know, then you will not care," and she lifted her gaze toward the far-off place wherein she was so long enslaved, "and children like me who still are there will be forgotten." She clutched her chest. "O, Karwana, I have not forgotten you, nor you, Hiba, nor Abi, or Kamal," and she closed her eyes and felt the ineffable pain of bad memories. The elderly woman gently squeezed the child's hand. "My friends, my sisters, my brothers—for who is a better brother and sister than those who suffer alongside you—are still in that terrible place." Her brown eyes shut. Her face became a map of sorrows, a physical map that re-created the great image of human suffering; not ordinary suffering experienced by ordinary people, but extraordinary suffering experienced by extraordinary people—people made extraordinary by their extraordinary suffering; she could see the GLA camp now, in her mind, and even smell the constant odors there from cooking and from the threat of pain and punishment for trespass of the children against their masters: she could see clearly where she and her friends had been held and how the trees and bushes stood on the perimeter and the noises of the forest as a reminder that she was still on Earth; she could see it all now and experience it all as her mind let loose its meager grip on present sanity and flowed back into that dark wilderness called insanity. Her grip on the old woman's hand tightened as her misty brown eyes opened.

"I remember the day I was taken. I was nine; I was getting water for my family at the well, and three men with guns came up to me and grabbed me and took me with them through a forest and to other raids where they took more children—mostly girls; then we moved again through the forest until we came to a camp that was hidden in the woods; when I arrived there I was thrown into a tent, where a Controller took me and raped me and then later he took me down to the river and threw me in and began to pray to his god that I might be purified by water, and on my head he poured water that was mixed with camouflage, and he chanted a chant that I might be purified; later, at the camp, I had shea oil put on my chest and back and forehead to further purify me and to protect me from evil spirits; and every time before this, he raped me, and every time after this, he raped me, and sometimes when he was angry or frustrated, he raped me, too—he raped me before battle and after battle and whenever he was happy: I was his little rape fix.

"Before we went into battle, we were instructed to pray so we might slay our enemies and purify the Acholi people of their sins; the soldiers were instructed always on our holy mission that Mulumba is following god's plan for finishing off his enemies, and we are taught that we were to burn down camps and villages and cut off the ears and lips of our enemies so they might follow god's biblical commands. Mulumba believes he is following the Ten Commandments, that the spirits move him and his soldiers to punish the Acholi, who he says are disobeying god's commandments.

"He thinks that the young girls he takes will be part of a new Acholi who will purify Uganda."

The sunshine of her mind still hid behind the darkest clouds.

"For the first year, I carried guns and ammunition for the soldiers, and cooked and cleaned for them, and mended their clothes, and dressed their wounds, and when I was eleven I became a soldier, too, even though I had been my Controller's wife for two years.

"We would go on raids and capture Ugandan troops and talk to them and cut off their lips and gouge out their eyes, and the little boys who had become soldiers with us were ordered to shoot these prisoners—those who refused were shot, so the captured soldiers always died.

"In camp, if a child ran away, a hunting party went after them and brought them back and laid them down inside the camp and then a boy was ordered to kill the runaway or be killed; but still, children ran away, and some got away; and I think the children would have still run away even if no children got away, because children always think they can succeed even though no one has before.

"Children are like that: they always think they can win, even when they have lost and don't know they cannot really win—and sometimes, they do win even when it shouldn't be possible. I remember Deborah."

A sliver of refreshing calm cut a slice of black cloud away and breathed a trickle of warm, golden sunlight into her pale mind. She reached out a slender right arm, which was cloaked by a white robe that covered scars from rocks and knife cuts and hot water scalding, and shut her eyes.

"There, Deborah sat in her Controller's tent, smiling at me when I first came into the camp, smiling whenever I needed a smile, hugging me whenever I needed to touch someone who would not hurt me; Deborah..." Her strained voice broke as her passions rose too humanly high to contain. "She," she began again, tempering her emotions as she had learned to do in the camps, "watched over me, and because of Deborah, I am here; because of me, she is not, for Deborah never thought of herself, but others; and she told me many times, 'Tumushabe, we are on earth to help each other; the one true God will take care of everything else.' And I wanted to believe her, even when she was beaten for bringing comfort to beaten children, and saying to me as she lay bruised and bleeding, 'we are only here for a little while, yet heaven is forever—how much pain can they give to me in so short time?' I remember her smiling when she said it, as if she were already there, in the presence of God."

A bolt of sunshine shattered the gloomy cloud and a burst of golden light adorned her healing mind.

"Deborah, our mother she was to us; lying for us, stealing for us, beaten for us, she took every blame against us and never cried out once, and never complained, no, not once, not our Deborah, our sister, our mother, our friend, our only real friend, who suffered so that others may live."

Her face was radiant with the bloom of love.

"A girl was supposed to kill a boy who would not kill an enemy soldier, and the girl was threatened with death unless she did so, and when the two soldiers raised their rifles to kill her, Deborah killed them with her own rifle, and she ran up to the girl and boy and hugged them both." Indescribable pain suffused the delicate texture of her face. "She hugged us for the last time, and kissed us for the last time, and sent us away, and I wept as I ran because I knew that I would never meet anyone again as good as she."

She opened eyes that had seen too much of those indelicate things that should remain unseen, and not enough of those good things that should be daily seen; her drifting voice raised one last decibel to proclaim as she wept, "I'm too old now, and have seen the last of my days, first in a world that should not be, and I know that no living Savior is coming for us."

The big man, whose very presence comforted the two children who stood behind him, grew rigid as his countenance animated grief and empathy; he wanted to stand up and say something, that he was here to fight for the forgotten and bring them back into the Light, but now he was on a respite, so won't you please be patient with him as he labored among the people to bring succor and charity. He watched, veiled in sadness, his large hand covering the small hands on his brawny shoulders, as the girl slowly walked away, wrapped in her private and tortured literature of horror and tragedy.

As the fortune of one falls because of injustice, and the fortune of another rises because of that injustice, there will never be true Justice.

This life just described—if deposited in the clean, pierced ear of a member of a civilized nation, an ear connected to a head free of lice and ticks and gunshot wounds, with a face absent of the impact of scattered rocks, sunburn, and diverse wounds, and eyes shielded from witnessing atrocities against Innocents, atop a body absent of a multitude of diseases and full of modern medicine and conveniences—would have crumpled them to the ground in a heap of sympathy, although transitory; but this story imparted to the present company was merely another grave dug alongside countless, unmarked others. The conversation soon turned to other things.

"Back again," the big man said, as he turned around and scooped up the two smiling cherubs, and placed them upon his broad shoulders, "so soon?"

"Yes, Mwindo," said Nabulungi, giggling.

"Yes, Mwindo," giggled Ojore, as Mwindo tickled the boy's bare belly with his head.

Mwindo understood that Nabulungi and Ojore needed time away from the societal blister that sat atop their hearts and bled pain and confusion every moment they were in this camp or on the road, and in order to heal that wound, he had not only to escort them but be with them as they left this living museum of mummified shame; therefore, they walked out of the camp and right into the forest, as they had done often, and where he taught the orphans the special character and consciousness of the land.

They walked, the giant and the two children, in this fragrant garden, this master gardener's paradise, among the spice-and sugar-bearing fairies of Nature, the boy and girl listening with care and excitement to the man's lessons concerning the secret lives of plants and insects and animals; he bequeathed to them those sagacious pearls a father pours upon his own son and daughter, to wit: how certain plants give life while others give death; how certain insects can lead to hidden food, and how others might be food; how certain animals lead to danger, and how others lead to life; and how Man has been commissioned to study and decipher the laws and customs of Nature or be subdued by it; it was in this untamed, unspoiled, pastoral utopia that he could rightly show the children how the world was supposed to operate, that there was balance in Nature, and where the wicked and avaricious living things were soon put to flight.

He never wanted to return to the camp after such journeys into the verdant hills, but it was an obligation to the children, for one day they might be rescued from their misery.

"Here," Mwindo said, smiling largely, as the travelers prepared to return, after plucking a pink blossom from a rosebush and placing the sweetly scented flower in the left side of Nabulungi's hair, "a flower for the flower of Africa, a treasure for the treasure of Africa." She hugged him as surely as if he were her own father.

"Here," Mwindo said, smiling, as he picked up a multicolored, radiant, shiny and smooth rock, and proceeded to lift it to the cerulean sky and allow its sparkles to fall upon the boy; and then he placed the precious stone in the boy's small hand, and said, "a treasure for the treasure of Africa, a gift for the gift of Africa." The boy hugged him as surely as if Mwindo was his own father.

"My Prince, my Princess," he said, solemnly, and nodding in approval, as he stood before them in the crown jewel of Nature. "What are your commands?" Both of them stretched their hands toward him, and presently he swung each one up, one upon his left shoulder, the other upon his right. "If only adults were so easily appeased," he thought as he walked back up the trail.

Nabulungi placed a colorful flower in front of him, and said, lovingly, "A flower for my King."

Ojore then placed a colorful flower in front of him, and said lovingly, "A flower for my King."

Mwindo took both of them, one in each arm, and embraced them as if they were his own children; and when he placed them back upon his shoulders, he silently wept with joy.

Once inside the IDP camp, and after depositing the children near the food station, he walked over to the people who inhabited the small huts he lived in. "So, my friends, tell me again—why do the children walk alone each night and every morning?"

A middle-aged man, who had been here for two years, said, "You can't have the whole camp leave every night."

"The children leave," Mwindo replied, frowning; "why must they be alone?"

"There is no reason for their mothers and fathers to go with them—it is the children who need to go."

"The children know how to survive," an elderly woman said; "the adults need to stay here."

"I will go with them," Mwindo declared, proudly.

"You will go," the man answered him, "but for what reason, I cannot say—for the children are safe."

Thus, Mwindo began to accompany the children on their nightly journeys, against the advice of some of the other Crusaders—as they had previously done—who were also in the same camp, some who argued that he must not expose himself to situations where he might be recognized.

One early dawn, when the newborn sky, like an elegantly polished crystal, spread its bronze prism and scarlet-streaked symmetry across the horizon like a rainbow wave, Nabulungi asked Mwindo the question he had feared to hear from her and had agonized on how to answer.

"Mwindo," she said, looking up at him with her soft, doe-like brown eyes, "what do I do if I am taken?"

He looked to Ojore, who was preoccupied with catching grasshoppers alongside the road, and then said to her, "Why do you ask, my little princess?"

She frowned and knit her eyebrows. "Can I be the flower of Africa if I am taken?"

He felt his great physique grow weak and his head become light. His voice had to be reassuring and full of certitude, without trepidation or worry at all. "You will always be the flower of Africa." He stated it as surely as the man who describes the assurance of sunrise following sunset to a frightened infant who is not certain it will happen again.

"And yet I have heard the stories of what happens to children—to girls like me—in the rebel camps, and I do not want such a thing to happen to me…"

"So, you must not be captured," he said, nodding approvingly.

"But many girls are taken often, and their fathers do not wish them to go."

His hard countenance softened, and then hardened again as he slapped his chest and proclaimed, "I will protect you."

She smiled, looked over to Ojore, who was scuttling along the edge of the dusty road searching for insects to capture. "I would not want him to go—it would not be good for one so young."

Mwindo smiled. "And for one so young—only nine—and yet, to be so wise," he said, nodding again.

"He must not go," she said, still looking lovingly at Ojore, and then she turned and looked up at Mwindo. "Promise me you will protect him first if they come for us."

He felt his heart grow numb. "No," he whispered, and shook his head strongly, "that I cannot and will not do—both of you will be safe with me forever."

She smiled and took his hand as she said softly, "You love us very much." He felt a great warmth spread inside him, the warmth of being loved, and he wanted to weep, but did not. "I know you love us, and we love you very much, but now you must show your love for me by promising to protect him first."

"I cannot lose either of you," he said, his voice absorbed by pathos, "it is like asking me which arm I would rather lose; what am I to say to that?"

"But it must be done, if you love us, and you do—so, you must promise."

"I will protect both of you," he murmured, looking into her guileless face. "I will, yet," but the words to come provoked no little emotional pain inside him, and he could not talk for a moment, and then said, after looking over at Ojore and back to her, "I will protect him first."

She kissed his hand, and as he knelt down and embraced her, Ojore came running and he embraced him too, for the longest, longest and longest of times, the same way a family, who wears the inviolate bonds of love, embrace each other.

Camp Life

Soft, furry white rabbits hopping down the bunny trail while chasing yellow and orange butterflies hear the clamorous roar of the predator approaching, so the silly white rabbits hop away from the noise into a small wire cage that Mr. Farmer-Gardener has provided for them, and then the trembling bunny rabbits hear the predators attack and see them gobble up the other innocent creatures of the forest, and watch the predators breach the silly wire barrier and turn their noses up at the silly, toothless guard dogs and snatch a sleeping rabbit here and there; and is it not the way of all things whenever we fail to slow the thundering step of the ravenous predator, when we accommodatingly step aside and fail to even place an obstacle in his way, not even a slick surface, a small hill of thorns, a blur of flashing signs, anything, and everything to give ample time for the prey to flee and the natural forces of goodness to prepare an adequate defense?

Life in the IDPs existed on a flat plain without probability of gain, and with the excellent possibility that any good thing could easily vanish; thus, any medicine one day was better than no medicine at all, and medicine two days in a row was a miracle; food came in batches when the cargoes weren't captured and sold by the rebels, so any food above a cup and a dash, or doused with spice or salt was a treat, and water, pure and fresh and clean, was a true revelation.

Disease, like cholera and dysentery, sudden and widespread, hung like a poisonous black cloud over them, replete with thunder and lightning that sat like a vulture over the crowded camp.

The Acholi were living in abject misery and extreme poverty, a rung higher than many on the outside; and as they knew the government troops were incapable of slaying Mulumba, and the government was incapable of providing them with even nominal subsistence, they could do nothing more than exist.

And then there were those unimaginable times when the Acholi felt as if more of their own bodies seemed to be disappearing into the harsh soil than there was adequate food to replenish it, when the nongovernmental organizations, the NGOs, involved in the pickup and transport of food and medicine to the camps, stopped coming, and although the World Food Programs, the WFPs, were involved in most food deliveries, the food supply was still reduced. The NGOs would not come if armed escorts accompanied the WFP shipment because it violated the textbook rules of nonviolence and noninter-ference; and so, when the WFPs did not come, nor the NGOs, the camps were stripped bare of their thinnest, remaining sanity.

It was at such times that the GLA would attack the camps and do what they believed their god had instructed them to do; but first, before the attack, the fighters prayed and sang for many days, and had their holy oil and water sprin-kled upon them, all in the hope of attaining god's blessing for their mission.

The GLA, on this particular day, first encountered a small elementary school that was run by three Catholic nuns; now, to them, this school was illuminated in the same fashion as an aboveground that is lousy with gold nuggets would be to a desperately poor miner.

Once the children, in their smart black and white uniforms, had been ushered out onto the dirt playground, three nuns pleaded for the leader of the GLA to have mercy on the school.

He frowned instead, and laughed, too. "But god," he said, in broken English, "has sent us to liberate these Acholi children from your Western prison."

Sister Francine, hands clasped in front of her rosary, her body attired in black and white clothes, her face pleading, spoke again. "I ask you, sir, to please consider the welfare of these poor orphans!"

The man shrugged his shoulders bare, black, bony shoulders. "I don't know what it all means," he returned, and then, waving his rifle toward his men, "but we need these kiddies." But the men were repulsed by the embold-ened nuns, and then the sister issued an impassioned plea.

"Must you take them, must you—why, why, take them; surely, God has not sent you here to take these poor children from us."

"Exactly! We're here to rescue them from you and purify them and teach them our faith and our sacred laws."

She shook her head, her clenched frown and clenched fists bobbing up and down in the languid air. "But they are innocent children and have no business in war."

The man, uncaring, shrugged his shoulders again. "They can carry a gun, they can cook, they can clean, they can do many chores." He waved to his man again, but once more, the nun let her hands direct them to stay. "Woman, we must be on our way." He waved them past her, and this time, the men lined up behind the fearful students.

The brown-haired nun stood up straight and loosened her fierce look. "I have read about you—you say you are a Christian, but Jesus would never kidnap children. He preached that we must protect them."

"We have," the man said, looking and counting, "forty-six new disciples—the Master will be most pleased."

"Is there nothing we can say to stop you?"

The man appeared lost in deep reverie for a while, rubbing his chin, then said, "I tell you what, Madam, because you love these children so," and he snapped his fingers, "I will take only twenty-three!" He slapped his thigh. "You choose, Madam!"

Once seeing that the leader of the GLA would not alter his offer, she and the two nuns stood before the students, unable to decide, but when the leader demanded that they choose within ten minutes' time, the nuns did choose, weeping as they did so, until twenty-three weeping students stood behind them and twenty-three weeping students with the soldiers.

"Good, good," the leader said, smiling as he smoked a fat, brown cigar, now, and he patted the nun upon her shoulders, "you have done good, and now we will do even better!" He grabbed the woman and threw her violently to the ground, as the soldiers did the same to the other nuns. "Now, you will learn that Mulumba is god's true messenger and prophet, and not you, you foreign invader!"

And so, he and his men proceeded to rip the clothes from the struggling and pleading nuns, and each man proceeded to rape each woman, while the soldiers forced the screaming and crying children to watch; and when this emotional and physical massacre was over, the leader bent down and whispered to the brown-haired nun, "So, when you meet God, you ask him who is right, eh?"

Her voice had the strength of a smashed eggshell. "I know now; I am saved by the blood of Jesus Christ, and you are lost, damned to hell if you do not repent of your wickedness."

He rose up, a sneer elevating him to stand boldly as he took out his long silver sword and swung it up and around and down upon the woman. The other women suffered the same fate.

The leader shouted to his men as he watched red blood drain from his victims, "Take all of the children," and he bent down and breathed his hot, obscene breath on the brown-haired woman. "It is so much more fun when you pretend to give your enemy a chance." He emitted a lusty laugh from deep within the recesses of his freak zone, wherein lay the gnarled, twisted perversions that creep into an injured soul because it leaks humanity and goes about unchecked and unaware, and proudly boasts of its malevolence. She expired, and he kicked her corpse, and shrugged his bony shoulders. He spat upon her. "And now we go and cook some Acholi—Mulumba will be pleased with Patrick today. I can tell you this."

She could no longer reply, and even if she were still alive, she would have known that heaven would give the ultimate answer.

This GLA unit moved out and wound its way with the weeping children through the weeping forest and soon deposited the youthful cargo at one of its own camps, and then turned north toward an IDP site.

So, the legion of iniquitous spirits was on the march, and would not be undone; no, they would not be swayed or discomfited by human compassion, could not be stopped, they believed, as long as they wore the sacred shea oil and armor of their fanatical religion, and every success curled into their laps was like a piece of bloody meat tossed into the gaping mouth of a sharp-toothed, man-hunting tiger.

Onward they moved, praying all the while, chanting their special protective song, revving their internal engines to the highest acceleration point until their hearts pounded loudly and their bodies poured heavy perspiration, anticipation of battle lying like succulent honey on their wagging tongues.

Then, in the broadest daylight, as the last bronze curtain of dawn lifted from the sky to reveal a full spectrum of light, they sighted the camp and, walking boldly down narrow slopes without care if they were observed, soon breached the perimeter and then set about their Master's dirty business.

The routine they had established while invading such a camp originated from the playbook of ancient savages, to wit: plunder, kill, murder and maim, while heeding no rhyme or reason, following no logic or course, listening to no internal guide or external source, merely obeying the dogmatic philosophy of their mongrel master, the bleating butcher, the amoral assassin as they executed their appointed errands; however, there is one sentiment of value that was found in their core paradigm as they moved through the camp like maddened bull elephants, and it was a fierce species of love—yes, a love of job, a love of toiling for divine rewards that, they reasoned, were soon to be handsomely distributed to them—love, passion, fury, lust, ecstasy, all of it emasculating their sense of mercy and a loving heart and compassionate mind.

They were the stalking Black Panther, to devour the staked sacrificial goat.

And so it all began.

When there was a hut, they transformed it into a heap of ashes; where there was a human being, they transferred him into a lump of mangled flesh; where anything moved or cried out, they punctured it and stabbed it and shot it, and where anything stood or lay, they set fire to it, but soon the whole place was an abomination of desolation, and the people who escaped from the slaughterhouse, first, the soldiers pursued them into the forest to establish the slaughterhouse there, and those caught suffered a longer and painful dying.

Thus, covered in the warm blood and tears of their victims, they ventured on to the next camp, disregarding any news that had spread of their misdeed, or any condemnation of the human carnage they left all about them, like a wolf carving its way through a chicken pen; therein lay the heavy religious fervor that cloaked them with what they perceived as invincibility—they did not care how outsiders perceived them.

As it was, they were to rendezvous with another GLA unit that was set to attack another IDP area a few kilometers away, and they made post haste to enjoin their brethren and celebrate the triumph together; and soon they saw the camp, and were pleased that their brethren were already there and creating havoc, and so joined in, the same way a crocodile joins in the killing of a young, helpless deer that has veered too close to the watering hole.

Now, there was a man in the hills above the second camp, and he was busy searching for a certain clump of cherry-red flowers and a batch of glittering rock, when he sensed that there was commotion down below; and so, coming out of the deep picket, where even no light could enter, he first noticed smoke from the first camp, and immediately alighted toward a tall Acacia tree that bore a small, round mark upon its brown-barked belly, and he quickly dug at its base and uncovered a brown cloth that, once thrown away, revealed the French FAMAS G2 assault rifle, which also shot grenades, and the Belgian FN Minimi machine gun; a lesser man would have suffered over the choice of weapons, heavy or light, close range or distance, but he merely hoisted the rifle strap over his left shoulder and tucked in an extra thirty-round box magazines into his now tightened waistband, and hoisted the machine gun strap over his left shoulder and slung several belted two-hundred-round box magazines next to it. He heard pounding footsteps, and did not have to even look up to know who it was. He stood up.

The first man to come running was cursing like a man on fire. It was Henry.

"Neutrality, ha!" he shouted, falling to his knees as he dug to reveal his hidden cachet of arms. "And I'm out of shape and weak from all this horrible food!" He was digging furiously with his KA-BAR Fighting/Utility Knife, as were the other men at the other sites. He looked up to see Mwindo running down the path, pell-mell. "Wait up, man! You cannot defeat them all by yourself!"

One of the Crusaders, lifting up his rifles, said, "No one has told him he cannot, and so he will." He was one of Mwindo's men.

The attack on the village by the GLA had just begun, and at this early infancy of battle, the soldiers would be at their most audacious and therefore their most vulnerable, for every soldier walks in the battle holding hands with his naked mistress, Fate, and hopes to win her over through selfless devotion to courage and camaraderie.

The token sunbathers, sightseers, gawkers, hands-tied-behind-their-backs UN officials were dispatched with the greatest contempt and violence, they having incurred not only a brutal and violent death but a gruesome one as well by the gleeful, prancing soldiers; it must be remembered that for the GLA to be doing what they were now was their greatest joy, as it came from serving their god and pleasing it, and by believing that no other action on earth could bring them more joy and personal claim than this cleansing of the sinful from their holy land.

The ability to extinguish the frightened life of their choice dressed the soldiers in a powerful armor that hardened every time they shot down an unarmed Acholi, and penetrated deeper into their bones and sinew every time they smashed down even a feebly armed Acholi, and melded with their very heart and mind whenever they put out the lamp of life in front of their kinsmen.

The Acholi were running anywhere and hiding everywhere. And mothers screamed as they held their babies and fathers grieved as their families ran unprotected, but what else could they do, but run until they were shot or cut down by the sword, or until they escaped?

Four soldiers were running in tandem, in synchronization concerning their choices of huts to torch and people to murder, and they consequently felt invincible, for everyone around them cowered before them, and everything around them was burning, and behold, they felt as if they were charged with a sacred task by their god to scorch the land of iniquity, as if they were chosen horsemen of the apocalypse; these soldiers turned a corner and found a family of seven huddling together, snared by the ravages of terror, and they shouted the death cry as they raised their blood-stained swords, as they felt this time the need to physically dispatch these heathens in close proximity; and so, they converged on the family and brought down their weapons, but a curious thing occurred this time, for they, these seemingly unstoppable spirits, froze, their backs arched, blood seeping out of their naked bodies, and lo, they did the seemingly impossible, they collapsed to the ground, they fell, dying in a river of blood, and when they had fallen, they gave a view to the reason for this miracle, and he stood looming large, like a redwood tree in a forest of bushes and shrubs.

"Mwindo," the family cried.

Indeed, it was he, the Chadian warrior, glistening sweat pouring off his body, his face awash in the ferocity of battle, his rifle extended, his other rifle slung over his massive shoulders, and then, like a gust of wind, he was gone, sweeping through the encampment in pursuit of the pursuers, launching grenades at them when no Innocents were near.

So, now the hunters had a hunter on them, the executioners had acquired a target upon their sweaty backs, and scores of them were slayed.

Mwindo, as he ran, searching for Nabulungi and Ojore, sighted one soldier here and so shot him and saw another there and so shot him and turned the corner of huts and beheld three soldiers and mowed them down like they were diseased rodents; but then he came upon four more soldiers and two more beside him and one behind him and still he set to work like the great craftsman he was, shooting the men afore and aft him as if he truly believed the other men would somehow not harm him; and yea, this came to pass, as the men about him were felled like he were merely chopping trees, and he did not hesitate to understand why, but moved on, his keen eyes surveying the horizon for soldiers carrying away children.

But there were more shots fired into the war zone, more than originally possible, and soon the answer crystallized itself on the periphery of the battle zone.

The Crusaders had arrived.

When the GLA soldiers had attacked the first IDP camp, they had attacked several Crusaders who were working there, and as the Crusaders escaped and retrieved their own weapons, they ran to alert their fellows, who were working in various refugee areas nearby, who had seen the smoke and were already on their way; and so, as Mwindo ran boldly through the camp, six Crusaders were behind him.

The GLA were, as they saw it, being ignominiously swept from their target prematurely, but as the Crusaders saw it, the GLA were being flushed out of the camp like a virulent disease seeping from a sick body.

Mwindo was following a group of twenty soldiers who had gained the periphery of the camp and were splitting off two diverging roads; he dared not shoot because several of the men had small children in their possession, but shoot he must, as the soldiers would soon disappear into the camouflage of the dense jungle.

His great strides captured big chunks of ground as he neared the fleeing soldiers. He sighted Nabulungi. He sighted Ojore. His heart leaped.

The children were being dragged down diverging roads.

He had promised, yes, he had promised her, he knew, a promise he had never considered, never once supposed would become reality, but a promise that now cleft his heart in twain.

He was nearing the two roads and was still taking down the running soldiers before him, when he looked down the left road and saw sweet, innocent Nabulungi being dragged along at a rapid pace, and as he looked down the right road, he saw sweet, innocent Ojore being carried along at a rapid pace, and he screamed in anguish and desperation; and he took hold of the FAMAS G2 rifle in his left hand and the Minimi machine gun in his right, and pulled the triggers on both weapons and watched as soldiers without a child fell; but soon his trail of bullets led up to the soldiers with children and he promptly let go of the triggers and with a booming shout he turned down the right road, with now a dozen Crusaders behind him, as others went down the left road.

Mwindo was running full tilt and firing rounds from the sniper rifle into the soldiers even as the soldiers were firing back at him, and the Crusaders flanking him were firing their weapons past him and peeling away the soldiers in the rear; and then the GLA soldiers struck into the deep cover of the thicket and tore off into different directions, and the soldiers who carried Ojore turned and held up the boy as a shield; and lo, then this soldier was greeted with two well-placed 5.56 x 45 mm bullets into his weasel-like brain.

"Done," Mwindo cried, and scooped up the crying boy; turning, he yelled to his comrades, "guard him as you would your own son," and he darted off toward the left.

He was weaving expertly through the brown brush and leaping over the verdant foliage and dodging hanging limbs as he followed the sound of gunfire ahead, and then the noise stopped, and he knew the battle was over. He would not think of the outcome, but ran faster, eclipsing any past land-speed records for himself as he came upon the Crusaders who were standing among the fallen soldiers.

He saw men, and children who were not whom he sought standing, but this, he knew, was impossible, for she had to be somewhere standing safely with a Crusader, behind a tree, sitting and being comforted by him, surely with a Crusader, with his valiant comrades; and so when he came upon the last group of dead soldiers, his eyes saw but did not behold, his mind acknowledged but did not accept, the small body lying next to them. He threw away his weapons and the bullets and then fell next to her and lifted up her bloodied body and held it to himself as he rocked to and fro and wept. He heard but did not listen to the Crusaders who told him that the soldiers had killed her for no reason, he did not, could not, not now, not as he held the precious pink blossom of Africa in his arms; and then he did say, his voice full of burning pathos, "She did not die for nothing, no, not my little princess, not my good, good girl." He stroked her forehead and wet black hair and, looking at her lovingly as he held her gently, he said, softly, "She lived for a reason, my little princess of Africa, and she died for a reason, my little daughter, my pink blossom of Africa," and he held her head to his breast as he held her fast and his warm, pious tears fell upon her like a soulful christening.

Mwindo buried Nabulungi, and Tumushabe, who had told the story about Deborah.

The Crusaders around him said nothing, but faithfully stood near him, for there was nothing any of them could say to undo what had been so wrongfully done; for it was war, and Innocents would die.

The Mission Rejoined

The Crusaders were together again, and this time they did not care who knew it, be it man, country, or world; they were hungry, some of them weak, and they were tired, some of them exhausted, from the sparse diet and hard labor of the camps in which they had volunteered, but it had been the way they wanted it, and now it was over, and they would reclaim their vigor and stamina once again, and put on the mantle of war.

Now, the Ugandan government managed to deduce that another group had fought their fight, and like any sovereign government, cast a jealous eye upon the foreign intruders, and so dispatched their helicopters and tanks and associated military bodies to the site of the battle; and the Crusaders, not wishing to fight them, and being informed of what was to come by a courier, allowed themselves to be surrounded by them, but would not put down their weapons, and so a standoff ensued, until a lone helicopter landed in their midst and out stepped a man they had never expected to see.

He was dressed in casual attire, consisting of long white cotton pants and a beige-colored short sleeve shirt and brown slip on shoes, and he did say, easily, without a commitment at all to the power of his presence, "I am President Obote."

It was time for Moses to speak, and his tone was born by the power of wrath, "The President of Uganda deigns to come into the presence of commoners."

Even the men on guard on the periphery of the small clearing were listening now.

The man with the round head and small black mustache nodded, and then smiled as he waved about, "And who are you to offer judgment, but mercenaries and rogue military who have broken international treaties and the laws of Uganda?"

Moses' countenance was hard and unyielding, like the good sentinel whose face has grown cold awaiting the arrival of reinforcements. "It is better to die on one's feet than live on our knees."

Obote laughed and gestured toward the youth. "Such bravery," he cried, and held out his hands, "but why not in your own home country of Kush— you are a Kushite, are you not, the inflection in your voice is unmistakable, and your features are recognizable—and you are from the South, I would guess."

It was youth emboldened by righteousness that served Moses' intellectual palette now, forging words of Justice and Virtue that swallowed the arrogant scent before him and treaded on the shrinking black shadows that cursed the light and hid in the darkness.

"We will fight everything that has no soul, as flesh without spirit is an offense to God, for in this poisoned continent, we have a great commission to protect Innocents from soulless rulers."

The clever smile of the President began to subside. "You have youth, that is all; you have naivety—where you spin fairy tales—your iron mistress, which you hide behind like a child." He expelled a long, exasperated breath, and said, smugly, "You are alive only because of Sir Robert Heimdall," and he suddenly pointed his jewel-laden fist at him, "and that is all."

A heavy sneer fell upon the youth's face. "You have used children to fight your wars, too, you have; you have power and wealth, that is all, and the people want Justice, not kings, and one day, you will fall as surely as the tyrants have before you."

The countenance of his comrades had evinced hope when the name of their benefactor was uttered in the midst of the steel trap; information of his influence here they had previous knowledge of, but when they heard their comrade accuse this widely acknowledged profiteer of human bondage of his crimes, their countenance fell, yet they did not subvert the authority of the speaker.

Rancor spat at Moses like venom from a brown-and-white checked, light-green Boomslang as the President spoke, heavy perspiration pouring off his shiny, bald cranium. "I would kill all of you if Sir Robert had not intervened; truly, I would have, but he has saved too many people in my country and our sister countries, and his political clout is prodigious." His face was grim. "You and your compatriots will be escorted to the northern border and released into Kush."

"Home," Moses retorted, unimpressed.

"Good! A reunion!" Obote threw up his arms. "You will start now." He waved his commanders over. "Escort these fine gentlemen to the northern border."

As the Crusaders moved out, Henry, highly amused by the astonishing rashness of Moses, and bridled now with a singular boldness not often accorded to the common man, paused next to the Ugandan leader, and said, smirking, "You know," but then he chuckled to himself as he dialogued with his own cynical cannon, "and you are the least of petty tyrants," and his voice fell an octave down to wrath as he issued a hard stare no common man would desire. "So, what awaits the worst of the thieves, pimps, liars, cheats and murdering scoundrels, eh?" He felt the impulse to press his knife right through the soft, flabby neck of the gloating man, but Abebe touched him, and he moved on.

Once at the border of Uganda and Kush, the Ugandan military began to withdraw.

"Good luck fighting," Horatius said, winking at them.

"Best of luck," Arjuna said; "you've been so successful in your endeavors thus far."

The two men slapped each other on the shoulder. The soldiers gave them a menacing look, but the two men, wrapped in this fleeing, political impunity, laugh uproariously.

"We will send you a bill for our services," Henry cried, walking away. "Please send U.S. currency." Abebe could not deter the stabbing jabs of his friend, who, as it was, sent out one last quick barb. "Remember, no currency with the faces of people who are still alive," and he pointed back to his antagonists as he turned around, still walking backward. "I like my money to keep its value longer than a week. Thanks! Bye!"

"You just couldn't help yourself," Abebe whispered, looking behind him.

"And I did help myself, didn't I?" Henry said, smugly, and smiling, and then gesturing with his hands. "And it tasted just fine."

Once the Crusaders were across the Ugandan border and into Kush, the Ugandan military—helicopters, trucks, tanks, and foot soldiers—turned around and moved for a while, but curiously halted their progression.

Tyr and Enkidu and two other scouts had managed to slip away from the military escort, Tyr and Enkidu going over the Kush border, and coming back, and the other two doubling back and going west and up past the Kenyan border and back to the Crusaders.

Tyr spoke first. "Company."

Enkidu spoke next. "Bad company."

Olaudah spoke. "Company."

Julius spoke next. "Bad company."

They had not used radio transmissions for fear that the Ugandan military might eavesdrop.

A War Council convened.

"The Kush government and the rebels come from the north, and the GLA from the south," Conall began, standing between Mwindo and Moses, and before the assembled men, and then he lifted up his gaze, "and before us lies salvation." Before them rose the Imatong Mountains. He placed his steady hand upon the shoulders of Moses. "Lead us."

Thus, the journey began, swiftly now, for the opposing forces ahead and behind them were even now approaching.

And as the men walked, many of them knew what Mwindo was doing was wrong, but dared not speak to him of it; yea, not even Conall and Moses spoke of it to him.

Thus, as the men marched into the wilderness of the Imatong Mountains, upon the shoulders of Mwindo sat the newest and littlest Crusader of them all, Ojore.

War is a wasteland of humanity,
cruelties, savageries, destruction, despair;
the human spirit seeks justification,
to restore love and affection,
lest it lose its liberty to believe

Through the Wilderness

The Crusaders ran, loaded with weapons and hope, with the greatest expedition through the brush, looking up to the upland regions ahead of them, for therein, Moses had said, lay salvation, amid the various vegetations the mountains wore, like thick wool on fat sheep.

The violent echoes of battle visited their ears as they hit the base of the green hills. Moses wondered whether the Ugandan Army now fought the GLA at the border as a natural consequence of the civil war, or if they fought them to aid the escape of the Crusaders. "Both," he whispered, hopping over a bush and heading down the path wherein lay a small tributary-son branching out from its mother-river.

The men ran along the shallow stream, following Moses and his native Kush men alongside the base of the hills and into the deep crevices of the range that was adorned by the Albizia and Terminalia woodlands, and semi-evergreens of the Khaya, up further to the montane forest of alpine and sub-alpine, and higher still into the Hagenia woodland with its Erica thicket and thick patches of green bamboo, giving the Crusaders the cover they needed against the obtrusive eyes of the coming enemy.

Reaching a small peak of four thousand feet, the men halted and spread out to take up sentry points and gather information, and within sixty minutes' time, the men, peering through spy glasses, reported enemy troop movements from the south, and no troop movement from the north.

"They haven't had time to send government troops," Moses said to Conall and Mwindo, "and the rebels are too far away, for now; President Mustafa will send planes this time, and the Militia will be here." He stood fully erect now, a fearsome sight, as his face bore up his great resolve. "The Egyptians could not long conquer us—in fact, we conquered them! Nor the British, and then the North sought to dominate us, but they are all foolish, and do not know history," and he looked knowingly at Conall; "a people internally who resist continually will never be conquered externally—never, it is the way of people to rule their own homeland; we do not want those Muslims who practice theocracy, and Arab neighbors telling us, Christians and animists, and even our Muslim farmers here how to live—we will not yield; and so it is time," and his face was lit by the force of his proclamation. "We will call upon the People's Liberation Army." His men, their eyes wide open and wet with joy, stood perfectly still.

The Kush Liberation Army, the KLA, had been the new voice and dagger for the people of the South, but since their leader, John Suliman, had signed a peace treaty with the government and become its Vice-President and subsequently sent his troops to fight the KLA, and dispersed them, many people had lost faith in the rebel groups; there was still the Kush Liberation Army and the Liberty League Movement, who, even though they gained more fighters from the defeated KLA, were not strong enough and well-armed enough to overcome the military might of the Kush government in the North.

"The KLA once ignored us, the LLM, too; but now, these last six months, they are in retreat, and are in need of victory; we shall give them that."

Four Kush men were dispatched with explicit instructions on a mission that would carry them far into the southern towns.

"We have three days," Moses said; "after that, they will sing of us as martyrs, and I am too young for that."

It was impossible for them to go forward now, as the government planes had been searching the area, or backward, against the GLA, who were marching now in a strong contingent of more than five hundred soldiers; so, wait in the many miles of mountainous terrain they would, and wait three days for rescue.

Thus, the siege began, and it was clocked at twilight.

The Crusaders, having adjoined their minds, were now confident of the plan, and, equipped with radios and binoculars, moved out all along the ridges of the mountains, some on Mount Kinyeti, at the highest point, some along the Kinyeti River, others on hillsides nestled next to alpine and silk trees, while others still were constantly roaming on firesides covering north, south, west and east entrances.

The GLA came as one sweeping gesture of arrogance, a moving mass on foot, truck and horseback, wearing their invincible attitudes like freshly burnt tattoos on their proud faces. They never once thought of defeat, but only of revenge against those infidels who had dared to defend the Acholi people. Mulumba walked with them, for he realized that his leadership was in peril if a victory against this apparent mercenary group was not swift and decisive.

The Crusaders knew that they must never allow the GLA to cause them to congregate and encircle them, that they must be constantly moving, a rapidly moving target, an invisible hummingbird-like creature that appeared and took a shot and then disappeared into the naturally camouflaged environs, on the rear and flank of the enemy, above him, below him, near him, inciting the enemy to frenzy and frustration and thus making him prone to error, provoking him to disobey rules of combat, to disperse, to be isolated, to be afraid and lose faith in his mission goal.

The purpose of engaging the strolling GLA in long-range fire was three-fold: the first, and the most obvious, was to minimize risk for the defenders; the second was to keep the GLA from ascertaining the defender's position; and the third, to reroute the GLA into areas more strategically advantageous for the Crusaders to combat them. Thus, it all began, the first shot being fired from Moses, who was paired with Jon Paul and Julius, who, with their leader, assumed the T-position on a hill and fired their weapons, and then the three men scurried behind a smaller intrusion, still rubbing on concealment paint to obscure even dark skin that would shine at night.

The GLA had been walking along the valley floor into long columns and now split up, charging either side of the hills, leaving close to fifty men with the two Jeeps that were each mounted with a Browning .50 caliber machine gun.

Three Crusaders appeared on the saddle above the Jeeps and briefly opened fire on the soldiers, who, in turn, returned fire, but as the Crusaders were on the top of the saddle, they sank below the horizon and beat a hasty retreat up the gentle, fern-covered slopes. Two more Crusaders, before the echo of bullets dug themselves into the soft soil, appeared on the hilltop opposite the ridge and tore a fury of rounds into the climbing men below them and then disappeared behind the peak.

The GLA soldiers were organized into ten divisions and then were sent all over the hillsides, but they found only flying lead fairies buzzing the warm, Spring air and often settling their cute, steel-tipped, button-noses into their soft, black flesh; forty-eight of the soldiers died in the first ten minutes of battle, and eight more in the next five, and one hundred and fifty more men were lured into a kill zone that was at the north-south entrance of a valley between two high-reaching ridges, where the surveillance team of ten Crusaders awaited, flanked on either side, behind Alpines, lying in trenches that had firing ports carved out at both ends, with their HK-416 rifles; and to ensure their safety, all the while the support team of eight Crusaders awaited above and beside them. Thus, it began: the surveillance team brought fire and brimstone upon the GLA soldiers, who returned fire, while the support team too fired upon the GLA and watched for movement from the north and south trails; soon, fifty-eight GLA soldiers lay dead or dying, and many Crusaders abandoned their positions and radioed into the three leaders who watched through their infrared binoculars on high hilltops.

The Crusaders rendezvoused a half-kilometer away and reloaded their weapons and released the next assault, and studied the hastily drawn maps and then moved out once more to designated areas; thus far, they had not lost a man or incurred a wound; however, the GLA, in the first hour, lost ninety-one men to death or physical destruction, and they had earned every dead body and bloody wound by reason of their prior training and tactics and strategy, which consisted of barreling boldly into small villages of helpless peasants in refugee camps wherein were houses of the sick and dying and defenseless, and appropriating any victims or booty they chose; thus, they were educated in the premier school of bullying, wherein their strategy was self-inflicted, self-inflating invulnerability; if a graph of chickens with their heads cut off that showed where they had run after the foul deed was super-imposed over the movement of the GLA soldiers in response to having the fat head of their mission cut off, the two nonsensical trails would be identical and essentially merging.

The Crusaders set up ambushes and executed them—sending squads forward with left and right security teams, and squads flanking the enemy—and once this was accomplished, moved on to the next rendezvous point, and in this fashion they managed to carve out huge chunks of this overstuffed, sloppy brigade of scared-and-bleating sheep.

By the rise of the golden-brown crust of a golden-baked dawn, painting its ostentatious self in the pale blue sky, the surface of the mountains resembled an epidemic of epic proportions, as there were now nearly two hundred enemy soldiers' bodies strewn in a disagreeable fashion on stream, rock and gravel, creating their own bloody menagerie. But then came hearty black Arab Militia in their smart green Jeeps and mounted machine guns and boyish enthusiasm to murder, yet, enthusiasm that was based on years of mutilating and slaughtering defenseless citizens, mostly defenseless men and women, and, of course, children too, and only minor skirmishes with the new and highly unorganized Freedom groups of Kush; so, too, by the night, after fruitless searches for their quarry, they found themselves now candidates for fertilizer for the thirsty soil and food for the greedy organisms who soon swarmed around these fresh new corpses. Then came the military planes, and the confused Militia and GLA soldiers pulled back as the jets dropped copious amounts of bombs again and again at the direction of Mulumba and his land pirates. This shelling lasted for five hours the first night, and when it was over, and the morning appeared like a blossom of pink petals stretched across the cloudy sky, the GLA and Militia stirred in their encampments and realized that many of the sentries had succumbed to a disease called "knife in the vital regions," and their rancor and wrath increased, and so mounted their pride and let revenge drive them once more into the maelstrom, yet only to incur the same, infuriating results of defeat and despair.

The mountains were scarred now, cratered, having their complexion darkened by strewn blood and black powder. The GLA and Militia fanned out among the hillside and began the coordinated search but found only futility. Kush government troops arrived, three divisions strong, one thousand men, and the effort to disgorge the mountains of their prey intensified, yet once more returned only more frustration; night fell like a black, velvet cloak over the land and the bombing began again in earnest.

The Crusaders paid no heed to the shelling, for they sat and ate in the exquisite shelter of the mountains, experiencing the charm and aroma of fine dining, good friends and wonderful stories, guests of a genteel host who had been found in secret times that were known only by those who fought this enemy.

In the Caves

There is a sense of surpassing superiority, and defiance toward harsh things, when one is a target of powerful explosives but instead sits peacefully and uninterested, sipping black tea and eating hard biscuits, and chatting with one's friends, as if at a pleasant social gathering; so sat the Crusaders, undisturbed by the shelling, as the mountain quaked in response to the bombs bursting on its resilient, sinewy, hard skin; they talked casually, as if the riptide of fury directed against them was as inconsequential as a tiny pebble landing on the head of a sleeping Nile Crocodile.

"This place," Moses said, amid a distant clamor of shelling, "was hard won after so much digging of the tunnels; and the springs," he nodded to the natural springs that inhabited the caves, "are cool and sweet; a man might come here for retreat anytime."

"Yes, from a nagging wife," said Arjuna.

"How would you know, eh?" Horatius said, mischievously, and took a sip of his tea.

"I know," Arjuna protested.

"Then, you are married, eh?"

"No, not that," Arjuna said, thoughtfully, "no, not that—now."

Horatius was curious, and when he was, he never let up until he found out the truth behind a failed secret. "So, tell us, Indian."

"There, you see," Arjuna declared, exasperated, throwing up his slender, brown arms, "you leave one nagging wife and inherit another!"

The men on guard at the entrance of the cave smiled and laughed, but were sure to keep their eyes directed on the outside.

"So, tell us how you managed to come to this cheery place," Henry said, eating his biscuit and red beans, just now recovering from a mania to kill the GLA, which had astounded his fellows.

Arjuna, his face pale now, and rigid, like the stone walls behind him, said, unblinking, his voice deep and sorrowful, "Yes."

"I was born in the little village of Bokapahari; it is, you might say, Eastern India." Arjuna was not yet looking at any of his audience, but the wet soil, his head bowed. "You could say I was born there, but really I was born when I left India: one is not alive when one is born into wretched poverty—no, it is not that; when one is born into poverty and the pit of disease—is this not enough for one to endure, one who is born into a caste where one is supposed to be content with one's status?" Interpreters did not have to transmit the genuine pain in his voice that billowed and smoked as it drifted to the sentries at the opening and out into the cool, dark night.

"The British, the industrious beggars," he continued, his voice soaked in venom as he shook his head, "took our India for a reason—they worked us like slaves to enrich their coffers—and the government today does the same, the beggars; the people are still slaves even though their master has changed." He was still gazing directly into the hard ground when a distant memory imparted a small smile. "Bokapahari sits atop a coal reserve the British mined and then abandoned, so poor people—aam aadami, 'the common man,' came there to take the coal and burn it to process it and take it to market—free money!" The smile was still there, and it slightly increased. "As a child, where you live, you live, you don't know anything else, living atop coal fires and breathing foul gases, and getting your feet burned in games of dare when walking over the hottest ground, and playing in the filthy dust; well, this is what we knew—and there were five children, too, and mother and father, living in a small, red-brick house; it was the only life I knew, and I didn't mind because my family loved me." He paused, let out a wistful "hmm" as his round head bobbed up and down, and then said, "I never knew we were poor." He paused again, then continued, "Some houses had fumes coming right through the ground, and some of them sank into the earth—people died." There, the smile upon remembrance died, too, as the frown of bitter memory climbed atop his monument of shame and shouted in bitter prose. "My father and mother earned about three dollars a day—enough for us to live on—mining the coal and placing it in straw baskets atop their heads and walking to market; oh, how black their faces were, every day, how dirty their clothes were; but wouldn't you know that despite my mother's long, beautiful, black hair being covered in this fine, powdery, black soot every day, she always kept it so very clean at night by carefully washing it for the longest time." And his voice became winsome. "I used to love watching my mother wash her hair and becoming the beautiful woman she always had been to me; my mother, and my father, they did what they had to for us to survive—I wonder if this is the way of all the world."

His frown increased, his voice bereft of any good thing of the past. "One night, I was sitting inside my house near the door reading a book, and suddenly my mother picked me up and threw me outside, where I lay there scratched and bruised, and confused; and when I turned around, I expected to see my mother's angry face, but I saw nothing at all—nothing." He stopped talking. No words came for him for nearly a minute. His gaze still poured itself into the dark soil beneath him, and then, he said, and in a dead whisper, "The house was gone, and so were my brothers and sisters, and my father," he hesitated, "my mother…" The men in the cave were silent and drained of all noise and commotion. "I was ten, what was I supposed to do, now…

"I started harvesting coal, too—because I wanted to eat—as I would do for so very long," he continued, almost immediately, as if the speaking of this new arrival in his life kept him from sinking beneath the soft earth, "One day in market, I met a man, a Dalit—one of the untouchables, they called them, of which I was—who said he was going to Khairlanji to work on his brother's farm, and would I like to come; I said yes, yes, sir, I would, and I left with him that moment. I was twelve.

"So, I went to Khairlanji and joined other Dalits there, who lived among Kunbi, the farmer castes, and Kalar, the trader castes, who are still below priests and rulers and warriors, and I lived with his family, and worked very hard on his rice farm, and began to save money, and went to school, and yes, I met a sweet girl—Aishwarya—and we married when we were both eighteen, and for my wedding gift, my benefactor gave me a small house next to his, and a small piece of the farm." He smiled again. "I felt like the wealthiest and luckiest man alive, and only wished that my family could have seen my good fortune.

"Well, Kunbis and Kalars in the village were always jealous of our good fortune, and used to call my benefactor 'Mahar,' which means carcass handler, a job the untouchables once were confined to do; when the people would insult me, I tried to ignore them, and told them to please address me correctly, but they only mocked me.

"My wife gave birth to twins—twins, a beautiful girl, Suhani; and a beautiful boy, Rohan; can you truly imagine such a wondrous thing happening to me, such a lowly fellow? I was beyond overjoyed, and I thought I had found paradise, but no," his voice once more sank into that morbid oblivion where the charred remains of tragic pasts reside. "The Kunbis and Kalars could not stand to see our good fortune, and tried to legally take our land from us, and when they could not, they set to attacking us, sending rocks through windows and smashing our doors and destroying our crops; well, I would not allow such a travesty, as you can well guess; so, I did the same thing to them—yes, I did, and then one night they came for us, the cowards came for us." His swarthy face now fell into his waiting, outstretched hands. "They came for all of the Dalits—five families of us—and I should not be here, I should not," he was sobbing now. "I should have died with Aishwarya and the babies, I should have—I should be dead now, I want to be dead now." His voice was rising like the advanced strokes of a violent storm. "They came for us at night and they stood in front of our homes, but then the mob came in and the police did not, and there were torches and clubs and guns and panic everywhere, and I thought I'd hidden my Aishwarya and the babies from them, and so I got away and I thought I would find them where they were supposed to be, but they were not there, and I asked myself did I abandon them, did I, to the evil spirits who came to devour us; and so I came back and I found Aishwarya," he was screaming now, for as his mind was there in the midst of the horror, he was there. "She was dead, she was dead, she was dead, and what they had done to her, the cowards, and what they had done to the babies—I could kill them all, I vowed to kill them all, and I found a gun," he held out his right hand, "I tracked them down and killed them, each one, killed them easily, it was no trouble at all watching them die—and my beautiful Aishwarya and my beautiful babies were still gone." His chest was heaving and his body was covered with cold perspiration as his face rose up and his head fell back, with eyes closed, as he cried, "I killed you, I killed you, I killed you!"

Now, even the translators had abated, as all the men, testifying to the horror of the narration, were stone still, and many were silently weeping.

He let his head fall to his chest as he sat, slumped. "The police hunted me, and I didn't care; and they caught me, and I didn't care; what reason does a man live anymore if what little bit of heaven found in this kingdom of sorrow leaves him forever and he knows he will never again smell its sublime scent? Let them kill me, I wanted to die, I would not fight them—the whole world had abandoned virtue and so had abandoned my family, so how can I calmly live in such an open prison?" A smile of wonder captured his aching countenance. "The police chief understood, he did, he had been a Dalit, I knew it, and he took me away—such things are done in places where the law is not dressed in universal language—and put me in the army, and I did not care, for I was dead already; so, I was in the army, and I didn't care where I went or why I went there or if I might die, as other men might, and so I was the perfect soldier, who would willingly volunteer for the most perilous missions and obey without question, and so when the opportunity came, I agreed to go to Kashmir."

He pursed his lips and his body tensed as a small tremble broke over him. "Kashmir, Kashmir," he whispered, "it is so cold, so unbelievably cold, temperatures drop as low as sixty degrees Fahrenheit—Kashmir, more than twenty thousand feet high—and so cold, so cold to a man who lived in the cradle of warmth his whole life—Kashmir," he smiled, "a place no man should live in, but people, like in Baltistan, they live there—just like our brothers in the desert live here," and he shook his head. "A better man is he who can live in either furnace or frost; the greater man is he who can live in both." He sat up and nearly looked askance at his audience, but stared straight on into the swirling black mist. "Pakistan and India fought over Kashmir many times—it is on their borders, you know; and they still struggle over a part of Baltistan—the Siachen Glacier: two nations fighting over a chunk of ice; so," he shut his eyes and held out his slender arms, "we Indians sit on one mountain of ice and shoot at the Pakistanis, who sit two miles away across the great divide and shoot back at us." He dropped his arms. "Men die in avalanches or fall into the pits or die of altitude sickness; it is a place for men to be buried, a place to bury your past, a place to forget the world." His black, brooding eyes narrowed. "It is in such bleak places where your soul is laid bare, foreign such places—like here—where you must be true to who you are so other men might recognize your real nature and decide if they are for or against you, and if they can trust you when their backs are against the wall." He stared into the ruin of his past, and yet he did smile. "But I found my way off that high Citadel and came back to my good mother, India, and I quit the army and took to wandering the towns searching for life, and I entered medical school because I decided that healing was a better prospect to pursue than killing, and once I became a doctor, traveled to many countries, and saw much bloodshed wrought by rebels and religious zealous, and my heart grew weary of not being able to stop such horrible violence; and then one day I heard a man— his voice was like a healing balm upon my wounds—and he spoke of fighting injustice in the world." He looked with fondness upon his brothers, and said, with great reference, "Conall," to which his brethren nodded in hearty assent.

The story was done now, and the hearts of the men were awakened from their deep reverie, especially Horatius', who wiped away tears, and were thus exposed once more to the inglorious proceedings of the world, where they were once again drenched in the gravity of sworn vengeance from a hard enemy; but no one, not a single man among them, heard or felt the hard shelling outside on this iron mountain, for the hard shelling they had heard and felt inside of their pious souls.

Remembrance of Things

In an accompanying cave, not more than several meters from the one in which Arjuna had narrated his woeful tale, the rest of the Crusaders sat, again, with men posted at the entrance, on the lookout for their persistent antagonists.

The man ate and drank and talked in low whispers, halting when any errant bomb burst close to the cave and sent violent reverberations through the dirt and rock anatomy, and resuming when the reverberations slowly glided away like ripples in a pond wherein a great rock was dropped; but to allow such discordant noise to upend their equanimity chafed the men, and so they sought to seek a path around this annoyance.

One man would ask a question of another man in the hopes that the answer would provide a stimulus that would prevail against the outer clamor, but no answer took hold: and so more men asked questions, or threw out more ideas, and one even attempted to sing an old drinking song, but was stared down in shame by the other men; still, the men tried and tried, but no idea or question or even lengthy answer seemed adequate to quench the fire of unrest above.

And then Miguel said, quite innocently, while stroking his thick, black beard, "I have heard tales of a priest protecting his flock with prayers and pistols, in Kenya," and then stopped the natural advance of probing questions, quite content to allow the other men to blow on the spark provided and fan it into flame. Yes, said one, I have heard of such a man who fought rebels and a corrupt government, and even was knowledgeable in medicine and often healed his flock; yes, set another, I too have heard how he fed and clothed the poor and would not yield to tyranny.

"I have heard," Yoshitsune said, his eyes narrowing as he looked across the darkened cave to the man, "he was Special Forces."

Now, the clocks of space and time inside began to slow as the men pondered this newest revelation.

Julius, a Kenyan, spoke now, and his contribution would seal the bidding for undeterred silence against the outside peril. "I am from the Great Rift Valley, and I have heard the stories, and I know them to be true, for relatives of mine saw him and met him and were helped—by this Father Joseph, the Irish priest."

There was no real reason for every pair of eyes to now cross over and stare at Finn McCool, but perhaps the always-meddling, deciphering, suspicious minds of the men, instinctively reasoned that one Irishman let loose in Africa must certainly know another.

"Well, Finn," Yoshitsune asked—nearly demanded, "have you any knowledge of such a man, eh?"

Finn, sitting against the rocky, curved stone wall, his long legs stretched out and his feet crossed, one hand behind his head, one hand holding the tin cup that held the hot tea, smiled briefly, and nodded his blond head, and said, "Aye," and there, the theater of the absurd beyond these thickly armored walls turned out its dark lights as the theater of the fantastic inside this dark hole turned on its luminous lights.

He sat upright and set down the tin cup and inhaled deeply and exhaled slowly and then recounted the history of the Irish priest. He faced his audience with certitude and boldness. "It is true that this Father Joseph was Special Forces, and it is also true that he came to Kenya to cleanse his soul of the damage that war does to a man; and forthwith he settled down in the small villages and tended to the poor and sick, giving succor to those in spiritual despair, but unlike other men of the cloth, he could not rightly close his eyes to the root of the suffering about him, any more than can a gardener who treats a diseased tree—he will cut out the rot to save the tree, and Father Joseph, although he could not cut out the rot, tried to stop the rot from devouring his flock.

"Where there was tyranny, he spoke out against it; where there was corruption, he spoke out against it; and where there was pain and suffering and horror caused by President Mboya and his loyal henchman, Paul Kaloki, he spoke out against it, so much so that his own brethren sought to silence him and move him about as if he were a leper, but he would not conform to the frail image they wanted in him, and so he stayed on.

"He was arrested five times and beaten and tortured but was always released, and when he came back to his flock he again took up the spirit of Truth and Freedom and accompanied journalists about the countryside and told the story of how this regime was destroying Kenya. One night, when he was sitting in his bamboo hut, soldiers and Jeeps came for him, to kill him, but he managed to escape; when he came back, he found one hundred and nine of his flock dead."

His words had been fluid and his tone even, with nary an alteration in pitch or volume, but now—now he choked on a barbed memory and his mouth bled pathos. The men had never known Finn to be one who hesitated to assemble ready-made words for any occasion, yet this narrative seemed cursory, containing huge gaps, obscuring hard facts; he was throttled and bound by passion, and no one was quite sure what to do while he sat in his sad embrace, silent, unmoving; nor could they decide if he was done, or if they should speak to him; and so, in the end, as men will in the company of powerful memories, they kept quiet and simply waited.

They did not have to wait too long.

His words dripped now with warm blood, as if they had been dragged through the thorny thicket, and scraped over every sharp rock and across every raggedy bramble bush and down every fluted, hard bark.

"What they did to the least of them, they did it to me—is this not what the sacred parchments say; what the virtuous voices of past and present say; what our hearts say, as we look about the fearful world with a clear conscience?" His voice was so unlike its normally cheery self, so arrayed in sorrow and sadness, so attired in sackcloth and ashes, that the men were frightened for his health. "How comes it that a man treats another as beneath him; from whence come this severe doctrine of infidelity to Equality and Freedom and

Justice?" The men had, not once, not ever, never, seen him cowed by doubt, but he was afraid now. "Is there no Love in the world, where Man feeds unrestrained on his own kind for the luxuries of excess, which can never be satiated? Is this abomination inherited from the loins of icy space, now better blown to bits and atoms, and rebirthed as virgin stars? What good is our race when we, to the very last, our own very marrow is hot with iniquity?" They thought they heard him cry, but it was too strange, they knew, to hear of it from him, just as if they were to hear a songbird weep.

The translators translated with great solicitude and quiet.

He was silent for a time, and his face was veiled in the inky vapors, and this was a good thing, too, for the men would not have wanted to see him now, for now his countenance was so unlike his usual cheerful countenance, and so like countenance of a wrathful man, that the transformation would have chilled the men to their very bones.

"And so," he began again, a strange zeal for anger perforating his voice, "as unclean men take up the sword to hurt the Innocent, so too will I pick up the sword to punish unclean men, thus releasing me of my vows of peace and chastity—no peace can there be when the wolves devour the flock, and no chastity of the flesh when the world abides such things; so, I will make love to war and I'll make violence upon the guilty, and no man can stand against me, because I am alone among men." He let slip a hurtful smile. "I released the dogs of war upon the murderers, and I carried with me no mercy or sentiment."

His face was a conflagration of seduction, his chest heaved, his body perspired as he nearly cried in a guttural heave of pathos, "And so I hunted the rapists and murderers and mutilators and slavers, and I committed great violence upon them," and here he gave graphic descriptions of his deeds, "and easily did I watch them expire beneath my heavy foot, and I was happy, and no man could dissuade me, for I was merely doing what no court or judge or jury would dare to—I was bringing Justice."

Thus purged of the discordant memory, his visage wore a mask of wonder. "Why one man," he said in a hoarse whisper, "and not another? Why one man who stands, and another who flees; why one man who accepts, and another who refuses? Why, why are not all men good? And as all men are not good—and we presume to know what is Virtue—Justice must be brought to bear upon those men who were not good, by men of Virtue, and if not, then the world is a Confederate, and Man, a contemptible seed—which he is, but is offered redemption, which most men scoff at, most men," he repeated, as if in a deep trance, "most men, left to their own devices, practice the art of sin, and tender no reasons for it." He thought of Major Dunham and Major Chikere, and his men, and the truce, but especially of Captain Haidar, and he mused, "I will not forget any of you, ever, lest I dishonor what we achieved, what we drank from when in the midst of the madness of war: the golden chalice of peace."

He was exhausted, of mind and heart, and the men were exhausted, too, and shocked and astonished, as they would never again behold him in the same light, as he was much bigger now, and much more human now, and much more like them now.

A Surprising Revelation

Yoshitsune had sat there on the cold, hard ground, cross-legged, hands palm up and resting upon his raised knees, absorbed as the others in these emotionally wrought stories; and then, on a sudden, when all thought no one else would speak, and certainly not him, he began, staring into the black void. "As you know, I am Japanese; I am Chinese." He was silent for a good time, and many thought that perhaps he was done, but then: "These two countries have in common that they were early on unified culturally and politically, a homogenous society with a profound distrust of outsiders, especially those from the West, and consequently, Japan isolated itself from them, and the world, while China—who, as we know, invented paper, gunpowder, clocks, and too many more to name—no longer sent out ships for trade, and actually discouraged innovation, and so lost its technological edge." Everyone looked to him, astonished, and when he said nothing more for a few seconds, they thought surely he was done, which would fit his normally taciturn self; but then, "My grandfather, when Japan began to assert itself in Asia, was a college student, and joined groups that protested against military hardliners in the government and this aggressive imperialism; but such as these were soon silenced, conscripted, and immediately sent to China in 1937." His face was still stolid; his gaze, piercing; his tone, hard. "He and several of his fellow university students all went together, and vowed they would never engage in the kind of cruelty they had heard about; and at first, they did so; but," he grunted, "humph; war is a persistent mistress, she will never yield in her attempts to make any man into the submissive slave she wants him to be, to serve her malicious purposes." He nodded, drawing in his thick lips. "Well, one of his friends, Hideo, was a shy, timid farmer, who had never even fired a weapon until he was in the Army, but once in the company of other Japanese soldiers who had been christened by this gross violence," he paused, and uttered a deep "hmm," and then, "in a month, he had joined those who freely killed, seemingly without a conscience." He shook his head and was quite for time; and then, "It is best I start at the beginning." He expelled a long breath, nodded, and with eyes closed, "I can still hear my grandfather, Ken'ichi, tell us the story; I can still hear his voice, even now." He was silent for a moment as he swayed side to side, where no one dared speak, and then he began again, his deep, baritone voice full of passion and pathos. He opened his luminous brown eyes.

"When Japan invaded China, it was not too much later, after the surprising fall of Shanghai, that Chiang Chung-cheng—you would know him as Chiang Kai-shek—leader of China, appointed General Tang Sheng-chih and his troops to stay and defend Nanjing, but as he began to fully understand how difficult it would be to contain the might of a civilization that had been long militarizing—who had taught their people that outsiders were barbarians, but in particular, that the Chinese were pigs, that the Japanese were a superior race destined to rule all of Asia—once he realized the city lost, he ordered Tang and his forces to retreat, thus allowing the Japanese troops to take the city and do as they pleased." He paused. "There were hundreds of thousands in the city who then moved into the 'Safety Zone': Chinese civilians, Chinese troops who had surrendered; and a very few brave international members who tried to stay the brutal hand of the conquerors, but for them, it was like a weeping child who tries to hold back the violent father beating its mother; no, it is like a meek man who tries to use logic to dissuade a tyrant from doing as he pleases; better yet, it is like a good man who uses virtue and sentiment as a tool to persuade an ogre from eating his normal fare: human flesh." He shook his head, still sitting motionless. "So, imagine this three-headed beast let loose amongst those it despised, and with a lust to not only kill, but murder emotionally, to destroy their heritage, whom they viewed as subhuman, to be enslaved, to be part of the new Empire of the Rising Red, these soldiers who were inoculated with this 'bushido' ethic, which was a complete willingness to die for the glory and honor of Mother Japan. So," and now, he began to look in the direction of his mesmerized audience, as the translators spoke in low, hushed whispers to their attentive listeners, "a Japanese soldier, who had heard his whole life about how dirty and sneaky and immoral, how animal-like, how deceiving, how unworthy were the Chinese of the inviolate gifts of life and liberty, and he, now, walking amongst these frightful people like a prince, when he sees one of his brethren freely kill a captured Chinese soldier, and his other brothers do the same, perhaps quenching some of their anger or anxiety, the bloodlust will likely take hold of him, and he will join in the slaughter, killing one, maybe two, even three more; and then, as it slowly becomes him, as many as he chooses, and every time, a piece of humanity leaves him, until he is nothing more than the wild beasts of the field he once believed the Chinese people were; and so, the massacres began, of hundreds of thousands—we will never know the real number—of prisoners executed, of citizens tortured, shot, stabbed, strangled, beheaded, bayoneted, their bodies dumped into the Yangtze River; into ditches, big and small; burned, and buried—and sometimes alive; an entire army free to do as they pleased with their enemy, and for every Chinese, a potential victim, with only those few brave international members, risking their very lives, constantly standing up to the conqueror worm—one was even a Nazi; can you imagine that...” He then displayed a disgusted mask. “And so began the rapes—the refuge of the coward, the miscreant, the soulless ghoul; it is the scurrilous badge of the invading army, to seek to humiliate and degrade the defeated, by seeking to dishonor their women, and never more so than in Nanjing.” His body was numb, chilled by the memory of what his grandfather had told him in such explicit detail. “No one knows the exact number, but the estimate is that hundreds of thousands of Chinese women were brutally raped, and often, killed afterward, mutilated, bayonets stuck into them, decapitated, sometimes their fetuses ripped out of their bellies.” His face became sour. “The noble Japanese soldier; ha! Looting and burning the city! Nothing more than a barbarous primitive, butchering, raping, torturing, as have all such conquerors, as in times past, present, and will be in the future; when God is absent in them, they show who they really are: sin incarnate.” He lifted his head. His voice was now strained with pain from an irrevocable past, where his audience imagined he should very much like to have visited with vengeance on his mind, as his hard countenance reflected his frustration that he could not do so. He continued, his voice becoming uncharacteristically inhabited by a flowing river of uninhibited emotion. “What possesses a man to do those things? How a mild farmer one moment, like Hideo, is then one who was soon killing captives and citizens, joining in gang rapes, trying to force fathers to rape their daughters, watching with glee as such fathers killed themselves instead;

watching in amusement as Chinese fathers drowned themselves instead of facing such horrible consequences, for they knew…" He took a long, deep breath, his chest rising and falling, his face covered in thick perspiration. "And what of my grandfather? Hmm." He shook his head. "He would not concede to this heinous behavior; he quit the Army, he escaped, he fled to the jungle, and it was there that he met she who would later be his wife, Ti; she was only seventeen, he twenty-one, a love forbidden by both sides, and one to be guarded with their young lives; so, once they were united in holy matrimony by a sympathetic American priest, my grandfather had to decide what to do next: stay in China, risking being caught, tried as a deserter, a traitor? Rejoin the Japanese army—join in the spreading horrors they perpetuated against Innocents? Or somehow, get back to Japan, and bring Ti, my grandmother, with him? Hmm."

He sat stone still, as if contemplating what his grandfather had to decide; and then, nodding, "He decided that to stay in a country that hated the Japanese was too dangerous, so he left, vowing to return, but first made sure he returned to his unit looking like a captive, and so, starved himself for several weeks, and actually jumped off a cliff into rocky, dense brush to injure himself, where he broke a leg and dislocated his shoulder, and sprained an ankle; and so, when he did arrive back to his unit, they believed his story, and he was praised as a hero for escaping—and somehow, dissuaded them from going after his 'captors,' by convincing them that he had been blindfolded all the time; and so, he was soon sent home to Mother Japan to convalesce, where he prepared for the inevitable invasion by the Allies, and the Soviets; all the citizens were supposed to be ready to fight to the death for the Emperor; then came August 6." He grunted, with even more perspiration collecting about his smooth face, but which soon seemed perplexed. "What human beings have done to each other; they will stop at nothing to win once this stampeding momentum to complete victory consumes them," and for the first time that anybody had ever heard, his voice cracked with emotion, and remarkably, now as if he were about to weep. "Is it madness that grips him? But from where? Is Man so ignoble that he cannot be redeemed? They can, but choose not to, so this pure and robust evil flourishes, because they choose to ignore the Light which illuminates their wicked deeds; then came August 9, and the horror of war was finally over, but for many it had only begun, like for my grandfather; so, even though he'd been hurt by the blast that was so tragic—" and now he closed his eyes again, as his tone became grave and full of profound sorrow, "people vaporized in an instant to heaps of smoking ash;

buildings flattened, rivers burned; and then came the sad tears from heaven, this lethal radioactive dust, this black rain, so horrible, so very horrible—he was now forever 'hibakusha,'" he opened his eyes once more, "the name given to survivors, who then wore this shameful brand into the next generation; and he never stopped trying to get back to China, to Ti; but how? An ex-Japanese soldier goes to China to bring his Chinese bride to live in Japan and live in peace? Impossible! It was much too early for such forgiveness; so, he had to wait for ten agonizing years to go back there, and when he did, he found her, and my father, born nine years earlier, living in a small village, Zhufan, in the Jiangsu Province, and brought them to Japan, and truly attempted to live in a remote village; but it was difficult for the ordinary citizen to overcome prejudice against the Chinese, but to have one of their own marry one—it was unforgivable to many, and so my grandfather and grandmother had to move often, until the tide of hatred lessened, and they finally made a home in Kiso, in the Nagano Prefecture. It was then that my father, Kaito, met Aki, my mother, and later, I was born. Hmm." He nodded, seemingly satisfied. "Now, you know I am also Chinese, a heritage I am proud of, as much as I am Japanese, for I do not allow the sins of the past to visit or represent me; I am my own man, a new man, who seeks to accept what was noble from the past—while not forgetting what was ignoble—to inhabit my soul." He nodded to Finn, who, so long ago it seemed now, had discerned upon their first meeting that Yoshitsune was a mixture of the two distinct peoples; and then he clutched his burly chest, "It is who I am, just as all of you are who you are." He surveyed his audience with a disturbed visage. "It is a curious world, that one people think themselves superior to another, for it means nothing to one who has the blood of many people in his veins," and he clutched his right wrist with his left hand and squeezed tight, "and maybe," he smiled, "if we were all a part of each other, there would be less pain and suffering in this mean world." But he was not done, for he had signaled nothing to indicate this, and then, "And for those meek farmers who transformed into butchers and rapists?" He shook his head. "They went back to their humble farms, many simply doing what they had done before, their crimes done; why? Why? How could this be? War." He grunted deeply. "It is an enigmatic force that slays the souls of men, or men who allow it to." He displayed as much of an unforgiving expression as they had ever seen in him. "That is why I will brook no excuses for any who commit crimes against Innocents; no excuses, now, not ever." He paused, looking around with a grave countenance. "Better to die now and save your soul from shame and humiliation, and bring dishonor to all who are with you, know you, and respect you, but were not able to see who you really were all along." He nodded, apparently satisfied that he had said all he desired to say, which was more than they had ever heard from him all at once; and upon smiting his huge thighs, this signaled the end of his sorrowful, yet, in the end, hopeful tale.

A Message Received

The Army of Kush, and the Militia of Kush and the GLA of Uganda had roosted for the night upon the Imatong Mountains, deliberating upon their strategies in expressing their hostilities toward their enemy therein.

The Captain of the Kush Army did not take kindly to the idea that a group of renegades could cripple his resources for days.

"Are you certain," the Captain shouted at Mulumba, "that these scoundrels have not migrated to a place more tactically friendly?" He waved his right hand at the hills. "Eighty kilometers of dirt to hide in—it is like chasing a rabbit down its hole!"

Mulumba smiled. "No man escapes Mulumba," he said, "because god reveals to me his hiding places!"

"Then god needs to do a better job at reconnoitering, and the quicker, the better!"

"The infidels will die," Mulumba said; "god has revealed this much to me."

The Captain smiled smugly. "Does god tell you things other than about your enemy?"

"No, Captain," Mulumba returned, his face tilted now, as if to reflect the verbal spears sent to him, "only about those who choose to disobey his divine will and do not believe in him."

"Oh, I had some hope for tips for a certain stock; oh well, so be it, then," the Captain said, smiting his own thighs with a slender, black, reed-like baton. "God is selective in his communiqués—like any superior commander." He let out a terrific "harrumph," and then cried, "But I do not believe this god would last in our army—he would be outranked!"

Kush scouts came pounding up to him and disgorged themselves of any findings.

The Captain, forthwith, slapped each scout on his outermost thigh and then smote his own thigh. "How can one wage war when the enemy is absent? I would argue that it is difficult, indeed!" He turned to his lieutenant. "It is like arguing against oneself on both sides of the question—not very attractive, and not very profitable, at that! No, no, gentlemen, I need an enemy to fight, or my job as commander of these meager forces is in question—do any of you disagree?" Curiously, no one did. "Good, good, then, so, you men," he said, waving to the now-timid scouts, "go that way," he pointed the baton north, "and find me someone to fight or you can just keep on going!" As the men turned to leave, he said abruptly, after smiting their thighs, "Now wait, you dogs, I want that you should take great leisure in finding someone to cure," and here he threw up his hands in an exaggerated plea, "my intolerable loneliness!" And as the men turned once more to leave, he once again smote their thighs with his nifty baton. "Why so anxious, eh?" He walked around them, eyeing them suspiciously. "You may take more men, if you please, to accomplish the mission—but be polite and tell them about our little arrangement concerning accommodations if you fail." The men stood at attention but hesitated to leave until the Captain once more whacked them upon their same sore spot. "Now, go, you foolish young men," and he nodded and smiled with amusement as he watched them run like frightened bunnies from the grinning coyote. "Oh, the young, how unfit their juvenile minds for their juvenile bodies; ha! But they will succeed this time, I would bet their very lives upon it! Ha!" He smacked the thigh of his lieutenant. "Motivation, lieutenant— motivation moves the mouse through the maze!" He stared longingly toward the north. "Ah, Europe—my adopted paramour!" He glanced at his bewildered adjutant. "Any schooling, Lieutenant?"

The man stood tall. "Sixth grade," he shouted, beaming pride.

"Ah, yes," the slender Captain said, nodding, "a shepherd among lost sheep—a herder among the dumb cows, am I," then he slapped his own thigh with the baton. "So be it! It is my destiny, an accursed strain in my genetic structure!" He looked to the lieutenant, and he laughed heartily. "I might as well be talking Yiddish, you gnat-like creature!" He perceived the still-puzzled look on the man's visage, and he shook his own round head. "And you are the best and brightest of them!"

"Sir," a sergeant yelled, coming up, then entered the rarefied shadow the Captain drew in close proximity about himself.

The Captain raised his eyebrows and the sergeant dug his heels into the dirt as if some unseen force had fairly reached up and grabbed them.

"Lieutenant," the Captain began again, never once looking at the now trembling sergeant, "you might think of me as a sovereign nation exerting hegemony over any tiny, little country," and held up his right hand and put together the index finger and thumb, "who contravenes any rule I have instituted in my own sphere of dominance," and he, with a calm visage, shot out his trusty black whip-like baton and slapped the sergeant on his skinny thigh. "My domination does not spread too far, for I am not yet too large, being only a small country, but my boundaries extend as far as my voice reaches—it is better to think of my words landing several meters in distance about me and thus setting up guard and post and encirclement to protect their lord and master," any he paused, peering into the searching eyes of his lieutenant. "Do you perceive it, sir—do you see any of it?"

The lieutenant, in a charitable act of his stalled and misused brain, somehow understood, and so he waved back the sergeant, who stepped away several feet.

"Humph!" the Captain shouted, "impressive! There is hope for you yet, you wild creature—aha! You are now a *Homo neanderthalensis*—oh, pardon me, you would know your descendant by his common, vulgar name on the evolutionary scale: Neanderthal; yes, yes," he looked to the north again, "a lower ranking than man—but progress for this poor, slumbering imbecile!" He turned toward the shaking sergeant. "What drops of alphabets formed into information could you possibly deposit that will not vex me, you heathen?" The sergeant trembled more so. "Speak, you simpleton!"

"The enemy, Captain—we have found him!"

"Humph!" the Captain cried. "Intrigue at last! Let us move out!"

The Captain surveyed the columns of undulating black hills rising on either side as the Jeep in which the entourage sat rumbled down the pebbled path, and whispered, "What marvels these hills, and to disinherit their magnificence through our puny differences," and as sentimentality began to wash over his petrified heart and softened its waxy, outer shell, he balked. "Bah!" And with an expression of scorn and a wave of his baton, he waved this emotional invader into evanescence. "Any enemy troop movement in the area?" the Captain asked of his tightly orbiting adjutant, who, after a brief consultation on his radio, reported in the negative. "Wonderful, just wonderful!" And presently, they drove down the rocky path.

"Well, what have we here?" the Captain said, stepping out of the green and brown Jeep and observing platoons of his army cluttering the steep side of a tall mountain.

"Caves, sir—we have caves."

"Caves," he said, nodding as he looked up, pursing his thin lips, "indeed—caves, and caves are what I too would have chosen; formidable, this foe."

The mouth of the adjoining caves was barely visible from his view, and he stopped short of allowing them to bring in a full portrait of themselves. "Tell me, how came you to this spot?" he said, to no one in particular, but expecting a particular answer while staring up at the natural fortress. "Serendipity or calculated move?" But he caught his superior erudition showing too much and quickly repealed it. "Did you stumble upon the spot or decide the foe was likely here?"

"By chance," one of his men said. "We observed a man near a cave."

"Ah, by chance," he said, nodding his head, and smiling. "Very careless, this formidable foe—have they negotiated with you?"

"No word, sir."

"No word," he repeated it as if the speaking of it aloud would help his mind affix a marker of clarity above this perplexing action. "Well, sirs, let us proceed up the face of this obtrusion and engage in discourse with our curiously accommodating enemy."

"Kill them all," a voice rose up behind him in a wild clamor.

He looked behind himself and frowned. "Mulumba, sir, do tell your hungry god to quiet himself—soon there will be sacrifices enough to please several gods; yours just might have to wait his turn."

"Why didn't you tell Mulumba you were coming?" he demanded.

The Captain, bemused, looked about. "Are there two of you? Listen, Mulumba, my fanatical guest—'guest' being a word you should well remember, and remember its connotations in another country: you take orders from me," and with a flick of the wrist of the hand wherein he held his dear baton, dismissed his unwanted human flea of a guest. Soon afterward, Mulumba disappeared, although his faithful troops remained.

"Well, let us forward," the Captain of the troops declared, and proceeded forthwith up the severely leaning-to-the-right mountain of stone. When he attained a position nearly halfway up, he borrowed the blue-and-white-plastic bullhorn from one of his adjutants and at once blew his mean sentiment into its electronic mouth.

"This is Captain Mohammed Samoei," he began, in perfect English, "of the Kush Army, and I wish to parlay with you." He turned to his lieutenant, and scrunched up his nose and shook his head. "No need to be rude, eh?"

A big man with a great mane of yellow hair and a perfectly composed, handsome face, like that of a princely warrior, appeared, and when he deigned to speak, the force of his words cut through the heavy air like a sharp knife.

"Speak."

"Orders—orders?" the Captain exclaimed, his face aghast with derision as he looked away from the powerful blond vision above him—but not at his men—and then did smile; "yet, I am pleased with such hubris—it shows spirit!" He looked at his men with a mischievous glare on his face. "It makes one wonder what he will say next—if there is anything other than bullets behind such flair!" He returned his gaze above, and began to speak, but held his tongue, conscious now of proffering too many words in contrast to the single utterance of his protagonist, thus establishing himself as the weaker vessel in this drama. "Surrender," he decided upon, and so shouted it into the high-volume bullhorn. "Tit for tat," he whispered, anxious for a rebuttal.

"We accept your surrender." The four words, clumped together like compacted explosions, sprang from the cave and landed on the mountainside and shattered the equilibrium there.

So shocked was the Captain that he was temporarily rendered mute and physically paralyzed, and then a blast of a smile born from amazement crossed his dark visage. "I had not considered that, no sir," he said, forcefully, whipping the air with his black baton, sending the men around him reeling backward. "Fantastic! He is of a single mind—that of a superior tactician and warrior, proud and confident; splendid!" He looked to his men for intellectual parrying, but frowned, and said to himself, "Drama at last in this dreary wasteland." He held the bullhorn up and shouted into it, "Sir, I do not wish to proffer false hope, but it is your immediate surrender I would cherish, if you would be so kind!"

There was a long pause between the two communiqués that populated the cool air with glowing tinders of anxiety. But then the blond-haired figure spoke again.

"You are surrounded, and although you deserve death, we will allow you to live."

"Ha," the Captain returned, "how gracious of you—from men doomed to die."

"Faith often saves an undoomed warrior when his courage endures."

"How's that? Eh?" He looked away, frowning, at the ground. "I know that quote, I do—yes!" He turned back and shouted, "Beowulf! You know Beowulf!"

The voice was a strain less than hard now. "In Old English, and I have seen the Nowell Codex in the British Library."

"No! Truly! I am beyond jealous! But, say ye, university educated?"

"Yes."

"Where?"

"Cambridge."

"No! This is too much to be believed—what good fortune! A fellow Cantabrigian! Fantastic! I too attended it, 'Hinc lucem et pocula sacra'— 'from here, light and sacred draughts.' My home sweet home." He paused, shaking his head in fond remembrance of his unrestrained and happy youth.

"I knew it—we're brothers, linked by great literature in this tawdry, academic desolation; oh, what a shame, to come upon a brother Cambridge man who is your sworn adversary—the bad luck of it all!" He smacked his thigh with his baton. He paused, his mind agog with ideas. "Must you persist in being so demonstrative? I will guarantee your safety here, I, Captain Mohammed Samoei, Cambridge man at heart and hearth."

"Yet, it is you who must endure the legacy of capitulation, for your army is but a mere gnat about to be swatted."

"You needn't be so harsh, sir; I assure you, you will be treated honorably—an educated man in this burning asylum is worth so much more than this silly skirmish."

"Check your perimeters."

The Captain signaled to his men to radio the guards at their posts, and the calls came back in quickly. "Nothing—nothing, sir, I implore you to yield on this disputed point and trust me."

There was silence from on high for a moment, then the big blond warrior spoke, assuredly, as if he spoke of things he knew right before him. "You have a phone call."

The Captain burst out laughing. "Soldier, you amuse me, but the longer we talk, the less confidence my men have in me; so, let us be reasonable, and accept my terms."

And then the blond warrior pursued a course least likely expected: he took to walking down the sheer mountainside toward the Captain, who, in his distress, was torn between going and staying; but upon further notation regarding encounters of glorious soldiers on the battlefield, he assumed the posture of the former, and so took flight toward his antagonist.

The two men presently stood face to face, each of them standing as firmly as if planted by the defiance and ego of their cause.

"So, brother Cantabrigian," the Captain began, smiling, "how came you to such a fearful spot, fighting another man's war?"

Conall nearly smiled. "Injustice against one man is the fight of every man."

"Yes, yes, so you should think, Westerner—with liberal ideas of Freedom and Justice."

"Justice for all men, even those disposed to injustice."

"The great doctrine of equality—a fearful campaign here, my friend, a dead seed sown in sterile soil."

Conall smiled briefly. "One man with a cup of water…"

The Captain nodded approvingly as he eyed the bold youth. "I agree with such principles, in theory only; in practice, it is a delicate rose in my thorny, weed garden."

"And you, Captain, how came you here?"

"Hmm." The Captain looked to the far horizon. "A most circuitous route, sir: a journey the gods gave me—and Ulysses—for past transgression, for my personal affronts to custom and culture."

"And yet, you stand with a government that seeks to bring genocide to its own people."

"So I have heard," he said, solemnly.

"What matters an education if a man's mind, heart and spirit do not benefit from it?"

"And your band of brothers are Knights of the Round Table, nobel vessels of succor for the poor, defenders of the weak, restorers of lost liberty; and where do tyrants come from but the revolutionaries who promise peace after the storm?"

"But we ask for nothing but Justice."

"Ah, heroes: 'heroism feels and never reasons and therefore is always right.'"

"And: 'one man's Justice is another man's injustice,' but slicing up Emerson is a poor conveyor of wisdom."

"A pleasure to converse with you, sir," the Captain said, enraptured, and bowing ever so slightly. "And it does pain me to escort your merry band of hoods to prison."

A small buzzing noise was heard, and Conall raised a big, bulky, black steel object before the Captain. "It is for you."

"I have heard about such things; they are satellite—sat phones—are they not!" the Captain cried in delight. Conall held out the phone to the Captain, who took it with a sly wink. "Hello?" he asked, amused, and so when the voice responded, he shrugged his slender shoulders and laughed, letting the phone drop to his side. "A modified radio phone, no doubt."

"Doubt," Conall returned, and so genuinely grim was the forecast of doom upon his countenance that the Captain once again placed the phone to his ear, incredulity still masking his face.

"Yes, I am listening."

A garbled but barely audible voice declared, "Watch, and learn."

Then it came, a low whistling sound approaching from a distance, soon becoming a high-pitched sound hogging the silence into its wide girth to announce its cargo; wham, the missile slammed some four hundred meters before the two men, and everyone standing about, save Conall, jumped and readied for battle.

The Captain stared at the common visage of the youth, and lifted the phone to his ear. "This is the Kush Liberation Army, and the Liberty League Movement, and you are absolutely surrounded."

"We are surrounded," the Captain murmured, "but my men may not agree with surrendering to men whose people they have killed."

"You are their leader, you decide," Conall said, taking back the latest device in communications technology, which had more range and innovations than similar products and had recently been improved by scientists of Robert Heimdall Industries.

"I know these rogues—they are wedded to war and the destruction of your allies; they feast upon the dead souls of such people." The Captain looked back to his adjutants. "Wait." He walked down the slope, uttered a few words to his lieutenant, and then walked back to Conall. "Let us go," and he proceeded to walk up the hill at an accelerated pace.

"What did you tell him?" Conall said, anxiously looking back at the animated men below.

"I told him he was now in charge."

Conall, who began to quicken his pace, gestured to the men above, who brandished their weapons. A brief firefight ensued, whereupon some of those below found themselves propelled backward by skillfully placed steel bullets.

Conall entered the cave.

"Who is he?" many of the Crusaders demanded.

"An inveterate coward," the Captain said, plainly, "and a scholar—the wrong amalgam for armor."

More of the men objected to the presence of the Captain, but Conall merely assigned two men to guard him, and then met with the other leaders to prepare for battle, albeit a brief one, for as the combined liberation forces advanced on the Imatong Mountain caves, the Kush Army and God's Liberation Army, aghast at the prospect of defeat, soon retreated, but their pursuers overtook them and excommunicated most of them from the recognized and, if possible, grateful face of the earth.

So, now, the Crusaders stood with the KLA and LLM, their leaders stood before the men, little Ojore sitting right before Mwindo.

Moses spoke, and his vision was dark, and mean, and without mercy. "It is time for revolution, so let us gather our forces from the East, the West, the North, and the South, and march on the capital, and free our people from tyranny."

"But who will rise up and lead?" one of the liberation leaders asked. "In Africa, one tyrant emboldens another, one gives birth to another, one revolution serves as vote for tyranny."

"The people will choose," Moses shouted. "No man or woman will assume office by violence."

"These are words of peasants with shovel and pick; yet a peasant in the throne of power, they are words of the tyrant with steel and power," another liberation leader cried.

"Let any man who aspires to acquire power through force be promised death by his brethren here!" Moses shouted. "Despotism in Africa must be bled from any ruler who is not elected freely and legally." He looked to Conall and a small smile was exchanged between the two men, and then he looked again to the good soldiers gathered before him. "We march now, for Freedom, for Truth, and for Justice!"

The men cheered, and no one abstained, not even the former Captain of the Kush Army, who was, incidentally, still under close scrutiny.

And thus, it all began.

Revolution

Break a people down to their barest essentials and then strip them even of that and step on them and brutalize them and humiliate them and leave them to flounder in the wide-open, boiling desert as if they were infected rodents to be wiped out or pesky insects to be eradicated, and they will momentarily grieve, they will generally admit defeat, they will gladly die, for to grieve is to be expected, and to capitulate is human and the want to die is begging for eternal rest; but allow these people a tiny lull to remember life, to remember freedom, remember family and friends and tradition, and celebrate the small joys, and they will begin to unfurl that bright flag of brotherhood that waves behind each of them as they live again from day to day without persecution; now, offer these battered and bruised people, as they seek to repair their broken homes and broken bodies, a chance to install a mechanism by which persecution might cease, even temporarily, and they will risk home and body to encourage such a movement. It was in this state in which the combined liberation armies and the Crusaders found the people of southern Kush, and the people gladly and confidently joined the marching soldiers on their journey toward the capital, Khartoum, where the government, now allied with the North, had established a Muslim theocracy and imposed its strict law on Muslims and Christians, and any other culture caught in this intent to establish its rigid rule.

It was the People's revolution, the People's war, the People's liberation, born of an indigenous pride and wanting of no foreign armies to intervene; and so the war raged on, for six months—for six long and arduous months, the two forces fought for the right to control southern Kush, which had been merely a puppet of the Kush Islamic government.

When the Crusaders entered into the campaign on the side of the rebels in the second month, they made it clear that they were an independent operating body and not to be subject to the rules and regulations of the discouraged, failing, disorganized rebels, who reluctantly agreed; and quickly, the rebels recognized the usefulness of their new allies in terms of tactics and strategies and organizational skills, as provided thusly, regarding effective military procedures in the field: when walking in proper formation, there will be three teams, one in front, one behind, one on the side, with squad leaders in each one, and machine gunners, and trailing security; or explicit instructions on sending advance platoons to ferret out the enemy and assessing its strength; and exact details on how to knock out bunkers by converging to their blind side while rebels fire from the front, where one man from the side tosses in grenades and another enters with his rifle to finish the job; or how to conduct a proper raid by sending the support team, with the patrol leader inside and next to machine gunners, with the assault team to their left, and more security outside of them; yet these were mere methods, the entire philosophy of winning the war much more complicated, and it went something like this:

It was now the war of the guerilla who slowly whittled away at the well-equipped, highly trained, well-numbered military of Southern Kush, a government that needed to protect its bases, its transportation systems—its roads, its railroads, and communication routes—its towers and bridges, military aircraft and heavy artillery, and industrial complexes and machinery, its precious natural resources, all of which the now-conjoined Freedom Forces, under the direction of the Crusaders, attacked and plundered at any time, or captured if need be, employing hit-and-run tactics and then evading, always able to retreat if the enemy was too strong, able to regroup and strategize, unlike the government, which was coerced to stand and fight. It was the Freedom Rebels who promised hope to the oppressed citizenry, but it was the government that continued to oppress the people, by punishing them when it reasoned they aided its enemy, but which drove the people deeper into accepting the rebels, and by so doing, supplying them with food, clothes, medicine and shelter and, just as important, crucial intel.

The Freedom Rebels had no timetable, content to slowly wear down the increasingly desperate and politically splintering government, which eventually yielded up the remote areas where it incurred too many casualties and could not effectively manage, and that were too costly; thus, the rebels slowly broke off small bits of the stranglehold of the government by claiming even small territories, and where the people now joined their liberators and began to widen this freedom ring as it expanded toward the capital. The people were given titles to land by this new, self-declared moral sovereign, and natural rights were restored, and the basic necessities for survival were provided to them.

The Freedom Rebels began to hold more and more territory, having established bases in the rural areas, and gaining more allies among the people, and arms and artillery captured from the abandoned military outposts; thus, this battle-strategy philosophy—of isolating the government troops, of the rebels engaging them only when they chose, and in small numbers of no more than one hundred, and where the terrain favored their strategy, and where they calculated they would lose the least amount of soldiers, both male and female, and attack when they knew they had a better chance for victory, and unconcerned with taking a village or town until the enemy was completely driven from the area, and resting the growing rebel army, and keeping up its morale, and celebrating its martyrs and victims, celebrating its victories and learning from its defeats, and praising its heroes, condemning its cowards, rewarding the common soldier for a job well done, and executing without hesitation any traitor—slowly began to triumph.

The final assault, after six months of fierce fighting from city to city, occurred on a hot August night, where the taking of buildings, one by one, had gone on for several bloody, savage weeks, and it went like this:

The building in question is approached by two rebel teams on either side at the lower entrance, if the rooftop, the preferred method, does not have adequate cover; so grenades of various breeds are tossed in, depending upon the situation, while snipers on other secure rooftops and on the ground are on the ready and grenades are launched into upper windows; then, the soldiers go in, some walking high, some crouching low, at different sides of the room and firing in opposite patterns to secure it, and shouting to their brethren once the room is deemed clear; so, building by building, the rebels expunged the government troops, bringing them closer and closer to the presidential palace.

And what of those wounded in mind or body? Arjuna, Finn and Julius were busy dressing wounds made from burns and bomb blasts and rocket and grenade fragments, splinting broken bones, and cutting out bullets, applying tourniquets, treating shock, and once, in the midst of heavy fighting, even delivering a baby of a citizen.

The last stage, a weighty foundation that was built by the blood and bones and sinew, and sacrifice and courage and determination, of the rebels, was now set, and so the final day of fighting, planned at night, commenced.

Aerial bombardments by the South Kush air force were minimal, as the majority of the planes had been captured or crippled by the rebels, and so, the government would rely on six armored columns moving from all points of the compass from about the capital city to drive the enemy to its center and crush them; however, three of the columns were pinned down by rebel forces, two were defeated in a seven-day battle that included jets and helicopters and tanks, and every kind of artillery, much of it now piloted by the rebels, leaving only one division to march upon them; it was here that many of the Crusaders became adept at using anti-tank weapons like the Javelin, destroying many of their tanks, thus clogging the passage of more artillery through the streets; once this was accomplished, and enemy soldiers were cut off from their unit, they were met with rebel firepower from atop buildings and inside them and in alleys next to them, and from behind vehicles and immobilized artillery. This final assault saw the worst casualties of the civil war: one thousand and seventy-two dead and wounded government troops, and six hundred and thirty-three Freedom Rebels killed or wounded.

Five Crusaders died in what must be classified as the never-ending struggle for people to dominate another: Albade Okonkwo, a Bororo of Niger, whose parents fought the repressive regime of the 1980s; Mahmoud Zbiri, a Berger, and one of the Tuareg brothers, whose older brothers had fought the Mali and Nigerian government only years before; Lei Zau of China, whose great-grandfather had fought against the Japanese in World War II, only to perish under Mao; Tarek Eikady of Egypt, who had fought against religious extremists in his own country and the Middle East; and Jeanne La Cour, a fierce female fighter, who was inspired to join by her heralded ancestry, foremost her great-grandfather, who fought heroically in the French underground during the Nazi occupation of her beloved country.

But who also died, and were grieved by the Crusaders as much, were Innocents, and not just those killed in the path of battle, but killed by accident by Crusaders as they fought their avowed enemy; but this unfortunate circumstance of war had been with them from their beginnings, and every time they had wounded or killed an Innocent, yes, they grieved, but would not internalize it, lest they were felled by the absolute horror of it, which would inevitably lead them to question their actions; yes, this was war, and they could not even let such tragedies prevent them from achieving a victory that would ultimately create a kinder and gentler society, and each of them knew that they still upheld the spirit and intent of the Law of Armed Conflict, even if it meant they might perish or be wounded.

It ended, as it always does when a despot rules a country, with massive defections by the Kush Army, once it realized that the greater majority of the people had risen up against their leader; yet, a small but loyal and lethal force still protected the stronghold and headquarters wherein dwelled the pseudo-president.

The Allies camped on a small hill several miles outside of the Imperial Palace. The Crusaders sat, many remembering their fallen comrades who had died during this conquest.

Conall stood with Mwindo in the hush of darkness.

"He will be occupied," Mwindo said, looking up at Moses, who sat near a small fire. "We will ask for forgiveness later."

"It is all planned, then," Moses said, as he approached them, "for tomorrow night." He laid out the map of the small city that contained the Imperial Palace and went over the plans once more, then left to speak to the other Allied leaders of the Kush Liberation Army and Liberty League Movement.

Captain Mohammed—he of the former Kush Army, he who had been the first officer to abandon his position and join the Allies, who had distinguished himself in combat these last six months, and by doing so had won the admiration and respect of his brethren—approached Conall and Mwindo.

"It is a shame but a necessity for him," he began, looking back at Moses, who was now busily collaborating with the leaders on the imminent plans, "to be absent for the last dance." He smiled as he spied the false mask of innocence provided by the two men. "Come, come now, I have learned your ways, and I know that he, Moses," and he pointed to him, "cannot be anywhere near the fall of the president—it would not write a good biography for one who seeks a leadership position; can you imagine a man in America involved in the killing or even capturing of a president, tyrant though the President might be, and then seeking that office? Oh, it just wouldn't do—and I know your sensibilities and sympathies—Western ideals!" He looked again to the animated Moses. "Yes, he will be good for our country when it is his time, and he must be protected," and he looked again to Conall and Mwindo. "I will help you in this deceit; it suits me well."

The next night came and the troops were in position around the Imperial Palace. The President of Southern Kush had not fled, for, as all dictators believe, the first war they win is the beginning of every war they will win, and so this war was just another war to win.

The leaders of the Allied troops stood together on the hill, but Moses was not among them, as he had been taken violently ill. "It seems like malaria," one of the physicians had said. No one in attendance would blame Moses for not partaking in the final battle.

The assault began.

The Allied troops had tanks now and guns now and all the proper modern equipment to properly engage a modern army, but the army they faced was largely absent, as was stated previously, and with them most of their strategic leaders and firepower, leaving a group of soldiers dedicated to corruption and looting as reward for loyalty; thus, in the final analysis, these palace guards stayed on the fragile premise of vast wealth if they prevailed in the fight, and vast power, land, businesses, unlimited access to governmental services and priorities. And fight these government troops did, each soldier thinking of riches in glory before he died, and die they did, one by one, by bullet or bomb, grenade or blade; they died where they stood, their bodies left where they were as a testimony to bad choices.

Conall and Mwindo slammed against the outside palace wall and crouched low. They waited for their men to attack the front and sides, and from the rear, they would proceed with twenty men. Bullets and bombs besieged the place, lighting up the night like magnificent fireworks, bursting through the thin air onto cement and dirt and bodies.

"Let's go," Conall shouted to his men on his two-way radio; the other teams signaled their readiness. They climbed over the walls on dangling ropes.

Resistance from the palace army was fierce but short-lived, and the soldiers died easily, leaving a natural path to the presidential suites unguarded. As Conall and Mwindo moved circumspectly up the winding marble steps, even though they were on high alert for the enemy, they could not help but notice the extreme opulence of the palatial grounds, for, after all, the palace had cost one hundred million dollars in US currency to build, and by a man who thought it would be his first home forever, his great pyramid of Gaza, his private Valhalla, his ornate Mount Olympus.

The two men and their fellows came to the suites and kicked open the heavy doors, and finally, in the last majestic room, they found the self-proclaimed President of Southern Kush, standing proudly in his military uniform, which was speckled and striped with shiny medals.

"So," the President, said disdainfully, "you have won."

"You have lost," Conall said.

Mwindo walked around the room. "Look at this," he shouted, opening a huge brown wooden chest that revealed sparkling diamonds—all diamonds, large and small, cut and uncut, but the finest diamonds in all of Africa. "And this," he cried, as he opened another chest to reveal deep layers of the world's reserve currency—the American greenback—but no ordinary greenback, one denoting one-thousand-dollar bills, tied in bundles of one hundred, being five hundred such tiny bundles; and lo, there were five more such brown treasure chests with the same currency and value of thousand-dollar bills.

"Rich uncle?" Conall finally said, looking away from the treasure and back to the glaring prisoner.

"This is my money—I earned it," the President declared, gesturing defiantly.

"The dead earned this," Mwindo said, standing tall and approaching the President, "and the living will get it back."

The other men, some carrying camcorders and cameras, were, as instructed by the liberation leaders, documenting all of the loot therein, and anything else of value.

The other Allied leaders came in.

The President of Southern Kush was clad in chains and led away under close supervision by twelve trusted soldiers.

And then came the journalists, both foreign and domestic, to further document what had really transpired here so that no man might later contravene the official report.

The war was over, but the dawn of a new Kush was the worst battle to come, for few had confidence in this government ever ruling justly; already, many of the Allied leaders wanted the South to finally and officially secede from the north, a region dominated by Islamic rule. But this was not the most pressing battle.

Moses, although not fully healed, in the morning came down from the hill, still weary and weak.

He walked into the palace grounds like a man who has journeyed a lifetime to see the magnificent eclipse of the sun from a high mountain but who arrives after it is all over; his pale face was fused with abandonment, his weak gait in tandem with disbelief as he surveyed the devastation.

The sky was a heap of deep blue strata populated by white, fluffy puffs of cumulonimbus calvus, lazily drifting clouds, and the orange sun was a congenial host for any activity under its golden umbrella when the Crusaders congregated on the hillside outside the ruins.

Moses walked up to Conall and Mwindo. His face was aflame with righteous indignation when he spoke.

"Betrayal," he smoldered—yes, his words were poured into a cauldron of lava, molded into daggers and then fired with smoke and ash dripping from the sharp edges. "You had no right to alter my history." The men said nothing. "I am done here," he said, as if the words meant something eternal, and must be buried in the thick skin of his audience with great force. He turned toward his men. "We have much to do for my country," he finished, his black eyes burning wrath, and he walked away with his men down the long, winding hill.

Conall and Mwindo said nothing.

Another Man Falls

There was famine in Ethiopia; there always seemed to be famine in some African country, and sometimes many people died because of a lack of food, and sometimes people died because of a lack of receiving available food.

There had been famine a decade before with President Zere in power, and the peasant farmers in the drought areas had been forced to sell their grain so the soldiers and towns had plenty of cheap food, but this had been only one strike against the farmers. The Ethiopian Democratic Forces in the north battled the government troops, and the government troops responded by destroying crops and livestock and pastures and grain stores, and block-ading food from reaching the area where the EDF fought. Western aid that came to Zere went, in large quantities, to his army, his gilt-lined pockets, his friends and relatives, and his business associates. Famine zones were restrict-ed to charitable organizations. People died. They died first by the thousands, and as the Zere noose wrapped tighter around the area where the EDF hid, the people died in the tens of thousands; when Zere called for a gala event to celebrate ten years of his rule and lavished more than one hundred million dollars on the festivities, on this perverted pomp and corrupt circumstance, hundreds of thousands of people died of starvation; and when the childish, ignorant people of the West sang their songs and raised one billion dollars for a relief fund to help the famine folk, money that went into Zere's gold-lined pockets and to his friends and relatives and business associates; and when Zere relocated the famine folk—to rid the rebel zone so he might defeat the EDF, and when the summer rain did not come—more people died, from lack of food, from the move, from corruption, for no good reason other than to appease the will of another Big Man of Africa, who would, disturbingly, unbelievably, when opposition forces closed in, merely flee to another country and live in absolute opulence, free from impunity, free to sneer at his enemies and all of mankind: free to live as a free man lives, chuckling at Justice and its fanciful adherents.

Still, there was famine in Ethiopia, and the Crusaders would go there to bring succor to the people, and rest their warrior bodies and warrior minds, and bleed their warrior bodies and warrior minds until they had relaxed bodies and peaceful minds; so, first they reached the Tigre plateau, where there was abundant wildlife and idyllic surroundings so they might briefly rehabilitate their wounds, and then more south, where the worst of the suffering people lay like toppled-over, withered plants in the simmering sun.

There were lakes here and plenty of flora and fauna to remind one of the great richness and diversity of life in Africa. The men set up camp and soon began to explore the region, and none of them would dare speak of Moses' departure.

Mwindo had grown very close to Ojore these past months, and the men recognized this as a threat to the stability of their leader, but they did not speak of it to him, for they decided that a great warrior such as he must be respected in his wishes.

The boy still did not speak, but Mwindo never seemed to mind, and on this day, the two played near the water's edge with sticks and stones and played hide and seek in the woods, where Mwindo pointed out the animals that inhabited the area.

"Now, Ojore, one day you will grow up big and strong like me," he said, flexing his big muscles while the boy sat atop his shoulders. "You must learn to live off the land, to survive when Man takes your daily bread," he continued, walking along the path inside the woods; and presently, he began, as he had in past regions, to deliberate on the survival techniques necessary for independent men of adventure, pointing to certain medicinal plants, and edible plants, and picking them and sharing their bountiful fruit with the child; touching tree bark and explaining how to retrieve sugary sap from within its hull; crouching low to show the boy poisonous creatures, standing high to show the boy stealthy creatures, and tiptoeing slowly to catch a glimpse of dangerous creatures. The boy giggled and smiled and patted the giant's head; he rubbed Mwindo's curly black hair; he clung to Mwindo's thick bull-neck; and he soon fell asleep in Mwindo's big, muscular arms. Mwindo would tuck the boy in under his woolen blanket at night and simply watch the boy sleep, and to him, this was worth more than freeing any people from their wicked ruler, for this was real, and long-lasting, and was now, he and the boy, and he could feel the love of the boy in his heart, and this was worth more than any revolution because it was an essential part of his being human; and because when he looked at him, he also saw Nabulungi.

The next morning, the two of them, man and boy, went adventuring once more into the wild, and soon Mwindo found a small brook and set up a small camp therein and he and Ojore went and picked wild berries and nuts, and came back and ate them while watching the silver fish swimming lazily in the bubbling water.

A sharp howl came to their ears, and instantly Mwindo was the warrior, gathering up his rifle and standing at the ready. "Hyena," he whispered, looking deep into the forest. "Very bad, Ojore, these hyenas—they take anything; they have no manners." He looked to his side. "There are too many here, Ojore." He bent down and stoked the fire. "Stay here—I shall only go a small distance." He stepped a few paces out so he might better see. The boy whimpered. "It is all right, Ojore," he said, turning around, and gesturing with his hand to reassure the child. "I will not leave you; I just need to see so I might get a good shot at one of the little beggars." He turned around and took a few more steps, and the boy once more whimpered, at which Mwindo once more turned around to reassure him that all was well; and thus this routine was established, until Mwindo sighted two of the wily creatures, and he instinctively raised his rifle and shot at them, driving them away. "See, Ojore, I have shown them manners," he said, proudly, but as he turned, he saw, to his utter horror, that the boy was no longer at the camp. He ran back wildly.

"Ojore," he cried, coming into the small clearing and expecting to see the boy, but, alas, he did not. "Ojore," he cried, and dove to the ground where the boy had sat, and smelled the scent therein, and then followed the small footprints as they traveled in the same direction he had walked out into the forest.

And then his mind blew up its equanimity, for the trail of light footsteps suddenly terrifyingly disappeared, replaced by the paw prints of his now sworn enemies. "No," he screamed, and so loud and piercing was it that the trees and shrubs around him reverberated with its awesome power. He sent repeated volleys of shots into the air to signal his comrades, who presently came running, only to see a crazed Mwindo crawling about, his nose to the ground, and eyeing the numerous, heavy animal tracks as he crawled deep into the forest. "Ojore has been taken! The hyenas have him!" he shouted, his face trembling with rancor and rage. "Find them, find them, my brothers! We must find them! There are too many tracks, too many; deeper here, deeper there, lighter here, lighter there!" The men fanned out, inspecting every broken branch and paw mark and crushed plant, searching for hours, and then far into the night, circling around and back onto the main trail and back again and carefully inspecting every square inch of terra firma in a one-mile radius, but they found exactly nothing, and by the morning they realized all was lost.

But Mwindo was undeterred.

"The boy must be found!" he hollered, he raved as he ran to and fro, looking for trail clues. The men could do nothing but continue the search, and far into the night and the next day, and the next, covering even a larger perimeter, laboring unceasingly for their warrior brother who had sacrificed for them and saved many of them time and again; and once again, they realized that all hope was lost, that the boy was gone, that Mwindo must pull away now from this dreadful haunt or he too was lost.

Conall stood next to Mwindo, his arm upon the giant's shoulder. "Come, Mwindo," he said, with great compassion, "it is time to go now."

"No," Mwindo shouted, pulling away from Conall, and his black eyes were wild with abandon. "We must find Ojore! He needs me! We must find him or life is lost! We fought for Ojore and Nabulungi! We fight for Ojore and Nabulungi! She died for a struggle, but he must not die for nothing! May it never be! Come, my brethren, we must find him or all is lost!"

What could the men do but stay by their wounded comrade and wait for his mania to subside?

Three days hence, and the search still proved futile.

Conall stood once more with Mwindo, and this time his words were forceful and without sentiment. "We will go now, Mwindo; we are needed elsewhere."

Mwindo, his face infuriated with outrage, cried out, "What greater need than this, here, for a child stolen? What about all of your lessons—that no greater love hath one than to lay down his life for a friend; this is what I do!" He puffed out his chest and pounded it. "I lay down my life for my boy, and I expect you to do the same."

Conall, unmoved, said, "We will go now," and he held out his hand to Mwindo, who struck it.

"Never! I stay faithful to our decree! And my men stay with me!"

His men did stay, even as Conall and the others implored all of them to leave with them.

Thus, the Crusaders, having gained many men in Kush, and Captain Samoei still among them, departed, now numbering one hundred and fourteen men, walking slowly toward the south, and continuously looking behind themselves in hopes of observing a miraculous vision of Moses and his men, and Mwindo and his men running happily toward them.

Yet, it was not to be, and the trail of sorrow lengthened, so that the men often thought they were walking the long, languid planks of perdition.

Honeymoon

It was a somber group of men who sat around the campfire. They had begun to believe their cause had been in a limited capacity for success and survival due to the disparate cultures of the Crusaders and the disparate cultures of the regions in Africa; yet, had they not succeeded where others had failed? Had they not done a greater good when others had never even tried? Had they not fought the good fight and been faithful to their credos and to each other and abstained from fleshly temptations and the natural greed for riches and the natural tendency for corruption that power brings?

Still, they sat, humbled, melancholy, dejected, silent and weary of the present circumstances. Miguel sang a sad song about home, and the men listened to his smooth, sonorous voice and bethought themselves in the sweet embrace of wife and child, mother and father, brother and sister, and began to yearn for the idealistic pastures of orderly, civilized, safe living, the death knell for a warrior.

And then Conall said, while the men were deepest in this melodic reverie, "I am going to send for Eleanor, so we might honeymoon in Tanzania for a little while, and then I will rejoin you."

It was over, the men knew, completely over and done with now, as their last leader was, albeit temporarily, departing. The men felt like quitting, wanted to quit, sought to stand up and declare their intent to do so, but each man waited for the others first; had it not been a long and difficult journey, they reasoned, had they not done their chivalrous best, could they not now return to their homeland and live happily in the memories of their noble gesture and be content and happy with that? How much more, they wondered, must they do, how long must they do this, when will the rest of the world, which stands idly by, and complaining, and proffering easy excuses and far-fetched, ignorant solutions to problems here, finally stand up and not aside? Must they alone carry the burden of fixing the woes of this region? Still, not one man, not one, as they contemplated such thoughts, uttered a single word about retiring from this sacred mission; and yet the time was right, perfectly tuned in for defection, and it would take only one brave man to stand tall and profess his desire to quit this infernal business and crawl back to the safety and serenity of protected, dull, stupid and comfortable living; there, the men knew, there was that warrior-crushing word—crawl! It would make them seem cowards to abandon their posts by crawling under the safety and security of their wives', or future wives', familiar apron strings, and fine cooked meals and sturdy houses and steady, ordinary jobs; so, no, they could not comply with such a radical declaration, not now, not yet, for it did not seem as if their hearts and minds were saturated with the struggle, as if there was too much room left for more battles, more aid for the meek, more helping the poor and defending the helpless; so no, they now knew, it was not time, not yet, but soon, yes, very soon; so, they resolved, each and every one in their own private thoughts, that after Conall returned—had he not said it would be just a little while—then they would discuss such weighty things, and all would be well again.

The next day, the Crusaders moved on South, toward the drought-stricken areas, and on the second day of their travels were met by Robert Heimdall, who was accompanied by his trusted assistant, Paul, and Eleanor.

Conall and Eleanor embraced and kissed as if they had been apart for an eternity.

Robert accompanied the men to the emergency areas where he had already set up relief stations and was coordinating with various charitable organizations from around the world. After a week there, Conall and Eleanor bid everyone farewell, and took the Jeep that Robert had come in, and drove away toward Tanzania.

Tanzania—land of the golden Lion, the mammoth gray Elephant, the brown, hulking Buffalo, the sleek black Leopard, the tough, gray-skinned, wrinkly Rhinoceros—is a survivor among the brutality and profligate waste of Africa; it has had its tyrants, and may have more, but it teeters less on the delicate balance beam than its stately brothers and sisters.

The two honeymooners came to rest in the lush, verdant Manyara region, home of the rotund and stubby-legged Hippopotamus, the black-and-white-striped Zebra, the brown-blotched and horned Giraffe, and their affluent cousins and assorted friends and neighbors.

Robert had found a small cabin near the shore of this magnificent pool of natural calm, far from the national parks and roads and political unrest and even the rocks of the Samburu or the Turkan or Boran peoples.

"Oh, look, zebras," Eleanor cried, as she and Conall drove along the narrow path toward the cabin.

"This terrain is better suited for us," Conall said, observing the vast, rugged landscape, his warrior sense constructing defensive positions along the way.

She smiled, and squeezed his hand, for she knew, she truly knew, who he was and would always be, the man she wanted to be with forever.

The log cabin was at the base of a small hill, and on either side of it was a plush meadow and Acacia trees and shrubs that stretched for miles; in front of the cabin was a long stretch of short, verdant grass that fluttered and waved in the gentle, warm breezes.

Conall stopped the Jeep and jumped out, ran to the other side, easily lifted his bride up over the steel green frame and proceeded to walk with her along the dirt path to the front, where he soon reached down and grabbed the brass knob of the wooden door and flung it open and kissed his darling wife as he walked over the threshold.

The cabin had a dirt floor, an old, black, potbelly stove, a wooden cabinet stocked with food and drink, a queen-size steel-frame bed, a small oak desk with a battery-operated lamp, and a hearth with a long chain descending from the stone chimney that ended with a big, black steel pot.

Love provided the cabin with those essential things missing.

Conall and Eleanor walked along the meadow, he picking bright yellow flowers and placing them in her blond hair, she picking bright purple flowers and making them into a laurel wreath and then placing them upon his blond head. They picnicked in this perfumed field of dreams, danced in the elegant sweep of the sweet grasses, and ran along the pristine shores of the silvery lake, for their hearts and souls were now conversing in a special language, and without this constant current of radiant energy flowing back and forth between husband and wife, no real love could grow, for no good fertile soil would be laid; it is in this way that the man and woman bond, this is the way they understand each other, how they communicate to each other with even the unspoken word, with a glance, a gesture, a gaze; and even words carry unique structures and meanings through tone and pitch and tenor, where these unique sound qualities build good or ill tidings and feed or starve the heart and soul of the giver and receiver; so, once this new architecture within the bodily host is properly constructed, might a husband and wife begin to grow and teach each other the ways of female or male, and how the world works through the eyes of man or woman; it is in this way they became whole and, becoming whole, became even one flesh, sharing the same thoughts— yes, even unto death; herein lies real love, not carnal love, but love raised on faith and trust and loyalty, real love that survives any outside forces of attrition, for it has been forged through the fire of man and woman opening themselves honestly and completely and emptying themselves honestly and completely and assuming a new identity that can never be torn down; soon, then, it is complete, and the two are now one, but no earthly person or matter should attempt to dissuade this blessed union, as the lurid, boasting, slithering creature or thing would only end up devouring its own gross, vacuous, scowling self.

Conall came back in from fishing one fine day, and after presenting a bouquet of red and white flowers to Eleanor, received a smile and a kiss. He plopped the Nile Perch down on the iron stove.

"How goes the reconnoiter?" she asked, innocently, picking up the fish but sure to watch his reaction with her sharp female senses.

He smiled, and as he did so, she smiled, and as she did so, he laughed, and she laughed, too.

"But I haven't even mentioned such a thing, Eleanor; how could you be so suspicious?" The huge smile of admission was still looming large upon his calm and light visage.

"Are you not a warrior still, my love? And if I were a gardener, O, the ideas I would have now! Maybe I shall start a garden!"

"So," he returned, slyly, "how goes the interior designing ideas? Will I come home one day when we have our own place and find a pink kitchen?"

"Blue, actually," she said, smiling. "Sky-blue, like the midday sky in Kush, under which we first met." He took her in his strong arms. "Never has any woman held a grander vision of man, when first I beheld you, my love." They kissed. "Conall, my darling husband, good husband, good father, I love you so."

He held her out from himself, incredulity on his face. "Father..."

She smiled brightly and nodded, and then he lifted her up and swung her about, and took her by the hand and ran with her outside to the lush blanket of silken flowers, shouting, and singing—if it is to be believed—of the virtues of his wife. "Wife, mother," he sang, dancing merrily around her. "Husband, father," he cried, and then took her and brought her down to the opulent cherry- and violet-drenched, honey-scented flower bed and gently rolled about with her. "Father and mother, it is too much joy to bear," he smiled, crying ecstasy to the great crystal-clear canopy of sky. "It is too much happiness in this undiscovered continent." He crept closer, grinning like a schoolboy, and after carefully touching her tender stomach, presently laid the side of his head upon her dress, which covered the growing world within. "Mama," he whispered, as she stroked his blond, curly, long hair. "Papa." He sighed, and rubbed her belly. "She will be greater than us."

"Yes, he will," she whispered, adoring him.

He sat up, still with his hand upon her heap of stomach, and kissed her; and then his joy fled, and his face grew sober. "You know who I am."

"I know."

He closed his eyes and lay down with her in the velvety clutch of the amenable flowers, stroking her long, soft, blond hair. His voice was soft and vulnerable. "If only the world was good..." They lay quiet, and wrapped in each other's intertwined rhythms and pulses, then he whispered to her, ardently, "I must go back."

"I know," she murmured, her head resting on his. "I have always known." She knew not to ask any more about his dedicated Mission, that it was his burden to speak of it.

"One day," he whispered, and kissed her soft hair, "I will know when it is over, although it will never be over; but one day it will be for us, and I will come back to you and set up our abode and will make our peace with the world." He looked up at the deep, icy, azure sky. "This is the way I make peace with the world, by living what I know I must do, and doing what is right for the world; it is the way I might hold my child in my arms and not wonder..." He let his hand rest upon her warm chamber of stirring life. "Some men wonder 'what if'; some men reason 'not them,' and flee; but I will know why, and I will know who I am, and why I am, and where I am supposed to be."

There were two square windows on either side of the front door, where Eleanor chose to place flowers that Conall had picked for her. The window had thick wooden shutters and they would lock the security against the harsh winds that often crept up around Lake Turkana. It was a Sunday now; morning had broken in brilliant shafts of burnished gold, and Eleanor was cooking on the potbelly stove, looking out through the open window and into the long expanse of beautiful foliage. Conall, being the good warrior he was, was cleaning his rifles, a constant duty of every soldier who wanted to live another day. He abruptly stopped.

It is said that a soldier who has tasted combat, who has engaged in a firefight, who has shot at the enemy and has been shot at, is forever altered, a new creature he, and forever so, even in peace; ever on the alert, forever extrapolating information around him and synthesizing it and contrasting it with known combatant situations; condensing it, mixing and shaking it and distilling it to its essential parts and then spreading out its labyrinth image and looking at it from top to bottom and side to side and from underneath and on top; yet, all this must take a swift moment and the soldier must quickly drop the whole suspicious matter or act accordingly, but to act accordingly means acting savagely, so he must be absolutely certain, and since most soldiers in peacetime do not encounter enemy combatants or even civilian ones, most of them let such episodes simply expire, and then proceed on with life, and no one around them is the wiser.

But now, Conall had stopped cleaning and looked up and out the window and closed his eyes and experienced something unnatural in the environs; there is a natural rhythm in Nature, an ever-present hum, a harmonious song sung by the animals and insects that interact with the wind and the land, that plays its singular malady for anyone who cares to listen and interpret its ascending and descending musical scales; so when a disturbance comes, yes, Man, into the natural symphony, the refined ear of the expert listener might detect a breach in this uniform wave of harmony—and there, Conall caught it, barely, for his warrior senses were just slightly dulled the past weeks here, but not enough to deplete his rich mine of highly honed skills.

"Down," he cried, and Eleanor immediately obeyed, just as the first barrage of bullets tucked their nasty selves into the thick wall behind her. He slammed shut the window and secured the door and checked her, and then, with his rifle still in his hand, loaded it. "Who is out there?" He raged in his mind. Silence was to answer him for the next hour.

There were no cell phone towers here, none like those that had been recently constructed by Robert Heimdall in other parts of Africa, and used by the Crusaders with their new and large, but necessary cellular devices, and here radio contact with anyone was out of range. The man and woman were alone.

There were small cross-like slits in the windows to peer through, but he could see nothing. In the second hour, a raggedy, oily, snake-like voice slithered into the cool air.

"You, Crusader, you, and your woman, you are going to die, and I want you to know who is going to kill you, you foreign meddler; you heretic—this is Mulumba, you savage," and then the voice screamed as if it were being crushed, "You, who killed my brothers and sisters! You must die now!"

A horrific explosion of bullets ripped into the thick height of the front of the log cabin, and then stopped. The voice began again, but the words were the same hate-filled, crazed-tone, fanatical words of the zealot, the self-deluded, self-appointed prophet, so the words were ignored.

Conall made preparations. He had six rifles and two thousand rounds of ammunition. He had nearly forgone the taking of such a load of weapons, but his immediate past history had provoked him to be cautious.

Eleanor had gently chided him when he carved out a small window in the back of the cabin, but she listened intently when he had said, "You must always have a clear retreat route." There was, indeed, a very narrow opening between the cabin and the hill behind it.

The hail of bullets would massage their maddened selves into the cabin for a frenzied few seconds, and then, like a burst of summer rain, swiftly die out.

Conall would stand next to one window, peering through the small slits, then move to the next window and look through it, and move to the back window and look through it. Sometimes the rapid bullets would break the lull, and sometimes the venom-tipped words-like-bullets would smack against the cabin fortress and incinerate the quiet.

The frequent words of his enemy were inane, molten shots of insane lead shot from the gaping mouth of a mad man, words that promised destruction and humiliation for his personal enemies; these malformed, jumbled, discursive words were fodder strewn in the wind, meaningless forays into hyperbole and fantasy and nonsense.

Night came, and with it, movement outside the cabin; the bullets came then, ferocious and unrelenting, hitting and cracking the walls and door and windows, and with this, the horrific clamor of noise, human, unrelenting, grisly noise, cackling, gurgling, maddening vocal bombs lacerating the place. The rush was on.

Conall put his Heckler & Koch G36 assault rifle with its 5.56 x 45 mm ammunition into the hold of one window, and the FN Minimi light machine gun, replete with its long 5.56 x 45 mm one hundred ammunition belt of the round magazine pouch dangling from its steel belly, sticking out from the other; and thus armed, he fired the FN Minimi at the enemy who approached or retreated at close quarters, and the G36 at the enemy who approached or retreated at faraway quarters; and yes, he had on his infrared goggles, as he had had the foresight to bring them, but no, he had not set up any kind of perimeter alert, as he would have done during any other recess from battle.

He had wanted this place to be a respite from war, but he knew that war has no rest, takes no prisoners, never sleeps, shows no patience, favors no one; for war uses anyone to feed its lusty self and to achieve its selfish goals, and when one man dies, another eager young fool merely slips into his walking grave and continues the merciless struggle for dominance—dominance over a people, a region, a land, a philosophy, a religion; dominance that is ephemeral and mutable, here today and strong, tomorrow usurped and weak and transformed into a new, reckless character that stretches out its attractive tentacles to embrace more tyrants, more despots, and even more ignorant, democratically elected leaders who mistake war as necessary for progress, who do not understand the fundamental concepts involved in reasons for war, but progress for their meaningless heritage, only.

A violence of bullets came pounding upon the back wall. Conall ran to it and stuck out his FN machine gun and let loose a burst to silence the obnoxious uninvited guests; and then more pounding came from the front and sides, and Conall rushed to one window and fired the FN and ran to the other window and stuck the FN into its slot and fired. He was always careful to allow the rifle butt of unused guns to not stick out of the slits when the enemy was close. Eleanor was lying flat on the ground against the front wall, helping Conall reload the guns—a skill he was sure to have taught her. The surge of the enemy continued, unbroken.

By 3 o'clock in the a.m., the enemy had quieted for a quarter of an hour, and Conall had fully reloaded his weapons, and sat next to Eleanor, holding her fast.

"You are magnificent, my darling husband," she whispered to him. "I am glad I have beheld your great prowess in battle."

He wanted so badly to just hold and pray both of them away, far away into a real cottage in a real meadow, as in the one he had often visited in Ireland, safe, protected, certain; but now, he had to keep alert, keep his mind sharp, agile, frosty, lest the enemy creep in unawares. He knelt and checked the slits. The outside assault began anew.

Everywhere now there were bullets pounding and objects pounding and voices pounding on the walls, and the strident echoes reverberated throughout the cabin and soaked into everything with its deafening roar. Conall fired through every window, running back and forth and forth and back, rearming, changing guns, running and running and, then, a bullet creased his right thigh but he did not fall; then a bullet tore into the top of the shoulder, but he was not deterred, still moving swiftly back and forth between windows and firing and firing and firing. The assault abated.

He knelt next to Eleanor. He felt warm blood. It was not his own.

"Eleanor," he cried, and gently picked her up and saw by the small electrical lamp that she was bleeding profusely from the chest. "Eleanor," he cried.

She reached up her right hand and put it to his lips, and in a small, quiet voice, a voice tiny but resonating a power from within of gentleness and peace and love, she said, sweetly and peacefully, "Conall, my love, Conall, my husband, do not grieve for me now, not now, my glorious husband, whom I am so proud of, for soon I and your son shall see you in Paradise; now, my good and faithful and kind husband, you have much to do, and must do it, famously." She smiled. "I love you so very much."

He kissed her to a profound sleep.

She died.

He closed his eyes, seeing only her, thinking only of her, spelling only her sweet fragrance, hearing only her sweet voice, feeling her gentle laughter, her healing words, feeling only her gentle touch; then he heard her last wish and he heeded it. He laid her softly upon the cool soil and kissed her and stroked her lovely blond hair and wet forehead, then let his hand fall upon her still stomach, and nodded his head, and smiled. "Soon, my loves, soon, I shall join you." He stood up, and his smile turned to one of a frightening resolve. "But I have a task to do first, for each one I fell is one less disciple of iniquity in the world." He stood up fully erect, and thought of his brethren. "Let this day serve them well."

The next attack began; this time, fire came to the cabin along with the others clamoring to get in, and a battering at the door.

Conall lifted up the one FN and hoisted it upon his right shoulder, and lifted up the other FN and hoisted it upon his left shoulder, both weapons being fully loaded, and he was fully ready. He thought now of his family, and his thoughts were insulated by the whaling away of the closing enemy. "Dylan, my brother; Rhiannon, my sister," he thought, his eyes closed, "learn from this." He opened his eyes and thus opened his mind to the ferocious din. "Eleanor, my love, and my precious son," he smiled, and then gritted his teeth, and turned around and beheld the walls ablaze and the door splintering and the shrill cry of the predator without, crying, "Fear not He who can kill the body, but fear He who can destroy both body and soul."

The door burst open. He opened up with both guns blaring in a brilliant shower of sizzling firepower.

Divided They Fall

After Moses and his men had departed from their adopted band of brothers, they met with the new rulers of southern Kush who attempted to appoint them to positions of authority within the new government, which also embraced the exclusive doctrine of repatriation of unwanted ethnic tribes in the territory by any means necessary, and broad powers to hunt down and exterminate any traitor, enemy, or rebel, perceived or otherwise; but Moses' conscience as a Christian, as a Crusader—lo, as a man—would not allow his desire for peace to subsume his heart and soul by agreeing to this; so, in agreement with his men, they departed from this new regime which, he could already see, was disorganized, unfocused, and splintering into rigid, divisive ideologies. The heart of Moses fell as he passed from Kush to Uganda. "Why do we fight, if only to bring victory to fools?" He sighed. "Conall and Mwindo, my good friends, you were wise, and I, the fool." Yet, it was his great pride that would not allow him to rejoin them, and decided to pursue the true enemies of his country on his own, as he had done in the beginning.

It was the radical regime, the radical groups, radical prophets, leaders, religious zealots that he pursued, for their immutable doctrine was the iron dagger that bled the heart of Kush, the widening fissure into which their dogmatic fanaticism pushed others; their unrelenting, power-hungry adherence to an intransigent belief that relegated all others as infidels who needed to die; absolute madness that robbed too many of the people's senses. Oftentimes, it seemed that his people had no choices for leadership but poor ones, and this was one of the primary reasons he had begun his journey to fight and clear the nebulous land of confusion, and allow the people to see plainly what good choices remained.

He and his men were now on the trail of the GLA, who had operated mainly in Uganda, but often leaked across the border into Kush and interfered in their politics, and along the way, leaving a trail of slaughtered victims who did not qualify to live according to their exclusive philosophy. Moses had fought the group before joining the Crusaders.

"We will camp here for tonight," Moses said, at the foot of the Rwenzori Range, after two of his scouts returned and reported that no tourists, police, or indigenous people were about.

"And what if we do encounter civilians—how can we properly fight this war with them about?" Henry said, exasperated. "They only get in our way; we cannot let these obstacles stop our momentum."

Moses simply stared at him, then went about settling down the horses.

"Maybe you have been too influenced by those white-skinned foreign interlopers," he fumed, standing near Jon Paul, Abebe, Julius, and Olaudah.

Moses turned around, anger on his face writ large by suffering one more vehement protestation by Henry, and his voice was ignited by wrath. "You are either here or there," he said, pointing first to the camp, and then to the Rwenzori Range; "wherever you are, do it quickly, and let there be an end of it."

"How many men did you see?" Henry asked the scouts, his voice firm.

The scouts looked to Moses, who nodded approval, and then walked away to attend to the horses. "Twenty," one of them said.

"Twenty? Bah! Each of us," and he said, lifting up his HK416 rifle, "is worth at least twenty of these rodents." He let out a loud "harrumph," and then stated, with authority, "I propose to scout further—who will go with me?"

The scouts looked to Moses, and one of them said, "We have done the reconnoiter," and he and his fellow scout turned away; "our horses are fatigued."

"Must I go alone?" Henry said, irritated now, looking at the other men, many who shrugged their shoulders and some who sought to dissuade him. "Bah! I will go alone, while you women get your beauty sleep! Warriors do not need rest when the enemy is at hand—do you think they would rest if they knew we were here? No! They would attack immediately! So too must we be as ruthless." He prepared his gear, and after feeding his horse, mounted up, and looked at the men, yelling, as he waved them away, "Bah!" and then sped off.

Abebe, looking around, anxiously, pleaded, "Will we just let him go? What if he is captured?"

"Then he will be, and we will be compromised," one of the older men said. "That is why we have a leader—to avoid chaos such as rode off just now."

Despite his most ardent pleas, he could not gain sympathy for his cause. "Then I will go," he said, harshly, and after readying his horse, and gear, he rode off after Henry, shouting, "I will not abandon my own."

"They will jeopardize the mission," Jon Paul declared; "they must be brought back," and after being joined by Olaudah and Julius, all of them, not so foolish as to neglect the care and feeding of the horses, and after preparing their gear, galloped away after the first two.

There were still forty-eight men in the camp, and when Moses returned from setting up a defensive perimeter with several guards, many of them pressed him on the matter of the five who had left.

"They have done what they have done, but we will not—for the horses need rest, as we do, nor do we have complete intel on this GLA unit."

"Why do we not go out to them?" one of the men asked.

"Should we follow a fool into the furnace to retrieve a coin, or wait for the fire to die?" The men were silent. "It is our hope and prayer that they will come back."

But another man spoke up. "Shall we let them die?"

"Shall we allow men who called themselves prudent to join a fool's errand? If Abebe cannot bring back Henry, no one can."

"And what if they meet the GLA?"

"Then I have erred tactically; and you want all of us to go on prepared, and perhaps be attacked by the GLA; I tell you, we are not ready to fight." He looked all around. "And in the future, if any of you have an itch, and you desire it scratched, and decide to break protocol, you want us to risk our lives for your whim? But I am done with this business now," and he set about improving the defensive perimeter.

Consequently, no other men, due to the irrefutable logic of Moses, departed to chase Henry; and so, the men set about the camp, silent, contemplative, restless, walking about, looking up at the Rwenzori Range, then to Moses, two figures they considered immovable, hoping for a stirring in their leader, who would somehow convince them that doing what seemed absolutely and strategically wrong and illogical, despite all of the perfectly acceptable and easily delineated reasons opposing such an action, still, somehow, in some mystical manner that only Moses could provide, would make, at least, a mystical "warrior sense," and provoke them to pursue their wayward comrades. But Moses did not provide them with an indication that he would relent, drop the tight reins on logic and discipline and strategy that had made him a successful leader, and embrace all that he disavowed, and raged against; "no," his body posture declared, as he was seemingly at ease, and nursing his body with fine food and drink; and by his relaxed body and placid face, this indicated an inner man pleased with his decision.

So, when it came upon an hour that marked the time Henry had ridden off, the men should have been surprised to see Moses leap up, affix his gear onto his horse, and, without a word, follow the same route as the five men before him; but, knowing Moses and his contemplative moods, they were not, and, naturally, quickly followed.

As it was, Henry, having soon been joined by his four comrades, and having dissuaded them of the notion of his return, instead persuaded them to stay, and so the five men continued on.

"Henry, now that you have convinced us not to quit you—" Jon Paul began.

"—And quit common sense," Olaudah declared, still anxious as he looked about the dense forest, listening to the noises therein.

"—You need to take the lid off the reason for your loathing of the GLA," Julius finally finished, too eyeing with suspicion his immediate surroundings.

Henry, looking at them disapprovingly, shook his head. "The GLA scum are three leagues from here—so said our scouts; rest yourselves, lest you shoot a flitting shadow."

The men seemed to outwardly relax, but inwardly, remained on the alert.

Henry let out a loud "humph," and then said, "You know I was born in Kush, that Moses and I are both from the south; and I should still be at the University in Kenya, talking to all the pretty girls and studying world history; instead, I am a warrior, fighting enemies who disgrace and bring shame to our beloved country, and even now, pursue an enemy who freely murders, and must be killed." He abruptly halted his narrative, as the stunned men listened to this revelation about his previously closely guarded past, which now began to pour out like a freshly dug spring.

"My parents still lived in the Taharqa region—good Masalit farmers they were, too—with my two little sisters and brother, living peacefully on the land, when I left for the university; but Africa could not let us be content, no! She had to bring a severe drought in the northern regions, chasing Arab herdsmen into our territory—well, you already know that history." His voice grew tense, and now the screech and song of the forest faded as the men focused on the familiar story of human tragedy they knew was coming.

Now, the voice of Henry became absorbed in bitterness. "Our government could have worked to solve the dilemma—two disparate groups can live together peacefully, but instead, the government threw their lot in with the Arabs, who began to chase us out by any means necessary; but our people would not allow such injustice, and that is how the Kush Liberation Army and the now disbanded Freedom League came about. I rode with the KLA and FL against the Arab Militia, before I joined the Crusaders." The other men were shocked. "And why, eh? Why did I leave the University and join the rebel groups? I would tell you, because when the government retaliated against the KLA and FL, and allowed the Militia and their allies to slaughter my people indiscriminately, my parents' house was visited one night…" Now, his voice was no longer bitter, but had been captured in an arcane mansion where it seemed it had no visual compass, as if it wandered about, detached from its host's body. "Zealotry blinds their humanity," he murmured, as his compatriots inclined their heads to hear him. "They are not even madmen—that is too lenient a pronouncement: they are demented spirits from another world—to murder anyone not resembling their poisoned doctrine; and so they swept in without any pity or mercy and murdered my parents, and kidnapped my brothers and sisters, and sold them into slavery." He stopped his horse as his narrative tumbled into a fierce storm where the wind that blew carried the crackling sounds of war, and the hard waves that crashed carried the gushing blood and guts of his enemies, and the boiling air carried the stench from the strewn, bloated, rotting carcasses of those fallen. "I gladly joined the KLA to pursue those who are responsible for killing my parents: the Militia, and the GLA—who don't even belong here, who just joined in the genocide. I joined the KLA and FL both to bring back the life they had so easily taken from me, to wreak vengeance upon the GLA and the Militia, to find my brother and sisters and restore what we had once had—life; life! But I never found them—never…" And his voice trailed off as he still looked into the violent reflection of this horror. "And what of the world's response? The UN and Western governments refused to 'interfere in the affairs of a sovereign nation,'" he whispered in a guttural tone, stone still upon his horse. "A sovereign nation, we? Had they eyes to see the wanton slaughter, ears to hear the pleas of our people? They could have stopped it!" he suddenly shouted. "But they stood by and let Innocents die—genocide; it was genocide—but they were too busy watching television in their air-conditioned homes." He looked down at the trail, and then around at the mesmerized comrades. "You know what the descendants of the Dutch—those insufferable foreigners—did to our brothers in South Africa, they brought an abomination from the depths of their wicked hearts: Apartheid; but I do not say we Africans are immune from sin—we are guilty of much, but we are better off without outside influence…redrawing the boundary lines that created unnatural boundaries and coerced disparate tribes to live as one artificial people." He shook his head, disgusted. "It is not who we are; I tell you this right now, we are the only ones who can fix what is broken inside of us." He paused for a moment of reflection, and then said, "It takes a zealot to defeat a zealot."

He was silent for a time, examining the tired horses, and then said, "I was wrong to come here, now; Moses was right." He looked about, worried. "Our position is exposed—I allowed my desire for revenge to betray my warrior sense; you are all good men to come after me." He smiled. "Let us go back before we bring too much anxiety to our—" He stopped, his thick eyebrows knit, his black eyes narrowed, his nose sniffing the air. "Down," he shouted, even as a hail of bullets appeared like an abrupt deluge of summer rain all about them.

Their horses were hit as the men, with the rifles slung over their shoulders, dove to the ground, and crawled into the thick brush to take up positions behind boulders and fallen trees; but to be more exact, they slowly crawled, and with great pain, as all of them had been hit—but to be even more precise, one had quickly crawled, as he had sustained no injury: Abebe.

Henry assessed the damage: Olaudah had taken bullets to his left thigh, and right shoulder; Jon Paul had two bullets lodged in his back; Julius had four wounds: right shin, left arm at the bicep, left shoulder, left lower rib cage; and Henry himself had three wounds: neck, left thigh, right forearm. "How is it that you are so lucky?" Henry shouted to Abebe, but the latter did not hear him, so clamorous was the gunfire as the dense thicket began to slowly yield up the number of GLA soldiers who surrounded them.

The horses were then killed by the GLA soldiers, who were still descending the sloping forest floor, taking up positions north and west, shooting furiously at their foes.

Henry knew what he must do, as their radio walkie-talkies still were in the saddlebags of their fallen horses and could not possibly be reached. "Abebe," he shouted, "Abebe," he cried, above the tremendous din, and Abebe, hearing him, crawled very low to him. "Abebe," Henry said, holding onto the youth's shoulder, "you need to go back for help."

"No," Abebe said, fervently, "I will not leave all of you!"

Bullets were shattering branches, splintering twigs, chopping off small chunks of boulders, smacking into tree trunks all about them, even as Olaudah and Jon Paul and Julius shot back.

"Abebe, you must leave now; you can do this, only you; we are counting on you, good and loyal friend."

"No," he said, but with less enthusiasm, shaking his head, and then continued in his soft-spoken tone, "I will not abandon you."

"You must, Abebe, good son," Henry said, as bullets blasted about him, and nodding his head, pulled the head of the youth against his shoulder, and then whispered, passionately, "you are a good man, Abebe; outrun them, but now, before more come." He pulled the youth's tear-stained face gently back, so that they saw the joy of brotherhood in the teary eyes of the other. "Now, Abebe, do what God made you for—to fight His enemies, and now, with your feet, which He gave you for a reason; make us proud, Abebe Rono," and knowing intimately this region they were in, continued, "with the noble

Crusaders at Thermopylae, regained." He nodded again, his face full of certitude. "And promise me, when this is all over, you will run again, yes?"

Abebe nodded, and barely murmured, "Yes, Henry Kimathi," and then looked to the others, and grabbed each of their hands, bidding them farewell, and to Jon Paul, he bid him, "Farewell, brother," and then, slipping down a few meters, waited for the signal from Henry, and once he received it, crouched low and began to run through the forest.

The firefight between the two groups was fierce, as Henry and his men provided cover for Abebe, who now was running full bore on the rugged trail. But every minute, more GLA soldiers, who had shifted their position right after the two scouts of Moses had left them, arrived, joining their comrades on every point of the compass, except east.

The GLA soldiers halted their shooting, and when Henry and his men did likewise, the GLA commander shouted, "Give up, Crusaders, you haven't a chance. Better to be a prisoner than dead."

"We shall need to stall for Abebe," Henry whispered to his men, who were still positioned within a ten-meter spread of each other.

"Look," Olaudah said, pointing to GLA soldiers moving stealthily down through the forest on the other side, "they're going after Abebe."

"Give it to 'em," Henry shouted, and he and his men opened fire on the five creeping GLA soldiers, killing them. And then Henry shouted, "That's our response, you GLA scum—Crusaders don't negotiate with murderers and butchers!"

"How far back to camp?" Jon Paul asked.

"About five miles," Julius said.

"Twenty-five minutes," Henry said. "We need that much time to give Abebe a chance to get safely back."

There, he had said it, what the men had known all along, that they were done, that they must now live to give life not only to Abebe, but for the other Crusaders. They checked their weapons and ammunition.

The GLA commander shouted, "When we are done with you, Crusaders, we will chop up your bodies and feed them to the vultures."

Jon Paul shouted back, "You should worry more about He who can kill the body and the soul," and then winked at his smiling fellows.

"You Christians…" Henry said, smiling, his smile disappeared like a fading rainbow. "I'm sorry."

Jon Paul, Olaudah, and Julius, smiling, nodded their heads; and then, in the midst of their special brotherhood, Henry cried out, as did the others, somehow, remarkably, in one ardent, unifying voice, "Force and right are the governors of the world; force till right is ready."

And then the battle, until one side was utterly destroyed, began in earnest.

Aftermath

The superiority of Abebe's genetic makeup, descended from the Kalenjin group as it relates to his uncanny ability to run seemingly for many miles with great speed and without exhaustion, was never more evident now, as he sped down the mountain trail, taking great, unbroken strides, his feet, as if sentient creatures, easily negotiating every bump and fissure, rock and branch, leaping over objects, dodging them, expertly spacing steps between them, without failure, and the more he ran at a full, blazing tilt, his rifle still securely slung over his back, the more he was able to masterfully execute this magnificent, seamless feat.

And then he heard in the distance hoofbeats from behind, but glancing back, could see no one coming. He thought of hiding in the thicket, but if he were discovered, he would have had no chance to survive; no, he decided, looking at his watch, the only chance was to reach within gunshot of his encampment.

The trail was serpentine, wrapping around the mountain like a set of snake coils, flitting in and out of dense brush, near steep precipices, strewn with bark, pebble and twig, narrow at some points, generous in others, twisting sharply here, along straight stretches there; and right now, he was expertly maneuvering abrupt turns with adroit leaps and bounds that no horse could easily do, and so he would gain time; but then he came onto an open stretch of trail that was barren of overhead growth, leaving him exposed to any approaching enemy within a quarter of a mile. He must traverse this distance faster than he ever had run, for he had begun to hear the hoofbeats coming closer. He took off like an ignited rocket, the sunlight shining upon him, lighting up his dashing figure for all of adoring Nature to see.

And now the thudding sounds were coming from, it seemed, all around him, but he did not break stride, for the trail was about to diverge, one leading up to the left, and up, and one to the right, and down, which would impart anonymity.

His feet were flying, his arms pumping hard, his breath fast, as he neared the end of this exposed path, and then he heard gunshots sizzle past him, digging into the path ahead; and so, just as he was about to turn and fight, he saw what was before him, a moving dream, and his mind, acting before his body could move, ordered it to dive into the heavy brush, which he forthwith did, thus allowing the riders before him to clearly discharge their weapons at those just appearing in the clearing, the GLA soldiers, who, presently, were felled from their horses, dead.

Without word or hesitation, Moses hoisted up Abebe onto his horse, Son of Al Khamasa, and continued on with his fellow Crusaders.

After Abebe told Moses of the circumstances surrounding his escape, Moses ordered the men to slow, and sent two men ahead by foot through the forest on the left and right flanks, about one kilometer from where Henry and the men had been; no gunshots were heard as they circumspectly traveled along the path, searching the terrain for any false movement.

The two scouts returned, and reported that they could see a contingent of sixty-three GLA soldiers at what was, presumably, the site where Henry, Olaudah, Jon Paul, and Julius had been; so, the Crusaders quickly dismounted, and moved cautiously up the trail, men on either flank and in the middle, until they beheld the enemy, who, curiously, were standing about, many smoking, some gesturing at something unseen in the bushes, others on two-way radios, and more of them in the bushes, assiduously hacking away at something long and bulky, although unseen.

Moses, bow and arrow in hand, motioned to his men to take up strategic positions to encircle their targets—to cut off all exits east, west, and south, but more importantly north, which would be secured, in the case of immediate failure; four men took to the forest, two on either side, to come around in front of the GLA soldiers.

Moses waited until the soldiers put away their walkie-talkies, and he knew that they had attempted to call their now-dead comrades, for he and his men had confiscated the devices from the fallen soldiers and, listening in, knew that the soldiers had also called in to their main division.

"Now, they suspect nothing," Moses whispered to the man next to him; "we must not allow other GLA who are coming to be ready for us." He raised his hand to signal readiness to launch the poison-tipped arrows from their self bows, weapons to be used now, as they had not the silencers on their rifles, and they needed to kill each GLA soldier with absolute silence—which they needed during an interval of precious seconds.

There may be thirteen time-honored steps in the sequence to firing an arrow, from the moment the target is sighted to finally loosing the arrow, but they must all be executed in a few intense seconds for those in combat—from proper stance to nocking the arrow to drawing the string and aiming and to releasing and following through, and to the warrior-hunter it was a rush from absolute calm to explosive fury; and it went something remarkably similar to this:

Before the shot, the body must be totally relaxed—the hands exert all the strength as you grab the bow with your left hand and the arrow with your right and nock it, and raise it and then set to release it; all of this occurs while you are slowly and rhythmically breathing in, and once loosing the shot, at the pause of the inhale, you then fully exhale; this pattern is to be repeated seamlessly and flowing like an undisturbed stream as the next arrow is grabbed by the right hand.

So, once the arrow is nocked, three fingers are to be used as you, totally relaxed, draw the string toward your chin—one finger rests above the arrow, and two below it; it is crucial that when you release the arrow at the highest concentration of tension, you stay relaxed as you stand, sideways, straight and tall, eyes forward, and that you are still pulling the arrow backward, keeping the hands still in their proper place and relaxed; so when you release it, you are still relaxed when the inevitable recoil occurs—you must still be in the proper position, your body not absorbing the jerk because your right arm has done so. This is the mystical and powerful way of the warrior-hunter as he prepares to confront human prey.

There were forty-eight Crusaders, and sixty-three GLA soldiers, and Moses motioned to his men to let fly their feathery-winged friends at a target each had chosen by hand gestures, so as not to shoot the same one, a tactic that they had deployed with rifles many times.

Moses had chosen two targets, who stood side by side, smoking cigarettes, talking, smiling, laughing; and then a triangular-shaped dagger sank into the soft neck of the first one, blood spurting out in a red stream, as he clutched his throat and sought to cry out, but could not; the man next to him momentarily looked at he who was hacking at something unseen, and then his disturbed mind's eye beheld an arcane vision, of flying, black blurs and more soldiers gasping at these eerie intruders that were now sticking out of necks, eyes, chest, and mouth; and as he completed the turn, saw the soldier still next to him, for a brief glimpse, impaled in the neck, blood flowing down his skinny chest; then, as he sought to cry out, felt something hot and burning sink into his own neck, and he too, joined his own kind in this macabre, silent, tortured, hands-waving-in-vain-for-something-tangible-to-grab dance; then more expertly shot arrows joined the others, and this was the beginning of the second round, the first one having peeled off men who were separated from their fellows, and not in direct eye contact with each other; so when they fell, they fell without a word or cry, and so, by the time the second round of flying daggers were let loose, the surviving soldiers, in those few seconds of elapsed time, had no real chance to recognize the danger, and the few who did were unable to do anything substantial about it.

Moses signaled to his men to move in, now with their rifles on the ready, which, they soon knew, was not necessary, for their handiwork had dispatched every GLA soldier to the kingdom of the ants, insects, and fungi, who were now their greedy masters, as the alarm had been sounded to let the tasty feast begin.

But there was no such celebration above them, for the Crusaders soon saw the object of the GLA soldiers' intense desire as they had hacked and swung their long swords—it was the mutilated bodies of Henry, Olaudah, Julius, and Jon Paul, now laid together, first killed by a massive barrage of bullets, then butchered until they were not even recognizable to those who had known them for so very long as brave and noble warriors.

Abebe fell down among his fallen comrades, clutching first one, then another, apologizing for returning alive and too late, crying in uncontrollable, soul-aching, heartbreaking sobs, as he lay with his arms wrapped around those whom he had considered his family, his brothers, his friends, who had guided him, watched over him, and ultimately helped him to become a man.

The other Crusaders stood, unmoving, their minds paralyzed as they beheld the inhuman carnage done to these men who had been as much brothers to them as any; those they had loved as only those can who live as warriors and fight not just for a sacred cause but for the protection of each other; for who can truly know what the world is, what a family is, or friendship, or filial piety, or love for a fellow human being, or what constitutes a definition of family; for, what is it, after all? Is blood the sole marker for family, if, from the beginning, all had one common father and mother, and to your left and right are really your brother and sister; in the same way, can people who are not immediately related by blood have a more fierce and insuperable bond of love, obtained through their generous, selfless acts for each other, by a willingness to care for, protect, cherish, nurture, and love each other, and display an eager willingness to lay down one's life for another? Is this tie that binds as strong as any blood tie, one born to heroic actions for a lengthy time during a severe crisis? This is precisely what the Crusaders felt as they saw their slain brethren so wickedly treated, so disrespected, their basic human rights so blatantly disregarded; yea, they felt as if a distant part of themselves had ceased to exist due to the loss of their own, as if they could feel themselves lying there with their comrades, as if their own world could never achieve the same quality of life again, as if their joy of happiness could never be filled, as if they could feel themselves sink deeper into the watery mire wherein hardship and pathos and suffering existed in perpetuum.

Now, as they buried their fallen brothers, they could not definitively say that their own consciousness rested inside their heads, that their minds peered through their eyes; but that their bodies felt nonexistent, and their thoughts were freed from their corporeal body and fed into the spongy body of the earth as it received into its bosom these cherished four warriors, graves that the Crusaders, now covered in the blood of those whom they still reckoned as brothers, had dug with the very swords of the murderers; and when the dead were secured deep within the soft soil, Moses raised up a bloodied sword to the high vault of heaven, and swore down vengeance upon those who had lived so wickedly and unabashedly and without mercy, as he considered those murderers no more than soiled scars, blemishes upon the human race, who had lost their right to live due to their aggressive, gross indulgence in barbarity, and love for the slaughter of Innocents. "So shall they be mocked, as they are mockers of God," he said, in a tone so bereft of any recognizable human voice that it would have frightened any ordinary citizen who was not familiar with the grieving and suffering which occurs when one loses a unique, vital, righteous bond with another through injustice, one that had been achieved through hardship and suffering, defeats and triumphs; yet, it is a high state reserved for the arms of Justice, which would propel these Crusaders onward to engage an enemy despite the overwhelming odds against them, to a higher plane reserved only for those who honor Virtue.

"Either we are God's chosen soldiers, to do social Justice on earth, or madmen, engaged in an endless campaign against tribes of madmen, indistinguishable no longer by stripe, creed, or tribe," Moses thought, and forthwith, hung his head low for some time, and then lifted up his hands eyes to the cerulean sky. "O Lord, grant us Justice against our enemies, and punish us if we do not do Your will, for my heart and mind and soul see only blood, and I choose not to condemn myself to human weakness that craves swift Justice." Here was, perhaps, one of his greatest talents: the ability to think rationally and clearly during a great trial, and in doing so, set himself apart from the majority of human beings.

But this was not such a time.

This time, he blocked out his Christian conscience, and now, cloaked in the fresh blood of those slain as his protective armor, as were his fellows, and swearing undying loyalty to those so courageously fallen in a righteous battle against so palpable an overwhelming evil, he could see no other light dawning upon him but the luminous light of hot, burning vengeance; lo, he breathed in the scorching fumes of lust for violence, and it inhabited his senses, and reimagined his desires, and settled like a new sky of a heavy, wet fog upon his heart, and captured it; and so, he was undone, and led his men on toward the mark, where he promised recompense for the evil deeds recently done.

There was no more talk, no more planning, no more debates, but to merely act, as in battle: the enemy attacks, and then they, the Crusaders, attack, without thought about the day before, or the day after, but only to obey the powerful will to satiate the awesome desire to destroy that which needs destroying, to purchase death for that which deserves no life, to uncreate the thing unfortunately created and allowed to live, to wipe clean the world's memory of it, to make desolate and forgotten the birthplace of it, to efface any record of its nefarious practices and philosophy, to bring a pestilence to those who embraced the perverted ideas of an aberration of Nature.

Moses and his men, having the radio devices of the dead men, monitored calls between the GLA camps, and quickly determined that a large contingent was coming down the trail to search for the soldiers who had not responded in an hour's time.

The supreme commander in battle has an intimate sense of when to engage, how, where, why, with whom, from which direction, and how to continue afterward, like any grand chess master, always twelve steps ahead, a talent gained in combat experience; yet, there is also the variable of momentum gained from a fresh victory, albeit brief, giving rise to optimism, and thus, coupled with the fervent desire of Moses to make evanescent the existence of the foe before him, he enlarged the entire equation, no part of it capable of being separated, lest the whole, living stratagem unravel.

So, when the first wave of marauding GLA soldiers, thirty in all, came boldly approaching, the Crusaders, their horses veiled within the border of the forest, were in readiness, on either side, some further south, others further north, all to catch escapees, and then they opened fire, but from the east side only; close to half of the GLA soldiers fell, and the remaining ones were struck down as they fled in a westerly direction, where the Crusaders dispatched them; and so the Crusaders, having once again confiscated more radios, mounted their own horses and continued on, unimpeded by anything mortal or natural.

The encampment of this division of the GLA, established after raiding parties on local populations, contained some three hundred and fifty-three soldiers who were now on high alert due to the absence of a reply from what they now knew were their dead accomplices; however, this particular clearing was not chosen solely for strategic reasons, but for recreation and relaxation, a temporary refuge from government troops, a place to merely drink to drunkenness, violate female prisoners, prepare for the next excursion into the lives of those they deemed unworthy to live; never had the site been molested by their enemies, and so was not considered a viable stronghold, but a veritable fun palace of debauchery and rejuvenation; so, it was with great alarm that they now panicked, and made for the narrow pass, where their guards were situated, to engage this approaching, unknown specter.

But, in the diverse body of the Crusaders, in their combined experience, there had to be one with intimate knowledge of the terrain, and it had been Henry, the very reason why he had been motivated to boldly ascend the path so blindly.

"Thermopylae, regained," Moses whispered, as he saw the two scouts come back, and reported that a similar narrow pass that Henry had made reference to, the small Greek division that had fought valiantly against the great Persian army, was indeed there.

"But we must move fast, as the GLA moves even now," the one scout said.

Moses, nodding to Abebe, who now rode a horse of his enemy, nodded back, and then the men rose, posthaste, up the trail, picking up other scouts who had stopped at various points, until they reached the towering cliffs. Moses gave the signal for his eight men, who had already climbed its height, to kill the enemy lookouts, which was done in expert fashion with bow and arrow, and consequently, after taking up positions with six other men on either side of the high-walled cliff, immediately shouted that the GLA were charging through the sandy ravine, and so fired upon them with their HK416 rifles; and then Moses and the other men still with him dismounted, and met GLA soldiers with an overwhelming amount of firepower that drove them back through the pass, leaving altogether forty-six dead and twelve wounded, while the latter were abandoned by their fleeing brothers, some of whom attempted to follow them, either on foot or horse, but none survived; nor did others who were lying on the rocky path.

Now Moses and his men, having ascended to the top of the cliff, their forces split on both sides, numbering forty-eight, surveyed the scene, debated the logistics, and regarded the future.

"More GLA will come," Moses began, talking to the men around him, "so the battle must be now." There was no talk of retreat to ensure their absolute safety, no consideration of it, no option. "I estimate that we have eight hours until more GLA soldiers arrive," he continued, looking up at the darkened sky. A plan was then devised, measured, debated, analyzed, and proofed, and then a man was sent to the other side to inform the other men, who wholeheartedly approved it. "So be it," Moses said.

The plan was simple: the Crusaders were leaving. But had they not rejected retreating outright? Yes, but this was no safe withdrawal, but a tactical change, for their current position was untenable; they could not possibly hold the pass against more GLA soldiers, could not rush the hundreds of GLA soldiers on the small plateau inside, and so, they would—seemingly, to the enemy—be retreating like a whipped dog, but, in reality, they would assume a position far enough away so as to avoid detection, and then follow the GLA to their stronghold, after having contacted the Kush Liberation Army and the Liberty League Movement, and thus seek to deal a death blow to their accursed enemy. This was Moses' signature strategy: patience, careful consideration of the confrontation, despite the urgency and the desperate need for vengeance, despite it all; above all, patience, and a singular ability to recognize any previous mistake and amend it; so, the Crusaders left, and soon the GLA within, and those without, coming up the trail, discovered the Crusaders' absence, and so mocked this perceived cowardice, and proceeded down the mountain, celebrating their own legendary fierceness.

The GLA had been active for ten years, led by Mulumba, and they were never totally defeated, always managing to escape their enemies to a refuge in the many countries who welcomed their lethal brand of radicalism; and why were they never defeated—were they great fighters, great tacticians, great heroes? No, no, no; they had in common the traits of so many faith-based zealots: lightning attacks on the helpless, lethal attacks on small numbers of foes, retreating after slaughtering Innocents, hiding, recruiting and kidnapping young boys and girls to enlarge their army, and receiving aid from like-minded countries and rebel groups.

But now, the GLA was the hunted, and not as a momentary course gained as a reaction to their most recent outrage, but a carefully plotted, strategic, purposeful design that described only one outcome as agreed upon by the pursuers: to blot out their existence from the face of the earth, upon which they were no longer worthy to walk, and had forfeited the right to do so, by the sanguinary and obscene acts of outrageous, unmitigated bouts of violence against their victims, and allowing themselves to indwell and thrive in unrepentant sins, which seemed inseparable from their bodies now, as if their souls fed on it in the same manner a budding flower nurses on golden sunlight; therefore, such a perversion, an abrupt fault in the spectrum of decency, a blazing conflagration in the path of Innocence, Moses decided, needed to be uncreated.

So, the three forces—Moses and his men, the KLA and LLM—stood, high upon a distant hill, poised to attack the remote stronghold of the GLA that Moses' scouts, by following the enemy soldiers back from the Rwenzori Range, had found. The KLA managed to send three hundred and fifty men, the LLM eighty-one, and with a small Crusader contingent, amounting close to five hundred men, and as they had an abundant supply of rifles and ammunition and grenades and RPGs, they were well prepared to take on the more than eight hundred GLA soldiers below.

And then one of Moses' scouts pulled him aside.

"When I was near the encampment," he began, referring to his reconnoiter to assess the GLA combat strength as he hid in the dense underbrush; he had heard two men talking. "There was one man, named Patrick, talking to another man, who is lean, and muscular, whose name was—Ahmed." Moses, for no logical reason, as "Ahmed" was a fairly common name here, felt the chill of terror rise up in him. "So, I took his picture." He had a small, compact, cellular device that was used for taking video and still pictures only, as there were no cell towers available yet in this region. The other scout had distributed his pictures of the camp to his comrades, but this scout had kept this camera private. He did not have to say who the second man looked very much like, and when he handed the camera to Moses, the scout could plainly see the astonishment in his eyes. He did not leave.

Moses stared at the picture for a duration past amazement and approaching shock, and he forced himself, feeling this discomfort rise up in him, to look away, and at the camp below. He had always thought of his own family, wondered what had happened to his brother and sister, searched for them, but after finding no trace of them, reasoned that they were long dead. He looked again at the picture; yes, it was his little brother, and the last time he had seen him was ten years ago, when the Militia had destroyed his village and set him off on his fateful path. He had to act quickly, for he mustn't let this opportunity go by. The scout told him exactly where he had seen Ahmed, and said there were more pictures on the camera of the surrounding area and the dangers therein.

"I will go," he told the scout; "tell no one; if I'm not back in one hour, do what you must."

Night was falling, misty plumes descending, streaks and speckles painting the pale sky, sooty vapors billowing over the land as Moses wound his way down the sloping, thick brush on the hill, and toward the enemy encampment.

Ahmed was alone on guard on the periphery of the GLA encampment, walking with his AK-47 rifle slung over shoulder, smoking a cigarette, looking about, at ease, expecting no one to interrupt his reverie. He heard a voice, and though it pronounced his name with a long-ago familiarity, and even though he could not see a person, somehow he knew it was a family voice; and then it said, "It is I," as a body appeared, unarmed, coming out of the dark shadows, a smiling, happy man, walking toward him, even as Ahmed raised his rifle and pointed it at the stranger, who was, even now, nodding his head.

And then revelation seized Ahmed. "Moses," he exclaimed and, dropping his rifle, ran to embrace his older brother, both of whom were weeping now. "Moses, Moses, you live," he said, pulling him back from himself. "I can hardly believe it—praise god!"

Moses was no longer a warrior: he had never been one, he had never killed, never waged war against tyranny, never walked nearly the whole length and breadth of Africa, experiencing diverse cultures and meeting and recruiting men of similar philosophies to form his small band of freedom rebels, and never had lost out on a normal life; all of it was gone now, for now he was fourteen years old again, and he was on his way home from school, and here was Ahmed, alive, his family, clearly alive, and here was authentic love and joy, and he no longer wanted to be a warrior and do what others would not do—he had had enough, he had done what he must, and now it was time for others to stand up.

After moving into safer cover, the two brothers sat upon a log and talked of their youth, avoiding the decisive moment when all had changed, and then Ahmed spoke of it. "The Militia took Samya to a different camp—I heard from people who were there that she was later killed, and I went there and confirmed it."

The two mourned.

"I was with the Militia for one year—they trained me to be a soldier," he continued on, and then gave a lengthy description of his life there, "and then I was sold to the GLA." He halted his tense narrative and, smiling largely, wiped away tears of joy; placing his arms upon Moses, he whispered fervently, "I can't believe it—both of us together again." He nodded, and then his smile faded. "I heard the name of 'Moses,' when men spoke of these Crusaders, but how could I know, eh? My big brother, a leader of men! It was too much to consider." He forced a smile. "But I have a command here." He looked forlorn as he saw the disappointment in the face of his Moses, and then said, impassioned now, "I believe in our cause—Mulumba is a true prophet of god; I've seen him perform miracles," and he witnessed to him of his faith.

The voice of another guard rang out, and Ahmed answered that he was temporarily indisposed, but would resume his guard duty momentarily. His voice had been rough, authoritative, angry, but when he spoke again to his brother, it was deferential, respectful, timid. "What do we do, Moses, what must be done? Tell me, for I do not know how we can both survive."

Moses had seen Ahmed not as one of an army of terrorists who committed atrocities and needed to be scorched from the earth and buried like they were nuclear waste, their memories effaced from the annals of history, but as little Ahmed, his brother he had cared for, and taught; his best friend, who had always looked up to him for guidance, even now; and even now, despite the conflict of who both of them had become, he knew what must be done; and so, looking into the big, brown eyes of his brother, which were eyes full of wonder as they used to be when Moses would tell him about his lessons at school, he began. "This is the way it must be, and will be." It was the sagacious, firm tone of the older brother that Ahmed now heard, who knew more, had seen more, who could win the day against all odds. "You will return to your people, and I, to mine; we shall, neither of us, utter a word of this, for this is our concern, not others; what we are is family, and despite what has happened from that horrible day until now, we are still one, and that cannot, and must not, be denied; it is a reality only we share, that only we are responsible for, and understand only by ourselves—because of who we are." He placed his hand upon Ahmed's shoulders. "Now, here, we are brothers, forever, and no one can take that from us." A brief smile of remembrance came to his searching visage. "When we depart, we leave this forced and alien world, and go back to one we created—but no one created this one here but God, our family, our mother, and our dear father, who did not long live, and Samya, and this is what lasts forever," and he placed his hand over Ahmed's heart, "in here," then over his own heart, "in here: one family, the Khalifa family, living in the hut of straw and mud, playing in the sand, helping Mother with chores." He nodded. "We will go now, and God will decide." And lo, Moses witnessed to him of his own faith.

They both stood up, weeping, and embraced. "Go now, little Ahmed," Moses said, gently, then the two brothers departed from each other, each returning to their respective people.

Now, Moses sat upon his brown Arabian steed, Son of Al Khamasa, silent, forlorn, observing the quiet below, even now disassociating himself from the brief interlude of family reunion that had so heartened him, quickly assuming the hard mask of the merciless warrior; and so, when he looked upon the KLA and LLM soldiers, sitting in their camouflaged-painted Jeeps, and to his own men on their horses, who eagerly awaited the word, he said, with final authority, "Let no man live; let no man escape; and let there be no deliberate killing of Innocents—thou should die first." He looked below, again. "So, let it be done to them, as they have so egregiously done to others."

And he rode down the narrow dirt path that led into the deep thicket, followed by his men, while the KLA and LLM followed, one of them flanked on the left, the other on the right; and when all were in position, Moses, using a two-way radio, signaled the beginning of the assault. The night was pitch black, and their every movement was shrouded in mystery.

The fighting was so fierce and brutal that there was no diminishing in intensity from beginning to end, where each soldier fought continually on foot, horse, or automobile, always reloading, always charging, never a chance to contemplate an alternative course; once the Crusaders, KLA and LLM gained the upper hand, the GLA began its retreat, using kidnapped hostages, mostly children, as shields; but the expert marksman of the Crusaders, with their M25, or M24 or SR-25 sniper rifles, were able to extract the proper target and leave the Innocents with minor wounds or utterly unharmed.

Moses the fighter shot at the enemy without hesitation, but as Moses the brother, hesitated for a fraction of a second as he eyed the soldiers through the FLIR scope; and then he saw Ahmed, holding a child up against his own body, and he shot, yes, but altered it to the extent that the bullet merely knocked Ahmed down, releasing the screaming girl.

Presently, Moses knelt beside him, observing the blood streaming from the left shoulder of his brother.

"I'm glad it was you, Moses," Ahmed whispered, as they clasped hands, and he smiled. "Do you think about what life would have been like, had not that horrible day happened?" Moses nodded, a small smile on his face. "Yes, as do I; but, O, Moses, what will become of us?"

Moses shared his faith with Ahmed again, and before Ahmed could respond, a perfectly horrific shot rang out, and a bullet exploded into Ahmed's head, and his blood and tissue splattered on to Moses, who, although stunned, stood up, and beheld a KLA soldier, sneering, approaching him.

"No prisoners," he said, snarling, and pointing his rifle at another fallen GLA soldier, shot him for good measure.

Moses stared at the man as if he were a perverse creature recently formed before him, and whispered, with great fervor, "He was an Innocent—as much as anyone; such is the power of divine forgiveness," and he presently shot the soldier dead, and as he stood over him, he whispered, "kill no Innocent, lest you die," and he spat largely upon the fresh corpse.

And returning to his fallen brother, gently kissed his forehead, and whispered lovingly, "One of us is still here, my beloved family, one who needs to do what must be done, then together, we will finally and eternally be."

He would not weep now for his brother, who was once thought dead in the body, then found alive, but dead in the spirit; and although now dead in the body, but alive in the spirit, was a celebratory event. "There is no reason to bury that which rots, for the soul is incorruptible."

And presently he rejoined his men, and learned that a few GLA members had indeed escaped, shouting vengeance upon the Crusaders, and that a squad of KLA and LLM soldiers had gone after them.

"So, many have prophesied our destruction," he replied, unmoved, "and no matter how many of us fall, ten more will take our place, and we will hunt them down, the few who will take the place of their dead; for such is the way of this world."

The next day, the KLA and LLM squad brought back one GLA prisoner, and set him before Moses.

"He is from another camp the GLA soldier went to," one of the KLA soldiers began, then shouted at the kneeling prisoner, "Talk, dog."

The prisoner, covered in bruises and cuts and purple welts, looked up to Moses, and then shouted, proudly, "We are going to kill your big man and his woman for what you've done; even now, Mulumba is on his way to kill them."

Moses, frowning, said, harshly, "Who?"

The man was still silent, smiling arrogantly, and, without prodding, boasted, "Your blond-haired prince and his bride will soon die!"

The face of Moses lost its equanimity, his body lost its strength, as he cried, "Where!"

The man laughed uproariously. "You cannot stop our Lord Mulumba from doing God's will," and he smiled like the man who knows he will always win, and then bit down on a poisoned pill, and died, forthwith.

Moses, still in shock, then motioned to his men, who presently mounted up.

Then Moses and the Crusaders commenced galloping away in terrain that could only be traversed by humans and horses, slow, torturous terrain, without a way to communicate to the other Crusaders, who had their own communications devices, still in a region he knew not where, and unable to contact Dylan and Eleanor; had he wings, he would fly, but he had none, and thus, frustration bled his heart dry.

Two More Come

World relief agencies, the kind that citizens enjoy disparaging so they can reason their way out of contributing to them, acted so swiftly and with such exceeding abundance of goods to the famine in Ethiopia, that the Crusaders were left with little to do but act as auxiliary helpers.

"It is all your doing," Yoshitsune said to Robert Heimdall, as he admired the competent operation within the relief camp. "We are mere nursemaids."

"I propose," Robert said, gesturing with his hand to an assistant director where to place a new shipment of food and medicine, "a brief visit to our lovebirds."

Yoshitsune frowned. "It has only been two weeks; I hesitate, with my life, to come unannounced upon a husband and wife who are becoming as one."

Robert placed his hand upon Yoshitsune's broad shoulders. "They will welcome us, Yoshitsune—did he not say he would return within a month? And, I have a surprise for all of you." He had planned the speech to coincide with the arrival of a large cargo plane that was just landing on the hard barren ground behind them.

The Crusaders quickly gathered around Robert and Paul and looked with great anticipation at the cargo doors coming down.

"Rakhsh!" Rustem cried, and as he began to run toward the plane, so did the others, and soon they reunited with their horses, an occurrence that would happen often.

Yoshitsune stood still next to Robert. "You have great power now, Robert Heimdall, and with that, acting on a great responsibility to help the world— it is as all great men begin; and bowing to great temptation—and that is how all great men end."

The two men walked toward the joyous men. "Yes," Robert whispered, "it is a burden I must bear; and that is why I must have good men and women around me."

The horses of Mwindo's men and Moses' men were to be ridden by the newest Crusaders, and the horses without riders were to be brought along in the hope of those men returning. As for Conchobar, Conall's horse, no one would ride it, as he would simply be brought along on the journey until his master was reunited with him.

Presently, the men, confident upon their trusty steeds, departed toward the South, and in two days' time, they were nearly at the border of Tanzania. They set up camp and found a lake nearby and set out to bathe and fish in it, leaving a few men behind to watch the horses that no one rode.

Horatius was sitting on a boulder and eating a plate of red yam and red beans and rice when a distant figure approached the camp. He picked up his rifle and called to Arjuna; soon, it was apparent that the figure was a young man, a blond-haired, muscular youth who wore a green backpack that had two sheathed swords fitted behind him.

Now, Arjuna and Horatius stared because a stranger approached, this much is true, but they stared with intensity because this youth resembled someone they knew intimately.

"Hello," the youth said, riding up and waving to the men, and smiling. "I am looking for Conall Cuchulain." The men still had their weapons drawn and aimed at him, yet he did not seem to mind as he dismounted, and held out his hand in genuine friendship as he walked toward them, looking at both of the men as if he knew something they did not know, and that would bring him a hearty welcome here. "I am Dylan, his brother."

"Of course," Horatius cried, smiling, and after dropping his rifle to his side and then shaking the strong hand of the youth, Arjuna did the same.

"What brings you here?" Arjuna asked, and laughing, "You look so much like him!" and slapped the youth strongly on his back.

"How did you find us?" Horatius added, and laughing, "And you are the spitting image of him! Ha!" And he too slapped the youth strongly on his back.

Dylan smiled. "My brother wrote to me often of your exploits, and I set out two months ago to find you," he said, nodding toward the men, "and you are Horatius and Arjuna," nodding toward each one correctly, "I would know both of you anywhere!"

"So, you know where he is now?" Horatius asked.

"Honeymooning," he said, shyly, "but I mean to surprise him!"

The three men sat down and broke bread together, and then Dylan told them of his adventures coming here.

"You are quite the traveler!" Horatius exclaimed.

Dylan blushed, as he was too humble to knowledge his accomplishments. "Do you know where in Tanzania he and Eleanor are?"

The men showed him exactly where his destination was on the map, then he asked excitedly about Conchobar, and the men took him to the black stallion. Dylan stood next to the magnificent head of the horse and stroked his thick, shining mane.

"The horse knows you, because it first knew Conall," Arjuna said.

And then another man came into view. "Do you know him?" asked Horatius of Dylan, who responded in the negative. In a few minutes, the man walked into the camp, and he too was greeted with the ends of rifles. He was Kush. He spoke English.

"I am looking for Captain Mohammed Samoei."

"Why?" Horatius said, suspiciously.

"I have a communiqué for him regarding one of his comrades."

After the man was searched, he handed the note to Horatius, who read it aloud. "'Captain Mohammed, it has come to my attention that the God's Liberation Army has found out where Conall and his bride mean to vacation.'"

Already, Arjuna was on the radio—not the cellular phones, for they had no towers in this vicinity yet—to the other Crusaders. Horatius heard a rustling sound, and looking up saw Dylan mount Conchobar and, turning the horse toward the South, beginning to ride away. "Wait," he cried, running after the youth, but it was to no avail.

In a few minutes, all of the Crusaders had come riding up, and gathering their weapons, sped off south.

In southern Kenya, a young woman had, only the day before, arrived at the airport, rented a car, and drove toward the north until the passable roads ended, and then, abandoning it, took off on foot along the path, wearing a green backpack and bearing two sheathed swords upon her slender back.

"I shall surprise them, I shall," she often thought, smiling as she thought it. "I shall prove to them I am grown up, I shall." She was not afraid to be alone in the wilderness, for she felt the presence of her sister and husband and Dylan closer and closer with every step she took. She took out the letter often and read it. "'Dearest Rhiannon,'" it began, "'Conall and I will honeymoon in Tanzania, at Lake Manyara, for nearly a month. I shall call you when we return. He is a great man, Rhiannon, and you must meet him soon. Love, Eleanor.'"

"Soon, Ellie," Rhiannon whispered, "I shall."

The Storm and the Fury

It was a brightly shining sun that extinguished the pale, black night and crowned the sky with a gold-studded, radiant dawn.

Dylan sped swiftly across the meadow and saw, and then inhaled the wispy molecules of the charred, black smoke. He felt a chill cut him to his very marrow. The cabin came into view, but before it was a mass of men, chanting and singing and dancing, and he charged Conchobar on toward the mark.

It was plain enough now to see that the small home was burned to the ground, and even through the hundred men still standing around it, and the hundred men lying dead around it, he could plainly behold the light-skinned bodies lying near the cabin. He knew.

"All of you will presently die," he cried, stopping Conchobar a good distance before the army, and dismounting and throwing off his backpack, grabbed the two swords, which he presently unsheathed: the two swords: the long one, being the katana, and the short one, being the wakizashi, with which he had trained using the ancient technique of Niten Ichi; and began to move toward his foe.

Many shots from on high rang out and the renegades, now checked in their bloody intentions, looked upon a small hill to behold a mass of men, rifles with grenades ready to be launched: it was Mwindo and his men, having intercepted two scouts of the GLA and extracting the intention of Mulumba here.

And then another voice was heard from behind the cabin.

"All of you will presently die," the voice proclaimed.

The renegades looked behind themselves to behold an auburn-haired woman who held two swords, the katana and wakizashi—for which she was also trained in the venerable Niten Ichi technique—in her lithe hands, coming toward them.

Mwindo cried from atop the knoll. "Drop your rifles and use swords, or die."

Mulumba merely sneered, then smiled, and was to signal his men to disoblige this order, when he happened to look up and see the Crusaders appear next to Mwindo and his men; and thus, he accommodated this wish, and his men dropped their weapons and raised their swords on high.

And thus it all began.

The army of men divided themselves up in the same fashion as tiny bits of ore heaped between two powerful magnets, half of them attracted to the protagonist behind them, the other half attracted to the protagonist before them.

This was no place for showy blows and feints, parries and ripostes, or dancing about for style, for Dylan was a mystical force of nature now, a heaving, whirling dynamo of a focused, magnificent array of combative skills that moved through his opponents like a devouring storm, using his short sword, the wakizashi, to block and his long sword, the katana, to attack, and he began crushing his opponents as if they were children with mere sticks, smiting them as if they were blind fools, tossing them and laying them low as a master to lethargic pupils; his blurring strokes, with these finely crafted, sharp blades, cut and slashed every man who neared him, first their feeble swords, then their feeble arms or legs or heads or bodies, filleting these human rodents into a mangled mound of blood and guts and bone, and not one or two or three of them could penetrate his magnificent aura of immense power and strength as he used their inferior techniques against them: if they used a large rhythm in their thrusts, he used a short rhythm; conversely, if they used a small one, he used a large one; and by quickly learning their forced and confined and crude tempo, he adjusted his technique to move around it and shatter its meager harmony; and by adjusting his pace to strike simultaneously, or when the opponent's sword was raised or lowered, in a hitherto unrecognizable maneuver, he was able to move around them and inside them and outside of them as their techniques were cast into disarray and their minds into mass confusion and desperation.

Rhiannon, her athletic abilities with sword and form beyond the reach of mere man, took out every comer, dispatching them with no mercy, no thought, no worry, her skill unheralded in this mortal sphere, and unexpected from one so young, but a surreal gift she commanded as easily as walking and moving her arms; and for every villain who dared approach her, she sent him down as a shade in Sheol with her signature mark upon their bloodied and wrecked bodies; no one could approach her and live long, no one could gain entrance near her and even attempt a blow against her, for she easily dispatched them, and then in a seamless, continuous motion moved one sword to another villain and another sword to another, and in this fashion she swept through the great mass of trembling soldiers like a churning scythe that was rotated and turned as if by supernatural force. She cut through them like a farmer cuts standing stalks of wheat and then separates it from the chaff; she cut them as if they were puffs of clouds; she cut through them as if she could not die, and die they must, by her steady and strong hand.

They, these blubbering men, came in twos and threes against two sword-wielding titans, and so, in twos and threes, they died; and when they came in fours and fives, so too they died in fours and fives, for it did not matter how many of them came against the swordsman and swordswoman, it only mattered that when they did, they would surely die, and then without mercy from their antagonists; for what they could never have understood is the inner symmetry and harmony these two youths brought to bear on this battlefield, a spiritual uniting, a completion of two halves now made into a dynamic and magnificent whole, each style complementing the other, so that when he stroked left, she intuitively stroked right, and when he cut high, she cut low, and as they stabbed and blocked and dashed about, they were herding their quarry into a quickly diminishing dimension where there was no safe place, where their minds were shattered and broken as if with every fall of their brethren, their minds and want to fight fell with them, and their spirits capitulated to what they recognized as being beyond their pitiable worldly comprehension.

The soil ran deep with the cold blood of these cold-blooded cowards until only a few of them still stood, like Patrick, and soon they too joined their kin in the cold recesses of oblivion; and then, only Mulumba stood, and he wore the burning mask of the still-prideful butcher.

The swordsman, covered in blood and guts, and with the swordswoman, too covered in the blood and guts of her dead enemies, stood on either side of the smiling, sword-holding, infamous slaughterer—the leader of God's Liberation Army.

"I will kill you both," he cried, wild-eyed, looking back and forth to them; "god will protect me!"

The swordsman, his face aglow with savagery, cried out, his voice aglow with vengeance, "There is only one God!"

And the swordswoman, her face aglow with savagery, cried out, her voice aglow with vengeance, "And He isn't protecting you!"

Mulumba turned and attempted, in his mania, to strike the swordswoman, who easily parried this and in return brought down her sword in a swift and powerful stroke against the man's scrawny neck, thus severing his head from his body; and then did the swordsman raise his sword against the still-standing corpse and then in a mighty stroke pulled it down, and in so doing, cut it in twain, and then it crumbled to the ground, and lay alongside its bloodied head.

And thus ended the history of God's Liberation Army, who finally found those on earth who could properly resist them; here, then, was the apocalypse, as it pertains to injustice, a fearful portrait painted by two master artists who never once thought that what they were doing was impossible.

The swordsman and swordswoman walked to the bodies of Conall and Eleanor, which lay side by side and had not been mutilated.

Dylan fell to his knees beside his valiant brother and, embracing him, wept.

Rhiannon, falling to her knees beside her brave sister, embraced her, and wept.

The Crusaders, and Mwindo and his men, walked up, stopping near the lamenting brother and sister, and each one of them, every man there, wept as if he too had lost his own brother and sister; but, of course, as it related to their world, they had.

The Eternal Struggle

"So, he shall have a Norse funeral," Dylan had said, and as no one debated the point, he dressed his brother in the garments of his ancient ancestors, which Robert Heimdall had given to them as a wedding gift.

"So, too, shall she have a Norse funeral," Rhiannon said, and as no one dissuaded her, she dressed her sister in the garments of this ancient people, replete with a white spring dress and a garland of yellow and red roses in her hair.

"Upon this funeral pyre I commit this soul to Thee, O Lord," Dylan said, lighting the bundle of twigs below the pyre, "even though he was Thine, long ago," and nodding gently toward his fallen brother, "resurgam." And then said, solemnly, "Mo dheartháir, mo chara, mo comhairleoir ciallmhar." My brother, my friend, my wise counselor.

"Upon this funeral pyre I commit this soul to Thee, O Lord," Rhiannon said, and lit the bundle of twigs below the pyre, "even though she was Thine, long ago," and nodding gently toward her fallen sister, "resurgam," and then said, solemnly, in the Irish Gaelic words she had recently commited to memory, "mo dheirifiúr, mo chara, mo comhairleoir ciallmhar." My sister, my friend, my wise counselor.

Dylan and Rhiannon stood back and watched the orange and yellow blaze. The Crusaders stood behind them, while Mwindo and his men stood next to them.

When the fires had drawn their last hot breath, Yoshitsune bid the man and woman to leave this place, to avoid confrontation with the authorities; and after Mwindo and his men, despite passionate protestations from the Crusaders, departed, the group moved north and into Ethiopia and back into their camp, and no one spoke aloud, yet all of them spoke to themselves of weighty matters, in the private environs of their minds.

Once there, the Council was summoned by Yoshitsune, and each man spoke in turn, proffering reasons for either leaving or staying. Dylan and Rhiannon, standing side by side, holding each other's hands, having refused to yet bathe or remove their battle dress, listened intently, their countenance grim.

This has been a cohesive unit that has unraveled, many of the men argued, a family that has lost its parents, a great sword smelted and refined in brotherhood that has shattered and cannot be reassembled. It is over, said one, we have done our best, said another; the mission is over, argued one, the vision is dead, said another; we have achieved miracles, said one, we accomplished much, argued one; we did more than most, said one, we fought the good fight, boasted another.

But we must carry on, began another; we have only begun to fight, cried one more; we must never quit until we are beaten, argued one; we will never be beaten, said another, so we must go on, for evil will continue to spread as long as good people do nothing, said many.

Yoshitsune, having kept quiet during the proceedings, looked to Dylan and Rhiannon, and witnessed their quiet yet proud demeanor and their fresh youth, erect posture, and their noble bearing, and his heart waxed nostalgic for a time that was not too far removed from now. "And what opinion do Dylan and Rhiannon have?"

Though no man there, after seeing the supernatural fighting skills of the two, would deign to demote them to the status of unacceptable warriors, many assumed them simply to be immature and naive, yet they would allow them to speak.

Dylan walked into the center ring amid the troop of the great warriors, his two hands resting on the two black sword hilts at his side. "I am honored to be in the presence of great men, who have fought against armies no other men would dare fight or can fight, men who have fought for the glory of Justice and Freedom alone, and not riches and power; such men as these are the true Light of the world, the guardians of Virtue, who have taken up the cross and bear the burden daily." He unsheathed the swords and held them on high. "These swords," he began, as pious tears formed in his eyes, which bore the color of the darkest evergreen trees, "I forged for Conall and Eleanor, to tell them I was here to join the Crusaders." He looked toward Rhiannon, who now joined him at his side, and she too unsheathed her swords and held them on high.

She said, "I forged these swords to give to Conall and Eleanor," and began to weep pious tears, "and to tell them of my yearning to join the noble Crusaders."

Dylan and Rhiannon plunged the swords into the soft, black soil, and instinctively joined hands.

"I will do what Conall did, with no great man beside me, or many, and one great new woman." He felt her squeeze his hand.

"I will do what Conall did, with no great Crusaders beside me, or many, and one great new man." She looked to the man now, and saw other passionate faces. "We are young, and full of spirit to fight; it is our destiny." Silence then came to her thin lips.

"I thank thee for fighting with Conall, and I will honor all of you the rest of my days," Dylan said, and then silence came to his lips.

"So," Yoshitsune said, "you will carry on, so we might retire, we, who are too old," and he began to laugh. "You two bear cubs are bidding the old bears go and sit by the stream and fish; very good!" He smote his thighs and threw back his head, laughing heartily, and then said, "You are so right!" and he waved about, "These men have fought well and are tired, but," he shrugged his shoulders, "I am not so tired, I am not so old; so, this warrior will accompany you for a little while until my old bones betray me," he finished, his head proudly held high, his hands prominently on his hips. He then walked to the middle and took out his sword and thrust it next to the other swords. "Three!" he shouted, "is a beginning."

Rustem stepped in.

Finn and Miguel, smiling knowingly, too walked into the middle, as did Tyr and Enkidu, as did all the original men of Conall's band of brothers, as did all the rest of the Crusaders.

Then did a group of men in Jeeps appear on the horizon, and after being alerted to this fact by the sentries, the Crusaders came to attention, and took battle positions.

Yoshitsune, looking through the binoculars, grunted. "He comes," he whispered, and then shouted, "Clear!"

And soon it was clear who they were as Moses and his men, after temporarily abandoning their horses with trusted villagers and borrowing these vehicles, and gaining information of the movements of their comrades, stepped out of the Jeeps and stood in front of their comrades.

"Where is Conall?" he asked, desperately. No one spoke. "Where is Conall?" he asked again, beginning to walk around, agitated, and then noticing Dylan and Rhiannon, said, "And whose pups are these?" He regretted it as quickly as he had said it, for the stature of the two told a tale that spoke otherwise of their deceptive youth.

"Who are you," Dylan demanded, "that you come here so brashly and asking for my brother?"

Moses nodded. "Yes, you are his brother—and I am Moses, and have returned."

"You are Moses, who betrayed us," Dylan cried, having been told of how Moses had departed, and so grabbed his sword hilts.

Moses ignored him. "Where is Conall?" he shouted, angry now.

"Dead!" Dylan cried. "Killed by men you should have killed! This is your continent, your world!" He was weeping now. "You were his brother here— you should have watched over him!"

"Conall—dead," Moses said, looking to the Crusaders for acknowledgment. "Where, when?"

Yoshitsune told him.

Moses and his men got into their Jeeps. "We will go there; wait for us," he said, and despite protests from Yoshitsune that it was unsafe to go, began to speed away.

"And keep going," Dylan cried, gesturing violently at Moses.

Moses slammed on the brakes, jumped out of the Jeep, ran toward Dylan and abruptly stopped in front of him, his face aflame with passion.

"Conall was my brother! We fought side by side in battle after battle! No greater warrior have I known than he, and no greater friend, no greater brother warrior! And as brothers do, we quarreled, and as brothers do, we forgave! And now I go to pay my respects to the finest man I have ever known! And then I shall come back here and we will fight again, as brothers! Even, you and I, if you are here to fight as your valiant brother did! I do not need your permission to go or stay, for you are as of yet without a voice!"

The two men stood wrapped in this combustible flame of friction, staring into the other's bare soul.

Rhiannon walked up to them and took each of their hands, and said gently, weeping, "Conall and Eleanor loved both of you."

Dylan felt his hardened heart soften. Moses felt his wrath leave him.

Moses said, without anger, to Dylan, "I go to honor your brother, a great and valiant warrior, who fought for all of Africa; and his wife, a beautiful woman who gave her life that Africa might live."

Dylan now could go longer sustain his enmity. He nodded his head.

Moses and his brethren departed, leaving Dylan and Rhiannon, holding hands still, and the other men, silent, and full of reverie, and deep sorrow.

The Battle Rejoined

Moses and his men came back, and after telling everyone how they had left a fractured coalition back in Southern Kush that was not yet ready to listen to their ideas for Democracy—thus, the Crusaders were reunited. A war council was held and it was decided the route to be traveled would be through Tanzania and into Zambia, where the Crusaders decided they were needed most, and then into Zimbabwe.

The camp was cleared and cleaned, the horses fed, the man and woman, rested—no man there would question Rhiannon's presence; and so the Crusaders set off once more on their mission quest, while along the way, Moses and his men retrieved their hoses. The quest was rejoined.

The Crusaders rode far east of Lake Manyara, wanting to avoid the Tanzanian authorities, but if they had ridden by, they might have seen a young man, who carried a brown wooden cane in his left hand, place the red roses he had in his right hand in front of two wooden crosses, weeping all the while; and an older man, who whispered as he bent down, "All my wealth, and influence, and power, all of it proved of no value—for I could not save you." He shook his head as the other man placed his hand upon his shoulders. "This must not happen again," and he placed a pair of white roses at the site where Conall and Eleanor had fallen, he too weeping all the while, and then murmured, after gesturing all about him, "And for those mighty heroes who have fallen, si monumentum requiris, circumspice."

Each country the Crusaders visited needed them; each country they fought in had people who vilified or welcomed them; each country they lived and died in needed more than them, they needed an outside force, but not a nation to invade them and impose their personal reforms upon them, no; they needed the spirit of Equality, the spirit of Justice, the spirit of Love, qualities the people had, qualities the people always have, for people are always willing to live in peace and embrace Freedom; no people want incessant strife and war and destruction, no; it is only the rulers who want such horrors and impose their intractable iron will upon the suffering people, and in doing so usurp the natural rights of the people and replace it with her own wicked philosophy; and some people rebel, and some fight, and some rebel and become the very image they are fighting; and some people fight and become worse than the image they are fighting; but then some people fight and rebel and dedicate their struggle to bringing Liberty to their beloved homeland. One country flourishes, another disintegrates; one man stands tall, another falls; one revolution comes, another goes, but what remains the same is the eternal struggle for the common people to throw off the ancient shackles of bondage, and it is here that certain citizens have found it necessary to take it upon themselves to leave their comfortable and safe homes and join the fight of the oppressed: this is the creed and mission of the Crusaders; and as they fought for the next five years, they found more men, and women, even Mwindo and his men joining in on occasion, who shared their noble vision of fighting injustice, so that their ranks grew to more than three hundred from many countries and continents; and they vowed, after all was said and done, that if any one of their brethren needed help anywhere in the world, that any who could come, would come to their aid; and if the stories of all their adventures were told, if all the battles waged by these valiant men and women were written down, their fantastic tales would fill up more volumes of books than a person could possibly read in a lifetime.

One More Thing To Do:
Promises to Keep

I was, of my own free will, the personal secretary for my cousin, Julien Ngbogo, who, as you no doubt know, was President and later self-proclaimed Emperor of the Central Republic of Africa, the CRA. Please do not judge me until you have heard my entire story, and then, perhaps, you'll render a righteous judgment.

Yes, I know what you are thinking: how could I voluntarily stay with such a notorious man, a horrible man, an absolute dictator who ruined my own beloved country? I do not yet know all the answers to such a difficult question, but I will briefly tell you how it all began and where it ended up; please, have patience with me, for life is never simple, especially in Africa.

I grew up with Julien in the small village of Guen, and because his mother and my mother were sisters, our two families lived next to each other; we were really like one large family, working together, eating together, playing together, celebrating together; Julien was one year older thanme, and I, having no older brother, looked up to him as one, and he was a good role model for me: charming, handsome, intelligent and, mostly, ambitious; where everyone else wanted to be a farmer, he dreamed of being a businessman, deriding farmers as "accommodating the servitude of the past." It was exciting to hear someone talk so boldly, especially when all one saw around oneself was poverty and suffering and frustration. He wanted more, much more—not just for himself, but for everyone, a desire that originated in his generous spirit.

He was always talking about bettering himself, that he wanted to rescue our land from the corrupt politicians and generals who had sprung up unnaturally after the end of colonialism; so, he went to university, and received many honors, and a PhD in political science, so that we had then to call him "Dr. Ngbogo," which, I tell you, we wanted to do, with much pride. No one else in the village had ever graduated from the university before. And, oh yes, I went with him there—not to attend school, which I eventually did: he insisted, you know, saying that all men should aspire to better themselves—but to attend to his needs, for already I considered him to be a great man, and destined for great things; and who does not want to be near such a phenomenon; is it not only human? When one looks hard at one's life in my country, and sees it as one of hardship and injustice because of those in power, and when a man whom you intimately know declares that he aspires to do better for all of us, well, you will follow that man and gladly give up your life to help him attain this selfless dream—our dream.

After being in local government and achieving phenomenal success, he sought political office for the presidency, vowing to fight the widespread corruption and stop the terrible civil war that was destroying our country and—can you believe it?—he won, and at the time, I thought it was due mainly to a presence of international peacekeepers who placed neutral observers at most voting sites so that the people would not be afraid when they cast their ballot; oh, how the village celebrated for weeks!

And Julien did what he had promised he would: he lowered inflation and dug out the rot of corruption, he created jobs, lowered unemployment rates, balanced the budget and increased trade, passed reforms to allow more political parties and individual freedoms, and created a CRA that was a leader among African nations—one of the first to thrive since that beast, colonialism, had breathed its last, vile breath.

How could other nations around the world not come calling, I ask you? How could other capitalist nations not come with their greedy fists full of cold, hard cash to invest in a vibrant and untapped economy—first the CRA, and then the rest of the continent—for such was the economic chatter that dripped from the salivating lips of western capitals; we were the darlings of Africa!

How could I not be his faithful and willing servant, I ask you? Would you not have been more than happy to be part of a societal revival of your own country, especially one that had been devoured and its boundaries reshaped by European imperialists, and then plagued by civil wars? Who would not have participated—I say you are dishonest if you would have declined to be involved in this rare honor; yes, you would have heartily approved, like everyone else—for our country was now a paradise compared to our other brothers and sisters on the continent who were ruled by strongmen and corrupt politicians.

And then what happened next, I honestly do not know—I do not, even now, when I think very hard about it, quite understand how all of it came about, as if it were either by some divine plan or a natural course when the affairs of natural jurisprudence are violated; as if people who looked like Julien and I were really the culprits for the calamity of what was to come.

You know, I was his personal assistant, his personal secretary, his most trusted intimate—who better to trust than family?—who knew all about his dealings. Well, one day, I came up to him, and said, "Julien"—he did not mind this at all, as long as I called him "my President" in the company of others, which I did not mind at all; in fact, I rather enjoyed it; can you believe it, my own blood—the President! Well, as I was saying, I was with him this day, and said, with the greatest naivety, "There is a memo you have signed that outlaws all other political parties; can this be correct?"

"Of course, Jonas, it is my decree; can you not see the logic of it? Dissension has already broken out, people are openly questioning my reforms, my intentions—can you believe it? I cannot have it; so," and he pointed to the decree, and then adjusted his white collar as he gazed admiringly into the big mirror with the diamond-studded trim, "there you have it! Do you not think it wise? Must we not stop our beloved country from sliding back into civil war?"

"Well, Julien, I had not thought of it that way—everything seemed to be going so well; but, of course, I trust your judgment: you are, after all, the one who has restored our country to greatness." I nodded my head. "Yes, you must be very cautious."

He put his big hands upon my shoulders. "You are a good man, Jonas," he smiled. "It is just a precaution; it is only a small thing to do, now." He nodded. "All will be well; you will soon see."

I nodded back, for this new law indeed seemed like a logical thing to do at the moment: he had to protect the CRA from internal chaos—was this not what had happened the last time internal discord was not assuaged—so we might not again have another horrible civil war, especially one that took the lives of so many innocent people? Yes, of course, he was right—it must not happen again, we must show the world we were better than that, that we did not need our white European fathers to hold our infantile hand or subjugate us, for us to exist; that we were a sovereign nation and had a natural right to exist, that we could live democratically and freely on her own, that we were indeed civilized, just as much as them. Yes, he was right, Julien was absolutely right: we mustn't allow our beloved country to fall; he had to be stern sometimes because of the artificial situation colonialism had left us in, the artificial borders it had created, forming countries where before there were none but tribes and villages living peacefully and independently.

A year later, he seized all the foreign-owned businesses and gave them to his family or friends; even I received one, a large plantation, which I told him I did not want, but he insisted I have, needless to say; but now I must say that this was the beginning of the end for us: the other decrees merely undermined our foundation, but now foreign investors were suddenly disinclined to invest in the CRA; and why should they, I ask you—so Julien, my cousin, could take their holdings from them? And then he nationalized all the businesses in the CRA.

When he took away private ownership of business, I was, quite frankly, astonished, for was this not one of the basic tenets of democracy? I, at first, did not believe it when he told me; he said it was all for the good of the state: no more greedy capitalists; this was a move toward a more egalitarian society. I did not know what to say. It was too much for me to believe; it seemed he was ruining everything, and for no reason at all; why, why did he have to do this?

Would you believe it, we still had foreign suitors courting us—giving us big money—and why? You will really not believe it: it was because Julien said he was anti-Communist! It was the era of the Cold War, you know, and the Americans and the equally paranoid European allies would give money to any tyrant or despot—no matter how many human rights violations they were guilty of—as long as they even said, and moved against, supposed Communists; and Julien was praised by them for this! And here he was at the same time suppressing his own people as he took away nearly all of his democratic reforms, and became just like those whom he had once vowed to defeat—and now he was being rewarded for it! And the more farms and mines he stole, as well as any business that caught his fancy, the wealthier he became; I should know, I put the money he robbed from his own people in his bank accounts across the world, and I justified it all by saying that he was trying to help our country avoid internal conflict; but I knew better as I watched him put down "imaginary coups," have political rivals tortured and sentenced for life in prison, or executed; and people whom he suspected of treason—even his own friends—were tortured, and anyone who voiced opposition to him disappeared; and I said nothing to him—nothing! Why? Where was the person I had once been?

He was always gentle and kind with all of his family and the relatives he trusted; he gave us marvelous gifts, businesses, positions of power—his generosity with his own kind was genuine, and he loved his wife and children very much. And with me, well, he treated me as a brother, showering me with praise, giving me many fine gifts, and putting me and my family in the magnificent palace he built in the jungle; we lived there, like royalty—like kings and queens of old: we had many personal servants, took rides on his private jet everywhere: if he wanted to go to Paris to see an opera, off we went—fantastic! Whatever we wanted, we had; there were no limits to his wealth—I should know, I kept his financial records. Yes, here he was visiting his former European conquerors as a reimagined vision of what they were—the illegitimate son becoming the still philandering great White Father. Money and power had done what patriotism and pride had not: it had made them true brothers.

And yet, he had made our beloved CRA into his own personal fiefdom, where he was supreme ruler, and any who dared oppose him were dealt with violently, especially during the great purges, where there were many jailings, murders, tortures, and where the army would move through unsuspecting towns arresting nearly everyone, and raping and killing with impunity; and I said nothing in opposition—ever! I justified his actions by agreeing with him that it was all necessary to avoid that ever-present terror in our minds: a civil war, the convenient whipping boy of past regimes, our mute accomplice, to avoid a take-over from unfriendly neighboring states, to keep out the Communists; and yes, he was still a darling to the West, a frequent visitor at the White House, praised and fawned over as they turned a "blind eye" to his horrible human rights abuses; but then the Communist countries fell, and the nations around us largely became democratic, and our people were being crushed every day; so how could I believe this oppressive rule was still necessary?

And, O, the terrible waste: the money he spent on a coronation to make himself Emperor, ten million US dollars for an event that did not feed anyone or fix any broken system; the exquisite palace in the jungle, which cost hundreds of millions of US dollars, which did not purify our filthy waters or bring shelter to the homeless; the theft of the treasury for his own bank accounts the world over, billions of US dollars, which could have stimulated our economy and brought many, many jobs; and while our people starved and workers in the public service were not paid, while our people suffered during epidemics of disease, while the majority of our people labored all day in the hot sun for low wages simply to finance the building of another château in one of the European capitals of his choosing—a place he might visit only a few times a year—no ordinary citizen could conceive of such a horrid opulence, not even I, who was in charge of the funding of it, the building of it, even, yes, flying out and engaging in the inspecting of it; O, what a tragedy: every penny stolen from my people that could have gone to a better infrastructure, more schools, better medicine, more hospitals, better hospitals, more social services, better social services—that should have gone to building a real democracy! And I was just as much to blame, as much fresh blood on my hands that I did not even recognize from my own!

And as the years passed, the CRA became all about him, his will be done, his blessed image alone on currency and coin, his image alone on banners in schools and churches and government buildings, on street corners: if you were caught taking one down, off to prison for you, and no, no trial, either—why? You had violated the sacred image of our holy father! There were songs about him, poems, stories, and films, too, all praising him and him alone, and no one else, lest the great God Julien let his wrath pour out upon you! And the worst of it all was that I went along with it, all of it, willingly, enthusiastically, benefiting from all of this horror! I praised him, too, I being his most passionate cheerleader, for I still loved him like a brother—and he in turn treated me like one—because I wanted to truly believe it could still be the way it had been in the beginning.

And then one day, it all ended; yes, a coup, by many of his generals who were supported by neighboring and antagonistic countries, and off Julien fled, with his family and mistresses, with me and my family, to Morocco, and there we lived surrounded by unimaginable wealth; and then the documentaries and reports of what his long rule of terror had accomplished began to come out, containing information, most of which I already knew, and yet, still, I was unmoved, until I saw a documentary on the "Kleptocrats of Africa," and I witnessed the atrocities of other corrupt leaders, and I soon recognized myself among them. Yes, I was shocked by the abuses of Julien's regime, as if I was an outsider and hearing it for the first time, what I heard about these atrocities—yes, for the first time I acknowledged them for what they were: atrocities against my own people; and there was I, being mentioned as his personal secretary, the man who had helped him keep power; but had I really done such a wicked thing, was it possible, was that really me, who had once been a little boy and who used to climb the Kapok trees in the forest with my big brother, my hero, Julien; where had it all gone wrong? Perhaps the worst of it was that Julien, as he listened to these stories, simply laughed; yes, he laughed, even at the claim that he had used a small group of crooked power brokers to "rig" his first election to win the presidency! He did not even get angry; no, not at all; and why should he have? He had won, he had raped and looted and pillaged his own country and then fled, to live in absolute luxury with the hard-earned money of those who had looked up to him and entrusted him to lead them faithfully and honestly, but instead he had enslaved them and subjected them to abject misery and physical and financial deprivations of all kinds; he laughed, yes, and why not! He had won; he had sanctuary, he had his family; he had won, I tell you, and I had helped him to do it; and he had even betrayed those who had helped him rise to power by allowing them to be caught by the new rulers, so we might get away; but did I tell you he treated me like a brother! I had sold my soul for filial piety. Why did it matter so much?

And, sadly, I soon realized that my wife was just like him: greedy, selfish, arrogant—no, she was not like the real person I wanted to believe she was! I could not even talk to her about all that; no, so after I sent our families away—on a feint—on vacation, I decided it was time to be a proud son of the CRA once more. My eyes were slowly opening to behold real Truth...

So, now I was ready to celebrate the day Julien and I, as very young men, had made a pact to be more than ordinary, to really matter in society; we were toasting each other in his suite, when suddenly the lights went out, and when they came back on, there were three more men in the room with us, but they wore masks, and held black pistols in their steady hands.

Julien, ever the man in charge, demanded to know the meaning of this rude invasion, and he shouted for his personal bodyguards.

One of the men then said—I will not give their names nor describe all of their physical characteristics in detail, for reasons of secrecy, you see (but I will tell you, each of these men appeared to represent a different "race," if that is still a scientific term that applies)—that it was time for Julien to come back to the Central Republic of Africa and face a court trial concerning the crimes he had been accused of.

Julien laughed uproariously, and I should not have been surprised, for here was a man who had never been held accountable for any infraction he had committed, great or small, while in power. He proclaimed himself a free man now, in a country that not only welcomed him and supported him, but had no extradition treaty with the CRA.

One of the men—a tall, big man, with coal-black eyes that burned with the fire of indignation; his face, even though covered, was itself a hard mask of resoluteness—then spoke, and in a decidedly foreign accent (I will tell you it was an Asian one, which will not reveal too much of his identity), "There is a higher court that ignores the absurd vagaries of finite Man, and he must needs answer to that."

Julien merely laughed, and how could he not, for here was a man who had not heard nor accepted a contrarian view in decades during his authentic rule; it would be like an imposing father who had ruled with an iron fist over his cowering children, when suddenly one of them dared to not only speak when not spoken to, but with force, and accusatory language; yes, Julien laughed the same way the father would have as he gripped the black leather whip and raised it in his own hand against his bold child; yes, Julien now reared up his hand to strike this interloper who had dared speak to him in what appeared to be an unheard-of act: pure insolence; but as he let it come down, another masked man, whose skin was black, his face and eyes shining with the same brilliance of defiance as his comrade, raised his hand quicker and caught the blow, and then his fiery words scorched the thick air.

"You will answer to the Court of the people of the Central Republic of Africa, first, and later; but even now, the Court of God judges you."

Julien wrenched his hand away. "Ha!" And he threw back his head proudly. "You are mistaken! I am a free man in a free country; no one here can touch me, no, not anyone," and he spat heavily on the grand Persian carpet before them. "Back in my ungrateful country, no one would dare touch the King," and his black eyes were illuminated by indignation. He turned toward me. "Jonas—summon my bodyguards; call the police, the embassy; they will know about this outrage!"

The third man, also tall, and white of skin, stepped up close to the now raging Julien—the once assured-leader-for-life of the country that once had not been, then came to be in misery, and even now yearned to be free—and his face shone with the same curious phenomena as his two brethren, his voice as passionate, and lethal with audacity. "The Court of Natural Justice," he cried, "calls out for you now, which you have built, stone by stone, every time you deprived your own countrymen of their universal rights."

A look of realization then came upon the face of Julien as he gazed at the men, as he nodded his head. "Yes, yes, I know you now; yes, yes, I recognize your arrogance; yes, I know you: mercenaries masquerading as champions of the people—ha! Self-righteous men and women who violate the sovereignty of nations; I won't debase myself by saying the insulting name your mercenary group has adopted from a distasteful past." He threw out his chest and reared up his head, his proud countenance sculpted by self-assurance, and he gestured against them. "I do not recognize your authority here; be off now, you peasant rabble, and be fortunate to keep your heads after this grave offense; imagine, common criminals, come to arrest a king; Jonas," he turned toward me, "quickly, call the authorities."

And then, in the hardest thing I've ever done in his presence, the only time I did not acquiesce to his demands, I, with great difficulty, began to move; and then, much to his astonishment, I came to rest next to the three men, and then…unbelievably, I faced him, I who had worshiped him as a true savior of my own country, whom now I perceived as its avowed enemy.

He was so far taken aback—his mouth agape, his eyes wide, his face razed by the tremor of white shock—that he was, for the first time I've ever known him, speechless; and, to make it all worse, I felt bad for him, and still sought to go back and join him, and somehow work it all out so that we all could survive this nightmare; but I had made up my mind, and it was now too late; I could never go back.

"You betray me, Julien?" he finally said, sorrowfully, and not with anger, but with a profound disappointment that cut deep into the very marrow of my bones, for here I had indeed betrayed my own kin. "What have I done to you, my brother? Have I not always treated you as such, as my own family, you and yours, sharing my wealth and fortune?" He was so sincere that I wanted to weep, and my head fell upon my chest in shame at what I had done; for all of what he said was true. "What does this mean? Have you truly joined these devious men," he gestured toward them, "who want only my money; is that it," he raised his thick eyebrows, mumbling "mmm," and then, "Are they not really here for my money? Show me a mercenary and I will show you a thief with a gun."

"No," I somehow said, dared to utter against he who had been the all-powerful Lord of all, "they are here for Justice." I wanted to say more, but my inner constitution failed me.

"Justice? Bah! Jonas—what Justice! I governed as others governed, I did as others did, as I saw fit, and the people benefited—we drove out the Communists, kept out the imperialists, stopped the beginnings of a civil war; the people do not want this for me—no! I will never believe it! They want me back; I did what I had to do, which cannot be judged as any wrongdoing, but simply as efficacious and necessary."

"Julien," I said, mournfully now, as I approached him, "the people of our country hate you—no, they hate us; we starved them, we murdered them, imprisoned them, took away their rights, denied them Justice; we destroyed the Central Republic of Africa, just like the white imperialists before us; don't you see, my brother, we are just like them." Yes, I knew then, when the actual words of liberation came from my own mouth, that I was not just betraying him now, but all those years when I had allowed him to be a tyrant, I had betrayed him by not stopping him then, and had betrayed the people; yes, I was the true traitor then, a traitor to Justice; but no longer. I began to weep. "You and I are wicked, Julien; we hurt so many people, our own people, the people we were sworn to serve and protect; so, now we must now pay for what we have done; yes, we must be brought back to the Central Republic of Africa and held up for the world to see, and prove that even we, a lowly African country, still seeking to free itself of chaos, is capable of doing what is right; we must be brave, and help heal the wounds we created."

"What are you saying, Jonas? Are you quite mad!" He began to shout, frowning mightily. "Me—stand trial? For what! Kings are above the law; we," and he thrust his hand up into the heavy air, "are the real lawgivers—it is these men before us, the ones who thrive on chaos and war, who should be put on trial!" He pulled away from me. "I will use my money to buy allies and then return in triumph to our country; and I will forgive you, Jonas, you are under much strain; it is my own fault—I put too much stress upon you; please forgive me, you whom I love as my own brother."

I was staring directly into his troubled eyes when I, with all the strength I had, said in a hoarse voice, "When I realized these men were seeking you—yes, I have my own network of spies, too; you taught me well—it was I who contacted them; I, Julien, your own blood, who betrayed you, because first you betrayed our people, and I freely with you."

"No, Jonas, no, that cannot be," he said in a guttural whisper as he held me fast, "not you, not my brother; why, why, Jonas, O, why, what did I do to you?" Then fear animated his face. "My money; what about the money," and he stared at me, wild-eyed, as panic and despair seized him.

"I gave it back to those from whom you unlawfully took it: the people, the poor, poor, persecuted people…"

"Fool!" he shouted, rushing to the computer on the gold-leaf-inlaid desktop, and checked the accounts. "Nothing, nothing, nothing! All gone, gone, given to peasants, to fools, to inferiors—and look at all of them now," he said as he turned to face me, "civil war again—and Jonas, why, why? It is because, without me to keep order—that is why," he slapped, and then beat his chest, "I brought stability, yes, with a price, but the people do not want weakness, they want strength—a strong ruler who does what must be done to keep the law."

"We are going back, Julien, my brother," I whispered, nodding, and no longer weeping; "we must go back like men and face our accusers."

"Who—those miserable autocrats, those greedy politicians?Never!" He pounded his fist on a solid jade table. "Jonas, you must save me, arrange it, mercenaries are vermin, buy off these miserable fleas," and he gestured toward the still-silent men; "get back my money and pay off those incompetent politicians, and you will see, yes, that what they think is so important and are so anxious about today will be gone tomorrow; I know, Jonas," and he gestured wildly, "man is corrupt; money can buy any soul, no matter how good they proclaim themselves to be."

I had forgotten about his knife.

He always carried a pearl-handled knife that I gave him when first he had become President; how could I have forgotten that, and now, he held it out toward us. "I will never go back as a prisoner," he cried, head held high, "but as a conqueror, I—a conqueror, do you hear me: the people need me, me," and he lifted his right hand, index finger raised, "to heal the wounds of civil strife; I am the only one who knows how to rule, and in order to be successful, you must be merciless!"

"Julien," I said, approaching, slowly, shaking my head, "it is over for you and I; we are a dying breed."

"Jonas, we will be triumphant once more! No one can stop us!"

I stood directly in front of him now, and took hold of his hand that held the knife. "No, Julien, my brother, no, no more—no," and as I gazed deeply into his desperate eyes, I saw what I most feared: madness, absolute, pure madness, and that is when I, with no resistance from him, drove the serrated knife into his chest, and then fell to the floor with him.

Did he allow me to do this—did the young and innocent Julien, in one last noble gesture, reach out from the distant past and help me end this?

"Jonas, my brother," he muttered, staring up at me, his face wrought by confusion, "what happened to us?"

As I leaned over him, holding his sweaty hands, I whispered, "We lost our way, Julien, my brother."

The masked men attended to him, but it was too late.

I gazed tenderly upon he whom I had once worshiped and loved. "He never would have understood what he had done, too long did he freely dine at the banquet of the wicked, until he was more them than us."

One of the masked men lamented, "No matter the treachery of Man, salvation is always at hand for those who believe."

I am writing this narrative from a prison that I voluntarily entered, so I might be held accountable for my crimes against the Central Republic of Africa; by writing this, I am in no way attempting to seek leniency for the inexcusable acts I perpetrated against my own people, and state that I, of my own free will, assisted Julien Ngbogo in persecuting them. It is also my intention to make clear that the three men who came to take Julien back to the Central Republic of Africa were in no way involved in his death, and were interested only in bringing him to Justice, part of which has been accomplished, but not by his death—for I do not believe even that can erase the pain and suffering we caused, nor words, but actions, perhaps, being the money he stole, most of which has been restored to its rightful owners, the people; not, I am proud to say, to bureaucrats who, no matter their best intentions, would no doubt squander much of it, but to international, neutral organizations which have seen that these monies are helping those with the greatest need, and going to the infrastructure, hospitals, schools, and other areas of great concern.

I have confessed not only for myself, but for all of the Central Republic of Africa, so that future generations may better know the terrible origins and consequences of tyranny that spread throughout Africa, and be inspired to seek democracy as the only path to Freedom, Equality, and Justice; and that Man can be redeemed no matter his offense against his fellows, and God; and that, even now, I believe, after all that has occurred, I would accept a righteous judgment from God.

Book Two

From whence comes poverty,
it comes from tragedy;
where was it before,
but in you and me.

<u>She</u>

There is a large concrete building; it is the color of golden wheat at harvest time; it has humble white letters sweeping across its uppermost section: "Family Outreach." It sits on a street that few people travel, and yet a great multitude of people visit this dwelling, often staying for indefinite periods.

People, unbeknown to themselves, are the same everywhere: if they are cut, they bleed; if they are physically hurt, they feel pain; if they are emotionally cut, they weep; if they are physically hurt, they seek remedy; if they are emotionally hurt, they seek rest; here, a doctor may heal the injury to the body; there, many seek, and many fail, to heal the heart hurt, the mind trauma, the soul wound, of their injured loved one; and so, when one is suffering in heart and mind and soul, and one cannot find solace in friends, acquaintances, or things, one may seek a place where serenity is its soul, harmony its heart, and love its mind.

There were no receptionists inside this particular building; there was no paperwork to complete, no questions to ask, no criteria to meet so one might receive assistance here; for here, there were only volunteers, here to help only, to engender a healing, if possible; and among all of the people there—the poor, the sickly, the mentally beaten, the physically beaten, and the volunteers—among all of these hustling about, and bustling about, there was a singular one: one woman, whose very physical presence by her elegant beauty and fit form, when seen through a glass clearly, might have served her boldly and crowned her with arrogance, yet her actions were humble, meek, and mild; but here she lowered her superior physical nature: the great mane of flowing, silky, auburn hair and the thick eyelashes and arched eyebrows and delicate, peaches and cream complexion; here she could have reigned a queen, yet behaved as an apprentice to equality with the seekers here; a courier of utter humility who had completely emptied her being of hubris, of a vaunted past, of a selfish purpose, to serve this urgent, pressing need, to tend to the slain, the subdued, the sinners, herein.

She was always here early and the last to leave, and she never complained to anyone, ever, and took verbal abuse from anyone without retribution against them, every time, as it was: a mother who was a heroin addict, and who had a heroin-cocaine-meth-addicted, alcoholic, adulterous, thieving, drug-dealing, no good, dirty, rotten husband, shouted at her just as if this mother, the better half of this accursed union of flesh and blood, had the right to, and she, whose face, void of the illusory makeup kit of modern woman, still outshone her nearest spray-painted rivals, merely smiled and embraced the mother and whispered to her, "Your struggle is my struggle, you are never alone," and presently set the woman down and allowed her to weep for the longest time and drain her sorrows away.

And when the long day finally ended and the volunteers retired into the clutch of night, she inspected the record books and prepared the place for the next day, and then went home. "I am young yet, I am doing what others cannot; and one day I will not do this, and another will take my place; it is the proper way of things."

She arrived at her small home in the rural territory outside of Seattle, and shortly thereafter her man came home, too; and presently, they were engaged in one of their various athletic disciplines. They practiced: fencing, martial arts, wrestling, which was preceded by a pre-workout meal, and followed by a long session of yoga stretching, and then a hearty meal, over a long period of time. "We educate our minds, as well as our bodies," she often said, and after this delicious meal, they read: she, at the moment, a book on psychology—to be specific, *The History of Psychology*—and he, a book on philosophy—to be specific, *Plato's Republic*—but then, she, not to be too tightly woven into this matrix of too-sober things, read, with great delight, *Gone With the Wind*, and he, dedicated to the vanity of luxury of time, read *War and Peace*; and after which both had completed their academic ventures, they strummed the last remaining chords of a serene night with a passionate endeavor that united their mind and body with each other, and then fell to rest.

And then the day began again; but they were still young, and vibrantly so, robust, energetic, fervently young, living every moment of youth as if they appreciated the precious gift of life; but every waking moment they were healthy and free and able to bring succor to the poor, the sickly, the elderly, they celebrated life in the same fashion an old soldier does who has lived through too much and realizes what ordinary folk will never know, that life is a precious gift, and liberty a precious blessing, and health a precious miracle, and to have a noble faith, a precious joy, and to have all four transcends words; these two lovers understood this wisdom, at an age where most people are too obsessed with the finer things life has to offer—at an age when youth finally realizes that their very industrious will can claim economic riches, fleshly riches, and recreational and power riches; but not these two, the young man with a straight, back combed, blond mane, thick and curly, and unadorned by modern finery; and the young woman, with a long, flowing mane of thick, curly hair, and unadorned by modern niceties; and the man, possessing muscles of great strength, muscles created through exploring the various athletic disciplines of the day, namely: parkour, martial arts, weight training, acrobatics, and many more; and of the past, namely: wrestling, fencing, running, swimming, combat, and many more; and as for she, she possessed a fine athletic physique, in tone and texture, musculature and agility, a body created from pursuing numerous sports and athletic activities of the day, namely: gymnastics, ballet, martial arts, weaponry, and many more; and of the past, namely: mountain and rock climbing, swimming, acrobatics, hunting and tracking, combat, and many more; and whenever one of them found and embraced a new athletic skill, the other inevitably did, too; for, just as a modern man, who has a passion for art, excitedly informs his wife of a new artist he has found, and she, as passionate for art, does the same for him, so too our two lovers had a shared endearment of the union of mind and body against seemingly insurmountable physical obstacles; thus, athletic endeavor was one of the ties that bound them inextricably to each other.

<u>He</u>
He often said, "ties that bind us must never hurt us"; and she, well-pleased, would respond: "ties that bind us must always benefit both of us," and to both propositions, they heartily agreed.

One day, after he had been practicing his parkour maneuvers on various objects, high and low, wide and deep, jagged and smooth, big and small, of diverse shapes and sizes, and had nearly dislodged his right shoulder, and cut his right leg, and had torn his clothes and nearly split his round head open like an overripe, brown coconut, as she bandaged his shoulders, she whispered, grieved to the heart, "My love, how does this benefit both of us?" Pious tears assembled in her lustrous, turquoise eyes.

To have studied his face, then, one would have believed he was in no physical pain at all; in fact, as he attended her trembling query, his face was tranquil, and joyous. "My love," he began, his luminous sapphire eyes sweeping over her magnificent facial array of high, rosy cheekbones and dark arched eyebrows and thin, sensuous lips and translucent skin, his heart bleeding his love into her, said, "My love, one day," he began, with a mischievous twinkle in his voice as well as his eyes, "I may have to rescue you from villains unknown, and my body must be in a high state of physical superiority."

She nodded, reluctantly, and, as she began to smile, suppressed it, still angry at seeing his injuries. "Yes, you are right; but how do you benefit—other than being sound of body?" She refused still to look up at his searching, intent gaze.

His proud smile did not subside, it increased; and then, he took hold of her right hand, and left hand, and held them, briefly, to his chest, and then lifting them up to his bloodied lips, kissed them both; now, she lifted her head; now, she smiled, and waxed passion, and felt his undying and unconditional love flourishing strongly in her. "Whatever brings your touch to me, I can boast of no greater joy."

She looked upon the multitude of scars that were carved upon his stomach and back, and she began to touch them. "These are the scars of love," she murmured, "earned proudly by men of might and right; woe to any man who has them not, visible or invisible."

"Woe to any man who has a woman not like thee," he whispered, caressing her beauteous face.

It was then that their ardent hearts beat as one, and their souls they shared, and they shared a mind built on the same paradigm that transcended daily life, the squabbles and meaningless events; and it was in this way that the friction caused by natural human differences dissolved and deferred to a greater cause, the cause of Equality; for no occurrence in their life could ever mute the inviolate cry of Freedom they had so long fought for; and no common occurrence could ever darken the effulgent light of Justice that they were once, and present, and future, eager and willing to fight for, had fought for, and would gladly fight tomorrow for.

"If I give up the good fight, it is one less voice to arouse the populace to battle," he had said.

And it was in this way that they were eternally united, if eternity can be drawn as time together on earth, a bond that exists when people must struggle against injustice, but a bond that is seldom used—a fierce bond of fidelity usurped by the evil axis: the bond of luxury, the bond of easy living, the bond of excess; therefore, these two people, entwined in heart, soul, and mind, saw deeper, further, and wider of the past, present and future, in more dimensions and from more angles than their contemporaries, because of what they had done, and were doing, and were prepared to do, to live faithfully according to their credo and philosophy; in fact, she, his darling wife, was Rhiannon Aquitaine, now Cuchulain, sister of the great Eleanor Aquitaine, wife of Conall; and he was her faithful husband, Dylan Cuchulain, brother of the great Conall, husband of Eleanor.

The Cycle of Life

From the two comes one
From the one, perpetuity

It is a melancholy truth that poverty brokers ill will in the resident mind and heart; but it is a humble and even honest truth that a certain breed of poverty—one appropriated through a selfless vow—will precipitate no ill will in the resident mind and heart; and if this fervent vow were to benefit the poor, the elderly, the sick, the dying, or the oppressed, then the resident therein might be granted a semblance of a passing joy; but a more enduring joy has a rare opinion on the subject, as it must compete with brutish natural forces of self, those being the pursuit of wealth and fleshly indulgences that obtrude into its inviolate borders, where joy is quite often bound and chained and tossed into an emotional purgatory by its egotistical conquerors.

"We have everything we want, which is each other, our health, and our faith," she often said, when that black heart, temptation, would creep around the edges of their sacred vows.

"We desire only those riches we can achieve through fidelity and love," he would answer her.

"The desire for what we do not need is the seduction of sin," she would say. "The certain road to ruin."

"Our fortunes, ourselves, each other," he would say, affectionately.

And then both of them would burst out a-laughing at the grave tones of their words, teasing each other that they sounded like "old, retired folks."

"A big screen television would look great right here," Dylan would say, as he, still laughing, walked over to the barren wall in the dining room of their small apartment.

"And a glass dining table and, naturally, a grand chandelier," Rhiannon would say, too still laughing, as she walked over to the middle of the small place, then pointed, "about here—with beige, high-back leather chairs."

Then they would both smile, knowing that the forfeiture of finer things was strictly transient, and had no barbed stinger to leave in their strong wills; this, they knew, was set, and could not be broached, by man or his petty machinations, and somehow, they knew, despite their brief tenure as adults, that the rigors of poverty would never subdue them and separate them from the blissful Light, that this—this cunning interloper, temptation; this infestation across the fragmented structure of society—would never be their story: Africa had seen to that; darling, accursed, blessed, fearsomeAfrica had swallowed the possibility of poverty ever threatening their union. It was the macabre, tragic vision of Africa that they carried in that tightly sealed container, their head; it was their daring exploits there had that built an iron resolution that they carried in that porous chamber, their heart, which would forever resist the encroaching darkness poverty bleeds onto its occupants; and they would oft say, "Where the greatest of noblemen and -women fell, to the rising tide of bitterness and gall." It was this transformative vision of Africa, too, that brought comfort when their daily lives seemed too tall or too cluttered or too busy, and they despaired. "For what is our lot in life, when, o'er the world, we see the most oppressed, and compare?" And yet, most of all, through the battles there, and the people there, and the Crusaders there—there, they had, despite the bloody wars and the horrible disease and unbound persecution and killing, seen hope; there, among the worst afflicted, given hope; there, to those who accepted it; and by their very selfless actions, brought about societal progress, and had fought and lived hard and loved their comrades, and understood what a family was and should be, and what is essential in life, and what brings envy and strife, and what brings peace and hope. They had forged a virtuous constitution in the conflagration of life's darkest crucibles.

A betrothal of serenity and happiness gazed upon them as they strolled underneath the cool shade cast over them by the tall Sugar Maple trees that had the Autumn leaves of gold and yellow and brown and red in this quiet and elegant park; they appreciated the perfumed breezes, and the lack of rancid smells from rotting corpses; they appreciated the elegance of quietude here, and the lack of cannon blasts and rifle fire; they appreciated the idyllic pasture here, and the lack of dense, dangerous terrain; here, they found no fear of malaria, sleeping sickness, yellow fever, cholera and dysentery, and parasitic infections, poisonous creatures, or ambush from rebels or government troops—just plush, scented, verdant scenery that cost nothing to appreciate, except a life well lived.

It is true that both of them had lived more in those five years in Africa than most people ever will live, but he was still young, and prone to fits of silliness: one moment, he was holding her hand, and in the next, jumping onto a low hanging branch and then leaping, while chattering, like a ridiculous monkey, and bounding, like a ridiculous young man, from limb to limb.

Rhiannon, tried not to smile as she shook her head, but she did, and turned away to hide her face, "Tsk, tsk, tsk," she said, still walking along the pebbled path as he followed her from high above, "still can't deny the little boy." She secretly smiled in delight.

An elderly couple came strolling along, hand in hand, down the shadowed lane; and upon spying Dylan in the branches, the old woman said to Rhiannon, "Is he your beau?"

Rhiannon looked up at him, and then said, innocently, "Oh, him? I don't associate with known tree-climbers."

The old woman smiled. "My man used to jump off buildings to impress me."

The old man smiled as he lifted up her hands to show their wedding rings. "It worked."

"Good luck with him," the woman said; "he is a handsome rogue"

"He is, isn't he?" Rhiannon said, trying not to smile, her head slightly tilted as she observed her swinging man.

As the elderly couple slowly walked away, the wife said to her husband, "It's her beau—young men are the same in every generation."

"Hey," Dylan shouted, swinging with incredible dexterity from one stout limb to another, his feet acting like a tree monkey's tail as it latched on, "remember the lemurs in the Congo? Do you?" He saw her repressing a smile as she looked at the ground. "Remember when they jabbered until Yoshitsune would growl at them in that great, sonorous Japanese voice: 'Silence!' And then those crazy monkeys would immediately stop their jabbering and look nervously around," and he imitated first Yoshitsune's deep voice, and then the ridiculous primate faces and sounds.

She laughed, she had to, for when Yoshitsune had been vexed beyond reason that the monkey noise precluded him from precious sleep, he would truly he let out a blast of noise that rivaled Rinaldo's immortal shout, and the monkeys would look so stunned, and so distressed, and anxious, that they would begin to hop about in a panic, many of them producing copious amounts of waste—and Dylan had appropriated every nuance of Yoshitsune's glorious shout, and the exact body language and noises of the bewildered monkeys, except the discharge of waste, which he said he omitted to spare her delicate female nature.

"You're so juvenile," she answered, attempting to cover her widening smile.

"You're jealous because I can climb better than you," he said.

"Oh, that's a lie, Dylan—you and Abebe were the best, but I was even better!"

"Prove it," he exclaimed, his feet crossed, his arms crossed, as he leaned against a thick branch and gazed mischievously down at her.

"Hmm," she murmured, "not today—maybe another day."

"Coward!" He laughed.

She began to walk again. "Maybe so, but I am not the one who was fearful of crossing the Congo River," she said, with an amused smile.

"There were crocodiles in there!"

"You're the great Dylan Cuchulain—slay them all; Moses did!"

He smiled. "He shot them all with his magnificent bow and arrows; Moses had some true courage, didn't he?" He was leaping again from branch to branch.

"Yes, he was brave—as I suppose you are too, my love."

"Oh, thank you," he said, bowing his head toward her, then lifting off an imaginary hat that he, with a wide gesture, swept toward her.

She stood still as she gazed thoughtfully up at him. "They were our friends."

"Yes, they are."

"Yes, they are," she whispered.

"So," he said, crossing his arms again, "I challenge you."

"Oh, not now, young warrior—maybe in a few months."

"Months? What kind of a warrior are you—how many months, Mistress Cuchulain?" and rejoined his wild climbing.

"Oh—I would say," she said, tilting her beauteous head, "in about nine months—well, actually, now, only about seven."

He abruptly abated his prancing and clowning, and stood still as a Spruce trunk. "Nine months—seven months!" And then he abruptly jumped off the limb and tucked himself under and rotated once in this graceful somersault, landed on his nimble feet, rushed to her and then stopped and gazed with wild wonder into her luminous, sapphire eyes. "You and me?" he stammered. "And... and..."

She nodded, and said, smiling, "...And baby makes three."

This was the essence of life, they knew, the very seed from which all good things grew: from man and woman joined in holy matrimony, there comes a conjoining of heart and mind and soul; it is an agency created from a consensual agreement to improve the worth of two to the merging of the two; to better the life of two to the fidelity of the two; to help two prosper intellectually, emotionally, spiritually, and physically, through the sharing of thoughts of the two; to create one mindset, one philosophy, one ideal from the intermingling of the hearts of the two; to alter the history and current path and future of the two for the better, through the living together of the two; to take one human being and magnify their talents and skills and virtues, to decrease their foibles, and sins, and tempers, to erase their shameful path, to set course on a clear road, to open a portal to a brighter tomorrow to the joy of the two and the trusting of the two and the never-dying, ever-increasing, always-present love of the two; through the two hearts that beat as one, through the two minds that think as one, through the two souls that became as one; this, then, was their life, and they had built it, and now, with her baby growing toward them, their seemingly overflowing bounty of joy was even fuller; they had God, their love for each other, their health, and now the baby; so, what was everything else to them but nonsense and intemperance.

As the baby inside her grew, so too grew the excitement and anticipation of this new life, this innocent, fresh soul that would forever unite the three as family and create a bond that would continue down the generations; one life to bring light into the dark, joy into sorrow, hope into despair, and so light and joy and hope reigned and made all things new again.

A baby room was created in the small den of their humble home, and gifts were given from without; baby books arrived, baby clothes, too, and baby toys and baby-raising advice and baby food and even baby names; in fact, all things baby filled up the minds of the young couple, and too the hallways and rooms of the old house they had recently moved into.

"We have earned this," Dylan said to her, as he lay next to her in the darkness, holding her one hand, and with his other, feeling her now-large stomach; "we have done what is right in the sight of God; this is a gift greater than Man or mammon could ever bestow upon us."

"This is all we want," she whispered, smiling, as she stroked his clean-shaven face. "This is all we need; what else can we hope for? What greater miracle can we want in this—and one that has been freely bestowed upon us; the greatest gifts are here for those who simply live a good life."

She grew pensive for too long, too quiet in the wrong place of a narrative or dialogue, and he sensed it, and now knew he must, unlike at other times, ask her why. "What is it, my love?"

She was frowning still, staring up through the open window at the smoky haze of the city. "Why are we so blessed? Why does it all seems so simple—and yet there is so much pain in the world?" And pious tears welled up in her soft eyes of beryl. "Why is it so easy for us?"

He kissed her fair brow, and then said, "It is man's fleshly lusts that bind him from gaining the true treasures of the heart."

"O, that Conall and Eleanor might have lived." She wept now, and quietly, without great fanfare, as was the way of her kin.

"Through us, my darling, they will live."

"… In our hearts and minds…"

"…And in our words and deeds."

She put her hands upon the life that beat so strongly with in her. "Their life through our child's life."

"Their life in our life."

"Their blood in our blood."

He laid his head upon the life that waited so patiently to join its loving parents. "Through our child, their name."

He lifted up his head and stared into her gleaming eyes, and his voice was tender, and sweet. "I see Eleanor's goodness in you every day, noblewoman."

Now, he wept, but slowly, and quietly, as was the way of his kin.

"The best of who they were, and who we are, in our child," she whispered, caressing his curly blond hair, and she kissed his head, and said, "Do we deserve so much joy in a world of so much grief?"

"For what we did, and do now," he whispered, gently stroking her round belly, "for in Africa, we wrote our future—in Africa, where we did not have to be."

"In Africa," she whispered, her eyes narrow, her brow furrowed, "where we left our mark, and even where we were, we chose to help and not turn away." She was silent now and he was silent, too, as they thought of this adventure that separated them from ordinary folk. "It is what we do now."

"We have chosen the continuing path our brothers and sisters began."

"We have not strayed."

"We have kept the faith."

She secretly smiled. "We are not perfect, but the baby…"

He smiled, too, and lifted his head to gaze at her radiant happiness. "But the baby will make us practically, nearly…"

"…Perfect," she giggled.

"Did you hear that, baby of ours, who is, but is not here, yet?" he whispered, smiling, as he gazed now at the protuberance that to them was so full of life and joy. "You will help us be great—we shall attain greatness, now, and it is all because of you." He felt a small flutter inside the wondrous, warm womb. "Did you hear that, Mama," he said, excitedly—and it was the first time he had named her, this. "Our child spoke."

"Yes, Papa," she said, looking with exceeding admiration at her husband—and it was the first time she had named him, thus.

"We have earned this because we have asked for nothing else."

"We have asked only for that which is our natural right and ordained by God."

"Yes, and nothing more."

They were quiet again, as lovers are who feel the same pulse of soothing thoughts in the other; but soon, she spoke, and now her voice was suffused with humility and deference.

"We must continue an exemplary life."

"It is necessary—this we must do."

"We must not throw away that which we fought so hard to gain."

He lay next to her, his face next to hers, gazing into her loving approval of him. "We have fought the good fight, and we have won."

She smiled largely. "We have, my darling, my love, my husband—my proud Papa."

He kissed her, and said, with equal fervor and affection, "We have, my darling, my love, my wife—my proud Mama."

And this was their life as they knew it had to be, could only be, should be—because of what they had done and were doing and were willing to do later, to contribute to the continuous Harmony and Peace and Joy of the world.

The New Arrival

The sun is exactly in the right geographical location as it relates to the earth—that is, in the habitable zone—so as to spur and maintain the growth of life; let it be just a little bit less back or a little bit less forward, and our spherical bauble in the mild-mannered Milky Way becomes a dusty, dirty ice planet or a boiling, baking fireball; it is often proximity that determines winners and losers, and opportunity and chance, as it relates to the meek and mild who have no authorship over their own lives; well, the sun is in the correct universal parking lot and does bathe our mortal failings in nourishing golden showers; and it is true that some folks enjoy this natural interlacing of light and flesh more than others, and it is ever more true that there are a few human beings who seem to fairly glow, from without and within, as they bask in this unfurling, blissful warmth; now, perhaps it is proximity, one place hotter than the next, or one colder; or perhaps, it is the person themselves, as if by their cheery disposition they have placed themselves closer to the sun in spirit—or perhaps it is their adoration of the simplest gifts in Nature and their faith in their chosen God.

There was one such couple who, when they walked hand in hand down the shaded park lane, and felt the presence of the sun cuddle their skin with warm kisses, fairly hummed, so happy were they to feel their sky-king companion bless them with this free gift; everything to them was joyous: every tree, every bush, every shrub, every flower was a boasting of the renewal of life, the promise of growth, the hope of progeny; the busy honeybee and his indefatigable insistence to extract nectar was a marvel, and even the common sunflower, with its velvety, soft, yellow petals flowing out from its cluster of seeds within its brown discs, was beautiful; the perfumed scent of the plush foliage was sweeter, the chirping song of the birds merrier; the deft watercolor of the atmosphere above, with its fertile blue field and soft, swirling patches of wispy clouds floating in its icy bosom, frostier bluer than blue and snowier whiter than white; the elderly couples passing by were more than friendly: they were kin now, good neighbors, good company on a shared journey they had already taken and that would now be taken by this young people; every gladness was magnified, and every sorrow was lessened; and life seemed fuller, death seemed impossible, and every obstacle seemed as if it could be surmounted; for life was more than precious, and blessed, and innocent life was streaming into the existence they had created through the willful acquiescence of the merging of two souls—it was love they so desired, and family, for the furtherance of their seed, to bring forth this fragile human creature and shape it and help it grow toward the Light; it was their obligation as people, citizens, inheritors of the planet, and they were ready and willing to serve, without doubt, without complaint, without hesitation, to serve a cause they felt as right as the magnificent sun above them and the earth below them and Nature all around them.

A human being who is treated with undue kindness and charity by another is slave to the idea of giving recompense to that person; it is the way of Creation: the rain nourishes the plants, the plants nourish the animals, and they all give back to the air and earth—it is the way we are; so, when the volunteers and the recipients at the Family Outreach were informed of the impending birth of Dylan and Rhiannon's child, they were delighted—it brings great satisfaction to a human being to give felicity to a person who has been kind to them.

There was a celebration for Rhiannon at her work, a surprise party for her held by her colleagues there, and also attended by those citizens whose lives she had so tirelessly labored to change for the better; and as for Dylan, he did not tell his colleagues of the impending birth of his child, for he did not crave the attention such information would bring; still, they did find out, and he was grateful for their sincere wishes; and playfully, they rebuked him for not telling them of his secret. On his way home from this pleasurable affair, he had pleasant memories of it in his thoughts, enough to satisfy any man of the genuine affection and enthusiasm of his fellows, but he was not taken in. His mood slowly grew somber. "They are well-meaning people, they are," he mused, walking on the sidewalk of the busy boulevard, "but they are as of yet untested, unproven—where is their worth? Is it not easy to offer congratulations when life is good? Who are they to me?" He stopped and looked about. "It is too easy here—here, a man can become lazy and corrupt." He gazed at the passersby. "Here, they are noncombatants, but in another land—who are they, then… It is men of enduring honor, men of great resolve, men of unceasing mettle, of those I marched with, and gladly would have died with." He recited this warrior's poem again, and then sighed as he beheld the excesses and spoils of civilization. "All is vanity," and he sighed; "to thine own self be true—so, even me."

Life was good for Rhiannon and Dylan, and getting better; they had paid their societal dues and more; they were far ahead of the unfurling chaos behind them and the road before them was made clear by the genuine caring and affection for each other, and for others.

"Are you happy, Rhiannon?" Dylan asked, as they ate their dinner.

She smiled, but then, upon studying him carefully, her eyebrows knit, and she said, curiosity suffusing her tone, "You know very well I don't answer rhetorical questions," and she proceeded to study his face as he slowly forked another chunk of the tender and delicious red sockeye salmon and placed it into his waiting mouth.

After some time, he said, not even looking at her, "Do you miss Africa?" He looked at her now, as if he had been afraid to see what her first reaction was.

She stopped eating. "Yes," she said, directly to him—and not to the side of him or over his head or to the past or future, but directly at the present situation. "I miss our life there." She knew that this question was merely the outer layer of a multitude of questions, and she must not anticipate his next query, for she knew that as he asked these questions, he was assembling another chapter of the narrative of Africa he had never let go.

"Why?"

She knew what was coming, this black storm, and to delay its fury, she knew, was folly. "We lived as we chose to live—with no worry of modern problems: rent, or bills, or problems at work—living like we were meant to live, at least for a little while, so we could know, once we came back, what life is supposed to be like, so we can measure this life against what we had; so, we will know what life can be, should be…must be." She paused. "We climbed the stairway to heaven, and came back."

He smiled a little bit, and then sniffed it out with a sober thought. "How can we live here among these people—who are they to us? We don't know them—will they hold true in a conflict?"

"Africa was a journey for us, but we came to rest here."

"And what about those still there? What about our vow?"

She stared in wonder at his passionate countenance. "We will always honor our vow."

"Really?" he said, quickly. "And what if our life becomes so soft, and easy, and—precious…" He shook his head slowly, and his voice was colored with the stain of the unknown. "What if we forget, Rhiannon; what if the baby weakens our resolve; what if the call comes and we say 'no.' What if we become," and he thrust his muscular arm toward the door, "like them—not willing to risk even a little of what they have so easily gained."

Her tone was harder now. "We fought hard for what we have gained—we will never forget."

He abruptly stood up and walked to the veiled window and stared at it. "I can't even open the windows and curtains at night without worry—why?" He turned toward her. "I walk far outside of corners—I am suspicious of people as they approach me. I am always thinking ahead of what catastrophe might happen, and how to react to it…planning a retreat from every place I encounter, ever ready to do battle."

Her face was hard and still as she said, "I am the same way."

"Who are we, then, Rhiannon? Are we those two young people who began life in Africa and should still be there, or are we now no wiser: just more mature people who now live among civilized people; where should we be, where do we deserve to be; who are we, then—are we who we were in Africa or are we who we are now?" He was quiet for a long time, and then smiled, and turned toward her and then walked about the room. "It is hard to watch a good person die, Rhiannon; it is so hard," as pathos filled his aching voice and made it whole; "a good person you have served with and who has fought bravely and well—but it is harder to watch an innocent man or woman die, whom you could have saved, as you took up the sword and did what was right in your heart and mind and spirit and did what you knew you must do—no matter the risk, no matter where or when—it shouldn't matter." He shook his blond head. "Why have so many forgotten this? We must not," he cried, "ever forget."

"We won't forget, Dylan," she began, too standing, and then walking up to him and taking his hand, "and by not forgetting, we shall never be seduced by material lust." She embraced him then.

"We paid a price," he whispered, passion trembling in his words, as he thought of the nightmares they still had, not of those who needed to die, but of those who did not, "but it was a ransom that had to be paid—someone had to pay it, and we were the ones."

"A ransom paid," she whispered, passionately, as she gazed into his burning eyes.

"And Conall…"

"…and Eleanor…"

"…and the fallen noble Crusaders."

The beauty of Courage, the elegance of Honor, the temple of Truth lifted them up and set them cleanly onto the pious current of their simple love, and there they stayed for the night, and where they healed their wounds of love, knowing there were no others near them who understood their own unique grief.

Human conception begets an adventure for the authors of the deed, and the adventure begins as the newly crowned mother and father join in the external dialogue of parenthood; from the first day of the announcement to the birth of the child, much needs to be done, for the way must be properly cleared for a life to flourish.

It is like this: unbound ecstasy springs from the heart of the mother and father on the first day of the discovery of a child to be born, and every day after that, the ecstasy soars on high, as if it rides upon a rising column of hot air—it goes straight up and never looks down; yet, nothing can sustain such a high volume of joy, and so down comes the ecstasy, and up goes the anxiety of the mother and father as they realize they will now be the sole arbiters in managing a new life, and how radically their own lives will be irretrievably altered; yet, soon they come to accept it, and embrace it—if they are prudent—and ready themselves for the coming miracle.

This, then, was where Dylan and Rhiannon were emotionally, and intellectually, and they were undaunted and unperturbed. She insisted on working even into her eighth month, despite his most fervent protestations; and every night, he insisted on meeting her at work and helping her to her car and opening the door and helping her in and running to the other side and jumping into the old Ford, the cherry-red Mustang, and then driving slowly away only after he had asked her several times if she was comfortable; and then driving as slowly as if she were indeed in agony; and she adored him and was proud of him, and boasted to her mother and father about his tenderness and solicitude for her; he cooked dinner for her, and did the house chores, and he even did the grocery shopping—until she protested, and cried and hollered, "I am reading *The Good Earth*—peasant women worked in the fields until they gave birth; and remember, we saw this ourselves many times in Africa; so, don't make me into something different from my sisters around the world, just because we're here, and not there, with them—for if I was with them still, I could not hold up my head high if I were so pampered." And then he relented, somewhat, and acquiesced, somewhat, but always mindful of her, "blessed, burgeoning condition."

"You are in love with having this baby more than me," she said one day, laughing all the while; "would you have it for me, too?"

He had stopped his cleaning, and stood up, his face perplexed. "No," he simply stated, and went back to his chores.

"So, you're doing all of this out of guilt?"

He stood erect once more, his face perplexed. "Yes."

She shook her head, and around, saying, "You can do all the chores," and sat down upon the fluffed-up white pillows he had prepared for her.

"All right," he mumbled, as he turned on the vacuum cleaner, "it's a bargain."

"What?" she cried.

"I said," he shouted, "pregnancy makes your hearing more acute."

She eyed him with deep suspicion.

He turned away, smiling in secret.

And so another month went by.

She was strong and healthy and eating a nutritious diet, and he was hovering above and around her like an old mother hen, so all was in readiness.

They were walking down the beautiful shaded path of the park they now accepted as a sanctuary, a place where they met other couples who often shared their experiences of child-rearing, and on this day, they were conversing with the elderly couple they had met when Dylan had climbed the trees. Joy abounded.

And then joy recoiled. It shrunk down and withdrew into itself, in response to a loud report that seemed to come from a long distance away.

"Oh my, what was that?" the old woman said, holding both sides of her face now. "It sounded like a gunshot."

The warrior sense in Dylan caused him to assess the area for camouflage, for refuge, for defense, for battle, and as he looked to his wife, he beheld a face of ashen white, and his eyes trailed down toward wherein the baby still nestled, and he saw, but could not properly process, a spill of red liquid that was spreading, impossibly, as if in a bleeding nightmare, from her abdomen; but it did not seem possible for such a horrific act to occur here, not here, not in the birthplace of democracy, not in this idyllic rural house, not in this remote, private path, where they were harming no one and no one could possibly see them or even care about them or consider them in any way an affront; yet, here it was, as he dropped to his knees and held her: reality, cruel, unjust reality, thousands of miles away from Mother Africa and her inherent strife.

And still, he had instinctively reached for the weapons at his side that had not been there for more than five years.

The old woman called in for help, the ambulance came, and Dylan carried his fallen mistress through the open white doors and then the winged angel of mercy sped away. The elderly couple wept as if it was themselves they had seen from decades past, shot.

"Would that bullet had found me instead; clearly would I have rejoiced," the old woman whispered, weeping, while her husband held her fast.

"What is availed through the violent death of youth, but tragedy," the old man said later; "so too irony, that we will not even consider the lessening of violence, for fear that the offender might one day repent," when he was informed of the origin of the fired bullet, and the players involved therein.

Dylan and Rhiannon were as one, husband and wife, one in all ways, regarding how to view a fallen world, one in inspiration, one in passion; yet, as he held her and beheld her silent form upon the hospital bed, he knew that she had shared a secret bond with the life within her, that such enigmatic contents could never be transcribed into human language, and now that bond was evanescent; and no matter how much emotion he effused, or the amount of time grieving for her, he would never fully comprehend this dissolution between who should have come forth and whom she would have loved and raised and watched grow up, and who would have given her great pleasure and pride; the life of who she might have been, little Eleanor, was unwritten, and wiped clean from the future annals of history.

When Rhiannon awoke, when she first was made aware that the protuberance that had brought glad tidings was no more, she wept, and he held her, and wept with her, and yea, what they had shared in happiness, they now mourned as one; what place they had prepared for this new life to go to, they now wept over; and so they wept for the loss of innocence, and for their precious daughter and for the bleak darkness that enveloped them, and the cold emptiness that broke over them, and the cruel hand of fate that christened them with unforgiving reality; and there was no enmity in their hearts, no rancor flowing from their grieving minds, no buttress against the unseen forces of destiny; and yet, when she was home again, and he had settled her in, with a relative and friend tending to her, he did go looking for the unwitting forces whom destiny had selected as killers, and he found nothing more than what the authorities had found: that a rival gang, unknown, its members in one car, had shot at another rival gang, unknown, who fled in another car, one shot only, a high-flying, errant missile that had sailed unimpeded for a short distance and then settled into the young woman's body; and so he came home, thwarted of intelligence for her.

When he, at last, heaped praise upon her mother, and cousins, and friends, and after these Angels of Mercy had departed, and Rhiannon had begun to heal in physical body as well as mind, she, as he stood before their bed while she lay in the veiled darkness, addressed him, in a tone bereft of sympathy for the pursuer or the pursued. "Did you," she whispered, in a cold, harsh voice, "find them?"

He did not hesitate, for it would only further magnify his failure. "No."

She gazed intently at him for a moment, as if she were considering her answer, and then said, coolly, "It doesn't matter—it was Providence."

His effusive blue eyes smoldered wrath. "Apparently, it matters to you."

She shook her head as she lay upon the clean white linen sheets. "No."

"Should I have abandoned you to visit vengeance upon them?"

She closed her emerald-colored, misty eyes, and turned her head. "No."

"Have I failed you?" he asked, in a rare, if not impossible tone of incertitude.

She inhaled deeply. "No."

"What would you have had me do," he said, anxious now, "flee the scene and capture the murderers?"

Her silence was too long now, too long after affixing her blessings of his failure upon his fragile heart. "You did what you could."

"But not what I might have done," he responded, quickly; "not what a greater man might have achieved."

She opened her eyes and stared at him, her countenance ruptured red by sorrow and colored a sooty, dirty mask, by despair. "Little Eleanor is dead."

His visage softened by her conciliatory tone, he moved close to her. "Little Eleanor, whom we loved." His face took on the tear-stained mask of her deep despair and sorrow.

"Eleanor, our precious child," she whispered, warm tears in her soft eyes.

"Eleanor, our darling child, whom we shall always love."

"Eleanor," she murmured, her arms open now, and embracing him. "Our beautiful child; O, Dylan," she sobbed, tears streaming down her face, "how I miss her so."

He held her out from him and gazed into her pious intent, and whispered, in a tender voice, "Whenever I behold you, dear wife, I will see her in you, noble mother."

She smiled through her sadness. "And when I behold you, dear husband," she murmured, searching his handsome visage, "I will see her in you, noble father," and they embraced once more, and let their shared pain, through their shared heart and soul and mind, begin to disassemble itself and return to the cradle of blind obedience wherein dwells loyalty and devotion.

Hope Abounds

The death of an unborn life is the death of hope, but not all hope, not the idea of hope, for true hope cannot be extinguished from a human being any more than joy, or desire, or love; for to do otherwise, is to crush the human will and destroy the human heart and in so doing, kill the human body; but our two lovers were young, and youth can never be harnessed or restrained longer than the time between the rising of the morning stars and setting of the red sun; but none of this really mattered, not their ebullient youth or stolid character, for what mattered most was their time thus spent—like time living inside an ancient manuscript that narrated the massive and unfettered iniquities visited upon the ancient tribes—in Mother Africa, and they nursing at her nourishing bosom, and in doing so, becoming as one with her, sharing her nourishing blood, feeling her deep sentiment, her history, her desires, and baptized now by her wars and famine and disease; and in so doing, forever understanding truly what is essential and honorable in this slowly, dying world.

Here, now, they dwelled in Beauty, living inside the peaceful Temple of Truth and Freedom,

and there, long ago, they had oft dwelled in horror, fighting inside the wild beast of injustice and iniquity.

From grief and suffering springs a new creature
a creature born of affliction, bolder and stronger
able to endure, and see what before was hidden.

We pass through this life, waiting to see what we can see, not seeing what was invisible, and visible only to those who purchased it through intense suffering; where once was gaiety and celebration of society, the burdened few now see a profligate lifestyle; where once there were exceeding riches of opulence of lifestyle, they now see sin and offense; but once the burdened few have opened the doors of revelation, they must unburden themselves of the guilt of living well; yet, when the unseen virtues are revealed, they are revealed slowly, and what often appears as one ideal is obscured, and mistaken for another; so herein lies wisdom, to study all things in great detail and study the mind as it navigates this new course with its new helmsman, its valiant captain: the human heart.

Rhiannon could not live in the city wherein her baby was murdered, this much Dylan knew, and he would not contend her want to leave; but she sought to settle in a city once named for the home of the Angels, but whose reputation now registered it as a place of dread and death.

"Los Angeles," he said, with furrowed brow, "Los Angeles," he repeated, allowing his strong Irish accent to take hold of the idea and subvert it; "why, Rhiannon, why?"

"I want to continue our work there."

"But where in that den of thieves and criminals—in the city?"

"I want to work with youth who have unwittingly become child soldiers."

They were in the family room, she sitting on an old, sagging sofa, and he standing, still, staring with incredulity stamped upon his rugged countenance; and every time he sought to speak, to restrain his words, and then edit their content and apply the final version to how his wife would react, he was dumbfounded.

She was watching him intensely, and she was applying what she saw in his visage to how he had reacted to disturbing news while on their great crusade in Africa; and she knew he was defeated, and so must offer him some kind of conciliatory gesture.

She stood up and embraced him. He was undone.

They started the search for a house as all searches begin, and this was at that outer rung of the concentric circles which radiated out from the target area; they found an apartment in Pasadena, and every morning would drive into the lair of darkness wherein the progeny of poverty corrupted themselves and practiced violence and debauchery; and along the way, they looked for areas to which one might safely retreat after a long, steamy day in the hot belly of the beast; when they found no good home in the city, they visited the peripheral areas that did not feel the sharp waves of violent energy detonated every day in the deadliest zones, and soon they happened upon a modest home in Rosemead, and saw its soft, blue, wooden body and pretty white trim, and inspected its immaculate sturdy rooms, and inspected the quiet, clean street it sat upon, and the quiet, clean neighborhood it belonged to, and the quiet, sometimes old, sometimes middle-aged neighbors; and they, at once, recognized their new home on this cul-de-sac, just as any of us who travel are able to recognize anyplace as home that speaks simply and truthfully to us.

They had been frugal in their handling of money, and this afforded them the luxury of time to visit those workplaces that had received their résumés, and impress upon them this young couple's willingness to work tirelessly for a cause that seeks to cure that which for so long has seemed incurable in society, and as for the origins of such ills, they were thus:

A cut, nearly too small to see, appears on the body of an apparently healthy youth, and because it seems innocuous, is ignored by the youth; but, by and by, the cut becomes deeper, and sometimes bleeds, and this disturbing event compels the youth for advice from an adult; now, the adult, having much experience with ephemeral wounds—and as he still lives—has plenty to say, and says it; but, alas, the cut worsens, and so the youth seeks counsel from a medical authority, who dresses the wound, but soon sees it is deepening still, and worse, even more wounds appear, and still more, and so she orders tests; but the tests reveal nothing, and more wounds appear, until the anxious youth is fairly covered with festering wounds; soon, specialists come in, and manage to cure one wound, even while another is created.

So, it is the same with the sharp daggers that are gangs, who create wounds of unlimited proportions in the heart of society; and just as a physical wound provokes the body's immune system to send agents of healing and reconstruction to the damaged site, so it is the same with the gangs, and there always seems to be an endless list of human agents who boast of their great healing and restorative powers, and it all begins with the local government.

One of the ways in which city officials react to the destructive presence of gangs is by creating gang intervention programs: anti-gang councils and panels, anti-gang training for police and community, anti-gang pamphlets and workers to seed the schools and communities with their message of hope and promise; the police create gang task forces, enact gang sweeps, and carry out anti-gang interventions in communities; the courts, lobbied by the police, issue aggressive rulings regarding the gangs, the correctional community develops strategies that concentrate on specific gangs and gather intel; and the state and federal officials talk and give limited funds to those who fight daily on the front lines; and lastly, there are the independent groups who create their own charters and beg for funds from large corporations and cities, to deter gang creation and curtail their proliferation.

It all ends with the neighborhoods and towns slowly being dissembled and eroded from their original intent—that is, hearth and home, safety and sanity, recreation and relaxation—into a violent, monolithic, multilayered, multigenerational creature that has no boundaries or mercy, that is dedicated to the proposition that whatever it wants is not to be contravened, its unyielding iron will be done.

Rhiannon and Dylan were like fresh soldiers walking onto a battlefield of exhausted combatants and proffering their services to fight—and not only willing soldiers, but expert ones, as well; therefore, they were pursued by a multitudinous list of suitors, and after much deliberation, they selected an agency that was supported by a coalition of churches and gang intervention agencies that advocated authentic lifestyles for troubled adolescents, named Community Youth Outreach, or CYO. After shaking their hands, the President of CYO offered the young husband and wife a seat, which they took, and a cool beverage, which they respectfully accepted, but did not drink; he studied their fair countenances as he sat across from them—not on the other side of his small wooden desk in a higher chair to give him a height advantage, but next to it—and acknowledged the Master's degree Dylan had in Military History and Tactics, and the Master's degree in Sociology that Rhiannon held. He smiled, an act of instinct. "Forgive me," he began, "both of you look like soldiers."

Dylan issued that peculiar small smile that accompanies responses to a flattering but errant remark. "We both work out," he said, as if to draw the truth away from this probing.

Rhiannon smiled, too, but it was a woman's gracious, thank-you smile, as she interpreted the remark differently. "We earn our food," she stated, as if to lead him farther away from his subtle digging.

He continued to study the scarred body of Dylan, the many scars from knife cuts and knife stabbing and gunshots on his bare arms that he refused to hide, the white scars on his face—the two on his temple and one down the left side, yet he could not see the many scars on his back and his stomach and legs; but he was able to see beyond the major fleshly wounds from combat: he beheld the piercing, still blue eyes—eyes like blue, blazing molten fire—boring into and interpreting his very soul; and he beheld the lovely Rhiannon and her luminous emerald green eyes, and her many scars: the two upon her arms, and two upon her face—one across her temple, the other next to her left ear—but he could not see the many scars on her back and her stomach and legs; and he saw a woman hitherto unknown to modern society: unafraid, a warrior, a woman who would not suffer poor manners from anyone, anywhere, anytime.

His smile enlarged. "It takes a soldier to know a soldier." He said it as if to choose his company of complicity in a cover-up, yet he had couched the wording inside a light tone—non-hostile, in soldier's speak. Dylan and Rhiannon returned nothing, offered no facial gestures, no recognizable body language; and then the man with the short, black, curly hair and full black beard said to Dylan, in an octave lower, in a tone harsher, in a world where weak combatants lay dead, "Good gracious, man, I feel as if I were to make a wrong move, you would leap on me like a panther and swallow me whole," and then he smiled, and smote his huge thighs. "Young people today—so passionate; I do love it so!" He abruptly stood up. "Stand up, would you, Dylan?" Dylan obliged. The man nodded. "Now, I am six foot five, about two hundred and sixty pounds, and in fairly good shape; but you—why, sir, even though I am obviously taller and weigh more than you, you seem bigger than me." They both sat down again. "I wish I could say that gang members respect a man's physique—they do, to an extent—but the tone of words and posturing and action are much more powerful to these boys than muscle; well, let me tell you about myself."

He had started out as a gang member, started his own gang, quit, gone to college and played football, was drafted, and while playing professional football, he had yearned for a greater purpose, and so quit, and served two tours in the last war that American politicians created through misunderstanding indigenous cultures and their history, and the basis for regional conflict, and more importantly, by bowing to prevalent concepts conceived through ignorance and avarice, and not understanding the few but distinct reasons a nation-state goes to war; but it had happened, as do foreign wars we do not understand and should not engage in, and happen often; and the young men had gone in with great energy and full of optimism, and ready to fight against presumed tyranny and to preserve the democratic ideal, or so they were told; and when it was over, or unplugged, so that the blood spilled was finally drained away, and the men, embittered now, came back to a country that had known all along the war was unnecessary, this had been too much for the soldiers to embrace—how can a soldier watch a comrade die and admit later it was for naught? This had embittered him.

"So, I came back here determined to make it right—fighting for something I knew was not clouded by political rhetoric: like, hey, we've got a problem in America, called gangs; I found something that I could fight that I'd helped create, how do you lose on something like that—it's called personal redemption." He let out a quick expulsion of breath as he shook his large, round head. "You wouldn't believe how ignorant the government is of its war within our own borders—that's right, a civil war, I'm not mincing words here, and I'll say the same thing to anyone, anywhere, anytime; it's a war here, plain and simple—we just will not admit it; I mean, look: we have armed combatants shooting other armed combatants, and oftentimes, non-armed civilians, and robbing them and raping them and harassing them—right here in our own very civilized country; right here," he cried, stabbing the air in a downward stroke of his heavily callused left hand, which finished up with pounding his desk. "How insane is that? And no one wants to address it as an indigenous army fighting for territory and power among their own countrymen; and that, my good friends, is the soldier's definition on the battlefield—not from some scholarly textbook, and nothing you'll ever hear from those thin-skinned, mealy-mouthed, weak sisters who run this great country of ours for their own benefit and the benefit of their own petty kind."

The visage of Dylan, normally stolid, despite the weight and amount of emotional debris thrown at it, became an eager receptacle for the revelatory nature of information cast upon him, and chose not to obscure its interest, either: his cobalt-blue, soul-bearing, heart-piercing eyes narrowed; his thin lips were pursed; his body language, fully erect, maintained a relaxed composure, and then his large hands swept through his long, thick, combed-back blond hair and then rested again upon his large, muscular thighs.

The face, the lovely, vibrant face of Rhiannon, was an undisturbed portrait of blissful Nature, allowed to mature without the restless hands of an immature and insecure woman that would vigorously scrub and tear and gouge her face, a fair complexion slowly receded from its darker period in Sister Africa, and painted now with light brown freckles and a smooth texture, as if some inner spectrum of guardians had assembled and protected her flesh from the ravages of harsh sun, wind, heat, and cold; she wore a ponytail now that hung lightly down her muscular back; it was this strong but feminine face that bled enthusiasm for the raw guts of this tale, which spread with every word dropped from the narrator's mouth; her eyes seem to acquire a special vision into the story, as if with the events described; she saw these horrific, tragic events where she seemed to transcend space and time and invade them and live them and smell them and taste them and weep over them safely behind the iron veil she had built during those hard five years, and evince only a slight protuberance, a small quake, a slight echo of this terror upon her fair face and form.

"War, in any guise, whether dead, whether alive, whether hidden and disguised, whether open and recognized, needs to be resolved, lest we sleep in a silent grave," he said. His fleshly, black face was emblazoned with righteousness that comes from practicing what one knows is Truth; and yet, his countenance fell, and he said, "And so many will brand me a fanatic, a rabble-rouser; well, sir, and Mrs., so be it, because I have seen it in one place and I see it in another—and they have not." He stood up, agitated. "Ah," he grumbled, "well, now I say, let it lie—so," he slapped his hands together, "how much do you know about gang intervention?" and then sat down again.

"We have read the Spergel Model in its entirety," Rhiannon said, in an authoritative tone that begged challenge.

"You're hired!" he replied, slapping his thighs, then looking at Dylan. "… And?"

"And it has its strengths, as does LA Bridges and the GREAT program, and the Riverside program, and the LA plan."

"Impressive, very impressive—and?" he cried, pure delight raising him out of his wooden chair.

"And, it isn't working," Rhiannon declared, coolly.

"So, what about DARE, eh?"

"Don't even get me started!" Dylan declared.

"Ha! A couple after my own blood," he cried, standing up and slapping their hands on high, and noting, on the sly, the hard resistance of their inner, coiled strength; too nervous and energetic to sit now, he roamed freely around the room, and then said, hesitantly, as if afraid to hear the answer, "And…?"

"And our conclusion is that there must be a better way, and someone who has established it, somewhere," Rhiannon said emphatically.

"Here," Dylan whispered.

A giant of a man held out his giant of a hand to one, then the other, jubilation settling upon his broad shoulders as he happily shook their hands. "The name is Samuel T. Longfellow; welcome home, pilgrims!"

How it Ends Before it Begins

The philosophy of CYO is that a gang is itself a child of the community, born, bred and raised there, a product purely of the faults and problems of it, mistakes that the child falls into and the established gangs then exploit; thus, the ubiquitous mission statement that has appeared everywhere in the latter twentieth century and early part of the twenty-first, which Longfellow was loathe to write, but bowed, this time, to convention, to satisfy his constituents, even though, once it was read, most folks merely shrugged their shoulders, and people who knew him merely said, "That's our man Longfellow, for sure"; anyway, it read: "Problems: we make 'em, we can solve 'em." But however simply it read, it observed the true discipline inherent in it.

"We will, as a community, organize and restructure our neighborhoods so that a gang will not be able to survive there and eventually not start there," he once said to a City Council member, who merely shrugged her shoulders and rolled her glazed-over, chocolate-donut eyes. "We gave birth to them, we can abort them." A male member, who had been dreaming of the salacious benefits that come with power, was offended that such an offending term as "abort" had infiltrated his private reverie, and so frowned, and then, looking at the other members who had disgust riding their rubbery visages, impregnated his own low-level disgust with scorn and condescension, as he, and the others, thought it inappropriate for their imperial rank in society to hear such an offense.

"And how do you propose to do this, Mr. Longfellow?" asked the Mayor, the don of this legal mob, upon intertwining his plump, red fingers together.

"By educating our community, neighborhood by neighborhood, on the power they have to effect change."

"And how will you 'abort' more youths turning to that unfortunate lifestyle—gangs?"

"We mean to dissuade them from enrolling in gangs by concentrating on those youths who display certain characteristics—like impulsivity, truancy and aggressiveness. I will concentrate on prevention and intervention; as for suppression, I leave that to others."

Samuel Longfellow, still standing, held up his two outstretched hands and brought them together, palms up, meeting at each little finger, in a supplicating gesture; and then he spoke, in a hushed tone, so much so that his audience had to lean toward him. "Imagine a rotting apple—rotten to the core—but pleasing still," and he smiled on the outside; and lifted up his left hand and turned it over with flair, and said, "Imagine, if you will, an apple peeling like so," and he imagined to peel that imaginary apple. "The outside layers of the apple are still fresh and edible; the majority of the apple—ah! At least until the poison spreads," and let his left hand gesture up and out, as if to flee from said poison. "This, then, ladies and gentlemen, is the fringe—the outside section—and what gangs are mostly: fringe members, not well-established at all, no sir," and he waved his left hand, forefinger extended, "and pliable—pliable! It is the hard," and his voice became hard, "mean," and his voice became mean, "inner core that holds the gang together—a minority group—the leaders, the ones least likely to change." He dropped his hands and nodded his head. "I propose to identify those youths who have the propensity to join gangs and redirect their energies into other projects; and by doing so, I believe we can stop many youths from becoming fringe members, and perhaps, even core members."

"Mr. Longfellow, are you saying you have given up on preventing our children from becoming your so-called 'core members'?" the Mayor asked, indignantly.

"No, sir, not at all—I am saying that when we take one thousand children and help them, if we prevent them from joining gangs, most would have been fringe members—and a gang with mostly core members doesn't last too long; after all, leaders can't lead if there is no one to follow."

"I am deeply disturbed by your 'perhaps,' Mr. Longfellow," one of the councilwomen said, sternly. "'Perhaps even core members,' you said—so, why not prevent all of them from becoming gang members?"

"Because it is just not possible."

"So, you have already given up on our children!" the Mayor cried, throwing his arms wildly about.

"No," he replied, calmly, "I am merely stating verifiable facts derived from massive amounts of peer-reviewed, researched in the field and verified, scientific research from sociologists and criminologists, US Department of Justice, Office of Juvenile Justice and Delinquency Prevention; US Department of Justice..." But he was abruptly cut short by the exaggerated appeal to the squeaky wheel by the Mayor.

"You are negative, sir, negative, and we don't see how the city can offer your program money if you're not fully committed to fully eradicating all chances of our children to join that scourge on society—gangs!" the Mayor shouted, even manufacturing a tear to impress those around him with his genuine outrage toward Longfellow and his own manufactured solicitous feelings for the troubled youth of the city, even though he really believed that young people needed no additional "programs and activities" to steer them clear of joining gangs, but that the position of seeming to care about wayward youth was politically correct. "And what about the gang leaders, eh," he continued, as if he were leading his quarry toward a deep pit with sharp stakes at its bottom.

"I have studied various efforts, like the Broken Windows theory, the Boston Miracle…"

"Broken Windows, ha!" the Mayor began, wanting to show off his knowledge about other programs his brother and sister officials around the country had considered; "it is surely a sham, sir—too many studies have disproved its 'supposed effectiveness,' citing other factors that came into play at the same time that Broken Windows was implemented, such as a dramatic drop in unemployment and drug consumption…"

"As I was saying," Samuel interjected, "from many programs, like Broken Windows and the Boston Miracle, I have taken the essential methods that worked—"

"Boston Miracle, eh?" the Mayor cut in again, confident still. "More coddling of these hard-core gang members—and hasn't its supposed effectiveness waned, yes? Yes." He looked at his colleagues for support, and received it with nodding heads and smiling faces or reassurance even as he spoke. "We have tried to work with these violent gangbangers, Mr. Longfellow—we have thrown in millions of dollars and manpower to 'try,'" and here he performed the double air quotes, "and save them," and he shook his balding head, "but all to no avail—these leaders are too far gone; but yes, I do believe in trying to save the young ones before they get in too deep; but everyone, do you understand, sir?" He was indignant now, as if to solidify his position. "And would you dare to help current gang members who qualify as fringe members, even core members?"

"Of course," Samuel replied, "that is where programs like Broken Windows, the Boston Miracle, Operation Ceasefire, which was part of—"

"Outrageous! You will do what our police and other agencies have been unable to do—save these criminals from themselves? Have you seen the crime statistics of this city lately—murder, rape, drug dealing, theft, robberies, assaults, all up, up, up—and why, because of the proliferation of gangs and the bleeding hearts who want to excuse them for their violent actions; and as we wasted time and money and effort to try and rehabilitate these fools, they took advantage of it, laughing in our faces, and continued on with their business—the business of crime; and why were we trying to help these poor, abused youth—because these poor gangbangers were not given enough love," and now he leaned over the table at which he sat, past the microphone, "because they did not have the best opportunites in the world—well, who does? Plenty of people are born into poverty and suffer, and they do not commit crimes, and even though they are exposed to gangs, they do not join them;

no, no sir, this governing body no longer believes in holding the hands of criminals—of children who might be led astray, yes, but that is all." And then he slowly leaned back, enwrapped in a condescending air. "And that is all for you, sir."

"You would deny my request on a mere fancy of yours?"

"Good day to you, sir," the Mayor finished, not even looking at the giant of a man who still stood before him, but instead looking at his itinerary for the day.

Samuel Longfellow did not have to edit and approve of his own political posture, or incendiary words that would soon came roaring out of his own mouth, for what he felt, he would lay naked before his judges. "Ignorant and stupid people are the best salesmen a gang could have—and no, no good day for you; no, decidedly no," and he turned and retired into the cold, bitter night.

A man, tall and slender, his hair and beard beginning to show streaks of gray, was waiting for him outside of the building, and introduced himself to Samuel, whereupon the two men shook hands, and walked together for many miles as they shared their ideas concerning the reality of gangs.

A month hence, Samuel had a building and resources to start CYO, and had been operating it successfully when Rhiannon and Dylan arrived for their interview.

"We work with schools," Samuel said, as he walked alongside the couple in the CYO parking lot weeks later. "We give out questionnaires to teachers, K-12; we pass out pamphlets and flyers announcing our presence and the services we offer."

"Is it working?" Dylan asked, innocently.

"Good question," he said, nodding his head; "even one child who is saved," and his voice grew strong with emotion, "is a world saved—a world—just like you or I; why are they any different? You know, I'll work day and night to save one child from wandering away from the path to the Good Life." His countenance fell as he stopped walking; and when he spoke again, his words were tender, and filled with sadness. "Who would walk past a drowning child—no one! Isn't that what is happening to our children: they are drowning, and people walk by, and they rationalize it because they say it isn't their child, so why help them, why get involved: so it is easier to walk away with their eyes closed and heads down." He closed his brown-as-burnt-coca eyes. "Do these people not hear the same sounds we hear?" He inclined his head toward the horizon. "There—do you hear the rustle of the Olive tree in the gentle breeze; do they not feel the same sensation we feel? There—do you feel the warm sunshine upon your face; do they not smell the same smells as we? There—do you smell the perfumed scent of the red, red rose; do they not taste the same substances we taste? There—do you taste the sweet aroma of Liberty? Do they not see the same world in its exact dimensions as we? There—do you see the great domed sky above us? And yet, when they walk by the drowning child, they do not hear his plaintive wail, do not feel the droplets of water he splashes about in his desperation, do not smell his fear, do not taste the bitter gall they swallow as they turn their face away from him, do not see a child in danger—anyone's child, a child of the community, a child innocent and beautiful—whose soul cries out in torment?" He was standing very still and very erect and his arms were raised on high as he murmured, "When did we stop having empathy for our own kind?" He shook his head as if, truly, it was an expression of his aggrieved inner man that bared its affliction upon the conflicted outer man. "Will we ever," he whispered, as if now his inner, private sanctuary had spilled the contents of its soul, "care again?" And then he sighed heavily. "Did we ever care, or did we just care enough about our own?"

Dylan and Rhiannon said nothing, for there was, they instinctively knew, nothing they could say; yet they could listen, and learn, as was their nature.

Samuel Longfellow opened his big eyes and lifted up his hands and stood on his tiptoes and shouted, "There is a world to conquer!" And he increased his strong gait and led his newest recruits into an institution whose mission was to offer a luminous path down the dark, treacherous, serpentine road that could lead to the exalted Good Life.

What Is Family

A community is like a living creature: it has a head, in the form of city officials; it has a body, in the form of a cluster of neighborhoods; it has arms and legs, in the form of an infrastructure; it has breath, in the form of those lives consumed and the resulting fumes; it has senses: eyes, ears, touch, smell, and sight, in the form of those who can see and hear and touch, smell and feel; it has a mind, in the form of those who can think and help, and those who take power and responsibility; it has a heart, in the form of those who sweat and toil and bleed their existence to achieve harmony every hot, stinking, long day and every cold, stalking, long night; it has a soul, in the form of those who care and seek change for the better and who will not lie down when adversity strikes them or long rest in the face of injustice; and yet, despite its whole body, it is formed from disparate parts, and so will never move harmoniously too long down any path that will benefit all of them to the greatest extent.

From man and woman joined in holy matrimony comes a child, and a family begins, and a house they inhabit becomes their home; and when another family comes and builds their home near them, and then another comes, and more, this, then, is the birth of community; and when all the rest come—the laws and the businesses and the schools and libraries and churches and hospitals and courts and banks and fire stations and various social services—the community is complete, and desirous to thrive; yet, every entity therein needs the cooperation of the other, and when one player falls, the community is broken; and as one player breaks, more break who had relied upon the first not to fail, and soon a break in the unity of intricately woven fabric appears, and a balance once revealed and adhered to is severed, and a fissure appears, and more threads are loosened; such is the fate of many places, and they are unborn, and should be unwritten, but it is too late, and refuse to simply not be, and so they go on, trying to establish that which whole cities do, but they do it badly; and the result is confusion and destruction and decay, and from this comes imbalance, and this therefore breeds corruption, the same way an open, dirty, sore breeds germs.

There is balance in Nature: lightning brings fire and comes to a forest of young and old trees: it consumes decaying growth and weak trees, and destroys various insects and diseases that were tormenting the flora, and leaves that blocked the rain from soaking into the fertile soil, and seeds fall from trees, and the remains of the burnt debris give the seeds nourishment, and precious light comes to older trees that had been crowded out by shade-loving trees; the wolf hunts the elk, but if the wolf were to be removed, the elks would eat too much of the rich vegetation that runs along the creeks, and disrupt the ecosystem there; any life-form that exists and dies within the forest aids other life, and when it dies, provides sustenance for them; it is a delicate ecosystem that cannot tolerate dissension. And then Man comes, who seeks to rebuild Nature in his own inflated image; and the trees easily bow to his sharp ax, and the plants yield to his heavy plow, and the animals submit to his gluttonous appetite, yet none of them understand what is to come; and so, Man builds his house from the subservient families of trusting and helpless

Nature, but he exceeds his basic wants, and the self-healing, self-protecting, self-sustaining mechanisms of Nature fail, and an imbalance is created and encouraged and bred by avaricious and blind Man.

When once there was one family in a cabin of wood, and a floor of dirt, and possessing a spirit of unity and peace and humility, Nature coexisted with Man in harmony, and blessed him, and he blessed the land, and did not take more than he needed; and lo, the father hunted and the mother cooked and cleaned, and the children helped; and the father planted crops, and the mother picked the crops, and the children helped and learned; and the people smelled the sweet bouquet of plants all about them, even inside their homes; and the children learned about what the world is, and the father taught them, and the mother taught them, and there were few temptations about them to commit sins against others, and so they learned what it meant to live with each other and depend on each other, and what a family is, and what is expected of them to survive and even thrive in the world. But this singular kind of marvel-world is dead in the crowded city.

When once there was a family in a cabin of earth and wood, there is now a house of concrete and steel, and the inhabitants do not remember Nature, and they do not need man and woman to stay together to survive—outside forces come in and dictate a new way of living—so a man can leave and the woman survives, and the children are loosed from the taut threads that bind the family, and their roles in the world become confused, the lessons they now learn are not in Nature's sacred manuscript or pour from the lips of their trusted mother and father, but from outside influences that seek their own domain to establish; and already, such a house is spiritually and emotionally dead, and the people in it should flee and begin anew, but they do not recognize their calamity, for all around them, too, is disharmony, disunity, social devolution, but they see it as harmony, unity, and social evolution.

One Home

There is one house that is encapsulated inside a social conflagration. It is the house of Moore.

Grandmother Moore does not sleep; well, she does lie down at night upon a small, clean, white cot, but her cluttered and busy mind is still living the events of the day and attempting to resolve the conflicts therein; so, she will close her tired gray eyes and begin—begin to sleep; and then her grazing mind, still not done mending the breaks in the family fabric she so carefully wove the year and month and day before, which she will weave tomorrow and the next month and year, awakens her and demands satisfaction; so, she lies there and thinks and thinks of how she will stave off those attacks from without that seek to destroy her loved ones within, and she does so with a memory of what was but knows shall never be again.

It is her clear and vivid memories of childhood, when she was irrevocably bound to Nature, that betray her now and color her assumption about the world. "When I was a child," she sometimes said to her own children long ago, "we didn't need none o' that ol' perfumey stuff—ya see, Nature perfumed us, and that's the way it is now, young 'uns; we done los' Nature and found chemicals—it ain't right; none of it." It was the simple and elegant times that had built her, and excess was unknown. "You lived on what you raised and earned and worked for—ain't no one give you nothin'.'"

Her children would merely sigh, and her eldest would say, "Mama, but it ain't like that now, we gots modern stuff, like them VCRs."

And she would shake her round head and frown. "And now," she said, her small hands on the bright blue apron around her slender hips, "you got luxuries like the white folk had when I was a youngster, and now you is like them—white! Why, if black folk go bad 'cause of luxuries, it would be better that they were still po', and good."

But her eldest would moan. "Mama, we ain't gonna go bad 'cause of no VCR thing—heck, we got medicines that save your life, not like back then; you got to take new things with temptation—it's the way of the modern world."

Rosa Moore had eleven children, which, as it turned out, was none too many, and one husband, and as that turned out, was none too many; three of the children died in childhood, one drowned, two were killed in car accidents, three more during the war, and one went to live in the well-guarded, big concrete house with his fellow non-compliants; as for her husband, well, one day, he just plain old looked around at his large family, and decided to pursue an alternate life with a twenty-two-year-old waitress, and so he fled with her back to Mississippi where he had relations and began another family of his own. But Rosa, as she knew she must, soldiered on, cleaning, cooking, working a job at the local diner; and sewing, washing, and working a job at the local factory, and denying herself diverse pleasures, all for the chance of acquiring a happy and productive life for her precious children, denying herself love, and recreation, and leisure, to right a wrong; and she knew she was right, and felt Virtue, like a seed, grow in her heart, and flourish every long, sleepless night and hard, toiling day, for even if a poor soul has no education and no skills of consequence and it seems they will never create modern marvels or hasten the great change in society, that poor soul actually is able to create modern marvels and create great change in society, through one simple lifestyle decision: of being Good, and responsible, and noble, and industrious in labor, to contribute a service or good, or good family, that sustains a quiet, solid harvest that keeps a community strong, where every person they save is one less burden on society.

So, she watched her children grow up and some take the left turn and some take the right turn and a few go straight on ahead toward the blessed mark that is the Good Life; but for her children who failed, and who also had children who were in danger of falling into a pit of obscurity—in foster homes or on the streets or swallowed whole by nefarious elements—she could not let them fall, no; so, she held out her old but still capable hands and caught them up and swept them under her protective bosom, and there they stayed.

She was recently retired but now she was a mother again of ten grandchildren; so, she stood up taller and sucked in her sorrow and un-retired and fell down onto her skinny knees and prayed to God above for the strength to raise these children and to raise them correctly. "Lord," she oftentimes said, in times of trouble and even in times of celebration, "I have been alone for a while, and the world done passed me by, but now I need to git modern again, so I kin understand these here youngsters."

In the early morning dawn, she awoke—which was entirely not true, as she had really never slept too long at once to qualify as something to awaken from; still, it was before the mighty sun had lifted its majestic, glowing face into the heavens and watched in amusement as the darkness fled before her army of golden-rayed cherubs; there were breakfasts to be made, and lunches, packed the night before, to distribute, and laundry for Rosa to begin; then the sleepy heads would wander from their rooms—five boys in one small room and five girls in the other—down the hallway, and prodded and pulled by routine: eat, watch television, the younger ones listening to Grandmother's instructions for the day, the older ones listening to the burgeoning tick-tock of adolescence growing louder in their brains which, with every stroke of the clock, severed another precious strand of fidelity that still connected them to innocence.

Grandmother watched all of them as they prepared for school, and she worried mostly about the ones who had been raised by her children who had failed miserably as adults and masterfully as parents. "They need extra looking after," she often moaned, remembering her own mischievous youth; "these kids today is sneakier than when I was young."

"Grandma," one of the eldest ones asked, "why do we have to eat here, when the school gives us free breakfast?"

She rose up like a swelling fire, her face aglow with pride. "You eat here and I know what you eating, and that you are eating—Tommy." She wrapped his name in accusatory color, and he shrank back. She embraced him and kissed his handsome face. "Grandma works hard so you can have the best." This was her constant refrain at the end of the epic poem with which she encircled them—that life was good and all they needed was love and each other, and all would be well; that they were emotionally rich and spiritually rich, and rich with love and family, and God's love, and these were the only riches they needed. So, when she saw the thirteen-year-old girl avert her eyes to the latest fashion as the family ambled like an army down the glossy tiles of the local shopping mall, when the fourteen-year-old boy admired the expensive shoes of other youth passing by, when the little ones stretched out their hearts and hands for flashy toys too far away from their tiny grasps, the leader of this small but growing sovereign state merely said, "We have all God's riches, in our hearts." This was rich material for the innocent heart in this family to wear, but the older ones, whose heads were finally raised above the dark and din that childhood so artfully weaves about their silly minds, their fleshly desires could not be so easily sated; but it was Grandma who was the tie that bound them, Grandma who watched over them and cradled them in their hurt, Grandma who seemed to know when to apply her motherly salve and when to pull back and let them grow—Grandma, who seemed sometimes so young and to understand their youthful minds and desires, but also was so wise to anticipate what they wanted and why, and how to make sure they received what they had earned; yes, it was all Grandma, all the time, unceasing, unwavering, unstoppable, a one-woman army who was unassailable to lurking enemies, and not to be overcome by any mere human obstacle.

In the Belly of the Beast

There is only so much habitable land in the world and oftentimes too many people inhabit it, and therein lies the genesis of misery; but this is as it is, and no amount of persuasion will interrupt the human flow from the isolation of idyllic country to the accessible prosperity of the city; thus, it is here we begin our next story—a story of urban living and how it strays from the absolutely acceptable and unbelievably ignored Golden Mean.

There lies a strip of land in the wide world, and by itself, in the beginning, had the benefit of coastal influences and desert region and lush mountains and scenic valleys, but much of the southern section was mostly arid and could sustain only a population who would not exceed the strict allotment of available water; and this the first people did, they existed there and were one with the land and the land blessed them and harmony fell like cool rain upon them from the clear, azure sky; but then came those who did not understand the land nor the union of the natives with the land, and still, the equilibrium continued, for the conquerors were too few, and the natives too many; but then the conquerors were conquered from within and without, and lost the land to new tenants who built more dwellings there; yet, the land was still as it had been, as strong, and as immutable, and not to be trifled with.

Then a different kind of master came and sought to conquer and settle the land, and again, the land was not to be conquered; but then the land, unbeknown to itself, innocently adoring its outer core in golden splendor for eons, allowed a knowing member of this new tribe to pluck a single stone from its silvery streams, a single nugget of no more innate worth than a cup of dirt but now arbitrarily assigned enormous value, due to its rarity, by ever-scheming Man; and so others came and swarmed over the land like a drought, plundering her great natural resources and carving into her life's blood like thieves, like cannibals—like humans; and still, the land endured, because these tenants could not too long alter its natural makeup; and so, it was still desert and valleys, and mountains and coasts, albeit wounded from the steel-tipped hands that gouged and ripped and tore at her trusting foundation.

But one day more sophisticated machines came, and with them, fears and new ideas, and ideas that begat grand visions, for these machines allowed Man to reach beyond his limited, feeble grasp and manipulate Nature; they allowed him to think of one thing hitherto unknown in reality, and make it real; they made him feel as if a god, a new force on earth, who could move mighty rivers and mountains and unravel the secrets of the land; and so he did, and his ravenous madness was unleashed upon the unsuspecting land, and the revolution began; and war was declared upon it, and its death knell was sounded from sea to shining sea as its brothers and sisters of Nature too felt the sharp, blind ax of their traitorous suitors sink deep into their collective hearts; and the earth wept salty tears at the destruction of what had taken millions of years to perfect; Her comely figure, disfigured, now stained, wrinkled, barren; Her natural balance, imbalanced, now deceased, catastrophic, disastrous; Her pious honor, dishonored, now shamed, scorned, and spat on; Her cosmic membership in the exclusive club of planetary sovereignty, now purged, and she was left ashamed, a mother grieving for her lost and wayward children.

So, the artificial stage was set, and many pinstriped, blue-suited actors appeared to perform, and a pressing horde of people crowded the arena to witness the spectacle; and the stage grew, as the waters came flooding down cement canals and aqueducts and tunnels from abundant water in the north; and lo, the precious liquid cargo brought possibilities and hope, so before where there had been sparse life in the desert areas, where before there had been a few homes, a few small towns, a requisite number of counties, where before the southern region had been fitting for only a few ranches and few metropolitan cities, this fresh flow of life-giving aqua enabled the dreamers and speculators to forge reality from their greatest fantasies.

Now the play would proceed, the first act was completed, and the first towns to exceed the limits of indigenous resources were constructed; so, now where before there had been desert, there was a desert oasis, and the gracious climate attracted people in the same manner that a strong-smelling flower attracts a searching honeybee to its scented, ultraviolet-bearing blossoms wherefrom it sucks the sweet nectar.

So, the cities grew, like potted flowers in hot sand, never knowing that outside their fragile infrastructures lay ruination and death, all the time crowding the poor clay pots until they fairly burst, one city surviving because the founders foresaw the necessary infrastructure, others because of a richer class of folk; many survived, physically—that is to say, they still exist, as homes, as businesses, as local government; but died spiritually—that is to say, they died for want of societal harmony, slowly killing their physical structures with unfettered chaos and gross incompetence.

Let us, then, examine one such city that began in the bosom of tranquility and never saw the slow, insidious creeping of expansion past natural resources that caused too many to fight for too few places under the warm southern sun, where the soothing aroma of budding life was strongest; and now let us say it is like a garden in good soil where the hardiest roses flourish and the weakest roses die and the laziest roses wither, and the beautiful ladybug devours the nasty aphids, and where weeds grow in the spaces of least resistance; but let us further say that there comes a gardener who enriches the healthiest roses and even the laziest ones and heaps nourishment on the weakest but also upon the weeds; so, our city now is like that, where those who, then, would have died had they been weak or lazy now survive, and the strong become even stronger and soon subject those beneath them to a peculiar tyranny of avarice and power and mammon, that says, thusly: "what you have, we have, and more; what you want, we want, and more; what you have, we will take from you, and what you want, we will take that, too; and still, you will willingly serve us, yea, we will take even what you do not have to give, and still, you will be glad of heart."

Where once there were empty sections in the garden, now exist people; where once there was order in the garden, now exists disorder—for the weeds were plucked and the good roses shorn and the unnaturally large ones are now larger, and so people became like weeds and filled the empty places, and the lovely ladybug was exterminated along with the pesky aphids; and yea, the gardener wears thick, black sunglasses, and tends the tall flowers by hand, and does not feel the small ones crushed as he steps upon them, for he wears thick, black boots and does not hear their plaintive wail, for he channels loud music into his bursting eardrums; and one day, after much prodding from the helpless and frustrated people, he removes all of the obstacles that hindered his senses, and when he sees the perversion of the natural order about him, he decides that it is good, as he has never seen clearly or heard correctly or felt others' suffering before.

So, now we have this broken model, in which the inhabitants do not even know they are broken, and imagine their way of living to be fitting and proper, as does every society in every garden, and thus are cultures born—out of wedlock, with no real name or direction—and so they create a name and a direction, and with no parent, so they parent themselves, and then is born whatever goes, without remonstration or successful opposition goes, and all those who do remonstrate are societally damned, and damned to banishment or societal death.

Now, the city we have spoken of: it is a city, like most cities, once born and bred in rustic revelry, but as it grew, it shed its humble origins and broke the barriers of the garden and consumed the vistas they had longed for; as the city grew up, the populace grew, and as the populace grew, so did their ambitions, and with ambitions, came more of a variety of everything, and a few of the people rose up with the city and settled at the top, and some settled in the middle, and the rest were weighted down by those above them, and so stayed deep, deep below them, and with every passing generation, sank deeper and deeper into the societal mire, and sometimes were helped along by their sad, self-pitying, martyred selves.

Inside the city are many communities whose customs have evolved inside a porous, rock-hard encasement, and some have good customs, and some have bad, and some neighborhoods have built impermeable barriers about them with their constant habits, so that what is often good and beneficial and remarkable in the world goes by them in a kind of sooty, thick fog. It is as if they sit in a forest darkly, and cannot see past each other, to see how others live, to distinguish between one act and another, to judge one against the other, and they feel no light from the dense thicket, and become accustomed to one spot, one surrounding, one small influence, and they think themselves wise.

Now it is time to examine just one neighborhood in this frozen revolution. Here, they sit, rooted to the ground just like a gnarled old oak tree with movable limbs, and meander about, going to and fro, as they accomplish their daily objectives; they have established routines: to work, to store, to friend's house, to entertainment, just like any occupant of any neighborhood, and rarely do they digress from it, even in the wake of a calamitous event; and they are dedicated to the neighborhood, which is their mother and nurturer, a provider of stability, and inventory of friends and relatives, local shops and familiar sites—it is home and they are attached to it the same way a baby is to its mother, and whither goes mother, so goes baby.

Ants, living sociably with another, comfortable in their simple polity, will march up and down all day long on a tree and gain home and nourishment from it; and were the mother tree to blow in the wind, the ants merely blow with it; and were the tree to be struck and then tilt, the ants would tilt with it; and were the tree felled but still alive, the ants would fall down with it, yet never would the ants know they were shaken or tilted or felled, as they can see nothing beyond the tree, thinking the tree one-half of the world, and they the other half; and if the tree were to die, and the ants to leave, they would surely seek a paradigm of mother-nurturer elsewhere and then re-create their own niche—so in this way, they are more like their long-lost, twice removed cousin, the common-variety garden snail, who hauls his house and hearth around. And wherever the ants do settle, they will call it home, and unlike covetous Man, not tarry, not argue, not fight for honor or glory, but toil for the good of the colony; so, the tree brings life to the ant by providing it with a cozy home and nourishment, and the ant, life to the tree by protecting it from nasty insects and perhaps fertilizing around it, and this is symbiosis; but Man is a reasoning creature, and yet, when his dominion is contaminated, and spoiled, and rots, often-times he is adverse to fleeing even a felled tree, all the while lamenting about the injustice and indignity he suffers, not able to see the folly of his contribution to his own misery; so he stays, and lives on the dwindling feasts of his labor and dines on the famine expressed so unkindly by his wayward neighbor and the decay and rot that his senses now consider as acceptable and normal.

This is a neighborhood of families—the basic unit that populates communities the world over, yet many of these families no longer fit the prescribed traditional makeup of father, mother, son, daughter, more often having a mother, son number one, son number two, daughter number one, and daughter number two; mother, boyfriend, perhaps a son, perhaps a daughter; mother, and a boyfriend, who comes and promises fidelity and then leaves and is replaced by another aspiring boyfriend-husband-wannabe, and a son or two, and a daughter or two; grandmother, a blush of boys—grandchildren, cousins, a giggle of girls—grandchildren, cousins, and aunties, and uncles; two families under one roof—broken families or no—but choosing survival for now; and in the end, there is an infinite variety of combinations in these houses, just as there are in the fields, of insects and bugs, and in the woods, of animals and plants; in the trees, of birds and reptiles—they all share their home with their own kind—it is symbiosis; it is survival.

When we choose to live and not to die in the wake of adversity, we admire our own perseverance and tenacity; when we choose to live as adversity strikes us down, only by denying pride and accepting succor from others, we humble ourselves; when we choose to live, while adversity digs its sharp talons into our bare backs and hoists us up and flies toward its nest to drop us into the yawning mouth of its hungry babies, humility and shame, by seeking out and easily accepting a partnership with corrupt individuals and the advantages it brings, we then choose to live ignobly, and when we close our eyes to what the mind and heart rightly see, we consume both body and soul.

So, now we have a neighborhood that is marooned on a boulder that sits atop a high cliff and teeters this way and that, and is easily moved by the gentlest breeze or weakest vibration; and slowly it slides toward the abyss below, for it has no societal tether to attach to other boulders, to anchor it and dig into the hard ground, no solid foundation to stem its fall—because it cannot see the other boulders, cannot see the need for an anchor, cannot see the necessity of foundation—for this neighborhood believes it is the exemplar of the universe, and whatever resides outside its borders is meaningless; so, they are the norm, the new Golden Mean, the wise Oracle, the Holy Writ; they establish morals, they create law, they create rights, for they are a new land unto themselves, where outsiders fear to tread.

This neighborhood is a civilization whose history has been forgotten and where the present is also the future; here, all that transpires ripples out like concentric circles but crashes into societal constructs built by the occupants, so that they absorb their own misery, see their own reflection in all things good and bad, rely solely upon their own energies for progress, and so the outside world is thwarted, and it has no influence here. It is a world inside other worlds that are layered to infinity, and very few precious parts of it ever touch any other world.

Once, this was fascist Japan; once, this was fascist Germany; once, this was the Communist United of Soviet Socialist Republics; and once, this was any ancient island people, isolated from the world; but now, it is in too many countries, as it lies spoiling like a decaying animal wherein dwells busy insects and fungus eating away at the carcass and never thinking of a day when the good eating will be gone.

Here, in this concrete bunker, this fortress of steel and stone, they awaken to find the bloodied carnage of the night previous, and for the fact that they survived, they then acknowledge their debt to the whims of Providence; so, the new day begins and they attend to chores, to work, to recreation, and living, loving, but not leaving—no, never leaving; and as darkness descends, so too the malevolent spirits of the night, and the people attend to chores, to work, to recreation, and living, and loving, but never leaving—no, never once considering leaving their kingdom come, their own will be done, here, only on earth, an earth they have created from their own shapeless, soulless, mindless vision, armor-reinforced, blood-filled, insane asylum they alone rule, gladly, and boast of it.

And who are the princes and prophets of this human stain, this moral blot, but jesters and beasts in this bastard hell; and who lives here but those compliant; who but willing slaves, and those complicit in the crimes of their masters, especially since there are no high walls to obstruct them, no iron chains to bind them, no indispensable jobs to hold them; thus, this place of dwelling is no longer a true menagerie, but a cluster of those who take much and those who are willing to be taken.

As the compliants lie down and are trampled upon by their taskmasters, they attire them in a king's fine linen, made possible by their own blood and sweat and fear, and give them a sorcerer's scepter that is crafted from their willingness to acquiesce to domestic terrorists, and in doing so, create real magic for these feigned rulers, and a seven-diamond-studded crown—each stone representing a moral abomination: avarice, depravity, debauchery, blasphemy, corruption, lechery, murder; and thus, the criminals become a tyrannical monarchy, reigning through unfettered, inhuman hyper-calibrated suffering draped in multiple layers over the citizenry like a suit of burning armor; and the doctrine of these carnivorous kingpins states the greatest power over the greatest populace, and the greatest amount of bloodied monies extracted from the greatest number of people; and their covenant is with immorality, and sin, and they cleave to it like a baby craves sweet mother's milk; and they have great passion for such moral atrocities, knowing it unhinges the already tenuous minds of the population, knowing it creates unworldly creatures in their own tattooed souls, they who lust for the blood and suffering of those they subjugate, like voracious wild dogs lust for the hot blood of a fresh kill; yet, none of these moral transgressions are grand enough, eloquent enough, lasting enough, and they had no fear of anything beyond themselves—they do not honor Goodness and Love and Virtue, do not tremble in the presence of divine beings, nor even fear God when they revile Him; so, it is as they say, they are utterly without conscience, and will do anything to anybody, for sordid gain, and are no longer members of the *Homo sapiens sapiens* species, but savage animals in the loose skins of human beings they have hollowed out with their own fanged teeth and sharp claws.

And as these petty kings battle for hegemony, they will never know, as they lie in their own cold-red blood, that the path they followed to gain freedom from imaginary restraints has made them slaves; and behold, for by what a man is overcome, by this he is enslaved.

And so, this is how it is, and the world acknowledges it as so, and reckons that every man must do his own fighting; consequently, those who will rise up and fight will say, good, let the battle begin.

Old Beginnings

It is day now, light is ruler, light is prevalent, it reveals the precious doings of every creature, and yet it subdues the habits of those who prefer to hunt in the thick veil of inky darkness.

In this particular neighborhood, the residents awaken and begin the day with nourishment and then forced labor and perhaps errands, and consummate it with a little rest and recreation; and then night comes and they fall off to sleep, and are then awakened the next day to begin the process anew; it is a cycle, like any cycle in Nature—water, carbon, rock—beginning and ending and renewing itself and continuing on until the organism is exhausted and expires, but whose body then contributes to other cycles—cycles feeding into cycles; no escape from the intricate connection of Nature's masterful network of carefully constructed processes where nothing is wasted and nothing is destroyed.

There is one group of inhabitants who move ponderously throughout the day, slinking about in the light like snakes under rocks, staying close to the sides of buildings, like spiders; casting nervous glances aside, bodies trembling, faces sweating, eyes twitching, they seek refuge inside where they rest their nerves, plotting, brooding, seething; many of these malevolent spirts do covert business, some work, others are lifeless entities awaiting the resurrection of their true natures with the blossoming of eventide.

And then the first sprinkling of night comes in streaks and bolts, slaying the effusion of light; it comes in waves and tiers, undressing the brilliant incandescence; it comes like a great eagle's wing covering the land, and light is smothered, it is suppressed, it is undone, dropping like fireflies, giving way to the dappled, speckled shadows, retreating like a beaten army, giving way to freckles of darkness, darkness raining, darkness pouring, darkness scouring the last vestiges of light, chasing it away into anonymity; and now the invasion is complete, and all who thrive in the greasy bosom of obscurity, in stealth, in confusion, come fully alive.

First, the insects come creeping out, their simple brains obeying the neurological impulses of their simple bodies, stirring around, looking for food and mates; and soon the reptiles, the hunter birds, and then the parasitic invaders come: the mushroom sprouts, and so too that scoundrel Man, and the least of him comes to prey upon the weak and infirm, the helpless, the meek, the gentle folk, and consumes his blood, and in its stead puts in fear; and consumes his flesh, and in its stead puts in terror; and consumes his sinew, and in its stead puts in horror, so that he would rebuild these Innocents as beaten and bowed, crawling and crying, groveling, pleading, trembling vessels whose very spirit is subdued, and chained and flung violently into the dominion of cowardice and a conquered people.

From whence comes evil: hath free will been corrupted to produce a wellspring of human depravity; hath supernatural forces infected humans either solely or in concert with their own foibles; is evil merely a social construct, absent in the wild; is it a perversion of our good nature, or part of our nature, naturally; what are the gradations of evil, and are all humans capable of each, and when is a human culpable, and how shall they be punished?

O, that all the world were good
how glad the world would be;
but then all the world would
be in heaven, eternally

But this dark domicile, inherited from the hot furnace of man's darkest desires, is not paradise, not malevolent, not innocent; it is hell, it is present, it is purgatory, and the characters of animus and condemnation and damnation.

The fallen angels of the sleeping community unscrewed their human masks and revealed the boastful abomination therein; they wiggled out of their flabby human skin and deposited it at their hairy, clawed feet, and set the reptilian minds to the task at hand, to wit: while roaming on their private hunting ground; now the looting, unfettered; now the raping, unbound; now the destruction, without limit, of their bountiful prey.

They boast courage, they cry might
they vow vengeance, they seek victory;
yet they are cowards, they are feeble
their vengeance an artifice, their victories impossible

And their words come from a bubbling lake of fire that is poured from a crooked sluice that inhabits their slanting minds, wherein the coarsest drops of their blood-lava are then caught on the tiniest protrusions, and soon collected and smelted and turned into verbal missiles by the derelicts and drunken overseers of the language of history.

They congregate at specifically arranged places: foreboding, secluded, dirty hovels, the refuge of scoundrels, miscreants and degenerates who flee the gentle stream of civilization and wade into the foggy bogs and murky swamps and lay down their vicious plans of annihilation in the company of eerie howls and long-ago banished monsters.

The talk is hushed, their gaze furtive, their bodies huddled, and so they speak boldly; for without, no decent citizen would tolerate such a moral dissension; but within, their bestial grunts and growling tones signify a brotherhood that breeds like violent germs in this steel chamber that is forged by vice and violence.

> They bethought themselves the elect,
> they imagined themselves gods,
> an army, they became;
> the world, to conquer,
> and mercy they conquered,
> but freedom, first.

They tossed mean words like grenades into the absent demeanors of their enemies, each word for loathing and arrogance toward the greater mass of the world; every sentence was a ticking time bomb detonated on the idea that someone had money they had not, power they had not, glory they had not, that others who tarry on the road and block these gleeful ghoul's naked ambition must die, to wit:

"Yo, man, yo, I mean, did you see dat fat gangster drivin' dat fine-looking car, and wid dat fine ho! And where did he get dat money—from dumb peoples; we should be takin' his money, huh?" one of them began; however, there will now be a forced suspension of this specific dialogue—this gutter-jubilee, dirty, rusty-jewel-encrusted, debauched twenty-four-karat, gold-plated, filthy landscape inhabiting artificial and inflated street-talk nonsense by choice, which is better heaped onto a mountain of rubble and buried one thousand leagues beneath the ocean floor—to allow a transfusion of words last dunked in festering boils, corrosive gangrene, and spittle-dung-rot to sink into the anxious mind of the reader, which spoke of the murder of a nine-year-old Innocent. To continue again: "I feel like killing him right now, like when we got his little punk cousin in the alley and I popped him dead—yeah, that right, we need to show 'em we ain't got no problem—capping no chil' ain't no worry to us, y'all." By the hearty echoes of his animated brethren, there seemed to be anonymity in agreement that what they did not have—and especially owned by a rival group—deserved to adorn their persons, their cars, their houses; and then the youth held up that which was a new extremity: cold, hard, glossy steel, perhaps more like a doctrine, a creed embraced; perhaps like a lover, a faithful lover who was silent when she needed to be an explosive and alive; perhaps a friend, a confidant, a brother, who will never betray the holder of its slick, slender, black body; it was an authentic member, a family member, solid, deliberate, deadly—it was an extension of their thoughts, a concrete materialization of what they yearned to be, a heartless, soulless, merciless machine who brooked no dissent and heeded no compromise, and took no prisoners and authoritatively and utterly finished all business without the complication of words and emotion and regret; it ejected its tumbling cylindrical cargo in an explosive burst and once it took flight—unlike the mess, the trap, the war of words—the little messengers of pain did not return to its exit point. It solved that which was hitherto unsolvable, without mediation, and swiftly grafting, like nails pounded and finally stitched onto outraged flesh, a distinct message, hark: the proprietor of said machine has no conscience, no fear, and no use for human speech, reason or compassion, to settle conflict.

The youth held up the weapon and turned it this way and that as if he were showing off some fine artwork he had meticulously crafted; and lo, all the youths admired the weapon as if it were a great sculpture, and they sang the praises of its magnificence, as if it were some great idol to be worshiped; and they felt reverence and awe in its presence, as if it were indeed a living god, one that heard their fervent prayers and transformed their rags of a proper existence into the silken purple robes of an exalted prince.

"Wid dis," the youth said, his countenance lit by smugness, "ain't nobody gonna mess wid us… You know what I'm saying, yo?"

And no rational person would face down such a device—a device that could make a cur, a king; a weakling, a warrior; a sane man, insane; a marvel that fashioned wealth and power from poverty and weakness, gave dominion over the masses, altered the pigment of one's soul, tarried the heart, blinded eyes; even a fool could caress its slender form and paint its terror against Innocents; and no education was needed here, no scholarly titles to pull the curved trigger, no exams to pass to hold it firm as the hammer pulled back and then rushed forward—only a sullen stare, a face full of folly, a mind full of vengeance, and a heart that never cared where the ministering steel assassins impacted or if they found the proper target or missed or who was hurt or who was killed—only that the deed was done without hesitation, without remonstrance, without anxiety from an innate, inner dialogue that never questioned the value of such actions.

"The Original Gangbangers is tryin' to take our hood from us, an' that ain't right, no-how," the animated youth continued, gesturing wildly about with the mean machine still in his sweaty grip, "dis is our hood, and we gonna defend it," and he flashed the weapon in front of his fellow members, "any way we have to—and this be the way, we have to; do you feel me?"

This fervor was met with equal enthusiasm, and so the brood continued to stroke their anger and rage toward their absent enemy; it must be stated, emphatically, that their enthusiastic avowal to destroy was aimed only at their nemesis, the Original Gangbangers—not at the night sky, or the cool, wet ground, or even the tall, verdant trees; not even at the alley cat or the scurrying rat, no, nothing like that; it was a high fever that could break only once the hearts of their enemies stopped beating forever; but this is not to say that anyone who stood as an obstacle in the plan was not also a target, and quickly eliminated, or anyone who stood against them as they conducted business would not be shot down as if they were rabid dogs, and as easily discarded as a dead dog. And anyone accidentally wounded or killed was never remembered by them. Their vision was clear and centered on one task and one overarching goal: the mastering of their territory through any means necessary, and without regrets.

Thus, enamored with the vigor of vengeance, and adorned with the war paint of imminent battle, they were primed and pumped to attack and destroy any and all in their path; and along came a midsized sedan.

It was gentle blue, the color of the slowly approaching car, a kind of baby blue that signaled mildness, a special kind of timidity of the occupants who rode in this family flagship. Inside, there was father gentleman, who was slightly embarrassed at the wrong turn he had taken that now took them down this narrow and darkened street; and mother gentlewoman, reassuring her husband by softly stroking his arm that all would be well; and mild daughter, playing with her ragdoll, and mild son, playing with his toy superhero, all of whom were like four innocent lambkins who had lost their way and now have come upon the ravenous wolf pack to ask for directions.

But father lambkin soon saw his error as he approached the youths who gathered in front of the slowing car, and he trembled despite himself, for he was no longer a driver lost, but a hero found, as all fathers and husbands need to be in such situation; and as he switched gears and attempted to beat a hasty retreat, the howling wolves with their big black eyes and drooling, greasy lips and their gaping, yellow-white teeth, upon seeing the kind of creatures they had ensnared, heaped glee upon their own feverish, hairy faces.

Every heart of this pit of writhing vipers was sodden with wanton destruction for the lives of these wayfarers, and every heart of these band of brother wolves beat in the same rhythm for them, and tuned to the same song that sang, "We kill Innocents, we kill anything, our dead souls without borders, or dead hearts without mercy; I kill for pleasure, I kill for gain, I kill for the pleasure of feeling other people's pain." It was fuel for their fire of existence, it was the narcotic that they ingested; their hearts pumped not oxygen to feed themselves, but poison; not nutrition, but disease; not blood, but bloodlust; their minds fed on the freedom to select and murder any life-form they chose; and they bethought themselves gods.

They, these misanthropes, these rude soldiers in peacetime, swarmed like army ants on a fluffy, fuzzy caterpillar, these derivatives from sin and suffering, surrounded like virulent germs this frightened family, their weapons drawn and their souls closed: how could a human heart rightly see such an authentic true crime such as this, so heinous, so cold-blooded and drained of any human features of morality and virtue? And they enclosed the now-stalled car, the car with the four family members who were one in Love and Joy and Innocence, who were now trapped inside the sharp-daggered and yawning mouth of the drooling wolf; and what epitaphs did they paint with their accursed tongues about their victims, what sacred truths and virtues did they forswear as they raised in earnest, like a crystal glass of champagne to toast the well-being of a brother, their cold steel against the trembling family? Horrors, horror of horrors built upon and inside filthy, rotten, dirty lies that spewed from their wagging tongues like excrement, like the foul dung of deceased rats, fell from their sanguinary souls, as they shouted hoarsely and cried fervently, weird chants, insensible narratives about 'hoods and power and money, vicious rants, execrable vows that were a weird, frightening collage of madness to the Family, who understood only the narrative of gentleness and love, and devotion to bettering the world—not this toxic exhaust, these toxic fumes that seeped into their ears and fed their minds with the promise of pain for no apparent reason other than for self-aggrandizement and the deviant glory of their captors; the Family were travelers now in an alien world where the manners and customs and actions of their hosts were utterly and irrevocably nonsensical and too many cold degrees from normal to possibly interpret.

And yet, despite all this calamity, the Family thought the outcome would favor them, for they had lain in the seed of despair before and somehow had always landed vertically and unmarked; after all, they had done nothing palpably wrong, they had merely stumbled into the wrong hemisphere of influence, and thought themselves protected by bearing no cultural or business antagonism toward their new captors; and also, they reasoned, their moral standing, in contrast with the moral ambiguity of this menacing brood, surely would protect them…

…And so too thought the poor white lambkin as he stood in the icy shadow of the dastardly wolf. "But kind sir, what have I done to offend thee?"

"Sirrah, you insulted me last spring."

"But I am newly born, sir," replied the lamb, "and have not yet seen the Spring."

"You trespassed into my pasture to eat of its good grass."

"But I have never eaten grass," replied the lamb.

"Then you drank of my well."

"No," cried the lamb, "thus far, I have drunk only the sweet milk of my kind mother."

But the wolf sprang upon the poor lambkin and devoured him, for "any excuse will serve a tyrant."

So, too, the Family expected their innocence to protect them as they cried in protest against the encroaching foe, but the human wolves sprang upon the poor lambkins and devoured them all, just to show they could, and would, to anyone, and for any reason, for no reason, to gain all, or nothing, and perhaps just for sport, out of spite, or jealousy, or plain savagery, for the joy of the kill, to evince what they had learned all their years alive, the sum total of learning from their hard pedagogues, and what they had learned was this: that they would do as they pleased no matter who, or what, or when, or where, or why, or the general circumstance, because it was their whim to do, and anyone who held a contrarian view would be devoured.

But whatever dread they spun like sticky silk over the place, it hung like a toxic fog, even as the black and white cruisers came upon the scene and discovered the badly perforated bodies of the now still, once very gentle and kind and loving Family who had wanted only to live in Love and Peace and Joy, and flourish, and contribute to the betterment of the world in which there exists the fine heritage of family found, family loved, family spiritual, that makes the world good, that binds the world's wounds with unconditional love, what is the human mortar for harmony, human glue for Peace, human sympathy for gentleness; and now they had been crushed too soon, like a budding flower trampled upon by a mob's riotous bloody claw, without care, without understanding by these perpetrators who had reached into their own soul and cut its dangling heart.

And what could the policemen—the human receptacles of all that is human soil and stain—do now but weep, for lost and gentle sheep; and who would properly avenge them, the men pondered, seeing the horrific slaughter before them; not us, they whispered, because we have sworn an oath to obey a law laid down in centuries past—who would assume the mantle of universal law and administer fair Justice to the outlaws of this crime, if not we? And so they wept more, as they knew there was no true social Justice, could be none, for society cannot function with a vigilante consciousness inside its delicate structure, for such a radical doctrine has no Constitution, no hierarchical structure, no sacred texts, no checks and balances. And so they forgot about such cataclysmic ideas and moved on through a disturbed night that was now a little less clean, less structured, and less innocent, and later embraced their own family longer, and thought more often of going far away from this cauldron of unrestrained human intemperance, and burying their roots in a richer, more fertile, healthier and happier soil.

A Heavy Yoke

No good idea lies smoldering in the grave until first its ripest fruits are tasted by someone other than its creator; the world is full of opinions, most of them bad, and the best ones are oft recognized by only a select few, many of whom are impotent to implement the virtues of it; they say a good idea is never lost, just embraced and dressed up and handed down to another generation, and there exploited until its fruits wither away and die. Now, the rich can take a fair idea and make people think it is good and unquestionably a necessary part of the people's furious lives; the rich can do this, indeed, they can plant subliminal plots and characters into the minds of those they consider dullards and blockheads, human chattel for their ever-increasing financial-monopoly empire, so that the desperate fools think themselves incomplete without this indecipherable plot that involves this and that fashionable trend, or this and that delicious decor, even that certain too-expensive something—and this, even though the fashion was really not so, the decor not necessarily so, the expensive something much too much and really not indispensable; it was this dark magic the rich played on the mediocre middle-class, witchcraft on the lower class, envy on their own kind, this startling power to control that which was impotent without the desire to belong and assimilate and be recognized.

There are, however, those wealthy few who move society one way or another for the good of the world, and they are divided into two categories: one that does this for charity while the other hand is in the till and does what is good for them; and then there are those who, with both hands—and heart—exposed, do what is good for people, and these are the true philanthropists, though even a poor man can do the same.

Even one person can move a small rock for good, and in doing so, effect change for the entire landscape; so every man has the burden to do what he can for his fellow brother and sister, leaving no excuses for those who say they have no power.

There is such a man, but a very rich man, who had done now what he must, whether he was rich or poor, healthy or sick, to bring succor to those in need. You might look upon him and see no value to his store-bought clothes, his faded blue jeans and long, cotton shirts of humble colors; no opulence in his old and comfortable cream-colored Acura, no power in his small offices, but the value was in what one could not see: opulence, the opulence of generosity; power, the power of humility; determination, the determination to succeed by prevailing against all known and unknown obstacles; it was the unseen, what he could do with his billions but chose not to do, because he would not direct any money toward things that did not increase for the better the lives of the poor. "How will a handmade cashmere sweater for myself, which costs thousands of dollars, assuage suffering?" he asked his assistant. "Those monies can feed an impoverished family for months—waste, all waste, and wrong." Such statements led him to further musings upon the current state of the world, and where it had been, where it was now, and where it was going.

He read many books on the origins of poverty, the status of poverty, world aid to impoverished nations, and the general effect poverty has on nation-states; and watched documentaries on poverty and researched it through the computer and his personal contacts; he read many books on crime, and its many offspring—gangs, drug trafficking, corruption, and a new breed of prison population—and watched documentaries on them, and researched them through the Internet and his personal contacts and university professors. Men such as he, who have great wealth, can, with a phone call, a nod of the head, a mere suggestion, gain access to anyone of importance in every level of society, as people want to be around such inordinate wealth, as if knowing such a man magnifies their aura and accentuates and raises their social ranking and status; consequently, he personally knew police superintendents and special agency directors, world-famous celebrities and CEOs, powerful politicians and bankers, heads of state, ambassadors and journalists; if he needed a favor, he had only to ask, for many he knew were indebted to him.

When he saw suffering, he sought to ameliorate it; when he saw pain, he sought to soothe it; when he saw injustice, he sought to impede it, for he felt their suffering, he felt their pain, he felt their injustice; and when he acted against a human cruelty, he acted as if he was the one cruelly dealt with, the one shamed, the one humiliated, beaten down, hurt, and bleeding, whether it was emotional or physical, for he loathed it all because he felt it all so deeply. How can I do less, he often thought, until this world surrenders to Goodness, or is swallowed by fire, and a new Creation is born; until then, it is the duty of all mankind to strive for the Perfect, and in doing so, bring some comfort to each other, for each man is important, and each woman valuable, and capable of doing great good to those around them.

So, to this righteous end, he lived his life, and to this maxim, he held fast: that a life needlessly ended by disease, or ignorance, that a life captured by war, or violence, is tragic; but it is unrighteous that a life that has no champion to struggle against these forces, and so the eternal struggle therefore goes on, the eternal lamp of Freedom still lit, to guide those few who still dare to stand against the flow of inequality and servitude and unjust war.

"As long as there is one I can bring succor to, I live on," he told his loyal aide one day. "We are all brothers and sisters—every man my brother, every woman my sister; it is the way we must view Creation: one Father, one Mother, one Family; and we must not let borders, or race, or creed, religion, gender, philosophy, polity, or wealth dim our vision of what we must do to minister to the poor, the sick, the elderly: those first, and as for those last, for certainly, the privileged do not need us, as they already worship in the house of their own god—that is, material things, societal invincibility and the power it brings, and the endless vineyards in the highest echelons of society where they eat ambrosia and drink nectar, and ichor flows through their blue veins; these Olympians, these Athanatoi who think we are their Thnetoi, who serve their divine will." He paused, and closed his eyes, and upon his face was a writ got from living, and experiencing life; and his voice became an echo chamber for the trial and tribulation he had seen. "Life is pain, it is suffering, and no man ought to cherish his fortune at the expense of another; and no man ought to covet his lot without helping another; no man who is able ought to rest easy, as long as there are those who do not."

The reader must not think that the aforementioned man was born a saint or christened one by society and thus set out to preach his loving gospel to the desperate world; no, for even now, as he stood there, he remembered a dark past that had illumined his present path.

No Excuses

A night time fury
of cold and wind;
the humble home
protects those within

and how do the homeless fare,
prisoners locked in open air;
nowhere to run or hide,
destined to slowly suffer or die.

In the house of records containing all the persons who have lived or who live, there are but few who can understand, with an uncanny sense of the subtle vagaries and nonsensical rhythms, and even the rigid rules and structure of that enigmatic heart of shadows and feints, that elusive, obtuse world of mean and cold business, whose narrow doors admit briefly those who ruthlessly rise to the highest echelons of power, and where they are kept aloft by the cease-less toil and sweat of the faceless and struggling laborers below; and who, once being consigned to Mount Olympus, will voluntarily lower themselves to the repressed and discarded class of those they impugn and degrade?

When one sees what the accumulation of vast wealth can do—what it can solve, what it can acquire, what it can move when other efforts fail; when it can alter the seemingly unalterable, reverse the irreversible, break the unbreakable, purchase the unpurchaseable, sell the unsellable, make possible the impossible, what man or woman can long turn away from it, abandon its magnetic power to shape society and imbue the mind with a conquering spirt and gratify the deepest desires of self—desires previously considered unimaginable and forbidden, and even frightening to realize?

When Robert Heimdall first earned a million dollars in a few months of extraordinarily brilliant tactical maneuvering and unrelenting hard work, he was amazed at the ease of it, and soon realized that he had forever set himself apart from average men, who could never do what he had done because they lacked the strength of will and uncanny business acumen and fierce determination and willingness to sacrifice to succeed; but also, as he lingered here in this exceptional zone where the wealthy people congregated and decided the fate of societies, they, he soon discovered, at least compared to him, were illiterate and incompetent and meager of will, and where any highly competent and extremely intelligent and literate man as he might consign these inferiors to a lower station on the corporate plateau. When he had entered the Massachusetts Institute of Technology on a full scholarship as a mere sixteen-year-old, a place he found himself entirely at home, he had made make personal connections to geniuses in all fields of science and technology; where he honed his innate talents for commerce and realized how different he was from the average man; a place where he had built a foundation of knowledge, and a direction on how to proceed into the complex and crowded marketplace with an increased chance of success; yes, in the beginning it was here that he gained the entrepreneurial-cultural mind-set, and read the proper books, and began to interview the appropriate leaders; not just here, but elsewhere, these captains of industry freely advised the youth and were happy to tell him the secret of their success, as they feared no one; so, as he built his first business, he had a rudimentary, and then a sophisticated, model of how to attract and keep the best employees, and who to hire, and when to fire; when to be aggressive with those within his corporation and those without; when to be kind, and when to condemn, and when to forgive; when to give a raise, and when to wait; how to negotiate, how to interact with allies, and perceived enemies, and how to neutralize them and win them over; what constitutes the characteristics of an effective owner and a successful business; and why businesses fail, why workers revolt, why they are loyal; and where to establish a business and a meeting with rivals, and a place for him to retreat to in times of those rare moments of needed rest.

Men such as Robert Heimdall knew that the following maxim holds true: the harder and more often need you toil—if you are capable and cunning, competent and relentless, innovative and imaginative—the more wealth and power you will amass; so, with this grand vision before him like a pulsating beacon of light, he wholly embraced it, as if in a fanciful dream.

If he worked twelve hours a day, he distinguished himself among men and women who were still dedicated to their families and therefore were tightly harnessed to a limited work schedule and accumulation of wealth; if he worked fourteen hours a day, he outdistanced himself even more from them, being free now to pursue those radical ideas that would fire his far-ranging ambitions; if he worked sixteen hours a day, six days a week, he rose up to the company of a precious few, those power brokers who resided on a rarefied level previously hidden to him; so, if he worked sixteen hours a day, seven days a week, and often slept at his office, he burst through into the private domain of those who manipulated the power brokers, those whom the public recognized as kings and queens, but were truly, he now knew, merely flawed dukes and duchesses, princes and princesses. It was at this level that names and places and events simply became facts and figures and fodder for someone to reckon with so as to increase the holdings of his expanding empire.

It was here, it was then, at the exalted and constantly renewing summit of illimitable power, that the very beating heart and vibrant soul of business became his intimate paramour and family, his trusted friend, his comforting ally; where he was finally content, and experienced joy, and solitude, and made sense of the world about him; now, this home, here in the high throne of radiant glory, in the grace of glittering wealth, in the Cathedral of coruscating power, it was where he knew he needed to be, his niche, his natural birthright realized, his place in an orderly universe: to be ruler of the masses, to move society forward by his desires and predilections and very resolute will.

And it was all just business to him, no matter what he did; when he regularly ordered the termination of the lowest-performing ten percent of his growing number of employees; when he terminated anyone in a managerial position who displayed weakness or ineptitude even for a moment in their performance—even if the aforementioned people had verifiable, recognizably valid excuses—as he accepted no excuses for himself when he erred or failed, and thus accepted none from anyone else; even when he closed divisions to save even a fraction of revenue that ultimately caused the loss of many loyal employees, he did not care—for it was all just business, and if it moved his company forward, he did it, without hesitation or regret, as all employees were simply data and statistics, and his creditors and rivals mere pawns and players to move around and flummox in order for his company to increase its profit margin.

Still, he was somewhat generous with employees he dismissed or laid off, generally giving them one month of severance pay, and always allowing them to plead their case to keep their job before him, even though he never relented in his prior decision.

He had no wife, he had no children; at least he maintained the generous notion that he could not be a proper husband or father; he had few intimate friends: his daily contact with his subordinates and fellow merchants satisfied his basic need for human interaction; this is not to say that he did not engage in frivolities, especially with women, who moved in and out of his life with the frequency and austerity of the changing weather, for they served their fleshly purpose, and, like anyone who attaches themselves to a rich patron, they were well compensated for their freely given and uninhibited services. His relationships with human beings were superficial and transitory, because his life was in the making of money and building his business into a far-reaching empire whose importance in society would soon be incalculable and irreversible.

Then there came a particularly cold and fearful night, when one usually seeks the comfort of home and hearth, but on which Robert found comfort in working; however, he eventually decided to quit near midnight, and headed toward one of his luxury homes in the city, driving one of his luxury automobiles. His attention was soon drawn to a scene where an abundance of police and firefighters had congregated in front of a massive warehouse that he happened to own. He pulled off the road, came up to the officers, introduced himself as the owner of the building, and offered help.

It seemed that there was a man atop this structure who was threatening to jump. "He says," the policeman in charge began, "that after he lost his job, he couldn't properly care for his wife and child, and after that they became homeless."

"What is his name?" Robert asked, staring up at the man who was teetering on the edge of the roof.

"Chad Castleman."

Robert nodded, his eyes screwed up, his brows knit, his lips pursed. "Perhaps I can help."

The policeman shrugged his shoulders. "It looks as if he is really going to jump, and that we will not be able to stop him; maybe if you offered him a job, it might help…"

Robert took the bullhorn, quickly identify himself to the man, and offered him a job and financial assistance.

The man burst out laughing as he moved along the edge of the rooftop. "You! You—of all people…"

The police officer, bewildered, looked at Robert. "What does he mean?"

Without looking at the officer, Robert said, "I recognize that voice, and the name; yes, he worked for me." He had a remarkable memory for employees, proud that he could recognize at least those he had terminated; but this man, Chad, had also plead his case before Robert, and so Robert intimately knew the voice, as well.

The police officer, frowning, took back the bullhorn, and said, disgusted, "You can leave now…"

The man atop the building screamed at the firemen on the rising ladder to desist their intentions or he would jump immediately, and then he shouted, "I want to talk to you, Mr. Heimdall—come closer… or so help me, I will jump right now!"

The officer in charge shook his head, and then said, "This is not a good idea…"

But Robert was not the type of man who took orders, but gave them, such was the authority he wielded and the respect he received from those in the city who knew of his immense importance and power. "I'll take the risk—if I am the man responsible for him being up there, then I am the man who is responsible for getting him down," he said and, grabbing the bullhorn, walked confidently forward until he was nearly directly underneath the high ledge.

The man again spoke, his voice choking with pathos. "You destroyed my life—you—you could have given me another chance to keep my job; I was missing days because my wife was ill—but no! You don't accept excuses!" he cried, rancor throttling his hoarse voice. "It's all on you, rich man—it's all about profit margins, isn't it; you know what you are, you're a bad man, and the sad thing is, you don't even know it, nor do you care how many lives you hurt or destroy," and then he looked around, looked up into the icy, black void, and then down again, and said, his voice now timid and forlorn, "and her death is on you." And then he jumped, flinging himself far out so that he might fall upon he whom he so hated; and Robert, perhaps the first time in his professional life, hesitated, so in shock was he at this unexpected event, and even as the police officer next to him moved him quickly away, he still heard the horrible smash-thud of the human missile as it embraced the hard concrete.

Robert stood behind the firemen and police officers who attended to the dead man, and he whispered, "What does he mean, her death?" He would not leave until this disturbing question was answered, and forced himself to stare at the face of the bloodied corpse.

Several minutes later, a relative arrived, and told the officer in charge that the man's wife had died giving birth to a baby girl—died as they attempted to get to the hospital without a car, and even taxi drivers would not allow them into his cab without money; died on the side of a dark, lonely road, in the cold and the rain.

Robert got back into his car and drove away, and three hours later, he was still driving, but aimlessly, his efficacious mind now cut loose by what he abhorred most—emotional upheaval, a state in which his mind was disheveled, off the well-oiled, constantly renewable, slick track on which he so adroitly cruised; therefore, he drove back to his office, thinking that once there, he might soon forget this unfortunate incident, just as if it had been a bad transaction, but found he could not, and soon became more obsessed with it. He looked up the case of Chad Castleman, and determined, to his satisfaction, that he could not possibly have foreseen such a disastrous circumstance. "I am not my brother's keeper," he declared, pounding his desk; "if a man fails, he picks himself up and tries again—am I condemned to keep any employee who fails to uphold this company's highest standards?" Yet, as he sifted through this and other records of terminated employees, his smug satisfaction slowly dissipated. "Why did this have to happen—why now, of all times?" Yet, this was the mindset of the consummate businessman who thinks that any interruption during any phase of a company's life—whether it is at the beginning or in the middle—is always the "wrong time," as any interruption in the constant growth of a company was always interpreted as an exception to be foreseen and avoided; but this affair with the wont of achieving only victories is called fanaticism, and it breeds people of a different stripe who look at the world from a high angle in a parallel universe hitherto unknown to the ordinary citizen.

He tried to work, but could not, for his mind was transfixed on the question that needed an answer, so he must provide one—it was what he did, and made him successful: he never backed down from a problem, and never quit until it was solved, this dogged perseverance being one of the hallmarks that had been ingrained within him.

"I cannot work until I am satisfied," he said, and called in his private secretary and then ordered her to contact human resources and have them to gather up files on employee terminations in the last year. "This all makes no sense, what I'm doing," he declared, after she had left, "but the sooner I get this itch scratched, the better; I guess it's called a 'conscience'—even though, technically, I have done nothing morally wrong." He shook his head. "I need to get back to the business of doing business." He pounded the heavy desk again, shaking his head, again. "I employ tens of thousands of people, give them a good salary and benefits; I help society remain stable; I contribute to the betterment of the world; I do my part." He tried to wave away this festering wound in his mind, which had opened a gash that allowed new elements of reality to slowly slip in, but, alas, he failed, for he still heard the awful cracking of bones as the body had smashed into the ground; he still saw the grimaced-in-agony face of poor, dead Chad Castleman.

Three days hence, after he had slept very little, reports on those employees he had so casually dismissed now lay in heaps upon his desk, and he promptly set about inspecting them, meticulously going over each case, until his eyes burned and ached and his head pounded and his mind was stuffed with more confusion. "I must know," he finally decided, and immediately set out to discover what results had occurred due to his initial actions of firing so many, so often, anytime, anyplace, as a matter of cold, unyielding policy.

After visiting numerous ex-employees, who were hostile to his presence at their home, he then instructed his driver to take him to the house of Harley Weil, and soon his luxury automobile—which cost as much as all the houses on this block—was parked in front of the small house of this humble neighborhood.

It was Winter now, and the snow was on the ground as Robert exited the car in his custom-made suit and shoes, and long, thick wool overcoat, and dark brown, leather gloves. He walked up to the door and knocked upon it; then he felt foolish—he, a CEO and owner of a Fortune 500 company, visiting an employee he had fired a year ago suddenly made absolutely no sense to him—what could he possibly accomplish here? Therefore, he turned and walked away, glad that no one had come to the door, relieved he had finally understood that it was just the unfortunate witnessing of the suicide that had caused a temporary feeling of guilt which he knew would slowly resolve itself. "And now," he thought to himself, "back to the business of—"

"Yes? May I help you?"

He, this big man in town, mover and shaker, possessor of vast power and riches, hesitated, fumbling for coherent words to convey as he turned around and faced the woman. "Well, you see—I was looking for Harley Weil."

The woman then asked politely, "May I ask who is calling upon him?"

"Why, yes, of course," he said, fumbling for a card with his name upon it as he approached her, and then upon handing it to her, said his name as if it was best she hear it from him, "Robert Heimdall...."

"Yes, Mr. Heimdall, I recognize you." She stared at him from inside the doorway, unmoving. "Has Harley done something wrong, that you would visit your mean countenance upon us one year removed from your firing him; yet, you are here?"

"No," Robert replied, wanting desperately to quit this unhappy place, but his adamant, newly acquired, and persistent "conscience" rooted him to this spot. "I seek only to speak to him, to inquire as to his employment now…"

"You jest?" She had detested this man for so long, and now to have him here, and seemingly disoriented—the farther afield he was from his citadel of glory, she observed rightly, the more he was inconsequential, and inept—that she sneered contempt at he who was once so powerful and now seemed so timid. "You fire him and now are concerned for his welfare? Are you offering him a job?"

"Well, no, but I…"

"Good day, then, sir," she said, and began to close the door.

"You are right, Mrs. Weil, I have no right to inquire, but indulge me for a moment."

She held the door open, still. But with a look of contempt and malice still upon her face, her head slightly tilted by disgust, she said, hands on hips, "Why should I?"

He, once again, the supremely efficient and normally bold businessman, fumbled for precise and coherent words. "Because I am interested…"

She frowned, shaking her head, and said, as if against her will, "Well, if you really are interested—and I can't leave you standing outside in the freezing cold," and she glanced to the driver inside the car as she opened the door wider. "Why don't both of you come in…"

"He's fine," Robert said, motioning toward the car, and then walked up to the door and came inside the home, such a small, comparable home he had not seen in many years, its size the same as one of the bathrooms in his many mansions that were scattered throughout the country.

She shook her head, and said, irritated, "You wouldn't even leave your dog in a car in this horrible weather; my house, my rules," and she walked up to the car, knocked on the driver's-side window, whereupon it opened, and soon out came the sheepish driver who came into the house with her; within minutes, she had poured each of them a cup of steaming hot chocolate as they sat upon the chocolate-brown sofa, whereupon they thanked her and both drank gratefully from the white ceramic mugs. Afterward, the driver attempted to go back outside. "Where are you going, Ed?" She, of course, already knew his name. He motioned toward the car. "You're staying here—you can go to another room if Mr. Heimdall prefers a private conversation with me."

The confused driver looked at Robert, who waved the idea away. "He can stay here." Ed sat down obediently, yet tentatively, as if ready to flee this uncomfortable scene at the slightest chance.

"So, Mr. Heimdall, say what you came to say," she stated, emphatically.

Robert, now in the presence of one of his own employees, was more cognizant of his role as superior, and consequently, was more assertive and more certain. "I am genuinely interested in the employment your husband has secured after his—after I let him go; how then has he fared…"

A brief smile of disappointment came to her face as she held her head askew. "We are in a recession, sir, I'm sure you are well aware of it, although your business is not as affected as the employees you fire." She paused. "He works at anything he can—but right now, you might be interested, he is visiting ex-employees of yours." She sat up straight, her face lit up now by pride. "I should like us to visit them, too."

And they departed, but, at her insistence, in her modest, old automobile, and presently they came upon a homeless shelter that was situated at the "perishable and disposable" end of town. "Now, come see the result of your callous handiwork," she said to Robert, and inviting Ed in too, they all entered into the building, with Robert not only feeling foolish and embarrassed and ashamed, but trailing like a worried and frightened schoolboy who has been lured out of his own known and safe element into an unsafe and unknown domain.

"Harley, look who came to visit," she said, upon finding her husband in the midst of this harrowing den of gloom and sorrow—for everywhere there seemed to be misery on the faces of the inhabitants as they sat stooped over while talking or eating, or resting upon sofa, bed or chair; these desperate people who consequently issued unkind and despising looks at the ostentatious wealth that they perceived as spreading so unashamedly and condescendingly before them.

"Eh? It's the King of the city, come to let the little folk touch the hem of his fine garments," one man said, sneering.

"Watch your mouth, you lousy boozer," Edward said to the man, flexing his muscles.

"We don't harass guests," Harley said to the man, as he approached Robert, whom he now looked at, and then frowned. "So, why are you here— could it be because of Chad Castleman?" He saw the astonishment in the eyes of his antagonist. "Yes, that's right—we poor folk network, and we're good at it, too, probably as good as rich folk, but our success is measured in compassion and empathy, and helping each other."

"Let us leave this bitter place, Mr. Heimdall," Edward said, looking about, and now looking at Harley; "this is no place for a real gentleman who truly wants to help."

"Help? You!" Harley said, laughing at Robert. "You've helped too much as it is; look about you: you have five of your ex-employees—and two of them with their families—in just this one shelter; just imagine, five, in just one place; oh, you're a piece of work, a real gem, you are…"

Robert made no reply, for no healthy dialogue could yet exist between two men where ill feelings dwelled so deeply; and so, he drifted among the populace, his mind taking in the terrible lack of proper accommodations that barely satisfied their basic needs; yes, he recognized his other employees, and saw, incredulous to him, their happy children, who were amusing themselves with simple games and silly talk and reading books. He found the manager of the shelter, and inquired as to the length of time and qualifications for one to visit such an unfortunate, but necessary establishment.

"At other times it has been one month, but now it is one week at a time," the woman replied, "but they need to apply, for we have limited room."

He frowned. "But that is absurd," he began, turning around and pointing to the outside, "how can you object to anybody seeking refuge, especially in this cold weather?"

She shook her head. "We need more shelters in the city, but with the budget cuts, I'm sure you are aware of…"

But, as was his nature, he persisted when he happened upon something he considered impractical and easily solved. "And what of those turned away, where do they go…"

She stared at him for a time too long for him not to interpret her simmering and unwavering indignation at all things indulgent and wasteful, and then said, her voice breaking with sorrow, "In whatever they can: cars, abandoned structures, with friends or relatives—and there is always the final resting place, the morgue."

"People freeze to death, here," he whispered, flabbergasted, screwing up his brown eyes, and pointing about, "in this city? I don't believe it—I don't believe we turn away anyone who seeks shelter from…"

But even as he spoke, she handed him a recent newspaper article about statistics concerning the death of homeless people in the last month, twelve in all.

"Are these poor souls mentally ill," he began, "drug addicts, those with criminal records who perhaps cannot gain entry into shelters? There must be reasons for this, someone must know…"

"It is the entire spectrum, sir; yes, some are addicts, some mentally ill, and some with criminal records whom no one will allow in; but not always, no, not always…"

Robert seemed unable to accept such illogical facts, and then said, quite unlike himself as the man of yesterday who cared mostly for business, but more of himself, the man of today, who cared more for the business of people, "Is there nothing one can do?"

She smiled, touched his hand, and said, sincerely, "Yes, you can care, which is good, but many care and do nothing; but to do good, ah, that is where a human being becomes real."

He was taken aback. "Who is she to tell me I am not good," he mused, staring at her; "I am more successful than she," and with this ineffectual and ultimately empty argument, he left with Edward, leaving the wife of the man, who had decided to stay and help, behind, and so they hailed a cab and went back to their car.

Once inside his safe and cozy and warm office, again Robert felt satisfied that he had quenched his desire to know what had haunted him, and so once more turned his attention to the world he knew best, commerce, and its assorted siblings: meetings, deals, acquisitions, bartering, firing, hiring; all those facets that invigorated him because he was the master of this realm.

A week later, sincerely believing he had flushed out the heavy sediment of the unfortunate incident of the suicide and its consequent delay of his duties, he met with a man who, after being notified of his impending termination by human resources, now stood before Robert to plead his case, but surprisingly, with few excuses, and a sincere promise of harder work, as he was lately married and now expressed a fervent desire to evince maturity and responsibility to his beloved bride.

Robert would have summarily dismissed this plea as typical and unmoving and mediocre, but now, for some reason he was not yet privy to, he was susceptible to its basic, emotional content, which before he would have considered fawning, and found himself, unbelievably, saying, "It is the inclusion of a promise to uphold your wedding vows that impress me; so, I will offer you a one-month probation to prove your merit," and then he leaned closer to the now-smiling man, "but do not disappoint your wife," and he lifted up the dismal report on the man's work, "and do not perceive my offer as weakness, as it is more a chance for restitution for mistakes made when we are young and still learning what is important in life." He shook the man's hand, and watched him leave, and mused, "I have now strayed from the good business practice that guides all accessible employers: cast out those who can no longer or will no longer work up to their potential, and I do not know where this is leading me…"

The next day, there were three more workers who had been handed termination papers, and he met them, two men and a woman, and after also giving them a thirty-day grace period, issued them a similar admonition as he had to the man the day before; ten more employees in similar circumstances came in the next week, whom he also offered the same opportunity, at which point he instructed his Head of Personnel to temporarily suspend any more firings of the lowest-performing employees until he could fully determine the justification of leniency toward them. A month hence, he, after closely observing these fourteen men and women at their stations and scrutinizing closely their work, noted they all had improved, except one, who quit on his own.

Months later, he then held a meeting in a warehouse, which many of his employees attended or watched via video, where he announced the temporary suspension of the automatic firing of the lowest-performing ten percent of his employees, and that he would now determine a worker's worth based on teamwork, productivity, punctuality, attitude, and effort. Grievances would be handled at local managerial levels before they reached him; but also, he was now instituting a work pay incentive: more productivity now meant more pay; more profits by the company meant more money for employees; childcare for employees with infants would occur as soon as the rooms were built; and exercise rooms at every plant and warehouse would be built; a five-percent pay increase across the board would take effect immediately; and another week of vacation for all would go into effect at the beginning of the next year. His employees cheered after a sufficient amount of time had elapsed and once they realized he was not being ironic or farcical.

What had occurred to Robert, you may ask, to prompt such radical reforms? He had returned to the homeless shelter a week later to interview all the people there, to find out how, and why, they were there, and how, and why, they were not leaving, and what might have been done to prevent their presence there; he wanted to know if his motto, "no excuses," held true for all, and not just for those who succeeded or failed on their own; he did not find any angelic creatures against whom life had plotted to destroy, nor did he find many lazy malcontents who refused to interact in society and raged against having a job and being responsible and living in a fine house and gladly paying bills and having a life of pleasurable consistency; but, he slowly realized, everyone was not him—he, a man who, if he simply wanted something, instinctively knew the route to take, and once there, took whatever he chose; that people were different in mind and body and spirit from one end of the spectrum to the other: gifted, smart, average, slow, ambitious, gluttonous, willful, meek, angry, happy, lazy, ambitious, misguided, obsessed, but nearly all, despite their varied and often seemingly insuperable differences, desperately yearned for the Good Life—they wanted to fit in and feel wanted and necessary and be part of a harmonious, happy society; but that some of them just needed help and perhaps a little nudge in the right direction as they navigated the many pitfalls along the way. He realized that all of them could not be princes and princesses of the business world, owners, movers and shakers, leaders, that most of them were destined to simply be workers, and that was good enough for them, as long as they could have friends and relations and a warm and safe place to live, and a family to come home to where they were unconditionally loved; this was their ambition, not just to merely survive, but thrive when surrounded by those familiar things and people who would enable them to realize their own human identity and find peace, joy and contentment in this fearful, bewildering world.

He personally visited every homeless shelter in the city—shelters that were too often filthy, bedbug-ridden, and sometimes violent places—offering jobs; and all those employees he had "let go" in the last year, offering jobs, too, to help him make the determination that sometimes a person needs a second chance, and that it was up to people like him, who had the power and money, influences and resources to offer this very important and quite often healer of sorrows. He would never see the world the same way again, as simply consisting of the haves and the have-nots, but through a new lens that asked why not them, why not all, and if not all, why not more—more lifted up not by charity alone, but by being offered another opportunity to succeed on their own and mend their broken lives and learn from their mistakes. But he did decide to abide by one very important notion that he had learned early in life: that one must work to earn one's daily bread; yes, he would offer shelter to those homeless, food to those hungry, and clothes to those in rags, but he would not simply give it away—no good father or mother would simply give money to their child, for they knew, in their adult wisdom, to simply give a child something for nothing was to spoil and allow him to think that this was a generally accepted theme in life—that one had only to hold out one's lazy hand and receive the result of another's hard work and sweat, and in so doing, never learn the value of working to earn an honest wage, so one can then buy and truly own what one possesses, so, yes, Robert would help those in need, but no, he would not allow them to gain what was necessary in life by asking for it and having it easily thrust upon them; so, as it relates to giving succor beyond a temporary aid—as it regards those physically fit and mentally sound—if the homeless wanted to live in a house, they would earn their keep; if they wanted to keep getting food, they would work for it; if they wanted to keep getting decent clothes, they would toil for it; and in this way, he reasoned, they would gain a sense of pride and begin to make their way back to a higher sense of self-esteem.

Later, he was to build more homeless shelters, and install portable toilets and showers throughout the city, create a support program for ex-convicts that would better prepare them for an easier transition from prison life, and finance training to master certain skills and talents that would enable the person to be more marketable, and offer jobs to anyone who would take them, but always with the promise that it was for a hardworking individual, and those who were irresponsible and lazy and malcontents would fall away. But now he was captured by compassion and empathy for those fallen souls around him, as it related to own spiritual awakening, as he now began to see the harm that avarice had done to his soul, that the want of money had separated him from seeing the world as it truly was; and he grieved, for his heart was heavy with the guilt of his selfishness and power-based, wealth-infused paradigm that the strong needs rule the weak; and he became disillusioned with making money simply to satisfy his outsized ambitions, for what was its end, he wondered; by making more money, how am I a better person? Am I a better person because I am wealthy and have more power? It seemed remarkable that he had now condemned his life's goals, but he could not reconcile his current lifestyle with what he now knew was the undeniable truth: that those he fired oftentimes were more alive, more happy, more loved, of more human value than he; that all of the love they felt from their family and relatives and friends was of more value than all of the money he had earned; and he realized that he had assigned human identities to abstract ideas and things, which had been his nourishing family. Once the veil of arrogance that he had deliberately and carefully sewn was thoughtfully removed, he now looked about the world and saw the misery and pain and suffering he had not seen or dismissed as a natural consequence of a misbegotten life while resisting the reality that some live in prosperity, and some in poverty not always of their own choosing; that some would succeed, and some fail; that some would live, and some would die, that it was simply life, and could not be altered—and this was what he had once believed, but as he spent more time away from focusing mainly on profits, and instead investigating the reasons for inequality and injustice that seemed not too terribly far away, but even right next door to him, he began to believe that it did not have to be this way, that many times people were caught up in extraordinary circumstances not of their own making, and as much as he now found satisfaction through helping citizens in his city who needed it, he found too many who simply had a lackadaisical attitude or propensity for drugs or crimes that they could not, or cared not, to properly struggle against; and so he turned his eyes elsewhere, to find those people who, through no fault of their own, had been evicted from a decent life they had fought hard to have, and who were now trapped in a dreadful, pitiable existence of violence and starvation, fear and disease that abused and chained them and oftentimes killed them.

So, one day, after taking several trips abroad and observing firsthand how indigenous people suffered at the hands of cruel and indifferent rulers, and finally realizing that he had allowed himself to be comfortable and content with the upper tier of society, and by doing so, had established a false belief in him that he not only belonged there but deserved to be there, turned over the day-to-day operations of his company to his capable assistants, instructing them to operate his company with his new philosophy intact, and that he would contact them on a regular basis; and then quietly and unceremoniously he joined the Peace Corps, and was soon sent to poor villages in Mexico to work with the local people, at first, teaching them basic business principles and helping them start their own enterprises and providing them with vocational training, and later, simply helping them to lead a better life.

A year later he joined the International Red Cross, and moved to Africa, where he met a young woman named Eleanor Aquitaine, and later, a group of men who had their own idea of how to administer Justice in an unjust world.

Upon his return, he found widespread corruption in the uppermost levels of management in his company, as these men and women, not having a basic understanding of who he really was, had thought him mentally too weak now and ineffectual as a leader, not someone who would be stronger psychologically and spiritually and morally, and intellectually sharper, and better equipped to lead simply because he was now undeniably more of what is considered a decent man; in fact, his company was nearly bankrupt, and after freeing his company of this brood of vipers, he revived it from its last breath, not only by his will alone, but also through the renewed faith and hope in his employees, who enthusiastically welcomed his return; and soon, with their renewed dedication of promise to work harder than ever before, his company became even more profitable and stronger than ever—even as he pursued his philanthropic endeavors here, such as establishing boys' and girls' clubs, where they might learn arts and crafts, play various sports, learn life skills and feel safe; and abroad, in sometimes short, and sometimes long absences, first to Africa, and then to Mexico, to help those select few who had risen up from the teeming masses by electing themselves as necessary to fill a void that was sorely lacking, of those willing to sacrifice all to fight the good fight and restore social equilibrium in the wide world.

A Journey Continued

As he stood in the lobby of the building he worked in, Paul smiled, holding his brown walking stick, gently nodding his round head, his brown eyes gleaming with pride to be with the man he considered above and beyond the intellectual and moral horizon of most men. "He is what all should aspire to be, but do not care to," he often thought about his good friend, "and use their own suffering as their excuse; but it is curious that he uses his own suffering as evidence that virtue needs spread."

"Shall we go for a walk," Robert had asked Paul this day, where it seemed too cold to venture beyond the confines of home and hearth, "and see what we can see?"

The two men, modestly attired, exited through the double glass doors, out to the cement sidewalk of which mostly the common folk partake, at least those enwrapped in the soiled cloak of indigenous lack of everything; and they walked on toward the main artery of town, where the boulevard of dreams was violently ripped apart, like a string of pink pearls, and flung in opposite directions: opulence in one way, as far from the dilapidated and decaying ghetto as the other, and where each player knew his part from birth, having rehearsed it to rote memory; face the center, all ye who are too poor, but not necessarily poor in spirit, and weak in body, but not necessarily weak in heart, proceed down the filthy path that leads to uncertainty, sorrow, and agony; and all who are too rich, but not necessarily rich in spirit, all who art strong and body, but not necessarily strong in heart, proceed wherever thou choose; but thou wilt choose the glittering route with the finer things, and easier ways, and exceeding abundance of opportunity to enrich thy coffers, by stepping on the bent but not bowed bodies of those they consider the dregs of society, and they themselves, the foam of society, if society be a fine wine, by oppressing instead of defending the spirit of their intended victims, and by overwhelming, and invading with lies, and worry and woe, the minds of those they spit upon, and cheat, and collude against with their aristocratic brothers and sisters; and thus, this silent war, unspoken in cold, hard glances, raged on, and fought by one desperate class while the other class never saw past their own brilliant reflection in their highly polished glass and marble towers.

This night was a walk of discovery, a journey the men took often in various parts of town wherein their other offices existed; and this night, they would not walk past at least some souls who appeared in the throes of mortal suffering and pain, and who were many times cut and torn, many times bandaged and repaired, and so many times having sojourned through this endless cycle where all hope seemed lost.

And they were everywhere, too, these lost and disheveled souls, wondering about in the cold periphery of mainstream society, just outside the public conscience, inside that disappearing glance one never seemed to catch and remember; so, drunkards, yes, of drunkards there were many, and mentally ill folk, and users of illicit drugs, and their illicit managers, or suppliers, and pimps in the company of dark shadows, their ever-watchful eye on their high-heeled, well-oiled, walking, talking, Barbie-doll machinery; and the pedestrians walked on by, minding their own business, and the authorities drove on by, minding their own business, amid the shops, the props and the never-changing, ever-emerging, ever-expanding story that is a twenty-four-hour spectacle, the constantly damaged, constantly repaired human circus. Our two friends visited, in succession, first a bag lady, a woman of considerable skill at distancing from herself others with verbal abuse and a smell so foul, one suspected that rotting meat hung from the inside of her long, filthy, mud-colored overcoat; and then, three homeless men, to whom they offered food, clothing and lodging for an honest day's work, but alas, the men turned their suddenly snobbish faces aside and cast a net of anonymity over the two men, who soon moved on. However, they did find success for three homeless veterans, who easily took the Freedom Shelter cards and pocketed them—two of whom would appear, ready for work, the next morning.

The Freedom Shelter was the grand experiment of Robert, a place not just to place citizens who temporarily failed in their quest to live a normal life, or to simply allow those who had failed and attempted to stay clean and sober in various intoxicating substances, but a place where they would be helped to deal with those foibles that had chased them from their warm homes and loving families and onto the cold, mean streets.

Now, as the two men carved a circuitous route through this turbulent sea of despair, the behavior attracted the attention of certain individuals who engage in peculiar economic strategies, namely, panhandlers, but the men merely passed out their beige cards, soliciting shaking heads from these professional and semi-professional and amateur beggars.

"One can never tell who is wearing a false face here," Paul said to Robert; "it is not so difficult in my country—everyone is genuinely impoverished."

Robert had been observing a man and woman who had been scrutinizing them from a safe distance. "Here comes a charade."

Paul anxiously looked up. "You challenge me, eh, Mr. Heimdall?" He smiled. "If I win, you give to my choice of charity. "

"And if I win, Paul?"

"Well," he responded, rubbing his black goatee, "you give to your choice of charity." Robert nodded, and smiled. "You do not," he said, frowning, "think what I'm doing is unkind?"

"No," he said, reassuringly, "this man and woman are like land sharks, and what they're doing is very, very wrong, for it displaces and disguises those who are really in need; and, after all, it is all for a good cause, for our charity."

"I have confidence, now, even though I lost the last two times," he whispered, glancing furtively at the nearing target, and so, he turned and walked swiftly up to the raggedy-dressed man and woman who were about to solicit sympathy and savings from the two friends, but the man had his scripted, imploring verse cut and baked and stuffed down his whiskered gullet by the quick-talking Paul. "Excuse me, sir," Paul began, never once allowing even a whisper of an open from his adversary. "My friend and I are looking for his daughter who was kidnapped three weeks ago, not far from here," and while he spoke stiffly, he held up a card with a picture of a young girl that was computer-generated. "We are offering a reward—two hundred dollars. Well, sir, what do you say—have you seen her?"

"Well, no, but I need—" began the man, wearing his much-practiced face of distress.

"No, no? Could you look again," Paul pressed on, holding up the computer-generated newspaper article about the kidnapping of a girl of a homeless veteran. "We are so desperate—two hundred dollars."

"We just need baby food for..." the woman pleaded, using her most attractive and sympathetic sad face.

"Oh, please, kind lady, could you at least pass around her pictures?" he said, handing them both a picture of the artificial imposter. "And think of all that money—you will share in the reward if someone you give the picture to has seen her."

"Two hundred dollars," the man frowned; "is that all?"

"We gave blood—we did, three times in the last week, each, and we work over at the construction site," and he pointed south, "until they no longer needed us."

"I don't think two hundred dollars will motivate anyone to look for her," the woman said, in earnest.

The countenance of Paul froze. "People will only do a good deed for a certain price? Is this true?" His profound sorrow portended tears.

"Why don't you promise more?" the woman asked, sincerely.

"We don't have more," he returned, nearly weeping, pulling on his thick, curly, black hair; and then he turned away, the sounds of sobbing attacking what little bit of humanity still existed within them. "I'm sorry for taking up your time." He walked away.

"Hey," the man said, with a pained expression, "here."

Paul turned to see two one-dollar bills extended from the hand of the man, and three one-dollar bills from the woman, and by the time Paul reached them, the generosity of the man had reached parity with that of the woman.

An authoritative voice rent the air. "Don't you need that money for baby food?"

The man hesitated, stumbled over his half-formed words, swallowed them back down, regurgitated them up, masticated them and finally said, "Well, no, not now."

The woman was as silent as a shamed child.

Robert spoke again after taking the money from Paul and giving it back to the two charlatans. "Those people, then," he pointed to a man in a wheelchair with no legs, and a woman in a wheelchair who had a missing leg, both of whom had previously accepted an offer of work from him, "find it rather difficult to use deceit to gain monetary sympathy." He watched the embarrassed couple pocket the cash. "When will you begin living a life your children will not be ashamed of?" He and his faithful aide walked away.

"There is a clean water project I have studied," Paul said; "it has authenticity about it—no ambitious plans, scientifically researched, endorsed by the locals and not likely to be abandoned by them, and very practical."

Robert smiled, and nodded his head, making a mental note of it; but then he turned around and saw the man and woman walking away from the man and woman who had been in the wheelchairs, the latter who now each possessed five dollars they did not have previously. Paul saw this too. "It seems that we both won, at least temporarily."

The adventure had just begun.

It is not difficult to find the nucleus of human suffering, for it is a bleeding sore, an oozing, infected cut, a blemish, a stinking wasteland of shameless, drifting, damaged individuals lost in their own shattered ambitions, drowning on dead dreams, suffocating on harsh realities; and when they congregate, as if one growing organism, they are like a rising tide of pollutants that causes all the other swimmers to flee pristine waters.

It is then that the greater mass of society desires this bubbling morass of failure and shame into a bottomless abyss; or perhaps, it is saying, "would that I were a hammer, and they a nail, that I might drive them into the hard ground, forever."

But some did go in, like a chunk of steel to a magnet, to indulge in those parts of their incomplete whole that was defective.

Was it drugs of an illegal nature that the deficient mind needed? They were there, in abundance. Was it the union of tantalizing flesh that was sought? It was, like a busy store, swarming with goods: fat and lean, young and old, healthy and diseased. What did the shaper of pleasures that was deemed illicit by culture and custom need? It was there, it was for sale; whatever the desperate wanted, they would get, for wherever there is a buyer, there too will be a seller.

And who of a noble character, as deemed by culture and customs, would dare trespass into the societal model and even conceive of bringing back at least one of these intemperate citizens who long ago had dissolved their innate barrier of restraint and lowered their moral drawbridge to allow in all kinds of impurities?

Presently, Robert was conversing with certain young ladies, their tantalizing flesh painted, scented, and scantily and provocatively dressed, one here, or by twos, there, whoever would listen and take what they perceived to be merely a small rectangular cream-colored card, but in truth, a life preserver that once grasped would keep their bodies from their sinking-into-the-muck hearts and minds. He was roundly rejected.

He approached a lone female who had distance herself from the other high-heeled, stiletto nightwalkers, far from the view of his recent defeats.

"Good evening, Miss," he began, in a soft and gentle voice, while Paul stood next to him, observing the periphery of this unsettling haunt. "My name is Robert, and this is Paul." He smiled just as if he were addressing a clerk behind a desk.

"So, what's good about it, eh, big boy?" replied the gum-chewing woman, now eyeballing her ready merchandise. "What's up with the formalities? Call me Ginger."

"Good enough, Ginger, may I speak with you?" he asked in the most polite and diffident tone possible.

"Hey, do I look like I'm here for small talk?" She smiled now. "How about you and me, and your man, going to my place for a good time—a little bit of vanilla and fudge?"

"Oh, really," Paul retorted, irritated, "why am I his 'man'—because of a contrasting of skin color?"

"Hey, Nelson Mandela, cool your jets—I was just slanging it," she said, rolling her green eyes, and then looking at Robert, "What about it, boss, just you and me without your lackey?"

Now Paul was indeed indignant. "So, now you have assumed I am his manservant because my skin is black? How arrogant of you! You must think he is my master from the plantation—"

She cut him off with a flick of her bejeweled hand. "Hey, Professor, skip the whining lecture," she said, shaking her black-haired head, and then looking at Robert, "so, it's just you and me; leave Mr. Happy to write those perky greeting cards."

Robert merely smiled. "You must have done well in school."

"So," she whispered, approaching him with that come-hither look, "you want to play school?"

"No, but maybe you should still be in one."

She frowned, halting her bold advance. "Gosh, Dad, where have you been my entire life?" And she shook her head, turned away, and then looked back at him. "Say, are you a cop?" And when she received a negative response, continued, "Well, how about it then, sweetie, do you want me tonight, or do you just want someone to lecture because you're lonely?"

"We have a Freedom Shelter for anyone who needs a refuge—"

"Oh, no, a preacher!" she shouted, cutting him off, exaggerating a look for his religious collar. "And no, I don't need it; so, just go away, I'm busy—I work for a living," and she quickly sauntered off.

"Did God create you so you could give your body to the lusts of men? Is that your destiny here—is there no other life for you?"

Now, she was indignant, and as she turned, her light complexion was crimson rage. "How would you know, huh? Where is your crystal ball? You don't know nothing about our lives out here—what do you know about living a life you don't want?"

Paul stepped from the comfortable shadows, and announced his country of origin, and then said, as if to twist in the knife he had just driven into her psyche, "That's right, Miss, one million dead, no place to run or hide; one million murdered, in a country where my brethren die mostly from starvation and diseases that are cured here by a simple shot of medicine," and despite her most ardent protestations and feigned indifference, he forthwith narrated the worst of the mass murders in the starkest, most unrelenting, graphic language allowable to his good manners; and then said, his face tremulous with anger, "and you dare say you have no choice—there is always a choice when there is more than nothing available." He stood still, staring at her, scorn having bested his normally placid visage. "She isn't worth it; let her self-pity have her." He shook his head. "Americans, and their sense of entitlement…" He walked away.

She looked to Robert. "Why are you," she said, trembling, "harassing me—what have I done to you?"

He looked at her with a countenance of concert with love. "It is the little innocent girl in you who still wants the good life, no matter what horrible things have happened to you, which has called me this beautiful night; it is she I heard weeping, who knows it is never too late."

She shook her head, frowning. "Are you for real?"

He held out the beige card. "Herein lies salvation; you have only to reach out."

There appeared the specter of a tear, having been shared from the hard core of bitterness against this untoward life she imagined. "Will you yet save each and every one of us?"

He fashioned a gentle, knowing smile. "I would be very proud if you were the first."

She wanted to weep, but forced herself to look away. "Well, thank you, really, I will consider that," she whispered, nodding, her voice rent with emotion, looking again at him, and easily taking his card, held it in a tight grip.

He proffered her his loyalty and honor, and then departed with Paul to continue their walk down the boulevard of illusions.

She said, seemingly to no one there, "Who was he?"

The voice in her right ear, the one that came through the tiny earpiece, responded. "Lieutenant Corcoran says he is the real deal—he regularly walks this area trying to rescue society's castaways; he has connections, too, Lola—very powerful."

She was still watching the two men walking away, and she was beginning to weep. "That two would think of others before themselves, in this misbegotten world," she murmured, and then said aloud, "Are we working with his organization?"

"I will personally," the male voice, softened too by hearing the words of the two men, "speak to the Chief about it."

She was sobbing now, and felt enlightened, and illuminated. "There is still a chance even now, when it seems the whole world has given up."

Perils of Youth

"Come on, Mr. Cuchulain, do that again!" cried the children at the city park. "One more time, man! That was bad!" Dylan smiled, looking at Rhiannon, who too smiled, and nodded, and the children, having watched the special exchange, cheered—these children who still believed in the impossibilities of the world, still held fast that magic was real, and to be pursued and gained, if only one truly believed.

Dylan always began a routine with a different feat—this time he fell to the verdant grass in a push-up position and proceeded to propel himself into the air, clap his hands in front of himself and then behind himself and then bring his hand back and clap once more before reaching the ground; then he went to one hand, and then did push-ups—and his audience applauded; he then lifted his body up to a vertical position and performed handstand push-ups, and then with one hand: applause again; he flipped backward and landed on his feet and then flipped forward to his feet and then leaped up so high a large sedan might have driven clear under him, and then landed on his hands and then flipped back to his feet and tore straight at a concrete wall, ran up its entire length, using the corners to gain the twelve foot top, where he briefly stood, then jumped off it and landed gracefully onto the thick green carpet, rolled, leaped up and kicked high into the air as if to kick an importunate fly off a giraffe's ear. He landed, facing his audience, and—more applause, to which he bowed graciously.

Rhiannon smiled proudly.

"It's your turn, Mrs. Cuchulain," the children cheered.

"Yes, I'm no glory hound," Dylan whispered, as he passed by her, smiling playfully, and touched her hand.

She faced the playground, and then bolted toward the swings—and with graceful ease, climbed the slanting steel gray pole; slid, hand over hand, atop the straight bar; and upon reaching the middle, began to move her legs back and forth until she had achieved sufficient momentum to propel herself up and out as she performed a beautiful double somersault and landed neatly on her feet in the deep sand—applause and cheers! She bowed graciously.

She then leaped up out of the sandbox, onto the grass, ran, and began six perfectly executed forward flips until she landed perfectly upon her feet, bounded up, extended her legs and arms, and then landed gracefully, like a softly falling white feather—more applause and wild cheers! She bowed graciously.

She then performed, in tandem with Dylan, martial arts forms of diverse kinds, also using Styrofoam sticks in their routine—more applause and wild cheers! They both bowed graciously.

"Will you teach us that, huh, will you Mr. Cuchulain?" asked Gerald, one of the older boys.

The rest of the boys echoed this in enthusiastic chorus.

"Will you teach us that, huh, will you, Mrs. Cuchulain?" asked Miriam, one of the older girls.

The rest of the girls echoed this in enthusiastic chorus.

"Well, Gerald, I don't know, I will have to ask your mother's permission," Dylan replied, winking at Rhiannon.

"She'll say 'yes,' I know she will," Gerald cried out in delight, as his twelve-year-old mind and body yearned right now for nothing more than to accomplish such astonishing physical maneuvers.

"You'll have to do all of your schoolwork, and be good," Dylan said, somber of mission now.

"I will, I will—I promise!"

"I promise, too," Miriam said, her swarthy countenance still lit by the magical aura of the elegantly symmetrical dance of athletic skills she had just beheld.

"You'll have to do all of your schoolwork—and be good," Rhiannon said, and facing the girls, "all of you." There were five in all.

"Hey, here comes Marvin," one of the boys shouted.

Marvin was indeed coming, walking slowly, a curious, confident walk for such a youngster, but he had earned this walk, every casual, easy step he had earned, like a sculptor that takes her time to perfect each section of a figure carved from solid stone; Marvin had carved every piece of his new self away from his old self with exceeding will and fury, sculpted his new mind and heart with fierce determination to leave behind an outer husk that in its passage on earth was filled with too much sorrow, pain and suffering for one so young to assimilate; thus, by his very iron will, he had done what few older adults do: he had created in his mind a new way of thinking, and reasoning; and in his heart a new way of living and loving; and in his soul a new way to view the world, and sought to bring peace and harmony to it.

Lo, once he had been lost, and now was found; yesterday, he was emotionally crippled, and today, his mind had a crystal acuity; now, he had removed the shackles of inevitability, opposing those who say poverty encumbers you and binds you and makes you; he was no longer bowing to the noisy histrionics of naysayers, soothsayers, charlatans and quacks who spun doom for such youth, its origins being thusly:

He had been a gang member in the making: first, being born into its midst; second, being a mischievious urchin to angry teenager; and third, being a bonafide, eager student of those pedagogues who practiced and promoted in youth the fine art of vice and diverse sin; and so proud and loyal to them was he, that he never once questioned their direction; nay, he boasted about his association with them, and recruited youth of a similar age to join him in their nefarious activities. It was a Friday, a hot, humid day, too hot to be in the direct and glaring power of the sun, and he and his homies, in their low-riding automobile, were following a rival gang member, eager to dispatch him for his ignoble deeds toward them; when the moment came, two of Marvin's older associates quickly disembarked from their grey Chevy, quickly approached the man, who was parked at the curbside in front of his house, and one pulled out a revolver and purposely wounded the man, the other, with a bottle full of alcohol, now lit the rag that proceeded out of it, tossed the bottle into the back seat, and the two of them quickly retreated, where they then joined Marvin from a safe distance to watch the result of their handiwork.

Marvin and his associates were laughing loud and hard at this cruel jest, and when one of them remarked that it was better than they had anticipated because the man's little daughter was in the back seat, Marvin lost his composure, but only briefly, as the riotous mirth of his comrades drowned out any concern he could deliver to the dead and dying before him, he rationalzing that this was war, and Innocents would die. But then, an hysterical woman emerged from the house that sat in front of the car, her baby daughter in her arms, running madly toward the conflagration, screaming like one whose mind was cracked and bleeding sanity; and when she was too close to the orange, sooty flames, and she could recognize the horror of those two trapped inside and now being burned alive, she raised her head toward heaven and let out a wailing cry, and then—then, she threw in her precious baby and jumped inside.

He who had been Marvin, a youth of fourteen years, died.

He felt his sacrosanct soul, one that had been piteously buried in iniquity, now come to life, shuddering in fear for its newborn life; he lost his happy countenance and felt his face grow hard and numb, as if now a heavy millstone were slung around his neck and pulling him into the sinking mire below; his entire being shook as he beheld the horror of Innocent blood shed by those he now perceived as ghouls, and he stepped away from them, first in his heart, and then in his mind, and now physically, as if viewing them from another place, a faraway, protected place where no evil thing might follow; he saw those whom he had formerly called family, still laughing uproariously at what he now knew was wickedess unclothed, wickedness he had helped give life to. Where had he been, he pondered, as he moved further away from these young men whose faces now seeped a sewage of sin, as he heard the blood-curdling screams of the victims in the burning sepulchure; how could he have been companion to them, consoled them when they were sad, worshipped their every deed and word, encouraged them when they sought revenge? And somehow, in some way, he now knew he was no longer one of them, and could never be again, and so, with this virgin insight gained from peering into the grieving soul of sympathy and empathy, he walked away from these now-tranformed alien beings, forever.

Marvin strutted with the assurance of a new man, though he was a mere youth of sixteen.

But he was not just young, but vibrantly so, electrifyingly and optimistically so, that he fairly burst with the fireworks and explosion of unbound enthusiasm for life.

Of course, he came bounding toward them, somersaulting, throwing kicks and punches, and upon entering the kid zone, climbing, somersaulting, flipping, so acrobatically precision-perfect that one would have thought him a lifelong practitioner of such a discipline, and not just a one-year pupil of the Cuchulains.

His black, muscular body glistened in the hot sun as sweat formed upon his tall frame, and when he had finished—applause and cheers, and this time, it also came from his proud mentors.

He was boastful to his adoring audience, but courteous; he was proud, yet humble as he talked to them about how his association with the Cuchulains at the Community Youth Outreach had given him hope and direction.

"I like school now," he said, hoisting one of the children upon his brawny shoulders. "I don't need the 'hood—neighborhood—to determine my identity," and he tapped his barrel chest, saying proudly, "I know who I am," and then, smiling, he took another of the boys on his shoulders and threw him up in the air, only to catch him as if the child were indeed a sack of towels. "And what's your name, smiley?"

"Tommy," the child said, laughing, "but everybody calls me Tommy-Gun 'cause I like guns so much."

A black pall was cast over the festive mood, so felt because the participants herein wanted to be there and wanted to be part of the joy, yet it was not only festive, but authentic, in that it was a sanctuary from what hitherto had been unsaid—that was creeping, like a poisonous fog, animated, like a spreading virus, and capable of injecting a sour mood, like a hard kick to their un-flexed guts, that omnipresent thing which seemed to be looking at all of them with its evil eye from the clutter and cloistered, stuffed together like dressing in a Thanksgiving turkey—that emitted this foul smell and grievous intent by its very untidy, obstinate character because it allowed said formation of hoodlums, criminals, and miscreants to not only exist but flourish; and now the small party was tainted by this unwholesome reminder, and its presence needed to be expunged, like a spreading blob of oil on a virgin lake.

Marvin burst out in a big, wide toothy grin that would cauterize the wound opened up by the innocent remark, as the cleansing had to come from a youth; and as his entire demeanor was heartfelt and genuine, and coming from one who had been there and came back again, rescued by himself first, his hands high in the air, and grabbed by willing rescuers around him, it could little be denied. "Well, Tommy-Gun," he cried, lifting up the smiling youngster onto his shoulders once more, "we're just going to have to change that name to—let's see…how about Tommy-Books, huh?"

"No, no, not books—they're boring," Tommy squealed in delight, as his human ride pranced about the group.

"Well, how about Tommy Champion, 'cause he wants to be the champ at everything he does—basketball, football, track and field, and getting good grades in school," Marvin said.

"Yeah," the boy assented, easily.

"Yeah," the children cried in jubilant chorus.

"How about Tommy the Champ," cheered Rhiannon.

"Hey," Marvin said, enthusiastically, endorsing an idea that was acceptable from an adult, "how about that—Tommy the Champ!" And he tossed the giggling boy into the air.

"Tommy the Champ," the children shouted.

So, this nickname was soon settled, but the other children, naturally, too desired a personal moniker to offset them from the daily news of a crowded life; and soon, all of them had a unique addendum to their name, which was based on a prominent characteristic of them, and these were: Sylvia the Munchkin, because her fifth-grade teacher said she looked like one of the ballerinas from the Wizard of Oz; Derek the Peanut Butter and Jelly Kid, because, well, it was obvious; Latisha the Giggler, due to her merry disposition; and Eduardo the Superhero, due to his desire to be a superhero upon transitioning from child to adulthood—and before that he was willing to be apprentice to Spiderman.

Darkness was soon effacing the light, and the setting of the sun was the universal signal communicated through responsible parent to child that no matter where you were or who you were with, you came home, forthwith; and so, these children departed, after listening to Marvin speak of the magic and wonder of the CYO.

The trio headed toward the business section of town, where Marvin had secured a job in a warehouse during the summer months.

"Mama is so proud of me because I'm working and not hustling," the youth began, as they found the sidewalk and walked slowly along the bustling shops. "My boss needs me to sign some papers and I will start tomorrow morning—my first real job," and he shook his head, looking down, and then looked up at his mentors, "and it feels real good to be at a job where you don't have to watch your back all the time." He smiled, nodded, and then said, slowly, "Dylan and Rhiannon, when you found me last year and I was making one thousand bucks a week running drugs for the gangs, how come I didn't know what I know now? How could I have been so wrong? How have I been able to change? And why haven't other guys like me quit, too?" He shook his large, well-shaped head. "You know, it feels real good, real, real good, to work for a living, and make honest money; that first dollar I'll make will be worth more to me than all that dirty money I ever made—'cause it was all dirty; the people who have to suffer so the gangs can get rich, I mean, it ain't—I mean, it isn't right, no sir, no ma'am, it isn't." His black eyes were misty, but he was young, and could easily repulse such sentimental episodes.

Rhiannon placed her strong yet supple hands upon the lad's shoulders. "You have been reborn in the spirit—that is why the body must obey."

He nodded sheepishly.

"You are able to influence many people around you," Dylan said, in his still-detectable Irish accent.

Marvin nodded again, for he was still in awe of two people who seemed so confident and relaxed about themselves and their great athletic abilities, which his commoner eyes—or few eyes, for that matter—had never beheld, and that such phenomenal warriors as they would humble themselves to work with underprivileged youth and not train the rich and powerful won him over to their side. He felt like he was a small boy walking next to his parents, and wishing, but secretly knowing, that with great dedication he might one day be as strong and brave and true as they were.

Then something ominous with wicked aspirations came thrashing its disruptive spirit into the conversation, to wit: an eardrum-splitting, car-rattling, glass-shattering DJ in a metal carriage came into view, with its smirking crew sporting their arrogant scowls. The leader of this loosely organized group of young adults came out, all decked in the ostentatious fashion of the bawdy night crawlers: white t-shirt; long, golden neck chain; baggy, low-riding pants; hands gesticulating all about; his countenance wrapped up in his pseudo-honor; and spouting street jive and begging for a verbal jousting.

His sneering black face was grave. "Hey, homey," he said, open hand up as he approached his target.

Marvin stood his ground despite the sudden intrusion of this flashy monument to excess and temptation and greed extending its once-tempting leash to him; in point of fact, he stood stone still, much to the displeasure of the self-crowned vassal of the city, so crowned by coercion, chicanery, and crime.

"Yo, man, where is yo manners?"

Marvin stood unimpressed, and when he spoke, it was with wisdom accompanying his words. "Why are you here, Leroy?"

Leroy smiled, looking him up and down, as if he were deciding the boy's fate. "Where have you been, Marvin?"

Marvin stood taller. "You know I don't roll with the Black Hoods anymore."

"Oh yeah, dat's right, y'all don' got educated," he drawled, looking with contempt at the two adults. "The white folk stole you from us, like they always bin doing."

"No one stole anyone from you—I left of my own free will; I didn't sign any contract."

"Wrong, loser—once in, in forever." His three adjutants stepped up next to him, as if to offer a menacing presence. He looked at Dylan and concurrently came to rest directly in front of him, and said in his hardest and meanest tone to him, "Punk—punk thief."

Yet, it was as if Dylan were watching a silly children's cartoon with silly cartoon villains, so unmoved was his smooth countenance.

"I know all about your organization, punk, rescuing neighborhood kids from the scary gangs—ooh," he cried, raising his hands in a mock fright, and then laughing uproariously.

"They don't talk about you, or anything else about gangs," Marvin said, emphatically.

"You'll excuse us," Dylan said, casually, as if he were in complete control of the situation, "we were just leaving."

Leroy blocked his path, akin to a kitten stepping in front of a jaguar to prevent its charge.

Then came a booming command from behind them, "Leroy Roberts!" and the bodies of the four youths jumped.

Everyone there looked up to see a handsome, tall, rugged-looking, mature man striding toward them as if he knew absolutely he would conquer, such were the magnetic coils he threw over them with his solid, determined, iron-forged, silver-encased, gold-stamped will. "What are you up to with these good folks, Mr. Roberts?" Samuel T. Longfellow said, in a voice teetering on play, but tinged with ferocity; and as he approached, he saw his little hyena caught in the majestic stare of the magnificent lion's golden aura, and he became more emboldened. "You aren't bothering them about Marvin, right, Leroy!" he continued, in a probing, digging tone, and as his frightened rabbit froze in response, he then injected a small dose of venom as he shook his large head, as he pursed his lips, as he grunted, "Oh no, tell me I'm wrong—please tell me." And there he was, daddy coming home unexpectedly to find this troubling little boy with his greedy little mind deep down in the brightly colored tin cookie jar—and no one was there to accommodate his ready lies and weeping fits to elude prosecution.

Here was someone who said what he felt as long as he truly believed it was the gospel Truth about how to live a better life, and absolutely did not care what anyone else thought about it.

He towered over these four in physical stature and charisma. "Leroy," he began, smiling, refusing to talk "gang speak" to gain any kind of common ground or respect from this agent of the glorified-in-the-movies 'hood; it was now tête-à-tête, and everyone else, beware. "Are you selling raffle tickets to the policemen's charity ball? It'd better be something innocuous like that, believe me."

Leroy, a.k.a. Crazy, Psycho, Insane, of the 122nd Street Black Hoods, having recovered shreds of his barely perceptible and formed manhood, gathered his nerve, and assumed the low-down posture-scrunch of his slender body, his hands close to his sides, a mean countenance, and appropriate hand gestures, to signify his proper "tough guy" response. "Hey, man," he frowned, heavily, looking around, as if bored, "you ain't my daddy."

"Maybe I should be, Leroy," he said, scowling.

"Man, what's that mean, huh?"

Samuel smiled out of sheer amusement. "You can talk better than that, Leroy; you have been educated."

Leroy cursed, and one that had been soaked in a thick solution of boiling gall and wrath.

The voice of Samuel boomed now like the crack from a hunting rifle. "Hey," and all the gangbangers looked up to the man, "you know I don't tolerate profanity of any kind—especially around women and children; and yes, Marvin is still legally a child." Thus far, this verbal barrage was simply expanding hot breath, until the all-important check for understanding came, and not as a question, but as a command: "Do you understand?" There was a barely perceptible nod of all four of the young men's heads. "Good, good, I know that it's hard work to break bad habits." First came the fine cracks he carved with his abrasive style, then came the genuine bonds he used to fill them in. "Now, Leroy, I'm not mad at you, I'm not; I know you're a good boy, I told your mother and grandmother the same this morning." Then came the first seal. "Your mother is a fine woman, a good woman, who has worked hard to raise her five children—and she is worried about you, so I promised her I would talk to you." Thus came the second healing seal, which started to form in the tiny breaks of wounded and embarrassed pride of the youth. "You wouldn't know it," he continued, winking at the other two mesmerized adults, "but Leroy here is one of the city's finest basketball players." Thus came the hard seal, which nearly filled the entire fissure. "In fact, I have some very good news—Coach Mitchell of LA College wants you to try out for his team." Done: the master brick-builder had repaired the damage he had purposely inflicted—a broken bone healed is stronger than before; but now, a top layer, a hard adhesive, was necessary. "And Junior," he nodded to one of the youths next to him, "and Lester, and Morris, and Tony too," he nodded to them. Now, it was complete—fait accompli.

He was now the master clay-maker, and the clay in the master craftsman's hands had been scarred by the same scars they bore—because he had been raised fatherless as he roamed the streets, had founded the 122nd Street Black Hoods, had been shot three times, stabbed five, hospitalized three, then left the dysfunctional family he had formed; he had played professional football for three years, then quit and joined the military, came out and acquired a Master's degree in Social Psychology, and then dedicated his life to disbanding not only all gangs, but in particular his old one, which had gone national, penal, and altogether bad. Every night he lay awake, crushed by regret, imagining all those Innocents being hurt by the organization he had once been so certain of and loyal to, as certain of and loyal to as he was now of his passionate crusade against them; and no amount of rationalizing—that those youths in his old gang would inevitably have joined another gang—could ameliorate his ever-pounding ache, inner torment, guilt, and incessant shame; he had erred greatly, and so greatly must he labor to undue his error. The law of reciprocity lived within him, like honor come to life.

So, in the community, he had been touched, in that he had sinned, but was now untouchable, in that he had repented, and proffered his blood, sweat, work and tears to all who needed him—and he never turned down a truly contrite citizen; and consequently, most folks—except most politicians—wanted to be near him, as if to be even in the periphery of his powerful, looming shadow brought them some sort of prestige and respect, as if to say: look, I know who is righteous, and humble, this good man, his noble cause; but, was the refrain, why so few?

> We all stand against the rising tide,
> and soon the tide is walled,
> but this tempest swell never falls,
> and soon there is no wall at all;

but perhaps there will be one to stand tall,
against the rising tide.

For too many had stayed too long in the dark shades of iniquity, and now felt the need to purify their souls of this foul stench, this apocalyptic vision, this malignant tumor in the heart of society; and some had so long been in the cold comfort of this mangled image of life that they reasoned their existence decent; they could not discern the slow degradation of virtue around them, so that they had become like frogs in a beaker of water that sits atop a slowly heated burner, who are lulled to a sense of safety and never jump out, and are thus boiled alive.

Are we no better than frogs? whispered those whose minds respect the vulgarity of such hidden analogies.

Samuel knew how these boys thought, and what motivated them and how they schemed to prosper every day, so he could easily—well, maybe not that easily—encircle them and overpower them and set his image between what was seen and not seen, and by doing so, gain acceptance into their artificial world of false pride, false honor, and false family values: because he was what they needed: a father; because he was what he was now to them: a friend who would not betray them; because of who he was and what they aspired to be, whether they knew it or not: a real man, and because of these three, he was not to be turned away from their incomplete healing, which was severed by day and devoured by night, for they yearned for harmony and joy, peace and love, as all people do who cherish and understand the Good Life—these youths may not have been able to articulate such revelations in their minds, but their hearts ultimately recognized a savior, and would not be deterred.

Yet they were still the curling black smoke that came from the consuming, roaring, fire; the fading, easily dispersed, carried-by-the-hot-wind soot and ash that might settle far afield from its instigator; they could be assuaged, they could be captured and cleansed, these youths, but the conflagration that gave them birth, life, and power, this blood-red cauldron in this burning furnace, had a heart inside it, of pure ice—a frozen, growing, jagged chunk with a dagger-tipped core, which burned ever so brightly every day that no one sought to quench its rage.

We are drawn to what is morally good and pleasing to the discerning eye, and in this way assure the species is perpetuated; it flourishes, as order is established; but to do otherwise creates disorder, and the survival of a species is threatened; so, how to consider that which is vile, not simply in the raw—even if a poisonous plant or snake can be classified as such, for they are simply obeying their biological instincts to survive—but by free will, as free as it can be, offered in a world compromised by willing villainy, who seek the collapse of innocence; who do the vile congregate with, and what is the origin of their altered state, and what should be done with them, and when, and for how long, and how many times must we judge them? Do these vile creatures—by nature or design—understand who they are and what they once were, if ever they were different, or might be, or could be, or should be? Do they know if they are right or wrong, and why they are the hunted, the shunned, and the shame of a free society? These are the naked questions Samuel Longfellow asked himself; even in his dreams, he was haunted by the specter of why the world is so cursed, why he had been a willing partner in its moral dissolution, why he had once abandoned it, and why others had never given up the good fight.

And so, when he drove behind the four 122nd Street Black Hoods to their home base, and exited his car, and walked up to the dozens of angry-looking young men staring at him as if they wished to tear his body apart limb by limb and feed it to their ferocious dogs, he wondered why he had to make this hard pilgrimage so often and alone; yet, he knew he was not truly alone, as long as good citizens such as the Cuchulains joined in the eternal struggle. He smiled, and thought, "And Robert and Paul, too."

He walked up to the present leader of one of the most feared gangs in East Los Angeles, and knew he was not alone, and felt confident that no matter what happened to him, others would take his place, because what was before him was a severe displacement in the time warp continuum of a democratic society, and for society to go forward and the good Earth to spin gently on its axis, this rift, he knew, must be constantly healing.

And he was truly not afraid as he strode straight into the lions' den.

Parallel Universe

Flesh and blood, muscle and bone,
of man is made, his upright home;
heart and soul, mind and spirit,
of man is formed, from a sacred script.

Seeking Nature's sceptered crown,
no loyalty or love, no honor, bound;
Man blindly tills the fertile ground,
planting seeds in a rising mound;

By greed and lust, he beguiles
towns increase by his crafty wiles
no paradise this, no idyllic isle:
rubbish deeds, in a rubbish pile.

What is land, this outer layer of our humble planet; what is it but dirt, and rock, soil and sand, plants, animals and insects, laying out its outer crust in one continuous spherical path, and life flourishes therein, atop this fifty-seven-million-square-mile life raft that floats atop a roiling, boiling, steaming lake of bubbling fire; and the other planets bowed before it, for they saw within themselves a sterile womb of ice or heat, and loneliness swept over them as they gazed upon the good green and blue planet; and the gas giants admired her stately glow and knew it outshone even their internal nuclear fission, for even one gram of pure organic life ranks higher than all the combined inorganic elements in the universe; yea, even a microscopic amoeba is mightier than them all—mightier than all the stars and planets, comets and meteors, dark energy and dark matter combined; and a small, living seed is so vast in importance and nobility, that its very presence is more precious than any molecule and atom that inhabits a lifeless palace of empty black space.

How much more than, in importance, in its essence, is an entire planet that is covered with diverse life-forms, trillions of living things, billions of different species, nursed by their white mother as they bathe in crystal-blue and green water and frolic on fresh, virgin land, and gracefully soar in a deep cerulean sky; how can its presence be measured—by what mere scale, a solar scale, a galactic scale, a universal scale, and perhaps, one may even consider a Godly scale.

And then Man comes, arrogant, selfish Man, whose every charging footstep is for his own ambition, his every cunning thought for his own needs, his every lustful deed for his own edification—ambition moves mountains, but this ambition is for more wealth; his needs must be met, but so too must his neighbors'; edification separates us from the animals, but it must, in its end, benefit others; grandiloquence has become Man; foolishness becomes Man; war becomes Man, because Man will not relent, will not be satisfied, will not be content. He spears his own equanimity with his uninterrupted, never-ending quest for more.

> The land is barren; the land is bleak;
> the land is weathering; Man grows weak;
> the land turns fruitful; the land gives life;
> the land is reborn, and so is Man

> Land needs no harvester, no maid or serf,
> no master or Lord to tend its turf;
> no thought or reason is needed here,
> its internal design, planted there.

The Golden Eagle does not cogitate upon its own actions, but obeys its own instinct; so, too, the White-Spotted Owl, the Bottle-Nosed Porpoise, the Monarch Butterfly, the Honeybee, the mighty Cypress tree; and some live, and some die, while others wither, and others magnify, but always, there is balance, a delicate ecosystem that has developed due to its complex, interwoven relations, there; trespassers will destroy us, reads a sign constructed by a species who might suddenly acquire thought, here.

But Man brings his own sign, in different languages, and plants it here and there, for different reasons, by different races, for one, a few, for many, for a nation, and no two signs are alike; in one forest, one man builds a home, in another, a family builds a farm, and in still another, a man builds a ranch, an empire, and other men come to live there; and so a school is built, a church, too, and soon a grocery store, a hotel, a bank, a restaurant; a doctor comes, and a lawman, and after all the players in the town are in their proper roles, a town is born; but the town grows, and more people arrive, and progress comes, and more homes are built, and sold, and one day the town is a city, which is within a county, within a state, within a country, within a hemisphere, within the Earth, within the solar system, within the Milky Way, within the universe.

The land is its own sovereign, its own master, and lord; it needs no owner, no guide, no overseer; one man opines you can't own it, and moves with the seasons from place to place; another man opines you can own it, and walls off a space, and now these two men quarrel; but the land cannot be bought, or sold, be rented or in bondage, for it is free, like the air; it is sovereign, like the water; it owns nothing to anyone; it cannot be altered or destroyed, just like sister water cannot; it cannot be captured or killed, just like brother air cannot, for the land and the sea and the air are one; no man would dare declare he owns this air, or this water, or this land, forever, for the land, water and air cannot be contained, and slips through the desperate fingers that hold them; neither can they be captured, just like time cannot; Man may chop them and bottle them and eat them, and desecrate them, befoul them, beat them and scrape them and redress them, and murder them, but they will rise again and carry on again and rejuvenate once more, and Man will never understand his folly and never stop trying to permanently conquer that which cannot be conquered—Creation.

There is a small patch of black soil. It exists independent of the rest of the world. It neither cries or quakes, begs or borrows, for it is complete, as all of its biological needs are generally met; sunlight, water, abundant soil, and freedom to grow. It needs no admirers; it is its own joy and triumph, ruler of its self—sovereign; left alone, it will live forever in this tranquil garden; it is part of a perfect union of animate and inanimate objects, part of the perfect arrangement of inorganic and organic, part of the perfection of Creation, unspoiled, untamed, undisturbed, a golden aura without blemish.

Then comes Man, who does not understand the delicate rhythm and cycle of harmony, and does not honor the delicate gossamer threads that hold together equilibrium, nor the delicate, explicit dialogue of Nature he must listen to and obey, or he will destroy himself and Nature; so, he plunders, he foils, he churns, for his own will, not for the will of all, and does not see that toiling in league with the subtle vicissitudes of Nature will bring vitality and robustness to all; he breaks things down that should be left standing, he does not repair what should be fixed, he abandons things that should never be left alone. Man, who is the usurper, the slayer, the coming storm: will he stay after his dissolution of perfection; will he ever know what damage he has done, or will he care? O Man—who should be as sensitive to his environment as if every movement is like a velvety-soft rose petal against his bare thigh— should stop and observe the carnage therein, and seek to repair or restore it, but plainly ignores it. The challenge of Man is to see how far he will go to achieve his own goals; how much damage will he create in a paradise where he dares exceed the natural boundaries in the pursuit of living a life of excess: does he care that seeking a grandiose life means the earth will feel his dagger plunging into its trusting bosom?

Man, that great harbinger of reason and riot, has conquered that which seems not to struggle against him, but is always struggling to regain that which he has lost: equilibrium, that Nature has already brought through an infinite number of ever-changing variables and constants, and through symbiosis and natural selection.

So, one man drives a wooden stake into the soft belly of the moist earth and it easily swallows it and grows around it and absorbs it; and the man abides there until his nomadic spirit chases him onward; and another comes, and pulls out the stake and puts in his own; and so this goes on for centuries, until the ground has swept over the claim of the first man with its wandering minstrels: leaves, dirt, rocks, insects, animals, and as they lay upon it, the plants fall on it with their bright, multicolored bodies, and now layer upon layer forms, even as another man drives a new steel stake into the spot where before stood his savage ancestors; and then more men come, and more, and then some who say you cannot own the land, and when they come back to visit their spiritual grounds, invaders, like virulent weeds, have come; and battles occur, and wars break out; and when this is settled, more men come and stake out more of the land, and build upon it magnificent buildings in which they will dwell; and years pass, and these men think this claim shall be etched forever in the heavens and carved in stone to be witnessed by all who dare trespass.

But the precious land beneath our restless feet is our sacrosanct bond and we fight to stay on it, and fight for more of it; the land is power, and can be secured without education, election, or by eloquent enunciation, but by mere force, and so that which the inhabitants thought was permanent was only temporary, as they flee to the faraway, rolling hills and look back at the swarming bands of looters and sackers.

And so it goes on, like this, ad infinitum, and as history records each bloody year—like a tree ring around its stout, fibrous waist—more of what was is covered up by more of what is, and what is easily erases the memory of what might have been forever, into fragments now, slivers of life, lost bits of a civilization floating in the torrid wind, down in deep, verdant valleys, in rushing, silver streams that empty into the crystal, glimmering-blue-and-green, vast ocean; gone, gone, forever gone, to be reassembled into countless shapes and sizes, filtered, reformed, redistributed, to be taken up by a new life, a new civilization, that will now hold up this new treasure and ask its exclusive and very private supernatural being to bless it and them; and so the cycle continues, yet each succeeding generation reasons it is the Almighty Creator of it all, the beginning and end, lord and protector, who will thrive for eternity.

And then another usurper comes and slashes and cuts and burns the once seemingly indomitable empire to soot and ashes and rubble, and too come the long-ago stories to be told by scattered and lost peoples for posterity.

So, now it is present day, and thus, is it possible that whoever is strongest enough to hold the land, gets the land? If this is not so, then, presently, whose land is it? Does it belong to those who lived on it thousands of years ago? Are they not dead? Is it a legal gift of passage—the ancestors of those long-ago owners now get the land? Who are they? And what of those who legally paid for it today? Is there a government involved? Did one nation conquer another to take the land? But once the war is over, to the victor goes the spoils, and if the vanquished wants the land back, they may seek it, and redress any wrongs they felt; this is, after all, how wars sometimes begin.

Imagine a house, with a family of six living inside its stone walls; one day, a family of seven comes along and evicts the family of six, and in so doing, they hurt some of the family of six; now, the family of seven begins its squatting reign, until a family of eight comes along and evicts them, and perhaps, in doing so, even kills some of the family of seven. This unfortunate history goes on for a considerable length of time.

After several generations, relatives of the first family knock on the door of this durable house and demand not only that the current owner vacate the premises but that it redresses any wrongs done to their ancestors; of course, the door is probably shut after an abrupt goodbye, for logic and reason have no acquaintance, and are no bedfellows with incoherence and insanity; thus, it is established: if wrongs need to be redressed, only the living offender may recompense the living offended.

And as for the analogy of the house as land, this maxim is hereby established: whoever is strongest enough to hold the land gets the land. There is no other logical recourse.

So, here we are in the present day on land that has had too many owners to record—and, after all, they are all dead, and their ancestors' ashes scattered to the four winds, like an angel's white puffy hair on a steady stream of hot air, and are, as we now know, not to be part of the present equation.

There is a neighborhood. It is like most other neighborhoods in this Western state, composed mainly of small, humble, well-kept tract homes, stretching for a few miles in either direction; during the day, it is reasonably quiet, as the elderly enjoy their sunset years, as the young mothers play with their children inside their small, gated front yards. There is not much worry now, for the scary Beast is still at bay, and the residents understand that he mainly prowls about at night, seeking his victims. The more intense the light, the brighter its beam, the more effulgent its glare, the more it empties the streets of human vermin; but once this incandescent fuse dims, once the sun turns her shining visage away, the land becomes littered with speckles and stripes of shadowy darkness, little dots and dashes, sprays of clustered darkness, tiny flecks and flakes, zealous fronds and frills of darkness descend, as disheartened light climbs into her comfortable bed, and obscurity releases her eager children, fog and fugue, injected like malevolent germs into a healthy bloodstream. The stage is set, the uncouth characters well rehearsed with their freely chosen lines, which state thus: this is our territory, we defend it from all invaders, both foreign and domestic; but they don't really mean it, no, they mean to murder anyone not like them, and that is all.

Now, these pseudo-soldiers have not asked the permission of other residents for their agreement to this bold proclamation; no quorum has been called, no forum announced, no town meetings held to discuss this violent initiative, this nasty proposition, where a few dictate an edict to the many, where they have fully embraced the newly formed maxim: whoever is strongest enough to hold the land gets the land. But they are in grave error, for the land is not theirs to hold, or represent—they are not a duly elected representative body, nor have they legally purchased it—for they have elected merely themselves rulers where they patrol the land like soldiers, act like soldiers, think like soldiers in their undeclared war; in patrolling their area, they form groups, and desire to protect their own territory; in acting it, they have their own unique language and dress and ranking to identify each other; in thinking it, they are ruthless, and take few prisoners. And sometimes, as in all wars, they kill Innocents, but in this war, they do not seem to possess a conscience about such catastrophes—for they are a new breed of warrior-criminal who heeds no universal, natural, or international laws, for they are a law unto themselves.

And in the city where this neighborhood exists, there are more than one thousand such pseudo-soldier confederations, mostly antagonistic to each other and worried about their own territories while vying for control of others, all antagonistic toward accepted and legally recognized authority groups, who, incidentally, wage their own frustratingly curbed, hemmed-in-by-soft-laws battles against these self-proclaimed warriors of the street.

Here comes a man, boldly, into this heart of darkness, into these border war, where exists darkness of heart, mind, and soul; he hath no fear, for peace and harmony resideth upon his broad shoulders—shoulders as wide as a Golden Eagle's wing span; peace like a white dove descended from the heavens with the green, ripe twig of hope and promise; and harmony like a beautifully written, beautifully orchestrated melody. He never once imagined a saboteur lurking behind him, or guns trained on him; never worried that young men threw their hard stares at him like sharp knives, for these mere reflections could not touch a man who had full faith in who he was and what he was doing and what he planned to do; for he had long ago and bravely confessed his sins and prayed for forgiveness, and for guidance to right his wrongs and to clear away the thorny bramble he had once planted in earnest; and to do now what he must, he feared no evil, for he considered the good he did was a shield, and if he were to die, then he would die righteously, and blameless, in the struggle at the appointed hour.

Samuel Longfellow walked up to the main gathering place of the 122nd Street Black Hoods as easily and relaxed as you and I would do when we walk along a fragrant path of blossoming flowers and abundant trees wherein no detectable harm lies, but peace, love, and joy reign.

The man who stepped out to meet him was the leader of the youths, as all of his subordinates about him, as he shook the hands of the founder, gazed on in intense wonder to see how he, without whom there would be no brotherhood, no family affiliation, would interact with he whom they now obeyed without question and with undying loyalty, especially since the two men were generally regarded in the community as two who were unstoppable, unmovable, and unshakable, and absolutely opposed to each other philosophically, morally, spiritually, and in every other measurable intellectual and ethical discipline; and here is where the magic of language transformation occurred: where before, only moments ago, the leader, designated by his homeboy scholars as the blood king, was engaged in the following conversation with his adjutants: "Yo, cuz, s'up? Ya know I be chillin' las night wit' my bloodette—you know we wuz rapping 'bout our homey we be bringing home las' night—man, dat was tight—beatin' and kickin' 'em, and all the time he took like a man," he had smiled, waving his muscular arms about, "yo, man, we got ourselves some mo' Gs, after we cap dem weak," and he proceeded to bathe his conveniently absent prey with venomous language that promised to cleft them in twain, burn them alive, and then scatter their ashes to the slimy gutter, and he had finally finished, "you know what I'm saying?"

When Samuel came upon the intimate gathering, it was not unlike the hunter-farmer stumbling upon the house-of-chickens-raiding foxes.

The youths stood still, moving closer together, becoming silent, cautious, offering their mean countenance to a man who, if they had known what such childish-amateur antics really meant to him, would have done it anyway; it was all they knew, the official posturing on the street, just like in the wild, when a threat is unknown or perceived.

Samuel saw the youths as mere youths, children, wearing grown-up masks, playing with grown-up toys that got them into grown-up trouble; and forthwith, he shook the hand of every youth there, saying the name of each one, sure to say something genuinely positive about them, something not hard, something not drenched in blood, not something that could be balanced on the head of a knife, a gun, or a needle; for he saw the boys as collected on the tip of a thick, yellow match head, each boy one flake of gunpowder, and when the match met friction created by their bad behavior, the first boy was lit up, and he, in turn, lit up his fellows, and so on, until the entire group was a choir of roaring, orange conflagration, and he, the cool liquid, stable staff that stood between them.

The two leaders walked out into the smoky veil of night. Samuel spoke first. "So, Tyrone, how is your mother?"

"Fine, sir," answered one of the most feared gang member-leaders in South-East Los Angeles, with utmost respect and admiration, and mildness, too, as if he were indeed talking to his father, whom he might as well have been talking to.

Tyrone's real father had never existed—only a mother, a hard-working mother who had worked two jobs for twenty years; her life had begun every day the moment she woke up at four-thirty in the a.m. to do household chores and prepare a breakfast for her two little boys and pack their lunches, kiss her little angels goodbye, walk them to her sister's house near the bus stop in the still-early cold dawn at five-thirty, and then journey one hour to her cleaning job, where she labored unceasingly until one-thirty in the p.m., at which point she took the bus home, picked up her children from school, walked them home, prepared snacks and dinner for them, got them started on their homework, and instructed them to "under any circumstances, never answer the door, until your Auntie comes over to over to get you." And then she would kiss them goodbye, walk to the bus pickup spot, ride that same downtown LA commuter, propane-fueled, white bus to her next cleaning job, where she would toil from four-thirty in the p.m. to nine o'clock in the p.m., and then take the same roundabout bus back home, creep quietly into her precious boys' room, pray over them, and then thank God that this family had survived another day; kiss them goodnight, go to the kitchen, eat a very light dinner, read her Bible, and watch some television, as the beaten-down woman fell asleep on the beaten-up, old, brown, sagging sofa.

And then she awoke at four-thirty in the a.m. the next day and the cycle began all over again; but she survived, and her boys survived, and thus far had beaten the intrusive system—all by herself, with no help from any dead-beat husband or handouts from the intrusive government, or keep-you-on-a-short-leash, know-it-all, contrarian-spewing, nosy relatives; she, a single black woman took on the whole wide world, which daily seemed to want to crush her, to place its big, black, iron boot upon her slender neck and push her into the hard ground and coerce a confession that she had failed, was a bad mother, a dangerous mother, a helpless victim of a broken system that demanded she pull out her lithe hands and beg for mercy and succor—but she had said, no, most emphatically, most undeniably, most spectacularly, no, not me, not this proud, young, uneducated woman who, yes, had become pregnant at age fifteen, but somehow had managed to raise the baby, and find another man—even though he soon abandoned her even when he knew she was pregnant with his own child; and then she had moved on, got these jobs, and got by; yes, she had fooled them, fooled them all, and felt as if she had been living this hard life for decades, an old woman locked into an endless routine of despair and hard labor, slowly whittled away by the pressures of every burden in the world on her small, delicate shoulders, her mind and body and spirit slowly being swallowed whole by this unseen, malevolent pred-ator that sunk its sharp talons into the infirm, the weak, the elderly of the swarming human herd—talons sharpened by every wrong move, every wrong action, behavior and emotion of its unwilling victims; and as she battled every day just to survive, at the end of the night she felt as if she had been through a long, drawn-out, vicious war, and she considered her failing strength, and reasoned she could not go on; but she would think of her small boys, her beautiful boys, her precious sons who gave her the will to live, to carry on, to stand up and be counted, to shout out, "I am here, me, little Tonya Simpson, and I will not give up, or go away, no, never; I will be strong for my boys, for them I will fight on, because they need that chance in this mean ol' world to grow up straight and true, and be somebody other than another dead-on-the-street-as-a-result-of-violence black youth—not my boys!" And then, only then would she feel herself being lifted out of this heavy malaise, out of the slimy, hard grip of the creeper, death, that increased when it sensed fear and weakness, and moved herself toward the resplendent light and the fresh, clean air, and finally, to touch the good green earth and by her own weighty resolve, pull herself clear from this dark abyss to stand tall and proud, and say, "I have survived another day, world—I have; one more day I win, and you lose, and my boys are safe once again, and nothing, nothing will ever stop me from what I know I must do, because it is the right thing to do, and as long as I do that, I am not ashamed, I am not hesitant, I am not sorry; and I am blameless." So, this was the secret to her success, that she woke and considered every day a brand-new day and a day to be fought and overcome and conquered like any other common enemy; for the past was past, the future unknown, and the present, everything that mattered—because she could see it, feel it, smell it, taste it, hear it, and if, she reasoned, as long as she could use her clear senses, she would never lose the prize that she held daily in her loving arms.

And she was only twenty-two years of age, then.

Samuel was walking along a well-trodden path with Tyrone now, one that led past the ascribed boundaries of the 122nd Street Black Hoods territory, and finally to the border, an artificial line as in any city, county, state or national border—and subject to change without any prior notice—where a new regime began: the Original Gangbangers, and where every pair of eyes, be it of a child, woman, or man, was an evil augury that purged the sensible mind of a rival gang; for it was the very potential of any connection between citizen and gangbanger, or gangbanger to gangbanger, which was the vital juice that fueled paranoia, and from this, sprung conflict—violence—the wellspring of their power.

The further afield of the electrified power grid that Tyrone's homies dwelled, the more his demeanor softened, and his defiant and violent posture began to wilt; this truth was held as long as his agile form drifted from the universal ideas of what a gang is, the natural idea of who or why it exists, toward the universal model of Nature, where the unnatural has no ready fortress and plenty of enemies, even though there are also plenty who will, even in the bosom of the wilderness, pervert the natural—it is not an elixir, a panacea for all of society's ills—but in this boiling cauldron, wherein too many reside within too narrow a living quarter, there are few chances to separate those who would thrive or those who would not, had they the chance to live in harmony with Nature. What we have now, though, is the hardening of his resolve, the stiffening of his thick neck, the screwing up of his coal-black eyes, his senses sharp as if he had entered a dark forest of predators, as indeed he had, for he had just crossed over into another sphere of influence, wherein the beast of a different stripe roamed.

Marshaun de Thompson, leader of the Original Gangbangers, boasting a membership of over one thousand strong, stood alone, wearing a steel mask of insolence and enmity, layered over the bitter years, riveted down through bitter tears, signed, sealed and delivered onto a hard-core platform that shouted, "Death to outsiders: no mercy, no rules, no forgiveness—and no regrets." It was a conscience not only subdued, but altered, baked and set in a hard cast that rewired the brain into a constant battle mode, although there was no palpable war raging; yet it was a self-imposed, self-made paradigm, even though every contextual clue around him offered the antithesis of his newly formed doctrine of apathy, hatred, and violence.

He fancied himself a human weapon, a living arsenal, a gun of muscle, blood and bone that had no emotions as it delivered its wicked cargo to its victims; he was cold steel inside his drone-like appearance, programed only for murder, mayhem, and mob rule, and he was your neighbor, the man next in line at the store, the one in the car beside you, the person passing you on the sidewalk; and what you never knew was that one wrong move, a tiny variation of an acceptable facial feature, and errant emotional outburst, the tiniest puff of outrage, the black smoke unfurling from your indignant mark—however brief, however fleeting its impact, even followed immediately by contrition, proffering brotherhood, an extension of a hand, genuine sorrow, regret, asking for forgiveness, it was already over for you, for he had marked you forever as one not worthy of life; but why, you ask, why? What had you done to deserve this burning death wreath tied around your neck? You had, simply, socially, grazed against the one who saw himself as a true lord, a king, a ruler of not only his own domain, but of all in his puny sphere of influence; by offending his highness, you were marking yourself as a future victim of a shooting, a stabbing, a vicious beating, because you had violated a law he had created from dust, from rot, from the fossilized ash and dung of long-dead totalitarian regimes, long-dead dictators who had ruled with a beast's merciless nature, an integrated system that existed only in uncivilized places, a way of thinking supposed to be quashed, sanitized and burned-out by modern living and natural human rights, that were presumably to spread with technology, like a soothing elixir, to all parts of the still-savage corners of the world; but it still existed here, this ancient philosophy of retribution and revenge against a misinterpreted glance, act, or behavior, and once vengeance set its sharpened teeth upon its victim, it was unrelenting; so, he was a red-eyed, ravenous wolf among sheep when there was no need anymore for the wolf to hurt them, as the wolf long ago had become extinct through connection of histories and stories and exchange of information around the globe, but the wolf could not be satisfied, and thought he still needed to set an example to keep those in line he thought deserved to be under his long, dark shadow—just as it was once practiced in the old and disturbing South.

"Yo, what up?" Marshaun said, in a deep voice, his practiced-to-perfection, mean-posture set, his demeanor hard, his words even harder. "You come to beg for mercy, or what…"

He might as well have pulled out a large stick and smacked Tyrone across his close-cropped, curly, black-haired, round head; now, it is a fact that youth such as Tyrone, the rich spices of angst and bitterness flowing like a mighty stream in their still young and plastic arteries, will emotionally combust faster than the time between the beats of a hummingbird's wings. Was this profile present when Tyrone was five years old: an innocent lad in kindergarten, full of life and excited by not only every new, precious letter of the alphabet he learned, but especially by "T?" This must come back as a resounding "no." Would he, that he lived so long, even to eighty years old, be so inclined to such emotional volatility? Again, there must be entered into the record a resounding "no." It was the perilous growing-up years in which blossoming youth gets lost, and turned around, and thus pursues the wrong path, where Samuel sought to either set them on the right path from the beginning, or turn them around now, no matter how hard the turn, no matter how many the attempts to nurture them along the tried-and-true, forged-in-trial-and-error road to the Good Life; to keep the youth out of harm's way until they reached their thirties and forties, when Samuel knew that most men who had practiced a life of sordid adventures began to naturally mellow, when their hyper-violent, hyper-aware lifestyle was tempered, when they thought more of raising a family and safeguarding them from people like their former, violent selves, was his goal; and as for Marshaun, well, he had been violent as a five-year-old, and his hysteria was to claim this ultraviolent feeling as righteous, just as someone might feel compelled to declare their gentle and peace-loving ways as righteous and even universally sought after, to achieve harmony and balance in this ruptured, unclean womb called life; Samuel knew that for this youth, it was like chasing a lit fuse—lit on both ends, and both traveling unimpeded and gaining momentum en route to large kegs of black gunpowder.

It is hard to keep apart that which feigns to embrace its polar opposite with all its fiery-hot blood and tempestuous soul.

Samuel Longfellow, however, had a unique feature, hitherto unknown to those youths, in that he was an authentic man, a big man, a huge man of great physical stature who could manipulate any youth such as these with a simple redirection of his muscular arms—like 150 mm howitzer cannons they seemed to an ordinary man, and hands that were so exceptionally large, any ordinary man's puny hand might have looked like a mere children's hand as it lay meekly against it; even among mature men he was like a giant, among big men he was still a breed apart, an evolutionary upgrade, a species separated by superior genetics; where for some men, genius or heroism made them like gods to the ignorant masses, he was a solid mountain of finely chiseled sinew that towered over, shadowed over nearly all mortal men. He had put his innate talent to use in his football career: an All-American in college all four years, and all Pro for his brief tenure in professional football, and then walked away from the fame and the money and the women and the glory, because he believed he needed to do more for the world; and then excelled in the Special Forces unit in the Army, and once he left, he continued his quest to find something that would satisfy his searching soul to give back and recompense even more to a world he had offended.

An inferior man, a man born of the rank of the physically average, when in the looming presence of a physically greater man, when he feels one hand from this behemoth upon his chest—no matter his chiseled pride, his muscles built from pushing heavy weights, he is still inferior, for no amount of post-birth strength training can ever match the DNA supreme structure of a true iron man—will naturally defer and relax any attempted forward motion. But Samuel performed this feat for both youths, simultaneously, and subsequently, they yielded, to this supernatural force before them.

He knew no words could soothe their raging fire, no calm words could assuage their wrath, no magical, script-ready, Hollywood-produced, grandiloquent, smooth-as-flowing water speech would turn their violent tide; so, he talked not to them, but about others, to let a small bit of light break through their callous exterior. He first cast his intense glare upon Marshaun, and held up a black and white photo of an infant hooked up to various medical instruments. "Marshaun, tell your brave gangbangers that when they shoot a child, they must make sure the child is dead, and not in critical condition, and expected to die soon—paying medical bills is not as easy as selling crack. Most people work and earn an honest day's wage."

"Man, we ain't killing no baby," he replied, frowning, moving his hands about the way he had been taught by his teachers on the street, as if to portray outrage and innocence.

"Really? Your little fleet of killers didn't shoot fifty-seven bullets at Tyrone's boys last week—and of course, they missed, as people do who just want to shoot at an object and don't care where the missed bullets go—and instead killed a mother and wounded the baby?"

"Nope," he returned, disgusted.

"How about that, Tyrone," he said, looking up upon the meek youth; "is there truth in Marshaun's response?"

"No," Tyrone said, feeling empowered, turning his head aside to evince his apathy.

"So, he shot at your loyal posse?" And when he received a positive reply, he continued, "When you were cruising where he lives—which is not his neighborhood, by the way; it is not his," and he looked to Marshaun, and then back to Tyrone, "and where you live isn't yours, either, any more than it is the social worker's who lives down the lane—so, you admit your homeboys were there, and were flashing signs, Tyrone?"

"Don't know; I ain't their daddy."

"Really? Because both of you seem to think you're their daddy, and more than that—their leader." His gaze was such that the two youths were held fast by it. "Let me tell you something, children—and that is what you are, children, until you do what a man needs to do: live a decent, honorable and responsible life."

"Man, why you always dissing on us?" Marshaun whined.

"Because you need it—and stop talking like you're a no-good, dumb, ignorant slave, which is what you are, by the way, as long as you talk and act this way; both of you think you're so smart, so free, so brave, when in reality, you're building chains and shackles around your feet and hands every time you pull that trigger or order someone to do the same; man, you two don't deserve freedom—you would be better off being slaves—at least, when your ancestors were slaves, they were better people, a more honorable people, a prouder people; if they could see what the black man has become after emancipation, they would clap irons on you in a heartbeat."

"Man, that be dumb," Tyrone said, sour faced. "I ain't never gonna be no slave."

"You will die in prison or on the streets, either way, serving your master."

"Man, that's messed up," Marshaun replied, his head bobbing up and down.

"Tell me how you help the community—go ahead," Samuel demanded, and not softly, either, not like a man attempting to negotiate out of fear, or weakness, nor attempting to pacify or reason first, but from a position of towering strength that was built on a foundation of eternal Truths that stung the corrupt soul. "Let me ask you something, Marshaun—yes, answer this—do you love thy neighbor; do you? Do you love your community?"

"Man, I love my homies—and that's all," he shouted, defiant. "They're all I need."

"Really?" He nodded as this information fed its disturbing images to him. "So, who are we to you?"

He held up his fingers, his comely black face shining with savagery and pride, and robbing them together, he said, "Green, man, green."

"And what about your family? Why are they to be protected, if the rest of us are just here for your pleasure?"

"'Cause I'm me," he cried, standing erect now, his voice sharp with wrath, banging his chest, "and I'm strong—and you're you," he thrust his pointed hand at his accuser, "and you're weak—you want to talk and try and help us; why do we need helping, huh, why? I is rich, man, rich—and powerful; I got an army at my command, and ain't nobody gonna stop us, no-how."

"What! Are you at war? With whom—the whole world, with anyone who isn't just like you?"

Samuel looked at the youth as if he meant to haul him up and throw him across his knees and give him a good ol'-fashion' whoopin'; but then, instead, he laughed, and hard too, the way an adult does when a child who has recently tasted of the fruit of the tree of knowledge of good and evil now thinks he knows more than his elders; it was a hearty laugh that was capable of deflating and ultimately rebuking any such nonsensical ideas thrown at him by the youth. Tyrone was quiet, but listening intensely.

Samuel stood now as a pedagogue and preacher, as a man; past and present, as a black man; a bright, shining beacon of hope for the future, as a universal man; and lo, his voice was magnificent, with a blooming pride; and penetrating, with humility and gentleness, and those who heard it trembled, as if some inviolate power unbeknown and unfathomable to them had been rendered into melodic, hypnotic, smooth human tones. "It is your ignorance that enchains you, you pathetic slave—and that is what you are, a slave; although you see no chains, I see them; although you think you are free, your actions have condemned you, and by so doing, you would better have remained as your great ancestors lived: enchained, but free; enslaved, but not broken; enchained, enslaved, but living in the bosom of goodness, and embracing God and living the life of noblemen and -women, although persecuted by those who are not fit to tie the straps of their sandals." He raised his long, big arms out as if to embrace the world. "We are finally free—free—and O Lord, what path do our youths follow? But the one so egregiously laid down so long ago by our persecutors. How comes this tragedy," he shouted, looking skyward, "where our youths so openly reject heaven, and prefer to reign in hell!"

But he was talking to mineral, without recognizable sentience; and to animal, without reasoning, love, or thoughts; two creatures so soaked in dread, so self-created, and self-regenerating without applied intelligence or compassion that these youths could only tremble at his enigmatic might, as if they felt the earth tremble and commence to consume their mortal failings, these wild creatures who were a weak assemblage of mind and spirit, bereft of heart and soul, left only with cunning and craft to navigate the wide world. They were savage beasts murdering each other for the juicy carcass, and mere words from anyone else fell on their sharp teeth that bit into tough flesh and bloodied hands that incessantly tore into their adversaries; this was their law: the law of survival without legal or moral parameters.

Tyrone's mind transposed a glimmer of this revelation onto his angry brain, and muttered, rather strictly, as if in a trance, momentarily, "We is soldiers, you know…sol-dyas—it's a war, y'all, a war," and gazing with a feverish desire at Marshaun, to whom he was long ago related by ancestral genes, but because of diverging paths, instead of a brother, was now an invented enemy, "and I plan on winnin', yo…"

Samuel felt an overwhelming compulsion to hoist the youths on high and shake them until all the senseless enmity and never-to-be-filled, phantom, make-believe vengeance, which was the fuel that sustained their feigned blood feud, shed from them as easily as dead skin cells—dead ideas that had festered and blistered to the point their streaming pus was the nourishment for their hearts.

"No enemy might have planned a greater vengeance upon the black man and dreamed of so great a success; little could he imagine we would willingly bring about our own moral and racial destruction." Samuel said this, but it seemed as if he reached into the chaos of history and ripped open a bloodied vein and let its destruction fall into his mind like an incendiary map of irony and tragedy; the pitch of his voice rose up and down like the clanging of a blacksmith's weighty steel hammer against an iron anvil whereupon he forged the sword of Liberty; the volume of his voice soared and fell like the rising and falling of a mighty wave; the tone of his voice was now like the taskmaster who awoke the slaves by the very harshness and promise of destruction in its cannon-shot-like expression. "Get up, you lazy darkies!" His body was never at rest; his hand in rhythm with his oratory; his athletic and graceful body moved to the power of his words; his strong facial features reflected the meaning of his message. "You have declared war on the struggle for Justice and Freedom and Equality that your forebears so mightily fought for, and died for—and for what?" He shook his head, as one immersed in a wakeful nightmare. "This is your kingdom come—this vast criminal wasteland you have built from ignorance; you, who have debased what and who came before you, and dishonored what they struggled to do, simply to survive so they might pass on the torch to later generations in the hope that freedom might one day be attained; and you have spit upon it." He rose up before them like a consuming fire, and although they did not comprehend a single metaphysical word that had fairly flared up like a raging conflagration before their vacuous minds, they sensed, even in their infantile brains, they had erred somewhere—but still would not embrace it. "You have condemned yourselves by your actions; repent, sinner, and be saved."

Samuel stood there, a human plowshare, having driven the blade deep into their fallow psyches, and he soothed himself. "Brother, I do call you brother—and I call any man my brother; do not mistake our common skin pigment as a reason to name you friend; certainly, you do not subscribe to even that—but I would argue that the time is at hand to consider your own position in this neighborhood."

Marshaun, now able to disassemble and reassemble some meaning, frowned. "Man, you do what you do, and I do," he said, forcefully, pointing to his big self, "what I do."

"Words—I have inoculated them with mere words they cannot see, or use, or hear," Samuel thought, disappointed that he had allowed emotion to capture his communication skills. "I am not at the pulpit." He thought of Frederick Douglass, E D Morel, WEB Du Bois, Eglantyne Jebb, Fridtjof Nansen, William Wilberforce, Dr. Martin Luther King Jr., and more he had studied: Lincoln, Henri Dunant, Gandhi, William Lloyd Garrison, and Booker T Washington, and the founding members of the society for effecting the abolition of the slave trade, which began the dismantling of slavery the world over, during the "Great Awakening." The world, he knew—at least the good people of the world—had risked life and limb to free, quite often, not only people of their own color, creed or religion, but all people not serviced with the inviolate rights promised to all men of all kinds by natural law, because, as they saw it, it was their moral duty to do so, whether the oppressed were workers, women, slaves, wounded soldiers, children, immigrants—the freeing of them had awoken and united the world to a sense of moral duty and righteousness. "To have come so far, to give Freedom to all, so they can destroy themselves with it—then it is better to be in chains than be free." He nodded in a profound acquiescence to himself as he thought this and then muttered, "Deeds, not words." He paused inside the intellectual realm in which the heroes of the past, whom he honored in his daily labor, resided, and acknowledged the supreme efforts they exuded while in the specific context of their era. "In one century, one man; and another century, another man; this century, many men; one past, one present, and one to plan the future." He thought of these powerful words as he beheld the two ordinary yet crucial players in the spiraling trajectory of so many youths, in the violent drama of this modern age.

He wrapped his arms around the shoulders of the youths, who were so physically imposing to ordinary men, so much so that he made them look like helpless teenagers.

"All right, boys and girls, let's—as my singing ancestors used to say—go walking and talking," he said, and escorted them on down the road as easily as a mother duck does her helpless little ducklings.

They now resided inside his giant shadow, a mystical place to them, for in here dwelled no dissension, no cruelty, no enmity, no retribution, but only love, faith, hope, beauty, joy and harmony; here, they were baptized with a gospel of humility, of tolerance, of sacrifice; here, no vile thing could come, no wicked idea, no venomous creature that was held captive by their master, the corrupter of flesh and bringer of sin, who needed the weakness of mind, body, and soul to thrive; and here, Samuel T Longfellow reigned supreme, for he had previously sacrificed those things that made Man weak and an open vessel to corruption: lust for self, lust for power and domination, lust for money. He could not be caught, tried and convicted for crimes he had already repented of, he reasoned, and forgiven of, he knew; and he knew he was not perfect, only stronger, and wiser, but still subject to temptation. "I have given up the temptation of this dark place; my words no longer build a steel cage to trap me; my actions no longer dig a grave with which to bury me; I stand apart from the fire that consumes man; I stand aside from the storm that sweeps men away; I stand firm when the land quakes, for my faith sustains me, and yet I am still tempted by the past. I am yet a man—my burden, our burden; our destruction, and salvation." He gazed at the two youths he carried along as if they were obedient children. "They may have no other like me, so I must be like no other, a man above reproach: the spirit is willing, but the flesh is weak."

When the trio approached the tall, white buildings, the two youths began to tremble, just as if this mass of structures emitted a kind of force field that bore straight into them and caused them excruciating pain. The big man felt their puny resistance, but merely increased his grip upon them, and soon, all were inside the somber, quiet palace of dread and melancholy. It was not the first time he had escorted these two gang leaders into this cruel resort to show them the ill-treats resulting from their senseless war campaign against their imaginary enemies: wounded citizens, in various conditions of physical distress: bullet holes in the abdomen, bullet holes in the head, bullet holes in the legs, bullets, bullets, once sprayed, landing everywhere, on everyone, and everything, and the two leaders had always stood tall, and firm, evincing that staid face of the unmoved warrior, the vacuous eye of the unrepentant soldier, the easy posture of the reassured assassin—now emboldened by their violent handiwork, now impressed by the fear in the eyes of their victims, now enthralled by the power that rose up in them, the power over the lives of poor people, ordinary people, extraordinary people, giving them over to a secret gospel they lived by, a holy scripture that read: with a gun, with no conscience, with no remorse, you could rule the streets, and gain what you lusted for, the things most desired.

The massacre of the latest gang free-for-all rivalry had occurred only late last night, but that day would offer its recurring nightmare to the victims for the duration of their lives.

Now, Samuel stood with those who were too powerful and too young to have so much power, too unintelligent, too immoral, to so easily destroy lives while dressed in the skin-tight garments of freely given impunity. "Now, we will see what we can see; and wonder why, you do not even know who lives or dies around you," he whispered to them, as they surveyed the human carnage while walking down the white-tiled corridor. No one paid attention to them; no family member worried about them as they gave their full attention to their own fallen loved ones.

The two gang-banging, standing-proud, smirking leaders felt invulnerable to this horror, as if they wore a special armor of invincibility that protected them from feeling anything, for they reckoned themselves merely good generals looking over war casualties, and they reckoned it simply a consequence of their private and whimsical predilections; yet, last night had been radically different, as they had targeted, to evince how hard were their hearts, certain Innocents, which Samuel recently had found out about.

And now, the human rock that was the first gangbanger-man came upon the victim of room 324a, this animated rock that was neither moved nor shaken, felt neither hot or cold, neither cared nor thought of those he hurt, beheld the life-giving IVs dangling from the slender black arms of the silent form of Tonya Simpson. Tyrone suddenly became flesh, and leaped to her side, weeping next to his little brother, who had recently left his college class to come here.

"Weak," Marshaun whispered, smirking again; "I don't care who I shoot—ain't no prob' of mine."

"Go," Samuel commanded, leading him on.

The two moved on, Marshaun swaggering as he walked, mumbling all the while about the concrete bunker in which his heart lived and thrived; but no man—no real feeling, capable-of-a-conscience man—can resist even the most basic of human compassion for those they love.

And there she was, in room 326a, a frail, old woman, her black face in agony even as she lay there unconscious, for bullets to the spine will do that.

"Grandma!" Marshaun screamed, and behold, he was a little boy again, as he knelt at her side and held her hand and kissed it and stroked it passionately.

Samuel closed his eyes, and whispered, "How many must die before we reclaim our humanity, O Lord."

A truce between the 122nd Street Black Hoods and the Original Gangbangers went into effect that dreadful day.

In the Nether World

The earth needs not Man, but Man the earth
the seed of harmony lives in earth and Man;
yet Man kills the seed, and casts his cunning eye,
and stretches out his powerful hand, his will be done;
he is god now.

What is the city, but a scar on the fertile skin of the planet, a festering wound, a blemish, a deepening fissure that gouges and bleeds the good faith of our good mother, Nature, an artificial construct that tears and bites the woody fields, a miserable assemblage of concrete and metal, a mindless conglomeration, a spreading contaminant, digging in, pulling up, cutting in, blowing up; putting nothing back, repairing nothing, recovering nothing; O Man, he who doth not sense the eternal rhythms of Nature's fluttering heartbeat; who has an ear, but does not listen; who has eyes, but does not see; who has hands, but does not feel; who has a nose, but does not smell the pure, refreshing scent of his environs; instead, his ears hear the music of his own reckless merriment; whose eyes see only his own imperfect creations; whose hands touch only his own labor, his own, whose nose smells only his own common scent, his own ambition, and thinks it divine; Man may lord over the land, over the flora, over the fauna, but is not its creator, its Fate, but merely its custodian, its protector, and has become its destroyer, its source of harvest famine; Man as patron of Nature has not allowed her to flourish, to grow, to mend, but sees her as a tasty morsel to consume, an agent to bribe, a body to rape, sack and pillage.

A metropolis disintegrates the earth as surely as a sharp knife in the back of a sleeping, pregnant woman; it threatens its existence, it sickens its womb, it creates in it, a fetid tomb.

There are many kinds of birds, but one species; many types of trees, but one species; many types of fish, but one species; many birds, possessing many personalities; many trees, possessing many forms; many fish, of diverse sizes; they live, they grow, according to the immutable laws of biology; they thrive, they die, according to the heritability of their genes; daily they live according to their environment, and daily they die; all fauna and flora, water and air, exist in an interdependent and intricate collage of constant interaction with each other, and thrive, achieve harmony, despite cataclysmic disruptions, despite violent death, despite change—they continue on, shaped by Nature, swaddled by Nature; are, in fact, Nature.

The mystical, sparkling jewel that is Sister-Sea dwells at the bottom of the world, constantly replenished and nourished through innumerable pathways that meander downward through Brother-Land, receiving clean, refreshing aqua pura to her blue-green body; and yet, as vast and grand as she is, she is still subject to the geological whims of her Earth mother; and so, at times, she is compelled, against her most desirous wishes, to rise up and send forth high-rising tendrils and forceful limbs, confident that her lustrous Brother-Land, with whom she long ago establishea delicate netword so he might survive such extravangances.

Yea, Sister-Sea may rise up and throw out a tempest swell and pound the foggy coastline, but Brother-Land merely shrugs, for in his bosom lay many bodies of water nearby, that greets these surges, thusly: "Come, friend, rest your blustery self in my gentle brake, where I shall absorb the impact of your power, and reduce your speed and depth, and spread out the raging flood therein; and do not fear, for my little children, who stand as mighty sentinels of sand at the shore, will absorb the impact of your forced impiety.

So, when the storms have subsided, the damage to Brother-Land is little, and he and Sister-Sea commune again like two cooing, Turtle doves.

But then comes Man—and he blindly smashes the ancient checks and balances that exist between Brother-Land and Sister-Sea, and sweeps up the natural land barriers, and fills in the natural water brakes, all to construct his precious buildings and develop the area; and then, most horribly of all, places people in them—all where the capable fortresses that protected Brother-Land from the high fevers of Sister-Sea once stood; and now, what happens when a blustering tempest comes—it wreaks havoc! And Man laments, he grieves, and wails: O God, why, why why! And Brother-Land and Sister-Sea, weep, "O Man, why, why, why!"

Yes, and then comes Man, and Nature loses her golden raiment, her lustrous shine, her noble purpose; for Man shapes, Man changes, Man disrupts, without clear thought, or magnanimous ideas, or solicitude toward others or the environment. He is, therefore, divorced from the land, another force that has usurped a simple and elegant design: he is a reckless power who will not clean even his own dirty house; he does not seek to repair and rebuild, to restore, to achieve that which was perfection, inviolate, glorious, for his conceit is that his own creations are perfection, inviolate, glorious; he is, therefore, truly blind, a blind god groping for guidance, and deciding what he touches and creates must be purposeful and good.

This, then, is Man, among many forms of life, Man in the artificial clothes of metal and concrete, Man living in the bubbling foment of grinding, intolerable civilization; yet, Man alone may attain a higher degree of nobility and understanding. It is solitary Man in the nurturing bosom of Nature who begins to understand who he is and why he is, and where he has gone and where he is going, what it is he will find there, and what he must do once he is there; here, a human being truly is born; it is here he can fully realize his greatest potential and direction and Destiny, where he may fully experience all the virtues and clearly recognize sin that has been obscured by the omnipresent moral pollutants of civilization.

What is a planet but what it absorbs, the precious minerals and vitamins and rain its roots and fine hairs take in, and the blessed warm rays of the yellow sun upon which it feasts, and the delicious air with his precious cargo;

what is it, but the total sum of its environs? Is Man any different? Yes, he may have many heritable traits that influence his decisions; yet Man considers himself a rational, thinking creature who has free will to pursue and claim what stands in the fore or the aft, to grasp what is above or below him, to turn left or right, to resist or agree, to help or abandon, to love or hate, to worship or dismiss, to study or forgo, to work or relax, to join or decline; this is Man, wandering through the pastoral hills of Paradise with singular speech and abstract thinking and his ability to alter his surroundings, creating sparks that land on the sweetest and most delicate life-forms.

A child reared in the midst of tranquility and beauty comes to know what it is to be human—that humans are to be as much a part of Nature as the flora and fauna; that he is Lord and Master, protector and custodian, observer and worker; but more than that, his very essence, his personality, his values, his notions, his actions, his behavior, are shaped by feeding into this complex web of interacting and interdependent organisms; for he was meant to delight in the resplendent gardens of multicolored, heavily scented blossoms, to be in awe of giant brown Sequoia trees, to admire the sleek and powerful body of the Black Panther; so, what cleaves his heart here and shrinks it; what torments his mind and spoils it; what here provokes him to violence, to hurt, to lie, to cheat, to steal, to turn away from his neighbor? This is not to say Man is a truly grand creature here, for poison anywhere is poison, be it prepared in a laboratory or grown deep in the black forest of a black soul; but here, Man may learn patience from the soft breezes that blow through the succulent bushes to cool the panting Lynx, and gentleness from the red-tailed doe as she gently suckles her newborn son; here, his imagination is shaped, his health heightened, his mind free to think about matters greater than self and profit. How, then, can Man live and be even considered a distant cousin to decency? He must live hard: a hard, backbreaking, labor-intensive, gut-busting life from sun up to sun down, then retire at night exhausted, eat, relax, retire early, and then rise the next day to once again plow the fields, plant the crops, pull up the stumps, move the rocks, gather the fruits and vegetables, prepare the meals, and then he will be free of the idleness that brings discontent, which leads to temptation and ultimately sin; but Man, given the chance to be a loafer, is; if given the chance to be gluttonous, is; if given the chance to be irresponsible, is; so, on the one hand, there are those who work hard and keep their minds and hands busy, and others who stray into that region where at one end trouble welcomes them, and at the other, iron chains and a cold grave to end them.

But Man will not live alone; he must live within the confines of civilization, he must, it is his reality, but it is a matter of degrees, and choices, and regions, and governments, and peoples; he must live within the blood-soaked, bodies-buried-to-the-sky borders of the polis, and therein breed discontent and frustration and every kind of iniquity.

In the city, in the very nucleus of the crowded city, a child is born, and he quickly learns the way of the world—his synthetic world—by exploring his environs; but where there is safety, there is also peril; where there is good, there is also bad; where there is prosperity, there is also poverty; but not so in the fertile forest—where things must be fertile to be equal or do not survive—where boundaries are invisible and rest upon creatures and places, but temptation is a burden one faces in a reflection in a crystal-clear pool. Evil is evil no matter its residence, no matter its face, no matter its guise, yet its voracious appetite is increased when temptation is eagerly ingested by its contemporary human cousins in the tenuous fortress of society.

A rat lives in a small, balanced, automated and naturally occurring wild ecosystem, where it has learned how to survive and thrive within this cluttered yet ordered, familiar environ; now, place the rat, the brown, long-tailed rat, in a foreign context, in the guts of a city, and its internal gyros are upset, its senses jumbled, its instincts battered; and instead of vegetable life and insects, it stumbles into the society's garbage, society's leftovers, society's dwellings, and becomes a new creature—hunted, conniving, gorging, cunning, dirty and diseased.

A child is born, but not in the elegant embrace of the silky sequence of perfumed flowers, but in the sterile, dreary, choking monolith called a hospital. His mother takes him home to her poor palace, one of many throughout the city; she is alone—her husband, having eloped earlier with hard narcotics and the disturbingly easy company of a disturbed sexual deviant, exploits this niche he has found, to wit: plasters his brain with hyper-abundant stimulants and plies his flesh with diverse carnal knowledge, so he might be in a constant and increasing state of ecstasy, and retreat from the harsh realities of having to be a responsible, caring, sacrificing, loving husband and father; and since he absconded with what little cash his wife had managed to keep him from pilfering for his perverted pleasures, the new mother has to rely on the kindness of a benign government, and the predilections of willing, financially able, prone-to-prostitute-their-girlfriends, guttersnipe men. Despite all of this, the baby survives, taking what it needed from the environment, but not what was necessary to thrive; if it was fed on substandard food with minimal nutritional value, then it absorbed what it could, and somehow it grew; if it was fed on environs awash with chaos and peril, then it absorbed what little calmness and sobriety it could, and went to school wherever and whenever Mama happened to be in the mood to take him there, and there he absorbed what little education he could, and his mind somewhat grew. If, then, he had food, it was sugary, fatty, salty, and stuffed with unnatural ingredients; if he had love, it was ephemeral, perhaps contrived, perhaps out of guilt; if he ventured outside, it was to associate with characters caught up in the maelstrom of inner-city machinations, characters running away from trouble, into trouble, creating trouble; if he attended school, it was to many schools in the same school year, and too often where he was just another faceless inhabitant sitting in the lonely shadows in the back of the crowded classroom and fading into darkness because he was never there long enough for anyone to help him. But human beings are remarkable in that they can adapt to the most rigorous and unforgiving circumstances; so, by the time he was an adolescent, he was quite strong physically, socially acceptable, and rather intelligent.

But his mother, her will to live a good life as society dictated, was now evanescent, and so she and her current john-boyfriend-human vampire, one cold, rainy, awfully windy night, without a care or solicitous thought about the boy, took a twisted turn toward the attractive light on the wild side of aberration and abomination, and were soon swallowed whole, just like a man drowning at sea might be swallowed—from wet head to soggy shoes—into the giant belly of a smiling leviathan.

And now Tommy was alone—yet, he was not alone, for Grandma Moore was still about, and she was not one to allow her blood relations to be swallowed by any creature, great or small, animate or in animate, real or imagined, that did not have his best intentions at heart; so, she swallowed up little Tommy, and he landed upright easily upon his two strong feet and came to rest next to his other abandoned, orphaned, forgotten relatives.

There was an old woman who lived in a shoe…

And Grandma Moore was fond of saying to her adopted children, when, in the early crisp, cool morning, she would have them sit in front of her so she might address them before they departed for school, a variant of her main message delivered: "Listen, children: if you have mouths, close them," and they would, swiftly; "if you have eyes, open them," and they would, widely; "if you have hands, fold them," and they did, amusedly to her. She would be pleased now at her little band of loyal troops. "Rose," she would ruminate, "you thought you was done, but the good Lord did nominate you again to raise a family, and I ain't one to shirk my Christian duty," and as she would stand up tall before her blessed youngsters, she felt an exorable pride bear up in her wiry, lean, and aged body, and her passionate, good, and loving soul.

"You children are my kin, and my kin are good—they ain't no slackers." The older children giggled at the idea that Grandma used modern slang. "All of us has been hard-working individuals, working hard is what you need—no one likes a loafer—and they is always in trouble, too," and then her small, black eyes widened at a long-ago memory, "and they is always aiming to get you involved in their danged mischief—misery loves company!" She walked up and down the quiet ranks. "When I was a young'un, if I was bad, and my neighbor don' caught me, they spanked me, and then told my mama, then I got me another whoopin'! But I don' believe in no whoopin's nowadays, jus' good ol'-fashion' groundin'," and she stared hard at the teenagers, "cause it's socializing you want, and if you do wrong, it's loneliness you gonna git—and you get to keep ol' Granny company." She would later hug them and they would kiss her, and off to school they would go; now, seven would leave that day, and three who were still too young would stay, and then she would attend to household chores and errands.

Her pious words flowed like a warm, soothing current in them while they completed their school-assigned tasks; her abounding encouragement encouraged them like a hot broth to a cold body; her loving heart wrapped them in a fine raiment of shimmering gold and silver to obscure, to catch, to deter any untoward missiles fired at them by any lurking, sinister forces that existed solely to destroy that which was conceived in Love, Beauty, and Faith.

Did the flaming arrow of temptation strike the eldest child, Latonya, who was in Rosa's care, then it struck a superior and elegant network of multilayered defense systems ultimately defined by its unique and simple design: faith in oneself, faith in one's guardian, faith in God, and so the miserable arrows, carrying a perverted gospel that was manufactured in the stinking gutter of filth and ungodliness, was easily extinguished; like a hard breath snuffing out a candle; like a strong hand deflecting an angry wasp; like agile feet leaping over piles of mud, as so: she was, Latonya, so young and beautiful and fresh, like a fully formed and newly opened iridescent and aromatic bud that had recently bloomed, and offering sweet, sweet, very intoxicating and generous stimulants to the embracing air, a walking, talking, living and breathing, luscious and soft, velvety, radiant flower she was, and males flew to her as surely as if they were bees and compelled—without any will to resist—to enter her rarefied house of nectar and assorted delights; alas, to them, she, unlike the insects of the land and air, and animals, too, had a will, seemingly unlike the men and women about her, and she exercised its greater portion to resist them, and by doing so, showed herself human, and able to use all of the resources available to her supposedly rational and thinking species, as evidenced from dialogue recently invested into the crowded, tear-stained journals and diaries of juvenile history:

"C'mon, baby," once more began the handsome black youth, who felt it necessary to explain himself again on a more enchanted level, "let's hook up, you know it'll be good for both of us—like a spiritual feast—c'mon, baby, you know I love you."

But she was steadfast to her declared philosophy toward all things physical between man and woman. "Rashon, you don't love me—you lust for me; you throw around words like 'love' to entice girls into your bedroom, where the sheets are still warm and crumpled."

He smiled at the naughty orgies he had plotted against his kin and kind. "Baby, I ain't hiding nothing—you know I ain't no saint; but I ain't," he began, and emphasized "ain't" quite heavily, with a wry grin, "no sinner. I don't believe in all that church-Bible-talking nonsense about waiting for marriage—for what? Who are we hurting? I use protection, shoot," he waved his muscular arms about, grimacing. "I don't believe in all that sin and stuff, anyway—it's just a guilt trip, so those rich old priests can take y'all money and scare you 'bout going to hell, 'n' all."

He was an aroused bumblebee flying madly around a delectable honeypot that he could not open, and he was bewildered, for the other honeypots were more than happy to accommodate his violent lovemaking and believe his fierce boast about how much he loved them and how he even had told his friends—something he said he never did—about how he always kept his word to his sweet little honeypots; but this particular honeypot refused to even open up her fragrant blossom one teeny-tiny molecule in response to his begging and pleading and absurd promise-making.

"Do I look like a fool, Rashon, do I? Do you really think I am going to be another unwed black woman—well, any woman for that matter—who gives birth and raises the child alone because his slacker-father is busy impregnating other equally dumb and gullible females? Do you think I'll be just another pimp's whore, with another whore's john? Is that who you think I am—no!" And she had stepped back from him just as if an epiphany had bored up into her feminine soul; and now she was waving her fingers at him, as if she needed to physically direct her wrath. "Is that what you are making black women into—fools?" She folded her slender arms and stepped back from him, then walked slowly around him, eyeing him with great care. "You're just a man, like any other man, and I know why women fall for your smooth lines," she continued, and then halted in front of him, having come full circle. "Black women—women," she said, solemnly, "women," she then said with such passion and with such finesse and totally as if to finally cleanse the idea that by "women" she meant "black women," but now meant "all women," that the youth looked around expecting to see a throng of such females; "can help the entire world if they would not allow men to avail themselves of the ready sexual services of these eager women, and just once think of the emotional and physical consequences of such an illicit union; hey, I think it's still called," and she did the "double quote" movement with her fingers, "'fornication,' by those old conservative folks: and you know what, I think they're really onto something." She nodded in reflection upon this supposed truth. "But it applies only to me, the founder of it," she mused, then shook her head, and walked away, triumphant and proud, recognizing Grandma Moore's wisdom in her private rebuke, a victory won, a victory for her world, a victory that would slay the enemy that had harassed and defeated her race and gender for centuries, and in so doing, abated this long-suffering lineage of poverty and ignorance, and the pity of self, and self as victim; and the victim without a resolution, for it was a full circle, a cruel circle that began with the head, which followed all around until it swallowed its own feet; still, it was difficult for her not to turn around, as she still felt his strong male scent embedded in her aroused female organs.

The male youth simply found another, and another, and still another honeypot, willing and too eager to hear his pleasing lies, to willingly open their long, pretty, jetty blooms, that day, and the next day, and the next, and after that, one more time, ad infinitum.

And then Grandma went and did something no one had expected or ever dreamed of, not even contemplated even for an instant, any more than one would consider the sudden erosion of a mighty monument that has always been in attendance in one's memory: Grandma up and died. She was eighty-two, but her legacy would live on.

It was Tommy—the other kids called him Tommy-Gun; Tommy the Champ had never taken hold, because he was always talking about guns and rifles and playing video games where he decided he was always the hero—who found her one early morning.

The rain had been coming down so hard and for so long that the people of the city had begun to believe the sun had capitulated to frosty winter for good and fled for the safety of other, warmer continents; but it was just the sun resting, they decided, the sun in its celestial bed, perhaps with a mild cold or maybe too much siesta—one can never tell with an entity that burns fuel for five billion years and knows there's another five billion ahead; it is simply a daunting task, and surely monotonous for eons on end; so when a mischievous yellow gas giant takes a well-deserved respite, who are we to argue?

The reflection of the streaming rivulets down the window pane covered her peaceful body in a watery veil as the oldest of the children—five of them—stared at her. The dead, at least those recently expired, who have not yet been exposed to the withering elements, are still victims of style and cultural norms; a dead body dressed in snow looks serene, while such a body that is naked and shameless, lying in the hot street, causes confusion and angst; but here, the rain shadow cast a severe mask upon her face that advanced the idea of a tranquil sleep; yet, all of this didn't matter because, in the end, she was still dead.

"Grandma can't be dead," Tommy whispered, holding the hand of his cousin, Latonya. His eyes narrowed. "She said she would always be there for us."

And then Latonya said something that might have formed on the lips of a prudent adult, and not delivered by a sixteen-year-old: "She will be," and looked to Tommy, a feeling of maturity swelled up in her breasts. "She is in us—here," she whispered, clutching her heart, and looking to her younger cousin, "she raised us, and we must carry on what she started."

"But if the police find out…" Tommy said, shock spreading over him like a cold, wet fog.

She said it as if she knew what was to be, and with surpassing certitude. "They won't," and she walked up to her grandmother, she who had raised her and given up her own peaceful life and now her very life, and kissed her gently on her wrinkled forehead. "Do not be afraid, children; it is only Grandma, asleep." And after the other four had kissed her beloved grandmother, Latonya continued on, as they all knelt down around her, "Now, you mustn't see her as this anymore—for she is in heaven, in a new body, and she waits for us."

"She'll have a long wait," Tommy said.

Latonya looked at him. "It is my intention to make it so." She smiled, and looked toward the only mother and father figure and giver of the family law and explainer of the mysterious ways of the world whom she had ever known.

"She gave us her heart, and it is up to us to survive," she whispered, and then instructed them to hold the hand of the others, so that the grandmother was now encircled by the symbol of love and unity and loyalty. "Let us pray, then," she whispered, and they bowed their heads. "God, give us the wisdom of your faithful servant, Rosa Moore, and love and protection and direction." Her cousins were astonished to hear her talk thusly—she who previously had seemed to talk only of boys and school and independence. "Jesus, we need a miracle—we cannot give up now, after we've come so far, when we are so close," and her voice grew heavy with sorrow, "just a little longer, Lord, and these children will be all grown up and good citizens—O Lord," but so great was her grief that she began to weep, and now, as if they had waited, the others wept too, around the woman who had never seemed like much to anyone outside of the small home except a humble old woman who seemed polite and quiet, but actually was a veritable Titan, a Hero in the grandest sense, who happily and selflessly spent her life-force in the pursuance of securing a joyous fate for her little brood of darling Innocents.

A Day in the Life of a Boy

Let's now peer into the innermost social order of Tommy and see what beats in the heart of city youths; but first, let us go across town and peek into a house of one of his best friends, LaShawn, as he prepares for school.

He awakens, alone, and alone moves through the small, cluttered department, rubbing his face as he sleepily makes his way to the refrigerator; he opens the door, grabs a plastic container that holds food—prepared by the finest assembly-line robots and their trusty human helpers, the idea of which was hatched by the most devious artisan body-wreckers in history, pumped and packaged by the finest assembly-line robots and their trusty human accomplices—and that will be his instantly gratifying breakfast: six small, white-frosted, sumptuous donuts, plus a long chug of milk, and—voila, his deep gut ache is appeased, for now; so, now, he moves on, still alone, dresses in yesterday's dirty, wrinkled clothes, removes himself from the premises, and heads off to school.

School is the destiny, but not the objective; first, he must stop by the apartment complex that houses his street brethren. "Yo, Kobe," he shouts at the window, "come on, man!" Kobe, two years his senior—fourteen, big and strong—comes bounding down the concrete steps, leaving behind a mother sleeping off another drunken night; he is dressed in saggy, baggy, black shorts, a local professional basketball team's purple decal decorating his long black-sleeved shirt, a baseball hat of the same fated description, and a long, imitation-gold necklace around his thick, black neck. The two youths slap hands, and in doing so, an invisible bond is reconnected and wraps its knotty rope around the tender mind and heart of the younger boy, who is now irretrievably bound to follow he who was just one more link between the known and the unknown, who will fill his curious mind about the wide world, an ever-present pedagogue whose lessons are never boring, trivial, or seemingly unrelated to reality.

A circuitous route is now taken to ensure each point of their intimate social compass is visited: first, to satiate their ever-present and enormous appetite, the local convenience store is visited, where they meet Tommy, and where they purchase a tub of soft drinks, a fistful of candy bars, a couple of donut packages; and second, to their more well-rounded, well-formed, well-established families, their elders' houses, to their city's elder siblings, their outside kin and role models and friends, their homies in the neighborhood. It is here they are hugged and embraced, it is here they exchange pleasantries, it is here that feel-good hormones are released as the youths harmonize their robust internal emotions to the exact rhythm of each other, so that all eventually will beat to the sound of the same war drum; here, they are all brothers—what need have they of biological brothers? Here, they are supplied all their teenager's needs and wants—what need have they of other friends? Here, they have all their questions answered—what need have they of outside pedagogues, or even parents?

Here, the thick cords of brotherhood are formed, ties that will bind them among virtually any outside forces, a movable entity now, a growing collective that thrives and exists on new blood feasting on the spilled blood of whoever opposes their unified consciousness.

There are no boundaries of time to imprison them here. The boys exit when the leaders exit, and so, perhaps the third destination, school, is visited then, and the security personnel of the school will listen to their excuses: "car broke down…mother is sick…overslept…" Such are the lies given to protect the brotherhood, to keep it vital and alive, to allow it to thrive.

The teacher talks his special talk, a message of hope and redemption crafted for his delinquent audience, but they are immune, for in this classroom are the eternal ideas and ideals, the formulas, the initial pouring out of the fount of knowledge to prepare one for a better future, and Kobe and Tommy, in their infantile minds, are locked into a moment of immediate gratification, the intoxication of seeing, acting and grabbing, and the resulting pleasure derived therein—to them, then, the man before them in this particular period is a loser, the next woman in the next period a loser, ad infinitum; thus bored, they duck out, and run pell-mell into the very hustle and bustle of the very alive and exciting city of Angels; to be specific, the east end, and a little bit south, too.

But LaShawn opts to stay, for that day he will try out for the basketball team, and after being accepted, will decide to dedicate his life more to academia than frivolity, and mischief; so, his brief profile in the ever-widening panorama of those who inhabit this teenage wasteland, will fade—because he will decide to wade out of the deepening pit before it swallows him whole.

Later on in the day, Tommy and Kobe walked along the boulevard of shops and restaurants on Wilshire Street, gazing in wild wonder at the delights therein.

"Man, I sure want some of them hot burgers," Tommy said, as he stared through the glass windows, "but I got no money—Grandma didn't give me none."

The cold weather encased the meaty, smoky aroma in a tempting cachet, its mouthwatering molecules wafting into the flaring nostrils of the two fragile captors, enticing them into its seductive lair.

A few minutes later, the youths came running out, laughing, holding the officially approved American dietary regimen: burgers, fries, and a soft drink in their hot little hands, but soon they were stopped as if ramming into an invisible barrier.

"All right, you two knuckleheads," Latonya began, taking them each by their ear, "come on."

As the trio entered the restaurant, the manager met them, his face flushed with red fury.

"Don't worry, sir, they are going to give the stolen goods back, and make restitution, aren't we, boys?"

"Yes, ma'am," each said, wincing in pain.

Ah, but the aforementioned fairy tale never happened; yes, the boys did enter the restaurant, order food and accept it, and exit without paying, but no, that omnipresent, fairy-tale guardian was not there to turn this defeat into victory; O, if this were a less populated town, or a clearing in a forest with a close community, or a familiar place to all, how different the world would be, if indeed, by remaining small, it never grew up at all.

So, as it was, the two, now fugitives, ran smiling and laughing down the crowded sidewalk, proud of this criminal offense, emboldened by their reckless action, thrilled by the rebuke of authority; and now equipped with this sense of liberation from society's strict standards of moral conduct, which had crowned them like thorns, they turned the corner from one domain wherein light and dark existed, side by side, to where the darkness, drawn by the inhabitants therein, pushed out the Light.

Once the conventions of society are shattered, the juvenile mind wanders outside of the unsigned but implied social contract, to wit: was there an old man struggling to regain his balance, then he was knocked down by the running pair; was there an elderly woman who had her black leather purse loosely dangling from her fragile, thin shoulders, then it was snatched, ripped open, money taken, and discarded like so much rubbish into the filthy gutter; and with this newly acquired money came a little stretching past the artificially imposed limits on what youth can purchase, but this did not last long: for a fool and his money are soon parted, and youth, crazy, vibrant, heedless youth, do not think beyond the exhilarating moment of the exalted "now," for they live in the ecstasy of the consuming fire, and seek to feed it, and fuel every second of every day, at any expense, no matter the cost, human or otherwise; so, those ostentatious objects that appeal to the immature eye were purchased by the youths—glitzy eyewear, sparkling clothes, rainbow-colored shoes, and more rocket fuel—a.k.a., junk food for fast-burning projectiles, their metabolisms.

Twilight, cool and majestic, ascended, and with it, the energy of the youths descended, the thrill of defying adult laws dissipating, their money gone; and then they saw Benny, who was stressed in his blood obligatory baggy pants and loose-fitting long-sleeved shirt, and sideways baseball cap, crossing Winchester Street.

"What up, Benny?" Kobe shouted, happy to see a familiar face.

The youths exchange handshakes, as if they were three brothers, Benny flashing them the gang sign of the Original Gangbangers—the manual alphabets of "O" and "G."

"Why don't y'all come wit' me to our hood?"

The two youths readily agreed.

The air was ripe right now with the bracing coolness that comes once the mighty sun yields to the dark canopy of night. The boys felt the chill of winter nip at their bones, so what better hot elixir than a steaming-hot drink of brotherhood?

The headquarters for the Original Gangbangers was a large white house located and purchased with money gained not by their own honest blood, sweat, and toil, but by making sure their victims bled, and perspired so they would give them the monetary result of their hard work.

There were plenty of disciples of the Original Gangbangers here, in various states of repose, most engaged in filling their bodies with hard liquor, hard drugs, and hard language; it was a time of getting high, getting ready, and talking of getting even; yes, there was always bravado talk of getting someone who disrespected their sacred brotherhood of self-proclaimed saints and demigods of the underworld; herein dwelled mortals who bethought themselves the highest forms of humanity, its greatest philosophers, summed up in the following: "it's us or them"; the thought of its greatest intellectuals, summed up in the following: "I don' need no college degree as long as I gits the guns and the green"; and its greatest philanthropists, summed up in the following: "I help my own." So, herein dwelled those who reasoned themselves the orb of society's power, rightful heirs to great conquerors from history past, the nexus in the evolution of hoarding riches and power by brute, unrelenting, unimaginative force; herein dwelled those who considered themselves the new Wall Street bankers, new legislators, the new and only political party. "We rule 'cause we can," they mocked, while they frolicked in the ever-widening pools of shed, red blood; and they proclaimed, as they unwittingly wore the green felt cap, with its jingling silver bells, of the court jester, and the egregious scowl of the madman, "We do what we do 'cause it is who we is, and who stop us, huh? Everyone afraid of us—and that's why—we do what we do." Therefore, they were Socrates, Plato, Aristotle, all newly interpreted and compressed into one, like a big gift package that explodes upon opening, but not into your mind, like philosophers of old, but burning shooting, hot shrapnel into the soft bellies and softer heads of fast-retreating modern ideals of policing and jurisprudence.

There was talk of business, of pleasure, of personal ambition in company of their loyal bloodettes, who would get pregnant at a moment's notice, commit a crime without hesitation, accept any order willingly; consequently, these youths had what they considered all in life, at least all that was necessary for their necessary happiness: constant indulgence of fleshly lusts, stimulating drugs, and the constant stream of money that fueled their recreational pursuit and personal ambitions and want of material things.

On business: "Yo, the good times keep rollin' on, y'all, you know what I'm saying?" One of the younger disciples began, rubbing his index finger and thumb together, and then rocking his skinny form back and forth. "Green is good."

"Man, you don' know nothing," his disgusted elder cried, crossing his hands in the air, "don' you listen? Them wetbacks from down south who supply our stuff, now they is moving in on our operation."

The youth shrugged his shoulders. "So," he said, making his right hand into the shape of the universally accepted form of a pistol, "just do 'em in, we know where they live."

"Brother, you is ignorant; I ain't talking about them dumb Mexicans across town, I'm talking about the Cartels—the Cartels ain't just another mass of crazy gangbangers: they is big and organized, and they is crazy violent, too; I heard stories about them crazy..." But then he let rip a shout that unleashed weighty cargo that hung over their heads, and spilled forth condemning articles of various kinds, thus allowing the dialogue to enter into the realm of discursive, meaningless rant; so, we move on to more instructive and fruitful ground.

On pleasure: there was talk of electrifying, sizzling moments of the ephemeral here and now, and we-must-live-every-day-as-if-it-is-our-last-day, and not nobly, or even acknowledged as ignobly, but simply obeying the desires of the hungry flesh; was there a fine young woman the typical youth desired here? Well, then, he had her; were there two fine young women he wanted? Well, then, he had them both, and riches and power were his side-kicks; was there a very shiny, brand-spanking-new, shining automobile with all the essentials enticing him? Well, then, he simply pulled out the thick wad of thousand-dollar bills and paid the salivating salesman; was there a home he wanted, jewelry, and various other expensive toys? Why then, he bought them, he bought them all, because he wanted them now, right now, because now the money was free-flowing, flowing in from the left, flowing in from the right, in steady streams, and uninhibited, falling down from the sky, flowing in with the wind into his greedy, outstretched hands, and it seemed never to stop, so why should he think it would? So, he spent as if there was a tomorrow that was just like today, which was the same as yesterday: money, money, everywhere, a turned on, wide-mouthed golden spigot that would never, ever drain itself, dulling his mind to ponder the how, the why, and the maybe, veiling his heart to what other worlds might occur, should occur, how they had occurred; darkening his soul with star-spangled lies, forever promises, and the fantastic guarantee of practicing sin without the avenging law ever coming knocking hard on his boasting, and dangerously arrogant, wide-open door.

On personal ambition: "I want," began the fervent sentence of the typical youth here, "I want to do this fo-e-va," and then, to be more specific, he expounded on this theme, in different verse, but all with the same rhyme, rhythm and reason. "I want to gang-bang with my homies, be here with my ladies, live this good life all the time," and was always followed by the wide, toothy grin only naive youth provokes when tomorrow is not seen as anything other than one long, uninterrupted, non-changing, continuous, magnificent, all-is-well today; here, they felt like a family, where they experienced family values, all things family: love, friendship, sacrifice, caring, pride, concern, worry, planning, imparting to them a sense of value, usefulness, meaning, as if this way of life was just as good as any other normal family. Their own families may have failed them, abandoned them, had even been there for them, but this family was their stepping out and away from their own birthright to establish their own identity, to pursue their own dreams, to find a place in the wide world and prosper there.

One man there, elderly by the standards of the ruler of this orphaned life, but in reality, thirty-five years of age, spoke not with booming clarity of boasting and the assertiveness of inflated pride, but with a voice that evinced respect for the past, caution for the present, and wariness for the future, a voice empty of rhetoric, replete with meekness and worry, two traits best left outside of this cauldron of narcotic thinking and testosterone nihilism. He leaned over closer to his woman when he whispered, "Will I still be here," his dark eyes pleading his passionate case, "when I'm sixty?" He searched her for even a glimmer of response, one that might be given to him in the quiet embrace of privacy, but not here, in this soldiers' palace, where he reigned supreme, and money, as common as paper, lining his gold-plated coffers. She gave a barely imperceptible shake of her round head. He had long thought of retirement after seeing his comrades in various states of physical agony: in the hospital, in wheelchairs, in the clutches of drug addiction; in various states of mental anguish in prison, in physical agony, in physical rehabilitation due to street violence; in diverse states of death: in bloodied heaps on the street, as unrecognizable, mutilated corpses in open coffins, in their final agonizing breath at the hospital: yet, his soldiers' platoon frowned on early retreats, especially when the soldier planned on living locally; so, he would move away, far, far away, to a land hitherto unknown to himself and his tribe, where people did not yet intimately have knowledge of the exploits of organized youth whose appointed activities savagely unwound the carefully woven tissue of a tranquil society, a quaint little community in Illinois called Decatur, where he longed to fulfill a long-held dream of being a farmer, where he might actually cause good things to grow, and not bad; and, while there, if ever there transpired a revival of the dying embers of this uncultured life, the three importunate bullets in his body were sure to douse that hot flame. He left the next week, untraceable, never to be heard of again, and was soon forgotten, like a ruined civilization that was buried under new layers of other dead souls.

One in, one out;
A two-way travel route;
a man dies, a child is born,
one we cheer, the other we mourn.

And that dark, pounding, hard-raining night, a man was born—as defined by an exclusive group in society—right there, in this ancient cathedral of idols, in the secretive world that resembled deep, maze-ridden catacombs.

Sacred rights began when man first sought the companionship of others, when first he examined his heart and saw loneliness, and uttered this proclamation of human need, "join me." And thus, rituals began, one people devising the union of a group with a handshake, others with a kiss, some with physical contests, mental tests, pledging allegiance, and never exactly the same from one hemisphere to the next, nor even county to county, state to state, town to town, as diverse as our flowers in the fertile forest; the women choose one path, the men another; warriors one way, intellectuals another; it may be in fashion to nod the head, agree to outrage, take all manners of abuse, sign documents, betray others, give money, defy the establishment, show bravery, abhor violence, honor God, dishonor God; and here, tonight, one such confederation of young men were obeying the contrived rules of the game to test the desire of one to be a member of their elite fraternity.

His false face of bravery he did not wear too well, as he stood trembling like a little boy before his imminent antagonists, for he was still, at heart, a little boy, although his aspirations had elevated him to desire the rewards and responsibilities of adulthood; as it was, Kobe stood before his inductors into this private club whose legion of admiring fans continue to grow around the known uncivilized world.

"Get 'em," one of the lieutenants cried, and his five waiting disciples dove in against the waiting youth.

Tommy watched in awe and fear as his friend took the sixty-second pummeling like a veteran fighter; five young men punched and kicked, pushed and shoved his friend, who valiantly swung, albeit blindly, against the kinetic flurry of fists and feet. And when it was over, Kobe was bloodied but still standing, and congratulated by his attackers and other onlookers, for he had passed the initial test. Tommy felt pride in knowing the potential newest member of the Original Gangbangers, and his own desire to be part of what he perceived as a wealth of older brothers and fathers increased, so much so that he thought he would fairly bust if he had to wait one more day to join them.

The Metabolism of a Culture

Juan Rodriguez was born in Mexico and came to America when he was still a boy, but unlike any ordinary American boy, his life was one of work and strife, like in Mexico, but unlike in Mexico, at least here he had the ample opportunity of going somewhere other than behind himself and walking backward; so, possessing a unique characteristic that allowed him to understand that the more you labored, the more money you made, and if he was prudent, the more he worked, the more he saved, compelled him to greater heights of financial independence; and thus, he had, by age twenty-two, shorn the iron shackles of debt his parents owed back in the mother country, and presently sent for them, and his little sister, too, and they all rented a modest home in a humble neighborhood of a small suburb of Los Angeles, where the collective tenor of the inhabitants was one of constant gratitude to have successfully escaped the tyranny of the perpetual inefficiency of a government that was unable to stimulate an economy past the level of unacceptable and outrage; incompetent to burn up, to sweep out, to finally wash away the centuries-old layers of sludge that is corruption, to a place not paradise and not perfect, but closer to paradise, and closer to perfect, than anything else they had ever experienced; and so, inhaling the sweet aroma of opportunity and hope, they set to work to ensure going back, or failing here, would never, ever happen.

The father and mother of Juan picked grapes and strawberries and potatoes and other available produce in every season, but sometimes in the boiling summer sun for twelve hours a day, never once complaining of their low wages or intensely physical labor; his sister worked as a bus girl in a restaurant during the day, and during the night as a cleaning woman in a professional building; Juan, now twenty-three, was an assistant manager at a fast-food restaurant, where he worked seventy hours a week. When the family was at home, together on Sunday, they went to church in the morning, had friends and relatives over in the afternoon, and went to bed early at night. On Monday, the family awoke, gathered and prayed, thanking God for their warm beds and sturdy house, and electricity, trash pickup, access to good health care, law-abiding neighbors, a refrigerator, America, a paycheck that did not disappear, that they would not be gunned down by criminals who have no fear of the authorities, and, yes, sewers, showers, and central air-conditioning and heating. Amen.

This was life for them and it was a good life, a joyous, peaceful, blessed life, and eventually the sister, Rosa, was married, and the family celebrated, and Juan married, and the family celebrated; then came grandchildren for the father and mother, and the family exalted. It was a good life they had earned, and they knew it, knew now that hard, unrelenting perseverance brings balance and financial solvency to a prudent family such as they who had invested their money in conservative institutions and each other.

And so, Juan and his wife, Sonia, had two children, two boys, and living not far from the homes of his parents and sister and her family, flourished as families do in a world that covets charity and virtue the same way a garden covets sunlight and rain. The eldest boy, Diego, was a distinguished scholar in high school, already taking pre-college courses in his senior year.

Tomas Rodriguez walked slowly behind his brother, as they approached the school.

"I'll see you at lunch," Diego said, deliberately looking back at his younger brother, "okay?"

"Yeah, sure," Tomas replied, seemingly uninterested.

Diego abruptly halted, turned around, and faced Tomas, who now displayed that irritated, bored look of the deserter—yes, the one who deserts education he perceives as a boring known, for the stimulating joyride of the outside unknown. "Tomas, you need to go to class."

Tomas, possessing that rare and dangerous too-early appetite to know that an older brother really isn't his superior, walked slowly up to him, head down, then defiant face up, never flinching as any ordinary younger brother would seemingly do, and was wont to do. "Get lost, D," and head down again, he walked past Diego, who knew what was to come.

"You need to go live with Grandfather and Grandmother Rios in Mexico," he said, angry now; "you don't know how good you have it."

Tomas shrugged his shoulders, halted, and turned around. "You want me," he began, eyeing a pretty girl walking past him, "to give up all this, huh? Well, you can do this school thing," and he pointed to himself, "but I don't like it—you like it," and he pointed at him, and then pointed at himself; "I want other things."

"It's not your right to want other things right now, you're a seven-teen-year-old—a minor; you do what your parents tell you."

"And what is that, Diego: go to school, get a safe job, and live in a safe neighborhood, and make enough just to pay the bills? I want more," he cried out, pounding the black leather jacket that covered his chest. "I don't want to play it safe," and he looked around in disgust at the scurrying students. "That is too easy—where is the challenge to just barely survive—I'm a winner, and winners take gambles."

Incredulity crossed Diego's swarthy countenance. "You're so naive, you're just talking like a punk."

He smiled the smile of ignorant youth that thinks it is wise. "Well, may-be I am."

"No," he replied, shaking his head, "you're just a gangbanger wannabe."

Tomas smiled again, holding out his arms in a defeated gesture. "Well…"

Diego was right atop him now, atop the white step above him, staring straight into the bemused grin of his younger brother. "If you want to play gangbanger, go right ahead, it is a free country to die in—but not while you live at home; if you want to throw your life away after you graduated, fine, go ahead and do it—but not in our house."

Tomas shrugged his shoulders again, raising his black eyebrows, mirth forming like an endearing play across his too handsome and rugged face, and then said, casually, too easy and too carefree, "Okay," and then turned around and walked down the cement steps and out of sight.

He did not come home that night, nor the next, and then a fortnight passed, and no word on his whereabouts, despite a missing person's report filed with the local police agency and councilman and youth organizations, and flyers put up around town, and Internet searches, and the church getting involved, and friends and relations, too, all looking, all hoping, all praying to find the gone youth, but as Juan and his distraught wife were soon to learn, it is very difficult to find such a boy who not only does not want to be found, but has also found what he considers a superior and permanent home, the kind a rebellious youth yearns for when first he flees the nest, which is the following:

The photo album of the inhabitants in the larger home on this private cul-de-sac would show young males tripped up in a style of dress that announced their loyalty to those with a Mexican heritage who had given an allegiance to a particular brand of consumerism. Every societal group seizes a stylistic attitude that separates them from the indistinguishable, blurring masses, and here, it was no different: bald heads, or straight-back, jet-black hair; oversized pants, short or long white socks pulled up to the knees, oversized white T-shirts, black leather belt buckle replete with letters that signified their gang, or other varied dress of their choice; multicolored tattoos aplenty: long, gorgeously drawn, colorful, storytelling pictures, of religion, family history, names of mothers, girlfriends, dead friends, on every imaginable body part; big business uses television, radio, newspaper and Internet sources to advertise, these men use their bodies, to admonish the public and other gangs, and to celebrate their proud membership.

The dialogue of the men, or ideology therein, was not much different from that of their rival brothers the 122nd Street Black Hoods, except that the presence of the Mexican drug cartels was a hard chestnut they could not crack with their usual threats and intimidation, as evidenced by the unhappy harvest the Cartels had recently picked, consisting of eight dead gang members.

One of the newest members, a youth who had easily survived his "jumped-in" initiation, spoke, boldly, in the midst of elders, with authority, supplanting his minor role and ritual of simply listening and learning while standing in the background.

"Do you know what the indigenous Indians did when the Americans came west—they fought them," the eager youth began, as if he expected his every word to be grasped with enthusiasm by his audience.

"No, brainiac, tell us," said one of the elders, who was covered with numerous well-earned prison tattoos, looking around at the fine homegirls.

"They fought them, and lost—and do you know why…"

"Hey, just cut to the chase, Professor," the same elder said, after taking a gulp of his ice-cold beer, and eyeing a very comely young lady.

"Because," the youth continued, undaunted, when he should have been very daunted, but as he was young, and thought himself experienced the ways in manners of this culture, he assumed his narrative must be embraced. "They were outnumbered, and destined to lose."

"And so, so…" the elder said, if only to irritate the youth, waving his hands around in a circle to irritate the speaker. The other listeners around him were smartly quiet.

"It is the same with the Cartels."

"What," the elder shouted, now armed with a reason to be truly outraged, "hey, tapado, you ain't even making sense here," and he issued formidable words of an obscene flavor at him.

The youth persisted, ignoring the grim countenances around him as a loud signal to cease and desist immediately from his equally powerless, still-too-young-to-vote brethren. "We're like the Native Indians, and the Cartels, like the American Cavalry; we need a different strategy."

Now, the elder, who really had been only half in and half out of the conversation he had deigned to enter only to occupy his time while scouting out his forthcoming flesh party, his spirit, infected with gangrene in the federal penitentiary, festered, and now erupted, with a lengthy display of illuminated, boisterous obscenities, and then finished with, "You're an idiot, ese."

The teenager still pressed forward with a speech he had already rehearsed. "Hey, we already use the Cartel's product, but that model has changed; now, they want to be here and run things and cut out the middleman—us—but I say we work with them; so, I say let's do it, and use them for protection against other gangs and the police, and we use them for information on our rivals, and then we…"

But alas, the swirling, cocaine-laced fog in the brain of the elder saw only a flashing red light before him, which had to be knocked out, and so he did, his face scrunched up and disgusted, his large fists, like giant hammers, presently pounding away on the defenseless boy. Blood flowed like a burst dam.

A man of superior rank stepped in, made peace, sent the elder on his way to his female target, ordered the onlookers to disperse, and helped the beaten youth to a brown, sagging sofa.

"Mijo, you need to keep a low profile," the older man began; "you don't shoot your mouth off around guys like Enrico, he's a hard-core prison vet. He don't mess around—if he don't like you and feels like punching you," he popped the air with his fists, "then he does; you need to stay clear of him—and guys like him—at least until you have proven yourself," and he shook his head, after giving the youth a tissue to wipe the blood from his forehead. "Man, right now, you're just a baby, a fresh-faced punk—you have no right here, no voice: you just take orders and listen; you can't go around showing off your education in front of guys like him, it's disrespectful; it's like an attack on his years in the gang; look, Tomas," he whispered, watching the boy feign to maintain a hard countenance, "we're taking a big enough gamble as it is with you, taking in a minor like you—remember, one of the reasons we took you in was because of your connections to good weed you found, and the cops and everybody else nosing around haven't been easy to get past; but, hey, you're a good kid," and he issued the boy a hearty slap on his slender shoulders. "Just keep a low profile for a while, and you'll be fine."

Tomas looked up at him, sniffing, still massaging his wounds. "So, Miguel, are you saying my ideas are no good?"

Miguel laughed long and hard, and taking the boy's head in a playful headlock, then releasing him, said, "That's what I like about you, mijo—you're young, and headstrong; reminds me of myself when I was your age, but," he said, serious now, "I knew when to quit—right?"

"Right," Tomas replied, smiling sheepishly.

"Good boy," Miguel said, nodding.

The Mexican Cartels that had surreptitiously moved far up north did not care about the subtleties of social graces, and continued to migrate, just like an invading tick, a spreading tumor, a foreign species intruding into the ecosystem, which ruins the delicate balance therein.

The local police agencies understood the indigenous gangs: they fought them, had task forces exclusively to mediate conflicts between them, had committees, special reports, explicit expense accounts, a whole history of working to suppress gang warfare; there were gang sweeps, gang injunctions against their meetings, special laws against gangs, school programs advocating against them, outside agencies receiving grants and additional funding to fight them; and when all was said and done, the local authorities were not certain if doing something was effective—for the gangs continued to grow and prosper—or if doing at least something kept down more of this explosive growth and prosperity; but in the end, they decided that they couldn't just lie down and do nothing, so, they did whatever they could.

The local police had a multitude of programs that targeted the gangs: they went into the neighborhoods to try and show their authoritative and comforting presence to neighbors; they copied other programs that were successful around the country, such as setting up boys' clubs, endorsing YMCAs and YWCAs, and encouraging the youth of the troubled areas to attend school and seek a safer future; and they went into schools in league with various anti-gang programs, and they worked with various youth organizations to help alleviate the blight and burden of this ever-increasing specter and spider's web that is the ancient idea and harsh reality of gangs.

The Cartels were not to be affected, as they were a resilient new power, and local matters were as irrelevant to them as a bug to a bulldozer, because they considered themselves a superior force, as much so as every conquering entity has done in history past: the Japanese thought the whole outside world mongrels; the English likened the aborigines to animals; slaves around the world were not considered worthy of citizenship among human beings; the young Americans decided the Indians were like irksome coyotes and put a bounty on their heads; and the Nazis, well, they considered just about everyone who was not like them unworthy of life. The Cartels had no history here: no affection for culture, no roots in the neighborhood, no respect for what had gone on before them and what would happen afterward; they were still an emerging Leviathan that had conquered its neighbors on the opposite end of the compass, and now was reaching its hungry tentacles into the vast riches of North America, with future plans to creep into the rest of the world.

Their philosophy in the promised land differed from any other present one as much as East is from West, to wit: conquer, destroy, loot, pillage, rape, and seek new business frontiers; and so, countries and uncooperative gangs intimately felt this new threat—the bold threat of a well-organized, well-financed, well-armed business monolith that was like a sovereign nation but was concerned only with gaining customers through acts of unfettered criminal conduct. They were an invading army, and would brook no prisoners.

> When hath the predator abated its hunt,
> at the behest of its prey,
> when hath the predator delayed
>
> When hath the predator compassion,
> at the behest of its prey
> when hath the predator walked away;
>
> When hath the predator become friend,
> at the behest of its prey
> when hath the predator become the hunted.

Four days after Tomas' ideas about an artificial conciliation with the Cartels were roundly rejected by his elders, four of his gang, and five of the

122nd Street Black Hoods, were found lying on the street in neat rows—like strips of freshly cut bacon—with tattoos spread over them with the following moniker: AC.

The regional war was on.

Rise of the Cartels

"There are no borders that separate countries, only ideas": spoken by a retreating immigrant who was between the growing prosperity of here, and the dwindling poverty of there.

"Where would Mexico be without the imperialist American?": spoken by a lamenting left-wing professor of Mexican history in the University of California system.

"Mommy, are there still Indians today?": spoken by a schoolgirl in the state of Oaxaca.

It is the same old story, and always will be a new story, and a future one, too, about the land, and who uses it and how it is used.

There is a particular continent: this time it is South America, and the region is the jungles and valleys of the Andes; an indigenous population explores the land and finds plants that will help them to survive in their harsh environs. There is one particular plant that bears greenish leaves, and when dried, taken by the finger to form a quid, and placed between the cheeks, with a tad of lime, produces the desired effect—teasing out the alkaloids that will deliver great vigor and endurance so the native may continue his arduous labor. It is the way it is, the plant grows freely in this area, free to be picked and used by its human coinhabitants in good faith, used in religious ceremonies, as much a part of the land as the pristine streams and wild berries and plentiful game—it serves its purpose in the life of the villages; it is part of the intricate design of Nature that the people have discovered to help them survive. It is as necessary to them as protein, fat, carbohydrates, vitamins, minerals; it is essential; it is a daily routine that nourishes their sleek and strong bodies. It is this way because Nature has secrets, and these people have found one.

Then foreigners came, and saw the plant's value, and after conquering the natives, encouraged the use of the plant to keep the people strong in their slave labor, and slowly, the fame of the plant grew: it was used in Europe as a tonic, in America as a beverage, but then scientists found that there was an addictive quality to consuming too much of this leaf, so the American company took out the alkaloid and simply used the leaf to flavor their soft drink; but now, the genie had been let out of its bottle—for anything with an addictive quality can be a mass marketing bonanza for smart businessmen with no scruples.

And so, those people who had taken it upon themselves to exploit any fleshly weakness of the human body in order to enrich their own bank accounts pricked up their ears at the news of this finding: addiction; they already had a lucrative business in selling human flesh and human toil, selling alcohol and cigarettes, managing various pharmaceutical drugs, and other hyper-concentrated forms of other plants; but now, this new one had them salivating just like the ravenous dog in an iron cage who has a bloody meat bone just outside his reach. They would do whatever was necessary to break free of the cage and consume that delicious meal until their swelling stomachs ached, whereupon they would vomit, and commence to eat more of the same.

It worked, of course it did, for "people in need are weak indeed," and citizens flocked to the new street drug like hungry seagulls on fresh abalone, and the historic stage was now set for three crucial players in the ensuing industry: concerning the authorities, there were seemingly ten more for every one that fell; concerning the growers, makers, distributors, and sellers, there were seemingly twenty more for every one that fell; and the customers, there were seemingly an unlimited line of them for every one that died or sobered up. It was a war for the deep pocketbooks of these desperate clients, no more different from the battle of companies to sell the most cars, televisions, or hamburgers. It was no different, after all, from what the arrogant European Colonial powers did in China during the ghastly and reprehensible Opium Wars.

Even as the war raged among the constituents in the sordid melodrama, countries that fought the makers allowed certain growers to grow and sell it to companies to be used in their household products.

And, of course, as previously mentioned, there was—and still is—the curious case of the global soft drink conglomerate that began using the whole leaf in their original soda pop but then had the alkaloids squeezed out—to be sold to pharmaceuticals—and then used only the stripped coca leaves in their product. And the natives say, Viva Coca-Cola!

Let us follow a leaf, magically transformed into one with a cognitive consciousness, from harvest to its final illegal destination. It begins thusly: we see the hearty coca plant plucked from its birth mother in the Andes region, and see it transported originally to Colombia, but now Mexico, where new entrepreneurs, having become fully invested in the idea that human beings are mentally frail, pathetic vessels who struggle daily to resurrect their misbegotten lives above the level of a corrosive, disjointed madness, need an artificial stimulus to keep their sanity buoyant, and were fully confident of the wealthy demographic and customs of their North American cousins, and so they labored ceaselessly to turn the humble leaf and its alkaloids into a white powdered barrel of emotional dynamite, where the stimulants therein had a newly christened name, cocaine.

And what of the first darlings of the illegal drug trade, marijuana and heroin and opium; were they jealous, but no, they evinced great affection for their newest partner, as they had grown lonely carrying the burden for so long of being the only golden children.

The cocaine was then packaged in a multitude of guises and set out on its way up north, to various checkpoints, where the local authority in place, accustomed to standing tall, now looked straight ahead—in point of fact, looked left and right, up and down, at any point of the compass other than at the incoming package, and curiously their income increased dramatically; score one for loafing and accepting any offer from the highest bidder.

By and by, the recently redesigned and redressed coca plant, hitherto unrecognizable to the South American native, after an air route, a land route, and a water route, or even a tunnel route, finally and eagerly reached its destination where, if the now super-normal plant—again, if it were capable of thought, and aware of the perverted virulent strain it had become and the unethical possibilities it would produce—might imagine its destination to be a horrible Communist-Socialist fortress: this America; some kind of gulag, a war zone, a plague-infested horizon for the citizens who were so mentally distraught that they needed a powerful stimulant to make it through another harrowing day in the chilling killing fields—at least equal to the same regions the coca leaf had passed along this circuitous route, and also in other routes, as related to it by its fairy brethren in distant lands (coca plants possess, like all living organisms whose lives are rooted in the rich soil, the singular ability to communicate to each other through the top layer of the earth by a process called "magnetic resonance concentric waves harmony" or MRCWH); but were nonplussed when the disturbing facts illumined their powdery white faces—America was not as it had supposed. And so, what, in fact, was America, the magic leaf wondered, and soon found out: a compendium of literate and illiterate fellows, as it relates to common sense, and finances, love, and family and folks, most of them dwelling next to and often with opportunity, but opportunity, often like a lover spurned, to wit: the little white powdered keg found its way into the nostrils of the very, very rich, or very, very poor, into the flaring nostrils of the famous, and the infamous, into the eager hands of the ambitious merchant, the famous athlete, the worker with the clean collar, the worker with one not so clean; it made its way into every intentional crack and unintentional hole, it did, burrowing in like an avaricious parasite and freely sucking the thick, red blood therein; but first, it needed a helping hand to simply get there, to those willing participants in this grand drug experiment; so entrepreneurs stepped up and put out their hands and closed their minds to the ensuing carnage, and in so doing, filled their silver-lined coffers with cash flows equal to the Fortune 500 companies: America, meet the newly crowned CEOs of industry, the captains of commerce, wonder boys and girls of, no, not Wall Street, but back street, where dreams come true at the expense of another's lust for a grandiloquent lifestyle.

So goes the illicit drug trade, so goes the increased prison population, littered and stuffed with a newly acquired paradigm of prisoner: first, that opportunistic leech, the pusher, and then, the addict, a danger to oneself and punished by the state, who is now father and mother, and wise counselor to its ever-growing family: so goes crime, bankrolling the operations of small-time, petty hoods and big-time, annihilating hoods. The coca plant blushed crimson embarrassment: "Is it my sin that these bipeds are as feeble as an injured bird?"

This one particular shipment of the mighty mind-altering plant, which fought extradition in its magical mind but lost, came to rest in the state of California, in the province of Los Angeles, in the east quadrant, in a dark, clandestine warehouse where brooding young men holstered with brooding black guns purchased it from their drug contacts from the South; the exchange being done, the two happy parties prepared to leave, when, upon a screaming report, the buyers yielded up their roles as interpreters of America's taste values, to the cold, wet grave, a longtime partnership now dissolved. It was, after all, Winter, and the ice-cold blizzard of rain and wind was howling like a banshee outside. The normally grim employees of the Azteca Cartel let down their guard to reveal a slightly sardonic mask as they acquired said white, powdered treasure and black suitcases of cold, hard cash; the red and white were now inextricably mixed, and the coca, hanging its collective stalks the world over, wept, as it recognized its intrusive companions, and murmured, "You have realized your fortunes in cannibalism of your own kind, who, with one taste, will never return to the land of the living."

The cycle is completed, the eternal beat goes on, and the world will seem even more incomprehensible and incorrigible; but, lo, those who have ears that truly hear, and eyes that see, see what others do not see, hear what others do not hear, and in so doing, live emotionally, spiritually, and intellectually so far ahead of their fellows, that they will seem like an aberration as they go about advocating for and constantly seeking a better world.

It Goes On

I look inside this steel mask
and see the ugliness within;
and I know the ugly world outside
comes from my world within

A boy who inhabits any secluded island will naturally explore his environs with his body and mind, the more with the body as he climbs and jumps and runs freely about, than his mind, if he has no one else there to educate him. His muscular strength is the easiest interpreter of what is heavy or light, his mind the best interpreter of what is safe or perilous, and when there is peril, it is his body that reacts and his strength that compels him to higher ground; his mind may devise a weapon, but it is his body that uses it. To meet another boy, it is a test of strength, wills, and endurance to see who survives on the island; it is the same with men, too, savage men on an island, where their bodies become the flagship that sails them through life—in war, in domination of lower species, and rituals, in rites, in contests and subjecting weaker humans—when there is no government, no faith, no civilization; but introduce civilization and it brings laws and stability, and Man should increase his mind to navigate the wide world while concurrently placing less emphasis on the physical—as commerce supplies needs, as cities provide protection, as states provide education, and mostly, this is so, the mind does share the stronghold the body had, to find its way through creepy, shadowy, dark places. But there are always exceptions.

There is a ritual among certain gangs in the modern age that is a mutated gene of earlier versions, to wit: I am a male, I am strong and brave; therefore, I will inflate my ego through the exercising of my great strength acts of derring-do, through endeavors in which the mind is less of an equal and more like an oarsman that merely stirs the body through its wild excursions.

Here is one such hallucinogenic episode played out in the fertile dens of youth's corrupted conscience: they, these feral creatures, unhinged from any universal law, any higher spiritual, philosophical, or moral authority, and certainly not acquiescing to any kind of societal ethics or acceding to jurisprudence, sought to placate their own furious impulse during this initiation, which was, to the host, violent beyond human comprehension, and also to the recipient by a random act of nonsensical violence; later, we shall witness the destructive results of this for one particular family. But for now, let us merely proceed with examining just one organization that was dedicated to abrogating such atrocities.

Charitable organizations, like schools and nongovernmental organizations, and other nonprofit organizations, have been infected with the bells and whistles, slogans and songs, advertisements, feints and dodges begun by the greatest trickster of the day: commerce; yes, it is the inbred chicanery of wealthy businessmen who have mated their poisonous tar pit of a diseased soul with the very world they mistreat, misrepresent, and mystify, and there is no worse case than their insincere proclamations regarding their lying intent, called the mission statement, which usually involves lofty ideals and a promise to adhere to higher standards. It is this they have so ignominiously passed down onto those they pat on the heads of the subjects they so despise. Every company has an illusory mission statement nailed above their mahogany doorways, enshrined on their gold-lined temples, and the nonprofits soon followed like blind lambkins, even though, once their vision was accomplished, no one at the worksite ever referred to the noble and impossible-to-follow declaration again.

There was no blaring mission statement above the outside doorway of the Community Youth Organization; no soaring rhetoric, no gilded prose, no fancy letters flashing loud—only the simple words in mellow yellow, "Youth Freedom Hall," for the name of the place was the vaunted prize, the allure, the magic within, and the brief words he had assigned there were gone forever.

Paradise needs no signpost, once its location has been firmly established.

Those in authority asked no questions of those who came there, required no money nor contracts signed, pressed no one to come back, and only in the case of minors did they pursue personal information, and, in this case, parental consent.

On any given day, the congregation of the faithful were ex-gang members, runaways, ex-convicts, and youth from local schools, who were free to come when they pleased, leave when they pleased, stay as long as they wished, and had only to follow one golden rule: honor thy neighbor. Any act of verbal violence resulted in a firm warning, and any physical violence by a member resulted in a permanent ouster.

This day, the man in authority was standing in the midst of twelve awestruck youth, demonstrating diverse athletic skills hitherto unknown to their city-bred, nourished minds.

Inside this immense building, there was a large section designated as the gymnasium—yet, here there were no basketball court, no weights, no police, but equipment that mimicked the plentiful exercise stations found in this spectacular font of nature; there were, in fact, a rock climbing wall; six long, two-inch-thick, thirty-foot manila ropes hanging from the vaulted ceilings, under which lay three feet of ultra-cushiony mats; six sets of kettlebells and sandbags of varying weights; power stations, replete with pull-up bars, tricep bars; and in the backyard: a salmon ladder; an obstacle course for parkour training, consisting of monkey bars, small towers, long metallic rails, and makeshift walls; and inside there was more, including a pommel horse, a balance beam, jump ropes, medicine balls, more manila ropes, truck tires and sledgehammers, an exercise mat for martial arts training—but no weapons as accessories.

Now, Dylan was about to ascend to a rope via the wall before him. "Here we go," he shouted, dramatically clapping his hands together quickly, and running straight at the vertical rise, he hit it first with his right foot, and then left foot, and then proceeded to run two more steps up it, propelled himself backward and out toward the ropes, which, upon hitting one, he grasped with his hands and legs, then let his head fall while concurrently lifting up his legs until they were straight; he held this dynamic position for a few seconds, then brought his legs down, swung out and grabbed another rope and, by extending both arms, performed a perfect iron cross.

His youthful fans went wild.

He then swung, as naturally as a monkey, from rope to rope, doing various feats of athletic derring-do, and then finished his performance by flipping gracefully and landing expertly on the brown mat.

As he was surrounded by his admiring audience, Rhiannon sat in the background, smiling largely and applauding.

"Mr. C, you're like Spiderman," Gerald gushed, as befitting his brief sixteen years on earth.

"Isn't he amazing," Miriam said, smiling widely, as she looked behind herself, "Mrs. C?"

Rhiannon, invested with a sense of pride only a wife understands, stood up, and said, evincing a silly grin, "Show-off!"

Miriam laughed. "Oh, Mrs. C, you can do the same things—only you can't now, 'cause of the baby."

Rhiannon stood up, smiled warmly and nodded as she held and rubbed the protrusion-shaped palace that housed the soon-to-be-born Prince of Cuchulain.

The girls of the club came over to her. "I'm so excited," Miriam said, "for you and Mr. C."

"Is he your first?" one of the girls asked.

The smooth countenance of Rhiannon flushed with a pain imperceptible to them but recognized by Dylan; and then she smiled briefly, and her words were soft and gentle, like the spirit of a people who have seen too much death and dying, and pray only for peace and prosperity. "No."

The girls, belonging to the ranks of this sacred sisterhood, possessed a unique sense of understanding regarding such things—such death tones, tones of sorrow, a mother's lament—and they grew silent, accordingly, honoring a woman who had sacrificed so much and so often to aid them in steering their wayward lives back on the course toward even a chance at the fabled Good Life.

Miriam, having a special relationship, and a longer one, with Rhiannon than the others, was quick to remedy the situation and quickly close the open wound. "Gosh, Mrs. C, how come you still look so beautiful, huh? I mean, most women I see get as big as a walrus!" And she donned her best "walrus costume" and forthwith waddled around, making walrus noises. Everyone laughed: so, mission accomplished by a mere fourteen-year-old, who had seen more and done more things no fourteen-year-old, or anyone, should ever experience.

Latonya walked in, seemingly alone, but in reality, bringing a whole history of her family with her, and with it, a generation in trouble.

"Has anyone seen Tommy?" she asked, hopefully, and when no one responded in the affirmative, her fragile equanimity broke its thin skin and burst trepidation over the place. "I think he's with his friend Kobe, and Kobe is in the OG now, and I think there's going to be trouble tonight with another gang."

Marvin, who had been putting away some equipment into the storage space, came up to her, and already hearing her distraught voice and seeing her distraught face, spoke to reassure her. "I'll find out, Latonya." And he could find out, having many other friends who were now on the breathable outside but still had an ear to the unbreathable inside of gangland.

"When did you see him last?" Dylan asked, approaching her.

"Yesterday morning—he got up and said he was going to a friend's house."

"When would you normally expect him back?"

"Well, it is summer, and we usually expect him home by supper."

"What about your grandmother?" asked Rhiannon. "What does she say?"

When Latonya hesitated, it would have been perceived to belie the truth known by her own kin. "Oh, she's so worried…"

"Why do you think there will be trouble?"

Latonya sighed, shaking her head, her face stricken with grief. "One of my old boyfriends told me," she paused again, more upset than before, "it's so frustrating—does every black youth have to be in gangs, or know someone in them? Praise God on high for your organization, Mr. and Mrs. Cuchulain." By now, Rhiannon had her arms around the young woman and was escorting her to a folding chair. "Thank you, you have been so good to Tommy, and my family, but now, it just seems that whatever was going to happen to him could not be stopped." She shook her head again. "He is, after all, a young black boy—isn't he supposed to die a violent death on the filthy streets? Isn't that with the statistics…" But she broke into sobs, and laid her black-haired head upon Rhiannon's shoulder.

By the by, after the other minors had left, Dylan and Marvin made numerous phone calls; in the immediate present, there arrived the one man they had come to cast upon their heaviest burdens.

Samuel T. Longfellow came striding through the open doors with the urgency and zeal of one who was searching for one of his own. "All right," he cried, clapping his large hands sharply, "let's roll!"

He had, during his fast track to the CYO, made a dozen phone calls on his cellular phone to various individuals who might have knowledge of the whereabouts of Tommy. "What I am hearing from my people in the know," he began, sure to address Latonya directly, "is that this is Kobe's initiation night—and you know what that means," he put his hands upon her small shoulders, "probably a drive-by, and maybe with Tommy in the car with him," and then he stated, emphatically, "though it seems unlikely—but we aren't taking any chances." He looked toward Dylan, and said, "I am pretty sure I know where they might be tonight," and the two convened alone in the office.

"Why not call the police?" Latonya appealed to Rhiannon.

Rhiannon, still holding the trembling girl, explained the philosophy of Samuel Longfellow. "We don't work with the police, nor against them; we don't work with the gangs, nor against them; yet, by doing what we do, we aid the police and help those who don't know they need help, and by doing so, help the community."

She shook her head. "I don't understand."

Rhiannon grew somber, her face placid and calm as she spoke. "We do not preach against the gangs or deliberately attempt to rescue children from them; what we do is offer this," and she gestured about the place, "to any neighborhood children—from any class, race, creed, or ethnicity; if they come from a good home or bad, the streets or a job, so be it, we accept them."

"And the gangs respect that?" Latonya asked, drying her tears with a white tissue Rhiannon had given her.

"We are no threat to them because we do not target them, any more than we target any group so ill-conceived," she continued, and then hugged Latonya, and looked about the center in awe and respect. "We welcome all comers—no one is turned away."

"You are like the church of the living God."

Rhiannon smiled, nodding. "I suppose we are," she said, and then whispered, "one more way in through His doors."

Samuel and Dylan exited the office. Marvin left to talk to his contacts.

"You stay here," Samuel said to Latonya; "we'll handle this."

Dylan bent down and kissed Rhiannon. "I'll be back tonight." He then kissed the house of the Prince of Cuchulain, and then said in an ardent whisper, "Be good to your mother, little Conall."

Latonya expressed her gratitude to the men, and watched them retire into the great unknown, the city streets.

"I think it's so sweet you call your baby by name," she said. "You're a lucky woman, to have so caring a husband." Rhiannon smiled in acknowledgment. "Do you worry," she continued, with furrowed brow, although hesitating, "about him?"

Rhiannon briefly thought of the sum and substance of her life in Africa, and when she spoke, it was as one with a special knowledge and authority on the subject. "Those who seek to hinder him, it is they who should worry." She closed her emerald-colored eyes. "And with Samuel, too—they are quite the heroes."

"Heroes," Latonya whispered, in reverence.

And with these sentiments deeply embedded in their bosoms, they rested easier.

Operation Rescue

In war, battle zones are clearly delineated: a soldier's uniform is different, usually; combatants and citizens are clearly separated, normally; buildings of the enemy and buildings of the Innocents are known, marked, and distinguished in battle, and respected by each side, hopefully; but in this silent and secret war on the streets, there were no clearly drawn lines anywhere involving anybody, anything, or anyplace. It was the new age of crime.

The enemy had no respect of person, place or thing, boundaries, babies, or bullets, only their own ambition, their will be done, their lustful flash be appeased; if they decided a violent act needed to be conducted on a particular night, it was done irrespective of surroundings, casualties of Innocents, retribution from their enemy; and when the misdeed was done, they hid in their homes, secure behind closed doors, guarded by weak laws, protected by compassionate judges and juries, benefiting from the same societal contract the rest of the populace benefited from: but the latter who believed that by doing what is right, right things will happen to you, and then you will enjoy the protection that is supposed to be inherent in modern civilization.

Imagine the horrible places a person flees from, the terrible places that emit frightening sounds and nasty epitaphs which produce fear in the minds of ordinary individuals; the kind of boiling, roiling, tempestuous pit of human refuse where every kind of indecent and vile act is indulged in and heralded as good and wondrous; this is the least traveled road our interested parties, Samuel and Dylan, were on now, willingly entering into this long-ago-discovered and quickly forgotten and abandoned residence where virtue lasted as long as a burning candle in a harsh wind.

Into this breach of decency they descended, with neither sword nor buckler, police nor officials, but Wisdom and Beauty they held, and Justice and

Love covered them, as they marched into this heart of embedded, spreading, seemingly unstoppable darkness.

> Whereunto this villain's castle, they marched upon
> for a noble purpose, for Innocents' salvation;
> for unto themselves, they were cast,
> last of noble knights, chivalry and honor their banner carried.

They were warrior's warriors, yes, warriors now, albeit peacetime warriors—the difference being here weapons were not guns, but words; not violent actions, but actions of good deeds; not noble gestures of warfare, but noble gestures of confidence, self-sacrifice, and humility.

There is a roadmap of every section of every town, an intricate detailing of the dealings of those just, and those nefarious, the former undisturbed as to their whereabouts and habits, the latter, furious and stealthy about their shadowy existence; yet, someone always knows even the most intimate of thoughts of even the most notorious of the cunning agents of chaos—useful information, like a continual advertisement, always for sale; thus, Samuel, with his many lifetime contacts throughout the city, knew precisely just where, when, and who was involved in the premeditated launching of Kobe's career as a generally accepted, hardened gangbanger.

There sat the automobile that would convey the four youths from point of innocence to the point of willing collaborator. Courage, the youthful faces spoke to each other while they opened the doors; courage, their eyes spoke as they entered the heavily tinted, plateless, black Cadillac, and then coolly pulled the doors shut; courage, their trembling bodies spoke, as they knew that an irreversible transition from boyhood to manhood would occur upon the successful completion of this challenging chore.

And wherefore was this anticipated jubilation from their elders; what good deed from these youngsters did they meditate upon? What noble deed, purpose or challenge had they in mind to usurp, to conquer, for the four youths to firmly establish their credentials and be finally recognized and accepted as worthy citizens who deserved an actual geographical region in the consecrated land of the Good Life? Would this hot night embrace four more college graduates; or four more youths, having decided against the "now" of the acquisition of instant gratification, ready to pursue charitable work; or perhaps four youths, through a passionate proclamation in deeds and words, who were now dedicated to the idea that equality is more than just a word written in ink on old, vacuum-sealed documents, but is a living word, which without constant care and feeding, and reaffirmation, and put to continual use, greased-up, powdered-up, and polished-up, is simply another useless ideal meant to appease the restless masses, and would now work tirelessly to promote such lofty concepts?

No.

Their mission was malicious; their target, human; their resolve, strong; they would, before this night had its sooty lamp extinguished by the rising of the yellow star, before they returned to their dragon's lair, execute members of a certain species they had been taught to loathe and want to murder on sight. Guns were cocked, smiles too; hearts were withdrawn, souls covered; minds were sharpened, knives too, on one bursting refrain: "Kill the dirty Mexican." Their homies swarmed the car, cheering the impending death of their I-don't-know-why-but-they-must-die enemy, incessantly egging their juvenile member-worshipers onward—and the scene was electrifyingly fluid, progressing from shattering, whooping yells to hard grunts of camaraderie. Finally, the time arrived, and came farewells and heartfelt handshakes through the open windows; encouragement was lobbed at the occupants like fragmentary grenades. The driver ignited the engine amid this joyous fever, like a fever at the start of a grand parade, of a family's long journey, of youths going off on a long voyage of discovery.

And then it all ended as abruptly as a dropped guillotine silencing a boisterous crowd.

There came upon the stunned populace of Gangsville, exclusive, two sauntering men, both physically large—not that it mattered much to these youths, but huge muscles still conveyed the message of dominant alpha male, and accrued even more currency with a tight culture that judged each other more on strength of body than on strength of mind. One man was black of skin, the other was white of skin; one was six feet four, known in his earlier bad ol' days as the black Hercules, due to a naturally gifted physique that resembled a dedicated bodybuilder—and this before he actually began to work out properly; and the other, about six feet tall, chiseled muscles, thick, long, blond hair, also walking with a swagger of surpassing equanimity and certitude.

The two sleek Panthers walked easily into the cluster of snarling, angry Coyotes, and were immediately surrounded.

"What you want, Longfellow?" one of the lieutenants bellowed.

Samuel said calmly, never flinching, never even evincing fear, as if he truly were picking up a package at a retail store, and sure to address only the clerk, "I am on an errand for the Moore family. They want Tommy home."

"Tommy who? Ain't no Tommy here," the appointed representative responded, looking about with his hands spread wide as if to seal his feigned ignorance.

Samuel, still in the same relaxed stance, continued on, "I appreciate you taking care of him while he was away, but his family misses him."

"You're wasting your time, man."

The engine of the wannabe death car idled low and mean.

"Kobe might want to come with him, as his mother is worried about him, too."

The speaker of this Gang House of Representatives laughed, as did many others. "Man, you got some nerve waltzin' in like some Special Ops dudes, askin' for what you got the right to ask fo'."

"But I'm not asking—their families are."

The speaker let out an expulsion of breath to show his disbelief. "Well, that's just too bad, 'cause we don't take orders from no flunky families."

"Well," Samuel said, lifting one corner of his mouth, "now, I am asking."

"This ain't your business, bleeding heart, or your white servant's business, either."

It was Dylan's impulse to reach for the long-ago serrated knife at his side, and his rifle over his broad shoulders, but he relaxed his posture, and trained his focus on the immediate goings-on.

"What—don't your big, dumb white ape talk?"

Dylan suppressed his warrior's rage and channeled it into the stolid, silent, severe, but most importantly, emotionally unmoved man he appeared before them.

"Hey, Longfellow, just go home, and play nursemaid somewhere else."

"I will not leave without Tommy and Kobe; I made a promise to their families."

"Well, you made a promise you can't keep—too bad for you, you just have to get used to disappointment."

"On the ready," Robert said, as he lay upon a faraway hill, looking through his infrared binoculars at the confrontation.

"I am ready to shoot," Paul responded, lying next to him, looking into the scope of the Accuracy International AX 338 rifle.

"I will tell you when," Robert whispered.

The speaker of this social gathering tried not to flinch, but he was as successful as a pink, fat pig waking up with the bear's wet snout in his face. "You got no reason to be here, Longfellow," he cried, alerting his loyal colleagues to gladly loosen the reins on restraint. "I won't tell you again."

"Steady," Robert whispered, "steady…"

Paul breathed in slowly, and exhaled just as slowly, resting his elbows on the soft, wet grass.

Dylan's brain began to release the frantic sense of savagery into his hot blood stream, now surging like an electrical storm throughout his body, igniting his lust for defending Innocents. He felt more than just alive, but necessary, meaningful, awakening a purpose he should never have let petrify. Regret encouraged him to act accordingly at the slightest provocation he was beginning to hope would happen.

And then one of the car doors opened, and out hopped Tommy, and then out hopped Kobe, and so out hopped the sinewy tension.

The two boys walked sheepishly up to Samuel and stood next to him just as if they were now who they truly were—just kids.

"Man, you can't be coming here and disrespecting us like this," the speaker raged, his hands gesturing wildly as he approached Samuel, "it ain't right, you cain't do that on our turf—you ain't no lawman; what you done is wrong, and you got to pay." He was encouraged in his rant and threats by his echoing loyalists.

Samuel remained emotionally unmoved. "Tell Marshaun I will speak to him."

"Man, Marshaun ain't here now—I am," the youth screamed, banging his chest, "and you have dissed our gang."

Samuel turned to leave, as did the boys, close in tow, as did Dylan, who still experienced the height of a soldier's readiness, and still aspired to create a wasteland of this bleak haunt.

Now, all of the other attendants were screaming and yelling evil portends, bellowing columns of rancorous smoke, alleging inevitable atrocities that would soon befall the two rescuers.

Paul calmly tracked the wild and frenzied youths through the black metallic scope, his fingers still lightly on the trigger of his rifle that shot .338 Lapua Magnum rounds and had a SOCOM 338-Ti sound suppressor on its snout, eager to obey the order to shoot.

There was an unseen barrier that lay like a heavy tarp over the confrontation, the barrier erected by Samuel once he stepped back into the life cycle of gangs and wove a path through their lives—all of them knew him, oft hated him, but respected him for what he had done for other brother members: appealing to parole boards, probation officers, and judges, for leniency for the youths, for compassion, for his promise to intervene and help the them, which he always did; they admired him, yet argued against his meddling when it did not directly benefit them; it was a barrier they could not cross now to hurt him, as if to do so would eliminate the last vestiges of humanity still available to them, a barrier he could not strain often; and so, that night, after he disappeared into that good cover of darkness and took the two boys home to their so grateful families, he knew he must certainly wait for the large breaks and tears of this thick barrier to heal once more.

Dylan, once at home again with Rhiannon, reflected upon his seething want to engage in physical combat. "Am I thus interned, once blood is drawn, am I no longer free?" He said nothing of this to his wife, whom he now doted upon selflessly.

Robert and Paul, back at the corporate offices of Heinlein Enterprises, stood before a model of the future of the skies.

"When will the X-1 Kitty Hawk be operable?" Paul asked, bending low and examining the small vehicle.

Robert nodded his head, as if to answer a burning question asked long ago on the field of battle. "When," he whispered, staring at the marvel his scientists had recently perfected, "it is necessary."

A Child, a Child is Born

They were both born with extraordinary athletic abilities and into middle-class families, both of them then sharpening their skills, both then taking a path not to elicit monetary gains from such talents, but for the gains of Freedom and Justice, Peace and Prosperity for others.

Dylan and Rhiannon, after returning from Mother Africa, to whom they still felt a warm attachment, certainly could have exploited their unique talents, but chose to continue their mission to bring Liberty and Equality to a world that, without people like them, would never yield up such inalienable rights. They cared not for riches, nor fame, self-glory, power, nor material things, but for each other, and treating their fellow man with respect and dignity. It was a fable easily written but hard to enact, and this was their challenge daily—not to stumble, not to break, not to grumble, not to take; they sought to give, to aid, to heal, to use their marvelous energy for good. It was all so elegantly simple, yet few would do so much for others while denying so much for themselves.

"How can one do wrong when one helps another?" Rhiannon mused one day, an answer to no spoken question.

"And you will be blessed, mother," Dylan had replied, kissing her hand.

So, they now knew what brought true Joy and Bliss, what values they needed to live and thrive, along with core institutions, and be exceptionally happy, and here was their secret: Faith and Health and Love.

Did she desire finer things than the sparsest of surroundings? Yes, she was a woman, who labored hard and never complained; did he desire finer things in the sparsest of surroundings? Yes, he was a man, who labored hard and never complained; yet, they had also had a singular gift bestowed upon them in Africa, the gift of seeing, not merely reading and hearing stories of the horrors of unfettered avarice, where corrupt rulers and aristocrats bled their people of what little monetary value the poor had and then stuffed their own overflowing, obscenely high and deep, endlessly long and wide, diamond-studded coffers: coffers built from the blood and bones and tissue of the very people they ruled, rulers who could not be called countrymen because they and assorted villains were not of the same noble breed as the poor, who were noble because they were persecuted and crushed and laid flat but somehow persevered and refused to yield to tyranny, and somehow carried on another day—always in the hope of a better life—to face these miscreants who were of a species having recently sprung up, like a nighttime fungus, identifying themselves as saviors and taking foreigners' loot, and pillaging local booty, a species easily tracked around the world through their egregious and overtly open actions, and not to be confused with ancient monarchs who made no outrageous excuses or hid their true affections for abundant riches and unlimited power.

Dylan and Rhiannon had seen this perverse imbalance of wealth distribution, witnessed its deleterious effects: the civil wars, the manmade famines, the torture and slaughter of Innocents so the ruler might preserve his petty temporal kingdom come, and it had sickened them, much in the same way a child gets violently ill on a particular food, which later can no longer be tolerated; so, toward this end, they were finished, having never begun a fanatical desire for the alluring seeds of mammon in the first place, and now this hard lesson learned at the proper beginning of adulthood enhanced their constantly evolving education.

And so they, by all those battles there, talked and reasoned about what was necessary, what might be included to procure their happiness and guard them against such assaults of human foibles from within—the want of finer things than was necessary to exist comfortably and in league with joy and happiness. Of course, this being said, they agreed there must be necessary, first of all, Faith, and Liberty, too, and making a decent living—for poverty imprisoned souls, they knew, and led to temptation; they also decided good health was foundational to their new creed, for without it, life could be a prison, so they exercised and ate a wholesome, natural diet, slept well, and refused stress to access their intimate lives. And they often wondered if Faith and health alone were sufficient to secure harmony.

And so, with their unwavering faith in God, their good health, and living in a fine democracy as America, and obeying the laws of the land, they easily adhered to their ideals, and were content to follow them the rest of their heavenly days. All of this was Bliss, and to add more seemed to tempt Providence, but there were essential ingredients still to be stirred into the fragrant stew.

Of course, they needed friends, and relatives, of course they did, and they communicated often with them: he, with his family in Ireland, and her, with her family in Rhode Island, and both of them with select friends here, and they were twice blessed; and yet, there was more to come that would flow into their never to-be-filled cups of Joy and Peace, their own family.

When little Conall was born, so happy were they, so deliriously happy, that all the power, all the glory, all the riches, and all the fame in the world could not be traded for one mere second away from this precious new creation of life that was now theirs—theirs to hold and raise, care for, worry about, teach, love, and cherish; this was, to them, life complete, adorned with every natural splendor under the sun, and to be offered any artificial stimulant now, would be antithetical to their very lives, and sinful.

So, when the new mother and father stood on the white cement steps of the hospital, bathed in the golden splendor of the early morning sky, with Samuel, Robert and Paul, and Rhiannon proudly holding the baby in soft, beige swaddling cloth, they knew, without even once thinking upon it, that with the baby now in their lives, it was better than any king's treasures, better than want for power, beyond the indefatigable desire for material things, beyond any temptation for worldly lusts; for here, in this tiny bundle of fresh life, was the completion of all they needed to truly safeguard themselves from self-immolation.

Samuel beamed so bright he was like a new father, too. "A boy," he cried upward, "a brand-new baby boy! Glorious! Thanks be to God!"

Mother and father were so proud that they did not want time to go forward, as they wished simply to gaze then and there forever upon a little bit of perfection, upon a free gift, that was so remarkable in its ability to bring happiness and joy to those around it with simply its miraculous appearance. Were they still in the physical world? Yes, certainly, but they did not feel its tepid forces around them. Did they still have problems? Yes, certainly, but they presently did not feel them. Did they have all the answers to all the world's problems? No, but the exultation they now felt certainly colored the world in warmer hues and tones, and gentler harmonies.

Robert had offered, knowing he would be politely turned down, a chauffeur, but the Cuchulains had insisted on using their very own ten-year-old, white Toyota Corolla.

Dylan found it difficult to turn his loving gaze from the child. "I will go and get the car now," he whispered to her, and when he managed to look at his wife, he felt even more bliss, and upon kissing her on her fair brow, murmured sweetly, "the two most beautiful creations on God's green earth." He began to walk toward the parking lot.

Dylan had a remarkably wide-field peripheral vision, equipping him to see any object advancing when others saw them not; so, when he turned to leave, and saw the streaming lines of cars in front of him still, the patients walking to and fro on the white-hot sidewalk, patients and their families still coming from the left and right, he saw one car uncharacteristically slow down, and then saw the same car letting its passenger-side window come down all the way.

Four men—who rendered themselves bold because they considered themselves to be breaking with convention— had just recently entered this dark-windowed, great metallic Chevy cruiser to embark on an errand of serving notice to those who dared live according to the dictates of common decency and respect for their neighbors; for today, they would trample such idyllic notions asunder and rebuild the smashed, lofty ideals into a high temple where they wished to be worshiped, and which had weird, rambling hieroglyphics decipherable only to themselves in the torn, broken conscience of the world.

Dylan was in Africa again, right there, right now, on the highest alert, fearing the loss of all; and so he turned toward Rhiannon and cried out a loud warning as he saw the black barrel of the rifle appear and heard the fiery blast and deafening sound, even as he reached the ground in front of her, even as he instinctively reached his for long-ago abandoned weapons. It was too late.

Blood was everywhere, and not one red drop of it was from an adult.

Pain and Suffering

Baby Conall was dead.

No one who knew of his birth could conceive of such a horrible plot against him, but it was nonetheless true.

Dylan, even in the history-altering event unfolding before him, wore his warrior's dress; he managed, immediately after this family holocaust, to pick up a large rock, aim and throw it powerfully at the quickly retreating black, unmarked sedan, the fast-moving projectile smacking the back window and placing a small mark upon its surface. There was nothing more to do. He turned toward Rhiannon.

She was covered in blood—her baby's blood on her beauteous face, sprinkling her auburn hair, splattering her white gown, drenching her senses, so that she was not sure of what she beheld. Dylan tried to take the baby, but she would not let go. He could not feel his body. She could not feel her mind.

Robert and Samuel were on their cell phones, calling for the authorities. Hospital officials, with security personnel, came and attempted to move the group back to safety, but Rhiannon would not, could not move, still staring at her newborn child, her mind swept into an incomprehensible world.

Paul wept as if he himself had lost his own.

The police arrived and barricaded off the incident with yellow caution tape. An ambulance came. Men in white uniforms attempted to move she who was still a mother. She would not move, still looking at her life, her beautiful love, her joyous future. The men attempted to physically move her, but then felt something odd, something they could not explain, a force so powerful and seemingly mystical, that they were fearful—and what was it? They then felt the left hand of Dylan ushering them away from his precious world. They looked at him in awe. He shook his head, covered too in the precious blood of his own lost, sinking world; so, he gently took her trembling form and helped her into the ambulance, as the still frantic Samuel, Robert and Paul got inside their respective cars and followed them, all the while making violent phone calls to all who might have intelligence on this repulsive, heinous act.

At nearly the same moment of the assassination of this Innocent, the Community Youth Organization Club that Dylan and Rhiannon managed and operated, and Samuel leased from Robert, was bombed and subsequently burned to the ground—and normally would have had many occupants in it, but had been closed early because of the momentous event at the hospital.

The war was on, yet no one had openly declared war against Samuel and the Cuchulains, for such cowards hide behind terror and anonymity.

Baby Conall was buried the next day.

Everyone who was there was supposed to be there—the father and mother, and their families, relatives and friends, Samuel, Robert and Paul, and Marvin, and the children from the community center, all of them grieving over the loss of one so special and so innocent.

Rhiannon and Dylan still wore the same clothes from the day before, both having not showered, letting their baby's sweet and innocent blood adorn them as an impassioned testament to their love and loyalty for him.

And after the visiting families finally went home, and the relatives and friends retreated far enough away and long enough to give ample time for the couple to grieve, there came a night when Dylan removed his blood-stained clothes, and instead of washing them, placed them in a black plastic bag, showered, and then put on fresh clothes; but Rhiannon did not; no, she decidedly did not, she wore the same blood-soaked white gown as she walked about the small home they owned.

And lo, she did not talk, had not talked since the massacre of her own dreams, his dreams, her reality, his reality, their hopes, their joys; nor did she look at her own husband long ere she turned away.

He would speak to her softly, gently, lovingly, and she would simply walk away, her face flaccid, as if her now lusterless eyes saw no good thing, as if her mind beheld no good reason to stay and listen.

On the seventh day after the death of baby Conall, she removed her clothes, placed them in a black plastic bag, showered, put on fresh clothes, but still embraced her cushioning silence, and widening aversion to listening to him and being around him.

Dylan was slowly coming undone.

As regards the house: where he went, she did not; where he sat, she stood; where he lingered, she moved on. If he went out to the backyard to work out, and found her there, she quickly left, head down, walking clear of him; if he ate in the kitchen, she ate in the living room; if he slept in their bedroom, she slept in the spare room, which she eventually made her own.

As regards conversation: when he happened to ask her a question, she ignored him; when he happened to address her with a concern, she looked past him; when he chose to confront her on these issues, she would then stop and simply look at him with such a blaring, unbowed intensity and such fierceness of mind, that her face assembled a red-hot glowing iron mask that had sat so long in the blazing fire its basic features seemed altered, and then she would abruptly walk away.

As regards travel: she would not leave the house. There was nothing more to say about it, she was now connected to their home, and dependent upon it for every good thing.

As regards the flesh: she would not allow him to touch her; nor brush up against her body, and no holding of her hand, no embrace of her, no stroking of her lovely, thick, long hair. When she moved about the house, she took great care to avoid any chance that he might even graze against her.

As regards the beautifully decorated nursery room: it stayed untouched, and she visited it often, and made it plain to him, through hard stares and hard gestures, that it was her sanctuary and memory palace, alone.

But this house was no prison, it was a home, their home, where they both lived, both ate, both slept, and she could not long refuse communication with him, so she did relent and wrote messages on paper, but when this did not suffice, she, writing, asked him to buy books and CDs on sign language, which they both learned quickly, but she still refused to communicate with him on matters of any importance.

But this was a marriage, a relationship built through many years of emotional, spiritual, intellectual, philosophical and physical bonding, and he would not suffer long her newly adopted, wayward direction.

"She cannot long keep up the silent war," he thought one day, about a month after the horrible incident, looking at her practicing the Kalaripayattu stick-fighting technique in the backyard that Arjuna had taught them, "of unilateral disarmament, and expect me to do the same—is this what she truly wants? Is she ashamed that I am attempting to live again? No! She blames me, she does! What does she want from me? How have I failed her? How?" The idea that she would just disarm him from what he considered honorable and acceptable incurred his wrath. "I have been the good and faithful husband who allowed her to grieve; I have given her time, space, and her will to grieve—and it hasn't changed. Well," and he looked again at her whirling image, "I am done with that!"

His story: he then marched straight out to the backyard, and after picking up a set of the bamboo fighting sticks, came to rest directly in front of her. "Let's go," he said, forcefully, and when she attempted to move away, he moved around and stood directly in front of her; when she attempted to leave, he blocked her, increasing her frustration. "Come on, let's spar, you and me." He could see the fury and fire rising in her flushed cheeks as he began to tap her sticks with his. "Right now, you and me; I can see you're getting rusty—let's go." He began to dance about her, nudging her sticks, smiling, posturing as she rooted her anger to the thick grass. "Afraid you've lost your edge…" This statement served to break the hold wrath had on her, and she fairly exploded, engaging him fully. She thrust, and swung, she parried, she attacked, she leaped, she flipped, she danced, she hit low, she hit high; and everywhere she hit, he met her, high and low, left and right, center and side; and they dueled like feverish combatants, each following long-ago established unscripted attacks and counterattacks, defenses, and calculated retreats, yet carefully designed not to injure the opponent. And when the long, fiercely contested session was over, he thought it was a way in.

"How about a drink of…" he began, still tired, and then watched her simply walk away after replacing the sticks in the cloth sheaths and hanging them upon the white walls inside.

He followed her. "Rhiannon," he cried. He had not said her name in a time too long to remember, and it served to hold her forward motion, like a magical lasso, freezing her to the brown hardwood floor in the hallway. He approached her with great hope. "Rhiannon," he said, softer, stopping just behind her back. She stood perfectly still. It was the first time since that terrible day that she had responded to a request of his that required her to listen. He wanted to say so much, but he felt there was only time for the most important thoughts now. "I love you, and I love our little Eleanor, and Conall."

She did not turn, did not acknowledge his declaration, made no sound, standing perfectly still for a few moments, and then walked quickly into the nursery room and shut the door.

"This isn't over," he mumbled to himself and, approaching the room, said aloud, "Rhiannon, we need to talk; we cannot live like this anymore." He stood in front of the door, his voice passionate. "We are still a family, you and I…" And despite his fervent please, she did not answer, and he began to feel as the fool, who thinks words can heal wounds. "Deeds, not words," Conall had always taught him; "every moment you talk about what you are going to do, you've lost the time in the doing of it."

"Deeds, not words," he murmured to himself, his head leaned against the door, and thought, "Rhiannon, what do you want from me?" instead of asking her, which he could not bring himself to do, for fear that he might fail her request.

That night, he was on his cellular phone, making calls, whispering, and when she happened to come out of her room, he stopped talking, or cut the call short, and then went elsewhere to finish the conversation. These stealthy phone calls continued, oftentimes followed by his abrupt departure and long absence, oftentimes resulting in his coming home in the early morning, leaving at any time, coming home at any time, and as time went on, more calls came, and he made more, and left more, and was gone more often.

Still, they had to eat, and when Robert had bought the material for another building, and Samuel, Dylan, and the older members of the CYO helped the professional builders build it, Dylan went back to work, but not Rhiannon, who still would not leave the house, never answered the phone, read the newspapers, listened to the news, watched television, movies, listened to music, wrote letters, or received visitors.

Her story: she would finish a strenuous weight workout, stretch, eat, go to her own room, sit down at her vanity, stare into the unlit mirror, and wonder, wonder why she had no tears. "Why have I no tears, why?" And she would think, holding fast her face, "Am I a bad mother? Have I no tears left for my own? What is wrong with me? Why can't I cry?" And she would grab her thick hair and pull at it, as if to draw answers from her reluctant mind. "My baby died, my own Conall," she thought, hoping the thinking of it would precipitate weeping, but this failed. "Who are you, what are you, what have you become, so cold, so angry; and then he comes to you, and you drive him away." And then she heard Dylan's voice at the door, and she walked softly to it and rested her face against it, listening to his vow to stay with her, to love, honor and cherish her; she heard his genuine love for their children, for her, and his dedication to her, that he would wait patiently until she decided to once again be who she was; and still, she shed no tears. "What is to become of me if I cannot weep for such a loss?" She slid down against the cool door and sat with her back to it. "How can I not weep at his devotion to me? Why do I treat him so horribly?" She sat once again at her vanity, studying her face, beseeching for the one act she so desired to authenticate her utter loss, to appease her doubts, to bury her shame, but alas, the tiny messengers of sorrow, conveyors of pain, deliverers from suffering, kept behind their emerald-colored prison, safely locked away until undiscovered emotional pain could be summoned. "Am I so horrible a person? Do I not feel agony like others? Am I yet stone?" she wondered, seeing her image, yet denying its reality. "Who are you, these days, to betray that which I so dearly love?" She shut her eyes and thought of her babies, dying, her babies dying now, for no reason, for no recognizable purpose, and she was certain that now she would weep within the deep confines of solitude, in the embrace of the comfortable dark, knowing who she was and what she had been through to still be alive, that she was a good person, who had shunned worldly pleasures and pursued a noble path. "Do I not deserve to weep, as other women do?" she raged internally. "Haven't I the same rights? Am I so different?" And when she opened her eyes again, there was nothing but the dry, smooth face that bore the pain of desperation and guilt. "Am I so condemned?"

Their story: he was sometimes gone—for an entire day, and would often come back in the dead of night, his subtle movements awakening her; and upon opening her door, she would find him standing there, his clothes perhaps torn, his arms perhaps bloodied, his countenance perhaps wild, and he would stare at her, and she at him, in total silence, until one or the other, or sometimes both, just drifted back into the safety and solace of nighttime shadows. This happened for months—for months he followed this mysterious schedule, and never an explanation came from him, nor did she demand one.

Is it a woman, she would ask herself; could it be? No, not he, not Dylan, not after going through so much together and losing so much—together; is he getting into fights? With whom? What have I done to him? He is such a good man, and I failed him—why, why am I doing this? What am I waiting for?

And many times he would come to her door and sit down and just talk to her as if she was sitting across from him and listening to his every passionate and true word, to wit:

He would smile. "You know, I dream about little Eleanor and Conall, and I imagine them as I know they would have been—Conall, so handsome, like his uncle, and Eleanor, so beautiful, like her aunt, and we are, all of us, playing together on the great savanna of Kenya—so happy, so carefree, so much in love with each other, because we understand that health is a special gift, as are Freedom, and Faith, and Happiness; and we are so, so happy, Rhiannon, and sometimes Conall and Eleanor are there too, with their child, with Felice, so beautiful like her mother, and all of us are so happy, the way it should have been, had we all survived, had this been Heaven." He paused, reflecting upon the harsh realities of life. "But this is reality, Rhiannon, and reality means experiencing good and bad, pain and joy, gain and loss—but we all must overcome that which we know God wants us to have but have lost, and be the stronger because of it—it is the way we grow, otherwise we are just shallow images flitting on a wall, and not to be believed."

On the other side of this artificial barrier of paint and wood, she too sat, her back against the warm door, her eyes closed, listening to his comforting narrative, her face lit by an ardent expression of affection and a longing for peace, but a smooth countenance that never lasted too long, for the horrible image of her baby's violent deaths would rise up and eclipse any good thing she heard, and she would consequently crawl away and lie in her bed and want to properly grieve, which meant, to her, to weep, which she still had not done. "What kind of cold person have I become, that I cannot grieve for the loss of my own? What good am I to him, now? He deserves someone better, someone who can—feel." It was then and there that she thought of leaving him, to free him of her unworthy self, to allow him to go forward without the weighty chain of her lost and pitiful self around his neck.

She packed her satchel bags one hundred times on different nights—always at night—and one hundred times walked out of her room and down the dimly lit hallway and out the front door and down the cement steps, only to pause as the silvery moonlight wrapped its silken dress around her trembling form, and always she would feel herself begin to weep but knew no tears would come, knowing that she could not possibly leave the only man she'd ever loved, could ever love, must ever love, no matter what happened, had happened, or could happen, that they were truly as one, if a man and woman could be one—and not simply through the saying of certain, carefully rehearsed words, but through the doing of good deeds, of living life together, of exploring the infinite menu of life's choices and selecting those that ultimately make a person more noble, more humble, more human; that by selecting to live in dire conditions and experiencing hardships for the betterment of others, instilled in both of them the kind of honor and nobility that can only be attained through self-sacrifice, and magnified even more when greater self-glory and riches could be secured in its stead, but denied; that by living for others instead of self taught a person why they are alive, gave them purpose to live, helped them understand one of the reasons for Creation; that by doing for those less fortunate than oneself, one was also doing for oneself: that this was a great secret long forgotten, though written in many languages, and many faiths, long ago, and remembered when practiced by those who truly believed it. They were blessed, and were at peace, and furnished with the essential qualities that without do not completely make one human—yes, she knew, to be physiologically human meant thinking and having a body; to exist meant living and breathing, communicating, and eating; to interact involved family, friends, recreation, relatives, and commitment; to be involved meant having your own family, job, responsibilities, relationships, marriages, and caring; but if one lived only for self and family, only for work and play, one was half, and not whole, a victim of seeing only what others with myopic goals see: the immediate, the present conflicts, the selfish self, blowing its own spoiled horn, that to ignore the plight of those who did not have the same opportunity to flourish was to never understand how and why it all came about, and how life once was so hard, and still is, and must be softened by those who have more, much more than they could possibly ever need.

She knew all of this—intellectually, emotionally, spiritually—and it was one reason she could not really leave him, the other reasons being her indefatigable love for him—a love born, nourished, and grown up through their African adventure—which was continually attacked, soured, questioned, and hurt, but always able to repair itself, always coming back stronger after fending off conflicts and assaults from every kind of enemy: temptation, in the form of greed and power; and lust, in the form of other comely flesh; and sorrow and pain, in the form of life; thus, it was a love forged from pain, enduring pain, and now it understood pain, and that caused it to thrive, and not be easily defeated. This was why she could not leave him, why she always turned back and unpacked her bags and soon found himself sitting on the small wooden stool in front of her vanity, for she absolutely knew she could no longer leave him than leave herself.

Still, this tenuous, and susceptible, and therefore dangerous cycle of events went on for Dylan and Rhiannon; and twine that is stretched can only go so far before one side shatters, never to regain its shape.

It Begins

Dylan would come home after work, stay a while, make a few secretive phone calls, and then leave; he would come back late at night, or early in the morning, often disheveled, bruised sometimes, or bleeding, his clothes ripped, his hair matted with blood, his demeanor like that during his time in Africa—and she knew it.

She would burst out of her room to find him in this distressing condition, he standing in the dark kitchen, tending to his wounds, sometimes eating or drinking, and she would just stare in amazement, and he would stare back, and then turn his back on her, and carry on with what he was doing.

"Is he a criminal now—no!" she would ponder, and then curse herself for such a slander. "Not him; then what, what! What is he doing?"

It was nearly Winter now, Winter with its unforgiving cold breath blowing relentlessly over the land, yet a mild breath, a very mild humor, this Winter's tale here in this southern region of the Americas, not a genuine winter, really, but imitation, not a significant change to qualify as a season, merely an alteration in the calendar weather—warmer to colder; little rain to simply more; no snow to, well, no snow: it was, after all, founded in an arid region, this sprawling county of Angels.

Now, it was raining, this dark night, when both of them were at home, hard rain, unrelenting, pounding, loud rain drumming on their tiled roof, the cemented walkway to their front porch, their back lawn, and he listened to it as he lay in his bed, and remembered; and she listened to it as she lay in her bed, and remembered, and both of them wondered what it would have been like had baby Eleanor and baby Conall lived, for this was the two-year anniversary—if an anniversary for such a tragic event should even have a marker—of baby Eleanor's death.

A kaleidoscope of memories was evoked in the walls of their minds: of people, places, and things that had happened, and people, places, and things not real, of possibilities that should have been, should have been given to them because they had labored so hard to do what they knew was right and honorable, but somehow, was denied them; and their reverie on this gloomy night, this torrential downpour of cold rain, moved over the casting of an unknown future, of what might befall them—what if more pain, more sorrow, more tragedy—and poured over two who had freely given up so much to help so many; did they deserve this suffering, did the past and immediate pain presage more agony, more emotional toil; had they brought this upon themselves by denying their true design in life, that of the true warrior prince and princess who needed to be honest about who they were, and who should desire no family, other than other warriors? How much more could they manage, and not be bitter? These thoughts they both had, for both, being together so long and through so many difficulties, and having to rely on each other—unlike the wealthy who so often rely on subordinates for too many important things—they had to learn to love each other; and unlike the rich and contented, they had to learn to compromise and understand what the other thought, and please the other, to want to please the other, and doing so, please themselves, and in doing so, find true love—unlike those simply wedded and kept bound by mere paper and mortgages and responsibilities; and by living, truly living, as they had endured hardship and risked life and limb, and denied self; and by the pursuit of bringing succor to others, they understood life, and in doing so, understood each other, and what the other needed to survive: love, loyalty, fidelity, respect, honor, courage; and so, as it was, they were truly the same person, although entirely separate as male and female in unique emotions and thoughts and physiology—but in what essential ingredients that binds us all as humans, they were as one.

And then a deep shudder took hold of her as she lay pondering their life, an electric jolt that rippled throughout her sleeping form and caused her to rise up and leap out of her warm bed. It was a new thought, posed to her from where she knew not, possessing such a radical new shape, of sound and fury, so dynamic, so ferocious, of power and determination, so shining and so seemingly new, but somehow so ancient, too, as if she had had this thought dedicated to her consciousness long ago through trial and tribulation; as it was, she knew what she must do now, and it was too late for a sensible mind to circumvent her actions.

She knew exactly what she had to do and did not care what anyone else would think about it, so, consequently, she simply banished all musings about it, and simply acted.

There she went: to the plastic bag wherein the bloodied gown of silent horror lay, and took it out, undressed, put it on, walked barefoot to the door, opened it, saw and heard the exuberant rain but cared not for its puny presence, and therein, leaped down the cement steps and began to run full tilt out into the black pitch of night.

O, how hard she ran, running full speed, and able to sustain it due to her magnificent shape, running unimpeded down soaked sidewalks, running madly, wildly, magnificently, not slowing down, not tiring, not deterred, boldly, toward her goal, thinking of only one thought, one idea that was driving her fiercely onward to where she must soon be, one hungry, all-consuming, powerful idea that must be consummated this very night.

She was there soon enough, leaping over the red-brick barriers and onto the soaked grass and running expertly through the stone markers, twisting, turning, and leaping, until she came upon it, and then felt her body grow numb as she finally stood before these memorials to those who were so wrongfully and spitefully taken from her; and she stared at the gray gravestones for several minutes, trembling in fury, and she then read the words aloud, "Here lies Conall Glenn Cuchulain II; here lies Eleanor Saoirse Cuchulain…" but she could not even speak the rest, and she began to weep pious tears that she could feel flow down her hot cheeks; and she trembled in her furious power, as she breathed in and out heavily, her lips quivering, her face flushed with sorrow, so full of wrath and vengeance was her usually soft and gentle voice, so hard and mean, so devoid of the very molecules of passion and caring that her mind and body united to protect her; and yea, as she spoke, her translucent tears became dark, red as blood, and smelled of a powerful narcotic, and colored her trembling countenance, and drew a grim picture of the mask of the resurrected warrior, in a voice that was trembling from unleashed and unrequited fury, "Promise me…"

He was standing behind her now, having too put on his bloodied clothes from the plastic bag, then running full bore and barefoot in his determined pursuit of her, and now staring at her extraordinarily defiant and erect posture.

Her voice seemed to possess a kind of supernatural thunder that exceeded the pale ordinary thunder of earth and sky, her rhythms and tones deeper and richer than the regular rhythms and tones of the rain, her voice seeming to light up the graveyard in bursts of conflagration brighter than the white lightning that crackled above them, for her voice came from a primal source that all Nature obeyed and bowed to, respected and wept for—it seemed that Nature was weeping for her loss too, her pain, her sorrow, that the icy rain was her pain, and the rain its silvery droplets of sorrow.

"Promise me," she cried, as he stood, panting still, behind her, and her tone became that of the Huntress: the howl of the Red Wolf, the roar of the Black Panther, the screech of the Golden Eagle as they set forth to find their prey, "you will kill them all." Her blood-red tears trickled down her blood-red gown, and the colors became as one.

He was no longer here in a civilized world, part of an organized community that tacitly agreed to obey laws where most sought to live together in peace and harmony, no; now, he was above and beyond them, back in Africa, back in the sharp talons of injustice and inequality that squeezed and tore at him to do what he knew was right and fair; he was the warrior again, activated by the revelation of tragedy, of harsh realities, of what should be and must be. "Yes, I promise," he cried, in a magnificent shout, and gazing upon the gravestones still, he, for the first time in many months, put his mighty arms around her, and then turned her around to search a face that was consumed with a pathos unimaginable, finding her volcanic-colored eyes glowing with an iridescent fire that had been burning since first Man heaped suffering upon his brother. "I promise you, upon our children's graves, I will kill all those who need to die."

They gazed into the blazing eyes of the other, but more than this: into his beaming soul, she saw; into her beaming soul, he saw; into his passionate heart, she journeyed; into her passionate heart, he journeyed; into his fervent mind, she was joined, into her fervent mind, he was joined; he into her being, her into his being, two minds, two hearts, two souls, as one, thinking as one, breathing as one, living as one, and dedicated to the principle that Justice would be meted out, by righteous means, by righteous judgment, in one clear, bold vision, sustained by an inexhaustible quest for Truth and Love; they would not this day nor ever again be denied the fulfillment of their true heritage, the heritage of every freedom-loving people, that all men and women are created equal, that they are endowed by their Creator with certain inalienable rights; that among them are life, liberty, and the pursuit of happiness and property—but that when it becomes evident that the government has failed to safeguard these rights, it is therefore necessary to provide new safeguards for their future security; as the present government had failed, this new entity just breathed into existence, in one bold union now, declared, "to protect our homes, our families, our businesses, we will do what others have tried to do, could not do, or would not do, and all have failed, regardless of their ambitions or excuses."

He took her now in his strong arms, his passion unbridled as he stared at her raw, sensuous beauty with a desire unimaginable, a desire to be one with her body, mind and soul, and as she stared upon his muscular presence, she felt a desire to be one with his mind, body and soul; and presently he kissed her, long and hard, and she kissed him, and they began to fall, as if they were uniting to a heightened state few lovers could ever attain, where their very essences commingled and dissolved into the other, to create one superior, complete human being who evolved for the betterment of the world.

And then, amid the still hard, unrelenting cold rain, they slowly and gently were falling, falling slowly to the ground and finally into the mud and slush; they lay, wrapped in a lovers' embrace of unbridled passion, kissing and hugging, stroking and holding; and yea, they consummated their love for each other, there, right atop the memories of their children, unafraid of where they were or who they were now or what they were about to do; and lo, when the fierce storm had passed and the night sky magician had torn away her carnivorous cloak to allow the first golden rays of a diamond-studded dawn to fasten its gossamer wings upon the land, this shaft of luminous light revealed those who lay prostrate upon their children's graves: her right hand holding his left, both of them staring up at the deep pools of this new azure sky, at the promise of a new dawn full of hope and redemption, both of them silent, but internally, set to do what few have ever dared to do.

And from this humble plot of land, a grand vision was born, which should never have been conceived had society done what must be done, long ago; and it was now too late to put back that which was recently given life, this bold creation called back into existence once more, for once the hallowed bells of Justice ring throughout the land, our aroused minds cannot be compelled to purge that which was newly acquired, and that sacred bell cannot be unrung.

Book Three

When first he realized Rhiannon was not to be so easily healed in mind, body, and spirit, Dylan instinctively knew what must be done—although he had refused entry of such a revolutionary notion to now usurp and tear his peaceful pilgrim's clothes that he had so humbly and gladly worn as of late and dedicated his life in the wearing of, which had been a symbol of an emerging new mindset that had evolved from having done good through physical battle—to once more weave the battle dress of the soldier and equip himself with the fearsome warrior's armor, which proclaimed, undeniably, irretrievably, war.

He had felt the desire, the necessity to walk back into the eternal conflagration he miraculously lived in and had once walked away from, for too many customs and laws had been recently broken, and he was not to be appeased.

"Who else is out there," he wondered, soon after the murder of little Conall; "we must be diligent, for unnatural forces have crossed into our heritage, who are no respecter of human life."

He loathed leaving Rhiannon alone, and whenever he did go, he was sure to have a confidant watching the place.

Of course, he would not do what he intended to do alone, knew he could not be the only one who had come to this conclusion about the world, not if they understood the world as he did: analyzing it from one extreme geographical point to another in terms of war, chaos, poverty, inhumanity, injustice, incessant political unrest, to tranquility, peace, harmony, opportunity, hope, democracy; and there were his travels that had enlightened him, and his growing up in the idyllic verdant harvest of Ireland's gorgeous pastures; he had seen much, and knew what he saw now did not have to be the way it was, it had just, he reasoned, become this way, and the solutions were too accommodating toward the wrongdoer, too societally correct, and therefore too judiciously tepid; but that is all about to stop, he decided, and I will do the stopping.

It is a great boast to challenge comfortable societal norms while one is riding a violent recoil from a senseless murder, for one in this circumstance vows to the stars and man, and God above, his resolute will to fight the perpetrators of the heinous crime and all who were willing participants of it, for it is hot passion taking its turn in the highest temple of righteousness, and who can deny the honor of this seemingly implacable vow?

No matter the degree of passion, despite its depths dug by moral outrage, its height seared and sealed by wrath, its wrath carved by bloodlust, it cools; like any good sword drawn from the blacksmith's pool of molten steel, it must reach equilibrium or melt from its own inner fire; but, Man, at least some men, some skilled men who have traversed o'er the hot coals of war, have learned how to rein in these passions and form them into a source of power that drives them and sustains their will to victory; but this harnessed passion cannot cool or heat, dwindle or expire, lest the host lose his desire or act imprudently; thus, nearly all men, in their lust for vengeance, rebuke their carelessness, and retire to the former comforts of safety, security, and satiation of spirit, while others go forward too fast with too little foresight, heeding no admonition, acknowledging no merit in patience, and so, most implode, or cause more harm than good, and as for those who succeed, it is too few to consider.

Dylan had learned forbearance from the fathers and mothers of forbearance—from whom he had also learned leadership, planning, responsibility, strategy, discipline, humility, the time to listen, the time to speak, the time to act, the time to advance, time to retreat—from his parents, his brother, the Crusaders, from his wife, and from those he fought for; so when he commenced any adventure, his mind was free of chaos, his heart in a simmering chamber, his soul humming and wanting battle.

He would not now, or ever could, relent once he set his mind to such a weighty task, any more than the sun could choose to no longer awaken man with its shining grin, and he drew his every ounce of wide-awake, powerful drive from a tiny, harnessed, bursting with energy, concentrated power source, and its name was Justice.

But no man is an island, no man an army, no matter his best intentions or his abilities, as he needs others of a like mind and will, honor and resolve; so, he called first the man with whom he had long ago existed in a seemingly forgotten—except for those who still live there—adventure on a faraway continent.

He met Robert and Paul sometime after that dreadful day of his son's death, who both expressed their hope that Rhiannon was well. He sat in Robert's home, on a small, inexpensive sofa; Paul, with his brown cane leaning against a chocolate-brown coffee table, sitting on a brown leather easy chair, in fact, now leaning back in seemingly quiet comfort, watching his guest intently, while Robert sat on his chestnut hardwood rocking chair, in fact, rocking back and forth, his eyes closed but his ears quite open, as he listened to Dylan expound on the merits and boundaries of his ambitions.

When Dylan had exhausted his plans, Paul said, rather heatedly, about those named culprits, "Were I the Emperor of this miserable planet, I would slowly drown them all."

Robert opened his eyes, stood up, walked up to Paul, placed a reassuring hand upon his slender shoulders, walked to the center of the living room, which was sparse with furniture, and faced the two men, speaking in a carefully scripted voice replete with a cool tone, volume, and cadence. "I do not believe it is healthy to sit on a construction of wood and cloth and leather that costs more than a middle-class family makes in a year, or might feed an entire poor village for a year—instead," and he suddenly dropped his arms as he barely whispered; "Zulu one," and he was presently bathed in a sparkling, pulsing being that radiated about his body. "Behold, the product of man's wondrous imaginings."

Dylan rose to inspect this modern engineering marvel, standing next to it, as if it were an alien species. "A force field of some kind…"

"Yes, and much more," he said, and nodded toward Paul, who now had a SIG Sauer P320 pistol with a SRD9 silencer in his hand, and without hesitation, fired at Robert, but then smiled mischievously as he watched Dylan's incredulous face.

"The bullet was absorbed into the energy field," Paul said, now standing next to Dylan.

"Yes, the Zulu project turned the expended energy of the bullet upon itself and consumed it—like a cannibal—and grew stronger," said Robert.

Dylan put his hand up to the whirling, streaming vortex.

"The Zulu project can be activated by only three signature voices: its creator," Paul intoned proudly, "and— Zulu one," and instinctively, he too was cloaked in its intricate web of pulsing light.

"Fantastic!" Dylan whispered, in awe as he closely observed the phenomenon.

"It is technology that drives an economy, Dylan," Robert began; "did you know that the economies of the world did not grow until the Industrial Revolution of the nineteenth century? Technology, like this," he whispered, as he walked, the molecular shield still encircling him, but it then abruptly lost its shine, and evaporated, leaving a faint aura around him. Paul then walked out of his. "Zulu is not complete, yet." Robert placed his hand upon the shoulders of Dylan, and gazed with utter solemnity into his eyes, and said, "Technology must be used for the betterment of society," he said, in earnest, and then smiled. "You're about a size large—six feet, I would say." Dylan nodded. "Let us counsel together, about what needs be done, and how to do it, and who will join us."

Paul said, fervently, "The fight is not just where tyrannical governments claim authority."

"No," Robert continued, "it is wherever the common people have no voice against any kind of social injustice; Dylan, we were as one in Mother Africa, as are we all now; where one seeks help, there we shall all be; where one falls, another rises."

"Our credo," Dylan whispered, in reverence, thinking of the Crusaders. "Force and right are the governors of the world…"

"And force until right is ready," Robert correctly responded.

"Eternal vigilance…" Paul said, proudly.

"Come," Robert said, at the same time moving toward the elevator, "and see what weapons the twenty-first-century soldier needs; and oh, yes, this room is soundproof, anti-eavesdropping, too," and then made a circle with his index fingers and thumbs and put each before an eye. "Technology, not leather chairs."

Robert breathed into a device located next to the elevator door, which activated an LCD screen, on which he placed his hand, and then spoke into a small black microphone next to it. "Beyond the pale," and then he spoke in the language of one of the African tribes that produces clicks, the Hadza of Tanzania. The elevator door promptly opened, as he said, grinning slyly, with a wink at Dylan, "So the help doesn't get lost…"

Once inside, Robert repeated the same process, and down the elevator went, some four floors. His demeanor became grave once more, as if the problems of the world had been placed around his neck. "It is a great responsibility to be wealthy—one can effect change for the betterment of society, but one must have the proper bearing or the money goes to waste." The elevator stopped, and he repeated the safety procedures.

Paul then said, his tone steeped in animus against the inferred contents of his words, "You don't have to be at war to prepare for war."

The door parted, and the future of urban warfare unfurled itself before them.

Tools of the Trade

"We're not in Africa anymore," Robert said, with a knowingly wry grin, as the three men looked out on the far horizon of fantastic state-of-the-art objects. "Tanzania 5, Operation Vigilante," he said, and the myriad of electrical alarms and locks, lasers and traps was disarmed. He put out his hand. "Let us proceed to what Paul calls 'the creator's room.'"

Indeed, as they moved forward, Dylan espied diverse kinds of hitherto unknown technological fancies: either real or imagined, in theory only, as an outline, a model of, in various stages of completion, completed but not tested, tested but not completed, and completely done, and usable, and hanging from wires, lying on tables, and propped up.

"I want to introduce you to some of our little friends," Robert said, proudly, and then, looking out across the vast stretch of worktables and stations, and computers and assorted machines, he said, low and sweetly, while holding his right hand slightly out and beckoning something hither, "Come, Betty Butterfly, come to Papa," and behold, from out among the darkened vistas came a cherry-red and deep-ocean-blue butterfly, moving straight toward him, until it landed softly on his hand. He turned toward Dylan. "You can pet her; she isn't shy."

Dylan reached out to touch the remarkable engineering feat, gently touching the fine sheath of red and blue wings as they slowly flapped back and forth, marveling at the slender carbon rods that held together the elastic capacitor films.

"Remarkable, isn't it? The butterfly is a simple yet elegant creature in Nature, yet it has taken us thirty years of concentrated scientific endeavors to make even a reasonable facsimile of it." He smiled as he gazed upon Dylan's awe.

"You must have some homing device on you," Dylan whispered.

"Very good, Dylan—yes, it is my ring," he answered, wiggling his hand with the computer chip in the ring on his little finger, and promptly tossed up the mechanical marvel, saying simultaneously, "Quadrant 4, Betty Butterfly," and off flew the graceful machine to its robotic sleep, and then whispered, "Ah, but hopefully her brothers and sisters will not need this kind of homing device..."

"You're on television," Paul said, mischievously, nodding his head at several LCD screens mounted on walls surrounding them.

Dylan saw images of the three men, from the vantage point of Betty Butterfly. "Surveillance camera, too," he whispered; "amazing."

Robert pointed to a distant workstation, and said, "Keep your eyes on that table, and watch the mannequin there," and he clapped four times in rapid succession, paused, then three times, and then winked, snapped his fingers twice, and something stirred.

"Can you guess what it is, eh, Mr. Cuchulain?" Paul asked, excitedly.

The gliding plane came slowly toward them at approximately twenty meters high, and showing images from below on the screens, when suddenly it emitted a pinpoint-width laser beam at the mannequin, knocking it backward with a powerful blast.

Dylan's voice was tinged in awestruck colors, when he whispered, "The future…"

"I am very curious to see how this latest innovation to technology that is decades-old suits you," Robert began, walking them over to a station where hung a unit resembling a miniature jetpack but with wings, and then said in deep reverence to its inventors, "the X-1 Kitty Hawk."

"A jet wing pack," Dylan said, inspecting the contraption. "I'm sure your people have made it useful and practical."

"Yes, for a machine invented so long ago," Robert replied, watching Paul help Dylan place the pack on him, "so very little was done to improve it—until now, and now it is virtually noiseless, far-ranging, reliable, and weapon-ready; you see, the wings are made of carbon fiber, the unit is powered by four of my specially designed jet engines and maneuvered by the flyer's body motions, but unlike earlier versions where the rocketeer had to parachute down, we have modified it so the flyer can now land safely and at his own speed; and then blast upward, if necessary, very quickly, and with cargo," and he pointed to a small platform attached at the base.

"Fantastic," Dylan murmured, feeling the incredibly lightweight material conform to his particular physique.

After Dylan removed the unit, the trio resumed the tour, and Dylan learned of many projects that were available only to certain intelligence agencies, or existed as skeletal ideas in science journals and abstracts, and science books; and many that were available on the free market from companies or universities were simply improved upon here, such as augmented reality.

And then they came to a table that contained the greatest innovation of his scientists.

"This," Robert waved over the device, like a proud father, "is the first, fully functional quantum computer, and operational at room temperature," he smiled, nodding his head; it is "amazing that we have come this far, from my friends long ago at MIT who first proposed such a special creature—it is so radically different from an ordinary computer whose memory is composed of bits that are either a one or a zero; but ah, here we have," and he bent down and looked at it fondly, "qubits, that can represent a one or zero, and virtually any state that exists in between, a kind of netherworld..." He tilted his head and closed his eyes. "O, with this computer, we shall uncover that which hitherto has remained covered—there shall be no encrypted code we shall not be able to decipher, such is the power of this miracle machine, for it will render all others as if an adult to infant in knowledge and power, and is not to be rivaled anywhere; we shall visit the Dark Web and see what artful deception these villains practice..."

"You see," Robert said, after they had viewed all of the projects on this particular floor, "the science to make the seemingly impossible possible, or the impractical practical, is quite often there, it's just that the people involved have ulterior motives to allow the idea to flounder or flourish."

"Money," Paul said, disgusted.

"Yes, and power, too—but we want these inventions to benefit Mankind, if it takes our very last penny."

"We were broke before and don't mind being broke again—on principle," Paul said.

Robert became serious. "In Africa, we had the luxury of acting like a sovereign nation, because there was no uniformity or stability, no recognized, legitimate government or authority to tell us to leave—we were like an army, but we happened to be moral, and obeyed universal mores in our dealings; but here, there are rules, so we must be very careful when we practice stealth that society frowns upon."

"O, if an Emperor I, I would suspend habeas corpus, and do what needs be done," Paul said, impassioned.

Robert smiled warmly. "Emperor Paul..."

Paul looked at Dylan. "I have been going to university here, I have learned what America was like, and what she should be—and I don't like what she is, now."

If before Robert was somber, now he became grave with a fervent will as he spoke once more to Dylan. "You must have wondered if I would have begun a new Crusade in the Americas against our common enemies even without your terrible loss." But he lingered now, and looked over the multitudinous array of state-of-the-art technologies. "A nation builds weapons during times of peace to prepare for war, keeps an army on the ready to prepare for war, but must be wary of engaging in a conflict unless an infraction among them warrants a prolonged series of battles—that leads to war." He nodded now, as if he were reflecting on the long-ago past, and then on the present, and thus, was silent for a while, and finally said, with malicious intent, "We finally have the technology to do what could not have been done twenty years ago; so," he paused, "now we will begin to move the second hand one tick away from twelve o'clock midnight, and perhaps gain a few seconds backward toward what so many have so long and bravely fought for…"

Crime Report

"Scholars are fond of saying that corporations, lawyers, and money rule the world—well, I have all three," Robert began, as the men, once again in his secured living room, sat on the humble sofas, "and I intend to use them to profit my own affairs, which then profits Mankind, especially those good people of sacrifice who have much endured much, especially those who have done so and have been unfairly punished by entities unworthy of the rights of Man." He nodded to Paul, and pointed toward a panel in the wall, then continued speaking to Dylan. "What I learned in Africa, and China, in India—in many countries—is that a robust economy can get more people out of poverty than all the foreign aid and charity combined."

"A free market in free societies allowed to flourish…" Paul said.

"Yes, free—but even then, we must also provide a chance to those who still need assistance," Robert continued.

Paul, having extracted the documents from the wall safe, walked back and handed them to Robert. "The police report," Robert said, solemnly, laying the manila folder on the glass coffee table in front of Dylan.

Dylan stared at the documents that contained the information which might expose the culprits behind the evisceration of his quiet, unassuming life, and for him to reach for it now was a declaration that he wanted to know who was responsible, and once knowing this, knew he must act. He picked it up, and read the three papers; presently, he put them down, his face a whiter shade of pale. "The Cartels…"

"Yes, this one particular Cartel—by ordering the hit through their gang affiliate, and burning down a building they thought full of children, sends a message of such maliciousness, on a scale of such unequaled magnitude of evil, that they establish themselves as players without a conscience, but also worthy of rebuke—and if not from our indigenous authorities, then from those who can, by our skills and resources, and will, by our ambition to right wrongs, right wrongs; there is no other choice, other than to drown in our own self-misery and inaction."

"The Cartels," Paul said, handing Dylan more manila envelopes, "have infested our country, like a virus unleashed."

"This will not, must not stand," Robert said; "not here, not in America— to allow them entry and become a fixture of crime would be a critical error of the intelligence community." He pointed to a confidential report. "As you know, the authorities are fighting them, but with limited success."

"The Cartels have moved across the borders in Texas, Arizona, California; they are into all forty-eight continental states—like a spreading contagion," Paul said, disgusted. "Crime rates are up."

"Yes," Robert said, "kidnappings, murder, assault, the sex trade, human trafficking, bribery—every filthy act connected with their initial global enterprise, the making and distribution of illegal drugs, has increased, but the authorities have to play by the rules."

Paul grinned, but it wasn't born from glee, but hope and satisfaction. "They think America is Africa—where even now they're invading; a continent to take as they please, to corrupt our politics, and buy everyone with their filthy lucre."

Dylan read the confidential report again, while Robert and Paul went into the kitchen to prepare refreshments. "Money," he mused, as he finished it, "can only buy that which is corruptible."

Robert and Paul returned with green tea and fresh fruit, and sandwiches, and now the men talked of what needed to be done; and when it was over, and the night had been too long drawn over the land, Dylan bade them farewell, and then, said, standing there, with no little difficulty, "I thank you for your prayers for Rhiannon," knowing the men had not seen her in over a month, and were curious about her absence at the new Community Youth Center. "She is a good woman, a strong woman…" But when he felt tears about to betray his sorrow, he abated, and turned away, as if to admire, and indeed, comment on some structural design inside the mammoth home.

Paul and Robert felt this flood of emotional distress, and too withheld their want to weep; presently, Robert handed Dylan one more document-filled manila folder, and after the men exchanged handshakes, and farewells, Dylan left, and soon arrived at his own home, and upon entering, saw Rhiannon come out of her room and look at him with confusion and concern.

Once inside the safety of his room, he opened the folder, and read aloud, in a guttural whisper, information not found in the police report, as his body went numb, his warrior spirit igniting his passion for revenge. "Herein are the details of the murder of Conall Cuchulain II, specifically the identities of the perpetrators; being the three members of the 122nd Street Black Hoods gang in the car: Jamaal White, LaShawn Brown, Henry Davis, who have been apprehended and admitted their role in this initiation for gang membership, and the Cartel responsible for ordering the murder: the Azteca Cartel, of Mexico, state of Azteca; but the name of their actual shooter has yet to be identified."

He closed his eyes, imagining the facial characteristics of his antagonists, allowing their malevolent properties to boil over, and then whispered in a voice as if blown by a furious, hot wind, "They are dead already—they just don't know it." And right there and then, he began to sup on, at the precise interruption in the history of peace, the thick meat and rich frothy drink of the cool, calculating, and cunning avenger.

Friendly Persuasion

Samuel Longfellow was not like other people as it concerns compassion; what the poor and diseased felt, their humiliation, their shame, he felt in kind; what miseries and discrimination they experienced, he felt in kind; what good things were absent in their lives, he felt, too, for although he was handsome, healthy, and of middle-class status, he felt more kinship with those who seemed to be forgotten by a prosperous society. "Deeds, not words," he would often tell himself, and often, as he was visiting and helping at the Children's Hospital, volunteering at the Veterans' Retirement Home, helping at the local homeless shelter; and with him now, whom he had recently met, was a woman, whose name was Florence McGuire, a young lawyer who specialized in defending the poor, the seemingly defenseless, and those once accused and now residing in jail—but after her long, detailed analysis, she believed to be imprisoned falsely. He had known, he had always known, even when long ago he was stepping off the path that leads to perdition, that he needed to be with his own kind, someone who believe wholeheartedly in his causes, his beliefs, his aspirations, and not with those lukewarm, Harvey Milquetoast, stay-close-to-the-wall-for-fear-that-being-out-of-the-shadows-might-expose-us-a-human-being-respon-sible-for-not-only yourself-but-your-brothers-as-well people, but people overflowing with love for those who could not quite seem to put one step in front of the other on the brightly lit, easy-to-maneuver road to the Good Life, and Florence McGuire was such a gentle and loving and caring soul. So, now he had a companion to aid him in his quest to bring succor to the fallen, and his strength was doubled, and his confidence boundless.

And then along came a spider, with a venomous bite, and its name was immorality, and its venom was a bullet, and the consequences tragic, bringing upheaval to his upwardly mobile plans to right wrongs and save the perish-ing-into-darkness day.

The death of baby Conall was like an insurmountable brick wall he crashed into full bore, at which point he was unceremoniously slammed to the unyield-ing, hard ground; now what—what should he do, forgive and forget this, too, forgive and forget, who? What was he forgiving, and forgetting? These things he contemplated, and this, too: how much more will we suffer, what else can these offenders do, and will I ignore it? What inhuman decrees can they enact, and will I still step aside? Who can they hurt, how many can they injure, what damage can they do, so that I will yet be a man and step up? But should I step up? Who am I to intercede? I have chosen to wade into the mire and attempted to retrieve those who wish to be rescued—what am I to do with those who have no conscience and prey upon the Innocent? Am I not only one man, who has no official designation to move against these indigenous terrorists? Have I not chosen to ignore their crimes and help the criminals to reform—how else will they be helped? Who am I to judge? Who am I to throw down the gavel and pronounce sentence? Do I help those who have committed this heinous crime? Absolutely not! But do I help those who have committed other heinous crimes to other people's children and ask for genuine contrition—absolutely yes! Aren't all children God's children; aren't all children our concern: your brother, my brother, your sister, my sister, your child, like my child—how is it any different?

If I refuse to help those who did this, I must quit now, pick up the sword and smite them all. But then he would hold his head on high: Yet, they must repent, and I will visit them in jail…

His past quarreled with his present, and his present condemned the future.

Life is never easy, he reasoned, when you care deeply, or, perhaps, care too much.

In the beginning, sometime after the funeral, when the world seemed to lose some of the gray pall that hung like a black funeral wreath over the land, he had wanted to visit Dylan and Rhiannon, but felt this too intrusive, and decided that they would reach out to him on their own; but as time went on, and they did not contact him, he worried, and asked Florence for her opinion on the delicate matter.

"You are their good friend, you have certain responsibilities and privileges," she said, as the two sat together in his modest home. "You have been through much with them, there is no casual acquaintance—there is a bond," and she intertwined her slender fingers.

He felt her gentle presence, her pleasing spirit wash over him like a warm balm, and he was reassured of his role.

As it was, when Dylan again assumed his role as coach and counselor at the rebuilt Community Youth Center, Samuel was sure to spend time with him alone.

"How is Rhiannon?" he asked, sheepishly, one day, as the two men sat in the office of the place long after the other adult helpers and children had departed.

Dylan, his stoic face unmoved, replied, "She is well," and offered nothing more, a universal signal between two men that the topic was private between husband and wife, and not to be discussed elsewhere—sealed from the outside in a tight marital world.

"How about you, Dylan—how are you?"

Dylan, his countenance still smooth, could have provided the same answer, but since he had recently met with Robert and Paul, offered more to make known the unknown feelings of Samuel. "It has been hard," he began, carefully, looking his compatriot full in his searching black eyes, "to forget."

There, this was what Samuel needed, an opening in the normally reticent culture of grieving men. "I hear you, brother, I do," he whispered, nodding slightly, but then saying nothing more, not wanting to risk a breach of his friend's delicate system of internal security walls.

Dylan continued in a more resilient tone, "You work hard and help those in need and this happens…" He let seep out a little more emotional carnage as an attractive lure, just enough to protect his male shield.

Samuel had to open the leak a tiny bit more. "So, what does one do when this happens?"

Dylan was quick in response this time. "A man has choices…"

"Capitulation or perseverance…"

Dylan resumed his stone-still image again, and let the heavy air around them breathe before he coolly said, "There are other choices."

The vague, flitting references, veiled and cast in hard, unyielding images and tones, needed a lucid illustrator, and Samuel began to draw them with his pointed words. "One can always join a monastery."

Dylan issued a half-smile, but it quickly vanished. "One could, but one could also do something."

Samuel felt a surge of worry bear up in himself, and hoping it was a false interpretation of Dylan's last connotation, lifted up a tiny pebble to throw into the unclear waters, and ushered forth a grin at this still-strong wall of imperceptible emotions. "Men such as we follow a calling—some call it Providence; it is a hard thing to abandon our destiny."

"Sometimes a man discovers his fate is on the peak of another mountain, after he has climbed one next to it—but a man must keep his eyes open."

Samuel knew about the death of a little Eleanor, and he feared that Dylan spoke of those things Samuel hoped Dylan would not do; still, he had to know, now, and so he said, with resoluteness, "So, what does one do now—climb the other mountain—and what if it is mined, and leading to a danger the man cannot yet perceive—and who should have stayed safe on the other mountain."

"The greater the risks, the greater the rewards…"

"Hey, no one said this job was easy, either—and the rewards are substantial."

"And for those who cannot conform to your efforts, nor the rules of society, do their heinous acts go unheeded by the proper authorities—what of they?"

Samuel knew now, could see clearly now, for the carefully constructed barrier of masculine vanity and ego of Dylan had hemorrhaged, and it bled a red, pungent aroma that burned and would confuse the senses of a weaker man; but he thought himself, by his own charitable actions and selfless deeds, too far above these renegade fumes to be influenced by them.

"The calling of men such as we is to minister to the fallen souls who seek our guidance, not to have them arrested." There, Samuel had emphatically stated his—their—unstated mission statement.

"And when does the peacekeeper realize there are those who truly do not want peace, and seek to destroy that peace, and the peacekeeper? Should the peacekeeper still give succor to those who need it, and give no comfort to those who would destroy an Innocent?"

"The role of the peacekeeper is to practice and keep peace, the practice of nonviolence toward an amelioration of aggression."

"In war, does not the International Red Cross give aid to fallen souls on both sides—because if one side does not respect the red armband, their soldiers may die unattended? It is the way of civilized nations, but I tell you this," he had spoken plainly and calmly, but now his volume increased as if stoked by anger, "this place is not truly civilized, and nonviolence only works in a true democracy."

The hot ash from Dylan's smoldering fire landed on Samuel's equilibrium and upset its delicate balance. "So, what would you have us do," he nearly cried, holding up both hands at an equal height, "on the one hand, help," and he lifted up his left hand, "and the other, declare war?" And he lifted up the other hand to the height of the other, his frowning face determined by a rising frustration and uneasiness that held an untenable position.

Dylan was about to declare the credo of the Crusaders, but yielded to its memory of something special still far removed from the understanding of civilized man; and when he did speak, his face was flushed with the pride and honor, his voice lean of calamity, and fat with passion, in words he would later recite to his fellows, "I will do what I must to ensure that this nation I now proudly call home is a home I can live in without fear of a criminal force that is all powerful because it has been allowed to prosper, because we acquiesced to it and thus fear it, and flourishing, because it knows our civilized breeding will not allow us to meet fire with fire."

Samuel had now to defend the historicity of a peacekeeper mission as solely noncombative, even when a malevolent enemy is about to massacre defenseless soldiers and the peacekeeper might prevent it with a single whisper of admonition, or tread violently upon his path from soldier and sinner, to peacemaker and protector. "And what if someone had met my fire with fire when I was young and foolish?"

Dylan was unmoved. "That is a future you will never know..."

"No, Dylan, no—wouldn't I just have been another casualty of war: a casualty on the street, a youth not given the chance to reform and give back to the community?"

"I cannot argue the present by an unknown past."

Samuel inclined his head ever so slightly. "What are you saying, Dylan— that we should not reach out to these wayward youth? I know you're not," he began, a slow fever beginning to heat up his words, and he gestured about, "because you are in here, working with these kids; that means you still believe in our mission."

Dylan knew he must elicit from Samuel a response that would define him as consummately committed to his non-passive reconciliation with the most hyper-violent criminal activists, but having at least a doubt, a reasonable doubt, a future possibility that might include a physical, proactive presence on the mean streets.

"I believe," so he began, his countenance smooth upon the surface, hiding his passions, "in offering chances," and here he reached out his right hand, palm down, which could crush a man's skull with one blow—a feat he had done oft in Africa—and turned it over slowly; "to every person, and if they reject it, I still keep out my hand," then he put out his left hand, palm down, and too turned that over; so, now he had two hands out that could hold down and squeeze a man unto death—a feat he had done oft in Africa; "and offer both hands to help anyone who seeks it, and this help I offer freely, and always will—and even when someone rejects my offer, I do not cry nor moan, but keep my hands out still, to the same ones, or anyone; it is what I must do now with hands such as these," and as he looked at his unusually large, white hands, he compelled Samuel to do the same: the fingers were thick, like knotted ropes, so that when he happened to make a fist, it seemed as if something fashioned from the heartiest twine of Nature extended from his wrist; the back of his hands were scarred, as were the palms, from sword cuts, bullet holes, knife slices, rope burns, bark abrasions, and venomous insect bites and stings, as if his hands were merely shells that had been pummeled and pounded, whacked and hacked, as they had led the body through the enemy-infested jungles. And then he said, solemnly, his tone the very essence of peace and forgiveness, "And for all who ask, I will lift them up, and I will not abandon them, no matter how many times they fall, for Man is a weak vessel, and seeks to do what is right, and ought to be given the chance to transcend his foibles; and as for those who seek to harm me—or my own," and with the last uttered word, his cobalt-blue eyes lit like a rising flame, and his tone became grim, like a coming apocalypse, "after first rejecting the free offer of society, and then freely rejecting my offer, they must know that there is Justice in the world," and as he raised his head on high, his posture straightened and his voice grew stronger, it seemed to Samuel that he had suddenly transformed into someone else, some figure he had rarely seen in his lifetime: the singular, highly polished, powerful glare of the warrior that can come only from tried-and-true experiences with the most dangerous and roughest opponent and terrain, and triumphant, in no uncertain terms, through a multifaceted arsenal of defense and offense, through hand-to-hand combat, and diverse weapons, a mesmerizing aura that he had seen only in Special Forces veterans who had been plunged into the very heart of darkness, and in order to survive, had performed all kinds of brutal and violent acts; and although Samuel knew nothing of Dylan's time in Africa, he had always understood there was some unyielding element hidden underneath his long, blond hair. At this moment, Samuel sensed—no, knew—that Dylan could lay waste to any man who dared oppose him; but then as quickly as this soldier's camouflaged cloth had been draped across Dylan's broad shoulders, it was loosened, the blinding light from his inner warrior dimmed, to reveal the soft-spoken, casual, easy-going man Samuel had always known.

"Justice will be meted out by the proper authorities. I cannot do both—I am either a peacemaker, or I use one; nor can I work for unity on the one hand," Samuel began, holding up his own right hand, palm up, and then the left one, palm up, "and on the other, work to punish those who do not conform."

Dylan smiled and slapped his friend on his big shoulders. "Well," he said, standing up, "we agreed to disagree, agreeably."

The two titans, for truly they were, then washed all of this discomfort away with talk of other manly things.

That cold, rainy night, Dylan made a few long-distance phone calls to a specialized breed of men who were of his exact persuasion in the way of the warrior.

The Future of Things

First, came the rock, and it caused bodily harm
then came the spear, and it could bring a body down;
next came the bow and arrow, and it pierced man's entrails;

last came the gun, and it changed the map of Man;
and now comes the future of designer annihilation
where there is no end, but the end of destruction

Dylan had come home late, bloodied and bruised, and Rhiannon glimpsed his wounds, but it was when they were emotionally derailed, and so he said nothing, but if he had, he would have explained that, perhaps, that night, he had been flying the X-1 Kitty Hawk jet wing and it had crashed more than once, or the lightweight, finely woven Kevlar armor he wore had not properly stopped all of the dummy bullets, or he had fallen from the great height he was scaling when the mini drilling platforms for scaling structures had given way, and he had saved himself only by holding onto the ridges of the wall before ultimately landing atop the foam mattresses he had not allowed Robert and Paul to place underneath him—but they had defied him, anyway; but these mishaps were quite necessary and expected, as they would be for any test pilot, pioneer, trailblazer, the kind of intrepid man who would not hesitate to strap himself in, on, or next to, to demonstrate efficiency, safety, and durability of the model, because he was not afraid, because he had a mission, because he would not be dissuaded from what he knew he had to do, must do, and would undoubtedly, undeniably, irretrievably, do. Was it a device in the preliminary stages and ruled unstable, and therefore, unsafe? He did it, unhesitatingly. Was it an instrument, if used wrongly, that might cause great bodily harm to him? He used it, unhesitatingly. Was it a weapon that might backfire and kill him? He did not hesitate. Why, why was he so seemingly reckless that even Robert and Paul were emotionally unhinged at the gregarious attitude of their too-willing guinea pig: it was because of her—because he had taken a vow to protect her and had led her to this sloping valley of pain into which they had imperceptibly fallen, and now he would bring them out of it, because of little Eleanor, and little Conall, and for Conall, and Eleanor; but more, for Rhiannon, because he knew it was what she would want, what she would do, what she would expect of him—to delay making swords into plowshares, and to take up the sword again when the staff was not enough, for the lion was not yet ready to lie down with the lamb, and no amount of begging, helping, and sacrificing, could change that.

But this would not have been the only reason to come home beaten and exhausted, for lately, it was also because of those who were coming.

When the Crusaders had ceased their campaign in Africa as a coordinated, carefully controlled, unified presence, they promised each other they would continue the good fight wherever they settled, whether as warriors of war or peace, but more importantly, they vowed to respond to any Crusader's request for help in their homeland, no matter the distance, hardship, or time.

It was a few months after the death of little Conall that Dylan stood in the comfort of his backyard and dialed the number on the special cell phone—which no expert eavesdropper could listen in on or trace—of the first Crusader, while he thought of his fallen children, while he thought of working with Robert and Paul, while he looked at Rhiannon moving as one dead around the house, that he first spoke to Yoshitsune, and then to Rustem, and Horatius, and Miguel, and many, many others the next night, and the next, until all was in readiness.

And thus, the second Crusade began.

War Council

Dylan had called only those Crusaders who were familiar with the United States of America: those who had lived here, like Yoshitsune; worked here on a visa, like Horatius; visited here extensively, like Rustem; who were comfortable with the specific customs and culture of the citizens, understood the themes and ideas that prevailed here, like Miguel; and so they came, and the mission began to take shape.

Those who arrived had to follow explicit instructions, to wit: they must have a carefully prepared and clearly stated purpose for the visit, which had no connection to their soldiering in Africa; they must not openly congregate with any of their fellows; they must stay clear of trouble; and once these details were established and adhered to, and after a grace period of three months had passed, their presence in or about the county of Angels occurred. They did assemble, but once again, they were careful to do what needed to be done to keep a cloak of anonymity around themselves; but also, to place certain devices over the license plates of their cars, which masked the true numbers and letters therein, thus frustrating any recognition software alongside the road, but if the authorities were to stop them and check the numbers on the plates, the officers would find nothing but a clear record; also, they wore certain glasses that obscured the true appearance of their faces, and wore false fingertips.

When it came upon them to unite once more, they followed a certain strategy, devised by Robert, which was thus: each of them were to go to a particular building, and that building, be it rural, city, or otherwise, was like the end of the maze, so from this point, they were to follow exactly a circuitous path that no intelligence agency, enemy—either foreign or domestic—might follow; as it was: take Miguel, who held an amused grin in one hand, and a fat, brown cigar in his other, walked into a remote warehouse in the deep-set, forest hills of San Bernardino, and upon entering said place was soon escorted by gracious, masked men—who also masked him, to which he did not in the least resist—to an elevator, which soon took them down four levels, at which point he exited and sat upon a railcar, was driven some distance, and taken up in an elevator to a garage, placed inside a black-as-pitch Cadillac, which was replete with all the accoutrements of the intelligence community, to wit: tinted windows, false plates, radar-slipping technology, and an engine that could outstrip the best of the police cruisers; and off he went for a good amount of time, until he was again in a warehouse deep, deep in the unbridled forest, far past any open land, and once more going down, down to another level, until he was finally unmasked and released by his still-amenable hosts, to whom, before he placed his wet cigar into his wide mouth, he said, "Muchas gracias, and good hunting," and soon turned his attention to the dim light and noise that trickled down the long, dark hallway before him. "The last one to the party," he whispered, amusedly, raising his thick black eyebrows, his handsome round head bobbing about as he walked the freshly polished tile floor in his beige snakeskin boots, "the last one to leave." He reflected upon this maxim for a moment as the noise sharpened into human talk, and the light leaking from the room grew brighter. "And that is me, as it relates to standing in one place too long, while my brothers and sisters are in bondage."

For the years previous, he had been, after Africa, visiting his family and relatives in Mexico, and then became ensconced in the struggle against the expansive Cartels in the countries below the border; and despite the lapse of time, as he neared the narrow portal that led to the great chamber inside, the voices, as they became more distinguished in their unique characteristics, attuned his memory to what had not too long ago had transpired, and he could see his comrades before him: now, on a grassy plateau overlooking an enemy encampment; now, on a rocky ledge, in a fierce firefight; now, on a leisurely march in the dense jungle swatting away insects; hearing his fellows' robust conversation, seeing their animated faces, sharing their dreams, their wants, their hopes; and here, as he turned the corner and came into the cast of a luminous glow, it was as if they had never departed, for those who joined the eternal struggle for Freedom, are, despite distance, race, culture, creed, gender, or social status, always on the same geological and societal map: the map of Justice.

He had planned to express himself in one way, then another, and still, some other witty remark, but decided it was risk to his esoteric reputation, and served poorly as an opening salvo to this somber occasion; so, as it were, as he faced his brethren, who were now standing, and then moving toward him, he merely said, with arms spread out, finally deciding that his valued past, and his valued presence here, spoke it all: nothing.

They expected nothing more.

And so, as they approached him, he saw Yoshitsune of Japan, late of Nepal; Finn McCool of Ireland, late of Egypt; Arjuna of India, late of Pakistan; Rustem of Iran, late of Iraq; Horatius of Italy, late of Egypt; Tyr of Germany, late of Egypt; Enkidu of Iraq, late of Egypt; Antonio Juan de Bolivar of Bolivia, late of Colombia; and Robert, and Paul, and Dylan; and he embraced each of them with an ardent fervor that can only be shared by warriors who have nobly fought the good fight, and are prepared to fight once more; and smiles were embraced, too; but careful, constrained smiles—smiles grown only by the special relationship of brotherhood, not of a celebratory nature, not with so grievous a challenge awaiting them, though most of them knew not what hard battles were to come; but these were only the first ones to arrive, and so they all sat down again and could not help but reminisce about absent friends, their families, their lives, but not yet about their African adventure—for this era of their lives they had already fully lived, that remarkable and audacious plot that had impossibly succeeded, but is not to be praised, not stroked, not admired, but remembered only to move them forward onto the next pages of the history of injustice where they would continue the endless battle, for great soldiers do not fondly remember fighting a great enemy, as it is their duty to have done so, not for glory, honor, or privilege, much as a father rescues his daughter from a swirling river, or a mother her son from a raging fire.

In time, more Crusaders came, and so, now, there were more than one hundred men and women filling the secured chamber, talking mostly of events current and of possible futures; and then she entered, and the clock that measured and ruled the lives of mortals stopped—whether they were husband, wife, brother, sister, friend, or worker—and the clock of the immortals began, of warriors, of dedicated soldiers, of heroic men and women.

Rhiannon, she who had relit the always-hot candle of battle, even with her mere suffering presence, stood before them; and she was adorned in a halo of shimmering piety, as all knew the reason for their being here.

The men arose and embraced and greeted her, in the individual tradition of their country, and the women, too; the women embraced her as no other could, and the men as friends and brothers, but all of them beheld her elegant, simple beauty, poise, and bearing, and allowed their intrigue to profit their inquiring souls.

When all of them were assembled in the brown leather chairs that were arranged in a semicircle that spun from a large nucleus as of hitherto unknown technology, to the outside from the multilayered, movable, interconnecting wooden floor, then did Dylan stand, possessing a steely determination that his fellows had seen in many leaders in many lands and too many revolutions; and as he perceived his fellow Crusaders, he gazed upon them as those who rightly held the sword of Justice and wielded it with impunity; and as he spoke, it was as if from the distant clamor of battles past, and present, wherein the forces of good battle the forces of evil, and yea, one voice arises, and leads those who are too weary, too desperate to continue and to stand up and heave back against the enemies of freedom; but they must, it is a humble mantle they have assumed, and wear, for it is their destiny to sacrifice all so that many might live in peace; they must win, or risk the death of freedom, of history, of mankind, of the earth itself, of faith in doing what is right, because they know, they absolutely, undeniably, incontrovertibly understand in their hearts and minds and souls—and who can know so deeply and keenly and spiritually but those who bear the brunt of the fight—that if they do not compromise, nor capitulate, or retreat, if they move forward, no matter the seemingly impossible odds or circumstances or outcome, they will, to the very last man and woman counted, secure victory; for every time that the spirit of evil conspires to conquer, they will lose if the spirit of Goodness arises and refuses to yield, and the loud bells of Liberty will then ring throughout the land, and once again that tumor of greed, the fever of conquest will have been subdued, and the people will have their triumph, that is solace and tranquility, and the right to live in peace.

"When nation-states no longer invade one another," he began, in earnest, standing atop a small platform near the entrance, "and democracy is practiced, when the peril from without seems gone, and the peril from within seems gone, then another invader comes: not religious, not ethnic nor political, but the iniquities that come of a settled, reawakened civilization, and there is no common ancestor here, except greed; no commander, except power; no unifying theme, except desolation of the citizenry." He raised his blond head slightly. "There is an undeclared war against a sinister rising tide, yet there is no undeclared army, only compromises; yet, I have declared war against this rising tide, and I have an army." He gestured with gushing pride toward his fellows. His voice blew an icy presage for those who had too long and without restraint lunged eagerly and often over the consensual, law-abiding line. "And who will make war against soldiers who fight against Innocents, who; who will fight soldiers who practice this deceit among the fair communities, who hide behind constrictive laws, who offer us sorrow as validation for their intolerable crimes? The state and locally recognized authorities must adhere to constantly wavering philosophies of jurisprudence and penal justice, but there is a philosophy of jurisprudence and a penal justice, that never wavers, never wanes, does not boast, does not hide, is not arrogant; rejoices with the truth, hopes all things, endures all things—because it is inviolate, sacrosanct, indivisible; it is universal law, an inviolate emblem of moral codes that guides our heart and mind and spirit." And now he began to move among the mesmerized listeners as if in an enigmatic, enlightened trance. "For no culture," he erupted, just like a fiery volcano, "no people, no place, accepts murder without a proper punishment," and he gesticulated wildly about; "no good home would accept such a violation of natural rights, and then, no town, no state, no nation-state should so accept such murders—or thieves, slavers, or kidnappers—but I am talking of those who practice crime in the same manner as we practice good parenting, good schooling, good solicitude; they practice perversion, and they are given unreasonable chances to reform because life is so easy, so comfortable, not hard, not manic; no pioneering culture would tolerate such a breach in societal etiquette to the point where manners and ethics and morals are evanescent and replaced by a nonsensical, doggerel display by professional criminals; and society seeks to recuse itself as judge, as they cite poor environment as inciting moral decay—well," he cried, "I say no more aiding and abetting those we have allowed to become masters at their heinous craft of deceit and cunning criminality: the war is on!"

What is a cheer, here, but the spontaneous eruption of approval for the host by an attentive audience, but a cheer here came from diverse sources, from varying ethnic, national and personal histories; so, here a cheer from the African, related to his fight for freedom and justice in his homeland; so, there, a cheer from the Mexican, related to his universal wanderings and search for peace and liberties; and a cheer from the Indian, related to his personal history and open declaration of a pursuit to free all people from the bondage of inequality and injustice.

"We must know the nature and character of this villain, who freely terrorizes the citizenry as a bold fox would the pen and unprotected henhouse," Dylan began again, now standing on the center platform, and facing his fellow apostles of Justice. "In every nation, they wear different apparel, but their black souls remain the same, and it colors their faces with a hideous mask." He stopped his monologue and slowly looked around at his enraptured believers, his faithful followers, and when he found the passionate and beauteous face of his beloved, gazed upon her. "The enemy here is the same as the enemy there, shielding themselves behind women and children, and the sick and the elderly, and the starving, and camouflaging inside the safe harbor of community, as is the wont and signature of cowards from every age and nation, for cowardice is a sin that unites all men under the same shameful banner, wherein it sits like a rapacious, living poison and ready to harass those whom it despises, those whom it sees as good, those whom it sees as a threat to its own ignoble purposes: greed, murder, avarice, lying, cheating, stealing—and so sets its black heart to rend those very virtues their black heart has emitted, a heart so black—black, with concrete oozing; thick with a oozing black that no good thing can now enter into its tangled and perverted domain—that being all common virtues and human joys, joy derived from caring, joy from loving, from sacrificing, for all, which, for you and I, is our trusted and most virtuous nature." He looked about his fellows, and their brightened countenances, every one, were instilled with more pride and brotherhood than ever before, and he continued his emboldened speech, more impassioned than ever before. "So, they must not be allowed to destroy that which is good, anymore, for that is sin, and for us not to aid those who are Innocent; to allow those are wicked to flourish and thrive, this too is sin—for we are to strive to be as perfect as humanly possible—a mighty sin that would soil our hearts and weigh it down with immense grief; so, we will wage war against the recreants who wage war against the Innocent; and we will not retire, nor capitulate, nor even rest, until the sincere credo we, the elect, have sworn an oath to follow: I will do what I must to ensure that this nation that I now proudly call home is a home I can live in without fear of a criminal force that is powerful because good people have done nothing to prevent it, that is confident because we acquiesced to it and thus fear it; and increasing, because it knows our civilized breeding will not allow us to meet fire with fire, blood with blood, face to face, and more than that," and as his voice suddenly was raised to an impassioned pitch, an enthrallment of what was to come, up rose his fellow Crusaders, who, in perfect harmony, recited their undying credo, "Force and right are the governors of the world, force till right is ready." And oh, how they cheered!

He was moving about them as one integral piece of a vibrant whole, where any vital piece missing would destroy the integrity of the whole, a phenomenon of unity, of bonding, through respect and trust and devotion learned through common trials and tribulations, an unbreakable bond held by an external cement of brotherhood that had first been learned when man assembled to bring about a better world, and one that might only be realized through revolution; learned when man first assembled to fight a common threat to their peaceful way of life; and learned when man first assembled to confront those malevolent forces who cannot be deterred by mere words alone, but by noble deeds, self-sacrifice, and a willingness of the oppressed to fight until the last dying breath for those sacrosanct ideals that keep lit the eternal fire which lights the path they travel on the road to peace, prosperity, and harmony: the Good Life. Thus, this faithful creed they have secured, and earned, this righteous emblem of goodness, decency, and virtue, which is their body's fuel, their heart's blood, their spirit's effulgent flood, it resideth in all men, and thus all men are responsible.

"But we are free men and women, are we not," he continued, letting fall slowly the fiery flare he had set off above their heads. "We are not chained to one man's thought," he uttered, nearly intoning, now igniting this spectacular torch above their hearts. "This war I have declared will not settle well in every heart; so, brothers and sisters, leave no path untrodden, spare no barbed arrow's flight; speak out in ungentle words, so when we finally stand, we stand united, doubt and worry having no authority over our actions."

The war council, having already been apprised of the enemy without, commenced in the animated conflagration of verbal jousting that had served them well in Africa. First, up stood Arjuna, who knew all too well the whims and appetites of the unbound, maddened mob. "It is as you say, we are free men and women—but so are the people of this country," he began; "I see no fetters on the feet of the citizenry, no UN troops, no refugee makeshift camps, no concentration camps, no death camps—like in Kush, like in the Congo, like in Uganda; where is that clear delineation of Innocent and soldier?"

"This is a civilized nation," Cyrus of Germany began, also standing. "How can we fight in the open, among communities, where there are too many Innocents who would be hurt?"

"And what of the laws of your land?" Ana of Honduras said. "Is it our task to fight criminals in every land? This is not our vision, nor our concern—it is as Arjuna says, a civilized country needs its own authorities and people to free themselves from the special bondage you speak of."

"How can we declare war on children? There are too many gang members who are but mere youths, trapped in the gang; how can we fight them—is it our right to fight them?" continued Arjuna. "Every industrial nation has a criminal entity, and must overcome them on their own terms—in Africa, we were Crusaders; here, we will simply be vigilantes, risking innocent lives on a mission that will have no discernible impact, for there are too many criminal groups—I have studied them, I have—and they have thousands, hundreds of thousands of members; it is too impossible to contemplate, and I say," he stated emphatically, "we cannot engage them all, especially since they are not unified, like a common army."

"I agree with Arjuna," said Sebastian of the UK; "we have gangs in England, but no one would even think of openly engaging them, for they will merely return no matter the scope of the victory; it is the way of human nature—youth will always have a common criminal element; I say this is beyond our credo."

Jorge of Argentina said, "But we saw the fate of children in Africa who were kidnapped by the rebel forces, who grew up in real poverty, who joined insurgency groups in order to survive; but it is not like that here: I find no way to excuse these gang members—whatever environment they grow up in here, it is not like in Africa. If we excuse their joining gangs in the richest country in the world, then we must excuse everyone else, too, including adults who began as minors in gangs—and adults and armies who terrorize and hurt Innocents; no, I cannot sympathize nor condone such immoral behavior." Many of the members agreed with him.

Thus, the firestorm of debate swirled about the Council, with much discussion on the merits or demerits of this impending fight, focusing mainly on the worldwide reality of gangs and the inability of governments to properly address them; of society's fault in allowing such groups to flourish; of the innocence of youth in these gangs; of the logistical problem of open warfare in settled, democratic communities; of the potential wounded and dead of the citizenry; of retribution of the gangs against Innocents; of the unhappy local, state, and federal authorities who would undoubtedly look unkindly on an undeclared, unsanctioned war on American soil; and with all these impediments, out flowed support for the mission, like freely flowing blood from an open wound; and every flaming arrow shot into the heroic request pierced its heart, so that it lost its fiery glow, and appeared not so mighty, to be brought down so easily; and every sharp-edged blade tore into its muscle, and tendons, so that it lost its strength and appeared not as strong, to be brought down so easily; and every crushing blow to the weakened body crushed its cartilage and bones, so that it lost its structure, and appeared defeated because it had been brought down so easily, and by its very own.

Two hours hence, and the Council had no common opinion, except divisiveness, which no good army might have and hope to succeed.

And then Dylan rose up, having sat in absolute silence during this lively debate, and now all eager eyes were upon his magnificent, muscular, Celtic form as he strode about, as a warrior king of old; then he stopped on high, and observing his fellows, he let fall back his blond head, standing fully erect, his massive arms lifting up, just as his voice lifted up in the passion and pageantry of his ancient people. "But I do not declare war upon the indigenous gangs of this great nation," and his azure eyes burned bright, like frozen diamonds in a lake of fire. "I declare war upon those who have already declared war upon us," and when he shouted, so great was it that his furious pathos swept into warrior spirit of everyone there. "I declare war upon the Cartels, here, in my home, and there, in their homes, and further still, in your homes, until they are utterly, undeniably, for all time, annihilated, defeated, and surrender unconditionally, unmercifully, to the forces of Justice."

This world, their world, the world of taking up the flaming sword of Truth and Freedom against the seemingly unrivaled and unconquerable forces of wickedness, came alive once more, the veil of uncertainty having been lifted, and the mission miraculously reborn.

The Mission

He had recaptured what had escaped—unity—and now set about to build upon this solid foundation.

He reached out his left hand, and declared, as if grasping something substantial, "I take the eternal torch of Freedom, first lit when brother rose up against brother, and Man stood, against such aggression," and passed the mystical emblem to his other hand; and lo, his voice became exceptionally hard, as if unveiled from a long-ago chivalrous past, and his voice became exceptionally proud, as if it too reflected the heroic standards of days gone by, "and now passed from warrior to warrior, fighting foreign invaders in his homeland: now, Israel, fighting heroically; now, the Scots, fighting heroically; now, the Irish, fighting heroically; now, the English, fighting heroically, now, the Americans, fighting heroically, and now," he continued, still passing the light of Liberty, "all men, all women, everywhere, who fought heroically against invaders both foreign and domestic, and fight even unto death," and then the sacred symbol was alone in his right hand and outstretched on high. "But not for themselves only, but for every freedom-loving people—today, yesterday, and tomorrow—for to capitulate is for Man to capitulate, but what is Man but a God-fearing, freedom-loving, peaceful creature who must not and will not be interred, enchained, and encircled—he must be free! He will fight day and night, in ice and rain, month after year, in heat and fire, and drought and famine, to live free," and he pulled his right hand back and shouted out again, "All honor and glory to those who fought, and died, and were wounded in every nation, every town, and village; and now, in Africa, in Mexico, and Asia, in the Middle East, and even in civilized places, where it is assumed that no war rages, rage silent wars, small wars, but wars indeed— wars of attrition by growing criminal organizations who lean against the once-safe structure and operation of Democracy, and rock its foundation," and his face was now disturbed unto a passionate fervor. "I smell the rot of murder and mayhem, the foul stench of injustice fills my nostrils, the inability and unwillingness of the world to legitimately oppose those who seek the destruction of the basic tenets of Democracy; this, we cannot let stand," and now his voice soared to hitherto unknown heights and depths of pathos and passion. "So, let our noble actions illumine the righteous road that others equally inspired may follow as a clear path, as we approach that sacred shrine of Freedom, where men and women of every land and kind may reside in the solace and harmony we desire." He cast his sparkling eyes about the room and affixed them upon his loving wife, and his voice shifted to a whispering roar, so that all needed to strain to hear its subtle inflections and zealous tones. "Is there not always one who stands tall against the rising tide—is there not always one? One stands, one falls, another picks up his staff, and moves forward; and once they are felled, does not another always bend down and take that good staff and raise it up and aim it on high as a beacon of Truth and Light against the forces of darkness, so that others may follow this clear path?

So, we must now do what others will not do, cannot do, are afraid to do," and he moved about, his voice enthralled once more, infused with the exhilaration of what was soon to come. "So, let us do what we know we can, and must, and are not afraid to do, for there is no other—and it is at this crucial hour that the scales of Justice must be weighed aright, or we allow the rising tide to prevail, and all men and women will suffer."

He looked at his fellows once more. "So, my brothers and sisters, the die is cast, the players established; so, speak your mind: let no one this day be unheard or dismissed."

Yoshitsune had only to stand, to quash the urgency of any others in the room; and then, his handsome visage burning bright and projecting unyielding boldness, declared, "Now," and he looked slowly round with that stern countenance, "we have an army to fight!"

This proclamation, having expressed the prevailing sentiment of his animated fellows, opened a new chapter in the struggle of democracies to keep intact their fragile and youthful existence, and keep safe their sleeping and trusting citizenry; and, had the Cartels south of the US border ears, they might have listened; but had they also feet, they should have run; but had they a commonsensical mind, they should have thought where to hide; had they even a modicum of intelligence, it would have fostered fear for their very lives; and had they even a sliver of a heart, they would have begged for mercy; and lastly, had they very real human souls, they would have repented in sackcloth and ashes.

But they hadn't, and so the war was truly on.

Book Four

Robert, with Paul at his side, now stood up, and all eyes swept to his humble posture.

He was still lean, having followed a strict regimen of vigorous exercise and a healthy diet; he wore a full brown beard underneath his kind brown eyes; he wore the clothes of the everyman, a person he had always felt he was, despite his prodigious wealth—comfortable clothes, like simple cotton jeans, and a beige, long-sleeve shirt, and well-built gray running shoes, as he never cared how he appeared to others, only how his deeds appeared to God.

Paul, attired in the traditional dress of his homeland, wore special glasses, as did Robert, but also wore a special hat, which Robert did not; and so it was Paul who motioned with his hand, and a loud buzzing noise came to the ears of the Crusaders, and then he waved his arms in certain geometric shapes and patterns, truly like equations; and behold, there appeared a great army of winged robotic messengers, of all manners and degrees of the insect and bird world: multicolored Monarch butterflies and humming birds, and honeybees, and dragonflies, and dull gray painted ones, and camouflaged ones, all carrying the same special glasses that Robert and Paul wore, now politely hovering and releasing their cargo to the now outstretched hands of their astonished guests, and then quickly flew back to their high stations to roost in their electronic nests. The Special Ops glasses were shaped like standard glasses and indeed contained a special glass, but also maintained a tiny microchip that projected written text on them, a video screen, the Internet, a video camera, turn-by-turn navigation, and sensors to read reactions to the pupil, and facial muscles, and lastly, phone capability.

"Technology, ladies and gentlemen," Robert began, walking among them, "moves economies—and those who do not adapt with it are felled by it; no good army succeeds without it; consider the discovery of various metals, from bronze to iron to steel, where armies discovered how to make better weapons, and their swords cut through the armor of opposing armies like hot knives through cold butter; the Cartels are using more advanced weaponry to match or exceed armies, so we too will use technology, but also such that no one has yet used." Therefore, he delineated, in great and lengthy detail, the technology available to them, and they, those warriors comfortable with rifle, rope, or bow and arrow, were entranced, and enthused, and struggled to see the images on the small screen before them; but they were flesh and blood, not mere machines, and after the session, they took a long break, eating, drinking, talking, remembering; and when all were regenerated in mind and body, the next session began.

Where before Robert was sober of mind, and slow of speech, he was now exceedingly grave, and each syllable was accented with a presage of urgency, though spoken carefully, slowly, and precisely.

"How many gangs have we in our liberal democratic nation; how many gang members? Some say thirty thousand gangs, and one million or so members—some say," he began, his heart heavy with a memory of past atrocities around the globe, from antiquity to the present, and especially consumed by those he had witnessed in person. "So, whence comes a gang? What is its definition? When man first joined together to bring harm to Innocents, there you have it; and now, gangs control governments, as we well know—they call themselves legitimate governments; well, I say to you, any coalition of individuals who do not hold to democratic principles as a governing authority are illegitimate, and are mere criminals supporting power and murdering anyone in their petty sphere of influence..." But he halted this classical rhetoric, this ideological criticism, and checked himself and restrained his emotions, for still—still, he saw too often, too many times awake, too many times asleep, the result of insanity, wickedness and avarice, so many dead, so many Innocents slaughtered for the bloated ego of megalomaniacal rulers who were stuffed with an unquenchable thirst for power over the lives and habits of their countrymen, who would gladly offer gratitude, loyalty and devotion to rulers who treat the citizen as Nature showed them, as sages instructed them, as God commanded them: humanely, compassionately, justly.

His voice softened, but still it rode hard on the battle-torn road upon which he daily trod. "In this state alone, we have more than six thousand gangs, and over two hundred and thirty thousand members, and most of them are situated in this region." He pressed on the small electronic device in his hand, and the map of this area appeared on the lenses of this audience. "You will experience difficulty adjusting to this technology," he said, observing those who were moving their heads about, and lifting up the glasses, "but there is no time like the present," and then proceeded to explain augmented reality, and demonstrated how their cell phones could project a virtual image onto any surface they chose.

"The history of gangs," he began once more, "an education," and he henceforth narrated their worldwide origins and their ultimate state of being today.

"The history of the Mexican and Colombian Cartels," he began once more, "an education," and he henceforth narrated their worldwide origins and their ultimate state of being today.

Session two ended, and once more, the Crusaders ate, relaxed, drank, reminisced, but never spoke of this current mission; and when the break was over, they returned to their leather seats, and prepared for the third session.

"All of this information is on your hard drives," Robert began, "and also contained in the physical documents before you; and now, what we need to know..." An acute tension appeared on the alert countenances of this elite group, for any history of an enemy is mere facts, but this was information of the present, and immediate future. "As you know, many illegal drugs come from the south, but now I will speak of cocaine: it is grown and shipped the Andes region in South America, and then smuggled by the Colombian Cartels to Central America to the Mexican Cartels, who have now taken over the business from the Colombians of shipping it to the most aggressive consumers," and he pointed, shamefully, downward, knowing his audience saw the routes and final destinations on their smart screens, and on their smart wristbands, which many preferred. "And everywhere along that route, crime has increased; and every country it passes through grows desperate, yes: like Costa Rica, Nicaragua, Colombia, El Salvador, Honduras; but Mexico is perhaps the most frustrated, for there not only have the Cartels taken control of many provinces, and even reign supreme over their predecessors, the Colombians, but the government has been unable to prevent them from spilling over our border—where even now our government officials have been unable to stop them."

He hesitated, for even his weighty resolve was loosened by the burgeoning scope of this proposal. "We cannot fight all the gangs here—the black gangs, the Latino gangs, Asian gangs, the biker gangs, the prison gangs—but we can fight them another way by depriving them of their primary income; what we resolve to do here is unprecedented, for us to declare war upon a foreign indigenous enemy is a crime the authorities will vigorously seek to dissuade."

Arjuna shouted, "It never stopped us before!"

"Here, here," his fellows shouted.

"We will fight in a sovereign nation—not in a civil war, not besieged by warlords, not shared by UN troops; in fact, in several sovereign nations."

"If not us, who else, then?" Tyr cried.

"Many here will be wounded, some will die, others perhaps imprisoned…"

Horatius shouted, "To die for a just cause is a warrior's glory."

"Here, here!" his fellows shouted.

Robert unfurled the full spectrum, from stem to stern, of the grand plan, with every unsavory tidbit and morsel, uninhibited and raw, and down and dirty; a plan so sweeping in its aim and purpose—the possible destruction of governments, the restructuring of society—that wars could result; and the response from the stalwart Crusaders?

They stood up, and cheered, raising their clenched fists in defiance of the epic struggle to come, ever confident of the battle to ensue, fearing nothing but doing no good deed that would allow this prodigious inequity to unleash its virulent and sanguinary soul across the entire globe.

Thus was the stage set, the players selected, the resources gained, and no good excuse to provoke them to delay.

This imminent war on American soil was officially and unanimously declared against an enemy whose sole purpose was to disrupt and destroy the lives and homes of Innocents the world over.

How It All Began

The truly wealthy are able to create a door anywhere, at any time, under any circumstance, where before there was simply no opening; this esoteric door that causes men to step aside, step back, bow down, grovel; this magical portal that leads to a citadel where those who have reasoned themselves the masters of the known universe.

Robert Heimdall, through the establishment of his pioneering concepts in microloans in Third World countries, financially aiding governments and companies in emerging democracies, purchasing millions of acres of land worldwide when the estate market had crashed, and selling it at its soaring peak; and after cashing in all of his stocks when they were unreasonably high, and waiting patiently for years for the market to completely and utterly exhaust itself, where people vowed they would never buy stocks again, where he knew this was finally the bottom, he had purchased millions of prime stocks, then sold them at a soaring and unreasonable peak; investing in young tech companies in the field of electronics and communication: artificial intelligence, cell phones, computers, smart software; working with the brightest and most innovative of scientists to create groundbreaking technology that went beyond creating marginal changes, such as safer cars or airplanes that merely flew further or computers that were smaller and faster, but devices and concepts realized that would shape society for the better and create fundamental changes, such as the quantum computer and cryptography, and helping developing better and more nutritious strains of plants that would tolerate bad weather and insects, and powered exoskeletons for people whose physical abilities have been compromised; drones for firefighting and surveying agriculture, and other practical uses; micro air vehicles for reconnaissance and other practical uses; body implants and prostheses, regenerative medicine, robotic surgery and tricorders, especially on the battlefield; and force field, stealth technology and a cloak of invisibility as it related to camouflage, to speak of only a few, had yielded him thousands of patents—many of which were shunned by universities or government agencies; and he was now so rich that he no longer counted it, and used it as a tool for the causes he had come to believe in. He was especially proud of profit that was procured from ultra-rich individuals and corporations, thinking that "every penny I take from them, I use for a noble purpose, like treating arsenic-laced wells in India; is this not a great struggle in the world?" He knew the statistics—he knew that the majority of land in many poor nations was owned by a small cluster of powerful families and corporations, and often had peasants farming it and paying rent, and though land reform was not his venue, he could at least buy the land when the market was low from these families who no longer wanted it, and then allow the poor to buy it back at a reasonable price. "After all, serfdom is long dead, is it not?"

So, when Robert Heimdall scheduled an appointment with the governor of any province, state, or district, or president of any nation-state, or CEO of any Fortune 500 company, or any at all, they made adjustments; and when these ambitious meetings were completed and agreements were reached, plans designed, stories told—money flowed more freely between countries, corporations, and citizens; and all who met him knew his passions, philanthropic history, and these inherent goals: by stimulating the economies of the most impoverished countries, which, he told them, did more to bring the poor up from squalor than mere financial aid alone, especially aid not smartly given; to build more facilities to treat drug users, which, he told them, did more to fight illicit drug use than the failing, failed, and destined-to-fail drug war; to decriminalize, first, marijuana, he told them, would do more to fight the drug lords and street gangs, and free up necessary resources that now are disproportionately aimed at arresting low-level users and sellers—but also cocaine, and other substances, too, if they were also government regulated and privately produced, and subsequently, priced reasonably low, so low that the prisons would have more beds available for real criminals, and people who had once acquired too much money growing, producing, shaping, selling, buying illicit drugs would have to get real jobs, or simply move over to another criminal enterprise—at least one, he would reassure them, that might be easier to combat.

Most of those he spoke to listened, but heard only what they wanted to hear: how they would profit from a joint venture with one of the richest men in the world; and of those who heard what he truly said, few agreed, or cared, for narcotic-laced mammon had long ago captured their want for greed, and of those who heard and agreed and cared, most thought him a harmless but powerful radical, tilting at windmills, an eccentric who used his vast economic network of influences to pursue his private but impractical societal goals; after all, they knew, this was a man who could gain an appointment with seemingly any king or queen, president or prime minister at a moment's notice—to pursue what they considered impossible, impractical, and illogical, and so he received few of their pledges; and of the rest who were also passionate about his want to bring succor to those less fortunate than they, he received their financial and moral support.

But he knew this was the unfortunate history of the sometimes unfortunate race called human beings, that those in power simply never saw the good or need to improve the lives of those emotionally ruined and economically deprived. One man, the CEO of one of the biggest Fortune 500 companies, was quite eager and frank in unveiling, like a proud peacock, his long-held philosophy on the matter of class structure.

"Don't fool yourself, Robert," the big man with the twenty-thousand-dollar suit began, inside his million-dollar-a-month-rent suite, as he offered his plainly attired guest—who politely refused—an alcoholic beverage, and his stark ideas on what he considered stark reality, as if he had only to speak them, and Robert, upon hearing them, would surely believe them. "All of this ridiculous historical narrative you hear about equal rights is a bunch of drivel from philosophers and religious figures preaching love and equality—it's not real, it's not practical, it plain doesn't work because it goes against nature; why, look around you: you see inherent differences in the races, and men and women, and one person to the next; so, it all comes down to what each individual does with his life: if you fail, you're a slave; if you succeed, you are a master; it is as simple as that; there have never been equal rights among people, and there never will be—it's all a sham to appease special interest groups and quiet the ignorant masses into thinking they really are just as good as you and I, and really can be happy—ha! Now, there's a laugh!" He then frowned the way a man might if someone had just told him his dog had filed a complaint against him in the lower courts for acts of unnecessary cruelty. "Look, Robert," he continued, as if he were addressing a social equal merely because the other man had as much vast wealth as he. "The world has changed since civilization was first formed—and we got it right at the start," and he moved to the window, which issued a spectacular view of the swelling empire of real estate his chicanery and ruthlessness had gained him. "Kings come about, well, because there will always be those who naturally would rule; we are kings, Robert, you and I, that's right, just like those Egyptian pharaohs, like the Kings and Queens of old Europe, like Caesar—but now, instead of kingdoms to rule, we rule much more; why, we rule other countries, too; we rule the rulers—without us, they fail; the strong rule the weak, is it not so? Just look at Nature! We're all animals, after all, and I am a shark, and the rest are guppies; our influence stretches beyond our natural borders— what we say goes, and so goes the world; we raise rates, we influence governments, we initiate wars; just look at the last few centuries—look at the wars brought about by imperialist conquests: first made by industry: the East India Company, which led to the British occupying countries; our American companies' excursion into South America led to invasions; Britain went to war against China over the opium trade; and what is imperialism but the quest for capitalist greed?" He was no longer addressing his guest, but his idols of the past, conquerors all. "It's all about economics, all of it: you can conquer all the nations you want, and in the end, it's all for goods and services—simple economics: trade, buying and selling; so, now, we don't have many physical wars where we invade sovereign nations; good, I say—it's bad press, after all; we don't need wars, anyway, we have a business acumen, good ol' business acumen," he nodded, sneering. "We still have kings and queens—it's just that slaves are better off—but we're still kings, and to keep them quiet, we give them just a little bit: the right to vote, own property, have a decent job, and if they benefit from us, it's incidental; we cut the pie we designed and they build, and when we eat it, if a crumb happens to fall to the ground, the suckers crush each other in a mad scramble for a crumb, like the dumb animals they are; well, maybe one day, soon, there will be less and less of the crumb for them to kill each other for—and if they're lucky, a few of them will be able to fight their way to the top." He uncharacteristically paused, shaking his head. "But they'll never get it, no, they never will: that they are our natural servants, each and every one of those poor, dumb fools—working for us, slaving for us, enriching our coffers while we break their precious unions, destroy their fat pensions, give them shoddy products—and they squawk, and whine, and protest, but in the end, what are they going to really do, huh? Nothing! They can't because they know who they are and deep down know they can't do what we do, so that is why they allow us to take the reins of power, and the risks and stress and abuse associated with it, and the defeats—and when our companies lose money, and we get a salary increase, and even a bonus, sure, they whine, and squawk, and protest, but in the end, what are they going to do about it, really? Rule? Run a billion-dollar empire, no! They haven't the guts, nor the brains, nor the business savvy; so, they sit back in their little comfortable homes, and work at their menial little jobs, and play it safe, and get their little salary, happy to have at least something—even if it is just a tiny piece of the now stale, old pie—while we, at the top, take great chances to improve this economy—us, the ruler supreme! Class division—bah! There are only two: the haves, and the have-nots; and we have all the juice—I mean real power, baby, undiluted power; so, we let them live their safe, easy lives, and give them a few liberal democratic laws, and they are happy; and I'll tell you what: we could take more from them if we chose—lower wages, fewer rights, worse living and working conditions, and I'll bet they wouldn't complain much; they always adjust to what little they have—I believe it is called, 'numbing oneself to the harsh reality of a failed life.'" He stopped, and his fiery, glowing eyes, lit by the incandescent lights of his many skyscrapers and corporations laid out before him, now dimmed slowly, and slowly, he came back to the world of the living. "So, I say let them kill each other—let them have their drugs, their booze, their petty crimes; it doesn't affect us, not one little bit—and let them have their omnipresent entertainment industry and social media to keep them really busy so they really will forget all about us." He turned to face Robert, who had managed, by much practice, to keep a stolid countenance. "I like your idea of drug treatment centers—it makes us look like we really care, even though we both know it is a colossal waste of time and energy; why, I have charitable organizations I contribute to, also; I have to, it's the thing to do when you have billions—at least, for now, anyway, it must be done; it's all about appearances, create the illusion that we really do care..."

Robert graciously thanked the man for his valuable time, and departed, designing a unique mental note to himself to go directly home and immediately get his humble self on his hands and knees and thank God that he was who he was, and to ask God to keep him humble in spirit and chastise him when he thought himself better than anyone else, and especially, when he sinned; and he prayed for guidance concerning this new tactical operation and wondered if he were in the moral wrong; and he wondered why this other man was who he was, and why, why everyone simply did not aspire to be good, which, when he was in the huddled darkness of his home and kneeling in genuine supplication, he decided it was that Man, left to his own devices, is led by his own selfish genes to dominate and covet his neighbor's possessions, human and otherwise; and still, every day, he struggled against the desire to capitulate to temptation that his great wealth had wrought.

The next day, he received his limited absolution and anointing of others on the streets, walking with Paul, continuing his mission to care for those who had somehow just got lost on the golden shining path to the hallowed Good Life.

So, too, did Dylan and Rhiannon resume their roles as administrators of their youth clubs, along with Samuel Longfellow, and again, all three went forth to proffer help to those who still needed and wanted and sought it.

Yet, there now was a difference: when Robert and Paul, and Dylan and Rhiannon, worked with the wayward souls of the streets, they not only listened, and soothed them, and asked questions, and offered help; now, they put this valuable intel into their growing databank.

And when the Crusaders met, more than one hundred strong, they studied real-time satellite video, public court records, local maps, gang histories and their affiliates and operations in and out of the state, and where the exact areas of coca and other illegal substances were packaged in the Americas, the exact routes the products took; the histories of these prodigiously growing drug traffickers: Mexican and Colombian, the betrayals therein, the unrestrained violence and bloodshed, the failure of indigenous governments to control the Cartels; the strategic points on the US-Mexican border, the tunnels, the drop-off points, the water routes, the shipping sites; the Cartels' excursion into US cities, where they were breaking through into states and slowly creeping into bigger cities and even smaller communities;

and the major headlines as of late, as if to bolster their bald position: Cartel influence increasing in Chicago, in Los Angeles, in New York; Cartel influence igniting violence in city streets; local authorities and the Federal Bureau of Investigation and NEA and other assorted intelligence agencies battled the increasing presence of the Cartels; state emergencies declared; National Guard deployment along the border; the President declaring a state of emergency; kidnappings, murders, extortions, fraud, all crime indices having risen—either related directly or indirectly to the increased presence of the now-ubiquitous Cartels.

"And still," Dylan said at one of their meetings, three months after the initial gathering in the underground house, "despite the slumbering bear being covered in filthy rats, he will not stand up and defend himself—why?"

"Because we—civilized nations," Yoshitsune said, "are soft on criminals: we do not treat them like enemy combatants, but as socially wrong individuals. If only they had the proper upbringing…bah!"

"It is like trying to kill a nest of wasps by killing only the outliers," Tyr said.

"Operation Pushback begins tomorrow," Dylan said, solemnly, "and let no man or woman go forth with doubt." No one in attendance gave the slightest indication of responding. "Let us revisit the mission once more…"

And so, everyone began the process of intimately describing the role and goal of every other Crusader, first in pairs, then in small groups, finally as a whole: then, the weapon and technology available was analyzed in the same manner as was the overall mission: its possible failures, possible retreats, options, safe houses, lawyers to call, doctors to visit, police officers to contact, reporters to know; hotspots, soft spots, where the local authorities, and the FBI and DEA, and other agencies loomed large and small; where police helicopter patrols flew, where there were friendly neighbors, unfriendly ones, people in the network, people in the know, people who could be trusted, people who were foes; escape routes, safe routes, dangerous routes; avoiding video detection, facial recognition detection, satellite detection, phone eavesdropping, license plate surveillance; every possible scenario devised by the minds of veteran combatants and scientists who came from diverse backgrounds was scrutinized, as were relevant nations, religions, ethnic groups, credos, and every possible and impossible scenario devised by men and women who had survived innumerable battles precisely because they always considered an impossible defeat becoming possible, and how to avoid it and, if forced to confront it, live.

Papers were given out: official documents, aliases, passports, lists of people, plans, things to memorize; equipment was passed out: spy, offensive, defensive, covert, overt; timelines gone over, destination points, procedures again and again, and phone numbers, addresses, names, codes, again and again—until, weeks later, all was in readiness.

First, came the immense delineation of data that had already been gathered and was still growing, to be untangled, unclogged and disseminated to the proper categories of the increasingly crowded map of the southwestern states in the lower regions of the Americas, in particular, Mexico, and to be specific, the hot zones where the Cartel presence had increased and indigenous people's frustration and anger had gained tenfold, information that at all times could be encrypted and sent to the cell phones, smart phones, vision glasses, special two-way communication wristbands, visually, as well as by audio, and also to the small communication devices each Crusader wore and expertly concealed in their ears; and this phase continued for many months.

Second came the first of many quick forays into the stable fabric of societal law that had been woven by centuries of generations, improved upon, agreed to, that was not about to be formally breached, to test its sensitivity to a new force that was self-sustaining and sovereign, stitched—no, singed by fire and sustained by blood into the burgeoning and awakening landscape.

The Mission Begun

The Rodriguez family was not unlike any other family on this ungentle planet—given the same disturbing circumstances of any close family unit—and they acted accordingly, to wit: with the disappearance, and complete submergence, of the youngest son Tomas into the parallel consciousness of the culture of gangs, they, to the surprise of no one who knew them, set out to reclaim him, and without relenting, or compromise, or charity toward all who got in there love-fueled generations-of-family-solidarity way.

Diego had set out on an earnest quest to locate his brother, but his circle of acquaintances and limited influence gained him no useful information; still, he was young, and felt that by refusing to capitulate, he would yet gain victory, and so started down that uncertain road that leads to people and places he had no worldly knowledge of, and where he might apply his limited skills of persuasion and passion.

Juan, being a man of practical means, appealed to the official authorities to find his son, and as that failed, he hired a succession of private detectives, all of whom soon begged off the case for fear of their very lives. But he was not a man to be undone by emotional tumult.

His wife, Sonia, put out flyers, roamed the neighborhoods, visited Tomas' friends, consulted with local anti-gang organizations, but received only more grief to fill her grieving heart.

And yet, none of them could stop, regardless of what Tomas had said or done, for he was their brother, their son, their family, and when they were all at home together, there was an emptiness and fresh memories there, which provoked them to search and never give up, because he belonged to them, despite what he thought, or where he was, for he was a child still, and they together, who were older and wiser, knew better.

The movements of individuals, as they journey throughout society, leave a distinctive mark, as it pertains to their unique habits, lodgings, acquaintances, and travels, as surely as any bullet spinning to the barrel of a gun picks up distinctive striations and thus can be distinguished by it. Tomas was so much like a discharged bullet still spinning and rampaging through life that to have seen one was to have seen the other; where the one seemed to have no conscience in his actions, neither did the other, though the former had no excuse, and the latter was merely a pawn of the shooter; where he had no direction except provoked by his master, so too the bullet; where he had no seeming will of his own, so too the bullet; where he had no discretion, no discrimination concerning his actions, so too the bullet once it left its home base; where he had no seeming remorse, no regret, no recourse for those whom he harassed, so too the bullet, so it was in this way that he was becoming more animal than human, or inanimate than animate, more machine than flesh; and every single day in the protective, soothing womb of his nurturing homestead, he was nursing on the vile milk of pure unrestrained violence, nonsensical violence, violence for violence's sake, for the sake of delivering pain, murder for the horrible sake of money, filthy, dirty, soul devouring of this almighty green anathema, all for the sake of the family gang, which he now called mother, father, sister, brother, aunt, uncle, nephew, niece, cousin, friend, wise counselor, confidant, priest, and omnipresent, omniscient, god.

It is easy to find the vapor trail of verbal intercourse and physical interaction of an ordinary person who is not hiding, nor in a tight cluster of a primitive society that shuns the daylight and operates within the borders of criminality—but, alas, Tomas was, and the private investigators had neared the inflammable boundaries of this bloody zone, only to find austere figures and diabolical goings-on, and they had fled pell-mell. Ambition and trepidation, it seems, have boundaries, too.

But the slivers and flakes of information that the investigators had at least gleaned, and the people who had responded to the flyers, imparted sufficient intel to the family to discover the exact whereabouts of the youth, and his parents began to draw up a plan for rescue.

Lo, Diego, having dethroned the short reign of common sense that resided within his immature mind, embarked, sans parents, friends, police, toward the palace of secrets, the territory of no man's land, the isle of forbidden fruits, emboldened by a sense of dignity, honor and moral righteousness.

"I am his brother, still; I will receive concessions," he reasoned, approaching the ordinary-looking residential house, but which was truly a well-guarded, secure fortress. He parked his gray sedan some distance away and began to walk toward the place, proud, pleased, and confident of his success. "Mama and Papa will be so happy," he thought.

And then he touched the incendiary hem of the insular world that had been heavily stitched with heavy armor by the inhabitants, therein.

"Hey, what are you doing, homey," a sonorous voice said, in no uncertain terms, which meant "go away" in any culture, by virtue of its actively pernicious sentiment, and was easily understood by the local people, but its subtle tones were missed by an immature mind that was penetrated and consumed with a fierce, proud determination.

He should have turned, and without directly responding to the guard, and walked away, but instead, he actually responded, thusly, as if the speaking of his name would automatically open shut doors, holster guns, and lower fists. "I am Diego Rodriguez; my brother is Tomas Rodriguez."

An older resident of the world would have recognized the severe discontent assembled in a fury upon the face of the guard of his dark realm, a sign to retreat and live another day, but Diego missed this social cue, and so continued on, undeterred. "I would like to see him."

Now, the countenance of the tall, muscular guard flushed red with anger at the impudence of the intruder, and so, in accordance with the customs and rituals of his singular culture, he responded, cursing, and then growled, as if more beast than human, "Hey, fool, what do you think this is, a workplace, eh? So, go home, while you can," and then added another specially wrapped and defined obscenity aimed at the offender's mother and father.

"No."

When Diego uttered it, it was drawn from a deep well of respect and confidence in his ability to reason with this man and defend his position, but what he failed to realize and appreciate was that the nature of orders given to him had no acceptable counterproposal.

The human sentinel reacted swiftly, both in mind and body, to dispatch his obstinate foe, when an absurd and astounding event occurred—he was attacked, and it was he who was too easily dispatched.

Diego moved around the man who was now screaming in agony as he tried to wipe off the thick film of heavy-duty, maximum-percentage pepper spray from his outraged face; Diego was now propelled forward but not alone, steeped in the influential philosophy of twenty-first century enlightenment that espoused the natural rights of man to freely choose his path and with willpower prevail against any manmade obstacle—if only because he was young, and brave, and righteous, and so could not be in the wrong, fail, or die; so he pressed on toward the winking sepulcher, which sank into more obscurity in the misty twilight.

He was not certain of what he would say or do, but rather, he would announce his presence boldly and expect the blooming tide of violent men to magically part for him and allow entry into their private kingdom to retrieve his brother—his little brother—to which they must acquiesce, because Diego meant no harm, was an Innocent, was protected by his very citizenship in the sovereign country of the United States of America, and was here only to take home a wayward child; surely, he reasoned, they would not dare dissuade him.

He knocked on the door as plainly and innocently as if you or I might ask for directions to church. The door opened, and with it, a parallel world hitherto unknown to him spilled out.

It was not a clearly recognizable public citizen he gazed upon, but a power-fed, specially designed, cut and dressed member of an elite killing force that was so far removed from his sensory input that it was like meeting an alien from another world.

The bald-headed, heavily tattooed, mean-looking man with severity and a grimace encrusted upon his pale countenance, stared at the youth in the same way a Bengal tiger might had he turned the corner only to come face to face with a doe-eyed deer—but a tiger who knew this deer had recently injured its mate.

A noise came from behind the greeter, and Diego saw an approaching man wave off the maddened figure of the running guard who was swiftly coming up to him, and then look back to Diego. "You have some real 'tripas' to come here," he said, and it was not meant to be interpreted as conferring any modicum of respect, "and stupidity…"

Diego, thoroughly undeterred, proceeded with his stated goal. "I am the brother of Tomas Rodriguez, and I'm here to take him home."

"Okay," the man said, rubbing his bare chin, "come on in, homey."

He walked into this gathering like he was walking into any residence, but still felt as a savior, the protector of his own innocence, and heritage, and enjoying the special privilege of his special relationship to Tomas.

But he was now in the remote and wild jungle where the fiercest predators do battle for their food and domination over their race and the subjugation of weaker species, and everywhere he looked, the hard faces of his unexpected hosts cast a dissenting glare at him, even as he followed the bald man, in the stifling, smoky, noisy, suffocating place.

"Here he is," the man said, as they came to rest in a bedroom, "your little brother," and he walked away; but it did not appear to be his brother, so little of him still remained.

His head was shaved, his body tattooed, his expression lost as he sat puffing on a huge glass bong, after having snorted pure white cocaine, after having indulged in an uninhibited orgy with two teenage girls, who were presently asleep next to him on the large white sofa. He opened wide his eyes and expressed a mild surprise. "Am I late for class?" he said, laughing.

"You're coming home with me," Diego said, disgusted, "right now."

"Mr. Goody Two Shoes, giving orders as always—well, no thanks," he returned, and took another long draw on his mystical giver of euphoria.

Diego knocked the still-smoking bong out of his brother's hands. "Get up!"

Tomas leaped up in a maddened fury. "You ain't in authority here, Diego," he cried, his face ablaze with wrath, and then he tapped his own chest, which was swollen to the top layer with multicolored tattoos; "here, I am in authority."

The brothers were now face to face: antimatter to matter, Ying to Yang, darkness to light, neither force giving in.

And then, a voice of real authority, and able to correct and reduce the irreducible quotient of obscenity until it deflated, broke over them like a tidal wave; yet, it was not strident, nor foreboding, evoking only power, and sensibility. "Sit down, Tomas." Tomas sat like an obedient dog whipped into submission. The bald-headed man looked toward Diego. "Come with me." His streetwise wisdom and equilibrium wrapped itself around the youngster and pulled him along to an empty room, with they now stood, toe to toe, man to man, foe to foe.

"Listen to me, Diego," the bald-headed man began, his countenance grave, "you are not at a college party in your dorm," and he thrust his tattooed hands toward the brown carpet, "like the sign says—you are here." He stared into the face of his listener as if he were now his father, now his mentor, now his wise counselor. "You are a guest in this place, and you have to observe the traditions practiced here."

Diego sought to speak, to defend his seemingly untenable position, but even with his undeveloped life skills, he was prescient of the repercussions of speaking when one should merely listen.

Miguel spoke further. "You have misplaced courage to come here," and here he spoke Spanish, "and ask for your brother's release," he continued, reasonably, and then stated, unreasonably, "Man, don't you know our customs? You are disrespecting our value as a family to exist for Tomas—he is eighteen now, legally an adult: he makes his own choices; look, Diego," and now he sounded reasonable, capable and willing of dialogue and compromise, "your coming here was allowed because you're Tomas' brother—but that was a one-time gift, son." The abruptness of this statement painted Diego into the extreme end of a very small corner. The violent mask of the oppressor faded for a moment and let flash a fallen world of humanity and innocence, but it was merely an old, dead memory, not able to hold onto anything substantial for long. "Look, man, you don't belong here," and then he pointed to the outside, "you belong out there," and then gestured all around himself, "your brother belongs here; look, you need to leave right now, and if you come back, there will be no mercy. I know you are smart enough to understand that."

But a righteous fervor is not easily subdued. "If it was your hermano— what would you do?"

Miguel wanted to say what he might have said had he still been among the living, and not the walking dead, but he merely responded, dutifully, "Adults are free to be whoever they choose to be," he shrugged, parting his hand in a wide gesture; "it is the way it is."

Diego wanted to say what he might have said had he still been among the living, and not the walking dead, but he merely responded, politely, "It is as you say," and he presently retired to the refreshing cool breeze of the wide-open spaces and past the still-fuming guard.

He was not repulsed by this failure any more than a good soldier would who repeatedly charges the same hill he believes can inevitably be taken—he was only more perplexed, and cogitating on a better extraction plan for the strayed black sheep of the Rodriguez family. "Once he is home again, he will be fine," thought he, who soon was to revisit this forbidden haunt.

He did not even wait to return until the next day.

I will come back this night, he decided, without even consulting his mother and father, so as to relieve them of any worry, and of a personal necessity to be the hero; and so off he ventured, into the wild black yonder, to rescue someone who did not wish it, in a place that was a citadel for the Los Surenos gang, and their recently merged partner, the Azteca Cartel; yet he, still wearing what he perceived as a badge of righteousness, feared no verbal recrimination or physical reprisals from his brother's captors.

Youth is not bound by the past—of past failures, of past conventionalities, of past winners—for it affords itself a new creation of every new generation, and a creation in itself; and invulnerable, because it is innocent; confident, because it is bold; unstoppable, because it is courageous, and it creates its own armies with its very will, and glorious speeches, and swift action! Youth be praised!

And so, flaming youth carried him past the lazy guards, and too easily back into the den of thieves, where "Open Sesame" was not required, where he might posit his role as a hero, exemplar.

The righteous man may practice his righteousness in the light, but the unrighteous man must practice his art of deception in the dark—and these days, he is surrounded by state-of-the-art surveillance systems.

The electronic monitors in this fortress of chaos swept up the approaching furtive figure, and the human monitor alerted the response team. This time, the influence of the bald-headed man was superseded by the prevailing code of the gang's credo: stay alive, show no mercy, all intruders are worthy of pain and destruction.

So, after he was caught, Diego received a severe, lengthy, and animated beating, as Tomas stood before him.

It was the creeping specter of the Azteca Cartel that placed the cold, hard steel hammer and sickle in the hand of Tomas, the electric jolt of which reverberated throughout him, promising unlimited power, glory, riches, importance—if only he were willing to obey without moral thought and execute orders like a seething savage filled with the opiate of madness.

And though he had done dark deeds,

and drunk the blood of Innocent sheep,
now a gentle lamb was he,
in the golden light of family.

Upon seeing Tomas hesitate to execute an order of judgment upon him to beat his beaten brother, Diego, heartened at the sight of his brother freshly returned to him, said in a voice angelic and testifying, "You have corrupted his flesh, but not his soul," and he looked at his captors without fear or trepidation, "and in that, we have won, and you will always lose."

He might as well have been waxing virtue in the midst of red-eyed ghouls of iniquity, blood dripping from their sharp yellow fangs, and expect understanding and mercy, for the response he received: bewilderment, confusion, then amusement, laughter, which landed upon him in big, generous portions, and finally, anger, wrath, resentment pouring over him in even bigger helpings; but his chosen instrument of combat in this constant war was his good heart, mind and soul, like his diplomatic ancestors, whereas his enemy had long ago and happily chosen brawn, bloodlust, and savagery, like their warring ancestors.

A noble word cannot defend against a crashing fist, nor a noble document against an invading army, but each man is allowed his own way of navigating the troubled world, and so noblemen let their capable brethren engage a scurrilous enemy.

As Diego had no proxy army here, only his noble words, he was thus disarmed by circumstance, and his kind heritage was undone; and presently, his antagonists presented him with a multitude of kicks and punches that not only enraged but curiously pleased them. Tomas, now a weakling in the smoldering eyes of his former employer who feigned to be family, received the same beating in kind, from those he had once embraced, as they pommeled their excommunicated fallen brother, for this must now be, they thought, to keep their tribe strong, and ensure no one will think even once of betrayal.

The two brothers were united in true brotherhood while in the steel jaws of this society that was anointed in infamy; and thus, as they were being driven to a remote site where they would draw their last breath, they held fast the other in a special bond no wicked mind could ever build or conceive, usurp or deny.

And so, did the brothers Rodriguez, still holding each other's bloody hand, finally embraced the tradition held so long in the glorious past of their family of pride, and virtue, and morality, which is worth more than silver, gold, and diamonds; that family, relations, and friends are of more value than power, glory, and wealth, where a world must have sacrifice, honor, and fidelity to survive, even if others fall to the temptations of excess, depravity, and indulgence; and so, in these last important moments together, they embodied the spirit of chivalry, bravery, and loyalty, which was begun, sustained, and fathered by the very spirit of the law of rebellion and revolution against tyranny and depression the world over.

It was Juan Rodriguez who identified the inhumanely shattered bodies that formally housed the souls whom he had so loved. He and his wife were undone, completely, and utterly, emotionally, and physically, and a stinking mist enveloped them, especially—especially dark, and brooding, seeping deep, deep into the very core of what was once suppressed in Man lest its rage be loosed upon the populace.

Juan was no soldier, no warrior, fighter, or trained combatant, but, yes, he was a man, and any man, once violently wronged to his very sacrosanct soul, soon becomes all of those things—and more, once he saw his wife fall into a black malaise of depression while smothered in the numbing pulse of shock, and he found out exactly who had fashioned this impossible horror out of their wicked hearts.

And this would prove very, very unfortunate for those who bethought themselves above and beyond the law, and had never once reasoned that any ordinary citizen would dare pick up the bloodied sword and shield against them.

They were wrong.

Connections

Everything was in readiness.

Operation Pushback had begun. No one in the assorted Cartels, not one of them; no one in the various crime syndicates, no, not one of them; no one in the multivarious affiliated gangs, no, not one of them, even suspected that there existed, outside of the universally agreed-upon and recognized and restrained-by-society laws, an elite group of highly trained operatives who were dedicated to a singular proposition: the abrogation of these criminal organizations by destroying their ability to buy and sell certain highly valued, stimulating drugs, and in so doing, deplete their finances, leading to the effacing of their heinous crimes, which included, but were not limited to: human trafficking, murder, kidnapping, bribery, extortion, blackmail, all types of sexual perversion, assaults—or, do as much damage as they humanly could manage until they died in the attempt.

When there were Crusaders needed, they were there: in Mexico, and Central America, in South America; on the sea, on the land, in the air, underground, under the sea, under the radar; in the city, in the country, in the wild, invisible, incognito, unknown; on the web, on the radio, on the cell phone, on the satellite phone; so, wherever they were, they moved the plan forward, like any good harmonious family of united workers dedicated to the survival of the community.

Now, at every point of the compass, they had the exact route the radically altered coca plant took, from planting to harvesting to processing to being moved to the suppliers, to the place where it would be secured by the sellers, and then sold to the salivating customers, this purified, intensified, bringer of intense euphoria. Each grid on the map was marked, each region tagged, each player accurately described as the product went to and fro.

One can read books and hear stories and read articles about a certain phenomenon, but one must truly witness its ongoing production to definitively argue with complete confidence about its true history, past, present, and even a speculative future.

As it was: there was a large swath of territory that mostly poor peasant people inhabited, who lived a life so sparse that they were barely able to maintain sustenance, but this is without describing the debilitating human and economic costs of disease, of illness, of natural disasters—and man-made ones, too; loss of labor, loss of land, loss of liberty: injustice, inhumanity, insanity, with no clearly delineated, illuminated line out of this miserable mire and onto the path that leads to a better life—which was an impossible dream as it was, for, as it was, living in such wretchedness did not exactly engender hope to join in on the carefree excesses of their mind-numbingly insulated, inured, and incredibly naive North American cousins. So, slaves they were, though no visible chains fell from their emaciated, sallow bodies, for history past and present made those economic chains, and it is called corruption. To wit:

You are born on the fertile land of your forefathers, you are raised on the ideas of hard labor as a way of life; you marry and raise your own family and continue to live as you have, and this is your world, with all of its titles and honors, its grand theater, its politics, literature, music, art—and its hard work, tragedy, and suffering—where there is joy beyond worry of money and illness and food, fleeting in the quiet moments of family gatherings and simple locations, warm smiles, but always something bad soon befalls them: rebels come, bandits come, and the government comes—is there a distinction between them, you ask, as they rape and pillage, plunder and sack what little precious goods and structures, and family, and land you have, and you know it is not right, but you are alone, and those who were supposed to protect you are even against you.

As you stand in amazement and observe the worsening condition you are in despite what you think you deserve, you see a flickering light that flashes around the blurry edges of this horror that has failed you and your kin, friends and relatives, a small packet of luminous energy that, once touched, seems to bring monetary reward, an absence of violence against the new owner, even protection, and this magic fairy dust beckons you; so, you touch it, and feel its exceeding abundance; and behold, as you plant it, and become part of the complex network of employees across thousands of miles, your lot in life improves: life is now good, the simple coca plant hath brought bright joy, where before only thick gloom existed.

But you are not only a poor farmer, but a worker at the docks, a guard at the border, a soldier, a police officer, but poor ones in a poor civilization that has this new and amazing font of riches for any who yield up their conscience to the prodigious appetite of the cocaine industry, and its highly stimulating relations, so you join, and you become, for all intents and purposes, rich and protected. Life is suddenly and appropriately good.

It is all so simple: the product comes, you help it along—you plant it, process it, package it, transport it, protect it, until it goes across the filthy rich American borders, and then the assembly line continues on.

Do you draw a paltry salary in exchange for hard labor at your regular employment? Do the traffickers offer more, plus protection? It is all so simple: you accept; are you an officer of the law sworn to uphold the law of the land? Do the traffickers offer more, plus benefits? It is all so simple: of course you accept. The pattern is the same, even if you are a federal investigator, judge, government official, police, military—the money seduces you; it is all too easy, only a fool, you know, would decline.

Oh yes, some of you actually openly resist, and you know what generally happens to them—the sepulcher reaches to the bottom of the hard mantle where the charred, bullet-ridden, mangled bodies of good men and women journalists, reporters, government officials, judges, officers, soldiers, businessmen, workers, farmers, guards, and yes, others decline, and live, and some of them fight, others flee, others simply remain, and come what may, but you know that "come what may" can be sung only so long on a sinking continent.

So, when law enforcement happened not to step aside but stepped up, and set its stern face toward the direction of the traffickers of cocaine, marijuana, heroin, methamphetamines, or any other recreational substance designed for mass consumption, they were met by a porous, unwieldy, flimsy corporate body of brother and sister officers that leaked and reeked of incompetence, inefficiency and, most maddeningly, corruption.

And even when El Presidente sent in the big hammer, the army, to bludgeon the enemy, the death count concerning the principal players, and "collateral ones," simply increased.

Thus, the Crusaders became as green leaves in a dense green forest, unmoving, patient, observing, trusting no one outside of their own, and soon, a route, with the drug-suppliers-players involved, was recorded, in the countries south of the United States; and soon, the same route was recorded for the states, all of this intelligence-gathering of the Crusaders came from fieldwork, accessing web information from certain individuals who were intimately involved, governmental websites, police agencies, nations' web pages, and anyone or any public entity that would yield up necessary information to ensure success.

Back in the States, it was a hot, humid, stinking, life-arresting night, when the horrible heat blankets you and befouls your mind and casts you into a black mood, and smothers you and runs you like a coward to the cool fumes of central air-conditioning; and those without, why, you merely suffered; and four Crusaders were sitting quietly, in two cars, near a house they suspected was a main repository for cash and cargo, and a crucial meeting place for the local gangs and the Azteca Cartel.

For six months, the Crusaders had prepared for battle, anticipated it, strategized, gathered information and analyzed it, run various scenarios and dry-runs, and staged actual rehearsals inside secluded, giant warehouses using paintballs for ammunition; had practice sessions devoted to answering every conceivable question that might presage some event, some catastrophe and unforeseen circumstance that seemed logical or illogical, and even unlikely and impossible, that would render them inert in the field, dead on the streets, confused and uncertain as how to proceed further; yet, this was no mere passing, but a daily ritual for them, as they waited patiently, stealthily, and ready to strike.

And yet, despite all of their carefully researched and prepared text on the business of preparing for every conceivable situation, they were about to learn that no amount of wide and varying intellectual cogitating on strategizing may prepare one for the inconceivable, as follows:

There was a middle-aged man walking straight down the middle of the road in an area, where no one comes out of their house after the sun goes down; but here he was, walking slowly, methodically, seemingly unafraid, obviously not concerned with the dangers about him, as observed by his large, erect posture and smooth, swarthy countenance. He appeared, to the curious Crusaders near him, as rather ordinary: not athletic, dressed in ordinary street clothes, having a two- to three-day growth of black beard, and possessed, as of yet, of a mysterious, but palpable, weighty resolve, as evidenced by his now strong gait, his steely gaze, his determined path in one particular direction—straight toward the house where flesh, bone and blood nightmares were born, raised, and thrived.

Tyr and Enkidu sat in one black sedan, totally anonymous, anti-intelligence recognition abilities abounding, their faces disguised by heavy makeup, false noses, and wigs, while Arjuna and Finn, similarly attired, sat in a similarly falsity-generating sedan some fifty meters behind them.

Tyr, using a state-of-the-art walkie-talkie system built and specially designed for them, not authorized by any official agency and on an anonymous radio frequency, using an encrypted code designed by Robert's quantum computer that was unknown to any intelligence group, and one that rapidly changed, sent a message and infrared copy of the man's face to command headquarters, which, once translated—and the longer it went on, the more it became punctuated with a heightened sense of urgency: "male innocent walking toward the target... with an iron resolve."

"Who could he be?" Enkidu whispered. "He cannot be what we seek..."

"You're right," Tyr whispered back, after finishing the message, and then texted Arjuna and Finn. "They agree."

"I say he is a madman, out for a walk," Arjuna declared, perplexed.

"No," Finn replied, spying the man as he slowly disappeared into the swirling black mist of night, "I have seen that iron will before."

"Where?"

Finn held up his head, inhaled slowly, and expelled even slower, reached over and grabbed the rearview mirror and aimed it at his friend.

Arjuna was not foolish enough to doubt a fellow warrior. He reached for his weapon. "Should we stop him?" This declaration required a new text of the exact question, which presently was sent to all the parties involved.

"No contact," Finn whispered.

Arjuna understood, too.

"No contact," Tyr whispered.

Enkidu understood, too.

"We have to wait," Arjuna said. "I don't like it." He was agitated now, watching the lone man nearing the house.

"No one likes it," Finn said. "It isn't in our nature."

"It isn't Africa."

Finn gave a barely perceptible nod of his blond head.

Tyr, looking through his mini black binoculars, whispered, "We have never waited so long—it is difficult, when the enemy is right before you..."

"Civilization," Enkidu replied, thoughtful, "is a muddle."

"Look," Tyr nearly cried.

"Look there," Finn whispered harshly.

Now, all of them were looking with the intensity of a battlefield soldier, for the man had lately separated himself from the casual citizenry who takes late-night walks. He had pulled a weapon.

Finn messaged to command center even as the first shots sliced through the sultry air.

"He took out a guard," Arjuna exclaimed.

"We can't stand down," Tyr shouted, looking at the screen of his walkie-talkie.

"But the mission..." Enkidu said.

They could plainly see the man whirling around to point his rifle at another fast-approaching sentry.

"How can we wait," Arjuna screamed.

"We must wait," Finn said, coolly, looking intensely at the luminous screen, "wait, wait..."

The response appeared on the screen. "Juan Rodriguez: two sons murdered by Cartel... fight."

A moment later, a few miles away, a blond-haired, muscular man strapped himself into an all-black, slender, sleeker version of the KH jet wing, and in one seamless movement, even as he adjusted the dials and hooked the wires to his own forehead, he ran, and as he leaped into the air, the silent engines ignited and propelled him into the grand temple of this moonless, light-less, black-as-pitch night.

The four men, finally feeling home again, disembarked from their cars and ran pell-mell toward the black mansion where even now a fierce gun battle had erupted.

The war had begun.

Juan Rodriguez

Daily and without ability to abate it, Juan watched his wife move closer to that room in which, once ensconced, few return from behind its encompassing darkness; and this was much worse than any sudden, tragic death, as he had experienced with his sons, for here he was impotent to alter the downward spiraling path that she seemed to want, that her brain seemed to thrive upon, and her heart to seek, to hide from the misery and despair she could not effectively understand and defuse. When the doctor finally pronounced judgment that Juan had already known, that she was in shock, near comatose, and needed round-the-clock care that was challenging him physically every day to provide—and he would not accept help from relatives and friends— and that she needed care that would bankrupt them, he knelt next to her as he stroked her moist face and stared at the woman he could still see only as his youthful, full-of-life, blushing bride of twenty. He murmured, not certain if she truly heard him, passionately, sweetly, adoringly, "My beautiful Sonia, my beautiful, beautiful bride," and looked at her expressionless visage, and wept. "I love you, Sonia, I will always love you." He kissed her warm forehead, and said, lovingly, "We shall not long be apart, and once again a family."

He would not stay with her much longer, for there were preparations to be made. As he readied himself for the imminent deed, he was as if one moving independently of his true self: for truly, he did not recognize this species of thinking of the external foreigner that now inhabited him—nor would he stop him from necessary chores, and not only could not stop him, but, rather, knew he must not stop him. "Would I not do the same?" he seemed to ask, from a great distance and separated by an energy, an indeterminate force he yielded to and followed like a faithful servant. "Where you go, so too go I," he heard his faraway self whisper, still watching with great curiosity as the intruder neared completion of his deliberate tasks. "He will restore that which I lost, and all will be well again; soon, we will be a family once more—it has only been a short time away from each other." He looked toward the room where she lived like one dead in the grave of this choking heat. "Soon, my love," he murmured, and then felt himself pouring through the door and out into the fresh air and then commence to walk, not drive, for there was something about an automobile right now that was too facile, too remote in its access, too connected to modernity, because his actions now were linked to a savage, primordial past, and no civilized artifacts save the cold steel hardware upon him need aid his mission.

And so he walked, calmly, smoothly, easily, down the long, lonely sidewalks and across empty streets and past deserted buildings and into a wasteland where live things go when first the thought of a torturous death trespasses away from their feuding thoughts. He had crossed the porous barrier between light and dark, between rich and poor, between law and lawlessness, and he felt emboldened, and protected, because he was a messenger of the Light, and the Light was good, and he feared no evil.

No sense of weariness or ache bore up in him, as his body was feeding on the fuel of an ambitious want to war upon creatures so undeserving of life, so that it sharpened his senses; finally, he turned a filthy corner and beheld the nest wherein the human filth was engendered, as if, in his mind's eye, he clearly saw, it was an open sewer pushing out rotten sludge; now, his slack body grew tense, his stoic face flushed crimson anger, his comfortable stride increased and quickened, for battle loomed, and he must needs be ready; but no longer did he feel he walked alone, but with brother warriors of glorious past, of noble warriors, and knights, of revolutionaries, who refused to accept the rule of unabashed criminal insurgents.

He was the deliverer now, and any and all who stood in his determined path must needs die. A guard appeared and accosted him, and then a brilliant flash as retort occurred, and the guard died. The man simply moved on. He was no longer just an outraged man, grieving parent, despairing husband, who bemoans his fate, and rages against injustice—just like every other despairing citizen who knows there is in fact no social justice in the world; he was, in fact, in his mind, creating Justice, with each pull of the trigger, leveling the playing field, honoring those who had heroically died so that others might live in true democratic freedom.

Another guard appeared, and fired, missed, and the man fired once, twice, and felled the guard. He moved on toward the mark. The lights in this house of horrors, which brought terror and operated in plain sight but somehow never died, came on.

Four men fairly exploded from two parked cars and ran hard toward the coming conflagration.

Juan Rodriguez entered through the open, narrow black doors with a Heckler & Koch 0.45 in one hand, and a MK 23 pistol in the other, twelve rounds ready in each, and several box magazines of twelve rounds inside his coat pants pocket, replete with suppressor; his Heckler & Koch MR556A1 rifle, with thirty rounds ready, and several box magazines of thirty rounds each inside his coat pockets, hung by a black leather strap over his shoulder. He shut the doors behind himself. It was a habit.

Two men with handguns appeared in front of him.

In a moment, two men with handguns lay in a bloody heap before him. He felt the scales of Justice rise a little bit as these bodies were heaped on one side and the other side with Innocents on it rose a bit. He moved on.

It was a large house, consisting of two stories and many rooms, which were filled with a mix of gang affiliates, card-carrying, flag-waving Cartel members, and young women who had long ago decided to donate their bodies to a heinous criminal organization for a lucrative lifestyle despite the intervening degradation of their eternal souls, in company with mounds of cash, highly stimulating drugs, weapons, tobacco, alcohol, and the euphoria from being around seemingly unlimited power.

It had certainly been an unusually celebratory night for the people here, because of the latest delivery of goods rendered, and the amount of cash taken in, and ensuing orgy of sexual congress, in concert with the copious amounts of alcohol, and cocaine, and heroin and marijuana they freely ingested, that so deviated from the norm that the parties involved were so exhausted and spent that they were absent in mind and body, and most were too sluggish to respond to a physical threat they had hitherto considered impossible.

Two of the lethargic, bloated, bewildered and higher-than-a-hot-air-balloon creatures appeared at the top of the stairs, albeit with loaded guns, but unfortunately for them, their fog-infested brains were more loaded, and the two barefoot gunmen were dispatched quickly by the intruder.

But not everyone was drowsy and just waking up. Five gunmen came rushing out of the kitchen, pistols firing.

And where were the four men on the outside? They were about to come inside.

But this was the makeup of the forces seen, not unseen, for this was, after all, the age of technology, and more forces were now involved, as we shall soon see.

Who Completes the Complications of Battle

It was the era of instant communication, no longer a scenario where commandos relied on pigeon, soldier, hot air balloon, or reflective light, where even the field radio and walkie-talkie gave way to their progeny, the cellular and satellite phone, and where widely disseminated information connected all the players together like strings on a harp—one pull and all felt the proper hum and vibration. There was, consequently, little time to think and plan an action; it was now just action.

So, when Juan Rodriguez thrust his avenging self into this stealth world of the Cartel-gangs, lines of communication had lit up: first, the members of this exclusive order signaled for more help; second, neighbors who had heard shots called the police; and third, the Crusaders sprang into action, and here, their story will be delineated first.

Firstly, every location where the Crusaders were present was considered a potential battlefield, and this meant a perimeter protection was drawn, circumscribed along specific borders, describing all possible scenarios and players involved, like a giant target, with the operatives the bull's-eye, and concentric rings of the key checkpoints radiating out from it, to wit: yes, the four Crusaders exited their vehicles at approximately one o'clock in the a.m., on a Friday, late in August, but from the outer ring, the command center, specific alerts and a sophisticated code were sent out to Dylan, whom we have already seen jumping into action, and to operatives manning stations that controlled the drones.

Secondly, the police came, a route known and mapped by the Crusaders, in two squad cars, with their sirens silent, officers requesting backup.

Thirdly came more of the Cartel-gang alliance members, from any and all directions, in cars and trucks, on motorcycles, on bicycles, with guns, with rifles, ready to kill, eager to kill, happy to kill.

Thus, when the four Crusaders moved cautiously through the doorway of the house, behind them was a fast-burning fuse that led to a mountain of black gunpowder that recently had been lit.

The five Cartel-gang "hybrid" members were firing in rapid succession at one who was firing in rapid succession back at them in this dark living room, now illuminated by sparks of gunfire. Juan was struck four times about his body, yet he still killed two of them. The Crusaders killed the other four.

When Juan turned around to see the reinforcements, they were already firing up at the three men who were firing at them from the top of the staircase. He felt a dull burning sensation in his body, but he cared not. Two more armed men came from the kitchen, and he dispatched one, while a Crusader killed the other. The five, united in purpose to survive, took to the sides of the living room wall.

Four men, two equipped with assault rifles, began to fire from behind the protective barrier of the other side of the two-tiered stairwell.

Tyr tossed a stun grenade, and Enkidu threw a noise blaster up to the hallway, and motioned to Juan to clap his ears, and shield his eyes, and they did the same.

In a moment, it was over; it wasn't really fair, this contest, where ordinary bully-terrorists used to gunning down helpless Innocents were up against four highly trained veteran soldiers who had special weaponry, but it was a battle, and fortune favors the prepared and the well-trained.

Three gunmen burst through the door, two rushed into the open sliding door from the backyard, and four more came rushing from the top hallway.

Tyr and Enkidu had already thrown stun and noise-blasting grenades and smoke grenades at every point of access to the present position, and so, as they crouched low behind furniture with their oxygen masks on, they and their comrades had no trouble dispatching the newcomers to this dead man's party.

And every sound that occurred, every scene, was relayed back to control headquarters and their fellows, through the micro video cameras mounted upon the four Crusaders' glasses, and the microphones on their lapels, and through tiny transmitters embedded in their ears, to which they continued to hear encoded communication.

Silence lived for a fantastic moment, as if to say, all was over, all was good, as it had been, that the fight was done, that the Crusaders had won, and the longer it breathed life and energy into the place, the higher the chance that it was all true—and then, it was aborted, and it died, as the men, anxious, sweating, breathing hard, listened, their countenances hopeful, felt the crush of the inevitable. It is never easy, each man heard himself whisper to his naive self. There it was—more Cartel-gang members about to crash through this momentary peace, and now police sirens, too, and they knew now, as they had already known, that this was merely the beginning.

But they were not alone, part of the whole, one layer of many members of the team, and no player acted independently of the other; so, yes, the enemy was moving in, their aggressive mood stabbing the silence with an evil augury, but, no, suddenly they stopped, and amid a great clamor and rapid succession of gunfire that roared like mighty thunder, and then, abruptly, as if the thunder's roar sufficed, the troublesome noise was quenched.

The Crusaders knew precisely what had happened.

"The drones," each of them thought, assuaging any residue of doubt that they would, as they always had, win.

They received their instructions to follow the plan that had been previously mapped out in just such a present occurrence in such a house: exit out the back and into the alley, where two Crusaders, each driving an unmarked, and unidentified and invisible—for all intents and purposes to law enforcement—car, were waiting, two men who had previously been part of a four-man backup unit—as was the rule in all such local operations—that had already dropped off two other men, who had taken the abandoned sedans and driven them clean away. But the police, after having issued their customary invitations to the guests inside to capitulate, entered into the slaughterhouse from, for now, the front.

The four Crusaders—wearing infrared glasses, and having already knocked out the lightbulbs that might be turned on to expose their whereabouts—and Tyr, helping a badly wounded and unconscious Juan, were in the large backyard, on the patio porch under the black canvas that extended several feet from the edge of the roof, when Juan struck a concrete table and fell, and then two uniformed officers came to the back doors of the house, yelling, "Halt! Drop your weapons," with their guns drawn and their senses lifted on high in a frenetic frenzy.

And then it was as if the inky, black darkness had an even thicker, sooty veil thrust over it, for the officers now saw not even a glimpse of the suspects, as they felt a rush of hot wind burst in front of them; and then, there, before them appeared the thick curtain of pitch-black, and a light humming noise that halted them, in a trance-like terror, frozen in their tracks; then they saw small, rotating lights whirring around as if in a halo, and they felt as if some supernatural presence was manifest before them; it was then the two officers fired several rounds into it, but it was like firing into sand.

Dylan, having landed precisely between the four retreating Crusaders and the fallen Rodriguez, had lifted up the special space-age, long, dark material that hung from his arms to mask what went on behind him, and then wrapped the man in it, and placed him onto a platform made from nanostructured ceramics, which jutted out from the base of the KH jet wing. The soft hum and whir of the engine spilled like a fantastic tale the officers were not too anxious to hear.

"Who," said the elder cop, weapon still on the ready, immersed in fear and trepidation, in a low, guttural whisper, "are you…"

The sound of more officers of the law sounded in the distance, and the wail of sirens, too, but the constant hum and whir before them seemed louder.

And then Dylan, in a robotic-filtered voice, let loose in an explosive and guttural shout, "Justice," and then he blew upward, with Juan safely in tow, shooting like a fast-rising rocket, as the stunned officers turned their weapons and beleaguered minds upon the ascending angel.

Finally, the junior officer, still in the tight grip of cold shock, asked, in a hoarse whisper, "What," but he stammered, and was unable to complete the sentence, and then managed to say, "what was it?"

The senior officer, still watching the incredible image receding into the thicket of a diamond-studded, hot black night, murmured, "The future…"

Recovery

The drones, having dispatched the moving fortress that was the Cartel-gang alliance, leaving a dozen corpses piled up on the sidewalk, on the front lawn, and on the street, were recalled by their master, and were soon safely within their protective and secretive nests, beyond the frustrated reach of the searching authorities.

Dylan, some two thousand feet above the ground, having secured a still-unconscious Juan to the KH, was communicating to his fellows in the command center, wary of police helicopters, low-flying aircraft, flocks of birds, radar detection, opportunistic shooters, and satellite photo detection; yet, the KH had radar slipping technology, invisibility cloaking, an electromagnetic force field generating anti-bullet safeguards, so that, even with the small rotating lights about their craft turned off, he was nearly an unidentified flying object.

The black helmet that Dylan wore had a video multi-screen that allowed him to see using the augmented reality technology, via satellite, the command center, surrounding images, television, Internet, or cable images, and the implant in his ear allowed him to hear information from a variety of sources; and the microphone in his helmet allowed him to speak, either to his crew, or, via voice-changing technology, to the exterior world—for he was, unbeknown to his foes, living inside a exoskeleton that had melded with the KH jet wing, making him the world's first fully functional flyer—independent of a traditional aircraft—capable of diverse maneuvers in the air, landing, and taking off, and fully equipped with weaponry, and other technology to combat the enemy soldier.

"All clear," he heard from command headquarters, as he traveled at a cruising speed of approximately one hundred miles per hour.

No good army, no good Special Forces unit—in fact, no good team of warriors—can properly function without having, at their immediate disposal, adequate and hopefully outstanding medical care; but due to the special nature of the Crusaders' mission, government and private health care facilities accessible to the general public were forbidden; so, a chosen few medical practitioners with allegiance to the Mission were recruited, and this was where Dylan now landed the KH, in the remote valley mountain region where a team of specialists had already assembled and were awaiting his touchdown.

Once Juan was removed, Dylan blasted off again, the KH nearly silent, issuing only a sudden gush of hot air; and then up he went, a streak of whooshing sound bleeding back down to his listeners. By the time he returned to the camouflaged headquarters in the wilderness region, he already knew that all of the Crusaders in this firefight were safe, the cars safe, but the Mission was imperiled; but just like a destructive wound, the Crusaders would work diligently to patch it, heal it up, and attempt to return the damaged site back to normal. The complicated process had already begun with a forensic team of computer experts scanning official police records for information on this brief battle and wiping clean any surveillance footage of the confrontation.

After a lengthy debriefing of the Crusaders who were still in the States, regarding the first battle of Operation Pushback, the Mission continued, but with more caution, for the local police agencies, baffled by the enigmatic Special Forces team that had successfully killed twenty members of the Cartel-gang alliance, and having no information on the illegal use of drones in United States air space, or the enigmatic rocket man, were soon, in their investigation, to be usurped by national security agency personnel, and other assorted police agencies assigned to investigate such internal affairs; and so for now, this file was dubbed "vigilante group unknown."

And what of Juan, what of he—of all the free people in North America who had witnessed the degradation and humiliation of being subjected to and conquered by an invading foreign force in league with the indigenous criminals to form an ever-expansive, multi-headed monster enterprise that was encroaching on the once-safe and formally guaranteed pursuit of life, liberty, and happiness; who had decided to take the dangling and unmanned reins of freedom and tighten them about his fists and raise the universal flag of rebellion? As he was a nobody, as it related to police records, his blood retrieved at the battle site was anonymous, and since his presence there was anonymous too, and his wounds tended to anonymously, he was not to be a suspect. He lived, yes, he did, and eventually returned to his wife, who, upon seeing his physical wounds, and tending to him, allowed her emotional ones to mend; eventually, they were both healed in mind, body and spirit, as much as could be gained where there existed an irreparable tear in their hearts, hearts that were achieved by the existence of loving each other and being loved in return; so that, soon enough—how long that is is not relevant anymore when one loses their precious children—they decided, without much deliberation, to sell their house, for which they received a rather handsome sum, if not, perhaps, for such a humble home, an amount that far exceeded their asking price.

The buyer, a middle-aged man, who sat in their house one early Saturday morning, after sipping homemade lemonade, explained it this way: that he was in the market for older homes to make them into safe houses for wayward youths, had the money to pay above market value, and, more importantly, enjoyed rewarding families like the Rodriguezes who were exemplars of the American dream.

Still, the Rodriguezes blushed; so much for so little, they said—it did not seem right; and then Juan had said, "My wife and I have talked it over, and we will take the money you're paying above our price, and set up a scholarship foundation for deserving boys and girls...to honor our two sons..." But he could not complete his word, so distraught was he, as he held his wife's hand.

"... Who recently died..." Sonia completed, as they squeezed each other's hand.

They did not see the imperceptible nod, the gleam of pride in the luminous brown eyes of the buyer. "I am sorry for your loss—I cannot imagine such a tragedy. It is a noble gesture, even when you grieve, you bring succor to others."

"What else can one do," Juan replied, "in this world, all we have is each other, and God, and if we would just listen to Him." He paused, lost in deep reverie. "We have replaced Him with arrogance and vanity, and knowledge—just enough to destroy us."

The man on the silver sofa nodded. "Wisdom is vindicated by her deeds."

The three of them would talk for some time after, exchanging stories and ideas about their long journey on the road to the Good Life; and when the sun dipped below the crimson horizon, it was a signal for the switch inside their bodies to turn on and call the day a day well done, and the night a night to be alone, so they all arose in unison.

Sonia wished the man well, and shook his hand. Juan walked out with him.

The two men stood side by side, silent, listening to the stirring echoes of that cowardly creeper, injustice, don its perverted mask: sirens racing about the evolving enabler, black gloom. Juan thanked the man, shook his hand, and wished him well; but then, he said, compelled by the wonders of good deeds immemorial, as he stared hard into the gentle face of the man, "Do I know you?" He felt the chill of revelation burst like raindrops of electricity over his tingling skin. He did not know why he had said this, but only knew he must.

The man smiled. "Those who care for people always recognize each other."

"No," Juan said, shaking his head, his black brows furled, his black eyes narrowed, and then asked, hopefully, "I mean—do you know me?"

Again, the man smiled, and this time placed his capable, large right hand upon the broad shoulders of Juan, and said, his voice full of the joy that the love of Justice brings, "When upon a place I stop and tarry, I seek rest and shelter of thee; when upon a place I call home, I give rest and shelter to those who ask of me."

Is it possible for two men, unknown to each other, in this case, to communicate in an unseen way, either physically, chemically, spiritually, or emotionally—it is not to be precisely known—so that what is not plainly written or plainly spoken, or plainly shown in some manner, is plainly and absolutely received and perfectly understood by their immortal souls?

It happened now, it happened, it did, this shimmering flare of eternal Truth and Justice bore into each man, because each man was willing to hear it and see it and listen to this now-uncovered sacred script; and they knew who the other was and who he had been, where he was going and why he was, and the crucible of the good fight he had willingly lifted upon his shoulders; so, this is true brotherhood, the recognizing of the other's good heart wherein a sacred duty lies to never relinquish the challenge of fighting to protect that which is noble, and proclaim without reservation and fear that which is holy, Holy.

And so, the two men departed, having firmly established a spiritual bond through a universal special language, forever connected, and elevated to a bridge they had once crossed so that one day they might live in a world where not even the stars need to shine, so great is the illumination from the glory and majesty of the essence of Goodness, Justice, and Love.

What Makes the Revolution Frozen

A poor man's life is a frozen fire;
the fire is the heart's desire;
yet this flame will never tire,
until it melts on Freedom's funeral pyre

You wake up and make your yellow tortilla and pinto beans, drink your black coffee from a faded tin cup, then stand on the front porch of your small domicile, and gaze first at what is nearest—the seemingly eternal, handed-down-generation-to-generation, archetypal poverty of yourself—and then at your immediate neighbor; and then you grasp the dearth of possibilities beyond that of more hovels, more shacks, more dumps to live in, more dismal landscapes, barren, sterile, weak, and you realize as you have every wet, cool, or hot, dry morning, that today is the same as yesterday, and will be the same shovelful of sorrow and regret tomorrow, and that into every hole you dig drops the same sweat and frustration of your ancestors. What is it all for, you ask yourself, why is it, what else is there, why me, and why not all of us? He looks back at his family: wife, four children, their hope in him, and he knows he must work, hard and unrelenting too, as has been practiced by his lineage from time immemorial, for he knows no other way of existence.

So, he does labor, harvesting the crops in the early, cool morning and into the sinewy waves of the merciless, scorching sun, until the last sprinkle of precious light, and now he is very tired, but he must prepare the produce for sale, must haul it to town on his lazy donkey, must take a low price from rich men whom he knows cheat and rob him and his fellow farmers, but what else can he do? He says thank you, and bows his head, averts his eyes, and leads the lazy donkey back home in the late, hazy, smirking dusk, and shares his minuscule fortune—any money made honestly and saved is a miracle and fortune to him—with his family; and so they will live yet another humiliating, degrading, suffering day; but is this this all there is, he wonders, as he stands on his wooden porch at the apex of a deep, dark, pitch-black night—was all the world conceived in such sorrow?

And then one particularly horribly cold and rainy day when you want to stay inside the toasty, warm, safe house, and not plow through the mud and slush of Nature's cruel jest, but know only the rich man can dare afford such "luxuries," you step outside and see that one of your forever-doomed-to-the-heavy-chains of poverty neighbors has achieved a hitherto unknown miracle: he has lifted up, in a time too brief to measure, the societal stones forged by his masters that so mercilessly weighed him down, and moved himself up the normally rigid, societal ladder.

So, you dare ask him—you cannot be dissuaded not to, so fantastic is the vision of him with a new, shining automobile, new clothes on his family, too, and now making a sign to stick on his weed-ridden front yard: "Take anything inside—it's yours. Pedro." And there were his children frolicking in the rain, exultant, as if they had recently had a life sentence communicated to instant freedom.

"What is it, Pedro, what has happened?" José asked, incredulous still.

"José, my friend," he returned, holding him fast by his slender shoulders, "good times have come to the Sanchez family—as I always knew it would," and handed him an American hundred-dollar bill, upon which José looked in shock. "I have many of these—really! Be happy for me—and yes," he suddenly cried, "it can all be yours, too."

José was fingering the money, turning it over and over as if to check its authenticity. "I have never…"

"Do you want to be rich, too, José? Huh? You can be, you know." His tone grew disdainful, as he gesticulated about in violent chops and waves. "No more living like our forefathers in this dead place; I mean, no more living like a peon—look, José, look: it's all about money," and he held out a thick wad of crisp, clean greenbacks of high denominations. "Money makes you proud—not this," and he spat, "this humiliating life—I'm tired of being just another poor Mexican farmer who has to beg the wealthy buyers for another peso; now," he thumped his chest, "I am as wealthy as they are—ha! What do you think of that, eh?" He stood fully erect, his chest out as he posed for his longtime neighbor. "I can hold up my head high and walk proud—well, what do you think?"

"But where—how did you get so much money?"

Pedro shrugged his shoulders and smiled. "It's also easy, José: I joined one of the biggest, thriving firms—with good benefits, high pay, and holidays off; one of the biggest in all of Latin America; they make hundreds of billions of dollars a year!"

"Who?" José answered, truly bewildered.

Pedro laughed. "The Cartels, José, the Cartels—but I have signed," he said, wiggling his head as he thrust out an invisible pencil in hand, "on the dotted line with the Alvarez Cartel—eh," and he shrugged his shoulders, "one is as good as the other—it's all the same; money is money."

José instinctively dropped the currency and watched it slowly drift into the puddled mire. "The Azteca Cartel," he murmured; "they are no good for Mexico."

"You'll pick up the money one day," Pedro said, nodding as he pursed his lips, "everyone else has, who is smart, and wants what he has always been denied; after all—it's just business…"

José said, still looking at the hundred-dollar bill that was now covered in small rivulets of mud, "What will you do for them?"

"Hey, it isn't like I'm killing people—it isn't what you think." He threw up his hands. "Everyone thinks we're only about killing—yes, people certainly die," and then his voice became stern, like a mentor's, "but only the ones getting in the way; look, we have a product to sell: cocaine, marijuana, heroin, meth—drugs! We have lots of customers," and he pointed decidedly north, "that way—and if people would just leave us alone, no one would get hurt."

"If…"

"Well, it happens, you know, and if I have to kill someone, I guess I'll have to—or maybe not, we'll see; but for now, I am just transporting shipments to the Mexican-US tunnel, that's all, and—boom—just like that, I am rich; can you believe it? It's a miracle!"

"No," he replied, gravely.

"Oh, cheer up, José—I won't forget you; I'll come for you and take you and your family out of this horrible place."

"I want out, I do, I want to take Ramona and the children away, but not like this…"

"José, you are an educated man—why do you stay on this miserable land? This is no time for a conscience; where is the conscience of our rulers who allow us—and want us—to live like peasant farmers? Everyone is on the take, anyhow," he said, hurriedly, observing José's frowning countenance. "Senior Suarez isn't just a Cartel leader—he helps out the province of Azteca. He gives us food, clothing and shelter; he builds schools, he builds churches, he builds roads—better than the local government, and they admire him, they work with him; the people love him and protect him because he only kills his enemies, not us," he pointed to the both of them, "not good Mexican citizens who work honestly for a living."

José looked closely at Pedro, his voice suffused with the grave pathos, long-ago established, buried and harvested, and passed down from generation to generation. "Is this the only way out?"

His answer came from a place in the soul that has already decided how to ditch the circuitous, hilly, mined path that is life, for a nice, smooth, straight one. "Si."

"I will pray for you, Pedro, on your travels." He held out his hand.

"I shall pray for you, too, José." The two lifelong, long-suffering neighbors shook hands in a firm grip, a link from the beginnings of this land that was first inhabited by their native American Indian ancestors and worked incessantly until this very moment, where for now the link had been dissolved for one of them.

As José watched Pedro drive away in his brand-new automobile, he happened to glance down, and saw the money nearly immersed by the thick mounds of muddy water, and as he turned and walked toward his own little house, which even now seemed like a sudden shock, the greenback completely disappeared into the thick ooze and brown muck.

As he toiled every day in the harsh environs of the state of Azteca, in the cruel heat, in the cruel cold, beside disaster, beside illness, where he was crushed by dishonest buyers, dismissed by local politicians, suppressed by unfair laws and trade agreements, he could not help but think of Pedro, the fabulously rich Pedro, who had been just like he from birth till just recently, but with one more "yea," than "nay," had assumed the bearing of a rich man, proud man, happy man; and also of his beloved country, which he had, as of late, begun to think had forgotten him and his kind, that someone else other than a true Mexican was now planning for his people. "It is as if bandits have taken our Mother Mexico and plundered her, and set her adrift," he thought, "and who shall we ask for salvation?" He could do nothing but shake his head as he plowed his fertile fields, as he took off his sombrero to pour cold water over his black, sweaty hair, and think, "But I am Mexico, I must be loyal to her, so when she is reborn, I will celebrate her; I cannot do this if I take the money—then I am no better than other men who have yielded to temptation, where we would be united by greed: a citizen of greed, a man without a country." But even as he said this, he did not believe it, and secretly yearned to live the bold and exciting life of Pedro, the hedonist. He did not even dare to tell his wife of such reprehensible ruminations.

So, he stayed on the land, despite his higher education, because his father had worked the land, and his father's father, and so far back that the direct lineage to the Yaquis on this very region could be established without too much difficulty; because his life in the city had been unsatisfactory, and he did not like the corruption he saw, the violence he saw, the sad disintegration of a once stable society he saw, which gave him over to profound despair, and compelled him to take his family back to the fertile fields of his forefathers. "I mustn't let the filth of the city accompany me here, for here, it is still unblemished; here, there are no murders, kidnappings, gang wars; here, there is only the land, and the peasants, and we are still unchanged, we are still Mexico, and we must stay here or Mexico will be no more."

> Winter arrives with a rattling chain, beating down Fall's refrain,
> establishing a heavy, despairing mane;
> Spring slices this curtain through, blowing in her perfumed breath;
> Man forgets what came before, this ethereal and welcomed fest;
> now Summer comes dressed in gossamer fare
> and soon Man remembers this scorching terror

It was a tinderbox of boiling heat that picked up the highest-thinking species and deposited them like helpless infants outside of their humid homes; so, there was José, sitting on the wooden porch of his home this humid night, playing with his children as he talked to his wife. Life was not a horror, he knew, nor was it exemplary, but manageable, as the crops had yielded him a decent profit this year. He yearned for neither treasures or power, but for serenity and harmony. And this, he thought, I planted in the green valley, where the world still exists as it was meant to be, where we have what most we treasure: each other, peace, health, and God.

And then, in the near distance, he heard a panicked moan, and then a desperate, shrill cry, followed by, and accompanied by, an urgent digging sound. He could see a small flashlight point toward his house, and with his curiosity piqued, he set forth to see what he could see; and he felt no fear, no worry, no reservation at all, as this was his kindred village, and his fellow farmers he had complete trust in, as was necessary for each other's survival.

"Hola," he said, casually, "buenos tardes, amigo," but the wounded voice that bled agony did not abate, nor the fast digging. He kept walking.

The night was altogether clear, and the bright, bold moon full, and the glittering white points of light so many that soon he could discern a man kneeling and using a small hand shovel, digging madly in the soft brown soil, his head thrust down toward the expanding hole.

"Pedro?" he whispered to himself, still watching the man widely attacking the ground with an hysterical fervor, and then, "Pedro…" He stared harder. "Pedro," he said, loudly, "it is José."

But Pedro heard only the cuts and thrusts of the silver-colored shovel, and his desperate ache, his chaotic need for resolution; and then, "Aha!" And there he was, holding up something in his hand as he became erect, still on his knees, entering the small flashlight upon it. "There you are!" And he kissed the dirty paper object, and sprang up, and began to dance merrily about the hole, singing and praising God on high.

"Pedro," José said, nearly upon his old friend now, "it is I, José."

"José!" he returned, standing still as he beheld him, a broad smile adorning his face. "José! My good, good friend," and he leaped into an enthusiastic embrace with him, and held him long and hard, all along, shouting, "José, José, tried and true, my good, good friend," and so he let him see the object he had so feverishly pursued, his face glowing with pride and joy, "you never took it—good, good for you; untouched, unclean—good, good José—yes! A virgin, still!"

What he held in his hand was the American one-hundred-dollar bill.

"José! I knew you wouldn't fail where I failed; let me hold you, let me see you, to know true goodness for one second, that it still exists," he began, still smiling, but then his happiness slowly dissipated, like golden rays of sun behind an immense dark and cloudy sky, and whispered, "Beautiful farmer José, and his beautiful family—are they still here? Yes! Good, good, I am so glad," and then the precursors of tears formed, "at least one of us—so much joy you must have; yes, so much joy I had…" And then he fell to the ground, as if struck by a powerful unseen force, and there, he dug his hands in the fresh, cool soil and then raised them up and smelled the rich, pungent humus as he gazed intensely at it and whispered, "I betrayed you, how could I," and smeared it over his sweaty, grimacing face. "I love you, and yet I gave my love to another; I did not have faith in you—faith; I let my desire for mere things darken my heart," and he began to weep, so much that his face was like a crimson mask upon a writhing sea; and then he murmured, drawn from self-pity, and want of self-instruction, "I'm no longer worthy of the heritage of my ancestors; I am an ancestor now to depravity..." And he fell forward and kissed the sweet mulch that brings life. "Take me back, take me back," he wept into the soft bosom of his once-blessed sanctuary and protector, Nature, his arms wrapped around himself, hugging himself tightly, murmuring, "Make it all go away, please, please, make it all go away, O dear God, make it all go away," and then began to press himself into the soft soil.

José gazed upon a man seeking to un-create himself. José grieved, yes, but he also feared, too, for the arcane narrative that began to slip from the man's wailing soul charted a slow, grinding course down the gloomy corridor that led to a secluded temple wherein resides the baser things of Man's nature.

Pedro was curled up fast now, shaking in a powerful paroxysm, holding himself fast, babbling loudly, and crying as if being thrust with daggers, but they were only daggers of his conscience, which he had once impaled and left to rot in the rubbish pile, but had regenerated itself from what little pieces had survived.

José sat beside him. "Pedro," he began softly, "where are Conchita, and Marco, and Lupe?"

"Dead," Pedro whispered, but it didn't sound like a human whisper, more like the growl of a wounded, wild animal trapped in a deep hole; but then he did not say anything more for a long time; and then he spoke again in the eerie, grunting, scrubbed-of-all-humanity voice, deep in tone, lost in regret. "Dead—I killed them."

José felt his body chilled head to foot, muscle to bone, heart to soul. "You mean—you left them alone, and they were killed..."

"No," he cried, "I killed them—I murdered them; O, if only that..."

José fell backward and stood up, and shouted, "What have you done?"

"I have tried to kill the soul of goodness, and yet, it whispers, 'Forgiveness,' to me..."

"No more riddles, Pedro—speak plainly!"

Pedro stopped his violent shaking, his body soaked in a waxy, yellow, stinking perspiration. "I acted as a stalking beast, killing not for sustenance, but for pleasure; so no," his tone moved sideways into a darker hue and at a decibel level few have dared to tread. "Even the beasts of the field kill for food; so, I am the worst of G..." But he could not pronounce such a holy name, now. "Free will is our hell."

José, frustrated still, cried out, "Did you kill Conchita and Marco and Lupe?"

"No," he sighed, lying on his bare back on the wet mulch, and examining his hands, "no, but I pulled the trigger that caused them to die."

José crouched down close to his friend's face. "Speak clearly, Pedro; speak the truth."

"The truth," he replied, eyes shut now, as the pain of memories left his mind. "I tried to kill it, too, but it wouldn't die—why? It seems so weak, so… innocent, but perhaps there is its simple greatness…"

"Start at the beginning, Pedro; tell me what happened right after you left."

"Hmm," he murmured, "yes, in the beginning—if only I could go back and stop myself from leaving," and then he said, passionately, "but I was so certain…"

Devolution

Pedro had taken his family to a comfortable home in the city of Alvarado, near other homes of his fellow playmates, and once disconnected from his family, he was free to ply this exciting new trade with all the vibrant energy and enthusiasm that still bubbles furiously in the heart mind of the young: his first employment was to simply accompany shipments of marijuana and heroin—two substances with a long history of cultivation and production in his home country—to the States, via land routes, and water routes, a journey made seamless and productive through the dismantling of potential human barriers: judicial, police, military, customs, and done so with a generous, steady flow of ever-increasing cash. He marveled at the ease of it all, and for the first few months, saw relatively few obstacles, as if, indeed, he were transporting nothing more than automobile parts, and not products responsible for the majority of crime in North America, and in Mexico itself, for much of the crime in Central America, and which fueled the coffers of criminal organizations around the globe, hundreds of billions of dollars a year in revenue that had contributed to the disruption of millions of lives, and deaths, and the ensuing chaos in every family it touched, every town, province, state, country, continent, and hemisphere, because of a human weakness for the products and the human greed to distribute them, human ignorance to preclude their reign of terror, and human fear to not step up to meet the challenge, and thus allow the disintegration of civilization, giving birth to new venture capitalists, the new dictators of modernity.

Pedro received no base pay, but flurries of cash given at times of exultation from his immediate managers, or simply for a job well done. But he saw the rewards of absolute dedication and loyalty to the boss of this El Narco, the Azteca Cartel. He saw other men issued greater cash for harder and riskier jobs.

"Jorge," he said one day to the fat man before him—one of many bosses between him and the big boss, the Capo—after thinking for a lengthy time on the proper words to elicit the best response from him. "I will do whatever job you need for me to do." It was a plain enough statement, and if made by an ordinary employee to his employer, might seem industrious, and be lauded for boldness and eagerness to better oneself, but here, in this job, without certain philosophical or moral absolutes, or limits, the possible outcomes were illimitable and therefore incalculable.

"In the city of Yermo, as you well know, a border town, which is very important for us," began Jorge Valenzuela, he who had grown fat off the insatiable appetite of the self-debauchery of others, "there is a man who is selling our product without our special license; consider it this way, mijo," he paused, as the two men sat at the round, wooden table on the veranda of the fine restaurant, as he heaped thick mounds of yellow butter atop his hot, brown muffin. "Coca-Cola sells Coca-Cola, and another vendor sells the same product, both with the name 'cola,'" he said, closing his heavy, big eyes and holding the steaming muffin to his thick lips and inhaling it like it was a sweet honey flower. "You think Coca-Cola might be understandably upset; oh, I think it is in the realm of possibilities," and he placed the soft, fluffy, heavily buttered wheat cake into his watering mouth and let it sit there for a few seconds, and then began to chew. "It is not right to take another man's brand he has worked so hard to maintain; in fact, it is just plain rudeness, I think," and he chewed some more, bobbing his head up and down and humming, then finally taking a swallow. "It is an improper upbringing: poor parenting, poor schooling—bad manners, all around; it cannot go without notice." He finished the tasty snack, and proceeded to devour the rest of his meal. "You see, mijo, we must protect our own special brand just like any other big corporation; and that is why we are big; we must also send a message to those miscreants about thieving another man's property in the form of a physical sign. Roderigo will guide you in this—he is most able." He chewed his tender bloodied steak and hummed for a while. "I spent four years at university as a business major, and now I intend to put it to practical use."

When Pedro was certain the man had dedicated a few minutes to the absolute science of gluttony, he dared ask, "But, Jorge, what of the police there?"

Jorge nodded his head, took a sip of his very expensive Chardonnay wine, and then replied, jabbing the air with his chubby hand, "I can see your naivete in that query, yes; ah, the police—but they are our police."

Pedro frowned. "But what of the military?"

Jorge nodded and took another sip of his magic elixir. "Ah, the military—but they are our military."

Pedro, more disturbed than ever, asked timidly, "But what of the courts there?"

"Hmm," Jorge murmured, and then smiled. "The courts, the military, the police—what are they but civil servants of the public, and are we not the public who pay our fair share of taxes? Don't you see, Pedro: Yermo is our town, is our district; Azteca is our state, and therefore, all civil servants serve the Azteca Cartel." He laughed. "Nosy journalists say these people are corrupt civil servants, but they would be mistaken in that assumption, for the only cause for their betrayal would be to align with an outside agency against—us." He smiled and flicked the air lightly. "You see, we are now," and his voice abruptly took on a mean stature, "the new revolutionaries and government of Mother Mexico; viva Mexico!"

The waiter who stood next to them, saw but did not hear, the bludgeoning dawn of a bold decree heralding in a new order, for, in the end, all he needed were his wages and a home in which to park his trembling form.

Later that night, Roderigo drove the black sedan that had no license plates and dark-tinted windows and a company sign upon the hood, which signaled to all who were interested parties to part and scatter like puffs of smoke in the wind.

"So, have you done this before?" Pedro asked, trying not to seem apprehensive and timid, but failing miserably.

"Look, man," the heavily tattooed, slender man replied, with a reefer hanging out of his mouth, "it's just an errand," and he reached back into the seat, grabbed an AK-47 rifle and handed it to Pedro. "Point, aim, shoot; that's it; ain't no more to it than that, then you go party."

"So, who is this guy..."

Roderigo broke into Pedro's question as if he knew it was coming, and had to be cut, captured, and strangled. "You don't want to know, believe me, man," and he cussed violently, as if the very thinking of their topic dredged up what he needed to suppress. "Hey, it's just a job—like delivering the laundry…"

"Live laundry…"

"Hey," Roderigo shouted, irritated now that his pupil had not heeded his good—as plain as his swarthy skin—advice, "listen up, Pedro," and now he was staring right at his pupil, who trembled as he observed his driver clutch even tighter his own black AK-47. "You don't need to know the name or his job or if he has a family; hey, Pedro, do you care if a cook who makes you a tostada is married—do you, huh?" Pedro looked at the road ahead and saw pedestrians in the crosswalk, and he meant to shout, but could not let slip, an admonition to him. "Hey, are you listening, or are you more concerned with how I am driving, huh?" Pedro waited for him to glance through the windshield, but he did not, as sweat crept in sticky waves through his own clothes.

Roderigo looked ahead, and seemed to recognize the danger, and then, without touching the brakes, looked again to his attentive student, with a wild mania and hitherto unknown scowl of contempt for life that petrified his partner. He stepped on the brakes. "Are they out of the crosswalk?" But he said it mockingly, to which Pedro replied, in a timid tone, in the affirmative. "Oh, I am so glad," he said, again glaringly in a mocking posture, and then abruptly, simply, stepped on the accelerator pedal.

The pedestrians fled like doves from a diving hawk. The car whistled by them.

Roderigo looked long and hard at Pedro, sneering, nodding his head, then looked to the road ahead, and suddenly laughed. "I love this job!" And let out a loud whoop and holler.

Pedro, already unhinged from a lifelong philosophy of conservative actions by his recent trespass into the world of the Narcos, now became afraid, for aiding an ultra-criminal, superpower, Fortune 500, card-carrying drug conglomerate who was responsible for the deaths of tens of thousands of lives and the destruction of millions of them—though he had no part in pulling actual triggers—still gave him a sliver of manufactured cushion between shame and horror, and merely a hand that got its slimy piece of the unsavory pie, and, to him, an accompanying guilt-free conscience. But now, his journey down the slippery slope was whipping hard the embattled host.

> Upon our birth, we freely roam
> upon the fresh fields of conscience's dome;
> and when we discover virtue's power,

we happily ingest its scented flower

We bring succor, compassion, faith
we find love, hope, and grace;
but when we see more of self,
temptation and sin reign in us;

When the god of reflection wanes
when the market of goods refrains,
we bring down our listed hand
a heavy bludgeon across a bloody land

We must keep our stolen treasure,
a stately life, on borrowed pleasure;
whatever must be done is done
and whoever, and whatever, is won
all else is damned and shunned;
our life now, a rolling stone of measureless fun

Pedro felt as if this car was driving too fast into his private inner hell of sin, yet he did nothing to dissuade the driver, or act to effect his own insatiable desire, so the journey continued on, and he sat motionless, knowing full well he was about to be handsomely rewarded for doing to another a great harm.

Thus, his mind and soul had crossed that great divide between rational and irrational, morality and immorality, caution and incaution, a chasm so vast and deep that for any man to successfully bridge it, he must labor ceaselessly and consciously and assiduously for a long, valued, linear length of concentrated time, energy and will.

Roderigo had long ago passed the citadel of reason to dwell in the house of ecstasy, and everything he did and possessed and valued most belonged to that subspecies of adventure called blood-rush, adrenaline-pumping, exceeding-the-boundaries-of-the-law, action He reached for the AK-47, the ubiquitous rifle of the Narcos, the comforter, protector, and fixer of all things uncertain and threatening, and nodded to his heavily perspiring companion. "Don't worry, ese, you just point and shoot—it's just like a camera," he spoke in earnest. He pulled the car in front of a small convenience store.

"Now?" Pedro asked, anxiously.

Roderigo abruptly laughed, gesturing wildly. "No! We're gonna come back at night, slinking around like cockroaches—yes, now!"

"I don't understand…in the daylight…without disguise…"

"Are you loco, are you?" he screamed, grasping again the black rifle. "Who do you think you work for—the Church? Look, man, we can go in there and waste that rat and come out and go across the street and order a taco and burrito and beer, and then watch the police arrive while we finish our meal; we leave when we want, because, amigo, we are the police."

"We are…"

"That's right, they don't arrest us, they arrest real criminals…" He opened the door. "Let's go and do it—the more you think about it, the worse it is— like right now."

When Pedro opened the door, he felt he was entering a dark corridor where any light entered did not escape; he heard nothing, for the bleak, cold blackness seemed to hum a macabre tune, where he was sure to be afraid, and blind, and the only light—a kind of eerily, filtered diffused light—that shone upon his face came from his partner, and the only comprehensible sound of life came from his mentor. He held his AK-47 tightly and followed Pedro, and then both of them walked through into the business.

The man they were sent to kill was having a party for one of his daughters, and all across the place were brightly colored balloons, and brightly colored smiles of the family, relatives, and friends, and everywhere there was joy and happiness moving in concert with the jubilant music; so, when the people turned and saw the armed men, and having lived in this terror-filled town, fear slew them.

"Well," Roderigo opined, sincerely, looking casually at the target, "you shouldn't have a family if you're going to cross the Azteca Cartel," and he lifted up the twisted tool of his misbegotten trade, aimed, and fired.

Pedro, as if connected physically to his pedagogue, raised his rifle when the other one was raised, pointed where the other one was pointed, and shot, though haphazardly, when the other one was shot. It was like he was not there, but physically removed, as in a movie, not killing—slaughtering a father and husband in front of his family, but in a book, not willing, not paid, but a prisoner, coerced, but he was there, and the horrific clamor awoke neighborhoods; then, after the bloodied corpses—people panic when unexpected horror puts its sweetheart pen on their blanched faces, and sometimes get in the way of intended targets—stopped their frenetic puppet dance, he simply followed his mentor out of the door, and now he sought not light, but darkness, and it fed him its grim nourishment, and yea, his eyes became aware, and he could vividly see, and the shapes and pulses and objects he saw appalled yet thrilled him.

Roderigo pulled the car across the street, whereupon the two got out and went into a fine restaurant and ordered a fine meal and watched, with dispassionate flair, as the police arrived thirty minutes later, and the ambulance sixty minutes after that, with amusement as a community quickly regained its senses, which were already dulled by the incessant hyper-violence, and soon all was as it had been just a few hours before.

"Yes, we are as gods," Roderigo said, after telling Pedro he needed to learn how to shoot properly, and that he would personally instruct him; and then, putting on his dark sunglasses as the men exited the restaurant, their bellies full of rich cuisine, "so says Arturo Suarez."

Pedro, shaking, heard but did not yet understand; he thought of his own precious family, and somehow, they seemed dispassionate and unrecognizable, and still, they were presently not to be dismissed, and the longer he thought of them, this song of love for them he began to see more clearly, and fondly, and believed himself still more a part of them than El Narco, when he murmured, "I'm doing this for you, my family," the nourishing lie that must be illustrated in fine etchings and elaborated upon with fine exaggerations until the truth no longer boldly dissects a lie, where a man is able to stand upon either moral tale and not know if he is here or there, or in one hemisphere or in the other. This is where the highly selective world of high-quality intoxicants is able to seal any ambiguities in the mind of oscillating vessels, and what better employer to work for, than one who majored in the selling of the products necessary for one's own atonement and generously supplied the ready cash to buy other mind-altering psychedelics and an accompanying, mirror-like, hallucinogenic lifestyle. He had been a simple man leading a plain, simple life in a settled region where life was not easy but manageable, where hard labor was necessary and responsibility great, and the values of people were practiced with high regard, lest the whole lot perish: brotherhood, loyalty, compassion, love, sacrifice, trust, faith, virtues born from waking up every day in an uncertain world, not one of convenience, where people existed in a community and lived or died oft on the union and loyalty of their good neighbors.

Now, months later, as the two sicarios cruised the streets in their black SUV, Roderigo had a swig of tequila to aid in the subsuming of his most vital organ, his conscience, and talked about more orders to kill interlopers and antagonists. "What did Jorge say about taking down the Judge, eh?" Pedro asked.

Roderigo shrugged as he turned the corner of the busy street and then parked their well-known death car. "He says to kill that big-mouth Judge first, but wait until we get more backup."

"For what? Who is going to stop us, eh? Who is going to go against the Azteca Cartel—no one, that's who, ese; I say let's kill that fat braggart today—but first this peasant woman," he said, disgustedly, as he looked at the hotel across the street, "and then that pig, Gomez."

Roderigo set up and looked admiringly at his anxious pupil, and then smiled broadly, with affection, then shared with him, as he had never done, a bottle of tequila from his own private stock; it is the private way of men to communicate friendship without words, a special language that unites them specifically with their animal counterparts.

This was now to be the seventh assassination Pedro and Roderigo had been assigned in four weeks, the first one being previously described, and the ones after, as follows: the second one was a petty drug dealer, whom they dispatched on the street; the third, an intrepid newspaper reporter, whom they killed in his home, and left a warning on his bloodied corpse; the fourth and fifth, two police officers suspected of informing on the Azteca Cartel; the sixth, an importunate journalist, who they gleefully gunned down in the broadest daylight possible and on the busiest street corner; and the seventh was to be a woman whose son had been murdered by some Cartel faction, and whether or not he was operating his own drug dispensary was unknown, but implied, yet it had not mattered to his grieving mother. She had been at the local newspapers, talking of plazas—the territories of particular Cartels— and other sensitive related Cartel jargon; she had done her research and trespassed into an automatic kill zone, where, once entered, the violators of Cartel law were scheduled certainly to die, but not on the particular clock of the organization offended.

She was to be held up as a deterrent for others who dared question the work ethic of the Azteca Cartel in this region. She had not hidden from any- one, proudly defiant in issuing incendiary statistics to the press at open con- ferences, on radio shows, on television programs. "I am not afraid," she would boast; "the truth will protect me—those murderers are afraid to kill someone who stands up to them. They would a kill a woman—cowards!"

"Sure," the boss of the local cells had said, upon listening to her pas- sionate refrain, "we are so afraid," and he had laughed then, thinking of the hundreds of people he had successfully targeted for assassination. "Señorita, you will get a midnight special."

Roderigo and Pedro watched the woman leave her hotel room, and enter a yellow taxicab that presently departed. They followed close behind, waited a while, pulled next to the automobile, whereupon Roderigo hopped out, black pistol in hand, ordered the woman out, who refused, then, opening the door, Roderigo grabbed hold of the struggling woman and hit her with the butt of his gun upon her pretty blond head, dragged her limp form from the car, and dropped her into the backseat of his car, he with her now, whereupon Pedro drove off.

"Oh, you're so brave," Roderigo said, smiling now, looking with excited lust at the full-figured woman. "So tough, to talk against our people—so macho!" he cried, working himself into a frenzy to open the loosely sealed chambers of reluctance that had once been nourished by virtue. "We have a special plan for you, you stupid whore," and he slapped her, just to hear the beginning of her dissolution of feminine mystique, demystified, vilified, knotted and tied, drawn and quartered, then stuffed and despised as something to be loathed and abandoned; a weighty task, this, first addressed by the devaluation of her gender worth, with the corrosive, sticking-like-hot-mud, scenery-rupturing "whore" missile—whore, the first line of offense against Woman to tear down her delicate feminine image and rebuild instead a salacious pageantry where she is paraded about like the wanton shrew who lures innocent virginal boys to their sexual and manly deaths; and done to give comfort to that relentless enemy, self-doubt, and its brother killers of men: jealousy, shame, and confusion, cousins to loathing, prejudice, and fear; so that which they did not understand, they choose to kill; so, now a loud rejoinder to the query "what else is woman but whore" needs more conspirators, and so too out comes "slut," which now Roderigo let splash all over the trembling woman, to paint her a rusty raiment and rub in their virulent spittle, and poisonous machismo paste, an orgy, a broad battery of words—be they words? Or wicked monsters animated to flesh by a union of savage cruelty, not fit to be seen, nor heard, nor written, but delivered back down the mouth of the utterer, this open grave, flowing with the sewer of sin that murders the Innocent if they are allowed to live in the fragrant bliss of Light; and tarnished was she now, boiling black tar and blood-soaked, plucked feathers upon her lithe form, for no champion contested their vulgar assault; she was primed to be dumped before one of the big bosses of the Azteca Cartel, a pristine cargo of unspoiled humanity to be defrocked at the feast of the living gargoyles, who crave scintillating flesh to blot out the smoldering dung heap upon which they so unconsciously thrive like squirming maggots on rotting trash.

El Jefe raped her first; it was his privilege—this was the first strike against her bare psyche, the next being the drugs that were injected into her and forced into her nose and the hard liquor they generously poured down her forced-open mouth; and third, all the other men in attendance gleefully violated her for five relentless, nauseating days.

"Come on, Pedro, get in on the party," Roderigo proclaimed, after expressing his machismo by having sexual relations with a woman who was screaming and crying, and tied down by ropes around her ankles, and wrists that were iron-pegged into the hard ground.

Pedro stuttered, frowned, and shook his head, and then said, nervously, while holding up his left hand. "I am married."

Roderigo laughed uproariously. "Ese," he said, bottle in hand as he pointed to their hysterical victim. "It isn't like she's a date—it's just business. She's just another stupid whore…"

"No," he abruptly shouted, trying not to look at her, "killing is one thing, but I took a wedding vow…"

Roderigo shrugged his slender shoulders. "I give you about a month…"

Three days hence, and a press conference was called, supposedly by this same woman, which many newspaper people daringly attended at the courthouse stone steps, and she did arrive, but it was more accurate to say that metaphysically, her body arrived; indeed, as she was unceremoniously pushed from the non-plated, unmarked black Cadillac, she was immediately and easily identified by the reporters as someone who had recently been physically traumatized, for she was stumbling about, bewilderment and confusion locked onto her smeared countenance as if some inner mechanism in her was broken; she was mumbling, her red lips palpitating, her face heavily made up with black eyeliner and long, false, black lashes, wild eyes flitting from place to place, and all the while she was dressed in the ostentatious gown of the bold prostitute: six-inch, black high heels; short black leather miniskirt; tight, low-cut black leather halter; several layers of deep rouge on her twitching face; her blond hair greased with long, colorful buns weaved atop it. She walked with frantic hands held out, as if she were seeking something only she recognized; as she neared the uneasy reporters, they could see, as a horrible chill ascended and descended their flexible spines, blood dripping down from the inside of her dress and streaming down her wobbling legs.

One would have thought they had beheld the plague, so hastily did they exit the area, leaving her to stand alone, turning slowly this way and that, with knit brow, and a prisoner's frown, looking for anything real to recognize and mentally hold onto.

But she was a neon sign now, a no-trespassing sign, a Judas goat, a free advertisement that screamed that with one so easily kidnapped and tortured and raped, and the subsequent failure of the authorities to do anything at all, no one was special, not sinner nor saint, politician nor police, judge nor jury, for all were clearly under the heavily stamped and sealed emblem of approval of the Azteca Cartel; it was, after all, their kingdom come, now, and they could alter the lives of any citizen within a hemisphere of power they wielded without any viable objection from any citizen, police organization, military branch, or sovereign nation.

This was the twenty-first century dressed in the clothing of barbaric antiquity around the world; one town free, one in chains; one state in chains, one free; one country obliterated and suffocated by tyranny, another a properly functioning, well-established liberal democracy; and the latter would say to the former, concerning the pleas of the undernourished, the imperiled, the imprisoned, as it relates to their rulers, "Fair fight! Fair fight!"

A correction, please, says the oppressed to the free, wealthy world; a fair fight implies a chance on both sides; give him, the oppressor, a rock, while I, the oppressed, also have a rock—then, we will see who is more accurate and can hit the mark and never give up.

But a correction, if you will, the free, wealthy world replies, and politely too, from behind its capitalistic ideology; the oppressed, that is you, have free will to determine your own social and political path—rise up and challenge your oppressor, create your own destiny, fight your own fight.

A rebuttal, if you please, reply the collective voices of the oppressed. You gained your sovereignty over many centuries of brutal warfare—we know, we too can read books; you also had many military alliances with foreign entities to secure your inevitable outcomes; so, please, do so with us—we are very willing, and eager to do so.

Once more, we respectfully require, and humbly ask—we who are so mighty—a clear and legal rebuttal; we will issue you medicine, clothes, food, and even weapons if you choose to fight your oppressor; but, excuse our candor, do you truly seek democracy, or are you really socialists, or religious people seeking a theocracy? Please explicate.

An honest reply, in blood and words: we desire the rights of all people to live with certain inalienable rights—Freedom, Equality, and Justice, as you can previously attest.

But, sir, do you claim that all peoples truly beg economic parity in democracy, or do many of you want a patriarchal/matriarchal ruler to establish law and order and make you feel safe and secure despite what you lose in human rights?

So formal now: that may be so for a prisoner—to his jailer—who fears other prisoners, and believes half the world is in his own station, and the other half the jailer, but not for any free prisoner who can truly see what opportunities the real world affords him.

You speak of opportunity again, citizen; so take it—free yourself; we will aid you.

You speak of democracy, so democratize the world.

We cannot interfere in the government of sovereign nations.

Geography crowns the victor.

Revolutions must come from within.

Pray, help us.

Citizen, heal thyself.

My compatriot is dead; now, where are we?

My compatriot has been elected to higher office; now, let us begin anew.

A month hence, after she told the authorities who had kidnapped and violated her, the woman was kidnapped by the same Cartel again, and suffered the same fate.

He Who Falls Must Rise, or Die Trying

A corrupt man creates its own fate, and by correctly predicting the same for another, he is a prophet for those who desire wealth through deceit; a good man is a prophet for no one who labors honestly and hard.

Roderigo and Pedro were soon assigned the coveted task of dispatching the aforementioned, irksome Judge Gomez, and, as an added bonus, by any method they chose, which was an indication from the bosses that they trusted this executioner duo. It was a prestigious honor for the two to have a free hand in dealing with the persistent and vocal Judge, and the pride they felt urged them on to exceed the expectations of their superiors.

"I don't understand people like the Judge," Pedro said to Roderigo, as they drove to the intercept point; "don't they know they are going to die for their obstinacy?"

"No," Roderigo replied, knitting his black brows and pursing his thin lips, his tattooed forearms resting on the wheel, and thinking himself very much the academic scholar. "They believe in Justice—the law," he gestured, "as if by talking about it to the people, they are magically protected."

"Where do they think they are—the United States?"

He let out a loud, "Ha!" And then he said, somberly, "But that is changing there, too; now, no one," he stated, emphatically, "is safe from us, anymore."

This fact—and also that he considered Roderigo an apostle whose epistles were gospel—emboldened him, making him feel as if he had correctly selected the fastest rising corporation, and was eager to ascend its corporate ladder.

For a delicate job such as this one, it was necessary to kidnap the victim on the road, preferably far from the city and any witnesses, thereby throwing a cloak over the kill, even though everyone would know who had done it, and why.

The Judge had a driver and a bodyguard, but such facts were amusing to veteran assassins. Roderigo had once said, smiling, "So, if they have two armed men, you simply," and he had held up his hands as if to gesture the obvious, "have four; if they have four, then you have ten—it's easy; they are stupid, and cheap, and we are smarter—and richer."

They had scouted the job for weeks, and studied the daily habits of the slightly overweight barrister.

"He's a buffoon," Roderigo had pronounced with finesse; "he doesn't alter his habits—doesn't he know we're going to kill his fat self?"

It felt good and right for Pedro to agree wholeheartedly. "Yes, yes, they are all the same—they deserve to die, especially the stupid ones."

So, the stage was set: the target was known, his humanity had been attacked by his impending killers, and lowered into the animal kingdom; his intellect shorn and left as someone so ignorant and imbecilic as to be a danger and deserving of death, the stark contrast carved in stone among the mighty monolith of the drug traffickers who feigned that they sought merely to get a quality product to market and preferred no obstacles, but any obstacle erected would be destroyed, as if to say, "It is not our choice, it is yours"; they who preferred the powerful nomenclature of "Cartel," even when the title, based upon reality, was really meaningless; but Cartel sounded so Fortune 500, as opposed to the lethal ordinariness of "drug traffickers," criminal organizations, super-criminals, that the effect was stamped into the consciousness of society, and law enforcement.

There is a hunter who hunts game for sustenance, while another hunts for sport, and yet another who hunts not only for sustenance—his own internal self-doubts to be stroked, and utterly spent—but for the thrill of tracking an opponent, the anticipation of the kill, but also how to kill the game, human or otherwise.

Roderigo and Pedro are as much lioness stalking the wildebeest herd as any hunter, and like the lioness, they did not hunt the strong and agile, but the weak and infirm, the too young and the old, and with a bloodlust that grew exponentially with every kill; and with every satisfying kill, they felt invigorated with a sense of righteous indignation against what they saw as a weak and stupid prey that needed to die—as if the sudden-come-to-human-thought lioness might justify why she picks off only those who cannot challenge her might. The power of taking, the ability to take life from not only ordinary folks but the rich, the powerful, the strong—many of whom they despised—was a narcotic to the men, so much so that it became like an addiction; the killing created a euphoria for them, which was followed by a sharp decrease in pleasure, then dumped into a deep depression, where the fever could only be cured by the next kill—and the more violent, the more ironic, the more important the target, the higher the emotional high, but was soon followed by an even lower emotional low; and the more dangerous the circumstances involving the kill, the more complicated, and the more possible problems encountered if executions were not just picture-perfect, achieved an even greater and sensuous high—like a fragrant feast of hot, spicy food to an unrepentant glutton.

Then came the animal to the slaughter.

The Judge had three bodyguards this time, in addition to his armed driver. Roderigo and Pedro flushed astonishment, then anger, then the thrill of a greater challenge, where they would overcome the unexpected, and thus impress their bosses by not bothering them and doing this alone.

"Why, that fat hog," Roderigo said, sneering uncontrollably, like a butcher who realizes his hog won't willingly stick his thick, pink neck under his long, sharp blade, "who does he think he is—more guards!"

Pedro, laughing now, and watching Roderigo laugh, too, as their car drove slowly behind the target, cried out, "If he really is afraid, why not ten guards, eh? Three? Three! Is that all! Why, the dirty swine, we'll teach him a lesson," and he gripped harder the already loaded magazine of the AK-47 with its thirty 7.62 x 39 mm bullets, as if it was his security blanket and good-luck charm; at such times, when he happened to think of his wife and children, he quickly banished this image—usurped, perhaps, by the thought of the enormous amounts of money he was making and the benefit it was to them. "I'll make enough so we will never have to beg again," he would seethe, to further placate his doubts. "After all, it's just business."

It was not too difficult to dispatch the three bodyguards—for the dirt road the cars traveled often encountered herds of goats, their master, and the shepherd dog; and so, when this occurred, the assassins simply pulled up next to the Judge's car, and opened fire on the three unsuspecting, now thoroughly dead, human shields, and the driver, also.

"Get out, you filthy pig," Pedro demanded, opening the door of the bullet-ridden black automobile, and he yanked the slightly wounded man out and into their car, then drove away to a special place where the voices of opposition to the drug kingpin's associates are muted, and buried.

It starts on a verdant rolling hill and then collapses down into a valley of beautiful flowers, this path traveled by these two specialists of death, a dark character in the world they had come to know intimately.

Death is no mystery in the country of the poor, infrequent guest, no coy friend, but constant friend and visitor, and a bold and intimate mistress, a known and expected commodity in which the entire community participates: unlike in the country of the rich, where death is suppressed, camouflaged and altered, boxed, and quickly buried so that its seemingly bleak residence is rendered temporary; and this is called the sterilization of death, wherein its place in the natural order of things has been lost and meticulously washed away, something to be abhorred, rejected, pitied, delayed to an absurd degree, as if more money alone might allay the illimitable fleets of funeral ships that dock incessantly at every human port; and when death does come, the rich feel compelled, as befits their superior caste in the whole wide world of inequality, to wail and grieve as if indeed the universe has never known someone to suffer so much over the loss of just one human being. But the poor and defenseless know better.

Death comes for the poor more often and stays longer, sitting upon a thick branch and hovering, an expected and frequent guest that is an intricate part of the landscape; comes life, then living, maybe disease, and finally death; but for the rich: comes life, living, disease, but doctors and machines, and elaborate schemes, and when death draws near, it is rudely ignored by friends, its black-draped arm pushed aside into the waiting hands of the federation of death merchants: the ambulance companies, the hospitals, the mortuaries, the cemeteries, the churches, the insurance companies, all with their hands out, and once the cash touches it, hands in; thus, the rich are not to be concerned, as they stand far away, a companion to health, a deserter in death, a flamboyant mourner in reality. But not so for the poor: it is they who care for and comfort the dying, and house their own dead, dress the dead, pray over the dead, dig and bury the dead; it is the cycle of life, it is recognized by the poor as the way of things, to be accepted, understood, embraced—and often, by injustice and justice, but also by easily preventable disease and war and crime, for no discernible reason, for no good reason, for good reason; in ones, in twos, in threes, in groups, in entire families; a village, a city en masse, a people, a race, genocides—this the poor suffer, and the rich think loss of income, or divorce, the equivalent moral angst; death in the land of the poor is intertwined daily, an integral factor to be dealt with as much as working the land and celebrating the joys of life, one more event in the unending, seamless march forward of time; but for the rich, it is a destroyer of lives, disruptor of schedules, a life-changing catastrophe that clips the senses of equilibrium and sends the mourners reeling down a dark path of deep depression.

Pedro and Roderigo knew death intimately—to kill a target meant nothing to them—for they were surrounded by it, smelled its ripe, pungent odor, saw its turgid state, watched it bleed and blacken unto dust; first, Pedro had seen it as a farmer, killing his own animals, burying his own relations and friends; and second, Roderigo, as a laborer in the fields, had seen dead workers, dead animals, death everywhere, and ignored by the owners, as the corpses rotted openly in the scintillating sun as the stench filled his nostrils for so long they no longer were filled by its malodorous expression, its stink like the odor of ordinary flowers now, like the smell of the sizzling heat in the crackling clean, dry air, like the elusive nymph called life; so, when they threw down the Judge under the spreading wings of twilight, they were not throwing down an important man, a man deserving of life, but a man who had crossed the immovable line in their private sandpile and disrespected the big bosses too often and ignored their too-palpable and numerous admonitions; the man was merely a peasant or animal now, his corpse to be left decaying in the heart of the community, just another dead body in a civilization where lately there seemed just so many that they had become ubiquitous—which some might interpret as the decline of that civilization.

So, they took the babbling, pleading, black-suited man—but now reduced, as far as they were concerned, to a fat, snorting pink pig—and placed him on his trembling, supplicating knees.

"I beg of you, please, please, do not kill me," the Judge cried, sobbing like a panicking child.

There is no such quite fully realized sneer of contempt like the one proffered by one formally thought oppressed but now a ruler, to the one thought to be the oppressor but now the oppressed, and this Roderigo delivered in powerful waves.

"You," he began, spitting hugely on the groveling, dirty man, "who lived off the hard labor of the peasants, you filthy, lousy bourgeoisie."

"Does he know that begging, although highly amusing," Pedro said, with a bemused smirk, "never works."

"Hey, Judge, Mr. Big Shot, who ruled against the farmers in land disputes with the land barons, have you ever read where whining like a dumb animal caught in a trap—a trap set to catch the dumb animal—has ever worked?"

"He thinks he can—because he's so used to having everything his own way, the bourgeoisie pig," Pedro said.

The AK-47s were pointed the entire time at the learned professor, lawyer, and Judge, who was sweating profusely as he bowed his balding head down to the hard, hot soil. Then, suddenly, he became still, like a geyser that has blown fiercely and abruptly stopped, causing an eerie silence about. He lifted his round head and stared first at Roderigo and then at Pedro, in utter astonishment, as if only now he recognized what his captors truly were, thus freezing any more tears.

"So," he said, his voice not so low as his body, "you want to humiliate me first," looking back and forth at his captors, and the longer he stared at them, the more revelation illumined his swarthy countenance. "No, no, you will not; you're corrupt—you are killers," he said, defiantly, beginning to rise as his confidence in his actions of the past did, "who have been hired to suppress the truth about your bosses." He propped himself up on one knee as he continued. "And I will not," and he fastened his posture upon both knees, "crawl like a beaten dog to your bosses," and he remembered who he was and what he stood for and why he had spoken out against the drug traffickers, now standing upon one leg; "for I," and then the other leg, and as he stood fully erect, so too did his voice, his head held high, his chest out, "represent the law, and the will of the people of Mexico—and they say you're murderers, thieves, corrupters of society, and are destroying our beloved Mother Mexico." He said it as if he did not care what they would do to them now. "Bourgeoisie—you don't even know what that means; you picked up the language of socialists, and the irony of it is, you are the true lumpenproletariat—look that one up when you've taken a break from your terrible murders for your masters—and if that is too difficult to remember, just remember that you are filthy plebians; and yet, you are the worst kind of capitalists."

"Look, a talking pig," Roderigo said, smiling contemptuously, delighted that his prey had now stood up against them, "I do like 'proletariat' better," he turned and said with a smirking smile toward Pedro; "it makes us sound humble."

The Judge looked at Pedro, whom we had decided was the weaker of the two. "You seek to denigrate me to the position of an animal, so your conscience will easily bear my murder."

"There is no problem with my conscience," Pedro interjected, "that money can't solve."

The Judge refused entry of this obtrusive remark, looking at Pedro. "So, you will kill me, that is established—but do you think you're so self-righteous..."

"It's a living," Pedro returned, dryly.

"And a very good one, too," Roderigo said, and then added, raising the rifle at the Judge, "the hour is getting late."

"You have invented an enemy," the Judge continued, undaunted, "to condone the horrible things you have done."

"We have a product to sell—it is no one's business to try and stop us. It is people like you who have created," Pedro cried, wildly gesticulating around, "all this violence; the army, and the police need to do other things, like protect us from real criminals..."

Roderigo looked to Pedro. "We don't have to explain..."

"There is a preacher in town, his name his Manuel Alberto de Ortega, talk to him..." the Judge said to Pedro, "when your immortal soul no longer can hold your sins that seem unforgivable..."

"Ready to die?" Roderigo said, aiming his rifle at the Judge.

The countenance of the Judge was sober now, and at peace, when he said, still to Pedro, "I want you to kill me."

Roderigo laughed. "You don't think he will, you dirty swine—bourgeois swine."

The Judge finally turned to face his antagonist. "You don't even know what the word means—you're the new bourgeoisie," and then turned back to Pedro. "You... kill me... and look me in the eyes when you do it."

"You don't think I will..."

"Oh, you will," the Judge replied, coolly now, having finally accepted the invitation to death, and he reached down and picked up the black leather wallet that Pedro had removed from him. "Do you have honor?"

"Kill this dirty, rotten pig," Roderigo exclaimed, brooding, knowing that he was only a witness now.

"Yes, I have honor."

"Good—you have honor, then be honorable, and send a message to my family," he said, unfolding the wallet to reveal family pictures, "that I died with honor, dying for what I believed in."

Roderigo had ventured into territory largely unknown to him, where the prey was free to speak for a prolonged period; and yet, instinctively he knew this was not his killing anymore, because of the curious request of the Judge, and his own curious internal honor that he had invented to keep at least one corner of his blushing soul unblemished.

"What will you do with my body?" asked the Judge. "To be displayed, headless, with a warning…"

"Yes," Pedro said, automatically.

The Judge reflected for a moment. "I am concerned only with He who can kill the soul." He stared hard into the face of his executioner. "Will you let me have my last statement…" And when he saw no reflection of resistance in the face of Pedro, he continued, "I am Mexico, you are Mexico," and he looked hard at Roderigo, whom he now could consume with his final moments. "You, too, are Mexico—but what you have wrought upon us, and the world, is our shame, our sorrow, and we do not bear it lightly; right now, you are not me, not yet; but later, after much killing, with much, too much blood that cannot be wiped from your hands, maybe then you'll realize that in money and power, you are weaker, and in poverty and meekness, you are stronger." He raised up his arms slowly, his visage calm, his body still, as if he were about to go where he needed to be, and without struggle, or woe, looking straight into the eyes of his killers. "God loves you, as do I."

Pedro pulled the trigger, but it was Roderigo who took the long sword he stored in the trunk, cut off the head of the Judge and, with the body, put them in separate black plastic bags, then placed them into the trunk with the sword; and the men drove them into town, silent the entire trip back; Roderigo stopped the car in the plaza, planted the bloodied head on a pole with the body propped in front of it, and a warning sign scrawled in blood: "This man caused innocent people to die, so he had to die. Sincerely, the Azteca Cartel."

Then, on the trip home, out came the hard liquor, to be swallowed like water, and when at home, out came the company product—purchased at a steep discount—to be ingested passionately and widely until the sins of the past were procured by the sins of the present. It was then that Pedro first committed adultery—then, when his mind was temporarily unhinged from the hard lock to which his mind was subject; it was then, to subdue and drown doubt with more physical pleasure, this thing, conscience, which man seeks to destroy when first he seeks to anchor his mind upon a murky and bottomless sea.

The two men did not speak of the incident with the Judge that night. Two days later, they killed two more "defenders of the sacred realm," this time permitting no talk from the victims, this time dispatching them with exceeding swiftness and then burning the bodies, and immediately thereafter, partying like it was the end of the world.

Yet it was the end of the world for these two men, who had not been born into the violence of war, not recruited nor kidnapped, but were willing volunteers, and not volunteers without options, for they had plenty: other states, other nations, other jobs, for, "no man is rooted inextricably to the ground, lest he perish by his own hand," and they had refused. They had sold their soul to not just anyone—not a corrupt local politician or merchant—but the grandest politicians and merchants of death. "You have two good feet," Pedro's wife had lately told him, slapping said legs; "use them to walk us out of the cold grave we're in," to which he would not reply; and then she had lately told him, "You have two good arms," slapping said arms; "use them to dig us out of the cold grave we're in," to which he could not reply; and then she had said later, "You have a good mind; think us out of this cold grave we are in," to which he did not reply, and so she further said, "Life is for the living, my husband, do what you must." The frustration and anger upon his visage was his reply—frustration that he had thrust his family into this conflict, anger that he could not seem to simply reach out and take them out of it; there is an illusory country no man with a family wishes to ever visit too long, for it emasculates him, keeping heavy stones upon his crawling form—stones that increase in weight the more he struggles and whines, stones that whisper in a sinister, arcane gurgle, "failure"—that permeates his prefabricated, easily penetrated exterior and settles on his waning male psyche.

Six months hence, Pedro and Roderigo had kidnapped seven more people for ransom, worked arms shipments from the United States and Central America, worked on the radio communications network, and murdered twenty-two people: six politicians, four police officers, four activists, three reporters, three journalists, and two small-time drug dealers, using the AK-47 and AR-15 rifles, decapitations, fire, gasoline with fire, drowning, and the ramming automobile as methods of execution. "Variety is the spice of killing," Jorge had encouraged them; "don't get bogged down by one method—be creative," and he had waved his chubby arms around. "What will our competitors think if we just shoot everybody," and after his hands made the figure of a rifle, he slapped his chubby fist upon the fine, redwood oak table. "I say no—emphatically no: change with the times; be modern—don't become stale," and he had whispered, as he leaned over toward his mesmerized audience, "it makes us look boring, and not innovative; if you don't change with the times, you get left behind; say," he tilted his big, round head, his bushy eyebrows raised as he leaned back, "what about acid to decompose bodies? Have you used it? I hear it's marvelous stuff! Well, then, by all means, go get some and try it out—and come back and tell me how it all turned out—yes? Good! And yes, by the way, the big bosses just love the job two of you are doing—they call you 'the dynamic duo, two men who are clean and thorough,'" and he then laughed uproariously, slapping his chubby thighs. "How do you like that—you have a nickname." Then he became deadly serious as he said, "Don't kid yourselves—the big bosses don't favor just anyone with a pet nickname," and he leaned over and whispered, hand to his mouth, "it makes the other sicarios jealous, you know," and he pointed his left finger index at them, a gesture to be used, the men knew, when he was genuinely sincere, "only when they really, really like you—and have plans for you, eh? Ha! You're on the way up in the organization—so, gentlemen, don't blow it: keep up the good work, and remember my motto," and he stood up, his right hand over his flabby heart, his fat face burning bright with honor, and said, in earnest, "follow orders, be enthusiastic and honest about your work, and you will be rewarded." He shook their hands in the same spirit as would a proud father who sends his worthy sons off to work.

Indeed, the big bosses, up and down the natural chain of command, had noticed the efficiency and effectiveness and professionalism of the two men's clean, quiet work, which enabled them, the bosses, to make more dirty, violent money—every peso they pocketed was stained in the blood of every person who was an obstacle to the growing empire and personally monogrammed by the consumers of the product, the latter whose height and breadth and width, if stacked one upon another, reached from one end of the earth to the other, and back again, and then beginning another fast-building route, eagerly laying down tracks for the drug-trafficking industry to move their cargo like the builders of the first continental railroads.

"Expectations," Jorge said to them some months, and dozens of executions, later; "the big bosses have given you control of Yermo province, overseeing the process and distribution of the product." He watched as Roderigo and Pedro sat up like two obedient, happy children listening to their proud Papa. "If you boys do good on this job, it could mean big promotions, and good benefits; hey, don't we take care of our own, you two," and he threw up his hands in affection, "men of machismo!" he smiled broadly, and leaned in closely to them, and whispered, "I spoke to El Jefe himself," and looked around, as if the very speaking of this name invoked supernatural forces, "and he has plans for both of you—that's right; so, mijos, do whatever," he emphasized, with a loud whisper, "you need to do to be successful—it will be good for all of us. Let us pray." Indeed, they prayed, mostly for protection against their main rival, the El Dorado Cartel, and just as passionately and sincerely as any good practicing Catholic, for Catholics they bethought themselves, new converts to the religion of the drug traffickers, wherein dwelled gods and their worshipers, and in between them: priests, Cardinals and Bishops—intercessors all to the chosen Cartel god, albeit in name only; and, it must also be stated, that each god was a jealous god, insisting that all other foreign gods were false, blasphemers, and for that, deserving of death.

Pedro allowed all the enthusiasm and energy in his youthful mind and body to dwell in the body and soul of his new responsibilities, working oft as much as twenty hours a day for a week, or not sleeping for days, and always, it seemed now, accompanied and counseled by the ubiquitous white powder, ubiquitous comfort women—he never knew how the latter happened, it just did, and by the time he really thought about how it juxtaposed with his family, he had been in league with this kind of soul-crushing creature for months. Had he really been a simple farmer with a simple wife and children, he thought, as he now counted his millions of US dollars, which increased in amount daily? Work harder, make more money, he often told himself—this is the real way of the world; once I was lost, now I am found—why does that sound so familiar, he asked himself, in between pumping inordinate amounts of the white toxicant into his jittery body and inordinate amounts of a never-ending, endless loop of loose and easy-to-manage females who were not too too terribly bright, but beautiful and willing to sell their bodies for pretty jewelry or cold, hard cash; occasionally, he would drop by his spectacular homestead, in the beginning arriving clean and sober, and in the middle dirty, and drunk, and in the end, arm in arm with the nasty goods—white powder and painted women; it just didn't seem to matter anymore, he sometimes thought, when his brain was not being washed, rinsed and dry-cleaned by the various stimulants that were staked through his inflamed brain. "I've got business to do, and I need my things whenever I go; my blow, my homies; well," he would think, and then say, "there is my woman—so pretty—and my children—how precious—but Papa has work to do; here is ten thousand dollars, mama, buy some clothes; children, buy some toys—why," he then gave them more rolls of greenbacks, "buy the whole store; I'll be back, when I am back…" And so forth, he babbled on, and he still managed, with Roderigo, to increase production and sales, adding a sense of competency, and to please his superiors, thus giving him over to a sense of satisfaction and pride.

His mind was traveling at one thousand miles an hour and he was doing exactly what he wanted, wherever he wanted, and he felt great, he reasoned; so when his good wife asked him to please lower the high-flying, frenetic lifestyle, and reconsider a calmer, simpler one, he was forced to laugh, thinking it made no sense to him. She is a crazy person, he told his comfort women, she's not practical, like you, who are here to please, and say nothing contrary to your man. I think I will not see her for a while.

Roderigo, after a brief vacation period, came upon Pedro one day in their luxury suite that overlooked the large-scale operations of cocaine production, bearing a countenance of a mortally wounded warrior.

"Do you believe in hell?" he asked Pedro, in a pleading, suffering voice.

Pedro, studying the accounts, looked at his partner, frowned, grabbed a large plastic bag of freshly rolled, highly potent marijuana, and threw it to him. "Smoke this, and you'll be in heaven," he said, half-smiling.

Roderigo dropped the product to the wooden floor. "No, I mean the hell you are in after you die because you have sinned against God."

Pedro closed the black book, folded his arms behind his head, leaned back in his leather chair, and addressed him with incredulity. "You need to stop listening to fairy tales," he began, solemnly and, pointing to his own head, "they mess with your mind," and then looking at his partner more carefully, "they mess with reality."

"I have talked to Manuel Alberto de Ortega," he stated, as if it were to mean something disturbing, his face having blanched a moment before.

Pedro took a long inhale of his unfiltered cigarettes, and then uttered, with absolute abandon, "So—who is he?"

"The preacher," he said, slowly, as if to scrutinize his friend's reaction, "the one the Judge spoke of."

"Oh," Pedro replied, smiling and then frowning, "really? Why?"

Roderigo felt naked, stripped of his old man and shining with a nascent transfiguration he was certain all could see. His speech was halting, secretive, obscuring inflection, shielding tones, as if he might reveal the inner workings of his recently regenerated, immortal soul.

"I thought—I thought about the Judge... what the Judge said..."

"What Judge—which one?"

"The Judge whom we let talk..."

"Oh, that fat pig," he responded, waving it all away with his hand that clasped the smoking cigarette. "Well, he's dead, isn't he, what good was his God to him, huh? But why are you so worried about it..."

"I wondered why a condemned man would give the name of a minister of God..."

"Who knows? Look," he said, shrugging his slender shoulders, "let's go over the shipment details."

Then, out it came, like the birth of an abrupt baby. "Do you believe in sin?"

"Sin? What are you talking about, amigo—sin?" He looked at him askance, squinting, with furrowed brow, too. "No, man, no, I don't—hey," he began, throwing down his diamond-studded pen, "if I did, I'd still be a lousy dirt farmer, his hands in the dirt, and rocks for cufflinks," and he waved about his fourteen-karat-gold, five-thousand-dollar-apiece cufflinks; "sin is for peons, and children, to keep them in line; you know that, Roderigo—you taught me as much."

Roderigo could only think of what the street preacher had told him, without condemning anyone or anything, but only the world. "God is love, God is goodness, God is virtue; can you stand in His divine light and face Him with your unrepentant sins? Can you hold your precious newborn baby—who has no sin at all—and boast about your sins, and hope he does the same? Who wishes their child to do or cause sin? You cannot dwell with He who is love, with sin encrusted on your soul; become like a child, and seek after the word of God." He had seen this preacher after he had telephoned the family of the Judge to tell them that the Judge had died with honor, because he had seen the picture of the grieving family of the newspaper, and yet he had no idea why he had called, except that he had stared very hard into the fierce, dark eyes of the Judge that fateful day.

"You killed my husband," the wife had said on the phone, sobbing.

"Yes," he had said, numb.

She was silent. "He died with honor…"

"Yes."

"Is there no sin in your world?" She was no longer sobbing.

He was silent. "I don't know." He had been certain it never existed.

"When will the killing end?"

"As long as we want… things…" He was thinking of himself.

She was quiet. "How can we raise our children in such a world?"

Roderigo thought of his own two children, and thought of the Judge's two children, and for a brief moment, it seemed like there was no difference between them. "You cannot."

"I will pray for you—so you might be saved, so the killing might stop; it is no good to hate—hate feeds the killing, you cannot murder without hating, without destroying yourself; love stops it and heals all things."

"Love," he said, in a trance, as if this magical concept had never been properly transported to his mind, "what can it do?"

"Love conquers all things—it will conquer you, if you let it."

He wanted to express his gratitude toward her for not condemning him, but he could not, and hung up the phone; he knew that if his bosses found out about this call, they would kill him, but curiously, now he did not care. "They have no love," he heard himself whisper, as if he were a man who been blind his whole life, and only now beheld a tiny sliver of gorgeous white light seeping into his privately and exclusively held darkness.

Roderigo looked not at Pedro, but into him, bouncing off his internal hardware like a ball bearing. "I called the wife of the Judge." He could not stop himself, for he had been stuck, stabbed a hundred times by the undeniable Truth, and the old man junk, the old man decay was flowing out of him like an unclogging sewer pipe recently burst.

Pedro stood up, his old man network, lit up like a lightning strike, his face catching the spark and now a burning fire. He cursed, and then cried, "What is wrong with you, Roderigo? Do you want to die?"

"Something inside me," he returned, strangely silent, "wants to… not to kill me—but to free me…"

"From what? What!" he screamed, throwing up his hands, and then waving them about. "From all this?" And he reached in and brought out a thick wad of thousand-dollar bills. "From this?"

"Yes."

Pedro threw back his head, massaged his face, shook his head, then focused his feverish black eyes on his friend and mentor; and upon further inspection of him, he ran his hands through his thick, black, wet hair, and stood even closer, his combusting eyes searching for fresh evidence. "What are you doing, Roderigo—what do you want?"

But the face of Roderigo, the man who had opened the door of illusions and allowed Pedro to see the mystical kingdom that power and money can buy, reflected now not the stalking wolf, but the gentle lamb. "Do you ever consider the families of those you have killed?"

He shook his head, and said, exasperated, "No, I don't."

"I do." He could feel more thick, oozing, oily junk come out of him, a false fuel that somehow had imparted to him a feeling of power.

Pedro was undone. "You're going to get yourself killed—and me too."

"I can't do this, anymore." It was curious, he thought, for the more he confessed and espoused contrition to one who knew his history, the freer he felt.

"You're loco, amigo—you've gone absolutely stark, raving mad."

"That is what it would appear to someone who does not see the Truth."

"What you mean, the Truth; if I didn't know better, I would think that your brain is fried," he said, angrily, pointing to his head as he began to pace back and forth; "it's that preacher, it's all his fault—he needs to go down…"

"It is not his fault—he is only a messenger. Can you kill God?"

"What God, Roderigo—the guy who allows us to suffer as peons every day, who allows injustice and suffering in the world?" He grabbed his security blanket, his newly bought brown and black AK-47, and held it up. "This is god," and he held up the money, "and this, piedra," and he grabbed a bag of cocaine, "and this," and he shook it in front of his friend's face; "this is reality, it's whoever is winning, is god, who sets the rules; god is the one who is rich and powerful—we are the new gods on earth: let someone try and stop us; look, man, the God you create and worship is the one on the winning side." He looked toward heaven. "God, you just go ahead and try and stop us—you can't, because you're not there," and he turned toward Roderigo again, "and I don't want him there—this life is too short, and I don't want to suffer at all; in fact, I want to feel good all the time, so, yes, you could say I like my life: the money, the power, the women—I'm finally somebody," and he pounded his chest. "I like this feeling of respect I have—you want something, you take it, let someone else try and stop me; we are successful because we are strong, the strong are here to rule the weak; we were weak because we believed we had to be, because our fathers and forefathers had been; but that can change—just look at us now! We are rulers! We deserve our wealth and power! The weak need us to tell them what to do—they want us to protect them and help: that is why they are so weak; look, Roderigo, some are destined to be strong; others weak; we know who we are, so let's be that—true gods on earth to be worshiped and feared; we have achieved the same greatness as of old."

The countenance of Roderigo never flinched during this verbal flood-bath of Pedro, and the calmer he felt in the face of such temptation, the lighter his burden, the easier the steel chains on his neck broke; and his voice was light and airy, like the song of the spheres. "When you're weak, you are strong; when you're strong, you're weak."

"What?" Pedro said, and then cursed, "What's that? Gibberish? Riddles? Have you been reading the peasant's book of myth and legend—the Bible?"

"You think you're strong, but it is strength that comes from man; when you're gentle, and kind, and loving, then you're truly strong."

Pedro picked up the AK-47. "I'm going to kill that preacher myself…"

"You are not strong, now; see, you think the only way to solve the problem is through violence."

But Pedro no longer heard him, and was on his way downstairs, and giving orders to his loyal and very brutal lieutenants.

He came back that night, carrying a big black sack, and when he came into the office, he woke up Roderigo by dropping the bloodied head of the preacher onto his chest and stomach. "There—now, who is stronger, you fool!" Roderigo rolled away, trembling, and then collecting his thoughts, calmed himself. "Now, see! This is the world, Roderigo—come out of this magic spell you're under! It's bad for business." He shook his head and then pointed to it, and said forcefully, "You kill God in here."

Roderigo was weeping as he crawled toward the severed head, staring at it. "You can't destroy the Truth with a mere bullet, Pedro," he whispered, and he smiled briefly, at the remembrance of a man who gave him the message that set him free. "You are in heaven now," he murmured; "soon, I will be with you, brother."

Pedro, perspiring heavily, and his heart pounding from heavy cocaine use, bent down next to Roderigo. "You need to pull it together, brother, before the big bosses find out."

"Let them find out—they need it, too; think of the good things they could do if they repented and believed."

Pedro cursed, stood up and began pacing the floor, knelt down, removed another object from the plastic bag, thrust it in front of Roderigo's face, and declared, "The Judge's wife; the Truth set her free, too, you fool!"

"Oh, no, no," Roderigo said, sobbing now, and shaking his head, as he sat, rocking back and forth, cradling her head, and then the other head, as well. "Too soon, too soon; what have we done to you, Mother Mexico—we have made you the whore of the Americas."

Pedro stood up, sober now, staring down at a man he realized he no longer knew; and in this business, he knew, that was a dangerous predicament, and survivors were those who took no chances that did not further their political and economic station, and did not risk relationships that were not totally soluble in the war mix of blood, money, and product.

"I am leaving this place forever," Roderigo whispered, still looking at and cradling the woman's frozen death mask.

Roderigo was still swelled with the sanguinary roots of bloodlust. His voice was emotionless, like his cold, hard stare. "I killed her children, too— she told them; you, who seems to care so much—you got them killed."

Roderigo abruptly stopped crying, his face ashen white, and looked up at him. "You're me—no, you're worse than me."

"No, I'm me—and the better part of what you were when we first met: strong, dedicated, merciless..." He crouched down next to Roderigo, arms resting on bent knees. "Tell me this is temporary insanity, Roderigo— remorse, regret, I don't know," he began, gesturing with one hand as he scrutinized his friend's pained visage. "Why don't you go home and sleep on it, and come back in the morning..."

"No, Pedro," he pleaded, "you don't understand—this is how I should have been; I can feel it; I know for certain."

Pedro cursed. "It's a spell, it must be; one day you're a stone-cold, hard killer, and now, you're a whipped dog who wants to be friends with the other dogs who want to eat him." He intuitively knew what must be done, such intuition that becomes one whose very action is measured by his current hyper-violent, conscienceless lifestyle, and that was to kill Roderigo, kill him right there and then, as he was damaged goods, not to allow him life, not to allow a rupture of the first principle of this business—take no unnecessary chances; and Roderigo was an unknown now, liable to stray off like a wayward missile and blow up the wrong target. Indeed, Pedro knew for absolute uncertainty that Roderigo had to be put down, like a crippled horse, like a rabid dog, like a bleeding-to-death soldier—that was who he was to Pedro now, bleeding to death, but unaware of it, and needing to die, but thinking he was going to live; yet, he could not kill the man whom he considered his brother and best friend and mentor; instead, he found him a safe place for him to hide, hired him help he could trust, and ran the drug operation by himself.

But on the small, overstuffed ladder, with too many men and women scrambling forward to vault up the slippery rungs, there was always someone watching and eager to find weakness in another and exploit it. A month hence, and Jorge called Pedro into his office.

"Pedro, sit, sit," he said, affably, like the happy manager of a fine restaurant, "here, have some corn tortilla, and coffee." Pedro, shaking like a child inside, rode a wave of cool and calm equanimity on the outside. "So, how his business, and where is Roderigo?"

For an entire month he had practiced his carefully scripted responses to every conceivable question. "Business is good, but Roderigo is not feeling well."

"Oh, I am sorry to hear that—he is a good man; very efficient and dependable; well, what exactly is his illness?"

"Exhaustion."

"Exhaustion, you say? I can see that; yes, I can—too eager to please; too much hard work, you say? Well, when do you suppose he will return?"

"Soon,"

"Soon, good, good; soon, yes, it will be good to have him back; call him for me so I can wish him well."

He had anticipated this last request. "He has no phone in his house—he doesn't want interruptions right now."

"Sure, sure, I can see that, too—no phone; and what about his family?"

"He visits them."

"Good man; yes, it is important to be with family." He abruptly stood up. "So, let's go visit Roderigo; after all, we are his family, too."

Pedro had anticipated this request, too. "He left for vacation yesterday. He didn't even tell me where he was going—he said he wanted to relax, and when he came back he would be fit and ready to go again." It was all true, except the last part.

Jorge was still standing, and then smiled, but in an amused way. "This Roderigo—he is a sly fox, eh? He knows how to get away from it all; as long as he returns soon, yes?"

"Soon, very soon."

"Soon; good, good, he's done such a great job, and deserves a little rest; but still, this Roderigo, I never would have imagined him needing a vacation like this," and he threw up his arms; "oh, well," he frowned, "you never can tell." He sat down. His phone rang, and he answered it. "Yes, yes, oh really, well, send him right through."

Roderigo walked in.

How the Uprising Began

He walked in covered in the same rough, snakeskin exterior and confident swagger known to his fellows in the industry.

"Roderigo!" Jorge exclaimed, standing up, and extending both hands, clasping Roderigo's outstretched hand. "Good to see you!" And he tilted his head, still smiling. "Looking good, eh? Pedro told me all about your little vacation—all rested now, yes? Sit, sit!"

Roderigo sat, casting a steely glance at Pedro. "My vacation is over."

"Rested your mind and body, yes? Well, to be honest, I have done the same from time to time—it must be done, you know," Jorge began, and here he became serious, pointing to his head. "Clears out the clutter; well," he drawled, clapping his hands, "let's get down to business, now that the dynamic duo are together again."

When Roderigo and Pedro exited this place, and were certain no electronic devices were secreted inside their car and any surveillance was unable to detect their speech from any distance, Pedro spoke first, asking his friend how he came to be with him.

"His master's dogs are always sniffing around when they sense something wrong," he said, gravely. "I noticed them in town near my home; I saw them when I visited my family, and they were there when I was about to leave for my respite."

Pedro listened intently and then asked, "Did your family get away?"

Roderigo was quiet for a duration past uncomfortable, but finally said, "I am not sure; I sent them away, but have not heard from them. I am worried."

Pedro felt the frightening chill that this unknown information, encased in this cold-blooded world of the Narcos, cast upon them. "And what about you?"

"I need to get away, too—Pedro, I can't do this anymore." He closed his eyes. "The more I read the holy word of God, the more I understand what I was: a body without a soul, who thought he was a man; but a savage creature, like a grizzly bear who acted like a man: now I have found a conscience—a Christian conscience, and I know that I could never murder again; it is who I am now, and I have wept every day, and asked God for repentance—and still, I do not feel that I can be forgiven for the horrible things I have done." He looked at Pedro with a pensive expression. "I pray for you, too—and for the Narcos, to stop their killing, and for the healing of Mexico."

Pedro no longer heard what he considered incoherent rambling from a man who was now a danger to him and his family, but still a friend, a loyal friend who had saved his life numerous times, helped him become rich, and never betrayed him.

A plan for Roderigo and his family to escape from Mexico was decided upon.

The next day, Jorge asked the men into his office and ordered them to kill two federal judges and their families in a nearby coastal town. The US DEA was involved, in conjunction with the Mexican anti-drug and crime agency, Organized Crime Unit Task Force, or OCUTF, that had been formed for the sole purpose of deterring, dismantling and destroying the Drug Trafficking Operations, or DTOs, within their borders.

"I give you ten good men to help you," Jorge said, gingerly, "for this ejecucion."

"We select our own good men," Roderigo returned, coolly.

"Not this time—the big bosses want a message sent, that we," he said, slowly, "have," and he extended his fat arms outward, "no boundaries—and don't fail, ever, even if you have to try, and try again." He smiled. "Don't worry, you won't lose the luster on your stellar reputations."

There was no reason to argue, for to do so was to debate the big bosses, and this was just not done; no infant argues with his father, no private with his general, no human with his god—as was this situation.

But crafty men survive in times of war due to superior tactics and strategy, and Pedro and Roderigo knew what must be done.

The assassin caravan took flight and set up camp a mile from the objective; maps out, radio walkie-talkies in use, which was the way Cartels communicated to each other during operational mode, using clandestine code; and when the guns and rifles were checked, ammunition loaded, the plan rehearsed, exit strategies recited, the word was then "go."

The twelve men were in position, high upon a hill, overlooking the white-stucco building in which the two families were sequestered, a safe house that was guarded by numerous officers—most of whom were on the payroll of the Azteca Cartel. At the designated signal, the assassins attacked the DEA and OCUTF agents, the traitorous bodyguards attacked their own, and soon the bloody deal was done: twenty members of two families and agents lay dead, or more rightly described as butchered beyond recognition.

Roderigo had been laid flat in the beginning of the assault by a bullet to his left thigh. He was the only casualty.

Jorge was ecstatic the next day in his plush office. "Fantastic work, boys, first rate, very professional." Then he looked at the bandaged leg of Roderigo, and frowned. "Bad luck, eh? Or good luck—only a good, clean leg wound— and you live again another day, eh?" A knock came to the door, and the face of Jorge lost a faint glimmer of gaiety, flecks of joy cells—like old skin cells— that decreased imperceptibly to any casual onlooker, but not to Roderigo, who, with his new restorative self, was able to screen the old man through this new special filter and saw the suspicious change, as if Jorge had been dealt a royal flush; he knew Pedro was as yet incapable of seeing this kind of treachery, and confirmed it in his calm countenance. He stood by and moved to a point behind the door, feigning leg pain.

Inconceivably, thrust through the door was the shooter Pedro and Roderigo had hired to wound the latter, his face beaten terrifyingly to a fine, meaty red pulp of broken bone and cartilage and swollen and cut flesh, fol- lowed closely behind by two armed men.

"Oh, a guest, how nice," Jorge began, but only as a ruse, for his persona of cordial host was merely a feint on his audience while he went about the dirty business of punishment, he himself coming up with a very wicked-looking, slick, black Glock pistol.

But Roderigo and Pedro had been entwined as killers too long for Pedro not to notice his partner in a coiled-up, about-to-strike position—it is the same way with any two who are in synchronization and social and business arrangements: they sense a shift in the other's behavior, they smell a sense of provocation, they see the shape of things to come, especially in soldiers who count on the other for survival; Roderigo shoved the beaten gunman toward Jorge's desk and jumped the two men trailing him, while Pedro went after Jorge, killing him instantly with the gun he had secreted in the waistband behind his back.

This was no fantasy sequence, no movie script, no misunderstanding, and when desperate men have guns in their sweaty hands, they do not barter, think, or plan, but act, much like a panther does with its dagger-like claws when faced with a lethal enemy. Gunshots were fired everywhere, a close-fitting firing range that blurred the senses for any amateur and terrorized the mind of all but professionals; when it was all over, only the two true warriors stood, unscathed, and they instantly fled, shooting their way out past more armed guards, then tore out of the rear of the plush office building and, making it to their car, sped quickly away.

However, what the two men had done was akin to two mean bees smacking into a hornet's nest, and then attempting to flee unmarked; and like the unified nest, any disturbance in the hive sent shock waves of dissonance throughout its compressed existence, where all of the souls seemed to have a shared consciousness; thus, quicker than a governmental response, the Azteca Cartel members, always carrying a radio walkie-talkie, began to swarm over the killing site.

Pedro and Roderigo had invested their daily income of human value in Azteca Cartel stock, and saith the philosopher: please, I beg thee, do not put all of your fragile, freshly laid eggs in the same powerbroker—for there are diverse kinds of powerbrokers; many unknown, a few unknown, many seen, some unseen; many deceptive, a few forthright, yet all only found out by allowing the heart to seek them, to wit: as the men fled into this maze, which shrank every moment and became more dangerous and confusing every second, they realized that the townspeople were as intolerable of them as the allies they had once purchased.

It should not come as a shock that no citizen would admit them willingly into their homes, businesses, or shelters, and quickly, working out via neighborhood gossip, and through Cartel megaphones atop cars driving throughout the city, it was known that the two ignominious figures were, like two caught foxes in the henhouse, lurking in the local vicinity, with a handsome reward being offered by their fuming employers.

It was at this wild juncture, for a certain group of concerned citizens, that this event became propitious, and oddly and refreshingly ironic, and the world for them became like a small crystal ball wherein all the participants, when shook, might come to rest where formally it had been impossible to land.

Javier, of this aforementioned group, was talking now, enraged, as he always was, as are all men who taste injustice, and have it often smeared in their faces and are forced to not only ignore it, but, when confronted by the perpetrators, smile and smell its rank odor and kowtow to it. "How long can we live like sheep in the war zone? They kill whom they choose, rob whom they choose, torture and rape anyone they choose—it is enough to emasculate a man." But his umbrage at his own delinquent shortcomings toppled him to the brown sofa, and there to settle into a teary-eyed, red-faced, simmering, active volcano holding back its fury. His wife had been beaten, raped, and murdered by three "police officers," her body unceremoniously dumped onto his front lawn, and all this for no apparent reason other than her beauty had caught the salacious eyes of those who practice no moral restraint, who knew there was no legal redress for their offense. "How long can we," he lamented, "live like this?"

"This isn't living," Hector, a middle-aged man began; "we have been invaded by an army of vicious gangsters, and when our country attempts to stop them, the gangsters merely buy them off, or kill them; it is too much to take."

"I say we fight them," Arturo shouted, standing up now, a young man whose burgeoning flame to resist all perceived tyranny had not yet been quenched by reality, and now clutching his burning breast; "we are more than them: more willing, more brave—more of us!"

"We are more of us, sure, but how many are willing to fight, eh?" Isabel, a woman of thirty-three, said. "Who will fight an army? How can we win a war when the police and soldiers don't really fight them, and the ordinary people are coerced to become police and soldiers?"

"I will!" Arturo shouted. "I will gladly wear the uniform of the proud soldier for Freedom."

The group of twenty men and women of the town of Yermo were in agreement about what they should do, as they had agreed some thirty times before in the last year; and always, they left with more dignity than they had coming in; and in this way, they were like an addict, getting a fix they knew was only temporary, but knew must happen again.

"We have weapons, we have courage, we have the will," Pablo said, calmly, a man who was nearly thirty years of age, yet, by his cool and measured speech, seemed more mature and wise beyond his years; he was a relative newcomer to the meeting, and then said something no one had ever heard; he condemned them directly, which seemed to deflate their injection of self-respect; "but we're happy to have El Narco rule us," and he sneered, a very unsettling act in the midst of the victims. "He is our big father, who gives us money for things; and we hold out our hands, like scared children," and as he held out his still hand, he mocked his countrymen. "Gracias, good father, for compensating our losses: the murders, the rapes, the looting; for buying us goods and services—muy bueno." He stopped and stared unabashedly at his shocked audience. "And when he does not, we pretend to be brave—machismo," he cried, standing up, and beating his chest. "I will fight—but who? Who do you fight? You—a dumb peon—fight El Narco, with his missiles and grenades and automatic rifles, and thousands of loyal troops, really? Look at yourselves, children—for that is who you truly are: the children of peons, who strut about and shout 'always the next time,' because it makes you feel better! Well, amigos, next time is now! We, the despised peons, who have fought back the Spanish, the French, our own corrupt leaders, to gain democracy—for this? For what—to be ruled once again by another foreign invader, who counts on our 'big speeches' in the safety and comfort of our humble homes, which aren't even safe and comfortable any-more, and our own fear that we might lose what precious little we have—which is what, eh? What do we have but what little we've worked and sweated for, until they choose to take it from us; and don't count on our military, our police, our politicians—they are not ours to court; and do not count on the United States, or other allies; we must clean our own dirty house."

When someone speaks the truth that is in your heart and mind, it is dif-ficult to condemn them.

Lorenzo, a man of fifty-two, heavyset, then spoke respectfully, "Have you lost someone because of El Narco?"

Pablo, still standing, looked at the man with great pathos. "Yes, I have lost—Mexico."

It was then that the loudspeakers atop the black and white police car announced. "Two men, Pedro Gomez and Roderigo Chavez, have escaped from jail; please be advised to stay in your homes. If you see these men, immediately notify the police; reward for their capture is twenty-five thou-sand US dollars apiece."

Everyone in the room knew what had really happened. There was the electricity of revolt in the rarefied air.

Providence Steps In

Where is there to go, when there is nowhere to go but straight ahead?

Thus, these were the narrow, perhaps nonexistent options facing Pedro and Roderigo as they drove up and down the city, finding streets blocked, members of their Cartel driving after them; and even street punks, now that a detailed description of the car and two drivers had been widely distributed, were taking wild potshots at them—them, two princes who had ruled the city as despots and boasted of their ability to terrorize with impunity; O, the fervent joy, the rapacious delight this created in their enemies, which was, practically speaking, nearly all the townsfolk.

Realizing that any exit from town had been effectively blocked, the two now-radioactive men initially had sought refuge in an abandoned warehouse they had formally frequented to torture their prey, and although this afforded them a small measure of safety, it also allowed their adversaries time to tighten this self-inflicted noose.

Night—innocuous, sweeping darkness—throws a cloak of invisibility to the innocent, a lifeline to the innocent, a restive curative to the innocent; yet lurking near them, the guilty acquaint themselves with the same nocturnal effects. Perhaps, one day, the guilty will have an aura about their bodies that is dark when others have light, and is light when others are dark; yet, in this town, villains, curiously, did just that in their cocksure and vulgar manners, as if this was the way of the new world now, and forever, Amen.

Let us now see, if the forces of Freedom reside in the hearts of even the tiniest folks in the most seemingly inauspicious and inconsequential towns.

Hell hath no fury like a Cartel scorned, especially when performed so brazenly by one of their own; and thus, they—not hell—set out to do what needs be done to bring their ex-offspring to their ever-malleable, artificially created justice.

"Do what e'er needs be done," the boss above Jorge instructed his legions, his name being Caesar Gonzalez, otherwise known as the Brute; "if we need to burn this dump to ashes and scatter the ashes, and then rebuild it in our own image," he whispered, so low that his lieutenants, fearing his repeating of the orders would bring unfortunate physical reprisals, leaned so far forward from their standing positions in front of his illustrious desk that they nearly fell over, "which is something," he gestured upward, looking upward, too, and then pursing his thick lips, "I should like to do one day soon; but I digress; you, Carlos, tell me what I just said about those two rats..."

Carlos, prone to daydreaming about his current sweetheart, let loose a few beads of sweat down his arched back. "Yes, Señor Gonzalez—you said to kill them, and that you want to burn down the town."

Señor Gonzalez stared at him as if addressing a fossilized creature that had no reason to be alive in his vicinity, and so, with malice aforethought, he quieted himself again. "And when we do burn this dump and rebuild it—oh, one caveat: it will be in my image—with the expressed consent of El Toro himself, of course; you know, he is a very generous man, always happy to share," he said, stroking his thick, full, black beard as he pursed his lips again and cocked his head. He smiled, but it was awkward, as it was far from genuine. He continued on, after marking in his little black book, "Carlos, you need to apply yourself more often at debriefings; how else," and he looked to his other eager-faced men, "how can you possibly hope for promotion? You want to go back to mixing cocaine in factories? I would think not; so, listen up when I talk to you, and learn." He fancied himself, as you will soon see, one of the finest practitioners of elucidation, by virtue of his exclusive high rank in the religious order of the blessed Azteca Cartel.

"Take heed, little ones," he began, in four-beat tempo, for truly, he thought himself a good conductor in the scheme of life, and those fleshly beings before him but accessories, interconnecting, dispensable members of the orchestra he moved with every perceptible wave of his large wand. "Jorge Gonzalez was as good a man as you'll ever meet—none of you are fit to tie his sandals, whether he is dead or alive—and he was betrayed by two soon-to-be-butchered-alive-like-pigs, who claimed to be our brothers, but were in reality filthy curs," he began, pausing to allow the force of his devouring discourse to flood their minds, "found out by their treachery—this Roderigo Chavez cracked like a pathetic schoolgirl and confessed his sins," he enunciated the last word as if he meant to jab it into their eyes, "to the wife of a Judge he and his other equally foolish partner, Pedro Gomez, had recently—and to give credit where credit is due—masterfully and cleanly executed; then Pedro, apparently still in total use of his mental faculties, finding out that the wife knew, killed her and the rest of the family—a good man, he, up to this point of this instructional narrative. Benito," he said, gazing confidentially at the now-quivering youth, "give me a summary." After Benito did so, successfully, Caesar marked it in his little black book. "Good, good, listening skills are so rare these days; ah, but I digress," which he stated, more due to how it sounded than actually saying it. "Yes, but it was too late, for the wife had told a newspaper editor, who knew a man in our organization had been spilling his guts to a street preacher, who, we now know, this Pedro—a good fellow corrupted by Roderigo—also killed, to wipe the nose of his—how do you put it—newly saved friend; but saved from what, for us to slice his yellow skin off cell by cell; well," he paused, frowning, "we heard about it from one of our reporters, and we took the editor, got what we wanted from him, dropped a literal grenade in his mouth and left his blown-to-bits body in his office; so, Jorge had the two traitors watched closely at the hit of the two federal judges' families, and as it turned out, Pedro had hired a man to wound Roderigo, who, apparently, is so meek now he refuses to kill for us—unless, of course, we get in his way—and he has no problem killing his own people who treated him like family; what a hypocrite: I have never heard of such a practicing Catholic—outrageous!" And he banged the table with his large-fisted hands like an outraged Cardinal, and the effect of this was carried over into verbal outrage. "I want the two rats caught and I want them brought before me in heavy iron chains, and I want to personally set them on fire and then toss their charred bodies into the town square with a big white banner that reads," and he held up his hands, looking at them, "'this is what happens to traitors of our own family; if we will do this to them, what will we do to you if you betray us?'" He cast a glaring eye at his captive audience to mine their awe and approval of his plan, and they, knowing what happens to those who remain quiet, heartily anointed it with shouts and whoops.

Caesar, feeling vindicated, said, with some weird species of affection, "Now, go out," he began, slowly and carefully, "and find those cowards, and do what you have to, and if that includes going house to house," he said, still methodically, but then sped up his dialogue, "do it; and if that includes roughing up some of the citizenry, so be it; and if that includes," and now he fairly shouted as he pounded his fists and stomped his feet as he arose, "burning this entire city to the ground to find out where they are hiding, so everyone will realize what we will do to achieve total victory—so be it," and then he blessed them, as they instinctively stood and bowed their heads, and then made the Catholic sign of the cross toward them. "God be with you," he whispered; "let us pray." And they did, in earnest too, to a god who would fortify their will and motivate their desire and aid them in the capture and murder of two orphaned Azteca Cartel children.

Thus, the band of hit men, some recruited from Southern California gangs, others locally—a few specialists from the state of Azteca—went forth with this mystical aura draped over their bodies like a supernatural shield; many of the men kissed their crosses on the way out, each of them thinking, if they were to capture the two villains, of the great rewards therein.

The intellectual misinterpretation of the nature and character of the poor by the rich has given them an unfortunate conclusion: that the oppressed poor will accept inordinate amounts of abuse upon their collective heads ad infinitum, and never do more than occasionally grumble, which can quickly and efficiently be eviscerated by the occasional ethnic, racial, political, or religious cleansing, as ordered and ordained by the oppressive rich; but these wealthy rulers are wrong: rulers, yes there are—even though they may not hold political office, this is but a mere case of semantics, for they hold sway over governmental policy as do the politicians, as the two groups work in tandem to tear down ghettos and slums, to make room for their gilt-lined ideas, and continue to enrich their obscene bank accounts and hidden corporations, ever-expanding in value and hidden around the world, and so slums and ghettos are simply moved elsewhere—wherever poor people congregate en masse to huddle close together and innovate to survive.

Imagine a boiling kettle—the poor being the kettle, and the water, their emotions—and a lid that increases in weight the more the kettle boils—the lid being the rich—so when the hit squad of dozens of eager sociopaths took flight about town for the two escapees, the irony of the situation gave the water sufficient force to blow that now-pathetic top right through the weakly thatched roof.

"It is our divine office to resist now," Pablo whispered, yet it was a whisper that was akin to a shout—the shout of liberty—which fed into the hearts and minds of his fellows as he bent over the too cocky-to-be-by-himself Cartel assassin, who had just taken four bullets from Pablo's ArmaLite AR-8 rifle as he had attempted to force open the door in his quest for the two wayward hit men. "That will teach you to knock first," he said, looking back at the shocked yet exultant citizens of this meeting.

The cell phones began to ring, as if all the other resistance members at their clandestine meetings had heard the glorious news of this audacious killing, as if they were an interconnecting neural network able to sense the thoughts and movements of the other.

As one of the men ran to answer the landline phone, and others their cellular phones, and the rest of them gazed with excitement and trepidation, they found themselves affixed in the same historical moment that confronts all suppressed people: if they're willing to resist, when; and if not now, why not, and what must occur for them to fight, and when will the conditions for rebellion be to their liking, and if they yield now, then when will they ever fight, or were they ever going to fight? Now, at this precise second in the annals of uprisings of the oppressed against oppressors, they stood fore to their ancestors and aft on this battle continuum, and at this precise juncture, they must have felt a sizzling dynamism that compelled them to seize the moment—unplanned, unprepared, without hope, without direction—and for once in their ill-begotten lives, be spontaneous, pick up the free-rolling ball of lightning and run as fast and far with it as possible until they were wounded or dead—and even then, pass it on to another as long as they had a fighting breath.

Thus, with one unified, cheering voice, the group shouted to their comrades through their phones, "The revolution has begun! Fight! Fight for your freedom and your rights to make a mark," and almost immediately, gunshots, like the blessed sound of the Liberty Bell, peeled out in melodic song throughout the suddenly revived town.

"We are more of us than them," Pablo shouted, as he faced the outside world, and this hue and cry became a national anthem in the struggle against the Azteca Cartel.

It was as if the guards had thrown the switch on the steel lock of all the prison cells, for the citizens, most armed with rifles, guns, clubs or knives, came streaming from their homes, their shops, their errands, a coordinated yet scattered army of Minutemen recently born, stitching together a strategy even as they moved against the enemy.

Was it the auspicious debut of spectacular, freeing, uninhibited battle after a lifetime of groveling restraint, a declaration of universal rights shouted from the highest citadel of Justice; could it have been the instinctive marvel of standing up for oneself and fighting what was formally thought invincible, wicked, merciless, that the people took no heed of their own safety and charged the marauding Cartel soldiers? And even though many citizens fell that fateful night, there were courageous more found to pick up their fallen comrades' weapons and valiantly carry on the good fight, battling this nine-headed beast with every precious inhale of freedom they breathed in, and every precious exhale of pride and self-respect they breathed out, fighting now as do valiant soldiers with devotion for the preservation of home and hearth, family and friends, standing in the hallowed light that resisting evil brings, sharing the noble spirit of kindred liberators past; these young women, these young men, these old women, these old men; these sometimes young boys, these young girls; these sometimes sickly men, and sickly women; any and all who could fight, who had dreamed of fighting, of throwing off the rusted iron chains of repression, as if in a sublime dream, as if in a supernatural miracle, who could not but take up arms and shout, "we are more of us, than them." Surely, vastly outnumbering the enemy, victory could be lost only by capitulation, and these people—beaten, robbed, raped, sold into slavery, extorted, murdered, intimidated—could not conceive of living in hell anymore when heaven finally beckoned to them. So, they fought on, maddened, in a maddened frenzy; grimly, wearing a dark, grim countenance; bravely, engaging the enemy with the armor of bravery, without care for personal safety, but for the safety and future of family and friends, for the future of she whom they loved perhaps more than each other, Mother Mexico, for whom they would gladly die if she might be restored to her glorious past, and be assured of a glorious future.

The war, for that was what it was, raged on throughout the fiery, swirling maelstrom.

> Where men and women of ordinary lives
> adorn themselves in extraordinary light,
> and fight the great nine-headed Dragon beast
> tooth and nail, in courageous feats
>
> And what can tyranny say to freedom,
> what can violence to peace;
> how long can vice endure,
> how can enmity conquer love,
> how can injustice conquer justice;
> when finally man decides
> to rise above the rising tide.

Heroes, the citizens became that sanguinary, burning night; heroes they made themselves through every furious rush against rocket launchers, and fragmentation grenades, and automatic rifles, with every refusal to retreat, or surrender, or rest from the weary task of driving out the serpents from paradise; how many stories were forged that magnificent night, of heroism by the barber, the baker, the furniture-maker; the teacher, the butcher, the shoemaker; the nurse, the doctor, the restaurant-worker; any man and woman with two good arms and legs, or one or the other, even seated, even dragging, even crawling, had to be there, in the heart of the magnificent conflagration—shouting, loading, shielding, tending, for none could miss this one shining adventure: eradicating a lifetime of disappointment and frustration, to be part of a stalwart history that would be told and retold by fathers to sons, mothers to daughters, for decades, for centuries, forever as long as the earth was covered with certain creatures who bethought themselves not only superior to other life-forms, but imposed their opinions and beliefs upon them through bloodshed, slavery, and war.

> And when good morrow came,
> at their feet lay their broken chains;

the villain defeated, victory won,
freedom adorned the golden dawn

All throughout the town, the neighborhoods, the streets, the shops, there was the evidence of a war zone: dead bodies, burnt and smoldering buildings, spilled blood, prisoners, damaged homes, the walking wounded, the helpful citizen, the victorious citizen-army patrolling the perimeter and inner city.

During the brilliant chaos, Pedro and Roderigo had made good their escape, having a superior knowledge of the city through their previous endeavors, where they had mapped out alternate routes for every possible confrontation, finally navigating their way past the battle, and once outside the city, shook hands, and each went to find their respective family.

When Pedro drove up to his opulent home, which was some sixty kilometers away in distance and was located in the rural mountains, and surrounded by an electrified gate, replete with security cameras, high-tech alarms, and four highly trained bodyguards, he knew—the iron gate was open, and then he saw the horror: two dead bodyguards on the spacious front lawn, lying near the giant fountain. He ran into the house, gun in each hand, knowing, but hoping nonetheless, against reality, that somehow they who now hated and hunted him would leave his family...

There they were beside the two other bodyguards: his beautiful wife, his precious daughter and son, dead, shot many times and then mangled beyond recognition, the cruel payback of his cruel ex-employers. He threw himself upon them and wept out the bad soil where his past life had rooted and rotted, until he fell asleep.

Voices awoke him, the same brutish voices he had heard echoing in the nightmare he had just had; the sneering voice of the predator who has no conscience and blind allegiance to carry out any and all orders from its master: he recognized this animal tone because he, for the first time, recognized it in his own shattered voice. "This is me—it is me sent to kill me, me coming to kill me," he whispered, lying still with his arms around his family. "Me who killed my family," he began to weep, and forced himself to utter the precious names of his family, even as the voices grew louder, and he kissed them gently; "and now they want to kill me too, because I am no longer like them," and he looked at his family, "now I am like you again, like I was once was and should have been all along," he lovingly said to his wife, and kissed her again, and then looking at his children, saying their names with all the love he prayed he could retrieve from his burned-out soul, and kissed them tenderly. The vicious voices and loud noises were nearly upon him, and then something inside his warrior's mind became reanimated, and he felt for the guns, readied them, just as the four assassins came bounding through the open door; and he was already firing, and even as they fired, it was to no avail, for even though they were all expert marksmen, he was the better of them; and so, presently, they were dead. Yes, Pedro was grieving, but he was still on high alert, and as he turned around, reloading his gun, three more men came blazing away, but he dispatched them, too. He forced himself to check the perimeter, and once this was done, he set about the task of burying his own flesh and blood, and he instinctively knew, his bloody sinful past must be buried with them; and when these deeds were done, he collapsed upon their fresh graves, and lay there for three days, senseless, sleeping, moaning, weeping, despairing, without food or water, in his own waste, remembering his humble past, his ignominious present, but not imagining a clear future, for he imagined himself dead. "Why should I live—how could I have lived and been so evil and not recognized the destruction of my dark soul so clearly lit in the loving faces of my family? Where was the man who raised a family on a farm, who worked hard but was happy and never knew it; O, for the days passed of pure joy—simple days, when love was all the riches you needed," and he thought of his darling wife's warm embrace, and the loving, innocent embrace of his children and how it had made him feel so proud and good that they loved him, and he, them; and now, what had he murdered them for— but for the opiate of easy mammon, for the insatiable desires of the lustful flesh: ephemeral feasts that fade and fail in the illumine of Truth; for they are not eternal, he now knew, they will not be extolled in heaven, practiced by the saints, spoken of dearly by children—these false sentiments, he now knew, could never save you, belonged to no one good, for they yielded only disharmony, and destruction and division. Is the world better with Love and Peace and Joy, or the lusts of the flesh fulfilled, he pondered, gazing up at the scarlet-streaked dawn, as his mind and body lay in a state of suspended animation, as if he were truly a hibernating animal, yet conscious, trapped in a foggy labyrinth that obscured the moral compass he was born with; yes, he felt as if his wretched soul was a bloody stump, cut so far down it would never grow back, yet he desired it to grow, to sprout one green stem of blossom, one pink bud, and yield a fragrant scent that might cleanse his horrible sins.

It is better to die than to live on with the coward's memory, a murderer's memory, he mused, for now, all those killings, and kidnappings, and sexual exploits with faceless prostitutes, and his marathon dance with the white lady, with mud, with crank, came into him as if he were the Pedro of old, and could not understand how this other Pedro, this false Pedro, could have committed such atrocities so casually, so nonchalantly, so habitually, so—unrepentantly, as if, he worried, to his horror, he truly had been a wild beast in human skin; but how, why, he prayed to God, why did this happen? I had paradise, and instead I tortured, shot, and buried it for the perversion of the sensuous now—where was my Christian conscience, O Lord! Did I murder that too! No, I never had one! Then, I need to die—I do not deserve life, so foul have I become," and he took his guns, but, alas, could not destroy himself, and simply wept and wailed even more.

On the third day, night finally overcame the light, and fastened its restful ebony shield upon him, cuddling him in its forgiving bosom. He was waiting for, hoping for, praying for death, when a distant sound came to him, and he did nothing, but murmured, through dry, parched and cracked lips, "Consuela, Antonio, Maria, forgive me for what I have done—God forgive me; I am not worthy of life, I am not worthy of forgiveness, I am not worthy of love," and he raised his weak arms to reach out into the celestial heaven where he knew his family dwelled; and behold, hands took his hands, and a soothing voice said, "Pedro, it is I, Roderigo."

Brother Summer yielded up its sizzling crown,
bowing before the dimming sun;
Sister Autumn swept in on scented breezes,
Bringing calm before the coming storm

The Story That Never Ends

The sun pressed a breezy kiss across the awakening sky and flavored it with spreading tinges of vermilion streaks and broad hyacinth strokes, as if to say: my part is done; it is your part now to enjoy!

José could think only of the incredible tale Pedro had just told him, and finally, he spoke, after a long silence from his friend. "What happened, Pedro—what happened then?"

"Then?" Pedro whispered, still lying upon his back, and staring up at the simple elegance of Nature's beauty. "Roderigo nursed me back to health, and told me he was going back into town."

"What?" José exclaimed, emboldened to ask more questions.

"Yes, he said he was going back into town and to make peace with the people there; I begged him, José, I begged him not to go, but he refused." He paused. "He has nothing to lose, and his family is murdered, too…"

"And so he went…"

"Yes, he went—but he did not ask me to go. I have not seen nor heard of him since, but that was three days ago."

"How did you get here?"

"I walked, avoiding the main roads." He paused, then looked at his friend. "Have you heard of trouble in Yermo?"

"Yes, we heard, but it is so far away—and yet, I did think of you and your family…"

"I should not have come here, Pedro, you are in danger now; a fool and a beast have I become." He closed his eyes. "O, but I should not have come here," he shouted; "what have I done?" He pounded his fist into the soft mud.

José waved this possibility away. "If they found out where you once lived, they will come anyway."

"But you must know that they will do anything—anything!" he cried, suddenly, as if he saw in his mind the atrocities he had committed but had never recognized, as if a thick veil had suddenly been lifted. "If they even believe you haven't seen me in so long, they will still kill you just to kill you—even if they believe you; O, José, I know this," he cried in horror, the pain and torment of a conscience repairing itself now thriving in him, as if to remove old clutter and make new material could not be done without payment due, "because I have done this, to people just like you—to beautiful women and children like your family," and he paused, and wanted to close his eyes, but would not allow himself to, and forced himself to gaze hard at his friend. "I know how they think and feel, how they move, and why, and why they do what they do," and his voice became grave and forlorn, "for I am them still." He grabbed his head as if it were to explode. "Kill me, José, while you can—I am no longer worthy of life! If I were not a coward, I would have done it!" And he punched the soft soil. "I've contaminated the good Earth with the innocent blood I have spilled," he cried, and he gazed upward at José with pleading countenance. "Kill me, José, kill me," he moaned, taking his black handgun from his waist belt and thrusting it into José's hands. "I no longer know who I am, or what I might do; I can no longer trust myself; once you have tasted the fresh blood of Innocents you have slain," his tone weakened, as if he were trapped in a phantom prison of despair and humiliation, shame and degradation—in league with all of these fallen emotions, and their suffering cousins, self-persecution, self-loathing, self-damnation, a cesspool of every self-inflicted, emotionally debasing pain and self-realized horror that would gnaw at his mind, heart, and soul until he was fairly consumed by unstoppable pain and suffering. "You never lose the desire to kill for power," and he sunk back into the mud, "for pleasure," he moaned, as if stabbed in the heart, "to make the pain go away, if only for a little while—the pain," he barely whispered, "of remembering, and thinking that I'll never find my way home again…" He closed his eyes and lay there as if one dead, so exhausted spiritually was he, and murmured, "Kill me like you would any wild animal who threatens your loved ones."

José called to his wife, and soon, they had taken Pedro, despite his most vehement protestations, and moved him into their domicile, where he presently fell fast asleep, and where he was tended to and cared for, for two days as he regained his strength.

By and by, Pedro was fully revived in body, but not mind, and his insistence on leaving won the day. He embraced José and his wife, thanked them for their kindness, and left on a hot summer's eve.

"Where will he go?" Ramona, who now knew Pedro's story, asked José hours later.

"Where he needs to," José answered, looking out the door, imagining where his friend was; "where he believes he can atone for his sins." He put his arms around her.

"Why doesn't he ask God for forgiveness?"

He shook his head. "He fears God will not forgive him—and then he knows he is lost forever."

A rustle was heard in the bushes at the perimeter of the yard, and José grew numb with worry, then saw it was Pedro, and at first he was relieved, but when he saw his face, he ordered his family out of the house and into the woods to their long-ago agreed-upon safe spot.

"They are coming, José," Pedro cried, running up like a madman to him. "They are coming—too many to count; O, José, what have I done?" And he came to rest next to him, breathing quickly.

"How do we know they are coming here—for you?"

"I know, I know—they did not follow me, but they must have found out where I once lived; we must flee from this place: they will kill everyone and burn down everything; I tell you, José, they're like fungus rot—they have no conscience like civilized people." He caught his breath. "What have I done— what have I done to you? Haven't I caused enough grief with my sins—sins that follow me, still…"

The two men moved quickly into the thick cover of the woods.

"You have your guns?" asked José.

"Yes, yes, but two guns against an army—useless! We need to go, now!" He was nearly mad with urgency, for he knew what was truly coming.

"The other farmers—what about them?"

"I told them to go, but they did not believe me—why should they; who am I to them but a mere memory; they're lost, lost—nothing and no one can help them now…"

But he cut off his own words when the sound of cars sank into the still night. Two red Jeeps and two SUVs pulled up, and a total of twelve men exited the vehicles, and immediately, as if acting with authority given to them by the consent of the people, began to disperse toward the various farms.

"South American thugs," Pedro whispered to José and his huddled, crouched-down family, and then pointed toward the assassins, "very bad men—you would know them from their ultra-violent tattoos of death and mayhem all over their bodies, showing many weapons and scenes of those they have murdered—they are like land sharks, killing everything in their path when they are hungry; and, José, they are always hungry."

They could hear the shouts of the men as they moved about the large area, and heard them on the two-way radio as they approached the Gomez farm.

"They will find no evidence of me being here," Pedro whispered, "but that won't stop them—the big bosses want results, and killing Innocents and burning down houses is at least some consolation they can bring back…" He let his head down in abject shame, and then murmured, "And to think I was like them, and there were probably families hiding—frightened—in the woods, when I would come to do my dirty business…"

Gunshots were heard, screams came with them, and the men seemed to be moving toward the center of the small community of farms.

And then a voice was heard—mean, hard, inhuman. "Pedro—hey, Pedro, you rotten, dirty, stinking, lousy traitor," it began, like a hail of bullets, followed by a hail of obscenities and vulgar waste, "you come out from hiding, you dirty, yellow, stinking coward, and we will not kill these fine farmers—your good friends, right, Pedro? What do you say? Do you want them to die because you're a yellow, stinking, no-good, dirty, rotten, backstabbing, traitorous weasel?"

Pedro felt the surge of the warrior bear up inside himself, knowing that if he had sufficient manpower and firepower, he could take them on; no, he would enjoy taking them and butchering them and torturing them as they begged for mercy; yes, he thought, it would be sweet revenge to take down men who bethought themselves so brave and strong only because they had weapons and hostages—and he knew, it would be like killing himself. "But I was no different," he understood, searching to find a memory where at least he had honor in a killing, "there was a Judge, who started it all… but there is no honor in such things…"

"Hey, Pedro, we know you're here, you filthy dog—these Mexican peons told us; come out, Pedro, and take it like a man." The leader of the hit squad, looking around, spat largely upon the ground, then spat out even larger disgust. "I will give you exactly one minute to come out—you know I'm not bluffing…"

Pedro felt the inexhaustible chill of destiny crawl down his sweaty back. He knew he must act, smartly, to avoid José holding him back; so, all of a sudden, he stood up, and moved so swiftly that José had no time to hold him, and soon, he was in the clearing.

"So, there you are, you worthless piece of trash, you little punk," the leader — with the shaven, round head, and densely laid green and black tattoos, like a second skin over his body — said in a low, mean, guttural discharge; and sneering now, "you should have known we would find you; and you knew we would kill you," and he nodded back to the trembling families, "and them, anyway—you know," he shrugged his shoulders, "that's the way it is."

"I know you," Pedro said, approaching the men, "and I know you are the coward—like I was, with a gun; you're just a punk with no soul."

The leader laughed uproariously, as did his minions. "Man, you are weak, but that won't be too much longer—wait until Suarez hears about you."

"Let the farmers go," Pedro said, stopping some thirty meters from the man, his hands still resting at his sides.

"You know better," the leader responded, as if this were his role to play, and he could quote from no other script, "you know it has to be done," and he motioned to his men to approach Pedro.

Pedro nodded, and at that moment, allowed the two guns—one up each long sleeve, to fall gently down the length of his arm and into his waiting, sure grasp. "I do know," he whispered, and as the men approached, he lifted up the guns so he might kill as many of his former selves as possible and thus liberate the world from that many bad seeds. He fired, both guns blazing.

The hit squads aimed their AK-47s.

And then, so much firepower erupted that José and his family could not even tell what was happening, so fierce was the clamor, so disruptive to the normal quietude of their daily lives that they could not discern the specifics of the action, so foreign was battle to them that all was a small theater of smoke, fire, and the horrendous din of destruction.

When it was all over, José could not believe what he saw, for there, unbelievably, stood Pedro, and the farmers, unscathed, but all of the South American gang members were completely obliterated, lying in a heap of smoking ash and splattered blood and bone and tissue; he arose, as if in a trance, drawn to this macabre yet miraculous scene; and as he approached, he could plainly see that Pedro was also shocked by the outcome, the smoking guns he held in his hands hanging limply at his sides.

Then the miracle explained itself.

"Pedro," a voice suffused the air, like a sweet-sounding songbird after a violent storm. "Pedro," it echoed, and soon, into the dimly lit clearing, appeared Roderigo, AK-47 rifle in hand.

But he was not alone. Four men and a woman, rugged, confident, handsome, came slowly and casually walking behind them, their mean-looking weapons tucked snugly under their arms.

The one man carried an IMI Negev, the other an FN Minimi, in addition to the HK417 rifles rifle of their compatriots, except the woman, who carried an HK416 A5, and all of them also carried a special sniper rifle, as if indeed their weapons were as normal for them to have as a hoe or shovel to the farmers they had just saved.

Came Finn McCool, of Ireland, late of Africa; and Ana of Honduras, late of Guatemala; Antonio Juan de Bolivar, of Colombia, late of Africa; and yes, he had the fat brown cigar in his mouth as he brought up the rear: Miguel Cervantes, Esq., of Mexico, late of Mexico; and Yoshitsune of Japan, late of Nepal.

The Crusaders had landed.

Book Five

There are set patterns in the world, and irrevocable cycles that nourish and replenish Nature: cool, oxygenated winds in the Arctic sink into the sea and travel to the warmer climates and deliver their precious cargo to the seabed; the circulation of carbon and nitrogen involving soil of plants, animals and air; the oxygen cycle between air, plant, and animal; the rock cycle, from deep within the earth: liquid rock, to solid rock, which then withers and goes back to liquid; the water cycle from ocean to clouds to rain, and down again to the ocean—molecules that were once the body of an American pioneer, in an ancient glacier, a dinosaur; the cycle of life: birth, infancy, toddler, adolescent, adult, death, and in death, there is no selfishness, only restoring precious nutrients back to the earth for those buried in her bosom; atoms disbursed to other life-forms, to other substances, atoms that once inhabited the tree, the Greek philosopher, the star; these are Nature's cycles, established and preserving, a boon to Man as it tends to its own enduring existence.

And then comes Man's cycles, necessary and unnecessary, artificial and natural, intelligent and unintelligent, namely: birth, happiness, love, job, house, marriage, family, celebration, death—it is the same everywhere; it must be so, or life ends; and inside this set and secure pattern are endless sub-cycles: arguing, love, arguing, love; sleep, eat, job, play, eat, sleep; marriage, birth, raising a child, nurturing the child, educating the child, the child becomes an adult, gains employment, leaves home, initiates the cycle of his parents; governments have war, and peace, and war, and peace again, like the fighting couple; the alcoholic drinks, quits, drinks, and quits again; money is spent, money is saved; all of these are daily habits, ad infinitum, but these are necessary to keep the entire mechanism well-oiled and working properly so all of the parts, and even the whole, thrive; human nature and societal nature, the inevitable and consistent. But then there are those occurrences that are not necessary, but occur, and can be broken, but the ones who break them are either deemed mavericks and revolutionaries benefiting society, or even harming it, this designation is often stamped with approval or disapproval by he who wins or who has the most power.

There is a man: he goes from breakfast to job to mistress to wife—it is not an inflexible schedule; there is the woman: she goes from breakfast to job to her beau—to drink—and then to husband; there is a contingency, and variables are involved, remedies can be administered; these behaviors are selective, like the man who steals at his work; they can be revoked, like the prosecutor who persecutes a man he knows is certainly innocent but seeks to keep his high success rate intact, and favors the job of Attorney General; "tough on crime," his poster will say, but more important for what it will not say: "we will solve any crime—show us a suspect, and will show you a conviction; voila!" It is, said the frontiersman, when the fertile land was young and innocent and he could not see the wretched future, "the land of opportunity." It is better, said the beaver—could he speak—as he watched in abject horror as his elegant domain was misappropriated by the giant, two-legged, pale-skinned creatures, "to learn how to live where you are, then we will talk"; but, as it was, the beaver and the rest of his family were humiliated, and forced to move downstream with their astute cousins, that sun-loving rascal the Woodchuck, and the Hoary "the whistler" Marmot.

There is a man, once more: he attends to a routine entirely bred by his lamentation of walking the trail strewn with the still heavy vestiges of those who might have been saved had they had someone like him to steer their course anew; this is where passion lies, in a dormant seed of one's own casual good life and then awakening it, and in doing so, looking around again at the world and seeing that not everyone is wealthy, healthy, and wise.

This man made a choice to leave the allure of self-promotion through the accumulation of riches, to seek the welfare of those unfortunate souls who fall in between societal cracks and remain nothing but clutter and debris, to be blindly and slowly swept away. Thus, armed with such good intentions, he founded an organization that reached out to troubled youth, namely: in the schools, elementary and middle schools, he helped collect books from outside sources and pass them along to families at the lower socioeconomic income level, his reasoning to the teachers, as follows: "What creates a poor, uneducated adult? Answer: a poor, uneducated child; if a child does not receive the proper intellectual stimulation—along with proper nutrition—then the brain may never develop correctly; they will forever remain a prisoner," and he would look at the statistics, "always, because of what they did not receive—now." He and his people presented gymnastics and various athletics at assemblies; had a building in town where neighborhood youth could engage in athletic activities, read books, learn about the world through the use of learning games, and listen to men and women from local Boy Scouts, Cub Scouts, Girl Scouts troops, the YMCA, YWCA, various sports leagues, and other youth-oriented associations. This was his mission, his blessed endeavor, his family, his decision; and yet, he could have simply thought, "No, I seek material objects only." He could have allowed the wayward youth to die on the streets, go to jail, remain criminals, but to him, "Every life I save is a beautiful life—one to be cherished and celebrated; every life won is one less lost, and there are few things more precious than saving a life."

Thus, this was Samuel T. Longfellow's cycle: always helping, never hurting, never condemning, always healing. "Look forward, see your new self; for your old self is behind you."

It was Summer again, the season that delighted him the most; for the children were out of school, and his youth organization was filled with those carefree souls who still believed in the magic of life because every day was an exciting adventure of learning about this big, mysterious world.

This was the cycle of his choice, which begat new life, which begat new families, which begat new communities.

Dylan and Rhiannon were instructing children and teenagers on gymnastics, and martial arts, and Samuel was in the learning library that he had recently built—with the assistance of the neighborhood kids, because he believed that they would have pride, and gain self-discipline by participating in such an endeavor that involved a place they frequented—proud as any father as he watched the children reading, using the interactive globe, discovery maps, and the map timeline that stretched across a large section of the wall. He felt protected. "This is good—no one will harm us; the other thing that happened, that was because of something—a response; that is not the way of things; this is America, and even the bad guys have rules..." He wanted to believe in it so much because he brought no threat to the criminal element. "Do they truly want their own in an early coffin?" He had talked to too many gang members who confessed they did not want the same life for their offspring. "But I know some do—but we are not in their way: after all, this is America." Such thoughts comforted him and placated his fears of more retribution, which he believed to be an anomaly, a specific reprisal expressed and related to a specific event, expressed through violent means and now purged, resolved and forgotten.

There was a lull in the ultraviolet spasms that seemed to shake the city like it was an infant, from the death of the Cuchulains' baby, and the burning of the Community Youth Organization, to the still-unresolved and fantastic gun battle at the headquarters of the Los Surenos and Azteca Cartel businesses, and the weird tales of a flying-man vigilante that had created excitement and hope in the city begging and praying for rescue; but then, nothing had happened: no clues, no more bloody uprisings, but gang truces, and so the people beheld the golden shaft of light once obscured, thought they felt the warm sunshine on their cold hopes, and dared to think that life could begin again, like the phoenix rising.

Samuel thought so, and became engaged to Florence McGuire now: because the storm seemed gone, the dikes holding, the rain dried up, and all of his and others' hard labor coming to fruition.

"We can effect change for the betterment of society," he told Florence the night he asked her to marry him; "it can be done, as long as people like you really care."

She smiled, marveling at his humility, holding his large hands. "You are an incredible man," she whispered. "I'm honored to be your wife," and she was wont to weep at his goodness.

"You inspire me, Flory," he whispered; "you have given up the life of excess to help those who never would have expert legal help; and as for me," he smiled, "well, I'm just a regular guy who knows the streets," and he gazed into her luminous eyes, "a lucky guy, to have a wife like you."

She held up a knife from the dinner table in his small home, held it briefly in the flame of the candle, and smiling slyly, whispered, "Shall we cut our palms and grasp hands, and declare a vow of poverty and a dedication to helping those oppressed?"

He laughed harder than she. "Yes—actually, yes, we should," he said, and picked up his knife, held it briefly in the flame of the candle, and held it to his palm.

She was taken aback, and whispered, "Or," moving closer to him, "we could just get married and let the ring do the binding."

He leaned over, and nearly touched her beauteous face with his. "But that is so old-fashioned; in today's world, this is more symbolic of trust and fidelity."

She cut her palm, and the blood flowed red.

He was shocked and amazed, but pleased, and immediately cut his; they clasped hands, and then kissed.

"You are a remarkable woman, Florence McGuire," he murmured.

"You are a remarkable man, Samuel Longfellow," she murmured.

It was a good life, a life they reasoned they deserved, and they felt protected because of who they were, what they had done, sacrificed, and fought for, establishing Justice and fighting tyranny for the teeming masses who were incapable of or not interested in bringing succor to the fallen.

The family of Rosa Moore was flourishing under the guidance of Samuel: Latonya was in college, Tommy in high school, and out of trouble; the other siblings were all well, all receiving good grades once Samuel had intervened to get the family to homes of their relations who finally realized that they could not let their own blood fall by the wayside. The harvest is rich, and bountiful, Samuel mused, but we must never give up, or all is lost; for, in the end, we are all the same family, who, once scattered long ago, must find each other again.

The truce between Tyrone Simpson of the 122nd Street Black Hoods and Marshaun de Thompson of the Original Gangbangers was holding, because Samuel intervened, as he helped unselfishly and guided, and was there to aid the youths when they came to him, and because Florence was there to proffer them legal counsel; they trusted him, listened to him, honored him. They are not all lost sheep, Samuel reasoned, and what shepherd, if one sheep wanders away from the flock of one hundred, does not go to look for that one? Each and every one of my sheep is precious to me, he mused.

Every reasoning man seeks a return to Paradise.

Emboldened by the success of the work outside of his home, and his upcoming wedding, and certain that his heart had discovered the entrance into Eden, he therefore sought to follow this path by more good works, so that, yes, even the hallowed Garden should appear before him. I must continue to deny myself, he often thought, as he worked with the troubled youth, it is a great miracle, that one can discover one's true intent only by abstaining from the pursuit of material pleasures, and untoward physical lusts; with Florence at my side, I will be able to take up the Cross and not allow it to fall so far that I cannot pick it up again.

He began to concentrate on establishing a rapport with the gangs of those citizens whose heritage was south, and often, farther south, of the American border, done through establishing his solid credentials as a man who worked tirelessly with schools to help all those who sought it—if they came to him, he did not deny them, nor ask for any vow or declaration of nonviolence, or willingness to receive counseling or drug rehabilitation. He was, as Florence once put it, there with his hand out to help any and all, unconditionally.

Heat will prostrate a person better than a hard, lucky punch, and you always see it coming; it is not inclined to deception as it slowly crawls over your skin and lays a thick, hot blanket on it; it trumpets its presence, gladly, like a confident general, because it knows that away from instruments of artificial cooling, and natural shade, you are its prisoner, and this is when—when you know you have abandoned all hope—that its scorching rivets bore into your brain and steal your equilibrium; yes, it is a marvel that this by-product of the sun, this handsome heat, actually is able to take a reasoning creature like man and coerce him into actions hitherto unknown to himself, to relieve himself of felicity, of charitable acts, of good intentions.

Samuel had street credentials because of his past and present good works as a negotiator of peace treaties, and a neutral presence in conflicts. He was, Florence once said, like the Swiss—you can always find refuge with him. Today, he had been invited to parlay by two of the most vicious and uncompromising gangs in the region: Los Magnificos Locos, and the Downtown Bangers. Dylan, wary of every step he and Samuel made as they approached the meeting place, had company, via a micro, two-way transmitter in his left ear.

The two men talked of many things: of Samuel's wedding, starting a new Community Youth Organization, the lives of youth they had helped, and then, as they walked past a group of four hard-looking boys, who were intending to betray a mean spirit, Dylan said, "And what of the Cartel's influence?" There was little else to say to prompt a response, for each knew what had happened the last few months; yes, the Cartels had transgressed the boundaries of drug-running in stealth operations while hiding in the bush, being carefully defensive and slowly seeking their place in the hierarchical wrong among society's villains by slowly laying a foundation, brick by brick, mud by mud, blood by blood; now, they sought to drop their palace of iniquity into the center of society all at once, in plain sight and broad daylight, by any means possible—without compunction to method or limit to madness— as they had in Mexico, and thus establishing themselves as the top act in all of North America: feared, indomitable, and so intimately entwined into daily life that to separate them seemed impossible.

What they had done in Mexico and Central America, they were now doing here; brash, bold operations preceded by expensive bribes for government officials and establishing a network of spies and communication so that they had real-time maps and screens of all the activities of any town or sector they chose to operate in—to be more precise: they had, in their ever-deepening pockets, banks, lawyers, judges, police officers, newspapers, taxi drivers, merchants, legislators, DEA agents, FBI officials, military personnel, the common man on the street, gangs, informants, petty criminals; they could get intimate details for just about any sensitive operation; they had surveillance cameras, satellite video, and were setting up radio towers for communication as they had done in Mexico. The die was cast, the players in place, the red button to be pushed for their own Operation Takeover, which was unofficially codenamed: Greenback USA.

Samuel took the query like a goalkeeper, pivoted nicely, and deflected this strike in his mind, then explained aloud. "You and I are the same, Dylan; I cannot live my life worried about who is around the corner or behind every tree; if I did, if," he said, forcefully, gesturing about himself, "we all did— then, the bad guys win; and just like that," he snapped his fingers, "that's all they would ever have to do, is show muscle, and the good guys—like us— fold, like sheep; but," he said, suddenly walking taller, his barrel chest thrust out bigger, his head held higher, "we are the good Shepherd, and we never abandon our flock."

Dylan smiled, slapping the big man's shoulder. "I would have been disappointed had you answered any other way."

The meeting place was set in Reagan Park on Manana Gloria Avenue at 12:00 p.m. Each side of the warring gangs was to send their two chieftains to decide the matter. At high noon, all of the principal players in this drama were in a location, chosen by Samuel, at faded, chipped, green wooden picnic tables in the shade of rows of olive trees; two heavily tattooed members of Los Magnificos Locos faced heavily tattooed members of the Downtown Bangers, while Samuel and Dylan, after shaking the hands of the men who stood before them, then moved in opposite directions, Dylan remaining close on the periphery of the parlay.

Samuel began, as the four chieftains used all the might of their hard glare at each other to establish an unyielding, uncompromising exterior that somehow must be melted into one common seal of peace, speaking as one with authority, in the sagacious voice of one who knows what was and what is, and the terror of what is to come. First, he set the ground rules: there would be no talk of the illegal activities that either side wished to pursue; each side would be given ample time to delineate its position; and each side would be expected to respect the speaker of the opposing group. He looked first to one group and then to another. "Wise men stand before me, who know that there are no winners in an endless war. This is strength, knowing that there will never be a victor, for no victory can be achieved in a war that never ends; both sides must be willing to the cease-fire, so that each side will then be victorious. Compromise must come, without the loss of face, in order to achieve this victory. Let us now discuss our grievances."

Los Magnificos Locos said that the Downtown Bangers had encroached on their territory, shot their homeboys, and interrupted other important activities that were instrumental to the survival of the gang, and, immediately, the Downtown Bangers said the same of the Los Magnificos Locos.

"Who here is a father?" Samuel asked them.

All of the chieftains raised their hands, and each pointed to pictures and names of their children so masterfully drawn on their bodies.

"Did you know, that right here," Samuel continued, pointing to the grass under their feet, "right here, was once the territory of Mexico, the land of your proud forefathers; there were big *haciendas* here, big *rancheros*, and *vaqueros* rode the range—and before them, what was Mexico, and more south of us now, was the land of Indians: Aztecs, Incas, Mayas, proud warriors, who built great cities and ruled for a thousand years." He deliberately paused, like any good teacher, to pique their interest, and then one of the Los Magnificos Locos chieftains asked what happened to them.

"They were conquered by the Spaniards, and by disease; and as the two people married, a new people were born," he paused once more, nodding toward them, "the Mexican; and they eventually won their freedom from Spain, and later lost land to the US in a war, and sold some to them later, too." He looked at them as if he sought to drive home his point straight into their stubborn brains. "You are descendants of great survivors: not only those in Mexico, but kin to great Indian tribes—Yuman, Chumash, Patayan, Serrano; people who traveled where we stand and roamed free for thousands of years— until the American came and took their land."

One of the Downtown Bangers exploded an obscenity bomb concerning America, and everyone watched the black smoke and felt the black tar and smelled the acrid scent settle upon them. He clapped hands with his brothers, and Samuel noticed the faint signature of pride on the faces of the other chieftains. He continued, passionate, urgent. "All of you are descendants of these proud warriors, and you feel," he clenched his large fists, "the need to stand tall and fight for what you think is yours and roam free for what you think is so rightfully yours; it is in your hot blood." He studied the faces of these men, who were not more than twenty-five years old, to see if they were following his story, and satisfied they were, he continued on. "Do you know what their biggest mistake was?" He waited, and one of the chieftains said that the Indians should have got together to fight the Americans. "Some did—but this did not matter, even though they were skilled riders: they wrote bareback on horses, and were masters of the bow and arrow, the tomahawk, and knew the terrain better than anyone; but in the end, it was simply more of them, than they; same for the Aztecs, Incas, and Mayas, and the disease that the Spaniards brought—technology too played a part, and so they were conquered." He looked intensely at both camps, and announced slowly, and carefully, gesturing outside of their small sphere. "There are more of them, than you—that is why you cannot win; and technology, too, now plays a part," and, he emphasized, "it did not help the Indians in Mexico or in America to fight each other—because you will never win that way, either, it just goes on and on…" He clenched his right fist and tapped the wood lightly. "Keep what you have, and be proud; no one has ever won a war on the streets by killing their opponent, and all it does is get them," he pointed outside again, "to come after," and he pointed them, "you." He looked at them as if he were their tribal chief. "What have any of you accomplished that your children will be able to share with their children?" He knew sentimental appeal was without merit any time except now, when they were vulnerable to accepting change. "Compromise: each side needs to give up something if you want to survive— it is the way we live; it is the way we have to live if we want our children to grow up without fear." He paused, nodding. "There is a wise saying: 'an old man in jail does not desire to be young again—he desires to be free.'"

And then these tough, hardened gang members, who had killed, robbed, and sold illegal substances on the street, who had been in jail numerous times, who drank heavily, who lived fast and hard, seemed like passive, obedient children playing nicely in the park—at least, the two chieftains of the Downtown Bangers dissolved into this weird, putty-like, too easily manipulated substance, while the other two merely stiffened and assumed a severe countenance as a yet unseen and menacing cloud passed over them.

Then, two long, black automobiles with heavily tinted windows came rolling up to the parking lot near the benches, and when the occupants exited, the above intransigence of the two other chieftains was explained, for as the eight men, dressed in black suits and ties, approached the private parlay, it was evident they were not here to help.

All of the men had the physical characteristics of the citizens just south of, or even further from, the California border. One of them, jet-black hair glistening in the sun, spoke as he came to rest in front of the bench.

"Gentlemen, allow me to introduce myself—I am Gustavo Calderon, an interested party for the Los Magnificos Locos," he began, mild-mannered, then placed his open hand upon his chest, "I'm terribly hurt that I did not receive my invitation for your little get-together—maybe it got lost in the mail, no?"

Dylan was watching the men, still wearing the special glasses that transmitted images to his control center, and then listening to messages that came back in his ear transmitter; and soon he knew who they were: representatives of the Azteca Cartel, three executives and two associates, along with three very large Central American bodyguards, the latter of whom were intensely watching him.

"So," the Cartel executive continued, feigning curiosity while he looked at all in attendance, and moving his hands about, "what have I missed? Who has the minutes? Have you already served tea?" He looked around, feigning surprise. "Oh, am I overdressed? Say, why all the long faces? Is this not merely a gathering of gentlemen of commerce to discuss their business affairs?"

One of the well-muscled, heavily tattooed, bald bodyguards walked over to Dylan and stood close to him, staring at him intensely. Dylan never flinched, looking still at the speaker, his face as cool and calm as one totally and serenely disaffected by his surroundings, in the same way a mountain of stone disregards a gnat that has landed upon its great girth.

"Is this a private affair? Oh, I know why all the curious faces," Gustavo continued, snapping his fingers, "you don't know why I am here—how perfectly rude of me. Well," and he rested a hand on each of the shoulders of his subordinate chieftains, and whispered, with a winsome look upon his swarthy face, "you might say I am their manager–financial adviser," and he looked at the two men with a sly smile, and a wink, "like their favorite uncle, and I have a vested interest in their affairs; so, what is this all about, eh?"

One of the Los Magnificos Locos referred to Samuel in the most abhorrent racist language available to the vulgar-trained, enthused mind, indicting him as the sole reason that they were being coerced to have a binding piece with their mortal enemies.

Gustavo frowned. "Tsk, tsk," he said, concerning his chieftain, "you should not refer to guests—no matter how well intentioned, no matter how wrong they are—in such derogatory terms; I believe," and he looked at Samuel; there was a glint of amusement in his own dark eyes, "we prefer the term 'negro,' is that not right, Mr. ..." And he walked over toward Samuel, his hand outstretched to accept a formal handshake.

The bodyguard was pushing hard against Dylan now, increasing the great force of his strong body against him, but found it was like a child who leans up against a man, and hopes to somehow move him.

Samuel, as was his nature, put out his hand, but Gustavo took his away, and a sneer formed on his face as he sniffed the air, and then asked, innocently, "Is it true you want my homies to be on an equal status with the Downtown Bangers? Well, maybe you didn't get the email, but we are bigger than they, and don't offer a truce to some small-time organization—it makes us look bad, see? Now," and he looked to the still-smoldering Bangers chieftains, "if they want to submit to us and join a much bigger and more important organization, they are more than welcome."

The bodyguard was pushing, without benefit of his arms, with all his might against what he could not perceive as an immovable object—for in his line of work, everything was movable, at least with his gun.

And then Dylan simply, and without warning, quickly moved back one step, thus allowing the bodyguard to go chasing the air with his flailing hands, which soon took the ground to keep him from completely falling. He arose immediately, and as he moved against his adversary, Gustavo waved him off; the latter looked to Samuel, who now spoke, looking directly at his obtrusive guest.

"We came here today in peace, and peace I offered them, and I offered to you," Samuel began, in a regal, prudent tone that was sown from experience and genuine sincerity; and he reached up, snapped off an olive branch, broke it into five pieces, handed one to the Bangers, who received it easily, two to the Locos, who refused them, and the last to Gustavo, who did not receive it.

Gustavo sighed, eyeing the branch, and then frowning, as he shook his head, said, "You know, this is really a noble gesture—truly," and he looked again at Samuel, and with both hands, crushed the twig, "but I am not noble the way you want me to be, which is weak." He let the crippled peace offering fall to the ground, and then he moved closer to Samuel, his scowl of contempt emanating not from this human soul, but from the soul of a stalking, wild beast.

The bodyguard was still glowering at Dylan, who still ignored him the way an adult tiger ignores an irksome cub, and then reacting to the burnt offering of Gustavo to his false god by allowing a shadow of the warrior to flash upon his face, ready to strike and destroy.

Gustavo summoned his chieftains to stand as he said to Samuel, "Let me give you some really good advice that you should really take to heart—and I only tell you this," he began, seemingly sincere, "because you seem well intentioned, but in reality, you're totally misguided," then he said it with a bothered smile; "don't play nursemaid with my people—we don't need our noses wiped by anyone, especially by the likes of you," and he let his scorn become a look of loathing, and then, after spitting largely at the feet of Samuel, he and his crew left.

One of the Downtown Banger chieftains said, standing next to Samuel, "I don't know why the Los Magnificos Locos came, when all along the Azteca Cartel controls them." He nodded his head and rubbed his whiskered chin, and then said, "I appreciate what you tried to do today," and he looked at the retreating cars, "but those punks won't leave us alone—it's the big dog calling the shots; hey, we ain't no angels, but these dudes the chieftains were with," and he lowered his voice, "are bad news, you know? Hey, Mr. Longfellow," his tone became soft, and humble, "I appreciate all you have done for my cousin Maricela, getting her that scholarship and all, and for my little brother, keeping him out of juvey," and his hardened heart cracked; so too did his hard exterior, and he was wont to cry, but held it at bay. "Well, you know, I needed to tell you about those other dudes, those bodyguards—hey, I ain't no saint, but those guys ain't got no soul…"

The other chieftain, who was standing next to Dylan, reached out to shake his hand, which the two did, and then said, smiling with admiration, "Man, what you did to that big, scary-looking dude—I'm down with that," but even the mere thought of the next subject dragged the fresh grin off his face. "But I wouldn't push it with them—not alone, you know what I mean?" He nodded, looking again with admiration at Dylan. "You know, I heard about the stuff you do at the youth center—where did you learn all that acrobatic and martial arts stuff?"

Dylan allowed a small smile to form for a mere second as he observed the cars driving away. "From pushing it with men such as they."

It was agreed by the remaining parties that it would be prudent for the Downtown Bangers to retreat from encroaching on the territory of the Los Magnificos Locos.

The very next day—not even a fortnight to throw off suspicion—but the next early morning, the two representatives of the Downtown Bangers who had come to the park were found butchered in their homes, their families similarly murdered, and their heads stuck on poles upon their lawns, with the same crayon-crawled-on-a-brown cardboard message: "stay in your own sandbox."

A month later, Samuel was to be married to Florence.

What is Best Served Cold

The concept of a family is more than the sum total of its parts—not just father, mother, a son, a daughter, or perhaps the extended members: grandfather, grandmother, aunt, uncle, niece, nephew; the more blood relatives who connect from the nucleus of the family, the greater the idea of the family, the greater the bond, the greater the pulse of the family heart; and the more difficulties overcome, the more tragedies endured, the more joy found, the sinews and bone of family strengthen, and the blood and spirit of the family thrive, and its soul takes residence in an exalted shrine—no matter how many mistakes made, or betrayals, or wrath shown; it becomes an enduring rock all cling to in any storm, something they must have no matter how bad the outside world becomes; the family united is a good light shining true to guide them home, where they will be welcomed no matter what they have done—for outside all is foreign; and inside they have already become as one, and not to be undone; every man and woman needs a safe harbor when the world seeks to crush them; and so, the family will forgive, and be forgiven, love, and be loved, find solace, and bring solace, for each member must do this for their own survival, and the survival of their family, if they seek to build through trust and love and patience, in this blessed sanctuary for all.

What is a family: only goodness and purity and love? Must a family be reflected by one grand concept that exists in the mystical lives of vaunted fictional characters, or are there endless variations?

There is one family that has a man, a woman, two boys, and one girl; they have many relatives, and friends, and often celebrate their union with festivals, as they once practiced in their home country in Central America; and what do they celebrate, but the success of their new life in America, and the freedoms and opportunities that come with it.

The husband, Edgar Castillo, had a beautiful wife, Eva, and three beautiful children, and was a successful and wealthy businessman who was generous with his money to his friends and relatives; everyone admired Edgar—he was humorous, intelligent, witty, and charming. He had come to this land with nothing, and became something, and prospered, was well respected, and loved; he was the embodiment of the American success story, as some would define it.

This night, there was a celebration of his newly bought house in the high hills, which was replete with the big backyard and plush with verdant plants, a swimming pool, the ornate fountain, the high-end barbecue station, the sauna, the sunroom, and the inside patio replete with bar and game room; and inside the house, there were six rooms, and a theater room, a recreation room, all lined with plush carpet and fresh paint and find wood, and tended to by a hard-working-for-low-wages, live-in maid, Lupe, who also took care of the children, who were with relatives this night; this maid, from south of the border, was herself slowly saving up enough money to send away for her two older children, whom she had not seen in five years. She had tried twice before to bring them here, but the human coyotes had simply stolen her payments and did not delivered their human cargo. She worked in silence around the Castillo family, much like a slave at a plantation, as a reminder of something not quite equal, a bad taste to be spat out, as a living testimony that it was better here than there; yet, of all the people in attendance, she was the only one who knew what Mr. Castillo really did to make so exorbitant a salary, for she, still being a commoner, could see and taste and smell certain things he did in this world that others here could not, because she could still, in her mind, smell and taste them in the world she had come from: arrogance, terror, and the increasing gloating that comes from excessive hubris.

It was twelve o'clock midnight when the lights of the house, and the sound system, and the surveillance system went dead, where no phone worked—no landline, no cell phones, even no computer, tablet, or walkie-talkie; it was if a master switch had been thrown and all electronic devices were now rendered unavailable to all.

But this was a momentary distraction to sever the ties of the people from their senses, and when the outside lights came on, there were more than a few uninvited guests now in the backyard; a dozen armed and massed intruders stood on the ready, surrounding the revelers, who were soon checked for weapons, and their cell phones and assorted electronic devices confiscated.

"Edgar Castillo," began one tall man in the black uniform of the Cartel assassins league, in a disguised, muffled voice, "you will tell us the whereabouts of Señor Vargas."

"I don't know what you are talking about," Edgar replied, more angry than afraid.

He signaled to another masked intruder, who grabbed a man and dragged him into the house, and immediately, a single, loud report came to the numb ears of the partiers. The masked man simply repeated his question, "Where is Mr. Vargas?"

"I don't know what you want," Edgar pleaded.

Edgar's wife, still clinging to him, trembling, cried out, "What do they want, Edgar? Who are these men?" As her disorientation increased and her comfort level decreased, she pointed toward her house, and cried out, "Did they just kill Carlos? What is going on?"

The leader signaled that the wife of the man just dragged in be taken, and in she went, followed by another loud report, and the other masked intruder came back outside, his automatic rifle still at his side.

Hysteria now swept the guests, albeit delayed, for the acts of retribution so swift upon the sudden appearance of the intruders, unhinged their senses, stunning them, as if they had been swept into a real-time nightmare.

The leader asked plainly once again, "Where is Mr. Vargas?"

"I don't know," Edgar cried, with an urgent pleading. "Who are you people?"

The leader signaled for four more attendees to be taken into the house, and soon, four loud shots were heard, and the other masked man came out to affirm the deed.

"I don't believe you've killed them," Edgar cried, waving his hands frantically about; "why are you taking them inside to be shot?"

The masked leader ordered the curtain to be drawn away from the family room, to reveal six bloodied, dead bodies lying in a heap on the plush carpet. "Take the maid," he said.

The remaining guests watched in horror as the screaming maid walked through the outdoor patio, into the family room that faced the backyard, and was placed before a man with a rifle, who subsequently raised it and shot her dead, for all to plainly see. The masked leader turned toward Edgar again, and said once more, "Where is Mr. Vargas?"

"Who sent you?" Edgar cried, worried now.

The leaders signaled for two more protesting, imploring guests toward the execution room, but these guests were the sister and brother-in-law of Edgar.

"Please don't kill them," Edgar cried, "I don't know anything."

"Maria Ortiz says you know where he is."

Edgar started, his face betraying his mind's eye. "I don't know who that is..."

"Who are you people?" his wife sobbed as she clung to her husband. "Why are you doing this to us?"

The leader motioned for the brother and sister-in-law to be taken away, but Edgar cried out, "Tell me what you want to know, I'll do anything."

The leader held up a cell phone with a picture of Edgar and a young pretty woman engaged in a series of amorous poses.

"Who is she?" his wife said, incredulous, as if the possibility of her husband being unfaithful had temporarily erased the horror of the moment.

Then the next picture became more graphic.

"Pictures can be altered," Edgar said, but his words were inauthentic.

And then came more pictures of other women, and men with him ingesting cocaine, and other men surrounding him who had a dangerous demeanor about them.

She pulled away from him. "What is going on, Edgar—please tell me!"

"Where," the leader said, creating an icy chill with the word, which was a prelude to death, "is Mr. Vargas?"

Edgar shook his head. The leader motioned for the brother and sister-in-law to continue into the killing field.

"Do you know, Edgar, do you—if you know, for goodness' sake, please tell them!"

"They'll kill me."

The leader of the masked men halted once more the funeral march of the sister and brother-in-law.

"What?" she cried, as her sister, and brother-in-law were taken into the family room, and she gestured toward them, "what about them?" And she grabbed her breasts. "What about your own wife?" A man came for her and grabbed her arm. "Edgar! What have you done—who are you?"

Edgar watched as his sister and brother-in-law were forced to kneel before a masked intruder, who then put a rifle to the back of their heads, pulled the trigger, and then faced the masked leader. "Did the El Dorado Cartel send you?" he asked, numb.

"Cartel?" his wife cried, as she was led away, as she continued to look behind herself, screaming at her husband. "Tell them, Edgar—for goodness' sake, please tell them anything you know!"

Edgar was thinking that if he could indeed somehow survive this night, he could always get another wife—but the children he must have, and then he replied to the masked man, "Tell Señor Alvarez: if he kills me, this is war."

"It already is," the leader said, dryly.

The screaming and yelling and protesting madly wife was dragged to the family room, kneeled down before a masked intruder, a rifle put back of her head, and then came the loud explosion, and there was blood everywhere.

"I can help your organization," Edgar said, looking around now at a place empty of all of the guests, desperately seeking the last remnants of equanimity, "I know things."

"You're a nobody; we don't need lower-level punks, eager lapdogs who fetch bones for their master."

"I am a contract killer—I have killed dozens of targets."

"Petty hits."

Edgar described some of them in graphic detail, and then said, "I can name them—I will kill anyone, anywhere: women, children, anyone! I can be invaluable to your organization; I can tell you about Mr. Vargas, and many others—they trust me."

The leader was still as unmoving as a marble statue. "Why should we trust a man who rats out his own people, and easily lets his own friend and family members die?"

"They're not my people—and the people here tonight were just acquaintances, or relatives forced upon me, and as for my wife, well..." He looked at that heap of bodies in the family room, and then back to the masked leader. "You're on top now, everybody knows you're taking over the drug trafficking here, and we are on the way out."

"I don't believe your story about killing anyone—you're simply a collector of garbage that spills out."

"You don't know! I have killed dozens—remember the Carson Street shooting? That was me and my boys! Three punk street pushers who got in our way—put down, just like that," and he snapped his fingers at them, "and there were three of your boys at the Lexington warehouse; and how about five of your men outside of the gambling casino, which was made to look like a robbery—that was me and my boys! I can give you the details." He gestured about himself. "How do you think I can afford to live like this, huh? I get paid a lot of money to do the dirty work for Vargas—work other guys don't want because they pretend to have a conscience; bah! They can buy my conscience for the right price—anybody or anything, just the way my bosses like it—no limits, no questions, no hesitation; that's how you become successful in my business."

"It is easy for criminals," the masked man replied, unimpressed, "to kill other criminals."

"Oh, yeah? Me and my boys blew up this Community Youth Center— yeah, that was us," he stabbed his own chest with his finger, his face animated as he waved his arms about, "and that bratty kid—that baby of those idiot do-gooders—that was me!" he yelled, boasting, more pride suffusing his voice. "Yeah, that's right, I drilled that little brat—boom, boom," and he pointed his hands, shaped like a gun, at them, stabbing the air twice, "no regrets, no worries, no cares, just like driving by and shooting rabbits from my car—I couldn't have cared less when I did it; and after it was done, and I got paid a cool one hundred thousand Gs—that's right: a cool hundred thousand, more money than a typical loser makes in a year—and tax free, too—and afterward I went out for a couple of beers with my boys to celebrate. I told you," he pounded his chest, his face reddening, "that's who I am, don't you understand? Whatever you need done, if the price is right, I'll do it, I'll be happy to do it, I love doing it—don't you get it, that's what I do, I'm good at it, and I really love it," and he became even more impassioned, "and I sleep real good at night, because I don't care who I kill, because my reward is all this, this," he shouted, waving about the place, "and, you know what, eh? You know what, when all is said and done—it makes me feel like a man." And he stood there with his hands open, as if expecting the masked man to embrace his emboldened spirit. And when this did not happen, he continued on, more desperate than ever, "I can give you details—anything you want to know; what do you say, huh?" And then, clapping his hands, looking around at the encircling masked men, he presently gave up the position and routines of the highest-ranking American drug lord of the Azteca Cartel, Caesar Gonzalez.

The lights went off again, and in a moment, when all of the lights at the luxury home came on, the men were gone. Edgar, bewildered, walked into the family room and was stopped cold in his tracks, for there stood all of the guests, and his wife, alive, soaked with fake blood and flesh.

"Eva, you're alive!" he cried, moving toward her, but she was having none of it.

Her face was like one who has seen what must not be seen, although has to be seen, and perhaps, even was somehow known, but was painted in rose-colored filters, where she felt crushed, suffocated, abandoned. "You are dead to me." She would not speak his name now, for she instinctively knew that the only way for her dead and buried self to be resurrected from the cold grave was to cut him completely out of her life, as if he were a malignant, fast-spreading tumor—this was no mere affair he had had, a misjudgment in business, or losing his job (her upbringing had been poor yet moral, unassuming yet proud, and no matter how much she had veered from this model as of late, his now-revealed true identity was still the antithesis of who she truly was); and now, she would plot a course back. She turned her back on him, as did the other guests, who quickly left, for anyone with any sense of the recent hazards in society realized what was presently to occur to him.

"Get out," she said, her rising voice concealed in venom.

"Eva, we need to work this out."

"Get out," she cried, her face trembling.

"We need to…"

She turned around, her face burning with wrath, her voice shrieking, "You're a monster—you were going to let as all die—and you're a murderer—for murderers, you're a monster! And everybody knows it now! And an adulterer! I can't believe it," she screamed, holding her head tightly to try and keep in the exploding pain, "how did any of this happen?"

Now, he was mad. "Come on, Eva, like you didn't know I was doing more than imports and exporting cars."

"Get out," she cried, pointing to the door, "you sicken me!"

The face he had always shown her, the face of the kind husband and breadwinner, good father and friend, was shorn by the predator beneath it. "Yes, I work for the Azteca Cartel, and I have killed many people, but now I am in charge of distributing the drugs…"

Her outrage cut into his words. "What! What! You got a promotion—no more murdering innocent people, no more killing innocent babies, just stick their faces in cocaine and heroin, and meth…" And she began to sob. "It's a nightmare—I should have known…" And when he tried to touch her, she violently pulled away from him, her entire body shaking. "Don't ever try and touch me again, and just get out!"

"We can't stay here, Eva, those men…"

"Yes, yes, those men," she turned around, realization illuminating her face, "what were they about? What do they want? Why didn't they kill us? What is going on?"

Shed now of his false exterior, he began to think as a soldier, talking in a trance, as if to his own kind. "Were they my own people, testing me? I have heard of it—maybe that's why no one was really killed; but if that is the case, I failed; maybe it was the El Dorado Cartel, really, but then they didn't kill anyone, and they would have; they are just like us; but maybe they were the Feds, trying to trap me." He shook his head. "But either way, my people will know I gave up Vargas, and we are dead."

"What you mean 'we' are dead? You are the killer, Edgar," she yelled, not meaning to say his name.

"Don't you get it, Eva—when my people go after someone, they kill anyone else connected to them; that's the way it is—it's called being safe."

She cursed at him, unlike even her most irate self. "You're insane—I'm calling the police." She moved toward that telephone, then became hysterical. "What about my babies, what about them—if they are harmed…"

He ran to the phone and dialed the house where his children were spending the night, and soon hung up. "They're safe—they'll be safe."

"How do you know, huh? You said these people kill anybody connected to the one they want to kill—look around, Edgar, that is you!" she screamed, pointing at him. "My life is a nightmare right now because I married a hitman—no, a man who is helping to destroy this country. I'm calling the police," and she moved again toward the phone.

He stopped her. "I am not going to jail, Eva." He said it in such a way that the threat of harm to all who stood in his way was buzzing in the electrified air. He picked up the battery phone, a backup to the cell phones that had been confiscated. He placed it in his pocket.

"Then I'll drive to the police station, Edgar—the police need to know what is going on if I'm going to have my babies protected."

"Your babies—what about 'our babies'?"

"You lost the 'our,'" she cried, in his face, "when you slept with whores," and she turned toward the door.

"I know how to fix this—I will go to the El Dorado Cartel." She responded to this statement by spitting upon him. "I will tell them about my people, and they will accept me—it happens, I am switching sides. I can be invaluable."

"Why don't you just quit, eh? Estupido!" she cried, slapping her forehead.

"Corpses, that's why, Eva—corpses." He tried to gently take her by the shoulders, but she broke free of him. "Don't go to the police, Eva, don't—it would only make it worse; believe me, the Cartel will retaliate against you. Let me take care of it." He went to the door, turned around, and said, with affection. "I trust you—and despite what happened tonight, I love you," and he retired into the misty night.

He was at the headquarters of the El Dorado Cartel in thirty minutes—the other side always knows where the opposition resides. He was frisked and then was allowed to walk into the office of a high-ranking El Dorado Cartel executive. He planned on not mentioning the incident at his house. He sat down on the black leather seat, about to light a cigarette.

The man behind the big steel desk said to him, "Here, let me help you with that," and then took the white cigarette and broke it apart. "Secondhand smoke is bad for your health—what are you trying to do, kill me?"

Edgar tried to dump an artificial smile into the uncertain air, but it rang false, so he subdued it. "I can be of service to organization," he stated, flatly.

The big man, seemingly uninterested, still working at his desk, did not reply for several minutes, then, looking up, said, "Paperwork—it never ends." He seemed now to notice Edgar again, and recognized his reason for being present. "So, tell me something I need to know."

He did: Edgar told the man many things he knew about the Azteca Cartel, enough for the El Dorado Cartel to temporarily win the turf war on US soil, which had been raging for over a year. The man took out some chewing gum, offered it to Edgar, who declined, popped it into his own mouth, sat back in his chair, playing with his fingers while he looked up at the white ceiling, then summoned his adjutant to come in to take the recording of Edgar's detailed narrative of the day-to-day operations of the Azteca Cartel operations here, and have as much of it as possible verified.

Ten hours later, while Edgar was still sitting patiently in the chair, after the men had left for several hours, the executive came back, sat down behind his desk, did more paperwork for several hours, and then looked up at a nervous and agitated Edgar. "Oh," he said, as if remembering only now that the man was still there, "most of what you said checked out." He simply stared at him.

Edgar felt great relief. "Good, good; now, let's talk about where I fit in your organization."

The man frowned. "Where you fit in?" He pointed to himself. "That is my question to pose; this isn't the sticks—we aren't bullies here; I will let you know where you fit." He sniffed the air like he was sniffing the scent of the man, and said, as if uninterested now, "You can go—my aides will help you get situated," and he continued his work.

Edgar celebrated, smiling and cheering as he walked out of the building. He immediately called Eva, and told her all was well. He got into his car and began to drive.

He was about halfway home when he received a phone call on the prepaid cell phone he had recently purchased. The El Dorado Cartel had a job for him. He was overjoyed.

In an hour, he was with two other men in a dark sedan, listening to them explain the hit on his old organization.

"Yes, that makes sense, yes, that is good," Edgar said, sitting in the back, as if his enthusiasm was necessary to win them over, as if it was necessary to approve of the job, "after all I told your boss, it needs to be done; good, good."

The car stopped at a remote spot in the hills. The hit was to come by in about half an hour, and Edgar should sit tight, the man with the dark sunglasses and tattoos said dryly. Edgar nodded, and said he needed a smoke. He opened the door and stepped out to light a cigarette.

Instead, the man with the tattoos lit up Edgar's head with six rounds of bullets.

When the rosy, freshly laundered sky smiled on the valley, a bloodied corpse was found on a remote street, with a sign that said, "Keep your rats in your own sewers."

A rat ran up and sniffed the stiffened corpse, turned its whiskered nose up at it, and then ran back to the sewers.

This tale is not yet over, for there were a few more players to follow. Let us see one of them now as she sat on a green park bench under the shady trees in Huntington Park.

"Hello, Lupe," a voice broke the tension about her.

She smiled, looking to where she thought the voice originated. "*Bueno*—hello."

"Edgar has met his fate. You are safe."

She sighed, and said, meekly, "Did you…"

"No—it was done by his own greedy, traitorous hand." The voice paused. "We could not have done this operation without you: information about the guests who would come, what they generally wore, pictures of them, who they were, having confidence enough in us to allow us to video you being 'killed.' You would make a good secret agent."

She nodded, still waiting for the good news.

The bodiless voice was somber. "It is a difficult thing to find and bring two children from another country—there is an unhealthy fear about immigrants now." She nodded again, wringing her hands. "There are legal barriers, societal obstacles—we did all we could." She tried to smile in acknowledgment, but it was not to be; one cannot seem happy when one's heart is genuinely breaking. "Of course, you will be paid."

"I don't care for the money," she whispered, nearly sobbing; "I care for my two babies."

The voice was silent for too long. "You are a good person, Eva, and your goodness will always serve you well; for there will always be those who recognize it and want to help you; it is the rightful heir of a soul to do so."

The voice became animated, and full of joy. "Behold, your goodness has saved you."

She was bewildered, but only for a moment, for in the next instant, she instinctively knew that she was not alone, and being alone for so long when you yearn for those whom you dearly love puts you into a state of being forlorn and experiencing misery that can be felt in suffocating waves about yourself; but now, she no longer felt trapped inside the oppressive shell of loneliness and sorrow, as it had ruptured and opened up and let in the warm sun, the fragrant air, the melodic song of the birds that she had long ago stopped feeling and smelling and hearing. She turned around, and what did she see?

She saw her darling, precious, life—her life's blood standing right there with the grandest smiles in the whole wide world on their young, shining faces.

"Mama," they cried together, and they ran toward her, and she toward them, and, O, how they hugged each other in authentic love, real, vital, life-giving love and happiness, two more halves, now whole; three more drifting souls, now on course; a community disintegrating, there, a community of family healed, here; the world right side up, balanced, thriving, for hearts once disjointed were joined, beating as one, and tranquility and peace was born afresh around them; and behold, it affected those who felt its warm sympathy, and felt its gentle touch, and they too remembered that love surpasses all things.

"Paul," Robert said, watching the family walk to their car, "you old romantic, you have become sentimental in your old age."

Paul smiled. "It is all your fault—you are my teacher."

Robert smiled. "You taught me today, Paul—what you said to Eva was very beautiful."

Paul blushed, and shrugged his shoulders.

"I will drive us home today, good and loyal friend," Robert said, putting his arms around him, and the two friends retired back into the secret layer of combating the underworld of this new organization of crime, but with the beautiful notion that, sometimes in battle, after the earth is scorched and the bodies charred and the blood has seeped into the ground, beautiful, golden flowers once again take their rightful place.

The blond-haired, blue-eyed man, who stood next to the bedside of the woman, would presently seal the last act in the aforementioned drama; he watched with the ardor and passion of a good and faithful husband who gazes upon a good and faithful wife. "In her, I trust," he mused, smiling as he observed the serenity and kindness of her beauteous face; and as he bent down, he murmured, ever so slightly, even so lightly, "It is done," and kissed her on her fair brow, then returned to a far corner of their house to concentrate on work that men like he had decided must be done, no matter the time, no matter the place.

And after he had retired from her, upon her fair cheeks, pious tears—produced from the most private house of sorrows—appeared, silent, warming, cleansing; and then she presently fell to rest, to dream of days passed, when there was more laughter in their hearts, and days future when what must be done would be finished, and where there might be more laughter in more hearts.

A Time to Celebrate

And now, let us slip back to a time before our five Crusaders departed for their Mexico adventure, and met a man, walking along a road, who had a most interesting story about a town called Yermo...

Tyr and Enkidu were stationed in obscurity on one side of the park, and Arjuna and Finn on the other, watching the peace parlay through a variety of tools: binoculars, scope of a rifle, luminous screen of a tablet that was emitting an extreme close-up satellite, real-time video of the park, and when the Los Magnificos Locos mice left with their brother-rat Azteca Cartel members, it was Tyr and Enkidu who briefly trailed behind one of the cars, with Tyr leaning out and firing a small dart with a tracking device, which would dissolve in one hour's time, that stuck on the back of the chrome bumper. It would have been easier to attach the dart while the cars were parked, but there had been three men left to guard them to keep a lookout for the authorities.

The location of the Cartel headquarters was established, and the four-man team of Crusaders began their vigil: Cyrus of Germany, with Horatius of Italy, alternating hours with Yoshitsune of Japan, and Rustem of Iran. Every nuance of the operation was noted: catalogued, put in the database, cross-referenced; facial recognition used on the residence and visitors; and their driving routes and places frequented and detailed.

It was a Friday morning, not too long after Samuel had told Dylan that Tyrone and Marshawn had informed him that the Azteca Cartel was planning something against Samuel. Arjuna and Rustem were parked two streets down from the Azteca Cartel building, when they noticed more activity than normal.

"Something," Yoshitsune uttered.

Rustem, knowing that his partner, saying little, meant saying much, radioed in to Control Central about suspicious activity. Twenty Crusaders were alerted, equipped, and ready to go in twenty minutes.

At approximately nine o'clock in the a.m., the sun had not yet reached its daily zenith of brightness, and the birds were texting the joyous message of the liberating power of the air, when carloads of dark-suited men loaded into dark-colored cars, preceded by other men loading black suitcases into the backseats.

"Something big," Yoshitsune uttered.

"It has begun," Rustem radioed in; "all operatives stand by."

The six large, black sedans crawled along the road like sleepy alligators coasting along the riverbank in the warm water, and like the alligator, when they sighted their target, they prepared to seize it and go into a death roll. Once a target was acquired, the masked men from the cars embarked and, armed with automatic weapons, moved around the red-brick building to secure any entry and exit point; once the men radioed that all was in readiness, they moved in to enwrap their victims in their suffocating grip and crush them.

None of the human alligators touched the hair on one unsuspecting human antelope come innocently to the waterhole, for they were met by an unmovable force that abrogated their position, authority, and life on earth; for there was no activity inside the building, but a sham event, where Crusader men and women were hosting an exact replica of a ceremony in the house of God, replete with cars parked everywhere and music coming from the inside, and now welcomed their guests as surely as the early bird catches the fat, lazy worm.

The plan, set out by Dylan after the parlay, was carefully orchestrated so that the Cartel would think this old church building was the wedding, and it had been advertised as such, until the morning of it, and then was switched to a mile away. Eleven Cartel associates now lay dead inside the building, and their bodies were then hauled into black plastic bags, placed in unmarked white vans, and driven for disposal to a site that was unknown to ordinary folks and even extraordinary ones. Even as this cleanup was occurring, a call came in.

"We're being hit," Rustem cried, amid the gunfire; he was stationed on the periphery of the church where the actual wedding of Samuel and Florence was, where one member of the glorious event never showed, as she had been kidnapped that morning and tortured until she had only recently told her captors where the real wedding was occurring, and was then murdered.

Twenty Cartel members had been deployed to take down every person in attendance, but had met heavy resistance by the primary Crusader force, which had been increased in number once the missing female friend of Florence was reported to Rhiannon. The members inside the church were ushered into the cellar while the gun battle raged around them. Police sirens were heard, close, numerous, and clamoring, as if to say, "SWAT is on the way."

The Cartel army dashed away into their armor-plated cars and raced away, taking two dead, four wounded, and their smashed-into-smithereens and dispersed-down-yellow-streaked backs, their true form, the cowardly bully.

The Crusaders also departed; so too the two Crusader technicians who had bled the loud wail of the sirens through the loudspeakers that sat above their car, which was parked only a block away, and also spoke "police chatter" on the radio frequency the Cartels were known to listen to; so when the real police arrived, there were nothing but shaken and alive wedding members, spilt blood, and frustration as to the identity of the vigilantes.

The wedding did take place, at the insistence of the bride and bridegroom, who later did leave, although in the midst of numerous armed police officers, with much joy, and pomp and circumstance, and journeyed on their honeymoon to a faraway place even their worst enemies could not find.

When Samuel returned, he came directly to the small house of the Cuchulains, sat down opposite them, and said, very plainly and succinctly, after telling them he and Florence were temporarily living in a rented house outside of town, "It was you," he began, looking at Dylan, "who convinced the minister to move the wedding." Dylan did not flinch whatsoever. "Do you know these vigilantes—no," he shook his head, cutting the air sideways with his big right hand; "are you with them—both of you; of course, where one goes, goes the other."

There was no reason to hesitate, for the man before him was either for them, or against them, and as Dylan already knew the answer, he answered, simply, while holding the hand of Rhiannon, who squeezed her assent. "Yes, we are who you believe we are."

"Good," Samuel cried, standing, his hand extended toward them, "where do I sign? You saved the lives of one hundred people—and many more before that." He shook the hands of both of them, and then embraced Rhiannon, tears pooling in his eyes. "I have had time to think about it all, I really have," he said, calmer now, and then in a tranquil, yet peaceful tone, "when I was a child, I used to speak as a child, think as a child, reason as a child; when I became a man, I did away with childish things."

The Crusaders were now three hundred and eighty-five, plus one.

Those Who Serve

The commander at the Los Angeles division of the Federal Bureau of Investigation stood before the august assembly of agents who had long ago taken an oath to serve the general public, ensure their well-being, and protect them from all harm, both foreign and domestic; and they all knew this pledge, once difficult but impossible to uphold, was slowly, like a yarn of promises to keep, unraveling strand by frustrating strand every single day; and yet, there was a roaring, cleansing fire of hope they were forced by law to undermine and vigorously oppose.

He was grim—he was normally grim, it was the position; but as of late, he had few celebratory reasons to negotiate joy upon his pale countenance; his voice was heavy as he began, but then, as he spoke, it lightened.

"Some of you know what happened last night, and for those who do not—well," he began, standing at the front of the small room, "Operation Roundup was to culminate in the arrest of high-ranking Azteca Cartel members who have been warring with the El Dorado Cartel; six months of investigation and surveillance, outstanding undercover work, led us to a house in the southwest area; look, we had this whole operation covered from A to Z, and when our men converged on the place, well, let's say we had our heads handed to us." He looked to the agent in charge of the operation, and said, respectfully, "I'm going to let Victor Fuentes take it from here," and he stepped aside, relieved.

Victor was nearly forty years of age, with jet-black hair combed straight back, an agent most of his adult life. He was not so grim, but he should have been.

"Our intel was good, our timing perfect, everything in place; but when we went in, it was as if we had been worked by the Cartel, as if it was their operation to take us down—but they did not succeed: no, they failed miserably," he began, in a clinically, emotionless recital of a factual event, but emotion broke his training and indifference. "It was an ambush: the houses were empty, and then forty well-armed Cartel soldiers began to fire upon us." His eyes narrowed, as if he saw the reflection of the past in a mirror, darkly. "But they did not long use their weapons, for in an absurdly short time, they were dead," and his face grew curious, as if he now saw the battle in a mirror, brightly, "for the Defenders had come, and with them, our salvation." He saw the possibility of his men's deaths, but in reality their lives, and he had been irrevocably captured by admiration and gratitude for the rescuers; but he was, still, sworn to uphold the law, despite his internal allegiance to a greater good. "Though we were saved by these men—and perhaps women—who presently vanished, they cannot be allowed to roam free to do as they see fit in a country governed by the laws of jurisprudence; we cannot forfeit our sworn duty to uphold the law to accommodate," he paused, looking at the animated faces of other agents, "lawbreakers, no matter what good they afford society."

There is always one man among any band of brothers who must state what ought to be; and now that man stood up. "Four times in two months the Defenders have intervened on our behalf—more than one hundred agents owe their lives to them." His brother had been saved.

"Vigilantes," the commander interjected, "are not excused, no matter what their benefits to society—we are the law," and he pointed vigorously to the realm outside the sacred hall; "not anyone who gets an itch to play marauder and superhero."

"Are they against us? Are they with the Cartels?" another agent responded. "Why can't we work with them?" He had been saved by them, too. "How much time will we spend trying to take down the good guys?"

"No—most decidedly no—they are lawbreakers." the commander said.

"But they know the Cartels better than we—we need them."

"That is enough, Agent Ferguson," the commander cried.

Agent Ferguson righted himself and respectfully assimilated back into the ranks of those who dutifully acquiesce no matter the orders or means to accomplish it.

But one man's spark is another man's fire.

Early the next morning, the commander called Victor at his home, and asked him if he would consent to go to a most unusual crime scene. He complied.

He came upon an apocalyptic vision normally reserved for Third World barbarity, for it was a house—or, formally the outward appearance of a house, its structure so shattered and buried by holes that it resembled more an ancient relic of a hyper-violent war. There was a man standing near it, being interviewed by local police, when Victor approached him and introduced himself, and shortly they shook hands.

"Rough night?" Victor asked, as if to separate himself from the probing questions he knew had pummeled the man.

The man smiled briefly. "Termites." But there was more than just a jocular response to mask anxiety or relief here, Victor noted; there was an element of abundant certitude and cockiness, and arrogance about the whole affair in the handsome visage of the man, which lit up his entire posture, as if this incident was a trifle, a mere annoyance.

Victor smiled at the audacity of the steely reserve of the man. "Tell me about these industrious termites."

The narrative was light and easy, drained of full facts, meant to obscure greater talents from prying eyes. The man began.

"It was about two o'clock in the morning. I was working on a project in the garage, when I heard a noise." This was a bald-faced lie; the man had been in his house. "I saw many men with rifles outside."

The man's face was placid, sincere, and cool, and Victor was having none of it. "How many men?"

The man had already rehearsed that lie well enough, and then said easily, "I am not sure—maybe about seven or eight." This was another willful lie—it had been fourteen highly trained, well-paid, camouflaged-wearing assassins. The man stopped his narrative—it was his way to draw out the queries of his interrogators, so he could concentrate on his seamless, false story.

"Then…"

"Well, sir," the man continued; the seemingly significant utterance of "sir" seemed sincere, as it related to respect, "luckily, I had just turned out the light, so I hid." This man had done the complete opposite of hiding like an average, frightened citizen; in fact, he had gone straight toward the danger.

Agent Fuentes nodded appropriately, his brown eyes narrowed as he studied the incredible physique of the young man. "What happened next?"

"Those men began shooting into the house—which was empty—so, I just stayed hidden." Actually, at the first detection of the assassins by his surveillance system, he had simply applied who he was: a warrior supreme.

"How long did they fire?"

"Oh, about two minutes, I guess." He seemed like an ordinary hick, a plebian in the sophisticated ways of combat; yet, he had been on these paid killers the moment they opened up on him.

Agent Fuentes, having already been briefed by subordinates about the incident, asked questions as if he knew only what the man related to him. "Did you hear them say anything?" The man answered in the negative once more. "Did you hear them going into the house?" The man answered in the negative. "Did you have access to a phone?" No, came out once again, one more patch of plaster upon the wall between him and the facts, filling in the holes and strengthening the foundation he had recently moved around to keep his quarry off balance. "They would check the garage to be thorough…"

The answers of the man reflected a tacit agreement that he pretended the agent had no idea of the outcome. "Well, I suppose I would not be standing here if not for my rescuers." Actually, he had killed every assassin by himself.

"You're lucky they were in the area—maybe they were at the local donut shop." He smiled briefly. "Well, tell me about it."

"I heard more gunfire—and screaming and shouting, and then silence; and then I looked up and saw men—I suppose it was men, although a woman might have been among them—dressed in all black, standing around the house, checking the bodies of the ones who had been shooting."

"How did you know they were different from the shooters—weren't all of them dressed in black?"

"Oh, yes, but the first group wore separate clothing—the new group looked like they wore a one-piece uniform."

"You have a keen eye."

"Well," he offered, shrugging his muscular shoulders, "I guess you notice things like that when there is a crisis."

"And then what happened?"

"My rescuers just left." There, he had finished his seemingly simple, naive story, as if he, an innocent, naive bystander, was lucky to be alive; when, in reality, he had been in the empty house—empty because he had recently moved his belongings from it—when the assassins had struck; two of them had come in, one from the front door, another through the back door, and he had taken out first one, then the other through his learned-on-the-job, hand-to-hand combat training, then acquired their AK-104 rifles and began to fire at them as they closed in.

"Do you have any idea why these men attacked you?"

The man, his face as stolid as ever, replied, equanimity still washing over his face like a mighty river. "I worked at the Community Youth Organization."

"Oh, yes, of course—it was burned down a few years ago; and there was a man whose wedding was attacked just the other day…"

"Samuel Longfellow—a good man, we work together."

"A good cause, your youth center; yes," he said, smiling, "we need more good men like you." He paused. "So, are you married? Well, thank goodness, she was not here." He looked around at the cataclysmic, unreal damage in so quiet and respectful a neighborhood. "But you are all right—hold on," he halted, as if in a genuine attempt to find answers, "wasn't there one more incident connected to the burning of the youth center..." He really did not remember, but suddenly, he gave light to this confounding mystery.

The man with the long hair the color of straw and the Irish accent said, slowly, "Yes, my little baby boy was killed by shooters." Nothing more escaped from his closely guarded, sacred memory.

"I am so sorry; yes, I remember now—I am so sorry."

But this day, those petty killers from the same cowardly clan of criminals would not have the slightest chance of survival against the boy's father.

"Yes, now it all makes sense; Mr. Longfellow spoke of the incident in the park—my guess is, this must be retaliation."

Now, Dylan had a virtual lock on the why, where, and what for, and the Crusaders, having arrived after the deed was done, had made it appear as if they had indeed been inside and outside the house as Dylan had been when the assassins were attacking.

Dylan had been in the house and saw the two men come in, disarmed them, killed them, took their weapons, signaled the Crusaders for help, and immediately commenced firing out the front window; then running swiftly to the back and shot through the window, while still holding the other rifle and shooting out of the front window; then, he ran to the opposite side, firing this rifle, then the other, but this did not deter two assassins, who burst into the back door, and one through the side window, all of whom he quickly dispatched; and confiscating their weapons, tossed the ones whose ammunition he had already used up, and continued running wildly about, shooting through every available window and door.

The surveillance camera showed ten men left, too many to manage alone outside, so he needed to invite more of them inside; thus, he continued firing, nonstop, helter-skelter, a steady stream of bullets spitting fire into the hot night; two more men crept in, each through a window and firing and all the while, but quickly brought down by his superior guile as he shot from a hideaway closet he had built in; and then six crashed through at various entry points, and Dylan, despairing that he had recently filled up the escape tunnel he had constructed in the back room, stealthily crept out of the back window, still seeing the infrared images of his surveillance camera through his special glasses. He could see the assassins' every move.

He killed one around the corner, and then seeing the man inside running to the front, he reversed course and, rounding of the other side, opened fire on three of them as he fell to the ground, killing all of them. That left four, who, apparently still not in charge of their faculties, elected to continue the battle; but Dylan knew their exact whereabouts at all times and, ascending to the shingled-roof, shot them dead.

Now, the sirens would come, but not before the Crusaders arrived, who had already caused a seemingly serious, but in reality, innocuous disturbance in another region to draw police away from this spot, and did what must done to cleanse the area of evidence of one man's incredible defense, and allow it to be contributed to the work of the Defenders, leaving Dylan, without a scratch, wound, or bruise, to narrate his tall tale to the authorities.

Curiously, no outside cameras captured the mayhem, Dylan's surveillance system having been taken by the Crusaders, and other systems in the area having their video being wiped clean; and no witnesses came forward, especially those neighbors whom the Cuchulains had bonded with by helping them with their emotional and physical woes. The law enforcement officials bade Dylan well, and left, after watching him drive away with Rhiannon, his car having been disabled by the unwelcome intruders, and Agent Fuentes, half-smiling and nodding his head, thought, with much amusement, "I may have been born at night—but not last night, Mr. Cuchulain."

Year of the Cartels

The complexion of a culture is determined from its origins, and through the intricate makeup of new arrivals mixed in with the indigenous population, the presence of norms and traditions expressed as societal sediment rests undisturbed; each country is uniquely different, and some are ever shifting as new people come in to disturb and color the existing sediment.

As it is, there is a pattern established to which society becomes accustomed: democracy, or despotism; capitalism, or socialism; peace, or war; poverty, or prosperity, justice, or injustice; but once a society acquires the golden standard of living and then exists in a satisfying and comfortable state of peace and harmony, it fights to keep it; and taken away, the fight is more fierce, but with more grief and outrage; if the people need a revolution, it is up to those who are willing to risk life and limb, property and family, friends and relatives, to convince their brethren that this is not only right, but necessary.

Americans love their law-abiding freedoms: go where they want, do what they want; date whom they choose, marry whom they choose; live where they desire, work where they desire; this is not the only nation where the true nature of Man needs to reside to obtain true tranquility, yet there are fewer better designs of civilization. These often-coddled citizens heard about the hyper-violence of other nations, cringed about the horrors there, indeed felt compassion for those living there; and then soon thereafter, sat down to watch another movie played inside their warm, comfortable homes, engage another video game, frequent another restaurant; hang out, relax, stroll; call, text, email; and live, uninhibited, unobstructed, and unapologetic for people who are free.

And so, despite absorbing new immigrants, new ideologies, new ways, because no matter who came, or how many, in the end, they came for what Americans were all here for: freedom and opportunity and hope, and so these new people were Americanized, despite retaining their own homegrown customs; christened into the American family by virtue of their willing compliance to live within the strict boundaries of jurisprudence, their hearts and souls baptized within the blessed waters of the promise of the Good Life, if only they belonged and behaved.

And then the awful Them landed.

When there is abounding opportunity, there will be crime—it is inevitable, just as any healthy garden has weeds, but a healthy garden chokes out the normal growth of those unwanted but ubiquitous invaders; but there are gardens that are unhealthy because the garden is weak and ineffective, and the plants therein are complacent and compliant, encouraging not only the spread of weeds, but breeding a virulent kind that challenges the garden for dominance; so, when this abomination of species is imported to a truly healthy and fertile garden, it is a battle of wills and a test of the resolve of the garden to survive.

When the first steep break upward in the normal curve of crime statistics hit the States, it was likened to a band of marauding barbarians marching into a peaceful nation and slaughtering the Innocents therein; as if, indeed, the clocks of history had been reset to an epoch of savagery and sin, or, as some opined in editorials, such aberrant behavior had simply been momentarily repressed by easier, modern life, and now let loose by what was Man's true nature.

There were more kidnappings of wealthy financiers in Chicago, New York, and Los Angeles; more kidnappings of the children of the wealthy for ransom; more murders of politicians and law officers; more sales of heavy-duty weapons to indigenous criminal organizations; more sales of illegal drugs; more assaults on newspapers that criticized the Cartels; more executions of petty drug traffickers and battles with gangs who would not join the Cartels; more assaults on public institutions, more bold gun battles in the streets; more incursions of the Cartels across the American-Mexican border; more human trafficking; more prostitution, more arson, more, more, more of everything sordid and transparently and patently false and exactly antithetical to the wants and needs of good, freedom-loving people; like a burrowed-in tick, the various Cartel organizations had arrived, and then dug fast their clawed feet and hooked hands, with no conscience, with no understanding of the culture into which they declared an unprincipled insurgency, and no desire to know it; and, like an invading army of old, they obeyed no universal laws of war, intent on doing whatever was necessary to increase the length, breadth and width of their fast-expanding and bloody empire.

America, to them, was simply one giant shopping mall, where everything was free, and if one truly desired its wealth, it just had to be taken by force, but the key tenet for this was to do so without any moral inhibition.

Josie Cudillo was a young woman raised in the tradition common to immigrants from around the world and forgotten by too many indigenous citizens: that through hard work and clean living, one gains pride and honor, self-confidence and self-discipline, but more importantly, character. This credo had been built into her as much as the necessity of attending school and working hard, a consequence of her parents ill-begotten heritage; they had fled the military junta in Guatemala and, upon coming here legally, soon realized that they were in some kind of fantasy world where it seemed that all one had to do to achieve success in life was free oneself from the natural tendency to slothfulness and temptation that led to an emotional and physical self-immolation, and then the American dream would magically materialize—it seemed too good to be true; yet, they had done it, and the facileness of it was suspicious, as if there were another process or step to attain afterward, that someone or something would then come to exploit their joy and take it all away from them and send them back to their homeland of chaos; but, it never came, and this miracle was eagerly handed down, like an heirloom, to the four Cudillo children; first, the two older brothers, who went to college, and thrived, and then to the younger Josie, who was not so much endeared to the idea of liberating frivolity through hard labor—but instead, adhered to the new American expectation of receiving monetary benefits from someone or something, for little or nothing; and then there was her younger sister, age fourteen, who was still attempting to figure it all out.

"You must work, Josie," her mother would caution the nineteen-year-old, upon watching her perform—literally, for the four hundredth time on this particular day, as the girl lay on the sofa—another electronic text, with all the eagerness and intensity of the former three hundred and ninety-nine. "You must get a job."

"But Martha and Lucia don't work—their parents told them they can stay at home and take all the time they need to get a job," she replied, in earnest, and then her face lit up after reading the next electronic reply. She giggled.

Her slender mother, who still worked sixty-hour weeks at the two local factories, frowned, and shook her round head. "Maybe you should go back to Guatemala—then you would understand."

Josie would easily repel, by now, this old threat. "Oh, Mama," she said, smiling, and then, rising off the sofa, kissed her mother, "don't worry, you know I will get a job soon."

Alas, employment was forthcoming for the young woman, for her heart's desire was for the ephemeral, the unfortunate curse of the Now generation, fed on the constant, invigorating flow of instant, premixed, no-work-necessary rewards of bliss that was derived from entertainment and social media. What, then, was work compared to the excitement of burying one's head in the affairs of the new American royalty, in one's ever-increasing social circle? O, the intrigue, the plot twists and turns, the sharing of it all! And, if need be, one must simply take it all to work!

But the parents of Josie were not just old school, they were old world, too, and "all play and no work makes Josie a lazy and corrupt girl" was texted to her teenage brain after they finally did what they knew they must. "Like I'm a criminal," Josie whined, when she knew what had happened, for her electronic leashes—her cell phone; her constant electronic companions: iPad, tablet, laptop computer; her getaway car; her allowance; her ability to sustain anything other than eating and living at the family home—had been confiscated. "I'm a prisoner now," she moaned; "you've ruined my life!"

"Good," said her mother, her self-proclaimed warden, while her husband was off at one of two jobs, "do you want to get out of jail? Good, then go out the door and get a job."

"I will—and then move in with my friends!" Josie cried, in her malformed angst.

She did, in all honestly, try, but failed miserably, only attempting to secure a job with three firms in her hometown of Meadow Vista, which offered the kind of lazy positions where central air-conditioning and heating were offered, no heavy lifting, and the chance to sit around and talk when what little work was required was done, but which was her ultimate downfall, as she was still a child of the current generation who thought work was for their parents, and fun, for themselves as their only pursuit, and birthright, as long as they desired it.

And then one day, one of her friends met a "very nice man," named Julio, who was looking for "pretty girls who wanted to be models..." If only Josie's mother or father could have heard this block pitch, all the following tale could have been avoided—at least, for her.

It was, to Josie, the perfect job, the "easy way out," and so she and her friend, Marianne, accompanied by high expectations and dreams of riches and fame, drove to the house of the man.

They went through the front door, but came out the back one.

Let us now follow the circuitous route that the two frightened friends took with their new handler, Marco, alias Julio, formerly of Mexico, and now a peddler of human merchandise, and in this instance, inspired by the whims of the Azteca Cartel personnel, who were separated from their sweethearts and wives, and needed to have their fleshly desires satiated.

The girls went into a van, where they were beaten lightly, driven fifty miles north, given to a madam, who again beat them, dressed them, set them with the other captured girls, and decided who was going to regular johns, who to the big bosses, and who would be shipped back to the old country for more diverse work.

It all seemed so unreal to the sobbing Josie, as she stood attired in the spangle and sparkle of the unrepentant prostitute, as she listened to the middle-aged-looking woman—who was really only thirty-three and who once had been recruited herself—berate her. And then she heard those immortal and ironic words spoken by any fool child around the world, in her numb mind, "If only I had listened to my parents..."

And the stories she heard from the other girls—many of whom were victims of debt bondage to the powerful syndicates, real debt that had been accrued through their transportation across borders, a service rendered to them they had fully intended to pay, or imagined debt that they could never repay except through the giving of their flesh to the men they serviced; and there were the tales of the perverted sexual acts the women did, and the powerful drugs they ingested, and the beatings they took, and the fate of women who attempted to escape; all day, many times a day, seven days a week, this was their life, for the girls were property now, victims of land pirates, slavers, beasts of prey who had no conscience—their conscience being formed from the accumulation of filthy, rotten money and power, and increased by the want of more of it.

She had fallen into this human sinkhole that was filled with the excrement of rotting, tarred souls, and there was seemingly no escape; even though it seemed like a dream, it played like a nightmare; seemed a farce, played like a tragedy; seemed like virtual reality, but was all too real; she was to be fed, mind, body, and emotions, to men who would not even recognize her humanity as they abused her flesh and mind and emotions to satisfy their own aberrant, carnal desires. Suicide seemed a reasonable ally, but she was too much of a coward, even though other girls had told her of girls who had killed themselves—many, many girls, and, all, all too often.

She imagined herself working real hard at a difficult job, and being a good little girl who pleased her loving parents, played with her little sister ,and who was safe, safe inside of her house and living a life of a silly, carefree, but now hard-working and mature young woman, but this illusion burst when she was loaded into the van with the other twelve girls, all of whom were dressed up for the lustful pleasures of men who would soon destroy their victims' virginal dreams of a white wedding.

Where were their heroes now, the girls wondered; where were their rescuers; how could this be happening in America, in the twenty-first century, in this modern age of civilization? Where were the police, the FBI; where was anyone who would prevent this horrible wrong, which never should have happened, not here, not anywhere; yet, all they heard was the boisterous laughter of the kidnappers in the front of the car, and the constant smooth ride on the paved road, which, with every movement forward, was bringing them closer to their ultimate, humiliating, impossible-to-be-happening-now-or-ever mental and physical destruction.

Maybe the van would stop, they thought; maybe it was going back to the house where the girls were kept; maybe it was all a bad dream; maybe it was like their silly hopes and dreams, which they had always known were hopeless, and a fantasy, much like their lives had been.

Then, the van stopped, and so did their collective hearts; the door opened into the hot, muggy night air, and the mean-looking men and their ugly, soul-washed-out-to-sea hag-of-a-madam horsewhipped them with her vicious attitude. Reality was now, not a game on a brightly lit screen. They were the prize of flesh peddlers, and were about to be introduced to their new jobs: comfort women, whores, prostitutes; prisoners of war with no pay, no benefits, no vacation days, no sick days, and no advocates for their early release.

What had once been felicitous, youthful, giggling girls were now transformed into high-class-looking, high-heeled, short-skirt-wearing hookers, with thick, oozing, multicolored layers of dark makeup applied, but children still—still, for a few minutes longer, for a few precious minutes longer they still had hope, and faith, for a proper rescue. They entered the huge two-story mansion, trembling, frightened, and wanting to die.

They were paraded like willing whores in a brothel in front of the effusively smiling, high-ranking Cartel executives, many of them middle-aged men with daughters the same age as these girls; they were anxious to rape and deflower this tender white flesh with as much gusto as they had for hard living.

Josie was selected first, by a fat, ugly, stinking, but stinking-rich man, who quickly took her to his bedchamber, where she sobbed all the while, still hoping and praying for rescue, that there was still time, that all was not lost. "Where are you?" she wondered, thinking of her parents, and doing her best to see them in her tortured mind.

The man attempted to console her, but she would have none of it, so, naturally, he being a man who took no nonsense from anyone, slapped her to the bed, and accused her of spoiling the special moment.

It is curious, the fact that a slight disruption in the constant stream of daily business affairs has on one who is immersed in it; for, suddenly, the man looked from his fallen prey toward the front room. Did you hear that, he asked rhetorically.

The door opened, and in walked hopes and prayers, and a miracle with it. "Why don't you try hitting a man," the voice rang true through the black mask, and when the fat man pathetically tried to effect physical success against this Grade A warrior, he got, as the vernacular of the time so succinctly puts it, his clock cleaned.

And Josie instinctively knew it was all over, despite her hysteria, for she somehow knew who stood before her, as the masked man gently helped her up.

"You are," she wept tears of joy as she leaped into his strong embrace, "one of the Defenders."

Yes, their fame, not to be contained in a world where too much evil was not, had spread.

"Yes," he said, somewhat hard, and then, "yes," he said, softly, as he, Yoshitsune, held the girl, who trembled with joy, close to his black clothes, as he thought of his own precious son, Ichirou, had he lived, "it is all over."

A month hence, there was a humble house in Meadow Vista where a teenage girl, upon awakening, eagerly checked her text messages, texted her friends back, ran downstairs, kissed her parents and sister, and then sang, "Happy buenos dias," hugged her parents and sister, ate some breakfast, read the newspaper, and then went back upstairs and prepared for the day's activities; went downstairs again, kissed her parents and sister once more, hugged them even longer than before, and skipped out the door to her new job—and behold, it was even a Saturday. "But work is work," she often said to friends, and never once did she complain of being a waitress at the restaurant, for, truth be told, she enjoyed meeting people and socializing with him. During the week, she attended courses at the junior college she had recently enrolled in. "My compass has been reset," she liked to declare to her friends; "you must have a goal in life," she would add, in earnest. And when her little sister would slack off in school, or at her chores at home, Josie would certainly express her dissatisfaction with her. "Don't you know how important it is to receive an education, little lady? Do you think Mama and Papa and I work all day so you can be a slacker? No way! Why do you think Papa and Mama gave up their other jobs—to spend more time with their children," and here, she would nearly weep, for she knew why they had done so; and then she would kneel down next to her sad little sister in a very wise and certain tone. "Maria, you know how successful Carlos and Miguel have been—the first college graduates in our family; and, now look at me, working and going to school; are we not living the American dream? Come on, Maria, you're a bright girl, you have to be responsible; don't get good grades for everyone else, do it for yourself; after all," and she kissed her forehead, "you're the only 'Maria' we've got!"

"After I study," Maria said, smiling now, "can we go shopping?"

"Of course," she returned, smiling, "a girl has to have some fun."

Josie had never been interested in anything outside of her own insular world, but, as stated earlier, she would actually read the morning newspaper now. She began to be interested in civic affairs; the civil rights of people, immigration issues, crime rates, the existence of poverty. "I have a social conscience now," she proudly said to her parents one day, "my professor of history told me so—because I want to 'get involved.' Isn't it wonderful?"

And at night, when the working world settles down to relax and unwind, and prepare for the next day, she was sure to stay at home, studying, being with her family, but not spending so much time anymore on "frivolous things," she often said, like texting and talking on the cell phone about "just anything," she would say. "After all, every moment is precious and dear." Then she would kiss her parents and hold them even longer than before, and kiss her little sister, and hug her, and then go to bed; and as she would lie there, she would often think of the awful thing that had happened to her, and she would grieve for the girls who would never learn life's valuable lessons no matter what, and how many untoward things happened to them; but then she would think of the wonderful things, too, and she would smile, and feel a spreading warmth inside, the special warmth that comes from knowing there is real goodness in the world, that there are those who do care, who will risk their lives to help anyone in peril; and that she, little Josie Cudillo, had been a recipient of that knowledge of goodness, and that it had placed a weighty burden upon her spirit—that once she had perceived such a miracle, she was now obligated to create it for others. "It is now my heirloom," she would whisper, as warm tears of piety flowed down her florid cheeks. "I know the truth now—how can I not help to make it grow in myself, and in others, as well? It is my obligation." She would smile, then, thinking of the big, strong man who had rescued her. "I will be big and strong, too," and she touched her heart, "in here," and she imagined what he looked like, "for him, because he would be so proud he has made me—just like him!" And she felt pride and honor bear up in herself, and then recited her nightly prayers, certain to include one for her courageous rescuers, and then whispered, "You just wait and see, world: little Josie will yet be a woman who'll be a force for Good—and," she paused, thinking of the articles she had recently read about the Defenders, "Justice," and with that life plan established, and confidence brimming inside her, she fell to rest, happy and content, one more meaningful, productive, and caring life saved, and certainly secure on the narrow road to the Good Life.

Operation Pushback

The monolithic border that exists between the sovereign nations of the United States of America and Mexico may be interpreted either as a dike or temptation. It is a two-thousand-and-thirteen-hundred-mile-long, serpentine line of separation from California to Texas, a division of cultures and traditions, economic and lifestyle philosophies; we on one side, they on the other. It is not unlike the border between homes, or businesses, or cities, meant to issue identity to a person, place, or thing.

> And if borders were not there,
> would we care;
> would we go back and forth,
> and let nature take its course
>
> No borders at all,
> none for homes, no more walls;
> would we remember in December
> what happened in September

The Mexican government does not largely patrol its borders with the United States, but the United States patrols its own side.

The US border patrol, under the auspices of the US Customs and Border agency, are looking for lawbreakers—those citizens from Mexico or their more southerly neighbors who attempt to cross without the proper credentials, or people or organizations who seek to bring in products or offer goods without legal authorization; but the border is very porous, and cannot effectively be patrolled on land and sea and air; and what of those who merely go around this invisible line of demarcation and travel into the free states?

There has been a wall built, but it has been climbed, and broken through; there is water, but the people brave it; there is dry, hot desert, but the people dare it; there is the danger of their own human coyotes, but they still come; and yet, they are merely people intent on leading a better life. So let us survey those who come with bad intentions.

Before the Colombia Cartels had handed over the day-to-day multi-billion-dollar operation of transporting illegal substances to their Mexican brethren, the border agents dealt largely with the steady flow of wayward citizens, but once the cocaine, heroin, marijuana, and now methamphetamine baton was transferred, it became clearly evident that this disruptor would soon outstrip their meager resources; thus, in the US were born special operation units—specifically, the Mobile Response Team, or MRT; the Border Patrol Tactical Unit, or BORTAC, to deal with increased threats to the security of the nation along the border; and the Border Patrol Search Trauma and Rescue team, or BORSTAR, at Port of Entries, or POEs; and the International Liaison Unit, or ILU, which is a joint venture between the US and Mexican government to keep borders healthy and free of human contagion.

The surveillance systems included FLIR—forward looking infrared, remote videos, mobile, thermal handheld ground centers, radiant detectors, radiant isotope identification devices, integrated fixed towers, and unmanned drones scanning the border. As it was, there were dedicated men and women aplenty, and courageous and skilled and bold enough, and possessing the most sophisticated and reliable equipment enough, to preclude the present threat that these agents and devices were gathered for: precisely to combat what the homeland security agency had seen, and forecast.

Let us, then, accompany these courageous agents on a routine mission as they peruse and thus seek to strengthen the integrity of the narrow but wide swath of real estate that adjoins two disparate peoples.

The agents of old moved about in groups and relied on their immediate weapons, and even when the two-way radio came, it was a distinct comfort; but now, the modern agent walks, rides, or flies with an arsenal of weapons and equipment that provide the eyes and ears of those who are ready and willing to protect, reinforce, and rescue, to be more specific: the unattended ground sensor detects a large, moving presence, and this information is then sent to an integrated fixed tower, which then relays it to the command center, where personnel can target the area in question with an unmanned aerial drone, which may capture the image of trespassers, an image sent to the command center and then to members of MRT, who respond in kind to the threat, arriving by land in all-terrain vehicles, horses, motorcycles, SUVs, cruisers, pickup trucks, and vans; or by air in AW139 helicopters, and Super King Air 350ER planes; and by sea in forty-foot Seahawk boats.

If at night, thermal imaging, night vision, and infrared are used to draw a direct line to any uninvited guests; so, let us a survey late-night mission, and see what we may see when an alert comes in.

It is indeed an intruder—three, in fact, a typical number for desperate immigrants risking possible death to get the land of opportunity; three, perhaps a mother and father, and an older child, a family bringing only those who can move faster and farther without suffering and slowing them down, and who might later send for the littler and weaker ones; or, mixed families—it is never the same combination, and besides, the majority, if caught, do not resist, but give into the defeat of the present; but not of the future, for that is something their innate push for freedom will not allow them to do, and they will only try again.

Now, say that they are not simply those seeking to work in earnest and to establish a better life for their family, but those seeking in earnest to establish a foothold in the States to increase the sales of their forbidden product; why, they are pounced on by the border patrol, maybe not as easily, but with more gusto and guns, for such runners are desperate and sometimes armed; but the overwhelming abundance of technology, personnel, and funds the US has can stare down any such minimal threat.

That was yesterday's scenario, and today, the red dawn ushers in a new equation, brought about by the insatiable greed for a grandiose, seemingly ever-expanding market of insatiable customers for any highly intoxicating, addictive, life-destroying, family-imploding, societal-disintegrating narcotic, which is planted, packaged, and sold by those self-appointed, self-aggrandizing, self-centered princes of crime, princes of thieves, princes of self-vanity, petty, egregious, and inclined toward psychotic, despotic and megalomaniacal nature, the diabolical resume of mad men, and financed by confused souls whose resolve scatters like white thistledown on puffs of a soft breeze. Welcome to the free market of the twenty-first century.

So, here come twenty of the ant-like men of one of the Cartels, adequately equipped with weapons, intel, and bravado, yet they are so repulsed by the superior forces of the border patrol, who if necessary, will work in tandem with the Office of Air and Marine Operations units, who themselves will bring high-volume, high-grade weapons to the fight: the Sikorsky UH 60 Black Hawk, the AW139 helicopter, the AS350 Light Enforcer Helicopter—no remote-controlled toys there, no playthings, no games of hide and seek, but search-and-destroy mean machines, as in wartime. No small contingent of feet-rooted-to-the-ground, running-like-scared-rabbits drug traffickers could possibly withstand such concentrated and focused firepower. But this was during the first chapter of the drug wars, in the heat of its birth pangs, where the enemy was feeling and groping its way into uncharted territory, where there did not already exist massive and uncontrolled chaos and corruption; now, let us see how chapter two begins.

There is a tale not twice told, but thrice; the eternal game of the slimy rat attempting to infiltrate the pantry and steal pastry and cheese; so, come the rats, bold and swaggering as ever; comes one, the sacrificial lead to be ensnared, and eaten to ensure the survival of his brother rat; come two, in pairs they storm, and threes, and fours, too, but nothing too daunting for the owner of the delectable food—who simply supplies more traps, more effort, more whacks; but then, come the rats in fives, sixes, and then a swarm, a brown, furry, moving ground of scurrying, hurrying rats—but not just rats, smart rats, who have bribed one of the owners with gifts and treats to allow them in, to show them the way, to describe the trap; and now, the rats reign supreme, and when the other owners come, it is too late, for even a lower life-form that is coordinated and can corrupt its enemies is a worthy opponent.

Battles are won by superior forces, superior tactics, superior weapons, superior will; if the enemy has twenty men, you bring one hundred; if they have a set stratagem, you learn it and usurp it; if they have limited weapons, as prescribed legally by combat on their own soil, you bring unlimited weapons only a true army should have.

The El Dorado Cartel moved this fateful day with a diversion on land, sea, and air, attacking stations, personnel, boats, planes, helicopters, as if they had all the sensitive information of the border patrol and other US response agencies so as to ensure its own victory.

It was July fourth, after the setting of the sun, after darkness had prevailed, when conditions would provide the best giant-screen viewing for all who wished to see this annual gala spectacular, when the assault by the El Dorado Cartel commenced.

It was to be their Pearl Harbor.

The border patrol responded to the usual suspects, a few moving bodies at a port of entry on the California-Mexican border line; as usual, men were sent out, a Black Hawk helicopter flew out; and soon, the men were located in a thick coat of brush. It was over, as usual, and then, as unusual, it was not. That was when the handheld RPG-7 rocket launcher let loose its cargo and swiftly embarked on its short journey and blasted into the helicopter and it fell in flames. The men on the ground were gunned down.

The door that for so long had been tightly shut had now been violently ripped open.

This was the lead breach opened by the El Dorado Cartel, the first strike into sovereign land intended to test the readiness of the various agencies assigned the task to keeping the border safe; first, they sent waves of immigrants in various ports of entry along a two-mile stretch, to create a diversion, a tactic they had taken many times before, but without following through with high truckloads of cocaine and marijuana and heroin, which they did this time.

Three hundred Cartel soldiers descended upon a border patrol station, knocking out towers, detection devices, and killing agents along the way, and soon, they had reached the perimeter of the station, an act previously thought impossible, for the BORTAC team normally would be called, the Office of Air and Marine Operations would dispatch a team, local law enforcement would come in—but the impossible became the possible, a transition begun and finished by one of America's most endearing products: US currency, which had bought the cooperation of key personnel to cut the flow of information to outside police agencies.

The one hundred and fifty personnel inside the border patrol station had no chance to survive as the rockets slammed into their buildings, as the machine-gun fire ripped into the walls and windows, as grenades were tossed through the gaping hole; yes, the border agents fought valiantly, but death was imminent.

There is a rhythm and flow in battle, a cadence that can be measured, the convulsion of noise, intermittent silence, the volley of shots, the surge of gunfire, a pattern established, like a rhyme that is entirely recognizable; but if less occurs, or more is added, then the ratio, the odds, or the ammunition have been altered. Now something happened—more clamorous noise, but this time, different, strange, affecting, methodical drilling, a mechanistic swarming of one clamor against another, as if to strip it of its awful power by swallowing it whole. It wasn't long, this rendering of noise to shrapnel of silence; this precision surgical cutting-and-splicing process; and soon, only pure, sweet and comforting silence prevailed, and the agents inside the building dared peer outside, and heard, through a megaphone, the following beautiful words, "The Defenders have contained the enemy."

The trembling agents looked out into the quiescent harvest of night, and saw many lifeless forms about the place, and the fleeting image of the tiny drones, and then, the Defenders, dressed in all-black clothes, and masked, wearing their body armor, and heavily armed, stepped out into the open as if to signal their brotherhood. Then a man descended from the dark sky with a jet pack and landed in front of them, and his voice, although altered, was still genuine, and full of pathos.

"We are sorry for your loss of such brave men and women." He paused, this enigmatic, silent figure. "Eternal vigilance is the price of democracy; your struggle is not yours alone; fight the good fight, and honor those who have fallen this night. May God protect you always." And with that, he blasted off, and the other Defenders slowly disappeared with him; sirens could be heard in the distance, the far, far distance; and soon, the cavalry did come, but if not for the Defenders, the agents told them, all would have been lost.

The Last Goodbye

The Crusaders—operating in New Mexico, California, Arizona and Texas, none of them ever associating with the others in public, instead meeting at various underground facilities owned by Robert—were transported by his private planes to obscure and hidden rendezvous points, and although many lived in the same city, they lived in many different cities, albeit still close enough to aid each other in time of need.

The single operations duties of the Crusaders had been reduced, and now they operated mainly as a squad, but sometimes in small groups, in California, Arizona, New Mexico, and Texas. They had established a presence in the latter three states before the Cuchulains and others moved there, to provide insulation against prying eyes. The Cuchulains settled in Arizona, close to the border; as did, incidentally, Samuel and Florence Longfellow, two realities no one could question or be suspicious of; and there, they established a Community Youth Organization, and dwelled for some time.

Though they were far away from the congregation of Cartel organizations in major cities, the fallout from the rivalry between these super-criminal network of drug traffickers, as they maneuvered to establish a presence in a particular territory, was not unlike that from a detonated nuclear bomb—instead of horrific black rain falling on innocent heads, now there were more gangs anxious to help themselves to more of the enlarging drug-buying opportunities; thus, there were more gang wars as each side aligned themselves with the Cartel they reasoned would triumph.

The unrestrained practices of the Mexican Cartels to achieve their assorted gains, so long used in their own native country—including, but not limited to, kidnapping, bribery, murder, extortion, arms-selling, arson, blackmail, human trafficking, selling any illegal substance of every known variety: marijuana, heroin, methamphetamine, cocaine, speed, LSD, and ecstasy, and virtually any other mind-altering substance that came along—behooved each Cartel, like a Leviathan swallowing whole a city, to corner that market; and, thus inspired other gangs, and even other criminal organizations who could no longer restrain their nefarious selves, to emulate them, either by joining them or seeking their own territory through bloodshed, which created a disturbing panic of chaos in the streets, and in communities, even where before no such disturbances could ever have been conceived of rearing their ugly, papule-and-boil-covered heads.

And truly, the Cartels thought, what we have joined—meaning they and the criminal confederations—let no man separate; yet, and where was—the man?

Now, as the preceding statement regarding the United States government, they were like an ass between two bundles of hay.

The stories that leaked out of the Oval Office, as if from a submerged and drowning zeppelin in a swamp, were, some say, too fantastic to believe, as the stories piled up on the World Wide Web, in the newspapers and magazines, and on the incredulous, happy-to-pass-it-along tongues of your average, my-community-is-under-assault-by-invaders-while   our-insulated-leaders-sit-on-their-finely-manicured-and-bejeweled-hands citizens; so, to be fair to each side, here are just some of those… tall tales?; so, were they apocryphal, curved as a windblown dart from the center of truth, or absolutely, totally, embarrassingly true? You, reader, must decide:

Did the Secretary of Defense, when all the Cabinet members were present in National Security Council meetings, really pick up the White House calico cat, and before releasing him from her slender, long fingers, declare, in earnest, "Whatever way Cubby jumps—be it west, we intervene; be it east, we declare a truce; be it north, we ignore it," and upon releasing said confused feline, saw, to her delight, that he ran south? "A good sign, that," she declared, wiping her pasty forehead; "anyone for bridge?"

She was roundly criticized for such an unproven strategy.

"Let me show you how it is done," the Chief of the Armed Forces proudly announced, taking out a collection of odd-looking, small white bones. "I have spent some good time with our American cousins south of the border—if you want to beat your enemy, know how he thinks!" He knelt with good intention, on the blue Oval Office carpet, and before throwing said bones onto the official seal that represents the greatness of America, said, solemnly and enigmatically, "Whichever way the bones fall, they will tell us the way to proceed," and after throwing them down, he gasped. "Troops, troops on the streets," he exclaimed, in wild wonder, throwing up his hands.

The Secretary of State, still pouting from the hard lambasting she had received, her arms folded, said, watching the obese gentleman struggling to rise, "How do we know your interpretation is genuine, General; hey, maybe those are from the bones of the chicken we ate last night; in that case, I think they are really saying, 'you need to cut back on the bread and gravy.'"

"Tut, tut," said the bemused FBI Head; "maybe we would have better luck to see which way the chicken ran with his head cut off."

The Ambassador to Mexico soothed the inflamed minds of his comrades, explaining that in order to understand the mind of a Mexican, one needs to study his past, his culture, and the family structure; presently, he took from a brown box a cage wherein lay a small, beige-colored Horned Toad, and sat it down and he with it; his voice became sincere, like the look of his fellow, confused creature, who, incidentally, looked sincere because he basically just wanted to go back home to the sandy and toasty desert. The Ambassador put his intense face next to the still toad, and whispered, "I have heard that the Comanche did this—I know it sounds unscientific, but there is always some modicum of truth in old superstitions; and this time, ah," he nearly cried, "if he moves toward the President, he favors his views: toward the Attorney General, his views; whoever he does go, that is our manifest destiny."

Alas, an hour later, everyone merely had sore feet, as they had been reduced to standing still, without shoes, around the Ambassador, who reassured them that walking about upset the toad, who, incidentally, had never moved.

"Sir, you have a hole in your sock," said the Ambassador to the President.

"My wife does not believe in darning socks," the President said, shaking his head, "and I'm just a victim—like with that absurd reptile; now, here is an Executive Order—no more reptiles in the Oval Office!" He promptly stomped his feet and put his shoes back on. "Here, let me do all this superstitious nonsense the good ol'-fashion' American way," he said, firmly, and he took out a half-dollar with the image of a long-ago predecessor, to whom he whispered, "What would you have done, Jack ol' boy, eh? Were your advisers a collection," and he looked up at them, "of fence-sitters—oscillating, hot and cold, stumble-bums?" He flipped the silver coin and caught it expertly flat down on his wrist, covered it neatly with his hand, and then said, mockingly, "Heads we use National Guard troops, tails we don't."

"Why, that is no choice!" the Head of the NSA exclaimed. "What about the alternative? What about the military? More police! Heck, at least the full power of the USA and FBI on them!"

The President frowned, shaking his head, the coin still covered. "What about it, Mr. Attorney General?"

"We have to worry about the legal ramifications, Mr. President," he responded, in his best legal fashion, "regarding any radical proposal. We simply cannot make our country into a war zone."

"By thunder, it already is," the General cried; "might makes right!"

"Gosh, I'm shocked that you're arguing for that," the Secretary of State said, still fuming, "you're a walking stereotype."

"And you," answered, smugly, "are an equal opportunity hire."

"Cat and dog fight," said the amused Vice-President, who, thus far, had been silent.

"Thank you for your invaluable insight, Charles," the President said, visibly irritated; "thank goodness you have surpassed the stereotype of the job of Vice-President as being about as useful as an empty canteen in the desert." He cursed, albeit a light one. "I want some answers!"

"Well, sir, what if you check the coin?" the Secretary of State said innocently, inciting everyone, who sought penitence, to agree.

The President of the most powerful country in the world, in response to this suggestion, well, truth be told, he did expel a long, very, very long, exasperated sigh. "I hope I am covering your ears, Jack," he looked at his still-covered wrist, as he frowned. "O, how those whom the gods seek to destroy, they first make mad."

"Say, what is that—from one of those fantasy video games? I sure do like 'em!" the General said.

The President went and sat down behind his desk. "Everyone sit, and no one leaves until we have a resolution." He spoke to his secretary through the communication device on his fine mahogany desk. "Sheila, order takeout— we're going to be here for the long haul," and then he looked up. "All right, she'll take your orders now, and hey," he shouted, smiling, "we're going Dutch here: we have to watch the budget; those snooping reporters, and ex-officials write memoirs for money—blast them all!"

The General laughed. "A little levity leavens the whole loaf, eh, Mr. President?"

The President, arguably one of the most influential leaders in the free world, expelled a long breath of frustration. "We need flatbread," he mumbled.

It has certainly been asserted, and with great force, that the aforementioned scenes might have been the intellectual property of a former White House official with a very sharp ax to grind: a skewering of the facts, a distortion of key phrases, a severe uptick in the buffoonery of any meeting of Cabinet members; still, the inaction on the street in response to increasing violence did nothing to deter the ordinary citizen from deciding that such ineptitude was not only possible but preferable at such high levels, for it allowed the power brokers to do what they do best—in response to threats that do not directly threaten them—absolutely nothing, and for as long as possible, or until the people rebelled, and then, only begrudgingly, and with little care, for truly they did not know what to do, unless they were forced to do it to survive.

But this scene had its debut in print before the advent of the Defenders, who were perceived as a kind of people's rebellion, which was wholeheartedly embraced and endorsed by an increasingly desperate citizenry; thus, as the eyes of the people turned from their elected leaders to those who elected themselves to do what the recognized authorities would not, the inevitable occurred: the former group became jealous, and outraged, and then, of course, finally acted now that they saw the course laid out—like a well-lit flight path—before them by true professionals. The National Guard was dispatched not only to the border—and no feint, this, as in times past—as well as in the street; yes, the first wave of saviors had come. Could the military be far behind, people wondered?

The Cartels were ready, just as they were in Mexico.

History will record that the ultraviolence in Mexico had its birth when the government increased its campaign against the Cartels; it is no mystery, this, for when an army increases en masse against another, the latter increases its army—might meets might.

Before the surge in government troops in Mexico, the violence existed, certainly, as the main Cartels battled each other for territory, these plazas, and petty rivals increased, and many Innocents were killed: but the government, not able to see an alternative to displaying military troops, increasing police forces and special anti-drug task forces, finally did so; but when they did, the Cartels, like any cornered animal, fought back, and those who paid the price most were anyone who lived in Mexico—anyone: citizens, Cartel members, soldiers, reporters, judges, policemen, journalists, public officials, special agents, lawyers—for when the Cartels earn enough money to manage a country, such power is not easily yielded up. The critics, like a hovering black cloud, moved in, complaining about the increased mayhem; conversely, doing nothing and keeping it status quo, albeit less violent, brought forth the same critics.

But almost no one was listening to the little voice of reason concerning the radical idea of legitimizing and decriminalizing the buying and selling of drugs, as if during times of great upheaval, sagacious words, logic and reason were none too easily recognized: take a regulated, legal, much-sought-after candy bar and sell it for a nickel, and it makes the grower of the ingredients, the supplier of the ingredients, the mixer of the ingredients, and the seller of the ingredients a shiny new penny for each sale; but make the unregulated candy bar illegal, and it now it costs one dollar, and all concerned make about twenty shiny new pennies—and criminals are apt to want to keep their new-found wealth, and hurt anyone who seeks to take it away from them, and fight others who wish to take a part of their market; so, make the nickel candy bar legal once more, and all returns to normal, and each party involved makes a shiny new penny; but there will always be those who will not have this, as they fashion a career out of fighting the candy bar cartels, and spending inordinate amounts of time and cash on finding those who would dare to sell such poison—which anyone can get—always, which cannot be stopped from being sold, legally or illegally; which people, once addicted to, will rob and kill for to get the money to pay such exorbitant prices; thus, bad laws beget violence, and put in jail these poor candy-bar addicts, and buyers of too many candy bars, and sellers of too many candy bars are left to rot.

"If the public wants cocaine, heroin, marijuana, LSD," began Robert Heimdall, testifying before Congress, a man who owned many detox centers for addicts—and any money made from them was put right back into the centers—that had begun in cities, thusly: when his vast network of highly trained staff went to city managers, they did not just offer a plan for the homeless drug addicts, but a place to stay where these lost citizens would detox, for, they would tell the city government, if not, then the problem is not solved, and you are simply housing people who will continue the same destructive behavior. He continued on, "Let the federal government legislate these drugs, the state regulate them, the appropriate agencies regulate them, the private companies sell them, and doctors prescribe them, if necessary—and soon they will be a commodity, like every other drug sold over-the-counter to an adult; it will take the profit away from the criminal, reduce violence, free up the prisons and jails, allow us not to put such disproportionate amounts of funds toward fighting it, and instead, put that money into treatment for addicts; and allow the police to concentrate on the criminal who is not breaking your home to steal a television to pay for his drug habit, or the teenager with an ounce of marijuana on his person, but the real, violent, hard-core criminals, and all the other criminals who have fallen between the cracks as we have put the majority of our manpower into fighting this lost drug war; and also, it will dissipate what is known as the 'iron law of prohibition,' where a drug that is vigorously contested by the authorities is soon replaced by a harsher and deadly strain of it—it is a reality with the nearest history, our failed prohibition against alcohol; one can easily attest to these aforementioned narratives with minimal research."

His testimony did not sit well with those who could only counter with the same tired refrain, "Illegal drugs are destroying our country," to which he calmly replied, "Senator, when will the drug war be won?"

And the reply came swiftly. "We cannot give in to the drug lords..." Ad infinitum.

Robert and Paul had left Washington DC that day, melancholy, forlorn, and dejected.

"Well, old friend," he said to Paul, aboard their private jet, "we have two choices now—and the one, I will not do."

"Yes," Paul had responded, "it is as you say—we do as our conscience desires, not so the will of crippled leaders."

Now, this had been in the not-too-recent past, exactly before the deployment of the National Guard; so, let us see how the drug trafficker-conglomerates welcomed their newest opposition.

There would be a squadron of armed National Guard members patrolling a neighborhood area that had been infected with the southern invasion forces. Cartel soldiers would appear and fire upon them, prompting the Guard to fire back, and when it was over, there were dead bodies everywhere. This went on, ad infinitum.

The more National Guard, the more police, the more DEA agents, the more FBI, the more special SWAT teams, the more US Marshals and other covert operatives, the more Cartel soldiers were hired from a seemingly never-ending pool of anxious candidates: where one hundred Cartel soldiers died, two hundred took their place; where one hundred gang members died, two hundred took their place; some were imported, citizens were converted, and bought and sold; allegiances were stitched together in black and white gunpowder: Cartels and gangs, Cartels against each other, citizens caught between the shootings, and no one could conceive of a truce, or the end of hostilities. The war was on.

September swept in, and found the streets covered in blood, bodies, and despair, and it wept ashes and dew over its dead and dying children.

Dylan was locking up the youth center on a Friday night, and about to leave, when a familiar voice came upon him. "Long time, Mr. Cuchulain."

Dylan turned around, and saw Agent Fuentes. He smiled gently. "Victor," he said, amiably, and shook the man's hand.

"I have recently been stationed here; so, Dylan, how are you adjusting to the Arizona climate?"

Dylan smiled. "It is the same everywhere—it is what you make it."

"True, indeed." Victor smiled, and then said, "How is the family?"

"They are well—thank you."

"Good, good," he said, smiling once more, but nearly out of such necessary conveniences. "How about dinner…"

"I would enjoy that."

Presently, the two men were dining in a quiet corner of a local restaurant, neither man speaking of the mean season that connected them.

They spoke of family, of jobs, of events that alter lives; and then Victor said, aiming everywhere but the center, "Any problems here?"

"No," Dylan replied, still, in the proper vein of the proper stone-faced, highly guarded and secretive warrior.

"Good; well, of course—you will let me know, considering the increased presence of the Cartels, and especially what happened to you; and as you know, I am sure, they don't like leaving loose ends…and we never picked up the bad guys on your case, so, it is still a great worry for me." He drank some more of his black coffee. "You know, if, by some miracle, it'd been you alone who had defeated those hit men—why, you wouldn't be safe anywhere." He tried to smile but it didn't have any genuine surface to cling to. "Thank goodness for your guardian angels—the Defenders." He raised his coffee mug. "A toast to the Defenders."

Dylan tried to smile, but, alas, it too had nothing to cling to, but he did raise his glass of green tea, which was lightly flavored with honey, and tapped the brown mug. "A toast." And as he drank his cold brew, and watched Victor drain his hot coffee, he smiled inwardly, thinking, "Rhiannon will be amused that I toasted to myself."

"And yet," Dylan said, quite without affection, "you count them as vigilantes, who must be brought to justice."

A shade more an agent of the FBI than casual acquaintance overtook him, and he sat up straighter, and raised his head higher, as his voice became deeper and harder. "Anyone who operates outside of the specified and agreed-upon law must be reined in."

"And prosecuted," Dylan added, staring directly into the judicial soul of a man dedicated to obeying and upholding the law of the land.

"Come what may," he replied. No more smiles dared to operate upon his grim countenance now. "Let the law handle the criminals." When Dylan did not directly reply, he pressed it with fervor. "Do you agree, Dylan?"

"I am curious about the crimes these Defenders have committed."

"Plenty," Victor replied, with knit brow, "operating on United States soil as an independent renegade group, specifically in California, Arizona, New Mexico, Texas, using prohibited firearms, the use of prohibited drones, endangering the lives of civilians, killing—or murdering..." He had tossed out and then accented the last word.

Dylan rested his elbows on the table, his arms raised up as he folded his hands against his bearded chin. "Sounds serious."

"Oh, yes, very serious—we must not have an independent army let loose on American soil, no matter their good intentions; after all, we don't need mercenaries here, no dogs of war here, no soldier of fortune—this isn't, for goodness' sake," and when he paused, he tried to penetrate the crystal-blue sea and the swirling galaxy that was Dylan's eyes, as he enunciated slowly and carefully, anointing each syllable with his unique position and status, "Africa."

Now, an amused Dylan smiled. "Do tell."

Now, an amused Victor smiled. "Dylan, you are quite the closed book," he shook his head, "but it is our job to open books."

"This is the age of information."

"Yes, it is," he said, the levity gently subsiding; he looked around at the people here, then outside through the window at the passersby, then thought about his own family, and then looked at Dylan. "When I read about the Crusaders," referring to the book that was written by a husband and wife team of reporters, Jon and Jenny Pierce, entitled "Twentieth-Century Crusaders in Africa," "and what they did: how they risked their lives, not for money, fame, or glory—but for a cause, a virtuous cause—and the lives they saved; what you and your brother did, and the other fine men and women there;

why, they changed the course of history of that continent; truly, a greater story no one could have written, than of those selfless and dedicated warriors who liberated the enslaved from tyranny—truly Knights of the Round Table, great men and women of our time; the stuff of legend." His emotional voice betrayed an awe and respect he could not humanly repress. "And to think I'm sitting in the company of one of those heroes—it is truly an honor," and he reached across the table, and shook the hand of Dylan. "I salute you, sir, and what your Crusaders, at first alone, and then inspiring others, above all other concerns, did for the oppressed masses, especially when it seemed that no one else could, or cared."

Dylan could not, would not, but more importantly, must not respond, and in its stead, he listened more, and waited.

The voice of Victor was grave now. "For the Crusaders to come to America and do such great feats, is to undo the very fabric of our civilization—but here—here," and he tapped the wooden table with the index finger of his right hand, "we have an established order, a Constitution, a law of jurisprudence, which cannot be undone—despite their best intentions, despite the will of the people, even despite the will of some officers of the law who have seen lives saved, even of their own; it simply cannot be."

It was time for Victor to allow his revelatory words to seep in and take effect on the man across from him. He drained his coffee mug, allowed the waitress to fill it again, turned his full attention to the Crusader before him, and spoke, in an authentic tone of honor. "I can think of few men I would want at my side in battle, than he who sits opposite me." His heart thus spoke; his mind, too; his spirit saying this praise; his soul in tune, too; but his pledge to abide, to protect and serve, this dedicated man of the police he proudly wore, this vow, this oath he loyally swore, was more.

He spoke, now as a representative of the highest police organization in the land, yet, he could not fully suppress the boy in him who admired heroes and now the adult man who honored anyone who valiantly did not step aside, or step back, or bow to, in the face of seemingly insurmountable tyranny, the temptation of power, and the enticement of avarice. "The Federal Bureau of Investigation must not allow an independent, rogue military force to operate within the borders of the fifty United States, or any of its territories." There, he had stated it succinctly and intelligently, just as his training had taught him. "The Defenders will be caught and prosecuted to the fullest extent of the law."

Dylan, ever the stoic, and due to no little anticipation of such conversation, replied, "We all do what we must to serve our conscience."

"Here, here," Victor said, raising his coffee mug, and drinking from it, and then set it down gently, and looked again to Dylan. "So, when do I get the grand tour of the youth center?"

"How about tomorrow at ten p.m.; I am certain the bad guys will give you the day off." He briefly smiled.

Victor smiled, too. "Of course, the bad guys need to rest after their strenuous week."

It was agreed, then, and the two guardians of the land spoke of other matters, none of which were too solemn, mostly about the joys of family, good friends, and the hope of a better world; it was necessary and good that they spoke of such lighthearted things, for men such as they—picking up the sword others will not made them hard men, and they instinctively knew that hard men most often die young, and alone, eaten up by the grind and gruesome tread of the daily fight.

They departed as they had earlier met, amiably, each going back to the world that sustained and kept them alive.

After carefully checking for surveillance equipment attached to his car or person, after talking to Rhiannon in hushed tones, he spoke to Robert on a secure cellular device—he was still in New Mexico and conducting operations in the four southwestern states, then flew in the next week to visit the youth center, which he, after all, owned, and visited often.

Robert and Paul, Dylan, Rhiannon, and Samuel—the latter of whom had been involved in a few operations lately, all met in the center after Dylan had swept it completely for surveillance bugs. It did not take long for an executive decision to be reached: the Crusaders, separately, and at different times, from different locales, in different transportation vehicles, would depart from the States and land in, at different times, from different locations, in different locations, the home of the current and seemingly unafraid enemy, Mexico.

All was arranged by them, and went exactly as planned, each step of the way plotted carefully, double-checked and triple-checked, each step taken as if stepping onto a minefield, each glance back and up, as if an enemy was closing in, each careful look ahead and sideways illuminating the path as if it were an illusion to their enemies, where everything that seemed to be was not.

The day after they arrived at their destination points and finally convened at a secluded, camouflaged, underground shelter, a package, an electronic and encrypted software, was sent to the headquarters of the FBI in Arizona, stating: "to Victor Fuentes, for his eyes only."

Victor read it in a secure room of the building he commanded, and was exhilarated and fascinated as he read thusly: the names of compromised agents in the four southwestern states of California, Arizona, Texas, and New Mexico, some even in his own building, and offering proof as to their traitorous action; names of Cartel executives operating here, and their exact whereabouts; transportation methods and routes to storage sites of the drugs by the Cartels; banks, courts, policemen, DEA agents compromised, and proof of their traitorous acts.

Victor was undone, as he sat back and contemplated the impact of this revelatory information on the ongoing fight against the Cartels.

"Dylan," he was even afraid to whisper, "where are you, these days..."

Were his thoughts wings, and took flight
they would find him, in Mexico
in company of the Crusaders,
to fight the good fight.

The Eagle Has Landed

After the demonstration of Crusader firepower to evince their fierce determination to accede to no tyranny on any soil, sovereign or no—as evidenced by the Cartel assassins heaped up on José's farm—they convinced all the parties involved of the necessity and immediacy of leaving. No one demurred. Once a safe haven was reached, the group—which included José and his family, Pedro, Roderigo and the five Crusaders, Miguel, Finn, Antonio, Yoshitsune, and Ana—was finally able to become acquainted.

Soon, Pedro briefly related his shameful life, and then his awakening. "As out of a deep slumber, aroused by conscience," he said, and then continued, desirous to create hope in the minds of his perceived brethren, "And then I met these five, fine travelers on my way back to town, and they somehow knew of my flight, and quickly offered to help me; it is a miracle from God."

"Who are you," José addressed the visitors, holding still his wife, as both of them sat in between the children, "that you would help a stranger?"

Ana spoke, undaunted by any query. "Are we not all brothers and sisters when we fight oppressors? Then, we are strangers no longer, but that I should call you friends."

"Are you military? And from where?" Pedro asked. "Are you United Nations soldiers?"

"No," Finn said, amused, tapping his rifle, "we actually use these."

"You are from Colombia, I can tell," José said to Antonio.

"Yes, I hail from Colombia—and now I am a citizen of the free world."

"And you," José's wife asked, politely, of Miguel, "from your accent, you are from the state of Azteca."

Miguel smiled, took out his brown cigar, took off his big hat, bowed toward her, and spoke to in her native tongue. "It is my home, and to think of it now grieves me, for robbers have set up dominion there, and I mean to drive them out."

"But how?" José asked. "You are only five, and the Cartels," he halted, as if the bushes and trees had eyes and ears, seemingly like the buildings and streets did in town, "are so many armies."

Miguel pursed his lips, tossed his head, and gestured with an open palm, as if to say, "We are not afraid," but he did say, "You see what is happening in Yermo—Mexico belongs to Mexicans, and they," he nodded toward the now-faraway scene where the dead bodies of the Cartel soldiers still lay, and said with disgust, "are not one of us."

"They have taken up arms against Innocents, and have forfeited their citizenship," Antonio added.

"Tell us all about the city you came from," Ana asked of Pedro and Roderigo.

When Pedro and Roderigo had told more of their story, the wife of José, and his children, felt the chill of terror creeping up their fragile equanimity, and even though the visages of the Crusaders reflected a different, inured tone, all of them were moved.

"We need to know everything about the Azteca Cartel," Antonio asked.

Ana said, "We have to get José and his family to safety."

"I want to fight," José said, standing up suddenly, his face awash with pride. "Mexico is my country, too."

But Pedro, rising, placed his hand on his friend's slender shoulders. "You are a good man, José, and you must stay that way," he said, and then, wistfully, "after all, when it is all over," and looking at the children, "we are fighting for ones such as these—and they must have a good father," and he looked at

Pedro's wife, "and good mother, to help them rebuild our beloved Mother Mexico."

Pedro and his family were escorted to a remote farming area, leaving Yoshitsune with them to keep watch, where they could reside in utter anonymity, far removed from influence of the Cartels; and then the Crusaders, and Roderigo and Pedro, came back to the farm of Pedro, to wait.

"Let us see what we can see, if even these reptiles will bury their own dead," Ana said, as the six of them crouched in the dense vegetation, each holding a radio walkie-talkie they had taken from the soldiers.

Pedro and Roderigo had explained to the Crusaders the importance of the walkie-talkies, and the shifting codes.

"These codes, they are impossible to break," Roderigo had stated, "with all the money the Cartels have, they have employed the best minds in the world of ciphers—it is how they manage to stay ahead of the authorities."

It was true. One of the most innovative ideas of one Cartel had led to the construction of a network of radio towers all throughout Mexico, which was accessed through walkie-talkies, and in addition to the World Wide Web, and the human ears, eyes, and mouth in every town, city, and province, and territory, they had an intelligence map of every movement of other Cartels, enemies, and the authorities; yet, they had also hired many brilliant minds in code-making and -breaking, establishing what they considered an ever-changing algorithmic code that seemed inconceivable to break not only to them, but to their frustrated enemies. Naturally, the other Cartels followed this lead of building towers, and soon, all of them were operating in this clandestine cloak with utter arrogance and near invincibility.

The Crusaders here communicated to their home base through technology that was hitherto unknown in the world of commerce—military, private, or otherwise, on satellite phones—wherein the only server existed in the command center of Robert Heimdall, thus allowing them to speak freely, albeit with codes supplied by the quantum computer on an encrypted algorithm that, as of yet, could not be reverse-engineered.

And, since no one knew what to look for, the Crusader's phone service was not detected, for no machine existed that could do so; also, their phones were activated by the individual user's voice, fingerprint, and retina scan, making them virtually useless in the hands of a thief, who, if he did manage to steal one, upon failing to follow the proper activation sequence, would find himself with a very big headache, and soon, company, as his failure would, before the phone had completely disintegrated, activate a specially encoded "peril" homing beacon.

Therefore, as communication flowed between the Crusaders as effortlessly as a sparkling stream flowing serenely downhill, the coordination of landing the Crusaders in Mexico commenced.

A week later, by land, sea and air they came, and all those who were ready to fight the Cartels on the soil of a sovereign nation had landed.

The first modern war between foreign entities in the North Americas was about to begin.

Operation Justice

In the selection of a name of an intelligence operation, it should not directly reflect the reason for the mission, simply because the enemy, in the event of intercepting any information, may see the name and understand its relevance to the war. Thus, in the case of the Crusaders, as they descended to Mexico, initially decided upon possibilities such as Operation Friendly Persuasion, or Operation Bueno Tardes, but, in the end, they relegated all of these to weaker positions not suitable for their mission, and reasoned that Operation Justice was so generic, and so fitting and proper, that there was little danger that if the title fell into the hands of the Cartel, or any police organization, much damage to the objective would occur.

Robert had purchased great amounts of real estate throughout the Americas in the last decade, especially here, and here, building specially designed and equipped, seemingly innocuous warehouses that overtly were managed by farm conglomerations and assorted businesses, but in truth housed underground lairs, which were made by highly skilled engineers and would serve as headquarters, meeting places and units to store technology; he also had diverse aircraft, and airstrips to accommodate them. Security forces numbered in the hundreds, as did his scientific staff, all hand-picked by himself, tried-and-true veterans of long, drawn-out wars, and possessing the virtue most necessary in this precarious business: undying loyalty to the cause of liberating the masses from tyranny.

In the state of Azteca, in the high mountains, where even the most hearty of adventurers were not fain to go—except, seemingly, wild burros and hearty cactus—sat one such set of buildings, undisturbed by the populace and criminals, so far removed from civilization it was; and even the Mexican government did not bother Robert, as he was so generous with aid to schools, and building youth community centers, and helping farmers so they might be more efficient, providing skills-training for young people, helping to modernize hospitals, and providing drug rehabilitation centers and housing for the homeless and the destitute; in fact, they ran as blockade for him if any local agency even so much as sneezed in his direction. He was, many said, "Saint Roberto."

This complex, as seen from a satellite, projected a false image that would never show the arrival of so many men and women, for the structure of the buildings was much like the invisible-to-radar stealth bomber aircraft; plus, surrounding the complex was a great swath of metamaterial, which once light entered, controlled the electromagnetic radiation that essentially rendered the objects around it invisible; and so, in its stead, a dull and mechanical image was projected: of employees coming to work, opening up the place, working, shutting its doors, and leaving it. High-tech radar units were planted around the perimeter, extremely sensitive motion detectors, video cameras, an electrified minefield close to the building that those who wore a special receiver could step on without activating, but anyone else who did would be rendered very unhappy through a high electrical voltage.

Slowly, the Crusaders arrived, and gathered in the lower level of the complex, where the men and women exchanged pleasantries and spoke of past adventures and their desire for battle; and then there came a commotion, causing all of them to look up at the elevator entrance, and see, to their utter surprise, a man who had experienced such a desolation of hope in his own country that they thought he would not come.

And then by all, as if as one, came a joyous shout, "Moses!"

Moses, indeed, stood on the high, wooden, circular flooring, smiling broadly, and descended to greet the others, and finally to the center, raised platform where Dylan and Robert stood, and they embraced.

Moses said, smiling still, to his two friends, "I should not like to miss a good fight!"

"Thou art a true warrior," Dylan returned, misty-eyed, "like kings of old, at the head of his armies."

It was true—although the Civil War in Kush waxed and waned, when wax it did, Moses, despite the most vehement protestations of his President and Cabinet members, still cast himself not only as a General, but a fighting one, as well; and perhaps his greatest regret now was that his birth family was not here with him to see the fabled land of milk and honey they had always heard of.

Once plans were carefully laid out by Dylan and Robert, a robust discussion followed, an exhilaration of give-and-take that could occur only where camaraderie exists in the highest degree, and thus, all of them created, in the final analysis, an overall agreed-upon stratagem.

From the Master Sun's Military Methods, or the Sun Zi, Dylan spoke of the need to know the terrain, the environment, to avoid a practical war, to be efficient, and to keep the inner equilibrium of the Cartels in chaos, and to know not only where to finish them off, but when; and he spoke of Jomini, and the need to maintain excellent communications among the Crusaders, to benefit from espionage, and to have a carefully thought-out battle plan; and he spoke of Clausewitz, and the need to understand that when probability and chance occur, to take full advantage; to realize where the most vital areas of enemy lie—this center of gravity—that will deal a death blow to them, and to know once the objective has been reached, to quit the battle; and he spoke of the need to be mindful of cutting communications, to take an indirect approach when attacking, and to keep one's objectives at the forefront, and strike and even consider an alternative objective. These philosophies and more he elaborated on, as he had spoken often in times past.

"It is what we have always done instinctively," he said to them, looking around at these fine and noble youths, "but here, in Mexico, we must be wary of its sovereignty, and the right of their armies to give chase, and to not cause an international incident," and then he paused, seeking the agreement of his fellows to his next proposal, which he reasoned he would receive by their intense countenances, then chopped the air downward with his right arm, as he declared, "but that has never stopped us before!"

Enthusiastic cheers erupted!

He nodded, and when he spoke, all was hush again. "When we do what must be done, what others fear to do: to bring Justice to those oppressed—no matter their geography—then we are a sovereign entity who operates under the sacred banner of Almighty God!"

Hearty cheers erupted!

"Let us begin, then, this grand mission, and liberate the people from the domination and tyranny of those wicked forces, that wherever we go will meet with the credo of the Crusaders."

And all of them arose as if one single organism, a complete family, by virtue of having every kind of leader, every variation of warrior, every nuance of courage, bravado, derring-do, all possessing a single devotion to the willingness to die for a belief they so vigorously fought for; and they shouted, undeterred, undaunted, united, "Force and right are the governors of the world; force till right is ready," and then an explosive pause occurred, and they finally cried, "eternal vigilance!"

How the Octopus Lost its Tentacles

Were humans eight-limbed
would grief four times increase
and giving four times decrease;
or might giving increase,
and greed finally be dimmed?

The giant tentacles of the octopus that was the Narcos was in constant motion, constantly moving its slimy, bloodsucking arms over anyone who offered up their own soul for regurgitation for more than the pitiful pay they currently earned; yet, what happens if one courageous soul stands up against the multi-tiered, nine-headed beast, just one man or woman—not an army yet, not a city, nor a country, but one—and wisely, and strategically. There exists one infinitesimally small space in the prodigious reign of Narco power not yet filled in and occupied, and not easily detected, and it is called loyalty to Mother Mexico; but a movement begun, a tiny resistance against easily succumbing to what seems unstoppable, unbreakable, unimpeachable, this was an unknown element; yet, who can conceive of victory, if alone stands one against the monolithic evil whose residence seems irrevocable?

The Fascists were beaten because more people loved freedom more than those who loved unrestrained and unchecked power; the Communists were defeated because they were self-refuting, their moral crimes exposed to the world, like an abscess; the petty dictators were destroyed because the time allotting power to unelected megalomaniacs was long past: too many citizens of the world had heard the eternal proclamation of Justice too often and seen its sublime glory in too many places and felt its soaring spirit speak to their fundamental desire to be free too many times, to not beg its absolution of sins from their land.

Yet, the people do not always arise and throw off the yoke of servitude, for often they need something to inspire them, and they look for a leader; for in every revolution, there has always been, and must be, that one noble soul who will boldly proclaim the transgression of their oppressors, and unite the people and lead them to the promised land.

Had an octopus not eight limbs but two, might his enemies fear him less, or perhaps, not at all?

The Cartels need certain raw and finished goods and services, like any corporation: raw material for cocaine, marijuana, opium, and other stimulants; suppliers, shippers, agents, sellers, customers, enforcers, alliances, an army; thus, trade routes were established: by sea, by air, by land, by underground to the salivating customers; to protect this commodity were needed local spies: street corners populated by loyal followers, businessmen, the World Wide Web, military, federal, police, judges; and to protect them, an arsenal that came from their North American cousins, the greedy gabacho, who would sell arms to the murderers of their own mothers for profit; and to communicate all of this was needed a superior communications network: a mobile communications system for the extensive radio network used by virtually all of the Cartels, and main installations where their entire radio network was coordinated and controlled; and yea, the Cartels needed one more commodity, one more easily purchased item to complete the transformation of pauper to prince: the exclusive capitulation of the people and government and police to the will of the Cartels, their complete cooperation, tacit or otherwise, through bribery or violence thrust upon them. Does a sovereign, Democratic nation, so easily yield, so easily break when choked and splintered, beaten and broken, by obscene, gross violence and corruption? No absolute despot would allow such internal chaos; only in free nations could such societal heresy arise; and any nation that cannot endure and prevail against such insurrection is too weak to last in any fashion, and must be undone, so that the survivors may construct a nation-state that will stand firm against further internal and external forces of rebellion and revolution.

A house built on sand will not long last against the rising tide.

Had the Mexican government intel regarding the exact routes of the drug traffickers, yes; had they destroyed or impeded many routes, yes; could they legitimately pursue these routes to a necessary destruction of them, no—and no, for too often those forces employed to wreak havoc on these routes were corrupt, and fed information to their wily masters; but suppose there was a dedicated team of dissenters lethal to the life-force of the drug traffickers, those who could not be bought by any means, replete with the technological equipment to gain explicit knowledge of these routes, bound by no niceties of civilized laws: O, the damage they might assert upon these unchained terrorists.

Using Heimdall's Unmanned Aerial Vehicle, the UAV, drone surveillance, and informants' intel, the exact methods of delivering the toxic cargo of the drug traffickers was discovered by the Crusaders, and when they demolished the Azteca routes, they were certain to post boasting Internet signs of an El Dorado victory; conversely, when they bombed the El Dorado routes, they were certain to post Internet boasts of an Azteca victory; and when the Crusaders intercepted arms shipments—after Heimdall's scientists had engaged the Dark Web and found the secretive websites and dialogues of the parties involved—from either Cartels, and often in tandem with the FBI, ATF and DEA, whom they surreptitiously informed about these routes from the US to Mexico, or from Central America to Mexico, they were certain to mock the other side, as if they were the enemy, thus driving an existing wedge even deeper between the two Cartels, so deep it seemed irretrievable, the resulting ill humor of both sides increasing considerably, resulting in more hits, and more shootings and more killings against each other. Nor did it help that when visiting the dreadful haunt of the Dark Web, the Crusaders, whenever they could, drained the bank accounts of the opposing sides (giving the money to charities), and were certain to leave a trail that blamed the other.

During this newly minted Operation Sequester, no Crusader was captured, but ten were wounded, and nine killed, including: Liam Martin of Canada, whose grandfather had fought against the Fascists during the Spanish Civil War; James Thackery of the UK, whose grandfather had fought against the Nazis in World War II; Lyle Rasmussen of the US, whose grandfather had fought in the South Pacific against the Japanese in World War II; Jian Liu of China, whose grandfather had fought in China against the Japanese in World War II; Emma Elliot of Australia, whose grandmother had been a nurse and served in the South Pacific in World War II; Florencia Cardozo of Uruguay, who was orphaned early in life, after her missionary parents were killed by rebels in a neighboring country; Santiago Rojas of Colombia, whose mother and father had been members of an elite squad that fought the Cartels there; Fabricio Huaman of Peru, whose family was killed in the crossfire between radical, leftist insurgent groups and their battle with government troops, who likewise committed human rights violations; and Eliseo Echeverria of Mexico, whose great-grandfather had ridden with Emiliano Zapata to free his country of tyranny.

As it was, the Giant Octopus that was and is the body and spirit of the two dominant Cartels in the North lost significant suction power on all of its massive tentacles; had two badly frayed in a horrific fire; and actually had one severed, but not clean through, and then cut completely in twain by its mean cousin, the Giant Squid.

What Has an Ending
Needs a Beginning

The border town of Yermo had once been an ordinary town, not unlike any other town, but with the advent of the rise of the drug traffickers, it had become a personal fiefdom for the Azteca Cartel, a sprawling slaughterhouse wherein the residents were like cattle, herded this way and that, and unlike the dumb beasts, were never certain if death would come their way; but, if they did possess a death wish, could be certain of it, if ever they crossed the Cartel. If the Cartel demanded protection money from business owners, and did not receive it, they simply murdered them; and oftentimes it was the police who were in on the hit, blocking off a region of the city to allow the motorcycle- or SUV-driving sicarios to do their dirty deed.

And where were the police after the murder of the target and the subsequent displaying of the dead body in town square, often with a dire admonition written in blood upon it? And sometimes the murder was performed by teenage sicarios, and oftentimes for a paltry sum, of perhaps two thousand pesos—one hundred and seventy US dollars, by youths recruited from the slums, these children who grew up in a city suffused with violence and mayhem and uncontrolled chaos, and no controlling or intervening checks and balances from governmental agencies, thus allowing people to sink to, and never seek to rise above, the instinctual level of the beast of the field, where the human becomes as the predator, killing at will, without conscience, for daily sustenance, and thinking it is all part of a bigger, similar world.

The stronghold of the Azteca Cartel lay in the northern province of Azteca and resembled a military base, the center of the spider's web from which all orders were given: a mammoth complex with a main white building surrounded by barracks and cement bunkers, huge warehouses packed with a multitude of weapons and aircraft, vehicles and artillery, its periphery mined, heavily barbed-wired, with guard towers and searchlights. From above, one could have easily mistaken it for a maximum security prison.

Inside the main building, inside the main room, on a ten-thousand-dollar handmade leather chair, wearing diamond-studded cufflinks, sat a big man, the big Capo, chomping on a big, brown cigar, listening to his lieutenant narrate the goings-on in Yermo.

"I tell you, El Toro, it is a revolution—the people are fighting like brave soldiers against us," the slender, dark-haired man began, shaking his round head. "It is very troubling—it cuts into your costs; maybe the El Dorado people are behind this, like in Zapote—they are unscrupulous, no? They have their plaza, but no, greed will be their downfall." He got up, lit a cigarette, and paced back and forth on the plush rugs his boss had personally made from the brown bears he had killed long ago. "And when the Federales come in—those we do not control—our reserve will certainly drop."

The big man with the thick, drooping mustache watched with amusement as his loyal adjutant nervously paced about, gesturing wildly, and quoting statistics about monetary losses.

"You're a good man, Hector, to be so concerned with this little skirmish; you are the most efficient bookkeeper of all the drug traffickers—numero uno."

Hector flashed a smile but it faded quickly. "We have to stop this before it spreads, Arturo—it could spread revolution," he cried, stabbing the air with his hand.

"Do not worry yourself so, Hector," he said, evincing genuine sympathy; "it is no good for the body; did you know stress can cause high blood pressure, and lead to strokes; and the lack of sleep you are having can lead to heart problems, diabetes, and obesity; I know these things, I have read about it on Wikipedia; oh," he gestured at the disturbing thought of it all, "it is all so depressing—but you can do something about it, my good friend: try meditation, or listen to soothing music, like I do—they are both very relaxing and invigorating."

Hector seemed to be somewhat soothed as he stopped and stared at his boss. "You are correct, it is very troubling, and I need to manage my health better," he said, even-minded, then his thoughts took a wild flight when he retook the crisis at hand. "But how can I worry about so little a thing, when this ridiculous revolution is cutting into core profits—oy!"

Arturo smiled, nodding easily. "You should not worry yourself too much over such trivial matters, Hector; first, it is not a revolution," he began, holding the Merriam-Webster collegiate dictionary in his large, finely manicured hands, finding the proper page, and studying the fine print as he put on his bifocals, "it does not appear to be a revolt—no, that is certain," he placed his thick index finger on the word, "oh, here it is: a rebellion—certainly, against their masters; why, yes," and he took off his glasses, looking again at Hector. "Do you know what they are, eh? Yes, they are like cockroaches; yes, dirty, filthy peons in the dark who have taken over one part of the kitchen tile—one measly little, filthy square—and think themselves clean! Ha! The poor peasants, they will soon know who owns and runs that city."

"Do you really think so, Arturo—that the revolution, I mean, as you say, this rebellion is an anomaly, and will not spread? What if the Alvarez scum are behind it? Then they are encroaching on our territory—it is unprofessional; they have their market, we have ours." He sighed. "It is bad enough that we fight them in the States." He smiled. "Good news there, at least, eh?... An expanding market that we can easily meet—increasing our profits tenfold by our presence there; no more middleman, yes? That was a grand vision of yours, Arturo, to go north and control day-to-day operations—but that is why you are," and he flexed his muscles, "El Toro!"

El Toro smiled affectionately. "We have come a long way since our days playing soccer in the streets of Zapote, and stealing and running errands for the Higuera syndicate before we started to sell marijuana ourselves; boy, you remember our first hit, yes?" Both men laughed. "That fool, Señor Hidalgo, Chief of Police, who got greedy with the Higuera brothers, remember?" His deep voice became grave. "It is a lesson I shall never forget: it is like an appetite—eat until you are full; any more than that," and he shook his head, "muy malo—it poisons the soul, so you cannot see clearly."

"Good business sense," Hector said, calmer now, and now sitting again, "those were the days of our youth; golden days, too."

El Toro suddenly became agitated. "And I will not become some hunted animal like Gutierrez or Cabral, hiding in a different house every day, always on the move, afraid of everyone and every little thing; what good is an empire if you're hiding out in underground tunnels and surrounded by not family and friends but impersonal bodyguards you may not be able to trust, anyway; where is the loyalty these days, I ask you?"

"Yes, it is too much like a moving prison."

"Exactly," he said, enthusiastically, "a prison without bars, and built by not having enough foresight."

"We have to effectively deal with these tiresome people—how about rock, papers, scissors, as we did in our youth?"

"*Hola*! Perhaps I will meet with Tomas Alvarez, and will settle our disputes the way children do," and he put out his fist, and each man thus shook their hands down three times, and, as usual, El Toro, ever the rock, lost to Hector, ever the paper. "Maybe it is not so good," he declared, laughing and, taking hold of his authentic, circa-late-1930s German pistol, he said, his voice like the banging of steel on steel, "I suppose we need to convince them another way."

"It is Providence," said Hector, smiling as he shrugged his shoulders, and adjusted his big, black, horn-rimmed glasses.

"Now, what about the Defenders, eh? Do we know who they are yet?"

"Ha," he returned, waving away the subject in disgust, "those pipsqueaks, those little gnats…"

"Those insignificant fleas…"

"Fleas, yes—that is exactly what they are; we will soon find and crush them."

"How about the local authorities, the FBI, the DEA, the NSA, DHS, the CIA—surely, they will help protect us from them; I laugh until I cry tears of joy when I think about it."

Hector closed his eyes and shook his head. "These Defenders are few, we are many; they can be in only so many places, and we can be anywhere we lay down an Uncle Sam greenback—don't worry, if we don't buy information, the American authorities won't put up with them."

"Ah, cold, hard cash—it brings out true loyalty in a man!"

"Viva, US currency!"

"Viva, US marketplace!"

"Our coffers overflow; we should invest in US savings bonds for security: the stock market is too much like a woman lately—too volatile!"

"Yes, buy a few millions—and don't let Conchita hear you talk like that, she will have your head, amigo."

"You are right, she is a woman of great emotions; ah, but a new car always soothes her anger; by the way, how is the family?"

"Bueno—the children are growing up so fast; one communion after another."

The two men talked now of family, of relatives and friends, of pride and honor, just as any two men might who have known each other for so long, and who had been best man at each other's wedding, godfather to the other's first child.

A cryptic code was delivered to El Toro, who quickly deciphered it. "Yes," he exclaimed, upon reading the message, "we have the best and brightest code men and women in all the world!" He handed the paper to Hector, folded his callused hands behind his head, leaned back, and put up his big, black boots on the beige desk. "The El Dorado scum are going after control of the Northwest—can't they leave well enough alone? We control it—they have the plaza, the Cardenas Cartel theirs; it was determined, agreed upon…"

"Gifts exchanged…"

"The words of gentlemen given…"

"First Zapote, and now the Northwest; this is intolerable, and inexcusable; what is wrong with that pig, Alvarez—does he want it all? Does he realize that if he begins this, it will be a breach of contract?"

"We want peace, they want war."

"Then war, they shall surely have," growled El Toro, feeling like the fearsome name he had earned in his wild, unrestrained youth, when once upon a time he was a matador.

In the next month, it was reported that the El Dorado Cartel attacked the Azteca Cartel supply line, cargo shipments, production sites, and demolished airstrips. El Toro saw red.

Far across the arid desert, and into another northern state, lay the palace of the El Dorado Cartel, where they too had many sprawling complexes that were the nucleus of their operation; but at only one resided their leadership, the other big capo in the area, deep inside a cement bunker, and surrounded by a phalanx of bodyguards, his private army. His enemies called him Señor Muerte, but his men called him Mr. Alvarez, even those who had known him when he was merely a punk drug-runner, assassin, terrorist, drug-grower. He refused even the niceties of the extravagant wealth and growing empire he controlled, eating plain frijoles, tacos and corn, and playing narco-corrido music that sang about the exploits of the major capos; presently, he was listening to a song written exclusively for him.

He signaled for his main adjutant to enter.

"Do you have the statistics I asked for?" he began, more like the snarl from a dog who is eating greedily and is disturbed by another dog.

"No, sir." Fear settled into his voice like a creeping virus.

Alvarez stood up and stared straight at the trembling man. "Really? Why is that?" He rarely used the names of his subordinates, so as to dehumanize them, to de-power and un-rank them.

"We did our best, sir." He knew it was unwise to proffer any more information than asked.

Alvarez moved around the desk and stood next to the young, dark-haired man, his voice somewhat milder. "How long have you been with me?"

"Two years, sir."

Alvarez frowned, and nodded to the small radio. "You hear that song—about me," he said, nearly calm. "They say I'm number one—the best and greatest El Capo of all time; you think that is true, Luis?"

Luis, feeling calmer, and sensing the desire for brotherhood offered by the pleasurable pronunciation of his name, replied, in earnest, "Yes, sir."

"Really? Why?"

Luis smiled. "You are fearless, sir; you aren't afraid to take on the other capos when they are invading our territory; and you're good to your own people." He was worried about the last statement, but it was too late.

Alvarez was smiling now. "How is that?" He enjoyed hearing praise about himself, and like the peacock, fancied displaying his colorful feathers of hubris.

"Sir, you fought the Azteca Cartel for Zapote, and then, without blinking, you took a plaza from the Arroyo Cartel," he began, knowing that his boss preferred exact descriptions listed instead of mere, general praise.

"And," Alvarez said, smiling still, "what else?"

Luis knew he had to keep feeding the tiger, or the tiger would turn on him. "You give food to the people, build churches, and schools; you help the community more than any other capo."

"I do, don't I; that's true, I do," he said, nodding, and nodded again at the brown wooden radio. "That is why they sing my praise; hey, I'm not telling them what to write." Actually, he had bankrolled several of the narco-corrido bands and had presently written some lyrics, such as the one currently playing, and so many others, he could have made a handsome loyalty.

"Sir," the emboldened aide stated further, "you only push back after they push you." But after he said it, he felt a shudder of regret, and tried not to blush or show weakness, for he knew the anxious tiger, sensing this, would attack.

Alvarez pondered this assessment for a long period, as the frightened adjutant stood quietly at attention, knowing he dare not utter a response without a question directed at him.

"You're right, Luis," Alvarez answered him, finishing his lunch, as the next narco-corrido song about him began. "They have begun this war, so I will finish it," which was a bald-faced lie, as he was like the free-roaming pit bull who attacks the bull pup in a box—only when there is a clear and tactical advantage two ways. "If they hit me with a twig, I hit with a branch; if they throw a rock, I threw a boulder; if they shoot a bullet, I shoot a rocket." His face fairly lit up as surely as if he were in the presence of the god of warfare who had blessed and christened him as the warrior king; and, indeed, it was true, he escalated any confrontation, even a simple skirmish that by the passion of prudence would best be left alone and forgotten, but where he would then pursue it until the other side capitulated or was destroyed; and if they capitulated, he would move in and slaughter all, and once they were destroyed, he would, as in the case of a slaughter, then consume all their operations; his goal, in point of fact, was to be not just number one, but the only one. "So, Luis," he continued, seemingly pacified, as if a tiger whose appetite was satiated, "where are the statistics I asked for?"

Luis felt the alternate effect of icy cold, whose previous successor was boiling hot, purchase his body for a searing moment; it seemed the tiger had another stomach. "We will have them soon." He knew no amount of reasonable and even factual excuses—reasonable, good and easily checkable excuses—would suffice.

"Well, get it to me when you can."

"Yes, sir," Luis replied, relieved, for now, and exited, grateful that his head was still secure on his slender shoulders, and immediately upon finding the accountants who were delaying the results, upbraided them for their dullness of mind and laziness of spirit, and cast their minds into dark fear; shortly, he returned with the reports, handed them to the purring tiger, who expressed its pleasure at receiving them and then invited Luis to sit before him.

"I want your opinion on something," Alvarez began. Luis shuddered, for whenever Señor Muerte, as he recognized him more often than not, sought his opinion on a matter of some import, it was like navigating a minefield; and so it was his objective to ask more questions than give answers, so as to push Señor Muerte in a particular heading, and in so doing, deactivate the language mines himself. "You know we have had reports of the Azteca Cartel," he began, as even he, like Arturo Suarez, now accepted this misnomer of the drug traffickers, "sabotaging and raiding our shipments, our supply lines, our airfields; what do you think ought to be done?"

This one is easy, Luis thought. "They hit you with a hammer, you hit them with a sledgehammer; they do not respect you." He was confident that the last sentence, albeit unsolicited, was acceptable.

Alvarez smiled. "You're right, Luis, absolutely right—they don't respect us." He used "us" only when he felt his followers loved him. "We need to hit them back hard. Do you think we ought to wait?"

An imperceptible bead of anxiety shot down the back of Luis, digging its way into his skin, planting the opiate of doubt. Opinions will be the death of me, he thought; what is his mood? "Sir, we should strike only when we are ready." He grimaced inside, knowing he misspoke.

"What? We're not ready?" Alvarez shouted, as if the peacefully sleeping tiger, who had been dreaming of juicy kills, had just been stepped upon. "You said yesterday we are at full force to take over even the army!"

"Sir, I apologize: I was stating the obvious—of course we are ready—but I mean battle plans."

The face of Alvarez was slowly becoming studded with an evil portend. "We don't have a strategy mapped out to counter these attacks?" he cried, pounding the desk with his fisted hands.

Luis felt himself sliding deeper into the abyss that had been dug with his own careless, loose tongue. "We are analyzing the weak points and establishing areas of attack."

The tiger grimaced. "What good is that if they attack us tomorrow—they need to be stopped now!" He didn't really mean it—he had no such timeline to impede the encroachment of the Azteca Cartel, who were, at the moment, a mere pest to him—but he refused to allow others to think anything contrary. He had prepared battle plans months ago; in essence, he oversaw every facet of the El Dorado Cartel: tactics, strategy, production, distribution; every nuance, the progenitor of all areas of decision-making—father, son, counselor, banker, general, merchant, accountant, designer—because he bethought himself so superior that he could not lower himself to allow advice from those whom he considered stuck in a permanently submerged, backward culture— a caste of peons, peasants, and pea-brained worker bees.

"I will make sure the department heads of tactics and strategy..."

Alvarez cut Luis' stride in twain with a zenith-reached, boiling-pot, blowing-the-lid-off, horrific shout. "Do I have to do everything around here? I don't want to hear anything about another department—you just do what has to be done and bring me the report by 8:00 a.m. tomorrow morning, or department heads won't have one!"

"Yes, sir," Luis said, quickly, realizing that explication in the stern face of unbridled wrath was a poor choice of response.

"Yes, sir—what?"

"You will have the plans on your desk by eight tomorrow morning."

"Good," he answered, and, now at peace, lost interest in the topic, and returned to the narco-corrido ballad, which now referred to Ruben Perez as numero uno, and he shook his head in disbelief, cursed. "You know what my ultimate goal is, eh," he began, rubbing his fat, black-whiskered chin, as he stared out into his private domain of power, "I will be like those animals who have certain—how do you say," and then he gestured with his hand, which grasped the book on wildlife, "universal appeal for other predators to 'back off,' which is to say, certain colors that mean poison, like that wonderful creature the Coral snake—nobody messes with him because they see his orange and black colors and they know he means business! But, you know what, Luis, I'll bet you did not know that other Coral snakes, who are not dangerous at all, have similar colors—and still, still, they gain respect from their enemies; well, Luis, I will not be the snake with the false sense of protection—his bluff will last only so long—but I will be the King of snakes whom they know, and if they tangle with me," he shouted now, and suddenly standing up, raised his hand in the air, "they know their end is near!" He let out a loud "Ha," and then, nodding his big head, sat down again, and mumbled another complaint about the song.

"Now, that song is certainly fiction," Luis interjected, hoping to steer Señor Muerte back into the black pitch from whence he had bubbled up. "Perez doesn't have initiative, or the nerve you have; or," he felt emboldened, prodding him to make up for his prior gaffe, "the superior knowledge."

There was a faint glimmer of a smile on the countenance of Alvarez, the crimson of which was slowly disappearing. "Really?" He intended to sound still angry, but flattery had disabled his private ship, its canvas sail with the "black skull and cross bones attitude" being surreptitiously lowered. "How?"

"Sir," Luis responded, now moving quickly to the point, "when he hesitates, you strike; when he ponders on repercussions for his actions, you act; and when both of you meet, he always loses." He was smiling inside now, as he had long since formulated such mood-bolstering bombs to lob at the vulnerable vanity of his master at precisely such tender and raw moments.

The visage of Alvarez had lost its hard-tacked-on leopard skin and his common humanity illuminated it. He sniffed the air, and sat up straighter, his fragile ego normally drowning in self-debasement and doubt, now feeding on this like a hummingbird to sweet nectar; but then he felt embarrassment that perhaps Luis had noticed his ready acceptance of these compliments, and so resorted, although in vain, to grumble, and mildly accept what his adjutant had just uttered, and then he said, "Well, Luis, just let me know when the reports are ready."

A concession, Luis thought, as he retired, wiping his brow; that evening, he saw that Alvarez had placed another million dollars in Luis's foreign bank account, and he smiled, albeit cautiously, just like the lady astride the striding tiger.

Where the Revolution Began

It is true that the ultraviolence occurring in Mexico had begun once the government had decided to unleash the fury of the combined strengths of the military and assorted federal agencies against the Cartels, so that what had once been a war between Cartels, and their crimes against citizens, increased tenfold. The choices of the government had been to let the sleeping dog lie, or attempt to kill the rabies-infected murderer of the other neighborhood dogs, and cats; but instead, now, bad dogs grew stronger, increasing their presence throughout the land, as it relates to power, wealth, influence, and absolute, unrestrained terror, and as it were, throwing fuel on the already-out-of-control fire.

It is said that revolts give rise to rebellion, rebellion gives rise to revolution, and revolutions begat revolution; so it was true in Mexico, land of revolutions, first against the Spanish, the French, then the petty tyrants, the tyranny of one political party, the tyranny of perpetual poverty, and now, just another dominant force trespassing against the fundamental rights of the ordinary citizen.

It is always curious to see the stronghold the few mighty in strength and arms have over the many who are weak and poor in weapons, be it through prison, politicians, businesses, or the minority oppressing the majority with little else but bluff and bluster; what wall yet made can prevent unhappy prisoners from storming a few guards and bringing themselves freedom; what gun yet made can prevent an unhappy nation from rising up against corrupt politicians; what executive speech yet conceived can prevent unhappy employees from demanding equitable treatment; what big fist yet conceived can prevent even a drove of weak bodies and minds—are not those even frail and stick, when combined, born now of a greater strength—from overpowering a batch of overcooked and too-well-stuffed bullies? Fear, is the sorry refrain, but not fear of what might befall the challengers, but fear of what little crumbs they daily collect from their master's greasy lips, what little heat escapes from the fire their master's wide girth blocks, what little income they gain from the avarice of their master's project.

The people of Zapote were trampled and spat upon, and weary of the bloodied battle between the El Dorado and Azteca Cartels, who acted like two squabbling, spoiled children who crushed everything in their path and who cared not for the troubles of others; they were weary of reading about the dead, tired of seeing their own dead, numbed from the burying of their own dead. Rebellion was a soothing ointment on the unemotional words of the living dead.

Thus, inspired by the uprising in Yermo, the residents of Zapote stood up as one, and as one took hold of the El Dorado tentacle strangling their beloved province, and swiftly cut it off, armed themselves for the coming of the enraged body, and then awaited the same fate facing the citizens of Yermo.

The retaliation of the El Dorado Cartel was swift, and a contingency of paramilitary members—mostly foreign, numbering two hundred, thought sufficient to restore the iron grip of the El Dorado Cartel—was sent, and soon reached the outskirts of the city, stopping briefly upon a verdant bluff, to reconnoiter.

The bluff was a designated geographical point on the relief map of the world, but on one particular map belonging to the Crusaders, it was marked in red, surrounded by crisscrossed lines and connecting dots, and other highlights in yellow and green, which formed zones of stop, yield, and go, a strategic map of all of northern Mexico where the Cartels thrived—or, like ants, moved along the same well-trodden trail—marked and designated by name; where their bases of operation lay, marked and highlighted and named; and where the cities and provinces they held were marked and highlighted and named; where the drug traffickers' routes were, where the federal troops traveled, where past ambushes were, struggles fought, battles waged; yet, this was no static map, but a living document, created through exhaustive research of historical records, of papers, and magazines, and books, and the World Wide Web, and eyewitness accounts, satellite photos and live video, and reconnaissance by the makers of it: but more importantly, there were the contributions of a stealthy eye in the sky, the B35 Drone Guardian, able to fly over 15,000 miles without refueling and examine over three thousand nautical miles at a glance, operating as high as 50,000 feet and constantly scanning the Mexican territory and sending real-time information back its human masters; yet, for outside sources, this was half of the intelligence gathered, the other half coming from the spoken words of the Cartels.

It has previously been stated that many of the Cartels used a massive collage of towers erected across the country to create their very own private radio network—at first, unbeknown to the police agencies; and while using encoded language, they were able to blanket every territory with vital information from informants and from police informants, using walkie-talkies to transmit signals to antennas in virtually every conceivable place: trees, roofs, towers, high-rise buildings, mountaintops; and so, in conjunction with the massive amount of information offered on the World Wide Web, they could track the whereabouts of friend or foe, shipment by sea or air or land, and surveil any incident. And even when the police eventually found out about these antennas and tore them down, they could not keep up with the number of new ones the Cartels would immediately place.

Thus, as these two hundred men, hungry for the kill, stood on this rocky bluff, armed with Russian Kalashnikov rifles—now with the more modern AK-103, they were eager to sharpen their skills as much as a swordsman wishes to sharpen a dull blade, though their skill was kept active and polished by the killing of not only citizens, but many citizens, and their desire to ingest more power was inflated by killing more obstinate, defiant citizens, and by the killing not only of other Cartel soldiers, but any soldier; and to ingest even more power, they sought to kill well-armed, highly trained soldiers; but as for the killing of federal soldiers, and police, as it regards the Cartel's intake of power, any kill, any destruction of a life that was in a uniform that represented law and order, peace and freedom, imparted to them the greatest pleasures of all; and so as they gazed down upon the seemingly peaceful town, they considered themselves the highest order of life on the human food chain, the supreme hunter who had no qualms, no morals, no reservations about who they killed, nor the why, when, how many, what age, what gender, or for what reason of it all—for they considered this callous belief so great an honor that they wore its sanguinary badge proudly upon their bronze skin and arrogant iron mask.

Whence comes the idea,
to a human predator, great;
O mighty hunter, hunter of fates
thou becomes the hunted,
and human Justice awaits

Thus, set in mind and spirit to restore harmony with bullets and blood, they were preparing to set off, when a deep, sonorous voice slipped through the mystical air like a whirling mask.

"Surrender," it stated, in the stark language of the warrior in battle, "or die."

The two hundred highly paid mercenaries looked around and saw no one, and so scoffed as they raised their rifles; and yet, had they been able to see the snare they stepped into, they still would have balked, as arrogance and power had rendered their common sense mute as well as dumb. The leader cursed the unseen voice.

Dylan, McMillan Tac-50 sniper rifle in hand, appeared on the hill above them, protected by large boulders. "Lay down your arms," he shouted in Nahuatl, the Spanish dialect of the region, "or die."

The leader instinctively let loose a barrage of bullets at the lone figure, who swiftly disappeared; the leader, knowing he and his men were exposed in this position, also knew the options for cover were few, and so he led his men down the embankment to hopefully reach a forest of trees; but instead of a forest of green, they soon beheld a force of masked men, with rifles on the ready, and as the running soldiers began to fire, they were swiftly cut down as easily as a swinging scythe against a field of dry grass.

Had the leader known the full truth—that the position they had previously obtained on the naked bluff was akin to a shark swimming into a steel net, setting off a stratagem to allow the shark to swim a little further until he knocked into a steel cage; that the bluff and the surrounding areas were mere plot points on the map of the Crusaders, previously described, who had carefully scrutinized the movements of these war dogs for months, knew how they operated, and where, and when, because these El Dorado assassins, fearing no reprisals, acted not as cunning soldiers in war, who constantly think of every move, and countermove, where to camp in safety, where to stop and rest in safety, but as soldiers who move freely about, thinking nothing of strategy and tactics any more than a pack of ravenous coyotes think of it as they attack a herd of fluffy, white bunny rabbits—they, curiously, still would have pursued the same foolhardy course.

Dylan, still masked, accompanied by an unarmed man, rejoined his fellows, standing next to the bloodied corpses, and then said, "Go, tell the other leaders of Zapote that they are yet safe; but it must be spread, as rumor, that the Azteca Cartel did this."

The Zapote rebel leader, still in awe at the precision killing and might of these enigmatic warriors, nodded, and said, "It is like herding rats over a cliff," and then, "yes, it will be done, as you say; we are grateful."

"You know the risks," Dylan continued; "the El Dorado people will send more—the Azteca will send more…"

"We will be prepared," the man responded, "it must stop, this war—we have allowed it to go on too long; as our country is unable, so we must be able, and there will be innocent blood spilled—but that cannot stop us from what freedom begs us forward to do."

"May God and Justice go with you," Dylan whispered, solemnly, placing his large hand upon the man's slender shoulders; and after watching him walk slowly down the hill to regain his town, turned toward his own comrades, "and now, the Azteca Cartel will get their due."

It was war, and frivolous talk was buried deep with each drop of spilled blood.

The Azteca Cartel sent its own death squad to rain bullets and terror upon the residents of Yermo, a squad of ruthless, soulless assassins thirsty to kill anything that was not as they were—barbaric, cruel, and merciless; but they too easily fit into the ready noose fashioned so neatly by the Crusaders, and they too were given the chance to yield and live, but this was as likely as a pack of hyenas yielding to prairie chickens; so, instead they yielded their bodies back into dust, and their souls up to Judgment.

The leader of the Yermo rebellion stood with Dylan as the other masked Crusaders stood guard. "They would have our lives, these virulent monsters," Pablo cried, spitting symbolically upon the whole rotting mass of dead men, and then snapped his fingers, "just like that, as if we were nothing more than insects." He stood erect as he looked out among his defenders. "I wish to fight with you."

"Yermo needs leaders right now," Dylan said, placing his hand upon the man's shoulder. "Mexico will need leaders to rebuild her when she rises from the ashes." Seeing the youth nod approval, he continued, "You must convince the people that the El Dorado Cartel was responsible for this."

"It will be done," Pablo returned, eagerly, and then said, thoughtfully, "how can you fight the Cartels alone—it is inconceivable, as the government has failed, the local police have failed, the people have failed; it is too much to consider, although I pray for it with all my heart, soul, and mind for you to succeed."

"You know the risk when the Azteca Cartel hears of this…"

"What of it, eh? What can they do to us that we have not already suffered? How can Freedom be won without the shedding of innocent blood?"

Dylan nodded. "You are a proud son of Mexico."

A week hence, with the world-wide news of the Yermo and Zapote uprisings against the Cartels, and the increased violent battle between the El Dorado and Azteca Cartels, the Mexican government was compelled to send troops to both towns.

There are no secrets that money cannot purchase, and when the people who are tempted are poor, even a sparkle of silver will loosen their reticent tongue; thus, when the troops came, where they came, how they came, so too knew the Cartels—yet, what they knew, so too did one more force, to them hitherto unknown.

The federal troops, merely to be the first wave, were to land en masse at an airstrip near Yermo, load up their trucks and SUVs with weapons and cargo, and then drive into the town and prepare an adequate defense of it.

The four Lockheed C-130J Super Hercules planes landed—one loaded just with vehicles—the two hundred and twenty soldiers in the green uniforms disembarked, secured the periphery of the airstrip, watched the plane take off, and commenced toward their destination; this was when the first rocket was launched at them, and all of the men sensed immediately that their lives were over, that the never-ending nightmare of Cartel infestation in domination of war against them would never go away; this, they conceived of instantaneously, for their minds had been nurtured on expecting bad news, regret, and pessimism at the first sight, sound, or shot of their seemingly invincible, eternal, and omnipresent enemy.

The airstrip was bordered by two high rising hills, and the Azteca soldiers, stationed on the left, armed with mostly AR-15 rifles, and AK-103s, and RPG-7s, had begun their attack; but, alas, as they watched the federal troops scramble for cover, the brief ride of their projectiles was cut short by small, energetic, how-do-you-do, winged Angels of Mercy, which originated from the other side.

Indeed, above the fleeing troops there existed a phalanx of crisscrossing bursts of high-energy laser beams that blanketed them so completely that nary a gnat might escape through this flashing flood of coruscating brilliance, this extravaganza of bursting light that repulsed and ripped apart rockets, bullets, and grenades.

It was the worldwide debut of the Iron Phalanx, direct descendant of the Centurion C-RAM, cousin of the Iron Dome, and brother of the Iron Beam.

Where salvation births, that is where my heart lies, sings the poet, and the federal troops were no different, instinctively running up the hill and diving over the side to a miraculous safe place, having lost only six men, who had panicked and not been under the narrow protection of the Iron Phalanx or the accompanied firepower of its human companions.

To him who owes his life, a bond of brotherhood, eternal and loyal, germinates as a seed, and such wisdom entered into the minds of the soldiers as they fell into the protective embrace of the masked guardians, who presently crouched all before them, and introduced themselves as allies.

"Why didn't they just blow up the plane?" asked the Major of the man who was foremost in front of them, as if by this miraculous act of saving them, this man knew all.

"They like the show," the masked man replied, coolly, "but we must needs be after them, to lay a death wreath at the closing door of the Azteca traffickers."

"Who are you?" the Major asked, in earnest, as his men continued, with the other masked men, shooting at the enemy. "You are not Cartel; you do not seem like mercenaries…"

Dylan stood still, his luminous blue eyes staring at the man, and then said, passionately, "Liberators."

Tyr and Enkidu had already taken twenty men each to flank the left of the ambushers, while Cyrus, Horatius, and Rustem, together with Moses, had taken twenty men to flank the bushwhackers on the right. Samuel and Rhiannon stood on either side of Dylan.

"You are not from here," the Major remarked about Samuel, as he grasped his rifle.

Samuel smiled. "Anywhere my brothers are in chains, it is my home."

"Spoken like a true revolutionary," the Major said, gesturing on high. "I can tell we will get along famously; I am Major Ramon Gonzales, of the Twelfth Army Infantry," he said, and shook the hands of the two men before him, and the woman, and then looked at the huge Iron Phalanx, and shook his head. "Why don't we have one of these, eh?"

Dylan said, looking at the magnificent weapon, "It is our child, alone," and then nodding toward the opposite side of the hill where gunfire erupted still, whispered, "We have work to do," and after cautioning the Major on the dangers of using a walkie-talkie that could be heard by the enemy, instructed him that this ambush of the Azteca Cartel must be blamed on the El Dorado Cartel.

Now, with the combined strength of the two forces, forever allies forged in life and death, they easily defeated the Azteca soldiers, who refused to surrender and instead relished charging their enemy, and died in a hail of bullets and grenades. Ten federal troops were slain, and six more wounded; three Crusaders were wounded, but were quick to recover and later rejoin their comrades.

Once the battle was won, and after the Major had called for extraction by his commanders, the grateful federal troops stood in the midst of their bene-factors and listened with respect and admiration as Dylan spoke of things that must necessarily be.

"Presently," he began, still masked, and loosely holding his McMillan Tac-50 sniper rifle, his HK416 strapped over his shoulders, as the Crusaders stood behind him, "you must not speak of this place, not to anyone outside of those who remain with us now; you cannot trust, as you know, anyone outside of this place, for fear of retribution against not only you, but your family, for you know how easily your enemy drinks at the wellspring of corruption."

But the Major must needs be the representative of a sovereign nation, no matter his admiration and gratitude toward his rescuers. "We are forever in your debt—Libertados," he began, and he hesitated, looking about at the valiant, steadfast Crusaders, and his breast swelled with pride. "Libertad— libertad!" he cried, and his men echoed his exuberant claim, but then he calmed himself, and continued, "Yet, you are, perhaps, foreigners on foreign soil, sovereign soil, and must operate within the boundaries of sovereign law."

Another Crusader stepped forward, and came to rest next to Dylan. "It is as you say," he began, in his clearly distinguishable Kushite accent, "we are seen as aliens in your land, just as your people are seen when newly arrived in America; but, good sir, I would respectfully quarrel with you," and he bowed, and upon lifting his hand up, removed his mask, and addressed the whole army. "When liberty is shackled, citizens murdered, the resolve of the government unques-tionable, but the resolve of the enemy stronger," and as he saw Dylan remove his mask, and beheld all the Crusaders remove theirs, his mind purchased the proper words to woo this suitor, "it is the duty of every Freedom-loving man and woman to band with those who are oppressed, and in so doing, become as they: of one people, one nation, one world, who vow to battle against tyranny anywhere it is, for we," he now cried, "once we unite to wage the good fight against those who would rule us without mercy, all are brothers and sisters, of one family, one creed, one faith, that will not rest as long as injustice prevails, and will fight the world over to pursue what we all love—Justice."

"Justice!" the Crusaders sang.

"Justice!" the federal troops rejoined.

"Justice!" all of them erupted together.

"We are your humble servants," Moses continued, once the furor had lessened, in a severe yet sincere voice that penetrated the hearts and minds of all in attendance. "We are here to serve you; we have a strategy, devised through much deliberation, the mettle of it tested and forged in battle; we offer you the stratagem, and we pursue it, with your good company, or alone, for fight we must to alleviate the suffering of your people, as we can do no other."

The Major instinctively shook the hand of the brave and bold Moses, and saluted him forthwith. "I yield to your good cheer, and understand your credo; but it is a great weight upon my shoulders to abandon my rank in service and enjoin the battle with thee—though we are as one—against this terrible Leviathan that seizes our country in its steel jaws and rips it apart." He looked about at the brave Crusaders, and his brown eyes misted over. "Thou art champions of Justice, brave Crusaders, o'er the world—for all have since heard of your exploits in many distant places, and that you come here is entirely our honor; yet, my heart is heavy when I declare," and he gestured toward them, "that I must yield to country and service, and humbly decline your gracious offer to enjoin your battle; but, neither shall I hinder you." He looked solemnly at Dylan and Moses. "On this, you have my word, and along with it, our undying loyalty and our very lives."

Thus declared, the ephemeral hope of fusing two armies into one having vanished, the two groups exchanged hearty embraces and handshakes, and bid each other, no matter the barrier of language or culture, a fond farewell.

"Where shall you go now, my good friends?" Major Gonzales asked Dylan and Moses.

"Where we are needed," Dylan replied.

"Good soldiering," the Major responded.

"I should like to give you a gift," Dylan said, handing the Major a cellular phone and earpiece; "you may speak freely on it."

"Fascinating!" the Major exclaimed, examining the odd-looking, circular device and then placing it into his ear.

"Call on us as much as you care to, Major Gonzales; I only ask, upon seeing the cessation of your life—God forbid it, and protect you—moving over you, that you destroy it."

"Undoubtedly—secrecy above all, my good friends."

The two shook hands, and the Major the hand of Moses. "I bid you fare-well," he said, "and to fight the good fight."

"We wish you the same," Dylan replied. "God be with you."

And the groups, united in purpose, but divided in loyalty, departed.

"He is a good fellow," Moses said to Dylan. "He would join our little party had he no country affiliation."

"Yes, I believe so," Dylan replied, "he has an impassioned heart." And looking to the west, he said, "Let us travel to our next adventure quickly, for Robert has signaled more trouble for the Major's brethren."

And so, the Crusaders, packing up the Iron Phalanx onto a camouflaged truck, got into the camouflaged SUVs, and rode away into the scenery of a sinking orange ball of hot gases and brilliant, celestial light.

Comrades in Arms

When an American has a cultural epiphany that his form of government is not oppressive, but open, not regressive, but progressive, that society is not closed, but open, where the natural rights of Man might germinate and flour-ish and thereby provide the opportunity of a Good Life for hard-working individuals who are willing to obey the law of the land, such a person may feel the need to serve his country in such a manner that befits his patriotic fervor, either through the communication of democratic ideals in educational, journalistic, or political positions, through jurisprudence, either as an officer of the court or police, or agents of Justice, domestically or foreign, or, just as important, simply by being a good and productive member of the community. All of these citizens contribute to the betterment of society by adhering to a strict moral code that is not reducible to the mere reflection of a gutter-life whose foul proceeds flow to a sewer that sweeps into a pristine sea.

There is a class of citizen who has decided that they can best serve their nation by becoming a member of one of the seventeen intelligence agencies that are dedicated to protecting the interests and security of America, but in particular, by joining one branch where highly trained agents in various countries operate overtly, or if need be, covertly, thereby maintaining an effective and authentic pulse on that country in the event of a threat arising from the indigenous population.

There is an old and established CIA station in Mexico City. The people who work there know the customs of the land nearly as well as the indigenous population, and have labored meticulously and diligently to create a harmonious relationship with the people and police. It is a relatively calm and peaceful existence, for Mexico is an ally, and there have not been many reasons for sleuthing and skullduggery and the assorted games that spies play. But that was business as usual, in the old days, and that dull-and-ordinary yesterday was now long, long gone, replaced by the-world-is-now-upside-down today, and things-are-only-getting-worse tomorrow, and the-apocalypse-is-coming-unless-we-do-something-drastic-right-now future.

Mexico had been invaded by a foreign element that sought to devour her, noble head to firm foot, swarthy skin and strong bones and sinew, and drink her hot blood and then recast her in its own cold and iniquitous shape; turn her inside out, upside down, pick her up and shake her and loosen all of her virtuous restraints and erase her noble history and then violently smash her to the ground until she obeyed and acquiesced to its every sinister command; who was this thing, what nation had trampled her asunder, what sinister army now occupied her sacred ground, and what of the government's response? Yet, it was no outside agency that had invaded her, no alien territory that sought to dominate her people, no faraway head of state who had ruthlessly and so deviously planned her destruction, for it had come from within the infected heart of those who had decided that gaining enormous amounts of wealth was worth more than the lives of everyone but themselves, and the infliction is called avarice, which soon fuels power, and the main commodity is highly stimulating drugs. So, when the aforementioned-in-plenty Cartels began to spread their steely talons across the border into the United States of America, the CIA operatives in their Mexico City station, who had been bored by paperwork and monotony, were soon awakened, and set about to work with other intelligence agencies, such as the Special Collection Service and the National Reconnaissance Office—you might call them eavesdroppers with big radar ears—to see what they could see, and do what they could do, to stem this increasing threat to the stability of the Americas.

But the men and women of this office are flesh and blood, not of celluloid or paper, and no one is magically writing a script which excludes them from the perils of dealing with a monolithic machine that has no compunctions about wiping out any and all adversaries despite their country of origin, be they man or woman, young or old, with family or no, regardless of the place, time, or event; yet, the CIA agents must needs abide by their own sworn code of ethics, and therein was a dilemma, for they had not yet attracted the revelatory and necessary-for-survival notion that this enemy would do anything to assure all obstacles were clear of a path ahead that behind them was already strewn with the bodies of every conceivable kind of sinner and saint.

It was a Saturday night, and there was a celebration for one of their agents who was retiring after thirty years of dedicated service, and it was in the home of one of his co-workers on this sleepy, clear, warm evening, when you could walk outside in light attire and see the stars in all their magnificent glory. It was a joyous celebration, and all of the families of the agents were there, as were many DEA agents, who were stationed near the CIA office, and had worked closely with them, as they had socialized on many occasions over the years, making the event even more memorable and enjoyable.

And into the merriment and laughing and reminiscing was cast a pallid and squalid scent, this being achieved by a bold and rude voice that broke over the revelry like a poisonous vapor, "Prepare to die, you filthy trespassers, you filthy police—die."

The CIA agents on the periphery of this home were now dead, leaving for the people inside no good way to properly defend themselves against a squad of fifty-three assassins who had been promised a huge bonus by the boss of the Azteca Cartel—who had been lately irritated by the local agents as they dug into his furtive affairs—if the foul deed was done with style and finesse, and an exceeding harshness toward his perceived enemies, for he strove to achieve a supreme level for himself of a "state of inert conscience," like it was a colorful and honorable brand he was selling to the fearful public and his wary competition.

The operatives inside had guns, but not an arsenal, and the backup they called for would undoubtedly come too late. Being pragmatists, they knew all was lost, and so prepared their families for it. It was not right, they reasoned, but they also understood that the rules of this sordid game had changed, and they had not changed with it to properly combat the new players. But it was too late to mourn for what they should have done, and so they prepared to die with their loved ones; but at least they would not go down without a fight, and so the fierce but limited battle began.

The assassins had brought big-league weapons to a small-time affair—RPGs, fragmentation grenades, rocket launchers, AK-47s—and a lust for the blood of any police and their kin, and so they fired into the modest home with the excitement and thrill of obliterating their mortal enemies, desperate to kill representatives of this superpower they despised and perceived as having a condescending attitude toward what they thought was still their country.

It was America dying in that two-story, beige-colored home, the innocence of America being murdered without any perceived reason, murdered by thugs, rogues, gangsters, sowing a new breed of super-criminal, but really just a resurrected kind of human butcher that had incorporated its unique killing style into the very fabric of society, and no one seemed strong or smart enough to stop them. In the meantime, the house was being blown to bits and pieces, and inhabited now by smoke and fire. It was to be a massacre that was meant to draw a portrait of a kingpin who would fearlessly murder anyone from anywhere and from any country without reservation or worry of retaliation, as if he were the general of an army larger and more dangerous than anyone or anything who could possibly defeat this self-proclaimed emperor of his self-proclaimed, ever-increasing, territorial empire.

The Chief of the Azteca Cartel had wanted his men to not just kill these interlopers, but massacre them; to go inside the dwelling and torture and humiliate them so that they would die with a death mask of pain and suffering as an admonition to future interlopers. It was to be his latest crowning glory as he continued to stab at the beating heart of America's self-inflicted wounds.

The agents inside the disintegrating house, now upstairs with their weeping families, knew exactly who was behind this attack, and it all seemed so wrong, so horribly, morally wrong that such a group of anarchists and murderers and beasts in human flesh should be able so easily to kill them, and seemingly with impunity, as they had done to their fellow countrymen for too long; O, what they would do had they lived, the plans they now had, but as the boasting shouts and raucous laughter increased and drew closer, they could only accept their own inevitable deaths. The assassins outside broke into the house, promising pain and agony for their victims.

The agents had weighed the idea that suicide would be preferable to an atrocity perpetrated by these "degenerate, low-life, murdering scum," such desperate ideas they whispered among themselves as they heard the approaching villains ascend the staircase.

It is a curious thing, war—and this is what this was, a war recently begun and only extended now to include those Innocents trapped inside as one more prize for the Azteca Cartel to hoist upon its ever-increasing trophy wall— when two mortal enemies battle each other, and one side has gained momentum and is near to victory, that the inclusive din and human cry of the combatants is the same everywhere, of desperate pleas to continue the fight on the one side, and the intoxicating urging on the other to finally destroy that which was so long and hard fought against; it is surely a closed system that has no possibility for outside influence to interfere in it, no outside players who will fall from the sky and upend what seems fixed, and no altering the mindset of either.

But then there occurred a singular event that violated the identity of an unalterable and circumscribed battle that had a limited number of players and a clear and inarguable position that there was already a declared obvious winner and loser—weren't the salacious taunts of the salivating enemy even now echoing up the stairwell?—and lo, it was a loud, penetrating voice that originated from outside, which pierced all the players involved therein, "Americans, fear not, and do not lose hope."

The agents inside could not refrain from looking outside, and what wild wonder did they behold, what miraculous vision did they see hovering before them, but a distinct figure in midair far out beyond the house, harnessed in a kind of jet pack, firing upon their nemesis below; and yes, now they recognized more gunfire, too much now, occurring outside, and they could plainly see their rescuers systematically wiping out the assassins, and now pouring into the house and causing an explosion of noise with such massive firepower that it fairly shook the building. The huddled families, frightened and trembling, waited for what seemed a lengthy time, staring at the door before them, when the magnificent voice that had spoken to them began again, "You are yet saved," and with great caution still, they gazed again through the window, only to see the incredible vision of the figure who hovered before their window, partially lit now by whirring, dim lights. There was a serene harvest of quiet now as his hundreds of fellows, dressed in their black garb, assembled underneath him, some of them limping along, being held fast by their comrades; and when he spoke further, although the voice was electronically altered, its compassion and kindness was infused in his every word. "Forgive us for not being able to stop the killing of the brave men who guarded you, for we only recently learned of this attack."

The senior agent who was retiring, his mind still unable to process this phenomenon, asked, "Are you the Defenders?"

"Yes."

"We heard that you may be here." He paused, looking at the masked men below, and then said something that came not from his CIA-or a DEA-approved manual, but from his practically minded heart, "How can we help you?"

The man in the air did not speak for a moment, and then said, "It is how we can help you—we have broken the communication codes of these human monsters, and much more do we have to offer you."

The man inside the house nodded. "What was done here shall remain with us all of our lives, and we shall honor you always." He paused. "And now, we will fight together."

The man in the air nodded. "It is what we hoped for," he said. "Presently, you will receive information to help you fight this spreading pestilence." He paused, then continued, "Go with God, good and noble men and women, and children, and we shall yet have victory," and he forthwith blasted away into the ebony sky, his brethren slowly disappearing into the black envelope of night.

Now came the warm tears of relief and the joyous laughter of the families, all of whom were unhurt, and when they finally heard the wailing sirens of the approaching police, they finally understood what had transpired, and what could not, in their hearts and minds, be undone, ever: that a unbreakable bond had been born between them and their rescuers, that nothing human could dissolve it, nothing untoward, not even something innocuous that appealed to their modest sensibilities, for this bond was conceived at the highest and most fervent level, where exist men and women of surpassing courage who are prepared to give their lives so that Innocents might live.

Unfriendly Friendlies

The geography of the United Mexican States, in the uppermost region, is a combination of mountains and their forests, plains and their rolling hills, and desert, punctuated by desert shrub, like the Acacia and Jojoba, many a variety of cacti, including the Saguaro, and the Prickly Pear; and within these ecosystems thrive the mighty Oak, and the Velvet Mesquite; and a cornucopia of bushes, such as the Creosote and Indigo, and flowers, such as the Verbena and Evening Primrose, and arid grasslands.

Rough terrain for a prudent army proves to be a better ally, but a scourge for others; the proper use of the land for them is as crucial as weapons and supplies; it is reinforcement when they pursue, refuge when they are attacked.

Tyr and Enkidu, along with four indigenous citizens who had lately become Crusaders and who knew the enemy and its intimate territory, had gone down months before to this arid desert to reconnoiter and extensively scout, and thus had a masterful understanding of the flora and fauna; their report, along with virtual topographical maps and designated routes and statuses of the housing and main complexes of their enemies, were made available to all the Crusaders; yet, it was reconnaissance wedded to technology: the scouts, as they traversed the terrain on horseback, on donkey, on foot, in Jeeps, shot into the ground, from a special pistol that had a large, oblong barrel, a dart-shaped tracking-video-audio sensor that was connected to satellite imagery—aptly called the Eva, which was abbreviated from "eavesdropper" by the scientist-inventors in Robert Heimdall's employ—that, once embedded, its tip jutting out, could detect any large movement, record any sound, videotape any creature within its 360° rotating lens; once the system was in place, an electronic map of its location showed up on any of several electronic devices: cellular, tablet, or computer, portraying a convincing roadmap of its exact presence, and offering a real-time update of all available data in every quadrant in which it sat, like mischievous imps, spying on those disturbing entities that required extra-special care.

The Crusaders, traveling in the roughest parts of any region they entered to avoid confrontation with federal authorities, were dressed in flame-resistant desert camouflage: MultiCam, patterned; olive-colored Enhanced Combat Helmets, capable of stopping, at close range, shots from high-velocity rifles; body armor capable of stopping rifle rounds; custom-made light brown combat boots; a hydration system that allowed the wearer to sip water from a straw. Most of them carried the HK417 rifle and a sniper rifle of their choosing, and the SIG Sauer P320 pistol, which chambered 9 x 19 parabellum rounds; some of the Crusaders carried the XM25 Counter Defilade Target Engagement weapon, which delivers grenades over an ensconced target, and, once exploding, rains fragments upon them; a SAT phone, complete with GPS, capable of sending and receiving images, texts, and continuous assorted data; but they abandoned the use of exoskeleton uniforms, and the movement toward more technology that would burden them, for they would not be the future soldier who is weighed down with so much wear and technology that his footstep, when it needs be light, is heavy, and his eyes averted to reading manuals, when they need to stay alert.

Now, although they wore the recognized dress of the combat soldier, and bore the weapons and accessories, too, they could not ostensibly troop around a modern nation so undisguised; instead, they wore easily detached casual wear on the outside, and stowed away their equipment in false compartments; as to their palpable reason to be here, they had the proper passports, and proper documentation and permits, alleging that they were indeed a movie crew replete with camera and props—which shielded a large weaponry—who, in fact, occasionally stopped to "film" scenes from an actual written script.

By the by, it soon became necessary, as related to by Tyr and Enkidu, and the other scouts, after arriving back from a long trek and having observed Federal Police in the vicinity, that the Crusaders, anchored on a remote hill, surrounded by dense brush and trees, must now prepare the ploy.

Dylan and Rhiannon walked hand in and among the green poplars, silent under their leafy, spreading hood, thinking of times past, when such repose was preceded by joy and brought tranquility and harmony. They sat down under a giant Oak and leaned against its thick, corrugated trunk.

Rhiannon spoke, with eyes closed and heart open, her voice suffused with the nostalgic longing of a long-ago, cherished past. "What would we be, if not for our elders? Would we have drawn the sword? Was our fate created in Africa or merely realized?" She leaned her lithe body against his, resting her head, with its long, straight, auburn hair, upon his brawny shoulders.

"Where we are," he returned, quietly, unassuming, "is where we must be: it is who we are—it is who Conall and Eleanor were." He felt the soft squeeze of her hand upon his. "It is who our children will be; it is our heritage." He felt a shudder cross from her body and touch his, and he felt great sorrow for her. "Conall taught me that if you are honest with yourself, you will know who you are, and what you are, and what you must be."

"Yes, yes, Eleanor often spoke of the same, and she would often say to me, 'Rhiannon, people can tell you what you might be and must be, and what to do, but those people may not even know who they are.'"

Had Dylan been able to breach the physical barrier of her heart and mind—not that he did not possess a true soul of the faithful husband, who is truly one with his wife; a singular talent to interpret her every move and nuance and therefore gain entry into her heart and mind—he would have seen the powerful hurt a mother bears when not only does she have no child to love and hold and raise, but having lost two babies already, an indescribable scar has been forged that is so painful and deeply embedded in her wounded psyche, that he could not fathom it. Had Rhiannon been able to breach the physical barrier of his heart and mind—not that she did not possess a true soul of a faithful wife, who is truly one with her husband; a singular talent to interpret his every move and nuance and therefore gain entry into his heart and mind—she would have seen the profound regret that he had failed her too many times, and in so doing, failed himself, thus wounding his pride and self-respect, but also, that he had failed his two precious, blessed children, imprisoning him in an abyss so deep and dark, and haunted by his own inflated and cruel failures, that she would not have recognized his tormented spirit. And it was this unbound, seemingly impenetrable anthology of unre-solved stories of horror and doubt that would not, must not be allowed to verbally penetrate the veil of gloom and announce its presence here. It was better that they held each other than talked, and caressed and soothed the other, and were near the other, to offer healing, and in so doing, keep the tragedies of the past, past.

And yet, they were in a war zone, and plans needed to be scrutinized, altered, and improved often, so the two departed as Dylan walked up to Moses, who was talking to Samuel, the latter two of whom had become fast friends.

"Rhiannon is a remarkable woman," Moses said, having seen the two depart; "you are fortunate to have so faithful a wife at your side—and in battle, too."

"And how is your beautiful wife, Sumiah, and your beautiful children, Uduru and Mohammed, the little rascal?" Dylan responded, still on the periphery of his deep reverie with Rhiannon.

"They are well, and they still talk about the remarkable collection of Kush artwork you sent last Christmas."

"Where would you get such fine gifts?" asked Samuel.

Moses smiled, and intervened, looking at Samuel with a wink, and then at Dylan. "He is sly, this one—the connections he made in between fighting rebels..."

Dylan smiled, thinking of the years in Africa after the death of Conall and Eleanor, and how he and Moses had healed their rift, and fought side by side, but especially in Kush, to keep the new democratically elected government in power; it was then that he and Rhiannon had met Sumiah. "It's a gift," he said, smiling, gesturing too; "what can I say?"

The three men gained the shade of a slow-moving caravan of tall Oak trees.

Samuel spoke first, his soft voice betraying his soft heart.

"I lived a certain ideal that claimed Man is redeemable by himself, and now I live an ideal that proclaims Man as irredeemable without God—and those who resist immorality must serve recompense upon those who do not and hurt the Innocent, or all is lost." He paused, and looked about the elegant landscape around him. "I must needs be here, or perish as a man."

"It is all about recompense," Moses said. "In my country, if a man does not stand up against the rising tide, not only will he be crushed, but his family, and friends, and his community, as well, for he is an essential link of the sword and shield of Justice."

Dylan smiled briefly. "You sound princely, sire," he said.

Moses' smile had nothing to attach itself to, no good soil to live on, no nutritious fertilizer to help it grow, and he closed his coal-black eyes. "The good men of my country—of any country—can never sleep; the conscience of a just man, a righteous man, who loves Liberty, and Truth, cannot allow iniquity to flourish; O," and his voice descended into despair and frustration, "the horrors of some nations, the horrors some men visit upon another—how can they, as human beings, commit such unspeakable atrocities? How can they yet be called human; do we dare call them human; shall they be afforded the rights and laws according to other men?"

The men were quiet for some length, and then Samuel spoke.

"I should like to visit your country, Moses, yes," he nodded, as if the speaking of it solidified this offer. "I and my wife should like that very much."

Moses extended his hand to the big man, and they shook hands. "I would be honored, Samuel Longfellow, by the presence of you and your wife in our humble land."

Tyr and Enkidu, and the four other Mexican scouts, came up to them, and nodded.

"Recompense," Dylan said, as he stood, "Nature has inherent balance; Man must have his own," and he looked with pride at his fellow warriors. "So, let those be removed who have created this too, too heavy scale of injustice, and let us right a wrong."

Every move the Crusaders made was carefully calculated and coordinated, every plan capable of modification, every operation explored for retreats, for lures, and the unexpected that would leave them to branch off in the safest route.

The Crusaders were in seemingly casual positions of filming when upon them descended a battalion of fifty black-uniformed Federal Police, all of them armed with AR-15 A3 Tactical Carbine, MP5 Heckler & Koch submachine guns, and Heckler & Koch USP pistols, and arriving in a dozen black SUVs. The officer in charge hopped out of his vehicle and approached the film crew.

"Who is in charge here?" he asked, casually.

"Here," Dylan responded, walking toward the Major, and he easily shook his hand. "I suppose," he said, smiling, "you need to see our permits and passports?"

"Well, yes, that would be necessary, but I'm really here to warn you about rebels in this area."

"Rebels, you say?" Dylan said, frowning. "Are you serious?" And he looked quizzically at his crew. "What would they want us? We mean no one any harm."

"Ah, yes, but these particular rebels—they mean anyone harm," the Major said, walking around, admiring the equipment. "Is it a movie you are shooting?"

"Why, yes, sir—low-budget, action movie; but yes, a movie, an action movie," he said, enthusiastically, holding up a mock rifle and pretending to shoot his amused crew. "We hope to at least get back a little bit more than we put into it, and then, you know, with a good crew—you guys are the best," he shouted as he turned toward them, and then turned again toward his guest, "perhaps we will start making a profit."

"Good, good," the Major said, "good for the economy of Mexico; good, more money with which to fight these irksome terrorists."

"Should we leave, sir, you really think we should?" Dylan asked, sheepishly.

"No, I don't think so," he returned, pursing his lips.

"Well, maybe we can film them, with their permission; of course, the way Pancho Villa was once filmed; wouldn't that just be spectacular!"

"Movie people," he said, shaking his head, and then, "we are monitoring this area," and with a smile, "we will let you know," and with that, he bid them a fond farewell, and after returning to his SUV, issued a hand gesture for his force to move on.

When they were clear of the periphery of encampment, and after the area had been swept for electronic listening devices, the other Crusaders had their fun with Dylan.

"What a ham!" Rhiannon said, laughing.

"An Academy award!" cried Samuel.

"Speech, speech," said Moses, smiling, and then laughing.

Dylan had to laugh, and then bowed. "This is merely the first act, fellow artists." These words dampened the levity of the moment. "Positions," he said, seriously now, "and we will see what wicked things this way come."

Soon, they did see this two-legged monster, but this time, they were not acting, and assumed their dramatic positions as the cameras rolled.

The duplicitous snake, it seemed, had sent its envoy, the spy, to precede it, and then reported back to its slithering master.

Along, then, came a contingent of fifty men, riding in open Jeeps, heavily armed, driving boldly straight up to the site where the sixty men and women were allegedly engaged in a mock firefight scene, and, upon seeing the caravan of mean-looking, camouflage-wearing, rifle-carrying men, halted.

The lead Jeep halted near Dylan, and a tall, bald, heavily tattooed, cigarette-smoking man, carrying an FN FAL semiautomatic rifle and packing an FN Five-seveN semi-automatic pistol in a black leather holster, stepped out and walked up, in a cocky, confident swagger, to Dylan, who was, after all, the one sitting in the director's seat.

"Hey, John Ford," he shouted, gesturing about, "are you the one in charge of *Gone With the Wind*, here?"

"Actually," Dylan responded, calmly, "Victor Fleming—after replacing George Cukor—directed *Gone With the Wind*."

The big man lifted his strong right hand to backslap he who dared back-talk his own grandiose person, but it would have been easier to hit a hummingbird with a soap bubble.

Dylan had already anticipated such an unruly action, and he lifted his left hand and easily caught and contained the large fist, and then he said in a calm voice accompanied by an amused smile, "Have you a business card? Are you an out-of-work actor? We have auditions tomorrow..."

The men behind their leader cranked up their weapons and directed them at the crew.

When the leader felt the concentrated power of his prey reduce his own strength to a paltry, quivering mass, and gazed upon the fire flashing in the cobalt eyes of his antagonist, he was unusually frustrated; but he yielded for the moment, letting down his hand, for he knew his game plan, and was satisfied with what he considered was a foregone conclusion. "You," he growled, "and your," and he, being consistent with his bestial nature, uttered harsh invectives toward the crew, "people need to vacate these premises."

Dylan was unmoved. "Really—such foul language—tsk, tsk; and yes, by whose authority do you storm in here and demand our hasty withdrawal?"

"Mr. Kalashnikov and Mr. Glock," he grunted, holding up first his rifle, and then withdrawing his black-pearled pistol.

"Good friends of yours, no doubt—how perfectly provincial of you," Dylan responded, dismissing the man as he, still standing squarely in front of him with Samuel and Moses on either side of him, looked at the other armed men; "a formidable group," and then to his main antagonist, "you have introduced me to your mute friends, but I do not have the pleasure of your acquaintance," and he reached out his hand.

The leader frowned in disgust upon this gesture. "We patrol this area for the government, see," he said, smiling now, as he pointed toward the Federal Police as they surrounded the grounds high up on the outside of the periphery.

"Oh, I see—bodyguards, or something to that extent."

"Yeah, something like that…"

Dylan feigned surprise. "Yes, yes, now I know—I have seen documentaries about this—your military contractors, that's it, isn't it; American ex-Special Forces chaps hired to protect the people from—who? The Narcos! How thrilling! I would love to film your daring exploits."

The tone of the man with the black goatee darkened into the deadly season of a killing field. "Hey, you know, pal, I would really love to chat with you, but," he said, firmly, pointing at him now, "you really need to pick up and leave."

Dylan, looking past him to the waiting Federal Police, gestured toward them. "Why don't you and your friends stay and protect us while we film? I might even put you in the—"

The man, unaccustomed to subordinates—anyone who was not with him was against him, and anyone who was, and was without a weapon, was a subordinate—shouted and let loose violent curses into the balmy air. "You need," he screamed, so that his face grew crimson with wrath, "to leave."

Dylan, his face as stoic as ever, his body relaxed, dared creep closer toward the man. "So, friend, why aren't you making us leave—you have the real guns."

The man was taken aback, and fumed momentarily, and then, issuing a loud "humph," said, in a sonorous voice, "Don't worry, we will."

Now, Dylan smiled that cunning, I-am-way-ahead-of-you smile, that, too-confident, satisfied, I-look-like-I-will-lose-in-a-situation-that-seems-desperate-but-in-reality-I-know-I-will-win grin.

Dylan said, "You're a soldier—no doubt a soldier of vigorous training, a veteran of many battles against many formidable opponents," he began, but his "pleasant, accommodating, yet mischievous voice" had been abruptly buried by the ax and replaced by the glittering sword, and the man before him felt it pierce his inner, surprised coward, which lives in all of us, especially those who suppress it by killing defenseless, innocent people. "I am wondering if you have ever fought someone you did not bushwhack, and how formidable you would be, then."

Now, the big man in the combat fatigues was pleased, and nodding, with a pile of scorn upon his big, meaty, ruddy face, he laughed when he said, "The real you," and then gave a genuine smile as he nodded. "I could have used a soldier like you—but we are on opposite sides of this one."

"I knew of a man like you once," Dylan said, musing about Africa; "he was a good man who chose the wrong side."

"And whose side is that, huh?"

"Anyone who is against us is on the wrong side."

The man smiled, then laughed. "I don't know who you are, but I have to hand it to you—you've got nerves of steel."

"How so?"

The man, still smiling, said, "You are surrounded by more than a hundred men who are heavily armed, and you're talking like you really are directing this picture."

"My plan, exactly," Dylan said, coolly, looking about; "we will be leaving soon, either walking unimpeded, or over your stinking corpses."

The man laughed uproariously, and now he looked about as he gestured toward the film crew. "Am I missing something here? Even if those are real weapons, you're outnumbered, are out in the open, and clearly have a tactical disadvantage."

"Just ad bellum," Dylan answered.

"Eh? What's that—Italian?"

"St. Augustine: 'it is the just recourse to war.'"

"Well, partner, very soon you will be able to ask him all about it."

His men, in earshot of this, laughed.

"Americans choosing sides in a conflict that begs no side to be chosen—shame on you."

The man shrugged his muscular shoulders. "Hey, when good ol' America isn't invading countries, a guy has to eat; so, we sell our expertise to the highest bidder."

"You betray your ideals for money—unless, of course, you never had any."

The man wasn't laughing now. "Your time has run out, Victor," he whispered, leaning toward Dylan, with a smirk. "So, what happened to this good man who dared oppose your sacred ideals?"

Dylan responded, in the assured tone of the commander, who, despite it being only the beginning of the battle, knows he has already won. "You'll be seeing him soon."

The man, grasping harder his ubiquitous surrogate, his rifle, shook his head in disbelief, and said, pointing his free hand at his antagonists, "Am I missing something here? You're delusional."

"Why didn't you kill us when you came upon our encampment?"

The man smiled, acknowledging the tone and tenacity of the remark with a small nod of his round head. "There is no one within a two-mile radius of here—our scouts have checked; wherever your other men are, they will not be able to help you."

"You had to be absolutely certain that the kill was clean; that is not war, it is hunting."

The man sneered. "You're mercenaries just like us, foreigners who came here for fortune, and it doesn't matter for which Capo or El Narco you are working; all I know is, you ain't working for mine, so, go, you will…"

"So, you will murder if the price is right."

"It's nothing personal, friend, it's just war—and you picked the losing side."

Dylan looked at the Federal Police in the spread-out formation, and the other mercenaries in their surrounding formation, and then back to the leader. "I will offer you salvation: one chance to live."

The man frowned, shook his head, looking down at the ground, breaking it up with his foot; and then looking up, smiling, he said, "Friend, I kept you alive this long because I was curious about your little troupe here; but, you know how that goes—once satiated," and assuming a hard look as he readied his rifle, "boredom sets in, and it's off to the next topic of interest."

"Mala in se," Dylan uttered, "'evil in and of themselves.'" He shook his head. "When this is over, tell your patron saint that he will need to build more accommodations soon." And then he said, "We won't resist," and waved to his comrades, who, after carefully tossing aside their weapons, presently lay down on their stomachs; and then he, as he lowered himself to the ground, solemnly declared, "You will have to shoot us—in the back—as we lie defenseless; I will make it easy for you."

"Hey, I have no problem with that at all; I appreciate a man who realizes he's lost, and doesn't beg, or resist needlessly; it shows professionalism," the big man said, amused, and then he raised his hand; but as he did so, before the murderous little accomplices could come crashing out of his and his men's weapons, there came a terrific explosion of bullets, loud and clamorous, like pounding hail magnified, so fierce that the Crusaders, with their Enhanced Combat Helmets still on, clapped their hands to their ears, and then simply waited until the deadly barrage was over; and then, with utter confidence, they stood up, unscathed, observing with little sympathy the bloodied and battered bodies of these once-aspiring butchers near them and on the periphery, where bodies lay in scattered clumps of blood and guts and smashed arrogance.

Dylan stood over the still corpse of the now suddenly much smaller leader, and crouching next to him, made a pronouncement: "Just ad bellum," he whispered; "that which decays and rusts purchased your soul for cheap; and in its stead, you lost the treasure that is life." He stood up as Rhiannon walked up and embraced him.

Samuel looked at the desolation of life. "How came these men to such tragedy and sorrow?"

Moses said, his voice hard and resolute, "They became who they truly were, no matter their environs; be it Kush, America, or here; such men needs be killed, or we allow Innocents to die."

And then they looked over to the ridge of trees wherefrom their rescuers had emerged.

"He forgot what a good soldier does before battle," Dylan said, watching the other Crusaders, and the federal Allied troops stepping out of their underground compartments.

"Yes—reconnoiter, early and often," Moses said, "and anticipate," as he watched a few men moving the Iron Phalanx from its deep hiding place.

Major Gonzales walked up to Dylan, black smoke still drifting out of the end of his hot rifle barrel. "This was a great chance, my friend, to prove a point."

Dylan, still looking down at the former big man and butcher of Innocents, said, "I know his modus operandi: he enjoyed meeting his worthy foes—gentlemen in a duel; but I know he was hesitant because of our reduced number, as he must have heard we were much larger; I know…" He looked at the Major. "You know, and now you know more so, how corrupt it has all become," and he gestured toward the dead Federal Police on high, "when the Narco insurgents can buy the government—then they become the de facto government, and law and order is from their perspective; they have captured the state, controlling territories, and although Mexico is not yet a failed state, anarchy is destroying the equilibrium and fabric of society, one strand inextricably bound to another, from the very bottom to the highest top."

"Yes, I agree; yes, you're quite correct; and even when you called me and told me of your plan—that the Federal Police and these mercenaries were stalking you—I did not want to believe how bad it had all become, even though," he suddenly cried, "this is my homeland, and I have seen her devoured by such ruthless men; and yes, yes, it all needs to end; and we pledge our loyalty to your just cause—our just cause; we will be one army now, son of Cuchulain—I pledge it!" And all of the Mexican troops, and the Crusaders, being lovers of Equality and Justice, cheered, as they felt the waking of the birth of Liberty in this lost land.

"So, tell me, Dylan, about these underground bunkers—fascinating!"

"Yes," Dylan returned, smiling knowingly, mischievously, "we have built them—everywhere."

"Fantastic," the Major said, "lure the enemy in and spring the trap—exquisite!"

Dylan no longer smiled, acknowledging information he had just received on his earpiece-com unit. "We will be generous in giving credit to the El Dorado Cartel for this massacre."

The encampment was vacated, leaving no resistance for the scavengers of the sky and land to dine on a plump, ripe meal of their own kind.

Pruning of the Sheep

The rebellion in Zapote was not unlike the rebellion in Yermo, in that it had begun spontaneously and spread prodigiously, until the rebels had pushed out the invaders and held the city; now, this had two consequences, one intended, and the other inevitable; it inspired the captive state to rebel against their master, and it aroused sympathy around the world for their just cause; yet, there were two more consequences, each highly predictable: the Cartels of each state sought to reestablish themselves, afraid to evince weakness to other Cartels, and the federal government sent troops to disarm the rebels, which, again, created another unanticipated consequence: the rebels, too long frustrated by the apathetic government response, and the incompetent and often timid response of their duly elected officials, politely refused to yield a stance that afforded them, for the first time in a decade, a position of power and dominion, and— more importantly—liberation from the daily stranglehold and relentless massacre by an army that held in its bloodied hands a rotten, broken moral compass.

As it was, federal troops, the crack Special Forces Corp, were being sent to disarm and then safeguard the citizens of Zapote, on the next day after the federal troops, led by Major Gonzales, had landed near Yermo; he, decidedly, had radioed in to his superiors of the attempted ambush, and admonished them to wait, or send more accompanying troops to Zapote; alas, what seems facile and commonsensical in the real world is a hard and complicated entanglement in the deeply bureaucratic world of the military and government; decisions that any intelligent analyst could make and initiate instantly were forced here through a bottom to top filter that, once scrutinized and debated and approved, were then sent back down the same unclean filter, where, perhaps now with a "yes," or perhaps a "no," and coupled with unnecessary questions and suggestions, now befouled the original intent of the information sent, so much so that the order for more reinforcements was unduly delayed, leaving those who waited for rescue to do what they had always done—fend for themselves.

The first contingency of two hundred and twenty troops were close to landing on the outskirts of Zapote when grenades launched by a handheld rocket found their way into the soft underbelly of the four C-130J Super Hercules—three with troops, one with equipment—disabling them, and forcing a hard landing, in which they crashed and slid on the dirt airstrip, finally coming to a rest in a blackened and smoking heap. The four hundred El Dorado Cartel soldiers continued in their zeal to pump hot lead and rockets into the now-burning planes. It was the kind of fight the Cartels were motivated by: ambush, unfairness, slaughter, no contest, brutality, no prisoners, the bodies mutilated afterward as a message that they were indeed capable of any inhuman act, if only to further their status as a meteoric force not to be reckoned with.

It was nighttime, dark as pitch, senses sealed in a black sea of thick and swirling fog, where one could not observe one's own hand right before one's own eyes, where the only light was coming from the burning of the wreckage and the flashes of fire from the hot barrels of the AR-15 or AK-103 or M24 carbine rifles of the El Dorado soldiers, or the M203 grenade launchers.

The airstrip had not been built with the idea of a quick discharge of troops into thick brush and small hills in the case of ambush; it had, simply, been built, in the wide-open spaces, where on each side there was a large swath of bare dirt that might possibly be trespassed by the swiftest runners in seven seconds, but in those precious seconds to enjoin a small protective mound and thicket, the hail of gunfire rained upon an individual would be terminal; so, now, the troops were trapped in the three C-130J transport planes with their steel hulls that were being replaced by steel bullets and fragments of rockets; or, they might chance for cover, and hope the enemy had no infrared scopes to impair their mad dash.

But the El Dorado soldiers had infrared heat sensors on the rifles, and systematically mowed down the escaping troops as easily as a bear digging for a honeycomb in a beehive.

"We are lost," thought each of the remaining men as they sat inside this one particular burning coffin, as they listened to the death song of the massive firepower smashing against the diminishing plane; "we are undone," they heard, when their Major shouted above the clamor that no immediate rescue could be effected. "We are sacrificed for nothing," echoed with each ricochet and powerful blast of projectiles ripping holes through the waning metal.

"Let us go out like proud soldiers in Mexico," the Major shouted to the shivering, frightened men; "they cannot kill us all before we get to the mound. We go out firing and die like proud soldiers of Mexico; we will not die like trembling mice hiding in a snake's hole—viva democratic Mexico!"

After putting on their infrared goggles, the men prayed, and crossed themselves, and bid silent farewells to family and friends, and prepared their mortal bodies to yield up their immortal spirit.

And then the Major's cell phone rang.

He held up his hands. "Providence," he cried, exalted, into the slender, oblong black object.

"No," the voice responded, "but close." He felt a deadly chill. "Tell your men to surrender their weapons, and come out." He noticed now, yes, he did, that the incessant, spitfire carnage of weaponry had ceased.

The Major was in disbelief. "Who are you?"

"Your salvation, Major; you and your men come out, and we will allow you to join the El Dorado Cartel: or, if you prefer, you may die a gruesome death. I do believe in giving a good soldier a choice."

"Conscription at the point of a gun?" he responded, outraged. "You're slaughtering my men, and then you seek reconciliation? We do not negotiate with terrorists, and neither will the men in the other planes!"

The voice was calm and relaxed. "Life or death—it isn't a very difficult decision; be glad I feel sporting today."

"If we live, we die for God and Country; if we die, we die for God and Country."

"Noble words, but that won't soothe your families when they stand weeping over your blown-to-bits, burnt-to-a-cinder bodies."

"A conscience less bruised is no conscience at all, but a justification for wrong."

"Bravo, Major—you are a philosopher, but soon to be buried with the epitaph, 'he died needlessly.'" He paused. "I will offer you and your men sixty seconds to think it over."

Three of the remaining sixty-five men had already contemplated the seemingly magnanimous gesture, and came rushing out the door, screaming, "We have no weapons—we accept your offer."

No subsequent gunfire was heard.

"We want to live," nearly half the men cried, out of their wits, trembling, some weeping.

"They will kill you!" the Major returned.

"We will die, anyway!"

"Tortured—mutilated!"

"We risk death!"

"We risk life!"

Seven more men charged outside, and after laying down their weapons, footsteps were heard, and no subsequent gunfire, an attractive inducement for the remaining men.

"Even if they let you live, you live as a murderer, a monster; and if you seek to leave, they will only hunt you down," the Major shouted. Five more men rushed past him. "Go, go, all of you cowards, traitors to your country, your morals..." But even before the Major could finish, twenty-two more men had rushed out, leaving only fifty-seven men prepared to die even at the hands of those recently called "brothers." "Mexico, thou art lost," he sighed, his body and soul heaped in a slump, "when treachery purchases life." The other men voiced their loyalty and willingness to die. "Perhaps it is better that you do live—if live they allow you, if being with them might be called living; and if you can flee from them and live with your marred conscience; alas,

I cannot." Tears of piety met his grateful heart. "We die as proud Mexican soldiers, who fight this villainy unto death; so, let us do this, and plant the seed of a conscience in those who continue the good fight, and in our ex-patriots, who, if alive, will be forced to kill those whom they recently loved." He nearly wept. "You are my incorruptibles," he whispered to his men, "your rewards will be great in heaven, as you are now soldiers of Christ, willing to die for what is noble and right; you have not lost your soul for the price of this corrupted world."

His cell phone rang.

"I gave you a chance," the voice said, arrogantly; "your men are safe with us—now they are more us, than you. Prepare to die for no good reason."

The Major and his men prayed fervently, and prepared themselves for the final battle.

"We die as men, they live as cowards," he said, looking with pride at his own, truly, his own family, as much a family as any father and his sons, a squad that had been together for years.

One may live a long life and never know who truly is a friend or foe because no fierce struggle or hardship befalls them; at least, these men had found true brotherhood, which could be counted as rare a gift as a day of peace on earth.

The outside enemy commenced firing in a heavy barrage, the enemy lurking inside having been displaced to join their newfound brethren, and thus, the fight had no compromise. The onslaught was tremendous, the noise deafening, like being inside of a fired cannon.

"We charge," the Major cried above the clamor; "we will not be found cowering. God save Mexico!"

His cell phone rang.

There was no reason to answer it, for he did not wish to hear any more mockery, but there was no reason for the commander outside to call, thought he, but on a sudden, shouted, "Salvation!" and signaling to his men to halt, picked up the phone.

"Major Guzman," the voice began.

Major Alfonso Guzman, so taken aback from the familiar tone of his voice, that he briefly could offer no reply; then, collecting his thoughts, answered, "Major Gonzales…"

Joining Forces

"We are saved," Major Guzman cried to his remaining men, whose faces were bathed in the exhilaration of a pardoned prisoner who had stood in front of a firing squad, "how many men have you?"

"Few in number, great in skill and courage," he said. "Stay where you are."

Now, Major Guzman could hear a firestorm from the thousands of bullets shot and the Iron Phalanx blasts that settled upon the unprotected bodies of the El Dorado soldiers, and their recent political converts, some of whom tried to get back into the plane.

The El Dorado soldiers had stationed themselves with as little foresight for defense as the large predator who stalks the weak prey but does not worry about who stalks it. When the Crusaders and their Mexican ally, with assault teams and support teams in the center—replete with machine gunners and platoon leaders, and right and left side security teams, and squads flanking on either side—charged, the enemy was soon dispatched. And then the men inside the C-130Js exited after Major Gonzales called to them, and after greeting their saviors, set about to look for their fallen comrades, and upon finding them, some of them wept, while others cursed, and then wept.

Major Guzman and Major Gonzales embraced, as if friends reunited from a long absence, although it only been one week.

The Crusaders were introduced to the newest collaborators, and all the congregation presently moved to a safer and more obscured landscape; in fact, in the recesses of a valley full of trees and shrubs and bushes.

"The Azteca Cartel will be assigned blame for the pile of human dung we have left behind," Dylan said to the men, who stood still in the inky darkness, in concentric circles around him. "It is a fool who fights two enemies, who also fight each other; it is always easier to increase the enmity of vicious and chained dogs against another—just loosen the chain bit by bit, antagonize them, allow them to go wild at each other, and then set them free."

"Hola! These dogs have devoured all the other pets, and are restrained by the master from devouring each other—but who is this master?" Major Guzman asked.

"Reason," Moses said, standing next to Dylan. "Each side in a conflict does not want to risk what actual power they have—to risk all for all is too much, except for the worst of despots. We must make them think that if they do not fight, and fight now, for all, then all is lost."

"Yes, they are like the mean dog with a big bone in his mouth, who sees his reflection in a lake, then drops his own bone to fetch the bone of the other dog," Major Gonzales said, and then, wistfully, "ah, the benefits of a liberal education."

"What we here do highly resolve, death celebrates and heaven baptizes," Dylan began once more. "It is a blood oath, a spiritual oath, born of mind, body, and spirit; it is the golden chalice of eternal Brotherhood we hold, and the drink is Justice, and Freedom and Equality; no man who drinks from it can then fall away, for it is an elixir forged when first Man stood against a wrong; and now we are the cupbearers." He poured out water from his canteen into a stainless-steel nesting cup, as did the others into their cups, either from their own canteen, or another, and held it up high, as did the others in the still bottom well of this verdant garden, where the luminous shafts of starlight barely trickled to its depths. "All who drink of it enter into a sacred bond that cannot be broken; yea, to partake of it is to join in the eternal struggle against tyranny and oppression, to forsake all others, if need be; to wage war against wicked principalities unto death; so, if we live, we live to fight; if we die, we die so the fight might not die with us but carry on with those who pick up our righteous sword," and they drank of the cup of the sacred promise of things to come, and by doing so, swore their allegiance to each other and others who fought for Freedom, and to never retreat from injustice.

When the Crusaders departed from the Mexican soldiers, it was merely a physical parting, as they were now a metaphysical extension of two spirits synchronized and harmonized as one.

Secrets Revealed

After the customary introductions, José and his family, albeit still stunned, invited all of the new arrivals into their home.

"I grew up in a house just like this one," Ana said, at once joining the other women, a natural separation from the men.

"I recognize your accent," José's wife said. "You are Honduran."

"Yes," she replied, graciously taking a cup of tea, and nodded back to the simmering slaughterhouse, "like those dogs rotting out there—who will now have the same accent in hell."

Ramona frowned. "Shouldn't we leave?"

"Oh, no," Ana said, confidently, "there won't be a second squad—the conceit of the Aztecas is so great they think that one band of butchers is all they need."

"But won't other Azteca gangsters radio those whom you killed?"

"Well, yes," Ana replied, admiring, and touching the craftsmanship of the wooden and expertly stained furniture, "but we will take care of that."

"Hmm," Ramona murmured, "and so, you are here, a woman," looking at the mean-looking black and green-brown, one-hundred-round beta-c-magazine holding Heckler & Koch 417 assault rifle that hung from the leather strap around Anna's shoulders, "you are not ordinary..."

"No more than you, surviving here, working the land and enduring hardships every day, just like my mother did."

"Where is she now?"

Ana shook her head, and her long, black hair moved across her bare, bronze back and over her bare, bronze shoulders. "My mother was an activist—leading groups of women in protest against foreign intrusion of oil pipelines—which she was victorious in," she smiled in fond recollection, "because the American company she and her villagers fought were reasonable—an extension of American diplomacy; but she became encouraged by this victory, and applied her philosophy of peaceful resistance to local, violent men." She rose up to full height and her beauteous face burned wrath. "Men of no conscience are not reasonable." There was a faint glimmer of sorrow that she masterfully hid. "I buried my mother when I was fifteen, and killed my first drug trafficker—the pero narcotraficante," and here she turned her head and spat through the open door, "when I was sixteen." She knit her dark brows, and seemed to look now into a long-ago hurtful pass. "I was not so reasonable, then." Her swarthy complexion grew darker, revealing a fearsome scowl. "I fought with the Honduran Interagency Task Force, battling El Narco for two years, and after one of my units was ambushed by drug guerillas, I followed them into Guatemala, and there I found the Kaibiles Commandos, who fight everything that is rotten in their land; I wanted to join them, but they were reluctant, until I showed them what I could do, saving many of them in a firefight with their enemies, and so I fought with them for four years; and then I met Dylan and his brother, Conall, and here I am."

"Do you have a family?"

She looked to the men, who were huddled and speaking and excited tones, and gesturing about. "They are my family."

"Have you never married?"

Ana smiled. "I am the bride of Justice, and to him, I am a faithful wife."

Ramona knit her dark, thick black eyebrows. "I do not understand..."

Ana shook her head, her black eyes glowing bright with the aura of great truths revealed to an immortal soul and the ramifications of this, therein: "I do what I must, when first I learned about injustice; and I can now do nothing else, once I learned of succor I bring to those oppressed, because—others do not."

Ramona was astounded at the pillar of strength in this woman, and said, "Where do you travel now?"

She somewhat smiled. "Where we are needed."

"We have to go," Yoshitsune said, approaching the women, looking to Ana, and then to Ramona, "and you will go with your family to Cypress."

"I wish I could join you," Ramona said to Ana.

"You can," Ana replied, watching her ready her children, "raise them in the bosom of Virtue and the divine light of God, and be their exemplar."

Ramona wept after she embraced Ana, a woman she barely knew, and as she left with José, she looked back to the five valiant soldiers, and felt as if she should have always known them, these people who existed in myth and legend, in fairy tales and folktales she had heard when she was quite young; these noble heroes, who willingly did not retreat and withdraw in the face of a terrible threat, but actually stood their ground, inspired others to join them, and willingly took the fight to the oppressor. She had stood in the company of legends, and could see the eternal torch of Liberty each held that had been passed to them by those who had come before them and who also had refused to compromise and bow before oppression. "Such men and women as these," she mused, moving slowly in the deep picket, "are the ties that bind us all to Freedom and Equality."

Yoshitsune, having recently spoken with Dylan on a secure cellular device, rejoined his comrades, and spoke to them, as Roderigo and Pedro stood obligingly off in the distance.

"It is time to take down the communication centers," he said, in a hushed tone, "and these men, being late of the Azteca people, may have intel that we need, but..."

"Do we trust them?" Antonio finished, looking at the men.

"The recently converted," Finn replied, looking into his own past, "are either great allies, or great dangers."

"I say we keep them on a short lease or strangle them with it," Ana said, to which all easily assented.

"The Aztecas came to put down this uprising in Yermo," Yoshitsune now said to Pedro and Roderigo. "What knowledge have you on the operation of the Aztecas?"

Roderigo said, hopeful, "There is hardly anything we do not know, for anyone who does the will of his master here is a fortunate son."

"Give us an army that is incorruptible," Pedro said, thinking of his dead family, "and I will show you the end of these monsters."

Yoshitsune nodded. "Tell us all."

The Crusaders heard intimate knowledge of the inner workings of the Azteca drug traffickers, never even evincing interest in any one revelation, but interrogating these two former enemies for every bit of information, much of which they already knew.

Yoshitsune asked about drug shipments, Ana about arms shipments, Antonio about the Azteca stronghold, and Finn, about the sophisticated radio network.

"Tell me more; it sounds primitive, and easily beaten," Finn said to Roderigo.

"No, no, it is their greatest weapon," Roderigo returned. "The Cartels—all of them—use radio walkie-talkies to communicate with each other, though some are now using radio-receiving cell phones; all the while, the big bosses use only the Internet to transmit their coded messages—on frequencies the authorities cannot intercept or interrupt—and even if they suspect eavesdropping, they simply change frequencies."

"The authorities merely find your towers, your antennas," Finn said, and broke said radio imagery equipment over his knee, "and no more games."

"Oh, but the Cartels hide the antennas everywhere, and when the antennas and towers are destroyed, why, they even have a squad dedicated to rebuilding replacing them—yes, as fast as they are torn down, they replace them; it is a game the authorities cannot win."

"Tell me more," Finn said, not looking elsewhere.

"Many of the communication centers are mobile—to confound the Feds—and from these, most of the network is controlled."

"Most..."

"Of course, there are two dozen centers in the mountains that back up all the other centers, but only one command center that controls them all."

Finn nodded. "Why haven't the Feds taken them out?"

Pedro smiled. "They don't know where they are, and if they do know, the Cartels either take the Feds out, or bribe them, but if some centers are blown up, they are able to manufacture more quickly."

"But we know where they are," Roderigo said, "and we have maps, and exact locations…"

Finn, to throw off suspicion that he was too interested, said, "Well, something to consider when this is all over."

"But why?" Roderigo said. "Knock them out, and the Cartels are deaf, dumb and blind."

"It sounds like a job for the Feds," Yoshitsune objected, sternly, lending credence to the apathy of Finn.

"Why? We can do it," Pedro said, sternly.

"Do you want to?" Ana asked, feigning anger.

"Yes, if it means taking down the network and helping our cause…"

"Our cause, amigo?" Miguel said, feigning astonishment. "My cause is to even the odds in Yermo, and move on…"

"But we can deal a death blow to the organization…"

Miguel, frowning, shook his head. "Amigo, who do you think we are—conquistadors? You would need an army for such foolishness."

"No, no," Pedro cried, frustrated, looking toward Roderigo, and then back to his unbelieving audience. "We worked in them—yes! In the mobile ones, in the command centers—we know the schematic design for survival against attacks."

"When you are one of them," Roderigo said, melancholy now, "when you do their bidding, when you kill, and maim, and kidnap, and mutilate, and rape without question—no, when you want to and look forward to it because of this horrible thing inside you, this spreading sickness encourages you to hold it close, so close you feel its vile heartbeat," he paused, having temporarily lost his moral equilibrium in the remembering of this insidious awakening once inside him, and then continued on, his voice shattered by regret and shame, "why, it drains your goodness, and replaces it with wickedness, and now this gives you warmth, and sustenance, and joy, and purpose for living, and your heart begins to be in rhythm with it. " He had only briefly told them of his past crimes; but now he disgorged all the violent memories of his worst sins in one passionate flurry, as if he had to, as if he wanted to; and his rapt audience, even Pedro, were swept into this human maelstrom of unfettered mayhem and bloodletting and insanity as if described by a rabid dog, a ravenous wolf, an incensed cobra; absolute madness supported by a keen sense of purpose and strategy. "Atonement," he whispered, choking back down the chaos and horror of his dead flash, "atonement," he pleaded, "nearly weeping, "O, God, I seek atonement, for my family is dead now, and I need to redeem myself..."

"So," Ana replied, impugning his character with the false mask of disgust, "you think by more killing it will ameliorate the guilt in your grieving soul; freely you chose to murder, and freely you will be punished."

"God has saved me," he cried, pleading now. "I loathe murder, but crave to kill those who still do, as if by their very deaths, I will begin to live."

"They are a blot," Pedro interjected, full of pathos, "they corrupt Nature herself; they have no place among decent people," and he then too divulged his shameful past, en total, sobbing like a creature who has sloughed off its old, filthy skin, and now feels joy and peace from new, pink skin.

"So, what will the both of you do for us, eh," Antonio said; "who are we to fight such a foe even the government cannot subdue?"

"Even the government is corrupt," Roderigo replied, shaking now. "Money has bought them; you cannot trust any soldier, officer, judge, or jury, for money and violence has destroyed our very nature."

"It is true," Pedro said, "the Cartels are everywhere—look at us: we were recruited and became monsters, just like them; but as we repent, ten more willingly take our places; that is why we are so invaluable to you..."

"We know things," Roderigo said, his eyes flashing with the fervor of anticipation. "We can bring them down to their bloody knees."

"And you can cut off the head of the snake," Pedro finished.

Yoshitsune remained unmoved, aloof. "We need to go to Yermo," and he turned to go.

"We can do this," Roderigo said, firmly. "Better Pedro and I die trying than live as free cowards, imprisoned within our minds."

Yoshitsune paused in reflection, and grunted, and then said, begrudgingly, "Show me."

And they did.

The Tunnels of Yermo State

The history of warfare is a road that began when one person first yearned for the possessions of another, a road that has been too often traveled, and littered with Innocents as the principals involved tore at each other; a road that will end only once all men are equal.

Just as verbal warfare has no limits, so too are there no limits in physical warfare, the difference being that the former always has everything necessary for war, making the fight between the combatants potentially fair, while the latter has to settle for technology favoring one side and condemning the other; sometimes it was geography that tilted the golden goblet of inventions to the inhabitants, sometimes it was culture, sometimes it was circumstances; so, Man started with stone and bone and stick, then knife and sword, but it was a type of sword: bronze, then iron, then steel; bow and arrow, and longbow, then crossbow; spear, ax and mace; gunpowder, then matchlock, cannon, then flintlock, then percussion cap; bolt action rifle, semiautomatic weapons, machine guns; automatic rifles; chloride and mustard gas, bombs; bacterial warfare; bigger bombs, bigger guns, bigger cannons; missiles, lasers; and finally holding hostage the poor little atom and ripping apart its most guarded secrets.

The uniforms have changed, from fur to cloth, to spun metal, and the color coordination, too, but the refrain has not changed; the world is divided into two ideological and philosophical halves, where one side seeks to dominate the other, and in so doing, announces its superiority and dominance.

The battleground of war seems apparent and limited; by land, sea or air, although some industrious individuals have ventured into the very air we breathe, to foul, the very water we drink, to dirty; the very black space we gaze in wild wonder at night, to pollute; yet, there are some stealthy armies who have ventured into places not normally pondered, to circumvent even the deadliest of conventional weaponry.

The good Earth will buttress the onslaught of bomb or missile, fire or bullet; the sweet, faithful Earth, she who is the protector of those who dive into her nourishing womb, and dig deep to create underground worlds for combatants, Innocents, and fleeing leaders, which soon become towns, fortifications, encampments, and entire cities; there is no dishonor in ducking a punch.

Robert Heimdall had previously bought inordinate amounts of Mexican soil in diverse areas, and strategically near the mostly traveled routes for businesses, and mostly built near the places where the Cartels visited to practice their foul deeds; and quickly, as a cover, he developed them in the guise as a contractor, builder, prospector, eccentric owner, American capitalist, and began the complex tunneling that would eventually crisscross for miles where a modified vactrain—a vacuum tube train system, which incorporated magnetic levitation—was used for transportation, as the workers built the bunkers that would soon be full of supplies: food, weapons, ammunition, technology, medicine, and a ready retreat for the Crusaders and their allies; and there were massive buildings constructed to mask the digging, and massive excavations of rock and soil, which was deposited throughout various isolated regions.

The first attack upon a regional communication network unit occurred weeks after Roderigo's enlightened confession to the Crusaders, and it went thusly: two homes in the suburbs of Yermo, holding radio equipment to coordinate communication among the Azteca locals, were hit, the electronic treasure trove destroyed, the men killed; a mobile unit parked on the road near Yermo was attacked by masked assailants who seemed to appear from nowhere during the night raid, and after destroying the digital receivers and other assorted equipment, they seemed to disappear into the same invisible vehicle that had brought them there—or so said one survivor who was allowed to live after promising to tell his Narco that the El Dorado Cartel was coming.

The attacks on the El Dorado regional communication center and mobile communication systems were less, as the intel the Crusaders had gathered on them, by monitoring their radio trafficking, yielded less fruit, but it was a bounty nonetheless, and clearly offered significant victories; and they also left certain El Dorado personnel alive to convey a declaration of the mysterious assailants: "Tell your Capo, the Azteca are coming."

It was at this point that the El Dorado and Azteca Cartels, normally only willing to trade mild insults and fewer bullets, increased their animosity toward the other, and the kindling so expertly late at their feet, they so graciously and cooperatively fueled with incendiary words.

A Tale of Two Bosses

Arturo Suarez, El Toro, head of the Azteca Cartel, was musing upon the increasingly disturbing events that negatively affected his empire, stroking his drooping, thick, black mustache, then said to his trusted aide, "What is going on in this crazy world, eh, Hector? Is there no order left? What will become of us if we cannot stop these greedy El Dorado anarchists from their death wish? What do they want, after all; if they fight, we fight, and one loses, one wins; or maybe, both become so weak, we are killed by the real Feds, or the other Cartels; don't they know that? That if we both let sleeping dogs lie, we both win; what is wrong with that maniac Alvarez, huh?" He cursed, disgusted. "It would be better to merge, like those big companies, combining resources, but he is," and he moved the extended finger of his right hand around the outside of his ear several times, "loco; he is a sociopath, I hear." He frowned, shaking his head. "You can't talk to him—he only understands war—so, war we will give that psychopath; you know," and pausing upon further recollection, "if he were just a reasonable psychotic, I could manage him—much like a man manages a crazy woman with good food and wine, and love—but this man," he cried, "loves to hate, I know it! He lives by the blood feud, I feel it! He desires to be wronged so he can destroy; I sense it! I taste it! I hear the machines of war crackling in his disturbed mind, giving him warmth, the same way a good woman gives a man warmth; he has no love, but the spirit to destroy, and that, Hector, will be his undoing; you must, in this game, be reasonable; that is why, when we send our armies into Yermo, we will not burn it to the ground, as he would. What purpose would that serve? We would lose a huge revenue base and a strategic border town. We can warn other rebellious cities with a good, old-fashioned cleansing; you know, it is too bad, Hector: I truly feel that I could have been brothers with Alvarez—perhaps together we could have taken over all the plazas in northern Mexico."

"Yes, sir, but, as it is, as you say, his greed will destroy him, and you will consolidate all the plazas—the godfather of the North, kingpin of them all, CEO of a far-reaching empire."

"Do you really think so, Hector—I mean, truly?" he asked, timidly. "I often pray for such a thing to that 'Powerful Lady,'" it was the La Dama Ponderosa, their patron saint of death who watches over her faithful, "our

Santa Muerte; it would be better for everyone—less bloodshed and violence—and I then can continue to help the poor people of Mexico by bleeding the rich Americans of the United States; it would be a good and proper swap, and I would be leaving a fitting heritage for my children, the next CEOs. What father would do any different for their beloved children, I ask you?"

"It is within your grasp, El Toro," he said, knowing that this illustrious moniker, provided at the right time, served as stimulus for his boss.

Emboldened now, El Toro spoke further, as if in a trance. "It is my vision, Hector, truly it is my birthright, to herald in a new age—one where Mexico is the premier supplier of drugs in the world, but run like a smoothly operating business: no violence, no bloodshed, no nothing; and even if the drugs were to be legalized, we would realize a short-term decline in profits, but once the market absorbed our model—unlimited, clean, pure, reliable products—we would turn a profit; yes, I can see myself a CEO, with a Board of Directors, and going public, and selling stocks; can you see it, Hector, you'd be my Vice-President, and we would be—legitimate! No more gamesmanship, no more bribes, no more hiding, no more wars, no more persecution, but respectability and admiration of the people; the economy of Mexico would be stimulated and we would be a great nation. But this is the micro part of business, just the beginning; so, we would start acquiring perfectly respectful businesses, in technology—maybe selling computers and televisions, buy a couple of sports teams; I have always wanted my own soccer team, and people can wear our brand on their hats! Yes! It is all about the macro part of the business, my good friend; but, ah!" And then he suddenly shouted, "but I forgot about men such as Dr. Death—he would not stand for such a radical paradigm, wanting instead conflict to feed off; he thinks better when he is conflicted; I know him, he would, even if it all were legalized, still kill for control—and he prefers it to be illegal, anyway, it suits his spider-like personality; every good thing he sees, he feels he must poison; any clean thing he sees, he feels he must make unclean; every easy road that is successful, he wants to make inaccessible, if only he can kill to solve it all." He paused, and looked upward to what he perceived as heaven. "Oh, Hector, he is so wicked—where there is harmony, he creates conflict, as if it is in his lifeblood." He looked in earnest at his adjutant. "Is it wrong to hate so unrepentantly? You think I have offended the saints?"

"Yes, El Toro—you must forgive Señor Death, if you want God to forgive you your sins."

"But tell me this: why do you think he's so mean? He is so implacable, it makes me furious; perhaps he needs a good woman, eh?"

"Perhaps, or maybe he is just a bad seed."

"You are right, my brother; this is why I listen to your wise counsel; I must pray about it; but, say, have you more information on those irksome meddlers, these Defenders, who I am truly beginning to despise?"

"Yes, El Toro, they did kill our military contractors, and our people at Yermo, and by the transmission we have intercepted, are in league with El Dorado."

"That monster, Alvarez—who hits our art drug and arms shipments, and our radio communications centers; just wait until our new men arrive, then we will see," he said, smiling, deviously, as he strummed the tips of his fingers of each hand against each other. "Well, he is truly Señor Death and, as for these Defenders—bah! They hit our operations in the States, and not the El Dorado scum, and the foolish press paints them as heroes—yes, if assassins and murderers be such; well, Hector, Señor Death is going to learn who is the only true El Narco of the northern states."

Is it possible that hurtful words can be transported through some hitherto unknown medium that connects said words with its subject—in this case, Tomas Alvarez, a.k.a. Señor Death, whose ears, during the exact procession of spiteful words riding on the hot breath of Arturo Suarez, could, in effect, be defined as "burning"? And in consequence of this imagined, infernal act, Tomas seized the nearest thing living to him—an adjutant—and created a wasteland of moral unseemliness by his huffing and puffing of polluted words and baser ideas, and their intent, at the poor, trembling creature; even the other men in the room, who had seen his worst, were slightly taken aback; but then, like the third beesting, they quickly got used to it.

"Is everybody incompetent around here?" Señor Death fairly exploded, looking about himself as if he sought someone to sacrifice to assuage—or perhaps increase his passion. "I asked for a detailed report on Azteca activity in three states, and I only have two!"

Silence was worse than responding, so the bravest one in the meeting said, "Sir, we have had distinct disruptions in radio communication."

The big, very big, potbellied, black-hatted, and black-booted—made of snakeskin from rattlesnakes he had personally caught and skinned—honcho of the El Dorado Cartel stood up and parked himself in the midst of the men, who knew that he walked about in meetings only when he was agitated and about to explode. "A caged tiger," they called him.

"Who is interrupting it?" he growled in a tone that begged for the answers he hoped for.

The same brave man spoke. "We have more information that the Azteca people are the ones who were attacking our drug and arms routes and shipments, and took out our people at Zapote."

Alvarez cursed, as he could do no other. "This Suarez—this smug," he began, disgusted, "punk, small-time street hustler, who wants to be the only El Capo, is going to get a war to end all wars," and he stood erect and put out his chest. "I am going to give him World War IV—I am skipping World War III—this stupid, ignorant peasant is going down." He paused, looking at each man with an intense gaze that threatened physical harm if they were not paying attention to the most minute detail, and when he spoke again, he was still looking at them as if he were inspecting their very thoughts. "Do you know why, Luis—do you know about the blue moon butterfly of Samoa, eh? No, of course you don't; there is no reason for you to; you are not a man of letters as I; well, get out your mental notebook," and he walked about, his hand holding the book that contained information about said moths. "This blue moth was being killed by a particular bacterium, and do you know what it did? No, of course you do not, you are not a scientist as am I; well, in just five or six years, it evolved a special gene that protected it against this bacterium—fantastic! Well, my friends, this is what we do to survive: we mutate to stifle the enemy, to survive, to outmaneuver them all." He abruptly stopped, to hear, as the Greek chorus once gave its recitation during a pause in the drama, his own, loyal posse-chorus now sing his praises.

They bellowed and barked, threatened and promised destruction to the Azteca Cartel, much to the ever-expanding and delighted ego of their leader.

His temper, having been somewhat reined in, allowed him to speak somewhat more calmly. "So, can anyone see reason why we should not take out this idiot with the infantile brain, this moron, this self-obsessed fool, and take over Zapote, and establish ourselves as the greatest drug traffickers in Mexican history—no, no, strike that, in the history of the world!" Of course, all of his queries in which he proffered grandiloquent ideas were rhetorical devices, a fact his men knew all too well.

All of his men were presently dismissed to ready the assaults, save his trusted lieutenant, Luis.

"Luis," Alvarez stated, as if by pronouncing the name with his vaunted authority gave it a special legitimacy and honor, "what do we do?"

Any other officer in the room would have panicked at such an open-ended question, but Luis was better than most, for no one could pass the rigorous scrutiny of questions that constantly changed topics, and answers, that changed in substance, and direction, all according to the fleeting whim of Alvarez.

Luis knew he must state his case succinctly, swiftly, and with sagacity, and then allow Señor Muerte to analyze, and transpose, if necessary, his own ideas upon the information just presented. "Zapote is our town, it needs to be taken; we need to strengthen our drug and arms routes; and we need to take down Suarez."

"I agree," Alvarez said, from behind his desk, pouring himself a glass of liquid-amber tequila and turning on the radio, to hear the latest narco-corri-do. The song now playing was about Suarez, and how good a man he was to the community. "Hey," he said, disappointed, looking at the clock, "my song is supposed to be on right now."

"The clock is fast, sir," Luis said, feeling as if he had just scored a point by relieving some anxiety of his boss.

"Yes, yes, it is; thank you, Luis." He was staring into the brown radio as if he were actually watching the men singing. "You think that Suarez is a better man than I am?"

"No, sir."

"Okay, you say 'no,' but why?" There was a tiny wave of increased violence in his tone, longing to break free.

Luis had spent the better part of his day anticipating what Alvarez might ask him and how to respond with minimal verbal repercussions. "He is a skinflint with his own people; he has no insurance plan for them like you do; his giving to the community is minimal compared to your contributions." It was all true.

"That's correct, isn't it?" he said, uncharacteristically smiling. "He is tight with the budget; we have both heard the same thing—you know the rumors, so it must be true."

Luis, seeing the rare joy upon the face of his boss, wanted him to feel more joy, for he was like any other person who wanted to be around people who are happy; so, he decided to kick the soccer ball from his own side of the field way down the opposing side. "He can't win this war because his men do not respect him the way your men respect you, and want to follow you—his men can be bought by the highest bidder."

The narco-corrido song about Alvarez came on, and he became even more animated. "That is off the topic; but you're right, Luis, I have talked to many of his officers who said he is just plain weak; officers who defected and are in our ranks, now."

The rambunctious song sang about the strength and vigor and bravery of Alvarez, numero uno, El Narco; and why should this verse not state it so, as he had written the lyrics.

"We have to talk tactics and strategy, Luis; we can't afford to make any mistakes—this is it: if we beat him now, we can own all of it; is it not amazing? Twenty years in the business, and we are about to own it all!"

He was, for perhaps the first time in a year, content; maybe not happy, but optimistic of the immediate outcome.

But now Luis was worried, for Alvarez was never so weak and wrong as when he was happy for too long; so, he reasoned, I must provoke him to rage, and we will be yet saved; I repent of my earlier yearning to make him happy; some people are just better off unhappy all the time; it is the fuel that drives their engine.

Unfriendly Persuasion

The federal government of Mexico—at once dealing with multiple uprisings in cities across the northern states, as well as the world press, who were spotlighting what the ambitious architects of armed vigilantes had accomplished so quickly that the government was seemingly impotent to ever do—now decided, by force of notoriety and desperate to hold onto office and act like a sovereign nation, and also one that met the criteria of a democratically elected country, to send in troops to disarm the rebels; but as we have already seen, the need for security had thus far evaded the military, having resulted in two squads being nearly slaughtered.

At the behest of the Crusader's plan, Major Gonzales and Major Guzman met with the President of Mexico, an enlightened official who had recently been successful in unifying its police forces under one jurisdictional body, as had some countries in South America that had recently been successful against their Narcos and reduced them to low-grade fever, yet still a viable threat.

"El Presidente," Major Gonzales began, humbly, and respectfully, while in the secure office of the presidential palace, "we are here to inform you of an opportunity to cut off the heads of two Cartels."

"You can destroy the Azteca and the El Dorado clans," Major Guzman said, with great deference, as if the speaking of it in such a humble manner was attempting to offer the credit to the President.

El Presidente, sitting behind his royal, round, polished maple desk, unaccustomed to being the last informed of matters of the state of great import, stared with great curiosity at these two uninvited interlopers. "Go on," he managed to whisper, like a hiss escaping from a boiling pot.

The two men, sitting opposite him in two uncomfortable wooden chairs that sank well below his level, continued.

"We have intel regarding the plan of the Azteca, en masse, to attack the El Dorado stronghold," Major Gonzales said.

"We can catch two rats in the same cage," Major Guzman finished.

El Presidente—democratically elected leader of Mexico, representative of the people, who had campaigned hard to bring down the Cartels, and who now listened to two mere subordinates, who were here due only to one of their having a certain relative who happened to be a high-ranking general and who now dared put forth a plan devised by whom he did not know, and would accomplish what he, the most powerful man in the land, had not accomplished in three years—was simply vexed to irrationality. "Well, well," he began, calmly, using a subterfuge known to all politicians even when the fires of wrath are stoked within, "you have breathed this plan, and feel satisfied that I will consider it; good day, gentlemen." He was pleased he had given them their little moment of importance, the general would be content, and they would now just simply turn around and go away.

The two officers looked at each other in unabashed astonishment.

"El Presidente," Major Gonzales exclaimed, betrothed to incredulity, "you are mistaken as to the intent of our visit; permit me, sir, to clarify our position: we mean to take down the Azteca and El Dorado Cartels in one grand strike—we need only the manpower."

"You are hard of hearing, mon ami," said El Presidente, still fuming about the foolishness of subordinates who ply their expired goods in his presence. "You are summarily dismissed—now go," and he flicked his right hand at them, raising his voice, "you have mistaken me for someone who has the need to repeat himself."

"Forgive me for politely refusing, but El Presidente is gravely mistaken," Major Guzman said, leaning forward, urgency written clearly upon his grave face. "We can deal a deathblow to two of our greatest foes, and not just the leaders, but their armies."

El Presidente smiled, as does one who holds the gun. "You will kindly leave now," he said, looking at one, then the other with indifference, "or leave unkindly." He pressed a button to summon his Secret Service.

Major Gonzales had not come to this meeting entirely unarmed, as it related to verbal warfare, for his cousin, the General, had given him adequate ammunition regarding the bombardment of El Presidente's weakest offenses; thus, he stood up, as did Major Guzman, clearly succumbing to disrespect. "You give away Mexico to criminal insurgents—Nero fiddling while Rome burns—because your foolish pride won't allow you to hear out the plans of people who are not like you—anyone in your inner circle; cuantas personas hay en esta fiesta—how many people are at this party! Los mismos de siempre—the same old thing; to which I say, innovaro morir, innovate or die; you were not born a king, but of peasant birth, as we all are now; you, who are supposed to be the mirror of a new democracy in the Americas; instead, a mirror cracked into scattered fragments." He raised his head on high and puffed out his chest, to signal his declaration that he was indeed the equal of the man before him.

And Major Guzman finished, his head on high, standing fully erect, "Pride goeth before the fall."

El Presidente waved away the two Secret Service agents who now stood behind the two men, and then turned his austere look to the Majors as he arose. "So," he began, striding quickly toward them, "you think yourselves capable of delivering strategic plans to the military that will achieve…despite all the efforts in the last years of my predecessors, and myself…you, two mere Majors, have the temerity to promise absolute victory when all we have known is disgraceful defeat; prove yourselves, or be court-martialed!"

Major Gonzales was secretly delighted at the shrinking violet that had just reared up and burst forth. "Strike while the iron is hot," he mused, remembering what the General had said about El Presidente: "He is like those creatures who thrive best in the hottest temperatures—passion! You must arouse his ardor and question his honor to truly converse with him; he is a wet powder keg—so, hermano, light him up!"

"Yes, El Presidente, we have the heads of the Azteca and El Dorado Cartels on one silver platter, these ignoble rulers—yes, you are startled, but I say they are rulers! Like conquering armies, they are—a country within a country cannot stand; and if you dismiss this opportunity, history will not be so kind."

"You deign to judge me—who are you to even opine on a policy that so affects this country!"

Major Guzman intruded, respectfully, like a good soldier in the presence of his commanding officer. He held up his hands in a firm gesture. "We are the heart of your policy, sir; we fight daily on what you say in mere words; we have seen the future, and it is now, within our grasp," and he upturned both of his hands, "you must hear our plan."

"You cannot possibly have a grasp on the complexities of our campaign against the Cartels," El Presidente cried. "With all of my great powers, even I and my military, and intelligence community, cannot solve this constantly evolving labyrinth."

"And now, I dig even deeper," bethought Major Gonzales, and then said, "It is not us alone, sir, but our allies too, who will bring down the ruin of the forces that threaten our nation's survival."

"And now you say we are in danger of failing as a state? I am disappointed in that assessment that is played so ignominiously by foreign diplomats—allies? What allies?"

"Are you aware of an independent body of men and women operating within our borders and fighting the Cartels?"

"What! What! Impossible! You are confused, Major—you speak of military contractors hired by the Cartels; yes, yes," he shouted, smiling triumphantly, "we know all about those rabble, and they will be taken care of."

"No, sir," Major Guzman said, strongly, "not them, for them," and he pointed toward the north, wherein, in imagination, he created a boundary that once crossed existed the enemy, and then allowed his hand to gesture about the room, "but us, for us—men and women who fight for Justice anywhere they are needed."

"Mercenaries! In Mexico! Are you mad! We are a sovereign nation, not a backward Third World country—and you know of these dogs of war and have not named them and announced them before your highest authorities before this: it is treason if I find out you knew before today!"

"It is treason if we know how to take out the Cartels and turn our backs and walk away," Major Guzman said, calmly.

"You're both as mad as hatters—locos como sombreros! Why am I still standing here talking to subordinates—it is too humiliating!"

"Anyone who fights the Cartels in Mexico is Mexican," Major Gonzales declared, "anyone who fights injustice is my brother, my sister, and I welcome them; is this not the vision of the United Nations?"

El Presidente, fervent supporter of the essential philosophical doctrines of the UN, was stung, but he would not relent. "We have been invaded, and with the complexity of our own troops—Dios nos salve—God save us! Is it bad enough that the Cartels have corrupted everything they touch; but now, our own people become corrupted as we fight them; it is too much to bear; O, Mexico, thou art the crucible of the Americas!" He turned from them, and sighed, and then uttered, "All is lost."

"All is won, sir," Alfonso said, approaching him, feeling no longer just a soldier, but a citizen more; "we have the means to rid ourselves of this unlikely scourge."

His voice was hard and mean, and his voice implacable. "And who might be these men and women you extol so—have they names?"

"Yes, sir, they do," Ramon said, approaching him now, feeling no longer just a soldier, but a citizen more, and facing him, as did Alfonso, in awe and respect, as if he could see something greater than what was perceived as ordinary and possible all about him, and knowing beforehand the certain impact of great magnitude it would have upon the subject; and thus, he spoke carefully, slowly, and with great passion, "The Crusaders."

Manuel Diaz, for he now felt more a citizen than a President, even a dynamic young man again who believed in the impossible if it would benefit humanity, was muted by this revelation, as he had oft praised the Crusaders to his admirers, even in his autobiography, as a beam of hope that shone even in the darkest places: brave men and women who risked life and limb to defend those would been disinherited from the good things of the world. "The Crusaders," he whispered, looking back and forth between the two men, "the Crusaders—here, in Mexico; in Mexico." His black eyes narrowed, his black brows knit, his swarthy countenance frowning. "Why! Why! In Mexico—is it possible," and here his voice lost an octave, but more than that, its ardor, too, "in our Mexico, here, is it yet possible." His almond-shaped eyes saw the misery and suffering of the worst of humanity, lost, forgotten, abandoned humanity, and he superimposed his beloved Mexico there. "The Crusaders, ah yes, they must also be the glorious Defenders we've heard so much of—si," he whispered, and felt the awe we all feel at the mention of fabled heroes; "they have come here; are we so abandoned of hope, so lost, so forgotten; we, is it so?" He walked to the window that allowed a grand vision of the palace estate. "The King in his royal garden, picking roses while his subjects wither from neglect," he said sadly, "but I am no King," and he turned to face his silent accusers. "We are not capitulating to the anarchy of criminal insurgents." He shook his head. "But I cannot allow even the Crusaders to operate here, for always I considered them a mere fancy more than real, in my mind, obscuring the reality of International Law." He walked up to the two men.

"What have you in his black bag to convince me I would allow their trespass, and by so doing, violate the laws of Mexico's sacred Constitution?"

"El Presidente," Gonzales began, pathos streaming from his voice like the dying wail of a wounded soldier, "Mexico is the nucleus of this monster that threatens the world; you know where the tentacles of this beast grow and thrive: in the US, and Central America, in Europe and Asia, and Africa—but it begins here and we can end it… here."

"Sir," pleaded Alfonso, who now regarded himself as an equal, "we are responsible for these unfortunate creatures—we reared them, raised them, gave them life, allow them to flourish; it is our burden to rein in our own wayward children, even with gun and cannon, if need be; it is our responsibility to the world, as citizens of the world, for we cannot disassociate ourselves from our brothers and sisters—around the world."

Diaz gazed upon the men as does the father who finally admits his own children are thieves and murderers, and he alone must destroy them, as only he can, as he is the only one who truly knows them. "What does your bag contain, sirs? What can you present to further convince me of your sincerity and accuracy, for I cannot ill afford a blunder now, or my enemies will seize upon it, and the next person to stand here will be negotiating with these shameful Narcos."

The two men removed many items, and after carefully placing them upon the large desk, first placed a video disc into the portable tablet they had brought, and immediately, a painful narrative appeared: for the Crusaders had video-taped the most egregious acts of the Cartels, including their own attacks of the two rogues military units; also, the Crusaders' confrontation of the military contractors and Federal Police, and the targeting of the drugs and arm shipment routes, replete with details of maps of these and other invaluable routes. The faces of the Crusaders had been digitally altered and masked.

"Invaluable intelligence, these locations," Diaz murmured, fascinated, while rubbing his clean-shaven chin.

"But then this is only the beginning," Gonzales said, and, taking out the other discs, put in the most damning of all and allowed it to speak for itself: the complete, unadulterated radio network scripts—the frequencies of the Cartels, which, truth be told, could be switched or jammed, but the Crusaders had a device that filtered out the jamming and focused on the switched frequencies, but most importantly, most shockingly, were the clear, crisp voices of the Azteca and El Dorado Cartels, yes, but rendered meaningless to all who heard them, due to the ever-changing cryptic code of the language, but now rendered meaningful, as the Crusaders' elite scientists had broken the code through their quantum computers, so that now, under the typed translation of the voice, was the actual meaning.

"Hola!" Diaz cried. "If this is authentic, this is a godsend; we will know all! We must strike!"

"Yes, El Presidente," the Majors chorused, pride illuminating their faces.

"You are my aides-de-camp now; you will coordinate with the military, and with all due stealth, sirs, and confidence; but we must tell no one where we go until the moment we step onto the battlefield; I will not squander this gift offered to me—history," he said, putting his once-royal but now humble hands upon each of their shoulders while he stood before them, "will judge us as men of action, and worthy of our esteemed rank and responsibility!"

"To battle!" they all cried, in unison, as if finally of the same mind on the ideas that united all of them: Freedom and Justice.

The Defense of Yermo and Zapote

The distance between Yermo and Zapote was the difference between entire worlds, not merely geographically, but culturally, politically, and socially; the citizens of Yermo considered themselves modern urbanites, born of the city, inheritors of the new face of Mexico, freed from the stagnant past in which peasant farmers toiled like serfs on the land of pale imitations of Lords of the Manor; they wanted to join the rest of the burgeoning, metropolitan world and partake of the riches therein; conversely, the people of Zapote still considered themselves country folk dealing with modernity, but intent on keeping their forested, mountainous surroundings as a vital part of their heritage; and yet, the physical distance between the two cities was only thirty kilometers, but in this short space, it was like crossing from one alien soul into another.

It must also be remembered that the El Dorado Cartel claimed Zapote as their own, much as imperialist powers in history claimed foreign territories as their own by right and might and country; the same was true for the Azteca Cartel, as they viewed Yermo's citizenry as merely a conquered people, who were henceforth given no plebiscite to approve the matter.

It was the appointed task of Miguel and Yoshitsune and Finn, Antonio and Ana, to provide a ready defense of Yermo, and for Roderigo and Pedro to lead them back to the town they had, of their own free will, slowly and meticulously mutilated, and with great ambition and delight.

All were silent as Roderigo drove, the Crusaders scanning the area before and aft, and to the sides, and checking the sensors in the ground for signs of their ubiquitous enemy; then, nearly there, the Jeep stopped, and they disembarked, and listened to Yoshitsune delineate the stratagem.

"We meet with the leaders Ana has contacted." Such names had been secured after a few of the mobile communication centers were blown up in Yermo, and the Crusaders had proven themselves warriors for the cause of liberation and had gained the confidence of the rebels. "They will be apprised of the coming conflict." He looked at the two outsiders. "You must remain on the periphery, where we will need you."

When the two men argued against this forced exclusion, each with a Bible in their hand, Ana cut her way through the testosterone- and adrenaline-fueled pitch. "We can bury you there, or you can prove yourselves worthy where we need you." She shook her head, her long, black hair swaying over her shoulder. "The repentant executioner comes back to the chopping block to proclaim his genuine contrition; no, sirs, you will lose your handsome heads, and endanger our relations with the people there."

The face of Pedro paled. "We cannot atone for sins by hiding in the bushes like whipped dogs," he began; "you need eyes and ears that see and hear as the enemy does."

"We can anticipate their every move," Roderigo said, with knit brow, "for we are still a greater part of them, because they took out our guts and remade us in their deplorable image."

"Let us do this," Pedro finished, "so we can no longer be part of them, and restore that which was lost."

"Has God not done that?" Ana asked, with firmness.

"Yes," Roderigo returned, shaking his Bible and then holding it to his chest, "but I need to do this, to return to me—to get me back; I want to be what I was before I became them."

Yoshitsune, having studied the faces of the two men, and the faces of his fellows, said with finality, "So all men must choose," and that was that.

Thus, the band of travelers carefully made their way into Yermo, and was first met by three armed gunmen on the northern periphery of the town.

"Who goes there?" said the voice in the dense darkness that hid in the veil of bushes. "Friend or foe?"

"Friend," Ana shouted back, in the Spanish dialect of the region.

"Well, then, friend—mercy for all, eh?"

Ana smiled. "Yes—even with a bullet."

"Ah, friend," the voice said, "come forward—but with hands up!"

The travelers came forward, and soon, the guards appeared. "We have to be safe," one guard said, "even if you know the password."

"I agree," a voice said from behind them, and the guards looked behind themselves to a small mound, upon which appeared Yoshitsune, rifle in hand, its long, black, steel barrel pointed directly at them.

"Ah, but you do not trust us," one of the guards said, disappointed.

"No, no," Ana returned, shaking her head, as the two groups stepped in front of each other, "but you never can tell who you're going to meet when a war is going on."

"This is true," said the guard; "caution is a better part of valor; well, you knew the password, but still, maybe you are Azteca, or El Dorado—how do I know?"

"You don't know," Ana said. "Neither do we know who you are."

"It is a messy business, this war; I liked it better when I had my little restaurant, serving customers, and talking about soccer, politics, and—women!" And then he rubbed his protruding belly, and shook his head. "I think I'm a better lover than soldier."

"Will we stand here all day talking of old times?" Ana said, graciously. "Or shall we move on, and get down to the business of killing that which needs to die?"

"It is up to you, I suppose," said the guard, who was about forty-five years of age; he fingered his bushy, black mustache, and looked at Yoshitsune, who was holding up a big yellow straw basket of wine, bread, and cheese the guards had brought. "I'm no soldier," and he shrugged his shoulders, "but a simple restaurateur."

Yoshitsune walked up to him. "Eat," he said, handing him the basket now, "and be vigilant."

"Si, bueno, I will," he returned, and upon eyeing the big man, "to think our cause has attracted so many to fight for Freedom," and the very saying of it made him nearly weep, and thus, he said no more; and presently, he and the other guards, after bidding the band of travelers adios, resumed their prior activity: that of eating hard cheese and dark rye bread, and sipping red wine, and talking of soccer, politics, and women.

Ana contacted Pablo, and set up a meeting with him at a burned-out restaurant.

Pablo and Roderigo were sweating and trembling like prisoners of war returning to their captors.

"Amigos," Miguel said to them as he waved them to fall back a few paces, "you cannot wear the skin of killers, it is too easily recognized. You must wear the skin of Innocents."

"But we are not," Roderigo whispered, hoarsely; "we murdered Innocents and tortured these good people relentlessly and greedily, without a conscience," and the very speaking of it made him want to weep.

"Si, good arguments—but you have declared your new faith; hath Christ died for nothing? Did he die only for the good and noble? No, there are none who are good, only God; so, do you think yourself so wicked that even Christ cannot redeem thee? For He came into the world to save sinners."

The men were silent, and their shaking and profuse sweating abated; and then Roderigo asked, timidly, "What will become of us now?"

"Whatever God chooses," Miguel said, nodding, and thinking of his own life, "and all you might do is His will, and, come what may, it is at least what is right and honorable, and might inspire other men to do good."

"You must be a believer," Pedro said.

"Si, I believe, I am a good Catholic, for I've seen enough evil to know that sin walks the earth like a man, and I've seen enough goodness not to know that Virtue walks the earth like a man; that the manifestation of evil is merely the child of its hateful father, and the manifestation of Virtue is a child of its Good Father; but more importantly, that both species of reality are easily recognized by Man, and no excuses can ever justify joining the wrong side." He halted abruptly and looked into their gleaming eyes. "I've seen wicked things no human being could justify in his mind and do in all his earthly desires; and too have I seen wondrously good things no human being could conceive of doing in all his earthly desires; pilgrims, we think ourselves gods, but we are mere echoes of our chosen Father, and not worthy of life except for the grace of Him."

Pablo was waiting, armed, with four men, equally armed, at the appointed place; cursory greetings were exchanged, and the plot unfurled.

"We verified your story," Pablo began, with the intensity and passion of a soldier eager for battle, looking first at Ana; "we found the dead Azteca assassins where you said they would be; so, you saved the army, and now us—but you know that will not last: the government wants to disarm us because we are a reminder that it has lost the drug war."

"Present tense," Finn interjected, "losing—and it is just a temporary transition..."

"... To winning," Antonio finished.

"And how will that happen?" Pablo said, visibly irritated. "When we know this time the Azteca won't send an army so easily defeated."

Yoshitsune frowned. "You are a warrior now, good sir; so, you must think like one, and know that superior strategy and tactics lead to victory. There is no retreat in a war such as this—it is death, same as defeat."

"What do you know?" he replied, scrutinizing Ana.

"I know you are not alone," she responded, nodding, with a confident smile; "your cause is not yours alone—it is the world's cause, this is why we are here; yes, this is why," she smiled, and paused, "your own government is sending troops to aid you."

He knit his thick dark brows. "You know this?"

"I know what I need to know, and tell you what you need to know; and it is this: that the Mexican army comes."

Pablo looked at the other men there, and his gaze stopped on Pedro, and then Roderigo, and he frowned. "Do I know you?" His tone was leaning toward a cliff that led to an angry and roiling sea.

"They are here to help," Yoshitsune said. "Without their intel, many more will die."

Pablo, like the bulldog that clamps its powerful jaws on an object of its mad desire and does not let go until it fashions a sense of satisfaction from it, suddenly leaped up, his rifle out and aimed at the travelers, his companions doing the same. The air was no longer smooth, but rough, and inflamed with desire.

The Crusaders arose slowly, as did Pedro and Roderigo.

"I know these murderers—these butchers, murdering butchers of the Azteca Cartel; they murdered our people for years," Pablo screamed, his body shaking, his face awash in furious indignation.

"The crimes they committed, they will pay for later," Yoshitsune said, calmly, looking squarely at Pablo; "now, they are here to fight our enemy."

"Fight? How can we trust them—no, how can we trust you? No, no, I say," he yelled, swinging his weapon's aim across the images of those before him, "you knew of their treachery, and yet you brought them here! How can you reconcile the slaughter of Innocents!"

Finn stepped forward, so close to Pablo that his chest touched the barrel of his rifle. "And you say this, he who asks forgiveness of God for your sins." Pablo was silent. "Is it not written in the Holy Scriptures, 'but if you forgive men for their transgressions, your heavenly Father will also forgive you. But if you do not forgive men, then your Father will not forgive your transgressions.'"

"I have not yet heard these human monsters speak," Pablo said, trembling still, in his spreading rage.

Roderigo dropped his weapon, stepped forward, and knelt before the representatives of Yermo, and Pedro did the same; and then he uttered, his head lowered, "I have committed the most heinous acts against you and God when I was not saved; but now I am saved, and have committed my mind, body and soul to the Lord Almighty, Christ be my Savior; in my redeemed soul, I can commit no wicked act that contravenes God's law; I pray thee, forgive me for my iniquity, and allow me to prove myself worthy, in battle, and atone for my trespasses against thee and thine."

"Why! Why!" Pablo screamed, sweat pouring off his dark face, as he pointed the gun barrel directly at Roderigo's head. "How can I forgive what so freely, and joyfully, and wickedly they did to our own people? They do not deserve to live!"

Pedro, contrition weeping down his lowered face, looked up his accuser. "Can man do something that is so wicked that even God will not forgive?"

The entire history of Mexico lay at the focal point created by the wrath of Pablo and the peace offering of the two men; the clash between two diverging cultures, the peasant class and the warrior class; the tension between rulers and ruled; the dissolution of a nation defined by corruption, lust, and power; in earlier times, the men might have been brothers, in later times, friends, but now, mortal enemies, in this transitory stage between peripheral civilization and settled civilization, where the jostling for power upended societal structure.

Pablo simply could not release the venom so insidiously injected into his heart. "You need to die for what you did," he shouted, his sweaty finger on the trigger and ready to pull.

Roderigo looked up at him. "I do—I do not protest that—and if you desire, after this is over, if we still live, kill me if your Christian conscience demands it; better in heaven with God, than here with those who hate and will not forgive."

Pablo looked to Pedro, who said, "It is so with myself; I am not worthy of life here: I prefer the company of the Lord and all his saints, where all of my tears will be wiped away," and his head hung down again, as his voice drifted to the ground, "I prefer the coward's way out, so shoot me if you desire."

Pablo looked to the Crusaders. "Why did you bring such evil men to our fight! Why!"

"They can help us with what they know," Ana said, carefully, "and save more lives than they ever took."

"No! It cannot be! They must die now, otherwise there is no justice in the world."

"No, there will be," Finn said, standing still squarely in front of him, "and this guarantee I now give: any man or woman, boy or girl, whom they harm, or kill, you may do the same to me." He could see a slight diminution of the anger that Pablo fought hard to sustain. "You must decide, or every moment we talk, Innocents will die—and on your munificent conscience."

In the interim that dwells between decision and indecision that affect ordinary mortals, Yoshitsune declared, assertively, "We go, now," he grunted, raising his rifle and walking past the Yermo citizens, "whether you kill them or not," and the other Crusaders fell in with him, leaving Pablo no outside influence; and yet, he could not execute defenseless men, so he exclaimed a painful hurt, and turned around, as did his companions, to join the others. Pedro and Roderigo soon followed, still clutching their Bibles, which they read as often as they could, especially when they felt the old man inside them seeking to return to his powerful seat of infamy.

Upon meeting with the other leaders, the Crusaders apprised them of the imminent threat to Yermo, and instructed them on how to set up defensive perimeters. Pedro and Roderigo were then recognized by the other leaders, and Pablo, unofficially bound by his unspoken word—which yet, in his own benighted mind, was claimed as a vow given—explained that they were his prisoners, held by their proclaimed honor to provide special knowledge of this battle, and that he vouchsafed their safe passage, until which time they reverted to their former station in life: murdering scum who were to be shot down like the scurrilous mad dogs they were. Although the people were not fully satisfied with this explanation, so great was their respect for Pablo that they begrudgingly agreed, and so great was their admiration for him that they would temporarily delay their lust for revenge and actually fight alongside what they considered to be dead men walking.

"When will the army come?" asked one of the men of Yoshitsune.

"When will the Cartel come?" asked one of the women of Yoshitsune.

Yoshitsune, standing tall and unmoved by any palpable uncertainty, said, in an authoritative voice, "When they will; and until then, we will ready ourselves."

The same story unfolded in Zapote, led by survivors of the federal troops whom the Crusaders had saved from a certain death by the Cartels, and thus, we have a tale of two cities, girding themselves for a coming conflict that would thus define their existence for generations to come.

Where the Throne of Power Resides

The most powerful man in the world, as judged by the military and economy of which he was chief, stood in the midst of the Directors of various intelligence agencies, and all the principal players of the National Security Council, listening with increasing frustration to the narrative of the unstoppable rise and influence of the Cartels, how they had penetrated all facets of American society; set up shop in nearly every major city, with corollary hubs in smaller towns; established solid ties with gangs and organized crime, private officials of the government, officers of the law, legislative representatives, representatives of the legal branches, et al.—anyone who cared for acquiring monetary excess and who were not loyal to indigenous or even universal life-affirming values; and how the violence, usually reserved for the territory south of the border, had been successfully imported to the land of milk and honey, and having spoiled and curdled it, created more chaos, and caught more people in the widening net of cash, corruption, and illegal drugs; and yes, despite the National Guard being deployed on the borders, and in the streets, and more money purchasing even more police to patrol, it was, the disturbing narrative said, like a blind man trying to catch a giant white shark with a guppy net and a cork gun.

When this impossible-to-imagine, but hard-to-dismiss, sad tale abated, the President, his hands clasped behind his back as he paced across the conference room with the red, white and blue carpet, said, forlornly, but not facing his audience, "And who even has a cork gun?" He turned around, and his advisers were stunned to see a countenance so wrapped up in vexation that they were afraid to speak. He cursed. "Do I have to declare war upon this subhuman species! So help me, with all the power invested me, I will do so; I will have the military deployed on the streets to stave off a collapse of Democracy—and on my watch—this, this travesty! How came this shame, and so quickly; was it not too long past that even though the Cartels shipped their unsavory product across the border, the violence stopped there; well, speak, you tin men and women; I want answers, not rhetorical tricks and pomposity; so help me, if this threat is not vanquished, heads will roll—and it will not be mine!"

His National Security Adviser spoke, actually, with calculated nerve and soaring confidence. "We have it under control, Mr. President; we have informants, leads, we have surveillance…"

When the leader of the Free World raises his hand as a function for the speaker to halt his trespass, you obey. "Excuse me, Harry," he said, incredulously, shaking his head and frowning, "this is what you call 'under control'? Mass beheadings, mass kidnappings, mass murder sprees, mass bombings, Cartel civil wars in our streets—and here is a newsflash: I no longer classify them as pushers of illegal drugs, mere traffickers, but now a criminal paramilitary complex; really, sir, I question your sanity." He pursed his lips as he approached the man, who shrank away from him with every incendiary word fired at him. "You had better come up with a better answer than that, by Jove."

The Director of the FBI spoke in an assuring tone. "Mr. President, we are doing everything we can to contain this mess."

The President swung around to face the newest speaker, his face in shock as if he had just been verbally, and possibly physically, assaulted. "These aren't answers, gentlemen—and gentlewoman—these are vacuous pacifiers you drop in Third World countries, where they cannot contain corruption, where there is no," and he cried, "Democracy! For goodness' sake, people, look around: this isn't 1800—we have technology, we have modern weaponry, we have nearly unlimited resources," and he put his open hands upon his hips. "Are you trying to tell me we can't get a handle on this invading storm—we, who have the most powerful army in the history of the world?"

The Director of the CIA spoke, somewhat cautiously, "Mr. President, whatever we have, they have too; the technological gap between master and slave has slimmed to the point it is nearly imperceptible; I guess you can attribute that to a free market."

The President cursed again. "Are you telling me," he said, looking about, "that we need martial law?"

No one dared answer.

"So help me, I'll do it," he said, in a passionate voice; "I'll declare it and put our army and marines on the streets and fight these filthy miscreants until every one of them is either imprisoned or dead; and I will suspend the right of habeas corpus, as Lincoln did—and, by the way, I won't give a hoot what the Court rules on later: it's what's now that gets the fire lit."

The Secretary of State finally broke the high tension. "Sir, I have a chicken in the next room, and if you cut off its head, the direction it runs will tell you…"

The look of her boss seared a hole right through her porous brain, and she, somehow, understood that to speak further in the same vein might give rise to the rebuilding of medieval dungeons wherein she would be buried at the lowest level, with the dirtiest vermin and fellow imbeciles who did not recognize when to shut their mechanically impaired brains.

The face of the President fell into his large hands. "What will become of us if this south-of-the-border peril is not defeated?" He looked up with a desperate plea upon his face. "It must be stopped here, people, and now—do you hear me! We, who saved Europe in World War I, and the world from destruction in World War II, with the mightiest military yet seen in history, now cannot stop thieves, and murderers—for goodness' sake, people, they're like the invading Huns, the Mongols, the Vandals who took out receding empires; is this what we are now, but a growing empire susceptible to internal rot set upon by these unconscionable rabble!" He paused again, feverishly. "Never let it be so! If we have to go toe to toe with these wicked beasts, put tanks and troops on the streets, do whatever we must to keep the lantern of Democracy lit," and he looked at one of the walls, whereupon hung the reminder of the greatness of his country, "so help me, Mr. Lincoln," he yelled, looking at the venerable portrait of the great man, "we will do it, sir, to stop the greatest threat to our nation security since the Civil War," and he stood next to the painting now, "you saved us, sir, you did whatever was necessary, so too, shall I—I will not fail you or drop the sacred torch that illumes the inviolate path for Freedom, nor forsake the American people; have confidence in me, that I will lead them to what must be, can only be, and that is certain victory!"

He turned around, and his countenance was fierce, like that of a general before battle; his face was suffused with the strength and vigor of unsurpassing certitude. "I suggest you pray, if you are men and women of faith; and if not, I suggest you gain faith now, as we are about to go to war." He looked to his generals of the military. "You have plans for me, sirs, drawn up some time ago, which could be executed now."

But before they could answer, and aide to the FBI Director came in, whispered into the Director's ear, and then left.

"Sir, we have… something."

"Something," the President said, nodding his head as he, with his hands clasped behind his back while he once again began to pace back and forth, "that is more than we have—now."

The head of the local FBI headquarters in the California, Arizona, New Mexico, and Texas areas walked in, and was presently introduced; and when politely offered a place to sit, politely refused.

"It would be more appropriate for you to sit, Agent Fuentes," the President said, slightly uneasy and not used to being denied, especially by those seemingly incapable of having the authority to do so.

"Sir, it would please me to stand as I speak to you, as it would not seem appropriate to deliver such momentous and revelatory news in a contented and relaxed position."

The President, intrigued yet agitated, spoke again. "You will call me Mr. President."

"Sir, I would call you Paul, for that is the Christian name given by your gracious parents, and not even by your honorable surname, Whitehead, a good English name, but still you would receive me, after the disclosure of the contents of my intelligence, with great accolades."

"Agent Fuentes," the President exclaimed, his patience having been exceeded by this bold underling, "you are a subordinate officer in the Federal Bureau of Investigation; I suggest that, in order to keep your petty wage and rank, and ensure an uninterrupted retirement income, you address the highest elected official land as Mr. President."

Agent Fuentes smiled, and his Director, who ached to box his ears, cringed. "Good sir," Victor began again, and looked around the room, as if he had just not had his job security threatened by this executive bully, "and gentlewoman," he smiled, and slightly bowed toward her, and then he turned his calm gaze toward the still-smoldering figure that was the President. "Sir, I have pursued a course least traveled by my colleagues—that is to say, by my own wit and intelligence—and I have gained the favor of those indomitable Defenders, or, as we know them, the Crusaders, and treated them as equals, to gain their trust, and, to be frank, to seek their favor in the future."

"Betrayal," the President shouted, still restraining himself in the same manner a cook holds down a rattling lid on a boiling pot.

"Ah, betrayal—during war, our darling; during peace, our head on a scaffold."

"Out with it, collaborator!"

He was carrying a brown leather briefcase. "While we fight the Cartels here, in the dark, like little, frightened children, and are happy when we trip over one of them, the Crusaders are in Mexico, doing what our good and able friends in the intelligence community cannot do—fighting them there."

"And, and—you infernal wretch—now speak it!"

Victor smiled, still amused, and began again, "Sir, the Crusaders," he said, looking at him calmly, "as you know, gave us invaluable places and routes in the US some time ago, which strongly helped us drive some of these immigrant swine into the corner and ensnare them; but now, yes, now, the Crusaders have given us arms shipment routes and drug routes, often videotaped, and all exquisitely mapped, from Central America to Mexico to America, and from America back down south again." He halted his tease, to observe his captivated audience upon which he held a taut string by his masterly skills as marionette, and would presently make them dance and sing on his personally built stage; even the President had, in his pale face, the light of forgiveness beginning to stream back.

Victor stepped away from those in attendance, so that he could fathom all of their faces when he announced, with uncommon restraint, "As you know, the Cartels operate on a radio network that has been beyond our grasp to control, and with a code that our very best people cannot begin to understand and crack; gentlemen," he looked around, certitude flush across his bold face, "not only have the Crusaders deciphered this code, and just now eagerly handed it to us," and he looked at his watch, and then back to the perfectly spellbound audience, "at this very moment, they will have destroyed the vast majority of the Azteca and El Dorado Cartel radio communication networks, thus rendering our two most vile enemies—who have taken up nest in America like rats carrying the plague on an Asian ship to Europe—effectively without the ability to coordinate their vast empires; but, I must emphasize, opening only a brief window of opportunity."

No one dared to speak, for this all seem too illusory, that the answer to their most fervent hopes and prayers might appear in so timely a fashion, and slowly, cautiously, their fears and doubts began to acquit themselves of prejudice for defeatism.

"Is that all," the President finally managed to utter, still taken aback.

"No, sir, that is not all; for, at this moment also, the Crusaders, those brave and valiant men and women, are about to engage in battle with the two aforementioned armies, to do the job that some sovereign nation ought long ago to have done."

The aide to the President then walked in, whispered in his ear, and left; the President, still held in the magical aura of the fantastic news just presented to him, moved, as if in a dream, toward the door, and opening it, invited the esteemed gentlemen in, and said, with great respect "Ladies and gentlemen, the President of Mexico."

El Presidente, after greeting everyone in the room, and hearing of the revelatory news, said, with the greatest urgency, "Mr. President, we need to talk."

Subterfuge

"Luis," Tomas Alvarez began, sullen, in the early tide of this balmy August morning, his white coffee mug of strong black Columbian coffee in his big, bony hands, "I want to know," he sipped the hot, steaming brew, "when those Azteca dogs are going to hit us," he paused, looking around the room; his face began to spasm, and contort, and then he proceeded to drag his surroundings into his foul mood with bitter implications and vulgar epitaphs, as he, the King, wasn't happy, so too must the world be unhappy; were they joyous, then they must be sad; had they what he had not, then they must lose it; had they satisfaction, then they must be unsatisfied; what he was, what he felt, what he believed in, if it were vexing, they must too feel, or suffer the consequences. "Why do I have to do it myself?" he screamed, banging his fisted hand upon the Redwood desk. "Why? Tell me why, Luis!"

Luis knew his role now, and it was simply as a human conduit, to siphon off the overwhelming antipathies directed at all living things by his lord and master.

"I want to know," Alvarez continued, having dislodged a certain amount of negative pent-up energy to allow his normal speech to flow, "when the Azteca dogs are going to launch an invasion."

"We have received communiqués, sir," Luis began, finding the time right to assume the role of the sole interlocutor here, a role few could assume in the hall of the drug king and live, "that signify a certain time and date."

"I don't believe this—it is too suspicious," he replied, his thick, black eyebrows knit as he received the manila folder from his adjutant, who knew it was now time to stand patiently and await further orders while Alvarez studied the documents. "Sit, Luis, you make me nervous."

Luis, much relieved, and honored, obediently sat, and then patiently waited; and after some time, the big man, twisting his mustache, frowning, grunting, groaning, hemming and hawing, said, "When did we crack their supposedly uncrackable code—wasn't it about one month ago?" He received an affirmative reply. "Wait—I can tell you: it was exactly one month and two days ago—I remember it because it was the same day I had Marciano killed."

"Good memory, sir."

Alvarez looked up, his deep-set black eyes looking out from under his bushy eyebrows, and continued on. "That's why I am still alive, Luis—other men in my position get sloppy." He pulled off his glasses. "Do you know that I can quote any statistic from our budget, any monthly income, expenditures—virtually anything! I know each route of our operations, the name of all my top men; I have traveled over these routes to the homes of my men, met their wives, been to birthday parties of their children, and their catechisms, quinceañeras of their children; I am godfather to five of them—it's all good PR, Luis; learn how to deal with people—treat them fairly; but," he threw up his arms, "if they betray you, or are incompetent, well, deal with them just the same—appropriately." He replaced his glasses. "Now—one month ago—do you think that was a ruse?"

"No, sir."

"Why?"

"We have hit their operatives too many times, and hurt them too often; no, they would have changed."

"Are they too arrogant to think we cannot break their code—which was difficult, don't get me wrong, and even though it is a sporadic decoding for now; but what about the two men we captured who just happened to have the crucial piece we needed?"

"Coincidence; and we worked hard to capture those two inside men."

"I think so, too." He paused. "Have they cracked our code?"

"No, sir; we have no indication they have. We have evidence that traitors—as you already know, and who are being taken care of, as you already know—within our organization gave up our routes and times and dates to Suarez, but it was done not by eavesdropping of their people."

"And what about these reports of these foreign dogs, these Defenders, being still alive?"

"They are working for the Azteca people, sir—and they will be killed, like everyone else who gets in our way; do not doubt it."

"Good; well, this invasion date—August twenty-ninth—is it authentic?"

"We have reason to believe so—in seven days, sir."

"We are in total readiness?"

"Yes, sir."

"Good." But he said it as if pronouncing the death sentence upon a convicted criminal.

And what was his nemesis, Arturo Suarez, contemplating at the same critical hour?

"Hector," he began, eating his staple breakfast of fresh, fertile, brown eggs, whole wheat toast, freshly squeezed orange juice, two brown juicy sausages, and straight black coffee, "have you had your breakfast?"

"Yes, sir."

"Good, good, it is the most important meal of the day, as my beloved mother always said; now, about those two men who were killed in a shootout—Alvarez's men?"

"Yes, sir."

"We know who the leaks are, si?"

"Yes, sir—all taken care of."

"And we have no evidence of Alvarez having cracked our code?"

"Not now, sir—it is too inconceivable: even the best and brightest decipherers we hired cannot crack it."

"Bueno," he said, nodding his head, his big cowboy hat bobbing up and down, and after he had eaten some more, he continued, "What about the donations to the hospitals, the schools, the churches?"

"Done."

"Bueno," he said and, after drinking his orange juice and savoring its weakness, he swallowed, and then continued, "and the priest," to which he received a positive reply, and then stabbed the thick, still-sizzling sausage and held it up and about, "and the politicians," he said again, and after receiving a positive reply, looked at the brown, chunky, dense cylindrical object of his desire. "You know, Hector, the sausage—the pig that this was—he, or maybe, she—no? Died for a reason," and he slapped his protruding belly, "to satisfy my lust to devour a living organism," and he bit off a large chunk of it and, closing his large, brown eyes, declared, "are they any different from people— all of us are here to serve a purpose or others; how could it be any different?" He shrugged his fat shoulders. "The strong rule the weak; the wealthy employ the poor; but the strong must rule fairly, and the wealthy must help the poor; this is my general philosophy, as it stands today." He finished the generous sausage. "Now, the politicians serve a purpose: we donate to his campaign, and he—or she; I certainly don't want to be sexist, especially these days— donates to ours; in this case, we use the wealthy and the strong, ruling the ones who think they are wealthy and strong, but in reality are weak and poor; but, we let him think it: it is better that he—or she—is this way, otherwise their sensibilities would be offended." He ate some more. "It is a good model, as long as everyone knows their place, si?"

"Si, El Toro."

El Toro smiled. "All is in readiness for the coming battle with our unfortunate friend, Señor Muerte? And what of these nasty Defenders I have heard about? I thought they were to be taken care of…"

"They are working for Alvarez, but they are nothing to worry over; they will be taken care of—like all the others."

El Toro smiled, and with great enthusiasm, finished the meal that stimulated his taste buds for fatty and greasy, sugary, salty, and hot and spicy sensations; and as far as he was concerned, he was now a complete man, in mind and body, for he had a roof over his head, and clothes on his back, and he had had his food—at least until lunch. "One meal at a time," he was fond of saying; "enjoy it like it's your last, and you will live longer."

El Toro and Señor Muerte enjoyed the benefit of speaking clearly and in an authentic voice to a person in their presence who was able to instantly verify the information by a verbal reply; unfortunately, such was not the case for those in both organizations who relied on electronic devices for verbal communication, as the extraordinary physicists in the employ of Robert Heimdall, who had created a time-cloaking device that was able to alter communication between two parties after knowing the frequency and code of both of the Cartels in question, and by listening in for months to the conversations of high-ranking officials and learning the rhythm and rhyme of their speech patterns, and understanding their distinct personalities, which was like a unique signature that often helped the listener verify the authenticity of the sender, and by creating a computer generated voice—which was achieved by analyzing the unique sound of the speaker's words, and then, like parts of a jigsaw puzzle that are interchangeable with other puzzles, these bits of sounds were then assumed to form new words—that could mimic the voice of the officials instantaneously, were able to create the following hitherto unknown mirage, now regarded as a miracle, with increasing ease and longer times:

A General of the Azteca army on the battlefield to a General at headquarters spoke thus: "We need reinforcements!" But this voice signal was blocked, captured, and re-sent as, "We do not need reinforcements," to which the receiving General would reply, "Understood, you are good to go," but which was blocked and captured, and re-sent as, "We will send additional troops immediately."

And when the scientists sought to allow the Cartels to eavesdrop on each other on a frequency and cracked code they had created, but which was more difficult to sustain and keep hidden from the enemy, the following scenario would occur:

A virtual avatar of a General of the El Dorado army would speak briefly on the invasion date to another phantom General on a supposedly secure but not "cracked" and "deciphered" frequency. "We will invade tomorrow at three a.m.," to which the other General would reply, "Confirmed, the invasion date is for tomorrow at three a.m."

It just goes to show you: you can't always believe what you hear.

His Story

The communication headquarters of the Azteca Cartel were nestled in the dense mountainous region of Azteca, surrounded by structures that contained a small army whose sole duty it was to protect the nerve center of their employer, which, incidentally, had never suffered an attack, mainly due to the complex constantly moving about from one locale to another; one year it was built here, before that two miles west, before that one mile east, and in one year, prepared to go south, one and a half miles.

A running target is harder to hit, often said Arturo Suarez, a man who, although, naturally, detested running and hiding like a sewer rat, did not mind imposing such a stratagem on his equipment, and the men who habitually worked and guarded it.

When the leaders of Yermo had firmly established the plan to defend their town, and established their people in the proper defensive parameters, and armed now with weapons that had not only been procured from the fallen Azteca soldiers in town, but acquired from the fallen Aztecas at the nearby airstrip, all, then, appeared to be in readiness, leaving the five Crusaders, along with Pedro and Roderigo, to pursue a rendezvous route.

In a short while, they came upon a seemingly deserted and open section of the hills, yet one that was teeming with human life.

"Going down," Finn said, half-smiling, as he approached the camouflaged opening to the underground tunnel, and opening the stone-handled door, which he laid aside, he allowed Ana to descend, followed by Roderigo and Pedro, and then Miguel, and Antonio, who were still on watch, and then Yoshitsune, who waved him aside; so Finn went down the dirt steps and into an actual fortress that extended some one mile in every direction; and presently, he followed those before him and joined them in the modified vactrain, marveling at the engineering construction of the place; the cement reinforcement of the sides, the wooden beams, the shaft lighted by carefully placed lamps; and presently, he found himself ascending up until he saw the blessed peak of light streaming through into the tunnel, and he followed his comrades up the last steps to the precious, sweet abode of, little thought of, but widely appreciated now, simple terra firma.

There stood Rustem, Arjuna, Tyr, Enkidu, waiting, in good humor, clasping the hands of their fellows, and too the two newcomers.

"Well, where is that big fellow, Yoshitsune," Arjuna asked, mischievously, "did he get lost?"

"He was right behind us," Finn said, "when last I left him above the entrance; I thought he meant to scout."

Arjuna, although smiling, was not smiling on the inside, and without so much as a word or frown, took to the depths.

"Is he all right?" Roderigo asked.

Finn, looking at Arjuna disappearing into the tunnel, and then enclosing it, said, assuredly, "Do the mountains disappear?"

Arjuna cleared the tunnel quickly, and with great solicitude, and with his black Glock pistol before him, opened the other hatch and inspected the immediate surroundings, and upon seeing Yoshitsune sitting with legs folded, his arms resting on his knees, his visage grim, sat beside him. "What say you, big man of Japan?"

Yoshitsune sighed deeply, and exhaled his breath slowly, while staring straight ahead. "We Japanese learn early on to hide our emotions, but it is a difficult thing when you are in the wide world, and you peer inside the soul of a great tragedy."

Arjuna was amazed that Yoshitsune spoke of himself, as he, nor the other Crusaders, had ever heard him mention his own history, and thenceforth, Arjuna sat perfectly still, and excited, yet anxious, for to see this great man act indecisively or so unlike his stoic self was frightening.

"When I was twenty-two years old, I had a wife—her name was Aimi," Yoshitsune began, and from his face was torn a piece of calm, "and a baby boy, one year old—Ichirou," and then, as if from a blunt instrument, a crack rippled across his darkening visage, expressing bitter sentiment. "I was a police officer, on the Special Units team; I had," and he paused, at the remembrance of it, "a life." He rose up, and then, seiza-style, tucked his legs underneath and then sat down, sitting on his heels, and then pursed his lips. "The big earthquake came when we were in downtown, and we happened to be inside a building; I can still hear it collapse," and he closed his eyes, "and hear the crash all around me, like the air itself was shaking me," and he tilted his head and frowned as his breath quickened, "and I can still hear the screaming of my beloved Aimi and Ichirou; but it was a miracle, when, after the tremor stopped, even though we were trapped beneath the debris—we still lived."

Arjuna was numbed to a chill by the anticipation of an encroaching horror, frighteningly described; he did not even move, or make his presence known in any way, as he observed the swelling of pain seal itself like an unhealthy infestation on the usually smooth countenance, and one now covered in copious sweat, of a man he had once thought was unbreakable.

"We were buried alive," he opened his eyes wide, pain inflicting itself across his face as if at the end of a cracked bullwhip, "no food, no water; we existed on our love for each other." His lips began to tremble, "Our good Ichirou, our good baby boy, he was so fragile, and so innocent," his normally controlled voice was evanescent and broken into fragments and waves of agony. "He died on the second day, he was so little." Tears of piety welled up in his coal-black eyes. "He died in my arms." Tears flashed down his flushed, still face, and then he shouted in that magnificently trained kabuki voice. He was unable to speak for several seconds. "I watched her die on the ninth day, I listened to her beg me to consume her flesh so that I might live; O, merciful heaven, how could I do such a shameful thing to survive, even to the lowliest human being?" He was unable to speak for several seconds. "O, she was a good woman, and kind to every soul… If anyone deserved to die, it was me; I who should have died to sacrifice myself for my family, it was my sacred duty to do so, and yet I failed…" He was silent for a moment, and his voice became even more melancholy. "And I could not—I did not—even tell her that I loved her; it is not so often done in Japan: we Japanese, you see, show our love for each other through actions, through everyday events, through caring for each other, so it is unnecessary to so often say 'Aishiteru,' for that special person knows it, feels it, experiences it; and yet, as she lay there in my arms, dying, looking up at me with those loving eyes, I felt the desire—I felt the need to say 'Aishiteru,' I love you, Aimi, I love you, as I do Ichirou, as I will never love anyone else again—never, for you two have been my life's blood, my honor, my joy; and yet, to my shame, I could say nothing, but merely look upon her beauteous face, and hoped and prayed that she knew…"

Arjuna had affixed his sorrowful gaze upon this giant of a man, who now collapsed in bits and pieces before him, and without restraint.

"I held them both for two weeks, until we were found." He was calmer now, but his voice was as if sent through a restrainer and reorganized into a disjointed, wondering calamity. "I resolved to honor them by helping those who were buried alive all around the world." He looked at Arjuna, and shook his head. "I cannot go into such a place," and he glanced toward the entrance, "and yet survive; if I cannot take the tunnels, I will endanger the mission; so, I must leave." He looked again at Arjuna. "I have brought dishonor to my name, for I knew of the existence of the tunnels, and should have withdrawn then; I'm a coward." He hung his head low.

Arjuna dared not ask him how he had survived those long two weeks without food or water. "You a coward—ha! Let it never be, great one! And you are kabuki," Arjuna began, looking at the knit brows of his friend. "You will play a role now, on a real stage, a world stage, where you are not merely a man, but a great man, whose presence brings life to Innocents and the Crusaders, but whose absence brings a dissolution of order to the Crusaders, and our deaths, and many more deaths to Innocents."

"I cannot, Arjuna," he replied, nearly pleading; "it is too much for me; I am mere flesh, not stone."

"None of us are mere flesh, my good friend; we're warriors, apart from humanity." He paused, gazing intensely into the eyes of his friend. "You will not do this fine deed for yourself, but for those whom you once held in your loving arms, and still love: for Aimi and Ichirou." He stood up, and put down his hand to him. "Close your eyes, and once more hold your beloved Aimi and Ichirou in your strong arms."

"I have never," he returned, in a deep, passionate tone, "stopped holding them—for they are the blessed memories that drive me forward."

"Then let them drive you now, through your trial, where they will be with you; see them now, Yoshitsune, as I see my beloved Aishwarya and Suhani and Rohan every waking day and sleeping night, and hold so dear in my heart, that without their presence," and he clutched his chest with his free hand, "I would die." Passion suffused his voice. "Honor them now—let their golden memory give you solace."

Yoshitsune was unlike most men, who must ponder and speculate, wait and procrastinate—he was either in or out, rushing forward or running backward; thus, his mind appeased, he took the hand of his comrade, closed his eyes, prepared his mind, opened his heart, and went into the pungent, dusty, consuming shaft.

On the other side, the Crusaders waited patiently, not once thinking of calling the two men on their special cell phone; and then, they heard a sound, and readied their weapons, but soon relaxed them, as first came out Yoshitsune, then Arjuna, both men seemingly fit and able; and with no further questions asked, the group moved on toward the mark. No one, save Arjuna, could see the internal upheaval of Yoshitsune that was reflected in subtle waves across his face.

While Roderigo and Pedro walked ahead, Arjuna spoke in a hushed tone. "You must destroy the communication center by twenty-one hundred hours, the same time the forces of Major Gonzales and Guzman are to take out the El Dorado command center."

"When will the military come?" Finn whispered, watching the two men ahead.

"At twenty-one hundred hours," Arjuna continued, "to each battle."

Yoshitsune forced himself to speak, calming his mind, stabilizing his voice, seeking to flatten out all opposition to harmony and tranquility. "We must trust the two men before us, for they know the structure intimately." However, he knew their thoughts, and then said, "Men change." No contrarian view was offered.

"Come," Yoshitsune said to the two men, as they responded quickly. The troop halted. Yoshitsune stood before the two men as a father to his wicked yet repentant sons. "We need your help in a great endeavor." The men stood up, Bibles in hand still, their posture reflective of their inner eagerness to please these stalwart warriors, and their inner eagerness to atone for the past. "We will blow up the main communications centers of the El Dorado Cartel tonight."

Although Roderigo and Pedro beamed joy and pride, Roderigo spoke first. "It will be my great honor to blow it to smithereens."

"I would delight in making mute our enemy," Pedro said.

"Good, good," Yoshitsune replied. "Now, tell us all that you know."

And they did, in fine detail, so that when the two former outlaws were done, the Crusaders felt as if indeed they had been to the very place they never seen, but after visiting it, were hopeful no one would see it as it was ever again.

Tyr and Enkidu, taking off their backpacks wherein were packed the high explosives, and handing them to Finn and Yoshitsune, who put them on, then took off in the direction of the target with José and Guillermo, two Crusaders who knew most of the terrain, disappearing quickly and silently into the dark embrace of the dense forest.

Pedro frowned. "How can they find their way in the dark? They know such terrain?"

Roderigo said, "They must have GPS and other tracking equipment."

Rustem smiled. "They are like the birds of the air: once upon a place, and taken far away, can find their way back, and even without the stars, if need be."

"Such gifts are bestowed upon us all," Antonio said.

"We need only to recognize them," Ana said.

"And use them wisely," Yoshitsune said.

"It is this that we realize there is more in ourselves than what we perceive with our eyes only," Finn said, "and begin to see with our open mind, who bestowed these fine gifts upon us."

The communication center could not be detected by satellite, as it had special reflectors, and paint properties atop and over it, to deflect the invasive eye of electronic surveillance, and it was also nestled in an entanglement of thick forest, so that its scattered, plain, soil-colored buildings blended in like giant boulders or earthen protuberances.

Tyr and Enkidu, and José and Guillermo, checked the electronic sensor moving system as they neared their objective, and seeing no presence, moved in until they beheld the five buildings on the raised hills, and scouted the entire circumference of it, taking pictures of it with their infrared cell phones and recording video with their special glasses, and after sending the information to their control center, presently returned to their fellows.

"Here is the main network," Roderigo said, looking at the pictures on Tyr's cell phone; "blow this, and they will be without a voice for a good twenty-four hours."

"What about backup systems?" Enkidu asked.

"They have hundreds of smaller communication units, but this is the main artery, and if cut…" Pedro said.

"How many men will we encounter?" Tyr asked.

"One hundred men, at the most," Roderigo said.

Yoshitsune looked at his watch. "It is nineteen hundred hours; the cell phone towers near here will shortly be blown, landline phone signals terminated, and satellite reception blocked," he said, solemnly. "Let's move."

As they walked, Finn, observing that Pedro and Roderigo were perplexed, inquired as to their anxiety.

"I do not understand why more of you were not sent here," Roderigo said, "for such an important mission."

Finn nodded, and smiled, and said, reassuringly, "You will soon see the worth of each of us."

As they crouched before the sprawling complexes, Rustem split off to the left, for he needed no other company, and Yoshitsune and Finn to the right, the former of whom was about to cut the outside video surveillance; Tyr and Enkidu, once again wearing the backpacks containing the explosives, along with José and Guillermo, went to the rear of the buildings; Miguel stayed where he was, unlike Roderigo, Pedro, and Antonio, and Ana, who walked easily and slowly into the heart of the enemy's tongue and mouth, which rendered ordinary speech most foul.

Communication Headquarters

"What are the chances they will have heard of your defection or seen your pictures?" Antonio asked Roderigo and Pedro. "We have not heard it spoken of on their radio chatter…" In reality, the moment Roderigo and Pedro had departed from their brethren, the Crusaders had immediately seized upon this moment, blocked any transmission of this rare phenomenon of betrayal outside of Yermo, monitored radio chatter constantly for any news of it, and, more importantly, made sure that Yoshitsune and the other four Crusaders would "accidentally" meet up with Roderigo in the forest.

"Very little," Roderigo said, "and considering the mobiles we have taken out…"

"Even if they had, they would think us dead," Pedro said.

"They have more to worry about than two rogue men," Roderigo said. "You may laugh, but I will check my latest online social websites, to see if anyone has posted anything." And when he, being the point man, walked a little further, he stopped, raised his hands, and then said, definitively, "They must have set up the landmines, too." It was the M18A1 Claymore anti-personnel mines that lay in abundance before them, but were slowly and methodically detected by the portable micropower impulse radar device that Yoshitsune held, which emitted microwave impulses from its antenna into the ground and brought back the signature marker for the hidden villain; and as he slowly moved forward, his comrades were close behind him.

But this was a conversation that only delayed the inevitable—no chances must be taken, and so the plan of the two men assuming the identity of two Azteca soldiers they knew intimately, but whom they had recently killed, would be adopted; thus, Roderigo and Pedro, having never before been to this particular communication center, but to many like it, and with their faces partially disguised by the clever hands of the makeup artists within the Crusaders, must now play their most important role.

Presently, as they made their way into the clearing, they saw the five guards at the central barbed-wire fence, who, agitated, began to shout in the direction of the travelers.

"Ho, there! It is Felipe Lopez," cried Roderigo, "from Jorge Valenzuela, with new orders we are to hand deliver to your commander, Leon Castillo."

"And Jaime Alatorre," shouted Pedro.

The five guards, somewhat appeased, still waited for confirmation.

"Jesus Malverde," Pedro cried.

"Si," one of the guards responded, "Señor Muerte."

"The password," Pedro whispered to the Crusaders; "ironic."

Roderigo and Pedro shook the hands of the guards, told them their orders, and then introduced their companions.

"We are hunting Alvarez's people in the area—you heard about the mobiles being blown up?" Roderigo said, casually.

"Yes," one of the guards replied, "that is why one hundred men arrived this morning to fortify us, but you too are welcome," and then he frowned. "How did you get past the landmines, eh?"

"We step very lightly," Ana said, sneering.

"Have you seen these Alvarez vermin?" asked one of the guards.

"No, but we think they're headed in this direction," Pedro said, once again wearing the cloak of vicious killer, "but it will be their last chance for Señor Muerte."

The guards were staring at Ana, taken in by her beauty, and one of them ambled up to her, and stood too close, when he said, "So, señorita, what are you doing tonight, eh?"

She smiled, and said, softly, "You mean, if you don't remove your ugly self from me? Well, watching you get used to walking with a cane."

The other guards laughed and howled as the guard, upon inspecting the authoritative scowl across her dark face, carefully stepped away from her.

Three more men were coming from the main building. "We lost outside video," one shouted.

Roderigo nudged Antonio twice, a prearranged signal that trouble may be coming.

Miguel then reported on the ear com that more Azteca soldiers were coming, and that the transmission of their approaching presence had been intercepted and substituted with one that gave out "enemy chatter" of El Dorado bent on destruction of this facility.

A chill then purchased the inner sanctum of the four travelers, and their compatriots, who listened in on the com units all of them wore in their ears; the mobile units and other housing units had been demolished only one day before, and they had taken the risk that not too many Azteca reinforcements would be sent here as a consequence.

Roderigo, upon seeing one of the three men staring at him—a man he knew—coughed, a prearranged signal that trouble visited them.

Antonio, seeing the direction in which Roderigo looked, and seeing the man in question take out his radio walkie-talkie, said, rather casually to this man, certain to gesture at him, "I sure am hungry for anything you have inside; walking in the woods and tracking scum will do that to you."

The coded message had been received by the Crusaders' position on the periphery of the hills. "Anything" meant kill any guards who were approaching from the complex, as the guards already met would grant safe passage inside for the four down there. "Woods" meant engage any approaching threat.

Miguel, using his FN Minimi 7.62, opened fire upon the five black SUVs coming from behind in the woods, and simultaneously, Finn and Yoshitsune took out the approaching guards from the complex, and the guard whom Roderigo had recognized.

"We're under attack by El Dorado soldiers," cried one of the sentries who had greeted the troop, as he and the rest of them ran pell-mell under a barrage of bullets toward the main building, while the four newcomers feigned providing cover fire.

Once inside, the full extent of the resistance force became apparent to the four, as they plainly saw the hundreds of Azteca soldiers scurrying for their weapons.

Leon Castillo, the commander of the complex, came up to the surviving guards.

"El Dorado soldiers are attacking—these four helped save us," the guard said, excitedly. "They have been tracking them. Felipe has orders from one of the big bosses."

"Who sent you?" the commander asked with suspicion.

"Jorge Valenzuela," Roderigo said, replicating his bravura, thug-like cockiness, "to wipe your noses—now, let's get going!"

"Call Jorge," the commander said to the guard, and waited.

"That may be a bit difficult," Roderigo said casually.

"No one answers," the guard said, hanging up the phone, but trying another frequency.

Roderigo smiled. "Maybe you don't know who I am; I am Felipe Lopez, and I am on my way up in the organization, and you, as you stand here worried about chasing phantoms, will be lucky if Alvarez—whom I personally know," and he pulled out a picture in which he and the big man were arm in arm, "will let you live, after I tell him we tracked the Black Death Squad, the Escuadrón de la Muerte Negro, from Guatemala for three days, and then came to this post, where they, although given reinforcements, were sitting on their hands and taking a siesta and trying to contact a man who is dead; that's right, dead—he was killed by traitors in the organization." He then, nonchalantly, gave the commander the latest access codes for this complex, which were known by only a select few, but had lately been provided to him by the Crusaders.

Leon Castillo was, after all, a lower-level peon, in charge of a remote complex that had never been attacked, much like a man who watches the dial on a nuclear reactor and waits for it to reach the dreaded red zone. Alarms were bringing a rare clamor to the room, screams and shouts of urgency were resounding everywhere, gunfire was heard all about, and the now shocked and perplexed commander was standing adrift, just dressed down by who he perceived as one of the mean, soulless Azteca soldiers, believers in violence as a creed, who had killed his way to the top, and he was, quite frankly, nervous.

The guard was finally able to make contact with an Azteca operative, and the commander heard the operative verify the identities of the four new arrivals, and the fact that the Black Death Squad was indeed on its way to attack the communications center. But it had all been a ruse—Heimdall's scientists had intercepted the communiqué, and had responded appropriately.

Leon looked over to Roderigo. "What do I do now?"

Roderigo smiled inwardly, thinking, "Are all the wicked so feeble and afraid when confronted with something that seems more wicked than they— was I?" And then aloud, with the peremptory percussion of a confident leader, "Set up a perimeter, send four teams in each direction, determine enemy strength in every quadrant, and for pity's sake, tell the men who we are so they don't shoot us."

The commander, as if seized in the head by a superior tactical mine, obeyed, barking out these exact orders.

"And find out why the surveillance cameras did not detect this encroachment," Roderigo said, firmly, knowing the Crusaders had taken them out, and then continued, "we are going to secure the six control rooms." And he and the three others moved out with a scowl as if prepared for battle, the main guard from the outside fence accompanying them.

There were nine rooms in this building, six containing the communication devices, the other a cafeteria, a recreation room and a leisure center. The long corridor they walked had numerous cameras, and checkpoints at doors, which could be opened only by plastic cards with codes, and a code to be punched in, by thumbprint, and iris scan. Men were rushing everywhere, and chaos reigned, as the technicians had previously experienced only drills.

Roderigo, knowing the entire layout, led the team to the back of the building, where there were two large metal exit doors, protected by four guards.

"I am about to block the interior video transmission," Yoshitsune said, his voice nearly smothered by the rapid gunfire. "Done."

Ana and Antonio aimed their Glock pistols down the corridor in each direction while Pedro placed his pistol to the head of the man.

Roderigo took the trembling guard to the back door. "Do it," he grumbled, and the guard obeyed, putting his thick card to the electric slot, punched in the code, and then used his thumbprint and eye for a scan. "Paranoid bunch," Roderigo whispered, bemused, and then after opening the door, he and Pedro went out into the darkness, shouting orders as to their identity, and ordering men to secure various parts of the compound to lock down the area.

Subordinates are there to obey especially in a panic, and obey these drones did, eager to please their new taskmasters; presently, from the uppermost tier of the forest were thrown two black nylon backpacks by José and Guillermo, which Pedro retrieved and quickly took in, followed by Roderigo, who then presented the explosives-filled packages to Ana and Antonio.

As they walked, the guard begged, "Will I live if I cooperate?"

"This much I know," Ana said, keeping the barrel of her pistol snugly in his back, "if you don't, you won't."

The first control room was breached via the cooperation of the guard; and when the technicians inside realized the visit was not benign, they stood up, hands in the air, when one of them said, as Antonio set the deadly explosives that had been created by Heimdall's scientists, about the circular room, "Don't kill us—we're only technicians; we haven't killed anybody."

"What say you," Ana began to her comrades; "they're here by accident, as if on their way to church."

"Yes, they did not hold the gun or pull the trigger," Roderigo said, his crimson countenance burning wrath, "but they held the target still in their long-helping hands," and he, and Pedro, proceeded to lock them into a back room.

The next five rooms were prepared in a similar fashion, and presently, the troops stood outside the last one.

Antonio said, his face grim, "Let's move."

The Crusaders on the periphery acknowledged the admonition code "let's move," which meant the explosives would burst their tight bubble in three minutes.

This was also a signal for what had previously been arranged as a retreat for the Crusaders on the periphery, except that they now could not do this.

Even though Yoshitsune, Finn, Rustem, José and Guillermo had held their own, in total dropping forty men with the sophisticated FLIR technology of their HK417 rifles—the ThermoSight HISS-XLR thermal weapon sight that has a range of two thousand meters—and had enjoined with Miguel to combat the newly arrived troops, they would soon be enveloped as surely as an encroaching fire devours dry, naked brush; there was no conceivable way out, and they, through more encoded language, related this to their comrades.

"We have them trapped on the ridge," the commander excitedly and proudly related to the returning Roderigo and company.

"Good," Roderigo answered; "I'll join them." And he led the cautious Crusaders on, still with the obedient guard, who was still needed to bypass any unknown barriers; and presently, they were outside, the great clamor of battle reaching like a vile sword into their warrior's hearts; and then, soldiers from inside the complex came charging out of the door, guns drawn, but were met with gunfire from Ana and Antonio.

"We are oppressed from both sides," cried Yoshitsune; "on my count—three, two…"

The Crusaders coming from the building, having moved in a westerly direction and taken cover behind large trees they had mentally noted on their way in, crouched down low, hands over their heads.

"One," Yoshitsune said—and then cried, "No, wait!"

The Betrothal of Power and Vanity

Arturo Suarez, Chief of the Azteca Cartel—one of the wealthiest men in all of Mexico, and beyond that, in all of North America; a man feared in his own country, by everyone of every rank and creed, color and importance; a man used to dealing with obstacles as easily as a child knocks down a castle of sand—was undone, not only by the persistent attacks on his arms shipments, his drug shipments, his mobile and stationary network communications, and on his towns, but the unrestrained, as he perceived, stupidity, arrogance, and avarice of his main nemesis.

"Hector," El Toro said, after removing his big black hat, and then massaging his thick, black mane, "this Alvarez is indeed a mad man! Such brashness, such ignorance of proper business transactions: to attack our private fortifications, to interrupt the flow of our product to market—caramba! The man is loco—Señor Muerte, as we know, is a good, good name for him because he can't leave well enough alone, so then he will be … dead!"

"Sir, he is, as you say, insane; and we have intercepted more communications from his people—they are planning even more raids everywhere; sir, I believe they intend to take over our very plaza."

"He is forcing me into a fight; well, Hector, so it is a fight he will have—in spades! Are all the men in readiness?"

"Yes, El Toro."

"Send in my generals." Ten of his top military advisers, many of whom had been bought from the Mexican military, walked in and sat before their supreme commander; he stood before a relief map of the northern province of Mexico. "Our force of five thousand men are poised to attack the stronghold of Tomas Alvarez, boss of the El Dorado Cartel; we have intel that he intends to attack us tomorrow, but we attack today; we leave an auxiliary of one thousand men, and I personally recruited others to join our cause in crushing this madman. All of you have your instructions."

"El Toro," one of the generals said, "have you considered that it might be a trap?"

"Yes, I have," he returned, walking in front of the gray steel desk that sat in front of the pull-down map, "but our informants, our breakers of their code, our interception of their radio signals—although it is intermittent for now—all tell us that they intend to strike tomorrow."

"What about the federal troops?" another General asked.

"Yes, what about them—we will have them occupied; I tell you, in truth, sirs, that after this victory, we will own all the drug business of North America—lock, stock, and drug barrel."

"El Toro," another General asked, boldly, "is it our battle to lose?"

"Yes, General, it is; you see," he began, stroking his fine salt-and-pepper goatee—he had shaved his beard and quit dyeing the goatee, telling his wife he preferred to look his age when the time came that he would allow photographers to take his picture—as he sat upon the desk, "as of now," he glanced at his humble watch, which had been given to him by his mother, "on August twenty-third, at four o'clock in the a.m., I am a mere prince, and a prince must know what his subjects think, and want, and how they feel about their sovereign; is he a legitimate prince, or a usurper to the throne? Is he lawful, or a bandit? Who gave him authority—himself or the people, or the government—who, presently, must be seen as operating outside of the sphere of popular opinion; you see, sirs, we need to be the new force in Mexico; it must be the Azteca Cartel the people come to see as the official government, and I intend to be the legitimate ruler here." He looked at the incredulity spreading like a tidal wave across their visages. "I will have my own as mayors, governors, police chiefs, legislators, editors, television and movie stars, singers, writers, newspaper and magazine people—and what makes up the face of society but these, eh? We will be the new imperial power that takes over Mexico; and why not, I ask you: does not any peasant people, in time, come to accept their rulers—and with every succeeding generation, forget where rulers come from, eh? In a generation, the Azteca Cartel will be a political party, will have the same legitimacy as the Institutional Revolutionary Party, the PRI—and by the way, what were they for decades but tyrants and dictators? We will do what the United Fruit Company oil companies did in Central America—use their power and influence to simply take what they desire—and who is to stop us: the military!" He thumped his barrel-like chest. "A government is only as strong as its military—but now, we are the military! It's all about dinero, gentlemen: you buy allegiance with money, and then back that up with power; soon, I will own even the presidency: there is nothing money cannot buy in this corrupt world; and, my fine sirs, when has Mexico ever seen an indigenous power take over—never! Where Villa and Zapata failed, and other supposedly democratic reforms failed, I, Arturo Suarez, will not; and the people will hail me as a conquering hero! Why? Because I will, after destroying all opposition, decrease the violence here, improve the towns: create better schools, better drinking water, sewers, health care, job conditions; I, Arturo Suarez, promise this to a people who will embrace me with open arms!"

The generals, as if possessed of one mind, stood up and applauded, as the heartfelt El Toro graciously bowed, and then whispered, reverentially, "Let us pray," and then, after they took off their hats, they all bowed their heads. "Lord, deliver our enemies into your hands, so we can unite this land and stop the bloodshed, and bring prosperity to the people."

Across the great divide that was created by a distinctly different brand of vanity, there sat, silent in the pitch-black darkness, Tomas Alvarez, hearing no sound but the sound of his war plans, and seeing nothing but the dead and dying of his war, tasting and feeling and seeing nothing but the great victories that awaited him when all was said and done. He called in his trusted adjutant.

"Yes, sir," the adjutant said, hesitant to move about in the dark room.

"Do not turn on the lights, Luis." Luis stood perfectly still. "This is a great moment for the El Dorado people, you know it."

"Yes, sir." Good, Luis thought; he is brooding.

"I'm going to crush that worm, Suarez."

"I pray it, sir." Ah, he thought, he is in the blood feud.

"I gave that worm a chance for reconciliation—I backed off on attacking his towns, his people, his market, and what does that ingrate do?"

Luis hesitated, not certain if he were to respond.

"He goes after my town, my arms shipments, my drug routes, my communication networks—that lousy, no-good, filthy, conniving ingrate."

"Good," Luis thought, hearing rancor bleed through the disturbed voice of his boss, "he is incensed; he is a fine general now."

"I am going to crush that dirty, filthy, rotten, greedy, low-life peasant trash; I want him caught—do you hear me, Luis, I want him captured; I will offer a ten-million-dollar reward—in American currency—for his capture, alive, so I can personally beat him to death with my bare hands." He paused, nodding his head as he studied his raised hands, analyzing his own thoughts, and then said, staring straight ahead into what he thought was his grand future, and massaging a book on the fascinating life of sea creatures, "There is a sea slug," he began, slowly, methodically; "it journeys to the seas to find one special rock to sit on, then eat food that passes near it; now, you know what that sea slug does then? Of course not—you're not yet an educated man like me." He massaged the glossy cover of the Nature book that sat before him. "Now, once the sea slug needs only its body and not its brain to acquire energy, can you imagine what it might do? Yes, it eats its own brain, because it's no longer needed to survive. Well, I've just described that imbecile Suarez; and oh, by the way, the rest of the human race, too—except me, of course."

"Splendid! Magnificent!" thought Luis. "He hates all people not like him—he is his most despicable and heinous self again! How can we lose now? It is a blessing; Señor Muerte is alive and well."

"The last batch of communications we intercepted say he is still planning to attack on the twenty-ninth; write this down, Luis—it will be inscribed on the scrolls of history: four a.m. in the morning, the day that cur thought he was going to destroy us; but we will lead him to his own destruction, that madman; you know what I'm going to do to that lowlife, peon, brown trash…"

"O, happy day," Luis thought, "he is who he really is: living to destroy, happy that others betray him, praying that others disobey him if only he can then destroy them, because he was long ago destroyed, somehow, by someone—ah, but that doesn't not matter now; what does matter is that, for this crucial moment, he is pure of spirit in his fanatical cause."

"When I am done with that ignoramus scumbag, there will be no trace left of him or his legacy and all of Mexico; not one skin cell, not a fingerprint, nothing," he said, still enraptured in a smoldering, spicy cloak of vengeance. "The memory of him, I will wipe clean from the annals of Mexico; no book will remember him, no song will sing of him, no child will speak of him; who will want to remember someone so ignominiously defeated in battle? Who, who will praise a pathetic loser, a disgraced leader who could have had a comfortable, good life, but his greed and stupidity were his downfall; if there is anything left of him, then, it will be a cautionary tale—how not to run a business. The scum, the human scum." He paused, for several moments, while Luis stood, silent as a statue, waiting for explicit orders. "The men know the orders; they know what they have to do: show no mercy, take no prisoners, never retreat, obliterate anything and everyone connected with those Azteca dogs; I don't want to hear about a single act of charity or, so help me, I will kill the weak fool myself." He paused again, staring into what he perceived to be the absolute future of his expanding empire and regime. "You know who we are, Luis? But Alexander the Great, Genghis Khan, Napoleon— marauding conquerors who exposed the errors of once-great empires of their complacency and soft living." He paused. "Our allies are ready." As Luis did not interpret this as a statement needing a response, he said nothing, and then Alvarez shouted, "Are our allies ready for the fight tomorrow?"

"Yes, sir."

"Outstanding," he answered, appeased, still tapping his fingers on the Redwood desk. "Is the plan for the federal troops understood?"

"Yes, sir."

"Excellent," he answered, still appeased, and, sniffing, nodded his head; and then, lifting up his big cowboy hat, he stroked his fine, black, thick hair, and then reached over to turn on the radio. "You can go Luis—and Luis, great job."

"Thank you, sir," Luis replied, and as he left to go, he could hear the song on the radio coming on, the latest narco-corrido, extolling the virtues of Tomas Alvarez, Señor Muerte, the greatest El Narco of all time, the bravest, most fearless, the most handsome, the fairest, and destined to be a legend—and most importantly, such lyrics written by the big man himself. Luis closed the door in good cheer.

"Tomorrow," Tomas Alvarez thought, "is destiny, and Mexico will be more me than them, and the better for it."

The praising music sailed on, painting a celebratory mural of glorious sights and sounds in the swirling black mist of the upcoming inauguration of the first and deserving King of the Northern Province.

Preparing for War

The Crusaders were under the shade of giant Ponderosa Pine trees, sitting amid their fallen green needles and brown cones, enjoying the anonymity and coolness so simply offered by these humble sprouts of Nature, going over the impending battle, each man and woman having a detailed map of the northern region, and the blueprint and exact location of the Azteca stronghold, the exact places where the attacks were to occur, and the estimated number of enemy troop strength expected.

"All is in readiness," Dylan said, addressing all of the four hundred and eighty-five of his fellows. "Once we obtained the deciphered codes of both Cartels, and then raided each of their operations, and used the captured radio walkie-talkies, and used their unique signatures on them, and sent reports of success, and of future attacks, which would allow them to intercept and halt them—and by allowing each side to think they had discovered the deciphered code of the other, so they might listen in; we have led them to believe the attack is nigh: the El Dorado people believe the Azteca will attack them on the twenty-ninth, the Azteca believe the El Dorado people will attack them on the twenty-fourth; we also know that the El Dorado are planning on attacking tomorrow, but the Azteca are attacking today; and we know, by surveillance eavesdropping, that the Azteca will be sending five thousand soldiers presently to attack the El Dorado fortress; we wait until it is confirmed, then our assault begins on an Azteca stronghold least guarded; Majors Gonzales and Guzman have confirmed that President Diaz will be sending troops to battle the main forces at the El Dorado stronghold; all is in readiness, God willing." He was standing in the familiar place of leadership, high upon a small mound, as they sat in concentric circles before him, their weapons stacked upon their laps. "Yes, this script we have written has faithfully been followed by all parties, but this is a false reading of future events—we must be ready to improvise." And he, forthwith, examined every conceivable lapse in Operation Justice, which would undo them. "We must expect that this enemy will employ hitherto unknown tactics," he continued, and then gave explication and speculation into such happenings. "Thus, we are prepared, and each of us knows our true worth, and our role, and what precedes us, and what goes behind us, once the war commences." He checked his watch. "Even now our team is close to disarming the main communication complex of the Azteca." But he was interrupted by an urgent message in his ear com from a technician who manned one of the surreptitious surveillance systems located high up in the hills. He looked up at their curious faces. "Suarez has sent one hundred more men to the main communications network, with more on the way."

This possible reinforcement, due to the demolition of the mobile and other smaller communications sites, was a known risk, and was, therefore, foreseen.

"Rescue Team," Dylan said, even as the twenty men stood, and then with a reassuring nod of his head and a smile, "hurry back."

"We don't want to miss all the fun," said Moses, and then he and his men set off immediately in the direction of their needful brethren.

The path to the woods was coordinated by two Crusaders who were knowledgeable of the land, and once they attained the point where the tunnels began, they ascended into them, and presently exiting, could already hear the ruckus of battle, the back-and-forth, give-and-take, siren wailing of soldiers wed in steel and armor to settle disputes; this team of twenty rescuers moved swiftly, albeit cautiously, listening intently to outside noise and to the intermittent narrative in their ear com.

When they were close enough to see the enemy ensconced behind trees and vehicles, Moses said urgently to his own, "Hold fast—guests have arrived."

It was then that Yoshitsune had issued his order to, "No, wait!"

Antonio, looking at his watch, cried, "Ten seconds!"

"We wait to detonate," Yoshitsune cried, "until after the ringing of the bell!"

It was a long interval between shooting and defending oneself in combat, and then stopping, and waiting, hoping, praying for a miracle, as the enemy closed in from both sides with bullets and scowls, a mere ten seconds in which all of the Crusaders here could conceivably die as they sat wrapped up in the shield of darkness.

There wasn't even a moment's hesitation between the ticking of the last second and the tick toward the next, when the magnitude of the explosion exposed its high decibels to the company of men and women.

A planned surprise of attack by one side is the bridesmaid of strategy, the daughter of tactics, the mistress of subterfuge, as it gives birth to hesitation, a flinch from the other side, a pause that allows a chance to alter circumstances, revive plans, move forward, and in so doing, turning the tide where before the tide was turning you.

The Crusaders, upon hearing the fierce report of the screaming blasts, rose up, unlike their enemy, who was crouched down, and unlike their enemy, who obeyed basic human signals to cover and be disoriented in mind and body, they advanced, together now because of the delayed detonation, and let the high-toned noise drive them like wind against an Eagle's wings; so, they fairly soared, like Eagles, straight ahead, sending in three groups of men—one straight ahead, two on the flanks, driving the enemy who were already pinned down, firing relentlessly, from fore to aft at the dreaded foe and squeezing them in a barrage of rapid gunfire. The rescue team fired at those who restrained Miguel and José and Guillermo, and they, with those on the periphery, fired at those on the ground, and he was soon joined by his fellows on the ground, who too bore their bullets into the soldiers all around them.

It was technology that won the day for the Crusaders in this small skirmish: FLIR goggles attached to their helmets allowed the Crusaders to see their targets in the dark by heat signatures; Miguel's FN Minimi 7.62, Finn's IMI Negev, the XM25s the rescue team carried, the M2010 Enhanced Sniper rifle of Yoshitsune and others, the Mk 12 Special Purpose rifle, which was standard issue for them, gave them an edge and advantage: a better-aimed bullet, a quicker dispatch of a target, allowing the shooter to move freely to more hostiles, causing frustration and terror in their enemy who they cut into smaller units, and into smaller ones, and once again, until there was hardly anything left for the survivors to grasp for orientation and sanity.

When the flame of the firefight died, and the clamorous sounds of battle had ceased, it was the Crusaders who had survived; and the guard, who was a hostage, had been killed as he fled in the awful din.

"Let us hurry," Moses said, looking as his watch, "for the main communication complex of the El Dorado is blown by Gonzales' and Guzman's men, and the assault on the Azteca stronghold has begun."

War Plans

The main communications network centers having been dismantled, thus decapitating the fanatical culture of instantaneous messaging among the two respective terrorist-crime syndicate-aspiring Fortune 500 Empire Cartels, brought curious changes in their moment-to-moment habits and thinking patterns, which is to say: when one is alone, one is able to formulate a thought based on self-reflection and a foundation of knowledge that includes prior experiences; however, when one is always in the company of the electronic chain that is the iPad, tablet, computer, cell phone, it is as if no one any longer has just one neural pathway, but a shared one; you talk, he talks, she talks; a moment later, the phone rings, and you talk, they talk, more talk; and a moment later, the same occurs, and the endless loop begins anew, thus establishing a lack of independence for the person who can no longer operate via his mouth and his gray tissue matter without the assistance of helper-friends, who are now in the same flooded, not to be raised, sinking boat.

So, the fruit of the fertile womb of the Cartels' communications network was abruptly dried up, a mammoth trunk of the towering communications tree was uprooted, and the sizzling air filled with radio waves no longer sizzled, but sputtered, leaving the subordinates, the cogs, the servants, the soldiers, the eavesdroppers, the shippers, movers, everyone connected, deafer, dumber, and more blind; but more importantly, unsure, and unafraid of what to do next. So much for modern technology—modern as it fits the time, but deleterious in its effects on its unwitting victim who actually has lost the basic communication skills that have been built and honed in the host's lineage-DNA over the millennia.

Yet, the plan of the Azteca Cartel had been in motion before the aforementioned calamity, and they had sent their main force to fight at the El Dorado fortress and headquarters, thus confining the battle between the two superpowers of the illegal drug industry here.

"We figured no more than a thousand men," Dylan said, as the Crusaders awaited orders to attack outside the large compound that had been carved out of the dense forest. "All of you have your orders, and know your assignment." He looked toward the direction where Moses had recently gone. "All is in readiness—their communication network has been destroyed."

The men cheered.

Contingency plans were once more discussed, and analyzed, and once this was done, the Crusaders set out to seize the Azteca headquarters.

Samuel walked alongside Dylan, the latter of whom wore an expression of deep reverie upon his countenance; Samuel was about to pursue questions from him, but relented, and merely kept silent, too; until, a few minutes from the first strategic point of confrontation, he put his giant hand upon his friend's shoulders. "Destiny awaits," he said, half-smiling; "let us go with God, and fear no evil."

Dylan, looking up, half-smiled, and then said, "God with us, we will achieve success; and oftentimes the road is not easy, but filled with obstacles; and that, I say, is true faith."

The Crusaders soon came upon the military-like compound, which consisted of a fifty-foot-high wall of reinforced steel and concrete, guard posts positioned in key places around the periphery, thirty barracks, four main buildings, three main ammunition rooms, two radar towers, three helicopter landing ports atop buildings, and barbed and electrified wire above the steel walls, and the M18A1 Claymore anti-personnel landmines surrounding all of it.

"Looks exactly like the high school I went to," Horatius said, smiling, putting those around him at ease.

One of the technicians came up to Dylan, and gave him his tablet. "Movement detected in these sectors," Jenkins, a Crusader from Canada, said nervously; "too many."

Dylan held up his hand to signal silence as he listened to a familiar voice in his ears. "Skye," Robert Heimdall began, using Dylan's code name, "we have picked up massive troop movement in every direction around you." The voice paused. "Four or five thousand."

Just then, the Crusaders who had blown up the Azteca communications network, and the rescue team, came rushing in, and gave information to Dylan.

Rhiannon, who would never left her husband's side, briefly held his hand, and then stood aside from him.

Dylan listened to more narrative of the battle at the El Dorado headquarters, and his face reflected not only this grave news, but the mind of the commander who, even as he interprets it, is divining a way to sabotage the reality of it, to prevail against it, to overwhelm and defeat it. He held up his right hand and waved in all around them.

"As you all know," he began, still wedded to a supreme equanimity, "the Azteca army was to attack the El Dorado headquarters, and after a victory was declared, the Mexican army, and Majors Alfonso and Gonzales, were to battle the victor; but the Azteca did not go alone, but with the Cardenas Cartel, as allies, and their combined forces have now met the Azteca army; and the El Dorado-Velazquez alliance has sent troops to impede the invasion of the Mexican army, who, even now, are pinned down and surrounded; as for us, the Azteca here have recruited the Cardenas Cartel to fortify their headquarters, and even now, we are surrounded." He paused, looking about at his brave comrades. "The Mexican military, who would have come to aid us, are also struck down miles away." He walked among them now, his stride strong, his face stronger. "There are four or five thousand of our enemy all around us, scouring the woods for an invasion force." He could feel the fear and dread radiate from their tremulous hearts. He now shouted in the magnificent voice, heralding something wondrous and supernatural, "Have faith in our Mission to liberate this land, this world, this age, from this terrible scourge; Crusaders," his face was lit now by a special revelation, "have faith, and the courage that faith brings, and will provide a victory to his faithful; lose not your faith now, in our darkest hour, when He tests us most—for the road we have traveled is never easy, but hard, as it must be when we fight the soul of iniquity and servitude; it is a high price we pay to sever the chains of those who otherwise would remain enslaved, who have no other champion, who await those commissioned by God to bring succor and Freedom to them." He was walking amid all of them now, his demeanor clear, and bold, as if transfixed by an unseen glory, and they were affixed in a tranquil trance, hearing his every word as if it was dropped from the mouths of great and noble generals past, and spoken directly to their very hearts. "Crusaders, this is our life, our journey, our purpose; we are the elect of history present to liberate those imprisoned and terrorized, to bring hope to the hopeless, to bring joy to the joyless; to stand against the armies of darkness, to battle them unto death, to die in the pursuit of Justice for all, to live and join the eternal battle another day; Crusaders," he cried, so forceful and true that it seemed as if he spoke to each of them individually, "we will fight, and God will grant solace whether we live or die—for live or die, we follow His Holy word: defend the defenseless, comfort those in need, help those who need help; so, therefore, whether we live or die, we do so for God on Most High. Let us pray," and he knelt down among them, and they did likewise, and all of them prayed their private prayer to the Almighty.

And having thus resolved in their minds that their lives were fashioned out of finer cloth and anointed for a greater purpose by their Creator, the Crusaders stood up and heard now the refined flow of words from their leader.

"Our enemy will come to their end this day—all we need to is to hold true to our Mission," he said calmly. "They do not yet know of our exact presence, or strength, of this I am sure; but they see, in their paranoia, a foe; so, a foe we shall give them," and he told them of his plan, and immediately, they were heartened. "Let us go."

As they moved out, no man signaled it, but all men sang it out proudly, "Right and force are the governors of the world; force until right is ready!"

Rhiannon stood next to him, and the two lovers, two in physical body, but one in heart and soul, gazed at each other in quiet adulation, and want of comfort; but Dylan could only nod and smile in affection, and she also, and then, knowing what must be done, and quickly, she turned around, and headed away with the majority of the forces, leaving behind a small remnant who would presently engage the vast and encroaching enemy.

The Battle Begins

So, in the time it takes for a mother to walk from her bedroom to the bedroom of her baby, pick up that precious child, and in so doing, comfort her, the Crusaders had vanished, like so many phantoms, like a trailing mist, into the quiescent chamber of the murmuring earth, leaving a few of them to exercise their free will to despoil the determined will of the enemy.

So, now, there was: Dylan, proud son of Ireland; Yoshitsune, proud son of Japan; Horatius, proud son of Italy; Tyr, proud son of Germany; Enkidu, proud son of Iraq; Finn, proud son of Ireland; Rustem, proud son of Iran; Arjuna, proud son of India; Miguel, proud son of Mexico; Moses, proud son of Kush; Ana, proud daughter of Honduras; and Antonio, proud son of Bolivia—all standing tall, with passive faces, and passionate hearts.

There were no words necessary to be exchanged for men and women who had so long fought side by side in every conceivable battle situation and using every conceivable stratagem and tactic to survive; they were now like brother and sister molecules of the mighty wind, as one moved one way, they all moved together; as birds in a mighty flock, as one moved one way, they all moved together; as brother and sister fish in a mighty school, as one moved one way they all moved together; sensing every thought and action, reaction and defense, feint and retreat, advance and offense, as if one, and in fact, they were one in warrior spirit.

When this League of Remarkable Warriors was about to set off to meet their foe, one more arose from the safe depths to join them: Rhiannon, proud daughter of the UK, late of America, and she came to rest next to Dylan, who cast a look of surpassing pride upon her proud and beauteous face; and so, the number fixed, they went forth, a few in number, but mighty in deeds and desire against the ferocious enemy, who was great in number, but who possessed a mind full of the squalor that is created when unbound hatred of all that is good is foremost, and a heart full of a deeply rooted moral dissension that comes from existing outside of what brings harmony and serenity and peace to the vulnerable world.

The sensors had been strategically placed around the Azteca stronghold many months ago in anticipation of this battle, and so intricate in its design that it could give the receiver of information an exact read on troop strength and location; and from above came more data: the satellite in the sky, the spy drone, and the biobots, like the live moth, which had electronic sensors embedded into it to control its flight, and a video camera mounted upon its brown back, and which then flew into the compound and relayed real-time video to Heimdall and his scientists, who then organized all of this information as a 3-D virtual map—able to be projected into physical space by virtue of augmented reality, and sent it to the special glasses the Crusaders wore, which now showed where their enemy soldiers were by their heat signatures, so much that it was now as a deadly game of hide and seek; however, the Crusaders were not alone.

"Set, motion, blue," Dylan spoke softly the coded transmissions, as he walked alongside Moses.

"We need such technology in Kush," Moses whispered.

"It's in the mail," Dylan whispered, nearly smiling.

"Blue team," Robert Heimdall responded, "go ahead; one thousand troops; quarter-mile out, platoon line, squads in column; heavily armed."

Dylan did not even produce a flinch at the number. "We must provide a spike through their lines to reach the rendezvous point."

All of the Crusaders, above and below ground, were privy to all transmissions.

"The robin flies toward the sun to find her home in the meadow that sits next to the blue lake," Robert continued, which, decoded, meant "go to grid 106' longitude and 30' latitude."

"Copy that," Dylan said, watching through the special glasses, which were also infrared, as his comrades shifted, according to the virtual map appearing before them, to accommodate the order. "Requesting a drop from our little friends," he said, looking to Rhiannon, and winking, and she winked back. Robert affirmed the request. "How much further to the shield?" One half-mile, Robert returned. "Copy that, out."

"Defensive posture," Dylan whispered, as he crouched, and all of them then crouched, too. "Prepare the spike," he said. No one said a word; it wasn't the time to talk, or gaze upon the other, but the time to view the inner sanctum of their warrior heart, and liberate its fierce spirit to inhabit all of their known, and perhaps even unknown, senses, into a kind of swirling mass that, strand by strand, wove their distinct senses into one singular sense—as if there had been only one sense all along, but which had been split into pieces onto inferior life-forms during times of peace; so, what the eyes saw, what the ears heard, what the tongue tasted, what the skin felt, what the nose smelled, they all saw, and heard, and tasted, and felt, and smelled; and nothing human, or earthly, could disrupt this magical electromagnetic loop that spun out in ever-increasing concentric circles to detect even the slightest alteration in the flora and fauna of the forest; was that the abatement of the bird's rhythmic call, the increased scurrying sounds of the brown squirrel, perfume in the wafting, cool breezes, the distant crunching noises of army boots they detected? And, in concert with their eyes peeled on the heat signature image that the spy drone provided above to their special glasses, this gave the Crusaders a complete picture, unlike a picture they gave to their enemy, as the clothes and Enhanced Combat Helmet and special covering for the face they wore were made with a substance that reduced their heat signature to nearly zero.

No more commands were necessary now, as the engagement of the enemy was about to commence with a magnitude of clang and clamor that would disrupt the senses of ordinary men.

The drones attacked.

It was not one form of drone, and even one elite form might have sufficed, but here, there was a family descending upon the inhospitable host, and stinging mad they were; there were baby drones shaped like birds, and mama and papa drones shaped like bats, and headmaster bats, shaped like, well... dive-bomber killing machines, all of them spitting either bullet or laser, or dropping an arsenal of diverse bombs: explosive, smoke, electromagnetic pulsing disruptors, mine bombs that dug into the ground and exploded in sixty seconds; bombs that exploded ten feet from the surface; bombs that rained down red-hot shrapnel; bombs that radiated ear-splitting, high-pitched noises; drones equipped with short range missiles, .338 caliber bullets, and false 3-D images of drones that swarmed everywhere; and mere surveillance drones to record all the action.

And, to bring more pieces to the war party, there were camouflaged smart sticks that the Crusaders had previously sunk into the ground, sticking out a good two feet, which not only sensed when gunfire erupted, but visually and audibly recorded at geographical intervals of one hundred meters, covering one square kilometer around the Azteca perimeter and then sending the information to the scientists, who then relayed it to the Crusaders.

As the visitors from above arrived and unloaded their deadly cargo, the Crusaders arrived just in time for these festivities to unload theirs.

The Crusaders let loose with a meaty, ravenous barrage that, once delivered, merged with a frighteningly loud, piercing scream of the winged messengers, thus splitting the efforts of the Azteca soldiers, who began to shout wildly on high, and on low; so, when the barrage of weapons was fired from the ground, the Azteca soldiers were now caught in a squeezing vice that felt like they were submerged in a fiery river, rendering them bewildered and prone to panic, which brings comfort to the maddened mind, an excuse to shift away from reality and abandon responsibility. The Azteca, although superior in number and weaponry, had no communication with the control center, could see no palpable human enemy, saw their fellows being sliced and diced like a carrot through a metal grater, secured no recourse from shooting at objects which did not seem to react to this onslaught, and so when the heavy fire came from behind them, and to the side, they began to fire at wherever they supposed was a viable direction, except down.

The Crusaders, having unleashed their weapons into the weak flank of the Azteca soldiers from their southwest positon, then took cover behind trees in the south, and thenceforth felt the stirred-up human bees unleash their stingers at them; meanwhile, the drones concentrated on disparaging the explicit orders of the Azteca soldiers, who, induced by panic, continued to fire from the east to drive their unwilling enemy west.

When no firepower originates from one direction, but from all others, even on high from these hundreds of daring and diving drones, and the soldier to your left is burned alive, and the soldier to your right is burned alive, and the soldier at your fore is split open like a ripe watermelon under a sledgehammer, and the soldier at your aft is blown to bits like he just swallowed a grenade; and when this purportedly tough, bad-to-the-bone, top-of-the-line, fearless-and-begging-for-combat soldier loses, incrementally, the adhesive inner quality that is his built-in glue holding together this company of murdering thugs, his mental processes begin to fray, and these soldiers, who had built a reputation of amassing a great number of their ruthless, merciless, well-armed selves against a small number of unsuspecting, regular folk, or average soldiers with typical weapons, both of whom were usually provoked into battle by a surprise, vicious attack, began to fall like easily knocked-over dominoes.

Panic and suffering reduces even the best of soldiers to children, running amok with only one thought—survival; it is one thing to encounter heavy artillery, another to encounter an obstacle with no clear distinction for rebuttal. Although these Azteca soldiers wore infrared goggles and could easily navigate the woods, the absence of an enemy to hold and slay infiltrated their despairing minds and cut it in twain; so, as they ran, with a whimper and whining of self-preservation as catalyst, the Crusaders aided this willy-nilly, hasty retreat, now offering them more hostile reasons to run for their frightened lives—a blistering army of well-trained, well-intentioned, mean packets of hot, burning lead, some guided by the laser sights attached to their special rifles that burst expansive packets of fire and daggers above the enemies' heads, like a suffocating black bag full of angry Yellow Jackets.

Yet, no small contingent of dedicated warriors, no matter their degrees of marksmanship and their valor, even in concert with electronic allies, can dig the graves of thousands of men strong on the ground and in a furious retreat; so, Dylan signaled help from his fellows, who, after measuring the chaotic course the Azteca pursued, regained their presence above ground and were covered in the hole they crouched in by the protective half-moon, lightweight, XSAPI plates—replete with gun ports—which attached around their shoulders and waists like a harness, and which also had a layer of Spectra body armour that reinforced it from behind, all of which were second-generation systems that had been highly modified by Heimdall's scientists; and whereupon they took aim on the fleeing soldiers and unloaded the ferocity of their weapons, after which the Azteca, still dogged by the hundreds of drones and bullets from the rear, fired forward and to the sides in anticipation of this new enemy, but found only more dread, and soon, many were dead or wounded, except for those few industrious ones who hightailed it back to the fortress; but, with the benefit of long vision scopes by marksmen such as Rustem, many of them too were felled.

It was not much time later when Dylan was standing with Moses, Yoshitsune, and Samuel, when Robert spoke, clear and excitedly, "Ten thousand more, half in, half out, and our little friends are at supper."

The Crusaders, near five hundred strong, not a man or woman dead or hurt, now faced an army of ten thousand strong, and the drones were not yet ready to fly again.

"The half out," Robert lamented, "is about you."

Roderigo and Pedro came up to Dylan and pleaded to go on a special mission, to which Dylan reluctantly agreed, having Arjuna and Yoshitsune go with them.

As it was, the Crusaders were surrounded, once more.

The Script Altered

The head of the Azteca Cartel—alias criminal paramilitary complex, alias a Fortune 500 conglomerate expanding its primary goods: cocaine, marijuana, opium, heroin, methamphetamine, and illicit drugs of all kinds; and seeking to invest even in legitimate businesses too: the entertainment industry, social media, sports teams; and its principle services: murder, kidnapping, arson, extortion, bribery, human trafficking, and corruption of all kinds, which had expanded prodigiously even to other continents; a growing market this, just as the world economic situation improved and allowed people to live better lives, yet somehow, this encouraged citizens to make allowances in their increasing budget to include the buying and ingesting of illegal substances to, somehow, celebrate their newfound wealth—was fuming like a betrayed groom. "Why, that El Dorado scum, that El Dorado rat, that El Dorado peasant, peon, that piker," he shouted, as if the shouting of it made it true. "He wants it all—that madman-psychotic-madman; I will crush him! He blew up our communications network, he sends killers here, he defies our treaties all of the other Narcos agreed upon; well, we will see who gets caught in his own trap, that pathetic, untrustworthy, backstabbing weasel!"

"Yes, El Toro, he will certainly be crushed—the fool," said Hector.

"Yes, crushed like a worm under my heel," he returned, and smashed his snakeskin boots to the tiled floor, and then looked to his assistant. "What do we know about this invasion force?"

"We are not certain, sir, how many—for our first wave was utterly defeated, and apparently, there are drones involved."

"That impossibly insane madman," Suarez lamented; "why is he so greedy? Does he not know a good thing when he sees it? Oh, well, he will be destroyed—utterly, you say?"

"Yes, sir—utterly."

"And we have the Cardenas soldiers cooperating with our men? And our plan to bring them n will not be detected even by surveillance from satellite or drone?"

"Yes, sir."

"And we have our own aerial surprises, do we not?"

"Yes, sir."

"Well, let us not delay the execution of the soon-to-be-dead Señor Madman, who soon will truly be Señor Muerte; so, let us pray," and he bowed his head, solemnly.

Hector smiled, stimulated by his fantasy of dipping his hand into mighty stacks of future and wondrous riches.

The parallel of this hot-house-variety drug trafficker, Señor Muerte—who had simply been grown in different fertilizer and with different parents, and ingested different nutrients that led him to lend his particular notions toward a different nourishing sun—was, if possible, truly beside himself, as if his human self had split off from his bestial self: good and decent to bad and merciless, and announced now by a robust form of dagger-filled, dynamite-tipped words of denunciation of all things that he did not believe in or care for; i.e., most of the known world and its inhabitants.

Alvarez would have strangled the air itself to arrest its oxygen so that the whole of humanity might gasp and choke until it pleaded for its glorified savior figure to save it; but, then, he often responded, upon reflecting on such a scenario in which they all died, who would I have to subjugate?

Luis, in awe, stood in this darkened room, observing the appearance of this infernal Beast before him, this creature with the heavily etched scowl that was scorched in crimson rage upon its mean countenance; and when Alvarez talked, it was more in grunts and growls, and his very words painted a grim picture of an abscessed soul conspiring for revenge against who and what he considered as betrayal, and to qualify, one had only to disagree with him about even the slightest participle, verb, or adjective of even a trivial thing; and beware to all, in his presence, who held even a vestige of something even approaching impatience about this whole affair.

"They're all going to die, you know that," he continued on, steeped in a violent brooding; yes, he now wanted them all to die, or rather, he had always wanted them to die: he had just been waiting for an excuse to murder these life-forms he considered beneath him in every measure of human capacity: intellectual, emotional, spiritual, and physical. "For I am a god, and the world, mortal," he often thought—perhaps not in explicit phrases, but in an honest rendering of it; "why am I better than everyone—why me, O Lord? The burden is sometimes too great!"

He sniffed the air like he was sniffing the acrid odor of the bloated carcass of his nemesis, his face scrunched up in a sour expression. "Arturo Suarez is a dead man," he said, in a definitive, matter-of-fact tone and pitch. "I'll kill that fat pig myself, stuff him and put him over my mantelpiece." He saw the final consummation of this morbid act, and he sneered. "I will rule first the North, and then we shall see what we shall see."

Luis secretly smiled. "He is at his most sanguinary—good, the monster unleashed, with no mercy or regret, and whose thirst for blood increases the more he kills and conquers; good, it is what we need, now."

"You know what slime molds are, Luis?" He would not wait for a reply, but for silence, and once retrieved, like a bone thrown from master to dog, he proceeded, his hand upon the latest book from which he had obtained such knowledge. "They are a colony of one-celled organisms—amoebas— that form a single organism when food and water is scarce, but when alone, they part; you know how people are, eh? They are the slime mold not just when their collective backs are against the wall, but all their pitiful lives, unable to do anything without their own weak kind, but being together, they are still weak; and that is how I see people—all people—slime molds, and myself a superior rank of evolution that is somehow separated from human- ity; I believe I am the next evolution of Man: smarter, faster, stronger, more resilient, more clever, because all I see around myself," and his hard demeanor reflected horror and scorn, "is slime."

Luis, unsure as to his role—either as holder of the bejeweled scepter of the King, or simply stooge and court jester—was, nonetheless, now silent during this rambling discourse.

"Well, Luis, what do you say for yourself—are you mere slime?"

Luis, safe within the boundaries of muteness, began to sweat as he felt the penetrating gaze of this intense master.

"Are you deaf?" Alvarez suddenly shouted, as he pressed him harder. "Are you slime?"

To admit his personage into the scientific kingdoms of the lower order of this nested hierarchy, particularly as a Protist, or perhaps, fungus, as some would say, he thought, was to diminish his reflection in his master's eyes for- ever; or, more accurately, merely establish where he was as his master beheld him. Perhaps, thought Luis, he is in a state of war against all humanity, and I, merely part of another, lumped into a tower of slime; ah, but who knows what he thinks, when he thinks it—maybe not even himself. Thus, so unde- cided, he declared, "The world may be divided into supermen and slime, but I, as your loyal and trusted adjutant, feel fortunate to tread neither here nor there—the only way I can confidently serve you."

Señor Muerte nodded his head, his eyes screwed up in contemplation. "Good answer, Luis."

Luis flushed with pride.

"Are the Zapote soldiers getting along with our men?"

"Yes, sir," Luis answered, still excited by the rare compliment directed toward him.

"Good, good—and the inept Mexican army and all the police forces: still pinned down at Ciudad Calderon?"

"Yes, sir."

"Good, good; all goes according to plan, the plan of a superior man when he deals with the minds of slime molds. Let us pray," and he nodded his head, solemnly.

Luis was silent, and overjoyed, having already secured a small, personal victory for the day.

The War Rages On

There are limits for even men of exceeding valor and cunning in war, and here, they were reached when the Crusaders heard that ten thousand or so soldiers now stalked them.

"We must all go underground," Dylan whispered to those around him, and soon, all were quickly descending to the recesses of this cold, damp inner sanctuary.

It was not too much later that the very ground upon which they had stood was occupied by the prowling army of ten thousand, who soon learned, by looking eastward, north, south, and up, that their adversary, like the last vapors of dying night, had vanished with the rising power of the cleansing sun; and presently, quit the place, leaving it all too quiet and peaceful again.

The early rays of a radiant golden dawn fell upon the forest and dressed it in what seemed harmony regained, despite the blood that had been spilled, and the fallen soldiers who had been carted away by their begrudging brethren back to their fortress.

But the plaintive, urgent cry of Robert split this quiescent harvest. "Something wicked this way comes, a wicked bird laying wicked storms."

"Helicopter," Dylan whispered to Rhiannon, in the dark corridor, "bringing a firestorm."

All of them were silent as they listened to the approaching noise of the helicopters, and then felt the awful reverberations of the wicked eggs hatched above them: napalm, rocket bombardments, machine gun fire, across the square-mile stretch of dense wood, hills, caves, valleys, and rivers, killing all exposed animal life, therein.

The Crusaders, wearing the oxygen gas masks that had been stored in the tunnels, could feel the violent quaking caused by the massive artillery upon the surface; they felt the abomination the scarring did to the earth's protective skin as they resided inside her protective womb, the awful shaking and shudder as it was attacked, the awful and painful reverberations, its murmuring and sad refrain, its hopeless refrain, its cry for mercy, its plea to leave it be, so all might live in harmony; this, the Crusaders felt, as if they had fought not only for the Justice of people, but the Justice of the Earth, who was assaulted daily by greedy entrepreneurs who happily cut down and dug up her children for fun and profit; by uncaring businessman who raped and plundered her for untold millions; by non-thinking citizens who dumped waste and poisoned substances into her increasingly polluted nest; by governments that were too weak to enforce laws, too corrupt to empathize, and too narrow-minded to regulate the proper care and feeding of their mother-nurturer.

When the hour-long aerial-bombardment ended, voices were heard atop: the hard voices of the combined Azteca and Cardenas Cartel armies, scouring the countryside for the remains of their enemies; but finding no one and nothing, they soon departed, albeit leaving sentries posted at key positions.

After all the concrete layers of the underground tunnels, which had polypropylene fibers and steel added for reinforcement, and the steel arches were checked, and the safety of the Crusaders assured, a War Council was called, in a huge, round room lit by electrical lamps; Dylan stood in the middle of them, Moses by his side.

Dylan began, a calm voice before the coming storm. "We are not where we should be, nor on the path we ought to have traveled, or even at the beginning of our journey, but knocked down, held back, trodden upon; the element of surprise lost, our advantage gone, our enemy vastly outnumbering us; and retreat—honorable retreat that says a good fight was won, but not the final fight, and live to fight nobly another day—beckons us; it would beckon the very best of warriors, the best of them, so too it beckons us; so, what do we say to that which aspires for our defeat, and asks us to return another day, or hand the torch of blessed Liberty to another brave army?"

"Go down hard," Moses cried.

"Ho!" the Crusaders rang out, the place echoing in thunderous appeal.

"No man or woman would fault us, no man or woman would expect us to go forward and die needlessly, die in a battle where we cannot prevail," he began again, his voice beginning to rise in pitch and passion. "No man or woman would say they could have fought better, or with more honor, than we, and all would welcome us home as heroes, if we quit this place now, even though our mission lies in the terrible smoke and ash of our enemy's hot breath. No one," he cried, "would say, 'yield, you? Capitulate, you?' But ourselves—we would condemn! For we know, we would yet fault ourselves, that we had abandoned what was our vow and pledge to complete—no one but us would feel with dishonor and disloyalty that we failed to bring about the great cause of Equality and Justice for which we have so long and hard fought, for the oppressed and helpless; only the Crusaders would feel shame and humiliation that we had fled a battlefield yet untried and unknown, that we might have won, and famously so; what would the world have in the birthplace of Freedom and Democracy if every righteous army fled when the enemy seemed insurmountable, but tyranny yesterday, tyranny today, tyranny tomorrow—so, never let it be said that we would allow it to flourish as long as we have the will, the courage, the blessings of God, to fight this iniquitous Leviathan from stem to stern, from one end of the earth to the other, across mountains and deserts and oceans."

"Africa!" Moses cried.

"Africa," the Crusaders echoed, enthusiastically.

"Across valleys, and open places," Dylan continued, in an unbroken, seamless narrative, as if Moses' outburst belonged rightly in this telling, "we will chase this villain and fight him wherever he stands and with whomever he cowers, and no matter the number of his cowardly ranks, we will fight; and live or die, we will have followed what conscience God has given us that we cannot easily ignore: do what is right, and without hesitation, or worry, for as we pick up the sword of Justice and do His will, we are the true Lord's army—and not religious zealots or fanatics who seek only to harm those unlike themselves; and so, if we live or die, it is His divine Providence." He been slowly turning around and around as he spoke thus, and when his blazing eyes met the proud eyes of Rhiannon, he cried, "What say ye, Crusaders—do we retreat or fight?"

"Fight," they all cried, in unison, the thunder of their brave response much finer in tone and louder than the artificial boasting of the previous barrage of armament above.

And amid the roar of the exuberant cheers, Dylan and Rhiannon gazed at each other with an aura of love and devotion that had grown every day since first they embarked on this sacred mission; and amid the clamor, he walked up to her, and held her hands, neither of them taking the eyes off the other.

And then she whispered, and which he somehow heard, plainly amid the hearty clamor, her face lit up by pride, her voice suffused with love, her eyes filled with tears of piety, "Conall would be so proud of you."

And then he whispered, and which she somehow heard, plainly amid the hearty clamor, his face lit up by pride, his voice suffused with love, his eyes filled with tears of piety, "And Eleanor would be so proud of you."

The Fate of Yermo

The four men, having with little difficulty passed through the porous, non-combat-ready, undisciplined line of the skulking united front of these Cartel soldiers, hurried on into the deep thicket wherein resided the cloak of night and anonymity.

"Bah!" Yoshitsune said, as they swept down a steep embankment, "I should like to engage those buffoons in a fight less unbalanced—the cowards, their only passage to a victory is by a clear advantage."

"Ten to one, at least," Arjuna whispered, and after slipping past this poorly constructed and sloppy line of defense, finished, "I am not so impressed."

"You have taken on greater opponents?" Pedro asked, leaping over a fallen log.

"Greater, and better trained," Arjuna said; "these men are mere bullies in the sandbox, with no one to stand up against them; all of them will not be long for this world—the forest is thirsty for the rich nutrients in their fat and lazy bodies." He paused. "All men here of this malignant strain will soon be vanquished."

"But how can you say that?" Roderigo asked, in earnest, leading the men, and moving aside from an overhanging branch. "There are a dozen Cartels, and hundreds of thousands of men. It is an attraction for the poor to join them; it is a constant source of recruits, especially children."

"Yes, it is so around the world," Yoshitsune said, mournfully; "I have seen it everywhere, even in wealthy countries."

"So, why will it end here?" Roderigo asked, sidestepping a rock.

"The world progresses," Arjuna said, solemnly. "It seeks balance and harmony—it will never decline for too long, but improve; for thus was the way of life in much of history: poverty, disease, violence, and early death, it was an integral part of existence; but modernity has changed all that," and he interlaced his hands. "We are too closely linked now, and once that begins, the prosperity of one country inevitably arouses the passions of another; it is too remarkable, but true."

"It cannot be stopped," Yoshitsune said; "it is Destiny; the ways of Democracy will inevitably triumph, and even though new threats arise, be they religious or ideological, the forces of Justice will band together and fight them."

It was time for Pedro and Roderigo to assimilate the wisdom of what they had heard, and time for Yoshitsune and Arjuna to listen to the faint echoes of their surroundings.

It was not too much longer that they approached the periphery of Yermo and encouraged the armed men to contact Pablo, who, in turn, by secret radio code, ordered the guards to allow the men to proceed; presently, they were within the border of the city, where the battle between the Azteca and Cardenas Cartels and the Mexican Army and Federal and other police and Special Forces Corps was being fiercely fought.

The four men were escorted into a holding where all the leaders and many armed citizens of the city were, who looked with disdain and scorn upon the four travelers.

"Speak quietly, murderers, and foreigners, we have much work to do," Pablo said, in Spanish, as he stood on the high wooden stage of the school cafeteria.

"What work is that, amigo?" Arjuna said, in the perfectly understandable, though peculiarly accented dialect of their region, as he stood with the other men in the middle of the tiled floor, amid the grumbling people.

"Defending our city against the Cartels," another of the leader onstage cried out; "this war you brought here!"

"I?" Arjuna said innocently, and pointed to himself. "Now, how did little ol' me do such a thing?"

"You interloper, foreigner—you are not from here, why don't you go back to where you came from," the same one shouted.

The people roared approval.

Arjuna smiled, unperturbed, and looked around. "And where might that be, eh? Where is this world where there is no war, no unjust poverty and suffering? I live on the same planet you do; therefore, we are all in this together."

"Mere words," another leader shouted, "but we are in a war for our very survival."

Then the inevitable occurred, as the faces of their once and present torturers and fiends now came into focus.

"It's them," one of the audience members cried out, "the sicarios of the Azteca Cartel," standing now, his accusatory hand outstretched toward Roderigo and Pedro.

"Murderers," another cried.

"It is them," more cried out, rushing to their feet, and beginning to shout and scream in utter shock.

"Kill them," more shouted, as the audience began to coalesce into a violent, non-thinking, driven mob, and one man raised his pistol and shot five times at Roderigo and Pedro, but missed. The men never flinched.

"I have spoken for them," Pablo shouted, without the microphone, his hands held up in the air against the rising mob, and such was their reverence for him that all became eerily quiet. "They live, for now—for now, we need them; I will say no more on it." He stood, an immovable monolith. The people acquiesced, reluctantly, and now turning to the men, he said, "Why are you here? All is lost."

Arjuna, perplexed, look around and said, "Why aren't you," and he pointed toward the Azteca stronghold, "out there?"

"Fight the Azteca Cartel at their fortress?" one of the leaders cried. "Are you mad? Look here, madman; look here, killers, do you know what goes on south of us? Even the Mexican army and Federal Police cannot come to our rescue."

"The Azteca and Cardenas Cartels stop even them," another leader cried, "and when that is done, all is lost—lost, because of what," and she pointed to Yoshitsune and Arjuna, first with her angry eyes and heart, and then with her outstretched hand, "you have brought here! We had won—won!"

"What shall I tell you," another leader cried, "these foreigners have brought two Cartels to our door, to burn us to the ground, which will no doubt serve a lesson if other cities resist."

The audience, acting as a conduit and encouragement for contrarian views against the four guests, howled and hissed approval.

Roderigo shook his head. "Are you people all mad? You're like children; thank goodness your own children are not here to see your cowardice." The populace ached to gnaw off his seemingly haughty head. He continued, with his bold impotence, tearing a bigger hole in the minds of his already outraged listeners. "You are like children to believe that by locking yourself in your bedroom, and hiding underneath your bed, your parents will not find you; well, I have a newsflash for you good citizens: with or without these brave men," he pointed to Arjuna and Yoshitsune, "the Azteca Cartel would have come back to punish you; why? Because the Mexican army and Federal Police do not live here," and he looked around at the faces of the worn-down people who had to admit the bald truth of his words, "and I know—believe me, I know—the Cartels would have come back: they always do for a weak people, just like any conquering army that comes back to take the spoils of a conquered people as tribute."

"But this time they mean to destroy us all," one of the leaders shouted, waving his arms about.

"Good," Pedro said, angry now.

"How dare you; this is not your fight—you're still one of them! How is this stinking butcher still alive our presence?" one of the leaders shouted, his face scarlet with the want of revenge, his pistol raised at them.

But Pablo once more shouted down the livid crowd, by reassuring them of a future that contained true Justice.

"It is my fight now," Pedro finally was able to say, eyeing with disgust those whom he considered cowards; and then he pointed to Arjuna and Yoshitsune, "it is their fight," and he gestured to all of them, "it is your fight now; so now, end all this —now, now you must stand up and fight! Even now, brave men and women," and he pointed north, "will die trying to save people who do not deserve saving."

"Sirs, sirs," one of the leaders asked, almost in a polite tone, addressing the two Crusaders, "why, then, are you here; why come here and fight that which cannot be destroyed, that even the armies and police of Mexico cannot defeat; why, why, sirs, please tell me—why? I don't believe you can; you are here as fools, on a fool's errand, to die, and you seek not to die alone; am I right, eh? Citizens, am I not right?"

This seemingly irrefutable accusation elicited wild cheers from the all-too-eager and willing audience.

Yoshitsune began to walk slowly around the room, looking sternly at the mesmerized, now quiet people, holding fast his rifle, which was snug between his massive, crossed arms; and when he had walked up and down every aisle, and finally leaped up to the stage, he walked slowly in front of every leader; and then, turning around, he faced the people, his rifle now resting snugly under his right arm. He said nothing for a while, and then, with great force, and eloquent enunciation, "We do not fight for you, only," he began, in his uniquely accented but perfectly understood dialect of the region, his face gripped by authority and pride. "We fight against injustice and tyranny the same way you fight against a flood, a famine, an illness." He paused, shook his head, and said forcefully, "We cannot force the people to accept the cause of Freedom and Justice—it is a great responsibility, and too many people would rather live in slavery and accept crumbs," and he held out his open palms, as if begging, "instead of daring to live with Democracy, and perhaps suffer worse," and then pointed to himself. "I cannot live such a life; if I cannot be free, free to live or die by the tenets and principles God has given me, and by my own hand prosper or fail, then I will fight whoever is against what the world needs to thrive: Freedom and Justice." He looked again at all of them as if for the first time, his animated face reflecting his utter disappointment; and when he spoke again, his voice was as from history past, in alliance with noble warriors before whom had loomed seemingly insuperable odds. "I would rather go back to fight with my brethren against tyranny and die, than stay here and live like a frightened slave, clinging to the periphery of a bare existence, afraid to stand up for what I believe in, lest someone knock me down." He grunted, and shook his head, and recited eloquently, "How different the world would be if all the world stood up to tyranny; for how many more of us than they; how long would it take but a day?" And he leaped off the stage and, taking his fellows, swept them into his momentum; exiting the doors, they began the trek back toward the battle to be.

The Death of One Brings Life to the Many

Throughout the long, hot day, the Crusaders could hear, at various times, through listening devices, footsteps, and see, through their spyware, soldiers with their menacing dogs and sophisticated detection equipment scouting and patrolling the forest.

"It seems that modern technology has blinded men to the possibility of a shovel," Finn said, in amusement, to Rustem.

"It has always been the same thing," Rustem replied; "as soon as a man picks up a rock, he forgets his fist; when he uses the bow, he drops the rock; now, the gun, so down goes the bow; now, the missile, so now the gun lies at his side; it is always the same thing."

"Fortunately for us," Antonio said, in between eating his hearty meal and drinking cool water from a tin cup, "it is always comforting to know your enemy is simply a savage who is capable of only pulling the trigger, but not thinking about what to do before or after—like most invading governments."

"When have tyrants ever had to worry that the little peon would rebel?" Samuel began. "This is why he is so incautious, and bold; he is confident that force and threat alone can hold back those whom he subjugates; it is always the same—I have seen it on the streets, I have seen it in gangs, I have seen it in families."

"Businesses, too, are sometimes like tyrants, eh?" Rustem said, snacking on an apple. "They take over without bullets and bombs—the effect is the same."

Such were the conversations the men and women had as they patiently waited and ate their warm, energy-sustaining meals, while exchanging ideas, histories, and philosophies.

"I am interested in Kush," Samuel to Ana; "tell me more." And she narrated a brief history of the fabled land, and how in the last ten years, since Moses had gone from freedom fighter to general, civil wars had broken out between the North and South, but had been quietly quenched; but she could relate to him in detail only about the last years when she had joined the Crusaders in Africa.

Dylan and Moses were sitting together in a small room that had surveillance cameras and electronic sensor system data, where they communicated with Robert and Paul, who were still with the other scientists and technicians huddled together on different and high, distant, secluded mountaintops.

And then Moses told him about the fateful day concerning Conall and Eleanor, how he blamed himself, and pious tears welled up in his black eyes, his countenance full of sorrow and suffering.

Dylan shook his head and, placing his hand upon Moses' shoulder, whispered, reassuringly, "Moses, my brother, such is the way of war; Conall and Eleanor were to die that day—not by your hand, but that God had summoned them home; it was His divine will, not ours; what is done is done, and noble men such as yourself, who follow His will, are not accountable."

The men shook hands, and Moses expressed his gratitude for the kind words of his friend, and then asked Dylan about his remarkable father and mother, whom Conall had once said he would tell Moses about, and so Dylan related the adventures of his parents, both of whom had been killed by rebel soldiers in Africa.

When he finished that narrative, he grew pensive, and then said to Moses, "How can I lead these brave men and women into slaughter? There are too many of them and too few of us; no matter what we believe in, or how right we are, there are battles that must be won another day."

Moses frowned. "You do not believe that, my friend."

Dylan let his head fall into his open hands. "I care nothing for my own life, but for Rhiannon; if not for her, I would gladly sacrifice myself to gain absolute victory."

Moses, his hand upon the broad shoulders of the youth, spoke quietly. "I believe you, Dylan." He sat back. "When first I met Conall," he continued, and as Dylan looked up, Moses violently banged his fisted hands together. "He and I clashed like two charging alpha male rams." He laughed, and Dylan smiled. "It is true; I'm afraid we did not like each other too much— each of us too idealistic, too unyielding, too impassioned—but the important thing was we were not too dogmatic, as we believed in the same grand vision; we just had to come up with a way so we could both arrive there together; remarkable." He paused. "Yes, we retreated many times in battle—many times it was necessary—but a prudent man knows when to fall back and resume the fight another day; it is true, very true—but just not now."

"I wish I could believe that."

"We have many of varying faiths here: some Muslims, and Buddhists and Hindus, and many Christians; some would say He is the same God, others say these Faiths diverge too much, especially those here who do not believe, or are still searching; yet, somehow, united we still stand."

"A divergence of some significance."

"Ha! Yes, as your brother used to say; but, still, we are all men of great faith: in our God, in ourselves, in our cause; it is what makes us unique in all the world."

"We have been through more than most," Dylan said, finally. "We have accomplished what others said was impossible."

"And you must continually ask yourself—why? Why have we succeeded where others never even dared to begin?"

"For we sought, while others bowed; we demanded Justice, while others were cowed."

"Yes," Moses said, excitedly, "it is the same the world over."

"Without such noble ideals, Kush would fall."

"Yes, it would; but I know someone who would come to her aid."

Dylan smiled. "An honor," he said, inclining his head.

Moses laughed. "We have no need of you yet, my good friend—it is the grumblings of the civil war again, more warlords and regional conflicts that are, for now, appeased through careful negotiations."

The countenance of Dylan was grim. "I cannot risk your death here—it is too reckless to ruin the future of a nation."

"Oh, bah," Moses replied, waving it away. "Kush must learn to grow up without me; one man does not a nation make."

"No, you are wrong, Moses; you are the face of the revolution; is it not so, that in revolution, the vision of one great person can change history—look at Lincoln, Gandhi, King: without them, history is an abyss, governments are chaos, no democracy to inspire other revolutions; you, Moses, are the burning lamp in the darkness in a nation that needs the Light before them."

"You give me too much credit; I am just a man swept along in the currents of destiny—others could take my place."

"Impossible,"

Dylan nearly cried, "You are not interchangeable: without you, Kush crumbles back into anarchy; it has been stable, because you are Kush."

"No, no, Dylan, you are wrong; I am but one of its leaders, yet I serve the people only."

"People who need to be led!"

"Yes, they need leadership, that is true; but to say I am the only one…"

"History will judge me correct, you will see; in every great movement, there must be one person who represents the ideas and will of the people: someone who is good, just, kind, and intelligent, someone who will fight relentlessly until they achieve their lofty goal, one who understands the suffering of the people; that is you, good sir."

Moses was quiet, and then smiled. "And it is you, good sir," he began, in earnest; "right now, right here, in this place, you are the force that can alter history; and you, without you, all of this," and he gestured about, "goes away; it is you, Dylan; and Conall and Eleanor, whom I loved as much as a brother and sister, would agree." He paused, and then said, solemnly, "And those we lost in Africa—they died for something; they died for what we still believe in, what they believed in and were willing to die for; we are still fighting their good fight, just as, one day, others will remember us and take that eternal torch of Liberty…"

Dylan nodded in hearty agreement, but then said, "But the Crusaders…"

Moses nodded reassuringly. "They understand the risks, and what must be done." He stood up. "There is not a man or woman among them who would not gladly die for this cause; your cause, my cause, our cause, the cause of the world, as you so rightly said—the eternal cause for Justice and Freedom; how can we not seek it until we have it, and must be willing to die for it, as we can do no other."

"Now is now," Dylan said, standing too.

"Now is now," Moses said, "and one day, even perhaps today, men and women such as we will huddle together and speak of plans to fight injustice, inspired by those who came before them; for it is as you say—we must not let the chain of resistance be broken; we must keep the flame of Justice burning brightly, so those far away can see its hopeful light, and be inspired to fight the good fight."

Dylan smiled, and put his hands on the shoulders of Moses. "You are a good friend, and wise counselor, Moses Khalifa."

"There is a war to be won," Moses whispered; "let us proceed."

And the two men made their way to the large room, where the Crusaders soon gathered.

"When darkness comes," Dylan began, solemnly, standing before them, "we begin; we may be alone, without Mexican allies, but we will march with virtue, for she is our sword and buckler." He told them in detail, using 3-D hologram maps emitted from his cell phone, of the plans to once more assault the compound of the Azteca Cartel, and, to their great dismay, without the presence of the two Sabra Mk II tanks and M3A1 84 mm anti-tank recoilless rifles that had been promised.

He knelt down, as did the others, and his voice was not a shout or a cry, but piercing, and magnificent in texture and tone. "I humble myself before no man, but only God; we go into battle against a great army, and as we keep God's commandments, as a chosen people," and now his tone became grave, and foreboding, his voice steeped in a passionate trance, "and the enemy will come out before us in one way, and flee before us in seven ways; we shall plow them into fields and lay waste to their spirit. It is not the number of soldiers before us—it is the faith in us; it is not just our divine belief, but the unbelief of the enemy; we shall be above, and they below; we shall be the head, and they the tail; our faith must not wither, must not waver, must not perish, or we will wither, we will waver, we will perish; the enemy before us has faith in a false god, the ruler of this world, the gods of mammon, injustice, violence, iniquity, and servitude; and they feel a great power, but it is a power incorrectly interpreted, for it is a radiant reflection of a bruise, a wound, inflammation that does not heal, and spreads, like a contagion, and devours the Innocent; they are snakes come out of their dank hole, to lick the dust and gain power from every vile thing before them; they will sow, but not reap; they are flesh without soul, creatures without reason, a crashing wave that will never reach the shore; a roiling sea whose beds will soon dry up, its false image buried by the blood and deeds of valiant warriors, upon which good things will one day bloom; so, we must rise up against this false power and unmask it and show the world that it is weak, and when destroyed, it is not to be part of the world, but a mystery that brings chaos, suffering, and death; yea, we are the last hope for a world begging succor. We must fight and wash our feet in the blood of the wicked, as the good conscience God gave us and instructs us to do no other; and now we must boast, to leave proudly with our shield, or leave it proudly upon the battlefield. Amen."

"Amen," resounded in the cave.

As darkness descended, it was no longer time for lofty words, but bold action.

Tyr and Enkidu and the other scouts came back at the cyclical rebirthing of twilight leading into darkness, a black, multi-layered, charcoal-saturated, opaque-shaded, bleak darkness that had begun two nights ago on this dark moon, and again a dark moon tonight. It was the exact cloaking sky Dylan had chosen for this mission.

"Many of the enemy troops have pulled out to join their brethren against the Mexican army," Enkidu began, excitedly.

"They have about half the strength from yesterday," Tyr said, also enthusiastic.

Dylan nodded. "These citizen-generals of the Cartels would do better to read Clausewitz, Sun Tzu, and Jomini, than merely throw numbers against numbers; ah, but all the better for us."

"Five thousand still is a formidable number," Finn said, "if they were against anyone else but us." He exited the hole.

"So true," Antonio replied, snapped his fingers as he rose up through the opening, and holding his head on high, as he stood breathing the fresh air, "we are worth twenty men apiece, at least."

"Lined up man to man," Tyr said, emerging slowly from the tunnel, "we encircle this enemy."

"It is the little angels in the sky they should fear," Ana said, as she began to walk toward the faraway fortress.

The Azteca stronghold was five miles in the distance, a path that would take the Crusaders up hills, down valleys, through thick brush, and then to the mammoth, high-walled fortification.

One mile away from the fortress, Dylan, in constant communication with Robert and Paul, who were still stationed high on one of the mountain tops, next to their loyal team of technicians and scientists who readied the little aviators, motioned for the Crusaders to halt, encircle him in a tight formation, check their ear coms, special glasses, weapons, and then listen.

"The little aviators are about to strike," he began, when all were attentive. "They will take out the land mines; the predator drone will target the steel-reinforced walls; this will draw their soldiers out; they do not have the patience to shoot at nothing; these are criminal soldiers not used to real combat. They are bloodthirsty and drones do not bleed."

"What about the Mexican Air Force?" Samuel asked.

"Their planes at Bautista Air Force base were sabotaged—their helicopters too," Dylan said, but then the might of certainty rose up in his face, "but we have made reservations for two, long ago."

"Miguel and Horatius!" the Crusaders cheered.

Indeed, at that very moment, Miguel and Horatius were nearing the small airfield that contained a small surplus of jet planes that had been put out to pasture, and used during air shows. Ten Crusaders accompanied them.

"I know the men here," Miguel said, as the men crouched down next to the barbed-wire fence. "I can talk to them."

Horatius looked at his watch. "Well, don't gossip too long—there's a war scheduled soon."

"Si," Miguel said, handing his trusty FN Minimi 7.62, with great reluctance, to Horatius. "Take good care of her—she gets lonely if I'm gone too long; and, by the way, she likes to be petted and fawned over," he said, smiling mischievously, as he slid through the now-cut steel wires, and then leisurely walked up to the hangers.

"Hola," he called out, "Sancho! Eduardo! Carlos! Anybody here?"

A rifle, sticking out from a crack in the airplane hangar, met him. "Who goes there?"

"It is I! Miguel Esteban Vega Cervantes, Esquire!"

"Miguel, the hero of Monterey? It is impossible—he died bravely fighting the rebels in Honduras," the voice from inside said.

"Sancho, is that you?" Miguel asked.

"No, fool—Miguel Esteban Vega Cervantes, favorite son of Mexico, died fighting like a great warrior against the death squads in Guatemala," another voice rang out.

"Eduardo, my amigo, it is I—Miguel!"

"Then you are a spirit," another voice shouted, and then with much emotion, "Miguel Esteban Vega Cervantes, pride of Mexico, died fighting injustice in Africa."

"Amigo, open the door, and see that I'm flesh, not spirit," Miguel cried out.

The hangar door slowly opened, and a light flashed upon him.

"It looks like Miguel Esteban Vega Cervantes, perhaps a little aged," said one of the men. "Carlos, go confirm it."

"I? Why not you, Sancho—you are the chief mechanic: for your top salary, you take the big risks!"

"I will go," Eduardo said. "I am the lowest paid; I will not be missed if the ghoul devours me like I was a meaty burrito."

"The Three Stooges," Miguel said, shaking his head, "it is no wonder you are all still here."

Eduardo, coming up to him now, was smiling, then laughing. "Of course we knew it was you, Miguel, do you take us for lazy, good-for-nothing, superstitious peasants!" And as he embraced him, the others came out and did the same.

"Reunion," cried Sancho, wiping his moist eyes, "it has been a lifetime!"

"We have to have some fun, you know," Carlos said, shaking the hand of his former boss.

"Unfortunately, I did not come here for festivities," Miguel said, somberly, "you know what is happening even as we speak."

"Yes, yes," Sancho said, slapping his chest, "who would want to blow up our planes, eh?"

"Wait!" Eduardo said, excitedly, touching his comrades. "Miguel must be here on a secret mission; is that right," he looked at Miguel; "is it a secret adventure—are you fighting the Cartels?"

Miguel nodded and waved them into a tight circle. "Si—top secret—and you know what I need."

"Our jets!" the mechanic sang out.

"Precisely."

"And to fight the Cartels?" Sancho asked, his face lit with anticipation.

"Si."

"Bueno!" Eduardo shouted.

"And you are not alone, I suppose; but with your fellow fighters?" Sancho asked, his countenance lit too by the thrill of anticipation.

"Si."

"Anything for the great pilot who recommended us for this easy life here!" Sancho said, cheerfully, while gesturing about.

"Just make it look like you forced us to cooperate," Eduardo said, thoughtfully, rubbing his stubble chin.

"It is like an action movie—how glorious! Spies, adventure, battle!" Carlos said, rubbing his hands together.

"Just what we needed," Sancho said; "it is too quiet around here."

"So," Eduardo whispered to Miguel, looking around, "where are your fellow spies, eh?"

Miguel whistled back toward the cut fence, and presently, the other Crusaders joined him, much to the astonishment and the delight of the three mechanics.

"The plot thickens—how splendid!" Sancho cried, shaking the hand of each of the newest characters in this ever-expanding adventure.

"Life is so boring around this place," Eduardo said, also shaking the hands of the men.

"We are part of history, now, eh?" Carlos said, smiling, as he too shook the hands of the men.

"Now, you three," Miguel began, in earnest, "por favor—tell me all the planes here are airworthy."

"Oh, Miguel—have faith," Sancho said, as the men walked into the hangar. "When do you need them?" he asked, innocently.

"Now!"

"Oh, well, that may be a slight problem," Carlos answered, timidly.

"How much of a problem?" Miguel said, cautiously.

"One jet may be ready, and those," and Eduardo shrugged his slender shoulders as he looked toward the hangar, "not so ready."

"One," Miguel cried, "but I called, and you said you would be here now, in the middle of the night, and ready to go!"

"Yes, you did; we know now it was you; but then—well, where is caller ID when you need it; and after all, this is no restaurant, one can't just ask to reserve jets over the phone," Eduardo said, mournfully.

"It is not our fault," Sancho said, calmly; "we have asked for replacement parts, but there is the problem of those irksome battles stopping our shipments."

"And bribing guards," Carlos added.

"And getting the right parts," Eduardo finished.

Miguel, ignoring them now, was inspecting the F-5F Tiger II fighter jet, the same type he had flown so often, so long ago; he felt the texture of the sleek metal, stroking it with affection as if it were his long-lost lover. "You and I have a date, beloved," he whispered to her.

"You will return her in good condition, Miguel?" Sancho asked.

"She will show her loyalty to Mother Mexico one last time," he whispered, still caressing her, as the three mechanics busily prepared the plane for travel.

"Tell them I will be in the air," Miguel said to Horatius, then looking at the mechanics, "in fifteen minutes—five more to reach the target." He gave a half-smile, as he looked at the Crusaders, "Go with God, my friends," and watched most of them leave.

"Miguel Cervantes," said Sancho, gravely, "this jet will not be sky-worthy in fifteen minutes—she will be naked, and too shy to fully spread her wings; it is not good to rush her toilet."

Miguel shook his head. "All right, you lazy good-for-nothings," he said to them, as they were tightening, lubing, and checking the internal guts of their ladylove, "let's get this señorita bonita up in the cool night air—she needs a long walk with her beau!"

"She is no coquette, this one," Sancho said, patting the underbelly of the aging jet, "and yet, she is a fiery lover; if," he gestured with his right hand up in the air, "you court her just right."

"And how are your families?" Miguel asked.

"Bueno, muy bueno," they all said, and thanked him for asking, and consequently asked him, to which he replied that his family was too large to comment on, but he appreciated their asking.

Soon, the F-5F jet was ready, and Miguel embraced the three mechanics, who were filled with great emotion.

"The hero of San Juan," Sancho said, watching Miguel get into the cockpit, "comes back to us, only to leave again; it is much too soon."

"A hero, once more," Eduardo said, warm tears in his eyes.

"A true defender of the nation," Carlos said, nodding his head, misty-eyed.

Miguel, from within the confines of the cockpit, looked fondly at them. "It is men such as you—good, kind men, with families; good, clean, hard-working men—who are the true heroes and defenders of our beloved Mexico." He saluted them, and they, in return, saluted back; and presently, the few Crusaders who had stayed back tied up the mechanics so it would look like they had been assaulted.

Back at the Azteca stronghold, an apparent lone Eagle appeared above it, at first drifting along on the warm currents, and then beginning to dive, a figure of no great concern to the inhabitants below.

In a moment, the Tiger II was airborne, flying at more than one thousand miles per hour toward its destination, cradling its passenger in its cool bosom, where Miguel felt passionately alive, as if he were in the soft embrace of a living thing, as if his life had been missing a vital piece, just as a man who lived in a forest and who has moved to the city revisits its pastoral richness once more, and feels safe within its perfume-scented tissue.

The lone Eagle then began to slowly change into another shape—an oblong shape.

"How could I have stayed away so long," he whispered, massaging the black instrument panel; "forgive me, and forgive me for what I am about to do; but you will be remembered for the part you played." He closed his eyes for a moment. "Roberto, this is for you, the true hero of San Juan."

The lone Eagle was no longer, but now an easily recognized oblong-bomb shape.

It was not too long for him to reach the airspace at an altitude of 10,000 feet as he neared the Azteca stronghold; and not having to fear reprisal from

Mexican aviation authorities, he cleared his mind and set his course on the kill zone.

The Eagle was composed of smart materials that could shape-shift and also screen out any technology that could detect what was truly inside of it, but once the second stage of transformation was complete, this filter disappeared and activated high explosives inside it, and when this hit the concrete bunker of the fortress, the element of surprise would be accomplished, thus delaying a few valuable seconds when the gunners would launch on the incoming plane.

When Miguel saw the twin incoming missiles fired from the SA-7 anti-aircraft weapon, it was really too late, for the radar was not properly functioning, and he had been essentially flying in good hope and faith that the enemy would not have anything so sophisticated to engage him; yes, he swerved, at a steep angle, pitching the Tiger II on its side, so that the first missile missed, but the second clipped his left wing; and still, when he leveled off, and reset his trajectory by mastery of the coordination of the night sky's ancient mapmakers, he was still able to keep a stable course, until the next two missiles appeared like uninvited and rude guests right before him. It was all he could do to maneuver the craft so as to manage avoiding a full on collision, so as the two missiles bit into his ladylove and gouged out large wounds, he lost control, and the jet began a downward, spiraling death roll.

He could see the Azteca compound close ahead and the fluorescent tracer bullets shot from the Oerlikon GAI-BO1 antiaircraft 20 mm cannons to maim and finish him to the ground, but he could think only of the mission, and of his brother, as he felt the icy chill of air that poured through the badly cracked cockpit shield and into his shrapnel-induced wounds. "God grant me that I can do what Roberto did, a better man than I; God grant me victory against your enemies, my faith rewarded in full."

He felt a great surge of power regained in the controls, and the jet suddenly became upright, and immediately he shifted direction even as the bullets charged all around her, tearing this, rupturing that; yet, she was undeterred, and the now-child within her to which she had recently given birth was undeterred, and so the proper angle of degree was established, and was not to be undeterred, as if Providence had ordained it, and no amount of pitiful protestations of Man could prevent it.

Smoke and fire bathed the F-5F as she plummeted down in a speeding dive. "God grant the Crusaders victory," the son in his now-mother's comfortable arms murmured. Pilots who are reared in a plane have an acquired instinct and reflex that is utilized in survival mode, and now, he obeyed this command, albeit against his most passionate wishes.

The fiery plane did just as she was conceived to do, assembled to do, trained and pampered to do as she crashed on target: she disfigured the enemy, and not just a portion of it, but the main building that contained the control center, creating chaos and a riot in the confused and disorganized ranks of the Azteca soldiers.

The pilot, having been unceremoniously bolted from the torn cockpit, lay in the perfumed embrace of the plush flora, the black parachute next to him. Voices soon landed upon him like gentle rain.

"Miguel," Dylan said, kneeling next to him and taking his right hand in his, and Ana knelt next to him and took his left hand in hers.

"Miguel," Ana said, weeping.

"Do not weep," he murmured, "unless it is tears of joy." His entire body shuddered, and convulsed; he looked to all the Crusaders around them. "You are the chosen people of God, who can war against you..." His hands squeezed, then he let go of the hands that held his, and let them fall to his side, and dug into the soft earth, and, bringing them up, mingled the good, fertile soil with his thick, red blood, and held the warm mix in his hands. "This is what we fight for, for the land and the blood of Mexico, for they are one; and Freedom and Justice and Equality abide in them; it is the same everywhere." His body stiffened and he grimaced so that he could not speak for a time; presently, he said, still looking about at his friends, "I am proud to have been with such noble warriors; but now, God takes me into His eternal rest." And lo, his face became as smooth as sleep, and serenity visit him, and his body relaxed; and he died, death having spared him the final disgorging of a hidden mask of gasping and desperate clawing for life.

The Crusaders knelt all around them, and prayed, silently; and then, after Ana had kissed the forehead of Miguel, Dylan arose, as did all his true noblemen and noblewomen; and lo, his voice was like the spirit of war; the clamor of war, the beat of the war drum, the shout of the brave warrior, yet it was not harsh, nor loud, but piercing in its honorable tone, righteous in its confident manner. "God give us victory," he said, and despite his low voice, all managed to hear, and then looked to the fallen warrior; "let us grant him his." He looked below to the volcanic eruptions of noise and cries of disarray in the fortress. "No vile thing can stand against us now," and as he moved—yea, all of them moved, as if of the same mind, and body, and spirit, and sharing the same vision, and creed, and devotion, as if one unifying force guiding them to act as one in strength, bravery, and certainty of triumph.

The Moment Upon Them

An army that considers itself invincible no matter its size or weaponry, and considers the position of the enemy untenable and its tactics and strategies without merit, has the quality of a superior force that has defeated greater foes, and can also be the portrait of zealous fools.

The Crusaders marched in tandem, brother with brother, sister with sister, emboldened, determined, refusing to yield, retreat and fight another day; for they knew the fight was now, despite the great numbers of soldiers awaiting them; but they had known such deficiencies before in combat, and never believed they had lost the divine protection that saved them from destruction; thus, though they descended into seeming defeat, they never wavered; though it seemed certain they could not survive, their hard stride spoke otherwise; though it seemed futile, and reckless, they never hesitated, never wavered in their passionate conviction that all they need do was go forward and fight bravely, and with their unwavering, steadfast faith, victory would be theirs.

Two Sikorsky UH-60 Black Hawk helicopters rose above the walls of this stronghold. "Javelin," Finn cried, and he loaded the missile into the Javelin that Yoshitsune held; and Arjuna loaded the missile into the one that Horatius held; and presently, the missiles were sent to the mechanical birds, who were quickly struck, and burst into flames, crashing into the square of the compound.

"Incoming," yelled Cyrus, as he saw the blips of rockets on the screen he held, and Moses, in the seat of the Iron Phalanx, let loose its stupendous assault of the thousands of rounds per minute of bullets that roared into the sooty pitch of night to intercept the projectiles and blow them up into fiery pieces.

And the Crusaders gained more ground, watching more missiles from their drones slam into machine-gun towers, and their aviator drones, carrying small explosives, and some armed with bullets and lasers, discharge their cargo against a disturbed and bewildered enemy.

Yet, it was not nearly enough, and a prudent army engaged in this offensive would have pulled back, satisfied with a small advance toward victory;

but the Crusaders would not, for they held the intuitive sense that this was to be won now, not when the enemy might regroup or call in reinforcements, for they had catapulted momentum and surprise against their foe, and had a surpassing faith that boasts of honor and loyalty to a just cause that pushes them forward despite the overwhelming odds; so, even though it seemed hopeless as they neared the smoke and ash and rubble of the broken walls, they had hope; even though it seemed that in the next few strides, no aid might arrive, yet they saw it, heard it, felt its bugle call sounding the charge.

All was in readiness: the Crusaders, behind the protective half-moon XSAPI plates, many of whom were equipped with Heckler & Koch 417 rifles, which fire a 7.62 x 51 mm cartridge, or the Special Operations Forces Combat Assault Rifle, the FN SCAR-L, Mark 17, Model 0, which fires a 5.56 x 45 mm cartridge and is also equipped with an Enhanced Grenade Launching Module, and wore gas masks, and special FLIR goggles, ear com, special Enhanced Combat Helmets, that were modified to absorb shock waves from explosions and thus prevent traumatic brain injury, and specially designed anti-fog faceshields to withstand injuries to soft tissues, but both further modified—this last faceshield design finally overcoming the negative effects of back blasts—to reduce the underwash overpressure phenomenon that occurs when the blast waves travel inside the helmet, and the special space-age Modular Tactical Vest; and thus equipped with such stellar weaponry and armor in this earthly sphere, and praying to the heavenly domain, they moved circumspectly into the open spaces.

And they were wearing a blend of the natural camouflage that utilized quantum stealth technology making them virtually invisible in the dark terrain; some of the Crusaders were carrying the XM25, which was fitted with a computer laser finder, and fired grenades that exploded above or near the target; for each Crusader carried a weapon with a designated purpose.

And they had already used the SOFLAM—the Special Operations Forces Laser Acquisition Marker—which "painted" the targets inside the stronghold so that the Javelin, launched, and the drones, flying, and the missiles, shot, could have something to hone in on.

They moved quietly, in scattered formation, moving in haphazard lines, their eyes ever trained on the prize before them; enjoying, at least for now, the anonymity that the special reflecting infrared clothing afforded them, allowing them to gain crucial ground upon the temporarily bewildered and disorganized enemy.

The high multitude of attack drones, now large, now small, tossing in incendiary bombs, bullets, and lasers, created havoc from above, and with sharpshooters surrounding the complex—Rustem, with his Barrett M107A1 sniper rifle, and forty other Crusaders, some using the Mark 20, Model 0 Sniper variant FN SCAR-H, which fires a 7.62 x 51 mm round, perched on small mounds and in trees surrounding the compound—threw a mild blanket of protection for the fellows who were just now breeching the smoking, crumbling walls.

Two heavily armed drones that were packed to the hilt with explosives rammed into the courtyard where a great cluster of Azteca soldiers were roaming, killing most of them; four more drones dropped huge containers that produced a specifically formulated smoke through which only those with special optics could see; more drones dropped smoke fragmentation grenades that disabled the senses of those near.

But this was not the most important function of the drones: by using quantum ghost imaging, Heimdall's scientists were able to project images from specially equipped drones of a multitude of fully equipped, moving soldiers and vehicles onto the great plumes of drifting smoke that encompassed all the battlefield, a phantom army that was dispersed all about the real Crusaders, and that would move along with them into the compound, a decoy that the enemy could not discern from its physical counterpart.

Moses still rode the mobile Iron Phalanx with a hard XSAPI shield that extended over him for protection, he at the front of the Crusaders, like a tank, firing rapidly into the fleeing soldiers before them.

Despite all this—the drones, the sophisticated weaponry, the element of surprise—there were still thousands of Azteca soldiers still anxious for a fight, and positioning themselves among these fourteen buildings, some of which were high, others low, some wide, others narrow, many long, others short, planted like separate gardens that now served as barriers in a sophisticated game of hide and seek.

Within one minute of moving into the compound, five Crusaders had died: Santiago Silva of Argentina, whose parents were political prisoners and had been killed during the military junta of the late 1970s; Reynaldo Contreras of Mexico, whose parents were part of a recent peasant uprising for civil rights in Chiapas; Mauricio Villalobos of Costa Rico, whose parents were missionary workers throughout South America; Santiago Mejia of El Salvador, whose father had been a chief negotiator between the guerillas and government during the 1980s civil war; and Rosel Matos of Cuba, who parents had fought against Castro in the early 1960s, and were jailed until their death; Ana was wounded, but still moved on, and twenty more were now down and unable to move, but their brethren moved on toward the mark, unimpeded by odds any other soldier might have despaired of.

The Crusaders used a quantum imaging camera to distinguish enemy soldiers from their own and from the holograph soldiers; they were able to recognize each other even in darkness, smoke, or storm, for the uniform of each man and woman had been treated with a particular phosphorescent dye that could be seen only through the specially designed optics they wore; so, when a mass of soldiers met in the dense haze and ebony-rich darkness, the Crusaders could instantly pinpoint the enemy, namely: that Finn and Arjuna, hiding behind a large building, were about to be attacked by six soldiers, but Rustem spotted the enemy, saying, "F and S in L," which meant a certain sector, and after dispatching them, "Forward section in L is now clear."

"Copy that," Finn replied.

Samuel and Yoshitsune, moving from behind the burning wreckage of a helicopter, were briefly surrounded, unbeknown to the ten enemy soldiers; but then Rustem, using his Barrett M107A1, and two other Crusaders sharpshooters, using EXtreme Accuracy Tasked Ordnance, EXACTO, sniper rifles, which guided its .50 caliber bullet—even if it veered off course—to its target, took out all ten. "S and Y, all clear," Rustem said.

"Copy that," Yoshitsune replied.

The Azteca army launched their rocket-propelled grenades, their missiles, their fury of bullets to blanket the dense smoke in confusion, more often hitting brick and stone and fellow soldiers, for by now, their foe had implemented the next phase in their plan: to fly upward. Nine more Crusaders were wounded.

The Crusaders went up the metal ladders that were on the side of the buildings, launching grenades with their HK417 rifles and XM25s, spraying the enemy with bullets and blood, even as their remote-controlled massive aerial army continued its unrelenting, pointed attack on the outpost; but the mission was still the same: destroy the command center, capture or kill Alvarez, disable all electronic equipment, destroy all military equipment, secure any vital information pertaining to the daily operations of the Azteca Cartel: personnel, routes, names, countries involved, and government agencies compromised.

Some of the Crusaders were cut off from ascending to the vantage point as the Azteca army scrambled about, shooting wildly, and launching multiple

RPG-7 attacks; in one such group, three Crusaders were killed, two by shrapnel, and the other by shock waves to his tissues and organs: Joseph tweed, of the USA, whose brother was a member of the Special Ops team that had brought down significant terrorists in the past decade; Harold Schmidt of Germany, whose grandmother had joined in a plot to kill the leadership of the Nazis; Benjamin Dayan of Israel, whose grandparents had fought against its hostile neighbors during the many wars for the independence of the Jewish state; and one survived: Rhiannon of the United Kingdom, late of the United States of America.

"Up the sides," Rustem cried, which meant the Azteca were climbing the ladders of the buildings, and even as he said this, he and the other snipers were picking them off. "Too many!"

Rhiannon was trapped as she crouched low with her HK416 in front of her, and crawled along the rim of the building before her. Two unfriendlies approached her and she shot them, then three more came from behind her, still stumbling as the teargas choked them, and the stun grenades dazzled them, and incessant bombardment confused them; they saw her, but she killed all of them, and then, reaching the edge, covered in hot blood and guts, saw, with her special optics, a building that she recognized from the blueprint all of the Crusaders had memorized, a multilayered steel-reinforced storage room for bullets and grenades, a reason the door was opened; and quickly checking the path to it, and the perimeter, she dashed for it as the enemy closed upon her.

She clutched the door as bullets continued to flash past her and, slamming it shut, broke the internal locking mechanism.

"Dylan," she cried, "I am trapped in the storage room in sector R!"

And then came the loud grunts and cries of the soldiers, like rabid dogs, scratching and banging at the door to get at her.

"Too many going up," Rustem shouted, after picking off five more climbers in succession.

"Rhiannon," Dylan cried, running to the edge of the building he was on, and looking to the faraway building she was in, "I'm coming!" He never even hesitated or looked around as he shouted, "I am going to the storage room from rooftop ten," and immediately leaped to the ladder, using his HK417 to shoot three men on their way up, his XM25, the Punisher, slung behind his shoulder.

When he jumped and cleared the last seven rungs, he hit the asphalt running and was at full speed in an instant, his rifle blazing away in front of him.

The Crusaders atop the buildings turned their magnificent firepower to anything not painted friendly all about his racing form, thousands of rounds of bullets and many grenades tossed and rockets launched before Dylan, behind and beside him, so that the entire path of fifty meters between him and his woman, and the twenty meters beside him, was illumined by a great burst of incendiary gunfire and bombs bursting from above, and with the concurrent reprisal firepower from the enemy below directed above and some below, all this ferocity fairly melted all sound and coherence about it, laying to waste the enemy in blood and fury—this, the greatest battle of the struggle; and as the rescuer was sprinting full straight ahead, he still heard her desperate voice, calling out to him; and this blessed essence of love was a beacon of loving light he followed, as he fired his weapon and took out dozens of men, while up above, his brethren and the drones took out hundreds more all around him, even as the howling banshees clawed and shot and vowed to break through the steel barrier and skin alive the female Crusader inside it.

I need you, Rhiannon whispered, her back to the stone cold wall inside the storage container, her HK416 aimed at the banging, incessantly fired-upon door that was being ripped to shreds of weakness. Dylan, my beloved, my husband, where are you; I need you so much; I love you, so much.

Bullets and bombs and lasers blasted and blared all about the valiant rescuer as he ran full tilt, then a huge explosion rocked the small courtyard, and he was temporarily stunned; but the fragments of the bomb were absorbed by a downed helicopter he had been near, and so he quickly regained his composure and resumed his hard run, this time without his helmet, even as those above him provided an intense array of bullets, grenades, and lasers, and Moses shot the Iron Phalanx's tiny saviors all about him to intercept any nasty metal aviators; and the drones with their fiery tails, and now spreading their lethal wings, darted and dived above to scatter and scour the enemy near him, so that, as he neared his whole world, there he was: running madly straight down the middle, amid the rapid bursts of deafening explosions and great heaps of time-altering thunder bolts of scintillating firepower that crisscrossed every section of space about him but not on him, and so he ran unimpeded, like Mercury, like Fate, like the Future, set; and as he neared the storage bin, let loose the 7.62 x 51 mm bullets of the HK417 he held fast in one hand, and the XM25 grenades in the other, and fairly blew away every stinking Azteca dog, every filthy, dirty, howling hyena: he blew them to bits and pieces and into the fiery Inferno below; and as he came upon the door, he yelled to she who was inside, she who was his entire world outside. "Rhiannon,

Rhiannon," and seizing the handle the door with his great might, wrenched it open, and charged in, his weapons at his side.

There were no words to be spoken for two who walked in flesh but were truly as one, two in love, but as one; two souls separate during the day, but truly as one at night, who now embraced, and as she wept, he held her tight; and as he held her tight, despite all that was, all that occurred outside, all the death, the dying, the wounded, the destruction, the mayhem, it seemed impossible, and far away, and misplaced, for now they were united in one spirit, the sacred spirit of love and fidelity, and nothing earthly seemed capable of preventing this.

And then she said to him, words that swept a joy and passion so great into his heart that he no longer heard even the rumblings and grumblings of a magnificently contested, aggrieved, outside conference of angry, battling peoples. "I am," she whispered, still with her head resting gently upon his strong shoulders, "with child."

He felt the glory of new life gather itself up in him and deliver him from this horrible place, and wipe away the tears of bitterness and sorrow of his past; he held her out from his bloodstained, dirt-covered self, looking at her with love that need not be spoken, but felt, and felt because of a life of fidelity and right action; and then he kissed her, and passionately so, amid the clamor and quaking of the real world still raging outside.

But he had to listen now, had to recover, and retrieve himself, and thrust himself back into the intense fray. "There are too many, too many," he heard, this plaintive hue and cry of his countrymen—citizens of the same country of Freedom and Justice they loved and breathed, and fought for.

And then, in the far distance, but not too far for a faint sound to alight upon airy wings and swiftly fly to the ears of the embattled. "Viva," it began, "Viva," it rang, "Viva la Mexico!"

What happened, then, what strange thing occurred, to fatigue the health of the enemy's heart, what clamor, what yells, what great joining of rebellious spirits?

Madness and panic seized the Azteca soldiers as their once seemingly impervious societal walls were breached and a mass of fresh troops now crashed through.

"They're coming," Rustem said, nearly cheering, "the people!"

It was true: the people of Yermo had amassed in the thousands, with weapons and pride, and were marching now on the battle, actually engaging many fleeing Azteca soldiers; and the hearts of the Crusaders were heartened, and they fought on with true courage and valor, fighting in the smoke and ash, blood and death, as they heard the soaring song of their new comrades: "More of us, than they."

And Dylan, after seeing that the section he was in had been cleared of the lurking debris of villainy, came out with Rhiannon, and then heard something else that stunned him. "They're coming," Robert said; "it is all over, and yet now has begun." A great mass of noise was upon them.

Dylan looked up at the great swell of a swirling, misty night sky, and beheld a multitude of familiar aircraft with certain vibrant colors that swelled his breast with pride: helicopters, and jets, flying overhead; and after the compound had been secured with an extreme display of firepower from the new allies, presently, a military helicopter landed near him, and out stepped Victor Fuentes; and in the mind of Dylan, it was as if he inhabited a surreal dream as the agent walked straight up to him, smiling, and saying, boldly, confidently, gravely, "The invasion of Mexico has begun."

The Revolution of the Masses

This hard-fought battle having now been won, secured by the US Army and Marines and the now-freed Mexican armies and Federal Police, Victor spoke with Dylan near an Apache helicopter.

"Rebellions throughout Mexico are occurring, not only in Yermo, but in Zapote, and in all territories held by El Narco, the people have taken up arms to fight the Cartels; even in the streets of America, the people are fighting back against the Cartels and their gang affiliates who took over their homes and neighborhoods." He nodded, as if to aid the mind of Dylan in this miraculous transition to believe this blossoming fairy tale. "It is true—Mexico has invited us to help them with this war; and, my friend, we aren't going to leave this time until we are triumphant—and this time, we have a long-term plan." He smiled. "What you and your Crusaders have done here is to bring about the rebirth of Democracy, a debt the free world cannot repay." He paused, looking up at the F-35 Lightning II fighter jets that streaked overhead. "What say you, noble Crusader; finish what you have started, what say thee?"

Dylan told him of Rhiannon's condition, and the face of the agent became soft, and caring; and immediately, he radioed in another chopper especially for her; and presently, after Dylan embraced Rhiannon, he and Victor watched as she was flown far away into a black, cool, starry, yet somehow freer and calmer, night.

"We have much to do," answered Dylan, who was now joined by his fellow Crusaders, while Victor was now surrounded by DEA, CIA and other intelligence agency operatives—all of whom stood uncharacteristically quiet, and struck by awe, as if in the presence of enigmatic and mighty warriors of old, "and we will care for our many wounded, and bury our many dead."

Nineteen brave warriors had died: Kostya Sergeyevich Brusilov of Russia, whose grandfather had been captured by the Germans during World War II, and because of this, was considered a "malicious deserter" and traitor, and so, after he was released, was sentenced to eight years in the Gulag in Siberia, joining his family who had been sentenced there years before because of their relations to him; Aleksandrina Kimovna Melnikov of Russia, whose parents had been involved in espionage during the Cold War; Riley Thompson of Australia, whose father was captured by the Japanese while he fought in the Pacific, and was a prisoner of war for three years in Formosa, one of the most brutal war camps; Marie Murro of the Philippines, whose grandmother was in the Filipino guerilla resistance during World War II; Jericho Tagaan of the Philippines, whose parents were involved in fighting against corruption in their government during the years 1972 to 1981, when martial law was declared on their island; Pablo Castillo of Spain, whose grandparents had fought with the Republican forces against the Nationalists during the Spanish Civil War; Javier Reyna of Honduras, whose missionary parents were killed in Nicaragua by rebels; Lucia Belloni of Uruguay, whose parents had fought against corruption in their government during the civil-military rule period of 1973 to 1985; Cristina Cordua of Nicaragua, whose two brothers and sisters had died from their injuries after the 1972 earthquake in her homeland due to the government stealing emergency aid that was destined to help the stricken areas; Manuel Ramirez of Venezuela, whose mother died in the Caracazo riots of 1989 in Caracas; Francis Palacio of Belize, whose mother was part of the movement that helped gain universal suffrage in her country in 1954; Sergei Michail Kulik of Ukraine, whose grandparents were arrested and starved to death during the Great Purge of 1936 to 1938; Ruben Pedrosa of Panama, whose older brothers fought against their corrupt government during the 1980s; Rosa Mendes of Costa Rica, whose grandparents fought in the Civil War of 1948, where they joined in the protesting of the results of the presidential election that, they believed, had been unjustifiably annulled; Alejandro Nervo of Mexico, whose older sister was kidnapped and killed by drug traffickers; Eric Jefferson of Texas, whose older brother was a soldier in one of the many wars that the US fought in the Middle East in the 2000s; Luke Torrey of California, whose older brother died in one of the many wars that the US fought in the Middle East in the 2000s; Aiden Hightower of California, whose father fought in Vietnam, was captured, and was a prisoner of war for five years; and Sylvia Vazquez of Arizona, whose mother served as a nurse in Vietnam.

"Where will all of you go now, with, of course, the official blessings of both governments?" Victor said, nodding his head.

"Where we are needed," Dylan replied, and looking about the blood-strewn place.

"Suarez escaped, but we will catch him," Victor said. "And we do have his records; we have it all."

Dylan nodded. "In Zapote, there are the Majors Gonzales and Gonzales."

"Yes, I know of them, and here's what I know."

And so he told them, and also, to what he told them, this too must be added: it was true that the Zapote people, simultaneously, as if by intellectual and emotional osmosis, as if by the phenomenon of pride and honor suffusing the geography of northern Mexico, had risen up against their oppressor, and joined the Mexican army and Federal Police in battling the combined forces of the El Dorado and Velazquez Cartels.

"More of us than them," was the battle cry of those who fought the chains of oppression from that day forward.

Señor Muerte—a.k.a. Tomas Alvarez, former street thug, punk, gangster, terrorist, opportunistic organism attaching himself to any seemingly benign and inoffensive life-form to suck it dry of life and liberty—had sat in the black bloom of despair, as he listened to his massive empire crumbling around them.

"My personal choppers are down," he said to Luis; "what are we going to do? How could this happen? Where were our planes and choppers and tanks? How can sheep rise up against their master and say 'no'?'"

Luis, staring, stood before him, silent, unmoving.

"We cannot lose, not now; Luis, not us, we are a superior race—genetically superior—fated to rule the weak, the infirm, the imperfect," he shouted, and suddenly turned on the radio; the next narco-corrido began to play. "He used to be the biggest man," joyfully the song began, as if a song of liberation, "and now he is just the littlest man, because the people no longer wish it so, because the people no longer let it go; so adios to Señor Muerte, reservation for you, in hell."

"What! What! I didn't write that! I did not authorize that!" Alvarez cried, standing up, even as a terrific explosion ripped and shook the building.

"I know who did," Luis said, his voice possessing an eerie calm, which perturbed his boss.

"Who?" he responded, agitated, and now suspicious.

"You know of the North American Wild Sheep?" he began, in a strangely insensitive, detached voice, holding a book on wildlife. "They are strong," he continued, and stood up taller, "tough, resilient, resourceful and smart; they are true warriors, living on the land, not becoming fat and lazy and stupid like our sheep."

"Eh, what's this? You give me my own kind of analogy…"

But Luis held up his hand to halt this interruption, and Alvarez, hoping that Luis had some miraculous news, was willing to submit to this impudent behavior for now, but later…

"You, Señor Muerte, did not evolve, as promised; you, instead, became the indolent sheep, content to simply graze on the same green pasture, never worried about the closing walls around him; pushing without limits, just another greedy, petty dictator, who didn't know how to compromise or know when to stop, destined to be usurped by the next fresh idea."

Alvarez reached for his gun and, holding it up, aimed it at Luis, and without hesitation, pulled the trigger; yet, somehow, Luis still stood, and then he said easily, "Yes, you grew fat and lazy," he said, smiling now, as does the wolf that, wearing the fine clothes of the sheep, has just eaten the plumpest one; and then holding out six bullets that belonged to Alvarez's gun, whispered, "This is why you failed—by failing to alter your habits, and by trusting anyone…" and he smiled, wistfully, "I will perhaps not be a hero, but exonerated of my crimes."

Alvarez stood up, cursing, screaming wicked invectives and promises of retribution against Luis, as if by this very steel projectiles of vulgar language, he indeed constructed a worthy defense against all weaponry, as if indeed he would still live.

Luis took out his pistol. "I evolve, and survive; it's what happens when the tide has turned; as for you—you are like the claustrophobic mole: he cannot do what he was meant to do, but can do no other; so, he is no longer good for anything, and as you are in an infinite regress, it is mercy I bestow upon you; adios, Señor Muerte," he said, half-smiling, and pulled the trigger, even as the big man, screaming and yelling vengeance, charged him, like a fat, lazy, woolly sheep charging the wily wolf, doomed to die in its own thick, oozing blood and guts and brain matter.

And so forth, the revolution spread; by World Wide Web, by cell phone, tablet, phone, press, radio, television, word-of-mouth; by screams, shouts, murmurs, and whispers of great deeds done and marvelous offensive engagement of the common people who began to regain their self-respect, and hope, and a way home again, and by pride restored in the unlimited possibilities of a rejuvenated Mother Mexico. Viva la Mexico!

Revolutions were in one place, Mexico; rebellions in another, America; perhaps better explained by what really happened when the President of Mexico entered the Oval Office that fateful day before the aforementioned battles.

Manuel Diaz, President-Elect of the sovereign country of the United States of Mexico, stepped into the private room of his North American cousin, with utter sincerity and trust.

"May I offer you some refreshments, Manuel?" the American President began, taking advantage of the unwritten convention that allows heads of state to prefer first names to wearisome titles.

"No, thank you, Paul," Manuel replied, also taking advantage of this social clause; "the refreshment I require pertains to the state of affairs between the two countries; enlighten me, and so, refresh me."

"Please, honor me with specifics; please," Paul said, extending his hand to a plush, red velvet-covered chair.

"I prefer to stand—sitting makes one complacent and lethargic," Manuel replied, politely.

"My wife picked out these chairs," Paul said, stroking the fine fabric of the high-backed chair; "she would be disappointed that a head of state cast doubt upon her taste in finer things."

"Life is full of disappointments, no? In my office, I have wooden chairs for guests—made by peasants—to remind them that such officials who momentarily dwell in them are not our betters, and to give them no little discomfort, both by the hardness of the chair, and the fact that they cannot sit in luxury in the highest office of the land."

Paul stared at the proud man. "I understand. I too was raised poor."

"I am well aware of your upbringing—in that case, we are alike; but in others, as far apart as North is from South."

"Please explain."

Manuel moved about, hands clasped behind his blue blazer, a woolen suit that had been carefully and expertly stitched by local peasant women. "What are your intentions toward the Cartels?"

"I intend," Paul responded, and confidently, "to decapitate this writhing beast."

"Splendid—and how?"

Paul smiled. "Why, by stepping upon their nest; it is useless to kill worker ants here," and he pointed down, "when, the problem is," and he pointed south, "there."

Beads of perspiration appeared on the swarthy face of the president of Mexico, but his voice belied his inner tumult. "And how, pray tell, will you accomplish that; have they moved their entire operations to the States in the last four hours?"

"No," the American President stated, matter-of-factly, "not that I know of; no, I believe they are still mainly headquartered in your country."

Manuel shook his head. "Please, do explain how you will accomplish this daring and seemingly impossible feat from so far..."

Paul, with pursed lips, and a frown, walked directly up to him, and announced, "Why, by invading your country, obviously."

"La arrogancia del Americano," Manuel cried, "and you tell me this like you're ordering drive-through!"

"It is no reason to lose one's temper, Manuel," Paul said, half-smiling; "of course, I will consult you first."

"Oh, first you tell me of your plans to invade another sovereign nation, and then proceed—how perfectly civil; and we are the peons!"

"Manuel, you misunderstand me: with your permission, of course—I would never believe in invading our good neighbor without his explicit consent and enthusiastic approval," he said, smoothly, and finishing with a smile.

"And, if I do not..."

"Well, then, we will not—it is just that easy, Manuel; look, we are democracies, we must respect borders."

"So, you plan to invade Mexico—when!"

Paul gazed at his watch, and calculated the numbers. "Today is Tuesday; well, by Wednesday, at the latest..."

Manuel removed his jacket and placed it over the red velvet chair. "And what if I refuse?"

"That is simple; then we simply stand down."

He raised his hands, clenched his fists, and then, shaking them violently, cried out, "I should not have ignored the reports about your unusual troop movement along our border!" He then stood still and composed himself, and said in a calm voice. "So, Paul, tell me honestly—how long have you planned this?"

"We are ready, that is the important matter, Manuel," Paul said, standing next to him. "Tomorrow, I declare martial law, curfews in all fifty states; I will place the military in the streets; such a thing has not happened since the Civil War; you think I accept such decisions lightly—may it never be! I'm swept along by the currents of history; we have met an intransigent enemy who seems to have no inherent conscience; this is intolerable, and I will not allow such seething iniquity to go unpunished; not here, not there," he pointed down to the well-groomed carpet, and then southward, and then gestured all about, "not anywhere; you think our European allies are not of one voice on such an illustrious venture? The Cold War is over, religious fanatics are being fought in other countries; but the Cartels are our regional foe, they it will not long last on our watch; this much I do know; now, of course, I should have consulted you earlier, but timelines were altered by unforeseen events; well, you must know: the Defenders—or, you may know them as the Crusaders—have proven to be invaluable allies."

"Yes, yes, I have made their extraordinary acquaintance through third parties."

"Well, there you have it; they operate within your borders, and with your explicit approval?"

"With my reluctant acquiescence..."

"So, you know of their present battles with the Cartels?"

"Yes."

"And of their breaking the communication network codes of the Cartels?"

"Si."

Paul frowned. "And of their heroic fight virtually alone?"

"I have lent them my troops..."

Paul frowned once more. "Who even now are compromised..." He lifted up his head, and looked askance at his honored guest. "So, Mr. President— why am I so honored by your presence today?"

Manuel smiled. "I thought you would never ask, Mr. President..."

And as the men stood face to face, as each recognized a glimmer of mischievousness in the gleaming eyes of the other, a radiant smile appeared on the face of the other, and then slowly, and inevitably, laughter occurred—much, much-needed joyous laughter, like a cool rainstorm in summer.

When the celebration of subterfuge and diplomacy was behind them, Manuel spoke. "One day, soon, Paul, maybe we will simply trust each other and say what is on our minds."

"Gradations," Paul said, "slowly, we will be true neighbors, yet, hopefully, with no fences."

"I will take that drink now…"

"Good," Paul said, "what shall you have? We have a long session before us."

"Green tea, with much wild honey; hot, if you please."

"Good enough," Paul said, and promptly ordered two hot teas, with generous amounts of wild honey.

Once both men were seated directly across from each other, not cut off by the desk or false borders, and tea in hand, Manuel said, "I have ideas on how to use your esteemed military, especially your elite units."

"Please," Paul said, politely, motioning to him with his hand, as if to say "be my guest," and then finished, "we have till twilight." He opened the spacious windows and inhaled deeply, and then said in a winsome voice, "Ah, the aromatic stimulus of a new Autumn, a good time as any to go a-warring."

Now, let us leave these two fine gentlemen, who were discussing the war against the Mexican Cartels and possible excursions into Central America, with the cooperation of those nations, and glide into the future, to settle the account of the fugitive, Arturo Suarez.

Suarez managed to escape, as Victor Fuentes said, in the initial assault, and fled to the nearby mountains, where he lived with various people; and then, when the Federal police came calling, he moved into valleys, and caves, and even attempted to cross over into the States, but was rebuffed by Border agents; and despite his extensive network of contacts, and his enormous funds, he was cut off, first by his many high-in-the-government contacts, who were presently unavailable, and then his high-in-the-world-of-organized-crime contacts, who were presently dead, imprisoned, or also on the run; and then by his ill-begotten, bloodstained monies, which were frozen and then confiscated, with the help of his records retrieved, and now very helpful acquaintances; so, Suarez became the hunted, finding few allies who would harbor a man with a twenty-million-in-US-dollars bounty, which was painted with an extra-large, phosphorescent red bull's-eye on his big, black and increasingly gray-haired head.

However, he could not long run in a country that had posted his picture on every social media register, and made him the greatest villain of the moment; and eventually, he was captured, found living in a filthy, dirty, rotten, broken-down wooden structure in the deepest folds of the Sierra Madre Mountains, turned in not by one who even knew him, but by a local farmer who thought that, by the man's scraggly and smelly appearance, he was nothing more than an irksome squatter, a typical vagrant, a common trespasser; and after two hundred Special Forces agents surrounded the cave where the former El Narco was hiding like a beaten, cowering dog, and after he surrendered—and still wearing his crocodile-skin boots—and the numerous television cameras were finally allowed to come forward, reporters asked him many questions, all which he refused to answer; but he did say, quite boldly, "I am too big to fail; I know things," and then with what little pride he yet had, "no jail could hold me."

The officer in charge, hustling Suarez to the awaiting military convoy, thought, "You are correct, but how about a strong rope, eh?"

Two days hence, in the high-security federal prison ensconced somewhere in the deepest wilds of the Sierra Madre Mountains, on a floor dedicated to holding only one newly arrived guest, and attended to by a score of guards and soldiers, where few had actual access to the occupied cell, the large body of the prisoner was found hanging from the light fixture by the curiously extra-thick drawstrings from his prison uniform.

"There is nothing like the craftsmanship of strong Mexican rope made by our noble peasants," mused the same officer who had led the capture of this now-dead super-criminal, watching with satisfaction as the bloated body was cut down. "One more head on a pole; perhaps we should write an accompanying note, this time; ha!"

What Comes After

A clean house breeds no rats.

The conditions that existed all over the world to encourage the growth of the drug cartels, like warmth to bacteria, still existed: poverty, corruption, lack of education, lack of opportunities, avarice, human weakness, a deep recess of human wickedness, and a seemingly inexhaustible flame of human desire for power and wealth, and an implacable desire by certain people to offer pain and suffering to others so they might obtain it; but this is a narrative not likely to alter soon, despite technology, reform movements, and new laws, unless those aforementioned laws are directed by those who understand what must be done to ensure history does not endlessly repeat itself in vicious cycles.

Human beings change not when times are good, as success brings little self-reflection, and neither when times are momentarily bad, as this usually brings anger and recrimination—but when there is a total inner destruction and overall breakdown of mental faculties, where the internal compass is obliterated, the mind disheveled, the heart ripped asunder, the soul smothered, the body broken; it can be the same for a family, traumatized; a neighborhood, wrecked; a city, devastated; an estate, buried; a nation, destroyed—but there must be leadership to bring about permanent change, or the same malady will simply rise again in the exact encouraging conditions and proportions.

Yes, the backs of the Mexican Cartels were broken, and no, the UN coalition forces did not travel south of Mexico to enter countries where less violence, less corruption, less mayhem was already achieved; yes, the Cartels were driven out of the United States of America, and the high-ranking collaborators who had sold their precious citizens' card to them were, for the most part, arrested; but no, the majority of gangs were still in place, and their power still resided either on the streets or in the prisons.

It must be remembered that the Mexican Cartels had taken over the operation of selling drugs from the Colombians, who had been reduced to suppliers, and the existing conditions in Mexico had created a waiting and anxious army: of poor children looking for money, poor young men and women with few opportunities, poor pay for law enforcement, corruption at every governmental level.

Robert Heimdahl was part of an international team that was selected to work with the Mexican government, and he gave this speech before the committee of foreign delegates at their first meeting: "We do not come here as representatives of countries and agencies who know what is best for Mexico, but because they need an ally; we do not come here to simply give them money, so as to cripple them as we have done in other countries, to render them incapable of doing for themselves; we are not their superiors, we are their allies, who come to offer advice on job training and schooling for any citizen who is in need of it, to plant the seed of education so they might secure a better job and escape poverty, and thus not be tempted to join nefarious organizations or simply fall prey to the lure of crime; we are here to offer aid to Mexico so it can become more self-reliant—as has been done in other countries, like Nigeria, where the farmers are receiving more education, and are using more modern techniques so they will be able to rely less on food assistance from other nations, so they might have pride in the knowledge that they are feeding their own people." It was his organization that had created this opportunity. "This is the burden of all First World countries—to work together with needful countries toward a common goal: self-reliance. We would want others to treat us so if we were in a similar situation, which we all have been in, both as people and countries; so, let us now come together, and work assiduously to help a good neighbor realize their dream of prosperity."

Yes, the head of the snake had been chopped off, but the two parts were not buried too far apart, and could easily, with a little help from their friends, reassemble; of all the reforms and laws necessary for bringing about permanent change, the most urgent one was addressed in the first months of Operation Rehabilitation: the cleansing of the Cartels from the landscape of modern civilization.

There were former leaders of nations who had always been willing, once their tenure in office had expired and their legacy and retirement fund secured, to casually speak out, and even sign a document of the same content, for the decriminalization and legalization of the harvesting, processing, and selling of certain plants that at the moment were considered illegal to sell—such a radical act hitherto unknown to sitting politicians. But the world had reached its nadir in its exasperation at the drug wars, and was wont to forgive and forget, and willing to listen to any and all ideas, a trend normally followed only after a victory over a formidable foe.

So, Robert Heimdall, billionaire, philanthropist, essayist on social issues, attempted to assemble an august panel of former world leaders—and yes, current world leaders, too, but of the latter, no one of great import seemed interested in accepting this invitation—here, in his World Affairs Think Tank complex, where he invited university historians, economic professors, social scientists, political scientists, anthropologists, newspaper and magazine reporters and editors, Drug Enforcement Agency personnel, drug reform representatives, heads of the FBI, CIA, NSA, National Security Council executives, and other relevant agencies and people and, more importantly, representatives of various ideologies within each group; and they talked of the illegal drug problem, its history, its present effects, its future; and when it was all over, there was still considerable argument and tension about the direction to pursue; the law enforcement agencies argued henceforth: they could not see a road ahead littered with sneering ex-crime bosses and street punks who would walk free because drugs were now legal. It is like asking, they argued, for a general to walk away freely from the enemy before them; after shaking his extended hand, to go home and contentedly play bridge with their spouse—how could they so easily give up what they had been so passionately resolved to fight with all their heart and might, while ignoring their family and watching friends die, only now to allow those responsible to go away, unpunished; this would seem inconceivable to them, and would, more importantly, proclaim that the death and suffering of their colleagues and citizens in this long fight had been in vain and a travesty of Justice; it is our existence to fight the palpable evil—we can conceive of no other reasonable existence, they argued; for we are the last vanguard, and we mean to stay; so, with every word, and syllable break, and gesture and sign, and allegiance to a past held fast by two hands, they etched on the fresh gravestone of progress and invariance: safe, understood, comforting; thus, they were the immutable drug, their far-flung anchor cut loose as they drifted rudderless, a rusted ship, without sail, direction, or captain, seeing nothing but what they had always seen, a vast network of conspiratorial actors, good versus evil, us versus them, white and black, a crystal-clear, delineated danger to empirically see and affirm and confront. What would we do had we not the calling to search and find and destroy; and if it is a lie, they reasoned, what will become of our past lives? Who can we then be, if all long, we were fighting under a false treaty? How can we go forward, if all along, we have been going backward? No! A thousand thousand times no! No! No! Let us do our job and let us be! We exist to battle the scourge of illegal drugs, and if we, the last guardians—in fact, the only guardians—fall away, everyone will have access to these powerful substances and society will go absolutely mad! And so they argued, and so they held fast to the dogmatic tradition they had held from the beginning, born of a refusal to even consider viable alternatives.

Those in favor of decriminalizing and legalizing all drugs, first stated that Netherlands, Portugal, the Czech Republic, and other bold nations around the globe, albeit different societies, after adopting drug laws that were less harsh, and therefore opening the market to virtually any adult, had lower drug use, lowered crime, and had created more successful rehabilitation centers; yes, such centers that could be built with the monies not used in battling criminals who were only powerful, only rich, only… rich and criminals, because they sold illegal substances.

If cigarettes were to become illegal, criminals would sell them at a higher price and become rich, they argued, and usher in violence to protect their newfound wealth; make cigarettes legal, and the criminals would go back to whatever illegal act, if any, they had been involved with before, and then we would fight them there; but do not waste inordinate amounts of time and manpower on some fool with a pot farm in his backyard; in its stead, spend it on protecting society from real acts of crime: burglary, theft, fraud, rape, assault, murder, over-intoxication of any stimulating substance; do not make some homegrown deadbeat, moronic-fried-brain hillbilly into a Midas because he decides to steal a batch of cold remedy pills, cook them up in his dirty bathtub with toxic chemicals, and then sell them for tens of thousands of dollars; this, they argued, is unnatural, breeds violence, brings in a harder criminal element to support the fool, and brings, also, a poisoned product, and seduces too many people who normally would not have been involved in such a nefarious endeavor. The much-discussed of late, hotly contested "Iron Law of Prohibition" was also put forth.

It was the same quarrel the politics of the right and left had had ad infinitum, and few on the right had deserted the position they considered indefensible, and few too would cross the roiling water from the left, so that no proper compromise seemed possible, as neither side wanted compromise, only consummate victory: an untenable position for the defeated.

Although Robert Heimdall, with Paul at his side, was the mediator, he could see the hopelessness of the matter, and was close to bowing before the weight of despair, when he was contacted by messenger, who forthwith led him to an outside foyer, where stood, to his utter surprise and delight, the President of the United States of Mexico, and the President of the United States of America, whom he both embraced, and then escorted to center stage to the considerable awe of those assembled.

The two men stood upon the stage, facing a hushed crowd, who were, to each man and woman, now unsure as to how each would vote on the matter set before them.

The President of Mexico spoke first, his voice calm, his face serene, his posture correct. "Ladies and gentlemen, I must act as my conscience guides me, as the conscience of all Mexico wants, or I want, to do what is right and proper to create a better society; and as a politician, I must concede that this is of more importance than political power or parties, for in a Democracy, what are we but the will of the people, and if not, then our own will, and no longer a Democracy, but a tyranny of degrees, and corrupted by power and money; if it is best for the people, I say yes; if it is best for the world, I say yes; to say no would be for political expediency; to say no would be for sordid personal gain, nor am I a mere ideologue; so, it is time to place the safety and security and well-being of the citizenry in front of personal ambition; therefore, I vote 'yes' on the progressive idea of decriminalizing and legalizing all presently designated-as-illegal drugs. I thank you for your time and attention."

The whole assembly was motionless, silent, waiting for the speech of the American President, who presently and solemnly began.

"Ladies and gentlemen, we have been at war, but have refused to recognize its pedigree: a war of attrition by an enemy dedicated to nothing less than the undermining of the principles of Democracy for the enrichment and empowerment of their criminal corporations—terrorist corporations, and paramilitary insurgent corporations; we have met the enemy, and he is all of us, for only a free people might engage in complicit and willful acts of destruction to favor such malignant forces; we are the enablers, allowing the antidemocratic ideas emanating from our avowed and accursed foe, giving them aid, comfort, and sanctuary by our every acquiescence to not step in and fight them wherever they tread; whether it is by land, sea, or air, we cannot allow these now-vanquished foes to arise, like an eternal phoenix, in the form of regenerated crime syndicates, and once again soil the sacred pages of our Constitution; we give them power by allowing them to influence the market; we give them power if we merely hope for change; we give them power when first we do not seize the poisonous snake by its head and chop it off and throw it and its body into separate fiery furnaces; but first, we must take out its fangs, and leave it to slither away and die, and only then can we truly address the social ills that allowed the snake to flourish, and build a coalition to determine how to aid a people who need succor to recover from their ailments that no good citizen begs for; so, ladies and gentlemen, I concur with my esteemed colleague, and good friend, Manuel Diaz, President of Mexico, when I say to you, I cast a definitive 'yes' vote to decriminalize and legalize all drugs currently designated as illegal; and for the first time, party politics be accursed."

The stubborn ideals of opposing forces had just been exposed to an historical interlude that burned a rare perfume of concession for a cause that would benefit them and posterity, and as the audience stood and applauded, the vagaries of power shifted, and the future winked in gratitude.

Mexico enacted a blanket amnesty for all lower-level indigenous employees of the Cartels, but none for foreign players: Central and South American and American gangs and assassins, military contractors, and high-ranking officials, and all other associates from any region.

Roderigo and Pedro, surviving the years-long battle with the Cartels, created the Forgiveness and Healing gatherings, where they went from village to town to city, to gather the people and have them speak of their lives that had been altered by the presence of the now-defunct Cartels; and, always, the two men spoke first, spelling out in stark detail their mass atrocities, much to the consternation of the rancorous crowd, but then attesting to the healing power of God and their honest contrition, and never was their job more difficult than in the city of Yermo.

It was in the small neighborhood streets where normally meetings were held, allowing the ex-dealers, the users, the abusers, the abused, to confront each other, where the accused wept and begged forgiveness, and often the accuser granted it; but this time, the rally was held in the town hall, at the behest of the Mayor.

The auditorium of the high school was lined wall to wall, chair to chair, with the local residents; and no sooner did the two hosts appear on stage than the Gordian knot tied tighter; O, the bestial hissing, snarling, growling; O, the human wailing, sobbing, shrieking; O, the screams, the shouts, the hysteria; O, how the threats, the curses, and maledictions flowed like molten lava from a spewing volcano.

"Kill the murderers," sang the choir of the gathered people. The hosts did not discourage them. "Hang the murderers," the choir sang. The hosts did not disapprove. "They need to pay for their sins; let them repent while they rot in jail," the rising voice of the clanging symbols of justice echoed. The hosts would not condemn them.

A man stood up, unafraid, with a pistol in his hand, and pointed it at the men on stage. "You deserve to die for what you did! You killed my brother; you killed my wife!" he shouted, such that his entire being shook, and his reddened and tremulous countenance reflected the outrage of his mind. "How can you stand there and talk about forgiveness? Of course you want forgiveness, you stinking, filthy, murdering dogs!" How could the people respond except with a hearty approval? "'An eye for an eye,' as the Good Book says," and he shot twice at the motionless targets, missing badly.

The street minister, who daily attended to the needs of his wounded flock, stood up. "The Good Book also says to put to death by stoning for acts you have committed; but, I must remind you, neighbor, that we read the Old Testament in light of the New Testament, and we are no longer under the Law, but grace has saved us."

"They deserve death, not sermons," the man cried, his hand shaking as he held tightly the black pistol; "everyone knows it, except you!"

"Convince God, and we shall render such judgment upon the sinners." The shocked man stared at the minister. "Talk to Him," he continued, looking up and gesturing on high, "talk to Him directly, and if you can convince God that these two men before you should be murdered by you, we will not intercede."

The proposed assassin was encouraged by the throbbing, maddened crowd, and thus stimulated, he commenced his passionate plea, lifting his eyes unto heaven. "God," he began, in earnest, and then shouted, "these two men murdered many people, and they admit it," much to the cheering pleasure of the assembly. "So, God, I say they need to die; so, I will kill them." He held up his arms as if to signal this was his only appeal, and the people signaled their rowdy consent. He looked to the minister. "God seems convinced."

"Really?" the minister said, moving toward him. "How do you know?"

"The people here, as good Christian folk, know God's will, and they agree with me," he cried, thumping his chest with the sweaty hand that held the pistol.

The minister looked around. "The people know the intimate mind of God—astonishing," he said, incredulous. "So, why have I not consulted such prophets before, eh? Where were they when we needed one who speaks to God so easily?"

"It is not like that, minister; it is that they know His sacred will," a woman nearby said.

"And who knows that, may I ask; who will speak for you on the authority of Scripture you act upon?"

Many of the assembled people quoted texts that were, as the minister said, irrelevant today; finally, one man did say, "Paul wrote: 'neither thieves nor murderers shall inherit the kingdom of God.'"

The crowd roared approval, just like the bloodthirsty lynch mob.

"Paul of Tarsus," the minister said, and began to walk about the place where the human conflagration dwelled, "yes, yes, Paul—his Roman name, but Saul, his Jewish name; yes, yes, Paul wrote that, guided by the Holy Spirit; yes, Paul—do you know he knew Stephen, who was brought before the Sanhedrin, who hated our Lord and his followers; Stephen, who proclaimed the gospel before the Council without fear, or worry; Stephen, who, as he stood before those who hated our Lord, when he was done speaking, looked up and saw the heavens open and saw the Son of Man standing at the right hand of God; and do you know what the people did then—acting as if one people; yes, as if one mind: they drove him out of the city and then laid their robes at the feet of a young man who was involved in persecuting the Church; and then began stoning Stephen, the first Christian martyr; and as he fell to his knees, he prayed thusly, 'O, Lord, do not hold the sin against them.' And he died." The people were silent. "And who was that man who stood by in agreement—yes, but Paul of Tarsus! Yes, yes, who willfully persecuted the Church, both men and women, putting them into prison, and casting votes to put them to death; Paul, to whom, while he was on the road to Damascus, our Lord appeared and chose to be a great witness to spread the Holy Scriptures." He was walking among them now and touching them and bending down next to them, searching their minds with his passionate gaze. "How can our Father in Heaven forgive you if you do not forgive others?" He was face to face with the proposed killer again. "You will be a murderer; you will be a judge, you will know the mind of God; you will be God," he whispered, so that many had to incline their head to hear, and he knelt down before the man. "You are the prophet of God; you can do no wrong; lead us not into temptation," he abruptly shouted, looking up at the trembling man. "And when you have stoned these two men to death," and he pointed at the men on the stage, "God will protect you from punishment—no prison for you; you will be His chosen one to execute more of those abominable sinners; so, start now and shoot, shoot," he shouted, and he stood up, "kill the bad men who once murdered but have now repented—like Paul—like the thief on the cross who repented next to our crucified Lord, whom the Lord promised would be in Paradise with Him that very day; so, with every bullet you fire, you add a new chapter to the Holy Scriptures; so Benito, new prophet of our Lord and Savior, shoot! Shoot! And build the slaughterhouse again with every bullet you fire!" He paused for a fiery, impassioned moment as he moved close to the man and face him straight on. "But Jesus proclaimed, 'You have heard that it was said, you shall love your neighbor and hate your enemy: but I say to you, love your enemy, and pray for those who persecute you; and if you love only those who love you, what reward have you?'"

By now, the mad revelry to interfuse the two men on stage with a just revenge had been usurped by the eerie quiet, as all in attendance looked upon the sweating, shaking, would-be-avenger.

When Nature's fire has burned itself out, the embers of it still can ignite nearby brush, and rain will finally subdue it—it is the way of things; but in the end, it seeds more wood; so too the human fire that flares up, then burns out, bringing forth new sprouts.

And then she came walking up the aisle, right past the man with the gun, never touching him or looking at him, and proceeded past him; and, ascending to the stage, she turned around, her face quite expressionless, and spoke, in a voice disconnected from the deep, penetrating, inexpressible sorrow she related. "These men kidnapped and raped me, and left me for dead; yet, who am I to judge them." She shook her head, and stated, matter-of-factly, "I am not God." She frowned and looked at all of those about herself. "You know those of faith by their fruits; these men have dedicated their new lives to bring peace after war, willing to die for their mistakes; how long must they be good in order to earn our forgiveness; how long must they be wicked to earn our scorn; and what must they do that will never allow them our forgiveness; but, seeking God's forgiveness, have it granted." And she looked to the men and then back to the crowd. "Who am I to judge their hearts? Am I mightier than God, wiser than God, who forgives them if they truly have repented, but not I?" When she looked behind herself again, behold, the two men had fallen to their knees, weeping, their faces down in their hands.

Her breast swelled with pride of love for all creatures, and then she placed a hand upon each of their bowed heads. "I forgive you, my friends, I cannot hold anger in my heart; I must forgive you, for how can the Father forgive our sins, if we do not first forgive others," she whispered, looking with great compassion upon them now. "Now, rise up and do the work of the Lord, as He has so obviously called you for."

And lo, the men did stand, and embraced her; and lo, she wept, for the first time since the abomination visited upon her by those two once-brutal, soulless, nightmarish assassins. Her husband presently joined them, and he too embraced the men.

And what of the man with the little black weapon of destruction? He fell down into an emotional heap and wept, and was comforted by those around him, first by the street minister, and then by others.

"If we cannot forgive and forget," the minister said, to all and to no one in particular, "then we are doomed as a race, and this is why we need God."

It wasn't too much later that Roderigo and Pedro visited the jail of Yermo. The Sheriff brought them into his office and offered them refreshments, which they politely declined, whereupon he poured himself a cup of strong, Colombian black coffee, took a sip, and then looked up at the men. "Well, sirs, what brings you here on such a fine Autumn day?"

Pedro frowned. "How do you not know us? We are the infamous killers of Yermo—we are the ones who have proclaimed our guilt."

"We are here to turn ourselves in," Roderigo said. "We have preached the Gospel of Forgiveness, and now we are prepared for a just punishment."

"I see," the Sheriff said, pursing his lips, and then after looking for a document on his desk and not finding it, went to his steel cabinet and, finding it there, declared, "aha!" and sat down again. "It is always somewhere…" He skimmed the paper. "Yes, yes—here is the appropriate sentence, yes: Hereinafter, no lower-level associates—as defined in Article 2 of this proclamation—of the Mexican Cartels will be charged with any crime before the below affixed date." He looked at the calendar, then back to the men, and finally stated, matter-of-factly, after folding his hands upon the desk, "It looks like you are free to go."

"No, that is unacceptable," Pedro said, irritated. "We are murderers—you don't pardon murderers; you execute them."

"Si," Roderigo said, "you put them in jail for life—you torture them, knowing they will never get out. Isn't that the point of prison, to punish them?"

"Hmm," the Sheriff answered, perplexed; looking at the document once more, and reading the appropriate sentence again, he said, "no, no: this document—approved by El Presidente and the Congress—is very specific, and says otherwise." He paused, looking again at both men. "You are free to go."

Pedro shook his head. "What kind of place is this, to allow murderers to walk away? How can you condone such a thing?"

"It isn't me—it's Mexico," the Sheriff said, gravely; "we want to get past what seemed would never go away."

Pedro replied, "But how can you allow murderers to go unpunished?"

The Sheriff took a gulp of coffee, then stared long and hard at the document on his desk, contemplating its significance. He again looked up at the two men, and said, carefully choosing his words, "It seems to me," he then knit his dark brows, pursed his lips, and clasped his hands again, "it seems to me, in your case, at least, that Justice is done."

"How can you say that?" Pedro answered, astonished. "We are guilty! Arrest us!" He slammed his Bible on the desk.

"It is your sworn duty—we killed freely, so freely should you kill us," Pedro cried.

"Hmm," the Sheriff began, frowning, "it seems like you don't even believe your own Gospel message." He looked at each man with a face of great expectation. "What about the exquisite compassion of forgiveness?"

"Yes, we are forgiven by our heavenly Father, but we still need to be punished for our earthly sins," Roderigo said. He held his Bible fast. "It is only right…"

"Well, sirs," the Sheriff continued, "hmm…" He knit his brows again, took another drink of the steaming-hot coffee, and then tapped his index finger on the document while he frowned. "Hmm…"

"Well, are you going to arrest us or not?" Pedro said, anxious. "We want to be punished for our crimes."

The Sheriff pointed at him, index finger extended while it bobbed up and down. "I'll tell you what," he looked at the clock, and then back to them, "it is eight-thirty in the morning; if by ten a.m. you still want to be arrested—I'll do it." The two men readily assented. "Bueno." He nodded his head, stood up and, after putting on his cowboy hat, said, "Follow me," and exited the door, with the men close behind.

As they walked down the sidewalk that still had faint red stains upon it—like the blood from the roots of a "societal tree," said one reporter—they passed many new structures that had been erected to replace the ones destroyed during the rebellion. He said to the men, "We began to build as quickly as possible so as not to be reminded of the unfortunate and recent past." He waved to nearby citizens and bade them "buenos dias."

He looked at the men. "But then, we decided that the burnt places were actually a reminder of what we had so improbably accomplished—and so we decided to take our time." They walked past stores that were still being rebuilt. "We have nothing to be ashamed of—we did what we had to do: we overcame evil." He looked directly at the men and said solemnly, "But that was yesterday, and yesterday is gone." They moved on.

As they toured the city, they met more citizens, he always treating them with respect and genuine friendship, and certain to tip his beige-colored, palm straw hat to the ladies. "We are a fine people," he said, after greeting a family that was heading toward the local school; "sometimes, we just need a little reminder."

But the people who greeted him also greeted Roderigo and Pedro with the same respect, which made the former proud, and the latter confused.

The men moved on. "Did you know," the Sheriff began again as they walked past a construction site, "that in the old, old, old days—in certain countries—there were no jails? Hard to believe, I know; so, do you know what happened to offenders? That's right, they were punished and then let go; so, if you stole, you had your hands cut off—well, you get the picture..." He shrugged his shoulders. "I like to read history when I'm not working; I seem to have more time on my hands lately..."

The men moved on, touring more of the ravaged but slowly rebuilding city.

As they walked past an elementary school, where the children were playing outside on the grass, the Sheriff said, "It is a new era—even better than the one before this curse came upon us." He smiled as he gazed upon the happy children, nodding his head as he observed them smiling and laughing. "My son and daughter attended here—my wife used to work here as an aide."

"Where are they now?" Pedro asked.

The Sheriff looked at him. "They are dead."

The color in the faces of Roderigo and Pedro was drained as if boiled away by their own shame and humiliation.

Roderigo asked, nervously, and cautiously, "How?"

"The rebellion," he said, mournfully; "it is the price of Liberty."

The men moved on, quiet for a long duration, and then the Sheriff stopped in the town square, where many victims of the reign of the Cartel had been displayed, but here now was a bronze statue of a group of male and female combatants who stood on the ready, with an inscription engraved on the golden plaque that was attached to the rock base. He read it thusly: "'The condition upon which God hath given Liberty to man is eternal vigilance; which condition if he break, servitude is at once the consequence of his crime and the punishment of his guilt.'"

He nodded. "It is a hard thing to forgive—I know." He looked at the men now. "It is a hard thing to forgive those who have wronged you, and sometimes even harder for those who have done the wrong to forgive themselves." He looked at the statue again, at the proud and noble figures with their rifles on the ready as they looked anxiously toward battle. "Everyone who sees this statue sees what they want to see—some see the town, some see the Crusaders, some see themselves; but they all see the truth: that we did not fail ourselves." He nodded, looked down, inhaled deeply, and exhaled slowly, and then looked up again at the statue as if from a different perspective. "We Mexicans will never be conquered; we have shown the world at least that." He looked at the men again. "And now I ask you—are you of more worth to Mexico dead or alive? And have you done all you can for God? Will He say, 'Good and loyal servants, come home, there is nothing good left for you to do for Me; no one left to witness to, no one left bring comfort to, no one left to bring succor to'?" He paused. "It is a coward who does not do what he knows will help others. Listen," he said, putting a hand on each shoulder of the men, "you have asked for forgiveness from God and man, and I know you have been forgiven by Him if you asked honestly and sincerely, and the people also forgive you; and now, you must forgive yourselves, and free yourselves from the prison you yourselves have built, and acknowledge that God has already taken His away." He turned around and took in a panoramic view of the town. "Yes, we want to move on; but no, we do not want permanent monuments of what horrors were visited upon us—we can remember well enough." He smiled as he nodded, and inhaled deeply the fresh, perfumed morning air, and then exhaled slowly. He then said, with surpassing honor, "This is modern Mexico, and we will not be overcome; after all, we are more of us than them." He smiled. "We will forgive those who trespassed against us; but will never forget what happened here, and in this way, we will keep our proud heritage close to our hearts, and let it and God guide us to a better tomorrow." He looked at the town as it continued to awaken, and then to the men. "Yes, there is nothing we can do to you that you cannot do better, for only you know who you are, what you must do to be at peace with your soul." When the clock struck ten o'clock in the a.m., he smiled briefly, nodding his head. "Ten o'clock—time for more rounds," and he extended his hand and shook each of theirs. "Vaya con Dios—go with God, señores, and you will redeem your souls." He turned and slowly walked toward the main shops.

Roderigo and Pedro, Bibles in hand, gazed upon him as he greeted the people—the resilient and now seemingly invincible people who were smiling and relaxed, as if this new morning had the high probability of becoming a good and productive day. They looked at the statue again, read the words once more, then both of them, as if of one mind, began to walk down the sidewalk that would connect them to a road that led to the next town, where they would soon decide that their next mission was to help those immigrants who rode El Tren de la Muerte, "the Death Train," or sometimes called La Bestia, "the Beast," who were coming from Central America in the hopes of making it to that fabled land, America. Both of them had heard stories of how hazardous the journey was: that there were many deaths and injuries— that, in fact, many of these travelers had become stranded in Mexico, only to have unscruplous people prey upon them; and they felt an abiding love and sympathy for these people who oftentimes had fled a nightmarish world in pursuit of a better life. So, they would go there and help those who were lost and frightened, and had given up all hope, just as they had, not too long ago.

And no one seemed to notice them at all.

The Nature of Things

After the Crusaders had long ago helped depose the corrupt ruler of Kush, after Moses and his men had left, unsatisfied with the political philosophy of the newly united rebel groups, it was Captain Mohammed Samoei who would eventually take the reins of power there, albeit with a modicum of adroit maneuvering to gently remove any other worthy opponents; O, the benefits of a liberal education! "Like a prince among savages," he confided to himself, for, as he saw it, he had no others he could possibly trust enough other than to say to them, "fetch my black baton," so he might administer a fair beating upon their unrepentant and obdurate, slovenly bodies.

Once in power, he fully intended to serve the people the best he could, and still experience the finer things in life that power brings, but a curious thing soon befell him: a conscience, a most importunate occurrence that gave him no little discomfort, prompting him to exclaim, "Dash it all, now I'll have to experience piety!"

It had all come about when he began to tour the devastated towns and temporary encampments of the refugees, where his soul began to bleed sympathy for those starved and ill, and those who had been beaten, and abused in every imaginable way; once this new feeling of compassion bore up in him like a bubbling, fresh spring in the hot desert, he considered all the good he could do with the enormity of influence and access to wealth and resources he had access to that had previously been hidden or suppressed; and when he began to heal the deep fissures that had been filled with the spilled blood of his people, he actually felt contrition for his past misadventures as he developed what he could only describe as "a crown of empathy, its thorns stuck firmly upon my round head." He soon became the People's Champion.

He took a wife, and begat a family, thus becoming totally respectful in the eyes of his adoring people, and achieving what before had seemed impossible in this Civil War–plagued country: peace and prosperity, and heading toward a more democratic way of existence with reforms he slowly and carefully instituted.

But this was not a country that had merely thrown off the yoke of tyranny of an oppressive ruler and then started anew, it was a nation of disparate groups seeking power and prestige, an incessant battle of words and weapons and uprisings that sought to unsettle the peace and hasten the storm of war; and even when this was quenched, even when the government put down the rebellions and regained its political equilibrium, it must be remembered that this was Southern Kush, having gained its independence from the Islamic government of Northern Kush, and when a country once united, even by despotism, has those who decide that two warring halves are inferior to an iron-fisted, united whole, there will be no end to the chaos until one political group absolutely, incontrovertibly, and irrevocably wins.

So, it was the forces of Northern Kush that fell upon the South again, driven by religious dogma, and bloody mammon, dreams of undiluted authority, and the need to conquer that which they felt was improper, inferior, and divisive, and antithetical to their fanatical way of life.

The Civil War of Kush began once more, and came then the horrors and terrors of when those who have no conscience are allowed to have weapons and the will to use them indiscriminately on soldier or civilian; and there was a severe drought in the South, and the aggressive rebel groups from the North were enthralled to make it worse for the indigenous people here by blocking incoming aid.

It was in the first month of this conflict that a battle of great significance occurred.

The antagonistic factions in the South had plotted with their sympathetic factions in the North to attack a particular residence with a full battalion, but they had been met with great resistance by the Special Forces unit of the South that had been personally trained by the General of the Joint Chiefs of Staff, whose forces eventually repulsed the enemy. It is here we must now visit two significant players in the history of this brief war, both of whom had just contributed significantly to battling their foe, where one of them now lay badly wounded.

"Mohammed, my President," Moses said, laying his friend upon a sofa in the presidential house, "you should not have fought..."

Mohammed smiled, holding his bloodied side, but coughed hard before he managed to say, "Mr. Prime Minister, you rascal, and hypocrite—fighting alongside me like a young lion!"

"Two young lions, sir," Moses said with surpassing pride.

Mohammed smiled again, then grimaced. "O, how I loathe these troublesome death scenes; it is always so difficult to decide what to say…" His wounds seized him for a moment as he fought to hold equanimity. "I do so want to say something memorable," he whispered, holding Moses' hand.

The medics had been killed, and the doctor sent for, but it would not matter.

"What you have done here is memorable, sir; what you have accomplished in our country is unprecedented, and will be recorded in history as a lasting monument to Liberty."

The countenance of Mohammed, absorbed in pain, struggled to free itself of it. "Do you really think so? The people are suffering so because of this drought, and I feel so helpless…"

"Yes, Mr. President. You have shown the world that our people desire the same freedoms all people deserve."

He closed his eyes. "Tell Grace how much I love her," he murmured, and now in his mind he beheld his beauteous wife; "and Favor and Alimah, those darling girls," and now in his mind he beheld his beautiful girls; "and Jean Paul and Alghaily," and now in his mind he beheld his beautiful boys, "how much I simply worship them all."

"Your legacy shall live through them, and inspire all freedom-loving people."

He smiled through the excruciating agony. "You flatter me, Moses," he whispered and, opening his eyes, looked at his friend with great respect; "you have served Kush well, and now must lead her…"

Moses shook his head. "No, it is not for me to say, Mohammed."

Mohammed placed his bloodied hand on the shoulder of Moses. "We both know you were born to lead us—and the people love you."

"They love me because first they love you."

Mohammed smiled, and tears of joy began to flow down his cheeks, and then he gazed intently at his brother-in-arms. "Do you really think I redeemed my loathsome soul?"

"Yes, Mohammed, you did; you served God well."

"With that, I am happy, my good and loyal friend." He closed his eyes, his body shuddering in its death throes, and then whispered, "Will you call them now?"

Moses smiled. "Yes, Mohammed, I will."

Mohammed smiled and nodded. "I wish I could see all of them again, when we were so young, and so certain of ourselves as we fought for Justice."

"Justice," Moses whispered, "you have served it well; you have been the bright, shining star of Africa, inspiring other leaders to seek Democracy." He paused, staring adoringly into the eyes of Mohammed. "All of our brother and sister warriors are so very proud of you."

Mohammed nodded. "Yes, as I am of them; and when we were so young, so very, very young, and all we had to do to be right was fight against tyranny; it made one beautiful inside..."

And then the President of Southern Kush died, and Moses wept for one who had risked all to keep his country safe from those diabolical forces that will never reconcile with the incontrovertible concept of the natural rights of man, who seek to usurp and destroy those things and people they hate and do not understand.

Settling Down

The mission having thus been completed, after the destruction of the Azteca and El Dorado Cartels, and their unfortunate Cartel allies, after a grueling long time of fighting alongside the two allied government troops, and after the Cartels were utterly destroyed, the Crusaders, having enjoyed absolute amnesty from the Mexican and American governments, returned to their respective homelands, or their previous residences, wherever their hearts and minds happened to lead them. The identity of the General Chief of Staff of the Kush military as adventure and freedom fighter was, due to the influence of Robert Heimdall, kept out of the official profile, as, amazingly, were the names of the Crusaders.

America settled down to the level determined by order and harmony in a Democratic Republic, as the gangs reassumed their role once again as misguided members obsessed with regional disputes and grander ideas of expansion, this time not having an opportunity to being led astray by super-criminal organizations who conflated a limited purpose of being with their perverted desire for power that stretched beyond reasonableness, thus creating an organism that could not contain nor relate to its newly acquired powers and wide-ranging influences; nor did they, these gangs, reconcile with their communities and don the green uniform of Boy Scout and proffer aid to little old ladies as they crossed the busy street; they soon reached their full capacity as it related to their limited role in society; and as it related to the youngest members: there were still many of these lost youth who were candidates for rehabilitation, and still capable of becoming productive members of society.

But, you protest, what about the lucrative, constant cash flow for the gangs from the sale of illegal drugs; what was that, you say, illegal drug trade? What century are you in, eh? You must still have your head wrapped around those wild gangster stories and hyper-violent drug-fueled movies that glorified mobsters and vilified politicians on the take; but that was before nearly every head of state in the world—who were, quite honestly, fond of signing pledges (reduce carbon emissions pledges, no more war pledges, no more nuclear weapons pledges)—this time, after the United Nations, as a result of much prodding by Robert Heimdall and other equally sincere, influential people, agreed to a special meeting called by the General Assembly of the United Nations to explore the past, present, history and possible future of illicit drugs, where the overwhelmingly consensus by the representatives was favorable toward legalizing and decriminalization them—signed a document in which this scenario could actually become reality, hark: legalize and decriminalize any and all drugs that were currently being grown, sold, distributed by one or more people who by doing so sought to make a profit, often through coercion and violence, that would lead to an unbalancing of power, and disarming society, such drugs including (but not limited to, relating to all drugs that may be concocted in the future): marijuana, cocaine, heroin, LSD, methamphetamines, and opium.

A ceremonial signature does not translate into action, nor affect legislative change, but it can bring to bear the incalculable forces of a burned-out society that will demand action of its governmental agencies to do something other than that what was formally done, which proved fatal; so, slowly, through the forces of societal erosion, protests on the streets and in letters, in public speaking and debates, in boycotts and voting; and then one politician accepting the challenge of decriminalizing and legalizing all drugs, as other politicians hid behind the pollsters and anxiously awaited the fallout; and when none came, when the daring rogue politician was held as a hero and not derelict of reason, others, like rats jumping back onto what they had perceived was a sinking ship, joined her in the slowly resurrected, slowly expanding boat now serving as a life raft that, on occasion, was being sabotaged by the sly rat who wore the false face of the deceiver.

It was a brave new world, where psychopaths could not create huge conglomerates that sold illegal and stimulating substances, and by so doing, threaten to destabilize nations and the long-established equilibrium of society, for duly elected governments of sovereign nations now allowed firms to sell these substances legally and doctors to distribute them; so, these emotionally unstable citizens simply instituted other goods and services into their repertoire: prostitution, kidnapping, theft, extortion, fraud, murder, and assorted mayhem; alas, a criminal mind seeks a prescribed level, and if it cannot profit by a substance no longer profitable or viable, it assumes the next human indulgence in the outer limits of human veiled sin, and takes from this perilous fringe and repackages the product and advertises it as necessary for sustaining a meritorious life, and, as a byproduct, hopefully corrupting as many youths and adults as possible along the way.

The crimes of a criminal are like his own skin: unless it is torn off layer by layer, and burned to dust and ashes, the criminal remains the same; thus, it is prudent, the government decided, in such severe cases, for the government to legalize, legislate, and regulate those goods and services previously in the unstable hands of the criminal network; most decidedly, it is called wisdom gained from experience, while others simply pronounce it progress, and pragmatism.

> When inside a broken mind,
> a shattered memory divides;
> when the old is once forgotten,
> and the future soon arrives,
> salvation comes slowly, when the new thing quickly dies.

War has the ability to produce in the mind of its participants, either willing or unwilling, a dissonant sound that tilts and allows it to then perceive the precious outline and intricacies of life hitherto unknown to it, as follows: that which was formerly important may be rendered unimportant, due to its trivial nature, or, acts once perceived as trivial are now seen as important, as they are exercised with loved ones: priorities shift from one realm to another, and align, so that a clearer vision is beheld, and a lofty scheme of goals is delineated, setting the person on a more exclusive territory to explore; and from this exalted place, one can exculpate all offenses, offenders, legitimate and illegitimate; one can embrace newfound ideals, virtues, purposes; one can scatter the illusions of self and refine the true image of being; all may be accomplished, if one can learn and grow and thrive after the dissolution of physical combat, though the combat of the mind may never cease.

Samuel Longfellow and his wife, Florence, at the behest of Moses, and in conjunction with a Christian charitable institution, moved to Kush, and settled in the southern province, and set up a school for children, who, due to extreme poverty and dissimulation from intermittent civil wars, had very little education. And whatever supplies or building materials or goods the humble red-brick schoolhouse needed, an anonymous donor from America filled, as, of course, did the former General of the Joint Chiefs of Staff, and now Prime Minister of Southern Kush.

Before the schoolhouse was erected, and the only setting was outside under a pitched canvas for shade, where the floor was dirt, and a wooden framed chalkboard with chalk on a metal stand was the only writing space for the Teacher, and chalkboards and white chalk for the students, the Longfellows were amazed at the dignity and respect shown to them by their quiet, eager, and seemingly happy students.

"It is a curious thing," Samuel said to Florence, in the second week of them being here, as they gazed lovingly at the children who, this day, with smiling faces, were eating their nutritious snacks that had been prepared by their Teachers, "to compare them to their counterparts in the States." The schoolhouse was still under construction, and they helped, as did the children, who were of all ages, faiths, creeds, and backgrounds.

"It is too profound," she said, also gazing lovingly at her students, "and revelatory, that children in two places can be so extremely different and manner and speech and behavior." She had been a teacher's aide while she attended law school.

"I do wonder," he replied, but then a female child ran up to him and hugged him, and then hugged her too, and he watched the innocent, youthful creature return to her playmates, "it is as if we are watching children as they truly are—unspoiled by the comforts of civilization; as they were intended to be."

And, as if not to be outdone, the brother of the girl who had hugged Samuel ran up to Florence, and the two embraced, and then he embraced Samuel, and then the smiling imp skipped back to his family and friends. "Children of wealthy countries have so much to offer the world," she said, "but we have ruined them for our own selfish desires by removing all obstacles in their way to try and make them perpetually happy—we think we are strong, but we are weak."

"Yes, I can see it all now—yes, Flory, yes," he said, with knit brows, "children," his voice grew pensive, "they are the true measure of our immediate world: how they live, how they act, how they grow up—it is they who reflect our surroundings: in excess, they are spoiled; in deficiency, but surrounded by the excess of others, they can be corrupted; in deficiency, here, they are noble; in violence, here, they shrink back and seek shelter; here, they are what we should be, once were, should be again: virtuous creatures who still have a moral conscience not yet diluted or devoured by wealth or power; yes, Flory, in their natural state, they are of a finer stuff than we."

"And every soul we save from destruction is a world saved: a child not in war, not stealing, not being sold into servitude; we have given them their chance; how can we do otherwise?"

"How can the world do otherwise?"

As the two adults conversed, the children were plotting; and then, altogether, the fourteen students of all ages stood up together, and with happy faces and joyous hearts, burst out in a song of their own making that spoke of their love and honor for their beloved Teachers.

Flory, who knew more Kush language than Samuel, did not have to translate much, for the adoration of these innocent hearts for their saviors poured through in every syllable and rhyme; and finally, each of the children approached the two, and presented them with a delightful drawing done in crayon on paper of the present schoolhouse, their Teachers, and future school, and each in turn then hugged the two, who were now gently weeping.

And when the impromptu ceremony was over, Flory clapped her slender hands together, and said, "All right, you silly little ones," not even having to tell them to clean up their messes, "back to work!"

In an instant, all was absolutely still, as the obedient children immediately plopped onto the cold ground, sitting cross-legged, hands folded in their lap, all eager eyes and grateful faces directed at the Teachers; but then, one of the older girls, age ten, with big, brown eyes, timidly raised her hand.

"Yes, Rana," Flory said, standing at the front of the class with Samuel.

"Madame Instructor," the girl began, slowly, "it is not all work."

"No?"

"No," the girl returned, smiling largely, "learning is so much fun!"

And then all of the children erupted into smiles and applause and much giggling.

Samuel hugged his wife. "They need us, so," she whispered to him as she felt the genuine joy of her students.

"Yes," he whispered, watching their honest gratitude and enthusiasm for learning diffuse throughout the place like a cleansing, perfumed storm, "and here we shall make our abode, and family," and then looked to her, where new life inside her had recently begun.

Ireland is geographically mountainous, with rolling plains, and rivers, lakes, and inlets, and bogs too; there is also plenty of vivacious green, a lush palace of thick, hearty, sweet-scented green descended from the virgin territories that gave birth to man here; and there are rolling hills of green, bush, shrubs and trees of spreading, luscious green; and tall, thick grass, covering the land in a skin of verdant green; and scented clusters of richly huge flowers decorating the scenery. The land is eternal, offering itself to any and all who would stay and harvest its secrets, and honor its vital essence.

Ireland, which endured invaders and civil wars and partition, only to see her own suffering during the potato famine, where the typical Irish ate nearly ten pounds of potatoes a day, and drank much milk; but when the potato blight occurred, to watch in dreaded silence as her own starved, and abandoned her dry breasts as they left for foreign lands, was nearly more than she could bear; and then to later see political and religious upheaval and animosity between her own children would have cleft her heart in twain had she one; still, she survived, albeit politically of two regions, but in reality, one whole, which were uniquely, faithfully, historically, Irish.

But now she was slowly dying—not in the land itself, for there she was flourishing, but as it concerned the people who were leaving: she grieved; for the industries to keep the young people tied to the Mother Country were on the wane, and in these days, just like in old days, they sought fortune and a stable future, but too many saw too few opportunities in their beloved homeland.

A conflict arises, and some men see what is, and accept it, and oft join it, and decide there is no reversing a rising tide; other men see what is, and do not accept it, and fight against the rising tide; why, why then do some capitulate, while others stand firm? Who can stop the bleeding of a slowly trickling exodus of indigenous folk from a country that was established nearly two millennia ago? Who can stem the allure and promise of a better life outside of her pastoral bosom, which is more powerful than the land that bore them?

There are always those who, when all others have fled the coming beast, for a reason they often cannot explain, must not retreat, and await what horror may come; without such valiant citizens, the world would fall into chaos, if all that were bad and evil in the world knew that their very unsettling and potentially destructive presence caused those who consider themselves just and good to flee to save their puny and insignificant lives.

I risk all, for a precious very little, the warrior declares in the face of the coming calamity; and from a precious little, new lands prosper, without the weak and treasonous to bring despair and disharmony that sows weakness and capitulation.

As it was, there were two among many who would not yield to what seemed the inevitable and unstoppable, two who had recently come to live in the ancestral home of the man, in Kerry County in Kenmare; but with these two, there came to visit Ireland a third and fourth who brought two more, and together, they formed an alliance that sought to stimulate the economy of Ireland.

"My ancestry came from Norway and Iceland," Robert Heimdall began on this cool, breezy summer day, in the open town center of Dublin, as the people gathered round to hear the enigmatic, philanthropist billionaire. "Our cultures preceded the culture of this world, our forebears having thus established the course of our lives by their innovations and daring; what they wrought so skillfully and arduously over the millennia, a foundation of hard labor and ingenuity that came from understanding our role as inhabitants and caretakers of these ancient lands, only we understand what has gone on before us; we know the sacrifices made, the pain endured, the victories won, so future generations might carry on this grand legacy—and it is only you who can do this, not to be confused with any other people, who have no birthright here, no inheritance, no genetic ties to this magnificent region; for Ireland can survive only if true Irishmen and true Irishwomen believe in her and pledge to work to save her from a miserly end; it is not up to her—she has done nothing but give back to her children—so it is to you who must keep her thriving." He paused, looking at the mesmerized people. "Therefore, I propose, after talking with your duly elected leaders, and gaining their consent, to help rebuild her industries; first, as it relates to encouraging more citizens to gain expertise in Information and Communications technologies, especially regarding engineering, software and computing, I pledge enough monies for the training of ten thousand men and women; second, as it relates to encouraging more young people to attend and graduate from university, I pledge enough monies for scholarships for ten thousand men and women; and third, with regard to farming—sheep, crops, and the like—I pledge innovation from the finest scientific minds at the finest universities, enough monies to employ, for now, ten thousand men and women; and fourth, as it relates to vocational training in diverse areas, I pledge enough monies for ten thousand men and women; and let these pledges be a beginning, and allow hard work to produce even more fruit."

So unexpected was this magnanimous announcement, that the hushed people in the square were astonished, and quite speechless, but knowing the reputation of the man, words not of an idle boaster, spontaneous applause soon resided among the throng.

Later that day, Robert and his wife, Patricia, and Paul, and his wife, Honoraine, visited a house near a pristine lake that was situated in the lush and verdant hills of Glendalough.

"Robert," Rhiannon said, embracing him, "Patricia," she said, embracing her, "Paul," she said, embracing him, "Honoraine," she said, embracing her, "please come in."

Dylan shook the hands of the four guests, and welcomed them into his home.

"And who is this, eh?" Paul said, upon buying a spying a small figure who hid behind the kitchen door. "Can it be—little Conall?" The toddler, giggling, ran up to him, and the two embraced. "Uncle Paul," he whispered, as Paul raised him up, "I love you."

"Oh, you are such a good boy," Paul said, hugging him now.

"Aunt Honoraine," the boy cried, upon seeing her, and Paul set him down so he could run to her and receive a warm embrace.

"Uncle Robert," the boy cried, excitedly, and ran into the arms of the crouched-down gentleman; and then, "Aunt Patricia," he cried, and ran to her waiting arms, telling all of them how very much he loved them.

"He is so handsome," the two aunts exclaimed.

"He is so innocent," the two uncles declared.

"Oh, have we been too noisy?" Patricia asked Rhiannon. "Where is the baby?"

Rhiannon smiled, and said, nearly in a whisper, "No, she is up—she always knows when there are visitors," and she led the four guests into the colorful nursery, where the three-month-old was stirring inside her white, wooden crib. Rhiannon gently took hold of her and lifted her up. "Eleanor, look who is here—your aunts and uncles." Soon, baby Eleanor was held by each of them, and told how beautiful she was, and fondled, and then gently replaced back in her private sanctuary of peace and comfort, and then the adults quietly tiptoed away as she fell back to a blessed sleep.

When all of the friends were settled in the family room, Robert and Patricia, and Paul and Honoraine told of their latest travels in those unpitied countries that still suffered from the blight of ignorance the world bestowed upon them; and Dylan told them about his martial arts studio, and his youth club, and Rhiannon about her work with the local communities to bring an institution for victims of domestic violence and the homeless; they also discussed, with much pleasure, the recent fifteen-hundred-meter race Abebe's oldest son had run in, where he had established himself as the leading candidate to win a gold medal in the upcoming Olympic games, which gave the men over to reminiscing in their minds about that great adventure once so zealously lived.

Then, the two genders, following the dictates of Nature, divided into separate groups, the ladies in the parlor, the men in the backyard on the porch.

Robert and Paul marveled at the idyllic, verdant pastures that diffused across the spacious, clean, fresh land in all directions, and saw the son of Conchobar grazing in the green pastures near the graves of Conall Cuchulain II and Elena Saoirse Cuchulain.

Dylan recognized the disquiet that lay upon the faces of his two friends. "Something," he said, and nodding.

Robert, setting down his herbal tea upon the glass table, half-smiled, and when he spoke, it was with the solemnity of the inevitable, "It is always something…"

Rhiannon, even from the parlor, saw the grave posture of her husband, and she and her guests came to the backyard.

Patricia and Honoraine, sensing the change in the countenances of the four, whose histories as the Crusaders they knew, excused themselves, and went to play with little Conall.

Rhiannon stood with them now, and now, not as mere friends together, but as the indomitable forces they had been, and still were.

"The eternal struggle," Robert began, then, walking out onto the thick, green grass, removed his shoes and socks. He smiled as he crouched down and put his large hands upon the soft, plush surface. "There is something beyond just feeling good when we place our bare bodies onto the living skin of Mother Earth." He looked out again at the unfurling, dense, aromatic pastures, and then stood up. "That some may live in peace, and know such bliss, others must join the eternal struggle against tyranny."

"Moses," Dylan said, "we have been waiting."

"Yes," Rhiannon said, as she placed her arm inside the arm of her husband, "I feel it."

"Moses," Paul said, gravely, "it is his time now; even now, Yoshitsune and Horatius, and Rustem, and Tyr and Enkidu, who have been there, as you know, helping him as advisers, are now preparing for the inevitable; and many others are arriving now and more are on the way."

"We will make arrangements," Rhiannon said.

Dylan looked at her, knowing it was futile to dissuade her from the coming adventure.

Robert and Paul excused themselves and went back into the stone house that Dylan's grandparents had built and in which his parents—whose inspirational lives were often honored and cherished—had lived and raised them.

Dylan and Rhiannon held each other as they stood, barefoot, as they normally went about the place, now in the sweet touch of the cool grass, and gazing at the bursting radiance of a blushing clear and crisp sky that was painted in bold strokes of scarlet, and drenched in dappled hyacinth.

"It is for the lives of those inside," Dylan said, solemnly.

"It is for the lives of those inside," Rhiannon softly said, and then, "it is for lives and the land outside."

"It is for lives and land outside," Dylan said, hugging her now, and then murumured, "an bhaile, ní mór dúinn a thuill, ní mór dúinn a chosaint i gconai." *This home we have earned, we must always protect.*

They said nothing more, as there was not much more to say, for all of it had been said before, and understood, and the two were in agreement about it; this is the way of True Love, that they are in absolute unity about matters of great importance, and so have a lasting and serene harmony; and they could know such things only because of what they had experienced, most often together, and knew what was important in life, and trivial; what was worth dying for, and what was not; and they intimately understood their own nature, and the nature of each other, and consequently, realized the soul of the other, for truly, they shared the same God-fearing soul—and thus, they were rebellious in this imperfect world, having long since joined in a sacred union not only for their love, but for their very nature, and deeds.

And now, it was time to once more put on the hallowed armor of their true warrior self, which they had never undressed, for every time they defended even the least of God's creatures from injury, it grew in size and stature, and encouraged its permanent residency upon them.

So it was, and so it will be, that there must always be those who, when the oppressive gauntlet of injustice is violently thrown down before a trembling and cowering people, will eagerly come forward, and upon picking it up, without fear, and with great courage, slap it hard across the harsh, implacable, sinister face of the aggressor.

It is the way of things, lest we all perish as the heavy black boot of tyranny stands upon our collective, weak and willing necks. And somewhere in the flaming heart of Africa, a child was born, and raised unto the high vault of celestial heaven by his father, who declared, "O God, bless this little child, my precious Mwindo!"

> There is always one who will not retreat,
> who will not cower;
> who will not bargain,
> and inspire others to join,
> in the eternal fight, against the rising tide.

-Finis-